PENGUIN CLASSICS

THE BROTHERS KARAMAZOV

FYODOR MIKHAILOVICH DOSTOYEVSKY was born in Moscow in 1821, the second of a physician's seven children. When he left his private boarding school in Moscow he studied from 1838 to 1843 at the Military Engineering College in St Petersburg, graduating with officer's rank. His first story to be published, 'Poor Folk' (1846), had a great success. In 1849 he was arrested and sentenced to death for participating in the 'Petrashevsky circle'; he was reprieved at the last moment but sentenced to penal servitude, and until 1854 he lived in a convict prison at Omsk, Siberia. Out of this experience he wrote *Memoirs from the House of the Dead* (1860). In 1861 he began the review *Vremya* with his brother; in 1862 and 1863 he went abroad where he strengthened his anti-European outlook, met Mlle Suslova who was the model for many of his heroines, and gave way to his passion for gambling. During the following years he fell deeply into debt. In 1867 he married Anna Grigoryevna Snitkina (his second wife) and she helped to rescue him from his financial morass. They lived abroad for four years, then in 1873 he was invited to edit *Grazhdanin*, to which he contributed his *Author's Diary*. From 1876 the latter was issued separately and had a great circulation. In 1880 he delivered his famous address at the unveiling of Pushkin's memorial in Moscow; he died six months later in 1881. Most of his important works were written after 1864; *Notes from Underground* (1864), *Crime and Punishment* (1865–6), *The Gambler* (1866), *The Idiot* (1869), *The Devils* (1871), and *The Brothers Karamazov* (1880).

•

DAVID MAGARSHACK was born in Riga, Russia, and educated at a Russian secondary school. He came to England in 1920 and was naturalized in 1931. After graduating in English literature and language at University College, London, he worked in Fleet Street and published a number of novels. For the Penguin Classics he translated Dostoyevsky's *Crime and Punishment*, *The Idiot*, *The Devils* and *The Brothers Karamazov*; *Dead Souls* by Gogol; *Oblomov* by Goncharov; and *Lady with Lapdog and Other Tales* by Chekhov. He also wrote biographies of Chekhov, Dostoyevsky, Gogol, Pushkin, Turgenev and Stanislavsky; and he is the author of *Chekhov and the Dramatist*, a critical study of Stanislavsky's system of acting. His last books to be published before his death were *The Real Chekhov* and a translation of Chekhov's *Four Plays*.

THE BROTHERS KARAMAZOV

FYODOR
DOSTOYEVSKY

TRANSLATED
WITH AN INTRODUCTION BY
DAVID MAGARSHACK

PENGUIN BOOKS

PENGUIN BOOKS

Published by the Penguin Group
27 Wrights Lane, London W8 5TZ, England
Viking Penguin Inc., 40 West 23rd Street, New York, New York 10010, USA
Penguin Books Australia Ltd, Ringwood, Victoria, Australia
Penguin Books Canada Ltd, 2801 John Street, Markham, Ontario, Canada L3R 1B4
Penguin Books (NZ) Ltd, 182–190 Wairau Road, Auckland 10, New Zealand

Penguin Books Ltd, Registered Offices: Harmondsworth, Middlesex, England

This translation first published in two volumes 1958
Reissued in one volume 1982
9 10

Made and printed in Great Britain by
Hazell Watson & Viney Limited
Member of BPCC plc
Aylesbury, Bucks, England
Set in Monotype Bembo

List of Contents

PART TWO

Book Four: Heartaches

Book Five: Pro and Contra

Book Six: The Russian Monk

PART THREE

Book Seven: Alyosha

Book Eight: Mitya

PART FOUR

Book Ten: The Boys

Book Eleven: Ivan Karamazov

DOSTOYEVSKY *began writing* The Brothers Karamazov, *his last and his greatest novel, in June 1878, and finished it in October 1880, about three months before his death.*

'*You can't imagine,*' *he wrote to the Slavophil poet and critic Ivan Aksakov on 21 September 1880, '*how busy I am at present. I am working hard day and night. Yes, I am finishing the Karamazovs and reviewing in my mind the work which I, at any rate, think highly of, for there is a great deal of my own in it. I am, as a rule, highly strung when working – my work gives me a great deal of pain and worry. When working hard, I am even physically ill. Now I am striking a balance of what I have been revolving in my mind for three years, drafting it and writing it down. It has to be done well, that is to say, at least as best as I can. . . . The time has come when it has to be finished and finished without any further delay. . . . In spite of the fact that I have been writing it for three years, I keep re-writing some chapters again and again. I write and reject. . . . Only the inspired passages come off at once, the rest requires a great deal of hard work. . . .*'

As a matter of fact, Dostoyevsky had been revolving the subject of his last novel in his mind for much longer than three years. All his four masterpieces are essentially murder stories, but each of them deals with a different aspect of murder. Crime and Punishment *revolves round the idea whether the murder of an evil old woman, an unscrupulous moneylender, can be justified if it helps to provide the means for a brilliant career of an impecunious student;* The Idiot *deals with murder as a result of carnal passion set against the Christian ideal of forgiveness; in* The Devils *the motive for murder is political, while in* The Brothers Karamazov *it is the most heinous form of murder that comes under close scrutiny – parricide, a subject that seems to have exercised a powerful fascination over Dostoyevsky since early childhood. '*As a boy of ten,*' *Dostoyevsky wrote to a correspondent on 18 August 1880, from Staraya Russa, where he usually spent the summer* months, 'I saw a performance of Schiller's Robbers and, I assure you, the powerful impression it made on me then had a very fructifying influence on my spiritual development.' Dostoyevsky's wife Anna records in her diary that while engaged in writing The Brothers Karamazov her husband again re-read The Robbers, and on one occasion read it aloud to his family. Schiller's play deals with the subject of parricide and the rivalry between two brothers.

This theme Dostoyevsky introduces at the very beginning of his novel by a direct reference to Schiller's play. 'This,' Fyodor Karamazov tells Father Zossima, pointing to his second son Ivan, 'is my most respectful Karl Moor, while this son of mine, Dmitry, who has just come in and against whom I am seeking justice from you, is my most disrespectful Franz Moor, both from Schiller's Robbers, which, I suppose, makes me the Regierender Graf von Moor.' The old man, though, made a mistake: it was Ivan and not Dmitry who, like Franz Moor, had been plotting his father's death and was in love with his elder brother's fiancée.

The genesis of The Brothers Karamazov, however, shows an even closer link with Dostoyevsky's past. For it was during his imprisonment in Siberia that he met a man serving a twenty years' sentence for parricide, who was to supply him with the central idea of the plot of his last novel. He relates this meeting in The House of the Dead, the first great work he wrote after his return from Siberia. The condemned parricide was, like Dmitry Karamazov, a retired lieutenant of a line regiment, by the name of Ilyinsky. (In the first drafts of The Brothers Karamazov the name of Ilyinsky occurs side by side with that of Karamazov.) In the first chapter of The House of the Dead, which appeared in 1861 in Time, the monthly periodical Dostoyevsky published with his elder brother Mikhail, he gives the following account of his meeting with Ilyinsky:

'There is one parricide in particular I cannot forget. He was of noble birth and was regarded by his sixty-year-old father as a kind of prodigal son. He led a riotous life and got himself heavily into debt. His father tried his best to restrain him and persuade him to change his mode of life. But his father owned an estate and was reputed to have money, and so his son murdered him in order to inherit his fortune. The crime was only discovered after a month. The murderer himself had informed the police that his father had disappeared and that his whereabouts were unknown. He spent the whole of that month in a most dissolute fashion. At last the police discovered the body in his absence. There was an open sewer, covered by planks, running across *the whole length of the yard. The body lay in that sewer. It was dressed and carefully laid out, the grey head was cut off and placed beside the trunk, and the murderer had put a pillow under it. He did not confess; he was deprived of his rank and sentenced to twenty years' hard labour in Siberia. All the time I spoke with him he was in a most cheerful frame of mind. He was a muddle-headed, thoughtless, and extremely irrational fellow, but not by any means a fool. I never noticed any special streak of cruelty in him. The convicts despised him not because of his crime, to which they never referred, but because of his folly, because he did not know how to behave himself. In his conversations with me he sometimes spoke of his father. One day, talking to me of the healthy constitution which was characteristic of all the members of his family, he added: "My father, you know, never complained of his health to the very day of his death." Such brutal insensibility is, of course, uncommon; it is a phenomenon, a sort of flaw in a man's make-up, a physical and moral deformity still unknown to science, and not just a crime. I did not actually believe in this crime. But people of his town who ought to have known all the particulars about him told me everything about the case. The facts were so clear that it was impossible not to believe.*

'The convicts,' Dostoyevsky concludes his account, 'overheard him shouting in his sleep one night: "Hold him! Hold him! Cut off his head, his head!"'

But in a subsequent issue of Time Dostoyevsky published the following correction in a note before Chapter VII of The House of the Dead:

'*In the first chapter of* The House of the Dead *I said a few words about a parricide of noble birth. The other day the editor of* Time *received news from Siberia that the criminal had been right all along and had served ten years of imprisonment for nothing; his innocence had been officially established. The real criminals had been found and had confessed and the unhappy man had been released from prison. The editor has no reason to doubt the authenticity of his information. . . . There is nothing more to be said. There is no need to dilate on the tragic significance of this fact and on the dreadful fate of the young man whose life had been ruined by that terrible accusation. The fact needs no comment: it speaks for itself.*'

Ilyinsky was the victim of a miscarriage of justice, which forms the main subject of Dostoyevsky's last novel.

The parricide theme, however, occurred to Dostoyevsky long after he had conceived the idea of writing 'a huge novel' dealing with another great theme of The Brothers Karamazov, *the theme of atheism and the existence of*

God. This idea of his proposed novel Dostoyevsky first discussed in a letter to the poet Apollon Maykov from Florence on 23 December 1868, ten years before he began writing The Brothers Karamazov.

'I have now in mind,' Dostoyevsky wrote, 'a huge novel under the title of Atheism (for God's sake this is strictly between ourselves), but before I can sit down to it I must read almost a whole library of books written by atheists, Catholics, and Greek Orthodox writers. Even if I get an offer for this work, it will be finished no sooner than in two years' time. I have the chief character. A Russian who belongs to our social set, an elderly man, not very well educated, but not entirely uneducated, either, a man of some rank, who suddenly in his old age loses his faith in God. All his life he was only interested in his job in the Civil Service, never left the rut, and had done nothing in particular up to the age of 45. (A psychological explanation, a serious man, a Russian.) His loss of faith in God makes a tremendous impression on him (the background and the action of the novel are conceived on a large scale). He gets mixed up with the younger generation, the atheists, Slavophils, and Europeans, Russian religious fanatics, monks, and priests; gets deeply involved, among others, with a Jesuit propagandist, a Pole; sinks as low as the sect of the flagellants and in the end – regains his faith in Christ as well as in Russia, the Russian God, and the Russian Christ, (for God's sake don't tell anyone about it: so far as I am concerned, I am going to write this last novel even if it kills me. I am going to speak my mind no matter what).'

Fifteen months later, however, he changed the title and to a certain extent the contents of his proposed novel.

'This will be my last novel,' he declared, as it turned out prophetically, in a letter to Maykov from Dresden on 6 April 1870. 'It will be as large as War and Peace and, I am sure, you would approve of the idea of it, at least that is what I have gathered from the talks I have had with you. This novel will consist of five long stories (about fifteen folio pages each; during the last two years the whole plan has matured in my head). The stories will be quite independent of each other, so that they could even be sold separately. The action of the first story takes place in the forties. (The general title of the novel is The Life of a Great Sinner, but each story will have a different title.) The main question that will be discussed in all the parts is one that has worried me, consciously or unconsciously, all my life – the existence of God. During his life my hero is at times an atheist, at times a believer, a fanatic, a dissenter and, again, an atheist. The second story will take place in a *monastery. I put all my hopes on this second story. Perhaps people will at last say that not everything I have written is a lot of nonsense. (I am telling this to you alone: I want to make Tikhon Zadonsky the chief character of the second story, under another name, of course, but he too will be a bishop living in retirement in a monastery.) A thirteen-year-old boy, who took part in a criminal act, precocious and dissipated (I know the type), the future hero of my novel, is put into a monastery by his parents (our own set, cultured), where he is to be educated. A wolf-cub, a nihilist, the boy makes friends with Tikhon (you know Tikhon's character and personality, don't you?). . . . It is true,' he concludes, 'I shall not create anything but only show the real Tikhon whom I have taken to my heart long ago. . . . The first story will deal with my hero's childhood. . . .'* (Dostoyevsky had made an attempt to introduce Tikhon in The Devils, and in June 1879 he paid a visit to the bishop at the Optina monastery, together with the young philosopher-poet Vladimir Solovyov. They spent a week at the monastery, and Dostoyevsky incorporated his impressions of his visit in the descriptions of the monastery in The Brothers Karamazov. Father Zossima, too, was modelled on Tikhon.)

Dostoyevsky wrote in almost identical terms to the critic Strakhov, concluding his letter by the assertion that he had decided to make 'this idea of mine into the culmination of my career, for I can't expect to live and write for more than another six or seven years'.

In the meantime however, the political events in Russia, where he had returned on 20 July 1871, and, particularly, the growing revolutionary terrorist movement there, made him postpone his plan of writing his 'huge novel' and write The Devils instead. He also resumed his journalistic work by editing the conservative periodical The Citizen, in which he began publishing his extreme reactionary views in his Diary of a Writer, which he subsequently published independently, the last two issues appearing shortly before his death. 'During these years,' a close friend of his records, 'he never regained the composure which is natural to people who carry on quietly with their work. His inner tension hardly ever left him. He was in a constant state of nervousness and irritability, especially during the last years of his life.' By the time he began writing The Brothers Karamazov he had become, according to the same authority, extraordinarily emaciated and the slightest effort exhausted him. He suffered from emphysema, and it was a burst blood vessel in his lungs, complicated by an attack of epilepsy, that finally killed him: he died on 9 February 1881.

Dostoyevsky jotted down the first draft of The Brothers Karamazov in the autumn of 1874, about four years before he actually sat down to write the novel. This draft follows closely the Ilyinsky episode, and contains most of the elements of Mitya's story.

'13th Sept./74,' Dostoyevsky wrote. 'Drama. In Tobolsk, twenty years ago, something like the Ilyinsky episode. Two brothers, an old father, one of the brothers has a fiancée with whom the second brother is secretly and enviously in love. But she loves the elder one. The elder brother, a young lieutenant, leads a riotous and foolish life. He quarrels with his father. The father disappears. Nothing is heard of him for several days. The brothers discuss their inheritance and suddenly the police arrive: they dig up the father's body from the cellar. The evidence points to the elder brother (the younger brother does not live with them). The elder brother is tried and sentenced to hard labour in Siberia. (N.B. He quarrelled with his father, boasted about his mother's inheritance, and other foolish things.) When he entered the room even his fiancée recoiled from him. He was drunk and said: "Do you, too, believe I did it?" (The evidence has been cleverly fabricated by the younger brother.) The public is not sure who the murderer is.

'The scene in Siberia. The convicts want to kill him. The prison authorities. He does not betray them. The prison governor reproves him for having killed his father.

'Twelve years later. His brother comes to see him. A scene in which they understand each other without uttering a word. Seven years pass after that meeting. The younger brother is a person of high rank and occupies an important post in the Civil Service. But he is greatly worried, a hypochondriac. Tells his wife that it was he who killed his father. "Why did you tell me that?" He goes to see his brother. His wife, too, arrives. The wife implores the convict on her knees not to tell and to save her husband. The convict says: "I'm used to it." They make it up. "You're punished as it is," says the elder brother.

'The younger brother's birthday party. The guests assemble. He comes in. "I am the murderer." They think it's a stroke.

'The end: the elder brother is released, the younger brother sent to Siberia. The younger brother asks the elder one to be the father of his children. "He has entered upon the right path!"'

At the time these notes were written Dostoyevsky was working at his novel The Adolescent, and it was during that period that he jotted down a great number of notes which he afterwards made use of in his plot of The

Brothers Karamazov. *In one of these notes he already outlines the life-histories of the three Karamazov brothers.*

'*Preparations for the marriage of the second brother Fyodor,*' he wrote. '*The younger one goes out and meets Lambert. Tells him about his family. "Is there a devil?" the third brother asks the elder one. Meanwhile the rebellion of the children. And so one brother is an atheist and in despair. The other one is a fanatic. The third – the coming generation, a living force, new men. (And the newest generation – children.)*'

The children theme is first elaborated in notes for a separate novel: '*A novel about children, only about children and the child-hero. N.B. (save a suffering child, stratagems, etc.). We found a child left on our doorstep. Fyodor Petrovich (a lover of children and wet nurses). Fyodor Petr., addressing the children after he had carried out their commissions, says: "Children, I've done what you told me and I'm going to give you a full account of it now." Or, "Children, I've read this or that book," and then he tells them about politics, etc. N.B. (he is a grown-up child himself and is full of the deepest and liveliest feeling of love for children). The children plot to organize their own children's empire. Children's arguments about a republic or a monarchy. The children get in touch with the delinquent children in prison. The children – fire-raisers and wreckers of trains. The children convert the devil. Children – debauchees and atheists. Lambert. Andrieux. Children – parricides (Moscow News No. 89. 12 April). A civil servant, his marriage, a foundling [illegible], home for delinquent children, he accepts a bribe, resigns.*'

The maltreatment of children is touched upon in the draft of yet another novel: '*A fantastic poem-novel: the future society, the Paris revolution and Commune, victory. 200 million heads, terrible sores, dissipation, destruction of the arts, libraries, a tortured child. Quarrels, lawlessness. Death.*

'*Children. Mother marries a second time. A group of orphans. Half brothers and half sisters. The champion of truth. Death of the worn-out mother. The children's protest. Run away? They go out into the street. The champion alone. Wanderings, etc.*'

In his notes for the year 1877 there are also indications that Dostoyevsky was contemplating writing novels under the titles of '*The Russian Candide*', '*A Book on Christ*', and '*The Forties*'. The last-named novel contains a number of notes that bear a direct relationship to some of the themes in The Brothers Karamazov: '*The Forties. Book of Wanderings. Ordeals (1, 2, 3, 4, 5, 6, etc.). Satan: We were all deceived. [Young man]: What maddens me most of all is that you have been appointed to look after me. . . . Why, you even accept God as something that has been cast off.'*

Another brief note contains the following chapter heading that must have been intended definitely for The Brothers Karamazov: 'The Devil. Ivan Fyodorovich's Nightmare.' A further note, later elaborated in the chapter of Ivan and the devil, reads: 'The man who shot himself and the devil, something like Faust. Can be joined to the poem-novel.'

The first mention of Lizaveta Smerdyashchaya occurs in Dostoyevsky's notes as early as in 1874–5: 'Lizaveta Smerdyashchaya. Send me, the stinking one, not to thee into paradise, but into hell, so that out of the torment and the fire I may cry to thee: thou art holy, holy, and I have no other love. . . . '

At first Dostoyevsky intended to deal with one of the main themes of The Brothers Karamazov, *the disintegration of the Russian family and the Russian State,* in a separate novel under the title of 'Disorder'. The note referring to it is dated 26 August 1875: 'The title of the novel is "Disorder". The whole idea of the novel is to show that universal disorder now reigns everywhere in society, in its affairs, in its leading ideas (which for that reason do not exist), in its convictions (which do not exist, either), in the disintegration of family life. If passionate convictions do exist, they are only destructive ones (socialism). There are no moral ideas left, not a single one remains, and the main thing is that he talks as if they never existed. "But you are religious, aren't you?" "You did not expect me not to be, did you?" '

All these themes, roughly sketched in the notes quoted above, Dostoyevsky finally incorporated in his last novel. But even when he began writing it, his idea of its ultimate form was still very vague. In his foreword to the reader, he reduced the five novels of his first plan to two, the second of which was to be the main novel and was to deal with the life of Alyosha Karamazov 'in our time', as he put it. But, as always with Dostoyevsky, his first intentions never worked out as he planned them. Alyosha, as he appears in the later books of the novel, plays quite an insignificant part in the development of the plot and becomes a very shadowy figure indeed when compared with the figures of his father, his two brothers Mitya and Ivan, and his half-brother Smerdyakov. It is obvious that Dostoyevsky himself lost interest in him, and that the few pages he devotes to him in Book Seven was all he had to say about him.

The idea that Dostoyevsky did not finish his novel, based on his rather *confused foreword to the reader, is entirely unsubstantiated. Dostoyevsky himself admitted it in his letter to Ivan Aksakov, quoted at the beginning of this introduction, and in another letter to one of his closest friends, written from Staraya Russa on 7 September 1880. 'In spite of the lovely weather,' he wrote, 'I sit day and night over my work – I am finishing the Karamazovs. I shall finish it by the end of September and then return [to Petersburg].' On the other hand, he realized more than anyone else perhaps that the novel in its final form was far from perfect. 'I know,' he wrote to a correspondent in April 1880, 'that, like many other writers, I have many faults, for I am the first to be dissatisfied with myself. . . . At the moment when I am trying to review my life's work, I often realize with pain that I have literally failed to express one-twentieth part of what I had wanted to, and perhaps could have expressed. The thing that comforts me is the constant hope that one day God will grant me so much inspiration . . . that I shall be able to express myself more fully, that, in short, I shall express all that is locked in my heart and in my imagination. . . . I cannot help feeling that there is much more hidden in me than I have hitherto been able to express as a writer. And yet,' he concludes, 'speaking without false modesty, there is a great deal that is true and that came from my heart in what I have expressed already.'*

The Brothers Karamazov, then, is, first of all, a picture of Russia as Dostoyevsky saw it in the turbulent years at the end of the seventies and at the beginning of the eighties of the last century. 'Combine all the four main characters [of the novel],' Dostoyevsky wrote to Katkov, the reactionary editor of The Moscow Herald, in which the novel was being serialized, 'and you will get a picture, reduced perhaps to a thousandth degree, of our contemporary educated Russia: that is why I regard my task as so important.' And in further letters to Katkov, he defined Ivan Karamazov's rebellion as 'the synthesis of our modern Russian anarchism', or, in other words, the Russian revolutionary movement of his day. 'The modern negationist,' he wrote to Katkov, 'declares himself openly in favour of the devil's advice and maintains that it is more likely to result in man's happiness than the teachings of Christ. To our foolish but terrible Russian socialism (for our youth is mixed up in it) it is a directive and, it seems, a very powerful one: the loaves of bread, the Tower of Babel (that is, the future reign of socialism) and the complete enslavement of the freedom of conscience – that is what the desperate negationist is striving to achieve. The difference is,' Dostoyevsky continues, 'that our socialists (and they are not only the hole-and-corner nihilists) are conscious Jesuits and liars who do not admit that their ideal is *the ideal of the coercion of the human conscience and the reduction of mankind to the level of cattle. While my socialist (Ivan Karamazov) is a sincere man who frankly admits that he agrees with the views of the Grand Inquisitor and that Christianity seems to have raised man much higher than his actual position entitles him. The question I should like to put to them is, in a nutshell, this: "Do you despise or do you respect mankind, you – its future saviours?"'*

In another letter Dostoyevsky quite openly declares that his main task in writing The Brothers Karamazov *was the defeat of 'anarchism', which he considered to be his 'civic duty'.*

Dostoyevsky's personal involvement in the social and political life of his country becomes even more evident in the last chapters of his novel in which he attacks the newly formed courts and trial by jury. Dostoyevsky shared the opinion of Pobedonostsev, the reactionary Procurator of the Holy Synod, whom he is known to have consulted on the various aspects of his novel, about the newfangled trials by jury as 'the talking shop of lawyers as a result of which the most terrible crimes, indubitable murders, and other grave felonies remain unpunished'. He was present at the famous trial in 1878 of Vera Zasulich, the twenty-seven-year-old terrorist, who was acquitted by the jury of her attempt on the life of the Petersburg Governor-General. Her acquittal was followed by a concerted attack on trial by jury by the conservative press, an attack in which Dostoyevsky joined. In fact, he went so far as to reproduce many of the incidents of the trial of Vera Zasulich in the trial of Mitya Karamazov. Thus, Mitya's trial for murder, we are told, 'had become known all over Russia', and, in spite of the fact that it was quite an ordinary, sordid case of murder without any political implications whatsoever, it had caused such 'an immense shock' that all sorts of 'distinguished personages' with 'stars on their frock-coats' (as at the trial of Vera Zasulich) travelled from Petersburg to Skotoprigonyevsk, the remote provincial town, which Dostoyevsky had given such an unsavoury name (the English equivalent of it would be Pigsty). The presence of many fashionable ladies at the trial was another of the features Dostoyevsky copied from the trial of the terrorist girl. But more significant still are Dostoyevsky's descriptions of the presiding judge, the public prosecutor, and the counsel for the defence, all of whom were recognizable copies of the judge, prosecutor, and defending counsel of Vera Zasulich. Dostoyevsky made his intention of satirizing the new trials by jury quite clear in a letter to Pobedonostsev in which he drew the Procurator's attention to the September issue of The Russian Herald.

'*In this September issue,*' he wrote, '*will be a description of a trial, of our public prosecutors and lawyers – and all this will be shown up in a special light.*'

Equally characteristic of Dostoyevsky's methods as a novelist is the great pains he took to check up on the sources of the different incidents in his novel. In one of his letters to Pobedonostsev he underlines the fact that in one of the most important '*books*' of his novel, Pro and Contra ('*blasphemy and the refutation of blasphemy*'), '*I have not betrayed the principles of realism even in so abstract a subject.*' He tells Katkov that he had sought the advice of two public prosecutors in Petersburg before he wrote the description of Mitya's trial, and had checked up on '*the medical condition*' of Ivan with medical specialists and the details of Father Zossima's burial with members of the Holy Synod. Smerdyakov's song in the chapter '*Smerdyakov with a Guitar*', he wrote to Katkov, '*was not composed by me, but written down in Moscow. I heard it forty years ago. It was composed by some Moscow shop-assistants and passed on to the footmen. It had never been written down by our collectors of folk-songs and it appears in my novel for the first time.*' The legend about the onion had also been written down by Dostoyevsky. '*I ask you particularly,*' he wrote to Katkov, '*to go through the proofs of the legend very carefully. This gem was written down by me from the words of a peasant woman and* quite certainly written down for the first time.' The stories of the maltreatment of children, too, were taken from actual life. '*Everything my hero (Ivan) relates in the text I am sending you,*' he wrote to Katkov, '*is based on actual facts. All the incidents about the children actually happened and were published in the papers, and I can show you where – nothing has been invented by me. The general who hunted down the child with his hounds and the whole of that incident is an actual occurrence published last winter in the* Archives, *I believe, and republished in many newspapers.*'

Dostoyevsky took particular care about the episode with the children, which he quite seriously intended to provide a solution to the political strife in Russia and which peters out so disastrously in the epilogue. '*In your letter,*' he wrote to a correspondent on 28 March 1878, '*I was particularly struck by the fact that you love children, that you spent a great deal of your time with them and that even now you are so often with them. And so I would like to ask you a great favour: I am soon to begin a new novel in which children are to take part, and particularly children between the ages of seven and fifteen. There will be many children. I am studying them and have* been studying them all my life. I am very fond of them and I have some myself. But the observations of a man like you would be invaluable to me. And so please write to me everything you know about children. (*Incidents, habits, replies, words, sayings, traits of character, attitude to their families, their faith, their misdeeds and innocence; nature and teacher, Latin, etc., etc., in short, everything you know.*) You will help me very much and I shall be very grateful to you. . . . ' For his chapters about the children Dostoyevsky also studied the works of Pestalozzi and Froebel, and read the articles on schools by Leo Tolstoy.

It was by these means that Dostoyevsky sought to deepen and widen the realistic features of his novel (realism, as can be gathered from Mitya's use of this term, was one of the most popular literary slogans of that period). In the creation of his characters, however, Dostoyevsky departed from the cruder forms of realism by which he sought to give authenticity to the various incidents in his novel. His aim as a creative writer, he declared in his diary, was 'to find the man in man. I am called a psychologist,' Dostoyevsky writes. 'It is not true. I am only a realist in the highest sense of the word, that is to say, I depict all the depths of the human soul.' There was a curious dichotomy in Dostoyevsky's nature; in his journalistic works, and especially in his Diary of a Writer, he expressed views and opinions which for sheer crudity and lack of vision can hardly be paralleled in the case of any other great writer, whereas in his creative works, and especially in The Brothers Karamazov, he achieves a profundity of thought that surpasses anything written in his or, indeed, any other time. He needed what he himself called 'inspiration' to overcome his petty resentment against his political enemies, his racial prejudices, and more particularly his hatred of his more successful literary rivals. In the Legend of the Grand Inquisitor, which Dostoyevsky himself characterized as 'the culminating point of my literary activity', he launched an indirect attack on socialism by making Ivan accept what he considered to be the ultimate policies of the Catholic Church. 'By the stones and the loaves of bread,' Dostoyevsky himself commented, 'I meant our present social problems. Present-day socialism in Europe and in our country as well sets Christ aside and is first of all concerned about bread. It appeals to science and maintains that the cause of all human misfortune is poverty, the struggle for existence and the wrong kind of environment.' But actually the Legend of the Grand Inquisitor transcends the political divisions of mankind and presents the problem of the human predicament in its universal aspect. Again, however controversial Dostoyevsky's idea of expiation of sin *through suffering may appear, it is fully justified when he puts it into the mouth of Dmitry Karamazov.*

It is through the fullest possible integration of idea and character that Dostoyevsky achieves his greatest triumph not only as a creative artist, but also as a profound and fearless thinker. Indeed, the paradox of Dostoyevsky as a writer is that he puts the case against what he himself stands for much stronger than the case for his own ideas and convictions. Father Zossima's pious platitudes are never as convincing as Ivan's 'blasphemies'. Even in Father Zossima's case, his ideas of Christian morality catch fire only when Dostoyevsky gives them a fictional form, as in Father Zossima's account of his dying brother's conversion, his duel, and the story of the mysterious visitor. In this lack of consistency between Dostoyevsky the creative writer and Dostoyevsky the man lies the great tragedy of his life, and it is this perhaps more than anything else that accounts for his irritable and suspicious temperament, which was such a trial even to his closest friends. After his triumphant speech at the unveiling of the memorial to Pushkin in Moscow in June 1880, he remarked sadly: 'The main thing about me they don't understand. They extol me for not being satisfied with the present political condition of our country, but they don't see that I am showing them the way to the church.'

In The Brothers Karamazov, *too, Dostoyevsky saw the solution of Russian troubles in the Greek Orthodox Church, but that is not why his novel is recognized as the greatest achievement of his genius. It is in the universal human drama that its greatness lies, and not in Dostoyevsky's ill-contrived attempt to transform Russia into a huge monastery.*

D. M.

To the Reader

IN beginning the biography of my hero, Alexey Fyodorovich Karamazov, I find myself in some difficulty. What I mean is that though I call Alexey Karamazov my hero, I know perfectly well that he is not by any means a great man, and for this reason I can foresee all sorts of inevitable questions, such as: What is so remarkable about Alexey Karamazov that you should have chosen him for your hero? What exactly has he done? Who knows of him and what is he known for? Why should I, your reader, waste my time studying the facts of his life?

The last question is the most vital one, for all I can say in reply to it is that perhaps you will find it out for yourself from the novel. But what if after reading the novel you do not? What if you do not agree that my Alexey Karamazov is in any way remarkable? I am saying this because unhappily it may turn out to be so. He is remarkable so far as I am concerned, but I doubt very much whether I shall be able to prove it to my readers. The trouble is that though, in a way, he is a man of action, he is so only in a vague sort of way, in a way that is not quite clear. Still, it would be strange to demand clarity from people at a time like ours. One thing, though, is beyond question: he is a strange, almost eccentric sort of man. But strangeness and eccentricity are more likely to give a man a bad name than a claim to attention, especially when everyone today seems eager to reduce personality to a common denominator and find some sort of sense amid the general confusion of ideas. An eccentric, on the other hand, is mostly a personality and an exception. Isn't that so?

Now, if you don't agree with my last statement and reply, It is not so, or, It is not always so, I might feel happier about the importance of my hero. For far from 'always' being a personality and an exception, an eccentric sometimes, on the contrary, expresses the very sum and substance of a certain period while the other people of the same period for some reason or other do not seem to belong to it, just as though they had been cast up by the tide.

I wouldn't have indulged in these highly uninteresting and obscure explanations, but would have begun simply without an introduction: if they like it, they'll read it as it is; but the trouble is that while I am dealing with one biography, I have two novels on my hands. The main novel is the second one – it deals with the activity of my hero in our own day, I mean, at this very moment. The action of the first novel, on the other hand, takes place thirteen years ago and is not really a novel but just a chapter out of my hero's adolescence. It is quite impossible for me to dispense with the first novel because without it a great deal in the second novel would be unintelligible. But this fact makes my original difficulty much more complicated: if I, the biographer, find that even one novel would be too much for such a modest and unheroic hero, then why on earth do I come out with two novels, and what is more: how do I explain such arrogance on my part?

Quite at a loss to find an answer to these questions, the best thing I can do is to leave them without an answer. No doubt the perspicacious reader has long ago guessed that that is exactly what I have been driving at and cannot help being vexed with me for wasting words and precious time. To this I can truthfully say that I wasted words and precious time first out of courtesy and, secondly, out of cunning: I have, so to speak, warned you in good time. As a matter of fact, I am glad that my novel has been split into two stories in spite of the fact that it really forms one whole; for having acquainted himself with the first story, the reader will be able to decide for himself whether it is worth his while to begin the second. No one, of course, is forced to do anything, and the reader can, if he likes, close the book after reading two pages of the first story and never open it again. But there are conscientious readers who will insist on reading to the end so as not to prejudice their impartial judgement. Such, for instance, are all Russian critics. Confronted with people of this sort I should feel easier in my mind if I told them that, in spite of their conscientiousness, I am only too glad to provide them with an excuse to give up reading the novel after the first episode. Well, that's all I have to say in my introduction. I quite agree that it is unnecessary, but as it is already written, it may as well remain.

And now to business.

THE BROTHERS
KARAMAZOV

Verily, verily, I say unto you,
Except a corn of wheat fall into the ground
and die, it abideth alone : but if it die,
it bringeth forth much fruit.

ST JOHN XII. 24

✦ PART ONE ✦

BOOK ONE: THE HISTORY OF A FAMILY

I

Fyodor Pavlovich Karamazov

ALEXEY FYODOROVICH KARAMAZOV WAS THE THIRD SON OF Fyodor Pavlovich Karamazov, a landowner of our district, who became notorious in his own day (and is still remembered among us) because of his tragic and mysterious death, which occurred exactly thirteen years ago and which I shall relate in its proper place. For the present all I shall say about this 'landowner' (as we used to call him, though he hardly ever lived on his estate) is that he was a strange sort of individual, yet one that is met with pretty frequently, the sort of man who is not only worthless and depraved, but also muddle-headed – though one of those muddle-headed men who know very well how to bring off their far from honest business deals and, it would seem, nothing else. Fyodor Karamazov, for instance, began with next to nothing. He was a very small landowner, who always contrived to get himself invited to dinner and persistently aspired to the role of sponger. And yet at his death it was found that he left as much as a hundred thousand roubles in hard cash. And at the same time he continued all his life to be one of the most muddle-headed and preposterous fellows of our district. I repeat: it was not stupidity, for most of these preposterous fellows are rather clever and cunning, but sheer muddle-headedness, and of a special national kind at that.

He was married twice and had three sons – the eldest Dmitry by his first wife, and the other two, Ivan and Alexey, by his second. His first wife belonged to the fairly rich old aristocratic family of the Miusovs, who were also landowners in our district. How exactly it came about that a girl with a dowry, a beautiful girl too, one of those girls of character and intelligence who are often to be found in this generation and were not uncommon in the last, could have married such a poor specimen of a man, as he was called by everyone, I won't even try to explain. Why, I knew a young girl of the last 'romantic' generation who had for several years been consumed by an enigmatic passion for a certain gentleman whom she could have married at any time without any trouble at all, but who, after inventing all sorts of insurmountable difficulties, in the end threw herself one stormy night from a high cliff into a fairly deep and rapid river and was drowned out of sheer caprice, simply because she wanted to be like Shakespeare's Ophelia. Indeed, had the cliff, which she had discovered long before and which had become her favourite spot, not been so picturesque and had there been a prosaic flat river bank instead, she would perhaps never have committed suicide at all. This is a true story, and I should not be surprised if during the last two or three generations there were not a few similar or identical occurrences. In the same way, Adelaida Miusov's action was, no doubt, a reflection of other people's ideas and the impulse of a mind cribbed and confined. She may have wanted to show her feminine independence, to challenge the social conventions and the tyranny of her class and her family, and an accommodating imagination persuaded her, let us say, only for a brief moment, that Fyodor Karamazov, in spite of his status as a sponger, was one of the bravest and wittiest men of that progressively improving epoch, while as a matter of fact he was nothing but an ill-natured clown. The affair acquired still greater piquancy from the fact that it involved an elopement, and this greatly appealed to Adelaida. As for Fyodor Karamazov, he was at the time very much disposed towards enterprises of this kind by his social position, for he passionately desired to make a career for himself by fair means or foul; and to insinuate himself into a good family and get a dowry was a very attractive proposition. As for love, there does not seem to have been any of it at all – neither on the part of the bride nor on his part, in spite of Adelaida's good looks. So that this was perhaps the only case of its kind in the life of Fyodor Karamazov, a most licentious man all his life, who was ready at a moment's notice to run after any petticoat at the slightest sign of encouragement. And yet this woman alone aroused no sexual desire in him whatever.

Immediately after her elopement Adelaida realized in a flash that she felt nothing but contempt for her husband. The results of the marriage consequently became apparent with extraordinary rapidity. In spite of the fact that her family got reconciled to her marriage fairly soon and gave the runaway bride her dowry, husband and wife began to lead a cat and dog existence and there were everlasting rows between them. It was said that during their quarrels the young wife showed much more generosity and high-mindedness than her husband, who, as is now known, cheated her out of all her money to the amount of twenty-five thousand roubles as soon as she had received it, so that after that she never saw a farthing of all those thousands. In addition, he tried very hard to transfer the little estate and the fairly substantial town house, which were also part of her dowry, to his own name by the drawing up of a deed of gift. He would most certainly have succeeded in his attempt merely, as it were, because of the contempt and disgust which he constantly aroused in her by his shameless solicitations and importunities, and also because she was so sick and tired of him that she would have done anything to be left in peace. Fortunately, however, Adelaida's family intervened and restrained the swindler. It is known for a fact that there were frequent fights between husband and wife, but according to the stories current in our town it was not Karamazov but Adelaida who did the beating, for she was a short-tempered lady, fearless, impatient, dark-complexioned, endowed with extraordinary physical strength. At last she left the house and ran away with an impoverished and destitute teacher, a graduate of a religious seminar, leaving the three-year-old Mitya to be looked after by her husband. Karamazov at once turned his household into a regular harem and took to giving disorderly drinking-parties; in between these orgies he used to drive almost all over the province, complaining tearfully to all and sundry of Adelaida for having left him and going into details that any husband should have been thoroughly ashamed to give about his married life. He seemed, indeed, to be pleased and even flattered to play the ridiculous part of an injured husband before the whole world, and went into lurid details of the injuries he had suffered. 'One would think you'd got a promotion,' the scoffers used to say to him, 'you seem so pleased in spite of your great distress.' Many even added that he was glad to appear once more in his role of a clown and that, to provoke even stronger outbursts of laughter, he pretended not to notice his ludicrous position. But who knows, perhaps he did it simply because he was rather naïve at heart. At last he succeeded in discovering the whereabouts of his runaway wife. The poor woman, it seems, was in Petersburg, where she had gone with her seminarist and where she had plunged headlong into a life of complete emancipation. Karamazov at once got busy and began to make preparations to go to Petersburg. Why? That, of course, he did not know himself. And he would perhaps really have gone; but, having made up his mind to go, he at once felt himself fully entitled to indulge in a most unrestrained drinking orgy so as to get the courage he needed for the journey. And just at that time his wife's family received the news of her death in Petersburg. She seems to have died suddenly in some attic, according to one version, of typhus, and another, of starvation. Karamazov learnt of his wife's death when he was drunk and, it is said, rushed out into the street, and, raising his hands to heaven in his joy, began shouting: 'Lord, now lettest thou thy servant depart in peace!' According to others, he sobbed aloud like a little child, so much so that, it is said, people were sorry to look at him in spite of the disgust he inspired. Quite likely both versions are true, that is to say, that he rejoiced at his release and wept for her who had given him his freedom – at one and the same time. In the majority of cases, people, even evil-doers, are much more naïve and artless than we generally assume. As, indeed, we are ourselves.

2

He Turns Out His Eldest Son

IT is, of course, not difficult to imagine the sort of father such a man would be and what upbringing he would give his children. As a father, he was exactly what one might expect him to be, that is to say, he completely abandoned the child of his first marriage, not out of malice, nor because of any injured matrimonial feelings, but simply because he completely forgot about his existence. While he was boring everyone with his complaints and tears and turning his home into a sink of corruption, Grigory Kutuzov, a faithful servant of the family, took the three-year-old Mitya under his care; if he had not done so at the time, there would not have been anyone to change the child's shirt. Besides, as it happened, the little boy's relations on his mother's side seemed at first also to have forgotten him. His grandfather, that is, Mr Miusov himself, Adelaida's father, was no longer alive; his widow, Mitya's grandmother, had moved to Moscow where she fell seriously ill, while Adelaida's sisters had all married, so that Mitya had to remain for almost a year under Grigory's care and live with him in the servants' cottage. However, if his father had remembered him (and he could not really have been entirely unaware of his existence), he would have sent him back to the cottage, for the child would still have interfered with his debaucheries. Just at that time, however, Peter Miusov, a cousin of Mitya's mother, happened to return from Paris. Afterwards he spent many years abroad, but just then he was still quite a young man, but one who, unlike the rest of the Miusovs, was highly cultured. He had lived in Petersburg and abroad and was, besides, all his life a European *par excellence*, and towards the end of his life a liberal of the forties and the fifties. In the course of his career he had come into contact with many of the most liberal men of his time, both in Russia and abroad. He had known both Proudhon and Bakunin personally and, towards the end of his wanderings, was particularly fond of recalling and describing the three days of the Paris Revolution of February 1848, hinting that he had almost taken part in the fighting on the barricades himself. That was one of the most delightful memories of his youth. He was a man of independent means, owning, according to the old way of reckoning, about a thousand serfs. His splendid estate was on the very outskirts of our small town and bordered on the lands of our famous monastery. Against this, while still a very young man, he began, as soon as he came into his inheritance, an interminable lawsuit about the fishing rights in the river or the wood-cutting rights in the forest, I am not sure which, but he conceived it his duty as a citizen and a man of culture to start an action in the courts against 'the clericals'. Having heard all about Adelaida, whom, of course, he remembered and to whom at one time he had even felt attracted, and learning about Mitya's existence, he took a hand in the affair in spite of all his youthful indignation and his contempt for Karamazov. It was on this occasion that he made Karamazov's acquaintance for the first time.

He told him bluntly that he would like to be responsible for the child's upbringing. Long afterwards he used to recount as a characteristic trait that when he mentioned Mitya to Karamazov, the latter looked for some time as though he did not understand what child he was talking about and even seemed surprised to learn that he had a little son somewhere in his house. If Miusov's story was somewhat exaggerated, there was still something in it that rang true. But all through his life, as a matter of fact, Karamazov liked to dissemble, to play some unexpected part before you, sometimes, moreover, without the slightest need for it, indeed even to his direct disadvantage, as, for instance, in the present case. This trait, however, is characteristic of a great many people, some of them very clever people, too, and not only of a man like Karamazov. Miusov threw himself warmly into this business and was even appointed (jointly with Karamazov) the guardian of the child, for after all there was a small estate, a house, and some land left by his mother. Mitya did, in fact, go to live with his mother's cousin, but having no family of his own, Miusov, after settling his affairs and making sure of the revenues from his estates, made haste to return to Paris, where he intended to spend a long time, and left the boy in the charge of one of his cousins, an old lady living in Moscow. It so happened that, having settled permanently in Paris, he, too, forgot all about the child, especially when the February Revolution broke out, which had made such a strong impression on his mind and which he could never forget for the rest of his life. The Moscow lady died and Mitya was taken in charge by one of her married daughters. It would seem that after that he changed his home for a fourth time. I shall not dilate on that now, particularly as I shall have to tell a great deal of Karamazov's first-born later on, but confine myself now to the most essential facts about him without which I could not even start my novel.

To begin with, Mitya was the only one of Karamazov's three sons who grew up in the belief that he, at any rate, possessed some property and that when he was of age he would be independent. He spent a turbulent boyhood and youth: he did not finish his course at the secondary school, entered a military college, was stationed in the Caucasus, promoted to a higher rank, fought a duel, reduced to the ranks, again obtained promotion, led a riotous life and spent, comparatively speaking, a great deal of money. He did not begin to receive money from his father until he came of age and till then ran into debt. He got to know and saw his father for the first time only after coming of age when he arrived in our town for the sole purpose of clearing up their misunderstanding about his property. Apparently he did not like his father even then; he did not stay long with him, but left in a hurry, having managed to obtain a certain sum of money from him and entering into some sort of agreement with him about the future receipt of revenues from his estate, an estimate of the value of which (a highly interesting fact that) he was quite unable to obtain from his father on that occasion. Karamazov noticed from the very first moment of his meeting with his eldest son (and this too must be kept in mind) that Mitya had an exaggerated and quite wrong idea of the value of his property. Karamazov, for reasons of his own, was very well satisfied with this. He came to the conclusion that the young man was thoughtless, violent, passionate, impatient, dissipated, and that, if he were given some money occasionally, he would at once be satisfied, though only for a short time, of course. It was this that Karamazov began to exploit, that is to say, he would fob him off with small sums of money, which he sent him from time to time. In the end Mitya, having lost patience, made an appearance in our town four years later in order to come to a final settlement with his father. It was then that to his great astonishment he suddenly discovered that he had absolutely nothing left, that it was quite impossible to say how much money he had received from his father, that what he had received from him already exceeded the value of his property and that he was probably even in debt to him; that because of certain transactions into which he had entered at certain specified dates of his own free will he had no right to demand anything more, and so on and so forth. The young man was stunned, suspected his father of lying and deceiving him, was almost beside himself and really seemed to have gone out of his mind. It was this circumstance that led to the catastrophe, the account of which forms the subject of my first introductory novel, or rather the external side of it. But before I pass on to this novel, I must say something of Karamazov's other two sons, Mitya's brothers, and of their origin.

3

Second Marriage and Other Children

HAVING got his four-year-old Mitya off his hands, Karamazov very soon married a second time. His second marriage lasted eight years. He took his second wife, Sophia Ivanovna, who was also a very young woman, from another province where he had gone on some small contracting business with some Jew as his partner. Though Karamazov drank and led a disorderly and debauched life, he never neglected investing his capital and was always successful in managing his affairs, though, of course, almost always in a rather mean and shabby way. Sophia was an 'orphan child', the daughter of some obscure deacon, who had been left without relations since her early childhood. She grew up in the wealthy house of her benefactress, her instructor, and her tormentor – an aristocratic lady, the widow of General Vorokhov. I do not know the details, I have only heard that the poor adopted girl, a meek, inoffensive, gentle creature, was once cut down after she had attempted to hang herself from a nail in a box-room – so hard did she find it to put up with the caprices and constant reproofs of this apparently far from ill-natured old woman who had become an insufferable, mean, and tyrannical woman through sheer idleness. Karamazov made her a proposal of marriage, inquiries were made about him, and he was sent packing; and it was then that, as in his first marriage, he suggested an elopement to the orphan girl. It is very likely that she too would not have married him for anything in the world, if she had found out a little more about him in good time. But it all happened in another province; and, besides, what could a sixteen-year-old girl be expected to know, except perhaps that she'd sooner throw herself into the river than remain with her benefactress. So it was that the poor girl exchanged a benefactress for a benefactor. This time Karamazov did not get a penny, for the general's widow was furious, gave them nothing and would have nothing more to do with them. But he had not counted on getting anything: he was greatly attracted by the remarkable beauty of the innocent young girl and, chiefly, by her air of innocence which made a powerful impression on a voluptuary like him, who till then had been a depraved admirer of only the coarser kind of feminine beauty. 'Those sweet innocent eyes cut my heart like a knife at the time,' he used to say afterwards, sniggering loathsomely as was his wont. However, in such a lecherous man that, too, might have been only a sensual attraction. Having taken her without any money, he did not stand on ceremony with her, and taking advantage of the fact that she was, as it were, 'guilty' towards him and that he had practically 'cut her down', as well as of her phenomenal meekness and lamb-like timidity, he did not hesitate to trample on the ordinary decencies of married life. Women of the streets used to come to his house while his wife was there, and they would have wild parties. To show what actually used to happen, I may mention that the servant Grigory Kutuzov, a gloomy, stupid and obstinate moralist, who had hated his former mistress, this time took his new mistress's side, defended her and quarrelled with Karamazov because of her in a manner that was hardly permissible from a servant, and one day he even broke up the party and threw all the hussies out of the house. Later on the unhappy young woman, terrorized since her childhood, contracted one of those women's nervous diseases which are most often found in the country among village women, who are called 'shriekers' because of it. This illness, accompanied as it was by terrible fits of hysteria, at times deprived her of her reason. Yet she bore Karamazov two sons, Ivan and Alexey, the first in the first year of marriage, and the second three years later. When she died, little Alexey was in his fourth year, and though it may seem strange, I know that he remembered his mother all his life, but of course as though in a dream. After her death, almost exactly the same thing happened to the two boys as to their eldest brother Mitya: they were completely forgotten and abandoned by their father and found themselves in the charge of the same Grigory and they also lived in his cottage. It was there that they were found by the tyrannical old widow of the general, who had brought up their mother. She was still alive, and all that time, all those eight years, could not forget the injury done her. About her 'Sophia's' mode of life during those eight years, she had the most exact information from confidential sources, and learning how ill she was and in what hideous surroundings she lived, she declared aloud to her poor relations: 'It serves her right. It's God's punishment on her for her ingratitude.'

Exactly three months after Sophia's death, the old lady made an appearance in our town and went straight to Karamazov's house. She only stayed about half an hour in our town, but she did a great deal. It was in the evening. Karamazov, whom she had not seen during all those eight years, came out to her drunk. It is said that as soon as she saw him, she instantly, without any more ado, slapped his face twice with all the force at her command, and pulled him up and down three times by the tuft of his hair. Then, without another word, she went straight to the two boys at the cottage. Noticing at the first glance that they were unwashed and that their linen was dirty, she promptly slapped Grigory's face, too, and told him that she was taking them away with her. She took them out of the cottage just as they were, wrapped a rug round them, put them into her carriage, and carried them off to her town. Grigory bore the blow like a devoted slave, without uttering a rude word to her. When he saw the old lady off to the carriage, he bowed low to her, saying impressively that God would reward her for looking after the orphans. 'You're an oaf for all that!' the general's widow shouted to him as she drove away. Thinking it over, Karamazov came to the conclusion that it was a good thing and did not afterwards refuse his formal consent on any point to his children's being educated by the general's widow. As for the slaps she had given him, he himself spread the story all over town.

It so happened that soon after this the general's widow, too, died, but in her will she left the boys a thousand roubles each 'for their education', stipulating, however, that while all that money should be spent on them, it should be made to last until they came of age, because even so small a sum was too much for such children, but if anyone felt more generous let him give more, and so on. I have not read the will myself, but I heard that there was something queer of this sort and that it was rather eccentrically expressed. The principal heir of the old lady, Yefim Petrovich Polenov, Marshal of Nobility of the province, however, turned out to be an honest man. After an exchange of letters with Karamazov, he realized at once that he could extract no money from him for the education of his children (though Karamazov never directly refused, but always kept putting off in such cases, sometimes, indeed, becoming effusively sentimental). He, therefore, took a personal interest in the orphaned children and be-came particularly fond of the younger, Alexey, so much so that the boy lived at his house for a long time and grew up as a member of his family. I should like to ask the reader to note this from the very beginning. And if the young people were indebted for their upbringing and education to any man, that man was Mr Polenov, one of the most honourable and humane men one is ever likely to meet. He kept the thousand roubles the general's widow had left each of the two boys intact so that by the time they came of age it had doubled by the accumulation of interest. He educated them at his own expense and, needless to say, spent far more than one thousand on each of them. For the time being I shall again not enter into a detailed description of their boyhood and adolescence, but will merely indicate a few of the more important circumstances. Of the elder, Ivan, however, I will only say that he grew into a rather morose young man, who was always withdrawn into himself. He was far from timid, but it seems that already by the age of ten he had become aware that they were living among strangers and on other people's charity, that their father was a man of whom one ought to be ashamed to talk, and so on. This boy began to show very early, almost in infancy (so at least it was said), quite an extraordinarily brilliant aptitude for learning. I don't know all the particulars, but for some reason or other he left Yefim Polenov's family when he was barely thirteen, entered a Moscow secondary school, boarding at the house of an experienced and famous pedagogue, a childhood friend of Polenov's. Ivan himself used to declare afterwards that it all happened because of the 'enthusiasm for good works' of Polenov, who was carried away by the idea that a boy of such brilliant abilities had to be educated by a brilliant tutor. However, neither Polenov nor the brilliant tutor was living when, after finishing school, the young man entered the university. As Polenov had failed to make the necessary provisions for the two boys and as, owing to the unavoidable formalities and delays so customary in Russia, the money they had inherited from the general's widow, which had increased from one to two thousand roubles, had not been immediately available, the young man was very hard up indeed during his first two years at the university and was forced to earn his own living all that time as well as carry on with his studies. It should be noted that at the time he did not even attempt to enter into a correspondence with his father – perhaps out of pride, out of contempt for him and, perhaps, too, out of a commonsense reflection which told him that he would never obtain any real assistance, however small, from his father. Be that as it may, the young man was not in any way discouraged and, in spite of everything, succeeded in getting work, at first by giving lessons at sixpence an hour and then by selling short 'stories' of street incidents to different newspapers under the signature of 'Eyewitness'. These 'stories', it was said, were always so interestingly and pungently written that they were soon in great demand, and in this respect alone the young man showed his practical and intellectual superiority over that large, indigent and unhappy section of our students of both sexes who live from hand to mouth and who, in our capital cities, are always in and out of the editorial offices of different newspapers and journals, unable to think of anything better than the constant repetition of one and the same request for translations from the French or for copying out articles. Having got an entry into the editorial offices, Ivan never lost touch with them, and during his last years at the university he began to publish brilliant reviews of books on various specialized subjects, so that he became well known even in literary circles. It was, however, only quite recently that he happened to have suddenly succeeded in attracting the special attention of a much wider public, so that a rather large number of people at once noticed and remembered him. That was a rather interesting incident. Having graduated from the university and preparing to leave for abroad on his two thousand roubles, Ivan published in one of the leading newspapers a strange article, which attracted the attention even of non-specialists, and, what was so extraordinary, on a subject on which he was apparently not an expert, since he had taken his degree in natural sciences. The article dealt with the question of ecclesiastical courts which was being widely debated at the time. After discussing several opinions which had already been published on this subject, he went on to express his own view. What was so striking about his article was its tone and its extraordinarily surprising conclusion. And yet many churchmen were convinced that its author was on their side. But quite unexpectedly not only secularists but even atheists expressed their agreement with his views. In the end several shrewd persons decided that the whole thing was nothing but an impertinent practical joke. I mention this incident especially because this article eventually found its way into our famous monastery, where they were greatly interested in the question of ecclesiastical courts which had arisen just then, and, having found its way there, it produced general bewilderment. On learning the name of the author, they were also interested in the fact that he was a native of our town and the son of 'that Karamazov'. And just then the author himself made a sudden appearance among us.

Why Ivan Karamazov had arrived in our town just then was a question that I remember rather worried me at the time. This so fateful visit which led to so many consequences remained a mystery to me long afterwards and, indeed, almost always. In view of everything, it seemed strange that a young man, so learned, so proud, and seemingly so cautious, should suddenly take up his residence in so disreputable a house and with a father who had ignored him all his life, who neither knew nor remembered him, who, if his son had ever asked him for money, would never have given him any under any circumstances. For he was always afraid that his sons Ivan and Alexey might one day come and ask him for money. And now the young man took up residence in the house of such a father, lived with him for one month and then for another, and both of them seemed to be getting on marvellously together. This last fact seemed particularly astonishing not only to me but to many others. Peter Miusov, of whom I have already spoken, a distant relative of Fyodor Karamazov by his first marriage, happened just then to be spending some time on his estate in the vicinity of our town, having arrived from Paris, where he had settled permanently. I remember that it was he who was most of all impressed, when he had made the acquaintance of the young man. Ivan interested him exceedingly and he sometimes engaged, not without inner pangs, in furious intellectual arguments with him. 'He's proud,' he used to say to us at the time about him, 'he'll always be able to earn his living, he has money even now, he can afford to go abroad – so what is he after here? Everyone can see that he hasn't come to his father for money, for his father would never give him any. He doesn't like drinking and whoring, and yet the old man can't do without him – so well are they getting on together!' And it was true. The young man's influence over his father was quite evident; the old man seemed even to obey him at times, though occasionally he still was extremely and even maliciously perverse; sometimes he even began to behave more decently. . . .

It only became known afterwards that one of the reasons for Ivan's arrival was that his elder brother Mitya had asked him to intercede with their father on his behalf. Ivan had met his brother for the first time almost at the same time and during that very visit, but before his arrival from Moscow he had entered into correspondence with him about an important matter that concerned Mitya more than himself. What it was the reader will learn in full detail in due course. All the same, even when I found out what this special business was, Ivan still seemed an enigmatic figure to me and his arrival in our town remained a mystery.

I may add here that Ivan was at the time trying to mediate between his father and his elder brother, who was just then at daggers drawn with his father and even instituted formal legal proceedings against him.

That family, I repeat, met for the first time just then and some of its members saw each other for the first time in their lives. Only the youngest son Alexey had lived in our town for the past year and had thus arrived there before his brothers. It is about Alexey that I find it most difficult to speak in this introductory story before bringing him on to the stage in my novel. But I'm afraid I shall have to give some preliminary description of him, too, to explain at least one very strange fact, namely, the fact that I am forced to introduce my future hero to the reader in the very first scene of my novel wearing the cassock of a novice. Yes, indeed, he had been living for the past year in our monastery and was apparently getting ready to take his vows and to spend the rest of his life there.

4

The Third Son Alyosha

HE was only twenty years old then (his brother Ivan was in his twenty-fourth year and their eldest brother Dmitry in his twenty-eighth). First of all let me say that this young man, Alyosha, was not at all a fanatic and, at least in my opinion, not even a mystic. Let me make myself absolutely clear from the very beginning: he was simply a precocious lover of humanity, and if he took up the monastic way of life it was only because at the time it alone appealed powerfully to his imagination and showed him, as it were, the ideal way of an escape for his soul struggling to emerge from the darkness of worldly wickedness to the light of love. And this way of life appealed so strongly to him only because just then he had met, as he thought, an extraordinary being, Zossima, the famous elder in our monastery, to whom he grew attached with all the warmth of the first love of his unquenchably ardent heart. Still, I do not deny that he was very strange even then, having been so, indeed, from his cradle. I have, incidentally, already mentioned the fact that, though only in his fourth year when his mother died, he remembered her all his life – her face, her caresses, 'just as though she were standing alive before me'. Such memories, as everyone knows, may be retained from an even earlier age, even from the age of two, but merely appear all through life like shafts of light out of the darkness, like a tiny corner torn out of a huge picture which has all faded and disappeared except for that tiny corner. So it was with him: all he remembered was an evening, a quiet summer evening, an open window, the slanting rays of the setting sun (it was the slanting rays that he remembered most of all), an icon in the corner of the room, a lighted lamp in front of it, and on her knees before the icon his mother, sobbing as though in hysterics, with screams and shrieks, snatching him up in her arms, hugging him to her breast so tightly that it hurt, and praying for him to the Virgin, holding him out in both arms to the icon as though under the Virgin's protection, and suddenly a nurse runs in and snatches him from her in terror. There you have the picture! At that moment Alyosha remembered his mother's face, too: he used to say that as far as he could remember it was frenzied but beautiful. But there were very few people, indeed, with whom he would share this memory. In his childhood and adolescence he was not effusive and he did not even like to talk a great deal, but it was not from mistrustfulness, nor from shyness or from morose unsociability; quite the contrary, it was from something else, from a sort of inner preoccupation, a preoccupation that concerned only himself and had nothing to do with anyone else, but so important to him that he seemed to forget others because of it. But he loved people: all his life he seemed to have complete faith in people, and yet no one ever took him for a simpleton or a naïve person. There was something in him that told you and indeed convinced you (and it was so all through his life afterwards) that he did not want to set himself up as a judge of people, that he would not like to assume the role of one who condemned or, in fact, to condemn anyone for anything. It also seemed that he tolerated everything without in the least passing judgement, though often grieving bitterly. Indeed, he went so far as not to be surprised or frightened by anything anyone did, and that even as a child. Arriving at the age of twenty at his father's house, which was a veritable den of the filthiest vice, he, chaste and pure as he was, simply withdrew in silence when it was unbearable to look on, but without the slightest sign of contempt for, or condemnation of, anyone. His father, on the other hand, having been a sponger once and, therefore, a morbidly suspicious man who was quick to take offence, had met him at first mistrustfully and sullenly ('He's much too silent and thinks too much', he thought) but finished up by constantly hugging and kissing him before a fortnight was out, with drunken tears, it is true, and with tipsy sentimentality, but it was evident that he had grown to love him sincerely and deeply, in a way no man like him could ever, of course, have been expected to love anyone.

But then, everyone loved this young man wherever he made an appearance, and that had been so from the earliest days of his childhood. When he entered the house of his benefactor and patron Yefim Polenov, everyone in that household grew so attached to him that they treated him as one of the family. And yet he had entered that household at such a tender age that it was quite impossible to suspect the child of possessing any calculating duplicity or pushfulness or any skill in ingratiating himself into anyone's favour or any knowledge of how to make oneself liked. So that his gift of arousing a special kind of love in people was, as it were, inherent in his very nature, artless and spontaneous. It was the same at school, and yet it would seem that he was one of those children who arouse the distrust of their schoolmates and are sometimes laughed at and even hated. He would, for instance, often fall into a reverie and he seemed to shun the company of others. Even as a little boy he liked to retire into some corner and read a book, and yet his schoolmates grew so fond of him that he could be described without fear of contradiction as a general favourite all the while he was at school. He was seldom playful or even merry, but one look at him was sufficient to make people realize that there was not a trace of moroseness in him, that, on the contrary, he was serene and even-tempered. He never attempted to show off before children of his own age. Perhaps that was why he was never afraid of anyone, and yet his schoolfellows at once realized that he was not at all proud of his fearlessness, but gave the impression of someone who had no idea that he was brave and fearless. He never bore a grudge against anyone. It often happened that an hour later he would reply to the boy who had offended him or speak to him with as trustful and serene an expression as though nothing had happened between them. And he did so without any indication that he had accidentally forgotten or deliberately forgiven the insult; it was simply that he did not think of it as an insult, and it was this that appealed so strongly to the children and made them like him. There was only one trait of his character which invariably aroused in all his schoolmates from the lowest to the highest form the desire to pull his leg, though not out of malice but because it amused them. This was his absurd and morbid modesty and chastity. He could not bear to hear certain words and certain conversations about women. These 'words' and 'conversations' are unhappily impossible to eradicate in schools. Boys who are pure in heart and soul, almost children, often like to talk in class in whispers and even aloud of things, pictures, or images of which even soldiers would hesitate to speak; moreover, soldiers do not know or understand a great deal of what is familiar to quite young children of our educated and higher classes of society. There is as yet no moral depravity, nor any real, corrupt, inner cynicism, but there is the appearance of it, and it is this kind of cynicism that they often consider as something refined, subtle, daring, and even worthy of imitation. Seeing that Alyosha Karamazov stopped his ears with his fingers every time they talked about 'that', they sometimes deliberately crowded round him, pulled his hands away from his ears by force and shouted obscenities into both ears, while he struggled to free himself, lay down on the floor, tried to hide his face, and he did all this without uttering a word, without quarrelling, bearing their taunts in silence. In the end, however, they left him alone and no longer teased him for being 'a silly little girl', and not only that, but they were genuinely sorry for him because of it. Incidentally, he was always one of the best pupils in the class, but was never singled out as the top boy of the form.

After Yefim Polenov's death Alyosha spent another two years at the secondary school. Almost immediately after his death, the inconsolable widow went for a long visit to Italy with her whole household, consisting entirely of women. Alyosha went to live in the house of two ladies, distant relatives of Yefim Polenov, whom he had never seen before, and he did not know himself on what terms. Another very characteristic trait of his character was that he never cared at whose expense he was living. In that respect he was in complete contrast to his elder brother Ivan, who had experienced extreme want during the first two years at the university and had had to earn his own living and who from his earliest childhood had resented the fact that he was entirely dependent on the charity of his benefactor. But this strange trait in Alyosha's character could not apparently be too severely condemned. For anyone who had only the slightest acquaintance with him was immediately convinced, whenever this question arose, that Alyosha was one of those young men who in a way resembled saintly fools and who, if they suddenly came into possession of a large sum of money, would not hesitate to give it away at the first demand either to some charity or perhaps simply to the first clever swindler who happened to ask for it. And, generally speaking, he did not seem to know the value of money, though not, of course, in a literal sense. When he was given pocket money, which he never asked for himself, he either kept it for weeks not knowing what to do with it, or was so very careless with it that it was gone in no time. Peter Miusov, who was very sensitive where money and bourgeois honesty were concerned, delivered himself of the following aphorism after he had got to know Alyosha better some years later: 'Here you have perhaps the only man in the world who, if he were left alone without a penny in a strange city of a million inhabitants, would never die of exposure or hunger because he would be instantly fed and given some job, and if not, he would find a job himself, and that would cost him no effort or humiliation, nor would he be a burden to his employers but, on the contrary, they would probably consider it a pleasure.'

He did not finish his studies at school. A year before the end of his course, he suddenly told the ladies with whom he lived that he was going to his father about a certain matter which had just happened to enter his head. The ladies, who were very fond of him, were unwilling to let him go. The journey was not an expensive one and the ladies refused to let him pawn his watch, a parting gift of his benefactor's family before they went abroad, but provided him liberally with money and even with a new suit of clothes and linen. But he returned half of their money to them, declaring that he had made up his mind to travel third class. On arriving in our little town, he at first made no direct answer to his father's question why he had come before finishing his studies at school, but was, I am told, quite unusually pensive. Soon it was discovered that he was trying to find his mother's grave. He had even confessed himself at the time that that was really why he had come. But it is doubtful whether that was the only reason for his visit. It is more probable that he did not know himself and could not possibly explain what it was exactly that seemed suddenly to rise up in his soul and draw him irresistibly towards a new, unknown, but inevitable, path. His father could not show him where his second wife was buried because he had never bothered to visit her grave after her coffin had been covered over with earth, and it had been so long ago that he had entirely forgotten where it was. . . .

A word about Karamazov. He had been living only a short time in our town before the arrival of his sons. Three or four years after the death of his second wife he had gone to the south of Russia and finally turned up in Odessa where he spent several years. At first he made the acquaintance, in his own words, of 'a lot of dirty, low-down Jews', but ended up by being received not only by 'dirty' but also by 'highly respectable' Jews. It can be reliably assumed that it was during that period of his life that he had acquired a special knack for making money and amassing capital. He returned finally to our little town only about three years before Alyosha's arrival. His former acquaintances found him terribly aged, though he was not by any means such an old man. He carried himself not so much with more dignity than before as with more arrogance. The former clown, for instance, showed an insolent predilection for making others appear as clowns. His behaviour with women was not just indecent as it had been, but somehow disgusting. Soon he opened many new public houses in the district. It was evident that he was worth perhaps a hundred thousand roubles or only a very little less. Many people of our town and district were not slow to borrow money from him – on the best possible security, of course. Of late he had somehow grown to look bloated. He seemed to have lost his balance and his self-control, he had grown rather inconsequential, beginning one thing and finishing another, letting his thoughts wander from one project to another, and was more and more often drunk. Had it not been for his servant Grigory, who had also grown quite old by that time and who sometimes looked after him almost like a nurse, Karamazov would perhaps not have escaped serious trouble. Alyosha's arrival seemed to have had a sobering effect on him even from the moral point of view, as though something had awakened in this prematurely aged man that had long been smothered in his soul. 'Do you know, my boy,' he often used to say to Alyosha, looking intently at him, 'that you're like her, the "shrieker", I mean?' That was what he called his dead wife, Alyosha's mother. It was Grigory who at last showed the 'shrieker's' grave to Alyosha. He took him to our town cemetery and in a remote corner of it showed him a cheap but decently kept grave with a cast-iron gravestone which bore the inscription of the name, social position, age, and date of death of the deceased. Below were even engraved four lines of ancient verse which is usually found on middle-class tombs. Surprisingly, this tombstone turned out to have been put up by Grigory. It was he who had put it up on the grave of the poor 'shrieker' at his own expense, after Karamazov, whom he had often annoyed by remind-ing him of the grave, had at last gone to Odessa, dismissing both the grave and all his memories. Alyosha did not show any particular emotion at his mother's grave; he merely listened to Grigory's sober and sensible account of the erection of the tombstone, stood there for some time with a bowed head, and walked away without uttering a word. Since then he had not visited the cemetery for, perhaps, the whole of the year. But this small episode had also had an effect on Karamazov – and a very original one, too. He suddenly took a thousand roubles to our monastery and ordered requiem masses for the soul of his wife, but not for the second, Alyosha's mother, the 'shrieker', but for the first, Adelaida, who used to beat him. In the evening of the same day he got drunk and abused the monks to Alyosha. He himself was far from religious; the man had probably never put a penny candle before an icon. Such individuals have very strange outbursts of sudden feelings and sudden thoughts.

I have already mentioned that he had grown very bloated. By

that time his face bore unmistakable traces of the sort of life he had led. In addition to the long fleshy bags under his little eyes, which were always insolent, suspicious, and sardonic, in addition to the multitude of deep wrinkles on his fat little face, there hung under his sharp chin a large Adam's apple, fleshy and longish like a little purse, which gave him a sort of revoltingly sensual appearance. Add to that a long, cruel, and sensual mouth with full lips, between which could be seen stumps of black and almost decayed teeth. He sputtered every time he began to speak. However, he liked to make fun of his own face himself, though he was apparently well satisfied with it. He used particularly to point to his nose, which was not very large but very thin and conspicuously aquiline: 'A regular Roman nose,' he used to say, 'and together with my Adam's apple a real face of an ancient Roman patrician of the decadent period.' He seemed proud of it.

It was shortly after finding his mother's grave that Alyosha suddenly told his father that he wanted to enter the monastery and that the monks were willing to receive him as a novice. He explained that it was his fervent wish and that he was asking his solemn consent as his father. The old man already knew that the elder Zossima, who was seeking salvation in the hermitage of our monastery, had made a special impression on his 'gentle boy'.

'That elder,' he said, having listened to Alyosha thoughtfully and in silence and not in the least surprised at his request, 'is, of course, one of their most honest monks. H'm – so that's where you want to be, my gentle boy!' He was half drunk, and suddenly smiled his slow half-tipsy smile, which was not without cunning and drunken craftiness. 'Well, you know, my boy, I had a feeling you'd finish up by doing something like that. You believe me, don't you? That's what you always intended to do, isn't it? I'm sure of that. Well, why not? You've got your own two thousand – there's your dowry, and I'll never leave you in the lurch, my boy. Why, I'll pay what's necessary for you there, if they ask me for it. And if they don't ask, why go begging them to accept my money? Isn't that so? Why, you spend money like a canary – two grains a week. H'm. There's a certain monastery, you know, with a cluster of houses at the bottom of the hill in which, as everyone knows, the 'monastery wives', as they are called, live, thirty wives in all, I should think. . . . I've been there, and you know, it's interesting, in its own way, of course, I mean just to relieve the monotony, you understand. The only awful thing about it is the terrible Russian patriotism of these fellows – not a single Frenchwoman among them, and they could have had them, for they have pots of money. I suppose, when they get to hear of it, they'll be coming along. Well, here there's nothing of the kind. No monastery wives, just two hundred monks. Everything above board. They keep their fasts. True enough. . . . H'm. . . . So you want to go to the monks, do you? You know, I really am sorry for you, Alyosha. You may not believe it, my boy, but I've grown very fond of you. . . . Still, I suppose it's all for the best: you'll pray for us, sinners that we are, for we have sinned quite a lot here, haven't we? I've always wondered who would ever pray for me. Does such a man exist in the world? My dear boy, I'm awfully stupid about such things. You do believe me, don't you? Awfully. You see, stupid as I am about these things, I keep thinking, thinking, not very often, of course, but I do all the same. Why, I say to myself, the devils will surely not forget to drag me down with hooks to their place when I die. Well, then, so I think to myself – hooks? Where do they get their hooks from? What are they made of? Iron? Where do they forge them? They've got some sort of workshop there, have they? You see, in your monastery the monks are quite certain that, for instance, there's a ceiling in hell. Now, I'm quite willing to believe in hell, but only if it has no ceiling – it makes it much more refined, more enlightened, more Lutheran-like, that is. But actually it doesn't make much difference whether hell has a ceiling or not, does it now? And yet the whole damned business depends on that alone! For if there is no ceiling, there can be no hooks. And if there are no hooks, the whole thing's a fake, which again is unlikely, for who would then drag me down with hooks? And if they don't drag me down, what's going to happen then? Where's justice in the world? *Il faudrait les inventer* – the hooks, I mean. Just for me. For me alone. For if you only knew, Alyosha, what a shameless wretch I am!'

'But there are no hooks there,' said Alyosha, gazing gently and seriously at his father.

'I see, I see, only shadows of hooks. I know. I know. This is how a Frenchman described hell: *J'ai vu l'ombre d'un cocher qui avec l'ombre d'une brosse frottait l'ombre d'une carrosse.* But how do you know there are no hooks, my boy? When you've been with the monks, you'll sing another tune. However, go by all means, get at the truth there and come and tell me: I daresay it will be easier going to the other world if you know for certain what it's like there. Besides, it is more seemly for you to live with the monks than here with a drunken old man and those young sluts. . . . Though, like an angel, nothing can touch you. Well, perhaps nothing will touch you there, either. You see, that's why I'm letting you go – that's what I hope for. You've got your head screwed on the right way. You're enthusiastic now, but you'll get over it – you'll be cured and come back to me. And I'll be waiting for you: for, you see, my dear boy, I feel that you're the only man in the world who hasn't condemned me – I feel it, you know. I can't help feeling it!'

And he even began to blubber. He was sentimental. He was wicked and sentimental.

5

Elders

SOME of my readers may imagine that my young man was a sickly, ecstatic, poorly developed character, a pale dreamer, a weak and emaciated little creature. On the contrary, at the time Alyosha was a well-built, red-cheeked, clear-eyed boy of nineteen, looking a picture of health. He was very handsome, too, slender, of medium height, with dark-brown hair, a regular, though a little elongated, oval face, a pair of wide-set sparkling, dark grey eyes, very thoughtful and apparently very self-composed. It may be said that red cheeks are not incompatible with fanaticism or mysticism; but I can't help feeling that, if anything, Alyosha was more of a realist than anyone. Oh, of course, in the monastery he fully believed in miracles, but in my opinion miracles will never confound a realist. It is not miracles that make a realist turn to religion. A true realist, if he is an unbeliever, will always find the strength and the ability not to believe in a miracle, and if faced with a miracle as an undeniable fact, he will sooner disbelieve his own senses than admit the fact. And if he does admit it, he will admit it as a natural fact hitherto unknown to him.

In a realist faith does not arise from a miracle, but the miracle from faith. Just because of his realism, a realist, once he believes, must admit a miracle. The apostle Thomas said that he would not believe till he saw, and when he saw, he said: 'My Lord and my God!' Was it a miracle that made him believe? Most probably not, but he believed only because he wanted to believe, and maybe he already fully believed in his innermost heart even when he said, 'Except I shall see, I will not believe.'

It will be said perhaps that Alyosha was dull-witted, undeveloped, that he had not completed his studies, and so on. That he did not complete his studies is true, but to say that he was dull-witted and stupid would be a great injustice. I shall simply repeat what I have said above: he entered upon this path solely because it alone caught his imagination and presented him all at once with an ideal way of escape for his soul from darkness to light. Add to that that he was to a certain extent a young man of our own times, that is, honest by nature, demanding truth, seeking it, believing in it, and, believing in it, demanding to serve it with all the strength of his soul, yearning for an immediate act of heroism and wishing to sacrifice everything, even life itself, for that act of heroism. Though, unhappily, these youths do not understand that the sacrifice of one's life is in most cases perhaps the easiest of all sacrifices, and that to sacrifice, for instance, five or six years of their life, full of youthful fervour, to hard and difficult study, if only to increase tenfold their powers of serving truth so as to be able to carry out the great work they have set their hearts on carrying out – that such a sacrifice is very often almost beyond the strength of many of them. Alyosha merely chose a path leading in the opposite direction to that of all the others, but with the same ardent desire for swift achievement. The moment he thought seriously about it he was overcome by the conviction of the existence of immortality and God, and he quite naturally said to himself: 'I want to live for immortality, and I won't accept any compromise.' Similarly, if he had decided that there was no immortality and no God, he would at once have become an atheist and a Socialist (for Socialism is not only the labour question, or the question of the so-called fourth estate, but above all an atheistic question, the question of the modern integration of atheism, the question of the Tower of Babel which is deliberately being erected without God, not

for the sake of reaching heaven from earth, but for the sake of bringing heaven down to earth). It seemed strange and impossible to
Alyosha to go on living as before. It is written: 'If thou wilt be perfect, go and sell all that thou hast . . . and come and follow me.' So
Alyosha said to himself: 'I cannot give up two roubles instead of "all
that thou hast" or just go to morning mass instead of "come and
follow me".' Perhaps among the memories of his childhood he also
preserved the memory of the monastery near our town where his
mother may have taken him to morning mass. Perhaps the slanting
rays of the setting sun reflected in the icon to which his mother, the
poor 'shrieker', had held him up, had also something to do with it.
He had arrived in our town looking thoughtful, and perhaps he
wished only to see whether to give up all he had or only two roubles
– and in the monastery he met this elder. . . .

This elder was, as I have explained above, the elder Zossima; but I
have first to say a few words here about what 'elders' are in our
monasteries and it is unfortunate that I don't feel sufficiently competent or expert to do so. I will try, however, to give a superficial
account of it in a few words. To begin with, competent experts assert
that elders and the institution of elders made an appearance in our
country and in our monasteries quite recently, not more than a
hundred years ago, while in the Orthodox East, and especially in
Sinai and on Mount Athos, they have existed for over a thousand years.
It is said that the institution of elders existed in Russia, too, in ancient
times, or at any rate that it most certainly ought to have existed, but
that owing to the troubled times in Russia, the Tartar rule, the civil
wars, the interruption of our former relations with the East after the
fall of Constantinople, this institution fell into decay and the elders
ceased to exist. It was revived in our country towards the end of the
last century by one of the great ascetics (as he was called) Paissy
Velichkovsky and his disciples, but today, even after a hundred years,
they are to be found only in a very few monasteries, and are sometimes even persecuted as an unheard-of innovation in Russia. It
flourished especially in Russia in the famous Kozelsky monastery.
When and how it was introduced into our monastery I cannot say,
but there has already been a third succession of elders there. Zossima
was one of the last, but he was ill and almost dying, and they did not
even know who was to take his place. It was an important question

for our monastery because until then it had not been renowned for anything in particular; it had no relics of saints, no wonder-working icons, nor, indeed, any glorious traditions connected with our history, nor was it known for any particularly great services to our country. It had flourished and its fame had spread all over Russia solely because of its elders, and crowds of pilgrims flocked to our monastery for thousands of miles from every corner of Russia to see and hear them. What, then, is an elder? An elder is a man who takes your soul and your will into his soul and will. Having chosen your elder, you renounce your will and yield it to him in complete submission and complete self-abnegation. This novitiate, this terrible discipline is accepted voluntarily by the man who consecrates himself to this life in the hope that after a long novitiate he will attain to such a degree of self-mastery and self-conquest that at last he will, after a life of obedience, achieve complete freedom, that is to say, freedom from himself, and so escape the fate of those who have lived their whole lives without finding themselves in themselves. This invention, that is to say, the institution of elders, is not based on any theory, but has evolved in the East from a practice that today goes back over a thousand years. The obligations due to an elder have nothing to do with the ordinary 'obedience', which has always existed in our Russian monasteries. The elder's disciples must always be ready to make confession to him, and there must be an indissoluble bond between the elder and his followers. It is said, for instance, that in the early days of Christianity one such novice, who had failed to carry out a command imposed upon him by his elder, left his monastery in Syria and went to Egypt. There, after a long series of great exploits, he was found worthy at last of suffering torture and a martyr's death for his faith. But when the church, already regarding him as a saint, was burying his body, the coffin, at the deacon's intoning, 'Depart, all ye unbaptized', broke away from its place and was cast out of the church, and this took place three times. And it was only then that they found out that this holy martyr had broken the vow of obedience and left his elder and that he could not therefore be forgiven without the elder's absolution, in spite of his great exploits. It was only after the elder, who had been summoned, had given him absolution from his vow of obedience that his burial could take place. Of course, all this is only an old legend, but here is something that happened quite recently: a Russian monk of our own day, who was seeking salvation on Mount Athos, was suddenly told by his elder to leave Athos, which he had grown to love greatly as a holy place and a haven of rest, and go first to Jerusalem to worship at the Holy Places, and then return to the north of Siberia. 'Your place is there and not here,' the elder told him. Cast down with grief, the astonished monk went to the Oecumenical Patriarch at Constantinople and begged him to release him from his vow of obedience. But the Oecumenical Patriarch replied that not only was he unable to release him, but that there was not, and could not be, on earth a power which could release him from his vow, once exacted by an elder, except the elder who had exacted it from him. Thus, the elders are in certain cases endowed with incredibly boundless authority. That is why the institution of elders at first met with something very like persecution in many of our monasteries. And yet the elders were immediately highly esteemed by the common people. Ordinary people as well as great aristocrats, for instance, flocked to the elders of our monastery, so that, prostrating themselves before them, they could confess their doubts, their sins, and their sufferings, and ask for counsel and admonition. Seeing this, the opponents of the elders cried that, in addition to other transgressions, the sacrament of the confession was being arbitrarily and frivolously degraded here, though the continual baring of their souls to the elder by the novice or the layman had nothing whatever to do with the sacrament. In the end, however, the institution of elders survived and is gradually taking root in Russian monasteries. It is, of course, true that this instrument of the moral regeneration of man from slavery to freedom and to moral perfectibility, which has stood the test of a thousand years, may be turned into a double-edged weapon, so that it may lead some man not to humility and complete self-mastery, but, on the contrary, to the most satanic pride, that is to say, to slavery and not to freedom.

The elder Zossima was sixty-five and came of a family of landowners. At some time in his early youth he had been in the army and served in the Caucasus as an officer. He had, no doubt, impressed Alyosha by some special quality of his soul. Alyosha lived in the cell of the elder, who was very fond of him and allowed him to stay with him. It should be noted that Alyosha, while living in the monastery, was in no way bound; he was completely free to go where he pleased and be away even for days on end. If he wore his cassock it was voluntarily, so as not to appear different from anyone else in the monastery. But, of course, he liked to do so. Perhaps the power and the fame which constantly surrounded the elder exercised a great influence on Alyosha's youthful imagination. It was said by many people about the elder Zossima that, by permitting everyone for so many years to come to bare their hearts and beg his advice and healing words, he had absorbed so many secrets, sorrows, and avowals into his soul that in the end he had acquired so fine a perception that he could tell at the first glance from the face of a stranger what he came for, what he wanted, and what kind of torment racked his conscience. Indeed, he sometimes astounded, confounded, and almost frightened his visitor by this knowledge of his secret before he had even had time to utter a word. But for all that Alyosha almost always noticed that many, almost all, who went for the first time to have a private talk with the elder, entered his cell in fear and trepidation, but almost always came out looking bright and happy, and that even the gloomiest face was transformed into a happy one. Alyosha was also greatly struck by the fact that the elder was not at all stern; on the contrary, he was almost always cheerful in his manner. The monks used to say about him that he invariably showed a greater attachment to those who were more sinful and that the more greatly a man had sinned the more he loved him. There were some among the monks, even up to the end of the elder's life, who hated and envied him, but they were becoming fewer in number and were silent, though some of them included quite well-known and important persons in the monastery, as, for instance, one of the oldest monks, who was greatly esteemed for his vows of silence and for the strictness with which he kept his fasts. But in spite of it all the overwhelming majority were undoubtedly on Father Zossima's side, and many of them loved him with all their hearts, warmly and sincerely; some were, indeed, almost fanatically devoted to him. These openly declared, though not in a very loud voice, that he was a saint, that there could be no doubt about it, and anticipating his impending death, expected instantaneous miracles. They hoped that the deceased would confer great glory on the monastery in the most immediate future. Alyosha, too, had absolute faith in the miraculous powers of the elder, as he had absolute faith in the story of the coffin that flew out of the church. He saw many who came with sick children or grown-up relatives and besought the elder to lay his hands upon them and offer up a prayer over them, return very soon afterwards, and some even the next day, and fall weeping on their knees before the elder, thanking him for healing their sick. Whether they had actually been healed or whether it was only a natural improvement in their health was a question that did not exist for Alyosha, for he fully believed in the spiritual powers of his teacher, whose fame he considered almost his own triumph. But his heart thrilled especially and he looked positively radiant when the elder came out to the crowd of pilgrims from the common people who were waiting for his appearance at the gates of the hermitage and who had flocked from all over Russia purposely to see the elder and obtain his blessing. They prostrated themselves before him, wept, kissed his feet, kissed the ground on which he stood, cried out to him in loud voices, the women holding up their children to him and leading sick 'shriekers'. The elder spoke to them, read a brief prayer over them, blessed and dismissed them. More recently he sometimes became so weak from his attacks of illness that he was scarcely able to leave his cell; and the pilgrims sometimes waited in the monastery several days for him to come out. Alyosha never asked himself why they loved him so much, or why they prostrated themselves before him and wept with emotion merely at the sight of his face. Oh, he realized full well that for the humble soul of the Russian of humble origin, worn out by toil and grief and, above all, by everlasting injustice and everlasting sin, both his own and the world's, there was no greater need and comfort than to find some holy shrine or person, to fall down before him and worship him: 'If there is sin, injustice, and temptation among us, then there is at any rate someone somewhere on earth who is holier and superior; he has the truth, he knows the truth, which means that it is not dead on earth and will therefore come to us, too, one day, and rule all over the earth, as it was promised.' Alyosha knew that the common people felt and even thought just like that. He understood it. But that the elder Zossima was this very saint and this custodian of God's truth in the eyes of the people – of that he had no doubt whatever, any more than the weeping peasants and their sick wives who held out their children to the elder. The conviction that after his death the elder would confer extraordinary glory upon the monastery took, perhaps, even deeper root in Alyosha's soul than in anyone else's in the monastery. Indeed, all during the last few months a sort of deep, ardent, inner ecstasy burned more and more fiercely in his heart. He was not at all troubled by the fact that this elder stood before him as a solitary example: 'It doesn't matter, he is holy, his heart contains the secret of a renewal for all, the power which will finally establish truth on earth, and all will be holy, and will love each other, and there will be no more rich nor poor, exalted nor humbled, but all men will be as the children of God and the real kingdom of Christ will come.' That was what Alyosha dreamt in his heart.

The arrival of his two brothers, whom he had not known at all till then, seemed to make a most powerful impression on Alyosha. He made friends with his half-brother Dmitry more quickly and more intimately (though he arrived later) than with his brother Ivan. He was very anxious to get to know his brother Ivan, but though Ivan had lived with his father for two months and though they had seen each other quite frequently, they did not seem to become intimate: taciturn himself, Alyosha seemed to be expecting something and to be ashamed of something, while his brother Ivan, though Alyosha had noticed at first that he looked intently and curiously at him, seemed soon to have lost all interest in him. Alyosha noticed it with some embarrassment. He ascribed his brother's indifference to the disparity in their ages and, especially, in their education. But Alyosha thought of something else: Ivan's lack of curiosity and sympathy with him might have arisen from some cause unknown to him. He could not help feeling for some reason that Ivan was preoccupied with something private and important, that he was striving towards some goal, perhaps difficult to attain, so that he had no thought to spare for Alyosha, and that that was the only reason why he paid no attention to him. Alyosha also wondered whether his brother, a learned atheist, did not feel a sort of contempt for him, a silly novice. He knew for a fact that his brother was an atheist. He could not take offence at his contempt, if, indeed, it existed, but all the same he waited with a sort of uneasy embarrassment, which he did not understand himself, for the time when his brother would want to become better acquainted with him. Dmitry spoke with the utmost respect of Ivan. He used to talk of him with a sort of special feeling. From him

Alyosha learned all the details of the important business which more recently had formed such a remarkably close bond between the two elder brothers. Dmitry's enthusiastic opinions of his brother Ivan were the more striking in Alyosha's eyes, since, compared to Ivan, his brother Dmitry was almost uneducated, and the two of them, put next to each other, seemed to present such a striking contrast both in personality and character that one could hardly think of two men who were more unlike each other.

It was at this time that the meeting, or rather the gathering, of all the members of this ill-assorted family took place in the elder's cell, a meeting which was to have a tremendous influence on Alyosha. As a matter of fact, the pretext for this meeting was not genuine. It was just at that time that the disagreements between Dmitry and his father about the inheritance and financial dealings had apparently reached a crisis. Their relationship had become intolerably strained. It was apparently Karamazov who first jokingly suggested that they should all meet in the elder Zossima's cell and, without actually resorting to his arbitration, somehow come to some sort of decent agreement, particularly as the dignified presence of the elder might inspire respect and lead to a reconciliation. Dmitry, who had never been at the elder's and had never even seen him, quite naturally jumped to the conclusion that his father was somehow trying to intimidate him with the elder; but as he secretly reproached himself for many particularly sharp outbursts in his arguments with his father recently, he accepted the challenge. It must be noted, incidentally, that, unlike Ivan, he did not live with his father, but by himself at the other end of the town. It so happened that Peter Miusov, who was at the time living on his estate near our town, jumped at this suggestion of Karamazov's. A liberal of the forties and fifties, a free-thinker and an atheist, he took a great interest in this affair, perhaps because he was bored, or, again, perhaps from a taste for light entertainment. He suddenly felt like having a look at the monastery and the 'saint'. As his old quarrels with the monastery still continued and his lawsuit with it about the boundaries of their land, the rights of tree-cutting in some woods and fishing in the stream, etc., still dragged on, he hastened to make use of it under the pretext of coming to an understanding with the Father Superior and finding some way of putting an end to their differences to their mutual satisfaction.

A visitor who came with such good intentions could, of course, expect to be received in the monastery with more attention and more courtesy than one who came out of mere curiosity. In view of all these considerations, the monastery authorities no doubt put pressure upon the elder, who had hardly left his cell of late and who refused to receive even ordinary visitors because of his illness. In the end the elder agreed to see them, and the day was fixed. 'Who has set me up to arbitrate between them?' was all he said with a smile to Alyosha.

When he heard of the meeting, Alyosha was greatly perturbed. If any one of these contending and disputing parties could regard this interview seriously, it would undoubtedly be only his brother Dmitry; the others would come only from frivolous motives, which might even be insulting to the elder – that Alyosha realized very well. His brother Ivan and Miusov would come out of curiosity, perhaps of the crudest kind, and his father perhaps to act like a clown and make some disgraceful scene. Oh, though he never uttered a word, Alyosha knew his father fairly thoroughly. I repeat, the boy was not at all simple-minded as people took him to be. He was waiting for the appointed day with a heavy heart. He was at bottom undoubtedly very anxious to see all these family disagreements come to an end somehow or other. Nevertheless, his greatest anxiety concerned the elder; he trembled for him and for his reputation, he dreaded that he might be offended, fearing particularly Miusov's refined and polite sneers and the supercilious reticences of the learned Ivan – so at least it seemed to him. He even wanted to take the risk of warning the elder and telling him something about the persons who might come to see him, but, on thinking it over, he said nothing. All he did was to send word the day before the meeting to his brother Dmitry, through a friend, that he was very fond of him and expected him to keep his promise. Dmitry was puzzled, for he could not remember promising him anything, but he replied by letter that he would do his utmost to control himself in the face of 'baseness' and though he had a profound respect for the elder and for his brother Ivan, he was convinced that the meeting was either a trap or an unworthy farce. 'All the same, I'd rather bite out my tongue than be lacking in respect for the saintly man whom you revere so much,' Dmitry concluded his short letter. It brought little comfort to Alyosha.

Book Two: An Inauspicious Meeting

I

They Arrive at the Monastery

IT WAS A BEAUTIFUL, WARM, SUNNY DAY AT THE END OF August. The meeting with the elder had been arranged to take place at about half past eleven immediately after late mass. Our visitors, however, did not put in an appearance at the church, but arrived at the end of the service. They drove up in two carriages; in the first, an elegant barouche drawn by two fine horses, was Peter Miusov with a distant relative of his, a young man of twenty, by the name of Peter Kalganov. This young man was about to enter the university, though Miusov, with whom he was for some reason staying at the time, was trying to persuade him to go abroad with him, in order to enter the university of Zürich or Jena, and take his degree there. The young man was still undecided. He was thoughtful and seemingly abstracted. He had a pleasant face, was of sturdy build, and rather tall. Occasionally there was a strangely fixed look in his eyes: like all abstracted people, he sometimes stared at you for a long time without seeing you. He was taciturn and rather awkward, but at times, though only when he was alone with someone, he would suddenly become very talkative, impetuous, and ready to burst out laughing at the slightest provocation, sometimes hardly knowing himself what he was laughing at. But his animation disappeared as quickly and as suddenly as it appeared. He was always well and even immaculately dressed; he had an independent income and expectations of much more. He was a good friend of Alyosha's.

Karamazov with his beloved son Ivan drove up in a very ancient, jolting but roomy carriage, drawn by a pair of old pinkish-grey horses, which lagged a long way behind Miusov's carriage. Dmitry had been informed the day before of the time of the meeting, but he was late. The visitors left their carriages at the inn by the monastery wall and entered the monastery gates on foot. With the exception of Karamazov, none of the three visitors had apparently ever seen a monastery, and Miusov had probably not been to church for thirty years. He gazed around him with some curiosity, not devoid of a certain affectation of ease. But, observant though he was, he found nothing to interest him within the precincts of the monastery, except perhaps the church and the domestic buildings, which were very ordinary anyway. The last of the worshippers were leaving the church, baring their heads and crossing themselves. Among the peasants were people belonging to the higher strata of society, two or three ladies and one very old general; they were all staying at the inn. The beggars at once surrounded our visitors, but no one gave them anything. Only Peter Kalganov took a ten-copeck piece out of his purse and, looking terribly nervous and embarrassed, goodness only knows why, hurriedly put it into the hands of a woman, adding quickly: 'Share it out among you.' None of his companions said anything to him about it, so that there was no reason at all for his embarrassment; but, perceiving this, he was even more embarrassed.

One thing was queer, though: they should, as a matter of fact, have been expected and perhaps received with a certain show of respect: one of them had quite recently made a donation of a thousand roubles and the other was one of the richest landowners of our district and, so to speak, a most cultured man, upon whom they were all in a way dependent, since their rights of fishing in the stream might be jeopardized as a result of some unforeseen decision of the court. And yet no official person met them. Miusov gazed abstractedly at the gravestones near the church and was about to remark that the graves must have cost a pretty penny to the relatives of the deceased for the right of burial in such a 'holy' place, but he said nothing: his habitual 'liberal' irony was turning almost into anger.

'Damn it, there doesn't seem to be anyone one could ask in this stupid place,' he muttered suddenly, as though speaking to himself. 'We'll have to do something, for time's getting on.'

Suddenly an elderly, bald-headed man with ingratiating eyes, wearing a bulky summer overcoat, walked up to them. Raising his hat and with a honeyed lisp, he introduced himself as Maximov, a Tula landowner. He immediately did his best to direct the visitors.

'The elder Zossima,' he said, 'lives in the hermitage – in the hermitage, gentlemen – in complete seclusion – just about four hundred yards from the monastery – through the wood – the wood. . . . '

'I'm quite aware of the fact that it's through the wood, sir,' Karamazov replied. 'But we don't remember the way. It's a long time since we were here.'

'It's through this gate, sir, and straight through the wood – through the wood. Follow me, sir. Please – er – I'm going there myself. . . . Yes, sir. This way, sir, this way. . . . '

They came out of the gate and walked in the direction of the wood. Maximov, a man of about sixty, did not so much walk as run alongside, gazing at them with a nervous, almost offensive curiosity. He stared at them with eyes starting out of his head.

'You see, sir,' Miusov observed severely, 'we've come to see the elder on private business. We've, as it were, been granted an audience by "that great personage", and – er – though we're grateful to you for showing us the way, we – er – cannot ask you to come in with us.'

'I've – I've already been there. . . . *Un chevalier parfait!*' and the landowner snapped his fingers in the air.

'Who is a *chevalier*?' asked Miusov.

'The elder, sir, the elder – the splendid elder. . . . The honour and glory of the monastery. Zossima, sir! Such an elder. . . . '

His confused speech was interrupted by a very pale and haggard little monk in a cowl who overtook them. The monk, with a very courteous and profound bow, announced:

'The Father Superior, gentlemen, invites you all to dine with him after your visit to the hermitage. In his rooms at one o'clock, not later. And you, too, sir,' he turned to Maximov.

'Thank you very much,' Karamazov cried, greatly delighted with the invitation, 'I shall be very glad to! Very glad, indeed. And, you know, we have all given our word to behave ourselves here. . . . What about you, Mr Miusov? Will you come too?'

'Of course I will. Why, I've come here for the express purpose of seeing all their customs. The only thing that bothers me is that I shall have to share your company, Mr Karamazov. . . . '

'Well, I can't see Dmitry anywhere. . . . '

'I hope he doesn't turn up. That would be splendid. You don't suppose I like all this disgusting business of yours, do you? And with you here, too? So we'll come to dinner,' he addressed the little monk. 'Will you please go and thank the Father Superior?'

'No, sir,' replied the monk, 'it's my duty to conduct you to the elder.'

'Well,' Maximov twittered, 'in that case I'll go to the Father Superior – I mean, I may as well, mayn't I?'

'The Father Superior,' the monk said hesitantly, 'is busy just now, but, of course, just as you like, sir.'

'A most tiresome old fellow,' Miusov observed in a loud voice after Maximov had run back to the monastery.

'Reminds me of von Sohn,' Karamazov said suddenly.

'You would say that! Why does he remind you of von Sohn? Have you ever seen von Sohn?'

'I've seen his photograph. Not by his features, but by something I can't explain. The very spit of von Sohn. I can always tell from the face.'

'Well, I daresay. You're an expert on that. But, look here, Mr Karamazov, you've just said yourself that we'd given our word to behave ourselves. Remember? I'm telling you – control yourself! For, if you start playing the fool, I've no intention of being dragged down to your level. You see the sort of man he is,' he turned to the monk. 'I'm afraid to visit decent people with him.'

A thin, quiet little smile appeared on the pale, bloodless lips of the little monk, a smile that was not without a touch of cunning, but he made no reply and it was all too evident that he said nothing out of a sense of his own dignity. Miusov frowned more than ever.

'Oh, to blazes with them all!' it flashed through his mind. 'An outward appearance carefully cultivated through the ages, but really nothing but nonsense and charlatanism.'

'Here's the hermitage!' cried Karamazov. 'We've arrived! The gates are shut.'

And he began crossing himself fervently before the images of the saints painted above and on the sides of the gates.

'When in Rome do as the Romans do,' he observed. 'There are altogether twenty-five saints seeking salvation in this hermitage, looking at one another and eating cabbage soup. What is so remarkable, though, is that no woman is allowed to enter these gates. And that's quite true, you know. But,' he suddenly addressed the monk, 'I've heard that the elder receives ladies. He does, doesn't he?'

'There are peasant women here, too, now. There, sitting on the ground near the wooden veranda. They're waiting. And for ladies two little rooms have been built on top of the veranda but outside the hermitage wall. You can see the windows up there. The elder goes to see them by an inner passage when he feels well enough. But, you see, it's still outside the wall of the hermitage. There's one lady waiting there now with her sick daughter. Mrs Khokhlakov, a Kharkov landowner. I expect he must have promised to come out to her, though lately he's been so weak that he's hardly gone out even to the common people.'

'Oh, so there is a secret passage from the hermitage to the ladies! Please, holy Father, don't think I'm suggesting anything. I'm just making a statement of fact. You know, on Mount Athos – you've heard of it, haven't you? – not only women but any creatures of the female sex are not allowed – no hens, no turkey hens, no calves. . . .'

'Look here, sir,' Miusov interjected, 'I shall go back and leave you here alone, and they'll chuck you out when I'm gone. I'm warning you.'

'I'm not interfering with you, Mr Miusov, am I? Look,' Karamazov cried suddenly, stepping inside the wall of the hermitage, 'look in what a vale of roses they live!'

And, indeed, though there were no roses now, there were a great many rare and beautiful autumn flowers growing wherever there was the least room for them to be planted. It was obvious that they were tended by a skilful hand. There were flower-beds also inside the walls of the churchyard and between the graves. The wooden, one-storied little house, with its porch in front of the entrance, where the elder lived also had flowers planted all round it.

'And was it like this in the time of the last elder Varsonofy?' asked Karamazov, as he mounted the front steps. 'I'm told he didn't like beautiful things and that he would sometimes jump to his feet and beat even lady visitors with a stick.'

'The elder Varsonofy did indeed seem a little strange sometimes,' replied the monk, 'but people tell all sorts of silly tales about him. He never beat anyone with a stick, though. And now, gentlemen,' he concluded, 'if you will kindly wait a minute, I'll announce you.'

'For the last time, sir, remember your promise,' Miusov managed to mutter once more. 'Do you hear? Behave yourself, or you'll be sorry.'

'Now I wonder why you're in such a state of excitement,' Karamazov observed sarcastically. 'You're not worried about your sins, are you? I'm told he can tell by a man's eyes what's at the back of his mind. And how seriously you take them – you, a Parisian and a man of progressive views! I'm surprised at you – indeed I am!'

But Miusov had no time to reply to this sarcastic remark. They were asked to come in. He walked in somewhat irritated.

'Well,' it flashed through his mind, 'I know perfectly well what's going to happen now. I'm angry, I'll start arguing, I'll get excited and – lower myself and my ideas.'

2

The Old Clown

THEY entered the room almost at the same moment as the elder, who came out of his bedroom as soon as they appeared. There were two monks from the hermitage waiting for the elder in his cell: one of them the Father Librarian and the other – Father Paissy, a sick man, though not old, and, it was said, a great scholar. Besides them, there stood waiting in a corner (he remained there standing all through the interview) a young man of about twenty-two, wearing ordinary dress, a seminarist and a future theologian, who for some reason was enjoying the patronage of the monastery and the monks. He was rather tall, fresh-complexioned, with prominent cheek-bones, and clever, observant, narrow brown eyes. His face wore an expression of absolute reverence, but decorous and without a trace of fawning. He did not even greet the visitors with a bow, not being of the same social standing as they, but in a subordinate and dependent position.

The elder Zossima came out accompanied by a novice and by Alyosha. The monks rose and greeted him with a very low bow, touching the floor with their fingers. Then they went up to him for his blessing and kissed his hand. Having blessed them, the elder replied with as low a bow, also touching the floor with his fingers, and asked each of them for his blessing. The whole ceremony was performed very gravely and not at all like an everyday rite, but almost with a show of feeling. It seemed to Miusov, however, that it was all done deliberately in order to impress them. He stood in front of the other visitors. He should – and he had considered it carefully the day before – out of ordinary politeness and in spite of his own ideas on the subject (since it was the custom there) have gone up to the elder to receive his blessing, even if he did not kiss his hand. But, seeing all this bowing and kissing of the two monks, he changed his mind in a moment. Looking very grave, he made a rather deep and dignified bow, as is customary in high society, and retired to a chair. Karamazov did the same, but this time mimicking Miusov like a monkey. Ivan bowed very gravely and politely, but also kept his hands at his sides, while Kalganov was so embarrassed that he did not bow at all. The elder dropped his hand, which he had raised to bless them, and, bowing to them once again, asked them to be seated. The blood rushed to Alyosha's cheeks; he felt ashamed. His worst expectations were coming true.

The elder sat down on a mahogany leather sofa of a very old-fashioned design and asked his visitors, all except the two monks, to sit down along the opposite wall, all four in a row on four mahogany chairs covered with badly worn black leather. The monks sat down on either side of the room, one by the door and the other by the window. The seminarist, the novice, and Alyosha remained standing. The whole cell was far from large and had a sort of uninspiring look. The furniture and everything in it was crude and of poor quality; there was nothing in it that was not absolutely necessary. There were two pots of flowers on the window-sill and a great number of icons in the corner, one of them of the Virgin, very large and painted long before the schism in the Orthodox Church. A lamp was burning in front of it. Beside it were two other icons in shining settings and, near them, carved cherubim, porcelain eggs, a Catholic ivory cross with a Mater Dolorosa embracing it, and a few foreign engravings of the paintings of the great Italian masters of past centuries. Next to these expensive and beautiful engravings were to be seen several very crude Russian lithographs of saints, martyrs, holy men, and so on, which were sold for a few pennies at all the fairs. There were also a few engraved portraits of Russian bishops, past and present, but those were hung on the other walls. Miusov threw a cursory glance at all these 'official' adornments and then looked intently at the elder. He had a high opinion of himself as a man who could judge a person merely by looking at him. It was an excusable weakness, considering that he was fifty, an age at which an intelligent man of the world of independent means always acquires a great respect for his own judgement, sometimes, indeed, quite involuntarily.

From the very first he could not help disliking the elder. And, indeed, there was something in the elder's face that many people besides Miusov would dislike. He was a short, bent little man, with very weak legs, no more than sixty-five years old, though looking at least ten years older because of his illness. His whole face, which was very thin, was covered with small wrinkles, particularly numerous round his eyes. His eyes were not large, light-coloured, quick and shining like two bright points. He had only a few grey hairs left about his temples; his beard was small, scanty, and pointed, and his lips, which smiled frequently, were as thin as two strings; his nose was not long, but sharp, like a bird's beak.

'To all appearances a spiteful, petty, and supercilious character,' flashed through Miusov's mind. He was thoroughly dissatisfied with himself.

The striking of the clock made it easier for them to start the conversation. The cheap little wall clock with two weights struck twelve rapidly.

'Punctually to the hour,' cried Karamazov, 'and my son Dmitry isn't here yet. I apologize for him, holy elder.' (Alyosha shuddered all over at the 'holy elder'.) 'I am always punctual myself, to the minute, remembering that punctuality is the courtesy of kings. . . . '

'But, thank goodness, you're not a king,' muttered Miusov, unable to restrain himself from the very start.

'Yes, that's quite true, I'm not a king. Strange as it may seem to you, Mr Miusov, I knew it myself. Yes, sir! And, you know, I always say the wrong thing! Your reverence,' he cried with a sort of sudden inspiration, 'you see before you a clown. Yes, sir, a real clown! That's how I'd like you to look upon me. An old habit, alas! And if sometimes I talk nonsense when I shouldn't, I do it deliberately, sir, with the express intention of being amusing and agreeable. One has to be agreeable, hasn't one? Seven years ago, sir, I happened to find myself in some filthy little hole of a town. I had some business there. Wanted to found a small company with some lousy merchants.

So off we went to the police inspector, the *ispravnik*, for we had to settle something with him first and invite him to dinner. Well, sir, so out he comes to us, a fair, tall, fat, morose-looking fellow – the most dangerous individuals in such cases: it's their liver, sir, their liver. I went straight up to him with, you know, the nonchalant air of a man of the world. "Mr *Ispravnik*," I said, "won't you be, as it were, our Napravnik?" "Napravnik?" he said. "What do you mean, sir?" Well, I could see in a flash that our affair had miscarried, for there he stood looking serious and unco-operative. "I'm sorry," I said, "I wanted to make a joke to amuse the company, for Mr Napravnik," I said, "is one of our famous Russian conductors and for the harmony of our enterprise we want a sort of conductor. . . . " A good and reasonable explanation, wasn't it? An apt comparison. "I'm very sorry," he said, "I'm an *ispravnik* and I won't allow puns to be made on my official position." He turned and walked away. I rushed after him. "Yes, yes," I cried, "you are an *ispravnik* and not Napravnik." "No, sir," he said, "since you said so, I am Napravnik." And, you know, our business deal fell through! I'm always like that. I'm always doing myself some injury by my politeness – always! Once, many years ago, I said to a highly influential person: "Your wife, sir, is a ticklish lady." I meant it, of course, in the sense of a highly honourable lady, a lady of high moral principles, so to speak. But he suddenly said to me in reply to my remark: "Why? Have you tickled her?" Well, sir, so I thought to myself why not be polite? "Yes, sir," I said, "I did tickle her." Well, so he gave me a proper tickling there and then. . . . It happened a long time ago, so I'm not ashamed to tell the story. I'm always doing myself an injury like that!'

'You're doing it now, too!' Miusov muttered in disgust.

The elder scrutinized them both in silence.

'Am I? Well, fancy that, Mr Miusov, I've known it all the time. You see, sir, I had a feeling I was going to do so as soon as I began speaking, and, what's more, I knew that you'd be the first to remark on it. The moment I see, your reverence, that my joke isn't coming off, my cheeks begin to stick to my lower gums and it's almost as though they were contracted in a spasm. I've had it since I was a young man, when I was living on noblemen's charity and, indeed, making a living by sponging on them. I'm an inveterate clown. A born clown. Just as if I were a saintly fool, your reverence. Mind you, I freely admit that there may be an evil spirit in me, too, but if there is, it's only a small one. Had it been a bigger one, he'd have chosen different lodgings, but not yours, Mr Miusov, for your lodgings aren't big enough, either. But I make up for it by believing – I believe in God, sir. It's only lately that I've had my doubts, but now I sit and wait for words of great wisdom. I'm just like the philosopher Diderot, your reverence. I suppose you know, most holy father, that the philosopher Diderot went to see the Metropolitan Platon at the time of the Empress Catherine. As soon as he went in, he blurted out: "There is no God." To which his holiness, the great patriarch, raised his finger and said: "The madman hath said in his heart there is no God." And the philosopher threw himself down at his feet at once: "I believe," he cried, "and I will be baptized!" So they baptized him there and then. Princess Dashkov was his godmother and Potyomkin his godfather.'

'My dear sir,' Miusov, unable to restrain himself any longer, said in a shaking voice, 'this is unbearable! You know perfectly well that you're talking nonsense and that that stupid story isn't true. Why, then, are you making a fool of yourself?'

'All my life I've had a feeling that it wasn't true!' Karamazov cried with enthusiasm. 'But I'll tell you the whole truth, gentlemen. Great elder, forgive me, I invented my last story about Diderot's christening just now, this very minute, while I was talking to you. I never thought of it before. Invented it just for fun. You see, Mr Miusov, I'm making a fool of myself so that people should like me better. Still, sometimes I don't know myself why I do it. As for Diderot, I heard this "the madman hath said in his heart" scores of times from the local landowners I lived with when I was young. I heard it from your aunt, too, Mr Miusov, as a matter of fact. They're all convinced even today that the infidel Diderot went to the Metropolitan Platon to dispute about God. . . .'

Miusov got up, having not only lost patience but looking as though he did not know what he was doing. He was furious, and he felt that that made him look ridiculous. What was taking place in the cell was really something absolutely incredible. For forty or fifty years, at the time of the former elders, visitors had gathered in the same cell, but never without a feeling of the most profound reverence. Almost everyone admitted to the cell realized, as he entered it, that a great favour was being shown to him. Many fell down on their knees and did not get up during the whole visit. Many people belonging to the 'highest' ranks of society, even great scholars, or, indeed, freethinkers who came from curiosity or for some other reason, entering the cell together with other visitors or alone, thought it to be their bounden duty – all of them – to show the most profound reverence and tact during the whole of their visit, particularly as there was no question of money, but merely love and kindness on the one hand, and, on the other, penitence and an eagerness to solve some difficult spiritual question or some crisis in one's private life. So that such sudden buffoonery as that shown by Karamazov, which was so disrespectful in such a place, bewildered and amazed everyone who was present at the interview, or at least some of them. The monks, whose faces, however, did not betray any emotion, waited with earnest attention to hear what the elder would say, but were apparently ready to get up, like Miusov. Alyosha was on the verge of tears and stood with his head bowed. What seemed to him particularly strange was that his brother Ivan, on whom alone he had relied and who alone had such influence with his father that he could have stopped him, sat now quite motionless in his chair, with his eyes lowered to the ground, apparently waiting with a sort of curious interest to see how it would all end, just as if he had nothing to do with it. Alyosha could not even bring himself to look at Rakitin (the seminarist), who was also almost an intimate friend of his: he knew his thoughts, and he was the only one in the monastery who knew them.

'I'm sorry,' began Miusov, addressing the elder, 'to appear to be also taking some part in this undignified tomfoolery. The mistake I made was to believe that even a man like Mr Karamazov would realize his obligations when paying a visit to so highly esteemed a person. I did not realize that I'd have to apologize simply for having come with him. . . .'

Miusov stopped short and, utterly discomfited, was about to leave the room.

'Please, do not distress yourself, I beg you,' said the elder, rising on his feeble legs and, taking Miusov by both hands, he made him sit down again. 'Don't worry, I beg you. I ask you particularly to be my guest,' and bowing, he turned back and resumed his seat on the sofa.

'Great elder, tell me please, do I insult you by my high spirits or not?' Karamazov cried suddenly, grasping the arms of his chair with both hands, as though he were ready to jump out of it if the reply was unfavourable.

'I beg you earnestly not to disturb yourself and not to be put out,' the elder said impressively. 'Do not be disconcerted, make yourself quite at home. And, above all, do not be so ashamed of yourself, for that is at the root of it all.'

'Quite at home? You mean be my natural self? Oh, that is much, sir, too much, but I accept it – touched to the core! Though, you know, blessed father, you must not let me be my natural self – it's too great a risk! As a matter of fact, I won't go as far as that myself. I promise you this just because I'm anxious to save you from un-pleasantness. Well, sir, as for the rest, it's still enveloped in a fog of uncertainty, though I daresay some people would like to say all sorts of nasty things about me. It's you, I mean, Mr Miusov. As for you, most holy being, I can only tell you that I'm overcome with ecstasy!' He got up and, raising his hands aloft, said solemnly: ' "Blessed is the womb that bare thee and the paps that gave thee suck" – the paps especially! By your remark – "Don't be so ashamed of your-self, for that is at the root of it all" – by this remark, sir, you seem to have seen right through me and read my innermost secrets. For it does seem to me every time I go to see people that I'm more con-temptible than anyone else and that everyone takes me for a clown. That's why I say to myself, "All right, let me play the clown! I'm not afraid of your opinion, because you're all without exception more contemptible than I!" That's why I'm a clown, great elder. I am a clown from shame. Yes, sir, from shame! It's my sensitiveness alone that makes me kick up a row. If only I could be sure when entering a room that everyone would accept me at once as the kindest and wisest of men – Lord! what a good man I'd be then! Master,' he cried, falling suddenly on his knees, 'what am I to do to gain eternal life?'

It was difficult to decide even now whether he was joking or whether he really was deeply moved.

The elder raised his eyes at him and said with a smile:

'You've known for a long time what you have to do. You've sense enough: do not indulge in drunkenness and incontinence of speech, do not indulge in sensual pursuits and, especially, in the love of money. Close your public houses, and if you can't close them all, close two or three at least. And most of all – do not tell lies.'

'You're referring to Diderot, aren't you?'

'No, not only to Diderot. Above all, don't lie to yourself. A man who lies to himself and who listens to his own lies gets to a point where he can't distinguish any truth in himself or in those around him, and so loses all respect for himself and for others. Having no respect for anyone, he ceases to love, and to occupy and distract himself without love he becomes a prey to his passions and gives himself up to coarse pleasures, and sinks to bestiality in his vices, and all this from continual lying to people and to himself. A man who lies to himself can be more easily offended than anyone else. For it is sometimes very pleasant to take offence, isn't it? And yet he knows that no one has offended him and that he has invented the offence himself, that he has lied just for the beauty of it, that he has exaggerated to make himself look big and important, that he has fastened on a phrase and made a mountain out of a molehill – he knows it all and yet is the first to take offence, he finds pleasure in it and feels mightily satisfied with himself, and so reaches the point of real enmity.... Get up, please. Sit down, I beg you. Why, all this, too, is deceitful posturing.'

'Blessed man, let me kiss your hand,' Karamazov cried, rushing up to the elder and imprinting a rapid kiss on his thin hand. 'Yes, indeed, it is pleasant to take offence. You've put it better than I've ever heard it before. Yes, indeed, I've been taking offence all my life till I glowed with pleasure, taking offence to satisfy my aesthetic feelings, for sometimes it is not only pleasant but also beautiful to be offended. That's what you, great elder, have forgotten to take into account: it is beautiful! I shall make a note of that! And I have been lying, I've indeed been lying all my life, every day and every hour. Verily, I am a lie and the father of lies! Though perhaps not the father of lies – I'm afraid I'm getting mixed-up in my texts. Let's say, the son of lies – that, too, will be enough. Only – dear angel – one may tell a lie about Diderot sometimes, mayn't one? Diderot will do no harm, but something else will. By the way, great elder, I was for-getting, but as a matter of fact I had made up my mind as far back as two years ago to find out here, I meant to come here on purpose to find out – only, please, ask Mr Miusov not to interrupt me. What I wanted to ask you is this: great Father, is the story told somewhere in the *Lives of the Saints* true, the story about some holy miracle-worker, who was tortured for his faith and who, when they cut off his head at last, stood up, picked up his head and "kissing it lovingly", walked a long way, carrying it in his hands and "kissing it lovingly"? Is it true or not, upright and reverend Fathers?'

'No, it's not true,' said the elder.

'There's nothing of the kind in the *Lives of the Saints*,' said the Father Librarian. 'What saint do you say the story is told of?'

'I'm afraid I don't know what saint. Haven't the faintest idea. I've been deceived. I was told about it. I heard it, and do you know who told it? Mr Miusov here who was so angry about Diderot just now. It was he who told the story.'

'I never told you it. I never speak to you at all.'

'It's true you did not tell me, but you told it when I was there. It was over three years ago. I mentioned it because you undermined my faith, sir, by that funny story. You knew nothing about that, but I returned home with my faith shaken and since then I've been getting more and more shaken in it. Yes, sir, you were the cause of my great fall! That, sir, is not just Diderot!'

Karamazov got excited and assumed a pathetic expression, though it was perfectly clear to everyone that he was play-acting again. But Miusov was deeply hurt all the same.

'What nonsense,' he muttered. 'It's all nonsense. I may have really said something of the kind some time or other . . . but not to you. I was told it myself. I heard it in Paris from a Frenchman. He said it was read at morning mass in our churches. He was a great scholar. Made a special study of Russian statistics. He had lived in Russia a long time. . . . I've not read the *Lives of the Saints* myself and – er – I'm not going to read it. . . . All sorts of things are said at dinner. . . . We were having dinner at the time. . . . '

'Yes, you were having dinner and I lost my faith!' Karamazov taunted him.

'What do I care about your faith!' Miusov shouted, but he suddenly checked himself and said with contempt: 'You literally defile everything you touch.'

The elder suddenly got up from his seat.

'Excuse me, gentlemen, for leaving you for a few minutes,' he said, addressing all his visitors. 'But I have people waiting for me who arrived before you. And you, sir,' he turned to Karamazov with a cheerful face, 'would do well not to tell lies all the same.'

He walked towards the door. Alyosha and the novice rushed after him to help him down the stairs. Alyosha was choking. He was glad to get away, but he was glad, too, that the elder was cheerful and not offended. The elder went in the direction of the veranda to bless those who were waiting for him. But Karamazov insisted on stopping him at the door of the cell.

'Most blessed man,' he cried with feeling, 'allow me to kiss your hand once more! Yes, sir, one can talk to you, one can get on with you. Do you think I always tell lies and play the clown like that? Well, sir, I want you to know that I was acting like that all the time on purpose so as to try you. I've been watching you carefully all the time to see whether one could get on with you. Whether there was room for my humility beside your pride. Let me hand you a certificate of honour: it is possible to get on with you. Now I shall hold my peace. I shan't say another word. I'm going to sit in my chair and hold my peace. It's your turn, Mr Miusov, to speak now. You're the most important person left here now – for ten minutes. . . .'

3

Devout Peasant Women

ABOUT twenty peasant women crowded all this time near the wooden veranda built on to the outer side of the hermitage wall. They had been told that the elder would at last be coming out and they had gathered in expectation. The two ladies, Mrs Khokhlakov and her daughter, who had also been waiting for the elder, came out on the veranda, but in the part set aside for gentlewomen. Mrs Khokhlakov, a rich woman who was always dressed with taste, was still quite young and very good-looking, a little pale, with very vivacious and almost black eyes. She was not more than thirty-three and had been a widow for five years. Her fourteen-year-old daughter suffered from paralysis of the legs. The poor girl had not been able to walk for the last six months and she was pushed about in a long, comfortable wheel-chair. She had a charming face, a little thin from illness, but gay. There was a mischievous gleam in her big dark eyes with their long lashes. Her mother had been intending to take her abroad ever since the spring, but they had been detained all summer by business connected with their estate. They had been staying in our town for a week, more on business than devotion, but had already paid one visit to the elder three days before. Now they had suddenly arrived again, though they knew that the elder was hardly able to receive anyone, and requested earnestly to be granted 'the happiness of seeing the great healer once more'. In expectation of the appearance of the elder, the mother sat on a chair near her daughter's wheel-chair, and two paces away from her stood an old monk, who did not belong to our monastery but was a visitor from a remote, little-known monastery in the north. He, too, wished to receive the elder's blessing. But, on appearing on the veranda, the elder at first went straight to the peasant women, who crowded round the three front steps leading to the low veranda. The elder stood on the top step, put on his stole, and began to bless the women who clustered round him. They pulled a 'shrieker' towards him by both hands. As soon as she caught sight of him, the sick woman suddenly began hiccuping, squealing in an absurd fashion, and trembling all over as though in a fit of convulsions. Putting the stole on her head, the elder read a short prayer over her, and she at once fell silent and calmed down. I do not know how it is now, but as a child I often happened to see and hear these 'shriekers' in the villages and monasteries. They were brought to morning mass, they squealed and barked like dogs so that they could be heard all over the church, but when the Host was carried in and they were led up to it, their 'raving' stopped at once and the sick women grew quiet for a time. As a child, I was greatly struck and amazed by it. But then I was told in reply to my questions by some landowners, and especially by my town teachers, that it was all a sham and staged to avoid work, and that it could be easily eradicated by suitable severity; and various amusing stories were told to prove it. But later on I learnt with astonishment from specialists that there was no question of any sham about it, that it was a terrible illness that afflicted women, apparently mostly in Russia, which bore witness to the hard life of our village women, an illness which was caused by exhausting work shortly after difficult, abnormal labour without medical assistance; it was caused, besides, by hopeless misery, beatings, etc., which some women are unable to endure in spite of the prevalence of such ill-treatment. The strange and instantaneous cure of the raving and struggling woman as soon as she is led up to the Host, which had been explained to me as shamming and, moreover, as a trick played on the people by the 'clericals', was also probably due to most natural causes. For the women who took the 'shrieker' up to the Host and, above all, the sick woman herself sincerely believed, as an undeniable truth, that the evil spirit who had taken possession of her could not stand it if she was taken up to the Host and made to bow down before it. And that was why it always happened (and, indeed, had to happen) that the nervous and, of course, mentally ill woman always suffered a violent shock at the moment when she bowed down to the Host, a shock caused by the expectation of the certain miracle of healing and by her implicit faith in its taking place. And it did take place, if only for a moment. It took place in exactly the same way now as soon as the elder covered the sick woman with his stole.

Many of the women who had crowded round him were so thrilled and moved by the sensational cure that they burst into tears; others strove to kiss the hem of the elder's robe, while still others started keening. He blessed them all, and spoke to some of them. The 'shrieker' he knew already, for she had been brought from a nearby village only five miles from the monastery and had been taken to see him several times before.

'And here's one from a long way off,' he said, pointing to a woman who was still quite young, but thin and worn out, with a face that was not so much sunburnt as blackened. She was kneeling and staring motionless at the elder. There was almost a frenzied look in her eyes.

'From a long way off, Father, from a long way off,' the woman said in a sing-song voice, swaying her head regularly to and fro and resting her cheek on her hand. 'Two hundred miles from here – a long way, Father, a long way.'

She spoke as though she were keening. There is among the

peasants a silent and long-enduring sorrow. It withdraws into itself and is still. But there is also a sorrow that has reached the limit of endurance: it will then burst out in tears and from that moment break out into keening. This is especially so with women. But it is not easier to bear than a silent sorrow. The keening soothes it only by embittering and lacerating the heart still more. Such sorrow does not desire consolation and feeds upon the sense of its hopelessness. The keening is merely an expression of the constant need to reopen the wound.

'You're of the artisan class, aren't you?' the elder continued, looking curiously at her.

'We're townspeople, Father, townspeople. We were peasants before, but we're townspeople now – we live in the town. I've come to see you, Father. We heard about you, Father. Aye, we heard about you. I've just buried my little son, and I've come to pray to God. Been in three monasteries, I have, and they told me to go and see you, love, at this monastery. And so I've come. I was in church here yesterday, and today I've come to you.'

'What is it you're weeping for?'

'I'm sorry for my little boy, Father. He was three years old – three years in another three months he would have been. I'm grieving for my little boy, Father, for my little darling boy – the last I had left. We had four, Nikita and I, four children, but not one of them is alive, Father, not one of them, not one. I buried the first three, I wasn't very sorry for them, I wasn't, but this last one I buried and I can't forget him. He seems to be standing before me now – he never leaves me. He has dried up my soul. I keep looking at his little things, his little shirt or his little boots, and I wail. I lay out all that's left of him, every little thing. I look at them and wail. I say to my husband, to Nikita, let me go, husband, I'd like to go on a pilgrimage. He's a driver, Father. We're not poor people, Father. We're our own masters. It's all our own, the horses and the carriage. But what do we want it all now for? My Nikita has taken to drinking without me, I'm sure he has, he used to before: I had only to turn my back, and he'd weaken. But now I'm no longer thinking of him. It's over two months since I left home. I've forgotten everything, I have, and I don't want to remember. And what will my life with him be like now? I've done with him, I have. I've done with them all. I don't want to see my house and my things again. I hope I'll never see them again!'

'Now listen to me, Mother,' said the elder. 'Once, a long time ago, a great saint saw a woman like you in a church. She was weeping for her little infant child, her only one, whom God had also taken. "Don't you know," said the saint to her, "how bold and fearless these little ones are before the throne of the Lord? There's none bolder or more fearless than they in the Kingdom of Heaven: Thou, O Lord, hast given us life, they say to God, and no sooner had we looked upon it than thou didst take it away. And so boldly and fearlessly do they ask and demand an explanation that God gives them at once the rank of angels. And therefore," said the saint, "you, too, Mother, rejoice and do not weep, for your little one is now with the Lord in the company of his angels." That's what the saint said to the weeping mother in the olden days. And he was a great saint and he would not have told her an untruth. Know, then, you too, Mother, that your little one is most assuredly standing now before the throne of the Lord, and is rejoicing and happy, and praying to God for you. And, therefore, weep not, but rejoice.'

The woman listened to him with a bowed head, her cheek resting on her hand. She heaved a deep sigh.

'My Nikita, too, tried to comfort me with the same words as you, Father. "Don't be foolish," he says, "what are you crying for? Our son is now with the Lord God for certain and is singing with the angels." He said that to me, but he cried himself. I could see that he cried like me. "I know that, dear husband," I says to him. "Where else could he be if not with the Lord God. Only he isn't with us here, is he? He isn't sitting beside us now as he used to before, is he?" Oh, if only I could look at him just once, if only I could have a look at him once again! I wouldn't go up to him. I wouldn't say a word. I would just keep quiet in a corner, only to see him for one little minute, to hear him playing in the yard. He used to come to me and call in his little voice, "Mum, where are you?" Oh, if only I could see him walk across the room on his darling little feet just once, only once. I remember hearing the patter of his little feet as he rushed up to me again and again, shouting and laughing. If only I could hear it again – I'd recognize it as soon as I heard it! But he's gone, Father, he's gone and I shall never hear him again. Here's his little belt, but he's no longer here, and I shall never, never see or hear him now!'

She drew out of her bosom her boy's little embroidered belt and as soon as she looked at it she began shaking with sobs, covering her eyes with her fingers through which the tears suddenly flowed in a stream.

'Behold,' the elder said, ' "Rachel weeping for her children refused to be comforted for her children, because they were not," and such is the lot bestowed upon you, mothers, on earth. And do not be comforted. There's no need for you to be comforted. Be not comforted but weep, and every time you weep be sure to remember that your little son is one of the angels of the Lord, that he looks down on you and sees you and rejoices in your tears and points them out to God. And for a long, long time you will go on weeping as all mothers have done since time immemorial, but in the end your weeping will turn into quiet joy and your bitter tears will be only the tears of quiet, tender joy, purifying the heart and saving it from sin. I shall mention your little boy in my prayers. What was his name?'

'Alexey, Father.'

'A sweet name. After Alexey the man of God?'

'Of God, Father, of God. Alexey the man of God.'

'He was a great saint! I shall mention him in my prayers, Mother, I shall. And I shall mention your sorrow in my prayers, too, and your husband that he may live and prosper. Only you should not have left your husband. You must go back to him and look after him. Your little boy will look down on you and, seeing that you've forsaken his father, he will weep over you both: why do you destroy his bliss? For, don't forget, he's living, he's living, for the soul lives for ever, and though he is no longer in the house, he's always there unseen beside you. How do you expect him to come home if you say you hate your house? To whom is he to go, if he won't find you, his father and mother, together? You see him in your dreams now and you grieve, but if you go back he will send you sweet dreams. Go to your husband, Mother, go back to him today.'

'I will, Father, I will do as you say. You've touched my heart. Nikita, dear Nikita, you're waiting for me, my darling!' the woman began keening, but the elder had already turned away to a very old woman, dressed like a townswoman and not like a pilgrim. It could

be seen from her eyes that she had come on some business and that
she had something to tell him. She said she was the widow of a non-
commissioned officer and lived in our town. Her son Vassily served
in the army commissariat, but had gone to Irkutsk in Siberia. He
had written twice from there, but now she had had no letter from
him for over a year. She had made inquiries about him, but she really
did not know where to inquire.

'Only the other day Stepanida Bedryagina – she's a rich merchant's
wife – said to me, why don't you go and give your son's name to the
priest and he'll mention it in his prayers in church just as if he was
dead. His soul, she said, will pine for you and he'll write you a letter.
It's quite true, she said, what I'm telling you. It's been tried many
times. Only I'm not so sure, Father. Tell me, please, is it true or not,
and would it be the right thing to do?'

'Don't think of it. You ought to be ashamed to ask me such a
question. And indeed how is it possible for a mother of all people to
pray for the peace of a living soul? It's a great sin, a sin akin to sorcery,
and it is forgiven only because of your ignorance. You had better
pray to the Holy Virgin, our swift intermediary and helper, to grant
him health and that she may forgive you for your wrong ideas.
And let me tell you this, too, Prokhorovna: your son will either soon
come back to you or he will be sure to send you a letter. I want you
to know this. Go now and don't worry any more. Your son is alive,
I tell you.'

'May the good Lord reward you, Father. You bring us good tidings and you pray for all of us and for our sins. . . . '

But the elder had already noticed in the crowd the two burning
eyes of a wasted, consumptive-looking, though quite young peasant
woman, fixed upon him. She gazed at him in silence. Her eyes were
beseeching him for something, but she seemed to be afraid to draw
nearer.

'What's your trouble, my dear?'

'Give me absolution, dear Father,' she said quietly and unhurriedly
and, kneeling, she bowed down at his feet. 'I have sinned, dear Father.
I'm afraid of my sin.'

The elder sat down on the lower step. The woman approached
him without rising from her knees.

'I've been a widow for over two years,' she began in a half-whisper, with a kind of shudder. 'My married life was hard, my husband was an old man and he used to beat me mercilessly. He lay ill and, looking at him, I couldn't help thinking what would happen to me if he got well and got up again. And that's when the thought came to me. . . . '

'Wait,' said the elder and put his ear close to her lips.

The woman went on in a soft whisper so that it was almost impossible to catch anything. She was soon finished.

'Over two years ago?' asked the elder.

'Over two years ago, Father. At first I didn't think about it, but now I've begun to be ill and I'm very worried. . . . '

'Have you come from far?'

'Over three hundred miles from here.'

'Have you told it to the priest at confession?'

'I have. Twice I've confessed it.'

'Have you been admitted to Communion?'

'Yes, Father. But I'm afraid. I'm afraid to die.'

'Do not be afraid of anything. Do not ever be afraid. And don't worry. So long as you remain sincerely penitent, God will forgive you everything. There's no sin, and there can be no sin in the whole world which God will not forgive to those who are truly repentant. Why, man cannot commit so great a sin as to exhaust the infinite love of God. Or can there be a sin that would exceed the love of God? Only you must never forget to think continually of repentance, but dismiss your fear altogether. Believe that God loves you in a way you cannot even conceive of. He loves you in spite of your sin and in your sin. And there's more joy in heaven over one sinner that repents than over ten righteous men. This was said a long time ago. So go and do not be afraid. Do not be upset by people and do not be angry if you're wronged. Forgive your dead husband in your heart, however badly he treated you. Be truly reconciled to him. If you are sorry for what you did, then you must love. And if you love, you are of God. . . . Everything can be atoned for, everything can be saved by love. If I, a sinner like you, have been moved by your story and am sorry for you, how much more will God be. Love is such a priceless treasure that you can redeem everything in the world by it, and expiate not only your own but other people's sins. Go and do not be afraid.'

He made the sign of the cross over her three times, took off the little icon from his neck and put it upon her. She bowed down to the ground to him in silence. He got up and looked cheerfully at a healthy peasant woman with a baby in her arms.

'From Vyshegorye, dear Father.'

'You've dragged yourself here for five miles with your baby. What do you want?'

'I've come to have a look at you, Father. I've been to see you before, or have you forgotten? You must have a bad memory, if you've forgotten me. They were saying in our village that you were ill, so I thought I'd better go and see him myself: now I see you and you're not ill at all! You'll live for another twenty years. So you will, really! And, besides, haven't you enough people praying for you? How could you be ill?'

'Thank you for everything, my dear.'

'By the way, I have something I'd like to ask you, Father. It's a small thing. I've sixty copecks here, take them and give them, dear Father, to someone poorer than me. As I was coming here, I thought to myself: I'd better give it through him. He'll know who to give it to.'

'Thank you, my dear, thank you for your kindness. I love you. I'll certainly do so. Is that your little girl in your arms?'

'Yes, Father. Lizaveta.'

'May the Lord bless you both, you and your baby Lizaveta. You've gladdened my heart, Mother. Good-bye, my dear ones, good-bye.'

He blessed them all and bowed low to them.

4

A Lady of Little Faith

WATCHING the scene of the elder's conversation with the peasant women and his blessing them, Mrs Khokhlakov shed silent tears and wiped them away with a handkerchief. She was a very sentimental society woman and a genuinely kindly one in many things. When the elder at last went up to her, she met him ecstatically.

'Oh, I've been through so much, so much while watching this moving scene. I . . .' she could not go on from excitement. 'Oh, I can see that the peasants love you, I love the peasants myself, I want to love them, and – and, besides, how can one help loving our wonderful people, so simple-minded in its greatness?'

'How is your daughter? You wanted to have another talk with me?'

'Oh, I've kept asking for it. I've prayed for it. I was prepared to go down on my knees and kneel under your windows for three days, if need be, until you let me in. We've come to you, great healer, to give full expression to our deep gratitude. You've cured my Lise, you've cured her completely, and you did it just by saying a prayer over her last Thursday and laying your hands on her. We've come to kiss those hands, to pour out our feelings and our veneration.'

'Cured her, have I? Isn't she still in her chair?'

'But her night fevers have completely vanished for the last two days, ever since Thursday,' the lady hurried on nervously. 'And what's more she feels much stronger in her legs. This morning she got up feeling well. She had slept all night. Look at her rosy cheeks, at her bright eyes. She used to be always crying, but now she laughs, she's cheerful and gay. Today she insisted on my letting her stand up, and she stood for a whole minute without any support. She has a wager with me that in a fortnight she'll be dancing a quadrille. I've called in the local doctor Herzenstube. He shrugged his shoulders and said that he was astonished and did not know what to make of it. And would you really prefer us not to disturb you, not to fly here, not to thank you? Lise, thank him – thank him!'

Lise's pretty little laughing face became suddenly serious; she raised herself in her chair as much as she could and, looking at the elder, put her hands together before him, but could not restrain herself and suddenly burst out laughing.

'I'm laughing at him, at him!' she said, pointing to Alyosha, childishly annoyed with herself for having been unable to restrain herself from laughing.

If anyone had looked at Alyosha, who was standing a step behind the elder, he would have noticed a quick flush suffusing his face. His eyes flashed and he dropped them at once.

'She has a message for you, Alexey,' the fond mother went on, suddenly addressing Alyosha and holding out her exquisitely gloved hand to him. 'How are you?'

The elder turned round and all at once looked attentively at

Alyosha, who walked up to Lise and held out his hand to her, too, with a sort of strange and awkward smile. Lise assumed an air of importance.

'Katerina sends you this through me,' she said, handing him a note. 'She asks you specially to go and see her, and as soon as possible, and not to let her down, but be quite sure to come.'

'She asks me to go and see her?' Alyosha murmured in great astonishment. 'Me see her? But why?'

He suddenly looked very worried.

'Oh, it's all because of your brother Dmitry and – all that's happened recently,' her mother explained hurriedly. 'Katerina has come to a certain decision, but – she simply has to see you about it first. Why? I'm afraid I don't know, but she asked you to go and see her as soon as possible. And you will, won't you? I know you will. Your feelings as a Christian will, I'm sure, tell you to do so.'

'I've only seen her once. . . .' Alyosha protested with the same perplexed look on his face.

'Oh, she's such a high-minded, such an incomparable creature! I mean, her suffering alone. . . . Just think what she's been through, what she must be going through now – think what awaits her now – it's all so ghastly, so ghastly. . . .'

'Very well, I'll come,' Alyosha decided after running through the very brief and enigmatic note, which, except for an earnest request to come, offered no explanation at all.

'Oh, that would be so nice and splendid of you,' Lise cried, growing suddenly very animated. 'I told mother you wouldn't come for anything because you were saving your soul. Oh, how splendid you are! I've always thought you were splendid, and I'm glad to tell you so now!'

'Lise!' her mother cried admonishingly, smiling at once though.

'You've forgotten us, too, Alexey,' she went on. 'You don't seem to want to come and see us. Yet Lise has told me twice that she's only happy when she's with you.'

Alyosha raised his downcast eyes, blushed suddenly once more and again smiled without himself knowing why. The elder, however, was no longer watching him. He had entered into a conversation with the monk who, as we mentioned before, had been waiting for him by Lise's chair. He seemed to be a monk of humble origin, that is, of the peasant class, with a narrow, unbending outlook, but a true believer and, in his own way, stubborn. He introduced himself as coming from the far north, from Obdorsk, from Saint Sylvester, a poor monastery, consisting only of nine monks. The elder blessed him and invited him to come to his cell whenever he wished.

'How do you presume to do such things?' the monk asked suddenly, pointing solemnly and impressively at Lise. He was referring to her having been 'healed'.

'It's a little too soon, of course, to talk about that,' replied the elder. 'Relief is far from a complete cure and could arise from other causes. But if anything did happen, it did so by no power except by God's will. Everything is from God. Come and see me, Father,' he added, 'but I'm afraid I can't see visitors at just any time. I'm ill, and I know that my days are numbered.'

'Oh, no, no,' cried Mrs Khokhlakov, 'God will never take you away from us – you'll live a long, long time yet. And what's wrong with you? You look so well, so cheerful, and happy!'

'I feel much better today, but I know it's only for a moment. I thoroughly understand my illness now. And thank you for saying that I look cheerful. You couldn't have said anything that would have made me so happy. For men are made for happiness, and he who is completely happy has a right to say to himself: I've carried out God's sacred will on earth. All the righteous, all the saints, all the martyrs were happy people.'

'Oh, how splendidly you talk,' cried Mrs Khokhlakov. 'What brave and lofty words. You say something and it seems to pierce one through and through. And yet – happiness, happiness – where is it? Who can say that he's truly happy? Oh, since you've been so kind as to let us see you again today, please let me tell you what I couldn't say last time, what I dared not say. Let me tell you all I am suffering from and have been suffering for so long, so long! I am suffering, I'm sorry, but I am, I am!' And she put her hands together before him, carried away by some ardent, uncontrollable feeling.

'From what specially?'

'I'm suffering from – from lack of faith.'

'Lack of faith in God?'

'Oh, no, no! I dare not even think of that! But life after death – it's such a mystery! And there's no one, absolutely no one, who can solve it. Listen, you are a healer, you're an expert on the human soul. I have no right, of course, to expect you to believe me entirely, but I give you my solemn word that I'm saying this not because I haven't thought it over carefully, but because this idea of a future life upsets me so much that it positively hurts me. It frightens and horrifies me. . . . And I don't know whom to turn to – I haven't dared to all my life. . . . And now I dare to turn to you. . . . Oh dear, what will you think of me now?' She clasped her hands.

'Don't worry about what I think,' replied the elder. 'I quite believe in the sincerity of your anguish.'

'Oh, I *am* so grateful to you! You see, I close my eyes and think: if everyone has faith, then where does it come from? And then I hear people say that it all arose at first from fear of the terrible manifestations of nature, and that there's nothing in it all. Well, I say to myself, I've been believing all my life, but what if I die and there's nothing at all and all that will happen is that, as one writer put it, "burdock will be growing on my grave"? It's awful! How, how am I to get back my faith? Mind you, I believed only when I was a little girl, mechanically, without thinking of anything. . . . But how, how am I to prove it? That's why I've come now to throw myself at your feet and ask you about it. If I miss this opportunity too now, I won't be able to get an answer for the rest of my life. How is one to prove it? How is one to be convinced? Oh, poor me! Everyone around me, almost everyone, doesn't seem to care one bit, no one worries about it now, and I'm the only one who can't stand it. It's dreadful – dreadful!'

'I daresay it is. But it's something one cannot prove. One can be convinced of it, though.'

'How? In what way?'

'By the experience of active love. Strive to love your neighbours actively and indefatigably. And the nearer you come to achieving this love, the more convinced you will become of the existence of God and the immortality of your soul. If you reach the point of complete selflessness in your love of your neighbours, you will most certainly regain your faith and no doubt can possibly enter your soul. This has been proved. This is certain.'

'Active love? That's another problem and what a problem – what a problem! You see: I love humanity so much that – would you believe it? – I sometimes dream of giving up all, all I have, leaving Lise and becoming a hospital nurse. I close my eyes, I think and dream, and at those moments I feel full of indomitable strength. No wounds, no festering sores could frighten me then. I could clean and bandage them with my own hands. I could nurse the sufferers and be ready to kiss their sores. . . . '

'That, too, is a great deal and it is well that you should be dreaming about that and not about something else. I shouldn't be surprised if by chance you really did do some good deed.'

'Yes, but how long do you think I could endure such a life?' the lady continued heatedly and almost frenziedly. 'That's the most important question! That's my most agonizing question. I close my eyes and ask myself: how long would you be able to bear such a life? And what if the patient, whose sores you're washing, does not at once show how grateful he is to you, but, on the contrary, begins to torment you with his whims, without noticing or valuing your charitable services? What if he should start shouting at you, demanding something from you rudely or even complaining to your superiors (as often happens when people are in great pain) – what then? Will you still go on loving him? And, you know, I came with horror to the conclusion that if there were anything that could instantly damp the ardour of my "active" love of humanity, it would be ingratitude. In short, I can work only if I'm paid. I demand payment at once. I mean I want to be praised and paid for love with love. Otherwise, I'm incapable of loving anyone.'

She was in a paroxysm of the most genuine self-castigation and, having finished, she looked with defiant determination at the elder.

'That's exactly the same sort of thing a doctor told me a long time ago,' observed the elder. 'He was an elderly and undoubtedly clever man. He spoke to me as frankly as you, though in jest, but in mournful jest. "I love humanity," he said, "but I can't help being surprised at myself: the more I love humanity in general, the less I love men in particular, I mean, separately, as separate individuals. In my dreams," he said, "I am very often passionately determined to serve humanity, and I might quite likely have sacrificed my life for my fellow-creatures, if for some reason it had been suddenly demanded of me, and yet I'm quite incapable of living with anyone in one room for two days together, and I know that from experience. As soon as anyone comes close to me, his personality begins to oppress my vanity and restrict my freedom. I'm capable of hating the best men in twenty-four hours: one because he sits too long over his dinner, another because he has a cold in the head and keeps on blowing his nose. I become an enemy of people the moment they come close to me. But, on the other hand, it invariably happened that the more I hated men individually, the more ardent became my love for humanity at large." '

'But what's to be done? What is one to do in such a case? Should one give way to despair?'

'No, for it is enough that you are distressed about it. Do what you can and it will be put to your account. And you've done a great deal already, since you've been able to know yourself so deeply and so sincerely. But if you've spoken to me so sincerely now simply to be commended by me for your truthfulness, as you have just been, then it goes without saying that you will achieve nothing in your attempts at active love. It will all remain a dream and your whole life will flash by like a phantom. In that case, you will of course forget all about the future life and in the end you will somehow or other find peace by yourself.'

'You've crushed me! Only now, at this very moment, as you spoke, I realized that I was really only waiting for you to commend my sincerity when I told you that I could not bear ingratitude. You've shown me the sort of person I am, you've seen through me, you've explained me to myself!'

'Do you mean what you say? Well, now after such a confession I believe that you are sincere and good at heart. If you do not achieve happiness, you must always remember that you are on the right path and try not to stray from it. Above all, run from lies, any lies, and especially from self-deception. Watch over your lies and examine them every hour, every minute. Avoid, too, a feeling of aversion towards others and towards yourself: what seems to you bad in yourself is purified by the very fact that you've noticed it in yourself. Avoid fear, too, though fear is only the consequence of every sort of lie. Never be afraid of your own cowardliness in attaining love, and do not be too much afraid of your bad actions, either. I'm sorry I cannot say anything more comforting to you, for, compared with romantic love, active love is something severe and terrifying. Romantic love yearns for an immediate act of heroism that can be achieved rapidly and that everyone can see. This sort of love really reaches a point where a man will even sacrifice his life provided his ordeal doesn't last long and is over quickly just as though it took place on a stage, and provided all are looking on and applauding. But active love means hard work and tenacity, and for some people it is, perhaps, a whole science. But I predict that at the very moment when you will realize with horror that, far from getting nearer to your goal, you are, in spite of all your efforts, actually further away from it than ever, I predict that at that very moment you will suddenly attain your goal and will behold clearly the miraculous power of the Lord who has all the time been loving and mysteriously guiding you. I'm sorry, but I can't stay longer with you. They're waiting for me. Good-bye.'

The lady was weeping.

'Lise, Lise, please, bless her – bless her!' she cried, suddenly coming to life.

'She doesn't deserve to be loved,' the elder said jokingly. 'I've seen her misbehaving all the time. Why have you been laughing at Alexey all the time?'

Lise had, as a matter of fact, been doing just that all the time. She had noticed long ago, since their last meeting, in fact, that Alyosha was shy with her and tried not to look at her, and that amused her immensely. She waited intently to catch his eye: unable to endure her fixed stare, Alyosha from time to time threw a quick glance at her himself, as though drawn by some irresistible force, and at once she smiled triumphantly straight into his face. Alyosha was thrown into confusion and was annoyed even more. At last he turned away from her altogether and hid behind the elder's back. A few minutes later, drawn by the same irresistible force, he turned again to see whether she was looking at him or not. He saw Lise, almost hanging out of her chair, looking at him sideways and breathlessly waiting for him to look at her. Catching his glance, she burst out laughing so loudly that even the elder could not resist saying to her: 'Why do you embarrass him so much, you naughty girl?'

Lise suddenly and quite unexpectedly blushed, her eyes flashed, her face assumed a very serious expression and she said nervously, speaking very fast in a warmly indignant and complaining voice:

'And why has he forgotten everything? He used to carry me in his arms when I was a little girl. We used to play together. Why, he used to come to us and teach me to read. Didn't you know that? Two years ago, when he took leave of us, he said that he would never forget me and that we should remain friends for ever and ever! And now he's suddenly afraid of me. I'm not going to eat him, am I? Why does he refuse to come near me? Why doesn't he want to talk to me? Why doesn't he want to come and see us? Don't you let him? You see, we know that he goes everywhere. I can't invite him, can I? He should have been the first to remember, if he hadn't forgotten. But no! He's saving his soul now, if you please! Why have you put that long cassock on him? ... If he runs, he'll fall down. ...'

And unable to restrain herself, she covered her face with her hands and shook terribly and uncontrollably with her prolonged, nervous, and inaudible laughter. The elder listened to her with a smile and blessed her tenderly; but when she began kissing his hand, she suddenly pressed it to her eyes and burst into tears.

'Don't be angry with me. I'm a silly and worthless girl and – and Alyosha is probably right, quite right, in not wanting to come to see such a ridiculous girl.'

'I will certainly send him,' the elder said firmly.

5

It Will Be! It Will Be!

THE elder was absent from his cell for about twenty-five minutes. It was half-past twelve and Dmitry Karamazov, on whose behalf they had all met there, had still not arrived. But they seemed almost to have forgotten about him, and when the elder entered the cell again he found his visitors engaged in a very animated conversation. Ivan and the two monks took a leading part in it. Miusov, too, joined in the conversation, and apparently with great warmth, but he was unlucky again: no one paid much attention to him and, indeed, they almost ignored his remarks, which merely increased his ever-growing irritability. He had, in fact, had several furious arguments with Ivan before and he could not endure his opponent's somewhat casual attitude towards him without losing his temper. 'Before at least,' he thought to himself, 'I've always been in the van of every progressive movement in Europe, but this new generation simply ignores us.' Karamazov, who had given his solemn word to sit still and be quiet, had actually been quiet for a short time, though he kept watching his neighbour Miusov with a sardonic little smile and was quite obviously pleased to see him so irritated. He had long been meaning to pay him back for something or other and he did not wish to let the opportunity slip now. At last he could restrain himself no longer and, bending over Miusov's shoulder, he taunted him again in an undertone:

'You didn't go away after my "lovingly kissing", did you? You did consent to remain in such indecent company, didn't you? You know why? Because you felt insulted and humiliated and you remained to show what a clever fellow you were and get your own back. Now you won't go before showing what a clever fellow you are.'

'You again? I'll leave now just to show you.'

'You'll be the last, the last of all to go!' Karamazov taunted him again.

That was almost at the moment of the elder's return.

The discussion stopped for a moment, but the elder, who had resumed his seat, looked round at everyone as though cordially inviting them to go on. Alyosha, who had come to know every expression of the elder's face, saw clearly that he was terribly tired and that it required an effort to stay with them. During the latter stages of his illness he had been subject to fainting fits from exhaustion. Now his face was almost covered by the same kind of pallor as before a fainting fit. His lips went white. But he evidently did not want to dismiss the company; he seemed to have some reason for it. But what? Alyosha watched him closely.

'We're discussing this gentleman's most interesting article,' Father Joseph, the librarian, said, addressing the elder and pointing to Ivan. 'There's a great number of new ideas in it, but they seem to cut both ways. I'm referring to the article on the scope of the rights of ecclesiastical courts in dealing with social problems, which Mr Karamazov published in a periodical in reply to an ecclesiastical authority who had written a book dealing with the same question.'

'I'm afraid I haven't read your article, but I have heard of it,' said the elder, looking sharply and intently at Ivan.

'His point of view is extremely interesting,' continued the Father Librarian. 'It seems that in dealing with the question of ecclesiastical courts he is against the separation of Church and State.'

'That's interesting,' remarked the elder. 'In what sense, though?' he asked Ivan.

Ivan, at last, answered, but not, as Alyosha had feared, with condescending politeness, but modestly and restrainedly, with true courtesy and apparently without any mental reservations.

'I start from the proposition that this overlapping of the elements, that is to say, of the essential principles underlying Church and State, taken separately, will of course go on for ever, in spite of the fact that it is impossible and that it will never be brought into a normal, nor indeed into any reconcilable relationship, because its very basis is false. In my view a compromise between Church and State in such questions as, for example, court jurisdiction, is by its very nature impossible. The ecclesiastic to whom I replied maintained that the Church occupied a well-defined place in the State. But I maintained that, on the contrary, the Church ought to contain the whole State and not occupy only a corner in it, and that if this is for some reason impossible now, it ought most certainly to be set up as the direct and chief aim of the entire future development of Christian society.'

'Quite right!' Father Paissy, the learned monk who had kept silent till then, said firmly and fervently.

'The purest Ultramontanism!' cried Miusov, crossing his legs impatiently.

'Ah, but we have no mountains!' cried Father Joseph and, turning to the elder, continued: 'He answers the following "fundamental and essential" propositions of his opponent who, mark you, is an ecclesiastic: first, that "no alliance of social organizations can or ought to arrogate to itself the power to dispose of the civil and political rights of its members"; secondly, that "criminal and civil jurisdiction must not belong to the Church and is not compatible with its nature both as an institution vested with divine authority and as a body of men established for the pursuit of religious aims", and finally, thirdly, that "the Church is a kingdom not of this world".'

'A most unworthy play on words for an ecclesiastic!' Father Paissy could not refrain from interrupting again. 'I've read the book you discussed in your article,' he added, turning to Ivan, 'and I was astonished at its ecclesiastic author for maintaining that "the Church is a kingdom not of this world". If it is not of this world, then it cannot exist on earth at all. In the Holy Gospels the words "not of this world" are not used in that sense. You cannot play about with such words. Our Lord Jesus Christ came for the sole purpose of setting up the Church upon earth. The Kingdom of Heaven, of course, is not of this world, but in Heaven; but you enter Heaven only through the Church which has been founded and established on earth. Therefore, irreligious ambiguities in this sense are unpardonable and highly improper. The Church is, in truth, a Kingdom, and has been ordained to rule and at the end will undoubtedly become a Kingdom on earth – for which, indeed, we have a divine promise.'

He fell silent suddenly, as though restraining himself. Having listened to him respectfully and attentively, Ivan went on with the utmost composure and, as before, good-humouredly and readily, addressing himself to the elder:

'The whole idea of my article is that in ancient times, during the first three centuries of Christianity, Christianity existed on earth as a Church and only as a Church. But when the pagan Roman State expressed the desire to become Christian, it necessarily came to pass that, having become Christian, it merely included the Church as part of the State, but itself continued to be a pagan State as before in nearly all its administrative functions. This, as a matter of fact, was bound to happen. But there remained in Rome, as a State, a great deal of the pagan wisdom and civilization, for instance, the very fundamental principles and aims of the State. On the other hand, Christ's Church, having entered the State, doubtless could not give up any of its fundamental principles, the rock on which it stands, and could only pursue its own aims, which had been once and for all firmly established and revealed to it by God himself, such as, for instance, to turn the whole world and, therefore, also the ancient pagan State, into a Church. In this way (that is, with regard to the future) it is not the Church that ought to seek for itself a definite place in the State like "any other social organization" or like "an organization of men for religious purposes" (as my opponent, the author of the book we're discussing, describes the Church), but, on the contrary, every

State on earth must eventually be entirely transformed into a Church, and become nothing but a Church, renouncing those of its aims which are incompatible with the principles of the Church. All this will in no way lower its prestige or deprive it of its honour and glory as a great State, nor of the glory of its rulers, but will merely turn it away from the false, still pagan and mistaken path to the right and true path which alone leads to the eternal goal. That is why the author of *The Foundations of Ecclesiastical Courts* would have been right if, in trying to discover and lay down these foundations, he regarded them as a temporary compromise, still necessary in our sinful and far from perfect times, and no more than that. But the moment the author of these foundations takes it upon himself to declare that the foundations he lays down now, some of which have just been enumerated by Father Joseph, are elemental, firmly established, and eternal, he is going against the Church and its eternal and firmly established vocation. That is the gist of my article, a fair and full summary of it.'

'Which, to put it briefly, means,' Father Paissy began again, emphasizing every word, 'that according to certain theories, which have become all too clearly understood in our nineteenth century, the Church must be transformed into a State, just as though it were evolving from a lower into a higher form, so as to disappear into it, making place for science, the spirit of the age, and civilization. If, however, it refuses to do so and offers resistance, it is allotted only a little corner in the State and that, too, under supervision – and this is to be everywhere in our modern European States in our time. But according to our Russian conceptions and hopes, it is not the Church that ought to be turned into a State, as from a lower to a higher form, but, on the contrary, the State ought to end by being worthy to become only the Church and nothing else. And so it will be, it will be!'

'Well, sir,' said Miusov with a smile, recrossing his legs, 'I must say you've reassured me somewhat now. As far as I can make out, all this seems to be the realization of some ideal, infinitely remote, at the second coming of Christ. That is as may be. A beautiful utopian dream of the disappearance of wars, diplomacy, banks, etc. Something like Socialism, I suppose. For a moment I really thought that all this was serious, and that the Church would *now*, for instance, try criminal cases and pass sentences of flogging and penal servitude and, for all I know, even sentences of death.'

'Why, if we had only ecclesiastical courts now,' Ivan said imperturbably and without batting an eyelid, 'the Church would never pass sentences of penal servitude or death. Crime and the idea of crime would undoubtedly have undergone a change in that case, gradually, of course, not suddenly and at once, but I daresay in a very short time. . . .'

'Are you serious?' asked Miusov, glancing at him sharply.

'If everything became the Church,' Ivan went on, 'the Church would excommunicate the disobedient and the criminal and not cut off their heads. Where, I ask you, would the excommunicated go to? Why, he would have to renounce the company not only of men, as now, but also of Christ. For by his crime he would have transgressed not only against men but also against Christ's Church. This, strictly speaking, is so even now, but it is not officially so, and our criminal today very often strikes a bargain with his conscience. "It's true I've stolen, but I'm not transgressing against the Church. I am no enemy of Christ" – that's what our criminals quite often say today. But when the Church takes the place of the State, he will find it difficult to say this, unless, of course, he denies the authority of the Church on earth: "All are mistaken, all have deviated from the right path, all belong to a false Church, I alone, a thief and a murderer, am the true Christian Church." This is a very difficult thing to say to oneself. It requires very unusual conditions, a rare combination of unusual circumstances. Now, on the other hand, consider the views on crime of the Church itself: should it not undergo a change from our almost pagan views of today, and from the automatic cutting off of an infected limb, as is done today for the preservation of society, be transformed fully, and not falsely, into the idea of the regeneration of man, his reformation and salvation?'

'What exactly do you mean?' Miusov interrupted. 'I fail to understand again. This seems to be another kind of dream. Something shapeless, something beyond comprehension. What do you mean by excommunication? I suspect you're simply pulling our leg, sir.'

'But actually it is the same thing today,' said the elder suddenly, and all turned to him at once. 'If we had no Christ's Church now, there would be no way of stopping the criminal from committing his crimes and no real punishment for them afterwards. I mean, of course, real punishment and not the automatic punishment which you, sir, have just mentioned and which in the majority of cases only exacerbates the heart, while real punishment, the only effective one, resides in the awareness of one's own conscience and inspires fear and brings peace to the soul.'

'How is that, may I ask?' Miusov inquired with lively curiosity.

'It's like this,' began the elder. 'All these sentences of hard labour in Siberian prisons, and formerly with flogging, too, do not reform anyone and, what's more, scarcely deter even one criminal, and, far from diminishing, the number of crimes are steadily increasing. You have to admit that. It therefore follows that society is not in the least protected, for though a harmful member is cut off automatically and exiled to some remote spot just to get rid of him, another criminal takes his place at once, and often two, perhaps. If anything does protect society even today and indeed reforms the criminal himself and brings about his regeneration, it is, again, only the law of Christ, which reveals itself in the awareness of one's own conscience. Only by recognizing his own guilt as a son of a Christian society, that is, of the Church, does the criminal recognize his guilt towards society itself, that is, towards the Church. The criminal today, therefore, is capable of recognizing his guilt only towards the Church, and not towards the State. So that if society exercised its jurisdiction as a Church, it would know how to return the ex-communicated evil-doer to the bosom of the Church. But now the Church, deprived of her powers of jurisdiction and enjoying only the rights of moral condemnation, refuses to have anything to do with the infliction of real punishment. She does not excommunicate. She merely does not refuse to give the criminal her motherly exhortations. Moreover, she does her best to preserve Christian communion with him: she admits him to Church services, to the holy sacrament, gives him alms, and treats him more like an enslaved than a guilty person. And what would happen to a criminal, O Lord, if Christian society, that is, the Church, cast him out just as the civil law casts him out and cuts him off? What would happen if the Church punished him by excommunication immediately after the laws of the State had punished him? Why, there could be no greater despair, at least for a Russian criminal, for Russian criminals still have faith. However, who knows? Perhaps a most terrible thing would happen then – the despairing heart of the criminal would lose its faith, and what then? But the Church, like a tender and loving mother, refuses to have anything to do with punishment herself, for the man found guilty by the courts is severely punished already, and there must be somebody to take pity on him. But the chief reason why the Church refuses to have anything to do with punishment is that the judgement of the Church is the only one that contains the truth and therefore cannot assume actual or moral responsibility for any other judgement, not even as a temporary compromise. There can be no question of striking any sort of bargain here. A foreign criminal, I understand, rarely repents, for the most modern social theories confirm him in the idea that his crime is not a crime but only an act of rebellion against an unjustly oppressive force. Society cuts him off in an absolutely automatic fashion by a force that triumphs over him, and accompanies this excommunication with hatred (so, at least, they say about themselves in Europe) – with hatred and the most complete indifference and oblivion about his subsequent fate, as their brother. All this, consequently, happens without the slightest pity on the part of the Church, for in many cases there are no more Churches left there at all, but only clergymen and magnificent church buildings, the Churches themselves having long ago striven to pass from their lower form as a Church into the higher form as a State, so as to disappear in it completely. This is, at any rate, the case in Lutheran countries, I believe. In Rome, of course, a State has been proclaimed instead of a Church for the last thousand years. And that is why the criminal himself no longer recognizes himself as a member of the Church and, having been excommunicated, sinks into despair. And if he does return to society, it is often with such hatred that society itself seems instinctively to excommunicate him. You can judge for yourselves how it all must end. In many cases, it would seem, it is the same with us; but the whole point is that, in addition to the established civil courts, we have also the Church, which never loses contact with the criminal as a dear and still precious son. Besides, there still exists and is preserved, though only in thought, the judgement of the Church, inactive though it is now, but still living for the future, though only in people's minds, and is, no doubt, recognized by the criminal himself instinctively in his soul. What has just been said here now is also true, namely that if ecclesiastical courts were to be really set up and the jurisdiction of the Church were really to be established in full force, or, in other words, if the whole of society were to be transformed into the Church, then the judgement of the Church would not only influence the reformation of the criminal, as it never does now, but perhaps also the number of crimes themselves would diminish to a quite unbelievable extent. Nor is there any doubt that the Church itself would understand the potential criminal and his potential crime from now, in many cases quite differently and would know how to bring back the excommunicated, prevent crimes, and regenerate the fallen. It is true,' the elder smiled, 'that Christian society is not yet ready and is only kept in existence because of the seven righteous men, but as their number never decreases it will remain stable in expectation of its complete transformation from a society almost pagan in its organization into a single universal and sovereign Church. This will be, it will be, even though at the end of time, for this alone has been ordained to come to pass! And one should not be troubled about times and fixed dates, for the secret of times and fixed dates is in the wisdom of God and in his foresight and his love. And what may seem still far off according to man's reckoning, may by God's predestination be close at hand and on the very eve of its appearance. And this will be, it will be!'

'It will be! It will be!' Father Paissy echoed reverently and sternly.

'Curious, extremely curious!' Miusov said, not so much with heat as with a sort of concealed indignation.

'What strikes you as so curious?' Father Joseph inquired cautiously.

'But, good Lord,' cried Miusov, as though suddenly losing his self-control completely, 'what are you talking about? The State is to be abolished on earth and the Church is to be raised to the position of the State! Why, it's no longer Ultramontanism, it's arch-Ultramontanism! It's more than Pope Gregory the Seventh dreamed of!'

'You've got it all wrong, sir,' Father Paissy said severely. 'It is not the Church that is transformed into the State. Please understand that. That is Rome and its dream. That is the third temptation of the devil. On the contrary, the State is transformed into the Church, it rises to it and becomes a Church all over the world – which is the complete opposite of Ultramontanism and Rome and your interpretation of it, and is only the great predetermined destiny of the Orthodox Church on earth. This star will shine in the East!'

Miusov was impressively silent. His whole figure expressed extraordinary personal dignity. A supercilious and condescending smile appeared on his lips. Alyosha watched it all with a fast beating heart. The whole conversation stirred him most powerfully. He cast a cursory glance at Rakitin, who was standing motionless in his former place at the door, listening and watching attentively, though with downcast eyes. But Alyosha guessed from the high colour in his cheeks that Rakitin was no less excited than he; Alyosha knew what was the cause of his excitement.

'Allow me, gentlemen, to tell you a little anecdote,' said Miusov suddenly with an impressive and a sort of specially dignified air. 'A few years ago in Paris, soon after the December revolution, I happened to meet a most interesting man at the house of an extremely important member of the government, an acquaintance of mine on whom I happened to be paying a call at the time. This individual was not just an ordinary detective, but the chief of a whole lot of security agents – a rather influential post in its way. Taking advantage of this chance meeting and being very curious to learn something of his work, I entered into a conversation with him. He had come to that house not as a guest but as a subordinate official (he had brought his latest official report with him), and seeing how well I was received by his chief, he was so good as to speak to me with some frankness – up to a point, of course; I mean he was polite rather than frank, as Frenchmen know how to be polite, particularly as he saw that I was a foreigner. But I understood him thoroughly. The subject of our conversation was the socialist revolutionaries who were, incidentally, persecuted at the time. Leaving out the main point of our conversation, I shall quote only one highly interesting remark that gentleman blurted out to me. "We are not particularly afraid," he said, "of all these socialists-anarchists, atheists, and revolutionaries; we are keeping an eye on them and all their moves are known to us. But there are several peculiar men among them, though only a few: these believe in God – they are Christians and at the same time Socialists. It is these we fear most of all. They are terrible people. A Christian Socialist is much more terrible than a Socialist who is an atheist."

These words struck me at the time, too, but now I couldn't help remembering them here for some reason, gentlemen.'

'You are applying them to us and you regard us as Socialists, don't you?' Father Paissy asked straight out, without beating about the bush.

But before Miusov had time to think of an answer, the door opened and Dmitry Karamazov, who had been so late in making an appearance, came in. They had, as a matter of fact, given up expecting him, and indeed his sudden appearance caused some surprise at first.

6

Why Does Such a Man Live?

DMITRY KARAMAZOV, a young man of twenty-eight, of medium height and pleasant appearance, looked much older than his age. He was muscular and one could see that he had considerable physical strength; and yet his face did not seem to be that of a healthy man. His face was thin, his cheeks hollow, and his complexion unhealthily sallow. There was apparent a hard, stubborn, but also somehow rather evasive look in his large, protruding dark eyes. Even when he was excited and talking irritably, his eyes did not seem to obey his inward mood and expressed something else, which sometimes had little to do with what was taking place at the time. 'It's hard to tell what he's thinking,' those who talked to him sometimes declared. Some people, who saw something pensive and sullen in his eyes, were occasionally taken aback by his unexpected laughter, which showed that his thoughts were gay and playful just at the time when he looked so gloomy. However, the somewhat sickly expression of his face at that moment was perhaps not difficult to explain: they all knew or had heard of the extremely restless and 'dissipated' life in which he had been indulging more recently in our town; his extreme irritation in his quarrels with his father about the money he claimed the latter owed him was also generally known. There were a number of stories already current in our town about it. It is true that he was irritable by nature, 'of an unstable and unbalanced mind', as our justice of the peace, Semyon Kachalnikov, characteristically described him at some public function. He came in impeccably and fashionably dressed, his frock-coat buttoned, wearing black gloves and carrying a top-hat. As an army man who had recently resigned his commission, he wore a moustache and for the time being only shaved his beard. His dark brown hair was cut short and combed somehow forward on his temples. He walked with the long, firm stride of the professional soldier. He stopped for a moment on the threshold and, with a quick glance at the company, went straight up to the elder, guessing him to be the host. He made him a low bow and asked his blessing. The elder got up and blessed him; Dmitry kissed his hand respectfully.

'I'm very sorry to have kept you waiting so long, sir,' he said with extraordinary excitement, almost with irritation. 'But Smerdyakov, the servant sent by my father, told me twice in reply to my repeated questions about the time of the appointment that it was for one o'clock. Now I suddenly learn —'

'Don't worry,' the elder interrupted him. 'It doesn't matter. You are a little late, but it's of no consequence. . . .'

'Thank you very much, sir. I could expect no less from your kindness.'

Having rapped out his apology, Dmitry bowed once more, then suddenly turning towards his father, made him, too, a similarly low and respectful bow. It was obvious that he had carefully considered this bow beforehand, and quite sincerely thought it to be almost his duty to make it and express his respect and good intentions by it. Karamazov, though taken by surprise, rose to the occasion in his own way: in reply to Dmitry's bow, he jumped up from his arm-chair and made his son a bow as low in return. His face suddenly assumed a grave and solemn expression, which, however, made him look absolutely vicious. After bowing silently to the rest of the company, Dmitry went up to the window with his long and firm strides, sat down on the only vacant chair, not far from Father Paissy, and, bending forward, at once prepared to listen to the interrupted conversation.

Dmitry's entrance had taken no more than two minutes and the conversation could not but be resumed. But this time Mr Miusov did not think it necessary to reply to Father Paissy's pressing and almost irritable question.

'Allow me to decline to discuss this subject,' he said with an air of well-bred casualness. 'It is I'm afraid a tricky subject, anyhow. Mr Ivan Karamazov, you see, is smiling at us. I suppose he must have something interesting to say about that, too. You'd better ask him.'

'I've nothing much to say,' replied Ivan at once, 'except to make a little remark about the curious fact that European liberals in general and our own liberal dilettanti in particular, have often, and for some time past, been mixing up the final results of Socialism with those of Christianity. This absurd conclusion is of course very characteristic of them. However, it is not only the liberals and the dilettanti who confuse Socialism with Christianity. In many cases the police – the foreign police, of course – do the same. Your Paris story is very characteristic, Mr Miusov.'

'I should again like to ask your permission, gentlemen, to drop the subject,' Miusov repeated. 'I will tell you instead another anecdote, a very interesting and most characteristic anecdote about Mr Ivan Karamazov himself. Only five days ago, at a certain social gathering, consisting mostly of ladies, he solemnly declared during an argument that there was absolutely nothing in the whole world to make men love their fellow-men, that there was no law in nature that man should love mankind, and that if love did exist on earth, it was not because of any natural law but solely because men believed in immortality. He added in parenthesis that all natural law consisted of that belief, and that if you were to destroy the belief in immortality in mankind, not only love but every living force on which the continuation of all life in the world depended, would dry up at once. Moreover, there would be nothing immoral then, everything would be permitted, even cannibalism. But that is not all: he wound up with the assertion that for every individual, like myself, for instance, who does not believe in God or in his own immortality, the moral laws of nature must at once be changed into the exact opposite of the former religious laws, and that self-interest, even if it were to lead to crime, must not only be permitted but even recognized as the necessary, the most rational, and practically the most honourable motive for a man in his position. From this paradox, gentlemen, you can conclude what sort of ideas our dear eccentric and paradoxical fellow has been propounding and, no doubt, will go on propounding in future.'

'One moment,' Dmitry suddenly cried unexpectedly, 'did you say, "Crime must not only be permitted, but even be recognized as the most necessary and the most intelligent result of the position of every unbeliever?" Is that so or not?'

'It is so,' said Father Paissy.

'I'll remember that!'

Having said this, Dmitry fell silent as suddenly as he had burst into the conversation. They all looked at him with curiosity.

'Is this really your opinion of what would happen if people lost their faith in the immortality of their souls?' the elder suddenly asked Ivan.

'Yes, that was my contention. There is no virtue if there's no immortality.'

'If that is what you believe you are either blessed or most unhappy!'

'Why unhappy?' asked Ivan with a smile.

'Because you most probably do not yourself believe in the immortality of your soul, nor even in what you've written about the Church and the Church question.'

'Perhaps you are right! . . . But all the same I wasn't altogether joking, either,' Ivan suddenly made this strange confession, though, it is true, he blushed quickly.

'You were not altogether joking – that's true. You still can't find the right answer to this question and you're very worried about it. But even a martyr sometimes likes to amuse himself with his despair, just out of despair. You, too, in your despair, are for the time being amusing yourself with magazine articles and discussions in society without believing in your arguments and smiling bitterly at them with an ache in your heart. . . . You have not made up your mind what answer to give to that question and therein lies your great grief, for the question urgently demands an answer.'

'But is it possible for me to make up my mind?' Ivan continued to ask his strange questions, looking at the elder with the same enigmatic smile. 'Can I answer it in the affirmative?'

'If you can't answer it in the affirmative, you will never be able to answer it in the negative. You know that peculiarity of your heart yourself – and all its agony is due to that alone. But thank the Creator who has given you a superior heart capable of such agony, "to mind high things and to seek high things, forasmuch as our dwelling is in heaven". God grant that your heart's answer will find you still on earth, and may God bless your path!'

The elder raised his hand and was about to make the sign of the cross over Ivan from his seat. But Ivan suddenly got up, went up to him, received his blessing and, kissing his hand, returned to his place in silence. He looked resolute and earnest. This action and all the preceding conversation with the elder, which was so unexpected of Ivan, seemed to impress everyone by its air of mystery and even by a certain solemnity, so that they all fell silent for a minute, and Alyosha looked almost frightened. But Miusov suddenly shrugged his shoulders, and at that very moment Karamazov jumped up from his chair.

'Most divine and most holy elder,' he cried, pointing at Ivan, 'this is my son, the flesh of my flesh, the dearest one of my flesh! This is, so to speak, my most respectful Karl Moor, while this son of mine, Dmitry, who has just come in, and against whom I am seeking justice from you, is the most disrespectful Franz Moor, both from Schiller's *Robbers*, which, I suppose, makes me the *Regierender Graf von Moor*! Judge and save us! We need not only your prayers, but also your prophecies.'

'Speak without fooling and don't begin by insulting the members of your family,' the elder replied in a weak, exhausted voice.

He was clearly getting more and more tired and his strength was perceptibly failing.

'A disgraceful comedy which I foresaw when I was coming here!' cried Dmitry indignantly, also jumping up from his seat. 'I'm sorry, Reverend Father,' he addressed the elder, 'I'm an uneducated man and I don't even know how to address you, but you've been deceived and you've been too good-natured in letting us meet here. All my father wants is a public scandal. He has his own reasons for it. He always has his reasons. But I think I know why —'

'They all accuse me, all of them!' Karamazov cried in his turn. 'Mr Miusov, too, has accused me. Yes, sir, you have, you have!' He suddenly turned to Miusov, though the latter was not thinking of interrupting him. 'I'm accused of hiding my children's money in my boots, taking the same amount from each of them. But, tell me, sir, isn't there a court of law? They'll count it up for you there, Dmitry, from your own receipts, your letters, and your agreements – how much you had, how much you squandered, and how much you have left! Why does Mr Miusov refuse to arbitrate? Dmitry is not a stranger to him. Why, because they are all against me. As for Dmitry, he actually owes me money, and not just a few roubles, either, but several thousand, sir! And I have all the documents to prove it! The whole town is in an uproar with his debaucheries! And where he served before, he had to pay a thousand or two for seducing respectable girls. We know all about that, sir,' he turned to his eldest son, 'all the most secret details of it, and I can prove it, sir! Most holy father, I know it sounds incredible, but he has turned the head of a most honourable young girl, a girl of good family and substantial fortune, the daughter of his superior officer, a gallant colonel, a man who has deserved well of his country, who has received the Order of St Anne with crossed swords. He compromised the girl by a proposal of marriage, and now she is here, an orphan, his fiancée, and yet before her very eyes he is running after a siren in our town. But though this siren has lived, if I may say so, out of wedlock with a highly respectable man, she is of an independent character, an unassailable fortress to everybody, just as if she were a lawfully married wife, for she's virtuous, sir – yes, holy fathers, she's virtuous! And Dmitry wants to open this fortress with a golden key, and that's why he's trying to bully me now, to fleece me of my money, and in the meantime he has spent thousands on this siren already. He's constantly borrowing money for that, and who do you think from? Shall I tell them, Mitya?'

'Shut up!' cried Dmitry. 'Wait till I'm gone. Don't you dare to besmirch the good name of a most honourable girl in my presence! The very fact that you've had the effrontery to mention her is an insult to her. . . . I won't permit it!'

He was gasping for breath.

'Mitya, Mitya,' cried Karamazov weakly, squeezing out a tear, 'does a father's blessing mean nothing to you? And what if I should put a curse on you? What then?'

'You shameless hypocrite!' Dmitry bawled furiously.

'That's what he calls his father – his father! How do you think he would treat others? Gentlemen, just listen to this: there's a poor but honourable man living here, a retired army captain, a man burdened with a large family, who got into trouble and was dismissed the service, but there was no public scandal, no court martial.

He left the army without a stain on his character. And three weeks ago, my son Dmitry seized him by the beard in a pub, dragged him out into the street and beat him mercilessly in public, and all because I employ him as my agent in a little business of mine.'

'It's a damned lie!' Dmitry cried, trembling all over with rage. 'It may appear to be true, but when you examine it closely it's a lie. Father, I don't justify my actions. Yes, I confess it publicly: I behaved like a brute to that captain and I'm sorry for it now and I loathe myself for my brutal anger. But this captain of yours, this agent of yours, went to the lady whom you've just called a siren and suggested to her in your name that she should take the promissory notes I had given you and sue me for the money. Your idea was to have me put away in jail if I kept pestering you to give me an account of my property. And now you're reproaching me for being in love with that girl, while it was you yourself who suggested to her that she should get me to fall in love with her. Why, she told me so herself. She said so to my face, laughing at you! And you want to put me in jail only because you're jealous, because you've begun pursuing that woman with your love, and I know all about it, and again she laughed – do you hear? – she laughed at you as she told me about it. So that's the sort of a man he is, holy fathers, that's the father who reproaches his dissolute son! Gentlemen, forgive my anger, but I had a feeling that this cunning old man would bring you together here to create a public scandal. I came here to forgive him if he held out his hand to me: I was ready to forgive and to ask forgiveness! But as he has just this minute insulted not only me, but also a most honourable young lady, whose name I dare not take in vain out of a feeling of reverence for her, I've decided to show up his game in public, though he is my father! . . .'

He could not go on. His eyes flashed and he breathed with difficulty. But everyone in the cell looked perturbed. They all, except the elder, got up from their seats uneasily. The monks looked stern, but waited to see what the elder would do. The elder, however, sat looking very pale, though not from agitation, but because he felt too weak and ill. An imploring smile played on his lips; from time to time he raised his hand as though wishing to stop the two raving men and, of course, one gesture from him would have been enough to end the scene; but he seemed to be waiting for something himself and watched them closely, as though trying to understand something that was not quite clear to him. At last Peter Miusov felt completely humiliated and disgraced.

'We are all to blame for this scandalous scene,' he said warmly, 'and yet on my way here I did not foresee it, though I knew perfectly well with whom I had to deal. We must stop it at once. I assure you, your reverence, that I had no real knowledge of all the details that have come to light here. I was loath to believe them and it's only now I've got to know about them for the first time. . . . A father is jealous of his son because of a disreputable woman, and himself plots with that creature to put his son in prison. And it is in such company that I've been forced to come here! I was deceived. I want to make it clear to you all that I was as much deceived as anyone.'

'Dmitry,' Karamazov suddenly yelled in an unnatural voice, 'if you were not my son, I'd have challenged you to a duel this very minute . . . with pistols, sir, and at a distance of three paces – yes, sir, across a handkerchief – across a handkerchief, sir!' he concluded, stamping his feet.

There are moments in the life of old liars who have been play-acting all their lives when they are so carried away by the part they're playing that they really do weep and tremble with excitement, in spite of the fact that at that very moment (or a second later) they could have whispered to themselves: 'You're lying, you shameless old fool! Now, too, you're just acting a part in spite of all your "sacred" wrath and the "sacred" moment of your wrath.'

Dmitry frowned threateningly and looked at his father with indescribable contempt.

'I thought,' he said in a kind of quiet and restrained voice, 'I thought that I'd come home with my sweetheart, my future wife, to look after him in his old age, and all I see is a dissolute voluptuary and a most contemptible clown!'

'I challenge you, sir!' the old wretch yelled again, gasping for breath and spluttering with each word he uttered. 'As for you, sir,' he turned to Miusov, 'I want you to know that there has perhaps never been a woman in your family more high-minded and more honest – do you hear, sir? – more honest than the woman you had the effrontery just now to call a creature! And you, Dmitry, have jilted your fiancée for that "creature", so that you must be perfectly clear in your mind that your fiancée is not fit to lick her boots – that's the sort of "creature" she is!'

'Shame!' Father Joseph could not refrain from exclaiming.

'It's a shame and a disgrace!' Kalganov, who had been silent all the time, suddenly cried in his boyish voice, trembling with agitation and reddening to the roots of his hair.

'Why does such a man live?' Dmitry growled in a hollow voice, almost beside himself with rage, raising his shoulders so much that he appeared almost hunch-backed. 'Tell me, can he be allowed to defile the earth by his existence?' he asked, glancing at each of them in turn and pointing to the old man.

He spoke slowly and emphatically.

'Listen, listen, monks, to the parricide!' Karamazov cried, rushing suddenly upon Father Joseph. 'That's the answer to your "shame", sir! Why shame? This "creature", this "disreputable woman", gentlemen, is perhaps holier than all of you who are seeking salvation in this monastery. She may have fallen in her youth, a victim of her environment, but she "loved much", and Christ himself forgave the woman who "loved much".'

'Christ did not forgive for that kind of love,' escaped impatiently from the gentle Father Joseph.

'Yes, for that kind of love, monks, for that very same kind of love! You're seeking salvation here by eating cabbage soup and you think you're righteous men! You eat gudgeons, a gudgeon a day, and you think you can buy God with gudgeons.'

'It's intolerable! Intolerable!' they cried from all corners of the cell.

But this scandalous scene came to an end in a most unexpected way. The elder suddenly rose from his seat. Alyosha, who had almost completely lost his head with anxiety for him and everyone else, was just in time, however, to support him by the arm. The elder stepped in the direction of Dmitry and, reaching him, went down on his knees before him. Alyosha at first thought that he had sunk down from weakness, but that was not so. Having knelt, the elder prostrated himself at Dmitry's feet with full, conscious deliberation and even touched the ground with his forehead. Alyosha was so amazed that he failed to support him when he rose again. A faint smile played on his lips.

'Forgive me! Forgive me all of you!' he said, bowing to his guests on all sides.

Dmitry stood still for a few seconds as though thunderstruck: the elder had bowed down to him – what was it all about? At last he cried: 'Oh, Lord!' and, covering his face with his hands, rushed out of the room. All the guests hurried out of the room in a crowd after him and in their confusion did not even take leave or bow to their host. Only the monks went up to the elder again for a blessing.

'What did he mean by kneeling at his feet?' Karamazov, who had grown quiet of a sudden for some reason, tried to reopen the conversation, without, however, daring to address anybody in particular. 'Is it symbolic of something or what?'

They were all leaving the hermitage at that moment.

'I can't answer for madmen or for a madhouse,' Miusov at once replied angrily, 'but I'm glad to say I shall rid myself of your company, and, believe me, sir, for good. Where's that monk?'

'That monk', that is to say, the monk who had invited them to dinner with the Father Superior, did not keep them waiting. He met the visitors as soon as they came down the steps from the elder's cell, as though he had been waiting for them all the time.

'Do me a favour, Father, and convey my deepest respects to the Father Superior and apologize personally for me, Miusov, to his reverence and tell him that owing to unforeseen circumstances I regret to be unable to be present at his table, much as I should like to,' Miusov said irritably to the monk.

'The unforeseen circumstance is, of course, myself!' Karamazov at once broke in. 'You see, Father, Mr Miusov doesn't want to remain in the same company as I, or he would come at once. And you will go, sir. Yes, sir, go to the Father Superior and – I hope you enjoy your meal! It is I who am declining and not you. Home, home, home – I'll eat at home, for I don't feel I could eat anything here, Mr Miusov, dear relative of mine!'

'I'm not your relative, sir. I've never been your relative, you contemptible man.'

'I said it on purpose to make you mad, for I know you refuse to acknowledge our relationship, though you are my relative, however much you try to shuffle out of it. I can prove it by the church calendar. I'll send a carriage for you, Ivan. You can stay if you like. As for you, Mr Miusov, good manners demand that you should go to the Father Superior. You have to apologize to him for our high jinks.'

'But is it true you're going home? You're not lying, are you?'

'My dear sir, do you really think I'd dare to lie after what's happened? Sorry, gentlemen, I was carried away! And, besides, I'm deeply shocked and ashamed, too! Gentlemen, one man has the heart of Alexander of Macedon and the other the heart of a little lap-dog. Afraid mine is like a lap-dog's. Lost my nerve! And, really, how can I go to dinner after such an escapade? Bolt the monastery sauces? I'm sorry, but I can't do it. I'm too ashamed!'

'What if he deceives us, damn him?' Miusov stopped, wondering and watching the retreating clown with a perplexed look.

Karamazov turned round and, noticing that Miusov was watching him, blew him a kiss.

'Are you coming to the Father Superior?' Miusov asked Ivan abruptly.

'Why not? Besides, the Father Superior specially invited me yesterday.'

'Unhappily, I really do feel almost obliged to go to this confounded dinner,' Miusov went on in the same tone of bitter irritability, without paying the slightest attention to the monk who could hear him. 'I suppose we ought to apologize for the disturbance we've made here and explain that it wasn't our fault. . . . What do you think?'

'Yes, we'd better explain that it wasn't our fault. Besides, father won't be there,' observed Ivan.

'Your father! That would have been the absolute limit! Oh, confound this dinner!'

And yet they all went. The little monk listened and kept quiet. Only once on their way through the wood did he observe that the Father Superior had been waiting a long time and that they were more than half an hour late. He received no answer. Miusov glanced at Ivan with hatred.

'Going to the dinner, damn him, as though nothing had happened!' he thought. 'A face of brass and the conscience of a Karamazov.'

7

A Seminarist-Careerist

ALYOSHA took his elder to the little bedroom and made him sit down on the bed. It was a very small room furnished with the bare necessities; the bed was a narrow iron one with a strip of felt instead of a mattress. In the corner by the icons was a lectern with a cross and the Gospel lying on it. The elder sank exhausted on the bed; his eyes glittered and he breathed with difficulty. Having sat down, he looked intently at Alyosha as though considering something.

'Go, my dear boy, go to the Father Superior,' he said. 'Porfiry will look after me. Hurry, you're wanted there. Go and wait at table.'

'Please, let me stay here,' Alyosha said in an imploring voice.

'They need you more there. There's no peace there. You'll wait and be useful. If the evil spirits arise, you can say a prayer. And remember, my son (the elder liked to call him that), that this is not the place for you in the future. Remember that, my boy. As soon as it is God's will to call me to him, leave the monastery. Leave it for good.'

Alyosha gave a start.

'What's the matter? For the time being this is not the place for you. I bless you for great service in the world. There is still a long road before you. And you'll have to take a wife, too. You will have to go through it all, before you come back again. There will be much for you to do. But I have no doubts about you and that is why I am sending you into the world. Christ is with you. Do not abandon him and he will not abandon you. You will know great sorrow and in that sorrow you will be happy. This is my last message to you: in sorrow seek happiness. Work, work unceasingly. Remember my words from now on, for though I shall talk to you again, not only my days, but my hours are numbered.'

Alyosha's face again showed great emotion. The corners of his lips trembled.

'Why are you crying again?' the elder said, with a gentle smile.

'Let laymen bid farewell to their dying with tears. Here we rejoice over the father who is departing. We rejoice and pray for him. Leave me, please. I must pray. Go and make haste. Be near your brothers. And not near one of them only, but near both.'

The elder raised his hand to bless him. It was impossible to protest, though Alyosha wanted very much to stay. He also wanted to ask the elder – and, indeed, the question was almost on the tip of his tongue – what was the significance of that deep bow to his brother Dmitry. But he dared not ask it. He knew that if the elder had thought fit, he would have explained it without being asked. But it did not seem to be his will. The bow had made a tremendous impression on Alyosha: he believed blindly that there was a mysterious meaning in it. Mysterious and perhaps also terrible. When he walked out of the hermitage to reach the monastery in time for dinner (only to wait at table, of course), his heart suddenly contracted painfully and he stopped dead: he seemed to hear again the elder's words foretelling his fast-approaching end. What the elder foretold, and with such exactness, too, must beyond all doubt come to pass. Alyosha believed that implicitly. But how could he be left without him? How could he go on without seeing and hearing him? And where would he go? He had told him not to cry and to leave the monastery. Dear God! It was long since Alyosha had felt such anguish. He hurried along through the wood which divided the monastery from the hermitage and, unable to bear the thoughts which oppressed him so heavily, he began looking at the age-old pines at either side of the path. He had not far to go – about five hundred yards, no more. At that hour he hardly expected to meet anyone, but at the first turn of the path he suddenly noticed Rakitin, who seemed to be waiting for someone.

'You're not waiting for me, are you?' Alyosha asked as he came up to him.

'Yes, I am,' Rakitin grinned. 'You're in a hurry to get to the Father Superior. I know. He's giving a dinner. Since he entertained the bishop and General Pakhatov, there has been no such dinner. I shan't be there, but you go and hand round the sauces. Tell me one thing, though, Alexey: what is the meaning of all this? That's what I wanted to ask you.'

'The meaning of what?'

'That business of prostrating himself before your brother Dmitry?
Knocked his forehead on the ground, he did!'

'You mean, Father Zossima?'

'Yes, Father Zossima.'

'His forehead?'

'Oh, I see, I've been speaking disrespectfully! All right, so I have.
Anyway, what is it all about?'

'I don't know what it means, Misha.'

'I knew he would not explain it to you. There is, of course, nothing extraordinary about it. Just the usual well-meant nonsense. But
there was some purpose in the trick. Now all the sanctimonious fools
in the town will talk about it and spread it all over the province,
asking each other what is the meaning of it. If you ask me, the old
man is a sharp one: he smells crime. Your house stinks of it.'

'What sort of crime?'

Rakitin was obviously eager to tell him something.

'It will be in your family – this crime will. It will happen between
your dear brothers and that very rich father of yours. That's why
Father Zossima knocked his head on the floor. Just in case it happens.
Then, when it does happen, people will be saying, "Ah, that's
exactly what the holy elder foretold – it was a prophecy!" Though
I'm hanged if I can see what knocking his head on the floor has to
do with prophesying. Not at all, they'll say, the whole thing was
symbolic, an allegory, and the devil knows what! They'll trumpet
it all over the place and they will remember it: Aha, he predicted the
crime and marked the criminal. It's always like that with saintly
fools: they cross themselves at the sight of a pub and throw stones
at a church. Your elder is like that too: he drives the righteous out
with a stick and bows down before a murderer.'

'What crime? What murderer? What are you talking about?'

Alyosha stopped dead; Rakitin stopped, too.

'What murderer? Don't you know? I bet you've thought of it
yourself already. That's jolly interesting, though. Look here, Alyosha,
you always tell the truth, though you never like to commit yourself.
Tell me, have you thought of it or not? Answer.'

'I have thought of it,' Alyosha replied softly.

Even Rakitin was taken back.

'What are you saying? Have you really thought of it, too?' he cried.

'I – I haven't actually thought of it,' Alyosha murmured. 'You see, as soon as you began talking about it so strangely, I couldn't help feeling that I'd thought about it myself.'

'See? And how well you've put it! So it was while looking at your father and at Mitya, that darling brother of yours, today, that you thought of a crime, was it? So I'm not mistaken, am I?'

'But wait, wait a minute!' Alyosha interrupted him uneasily. 'What has made you see it all? And why does it interest you so much? That's what I'd like to know.'

'Two separate but natural questions. Let me answer each of them in turn. Why do I see it? I shouldn't have seen any of it, if I hadn't suddenly understood your brother Dmitry today. Seen through and through him all at once. Grasped his whole character from one significant little point. There's a point beyond which these very honourable but voluptuous people must not pass. Otherwise – otherwise he won't hesitate to stick a knife into his own father. And his dear old father is a drunkard and an intemperate old rake, who never knows where to stop, so they won't be able to restrain themselves and bang! into the ditch the two of them.'

'No, Misha, no, if that's all, you've reassured me. It will never come to that.'

'Then why are you trembling all over? Do you know what? Your Mitya may be honest (he's stupid, but honest) but he's a sensualist. That's the definition and the inner essence of him. It's from his father that he has inherited his disgusting sensuality. Why, I can't help marvelling at you, Alyosha: how is it you're still a virgin? You, too, are a Karamazov, aren't you? And in your family sensuality has reached a point where it becomes a devouring fever. So these three sensualists are now constantly watching each other – with a knife stuck in the leg of their boots. They're knocking their heads together, the three of them, and, for all I know, you may be the fourth.'

'You're mistaken about that woman. Dmitry – despises her,' Alyosha said, with a sort of shudder.

'Grushenka, you mean? No sir, he doesn't despise her. If he really has openly jilted his fiancée for her, then he does not despise her. There's something here, my dear chap, that you can't understand yet. You see, if a man falls in love with some beautiful woman, with a woman's body, or even with just one part of her body (only a sensualist can understand that), he'll sacrifice his own children for her, he'll sell his father and mother, and his country, too. If he's honest, he'll go and steal, if he is gentle, he'll kill, if he is faithful, he'll deceive. Pushkin, the singer of women's beautiful feet, sang in praise of women's feet in his verses; others do not sing their praises but cannot look calmly at women's feet. But, then, it's not only their feet. . . . In this business, my dear chap, contempt is no help, even if he did despise Grushenka. He despises her, but he can't tear himself away from her.'

'I understand that,' Alyosha suddenly blurted out.

'Do you? Well, I suppose you do understand it all right if you blurt it out at the first word,' Rakitin said spitefully. 'You see, you've blurted it out without thinking. It just escaped you against your will. Well, your confession is all the more valuable. So it's a familiar subject to you, is it? You've thought about it already, of sensuality, I mean. Oh, you virgin! You are a quiet chap, Alyosha, you're a saint. I agree. But quiet as you are, one can't tell what you haven't thought about, or what you don't know already, can one? A virgin and already plumbed such depths! I've been watching you for a long time. You're a Karamazov yourself, a full-blown Karamazov – breed and natural selection do mean something then. A sensualist after your father and a saintly fool after your mother. Why do you tremble? It's true what I'm saying, isn't it? Do you know what? Grushenka said to me, "Bring him to me (she meant you) and I'll pull his cassock off his back!" She kept begging me : "Bring him! Bring him!" I just couldn't help wondering why she should be so interested in you. You know, she's quite an extraordinary woman, too!'

'Give her my regards and tell her that I won't come,' Alyosha said with a wry smile. 'Finish what you were going to say, Mikhail. I'll tell you what I think afterwards.'

'What is there more to say? It's all clear. All this, my dear chap, is an old story. If you, too, are a sensualist at heart, then what is your brother Ivan? He, too, is a Karamazov, isn't he? That's what the Karamazov problem boils down to – sensualists, money-grubbers, and saintly fools! Your brother Ivan is writing theological articles at present as a joke and for some unknown idiotic reason, for he himself is an atheist, and this Ivan, this brother of yours, himself admits that what he is doing is mean and despicable. In addition, he's trying to get Mitya's fiancée for himself, and in this, I believe, he'll succeed. Why, he'll get her with Mitya's consent, because Mitya is letting him have her himself, just to get rid of her and go to Grushenka as quickly as possible. And, mark you, he does it all in spite of his high-mindedness and disinterestedness. It's people like that who're the most fatal of all! I'm hanged if I know what to make of you after that: he admits his own mean actions and goes on doing them! Now, listen: that old wretch of your father is now in Mitya's way. For the old goat has suddenly gone crazy about Grushenka. His mouth waters the moment he looks at her. He raised such a hullabaloo in the cell just now only because of her, only because Miusov dared call her a "loose creature". He's head over ears in love with her. At first he employed her at a salary in some shady business deals of his and in his pubs, and now he suddenly realizes what a lovely creature she is and he's worked himself up into a state of raging fury, keeps making her all sorts of offers, not honourable ones, of course. Well, so father and son are going to run into each other on that slippery path. Meanwhile, Grushenka does not seem to be particularly keen on either of them. For the time being she's sitting on the fence and teasing both of them. She's trying to make up her mind which of the two could be more useful to her, for though she could grab a lot of money from the old man, she knows he won't marry her and may even end up by turning stingy and tightening his purse-strings. In that case, Mitya, too, has his value. He has no money, but he's quite capable of marrying her. Yes, sir, he's capable of marrying her! Of jilting his fiancée, a girl of rare beauty, a rich noblewoman and the daughter of a colonel, and of marrying Grushenka, a former mistress of the mayor Samsonov, a lousy old merchant, a debauched peasant. And this may quite well lead to one of them committing a crime. That's what your brother Ivan is waiting for. If that happens, he'll be in clover: he'll get Katerina, for whom he is pining away, and get hold of her dowry of sixty thousand. To a small man who has not a penny to bless himself with this is not so bad for a beginning. And, mind you, far from hurting Mitya's feelings, he'll be doing him a great favour. For I know for a fact that last week Mitya, who had got drunk in a pub with some gipsy girls, was shouting that he did not deserve to marry a girl like Katerina but that his brother Ivan did deserve to marry her.

And Katerina, of course, will not in the end refuse such a fascinating fellow as Ivan, for even now she's already hesitating between the two of them. And what is so marvellous about this Ivan of yours that you should all be so taken with him? Why, he's laughing at you! He's in clover and having a jolly good time at your expense!'

'How do you know all this?' Alyosha asked suddenly, sharply, and frowning. 'Why are you so sure of it?'

'And why are you asking me now and why are you so afraid of my answer? It shows that you know yourself I'm speaking the truth.'

'You don't like Ivan. Ivan would not be tempted by money.'

'Wouldn't he? And what about Katerina? She's very beautiful, isn't she? It's not only the money, though sixty thousand isn't to be sneezed at.'

'Ivan has higher things in mind. Ivan wouldn't be tempted by any amount of money. It's not money or security that he is after. Perhaps it's suffering he is after.'

'What nonsense is this? Oh you – aristocrats!'

'Oh, Misha, his is a stormy spirit. His mind is in bondage. He's obsessed by a great, unsolved problem. He's one of those who don't want millions, but a solution of their problem.'

'Plagiarism, my dear chap. You're trying to paraphrase one of your elder's sayings. Hell, what a riddle Ivan has set you!' Rakitin cried with undisguised malice. He even changed countenance and his lips twitched. 'And the riddle is a stupid one. You can guess it easily. Use your brains and you'll understand. His article is absurd and ridiculous. You've heard his stupid theory, haven't you? "If there is no immortality of the soul, there is no virtue, which means that everything is permitted." (And dear old Mitya, you remember, cried out: "I'll remember that!") An attractive theory for scoundrels. . . . Sorry. I'm being abusive – that's silly. It's not a theory for scoundrels, but for bragging schoolboys with their "profound, unsolved problems". He's a dirty little boaster, but what it all comes to is that "on the one hand, we cannot but admit, and, on the other, we cannot but confess". His whole theory is nothing but a dirty trick! Mankind will find in itself the strength to live for virtue even without believing in the immortality of the soul! It will find it in love for freedom, equality, fraternity. . . .'

Rakitin grew excited and could scarcely contain himself. But, as though remembering something, he suddenly stopped short.

'Well, that's enough,' he said, smiling even more wryly than before. 'What are you laughing at? You think I'm a vulgar fool?'

'No, it never occurred to me to think you were a vulgar fool. You're clever, but – let's drop it, it was silly of me to laugh. I realize that you're capable of getting excited about it, Misha. From your excitement I guessed that you were not indifferent to Katerina yourself. You see, my dear fellow, I suspected it long ago. That's why you don't like my brother Ivan. You're jealous of him, aren't you?'

'Am I jealous of her money, too? Why not say it?'

'No, I won't say anything about money. I'm not going to insult you.'

'I believe it, since you say so, but to hell with you all and your brother Ivan! You won't understand that one can dislike him very much quite apart from Katerina. And, damn it all, why should I like him? Doesn't he do me the honour of abusing me himself? Why, then, haven't I got the right to abuse him?'

'I've never heard him say anything good or bad about you. He doesn't speak of you at all.'

'But I heard that the day before yesterday he was reviling me for all he was worth at Katerina's – that's how much he really is interested in your humble servant. And who is jealous of whom after that I don't know, old man. He was so good as to express the opinion that if I hadn't made up my mind to take up the career of an archimandrite in the very near future and become a monk, I would quite certainly go to Petersburg and become a contributor to a periodical, and quite certainly as a literary critic, and write for ten years and in the end transfer the ownership of the periodical to myself. Then I'd go on editing it and quite certainly in a liberal and atheistic spirit with a Socialist tendency, with ever such a tiny gloss of Socialism, keeping my ear to the ground, or, in other words, actually having a foot in both camps and hoodwinking the fools. The whole purpose of my career, according to your brother, is not to allow my Socialist tendency to prevent me from putting my subscribers' money into the bank and investing it at the first opportunity with the advice of some Jew, till I have enough capital to build a large house in Petersburg, transfer my editorial offices to it and let out the other stories to tenants. He has even chosen the place for it: by the New Stone Bridge across the Neva, which they say is being planned to connect the Liteyny Avenue with the Vyborg suburb. . . . '

'But, Misha, that's just what will happen, you know, every word of it!' cried Alyosha suddenly, unable to restrain himself and laughing gaily.

'So you too, sir, are getting sarcastic, are you?'

'No, no, I'm joking. I'm sorry. I've something else on my mind. But, tell me, who could possibly have given you all those details? Who could you have heard them from? You couldn't have been at Katerina's yourself when he was talking about you, could you?'

'I wasn't there, but your brother Dmitry was, and I heard him tell it with my own ears. Well, as a matter of fact, if you must know, he did not tell it me, but I overheard it, by sheer accident, of course, because I was in Grushenka's bedroom at the time and could not leave while Dmitry was in the next room.'

'Oh, yes, I forgot. She's a relative of yours, isn't she?'

'A relative? Grushenka a relative of mine?' Rakitin cried suddenly, flushing all over. 'Have you gone off your head? There must be something wrong with your brains.'

'Why? Isn't she a relative of yours? I heard she was.'

'Where can you have heard it? Oh, you Karamazovs! Giving yourselves airs as though you were great noblemen of ancient lineage, while as a matter of fact your father used to rush about playing the fool at other men's tables, and was given some job in the kitchen as a favour. All right, I may be only the son of a priest and a louse compared with you noblemen, but don't you insult me so lightheartedly and so wantonly. I too have a sense of honour, sir. I couldn't be a relative of Grushenka, a street walker, please understand that!'

Rakitin was beside himself with rage.

'I'm awfully sorry, I had no idea – and, besides, why a street walker? Is she – that kind of woman?' Alyosha said, suddenly blushing. 'I repeat I heard that she was a relative of yours. You often go to see her, and you told me yourself that you're not having an affair with her. You see, I never thought that you of all people despised her so much! Does she really deserve it?'

'If I visit her, I must have some good reason for it, mustn't I? That should be enough for you. As for being her relative, I daresay your brother or even your father is much more likely to make her your relative than mine. Well, here we are. You'd better go to the kitchen. Good Lord, what's up here? What's this? Are we late? They couldn't possibly have finished their dinner so soon! Or have the Karamazovs been up to something again? I'm sure they have. Here's your father and there's Ivan running after him. They've rushed out of the Father Superior's. And there's Father Isidore shouting something to them from the front steps. And your father, too, is shouting and waving his arms. Swearing, I suppose. Ah, there's Miusov, too, driving away in his carriage. He's driving off, you see. And there's the landowner Maximov running – why, there must have been a real brawl. So there's been no dinner! They haven't given the Father Superior a beating, have they? Or have they, perhaps, been given a beating themselves? It would serve them right!'

Rakitin was not exclaiming without good reason. There really had been a scandalous, unheard of, and unexpected scene. It all happened 'on the spur of the moment'.

8

A Scandalous Scene

WHEN Miusov and Ivan Karamazov were entering the Father Superior's room, Miusov, like the highly respectable and refined gentleman that he was, went rapidly through a highly refined process of a certain kind: he felt ashamed of being angry. He could not help feeling that he really ought to have had so little respect for a worthless wretch like old Karamazov that he should not have lost his temper in the elder's cell and so forgotten himself as he had done. 'The monks at least cannot be blamed for anything,' he decided suddenly, as he mounted the steps to the Father Superior's rooms. 'If here too there are decent people (I believe Father Nikolai, the Father Superior, is himself a nobleman), then why not be nice, kind, and courteous with them? . . . I won't argue, I shall do my best to agree with them, I shall win them over by being polite to them – and – after all, I'll show them that I have nothing to do with that absurd clown, that Pierrot, and have been merely taken in like the rest of them. . . .'

As for the disputed woodcutting and fishing rights (he did not know himself where the stream and the woods were exactly), he made up his mind to drop his court action against the monastery and let them have them finally, once and for all, and that very day, particularly as all that was not worth a great deal.

All these excellent intentions were strengthened when they entered the Father Superior's dining-room. The Father Superior did not really have a dining-room, for, strictly speaking, he only had two rooms, though they were much larger and more comfortable than the elder's. But the furnishings of the room were not particularly sumptuous, either: the furniture was of mahogany, covered with leather, in the old style of the twenties; the floors were not even stained, but everything was spotlessly clean, and there were many choice flowers in the windows; but the most sumptuous thing in the room at that moment was naturally the sumptuously laid table, though, of course, even that was comparatively speaking: the table-cloth was clean, the silver was brightly polished; three kinds of wonderfully baked bread, two bottles of wine, two bottles of excellent monastery mead, and a large glass jug of monastery *kvas*, famous throughout the neighbourhood. There was no vodka at all. Rakitin related afterwards that this time it was a five-course dinner: fish soup or sterlets served with fish patties; then boiled fish excellently prepared in a special way; then salmon cutlets, ice cream and stewed fruits and, finally, a fruit jelly. All this Rakitin sniffed out, for he could not resist the temptation to have a special look into the Father Superior's kitchen, where he also had his connexions. He had connexions everywhere and had a spy everywhere. He had a very restless and envious disposition. He was perfectly well aware of his considerable abilities, but he exaggerated them painfully in his self-conceit. He knew for certain that he would become a public figure of some sort, but Alyosha, who was greatly attached to him, was worried by the fact that his friend Rakitin was dishonest and did not seem to be in the least conscious of it himself. On the contrary, he considered himself to be a man of the utmost integrity because he knew that he would not steal money lying on a table. No one, let alone Alyosha, could do anything about that.

Rakitin, a person of little importance, could not be invited to the dinner, but Father Joseph and Father Paissy and another monk were invited. They were already waiting for the Father Superior in the dining-room when Miusov, Kalganov, and Ivan Karamazov arrived. Maximov was there, too, waiting in a far corner of the room. The Father Superior stepped into the middle of the room to welcome his guests. He was a tall, spare, but still very vigorous old man, with black hair streaked with grey and a long, grave, pious face. He exchanged bows with his guests in silence, but this time they all went up to him for his blessing. Miusov even went so far as to try to kiss his hand, but the Father Superior snatched it away in time, and the attempt miscarried. Ivan Karamazov and Kalganov, on the other hand, went through the full ceremony, that is to say, they gave the Father Superior's hand a resounding kiss as simple-hearted peasants might have done.

'We must offer you our most humble apologies, your reverence,' began Miusov with a wide, courteous smile, but still in a dignified and respectful tone of voice, 'for having arrived without Mr Karamazov, whom I believe you have also invited. I'm sorry to say he felt obliged to decline your hospitality, and for a good reason. Carried away by his unfortunate feud with his son, he uttered certain words in the cell of the reverend Father Zossima which were – er – hardly to the point. I – I mean, they were quite unseemly as – er – I believe' (he shot a glance at the monks) 'your reverence has been informed already. And, therefore, realizing that he had been at fault and being sincerely sorry and unable to overcome his feeling of shame, he asked us, that is to say, his son Ivan and myself, to convey his sincere apologies to you and to tell you how very distressed and sorry he is not to be able to come. In short, he hopes and desires to make amends for everything later and asks your blessing and begs you to forget what has taken place.'

Miusov fell silent. As he uttered the last words of his tirade, he felt so satisfied with himself that not a trace of his former irritation remained. He again fully and sincerely loved mankind.

The Father Superior listened to him with dignity and, with a slight inclination of his head, said in reply: 'I am very sorry he cannot be here. Perhaps he'd have learnt to love us at our table as we love him. Pray, gentlemen, be seated.'

But first he turned to the icon and began to say grace aloud. All bowed their heads reverently, and Maximov bent forward zealously, putting his hands together with special fervour.

And it was at that moment that Karamazov played his last prank. It must be observed that he had really intended to go home, realizing how impossible it was to go to dine with the Father Superior as if nothing had happened after his disgraceful behaviour in the elder's cell. Not that he was so very much ashamed of himself or blamed himself; quite the contrary, perhaps; but he still felt that it would be unseemly to go to dinner. But as soon as his rickety carriage had driven up to the front steps of the inn and he was about to get into it, he suddenly stopped short. He remembered his own words at the elder's: 'It does indeed seem to me every time I go to see people that I am more contemptible than anyone else and that everyone takes me for a clown – so that's why I say to myself, all right, let me play the clown, because you're all without exception more stupid and more contemptible than I.' He wanted to revenge himself on everyone for his own filthy tricks. At that moment he suddenly recalled how a long time before he had once been asked: 'Why do you hate that man so much?' And, in a fit of his clownish shamelessness, he had replied: 'I'll tell you why. It's true he has done nothing to me, but I played him a dirty trick, and as soon as I had done it I at once hated him for it.' Recalling it now, he gave a quiet and malicious chuckle as he hesitated for a moment. His eyes flashed and even his lips quivered. 'Having started, I may as well finish it,' he suddenly decided. His innermost feeling at that moment could be expressed in the following words: 'I couldn't possibly regain my lost reputation now, so let me be as beastly to them as I can: I don't care a hang, so there!' He told the driver to wait, while he returned with rapid steps to the monastery and went straight to the Father Superior's. He still did not quite know what he was going to do, but he knew that he could not control himself and that at the slightest provocation he might be driven to do something utterly abominable, but only that and certainly not anything criminal or something for which he could be convicted in a court of law. When it came to that, he knew how to control himself, and he was often surprised at himself for being able to do so. He appeared in the Father Superior's dining-room exactly at the moment when the prayer was over and they all moved to the table. Stopping in the doorway, he glanced at the company and gave his protracted, impudent, and malicious chuckle, looking them all boldly in the face.

'And they thought I'd gone, but here I am!' he cried in a loud voice.

For a moment they all looked straight at him without uttering a word, and suddenly they all felt that something revolting and grotesque was about to happen, something that was sure to end in a scandalous scene. Miusov at once passed from the most good-humoured mood to the most fierce. Everything that had died down and subsided in his heart at once revived and rose to the surface.

'No, that I can't stand!' he cried. 'I simply can't and – I absolutely can't!'

The blood rushed to his face. He even stammered, but he was beyond worrying about his style and snatched up his hat.

'What is it he can't stand?' cried Karamazov. 'He absolutely can't, he simply can't! Your reverence, may I come in or not? Will you receive me as one of your guests?'

'You are welcome with all my heart,' replied the Father Superior. 'Gentlemen,' he added, 'I appeal to you with all my heart and soul to give up your temporary feuds and unite in love and harmony as relatives should, with a prayer to God at our humble table. . . . '

'No, no, it's impossible!' Miusov cried, beside himself.

'Well, if Mr Miusov finds it impossible, then I find it impossible, too, and I won't stay. That's what I came for. From now on I shall always be with Mr Miusov: if you go away, sir, I will go away, too, if you stay, I will stay. You've hurt his feelings very badly, your reverence, by mentioning family harmony, for he refuses to recognize me as his relation. That's right, von Sohn, isn't it? That's von Sohn standing there! How do you do, von Sohn?'

'Are you addressing me, sir?' muttered Maximov in surprise.

'Of course, you,' cried Karamazov. 'Who else do you think? The Father Superior couldn't be von Sohn, could he?'

'But I'm not von Sohn, sir. I'm Maximov.'

'Oh no, sir, you are von Sohn. Do you know what von Sohn is, your reverence? It was a famous murder case: he was killed in a house of ill-fame – that's what you call those places, I believe – he was killed and robbed and, in spite of his venerable age, he was shoved into a box, nailed down and sent labelled in a luggage van from Petersburg to Moscow. And when they were nailing him down, the harlots sang songs and played the psaltery, I mean, the pianoforte. So this gentleman here is that very same von Sohn. He has risen from the dead. Isn't that so, von Sohn?'

'What's all this? What on earth — ?' voices were heard from the group of monks.

'Come, let's go!' cried Miusov, addressing Kalganov.

'No, sir, one moment, please!' Karamazov broke in shrilly, taking another step into the room. 'Let me finish. There in the cell I was put to shame for having behaved disrespectfully by shouting about gudgeons. Mr Miusov, my relation, likes to have *plus de noblesse que de sincérité* in his words, whereas I, on the contrary, like *plus de sincérité que de noblesse* in my words – and to hell with *noblesse*. That's right, isn't it, von Sohn? Excuse me, your reverence, but though I'm a clown and play the clown, I am a knight in shining armour, and I want to speak out. Yes, sir, I'm a knight in shining armour and Mr Miusov is a man of morbid sensitivity and nothing more. I came here today perhaps to have a look round and to speak out. My son Alexey is saving his soul here. I am his father. I care for his future and, indeed, it is my duty to care for it. I've been listening and playing a part but I've also been quietly observing things, and now I'd like to give you the last act of the performance. How are things with us? Well, sir, with us, if anything falls down, it just lies there for ever. With us if a thing has once fallen down, then it must lie there for ever. But that's not as it should be! I want to get up. Holy fathers, I'm indignant with you. Confession is a great sacrament, which I revere and before which I'm ready to prostrate myself, but there, in the elder's cell, everyone suddenly goes down on his knees and confesses aloud. Is it permitted to confess aloud? The holy fathers of the Church laid it down that a confession should be whispered in the priest's ear. Only then does your confession become a sacrament, and so it has been since ancient times. For how else can I explain to him before everyone that I, for instance, did this and that – I mean to say, this and that, you understand, don't you? You see, sometimes it's improper even to say it. Why, it's really scandalous! No, Fathers, for all I know you may even start practising flagellation in your monastery here. . . . I shall write to the Holy Synod about it at the first opportunity, and I shall take my son, Alexey, home. . . .'

Here it must be observed that Karamazov had heard all sorts of disreputable stories about the goings-on in monasteries. All sorts of malicious rumours had been current at one time, and they had even reached the bishop (not only about our monastery, but about other monasteries where the institution of elders had been established), to the effect that too much respect was paid to the elders, even to the detriment of the authority of the Father Superior, and that, among other things, the elders were abusing the sacrament of confession, etc., etc. Absurd charges which at the time died down of themselves both in our town and everywhere else. But the foolish devil, who had caught up Karamazov and was carrying him along on his nerves deeper and deeper into the pit of dishonour, prompted him to repeat the old accusation, of which he did not understand a single word himself. And he could not express it intelligently, particularly as this time no one had been kneeling and confessing aloud in the elder's cell, so that he could not possibly have seen anything of the kind and was merely repeating old rumours and slanders, which he only vaguely remembered. But having uttered his stupid accusation, he at once felt that he had been talking absurd nonsense, and he suddenly wanted to prove to his audience, and most of all to himself, that he had not been talking nonsense. And though he knew perfectly well that with each word he spoke he would be adding more and more absurdities, he was unable to restrain himself and plunged headlong, regardless of consequences.

'How despicable!' cried Miusov.

'Forgive me,' the Father Superior said suddenly, 'but it was said of old, "Many have begun speaking against me and saying many evil things, and, hearing it, I said to myself: it is the medicine of our Lord Jesus and he hath sent it to heal my vain soul." And therefore we humbly thank you, our dear guest!'

And he bowed low to Karamazov.

'Tut-tut-tut! Sanctimonious old phrases! Old phrases and old gestures! Old lies and conventional obeisances! We know all about these bows! "A kiss on the lips and a dagger in the heart", as in Schiller's *Robbers*. I don't like falsehood, Fathers. I want truth. But truth is not to be found in gudgeons, and I proclaimed it! Fathers, why do you fast? Why do you expect a reward in heaven for it? Why, for a reward like that I, too, will go and fast! No, holy monk, first be virtuous in life, be useful to society, without shutting yourself up in a monastery at somebody else's expense and without expecting rewards from up there – you'll find that a little harder. I can talk sense, too, Father Superior. Let's see what we have here,' he said, going up to the table. 'Old port wine, Médoc bottled by the Brothers Yeliseyev – well, well, Fathers! That doesn't look like gudgeons, does it? Look at the lovely bottles the fathers have put on the table – heh-heh-heh! And who has supplied you with it all? The toiling Russian peasant bringing you the farthings earned by his horny hands, wresting them from his family and the requirements of the State! Why, Holy Fathers, you suck the blood of the people!'

'That's quite unworthy of you!' said Father Joseph.

Father Paissy kept obstinately silent. Miusov rushed from the room, and Kalganov after him.

'Well, Fathers, I will follow Mr Miusov! I shall never come to see you again. You may beg me on your bended knees, but I shan't come. I sent you a thousand roubles, so your eyes are popping out of your heads again, heh-heh-heh! No, I won't give you another penny. I'm taking my revenge for my past, for my humiliation.' He thumped the table with his fist in a paroxysm of simulated feeling. 'This monastery has meant a lot in my life. I have shed bitter tears for it! You used to set my wife, the shrieker, against me. You cursed me with bell, book, and candle. You spread stories about me all over the district. Enough, Fathers, this is the age of liberalism, the age of steamers and railways. Not a thousand, not a hundred roubles, not a hundred copecks will you get out of me!'

It must be observed again that our monastery had never meant anything in particular in his life and he had never shed bitter tears for it. But he was so carried away by his simulated tears that for a moment he almost believed it himself; indeed, he nearly wept, so moved was he; but at the same moment he felt that it was time to beat a retreat.

In reply to his malicious lies, the Father Superior bowed his head and said again impressively: 'It is written again: "Suffer circumspectly and gladly the dishonour that befalleth thee, and be not confounded and hate not him who dishonoureth thee." We shall do likewise.'

'Tut-tut-tut! Considering thyself – and the rest of the balderdash! Consider yourselves, Fathers, and I'll be off. And I'm taking my son Alexey away from here for good by my authority as his father. Ivan, most dutiful son of mine, permit me to order you to follow me! Von Sohn, what do you want to stay here for? Come along with me now to the town. You'll have a good time there. It's only about a mile from here. Instead of lenten oil, I'll give you sucking-pig with stuffing. We'll have dinner. I'll get out the brandy, then a liqueur – I've got wild raspberry liqueur. Come on, von Sohn, don't miss your chance!'

He went out, shouting and gesticulating. It was at that moment that Rakitin saw him and pointed him out to Alyosha.

'Alexey,' his father shouted from a distance, catching sight of him, 'come home today for good, and bring your pillow and mattress, too! Mind I don't catch you here again!'

Alyosha stopped dead, observing the scene intently and in silence. In the meantime Karamazov got into the carriage. Ivan was about to get in after him in grim silence, without even turning round to say good-bye to Alyosha. But at this point a grotesque and almost incredible scene took place which gave the finishing touch to the episode. Maximov suddenly appeared at the step of the carriage. He ran up, panting, afraid of being late. Rakitin and Alyosha saw him running. He was in such a hurry that in his impatience he put his foot on the step on which Ivan's left foot was still resting and, clutching the box, was about to jump in.

'I'm coming too! I'm coming, too!' he cried, dancing about and laughing with bursts of gay, staccato laughter and a blissful look on his face, ready for anything. 'Take me, too!'

'There, didn't I say that he was von Sohn!' Karamazov cried delightedly. 'That he is the real von Sohn risen from the dead? But how did you manage to tear yourself away? What did you do there, you wicked old von Sohn, and how could you of all people get away from the dinner? One would have to have a face of brass to do that. I have one, but I must say I'm surprised at your impudence, old man! Come on, jump in. Let him, Ivan. We'll have fun. He can lie down somewhere at our feet. You will, won't you, von Sohn? Or shall we find room for him on the box with the driver? Jump on to the box, von Sohn!'

But Ivan, who had already taken his place in the carriage, without uttering a word, gave Maximov a violent push in the chest, which sent him flying three yards. If he did not fall, it was only by accident.

'Drive on!' Ivan shouted angrily to the coachman.

'What's the matter with you? What's the matter? Why did you push him away?' Karamazov broke out, but the carriage had already driven away.

Ivan made no answer.

'Good Lord, man,' Karamazov said again after two minutes, looking askance at his darling son, 'the visit to the monastery was your idea, wasn't it? You suggested it. You approved it. So why are you so angry now?'

'Stop talking nonsense,' Ivan snapped sternly. 'Have a bit of a rest now.'

Karamazov was silent again for two minutes.

'It would be nice to have a glass of brandy now,' he observed sententiously.

But Ivan made no answer.

'You'll have some, too, when we get home.'

Ivan was still silent.

Karamazov waited another two minutes:

'I'll take Alyosha away from the monastery all the same, much as you may not like it, most respectful Karl von Moor.'

Ivan shrugged his shoulders contemptuously and, turning away, began staring at the road. They did not speak again all the way home.

BOOK THREE: THE SENSUALISTS

I

In the Servants' Cottage

FYODOR KARAMAZOV'S house was some distance from the centre of the town, but it was not quite on its outskirts, either. It was rather old, but of a pleasant exterior: it was a one-storied house with an attic, painted grey and with a red iron roof. It was spacious and snug and there was no reason why it should not last for a long time yet. It had all sorts of box-rooms, hidden passages, and unexpected staircases. There were rats in it, but Karamazov was not altogether cross with them: 'Anyway,' he used to say, 'one does not feel so bored in the evenings when one is left alone.' And it was indeed his habit to send the servants away to the cottage for the night and shut himself up alone in the house. The cottage was in the yard. It was a large and solid building; Karamazov had his kitchen there, though there was a kitchen in the house; he disliked the smell of cooking, and the dishes were carried across the yard in winter and summer. The house was built for a large family, and there was room in it for five times as many people, masters and servants. But at the time of our story only Karamazov and Ivan lived in it, and in the cottage there were only three servants: old Grigory, his old wife Marfa, and the servant Smerdyakov, who was still a young man. We shall have to say a few more words about these three servants. We have already said enough about old Grigory Kutuzov. He was a resolute and steadfast man, going stubbornly and undeviatingly to his goal, if this goal for some reason (often a surprisingly illogical one) appeared to him as an immutable truth. He was, generally speaking, honest and incorruptible. His wife Marfa, though she submitted to him absolutely all her life, nagged him terribly. After the liberation of the serfs, for instance, she kept asking him to leave Karamazov, settle in Moscow and start a small business there (they had some money of their own); but Grigory decided then once and for all that the woman was talking nonsense, 'because every woman is dishonourable', and that they ought not to leave their old master, whatever he might be, because that was 'their duty'.

'Do you understand what duty means?' he asked Marfa.

'I understand what duty means, Grigory,' Marfa replied firmly, 'but why it is our duty to stay here I shall never understand.'

'You don't have to understand, but it shall be so. Hold your tongue in future.'

And so it was: they did not go away, and Karamazov gave them a small salary and paid it regularly. Grigory knew, besides, that he had an indisputable influence on his master. He felt it and it was quite true: Karamazov, a cunning and obstinate clown, a man who had a very determined character 'in certain things in life', as he put it, was, to his own surprise, rather weak in some other 'things in life'. And he knew himself in which. He knew it and was afraid of many things. In some things in life one had always to keep a sharp look-out, and that was difficult without a trustworthy servant, and Grigory was a trustworthy servant. It even happened that Karamazov had been in danger of being thrashed, and that soundly, too, many times in the course of his life, and Grigory had always come to his rescue, though every time he gave him a lecture afterwards. But blows alone would not have frightened Karamazov: there were more serious cases, very intricate and complicated ones, when Karamazov himself would not have been able to explain why all of a sudden he quite unaccountably felt that at that very moment he was in great need of the presence of a trustworthy and devoted servant. Those were almost painful cases: a most licentious man and, in his lust, as cruel as a vicious insect, Karamazov, when drunk, sometimes felt suddenly overwhelmed by irrational terror and moral shock which had an almost physical effect on him. 'At those moments,' he used to say sometimes, 'my heart is in my mouth.' It was then that he liked to have near him, though not in the same room but in the cottage, a man who was faithful and as firm as a rock, who was not at all licentious like himself, who, though he had seen the sort of debaucheries that were going on and knew all the secrets, tolerated it all out of a sense of loyalty, did not object to it, and, above all, did not reproach him or threaten him with anything, either in this world or the next; and who, in case of need, would have protected him – from whom? From someone unknown, but terrible and dangerous. What he wanted was the presence of *another* man, an old and tried friend, upon whom he should be able to call in his sick moments in order to look at his face, or perhaps exchange a few words, a few quite irrelevant words; and if that man did not protest and was not angry, he felt easier in his mind, and if he was angry, well, then it just made him feel more melancholy. It even happened (though rather rarely) that Karamazov went at night to the cottage to wake Grigory and ask him to come to the house for a moment. Grigory came, and Karamazov would start talking about the most trivial things and would send him back soon, sometimes even with a sarcastic or jesting remark, while he would go to bed with a curse and sleep the sleep of the just. Something of the kind happened to Karamazov after the arrival of Alyosha, too. Alyosha 'touched him to the quick' by 'living with him, seeing everything and condemning nothing'. What is more, he had brought with him something Karamazov had never experienced before: a total absence of contempt for him, the old man, whom, on the contrary, he treated with invariable kindness and with perfectly natural and single-minded devotion, which he so little deserved. All this was a complete surprise for the old profligate, who had lived apart from his family; it was entirely unexpected to a man like him, who till then only liked everything that was 'rotten'. After Alyosha had gone, he confessed to himself that he understood something he had hitherto not wished to understand.

I have mentioned already at the beginning of my story that Grigory hated Karamazov's first wife Adelaida, the mother of his first son, Dmitry, and how, on the other hand, he protected Sophia, the shrieker, from his master and from everyone who happened to speak ill or flippantly about her. His sympathy for the unhappy woman had become something sacred to him, so that twenty years later he would not tolerate any disparaging remark about her from anyone and would at once challenge the offender. Outwardly Grigory was cold, dignified, and taciturn. He delivered himself of weighty and trenchant words and never expressed himself in a frivolous manner. In the same way it was impossible to tell at the first glance whether he loved his meek and submissive wife or not, and yet he did love her and she of course knew it. Marfa, indeed, was far from stupid, and was probably much more intelligent than her husband, at least much shrewder in worldly affairs, and yet she gave in to him meekly and without protest and unquestionably respected him as her spiritual superior. The remarkable thing was that both of them spoke very little to each other all through their lives and only about the most necessary daily affairs. Grigory, dignified and majestic, always thought over all his affairs and troubles alone, so that Marfa had long realized that he did not require her advice. She felt that her husband valued her silence and took it as a sign of her intelligence. He had never beaten her, except once, and that, too, only a little. Once during the first year of Karamazov's marriage to Adelaida, the village girls and women, who were still serfs at the time, were collected before the country house to sing and dance. They began with 'In the Green Meadows', when Marfa, who was still a young woman at the time, leapt forward in front of the choir, and went off into the 'Russian' dance, which she danced in quite a special way, not as the village women used to dance it, but as she had danced it when she was a serf girl at the private theatre of the rich Miusovs, where the actors were taught to dance by a dancing master from Moscow. Grigory saw how his wife pranced through the dance and an hour later, at home in his cottage, taught her a lesson, dragging her about by the hair a little. This was the first and last time that he chastised her, and, besides, Marfa had forsworn dancing ever since.

God had not blessed them with children. They had one child, but it died. Grigory was very fond of children, and did not conceal it; that is to say, he was not ashamed to show it. When Adelaida had run away he took charge of Dmitrý, who was three at the time, and looked after him for almost a year, combing his hair and washing him himself in a tub. Afterwards he had taken care of Ivan and Alyosha, for which he had his face slapped; but I have already related all that. His own child made him happy only in anticipation of his birth, while his wife was pregnant. When it was born, it struck his heart with grief and horror. For the boy had six fingers. When he saw it, Grigory was so crushed that he not only kept silent till the day of the christening, but used to go away to the garden to be quiet. It was spring and he spent three days digging in the kitchen-garden. On the third day the child was to be christened; but by that time Grigory came to a decision. Going into the cottage, where the clergy, the guests and, finally, Karamazov himself, who had appeared personally in his rôle as godfather, had all gathered, he suddenly declared that the child 'ought not to be christened at all'. He had announced it quietly, without any explanation, letting his words escape him slowly and gazing dully and intently at the priest.

'Why ever not?' the priest asked with good-humoured surprise.

'Because,' muttered Grigory, 'it's a dragon, sir.'

'A dragon? What sort of a dragon?'

'It's a confusion of nature,' he muttered, though rather vaguely, but very firmly, evidently not wishing to dilate on the matter.

They laughed, and the poor baby was of course christened. Grigory prayed earnestly at the font, but did not change his opinion of the new-born child. He did not interfere, however, but he never looked at the sickly child during the fortnight that it lived and did not even wish to notice it, keeping away from the cottage most of the time. But when at the end of the fortnight the baby died of thrush, he laid him in his little coffin himself, gazing at him with deep anguish, and when his little shallow grave was filled up, he went down on his knees and prostrated himself before it. Since then he had never once mentioned his child; neither did his wife Marfa speak of her baby in his presence, and when she did happen to talk to someone about 'her darling child', she did so in a whisper, even though Grigory was not present. According to Marfa, Grigory had been occupied with 'religious matters' ever since the burial, mostly reading the *Lives of the Saints* in silence and when he was alone, always putting on his large, round, silver spectacles. He seldom read aloud, except perhaps in Lent. He was fond of the Book of Job, got hold of a copy of the sayings and sermons of 'our God-bearing Father Isaac the Syrian', which he read religiously for many years, without understanding scarcely a word of it, but perhaps prizing and loving it all the more for that. More recently he had begun to listen to, and show a great interest in, the doctrines of the flagellants, taking advantage of the presence of some members of that sect in the neighbourhood. He was visibly impressed, but did not think it worth while adopting the new faith. His assiduous reading of the 'religious' tracts lent an even greater gravity to his face.

Perhaps he was inclined to mysticism. And, as though by design, the appearance in the world of his six-fingered child and its death coincided with another very strange, unexpected, and quite exceptional event which, as he himself put it afterwards, had left 'an indelible mark' on his soul. It so happened that on the very night of

the funeral Marfa was awakened by what seemed to her to be the
cries of a new-born baby. She got frightened and woke her husband.
He listened and said that it sounded to him more like someone groaning, 'a woman perhaps'. He got up and dressed; it was a rather warm
May night. As he went outside, he distinctly heard the groans coming
from the garden. But the garden was locked up for the night and one
could not get into it except from the yard, for it was surrounded by a
strong high fence. Grigory went back into the cottage, lighted a
lantern, took the garden key and, taking no notice of the hysterical
fears of his wife, who was assuring him that it was a baby crying
and that she was sure it was her own baby crying and calling to her,
went out into the garden without uttering a word. There he realized
at once that the groaning was coming from their bath-house, near
the garden gate, and that it was indeed a woman who was groaning.
When he opened the door of the bath-house, he saw a sight which
completely dumbfounded him: the idiot girl who wandered about
the streets and was known all over the town as Stinking Lizaveta
(Lizaveta Smerdyashchaya), had broken into the bath-house and had
just given birth to a child. Her baby lay beside her and she lay dying
beside it. She said nothing, for she had never been able to speak,
anyway. But all this must be explained in a separate chapter.

2

Stinking Lizaveta

THERE was one special circumstance here which deeply shocked
Grigory, having finally strengthened an unpleasant and revolting
suspicion he had had for some time. Lizaveta Smerdyashchaya was an
undersized girl 'just under five feet', as many pious old women of
our town touchingly described her after her death. She was twenty
and her healthy, broad, red face bore an expression of complete
idiocy; she had a fixed and unpleasant look in her eyes, though it
was meek enough. She walked about barefoot all her life, in winter
as well as in summer, wearing only a hempen shift. Her very thick,
almost black hair, curling like lamb's wool, formed a kind of huge
cap on her head. It was, besides, always matted with mud, and had

leaves, splinters of wood, and shavings clinging to it, for she always slept on the ground and in the dirt. Her father Ilya was a homeless, sickly artisan, who had lost all his money and was perpetually drunk. He had been living for many years as a workman with some well-to-do tradesmen, also artisans of our town. Lizaveta's mother had long been dead. Ilya, always ill and in a bad temper, used to beat Lizaveta unmercifully whenever she came home. But she came home very rarely because she used to be fed by everybody in the town as a saintly fool. Ilya's employers, Ilya himself, and many other compassionate people in the town, especially merchants and merchants' wives, tried many times to clothe Lizaveta more decently, and towards winter always put a sheepskin and boots on her; but, although she let them put everything on her without protest, she used to go away, preferably to the cathedral porch, and take off everything she had been given – kerchief, skirt, sheepskin, or boots – and leave it there and walk away barefoot and in her shift as before. It happened on one occasion that our new provincial governor, on his tour of inspection of our town, caught sight of Lizaveta and was deeply hurt in his tenderest feelings. Though he realized that she was a 'saintly fool', as indeed he was officially informed, he insisted on pointing out that for a young girl to wander about the streets in nothing but her shift was a breach of the proprieties and that it must not happen again. But the governor departed, and Lizaveta was left as she was. At last her father died, and she became even dearer to all the pious people in our town as an orphan. Indeed, everyone seemed to like her and even the boys in the streets did not tease or molest her, and the boys of our town, especially the schoolboys, are a mischievous lot. She would walk into strange houses and no one drove her out; on the contrary, everyone tried to be nice to her and give her a penny. If she were given a penny, she would take it and at once drop it into some alms-box in a church or outside the prison. If she were given a roll or bun in the market, she would go away and give it to the first child she came across, or else stop one of the richest ladies in our town and hand it to her; and the ladies were very pleased to accept it. She herself lived only on black bread and water. If she went into an expensive shop and sat down there, the proprietors took no notice of her, though there were costly goods and money lying about, for they knew that even if they put thousands of roubles before her and forgot all about it, she would not take a penny. She very rarely went to church, and slept either in a church porch or, climbing over some wattle fence (we have a great number of wattle instead of wooden fences in our town even today), in a kitchen-garden. She used to make an appearance 'at home', that is, in the house of her late father's employers, about once a week, and in winter every day, but only at night, and slept in the hall or the cowshed. People were amazed that she could survive such a life, but she was used to it; though she was so small, she had an incredibly strong constitution. Some people in our town maintained that she did all this from pride, but somehow it did not make sense: she could not speak a single word and only from time to time did she utter an inarticulate grunt – what sort of pride was that? Now it happened – ever so long ago – that one bright and warm night in September (it was full moon) a company of drunken gentlemen of our town, about five or six gay bucks, were returning in high spirits home from the club by the 'back way' at what to us provincials seemed a rather late hour. There was a wattle fence at either side of the narrow lane, behind which were the kitchen-gardens of the adjacent houses; the lane led out on to the little bridge across the long, stinking puddle which it was our custom to call a stream. At the wattle fence, among the nettles and burdocks, our gentlemen caught sight of Lizaveta asleep. The merry bucks stood over her, laughing uproariously, and began cracking jokes of a quite unprintable character. It suddenly occurred to one young gentleman to put a highly whimsical question on an absurd subject: 'Could anyone,' he asked, 'regard such an animal as a woman, just now, for instance,' and so on. They all decided with lordly disdain that it was impossible. But Karamazov happened to be among the company and he at once volunteered the opinion that it was possible to regard her as a woman, very much so, indeed, and that there was something piquant about it, and so on and so forth. It is true that at that time he seemed extremely anxious to play the part of a clown. He liked to thrust himself forward and entertain the gentlemen, pretending all the time, of course, to be their equal, though, in fact, acting in their company in a manner that befitted a country yokel rather than a gentleman. Just then he had received the news of his first wife's death and, with a crape upon his hat, drank and behaved in such an unseemly fashion that many people in our town, even the most licentious ones, were nauseated at the sight of him. The whole crowd of course laughed at this startling opinion, and one of them even tried to egg him on to act upon it, but the rest began expressing their disgust in even stronger terms, though still with the utmost hilarity, and at last they went on their way. Afterwards Karamazov swore that he had gone with them; perhaps it was so, no one knows for certain and no one ever knew. But five or six months later everyone in town was discussing with sincere and intense indignation the fact that Lizaveta was pregnant and kept asking each other who was the man who had wronged her. It was then that a strange rumour spread through the town that the scoundrel was no other than Fyodor Karamazov. Where did this rumour spring from? Of that company of drunken gentlemen only one was left in our town by that time, an elderly and respected State Councillor, who was the father of grown-up daughters and who most certainly would not have spread such a rumour even if there had been anything in it; the rest, about five men, had all left the town. But rumour pointed straight at Fyodor Karamazov and persisted in pointing at him. Karamazov, of course, was not very much upset by it: he would not have troubled to answer the allegations made against him by some merchants or artisans. He was very proud in those days and never spoke to anyone except to his own circle of civil servants and noblemen whom he entertained so well. It was just at that time that Grigory stood up for his master energetically and not only defended him with the utmost vigour against all these slanders, but also abused and quarrelled with his accusers and forced many people to change their minds. 'It's the hussy's own fault,' he used to say emphatically, and her seducer was none other than 'Karp the Jemmy' (that was the name of a dangerous convict, well known to all of us, who had escaped from prison just then and had been living in hiding in our town). This conjecture seemed plausible enough, for the memory of Karp was still fresh in everyone's mind, and he was remembered so well because he had been loitering about the streets during those autumn nights and had robbed three people. But this affair and all these rumours did not alienate the sympathy of the townspeople from the poor idiot girl, who was taken care of and looked after more than ever. Mrs Kondratyev, a well-to-do merchant's widow, took all the necessary steps at the end of April to keep

Lizaveta at her house and make sure that she was not let out until after the confinement. They kept a constant watch over her, but, in spite of their vigilance, Lizaveta stole away from Mrs Kondratyev's in the evening of the very last day and found her way into Karamazov's kitchen-garden. How she managed in her condition to climb over the strong, high fence remained a mystery. Some said that she had been 'lifted over' by somebody, and others that she was 'lifted over' by some supernatural power. It is more probable, however, that it all happened in a very natural, though perhaps tricky way, and that Lizaveta, who was used to climbing over fences to spend the night in other people's kitchen-gardens, somehow or other managed to clamber over Karamazov's fence, and, in spite of her condition, to jump down into the garden, though, it is true, not without injuring herself. Grigory rushed to Marfa and sent her to look after Lizaveta, while he ran to fetch an old midwife who, fortunately, lived close by. The child was saved, but Lizaveta died at dawn. Grigory took the baby, brought it home, told his wife to sit down and put it on her lap, right against her breast. 'A child of God,' he said, 'an orphan is everyone's kin, and yours and mine all the more. Our little baby has sent us him, and he has been born of the devil's son and a holy innocent. Feed him and weep no more.' So Marfa brought up the child. He was christened and given the name of Pavel, and as for his patronymic, everyone began to call him quite naturally Fyodorovich. Fyodor Karamazov raised no objections and even found it all very amusing, though he continued to deny it all vehemently. The people in our town were pleased that he had taken care of the foundling. Later on, Karamazov found a surname for the child: he called him Smerdyakov, after the surname of his mother, Lizaveta Smerdyashchaya. It was this Smerdyakov who became Karamazov's second servant and lived, at the time our story begins, in the cottage together with Grigory and Marfa. He was employed as a cook. I should really say something more about him, but I am ashamed to keep my reader's attention occupied with common servants too long, and I am therefore going back to my story in the hope that all the relevant facts about Smerdyakov will somehow or other emerge in the course of it.

3

The Confession of an Ardent Heart in Verse

AFTER hearing the order his father shouted to him from the carriage after he had left the monastery, Alyosha remained standing for some time in great perplexity. Not that he stood still in one place for long – he was not in the habit of doing that. On the contrary, in spite of his great uneasiness, he managed to go at once to the Father Superior's kitchen to find out what his father had been up to upstairs. Then he set off for the town in the hope that on the way he would somehow or other be able to solve the problem that was troubling him. Let me say at once: he was not at all afraid of his father's shouts or his order to return home with his 'pillows and mattress'. He realized very well that the order to return home, shouted in so ostentatious a way, was given 'in a moment of passion' and, as it were, for the sheer beauty of it – just like the tradesman in our town who, when recently celebrating his nameday, not wisely but too well, had got angry at not being given more vodka and suddenly began in the presence of his guests to smash up his own crockery, to tear up his own and his wife's clothes, and, finally, to break his windows, and all for the sheer beauty of it, and the same thing, of course, had happened now to his father. Next day, of course, the drunken tradesman became sober and was sorry for the broken cups and saucers. Alyosha knew that his father would let him go back to the monastery next day or, indeed, even that very day. He was, besides, sure that while his father might hurt anyone's feelings, he would be loath to hurt his. Alyosha was convinced that no one in the world would ever wish to hurt him; indeed, that no one ever could hurt him. That he regarded as an axiom that could be accepted once and for all without argument, and that was why he went on his way without any misgivings.

But at that moment he was vaguely obsessed by another fear, a fear of quite a different kind, and all the more agonizing since he could not define it himself. It was the fear of a woman, namely Katerina, who, in the note handed to him by Mrs Khokhlakov, had so urgently besought him to go and see her about something. This request and the necessity of going there immediately aroused a strangely poignant feeling in his heart, and all the morning, as the hours passed, this feeling grew into a more and more intensely aching pain in spite of the scenes and adventures in the monastery, and now at the Father Superior's, etc. etc., which followed so closely upon each other. He was not afraid because he did not know what she was going to talk to him about and what answers he would have to give her. And it was not the woman in her that he was afraid of: of course, he knew little of women, but all the same he had spent all his life, from early childhood till he entered the monastery, entirely with women. He was afraid of that woman alone; he was afraid of Katerina. He had been afraid of her ever since he first saw her. He had only seen her once or twice, or perhaps three times, and had even exchanged a few words with her once by chance. He remembered her as a beautiful, proud, and imperious girl. Yet it was not her beauty that troubled him, but something else. And it was just the inexplicable nature of his fear that increased the fear itself. The girl's aims were of the noblest – he knew that: she was trying to save his brother Dmitry, who had treated her badly, and she was doing so out of sheer magnanimity. And yet, in spite of the fact that he could not but appreciate these beautiful and magnanimous feelings of hers, a chill ran down his spine the nearer he drew to her house.

He realized that he would not find his brother Ivan, who was on such intimate terms with her, at her house: Ivan was most certainly now with his father. And he was even more certain that Dmitry would not be there either, and he had a pretty good idea why. So they would have their talk in private. He wanted very much to go and see his brother Dmitry before that fateful talk. Without showing him the letter, he could have a few words with him. But Dmitry lived far away and he, too, was sure to be out now. After standing still for a minute, he at last came to a final decision. Crossing himself with accustomed rapidity and at once smiling at something, he walked resolutely in the direction of the house of the young lady he was so much afraid of.

He knew her house. But if he went by the High Street, then across the square and so on, it would be rather a long way round. Our little town is very scattered and the distances between streets are rather long. Besides, his father was expecting him. Perhaps he had not yet forgotten his order and he might be in a temper and, therefore,

Alyosha had to hurry to be in time in both places. As a result of all these considerations he decided to take a short cut, for he knew all the byways in our little town like the back of his hand. To go by the back-way meant avoiding the streets, walking along deserted lanes between fences, and sometimes even climbing over fences and walking through people's back-yards, where, however, everyone knew him and greeted him. In this way he could reach the High Street in half the time. In one place he had to pass very near his father's house, past the garden adjoining his father's, belonging to a tumble-down little house with four windows. The owner of this house, as Alyosha knew, was a bed-ridden old tradeswoman, who lived with her daughter, a 'civilized' parlour-maid who had till recently been employed in Petersburg in generals' homes, but had returned home because of her mother's illness about a year ago and who liked to show off her smart dresses. The old woman and her daughter, however, had fallen upon evil days and had to go every day to Karamazov's kitchen for soup and bread, which Marfa gave them readily enough. But though coming for the soup, the old woman's daughter had not sold a single one of her dresses, one of which even had a long train. Alyosha had learnt this quite by chance, of course, from his friend Rakitin, who knew absolutely everything that was going on in their town, and naturally at once dismissed it from his mind. But as he came alongside their neighbours' garden, he suddenly remembered the dress with the train and, quickly raising his downcast head, bowed in thought, suddenly came across someone he never thought of meeting there.

In the garden, on the other side of the wattle fence, stood his brother Dmitry, perched on something and leaning over the fence. He was gesticulating violently, trying to attract Alyosha's attention and apparently afraid not only to call out but to utter a single word for fear of being heard. Alyosha at once ran up to the fence.

'It's a good thing you looked up or I would have had to call you,' Dmitry whispered to him joyfully and rapidly. 'Climb over here! Quick! Oh, I'm so glad you've come! I was just thinking of you. . . .'

Alyosha was delighted, too, and was only wondering how to climb over the fence. But Mitya caught hold of his arm with his powerful hand and helped him to jump over. Tucking up his cassock, Alyosha jumped over with the agility of a bare-legged street urchin.

'Well done! Come along now!' Mitya cried in an enthusiastic whisper.

'Where?' Alyosha, too, said in a whisper, looking round and finding himself in a deserted garden in which there was no one except themselves. The garden was not very large, but the little house was at least fifty yards away. 'But there's no one here, so why do you whisper?'

'Why do I whisper? Damn it,' Dmitry suddenly cried in a loud voice, 'why *do* I whisper? You see how a chap can get all muddled up. I'm here in secret and am keeping a secret. I'll explain everything in a minute, but, knowing it's a secret, I suddenly began talking like a conspirator and whispering like a fool, when there's no need for it. Come on! Over there. Not a word till then. Oh, I could kiss you!

> Glory to the All-Highest in excelsis,
> Glory to the All-Highest in me!

I was just repeating that, sitting here, before you came. . . . '

The garden was about three acres in extent, but it was planted with trees only along the four fences – apple-trees, maples, lime-trees, and birches. The middle of the garden consisted of a grass patch which provided several hundredweights of hay every summer. It was let out for a few roubles in spring. There were also beds of raspberries, gooseberries, and blackcurrants along the fences; the vegetable beds were near the house, but they had only been planted recently.

Dmitry took his visitor to one of the remotest corners of the garden farthest from the house. There amid the thickly planted lime-trees and old blackcurrant bushes, elder, guelder-rose and lilac, stood an old tumble-down green summer-house, its latticed walls blackened and sagging with age, but with a roof that was still intact and could give shelter from rain. The summer-house was built goodness only knows when, at least fifty years before, according to popular belief, by a retired Lieutenant-Colonel, a certain Alexander von Schmidt, who had owned the house. But it was all decayed, the floor was rotting, the floorboards were loose, and the woodwork was musty. There was a green table in the summer-house fixed in the ground, and round it were green wooden benches on which it was still possible to sit. Alyosha at once noticed his brother's excited state, but as he entered the summer-house he saw half a bottle of brandy and a glass on the table.

'Brandy!' Mitya burst out laughing. 'I daresay you're already saying to yourself: "He's drinking again!" Do not believe what you see—

> Do not believe the foolish, lying crowd,
> Cast aside your doubts. . . .

I'm not tippling, I'm only "indulging myself a little", as that swine of a Rakitin of yours says. He'll be a State Councillor one day and he'll keep on saying, "I'm indulging myself a little". Sit down. I'd like to press you to my bosom, Alyosha, my lad, and crush you against it, for in the whole world I actually – ac-tu-al-ly (understand this! understand this!) love no one but you!'

He uttered the last words almost in a sort of frenzy.

'No one but you, and one other person, a slut I've fallen in love with to my own undoing. But to fall in love doesn't mean to love. One can fall in love with a woman and hate her at the same time. Remember that! For the time being I'm talking cheerfully! Sit down. Here at the table. I'll sit beside you and look at you and go on talking. You'll keep quiet and I'll go on talking, for the appointed hour has come. Still, you know, I think it might be more advisable to keep our voices down because here – here – you never know who may be listening. I'll explain everything – I told you: the continuation follows. Why do you think I was dying to see you all these days? Why was I longing to see you just now? (It's five days since I cast anchor here.) All these days? Because it's to you alone I'm going to tell everything, because I have to, because it's you I need, because tomorrow I'm going to take a header from the clouds, because tomorrow my life is ending and beginning. Have you ever felt, have you ever dreamt what it is like falling from a mountain into a chasm? Well, that's how I'm falling now, but not in a dream. And I'm not a bit afraid, and don't you be afraid, either. I mean, I *am* afraid, but I love it. I mean, I don't love it, but I feel excited. . . . Oh, to hell with it. It's all one to me, whatever it is! A strong spirit, a weak spirit, a womanish spirit – whatever it is! Let us praise nature: see how bright the sun is, how clear the sky, how green the leaves – it's still like summer, four o'clock in the afternoon, everything so still! Where were you going?'

'I was going to see father, but I meant to go and see Katerina first.'

'Going to see her and father! Good Lord, what a coincidence! Why, who do you think I was waiting for, what was it I wanted, yearned, hungered, and thirsted for so much with every fibre of my soul and every curvature of my ribs? Why, to send you to father and then to Katerina with a message from me and so finish with her and with father. To send an angel. I could have sent anyone, but I had to send an angel. And here you are on your way to her and to father.'

'Did you really mean to send me?' Alyosha could not help asking with a pained expression on his face.

'Wait! You knew it, didn't you? I can see you understood it all straight away. But not a word – not a word now. Don't be sorry for me and don't cry!'

Dmitry got up, pondered, and put a finger to his forehead: 'She's asked you to call on her herself, hasn't she? She's written you a letter or something and that's why you were going to her. You wouldn't have gone otherwise, would you?'

'Here's her note,' said Alyosha, taking it out of his pocket.

Mitya quickly glanced through it.

'And you went the back-way? Ye gods, I thank you for sending him the back-way so that I could catch him like the old fool of a fisherman caught the golden fish in the fairy-tale. Listen, Alyosha, listen, my dear fellow. Now I mean to tell you everything. For I have to tell someone. I simply have to. I've told it to an angel in heaven already, but I have to tell it to an angel on earth, too. You are an angel on earth. You'll hear, you'll judge, and you'll forgive. . . . For what I need is that someone higher should forgive. Listen: if two people suddenly break away from everything earthly and go off on some wonderful adventure, or at least one of them does, and before going off or perishing, he comes to someone and says, Do this or that for me – something no one is ever asked to do by anyone except on one's death-bed – would the other one refuse if – if he's a friend or a brother?'

'I'll do it, but tell me what it is, and tell me quickly,' said Alyosha.

'Quickly. . . . Mmm. . . . Don't be in a hurry, Alyosha: you're in a hurry and you're worried. There's no need to hurry now. Now the world has struck out along a new road. Oh, Alyosha, what a pity you've never had any idea of what ecstasy means! But why am I

saying this to you? You of all people don't know what it means?
What a silly ass I am! I say:

Be noble, O man!

Whose verse is this?'

Alyosha decided to wait. He realized that all his business was perhaps really here. Mitya pondered for a minute, his elbows propped
up on the table and his head resting on his hand. Both were silent.

'Alyosha,' said Mitya, 'you alone will not laugh! I should like to
begin my confession with – with Schiller's Hymn to Joy. *An die
Freude*. But I don't know German. All I know is *An die Freude*. Don't
think I'm just jabbering away because I'm drunk. I'm not at all drunk.
Brandy is brandy, but I need two bottles to make me drunk.

And Silenus, red of face,
Upon his stumbling ass —

You see, I haven't drunk a quarter of a bottle and I'm not Silenus.
I'm not Silenus but I am *silen*, I'm strong because I've made a
decision that is final and irrevocable. Forgive the pun. You must
forgive me a lot today, let alone a pun. Don't worry, I'm not spin-
ning it out. I'm talking sense and I'll come to the point in a minute.
I'm not going to keep you in suspense. Wait, how does it go? . . . '

He raised his head, thought a moment and suddenly began to recite
ecstatically:

Timid, naked in his den
Hid the savage troglodyte,
Over plains there wandered men
Spreading ruin to all in sight.
The hunter with his spear and arrow
Through the forests made his way . . .
Woe to any who in sorrow
Were cast upon that shore – a prey!

From the Olympian heights has flown
Mother Ceres swift to find
Her dear lost Proserpine, her own:
Bare and waste the land unkind,
Nothing there to ease and cherish,
No temple there to gods above,
No harvest of field nor burden lavish
Of vine to grace the feast of love.

> Nothing but the blood of wretches
> Steams from altars crude and bad,
> Nothing but the flesh of corpses
> Greets the eyes of Ceres sad.
> Sunk in deepest degradation,
> Vileness everywhere displayed,
> Foulness meets her woeful vision,
> Men their loathsomeness parade!

Mitya suddenly burst into sobs. He seized Alyosha by the hand.

'My friend, my friend, in degradation, in degradation even now. Man has to suffer a fearful lot on earth. There's a fearful lot of calamities for him there. Don't think that I'm just a boor of an officer who does nothing but drink brandy and leads a life of lust and depravity. I scarcely think of anything but of this degraded man, if only I'm not deceiving myself. Would to God I was not deceiving myself or showing off just now. For, you see, I think of that man because I'm such a man myself.

> That from the worst unto the better
> Man his soul may raise up high,
> He must join his ancient mother,
> Mother earth his best ally.

But the trouble is, you see, how am I to enter into an alliance with earth for ever? I don't kiss the earth, I don't cut open her bosom – so what am I to become: a peasant or a shepherd? I go on and on and I don't know whether I shall find myself amidst stench and shame or light and joy. That's the trouble, old man, for everything in the world is a mystery! And every time I happened to plunge into the very depths of the most shameless debauchery (and that was the only thing that did happen to me), I always read that poem about Ceres and man. Did it reform me? Never! For I am a Karamazov. For if I am to precipitate myself into the abyss, I shall do so without a moment's reflection, head over heels, and indeed I shall be glad to fall in such a degrading attitude and consider it beautiful for a man like me. And it is at this very moment of shame and disgrace that I suddenly begin to intone this hymn. Let me be damned, let me be vile and base, but let me kiss the hem of the garment in which my God is clad; let me be running after the devil at that very moment,

but I am still thy son, O Lord, and I love thee, and I feel the joy
without which the world cannot be and exist.

> The soul of all creation
> Blessed joy eternal fills,
> The secret force of fermentation
> With fire the cup of life instils;
> It lures sweet grasses to the light,
> And from the far-off outer spaces,
> Beyond the ken of furthest sight,
> Suns come out and take their places.
>
> At the breast of bounteous Nature
> Everything that breathes is glad;
> All nations, all creatures seek her pleasure,
> She gives to man a friend when sad;
> She gives the juice of grapes and garlands,
> And lust in lowly insect fires,
> But up above the angel stands
> In sight of God – his joy admires.

But enough of poetry! I've shed tears, so please, do let me cry. It
may be foolishness at which everyone will laugh, but not you. Your
eyes are shining too. Enough of poetry. I want to tell you now about
the 'insect', about the insect God has endowed with lust.

> And lust in lowly insect fires!

I am that insect, old man, and this has been said of me specially. And
all of us Karamazovs are the same kind of insect, and that insect
lives in you, too, my angel, and raises storms in your blood. I mean
storms, for lust is a storm – worse than a storm! Beauty is a fearful
and terrifying thing! Fearful because it is indefinable, and it cannot
be defined because God sets us nothing but riddles. Here the shores
meet, here all contradictions live side by side. I'm a very uneducated
fellow, old man, but I've thought a lot about it. There's a fearful lot
of mysteries! Too many riddles oppress man on earth. Solve them as
you can, but see that you don't get hurt in the process. Beauty! It
makes me mad to think that a man of great heart and high intelligence
should begin with the ideal of Madonna and end with the ideal of
Sodom. What is more terrible is that a man with the ideal of Sodom
already in his soul does not renounce the ideal of Madonna, and it

sets his heart ablaze, and it is truly, truly ablaze, as in the days of his youth and innocence. Yes, man is wide, too wide, indeed. I would narrow him. I'm hanged if I know what he really is! What appears shameful to the mind, is sheer beauty to the heart. Is there beauty in Sodom? Believe me, for the great majority of people it *is* in Sodom and nowhere else – did you know that secret or not? The awful thing is that beauty is not only a terrible, but also a mysterious, thing. There God and the devil are fighting for mastery, and the battlefield is the heart of man. Still, one can only talk of one's own pain. Listen, now to business.'

4

The Confession of an Ardent Heart in Anecdotes

'I LED a riotous life there. Father said this morning that I had spent several thousand roubles in seducing young girls. It's a filthy delusion. I never did anything of the sort, and if anything did happen, I didn't need any money just for *that*. With me money is an accessory, a fever of the heart, the background. Today it's a society woman, tomorrow a woman of the streets takes her place. I give them both a good time. I throw money about by the handful, music, noise, gypsy girls. If necessary, I give her money too, for they all take it. They take it with avidity. That I must admit. And they're pleased and grateful, too. Young society women have been in love with me, not all of them, but some – some; but I always liked the back streets, the deserted, dark back lanes, behind the square – there you find real, true adventures, real, genuine surprises – gold nuggets in the dirt. I'm speaking allegorically, old man. In the filthy little town I lived in there were no such back streets, but there were moral ones. If you were like me, you'd understand what it means. I loved vice and I loved the feeling of shame that vice gave me. I loved cruelty: am I not a bug, am I not a vicious insect? I told you – I'm a Karamazov! Once we went on a picnic – the whole town practically, in seven *troikas*. In the dark, in winter, in the sledge I began squeezing a young girl's hand, and forced her to kiss me. She was the daughter of a civil servant, a poor, sweet, gentle, meek child. She let me, she let me do much in the dark. She thought, poor thing, that next day I'd come and propose to her (you see, they thought a lot of me there as an eligible young man). But I never exchanged a single word with her after that. Never a word for five months. I could see how her eyes followed me about from a corner of the room at a dance (we were always having dances). I saw them glowing – glowing with gentle indignation. But this game only amused the insect's lust I nurtured inside me. Five months later she married a civil servant and left the town – angry and still perhaps in love with me. Now they live happily. Mind you, I told no one about it. I did nothing that might injure her reputation. I may have low desires and I may love low things, but I'm not dishonourable. You're blushing, your eyes flashed. Well, you've had enough of this filth, I think. And all this, understand, is only a beginning, it's only, as it were, Paul de Kock flowers, though the cruel insect was already growing – growing stronger and stronger in my soul. Here, old man, you have a whole album of reminiscences. May God bless them, the sweet darlings. I never liked to quarrel when breaking off a relationship with a woman. And I never betrayed any of them, never did anything to injure their reputations. But enough of that. You don't think I asked you to come here just to tell you all this nonsense? No, I've a much more interesting thing to tell you. But don't be surprised that I'm not ashamed before you, that, indeed, I'm even glad to tell you all about it.'

'You say that because I blushed,' Alyosha observed suddenly. 'I did not blush at what you were telling me, nor at what you've done. I blushed because I'm the same as you.'

'You? You're putting it on a bit, aren't you?'

'Not a bit,' Alyosha said warmly. (The idea had obviously occurred to him long before.) 'The steps are the same. I'm on the lowest one, and you're above, somewhere on the thirteenth. That's how I look upon it. It's one and the same thing. Absolutely similar. Anyone who has put his foot on the bottom step is bound to go up to the top one.'

'So you think one shouldn't put a foot on it at all, do you?'

'Anyone who can help it – shouldn't.'

'And can you?'

'I don't think so.'

'Not another word, Alyosha, not another word, old man. I'd like to kiss your hand, I'm so touched. That clever she-devil Grushenka is quite an expert on men and she told me once that she'd eat you up one day.... Sorry – sorry.... From these filthy abominations, from this field befouled by flies, let us pass on to my tragedy, also a field befouled by flies, I mean, by every kind of vileness. You see, the point is that though that beastly old man talked a lot of nonsense about the seduction of innocent girls, there actually was something of the sort in my tragedy, though it only happened once, and even then it didn't come off. The old man, who has reproached me with these cock-and-bull stories, doesn't know about this one – for I've never told anyone about it, you're the first I'm telling it to, with the exception of Ivan, of course, for Ivan knows everything. He knew about it long before you. But Ivan is as silent as the grave.'

'Ivan – silent as the grave?'

'Yes.'

Alyosha listened very attentively.

'You see, though a lieutenant in the battalion of the line regiment in which I served, I was really under constant supervision, just as though I were a convict. But in the little town where we were stationed I was very well received. I flung money about, everyone thought I was rich, and I thought so myself. Yet I must have pleased them in some other way, too. Though they shook their heads, they really liked me. But my commanding officer, a Lieutenant-Colonel – an old man – took a sudden dislike to me. He kept finding fault with me. But I had powerful friends and, besides, the whole town was on my side, and he couldn't do much to me! I was to blame myself, for I deliberately refused to treat him with proper respect. I was proud. This obstinate old man, who was not a bad sort at all and, indeed, a most kindly and hospitable fellow, had been married twice, and both his wives were dead. The first one seems to have been of humble origin and she left him a rather plain daughter. When I joined the regiment she was a young woman of four and twenty, and she lived with her father and aunt, a sister of her late mother. The aunt was meekness and simplicity itself, and her niece, the colonel's eldest daughter, was simple but pert. Talking of that girl, I'd like to put in a good word for her – I've never, old man, known a more charming character than that girl. Agafya her name was. She wasn't too bad-looking, either. A typical Russian girl: tall, plump, with a full figure. Her eyes were beautiful, but her face was perhaps a little coarse. She was not particularly keen on getting married, though two men had proposed to her. She refused them, but lost none of her gaiety. I became intimate with her – not in the sense this is usually understood. No, there was nothing of the kind there. I mean we were just good friends. You see, I often became intimate with women without making love to them, just in a friendly way. I used to say quite shockingly frank things to her, but she only laughed. Many women like frankness – make a note of that, and she was, besides, a young girl, which made it all the more amusing. And another thing. You could not possibly call her a young lady. She and her aunt lived in her father's house, but they seemed to put themselves in a humiliating position of their own accord, refusing to consider themselves on an equal footing with the rest of society. Everyone liked her and everyone was in need of her help, for she was an excellent dressmaker: she had a talent for it, but she demanded no payment for her services, she did everything out of kindness, but when people gave her money, she did not refuse it. But the Lieutenant-Colonel was quite a different kettle of fish! The Lieutenant-Colonel was one of the most prominent personalities in our town. He lived on a grand scale, entertained the whole town, gave dinners and dances. When I arrived and joined the battalion, it was common talk in the town that his second daughter, a girl of great beauty, would soon arrive from Petersburg, where she had just finished at a most fashionable boarding-school. This second daughter is Katerina, and she was the child of the Lieutenant-Colonel's second wife, who came from an aristocratic family. She was the daughter of a rich general, though I know for a fact that she did not bring the Lieutenant-Colonel any money, either. She came of a good family, and that was all. She may have had some hopes of inheriting money, but had not a penny in hard cash. And yet when the young lady arrived (on a visit, and not to stay), the whole town seemed to come to life. Our most aristocratic ladies – the wives of two generals and one colonel – and the rest after them at once showed a great interest in her. All took her up, gave entertainments in her honour, and she became the queen of the balls, picnics, and the *tableaux vivants* given in aid of some distressed governesses. I showed no interest. I carried on with my debaucheries. In fact, I had just done something so utterly disgraceful that the whole town was talking about it. One evening at the battery commander's I saw her sizing me up with her eyes, but I didn't go up to her – not interested! I went up to her only a few days later, also at a party. I said a few words to her, but she barely glanced at me. Compressed her lips scornfully. "Ah," I said to myself, "you wait! I'll get my own back one day!" I was an awful boor at the time when faced with a situation like this, and I was aware of it myself. What I felt was that "dear Katya" was not a silly little schoolgirl, but a person of character, a proud girl of high moral principles and, what's more, a person of intellect and education, while I had neither the one nor the other. You think I wanted to propose to her? Not a bit of it. I just wanted to revenge myself on her for not realizing what a fine fellow I was. Meanwhile, I went on leading a life of riotous dissipation and in the end the Lieutenant-Colonel put me under arrest for three days. It was just then that father sent me six thousand roubles in return for a formal renunciation of all my claims upon him, that is to say, for a written acknowledgement that we were "quits" and that I would not demand a penny more from him. I didn't understand a thing then.... You see, old man, up to the day of my arrival here, up to the last few days and perhaps, indeed, up to today, I didn't understand anything of my financial disputes with father. But to hell with it. We'll discuss it later. At the time, having received the money, I suddenly received a most interesting piece of news from a friend of mine, who was a most trustworthy fellow. It seemed that the authorities were dissatisfied with our Lieutenant-Colonel, that they suspected him of irregularities, in short, that his enemies were preparing a little treat for him. And, to be sure, the commander of the division arrived and hauled him properly over the coals. Then, shortly afterwards, he was asked to resign. I won't go into the details of how it all happened. He certainly had enemies, but all of a sudden there was an unmistakable coolness in the town towards him and his family, and everyone seemed suddenly to desert him. It was then that I played my first trick on Katerina. I met Agafya, with whom I'd always kept up a friendship, and said to her: "Do you know your father is short of four thousand five hundred roubles of government money?" "What do you mean? Why do you say that? The general was here not long ago and all the money was there." "It was there then, but it isn't there now." She was terribly upset: "Don't frighten me, please," she said. "Who told you that?" "Don't worry," I said, "I shan't tell anyone. You know perfectly well that in a matter of this kind I'm as silent as the grave. But I'd like to add, just in case, that when they demand the four thousand five hundred roubles from your father and he hasn't got them, then to prevent him facing a court-martial and being reduced to the ranks in his old age, he'd better send your educated young lady to me in secret. I've just had money sent me and I may let her have four thousand, and I swear to keep the whole thing a dead secret." "Oh," she said, "what a cad you are!" (She actually said that.) "What a horrible cad you are! How dare you!" She went away terribly indignant, and I shouted after her again that the secret would remain sacred and inviolate. The two silly women, I mean Agafya and her aunt, I may as well tell you at once, behaved like perfect angels all through this business. They really adored that proud girl Katya, humbled themselves before her, and waited on her as if they were her maids. . . . Only Agafya told her all about it, I mean, about our conversation. I found it out for certain afterwards. She didn't conceal anything, which, of course, was what I wanted.

'Suddenly the new Major arrived to take over the battalion, which he did. The old Lieutenant-Colonel suddenly fell sick, took to his bed, didn't leave his house for two days, and didn't hand over the government money. Our Dr Kravchenko assured everybody that he really was ill. But this is what I knew confidentially for a fact, and I had known it for a long time: during the past four years the money, every time after the authorities had been through the accounts, used to disappear for a time. The Lieutenant-Colonel used to lend it to a merchant of our town, an old widower by the name of Trifonov, a man with a big beard and gold spectacles, whom he trusted implicitly. Trifonov used to go to the fair, do some business there and on his return immediately return the whole sum to the Lieutenant-Colonel, bringing with him a present from the fair and with the present the interest on the loan. Only this time (I learnt all about it quite by accident from Trifonov's slobbering young son and heir, one of the most dissolute young scamps the world has ever seen), this time, I say, Trifonov, on coming back from the fair, did not return anything. The Lieutenant-Colonel rushed to his house, but all the reply he got from him was: "I've never received any money from you, and couldn't possibly have received any." So there our

Lieutenant-Colonel sat in his house, with a towel round his head, while the three of them kept putting ice to it. Suddenly an orderly arrived with the book and the order to hand over the battalion's money immediately, within two hours. He signed the book – I saw his signature in the book afterwards – got up, said that he was going to put on his uniform, rushed into his bedroom, took down his double-barrelled shot-gun, loaded it, rammed in a service bullet, took off his boot from his right foot, pressed the gun against his breast, and began feeling for the trigger with his foot. But Agafya remembered what I had told her and, suspecting what her father might do, stole up to his bedroom and was just in time to see what he was up to. She rushed into the room, seized him from behind, threw her arms round him, the gun went off and the bullet hit the ceiling. No one was hurt. The others ran in, took away the gun, and held him by the arms. . . . All this I learnt afterwards to the last detail. I was at home at the time, dusk was falling, and I was just about to go out. I had dressed, combed my hair, put some scent on my handkerchief, taken my cap, when suddenly the door opened and there before me, in my own lodgings, stood Katerina.

'Strange things do happen sometimes: no one had seen her in the street and no one had noticed her entering my lodgings, so that no one knew of it in our town. I rented my flat from two widows of civil servants, two ancient old ladies who waited on me. The two old girls had a great respect for me, they did everything I told them and, at my request, they were afterwards as silent as two posts. Of course, I grasped the situation at once. She came in and looked straight at me, her dark eyes gazing resolutely, even defiantly, but I could see from her lips and the lines round her mouth that she was far from resolute.

' "My sister told me that you'd give us four thousand five hundred roubles if I came for them – if I came alone. I have come. . . . Give me the money!" she said, but she broke down, her breath failed her, she was frightened, her voice gave out, and the corners of her mouth and the lines round it quivered. Alyosha, are you listening to me or are you asleep?'

'Mitya,' Alyosha said in agitation, 'I know you will tell me the whole truth.'

'I was going to. If I'm to tell you the whole truth, then this is how it all happened – I'm not going to spare myself. My first thought was – a Karamazov one. Once, old man, I was bitten by a centipede and was laid up for a fortnight with a high temperature; so now, too, I suddenly felt as though I had been bitten in the heart by a centipede – a noxious insect, understand? I looked her up and down. You've seen her, haven't you? She's beautiful, isn't she? But she was beautiful in a different way then. At that moment she was beautiful because she was noble, and I was a cad. Because she was standing then in all the grandeur of her sacrifice for her father and I was a bug! And she was *entirely* dependent on me, a cad and bug, dependent upon me altogether, body and soul. That was her position. I tell you frankly: that idea, the idea of a centipede, possessed my heart so much that it almost stopped beating with suspense. It seemed that there could be no question of any struggle: I simply had to act like a bug, like a vicious tarantula, without a spark of pity. . . . For a moment I felt breathless. . . . Listen. Next morning, of course, I should have gone to ask for her hand so as to end it all, as it were, in a most honourable way, so that no one should or could know anything about it. For though I'm a man of low desires, I'm honourable. But just at that very second someone seemed suddenly to whisper in my ear: "Why, a girl like that, when you come to propose to her tomorrow, will not even come out to see you, but will order the coachman to kick you out of the yard. Defame me all over the town – I'm not afraid of you!" I glanced at the girl, my voice had not deceived me. I should be kicked out. I could tell that from her face. I was furious. I felt like playing her a filthy, swinish trick, the sort of trick some low merchant might have played on her: to look at her with a sneer and, as she stood before me, bowl her over with the tone of voice that only some dirty shopkeeper knows how to use: "The four thousand, madam? Why, madam, I was only joking! Really, madam, you've been too credulous to count on it. Now, two hundred I might let you have with pleasure and gladly too. But four thousand, my dear young lady, is a bit too much to throw away on such frippery, don't you think? I'm afraid you've put yourself to unnecessary trouble."

'You see, I shouldn't have got anything out of it, for she would have run away, but it would have been an infernally sweet revenge and it would have been worth all the trouble it caused me. I knew I should have howled with remorse all the rest of my life, but just then I felt that if I could bring myself to say that, it would be worth it! I tell you this sort of thing never happened to me with any woman before, not with one. I mean that I should look at her at such a moment with hatred – and I swear to you I looked at her just then for three or five seconds with terrible hatred – with the sort of hatred that's only a hair's-breadth removed from love, from the most insane love! I went up to the window and pressed my forehead against the frozen pane. I can still remember that the ice burned my forehead like fire. I did not detain her long, don't worry. I turned round, went up to the table, opened the drawer, and got out a five per cent letter of credit for five thousand roubles which had not been filled in (I kept it in my French dictionary). I showed it to her in silence, folded it, gave it to her, opened the door into the passage for her myself and, taking a step back, made her a deep bow, a most respectful bow – believe me! She gave a violent start, looked at me for a second, turned terribly pale – she was as white as a sheet, I tell you, and, suddenly, also without uttering a word, not impulsively, but very gently somehow, she bowed deeply, quietly, and went down on her knees at my feet – with her head touching the floor – not the sort of thing you would expect a girl from a finishing school to do, but in the true Russian fashion! She jumped up and ran away. When she ran out, I was wearing my sword – I drew it and was about to stab myself to death with it – I don't know why. It would have been damn silly, of course, but I expect it was in the ecstasy of the moment. Do you realize that one might kill oneself in certain moments of ecstasy? But I didn't kill myself. I only kissed the sword and put it back into the scabbard – which I suppose I needn't have told you. And indeed I can't help feeling that in telling you about all these inner struggles of mine, I've exaggerated a little in order to show you what a fine fellow I am. But, all right, let it be like that and to hell with all those who pry into the human heart! So much for the "incident" with Katerina. So now Ivan knows about it and you – no one else!'

Dmitry got up and took a step or two in his excitement, took out his handkerchief, mopped his brow, then sat down again, but not in the same place as before, but on the bench opposite, along the other wall, so that Alyosha had to turn round completely to face him.

5

The Confession of an Ardent Heart:
Head over Heels

'NOW,' said Alyosha, 'I know the first half of this business.'

'You understand the first half – that was a drama and it took place then, in that town. The second half is a tragedy and it will take place here.'

'So far I can't understand anything of the second half,' said Alyosha.

'And I? Do you think I understand it?'

'Wait, Dmitry. There's one important question here. Tell me, you are her fiancé, you still are her fiancé, aren't you?'

'I did not become her fiancé at once, but only three months after that incident at my lodgings. On the next day after it had happened I told myself that the incident was closed, over and done with, and that there would be no sequel. To propose to her after that seemed to me a low-down thing to do. For her part, she did not communicate with me by a single word for the rest of the six weeks she remained in our town. Except, indeed, for one thing: the day after her visit their maid slipped into my room and, without uttering a word, handed me an envelope. It was addressed to me: I opened it and found the change from the letter of credit for five thousand. All they needed was four thousand five hundred, but they had to spend more than two hundred roubles to cash it. She therefore sent me back, I believe, only two hundred and sixty roubles. I don't remember exactly, but there was only the money in the envelope. No note, no explanation. Not a word. I searched for a pencil mark on the envelope – n-nothing! All right, so I went on a spree with the rest of my money and the new Major was forced in the end to reprimand me. Well, the Lieutenant-Colonel handed over the battalion's money – without trouble and to everyone's surprise, for no one believed that he had the whole sum intact. He handed it over and fell ill, took to his bed, spent about three weeks there, then softening of the brain suddenly set in, and five days later he was dead. He was buried with military honours, for his resignation had not yet taken effect. Soon after the funeral, Katerina with her sister and aunt left for Moscow. And it was only before they left, on the very day of their departure (I had not seen them and did not see them off), that I received a little note, on fine blue paper, with only one pencilled line: "I'll write to you. Wait. K." And that was all.

'Let me explain it to you in two words. In Moscow their affairs took a turn for the better with lightning rapidity and with the unexpectedness of an Arabian tale. The General's widow, their relative, suddenly lost her two heiresses, her two nieces who were next of kin – both died of smallpox in the same week. The grief-stricken old lady welcomed Katya with open arms just as though she were her own daughter, her star of salvation, and at once changed her will in her favour. But that was in the future; in the meantime, she gave her eighty thousand roubles for her dowry, to do with as she liked. A hysterical old girl. I had a good look at her afterwards in Moscow. Anyway, suddenly I received four thousand five hundred roubles by post. I was bewildered, of course. Struck dumb with surprise. Three days later the promised letter arrived. I've still got it. I always carry it about on me and I shall die with it – do you want me to show it to you? Yes, you must read it. She proposed to me. She herself made me a proposal of marriage: "I am madly in love with you," she wrote. "I don't care if you don't love me. It makes no difference, only be my husband. Don't be afraid, I'm not going to be in your way. I shall be your furniture, I shall be the carpet under your feet. . . . I want to love you always. I want to save you from yourself. . . ." Alyosha, I'm not worthy to paraphrase those lines in my own foul words and in my own vile tone of voice, always in the vile tone I could never get rid of! That letter touched me to the quick, as it still does, even today, for you don't think I'm happy now, that I'm happy today, do you? I wrote her an answer at once (I could not possibly go to Moscow just then). I wrote it with tears. One thing I shall always be ashamed of: I mentioned that she was a rich girl now, a girl with a dowry, and that I was just a coarse, ignorant pauper – I mentioned money! I should have kept it to myself, but it slipped out. Then I wrote at once to Ivan in Moscow and explained everything to him, as much as I could in a letter – a letter of six pages it was – and I sent Ivan to her. What are you looking at me like that for? Yes, of course, Ivan fell in love with her. He is still in love with her. I know that. In your opinion, in the opinion of the world, I did a silly thing, but perhaps that silly thing may save us all now! Good Lord, don't you see what a lot she thinks of him, how she respects him? Can she, comparing the two of us, possibly love a man like me, and particularly after all that's happened between us?'

'I'm quite sure that she does love a man like you and not a man like him.'

'She loves her own virtue and not me,' Dmitry blurted out involuntarily and almost spitefully.

He laughed, but a moment later his eyes flashed, he blushed all over and struck the table violently with his fist.

'I swear, Alyosha,' he cried with sincere and terrible anger at himself, 'you may believe me or not, but as God is holy and as Christ is our Lord, I swear that though I sneered at her higher feelings just now, I know that I'm a million times more worthless in spirit than she, and that these better feelings of hers are as sincere as an angel's in heaven! That's the tragedy of it, I mean, that I know that for certain. What does it matter if a man declaims a little? Am I not declaiming? But I am sincere. I'm sincere! As for Ivan, I quite understand how he must be cursing nature now, and with his intellect too! To whom has preference been given – to what? It has been given to a monster, who even here, when already engaged and when the eyes of everyone are fixed on him, can't refrain from his debaucheries – and that before the very eyes of his own fiancée, before his fiancée. And a man like me is preferred, and he is rejected. And why? Because a girl wants to throw her life and her future away out of gratitude! Ridiculous! I've never said anything of the kind to Ivan. Neither did Ivan of course say a word of it to me. He never so much as hinted at it. But destiny will be accomplished, and the deserving man will occupy his rightful place and the undeserving one will vanish into his back-alley for ever – into his filthy back-alley, into his beloved back-alley, a fitting place for him, and will perish there in filth and stench of his own free will, and like it. I'm afraid I've been talking rather wildly, my words seem to have all grown threadbare, I seem to be uttering them at random, but as I've decided, so it will be. I'll rot away in the back-alley, and she will marry Ivan.'

'Wait, Dmitry,' Alyosha interrupted again with great uneasiness, 'you've still not explained one thing to me: you are her fiancé,

aren't you? You're still engaged to her. So how can you break off
your engagement if she, your fiancée, doesn't want to?'

'I am her official fiancé. We were formally engaged. It all happened in Moscow, after my arrival. We had a full-dress engagement,
with icons, in the grandest possible style. The general's widow gave us
her blessing and actually congratulated Katya. "You've chosen well,"
she told her. "I can see through him." And – would you believe it? –
she didn't like Ivan at all and was not nice to him. I had long talks
with Katya in Moscow. I told her all about myself, honourably,
exactly, sincerely. She listened to everything –

> There was sweet confusion,
> There were tender words —

As a matter of fact, there were proud words, too. She made me
promise her solemnly to reform. I gave my promise. And now —'

'Now what?'

'And now I called you and dragged you over here today – this
very day – remember that! – to send you – this very day – to Katerina and —'

'What?'

'Tell her that I shall never come to see her again. Tell her I sent you
to say good-bye to her from me.'

'But is it possible?'

'Why, the reason I'm sending you to her is that it is impossible.
For I can't very well tell her that myself, can I?'

'And where will you go?'

'To the back-alley.'

'You mean to Grushenka!' Alyosha exclaimed sorrowfully, clasping his hands. 'Could Rakitin really have told the truth? And I
thought you'd just been to see her a few times and that it was all over
now.'

'A fiancé to visit a woman like her? Is that possible? And engaged
to a girl like Katerina and before the eyes of the whole world? I've
still got a sense of honour, haven't I? As soon as I began visiting
Grushenka, I ceased to be engaged to Katerina. I've ceased to be an
honest man. I realize that all right. What are you glaring at me for?
You see, at first I went to beat her. For I knew then and I know now
for a fact that the captain, father's agent, had given Grushenka my

promissory note so that she could summons me. This was done to make me give up bothering father. They wanted to frighten me. So I went off to Grushenka to give her a beating. I had seen her a few times before, but only in passing. There's nothing particularly striking about her. I knew about her old merchant – he's ill and bed-ridden now, but I suspect he'll leave her a tidy sum all the same. I also knew that she liked to make money by lending it at extortionate rates of interest, that she was a pitiless, cunning she-devil. I went to beat hell out of her and I stayed there. A thunder-storm broke, a plague struck, I got infected and I'm still infected, and I know that all's over and done with and that there'll never be anything more for me. The wheel has come full circle. That's how things are with me. And, as though on purpose, I just happened to have three thousand roubles in my pocket just then. A beggar like me, too! I went with her to Mokroye, about twenty miles from here. Got gipsies there, champagne, made all the peasants drunk on champagne, all the women and girls, too, threw thousands away. Three days later I was stripped to the bone, but still as proud as can be. Do you perhaps think the proud fellow got anything out of it? Not a chance. She never let me come near her. I tell you it's those damned curves of hers. That she-devil Grushenka has a kind of curve of the body which can be detected even on her foot. You can see it even in the little toe of her left foot. I saw it and kissed it, but that was all – I swear! She says to me, "I'll marry you, if you like, for you're a pauper. Promise not to beat me and to let me do anything I like, and perhaps I'll marry you." She laughed. And she is laughing still!'

Dmitry got up from his seat almost in a sort of fury, and all at once looked as though he were drunk. His eyes suddenly became bloodshot.

'And do you really want to marry her?'

'If she wants me to, I shall marry her at once, if not, I shall stay with her just the same. I shall be the caretaker in her yard. You – you, Alyosha,' he cried, stopping suddenly in front of his brother and, seizing him by the shoulders, began shaking him violently, 'do you realize, you innocent boy, that this is all a crazy dream, an impossible dream, for what we have here is tragedy! I'd like you to know, Alexey, that I can be a base man, a man of low passions that may only lead to ruin, but Dmitry Karamazov can never be a thief, a pickpocket, a little sneak-thief! Well, then, I'd like you to know now that I am a miserable little sneak-thief and pickpocket! For that very morning, just before I went to beat Grushenka, Katerina sent for me and asked me, in great secrecy, for she did not want anyone in our town to know anything about it for the time being (why, I don't know, I expect she had a good reason for it), to go to the county town and post three thousand roubles to Agafya in Moscow from there. It was with those three thousand in my pocket that I had gone to see Grushenka. It was this money that I took to Mokroye. Afterwards I pretended that I'd been to the town, but I didn't give her the post office receipt. I told her I had sent the money and would let her have the receipt, but I haven't done so yet – I've forgotten all about it – see? Now, tell me what do you think is to be done? Suppose you go to her today and say, "Mitya asked me to say good-bye for him." And she'd say, "And what about the money?" You might, of course, have said to her: "He is a low voluptuary, a vile creature with uncontrollable passions. He never sent your money, but spent it, because, low animal that he is, he could not restrain himself." But you might also have added: "He isn't a thief for all that. Here are your three thousand, he returns them to you, send it to Agafya yourself. All he wants me to do is to say good-bye to you from him." But now all she has to say is: "And where is the money?"'

'Mitya, you're unhappy, aren't you? But still things aren't as bad as you think. Don't give way to despair. Don't!'

'Why, you don't think I'm going to shoot myself if I don't raise the three thousand to give back to her, do you? That's the trouble, that I won't shoot myself. I haven't the strength to do so now. Afterwards, perhaps. But now I shall go to Grushenka. I don't care what happens to me!'

'And what will you do there?'

'I shall be her husband, I shall achieve the high distinction of being her spouse, and when her lover comes, I shall retire to another room. I shall clean the dirty galoshes of her boy-friends, I shall kindle her samovar, I shall run errands for her. . . .'

'Katerina will understand everything,' Alyosha suddenly said solemnly. 'She'll understand the full extent of your unhappiness and be reconciled to you. She is a highly intelligent woman. She will realize herself that no one could be more unhappy than you.'

'She won't be reconciled to everything,' Mitya grinned. 'You see, old man, there's something here that no woman can be reconciled to. Do you know what would be the best thing to do?'

'What?'

'Give her back the three thousand.'

'But where are we to get it? Look here, I've got two thousand. Ivan will give you another thousand – there's your three thousand. Take it and give it back.'

'And when are we going to get your three thousand? You're still a minor, and you know it's absolutely essential that you should go and say good-bye to her from me today, with or without the money, for I can't put it off any longer. That's the position. Tomorrow it will be too late. Too late. I'll send you to father.'

'To father?'

'Yes, to father first. Ask him for the three thousand.'

'But he won't give it, Mitya.'

'Of course not. I know he won't. Do you know the meaning of despair, Alexey?'

'I know.'

'Listen. Legally he owes me nothing. I've got everything out of him, everything. I know that. But morally he does owe me something, doesn't he? For he started with my mother's twenty-eight thousand and made a hundred thousand with it. Let him give me only three out of her twenty-eight thousand, only three, and he'll snatch my soul out of hell, and many of his sins will be forgiven him for that! And I'll be satisfied with the three thousand – I give you my solemn word – and he'll never hear of me again. I give him a last chance to be a father. Tell him that God Himself sends him this chance.'

'Mitya, he won't give it for anything.'

'I know he won't. I know it perfectly well. Now, especially. And that's not all. I know something else. Only the other day, or perhaps even yesterday, he found out for the first time *definitely* (underline definitely) that Grushenka may not really be joking and may be too glad of the chance of marrying me. He knows the sort of woman she is. He knows the cat. So how can he be expected to give me the money and so assist in bringing this about when he's madly in love with her himself? But that is not all, either. I can tell you something else. I know that five days ago he took three thousand out of the bank, changed them into hundred-rouble notes, packed them into a large envelope, sealed with five seals and tied across with a piece of red ribbon. You see I know every little detail of it! And the inscription on the envelope reads: "To my angel Grushenka, in case she decides to come." He scrawled it himself, in dead secret, and no one knows he has all that money in the house except his servant Smerdyakov, in whose honesty he believes as he believes in himself. So there he is waiting for Grushenka for the last three or four days. He hopes she will come for the envelope. He let her know about it and she has sent him word that she might come. Well, then, if she goes to the old man, I can't marry her, can I? Do you understand now why I'm sitting in hiding here and what exactly I am keeping watch for?'

'For her?'

'For her. Foma has a room in the house of these sluts here. I know him. He was a private in my battalion. He does odd jobs for them. He's their watchman at night, and in the daytime he goes shooting blackcock. That's how he earns his living. So I've taken up my quarters in his place here. Neither he nor the women of the house know my secret, I mean, that I'm keeping watch here.'

'Only Smerdyakov knows?'

'Yes, only Smerdyakov. He'll let me know if she comes to the old man.'

'Was it he who told you about the envelope?'

'Yes. It's a dead secret. Even Ivan doesn't know about the money or anything. The old man wants Ivan to go to Chermashnya for two or three days. Someone seems to be offering eight thousand for the timber of the copse there. So the old man keeps asking Ivan to help him by going and arranging the sale. It will take him two or three days. He wants it so that Grushenka can come when he's away.'

'Then he's expecting Grushenka today too?'

'No, she won't come today. There are signs. It's quite certain she won't come!' Mitya exclaimed suddenly. 'Smerdyakov thinks so too. Father's drinking now. Sitting at table with Ivan. Go on, Alexey, go and ask him for the three thousand.'

'Mitya, what's the matter with you?' Alyosha exclaimed, jumping up from his place and staring at Dmitry's frenzied face.

For a moment he thought that Dmitry had gone mad.

'What do you mean?' Dmitry replied looking intently and even solemnly at his brother. 'I'm not mad. Don't be afraid. I'm sending you to father and I know what I'm saying: I believe in a miracle.'

'In a miracle?'

'In a miracle of God's Providence. God knows my heart. He sees my despair. He sees it all. He wouldn't allow something awful to happen, would he? I believe in a miracle, Alyosha. Go.'

'I'll go. Tell me, will you wait for me here?'

'Yes. I realize it will take some time. You couldn't just go and blurt it out, could you? He's drunk now. I'll wait three, four, five, six, seven hours, but please remember you must go to Katerina today, at midnight, if necessary, *with or without the money*, and tell her that I've sent you to say good-bye to her. I want you to repeat it word for word: "He asked me to say good-bye to you." '

'Mitya, and what if Grushenka should come today, or if not today, then tomorrow or the day after tomorrow?'

'Grushenka? Why, I'd soon discover it and I'd rush into the house and prevent it. . . . '

'And if . . . '

'And if – there's going to be murder. I could not bear *that* to happen.'

'Whom will you murder?'

'The old man. I shan't murder her.'

'What are you saying, Mitya?'

'Oh, I don't know – I don't know. . . . Maybe I won't kill him, maybe I will. I'm afraid he'll become so hateful to me with that face of his at that very moment. I hate his Adam's apple, his nose, his eyes, his shameless sneer. I feel a physical aversion. That's what I'm afraid of. So I may not be able to control myself. . . . '

'I'll go, Mitya. I believe God will settle it for the best, so that nothing terrible happens.'

'And I'll sit here and wait for a miracle. But if it doesn't happen, then — '

Sunk in thought, Alyosha went to see his father.

6

Smerdyakov

HE really did find his father still at table. The table was as usual laid in the drawing-room, though there was a dining-room in the house. This drawing-room was the largest room in the house, furnished with a sort of outmoded pretentiousness. The furniture was white, very old, and upholstered in faded red silky material. On the walls between the windows there were mirrors in elaborate frames of ancient scroll-work, also white and gilt. On the walls, covered with white paper, which was cracked in places, hung two large portraits, one of some prince, who about thirty years earlier had been Governor-General of the province, and the other of some bishop, who had also been dead for many years. In the corner opposite the door were a few icons, before which a lamp was lighted at night . . . not so much from reverence as to light the room. Karamazov went to bed very late, at about three or four o'clock in the morning, and till then he used to pace the room or sit in an armchair, thinking. He had formed such a habit. He often slept quite alone in the house, sending his servants off to the cottage, but mostly Smerdyakov stayed with him at night, sleeping on a chest in the hall. When Alyosha went in, dinner was over, but coffee and jam had been served. Karamazov liked to have sweets with his cognac after dinner. Ivan was also sitting at table and drinking coffee. The servants Grigory and Smerdyakov were standing at the table. Both masters and servants seemed to be in quite extraordinarily high spirits. Karamazov was roaring with laughter; already in the hall Alyosha could hear his father's high-pitched laughter he knew so well, and at once concluded from the sound of it that his father was far from drunk, but was for the present quietly enjoying himself.

'Here he is! Here he is!' Karamazov yelled, highly delighted at seeing Alyosha. 'Come on, my boy, join us. Sit down. Have a cup of coffee – it's all right. It's lenten, but lovely and hot! I won't offer you brandy as you're keeping the fast, but you'd like some, wouldn't you? No – I'd better give you some liqueur – our excellent liqueur!

Smerdyakov, fetch it from the cupboard. It's on the second shelf to the right. Here are the keys. Be quick about it!'

Alyosha began refusing the liqueur.

'It will be served, anyway. If not for you, then for us,' Karamazov beamed. 'But wait, have you had your dinner?'

'Yes,' answered Alyosha, who as a matter of fact had had only a piece of bread and a glass of *kvas* in the Father Superior's kitchen. 'But I will have a cup of hot coffee, if I may.'

'Capital, my dear boy, capital! He'll have some coffee. Shall we warm it up? Oh no, it's still boiling. Excellent coffee. A Smerdyakov specialty. Smerdyakov's an artist at coffee and fish-pies, and fish-soup, too. Yes, indeed. Some day you must come and sample his fish-soup. Let me know beforehand. . . . But wait, wait! Didn't I tell you this morning to come home today for good with your pillows and mattress? Have you brought your mattress? Heh-heh-heh!'

'No, I haven't,' Alyosha, too, grinned.

'Oh, but you were frightened this morning, weren't you? My dear boy, you don't think I would hurt you, do you? I say, Ivan, I just can't see him looking at me like that and smiling. I can't. My belly starts shaking with laughter at him. I love him! Come, Alyosha, let's give you a father's blessing.'

Alyosha got up, but Karamazov had already changed his mind.

'No, no. I'll just make the sign of the cross over you now. So. Sit down. Well, now we've got a treat for you, and in your line, too. You're going to have a good laugh. Balaam's ass has begun talking to us, and how he talks, how he talks!'

Balaam's ass, it appeared, was the servant Smerdyakov. Though still a young man of twenty-four, he was quite extraordinarily unsociable and taciturn. Not that he was in any way shy or bashful – no, quite the reverse. He had a supercilious character and seemed to despise everyone. But it seems we simply must say a few words about him, and without delay too. He was brought up by Marfa and Grigory, but the boy grew up 'without a spark of gratitude', as Grigory expressed it, a wild boy with a furtive look. As a boy he was fond of hanging cats and burying them with ceremony. He used to dress up in a sheet, to represent a kind of surplice, and chant and swing something over the dead cat, as though it were a censer. All this he did on the quiet with the greatest secrecy. Grigory caught him once at this exercise and birched him severely. He retired to a corner and glowered at them for a week from there. 'He doesn't care for you or me, the monster,' Grigory used to say to Marfa. 'He cares for no one. Why,' he addressed Smerdyakov, 'are you a human being? No, sir, you're not a human being. You came from the bathhouse slime, you did. That's what you are. . . .' As it appeared afterwards, Smerdyakov could never forgive him those words. Grigory taught him to read and write and, when he was twelve, began teaching him the Scriptures. But that came to nothing almost at once. One day, at the second or third lesson, the boy suddenly grinned.

'What are you grinning at?' asked Grigory, looking sternly at him from under his spectacles.

'Nothing, sir. God created the world on the first day and the sun, the moon and the stars on the fourth. Where did the light come from on the first day?'

Grigory was dumbfounded. The boy looked sneeringly at his teacher. There was even something supercilious in his look. Grigory could not control himself. 'That'll teach you where!' he shouted and struck the boy a violent blow across the cheek. The boy took the blow without a murmur, but hid in his corner again for a few days. It so happened that a week later he had his first epileptic fit, a disease to which he was subject all his life. When Karamazov heard of it, he seemed suddenly to change his attitude towards the boy. Before, he used to regard him with some indifference, though he never scolded him and always gave him a copeck when he met him. When in a good mood, he would sometimes send the boy something sweet from the table. But having learnt of his illness, he began to take a great interest in him. He called in a doctor to see if he could be cured, but apparently his illness was incurable. On the average, the boy had a fit once a month, but on different dates. The fits, too, varied in violence: some were light and some very severe. Karamazov gave strict orders to Grigory not to beat the boy and allowed him to visit him upstairs. He also forbade him to be taught anything for the time being. But one day, when the boy was fifteen, Karamazov noticed that he was always walking up to the bookcase and reading the titles through the glass. Karamazov had a fair number of books, over a hundred volumes, in fact, but no one had ever seen him reading one.

He at once handed the key of the bookcase to Smerdyakov. 'Read, if you like. You'll be my librarian. Instead of hanging about the yard, you'd better sit and read. Here, read this one,' and Karamazov gave him *Evenings on a Farm near Dikanka*.

The boy read it, but did not like it. He didn't once smile. On the contrary, he finished the book with a frown.

'Well?' asked Karamazov. 'Isn't it funny?'

Smerdyakov said nothing.

'Answer, you fool!'

'Not a word of it is true,' mumbled Smerdyakov with a grin.

'Well, to hell with you, then, you're a born lackey! Wait, here's Smaragdov's *Universal History*. That's all true. Read it.'

But Smerdyakov did not read even ten pages of Smaragdov. He thought it dull. And so the bookcase was shut again. Shortly afterwards Marfa and Grigory reported to Karamazov that Smerdyakov was beginning to show signs of quite extraordinary squeamishness: before having his soup, he would look for something in it with his spoon, bend over it, examine it closely, take a spoonful and hold it up to the light.

'What is it? A cockroach?' Grigory would ask.

'A fly, maybe,' Marfa would observe.

The finicky youth never answered, but he did the same with his bread, his meat and anything else he ate: he would, for instance, hold up a piece on his fork to the light, examine it as though under a microscope, and after a long period of indecision at last decide to put it into his mouth. 'A little gentleman, forsooth!' Grigory muttered, looking at him. When Karamazov heard of this new side of Smerdyakov's character, he at once decided that he ought to be a cook and sent him to Moscow to be trained. He was in training for several years and came back greatly changed in appearance. He seemed to have grown suddenly old, prematurely wrinkled, sallow-faced, and began to look like a castrate. Morally, however, he returned almost the same as he had been before his departure for Moscow: he was as unsociable as ever and felt no need for anyone's company. In Moscow, too, as we heard afterwards, he was always silent; he seemed to take extraordinarily little interest in Moscow itself, so that he learnt little of it and paid no attention to anything else. He went to the theatre once, but came back silent and dissatisfied. On the other hand, he returned to our town from Moscow well dressed, in a clean frock-coat and clean linen, brushed his clothes very methodically twice a day, and was very fond of cleaning his smart calf-boots with a special English polish so that they shone like mirrors. He turned out to be an excellent cook. Karamazov paid him a regular wage and Smerdyakov spent it almost entirely on his clothes, pomatum, scents, etc. But he seemed to despise women almost as much as men, and was grave and almost unapproachable with them. Karamazov's attitude towards him changed somewhat. For his epileptic fits had grown more frequent and during those days the meals were prepared by Marfa, which was not at all to Karamazov's liking.

'Why do you get your fits more frequently now?' he sometimes asked, looking askance at his new cook and peering into his face. 'Why don't you get married? Want me to get you a wife?'

Smerdyakov merely turned pale with vexation at these words, but said nothing in reply. Karamazov would leave him alone, dismissing him as a bad job. The important thing was that he had no doubts whatever about his honesty. He knew for certain that Smerdyakov would never take or steal anything. It happened once that Karamazov, walking across his courtyard when drunk, dropped three hundred-rouble notes he had just received in the mud. He discovered his loss only on the following day: he had scarcely begun fumbling in his pockets for them when he saw them lying on his table. How did they get there? Smerdyakov had picked them up and had brought them the previous evening. 'Well, I must say,' Karamazov snapped, 'I've never met anyone like you,' and he gave him ten roubles. It must be added that he was not only convinced of Smerdyakov's honesty, but he was also fond of him for some reason, though the fellow looked askance at him as much as at everyone else and was always silent. It was very rarely that he would start talking. If it had ever occurred to anyone at the time to ask himself, as he looked at Smerdyakov, what the fellow was interested in and what was more predominantly in his mind, he would have found it quite impossible to tell by looking at him. And yet he used sometimes to stop dead in the house, or the yard, or in the street and ponder, and he would stand still like that for as long as ten minutes. A physiognomist, looking closely at him, would have said that he did not think of anything in particular, but was just vaguely contemplating. The painter

Kramskoy has a remarkable picture, called *The Contemplator*. It depicts a forest in winter, and on the roadway in the forest a little peasant stands quite alone in a torn coat and bast-shoes. He seems to have wandered there by chance and seems to be standing there thinking, but he is not really thinking but only 'contemplating' something. If you were to nudge him, he would give a start and look at you as though he had only just woken up, but without understanding. He would, it is true, have come to life at once, but if you asked him what he was thinking of while standing there, he would most certainly not remember anything. But he would most certainly never forget the sensation he had experienced during the time of his contemplation, but would always keep it hidden away inside him. Those sensations are dear to him, and he is doubtlessly accumulating them imperceptibly and without being aware of it – why and for what purpose, he does not know, either: perhaps, having accumulated such impressions in the course of many years, he will suddenly give up everything and go on a pilgrimage to Jerusalem in search of salvation, or, perhaps, too, he will suddenly set fire to his village, and, again, perhaps he will do both the one and the other. There are many people who are given to contemplation among our peasants. And Smerdyakov was no doubt one of them and he, too, no doubt, was accumulating his impressions greedily, hardly knowing himself why.

7

The Controversy

BUT Balaam's ass suddenly broke into speech. The subject was a strange one: Grigory, while shopping at the merchant Lukyanov's that morning, had heard from the shopkeeper the story of a Russian soldier who had been stationed on the frontier in some remote part of Russia and had been taken prisoner by some Asiatics. Threatened by them with immediate and agonizing death if he did not renounce Christianity and adopt the Mohammedan faith, he refused to betray his religion, was flayed alive and died a martyr's death, praising and glorifying Christ. The story of his act of heroism had been published in the newspaper of that day. Grigory had told them about it at dinner. Karamazov always liked to laugh and talk over the dessert after dinner, if only with Grigory. This time he was in a particularly light-hearted and pleasantly expansive mood. Sipping his brandy and listening to the story, he observed that a soldier like that should be immediately canonized and his skin sent to some monastery. 'I can imagine,' he added, 'the crowds that would flock there and the money the monastery would make.' Grigory frowned, seeing that Karamazov was not at all moved by his story but, as usual, was beginning to blaspheme. At that moment Smerdyakov, who was standing at the door, suddenly grinned. Smerdyakov had often been allowed to wait at table before, though only towards the end of dinner. But since the arrival of Ivan in our town he had begun appearing at dinner almost every day.

'What are you grinning at?' asked Karamazov, noticing the grin at once and realizing, of course, that it referred to Grigory.

'You see, sir,' Smerdyakov said suddenly and unexpectedly in a loud voice, 'I can't help thinking that even though the praiseworthy act of that soldier was so very great, he'd have committed no sin if in an emergency like that he had renounced, if I may say so, sir, the name of Christ and his own baptism, so as to save his life for good deeds by which to atone in the course of years for his cowardice.'

'What do you mean he would have committed no sin?' Karamazov broke in. 'You're talking nonsense, my lad, and for that you'll go straight to hell and be roasted there like mutton.'

It was at this point that Alyosha came in. Karamazov, as we have seen, was highly delighted by his son's appearance.

'In your line, in your line!' he tittered gleefully, making Alyosha sit down and listen.

'So far as mutton is concerned, sir,' Smerdyakov observed gravely, 'that is not so, and, if I may say so, sir, there won't be nothing of that there for this and there oughtn't to be, neither, in all fairness.'

'What do you mean: in all fairness?' Karamazov cried more gaily, nudging Alyosha with his knee.

'He's a scoundrel, that's what he is, sir!' Grigory blurted out suddenly, looking Smerdyakov angrily in the face.

'Don't be in such a hurry to call me a scoundrel, Mr Kutuzov, sir,' Smerdyakov parried quietly and with the utmost composure. 'You'd better consider it carefully. For once I'm taken prisoner by the enemies of Christians who demand that I should curse the name of God and renounce holy baptism, I'm fully authorized to do so by my own reason, since there wouldn't be no sin in it at all.'

'You've said that already,' cried Karamazov. 'Don't keep on about it. Prove it!'

'Broth-brewer!' Grigory whispered contemptuously.

'You needn't be in such a hurry to call me a broth-brewer, either, Mr Kutuzov, sir, but consider it carefully for yourself before you starts calling me names. For as soon as I says to my torturers, "No, I'm not a Christian and I curse my true God," I become by God's high judgement, immediately and specially anathema, accursed and excommunicated from the Holy Church, just as if I was a heathen, so that at that very instant, sir, not only when I says them words, but just as I thinks of saying them, so that before even a quarter of a second has passed, I'm excommunicated. Isn't that so, Mr Kutuzov, sir?'

He addressed himself to Grigory with unconcealed pleasure, but he was really answering Karamazov's questions, and he realized it very well, though he deliberately pretended that Grigory had asked the questions.

'Ivan,' Karamazov cried suddenly, 'bend over, I want to whisper something to you. He's doing it all for your benefit. He wants you to praise him. Come on, praise him.'

Ivan listened very seriously to his father's rapturous communication.

'Wait, Smerdyakov, shut up for a moment,' Karamazov cried again. 'Ivan, bend over to me again.'

Ivan again bent over with the utmost gravity.

'I love you as much as Alyosha. Don't think I don't love you. More brandy?'

'Thank you,' replied Ivan.

'You're well plastered,' Ivan thought to himself, looking intently at his father. He was watching Smerdyakov with great interest.

'Anathema! You're already accursed now!' Grigory suddenly burst out. 'And how dare you argue, you scoundrel, after that, if —'

'Don't call him names, Grigory, don't call him names!' Karamazov interrupted.

'You'd better wait a little, Mr Kutuzov, sir, and listen to what

I've got to say, for I haven't finished yet. For, you see, the moment I'm accursed by God, at that very moment, at that highest moment, sir, I become entirely like a heathen, and my baptism is taken off me and is considered null and void – that is so, isn't it, sir?'

'Finish, my lad, come on, hurry up and finish,' Karamazov hurried him, taking a sip from his glass with relish.

'Well, sir, if I'm no more a Christian, then I can't be telling no lies to my torturers when they asks me whether I am a Christian or not, for God himself has stripped me of my Christianity on account of my intention alone and even before I've had time to say a word to my torturers. And if I've already been degraded, then in what manner and with what sort of justice am I to be called to account as a Christian in the next world for having denied Christ, when for my intention alone I've been stripped of my baptism even before I had denied him? If I'm no longer a Christian, I cannot possibly deny Christ, for there's nothing more left for me to deny. Who in heaven, Mr Kutuzov, sir, would hold even an infidel Tartar responsible for not having been born a Christian and who'd punish him for that, seeing as how you can't take two hides off one ox? Why, Almighty God himself, even if he did hold the Tartar responsible, when he dies, would, I think, only give him the smallest possible punishment (for it's impossible not to punish him), arguing that he can't be blamed for having been brought into the world by infidel parents. Surely, God when he has a Tartar before him can't be expected to say that he too was a Christian, can he? For that would mean that Almighty God would be telling an absolute lie. And can God, the Almighty Ruler of heaven and earth, tell a lie, even by one word, sir?'

Grigory was dumbfounded and looked at the orator with his eyes almost starting out of his head. Though he did not quite understand what was said, he did grasp something of all that farrago of nonsense and stood still like a man who has suddenly knocked his head against a wall. Karamazov emptied his glass and burst into a high-pitched laugh.

'Alyosha, Alyosha, what do you think of it, eh? Oh, you casuist! He must have been with the Jesuits somewhere, Ivan. Oh, you stinking Jesuit, who taught you? But you're talking through your hat, casuist! You're talking through your hat! Don't cry, Grigory, we'll reduce him to dust and ashes in a moment. Tell me this, you ass: you may be right before your torturers, but you've all the same renounced your faith in your own mind and you say yourself that at that very moment you become anathema and accursed. Well, then, if once you are anathema, they won't pat you on the back for it in hell, will they? What have you got to say to that, my fine Jesuit?'

'There can't be no doubt, sir, that I've renounced it in my mind, but all the same there's no special sin in it, sir, and even if there was a sin, it would be of the most ordinary kind, sir.'

'What do you mean: of the most ordinary kind, sir?'

'You lie, c-curse you!' Grigory hissed.

'Consider yourself, Mr Kutuzov, sir,' Smerdyakov went on, gravely and imperturbably, conscious of victory, but as though trying to be fair to a defeated enemy, 'consider yourself: it is said in the Scriptures, that if you've got as much faith as a grain of mustard and if you tell the mountain to move into the sea, it will move without a moment's hesitation at your first word of command. Well then, Mr Kutuzov, sir, if I haven't got no faith and you've got so much faith that you keep swearing at me continually, why don't you tell that mountain to move not to the sea (for it's a long way from here to the sea, sir) but just to the stinking little stream which runs at the bottom of our garden, and you will see, sir, yourself at that very moment that it won't move an inch, sir, and everything will stay as it is and just where it is, however much you shout at it, sir. And that means that you have no faith, sir, properly speaking, that is, but merely keep abusing others as much as you can. And what's more, taking into consideration the fact that no one in our time, not only you, sir, but no one at all, from the highest person in the land to the lowest peasant, sir, can push a mountain into the sea, except perhaps one man in the whole world or, at most, two men, who are perhaps saving their souls in secret somewhere in the Egyptian desert, so that you would not be able to find them at all – if that is so, sir, if all the rest seemingly have no faith, will God curse all the rest, that is, the population of the entire world, except them two hermits in the desert, and will he not forgive one of them in his well-known mercy? And that is why I, too, hope that, having once doubted, I shall be forgiven if I shed tears of repentance.'

'One moment!' screamed Karamazov in a transport of delight.

'So you think there are two men who can move mountains, do you? Ivan, make a note of this extraordinary fact, write it down. There you have the Russian all over!'

'You're quite right in saying that this is a characteristic feature of the people's faith,' Ivan agreed with an approving smile.

'So you agree! Well, then it must be so if even you agree! Alyosha it's true, isn't it? Russian faith is like that, isn't it?'

'No, Smerdyakov hasn't got the Russian faith at all,' Alyosha said, quietly and firmly.

'I'm not talking about his faith, I'm talking about this characteristic, about those two hermits – just about that little characteristic feature: that is Russian, isn't it?'

'Yes,' Alyosha smiled, 'that is a purely Russian characteristic.'

'Your words are worth a gold coin, you ass, and I'll let you have it today. As for the rest, you're talking through your hat. Yes, sir. You should know, you fool, that here we do not believe merely out of thoughtlessness, but because we haven't time: in the first place, we're too busy with our affairs, and, secondly, God has given us little time, only twenty-four hours in the day, so that we have scarcely time to have a good sleep, let alone repent of our sins. And you've renounced your faith before your torturers at a time when you had nothing to think of except your faith and just when you ought to have shown your faith! So that, my dear fellow, it does certainly constitute a sin. Am I right?'

'It may constitute a sin, but consider yourself, Mr Kutuzov, sir, that if it does, it only makes it easier. For, you see, sir, if just then I had truly believed as one should have believed, it would really have been sinful if I had not suffered torture for my faith and had gone over to the vile Mohammedan religion. But, in that case, there wouldn't have been no question of torture, for all I had to do was to say at that moment to the mountain: Move and crush my torturer, and it would have moved at that same moment and crushed him like a black-beetle, and I'd have gone forth just as if nothing had happened, praising and glorifying the Lord. But if at that same moment I'd tried it all and deliberately cried to the mountain: Crush my torturers, and it did not crush them, so how, tell me, shouldn't I have doubted at the time and at such a dreadful hour of great and mortal terror? Knowing, as it is, that I shouldn't attain altogether to the Kingdom of Heaven (for the mountain had not moved at my word, which can only mean that they don't think much of my faith up there and that I can't expect no great rewards in the next world), why should I let them flay me as well and to no good purpose, neither. For even if they'd torn my skin half off my back, even then the mountain wouldn't have moved at my word or at my cry. Why, at such a moment a fellow might not only doubt, but even lose his reason from fear, so that he wouldn't be able to think at all. So why should I be specially to blame if, seeing as how I shan't get no advantage nor reward here or there, at least I save my skin? And, therefore, putting my trust in God's mercy, I can only hope, sir, that one day I shall be altogether forgiven. ...'

8

Over the Brandy

THE discussion was over, but, strange to say, Karamazov, who had been so full of high spirits, suddenly began to frown. He frowned and emptied his glass of brandy at one gulp, and that was already a glass too many.

'Get out of here, Jesuits,' he cried to the servants. 'Clear out, Smerdyakov. I'll let you have the promised sovereign today, but be off with you! Don't cry, Grigory. Go to Marfa. She'll comfort you and put you to bed. The swine won't let us sit in peace after dinner,' he suddenly snapped out vexatiously after his servants had promptly withdrawn at his word. 'Smerdyakov pokes his nose in here every time at dinner,' he added to Ivan. 'It's you he's so interested in. What have you done to make him so fond of you?'

'Absolutely nothing,' replied Ivan. 'Got it into his head that I'm a great fellow. A boor and a lackey like him! First-class material, though, when the time comes.'

'First class?'

'I suppose there will be others and better ones, but there'll be fellows like him, too. At first there will be fellows like him. The better ones will come after.'

'And when will the time come?'

'When the rocket goes up, but perhaps it will fizzle out. So far the common people are not very fond of listening to these broth-brewers.'

'There you are, my dear fellow. A Balaam's ass like that thinks and thinks, and the devil only knows what sort of ideas he'll think of in the end.'

'He'll get all sorts of ideas,' Ivan laughed.

'You see, I know very well that he can't stand me any more than he can stand anybody, and you, too, though you may think he's got it into his head that you're a "great fellow". And particularly Alyosha. He despises Alyosha. But, you see, he won't steal anything, he doesn't gossip, he holds his tongue and he won't wash our dirty linen in public. Bakes lovely fish-pies, too. But to hell with him. He isn't worth talking about, is he?'

'Of course he isn't.'

'As for the ideas he might get, the Russian peasant, generally speaking, ought to be flogged. I've always maintained it. Our peasants are rogues, they don't deserve to be pitied, and it's a good thing they're still sometimes thrashed even now. Russia is strong because she has lots of birch trees. If the forests were destroyed, Russia would perish. I'm all for clever people. We stopped flogging the peasants because we've got a little too clever, but they go on thrashing each other. And a good thing too. For "with what measure ye mete, it shall be measured to you again", or how does it go there? In short, it shall be measured. And Russia is just swinishness. My dear boy, if only you knew how I hate Russia. . . . I mean, not Russia, but all these vices – but I daresay Russia, too. *Tout cela c'est de la cochonnerie*. You know what I like? I like wit.'

'You've had another glass. You'd better stop.'

'Never mind, I'll have one more, and then another, and then I'll stop. No, wait. You've interrupted me. On passing through Mokroye I asked an old peasant about it and he said to me: "What we likes best of all, sir," he says, "is sentencing girls to be flogged and we lets the boys flog them. For, you see, sir, the girl he has flogged today the lad will marry tomorrow, so that," he says, "it suits the girls down to the ground, too, it does, sir." What do you say to these Marquis de Sades, eh? But, say what you like, it's witty. We ought to go and have a look at it, don't you think? Are you blushing,

Alyosha? Don't be bashful, my boy. A pity I didn't dine with the monks at the Father Superior's today. I'd have liked to tell them about the Mokroye girls. Don't be cross with me, Alyosha, for having offended your Father Superior. You see, my boy, I can't help feeling vexed. For if there's a God, if he exists, then of course I'm to blame and I shall have to answer for it, but if there isn't a God at all, they ought to be treated a hundred times worse, your Fathers, I mean, oughtn't they? For then chopping off their heads isn't enough punishment for them, for they impede progress. Believe me, Ivan, *that* hurts my feelings. No, you don't believe me. I can see it from your eyes. You believe the people who say that I'm nothing but a clown. Alyosha, do you think I'm nothing but a clown?'

'I don't think so.'

'And I believe you don't and that you're sincere. You look sincere and you speak sincerely. But not Ivan. Ivan is high and mighty. All the same, I'd make an end of your monastery. I'd get rid of this mystic stuff. Do away with it at one blow, all over Russia, so as to bring all the fools finally to reason. And think of the silver and gold that would flow into the mint!'

'But why get rid of it?' said Ivan.

'So that truth should prevail more quickly – that's why!'

'But if this truth were to prevail, you'd be the first to be robbed and then – liquidated.'

'Good Lord, I do believe you're right! Oh, what an ass I am!' Karamazov exclaimed, striking himself lightly upon the forehead. 'Well, in that case, your monastery may stay where it is, Alyosha. And we, clever people, will live in comfort and enjoy our brandy. You know, Ivan, I shouldn't be surprised if God hadn't arranged it all on purpose! Tell me, Ivan: is there a God or not? Wait: tell me the truth, tell me seriously! What are you laughing at again?'

'I'm laughing at your witty remark about Smerdyakov's belief in the existence of two elders who could move mountains.'

'Why? Am I like him now?'

'Yes, very.'

'Well, that means that I, too, am a Russian and I too have this Russian characteristic. And I daresay one can catch a philosopher like you also in some characteristic of your own of the same kind. And so I shall. I bet you I shall catch you out tomorrow. But tell me all the same: is there a God or not? Only, seriously, mind! I want it seriously now.'

'No, there's no God.'

'Alyosha, is there a God?'

'Yes, there is.'

'Ivan, is there immortality, I mean just of some sort, just a tiny little one?'

'No, there's no immortality, either.'

'None at all?'

'None at all.'

'You mean absolutely nothing, or is there something? Perhaps there is just something. Anything is better than nothing.'

'Absolutely nothing.'

'Alyosha, is there immortality?'

'There is.'

'God and immortality?'

'Yes, God and immortality. In God is immortality.'

'I see. More likely Ivan's right. Lord, to think how much faith and what strength man has sacrificed for nothing for that dream, and for how many thousands of years! Who could make such a fool of man? I say, Ivan, tell me for the last time and categorically: is there a God or not? I'm asking you for the last time.'

'And for the last time there isn't.'

'Who then is laughing at mankind, Ivan?'

'The devil, I suppose,' Ivan said with a grin.

'And is there a devil?'

'No, there isn't a devil, either.'

'A pity. Damn it all, what wouldn't I do to the man who first invented God! Hanging's too good for him.'

'If God hadn't been invented, there'd be no civilization.'

'Wouldn't there? You mean, without God?'

'Yes. And there would be no brandy, either. I'm afraid I shall have to take the brandy away from you all the same.'

'Wait, wait, wait, my boy! Just one more glass. I've offended Alyosha. You're not cross with me, Alyosha, are you? My darling Alyosha, dear little Alexey!'

'No, I'm not cross. I know your thoughts. Your heart is better than your head.'

'My heart is better than my head? Good Lord, and it's you who say so? Do you love Alyosha, Ivan?'

'I do.'

'Yes, love him.' (Karamazov was getting very drunk.) 'Listen, Alyosha. I was rude to your elder this morning. But I was excited. That elder has got wit. What do you think, Ivan?'

'I daresay he has.'

'Yes, he has, he has, *il y a du Piron là-dedans*. He's a Jesuit, a Russian one, that is. He's hiding his indignation at having to pretend and – and putting the garment of saintliness upon himself is too much for him, for he is an honourable man.'

'But he does believe in God.'

'Not a bit of it. Didn't you know that? Why, he tells everybody. I – I mean, not everybody, but all the intelligent people who come to see him. He told Governor Schultz quite frankly: *credo*, but I don't know in what.'

'Go on!'

'He certainly did. But I respect him. There's something Mephisto-phelian in him or rather something of *A Hero of our Time* – Arbenin, or whatever his name is – that is, you see, he's a sensualist. He is such a sensualist that I'd be afraid for my daughter or my wife if she went to confess to him. When he begins telling stories, you know. . . . The year before last he invited us to tea – with liqueur (the ladies send him liqueur). You should have heard him describing the old times! We split our sides laughing. . . . Especially how he once cured a paralysed woman. "If my legs were not bad," he said, "I'd perform a dance for you." What a man, eh? "I'm afraid," he said, "I've done a lot of copulating in my time." He got sixty thousand out of Demidov the merchant.'

'You mean, stole it?'

'Well, Demidov brought him the money as to a man who was honest. He asked him to take care of it because he expected the police to raid his place next day. So he took care of it. "You've donated it to the Church," he declared. I told him he was a scoundrel, but he said, no, he wasn't, he was merely broadminded. But I don't think it was him, after all. . . . It was someone else. I'm afraid I've got him muddled with someone else – er – without noticing it. Well, one more glass and I've done. Take away the bottle, Ivan. I've been talking a lot of nonsense. Why didn't you stop me, Ivan? Why didn't you tell me I was talking nonsense?'

'I knew you'd stop yourself.'

'You did not. You did it out of spite against me – out of sheer spite. You despise me. You've come to live with me and you despise me in my own house.'

'Very well, I'll go away. You've had too much brandy.'

'I begged you for Christ's sake to go to Chermashnya for a day or two, and you don't go.'

'I'll go tomorrow, if you really insist.'

'You won't. You want to keep an eye on me here. That's what you want. You're a spiteful fellow. That's why you won't go, isn't it?'

The old man just would not quieten down. He had reached that state of drunkenness when some drunkards, till then subdued, are suddenly overcome by an irresistible desire to fly into a rage and assert themselves.

'What are you staring at me for? You know what your eyes are like? Your eyes are looking at me and saying: "What a drunken rotter you are!" Your eyes are full of suspicion. Your eyes are full of contempt. . . . You've come here with some crafty plan in your mind. . . . Look at Alyosha. He, too, is looking at me, but his eyes are shining. Alyosha does not despise me. Alexey, you mustn't love Ivan. . . . '

'Don't be angry with my brother,' Alyosha suddenly said, insistently. 'Stop insulting him.'

'Oh, all right. Ugh, my head aches. Take away the brandy, Ivan. It's the third time I've told you.' He fell into thought and suddenly a cunning smile spread all over his face. 'Don't be angry with a feeble, stupid old man, Ivan. I know you don't love me, but don't be angry with me all the same. There's no reason why you should love me. You go to Chermashnya. I'll join you there myself and bring you a present. I'll show you a lovely little girl there. I've had my eye on her a long time. At present she's still running about barefoot. But don't fight shy of barefooted little girls – don't despise them – they're pearls.'

And he kissed his hand with a smack.

'So far as I'm concerned,' he went on, becoming animated all at once, as though growing sober for a minute as soon as he got on to his favourite subject, 'so far as I'm concerned – oh, you children, my dear children, my little sucking-pigs, so far as I'm concerned – there hasn't been an ugly woman in the whole of my life – that's been my rule! Can you understand that? But how could you understand it? You've still got milk and not blood flowing in your veins – you haven't hatched out yet! According to my rule, you can find in every woman something – damn it! – something extraordinarily interesting, something you won't find in any other woman. Only you must know how to find it – that's the point! That requires talent! For me ugly women do not exist: the very fact that she's a woman is half the attraction for me – but how could you understand that? Even in old maids you sometimes find something so attractive that you can't help marvelling at the damn fools who've let them grow old without noticing it! The first thing to do with barefooted girls and ugly women is to take them by surprise – that's how one should deal with them. You didn't know that, did you? They must be surprised till they're enraptured, till they're transfixed, till they're ashamed that such a gentleman should have fallen in love with such a swarthy creature. What's so wonderful is that so long as there are peasants and gentlemen in the world – and there always will be – there will also be such lovely little scullery maids and their masters – and that's all one needs for one's happiness! Wait – listen, Alyosha. I always used to surprise your mother, only it was in a different way. I never caressed her, but all at once, when the right moment came, I'd dance attendance on her, crawl on my knees before her, kiss her feet and always, always – I remember it as though it were today – I'd make her burst out into a quiet little laugh, a crisp, tinkling, soft, nervous, peculiar kind of laugh. That's the only kind of laugh she had. I knew that her attacks always began like that, that the next day she'd begin shrieking, that her present little laugh was not a sign of delight. But though deceptive, it sounded like delight. That's what it means to be able to find the typical in everything! There was that Belyavsky – a handsome fellow and rich too – who fell in love with her. He used to visit us almost every day. Suddenly, during one of his visits, he slapped my face, and in her presence too. And she – such a sheep – why, I thought she'd beat me black and blue for that blow. How she set upon me! "You've been thrashed, thrashed," she kept saying. "You've had your face slapped by him. You were trying to sell me to him," she said. "And how dared he strike you in my presence! And don't you ever dare come near me again! Go at once and challenge him to a duel! . . . " So I took her to the monastery to teach her meekness. The holy fathers read prayers over her. But I swear to you, Alyosha, I never did anything to offend my poor shrieker! Once only, perhaps, only once! It happened during the first year of our marriage. She used to pray a lot then and she was especially keen on keeping the feasts of our Lady. She used to drive me away from her then to my study. Well, I thought to myself, let's knock that mysticism out of her. "You see," I said to her, "you see your icon – there – well, look, I'm going to take it down. Now watch me. You think it's a miracle-working icon, don't you? But I'm going to spit on it in front of you and nothing will happen to me!" As soon as she heard me, good Lord, I thought she'd kill me on the spot. But she only jumped to her feet, threw up her hands, then covered her face with them, began shaking all over and fell on the floor – fell all of a heap. . . . Alyosha, Alyosha, what's the matter?'

The old man jumped up from his seat in alarm. From the moment he began talking about his mother, a gradual change came over Alyosha's face. He flushed, his eyes glowed, his lips quivered. . . . The drunken old man had gone on spluttering and noticed nothing till the very moment when something strange happened to Alyosha – exactly the same thing, in fact, as had happened to the 'shrieker' when he threatened to spit on her icon. Alyosha suddenly jumped up from his seat, exactly as his mother had done, threw up his hands, then buried his face in them and trembled all over in a sudden fit of hysteria, shaking with silent sobs. The old man was particularly struck by his extraordinary resemblance to his mother.

'Ivan, Ivan! A glass of water, quick! It's like her, exactly like her! Just as his mother was then! Spurt some water on him from your mouth. I used to do the same to her. He's upset for his mother, for his mother . . . ' he muttered to Ivan.

'But his mother was my mother, too, wasn't she?' Ivan suddenly burst out with uncontrollable anger and contempt.

His flashing eyes made the old man start. But here something very strange had happened, though perhaps it lasted only a second: the fact that Alyosha's mother was also Ivan's mother seemed to have slipped Karamazov's mind completely.

'Your mother?' he muttered, uncomprehendingly. 'What are you talking about? What mother are you.... Was she really? Why, damn it! Of course, she was your mother too! Damn it! I'm sorry, my dear fellow, I didn't know what I was saying.... This never happened to me before. I'm sorry. I was thinking, Ivan – heh-heh-heh!'

He stopped short. A broad, drunken, half-witted grin spread all over his face. And that very moment a terrible uproar broke out in the hall, violent shouts could be heard, the door was flung open and Dmitry burst into the room. The old man rushed up to Ivan in terror.

'He'll kill me? He'll kill me! Don't let him get near me, don't let him!' he screamed, clutching at the skirt of Ivan's coat.

9

The Sensualists

GRIGORY and Smerdyakov ran into the room immediately after Dmitry. They had been struggling with him in the hall, trying not to let him in (acting on the instructions given by Karamazov himself some days before). Taking advantage of the fact that after bursting into the room Dmitry had stopped dead for a moment to look round, Grigory ran round the table, closed the double doors on the opposite side of the room leading to the inner apartments, and stopped before the closed door with his hands crossed, ready, as it were, to defend the entrance to the bedroom with the last drop of his blood. Seeing that, Dmitry did not so much shout as scream and rushed at Grigory.

'So she's there! She's been hidden there! Get out of my way, you blackguard!'

He tried to pull Grigory away, but Grigory pushed him back. Beside himself with fury, Dmitry raised his hand and struck Grigory with all his might. The old man collapsed in a heap on the floor, and Dmitry, jumping over him, burst open the door. Smerdyakov remained at the other end of the drawing-room, pale and trembling and clinging to Karamazov.

'She's here,' shouted Dmitry. 'I just saw her myself turning towards the house, but I couldn't overtake her. Where is she? Where is she?'

The shout: 'She's here!' produced an astonishing effect upon Karamazov. All his terror left him.

'Hold him! Hold him!' he yelled, rushing after Dmitry.

Meanwhile Grigory had got up from the floor, but he still seemed dazed. Ivan and Alyosha rushed after their father. In the third room something was suddenly heard to fall to the floor with a crash: it was a large glass vase (an inexpensive one) on a marble pedestal which Dmitry brushed against as he ran past it.

'At him!' yelled the old man. 'Help!'

Ivan and Alyosha overtook the old man and forced him to go back to the drawing-room.

'What are you running after him for?' Ivan shouted angrily at his father. 'He really will murder you there!'

'Ivan, Alyosha, my dear boys, she must be here then. Grushenka is here. He said he saw her himself running into the house.'

He was gasping for breath. He was not expecting Grushenka that day and the sudden news that she was there drove him out of his mind. He was trembling all over. He seemed to have gone mad.

'But you've seen yourself she hasn't come!' Ivan shouted.

'She may have come by the back entrance.'

'But it's locked – the back entrance is locked, and you've got the key.'

Dmitry suddenly appeared in the drawing-room again. He had of course found the back entrance locked, and the key actually was in Karamazov's pocket. The windows of all the rooms were also closed; Grushenka could not possibly have got into the house from anywhere, nor could she have run out from anywhere.

'Hold him!' screamed Karamazov as soon as he caught sight of Dmitry. 'He's stolen my money from the bedroom!'

Breaking loose from Ivan, he again rushed at Dmitry. But Dmitry raised both his hands and suddenly seized the old man by the remaining wisps of his hair, gave a pull and flung him with a crash on the floor. He had just time to kick him two or three times in the face with his heel. The old man let out a piercing moan. Ivan, though not as strong as his brother Dmitry, flung his arms round him and dragged him away from the old man with all the force at his command.

Alyosha, too, helped him with all his feeble strength, clasping his brother round the waist.

'Madman, you've killed him!' shouted Ivan.

'Serves him right!' Dmitry cried breathlessly. 'If I haven't killed him now, I'll come back and kill him. You won't be able to protect him!'

'Dmitry, get out of here at once!' Alyosha shouted peremptorily.

'Alexey, tell me, please, you're the only one I'll believe – was she here just now or not? I saw her myself a minute ago stealing past the fence from the lane towards the house. I shouted and she ran away.'

'I swear she hasn't been here and no one expected her to come.'

'But I saw her. . . . So that she – I'll find out at once where she is. Alexey, good-bye. Don't tell the old swine about the money now. You must go to Katerina at once and tell her that I told you to bid her good-bye, bid her good-bye. Yes, bid her good-bye. Tell her that. He bids you farewell! Describe this scene to her.'

Meanwhile Ivan and Grigory had raised the old man and seated him in an arm-chair. His face was covered with blood, but he was conscious and he listened eagerly to Dmitry's shouts. He still seemed to think that Grushenka was really somewhere in the house. As he left the room, Dmitry gave him a baleful look.

'I'm not sorry to have spilt your blood!' he cried. 'Take care, old man, take care of your dreams, for I too have dreams! I curse you and disown you entirely! . . .'

He ran out of the room.

'She's here! I'm sure she's here! Smerdyakov, Smerdyakov!' the old man wheezed almost inaudibly, beckoning to Smerdyakov with a finger.

'She is not here, she isn't, you crazy old man!' Ivan shouted at him spitefully. 'Good Lord, he's fainted! Water! A towel! Be quick about it, Smerdyakov!'

Smerdyakov rushed out for water. The old man was at last undressed, taken to the bedroom and put to bed. A wet towel was wrapped round his head. Weakened by the brandy, the violent sensations and the blows, he shut his eyes and fell asleep as soon as his head touched the pillow. Ivan and Alyosha went back to the drawing-room. Smerdyakov was carrying away the pieces of the broken vase and Grigory stood at the table looking down gloomily at the floor.

'Don't you think you'd better put a wet towel round your head too and go to bed?' Alyosha said to Grigory. 'We'll look after him here. My brother must have given you a terrible blow – on the head.'

'He dared do this to me!' Grigory said gloomily and distinctly.

'He "dared" do this to father, too, not only to you,' Ivan remarked with a wry smile.

'I used to wash him in a tub and – he dared do this to me!' Grigory repeated.

'Damn it all, if I hadn't pulled him away, he'd probably have killed him. It wouldn't take much to do the old fool in,' Ivan whispered to Alyosha.

'God forbid!' cried Alyosha.

'Why?' Ivan went on in the same whisper, with a malicious grin. 'One reptile will devour another reptile, and serve them both right!'

Alyosha shuddered.

'I won't of course let him be murdered as I didn't just now. Stay here, Alyosha. I'll go out for a breath of fresh air. I've got a headache.'

Alyosha went into his father's bedroom and sat down at his bedside behind the screen for about an hour. The old man suddenly opened his eyes and gazed silently at Alyosha for a long time, evidently remembering and pondering. Suddenly there was a look of extraordinary agitation in his face.

'Alyosha,' he whispered, cautiously, 'where's Ivan?'

'He's gone out into the yard. He's got a headache. He's keeping watch over us.'

'Hand me the looking-glass. It's over there. Give it me!'

Alyosha handed him a little, round, folding looking-glass which stood on the chest of drawers. The old man examined his face in it: his nose was rather badly swollen and there was a purple bruise on his forehead over the left eyebrow.

'What does Ivan say? Alyosha, my dear, my only son, I'm afraid of Ivan. I'm more afraid of Ivan than of the other. You're the only one I'm not afraid of.'

'Don't be afraid of Ivan, either. Ivan's angry, but he'll protect you.'

'Alyosha, and what about the other? He's run off to Grushenka! My dear boy, tell me the truth: was Grushenka here just now or not?'

'No one has seen her. It's not true. She wasn't here.'

'You know, Mitya wants to marry her – he wants to marry her!'

'She won't marry him.'

'She won't, she won't, she won't, she won't, she won't marry him for anything in the world!' the old man cried, starting with joy, as though nothing more comforting could have been said to him at that moment.

In his delight he seized Alyosha's hand and pressed it firmly to his heart. Even tears glistened in his eyes.

'Take your mother's icon of the Virgin – the one I was telling you about – take it home with you. And I'll let you go back to the monastery. . . . I was joking this morning – don't be angry with me. My head aches, Alyosha. . . . Alyosha, comfort me, be a good boy, and tell me the truth.'

'Are you still harping on the same thing?' Alyosha said sorrowfully. 'Has she been here or not?'

'No, no, no, I believe you. What I want you to do is this: go to Grushenka yourself or try to see her. Find out from her as quickly as possible and find out for yourself which one of us she will have, me or him? Eh? What? Can you do it or not?'

'If I see her, I'll ask her,' Alyosha murmured, looking embarrassed.

'No, she won't tell you,' the old man interrupted. 'She's a flirt. She'll start kissing you and say that it's you she wants. She's a cheat, she's a shameless slut – no, you mustn't go to her, you mustn't!'

'And it wouldn't be nice, father. It wouldn't be nice at all.'

'Where was he sending you just now when he shouted "Go there!" as he ran out of the house?'

'To Katerina.'

'For money? To ask her for money?'

'No, not for money.'

'He has no money. Not a penny. Listen, Alyosha. I'll stay in bed tonight and think things over, and you can go now. Perhaps you will meet her. Only be sure to come and see me tomorrow morning. Be sure to. I'll tell you something important tomorrow. Will you come?'

'I will.'

'When you come, pretend to have come of your own accord to

see how I am. Don't tell anyone I asked you to come. Not a word of it to Ivan.'

'All right.'

'Good-bye, my boy. You stood up for me just now. I shall never forget that. I'll tell you something tomorrow – only I have to think it over first.'

'And how do you feel now?'

'Tomorrow, tomorrow I'll get up and go out. I'm very well, very well, very well.'

As he crossed the yard, Alyosha saw his brother Ivan sitting on a bench by the gate: he was writing something in pencil in his notebook. Alyosha told Ivan that the old man was awake and conscious, and had let him go back to spend the night in the monastery.

'Alyosha, I'd very much like to meet you tomorrow morning,' Ivan said affably, getting up from the bench.

His affability took Alyosha completely by surprise.

'I shall be at the Khokhlakovs' tomorrow,' replied Alyosha. 'I may be at Katerina's tomorrow, too, if I don't find her in now.'

'So you are going to Katerina's now? To "bid her a last farewell"?' Ivan suddenly smiled.

Alyosha looked embarrassed.

'I think I understood everything from his exclamations a short while ago and something of what went on before. Dmitry, I suppose, has asked you to go and see her and tell her that he – well, in short – that "he bids her a last farewell"?'

'Tell me, Ivan, what will be the outcome of this horrible situation between father and Dmitry?' Alyosha cried.

'It's impossible to say for certain. Perhaps nothing will come of it: the whole thing will just peter out. That woman is a wild animal. In any case, the old man must be kept at home and Dmitry must not be let in.'

'I'd like to ask you one more thing, Ivan: has any man a right to decide who deserves to live and who doesn't?'

'Why try to decide who deserves to live and who doesn't? This question is more often decided in men's hearts not on the basis of whether a man deserves to live or not, but on quite different grounds, on much more natural grounds, I would say. As for the right to decide – who hasn't the right to wish?'

'Not, surely, the death of another man?'

'Why not even the death of another man? Why lie to yourself when all people live like that and perhaps cannot live otherwise. Are you referring to what I said just now about two reptiles devouring each other? Let me ask you in that case: do you consider me capable, like Dmitry, of shedding the blood of that crazy fool, I mean, killing him?'

'What are you saying, Ivan? The idea never entered my head! I don't think even Dmitry — '

'Well, thanks for that, anyway,' Ivan smiled. 'I'd like you to know that I'll always protect him. But as for my wishes in this case, I reserve for myself the right to think as I please. Good-bye till tomorrow. Don't condemn me and don't look upon me as a criminal,' he added with a smile.

They shook hands warmly, as never before. Alyosha felt that his brother had taken the first step towards him and that he did so most certainly with some kind of intention.

10

Both Together

ALYOSHA left his father's house feeling more depressed and crushed in spirit than when he entered it. His thoughts, too, seemed disjointed and scattered so that he could not help feeling that he was afraid to piece them together and form a general idea from all the agonizing contradictions he had experienced that day. He was almost on the verge of despair, something which had never happened to him before. Over everything towered like a mountain the main fatal and insoluble question: what would be the end of the affair between his father and his brother Dmitry and that terrible woman? Now he had been a witness. He had been there himself and he had seen them facing each other. However, it was only his brother Dmitry who could be made unhappy, terribly unhappy: he was certainly in for some trouble. There were also apparently other people who were concerned in all this and perhaps more than Alyosha first imagined. Indeed, there seemed to be something mysterious about it all. Ivan had taken a step towards him, which Alyosha had long been wishing for. But for some unknown reason he now felt that he was frightened by this step towards a closer understanding between them. And those women? It was certainly strange: only a few hours before he had felt greatly embarrassed when he set out to visit Katerina, but now he felt no embarrassment at all; on the contrary, he was hurrying, as though expecting to find some solution to his problems at her place. And yet it was evidently more difficult now to give her his brother's message than before: the matter of the three thousand roubles was finally decided, and nothing, of course, would stop Dmitry now that he felt himself dishonoured and without hope, however great his downfall. He had, besides, asked him to describe the scene at his father's to Katerina.

It was already seven o'clock and it was getting dark when Alyosha entered the very spacious and comfortable house Katerina occupied in the High Street. Alyosha knew that she lived with two aunts. One of them, however, was only the aunt of her half-sister Agafya, the taciturn old lady who looked after the two sisters in their father's house after Katerina had returned from her boarding-school. The other aunt was a grand Moscow society woman, though in reduced circumstances. It was rumoured that both of them did everything Katerina told them and that she kept them merely as chaperons. Katerina herself did only what she was told by her benefactress, the general's widow, who had stayed in Moscow because of illness and to whom she had to write two letters a week with a full account of herself.

When Alyosha entered the hall and asked the parlour maid, who had opened the door, to announce him, the ladies in the drawing-room evidently already knew of his arrival (perhaps they had noticed him from the window), for he suddenly heard a noise, the sound of running footsteps and the rustle of skirts: two or three women, perhaps, had run out of the room. Alyosha thought it strange that he should have created such a commotion by his arrival. He was immediately shown into the drawing-room, however. It was a large room, elegantly and substantially furnished, not at all in provincial style. There were many sofas and settees, little ottomans, big and little tables; there were pictures on the walls, lamps and vases on the tables, there were lots of flowers, and there was even an aquarium by the window. Because of the twilight it was a little dark in the room. Alyosha noticed a silk shawl thrown down on a sofa, where people had evidently just been sitting, and on a table in front of the sofa were two unfinished cups of chocolate, cakes, a porcelain saucer with blue raisins, and another with sweets. Someone was being entertained. Alyosha guessed that he had interrupted visitors and frowned. But at that moment the curtain over a door was raised and Katerina came in with quick, hurrying footsteps and held out her hands to Alyosha with a joyful and rapturous smile. At the same moment a maid brought in two lighted candles and put them on a table.

'Thank God, at last you've come too! I've been simply praying to God for you to come all day! Sit down, please.'

Alyosha had been struck by Katerina's beauty even before, when Dmitry, three weeks earlier, had brought him, at Katerina's special request, for the first time to be introduced to her. During that meeting, however, they had not talked a great deal. Thinking that Alyosha was very shy, Katerina seemed anxious to spare him and had talked all the time to Dmitry. Alyosha had been silent, but he had seen through a great deal. He had been struck by the imperiousness, the proud casualness and self-assurance of the haughty girl. And his suspicion was confirmed. Alyosha felt that he had not been exaggerating. He thought her large glowing black eyes were very beautiful and suited her pale, even yellowish pale, elongated face. But there was something about those eyes and even about the lines of her exquisite lips with which his brother might well have fallen passionately in love, but which perhaps one could not love for long. He nearly expressed this thought frankly to Dmitry, when, after the visit, his brother implored him persistently not to conceal his impressions after seeing his fiancée.

'You will be happy with her, but perhaps not – serenely happy.'

'There you are, old man! Such women always remain the same. They never give in to fate. So you don't think that I shall love her for ever?'

'I don't know. Perhaps you will, but perhaps you won't be always happy with her. . . .'

Alyosha had given his opinion at the time, blushing and vexed with himself for having given in to his brother's entreaties and expressed such 'stupid' ideas. For his opinion had seemed awfully stupid to him the moment he had put it into words. Besides, he felt ashamed to express an opinion about a woman in such emphatic terms. He was even more surprised now, at the first glance at Katerina as she ran into the room, that he should feel that perhaps he had been entirely mistaken. This time her face shone with unaffected, good-natured kindliness, and genuine and fervent sincerity. Of all her former 'pride and haughtiness', which had struck him so forcibly at their first meeting, he was now aware only of her brave and generous energy and of a sort of serene and strong faith in herself. Alyosha realized at the first glance at her, from the first words she uttered, that the whole tragedy of her position in regard to the man she loved so much was no secret to her and that she probably knew everything, absolutely everything. And yet, in spite of that, there was so much brightness in her face and so much faith in the future that Alyosha suddenly felt that in some grave and premeditated way he had wronged her. He was conquered and won over at once. Besides all this, he noticed at her first words that she was in a state of great excitement, which was perhaps quite exceptional in her – an excitement that was almost indistinguishable from ecstasy.

'I was so anxious to see you because I can learn the whole truth only from you – from you and no one else!'

'I've come — ' Alyosha murmured, stammering, 'I've – he sent me. . . .'

'Oh, he sent you! I had a feeling he would! Now I know every-thing, everything!' exclaimed Katerina with suddenly flashing eyes. 'Wait a moment, I'd better tell you first why I wanted to see you so much. You see, I know perhaps much more than you do yourself. It is not news I'd like you to tell me. All I want you to tell me is this: I want to know your own, personal, last impression of him. All I want is that you should tell me frankly, simply and even coarsely (oh, as coarsely as you like!), what is your opinion of him and of his condition after your meeting with him today. That would be much better perhaps than if I, whom he doesn't want to see any more, had a personal explanation from him. Do you understand what I want from you? Now tell me plainly what was his message to me (I knew that he would send you to me!). Tell me every word of his message, please!'

'He asked me to say – good-bye to you and that he would never come again – but first to say good-bye.'

'Say good-bye? Was that how he put it?'

'Yes.'

'Perhaps he accidentally made a mistake in the word? Perhaps he did not use the right word?'

'No, he asked me most definitely to give this message – "to say good-bye". He asked me three times not to forget to tell you that.'

Katerina flushed.

'Please, help me now, Alexey. It is now that I require your help most. I'll tell you what I think, and you must tell me simply whether I'm right or not. Listen, please: if he had told you to say good-bye to me unreflectingly, without insisting on your repeating the exact words, without emphasizing them, then that would be the end – the end of everything! But if he particularly insisted on those words, if he asked you specially not to forget to say his good-bye to me – then he must have been in a state of excitement, perhaps beside himself. He had made his decision and was terrified of it! He was not walking away from me with a determined step, but taking a headlong leap. The emphasis on that word may have been simply bravado.'

'Yes, yes!' Alyosha agreed warmly. 'I think so myself now.'

'And if that is so, he is not lost yet! He's merely in despair and I can still save him. Wait, though. He didn't by any chance tell you anything about money – about three thousand roubles?'

'Why, of course he did, and that perhaps more than anything is making him so unhappy. He said that he had lost his honour and that he did not care what happened to him now,' Alyosha replied warmly, feeling with all his heart the dawn of a new hope and that there might really be a way of escape and salvation for his brother. 'But do you know about – that money?' he added and suddenly stopped short.

'I've known about it a long time – and I know all the particulars. I telegraphed to Moscow and I've known for some time that the money had not arrived. He hadn't sent the money, but I said nothing. Last week I found out how much he needed the money and that he still needed it. There's only one thing I want: that he should know to whom to turn and that I'm his true friend. But he doesn't want to believe that I'm his true friend. He doesn't want to know me. He looks upon me only as a woman. I've been terribly worried all this week. I wondered what I could do so that he shouldn't be ashamed before me for having spent that three thousand. What I mean is, let him be ashamed before everyone and before himself, but don't let him be ashamed before me. He tells everything to God without being ashamed, doesn't he? Why, then, doesn't he yet realize how much I'm ready to bear for his sake? Why, why doesn't he know me? How did he dare not to know me after all that has happened? I want to save him for ever. Let him forget that I'm his fiancée! And now he fears me because his honour is at stake! He was not afraid to be frank with you, was he? Why then haven't I yet deserved to be treated in the same way?'

The last words she uttered in tears: tears gushed from her eyes.

'I must tell you,' said Alyosha, too, in a trembling voice, 'what happened just now between him and my father.'

And he described the whole scene to her, told her that he had been sent for the money, that Dmitry had burst into the room, had assaulted his father, and after that had begged him specially and earnestly to go and bid her 'good-bye'. . . .

'He's gone to that woman,' Alyosha added softly.

'And do you think I won't put up with that woman? Does he think I won't? But he won't marry her,' she went on, suddenly laughing nervously. 'Could a Karamazov burn with such a passion for ever? It is passion, not love. He won't marry her because she won't marry him.'

Again Katerina suddenly smiled strangely.

'He may marry her,' said Alyosha mournfully, dropping his eyes.

'He won't marry her, I'm telling you! This girl is an angel – do you know that? Do you know that?' Katerina exclaimed suddenly with extraordinary warmth. 'She's one of the most fantastic of fantastic creatures! I know how fascinating she is, but I also know how good, how firm and noble she is. What are you looking at me like that for? Are you perhaps surprised at my words? Don't you believe me? Grushenka, my angel,' she shouted suddenly to someone, peeping into the next room, 'please come in. This is a very nice man. This is Alyosha. He knows all about our affairs. Come and meet him!'

'I've only been waiting behind the curtain for you to call me,' said a gentle, one might almost say, a sugary, feminine voice.

The curtain parted and – Grushenka herself, laughing and looking very pleased, walked up to the table. Something seemed to turn over in Alyosha. His eyes were riveted upon her and he could not take them off her. So there she was, that terrible woman, the 'wild animal', as Ivan had angrily called her half an hour before. And to look at her it would seem that a most ordinary and simple human being was standing before him – a nice, kind woman, beautiful, to be sure, but how like all other beautiful but 'ordinary' women! It was true that she was very, very good-looking indeed, a typical Russian beauty so passionately loved by many men. She was a rather tall woman, though a little shorter than Katerina, who was exceptionally tall – plump, with soft, almost inaudible movements of the body, which also seemed so delicate as to be, somehow, specially sugary, like her voice. She went up to him not as Katerina had done with a vigorous, bold step, but, on the contrary, noiselessly. Her feet made absolutely no sound on the floor. She sank softly into an arm-chair, with a soft rustle of her gorgeous black silk dress, delicately wrapping an expensive black woollen shawl round her plump, milk-white neck and ample shoulders. She was twenty-two years old and she looked exactly her age. Her face was very pale, with a pale pink tint on her cheekbones. The outline of her face seemed rather broad and her lower jaw even protruded a trifle. Her upper lip was thin, her slightly prominent lower lip was twice as full, just as though it were a little swollen. But her magnificent, abundant dark brown hair, her dark sable-like eyebrows, and her exquisite grey-blue eyes with long eye-lashes would have made the most indifferent and absent-minded person, meeting her in a crowd, on a promenade, in a crush, stop dead suddenly at the sight of her face and remember it long after. Alyosha was most of all struck by the childish, good-natured expression of her face. She had the look of a child, she expressed her delight like a child, she came up to the table 'looking delighted' and as though expecting something to happen immediately with childish, impatient and confiding curiosity. Her expression gladdened the heart – Alyosha felt that. There was something else about her, which he could not and would not know how to describe – but which he, too, must have been aware of unconsciously – that was again her soft-ness, the delicacy of her movements, the cat-like noiselessness of those movements. And yet hers was a powerful and ample body. Under her shawl could be discerned full, broad shoulders and a high, still girlish bosom. Her figure gave promise of becoming in form a Venus de Milo, but already in somewhat exaggerated proportions – one could see that. Looking at Grushenka, connoisseurs of Russian female beauty could have foretold unmistakably that this fresh, still youthful beauty would lose its harmony by the age of thirty, would spread, that her face would become puffy, that wrinkles would very rapidly appear round the eyes and on the forehead, that her complexion would grow coarse and red perhaps – in short, it was an ephemeral beauty, a beauty that does not last, which one meets so often among Russian women. Alyosha did not, of course, think of this, but though fascinated, he could not help asking himself with a sort of unpleasant feeling and as though with regret why she drawled like that and why she could not speak naturally. She did so evidently because she thought this dragging out of the words and the exaggerated and sugary modulation of syllables and sounds was attractive. That was, of course, a bad, ill-bred habit that showed bad education and a vulgar understanding, instilled in childhood, of what constitutes good manners. And yet this enunciation and intonation of words struck Alyosha as almost incredibly incongruous with the childishly ingenuous and gay expression of her face and with the soft, childishly happy radiance of her eyes. Katerina at once made her sit down in an armchair opposite Alyosha and kissed her rapturously a few times on her laughing lips. She seemed to be in love with her.

'This is the first time we've met,' she said to Alyosha ecstatically. 'I wanted to know her, to see her. I wanted to go to her, but no sooner had I expressed the wish to see her than she came to me. I knew we should settle everything, absolutely everything. I felt it in my heart. . . . They begged me not to take this step, but I felt that it would turn out for the best and I was not mistaken. Grushenka has explained everything to me. She has told me all her plans. She flew down here like a good angel and brought peace and joy with her. . . . '

'You were not too proud to see me, my sweet, good young lady, were you?' Grushenka drawled in her sing-song voice and with the same charming, happy smile.

'You mustn't speak to me like that, my enchantress! Too proud to see you, indeed! Let me kiss your sweet lower lip again. It looks as if it were a little swollen, well, let it be a little more swollen, and more, and more. . . . Look how she laughs, Alexey. It does one's heart good to see such an angel. . . . '

Alyosha blushed and a faint, imperceptible shiver kept running down his spine.

'You're so sweet to me, my dear young lady, but perhaps I don't deserve your kisses.'

'Don't deserve them! She doesn't deserve them!' Katerina cried again with the same warmth. 'Do you know, Alexey, we've got such a fantastic little head and such a wilful and proud little heart! We're noble, we're generous – you didn't know that, did you? We've only been unfortunate. We were too ready to make every sacrifice for a man who was perhaps unworthy or fickle. There was one such man, only one, also an army officer. We fell in love with him, we sacrificed everything for him – it was a long time ago, five years ago, and he has forgotten us, he has married. Now he's a widower, he has written, he's coming here – and, please, don't forget it's him alone we love, no one but him. We've loved him all our life and we love him still. He'll come and Grushenka will be happy again, for she's been so unhappy during the last five years! But who can reproach her? Who can boast of her favours? Why, only one bedridden old man – a merchant, but he was more like a father to us, he was our friend and protector. He found us then in despair, in agony, deserted by the man we loved so much – why, she was about to throw herself into the river at the time and it was that old man who saved her – he saved her!'

'You're so kind to defend me, my dear young lady. You're a little too much in a hurry about everything,' Grushenka drawled again.

'Defend you? Who are we to defend you? And have we a right to defend you? Grushenka, darling, give me your hand. Look at this charming, chubby little hand, Alexey. See it? It has brought me happiness. It has given me a new lease of life, and I'm going to kiss it, inside and outside, here, here, and here!'

And she really did kiss Grushenka's charming and perhaps a little too chubby little hand three times in a kind of rapture. Grushenka held out her hand and watched the 'dear young lady' with her charming, ringing, nervous little laugh, and she was obviously pleased to have her hand kissed like that.

'Perhaps there's a little too much enthusiasm,' it flashed through

Alyosha's mind. He blushed. All the time he felt peculiarly uneasy at heart.

'You make me feel ashamed, my dear young lady, kissing my hand like that before Mr Karamazov.'

'But you don't think I wanted to make you feel ashamed, do you?' said Katerina with some surprise. 'Oh, my dear, how little you know me!'

'But perhaps you don't quite know me, either, my dear young lady. Perhaps I'm much worse than you think. I have a wicked heart. I'm headstrong. I turned poor Dmitry's head that time just for fun.'

'But, then, you're going to save him now, aren't you? You've given me your word. You'll make him see sense. You'll tell him that you love another man, that you've loved him for a long time, a man who is now offering you his hand.'

'Oh, but I never promised you to do that. It was you who kept telling me all that. I never promised you.'

'I must have misunderstood you then,' Katerina said softly, turning a little pale. 'You promised — '

'Oh no, my darling young lady, I've promised you nothing,' Grushenka interrupted her, softly and equably, with the same gay and innocent expression. 'Now you can see at once, my dear young lady, what a bad and wilful woman I am compared with you. If I want to do something, I do it. I may have promised you something a little while ago, but now I can't help thinking: what if I should take a fancy to him again? You see, I did like Mitya very much once – I liked him for almost a whole hour. So perhaps I'll go and tell him now to stay with me from this day. . . . That's how inconstant I am. . . . '

'Just now you said – you said something quite different . . . ' Katerina whispered faintly.

'Oh, just now! You see, I'm so tender-hearted. I'm so silly. To think what he's gone through because of me! What if I should suddenly feel sorry for him when I come home – what then?'

'I never expected — '

'Oh, my dear young lady, how good and noble you are compared with me. I daresay you'll hate a silly creature like me now that you know what I'm really like. Please, give me your hand, darling young lady,' she said tenderly, and she took Katerina's hand with a kind of reverence. 'You see, my dear young lady, I'm taking your hand and I'm going to kiss it as you did mine. You've kissed mine three times, and I really ought to kiss yours three hundred times for us to be quits. Very well, I'll do it, and then let it be as God thinks fit. Perhaps I shall be your obedient slave and do my best to please you like a slave. As God thinks fit, so let it be, without any agreements and promises. What a lovely little hand you have, my dear, beautiful young lady!'

She slowly raised Katerina's hand to her lips, with the strange intention, it is true, 'to be quits' with her in kisses. Katerina did not take her hand away: she listened with timid hope to Grushenka's rather strangely expressed promise to please her 'like a slave'. She looked tensely into her eyes: in those eyes she still saw the same good-natured, confiding expression, the same serene gaiety. 'She's perhaps a little too naïve,' thought Katerina with a glimmer of hope in her heart. Meanwhile Grushenka, as though enraptured by 'the sweet hand', kept raising it slowly to her lips. But having raised it to her lips, she suddenly held it there for two or three seconds as though considering something.

'Do you know what, my sweet young lady?' she drawled suddenly in her soft and most sugary little voice, 'Do you know what? I don't think I'm going to kiss your hand after all.'

And she laughed her gay little laugh.

'As you please. . . . What's the matter with you?' asked Katerina with a sudden start.

'You see, I want you to remember always that you kissed my hand, but I didn't kiss yours.'

There was a sudden flash in her eyes. She was looking with terrible intensity at Katerina.

'You insolent creature!' Katerina cried all of a sudden and, as though suddenly realizing something, she flushed all over and jumped up from her seat. Grushenka, too, got up, but without haste.

'So I shall tell Mitya how you kissed my hand and I didn't kiss yours at all. And how he'll laugh!'

'You dirty slut! Get out!'

'What language, my dear young lady, what language! Really, you ought to be ashamed of yourself! A young lady like you didn't ought to have used such language!'

'Get out, you filthy prostitute!' screamed Katerina. Every muscle was quivering in her terribly distorted face.

'A prostitute, am I? Didn't you used to visit gentlemen in the evening for money yourself? Offered your beauty for sale, didn't you? I know all about it, you see.'

Katerina uttered a shriek and was about to rush at her, but Alyosha held her back with all his strength.

'Not another step! Not a word! Don't speak, don't answer her. She'll go away. She'll go at once.'

At that moment Katerina's two aunts ran into the room, followed by the maid. They all rushed up to her.

'I will go away,' said Grushenka, picking up her shawl from the sofa. 'Alyosha, darling, see me off home, please.'

'Go away, please, go away at once!' Alyosha besought her, clasping his hands together beseechingly before her.

'Darling Alyosha, do see me home! I've got something very, very nice to tell you on the way. I've staged this scene especially for you, Alyosha, dear. See me home, darling. You'll be glad of it afterwards.'

Alyosha turned away, wringing his hands. Grushenka rushed out of the house, laughing loudly.

Katerina had a fit of hysterics. She sobbed and shook with convulsions. They were all fussing round her.

'I warned you,' said the elder of her aunts. 'I tried to prevent you from taking this step. You're too impulsive. How could you do such a thing? You don't know what these creatures are like, and they say she's worse than any of them. You are too headstrong.'

'She's a tigress!' Katerina screamed. 'Why did you hold me back, Alexey? I'd have thrashed her within an inch of her life!'

She was quite incapable of controlling herself before Alyosha, and perhaps she didn't want to.

'She ought to be flogged in public by the hangman on a scaffold!' Alyosha backed towards the door.

'But, good Lord,' Katerina cried suddenly with a despairing movement of the hands, 'what about him? How could he be so dishonourable, so inhuman? Why, he actually told that horrible creature what happened on that dreadful day, on that hateful, for ever hateful day! "You went there to sell your beauty, my dear young lady!" She knows all about it! Your brother is a cad, Alexey!'

Alyosha wanted to say something, but he couldn't find the right words. His heart contracted painfully.

'Please go, Alexey. I feel so ashamed, so horrid! Come tomorrow – I beg you on my knees, come tomorrow. Don't think badly of me. Please forgive me. I don't know what I'm going to do with myself now!'

Alyosha went out into the street almost staggering. He, too, felt like crying as she did. Suddenly he was overtaken by the maid.

'Miss Katerina forgot to give you this letter from Mrs Khokhlakov, sir. She's had it since dinner.'

Alyosha took the little pink envelope mechanically and almost unconsciously put it into his pocket.

11

Another Ruined Reputation

IT was not more than a mile from the town to the monastery. Alyosha walked hurriedly along the road, which was deserted at that hour. It was almost night and too difficult to distinguish anything thirty yards ahead. There were cross-roads half-way along the road. At the cross-roads a figure loomed into sight under a solitary willow-tree. As soon as Alyosha reached the cross-roads the figure detached itself rapidly from its place, rushed at him and shouted in a fierce voice:

'Your money or your life!'

'So it's you, Mitya!' cried Alyosha in surprise, violently startled, however.

'Ha, ha, ha! You didn't expect me, did you? I wondered where to wait for you. Near her house? There are three roads leading from there and I would have missed you. At last I decided to wait for you here. You were quite certain to pass here, for there's no other way to the monastery. Well, tell me the truth. Crush me like a cockroach. But what's the matter with you?'

'Oh, nothing, Mitya. You gave me such a fright. Oh, Dmitry, this afternoon father's blood' – Alyosha began to cry, he had been on the verge of tears for a long time, but now something seemed to snap inside him. 'You nearly killed him – you cursed him – and now – here – you're making jokes – your money or your life!'

'Well, what about it? Improper, is it? Doesn't it fit the situation?'

'Why no – I merely —'

'Wait a moment. Look at the night: see what a dark night it is! Look at the clouds! What a wind has risen! I hid here under the willow, waiting for you, and suddenly – God's my witness! – I thought to myself: why go on like this? What am I waiting for? Here's a willow, I have a handkerchief, I have a shirt, I can twist them into a rope in no time, and a pair of braces too, and – no longer burden the earth, no longer dishonour it with my vile presence! And then I heard you coming and – Lord, it was as if something had dawned on me suddenly: so there is a man whom I love – there he is, that dear man, that dear little brother of mine whom I love more than anyone in the world and the only one I love! And I loved you so much, I loved you so much at that moment, that I thought: let me fall on his neck at once! Then a stupid thought struck me: Let me amuse him, let me scare him! And so I shouted like a fool: "Your money!" I'm sorry for my tomfoolery – it was stupid – as for what I really feel – that, too, is quite proper. . . . But to hell with it. Tell me what happened there? What did she say? Crush me, strike me down, don't spare me! Was she furious?'

'No, it wasn't that at all. . . . There was nothing of the kind there. There – I found them both there.'

'Both who?'

'Grushenka was at Katerina's.'

Dmitry was thunderstruck.

'Impossible!' he shouted. 'You're raving! Grushenka at her place?'

Alyosha told him all that had happened to him from the moment he entered Katerina's house. He was describing it for ten minutes. It cannot be said that he did so fluently or coherently, but he went over everything as clearly as possible, recounting the most significant words that had passed between the two young women and their feelings at the time, and describing his own feelings vividly, sometimes by a single characteristic detail. Dmitry listened in silence, staring straight at him with a look of terrible immobility, but it was clear to Alyosha that he had understood everything and had grasped every fact. But his face, as the story went on, became not so much gloomy as menacing. He knit his brows, he clenched his teeth, his immobile stare grew even more immobile, more intent, more terrible. . . . It was therefore all the more surprising when, with indescribable rapidity, his face, till then angry and fierce, suddenly changed, his compressed lips parted, and he burst into the most uncontrolled and unforced laughter. He literally shook with laughter and for a long time he could not speak for laughing.

'So she didn't kiss her hand! So she didn't kiss it! So she ran away!' he kept shouting with a sort of morbid delight, with insolent delight, one might almost have said, if his delight had not been so unaffected. 'So the other one shouted she was a tigress! Well, she is a tigress! So she should be whipped by the public hangman! Yes, yes, so she should, so she should! That's exactly what I think – she should have been – she should have been long ago! You see, old man, I don't mind her being whipped by the public hangman, but not before I get over my infatuation. I quite understand the queen of impudence – that's her all over, she's revealed herself entirely in that hand-kissing episode – the she-devil! She's the queen of all the she-devils that you can imagine in the world! She's delightful in her way! So she ran home? I'm going to – oh – I'll run to her at once! Alyosha, don't blame me. You see, I quite agree that strangling is too good for her!'

'And what about Katerina?'

'I can see her too! I can see through her. I see her as I've never done before! What we have here is a discovery of all the four continents of the world – of the five, I mean! What a thing to do! And that's the same little Katya, the little schoolgirl, who was not afraid to beard an absurd, coarse army officer in his den and risk a mortal insult because of a generous idea to save her father! But her pride, the need for taking the risk, the challenge to fate, the boundless challenge! You say her aunt tried to stop her? That aunt of hers, you know, is a despot herself. She's the sister of the general's widow in Moscow. She used to look down her nose even more than her Moscow sister, but her husband was caught stealing government money, lost everything, his estate and all, and his proud spouse had to get off her high horse and could not mount it again ever after. So she was trying to hold Katya back, but she would not listen to her. She thinks she can conquer everything, that everything must give way to her, that she had only to wish and she could bewitch Grushenka. And who is to blame if she believed so much in herself and was so proud of herself? Do you think she kissed Grushenka's hand first on purpose, with some crafty design of her own? No, she really did fall for Grushenka, or rather not for Grushenka, but for her own fantastic dream, her own crazy scheme, because, you see, it was *her* dream, it was *her* crazy scheme! Poor Alyosha, how did you get away with your life from those two females? Tucked up your cassock and ran, eh? Ha, ha, ha!'

'But, Mitya, you don't seem to have realized how much you've insulted Katerina by telling Grushenka about what happened that day. You see, Grushenka immediately flung it in her face that she had gone "to gentlemen in secret to sell her beauty". Could there be any greater insult than that, Mitya?'

Alyosha was most of all worried by the thought that his brother seemed to be pleased with Katerina's humiliation, though, of course, that could not possibly be true.

'Good Lord!' Dmitry frowned fiercely and clapped his hand to his forehead.

He had only now realized it, though Alyosha had told him about the insult and Katerina's cry: 'Your brother is a cad!'

'Yes, perhaps I did tell Grushenka about that "dreadful day", as Katya called it. Yes, I did. I did tell her. I remember it now! It was at Mokroye. I was drunk, the gipsy women were singing. . . . But I was sobbing, I was sobbing then, I was on my knees, praying to Katya's image, and Grushenka understood it. She understood everything then. I remember, she cried herself. . . . Oh, damn! But it couldn't have been otherwise now, could it? Then she cried, but now – now "a dagger in the heart"! It's always like that with women.'

He dropped his eyes and sank into thought.

'Yes, I am a cad! A thorough-going cad!' he said suddenly in a gloomy voice. 'Makes no difference whether I cried or not, I'm still a cad! Tell her I accept the name if that's any consolation. Well, that's enough. Good-bye. What's the use of talking? It's not a particularly cheerful subject, is it? You go your way and I'll go mine. And I don't want to see you again except as a last resource. Good-bye, Alexey!'

He pressed Alyosha's hand warmly, and still looking down and without raising his head, as though tearing himself away, walked off in the direction of the town. Alyosha gazed after him, unable to believe that he had gone off so suddenly.

'Wait, Alexey!' cried Dmitry, suddenly turning back. 'I've another confession to make to you alone. Look at me! Look at me closely: see, here, here – a terrible disgrace is being prepared for me. (As he said 'here', Dmitry smote his chest with his fist and with so strange an expression as though the disgrace was actually lying on his chest, in some place, in a pocket perhaps, or hanging in a sewn-up bag round his neck.) You know me now: I'm a scoundrel, an acknow-ledged scoundrel! But know that what I may have done before or may do in the future, nothing, nothing can compare in baseness with the disgrace which I am carrying now, at this very moment, here on my breast – here – here, which is about to be carried out, but which I have the power to stop – I can stop it or I can carry it out, make a note of that! Well, then, I want you to know that I shall carry it out, that I shan't stop it. I told you everything just now, but I didn't tell you that because even I am not brazen enough to do so! I can still stop myself; if I do I can retrieve half of my lost honour tomorrow. But I won't do it. I shall carry out my despicable plan, and you can be a witness that I told you so beforehand and that I'm fully aware of what I'm doing! Death and perdition! No need to explain. You'll find it out in your own good time. The stinking back-alley and the she-devil! Good-bye. Don't pray for me. I don't deserve it. And, besides, it's unnecessary. It's quite unnecessary – I don't need it. Away! . . .'

And he was suddenly gone, this time for good. Alyosha went towards the monastery. 'What does he mean by saying that I shall never see him again? What is he talking about?' The whole thing seemed utterly absurd to him. 'I shall most certainly go and see him tomorrow. I'll find him. I shall make a point of finding him. What is he talking about? . . .'

*

He walked round the monastery and went straight to the hermitage through the pine-wood. The gate was opened to him, though at that hour no one was admitted. His heart trembled when he entered the elder's cell: Why, why had he gone out? Why had the elder sent him into the world? Here was peace. Here was holiness, and there was confusion, there was darkness in which one went astray at once and lost one's way.

In the cell he found the novice Porfiry and Father Paissy, who came every hour to inquire after Father Zossima, whose condition, Alyosha learnt with consternation, was getting worse and worse. This time he could not even hold his usual evening discourse with the monks. As a rule, the monks gathered in the elder's cell before retiring to bed every evening after service, and everyone confessed aloud his sins of the day, his sinful dreams, thoughts, temptations, and even the quarrels among themselves, if there had been any. Some of them confessed kneeling. The elder settled their difficulties, reconciled, exhorted, imposed penance, gave his blessing and dismissed them. It was against these 'confessions' that the opponents of the institution of elders protested, claiming that it was a profanation of the confession as a sacrament and almost a sacrilege, though it was not so. They even represented to the diocesan authorities that far from attaining a good end, such confessions actually and deliberately led to sin and temptation. It was asserted that many monks were loath to go to the elder, but went against their own will because everyone went, afraid lest they should be accused of pride and a rebellious spirit. It was said that, before going to the evening confession, some monks agreed beforehand what to say: 'I'll say that I lost my temper with you in the morning, and you confirm it', so that they would have something to say in order to get it over and done with. Alyosha knew that it really did happen sometimes. He also knew that there were monks who deeply resented the fact that, according to custom, they had first to bring their letters from home to the elder to be opened and read by him before they themselves could do so. The idea was, of course, that all this should be done freely and sincerely and without the slightest reservation, for the sake of voluntary submission and salutary guidance, but actually the whole thing sometimes turned out to be highly insincere, false, and affected. But the older and more experienced monks stood their ground, arguing that those who had come within those walls in order to obtain salvation would most certainly find all these acts of obedience and self-denial salutary and of great benefit; those, however, who protested and found it too hard to comply were no true monks, anyway, and their proper place was not in a monastery but in the world. 'One cannot protect oneself from sin and the devil neither in the world nor in church, so that there is no need to encourage sin.'

'He's grown much weaker, a drowsiness has come over him,' Paissy told Alyosha in a whisper after blessing him. 'It's difficult to rouse him. But there's no need to wake him. He was awake for five minutes, asked to send his blessing to the monks and requested the monks to say prayers for him at night. He intends to take the sacrament again in the morning. He remembered you, Alexey, and asked whether you had gone away. He was told you were in town. "That was what I blessed him for. His place is there and not here for the time being" – that was what he said about you. He remembered you lovingly, with anxiety – do you realize how greatly you've been favoured? But why did he decide that you should spend some time in the world? He must have foreseen something in your destiny! Understand, Alexey, that if you return to the world it will be to fulfil the duty imposed upon you by the elder and not for vain frivolities and worldly pleasures.'

Father Paissy went out. That the elder was dying, Alyosha did not doubt, though he might live for another day or two. Alyosha firmly and ardently resolved not to leave the monastery next day, but to remain with the elder to the end in spite of the promises he had given to his father, the Khokhlakovs, his brother, and Katerina. His heart was ablaze with love and he reproached himself bitterly for having been able to forget in town for one moment him whom he had left in the monastery on his death-bed and whom he revered more than anyone in the world. He went into the elder's little bedroom, knelt down and bowed to the ground before the sleeping old man. Father Zossima slept quietly, without stirring, breathing regularly and almost imperceptibly. His face was peaceful.

On returning to the other room, where the elder had received his guests in the morning, Alyosha, without undressing and only taking off his shoes, lay down on the hard and narrow leather sofa, on which he had always slept, every night, for a long time, bringing only a pillow. The mattress, about which his father had shouted in the morning, he had long forgotten to put under him. He merely took off his cassock and used it for a blanket. But before going to bed, he fell on his knees and prayed a long time. In his fervent prayer he did not ask God to clear up his confusion, but only craved the joyous emotion, the emotion that always came over his soul after praising and glorifying God, of which his prayer before bedtime always consisted. The joy that came over him always brought him a light and peaceful sleep. While saying his prayers now, he accidentally felt in his pocket the little pink note which Katerina's maid had handed him in the street. He was troubled, but he finished his prayer. Then after a moment's hesitation he opened the envelope. It contained a letter for him signed by Lise, Mrs Khokhlakov's young daughter, who had laughed at him in the morning in the presence of the elder.

'Dear Alexey,' she wrote, 'I am writing to you unknown to everybody, even Mother, and I know how wrong it is. But I can't live without telling you what has arisen in my heart, and this no one but us two must know for the time being. But how can I tell you what I want so much to tell you? Paper, they say, does not blush, but I can assure you that it is not true and that it is blushing now just as I am blushing now all over. Dear Alyosha, I love you. I have loved you ever since I was a little girl, since Moscow, where you were not at all as you are now, and I will love you all my life. I have chosen you with my heart, to unite with you, and to end our life together in old age. Of course, on condition that you leave the monastery. As for our age, we shall wait, as long as the law prescribes. By that time I shall certainly be well and be able to walk and dance. There can be no doubt about that.

'You see how I've thought it all out. But there is one thing I can't imagine: what you will think of me when you read this? I am always laughing and being naughty. I made you angry this morning, but I assure you that just now before I took up the pen, I prayed before the icon of the Virgin, and even now I am praying and almost crying.

'My secret is in your hands. When you come to see us tomorrow, I don't know how I shall be able to look you in the face. Oh, dear Alexey, what if I shan't be able to control myself again and burst out laughing, like a silly girl, as I did this morning when I looked at you? I'm afraid you will think me a bad girl who is only making fun of you and you won't believe my letter. And that's why I implore you, my dearest, if you have any pity for me, not to look me straight in the face when you come tomorrow, because when my eyes meet yours, I may burst out laughing, and especially as you'll be wearing your long cassock. . . . Even now I turn cold all over when I think of it. So that when you come in, don't look at me at all for some time, but look at Mummy or at the window. . . .

'There, I've written you a love letter. My goodness, what have I done? Alyosha, don't despise me, and please forgive me if I've done something very bad and annoyed you. Now the secret of my reputation, which has probably been ruined for ever, is in your hands.

'I'm sure I'm going to cry today. Good-bye for now, till our *terrifying* meeting. Lise.

'P.S. Alyosha, you must, must, must come! Lise.'

Alyosha read the note in amazement, read it through twice, thought it over, and then suddenly burst into a soft, sweet laugh. He gave a start: his laugh seemed sinful to him. But a moment later he laughed again just as softly and happily. He slowly replaced the note in the envelope, crossed himself and lay down. The perturbation of his spirit suddenly passed. 'God have mercy upon all of them, save and preserve them, the unhappy and rebellious in spirit, and set them on the right path. All the ways are thine: save them according to thy ways. Thou art Love, thou wilt send joy to all!' Alyosha murmured, crossing himself and sinking into tranquil sleep.

PART TWO

Book Four: Heartaches

I

Father Ferapont

ALYOSHA WAS ROUSED EARLY IN THE MORNING BEFORE DAWN.
The elder woke up feeling very weak, though he wished to get
out of bed and sit up in an armchair. He was in full possession
of his faculties; his face, though it looked very tired, was bright,
almost joyous, and there was a cheerful, cordial, welcoming look in
his eyes. 'Perhaps I shall not live through this day,' he said to Alyosha;
then he expressed the wish to confess and take the sacrament at once.
His confessor had always been Father Paissy. After the communion
came the ministering of extreme unction. The senior monks assembled
and the cell gradually filled up with the lesser monks of the hermitage.
Meantime it was daylight. Monks began arriving also from the
monastery. When the service was over, the elder wished to take
leave of everyone and he kissed them all. The cell being so crowded,
those who had come first went out and made room for others.
Alyosha stood beside the elder who was again seated in his armchair.
He spoke and taught as much as he could. Though weak, his voice
was still fairly firm. 'I have been teaching you for so many years,
beloved Fathers and brethren, and I've been talking aloud for so
many years that I seem to have acquired the habit of talking and
teaching you while I talk, so much so, indeed, dear Fathers and
brethren, that it's almost harder for me to keep silent than to talk,
in spite of my weakness,' he joked, gazing with deep emotion at
those who crowded round him. Alyosha remembered afterwards
something of what he said at that time. But though he spoke distinctly

and though his voice was sufficiently firm, his speech was rather incoherent. He spoke of many things and he seemed to be anxious before the moment of death to say everything he had had no time to say in his life, and not merely for the sake of instructing them, but as though craving to share his joy and rapture with all men and all creation and pour forth his heart once more while he yet lived. . . .

'Love one another, Fathers,' the elder taught (as far as Alyosha could remember afterwards). 'Love God's people. We are not holier than the laymen because we have come here and shut ourselves up within these walls, but, on the contrary, everyone who has come here has by the very fact of his coming here acknowledged that he is worse than all the worldly and than all men and all things on earth. . . . And the longer the monk lives within the walls of his monastery, the more deeply must he be conscious of that. For otherwise he would have had no reason for coming here at all. But when he realizes that he is not only worse than all the worldly, but that he's responsible to all men for all people and all things, for all human sins, universal and individual – only then will the aim of our seclusion be achieved. For you must know, beloved, that each one of us is beyond all question responsible for all men and all things on earth, not only because of the general transgressions of the world, but each one individually for all men and every single man on this earth. This realization is the crown of a monk's way of life, and, indeed, of every man on earth. For a monk is not a different kind of man, but merely such as all men on earth ought to be. It is only then that our hearts will be moved to a love that is infinite and universal and that knows no surfeit. It is then that each of you will have the power to gain the world by love and wash away the sins of the world by his tears. . . . Each of you must keep constant watch over your heart and confess your sins to yourselves unceasingly. Be not afraid of your sins, even when you perceive them, provided there is penitence, but make no conditions with God. And I say to you especially – be not proud. Be not proud before the small, and be not proud before the great. Hate not those who reject you, who defame you, who abuse and slander you. Hate not atheists, the teachers of evil, materialists, even the most wicked of them, let alone the good ones, for there are many good ones among them, particularly in our own day. Remember them in your prayers thus: Save, O Lord, all who have no one to pray for them, and save those, too, who do not want to pray to thee. And add: It is not in my pride that I beseech thee, O Lord, for that, for I am myself viler than all men and all things. . . . Love God's people, let not strangers drive off your flock, for if you fall asleep in your sloth and censorious pride, and, worse still, in covetousness, they will come from all countries and will drive off your flock. Expound the Gospel to the people unceasingly. . . . Be not usurious. . . . Do not love silver and gold, do not hoard it. . . . Have faith and hold fast the banner. Raise it on high. . . .'

The elder, however, spoke much more disjointedly than it is stated here or than Alyosha wrote down his words afterwards. Sometimes he broke off altogether, as though husbanding his strength, his breath failing him, but he seemed to be in a kind of ecstasy. They heard him with emotion, though many wondered at his words and found them obscure. . . . Afterwards they all remembered his words. When Alyosha happened to leave the cell for a moment, he was surprised by the general excitement and the air of expectation in the crowd of monks in and near the cell. Some of them looked almost anxious and others solemn. They were all expecting some miracle to happen immediately after the elder's death. This expectation was, from one point of view, almost frivolous, but even the most austere of the monks were affected by it. Father Paissy's face was the sternest of all. Alyosha had left the cell only because he had been mysteriously summoned through a monk by Rakitin who had arrived from town with a strange letter from Mrs Khokhlakov. The letter contained a very curious and opportune piece of news. It concerned the old woman of our town, a sergeant's widow, called Prokhorovna, who the day before had come with the other devout women of the people to receive the elder's blessing. She had asked the elder whether she might order prayers for the soul of her son Vassya, who had been stationed far away in Siberia, in Irkutsk, and from whom she had had no news for over a year. But the elder had told her sternly that she must not do anything of the sort, calling such a prayer a kind of sorcery. But he then forgave her on account of her ignorance, adding 'as though reading the book of the future' (as Mrs Khokhlakov put it in her letter), in consolation that 'her son Vassya was most certainly alive, and would either come himself very shortly or write to her and that she was to go home and wait there'. 'And what do you think?' Mrs Khokhlakov added ecstatically, 'the prophecy has been fulfilled, indeed more than fulfilled.' Immediately on her return home, the old woman was handed a letter from Siberia which had been waiting for her. But that was not all: in his letter, written on the road from Yekaterinburg, Vassya informed his mother that he was returning to Russia with an official and that three weeks after the receipt of the letter he hoped 'to embrace' his mother. Mrs Khokhlakov begged Alyosha urgently and warmly to report this newly performed 'miracle of prediction' to the Father Superior and the monks: 'Everyone, everyone ought to know of it!' she exclaimed at the conclusion of her letter. Her letter had been written in great haste, and the excitement of the writer could be perceived in every line of it. But Alyosha had no longer anything to tell the monks, for all of them knew already: Rakitin, having sent the monk to Alyosha, had also commissioned him 'to inform most respectfully his reverence Father Paissy, that he, Rakitin, had something of such great importance to tell him, that he dared not put it off for a single moment and begged him humbly to forgive him for his presumption'. As the monk had told Father Paissy of Rakitin's request before he saw Alyosha, there remained nothing for Alyosha to do after reading the letter but to hand it to Father Paissy merely as a further written confirmation of the 'miracle'. And even that stern and mistrustful man, though he frowned as he read of 'the miracle', could not wholly restrain a certain inward emotion. His eyes flashed and a grave and rapt smile suddenly appeared on his lips.

'Who knows?' it seemed to escape him suddenly. 'We may see greater things yet!'

'We may see greater things yet!' the monks kept repeating around.

But Father Paissy, frowning again, asked them all not to speak of it to anyone 'till it be more fully confirmed, for there is a great deal of thoughtlessness among the worldly and, besides, the whole thing might have occurred naturally,' he added cautiously, as if to salve his conscience, but scarcely believing his own mental reservation, which his listeners very clearly perceived. The 'miracle', of course, became known immediately to the whole monastery and to many people from outside who had come for mass. But it would seem that the man who was most struck by the miracle was the visiting little monk from 'Saint Sylvester', the small monastery of Obdorsk in the far North. He had come to pay his respects to the elder the day before, and it was he who, standing beside Mrs Khokhlakov and pointing to the 'cured' daughter of that lady, asked Father Zossima with much feeling, 'How do you presume to do such things?'

As a matter of fact, he was now somewhat bewildered and almost did not know what to believe. The evening before, he had paid a visit to Father Ferapont in his cell in the hermitage, standing apart behind the apiary, and had been greatly struck by that meeting which had made quite an extraordinary and terrifying impression on him. This Father Ferapont was the aged monk, the great observer of fasts and silence, whom we have already mentioned as one of elder Zossima's opponents and, most of all, an enemy of the institution of elders which he considered a harmful and frivolous innovation. He was a very dangerous opponent in spite of the fact that, as one who had taken the vow of silence, he scarcely uttered a word to anybody. He was so dangerous chiefly because a great many monks shared his opinion and because many of the people who came to visit the monastery looked upon him as a great saint and ascetic, although they had no doubt that he was a saintly fool. But it was just the fact of his being a saintly fool that fascinated them. Father Ferapont never went to see the elder Zossima. Although he lived in the hermitage, they did not worry him unduly by their rules, just because he behaved like a saintly fool. He was seventy-five, or perhaps more, and he lived behind the hermitage apiary, in a corner of the wall, in an old, almost dilapidated wooden cell, which had been built a great many years ago, in the last century, for Father Jonah, another great observer of fasts and silence, who had lived to a hundred and five and of whose exploits many curious stories were still told in the monastery and in the neighbourhood. Father Ferapont had at last succeeded seven years before in obtaining permission to take up his quarters in the same solitary little cell. It was simply a peasant's hut, but it looked like a chapel because it contained an extraordinary number of icons with lamps perpetually burning before them – all gifts brought by people outside the monastery. Father Ferapont was supposed to look after them and keep the lamps burning. It was said (and it is quite true) that he ate no more than two pounds of bread in three days; the bee-keeper, who lived close to the apiary, brought it to him every three days, but Father Ferapont rarely spoke a word even to the bee-keeper who waited upon him. The four pounds of bread, together with the Sunday wafer, which the Father Superior regularly sent him after late mass, made up the whole of his weekly rations. The water in his jug was changed every day. He rarely appeared at mass. Those who came to do homage to him saw him sometimes kneeling in prayer all day long without looking round. If he did occasionally enter into conversation with them, he was brief, abrupt, strange, and almost always rude. On very rare occasions, however, he would talk to visitors, but mostly he would just utter one strange saying, which always greatly puzzled his visitor, and, in spite of earnest entreaties, refused to utter another word in explanation. He had no priestly rank and was only an ordinary monk. There was a very strange rumour, though only among the most ignorant people, that Father Ferapont was in communication with heavenly spirits and conversed only with them and that was why he was silent with men. The Obdorsk monk, having got as far as the apiary at the direction of the bee-keeper, who was also a very surly and taciturn monk, went to the corner where Father Ferapont's cell stood. 'He may speak to you as you are a newcomer, but perhaps you won't get a word out of him,' the bee-keeper had warned him.

The monk, as he related afterwards, approached the cell in the greatest trepidation. It was rather late in the evening. Father Ferapont was sitting this time at the door of his cell on a low bench. An old elm was rustling faintly over him. A cold evening breeze was blowing. The Obdorsk monk prostrated himself before the saintly fool and asked his blessing.

'Do you want me to prostrate myself before you, too, monk?' said Father Ferapont. 'Get up!'

The monk got up.

'Blessing, and having been blessed, sit down beside me. Where have you come from?'

What struck the poor monk most of all was the fact that Father Ferapont, in spite of his undoubtedly strict fasting and great age, still looked such a vigorous old man. He was tall, held himself erect and did not stoop, and had a thin face, but a fresh and healthy complexion. There could be little doubt that he was still very vigorous. He was of athletic build. In spite of his advanced age, he was not even quite grey, and still had thick hair and a full beard, which had once been black. His eyes were grey, large, and luminous, but so prominent that one could not help being struck by it. He spoke with a strong northern accent. He was dressed in a peasant's long, reddish coat of coarse convict cloth, as it used to be called, and had a thick rope round his waist. His neck and chest were bare. His shirt, of the coarsest linen and almost black with dirt, not having been changed for months, showed from under his coat. It was said that he wore iron chains weighing thirty pounds under his coat. On his bare feet he wore a pair of old shoes which were almost falling to pieces.

'I'm from the small Obdorsk monastery, from St Sylvester,' the visiting monk answered humbly, observing the hermit with his sharp, inquisitive, though rather frightened little eyes.

'I've been at your Sylvester's. Stayed there, I have. Is Sylvester well?' The monk hesitated.

'You're a lot of fatheads! How do you keep the fasts?'

'Our fare is regulated in accordance with the ancient monastic rules. During Lent there are no meals provided on Mondays, Wednesdays, and Fridays. On Tuesdays and Thursdays the monks have white bread, stewed fruit with honey, cloudberries or salt cabbage, and oatmeal porridge. On Saturdays white cabbage soup, pea soup with noodles, thin porridge, all with vegetable oil. On weekdays we have cabbage soup, dried fish, and porridge. From Monday till Saturday evening, during the six days in Holy Week, we have bread and water, and that, too, sparingly, and no other food is cooked; taking no food every day, if possible, but as it is ordered for the first week in Lent. On Good Friday nothing is eaten, and likewise on the Saturday nothing is eaten till three o'clock and then only a little bread and water and a cup of wine afterwards. On Holy Thursday we have something cooked without oil and we drink wine, or we have something not cooked at all. Inasmuch as it is laid down by the Laodicean Council for Holy Thursday: "It is not seemly to break your fast on the Thursday of the last week in Lent and to dishonour the whole of Lent." This is how it's done at our monastery. But,' added the monk, plucking up courage, 'what is that compared with you, Father? For you have nothing but bread and water all the year round, and even at Easter, and you consume as much bread in a week as we do in two days. Verily, such great abstinence is a wondrous thing to behold.'

'And mushrooms?' Father Ferapont asked suddenly.

'Mushrooms?' the little monk repeated in surprise.

'Aye,' replied Father Ferapont, 'I'm thinking of giving up their bread, for I don't need it at all, and going away into the woods and living on mushrooms or wild berries. They can't give up their bread here, and so they're still in bondage to the devil. Nowadays the infidels say there's no need to fast. Haughty and impious is this judgement of theirs.'

'Aye, that's true enough,' sighed the monk.

'And have you seen devils among those?' asked Father Ferapont.

'Which "those"?' the little monk inquired timidly.

'I went to the Father Superior's on Trinity Sunday last year, and haven't been there since. I saw a devil sitting in one monk's bosom. Hiding under his cassock he was, only his horns poking out. Another had one peeping out of his pocket. Such sharp eyes he had, too. Afraid of me. Aye, he was that. Still another had one in his stomach, inside his unclean belly, and another had one hanging round his neck, clutching at it, and he was carrying him about without seeing him. . . .'

'And you – you see them?' inquired the little monk.

'Aye, I see them. I see through them. As I was coming out from the Father Superior's, I saw one hiding from me behind the door. A big one he was, three feet and more in height. Had a thick, long, brown tail. Just then he got the tip of his tail in the crack of the door and, well, being no fool, I slammed the door to suddenly and pinched his tail in it. You should have heard him squealing! Began struggling, he did, but I made the sign of the cross over him three times and that was the end of him. Died on the spot, he did. Like a crushed spider. I suppose he must have rotted away by now there in the corner and is stinking the place out, but they don't see and don't smell it. Haven't been there for a year. I'm telling you this, as you're a foreigner.'

'Your words are dreadful, Father! And, great and blessed Father,' the little monk grew bolder and bolder, 'is it true – the great things they tell about you even in distant lands, I mean, that you are in constant communication with the Holy Ghost?'

'Aye, he does fly down. It happens sometimes.'

'How does he fly down? In what shape?'

'As a bird.'

'The Holy Ghost in the shape of a dove?'

'Aye, there's the Holy Ghost and there is the Holy Spirit. The Holy Spirit is different. He can appear in the shape of some other bird: sometimes as a swallow, sometimes as a goldfinch, and sometimes as a tom-tit.'

'How do you know him from an ordinary tom-tit?'

'He speaks.'

'How does he speak? In what language?'

'In human language.'

'And what does he tell you?'

'Well, today he told me that a fool would come to see me and ask me unseemly questions. You want to know a lot, monk.'

'Your words are dreadful, most blessed and most holy Father,' the monk said, shaking his head.

There was, however, a look of incredulity in his timid little eyes.

'Do you see this tree?' asked Father Ferapont after a short pause.

'I do, most blessed Father.'

'You think it's an elm, but it looks different to me.'

'What does it look like to you?' the little monk asked after a pause, in vain expectation.

'It happens at night. See those two branches? At night it is Christ holding out his arms to me and seeking me with those arms. I see it clearly and tremble. It's terrible, oh, terrible!'

'What's there so terrible about it if it's Christ himself?'

'He may snatch me up and carry me into heaven.'

'Alive?'

'In the spirit and glory of Elijah. Haven't you heard? He'll put his arms round me and take me up.'

Though after that conversation the Obdorsk monk returned to the cell he was sharing with one of the monks in great perplexity of mind, his heart was undoubtedly more with Father Ferapont than with Father Zossima. The Obdorsk monk stood first of all for fasting, and it was not strange for so great an observer of fasts as Father Ferapont 'to see marvels'. His words, of course, sounded rather absurd, but God knows what meaning lay hidden in them, and, besides, the words and actions of the saintly fools who lived by begging were a great deal stranger. As for the story of the devil's pinched tail, he was quite ready to believe it not only figuratively but literally. Indeed, it gave him great pleasure to believe it. Besides, he was greatly prejudiced against the institution of elders even before his arrival at the monastery. He had known about it only from hearsay and, like many others, regarded it definitely as a harmful innovation. But after spending a day at the monastery, he had discovered that a number of thoughtless monks who were opposed to the institution of elders were murmuring in secret. He was, besides, by nature a meddlesome and nimble-witted monk, with an insatiable curiosity about everything. That was why the great news of the fresh 'miracle' performed by the elder Zossima threw him into a state of great bewilderment. Alyosha recalled afterwards the figure of the inquisitive Obdorsk visitor darting to and fro among the groups of monks crowding inside and round the elder's cell, listening and asking questions. But he paid little attention to him at the time and only remembered everything afterwards. . . . And indeed, he had other things to think of just then, for the elder Zossima, who had felt tired again, had gone back to bed and, as he was closing his eyes, he remembered him and sent for him. Alyosha came running at once. There were only Father Paissy, Father Joseph, and the novice Porfiry in the cell at the time. The elder opened his weary eyes and, looking intently at Alyosha, suddenly asked him:

'Are your people expecting you, my son?'

Alyosha hesitated.

'Have they no need of you? Did you not promise yesterday to see some of them today?'

'I did – to my father – my brothers and – others too.'

'Well, you see. You must go. Don't grieve. I shall not die without saying my last word on earth in your presence. I shall say that word to you, my son. I shall bequeath it to you. To you, my dear son, for you love me. But now go and see those you've promised to see.'

Alyosha immediately obeyed, though it was hard for him to go. But the promise that he should hear his last word on earth and, above all, that it would be bequeathed to him filled his soul with rapture. He made haste so as to finish his business in town and be back as soon as possible. As it happened, Father Paissy, too, uttered a few parting words to him which impressed and surprised him greatly. That was when the two of them had left the elder's cell.

'Always remember, young man,' Father Paissy began at once

without any preliminary introduction, 'that secular science, having become a great force in the world, has, especially in the last century, investigated everything divine handed down to us in the sacred books. After a ruthless analysis the scholars of this world have left nothing of what was held sacred before. But they have only investigated the parts and overlooked the whole, so much so that one cannot help being astonished at their blindness. And so the whole remains standing before their eyes as firm as ever and the gates of hell shall not prevail against it. Has it not existed for nineteen centuries and does it not exist today in the inmost hearts of individual men and the masses of the people? Why, it is living in the hearts of the atheists who have destroyed everything, and is as firmly rooted there as ever! For even those who have renounced Christianity and are rebelling against it, are essentially of the same semblance as Christ, and have always been that, for so far neither their wisdom nor the ardour of their hearts has been able to create a higher ideal of man or of man's dignity than the one shown by Christ in the days of old. And any attempts that have been made resulted only in monstrosities. Remember this especially, young man, for you are being sent into the world by your dying elder. Perhaps when you recall this great day, you will not forget my words, given you as a heartfelt send-off, for you are young and the temptations of the world are very great and beyond your strength to withstand them. Well, now go, my orphan boy.'

With these words Father Paissy blessed him. As he left the monastery and thought over Father Paissy's parting words, Alyosha suddenly realized that he had found a new and unexpected friend in the monk who had been so severe and stern to him before, a new guide who loved him warmly, just as if the elder Zossima had bequeathed him to him before his death. 'Perhaps that was what had passed between them,' Alyosha reflected suddenly. The unexpected learned discourse which he had just heard – just that and not something else – merely bore witness to the warmth of Father Paissy's heart: he was in great haste to arm the young man's mind for a fight against temptations and to fence in the young soul bequeathed to him by the strongest fence he could imagine.

2

At His Father's

FIRST of all Alyosha went to see his father. As he approached the house, he remembered that the day before his father had insisted that he should enter it without being noticed by his brother Ivan. 'Why that?' Alyosha thought suddenly now. 'If father wants to tell something to me alone in secret, then why should I go in in secret? I suppose in his excitement yesterday he wanted to say something else, but did not manage to,' he decided. He was nevertheless glad when Marfa, who opened the gate to him (Grigory, it seemed, was lying ill in the cottage), told him in reply to his question that Ivan had gone out two hours before.

'And my father?'

'He's got up, sir, and is having his coffee,' Marfa replied somewhat drily.

Alyosha went in. The old man was sitting alone at the table, in his slippers and an old overcoat. He was looking through some accounts, just to pass away the time and without apparently paying much attention to them. He was quite alone in the house (Smerdyakov had also gone out to do some shopping for dinner). But it was not the accounts that interested him. Though he had got up early and done his best to keep up his spirits, he looked tired and weak. His forehead, on which huge purple bruises had come out during the night, was tied round with a red handkerchief. His nose, too, had swollen up terribly in the night, and it, too, was covered with a few small bruises, which certainly gave his whole face a peculiarly spiteful and irritable appearance. The old man was aware of it himself and he glared in an unfriendly way at Alyosha as he came in.

'The coffee's cold,' he cried brusquely. 'I'm not offering you any. I shall be having nothing but lenten fish soup myself today and I'm not inviting anyone to dinner. What have you come for?'

'To find out how you are,' said Alyosha.

'I see. But didn't I tell you myself yesterday to come? It's all a lot of nonsense. You shouldn't have bothered. I knew, though, that you'd drag yourself here at once.'

He said this in a most unfriendly way. Meanwhile he got up and looked anxiously at his nose in the looking-glass (perhaps for the fortieth time that morning). He also began adjusting the red handkerchief on his forehead more becomingly.

'A red one's better,' he remarked sententiously. 'In a white one it would have looked like a hospital. Well, what's been going on at your monastery? How's your elder?'

'He's very bad, he may die today,' replied Alyosha, but his father had never bothered to listen and had forgotten his question at once.

'Ivan's gone out,' he said suddenly. 'He's doing his damnedest to get Mitya's fiancée for himself. That's why he's staying here,' he added spitefully, making a wry face and glaring at Alyosha.

'He didn't tell you that, did he?' asked Alyosha.

'He did. Long ago. Three weeks ago, as a matter of fact. He hasn't come here, too, to get me murdered in secret, has he? He must have come for something!'

'Good heavens, why do you say such things?' Alyosha said, looking terribly embarrassed.

'It's true he doesn't ask for money, but he won't get a penny from me all the same. You see, my dear Alexey, I've made up my mind to go on living as long as possible. Don't make any mistake about that. That's why I need every penny I have. And the longer I live, the more I shall need it,' he went on, walking from one corner of the room to the other, his hands thrust in the pockets of his loose, soiled coat made of yellow summer calamanco. 'At present I'm still a man in the prime of life. I'm only fifty-five. But I'd like to go on being a man in the full sense of the word for another twenty years. When I grow old, I shall be no damn good any longer. No woman will come to me of her own accord. It's then that I shall need money. And that's why I'm saving up now more and more for myself alone, sir. Yes, dear son, make no mistake about that. I intend to carry on with my filthy kind of life to the end. Get that into your head once and for all. This filthy kind of life is sweet, sir: everyone abuses it and everyone lives it, except that they all do it surreptitiously, while I do it openly. It's because I make no bones about it that all the filthy swine are attacking me for being so simple-minded. As for your paradise, my dear sir, I want none of it. Make no mistake about that, either. Besides, your paradise is no proper place for a decent fellow, even if it does exist. In my opinion, a man falls asleep and doesn't wake up, and that's all there is to it. Order prayers for me in church, if you like. If you don't, to hell with you! That's my philosophy. Ivan spoke well here yesterday, though we were all drunk. Ivan's a boaster, and he has no real learning . . . nor any particular education, either. Keeps silent and grins at you without uttering a word. That's the only way he makes people think he's so clever.'

Alyosha listened to him in silence.

'Why won't he talk to me? And when he does talk, he gives himself airs. Your Ivan is a blackguard, sir! And I'm going to marry Grushenka any time I like. For, you see, my dear sir, a chap who has money has only to want something and he'll get it. That's what Ivan is so afraid of. He keeps watch over me to prevent me from marrying her. That's why he's egging on Mitya to marry Grushenka: he thinks he'll prevent Grushenka marrying me that way (as though I'd leave him my money, if I don't marry the slut!). Then again if Mitya marries her, Ivan will get his rich fiancée – that's what he is counting on! He's a blackguard, your Ivan is, sir!'

'How irritable you are!' said Alyosha. 'It's because of what happened yesterday. You'd better go and lie down.'

'You see,' the old man observed suddenly, as though it had occurred to him for the first time, 'you say that and I'm not angry with you, but if Ivan had said it, I'd be angry. It's only with you that I've had my good moments, for I'm a vicious man by nature.'

'You're not vicious, but warped,' said Alyosha with a smile.

'Listen, I had a good mind to have that bandit Mitya locked up today, and I'm not sure even now what I shall decide. Of course, in our modern times it's the fashion to regard honouring your father and mother as a prejudice, but I believe that legally it's not permitted even in our enlightened times to drag one's father about by the hair and kick him in the face on the floor in his own house and come and brag about murdering him – and all that, mind you, in the presence of witnesses! If I wanted to, I'd make him suffer all right. I could get him locked up for what he did yesterday.'

'So you don't want to tell the police, do you?'

'Ivan has dissuaded me. I shouldn't have taken any notice of Ivan, but there's something else to consider.' And bending over Alyosha, he went on in a confidential undertone: 'If I got the scoundrel locked up, she'd hear of it and run to him at once. But if she hears today that he has thrashed me, a feeble old man, within an inch of my life, she may give him up and come to see me. . . . That's the way we're made – we do everything contrary to what's expected of us. I know her through and through! Well, you'll have a drop of brandy, won't you? Pour yourself out a cup of cold coffee, and I'll pour a quarter of a glass of brandy in it. Makes the coffee taste twice as good.'

'No, thank you, but I'll take that roll, if I may,' said Alyosha, and taking a halfpenny French roll he put it in the pocket of his cassock. 'And you'd better not have any more brandy, either,' he suggested cautiously, peering into the old man's face.

'You're right, my boy. It merely irritates but doesn't soothe me. But, perhaps, just a little glass. . . . I'll get it out of the little cupboard. . . .'

He unlocked the 'little cupboard', poured himself out a glass, drank it, then locked the cupboard and put the key back in his pocket.

'That's enough. One glass won't kill me.'

'You see, you're a much kinder man now,' said Alyosha, smiling.

'Well, I love you even without brandy, but with blackguards, I'm a blackguard, too. Ivan isn't going to Chermashnya – why not? Because he has to spy on me. Wants to see how much I'll give Grushenka if she comes. They're all blackguards. I don't care a damn for Ivan. You see, I don't know Ivan at all. Don't know what sort of a fellow he is. Where did he spring from? He isn't our kind at all. And does he really think I'm going to leave him anything? Why, I won't make a will at all – make no mistake about that! As for Mitya, I'll crush him like a black beetle. I squash black beetles at night with my slipper: it crunches when you step on it. Your Mitya will crunch, too. *Your* Mitya, because you love him. You see, you love him, and I'm not afraid of your loving him. But if Ivan loved him, I would be afraid of it. But Ivan loves nobody. Ivan is not one of us. People like Ivan, my boy, are not like us – they're like dust driven by the wind. When the wind blows, the dust will be gone. I had a silly idea in my head yesterday when I told you to come today: I wondered if I could find out about Mitya through you. I mean if I let him have a thousand, or maybe two thousand, now, would the dirty pauper agree to get out of here altogether for five years or, better still, for thirty-five? Without Grushenka. Give her up alto-gether. What do you think?'

'I – I'll ask him,' Alyosha murmured. 'If you gave him three thousand, he might perhaps —'

'Nonsense! You needn't ask him now – no need to say anything to him! I've changed my mind. I got that silly idea into my head yesterday in a silly moment. I shan't give him anything. Not a damn thing. I want my money myself,' cried the old man, waving his hands. 'I'll crush him like a black beetle without it. Don't say any-thing to him or you'll be raising his hopes. And there's nothing for you to do here, either. You can go now – go! Is that fiancée of his, whom he has been hiding from me so carefully, going to marry him or not? Katerina, I mean. You went to see her yesterday, didn't you?'

'She won't leave him for anything in the world.'

'Aye, it's fellows like him that these nice young ladies love – rakes and blackguards! Rubbish – that's what these pale young ladies are, I tell you. Of course, if – oh well, if I'd been as young as he and if I had the looks I had then (for I was a better-looking man than he when I was twenty-eight), I'd have made the same conquests as he. The dirty swine! But he won't get Grushenka all the same. No, sir! . . . I'll rub his nose in the dirt! . . . '

He got into a rage again at the last words.

'You'd better go, too,' he snapped out harshly. 'There's nothing for you to do here today.'

Alyosha went up to say good-bye to him and kissed him on the shoulder.

'Why did you do that?' the old man asked with some surprise. 'We'll see each other again. Or don't you think so?'

'Not at all. I did it without thinking.'

'I didn't mean anything, either. I, too, said it without thinking. I say, I say,' he shouted after him, 'come again soon, I'll have a fish soup for you, a special one not like today. Be sure to come! To-morrow – you hear? – come tomorrow!'

And as soon as Alyosha had gone out of the door, he went up to the cupboard again and knocked back another half glass of brandy.

'No more!' he muttered, clearing his throat.

He locked the cupboard again, put the key in his pocket, then went into his bedroom, lay down exhausted on the bed and fell asleep at once.

3

He Gets Involved with Schoolboys

'THANK goodness he didn't ask me about Grushenka,' Alyosha thought in his turn as he left his father's house and turned towards Mrs Khokhlakov's, 'or I might have had to tell him about my meeting with Grushenka yesterday.' Alyosha felt painfully that since the night before the combatants had gathered new strength and that their hearts had hardened again with the coming of daylight. 'Father,' he thought, 'is exasperated and spiteful. He's hatched out some plan, too. And what about Dmitry? He also had grown more determined overnight, and, I suppose, he also is exasperated and spiteful and, no doubt, he's got some plan, too. Oh, I simply must manage to find him today!'

But Alyosha's thoughts were soon interrupted: he became involved in an incident on the way which, though apparently of no great consequence, made a great impression on him. As soon as he had walked across the square and turned to cross the bridge leading into Mikhailovsky Street, which runs parallel to the High Street but is separated from it by a ditch (our whole town is criss-crossed by ditches), he saw on the other side of the bridge a small group of young schoolboys between the ages of nine and twelve. They were going home from school with their satchels on their backs or with leather bags slung over their shoulders, some in school tunics, others in overcoats, and some even wore high boots turned over at the top, in which small boys, spoilt by well-to-do parents, particularly love to show off. The whole group was discussing something animatedly and apparently holding a consultation. Alyosha could never pass by children without feeling interested in them. That had happened to him in Moscow, too, and though he was particularly fond of children of three years old or thereabouts, he also liked children of ten and eleven. That was why, greatly worried as he now was, he felt a sudden desire to go up to the children and start a conversation with them. As he drew close, he scrutinized their rosy, animated faces and all of a sudden noticed that all the boys had one or two stones in their hands. Behind the ditch, about thirty paces from the group, another boy was standing by a fence. He, too, was a schoolboy with a bag at his side, about ten years old or perhaps less, pale, delicate-looking, and with flashing black eyes. He was watching the group of six schoolboys attentively and searchingly. They were obviously his schoolmates who had just left school with him and with whom he evidently had a feud. Alyosha went up to them, and addressing a fair, curly-headed, rosy-cheeked boy in a black tunic, observed after examining him closely:

'When I used to wear a bag like yours, I always carried it on my left side so as to be able to reach it with my right hand. You've got yours on the right side and you'll find it inconvenient to get at it.'

Without any premeditation or guile Alyosha began straight with that practical remark, and indeed a grown-up person could not begin in any other way if he wished to gain at once the confidence of a child and, especially, of a whole group of children. One must begin in a serious and practical manner so as to be on a perfectly equal footing. Alyosha understood it instinctively.

'But he's left-handed, sir,' another high-spirited, healthy-looking boy of eleven answered at once.

The other five boys stared at Alyosha in silence.

'He even throws stones with his left hand,' a third boy observed.

At that moment a stone flew into the group, grazing the left-handed boy, but missing them, though it was carefully and vigorously aimed by the boy on the other side of the ditch.

'Let him have it! Give it to him, Smurov!' they all shouted.

But Smurov (the left-handed boy) was not slow in retaliating: he threw a stone at the boy on the other side of the ditch, but missed him: the stone hit the ground. The boy on the other side of the ditch at once flung another stone at the group, aiming this time straight at Alyosha and hitting him rather painfully on the shoulder. The boy on the other side of the ditch had his pockets stuffed with stones. That could be clearly seen from the way his pockets bulged.

'He aimed at you, sir, at you, he did it on purpose,' the boys shouted, laughing. 'You're Karamazov, aren't you, sir? Come on boys, all together – fire!'

And six stones flew from the group all at once. One struck the boy on the head. He fell down, but immediately jumped to his feet and began throwing stones ferociously at the group. Both sides began exchanging shots incessantly, many of the group having their pockets full of stones as well.

'What are you doing?' cried Alyosha. 'You ought to be ashamed of yourselves! Six against one? Why, you'll kill him!'

He leapt forward to meet the flying stones and shield the boy on the other side of the ditch. Three or four boys stopped throwing stones for a moment.

'He started it, sir!' shouted a boy in a red shirt in an exasperated, childish voice. 'He's a beast! He stuck his penknife into Krasotkin in class today and drew blood, sir. Only Krasotkin didn't want to tell on him, but he must be given a good hiding.'

'But whatever for? I suppose you tease him. Don't you?'

'Look out, sir, he's hit you in the back again. He knows you, sir,' the boys shouted. 'It's at you he's throwing now, not at us. Come on, boys, all of you, at him again. Don't miss him, Smurov!'

And another exchange of stones began, and a very vicious one this time. The boy on the other side of the ditch was hit in the chest. He uttered a scream, began to cry, and ran away uphill towards Mikhailovsky Street. The boys yelled after him: 'See, he's funked it! He's running away! Bast-sponge!'

'You don't know, sir, what a rotter he is,' the boy in the tunic, who seemed to be the eldest in the group, repeated with flashing eyes. 'Killing's too good for him.'

'Why, what's wrong with him?' asked Alyosha. 'Is he a tell-tale?'

The boys looked at one another as though in derision.

'Are you going that way, too, sir? To Mikhailovsky Street?' went on the same boy. 'You'd better catch him up. You see, he's stopped again. He's waiting and looking at you.'

'He's looking at you! He's looking at you!' the boys echoed.

'You ask him if he likes a bath bast-sponge, a tattered one. Please, ask him that.'

There was a general outburst of laughter. Alyosha looked at them and they at him.

'Don't go near him, sir, he'll hurt you,' Smurov cried warningly.

'I'm not going to ask him about a bast-sponge, for I expect you must be teasing him with that. But I am going to find out from him why you hate him so much.'

'Yes, sir, find out, find out!' the boys laughed.

Alyosha crossed the bridge and went up the hill by the fence straight towards the ostracized boy.

'Look out, sir,' the boys shouted after him warningly, 'he won't be afraid of you. He'll stick a knife into you when you're not looking, just as he did into Krasotkin.'

The boy waited for him without budging. Coming up to him, Alyosha saw a boy of no more than nine years old, undersized and weakly, with a longish, pale, thin face and large dark eyes, looking vindictively at him. He was dressed in a rather threadbare old overcoat, which he had monstrously outgrown. His bare arms protruded from his sleeves. There was a large patch on the right knee of his trousers and a large hole, obviously heavily blackened with ink, on the right boot where the big toe was. Both pockets of his overcoat were bulging with stones. Alyosha stopped within two paces of him and looked at him questioningly. Realizing at once from Alyosha's eyes that he had no intention of beating him, the boy, too, dropped his defiant air and himself opened the conversation.

'I'm one and they're six, sir,' he said suddenly, with flashing eyes. 'I'll beat them all by myself.'

'I expect one of the stones must have hurt you badly,' observed Alyosha.

'And I hit Smurov on the head!' cried the boy.

'They said that you knew me and you threw a stone at me for some reason. Is it true?' asked Alyosha.

The boy looked darkly at him.

'I don't know you. Do you know me?' Alyosha went on with his interrogation.

'Leave me alone!' the boy suddenly cried irritably, without, however, stirring from his place, as though waiting for something and again with a malicious flash in his eyes.

'Very well, I'm going,' said Alyosha. 'Only I don't know you and I don't tease you. They told me how to tease you, but I don't want to tease you. Good-bye!'

'A monk in fancy trousers!' cried the boy, watching Alyosha with the same malicious and defiant look and taking up a defensive attitude, thinking that Alyosha would most certainly attack him now. But Alyosha turned back, looked at him, and walked away. But before he had gone three steps, a huge stone, the biggest one in the boy's pocket, hit him a painful blow in the back.

'So you'll hit a man from behind, will you? So they're telling the truth. You do attack people when they're not looking!' Alyosha said, turning round again.

But this time the boy, in a rage, threw a stone straight in Alyosha's face, but Alyosha managed to shield himself in time, and the stone struck him on the elbow.

'Aren't you ashamed of yourself?' Alyosha cried. 'What did I do to you?'

The boy waited defiantly and in silence, expecting that now Alyosha would most certainly attack him; seeing, however, that he made no attempt to do so even now, he grew vicious like a little wild beast: he dashed forward and flew at Alyosha himself, and before Alyosha had time to move, the vicious boy lowered his head, and seizing his left hand with both of his, bit his middle finger painfully. He dug his teeth into it and did not let go for ten seconds. Alyosha cried out with pain, trying with all his might to pull his finger away. The boy let go at last and jumped back the same distance. The finger had been badly bitten to the bone, close to the nail; it began to bleed. Alyosha took out his handkerchief and tied it firmly round his injured hand. It took him a whole minute to bandage it. The boy stood waiting all the time. At last Alyosha raised his gentle eyes and looked at him.

'All right,' he said, 'you see how badly you've bitten me, don't you? You're satisfied, aren't you? Now tell me what have I done to you?'

The boy looked at him in surprise.

'Though I don't know you at all and see you for the first time,' Alyosha went on in the same quiet tone of voice, 'it's quite impossible that I shouldn't have done something to you. You wouldn't have hurt me like that for nothing. So tell me, please, what I've done and how I've wronged you.'

Instead of answering, the boy burst out crying loudly, at the top of his voice, and suddenly ran away from Alyosha. Alyosha walked slowly after him towards Mikhailovsky Street, and for a long time he saw the little boy running in the distance, without slowing down or turning round, and probably still crying at the top of his voice.

He made up his mind to find him as soon as he had time and solve the mystery which had struck him so forcibly. Just now he had no time.

4

At the Khokhlakovs'

HE soon reached Mrs Khokhlakov's house, a beautiful, two-storied stone house, one of the best houses in our little town. Though Mrs Khokhlakov spent most of her time in another province, where she had an estate, or in Moscow, where she had a house of her own, she also owned a house in our town, inherited by her fathers and fore-fathers. The estate she owned in our district, too, was the largest of her three estates, and yet she had hitherto visited our province very rarely. She ran out to Alyosha in the hall.

'Have you received my letter about the new miracle?' she said rapidly and nervously. 'Have you? Have you?'

'Yes.'

'Did you show it to everybody? He restored the son to his mother!'

'He will die today,' said Alyosha.

'I've heard. I know. Oh, how I long to talk to you! To you or to anyone else about it all. No, to you, to you! And what a pity I can't see him again! The whole town is excited. Everyone's expecting something to happen. But now – do you know that Katerina is here now?'

'Oh, that's lucky!' cried Alyosha. 'So I'll be able to see her here. She told me yesterday not to fail to come and see her today.'

'I know everything, everything. I've heard all the details about what happened at her place yesterday and – and the dreadful trouble she had with that – that horrible creature. *C'est tragique*, and if I'd been in her place – I simply don't know what I'd have done if I'd been in her place! But your brother Dmitry, too, has behaved dis-gracefully – oh dear! I'm afraid, Alexey, I'm in a dreadful muddle. Do you know who's here? Your brother – I don't mean that dreadful brother of yours, but the other one, Ivan. He's sitting with her and talking – they're having a most important conversation. . . . Oh, if you knew what's happening between them now! It's simply awful!

It's a heartache, I tell you. It's like some frightful folk-tale which it's quite impossible to believe: they're both ruining themselves, goodness only knows why. They realize it themselves and they seem to enjoy it. I've been waiting for you! I've been longing to see you! You see, I simply can't bear it. I'll tell you all about it presently, but I've got to tell you something else now, something frightfully important – goodness me, I'd quite forgotten that it was so important. Tell me, why is Lise in hysterics? The moment she heard you coming in, she began to be hysterical.'

'It's you who're hysterical now, not me, Mother,' Lise's sweet voice was heard saying rapidly through a tiny crack of the door of one of the rooms.

The crack was very tiny and her voice, too, had a catch in it, just as though she wanted terribly to laugh, but did her utmost to suppress it. Alyosha at once noticed the little crack in the door, and Lise must have been trying to look through it at him from her wheelchair, but that he could not see.

'I shouldn't wonder, Lise, I shouldn't wonder. Your caprices will drive me into hysterics too. But then, dear Alexey, she's so ill. She's been so ill all night, feverish and moaning! I could hardly wait for the morning and Herzenstube. This Herzenstube always comes and says he can make nothing of it and that one has to wait. As soon as you approached our house, she uttered a scream, had an attack of hysterics and told me to wheel her back into her old room here. . . .'

'I had no idea he was coming, Mother, and it wasn't at all because of him that I wanted to be wheeled into this room.'

'That's not true, Lise. Julia ran to tell you that Alexey was coming. She was on the look-out for you.'

'Darling Mother, that's awfully silly of you! And if you want to make up for it and say something awfully clever, Mother dear, then you'd better tell Mr Alexey Karamazov, who has just come in, that he has shown how little clever he is by deciding to come to see us today after what happened yesterday and in spite of the fact that everyone is laughing at him.'

'Lise, you go too far and I'm afraid I shall have to be very severe with you. Who's laughing at him? I'm so glad he has come. I need him, I simply can't do without him. Oh, my dear Alexey, I'm terribly unhappy!'

'But what's the matter with you, Mother darling?'

'Oh, Lise, all these caprices of yours, your restlessness, your illness, that frightful night of fever, that frightful and everlasting Herzenstube, everlasting, everlasting – that's what's so awful! And everything, in fact, everything! And even that miracle, too! Oh, my dear Alexey, I can't tell you how that miracle has upset me, how it has shattered me! And now that tragedy in the drawing-room there, which I simply can't bear. I can't bear it, I tell you, I can't bear it. A comedy, perhaps, not a tragedy. Tell me, do you think Father Zossima will live till tomorrow? Oh dear, what is happening to me? I keep closing my eyes and I can see that it's all nonsense, a lot of nonsense!'

'I wonder if you would mind giving me a clean rag,' Alyosha interrupted suddenly, 'to bandage my finger with. I've injured it badly and it hurts me very much now.'

Alyosha unwound his bitten finger. The handkerchief was soaked with blood. Mrs Khokhlakov uttered a scream and screwed up her eyes.

'Good heavens, what a wound! This is frightful!'

But as soon as Lise saw Alyosha's finger through the crack, she flung the door wide open.

'Come in, come in here at once,' she cried, insistently and peremptorily. 'No nonsense now, please! Goodness, how could you stand there all this time without saying anything? He might have bled to death, Mother! Where did it happen? How did you do it? First of all, water, water! You must wash your wound thoroughly. Simply put it in cold water to ease the pain and keep it there, keep it there all the time. Quickly, quickly, some water, Mother, in a basin. And do hurry, Mother!' she concluded nervously.

She was terribly frightened; Alyosha's wound completely unnerved her.

'Shouldn't we send for Herzenstube, dear?' Mrs Khokhlakov cried.

'Mother, you'll be the death of me. Your Herzenstube will come and say that he can't make anything of it! Water, water! Mother, for goodness' sake, go yourself and hurry Julia. She's got stuck somewhere and she never can come quickly! But do hurry, Mother, or I shall die. . . .'

'Why, it's nothing!' cried Alyosha, alarmed at their alarm.

Julia ran in with water. Alyosha put his finger in it.

'Mother, for goodness' sake, fetch some lint, lint and that muddy caustic lotion for wounds – what do you call it? We've got some, we've got some, we've got some! You know where the bottle is, Mother. In your bedroom. In the medicine box on the right. There's a big bottle of it there and lint.'

'I'll bring everything in a minute, Lise, only, please, don't scream and don't fuss. You see how bravely Alexey bears his pain. And where did you get such a frightful wound, Alexey?'

Mrs Khokhlakov left the room hurriedly. This was all Lise was waiting for.

'First of all, answer my question,' she said rapidly to Alyosha. 'Where did you manage to get that dreadful wound? And then I shall talk to you about something quite different. Well?'

Feeling instinctively that the time before her mother's return was precious to her, Alyosha told her quickly and briefly, leaving out all the inessentials, but clearly and precisely, about his strange encounter with the schoolboys. Having heard him out, Lise threw up her hands in astonishment.

'But how could you, how could you get yourself mixed up with little schoolboys, and in that dress, too?' she cried angrily, as though she had a right to exercise her authority over him. 'Why, you're only a boy yourself after that, just a little boy, as little as can be! Still, you'd better find out what you can for me about that horrid little boy, and tell me all about it, for there's some mystery there. Now, something else. But first a question: can you, Alexey, in spite of your dreadful pain, talk about something quite unimportant, but sensibly, mind?'

'Of course I can, and, besides, I don't feel much pain now.'

'That's because your finger is in the water. It will have to be changed presently, because it will get warm. Julia, go and fetch some ice from the cellar and another basin of water. Well, now that she's gone, to business: please, dear Alexey, let me have the letter I sent you yesterday at once – at once, please, for Mother may be back directly, and I don't want her —'

'I'm awfully sorry, but I haven't got it on me.'

'That's not true. You have got it. I knew you'd say that. You've got it in that pocket. I've been regretting that silly joke all night. Please, let me have my letter back at once! Give it me!'

'I've left it at the monastery.'

'But I hope you don't think I'm a little girl, just a silly little girl, for having sent you a letter with such a stupid joke! I'm sorry for that stupid joke, but you must bring me the letter, if you really haven't got it now. Bring it today. Without fail, you hear?'

'I can't possibly bring it today, for I must go back to the monastery and I shan't be able to come and see you for two, three, or even four days, because the elder Zossima —'

'Four days? What nonsense! Listen, did you laugh at me very much?'

'I didn't laugh at you at all.'

'Why not?'

'Because I believed every word of your letter.'

'You're insulting me!'

'Not at all. As soon as I read it I thought that it would all be like that, for I have to leave the monastery as soon as Father Zossima dies. I shall then carry on with my studies, pass my exams, and when you've reached the legal age, we'll get married. I shall love you. Though I haven't had time to think about it, I don't expect I could find a better wife than you, and the elder tells me I must marry. . . .'

'But I'm a horrible cripple. I'm wheeled about in a chair!' Lise laughed, colouring.

'I'll wheel you about in a chair myself, but I'm sure you'll be well by that time.'

'But you're mad,' Lise said nervously, 'jumping to such a silly conclusion from such a joke! Oh, here's Mother – just at the right moment, too, perhaps. Mother, you're always so late! How can you be so long? Here's Julia with the ice, too!'

'Oh, Lise, don't scream – please, don't scream! Your screams drive me — What was I to do if you put the lint in another place? I've been looking and looking for it. I expect you did it on purpose.'

'But how was I to know that he'd come with his finger bitten through? If I had, I might really have done it on purpose. Darling Mother, you do say such clever things.'

'Clever or not, Lise, but must you make such a fuss about poor Alexey's finger and everything? Oh, my dear Alexey, what's worrying me is not one particular thing, not Herzenstube, but everything together. That's what I simply can't bear!'

'That's enough, Mother, enough about Herzenstube,' Lise cried with a happy laugh. 'Give me the lint quickly, Mother, and the water. This is simply a zinc lotion, Alexey. I've just remembered what it is, but it's an excellent lotion. Just fancy, Mother, he's had a fight with some boys in the street on the way here, and one boy bit his finger. Isn't he just a little boy himself, and is he fit to be married after that? For, just imagine it, Mother, he actually wants to be married! Just imagine him a married man! Isn't it laughable? Isn't it awful?'

And Lise went on laughing her thin, nervous laugh, gazing mischievously at Alyosha.

'But why should he marry, Lise? And why talk about it now? It's hardly the right occasion, dear, when – I mean, when that boy may have had rabies?'

'Goodness, Mother, do boys have rabies?'

'But why not, Lise? Don't look at me as though I'd said something stupid. Your boy might have been bitten by a mad dog and he would get mad and bite someone in turn. How beautifully she's bandaged your finger, Alexey! I should never have been able to do it. Does it still hurt?'

'Only a little.'

'And you're not afraid of water?' asked Lise.

'That will do, Lise. Perhaps I was a little hasty in talking about the boy having rabies, and you're already jumping to conclusions. The moment Katerina learnt that you were here, Alexey, she simply pounced on me. She's dying to see you. She's simply dying to see you.'

'Oh, Mother, you'd better go there alone. He can't go now, he's in such pain.'

'I'm not in pain at all,' said Alyosha. 'I'm quite fit to go there.'

'What? Are you going? So that's the sort of man you are!'

'But why not? When I've finished there, I'll come back and we can talk again as much as you like. I'd very much like to see Miss Verkhovtsev now, for I'd like to be back at the monastery as soon as I can today.'

'Take him away quickly, Mother. Don't trouble to come and see me afterwards, sir, but go straight back to your monastery – and a good riddance! I want to go to bed. I haven't slept all night!'

'Oh, Lise, you're just joking, I know, but I wish you really would go to sleep!' cried Mrs Khokhlakov.

'I don't know what I've — ,' muttered Alyosha. 'I could stay another three minutes – even five, if you like.'

'Even five! Take him away quickly, Mother! He's a monster!'

'Lise, you've gone out of your mind! Come along, Alexey. She's very capricious today and I'm afraid to irritate her. Oh, my dear Alexey, the trouble one has with nervous girls! But perhaps she really does feel sleepy. How quickly you've made her sleepy and how fortunate it is!'

'Oh, Mother, how nicely you talk! I'd like to kiss you for that, darling Mother!'

'Let me kiss you, too, Lise, dear. Listen, Alexey,' Mrs Khokhlakov said gravely and mysteriously in a rapid whisper as she went out of the room with Alyosha, 'I don't want to suggest anything to you. I don't want to lift the veil. But you'd better go in and see for yourself what's going on there. It's dreadful! It's a most fantastic comedy. You see, she loves your brother Ivan, but she does all she can to persuade herself that she loves your brother Dmitry. It's simply dreadful! I'll go in with you, and if they don't turn me out, I'll stay to the end.'

5

Heartache in the Drawing-room

BUT in the drawing-room the conversation was already coming to an end. Katerina was in a state of great excitement, though she looked determined. At the moment when Alyosha and Mrs Khokhlakov came in, Ivan was getting up to go. His face was a little pale, and Alyosha looked at him uneasily. For one of the things that puzzled him, a problem that had been worrying him for some time, was about to be solved now. It had been suggested to him several times a month before by all sorts of people that Ivan was in love with Katerina and, what's more, that Ivan really meant 'to take her away' from Mitya. Up to the last moment that seemed a monstrous insinuation to Alyosha, though it had worried him a great deal. He loved both his brothers and was afraid of just such a rivalry between them. And yet Dmitry himself had told him plainly the day before that he was even glad of Ivan's rivalry and that it would be of great help to him. Be of great help for what? To make it possible for him to marry Grushenka? But that Alyosha considered a last and most desperate step. Besides all this, Alyosha had been absolutely convinced up to the previous evening that Katerina was passionately and truly in love with Dmitry – but he had believed it only till the previous evening. Moreover, he couldn't help feeling for some reason that she could not possibly love a man like Ivan, but loved Dmitry exactly as he was, in spite of the utterly monstrous nature of such a love. But in the scene with Grushenka the night before he had seemed to be dimly aware of something else. The word 'heartache' which Mrs Khokhlakov had just used, almost made him start, because it was during the previous night, half awake at daybreak, that, as though in reply to a dream he had had, he had said aloud: 'Heartache, heartache!' He had dreamt all night of the scene at Katerina's. Now Mrs Khokhlakov's unmistakable and dogmatic assertion that Katerina loved his brother Ivan and was only deceiving herself on purpose, for the sake of some fanciful idea of her own, because of 'heartache', and tormenting herself by her imagined love for Dmitry out of some apparent feeling of gratitude – struck Alyosha very forcibly. 'Yes, perhaps what she says is quite true!' But in that case how awful Ivan's position was: Alyosha felt by some sort of instinct that a woman like Katerina had to exert her power over people, and that she could do so only with a man like Dmitry and most decidedly not with a man like Ivan. For only Dmitry could (though perhaps after a long time) submit to her at last 'for his own happiness' (which Alyosha, indeed, desired), but not Ivan. Ivan could never submit to her, and, besides, submission would not have made him happy. Alyosha had for some reason involuntarily formed such an idea about Ivan. And now all these arguments and hesitations flashed through his mind the moment he had entered the drawing-room. Another thought, too, flashed through his mind suddenly and irresistibly: 'And what if she did not love anyone, neither Ivan nor Dmitry?' I must observe that Alyosha seemed to be ashamed of his thoughts and had reproached himself for them when, during the past month, they happened to occur to him. 'What do I really know about love and about women and how can I possibly come to such conclusions?' he thought reproachfully every time such a thought or conjecture occurred to him. And yet he could not help thinking about it. He realized instinctively that, for instance, this rivalry between his two brothers was now a highly important matter upon which too many things depended. 'One reptile will devour the other reptile,' Ivan had said the day before when speaking with irritation about his father and Dmitry. So he thought Dmitry a reptile and perhaps he had been thinking him a reptile a long time! Was it since the time Ivan had met Katerina? Those words, of course, had escaped Ivan involuntarily, but that made them all the more important. If that was so, then what kind of peace could there be between them? Were there not, on the contrary, new reasons for feuds and hatreds in their family? And, above all, whom was he, Alyosha, to pity? And what could he wish each of them? He loved them both, but what could he wish for each of them among so many contradictions? One could easily lose oneself in that confusion, and Alyosha's heart could not stand uncertainty, for his love was always active. He could not love passively. When he loved someone, he at once set about helping him. But to do that he had to know what to aim at, he had to know what each of them needed and what was good for them, and having become convinced of the correctness of his aim, he would naturally help each of them. But instead of some fixed, steady purpose everything was vague and confused. 'Heart-ache' – that was the word spoken just now. But what on earth was he to make even of this heartache? He did not understand a single thing in all this confusion!

On seeing Alyosha, Katerina said quickly and joyfully to Ivan, who had already got up to go:

'One moment, please. Stay for another minute. I'd like to hear the opinion of this man whom I trust completely. Mrs Khokhlakov, please don't you go, either,' she added.

She made Alyosha sit down beside her and Mrs Khokhlakov sat down facing her beside Ivan.

'Here,' she began warmly in a voice trembling with genuine, anguished tears, which made Alyosha's heart go out to her, 'here you are all my friends, the dearest friends I have in the world. You, Alexey, were present at yesterday's – horrible scene and you saw the state I was in. You, Ivan, did not see it. He did. What he thought about me yesterday, I don't know. All I know is that if the same thing had happened now, today, I should have expressed the same sentiments as I did yesterday – the same sentiments, the same words and the same actions. You remember my actions, Alexey, don't you? You restrained me from one of them.' (She reddened as she said this and her eyes flashed.) 'I tell you, Alexey, I cannot be reconciled to anything. Listen, Alexey. I don't even know that I love *him* now. I'm sorry for him, and that's a bad sign so far as love is concerned. If I'd loved him, if I'd gone on loving him, I shouldn't perhaps have been sorry for him now. I should have hated him. . . .'

Her voice trembled and tears glistened on her eyelids. Alyosha shuddered inwardly: this girl, he thought, was truthful and sincere and – and she no longer loved Dmitry!

'Yes, yes, it is so!' Mrs Khokhlakov cried.

'Wait, my dear Mrs Khokhlakov. I haven't told you the most important thing. I haven't told you what I decided last night. I can't help feeling that this decision of mine is perhaps a terrible one – for me, but I know I shall never change it – not for anything in the world. All my life it's going to be like that. My dear, kind, generous adviser and the only friend I have in the world, Ivan Karamazov, a man who has a profound knowledge of the human heart, is entirely of my opinion and approves my decision. . . . He knows it.'

'Yes, I approve it,' Ivan said in a soft but firm voice.

'But I want Alyosha too (I'm sorry, Alexey, to have called you simply Alyosha), I want Alexey, too, to tell me now in the presence of my two friends whether I'm right or not. I feel instinctively that you, Alyosha, my dear brother (because you are my dear brother),' she repeated rapturously, seizing his cold hand with her hot one, 'I feel that your decision, your approval, will set my mind at rest, in spite of all my sufferings, because after your words I shall calm down and reconcile myself to my fate – I feel it!'

'I don't know what you're going to ask me,' Alyosha said, colouring. 'I only know that I like you and wish you more happiness at this moment than I wish myself! But, you see, I know nothing about these things,' he suddenly hastened to add for some reason.

'What is important about these things now, Alexey, is honour and duty, and I don't know what else, but something higher, something higher perhaps than duty itself. My heart tells me about this irresistible feeling and it draws me on irresistibly. However, the whole thing can be put in a few words. I've made up my mind already. Even if he marries that – that – creature,' she began solemnly, 'whom I can never, never forgive, *I shall not leave him all the same!* From this day on I shall never, never leave him!' she declared with a sort of heartache and a sort of pale, agonizing rapture. 'I don't mean, of course, that I'm going to trail after him, catch his eye every minute, torment him – oh, no! I'll go away to another town, anywhere you like, but I shall keep watch over him all my life, all my life, without ever tiring of it. And when she makes him unhappy, which she is sure to do, and very soon, too, then let him come to me and he'll find a friend, a sister. . . . Only a sister, of course, and that will always be so, but at last he'll be convinced that this sister is really *his* sister, who loves him and who has sacrificed all her life for him. I'll see to it. I shall insist that at last he shall know me as I am and tell me everything without being ashamed of it!' she cried, as though beside herself. 'I shall be his goddess, to whom he will offer up prayers – that at least he owes me for his treachery and for what I went through yesterday because of him. And let him see all through his life that in spite of the fact that he was untrue to me and betrayed me, I shall be true to him all my life and faithful to the word I gave him once. I shall – I shall be only the means of his happiness or – how shall I put it? – the instrument, the engine of his happiness, and that all my life, all my life, and let him know that beforehand all through his life! That is my decision! Ivan is entirely in agreement with me.'

She was choking. She may have wished to express her thought in a much more dignified, more skilful and more natural way, but it turned out to be too hurried and much too obvious. There was a great deal of youthful lack of self-control, a great deal of it was the result of her exasperation of the day before, of her need to hold up her head, and she was conscious of it herself. Her face suddenly seemed to become overcast and there was an angry look in her eyes. Alyosha noticed it all at once and his heart was touched with pity. And just then Ivan put in his word, too.

'I've merely expressed my opinion,' he said. 'With any other woman all this would be morbid and neurotic, but with you it isn't. Any other woman would have been wrong, but you are right.

I don't know what reason to give for it, but I can see that you're as sincere as it's possible to be, and that is why you are right. . . . '

'But that's only at this moment,' cried Mrs Khokhlakov, unable to restrain herself, though obviously not wishing to interfere, but suddenly hitting the nail on the head. 'And what is this moment? Why, it's simply yesterday's insult – that's all it is!'

'Quite true, quite true,' Ivan interrupted with a kind of sudden passion and visibly furious at being interrupted, 'quite true! With any other woman this moment would be only the result of yesterday's impression, and it would be only a moment, but with Katerina's character this moment will last all her life. What for others is only a promise, is for her an everlasting, a heavy, perhaps a grim, but an unremitting duty. And she will be sustained by this feeling of fulfilled duty! Your life, Katerina, will now be spent in a martyr-like contemplation of your own feelings, your own heroism and your own sorrow, but later on that suffering will be alleviated and your life will be transformed into sweet contemplation of a steadfast and proud design carried out once and for all, a truly proud design of its kind, desperate in any case, but which you've carried out triumphantly. And the consciousness of it will at last bring you the fullest possible satisfaction and will reconcile you to everything else. . . . '

He said it quite unmistakably with a sort of malice, obviously on purpose, and perhaps without even meaning to conceal his intention, that is to say, of saying it on purpose and derisively.

'Oh dear, it isn't like that at all!' Mrs Khokhlakov cried again.

'Tell me what you think, Alexey! I'm so anxious to know what you will say!' exclaimed Katerina, suddenly bursting into tears.

Alyosha got up from the sofa.

'It's nothing, nothing!' she went on, weeping. 'It's because I'm upset, it's because of what happened last night. But by the side of two such friends as you and your brother, I still feel strong. For I know that – that you two will never desert me.'

'I'm afraid,' Ivan said suddenly, 'that unfortunately I may have to go to Moscow tomorrow and leave you for a long time. And – er – unfortunately I can't do anything about it.'

'To Moscow – tomorrow!' Katerina cried, her whole face suddenly becoming contorted. 'But – good heavens, how fortunate that is!' she exclaimed in a completely changed voice and in a flash wiping away her tears so that not a trace of them was left.

This remarkable change in her, which greatly astonished Alyosha, took place in a flash: instead of a poor insulted girl who a moment before had been weeping as if her heart would break, there suddenly appeared a woman who was in complete control of herself and who even seemed to be extremely self-satisfied, as though she were suddenly glad of something.

'Oh,' she seemed to correct herself suddenly with the charming smile of a woman of the world, 'I don't mean it is fortunate because I must take leave of you. A friend like you can't possibly think that. On the contrary, I'm very unhappy to lose you' (she suddenly rushed up impetuously to Ivan and, seizing him by both hands, pressed them warmly). 'What is fortunate is that you will now be able to tell my aunt and my sister Agafya personally about my present situation, about the awful state I'm in now, and I hope you'll be absolutely frank with Agafya but spare my dear aunt, for I'm sure you will know best how to do it. You can't imagine how unhappy I was yesterday and this morning trying to think how to write this awful letter to them – for it's quite impossible to tell them everything in a letter. . . . But now I'll find it easy to write because you'll be there to explain everything. Oh, I'm so glad! But, please, believe me, I'm only glad of that. You yourself are of course quite indispensable to me. I'll go at once and write the letter,' she suddenly concluded, and even made to leave the room.

'And what about Alyosha?' cried Mrs Khokhlakov. 'What about Alyosha's opinion which you were so anxious to hear?'

An angry and caustic note could be heard in her voice.

'I haven't forgotten that,' said Katerina, stopping suddenly. 'And why are you so unkind to me at such a moment, Mrs Khokhlakov?' she cried with warm and bitter reproach. 'I stand by what I said. I must have his opinion and, what's more, I must have his decision! I shall do as he says. That's how much I long to hear what you have to say, Alexey, but – what's the matter with you?'

'I never thought it possible!' Alyosha suddenly cried sorrowfully. 'I couldn't have imagined it!'

'What? What?'

'He's going to Moscow and you cry that you're glad – you said

that on purpose! Then you began explaining that you were not glad
he was going, but that you were sorry to – to lose a friend, but that,
too, you were acting on purpose – you were playing a part in a
comedy – as on the stage! ...'

'On the stage? What? What do you mean?' Katerina exclaimed in
great astonishment, flushing all over and frowning.

'Why, however much you assure him that you're sorry to lose a
friend in him, you still persist in telling him to his face that it's
fortunate he is leaving,' Alyosha said, almost choking with excitement.

He was standing at the table and did not sit down.

'What are you talking about? I don't understand. ...'

'I hardly know myself. ... It's as though I had a sudden illumination. ... I know I'm putting it badly, but I'll tell you everything all
the same,' Alyosha went on in the same trembling and faltering
voice. 'My illumination consists in the realization that perhaps you
don't love my brother Dmitry at all ... that you've never loved him
from the very beginning. And Dmitry, too, perhaps doesn't love
you at all and has never loved you – from the very beginning. He
only respects you. I – I really don't know how I dare tell you all
this now, but I must tell the truth to someone because – because no
one here wishes to tell the truth. ...'

'What truth?' cried Katerina, and there was a hysterical note in
her voice.

'This,' murmured Alyosha, as though jumping off a roof. 'Call
Dmitry now – I'll fetch him – and let him come here and take you
by the hand and then take Ivan by the hand and join your hands.
For you're torturing Ivan only because you love him – and you torture
him because, having worked yourself up into an emotional state of
heartache, you imagine that you love Dmitry – but you don't love
him – you've only persuaded yourself that you do. ...'

Alyosha broke off and was silent.

'You – you – you're a little religious halfwit – that's what you are!'
Katerina suddenly snapped out, her face white and her lips contorted
with anger.

Ivan suddenly burst out laughing and got up. His hat was in his
hand.

'You're mistaken, my good Alyosha,' he said with an expression

Alyosha had never seen on his face before, an expression of a sort of youthful sincerity and powerful, irresistibly frank emotion. 'Katerina never cared for me! She knew all the time that I loved her, though I never said a word to her about my love – she knew, but she did not care for me. Neither have I ever been her friend – not once, not for a single day: she's a proud woman and did not need my friendship. She kept me at her side out of a constant desire for revenge. She revenged herself on me and with me for all the insults which she continually had to bear all the time from Dmitry, ever since their first meeting. For even the memory of their very first meeting remained in her heart as an insult. That's what her heart is like! All I heard from her was about her love for him. I'm going away now, but I'd like you to know, Katerina, that you really love only him. And the more insults he heaps on you, the more you love him. That is your heartache. You love him just as he is. You love him even while he insults you. If he reformed, you'd at once throw him over and fall out of love with him entirely. But you need him in order to be able to contemplate continually your great act of faithfulness and to reproach him for his unfaithfulness. And all this because of your pride. . . . Oh, there's a lot here of humiliation and humility, but it's all because of your pride. . . . I'm too young and I loved you too much. I know that I shouldn't have told you that, that it would have been more dignified of me just to leave you. It would not have been so offensive to you. But then I'm going far away and I shall never come back. It's for good. . . . I do not wish to stay beside a woman suffering from heartache. . . . However, I don't know what more I could say. I've said everything. . . . Good-bye, Katerina. You mustn't be angry with me, because I've been punished a hundred times more than you: punished by the very fact that I shall never see you again. Good-bye. I don't want your hand. You've tortured me too deliberately for me to forgive you now. I shall forgive you later, but I don't want your hand now.

Den Dank, Dame, begehr ich nicht!'

he added with a wry smile, having proved, however, quite unexpectedly that he, too, could read Schiller to be able to quote him, which Alyosha would not have believed before.

He went out of the room, without even taking leave of the hostess, Mrs Khokhlakov. Alyosha clasped his hands in dismay.

'Ivan,' he shouted after him, miserably, 'come back, Ivan! No,' he exclaimed again in a flash of grief-stricken illumination, 'he won't come back for anything now! But I – I am to blame for that. I began wrongly. Ivan spoke unfairly and spitefully. He must come here again. He must come back. He must!' Alyosha kept crying like one demented.

Katerina suddenly went into the other room.

'You've done nothing wrong, you acted beautifully, like an angel!' Mrs Khokhlakov whispered rapidly and rapturously to the grief-stricken Alyosha. 'I'll do all I can to prevent Ivan from going away.' Her face, to Alyosha's great distress, was radiant with joy. But Katerina suddenly came back. She had two hundred-rouble notes in her hands.

'I have a great favour to ask of you,' she began, addressing herself straight to Alyosha in an apparently calm and level voice, as though nothing had really happened a moment before. 'A week ago, yes, I believe it was a week ago, Dmitry was guilty of a very hasty and unfair action, a very ugly action. There's a very low-class public house here. There he met that retired army officer, that captain your father had employed on some business of his. Losing his temper with the captain for some reason or other, Dmitry seized him by the beard and dragged him out into the street in that humiliating state, and dragged him for a long distance. I'm told that a boy, the son of this captain, who is at the school here, quite a child, saw it all and ran behind them crying and begging for his father, appealing to every-one in the street to defend him, but everyone laughed at him. I'm sorry, Alexey, but I cannot recall without indignation this disgrace-ful action of *his* – one of those actions which only Dmitry would be capable of in his anger and – in his passion! I cannot even tell you about it. I can't bring myself to. I cannot find the right words. I've made inquiries about the injured man and I found out that he is very poor. His surname is Snegiryov. He seems to have committed some offence in the army and been discharged. I'm afraid I can't tell you anything about it. Now he and his family, his unhappy family of sick children and a sick wife – I believe she is insane – are absolutely destitute. He's been living in this town a long time, he used to do some work as a copying clerk in some office, but now he isn't paid anything. When I saw you, I – I mean, I thought – I don't know –

I'm afraid I'm rather confused – you see, I wanted to ask you, Alexey, my dear Alexey, to go and see him. Find some excuse to go there, I mean, to that captain – oh dear, I'm so muddled – and delicately and courteously, as only you can do it' (Alyosha suddenly blushed), 'I mean as only you would know how to, give him these two hundred roubles. I'm sure he'll accept it – I mean, you'll persuade him to accept it. Or rather how am I to put it? You see, I'm not giving him the money because I want to conciliate him and keep him from going to the police (as I believe he was going to do), but just as an expression of my sympathy, of my desire to help him. From me, from me, Dmitry's fiancée, and not from Dmitry. . . . In short, you'll know how to do it. He lives in Lake Street, in the house of a Mrs Kalmykov. Do me this favour, Alexey, for heaven's sake, and now – now – I'm afraid I'm feeling a little tired. . . . Good-bye. . . . '

She turned round and again disappeared behind the door curtains so suddenly that Alyosha had no time to say anything, and he wanted to speak to her. He wanted to ask her forgiveness, to blame himself – just to say something, for his heart was full and he was unwilling to leave the room without it. But Mrs Khokhlakov seized him by the hand and led him out of the room herself. In the hall she stopped him once more as before.

'She's proud, she's struggling with herself, but she's so kind, so charming, so generous!' Mrs Khokhlakov kept exclaiming in an undertone. 'Oh, how I love her, especially when – and how glad I am of everything, simply of everything now! Dear Alexey, I don't think you knew it, but now I can tell you that all of us, her two aunts and I, I mean, simply everyone, even Lise, have been praying that she should give up your favourite Dmitry, who doesn't want to know her and doesn't love her, and marry Ivan, who is such a cultured and nice young man and who loves her more than anything in the world. You see, we've been hatching a regular plot here, and that's perhaps why I'm staying here. . . . '

'But,' Alyosha exclaimed, 'she's been crying, she's been humiliated again!'

'Do not believe a woman's tears, dear Alexey. In a case like this, I'm always against the woman and for the man.'

'Mother, you're spoiling and ruining him,' Lise's thin voice was heard again behind the door.

'No, I'm the cause of it all, I'm to blame for everything!' the disconsolate Alyosha kept repeating in a fit of agonizing shame for his outburst, and even covering his face in his shame.

'On the contrary, you acted like an angel, like an angel. I don't mind repeating it a hundred thousand times.'

'Mother, why was he acting like an angel?' Lise's thin voice was heard again.

'Seeing it all, I imagined for some reason,' Alyosha went on, as though he had not heard Lise, 'that she loved Ivan. That's why I said that stupid thing – and what's going to happen now?'

'But to whom – to whom?' cried Lise. 'Mother, I'm sure you want to kill me. I'm asking you and you don't answer.'

At this moment the parlour maid rushed in.

'Miss Katerina is ill. She's crying – she's in hysterics, she's having convulsions!'

'What's the matter?' cried Lise, with real alarm. 'Mother, I'm going to have hysterics, not her!'

'Lise, for heaven's sake, don't scream and don't upset me so. You're much too young to know everything grown-ups know. I'll come presently and tell you everything you can be told. Oh, good heavens, I'm coming, I'm coming! She's having hysterics – that's a good sign, Alexey. It's wonderful that she's having hysterics. It's just what she needs. In a case like that I'm always against women, against all these hysterical fits and tears. Julia, go and tell her that I'm coming to her. And she's only herself to blame that Ivan has gone out like that. But he won't go away. Lise, for goodness' sake, don't scream like that! Oh dear, you're not screaming at all, are you? It's me who's screaming. Forgive your mother, darling, but I'm delighted, delighted, delighted! And did you notice, my dear Alexey, how young, how young Ivan looked when he went out, when he said all that and went out? I thought he was so learned, so scholarly, and suddenly he spoke so warmly, so warmly, so frankly, just like a very young man, a very inexperienced young man. And how wonderful it all was! How wonderful, just as if it were you. . . . And he recited that German verse just like you too! But I must fly, I must fly. Do hurry up with her commission, Alexey, and come back quickly. Lise, you don't want anything, do you, darling? For goodness' sake don't keep Alexey a minute longer. He'll come back to you presently. . . .'

Mrs Khokhlakov ran off at last. Before leaving, Alyosha was about to open the door to see Lise.

'Not for anything in the world!' cried Lise. 'Not for anything in the world now! Speak through the door. Why are you an angel? That's all I want to know.'

'Because I did something terribly stupid, Lise. Good-bye.'

'Don't you dare to go away like that!' cried Lise.

'Lise, I am terribly unhappy! I'll be back presently, but I have a great, great sorrow!'

And he ran out of the room.

6

Heartache in the Cottage

HE really was very unhappy and it was something he had rarely experienced before. He had rushed in and 'put his foot in it', and in what sort of business: in a love affair! 'What do I understand of such things?' he asked himself for the hundredth time, blushing. 'How can I be expected to make sense of such an affair? Oh, shame wouldn't matter, shame is nothing but the punishment I deserve. The trouble is that I shall now be the cause of more unhappiness. . . . And the elder sent me to reconcile and bring them together. Is that the way to bring them together?' Here he again remembered how he 'joined their hands' and he again felt terribly ashamed. 'Though I did it in all sincerity, I must be more intelligent in future,' he concluded suddenly and did not even smile at his conclusion.

Katerina's commission took him to Lake Street and his brother Dmitry lived not far away, in a lane near Lake Street. Alyosha decided in any case to go and see him before the captain, though he had a feeling that he would not be in. He suspected that he would perhaps somehow deliberately try to avoid him now, but he had to find him at all costs. Time was passing and the thought of the dying elder had not left him for one moment ever since he had left the monastery.

There was, besides, one thing in Katerina's commission that interested him particularly: when she mentioned the little boy, the schoolboy who had run crying loudly beside his father, the thought had suddenly flashed through Alyosha's mind that that boy was quite certainly the schoolboy who had bitten his finger when he had been trying to find out how he had wronged him. Now Alyosha was almost sure of it, though he did not know why himself. Having become thus absorbed in another train of thought, he felt better and decided not to think of 'the trouble' he had just caused, not to torture himself with remorse, but to carry on with what he had to do regardless of the consequences. That thought restored his good spirits. At the same time, turning into the lane where his brother lived and feeling hungry, he took out the roll he had brought from his father's and ate it on the way. This fortified him.

Dmitry was out. The owners of the little house where he lived – an old carpenter, his old wife, and his son – looked at Alyosha with suspicion. 'He hasn't slept here for three nights, perhaps he's gone away somewhere,' the old man replied to Alyosha's repeated questions. Alyosha realized that he was replying in accordance with Dmitry's instructions. When he asked whether Dmitry was at Grushenka's or whether he was again hiding at Foma's (Alyosha spoke frankly of these confidential matters on purpose), all three of them looked at him with alarm. 'They must be fond of him,' thought Alyosha. 'They're on his side. That's good!'

At last he found the house of Mrs Kalmykov in Lake Street. It was a ramshackle little house, lopsided, with only three windows looking on to the street, and a filthy backyard, in the middle of which stood a solitary cow. The entrance to the house was from the yard straight into the passage and on the left of the passage lived the old landlady with an old daughter, both of them apparently deaf. In reply to his inquiry about the captain, which he had to repeat a few times, one of them at last grasped that he was asking about their lodgers, and pointed to the door of the living-room across the passage. The captain's lodging really turned out to be simply the living-room of the cottage. Alyosha took hold of the iron latch to open the door when he was suddenly struck by the unusual silence behind it. He knew, however, from what Katerina had told him that the retired captain had a family. 'They are either all asleep or they may have heard me coming in and are waiting for me to open the door; perhaps I'd better knock first,' and he knocked. An answer came, not at once, though, but after an interval of about ten seconds.

'Who's there?' someone shouted harshly in a loud and angry voice.

Alyosha opened the door and crossed the threshold. He found himself in a fairly spacious room, cluttered up with furniture and household things of all kinds. There were a number of people in it. To the left was a large Russian stove. A line with all sorts of washing was stretched across the whole room from the stove to the window on the left. Along the two walls on the left and right stood beds covered with knitted blankets. On the left one was a heap of four cotton pillows, each smaller than the other. On the right one, however, only one very small pillow could be seen. The opposite corner was screened off by a curtain or a sheet, hanging over a rope stretched across it. Behind the curtain could be seen another bed made up of a bench and a chair. A plain, square wooden table of the type found in peasants' cottages had been moved from the corner to the middle window. All the three windows, each consisting of four green, grimy little panes, let through very little light and were tightly shut, so that the room was rather stuffy and dark. On the table was a frying-pan with the remnants of fried eggs, a half-eaten piece of bread and, in addition, half a pint with the dregs of earthly cheer on the very bottom. On a chair beside the bed on the left sat a woman of genteel appearance wearing a cotton dress. Her face was very thin and sallow and her exceedingly hollow cheeks showed at once that she was ill. But Alyosha was most of all struck by the look the poor lady had given him – a questioning and at the same time very haughty look. And until the woman spoke herself and while Alyosha was explaining the reason for his visit to the captain, she kept glancing from the one to the other with the same questioning and haughty brown eyes. A rather plain-looking young girl, with thin, reddish hair and poorly, though neatly, dressed, stood by the left window near the woman. As Alyosha came in, she looked him up and down with unconcealed revulsion. There was another girl sitting by the bed on the right. She was a very pitiful little thing, a young girl of twenty, but a hunchback, and, as Alyosha was afterwards told, with withered legs. Her crutches were beside her, in the corner between the bed and the wall. The remarkably beautiful and tender eyes of the poor girl looked at Alyosha with a kind of meek serenity. At the table, finishing the fried egg, sat a man of about five and forty, of medium height, spare, weakly built, with reddish hair and a thin, reddish beard which bore a striking resemblance to a bast-sponge (this comparison and particularly the word 'bast-sponge' for some reason flashed instantaneously through Alyosha's mind – he recalled it afterwards). It was evidently that same man who had shouted, 'Who's there?', for there was no other man in the room. But when Alyosha came in, he seemed to leap from the bench on which he was sitting at the table and, hastily wiping his mouth with a tattered napkin, rushed up to Alyosha.

'A monk begging for his monastery,' the young girl standing in the left corner said in a loud voice. 'He came to the right place!'

But the man, who had run up to Alyosha, at once spun round to her and answered her in an excited and a sort of shaky voice:

'No, madam, it's not that at all. You're wrong! May I ask you, sir,' he suddenly turned round to Alyosha again, 'to what I owe the honour of your visit to this – er – humble abode?'

Alyosha looked at him attentively: it was the first time he had seen the man. There was something angular, flurried, and irritable about him. Though he had obviously been drinking just now, he was not drunk. His face expressed a sort of extreme arrogance and, which was so strange, at the same time unconcealed cowardice. He looked like a man who had for a long time been at the beck and call of other people and had suffered a great deal, but who had suddenly jumped to his feet and tried to assert himself. Or, better still, like a man who wanted terribly to hit you, but who was terribly afraid that you might hit him back. There was a sort of weak-minded humour in his words and the inflexion of his rather shrill voice, spiteful and timid in turn, but unable to keep it up for any length of time and faltering continuously. His question about 'the humble abode' he asked with protruding eyes and as though trembling all over, and rushing up so close to Alyosha that he unconsciously recoiled a step. The man was wearing a dark, rather threadbare overcoat of some nankeen material, stained and patched. His trousers were of a very light check material, which had not been in fashion for a long time and which were so crumpled at the bottom that they looked as though he had worn them as a boy and grown out of them.

'I'm – Alexey Karamazov,' Alyosha said in reply.

'That, sir, I'm perfectly well aware of,' the man at once snapped out to let him know that his identity was no secret to him. 'And I, sir, am Captain Snegiryov, sir. But I'm still anxious to know, sir, to what I owe the honour —'

'As a matter of fact, I haven't come for any special reason. I just wanted to have a word with you, if you don't mind.'

'In that case, sir, here's a chair and do me the honour of being seated. That, sir, is what they used to say in the old comedies: "do me the honour of being seated".'

And with a rapid gesture the captain seized an empty chair (a plain, deal, unupholstered chair), and put it almost in the middle of the room; then, seizing another similar chair for himself, he sat down facing Alyosha, and, as before, so close to him that their knees almost touched.

'Nikolai Ilyich Snegiryov, sir, a former captain of Russian infantry, sir, and though disgraced by his vices, still a captain, sir. I should perhaps have introduced myself as Captain Sir and not as Captain Snegiryov, for it's only during the latter half of my life that I have begun saying "sir" to people. The word, "sir", sir, one acquires only when one has come down in the world.'

'That is so,' Alyosha smiled, 'but does one acquire it voluntarily or involuntarily?'

'God knows, involuntarily. I never used to say it, all my life I never used to say "sir", but suddenly I fell and got up with "sir" on my lips. That is brought about by a higher power. I can see that you're interested in contemporary problems. But how could I have aroused your curiosity, living as I do in surroundings in which the exercise of hospitality is impossible?'

'I've come about – that business.'

'About what business?' Snegiryov interrupted impatiently.

'About that encounter of yours with my brother Dmitry,' Alyosha blurted out awkwardly.

'What encounter, sir? You don't mean *that* encounter, sir? Are you referring to the bast-sponge, the bath bast-sponge?'

This time he moved so close to Alyosha that their knees positively knocked against each other. He compressed his lips so tightly that they seemed almost to disappear.

'What bast-sponge?' murmured Alyosha.

'He's come to complain to you about me, Daddy,' cried a voice familiar to Alyosha, the voice of the schoolboy, from behind the curtain. 'It was me who bit his finger this afternoon.'

The curtain was drawn aside, and Alyosha saw his old enemy lying on the bed made up on the bench and the chair in the corner under the icons. The boy lay covered by his overcoat and an old quilt. He was evidently not well and, to judge by his burning eyes, in a fever. He looked fearlessly, and not as he had done earlier, at Alyosha, as though he wished to say: 'You won't dare touch me at home!'

'Bit his finger?' Snegiryov cried, half rising from his chair. 'Did he bite your finger, sir?'

'Yes, I'm afraid so. He was exchanging volleys of stones with the boys in the street. There were six of them against him alone. I went up to him and he threw a stone at me, then another at my head. I asked him what I had done to him, but he suddenly rushed up to me and bit my finger badly. I don't know why.'

'I shall give him a hiding at once, sir. This very minute, sir!' Snegiryov now really did jump up from his chair.

'But I'm not complaining at all. I merely told you what happened. I don't want you to give him a hiding. Besides, I believe he's ill now. . . .'

'And did you really think I'd give him a hiding, sir? That I'd take my darling boy and thrash him in front of you for your greater satisfaction? Do you want me to do it immediately, sir?' said Snegiryov, turning suddenly to Alyosha as though about to hurl himself upon him. 'I'm very sorry, sir, for your poor finger, but, before thrashing my boy, wouldn't you rather I chopped off four of my fingers in front of you with this knife for your still greater satisfaction? Four fingers, I should think, sir, should be enough to satisfy your thirst for revenge. You won't demand my fifth one, too, will you?'

He suddenly stopped short as though out of breath. Every muscle of his face jerked and trembled, and he looked with the utmost defiance at Alyosha. He seemed beside himself.

'I think I understand everything now,' Alyosha replied quietly and sadly, without getting up. 'So your little boy is a good boy. He loves his father and attacked me because I'm the brother of the man who insulted you. I understand it now,' he repeated musingly. 'But my brother Dmitry is sorry for what he did. I know that. And if he could only come to see you, or, better still, if he could meet you in the same place, he'd apologize to you before everyone – if you wish it.'

'You mean, he pulled out my beard and now he's going to apologize for it? Everything fair and square. Is that what he thinks?'

'Oh, no. Quite the contrary. He'll do anything you like and as you like.'

'So that if I, sir, should ask his lordship to go down on his knees before me in that same pub – Metropolis it's called – or in the square, he'd do so, would he?'

'Yes, he would.'

'I'm deeply moved, sir. Deeply moved. Moved to tears, sir. I feel it, sir. I do, indeed. Allow me to introduce my family: my two daughters and my son – my litter, sir. If I die, who will care for them? And while I live, sir, who but they will care for a dirty wretch like me? This great thing the good Lord has arranged for every man of my sort, sir. For it's necessary that a man of my sort, too, should have someone to care for him, sir.'

'Yes, that's quite true!' cried Alyosha.

'Oh, do stop playing the fool!' cried the girl at the window unexpectedly, turning to her father with an air of disgust and disdain. 'Some idiot comes along and you have to put us all to shame!'

'Wait a little, Varvara, let me show myself in my true colours first,' cried her father in a peremptory tone, but looking at her quite approvingly. 'That's the sort of character she has, sir,' he turned again to Alyosha.

'And in all creation there was naught
To which his blessing he would give.

'I really should have put it in the feminine: to which her blessing she would give. But now do let me introduce you to my wife, Arina Petrovna, a lady with bad legs. She's forty-three. She can move her legs, but only a little, sir. She's of humble origin, sir. Smooth your brow, madam: this is Mr Alexey Karamazov. Get up, sir,' he addressed Alyosha, taking him by the hand and pulling him up with quite unexpected force. 'You're being introduced to a lady, sir, so you have to get up. It isn't the Karamazov, Mother, who – well –

and so on, but his brother, shining bright with lowly virtues. Allow me, my dear, allow me, Mother, to kiss your hand first.'

And he kissed his wife's hand respectfully and even tenderly. The girl at the window turned her back indignantly on the scene. An expression of extraordinary tenderness suddenly came over the disdainfully questioning face of Mrs Snegiryov.

'Good afternoon, do sit down, Mr Chernomazov,' she said.

'Karamazov, Mother, Karamazov! We're of humble origin, sir,' he again whispered to Alyosha.

'Well, Karamazov, or whatever it is, but I always say Chernomazov. Sit down, please. Why has he made you get up? A lady with bad legs, says he, but I've got legs all right, only they're swollen like buckets, while I'm all wasted myself. Used to be ever so fat before, but now I'm as thin as a rake.'

'We're of humble origin, sir, of humble origin,' Snegiryov whispered again in explanation.

'Oh, Father, Father!' the hunchbacked girl, who had been silent till then, said suddenly and hid her eyes in her kerchief.

'Buffoon!' the girl at the window snapped out.

'You see the sort of news we have,' said the mother, spreading out her hands and pointing to her daughters. 'It's just like clouds coming over: the clouds pass, and again the same music. Before, when we were army folk, we had many such visitors. Comparisons are odious, my dear sir. If anyone loves someone, let him love him, I says. The deacon's wife used to visit us and, "Alexander Alexandrovich," she says, "is a most excellent man," she says, "but Nastasya Petrovna is a fiend of a woman." "Well," I says to her, "everyone to his taste," I says, "but you, my dear," I says, "may be a little thing, but you smell bad." "And you," she says, "must be kept in your place." "Oh," I says to her, "you common dirt, who have you come to teach?" "My breath," she says, "is sweet and yours is foul." "Well," I says to her, "you'd better ask the gentlemen officers whether my breath is sweet or foul." And ever since I can't get it out of my mind. A few days later I was sitting just as I'm doing now, when the general who came at Easter comes in: "Sir," I says to him, "ought not a lady to breathe fresh air?" "Why, yes," he says, "only you'd better open a window or the door because," he says, "the air here is not fresh." And they all go on like that! And why make such a fuss about my breath? The dead smell still worse. "I'm not befouling your air," I says to them. "I'll order a pair of shoes and go away." My darlings, don't blame your own mother! Nikolai, dear, haven't I done everything to please you? I've only got darling Ilya who comes home from school and loves me. He brought me an apple yesterday. Forgive me, my darlings, forgive your own mother, my dears, forgive a lonely old woman. And why has my breath become so repulsive to you?'

And the poor woman burst out sobbing, her tears gushing out of her eyes. Snegiryov dashed up to her.

'Stop crying, my dear, stop crying, darling! You're not a lonely old woman. We all love you. We all adore you, my dear!'

And he began kissing her hands again and stroking her face tenderly with both hands. Snatching up the table napkin, he suddenly began wiping her tears. Alyosha fancied that he, too, had tears in his eyes.

'Well, sir,' Snegiryov suddenly turned to him fiercely, pointing to the poor feeble-minded woman, 'seen her? Heard her?'

'I see and hear,' murmured Alyosha.

'Father, father, you're not appealing to him, are you?'

'Leave him alone, Daddy!' the boy cried suddenly, sitting up on his bed and looking at his father with burning eyes.

'It's high time you stopped playing the clown and showing off your silly tricks, which never lead to anything!' cried Varvara from the corner of the room, losing her temper completely and even stamping her foot.

'You're quite right to lose your temper this time, madam, and I shall instantly satisfy you. Put on your cap, sir,' he addressed Alyosha, 'and I'll put on mine and let's go, sir. I've something important to tell you, but outside these walls. This girl sitting here is my daughter Nina, sir. I'm afraid I forgot to introduce you – she's an angel incarnate who – er – who's flown down to us mortals – if – er – you see what I mean, sir. . . . '

'Look at him, shaking all over, as though seized with spasms,' Varvara went on indignantly.

'And that one who's stamping her feet at me and called me a clown, sir, is also an angel incarnate, and she was right, sir, to call me that. Come along, sir, we must get it settled. . . . '

And seizing Alyosha by the hand, he led him out of the room into the street.

7

And in the Open Air

'HERE the air's fresh, sir, but I'm afraid I can't say as much for the air in my castle in any sense of the word. Let's walk slowly, sir. I'd very much like to enlist your interest, sir.'

'I too, have to discuss a very important matter with you,' observed Alyosha. 'Only I don't know how to begin. . . .'

'I realize, of course, that you have some business with me, sir. You'd never have come to see me if you had no business. You didn't really come to complain about my boy, did you? That would indeed be highly improbable. By the way, about my boy, sir. I couldn't explain it to you in there, but now I can describe the scene to you. You see, sir, only a week ago my bast-sponge was much thicker. I'm referring to my beard, sir. It's my little beard they nicknamed a bast-sponge, sir. The schoolboys chiefly. Well, then, sir, so there was your brother Dmitry dragging me by my beard. Dragged me out into the square, sir, and just then the schoolboys were coming out of school and Ilyusha with them. As soon as he saw me in such a state, he rushed up to me: "Daddy," he cried, "Daddy!" He caught hold of me, flung his little arms round me, trying to free me and shouting to my assailant: "Let him go, let him go! It's my Daddy! Forgive him, sir!" Yes, indeed. "Forgive him!" he cried. He clutched at him with his hand. He kissed his hand. That same hand – yes, sir, he kissed it! I remember what his face looked like at that moment – I haven't forgotten it, sir. I shall never forget it!'

'I swear,' cried Alyosha, 'he'll apologize to you with the utmost sincerity, with absolute sincerity, even if he has to go down on his knees in that same square. . . . I shall make him do it, or he's no brother of mine!'

'Oh, I see! So that's still only a suggestion! It doesn't come from him, but only from the generosity of your own warm heart, sir! Why didn't you say so before, sir? Well, sir, in that case let me, too, tell you of your brother's highly chivalrous and soldierly generosity, for he showed it to the full at the time. After he'd left off dragging me by my bast-sponge and had set me free, he said to me: "You're an officer and I'm an officer. If you can find a decent fellow to be your second, send him to me, and I'll give you satisfaction, dirty rotter though you are!" That's what he said, sir. A truly chivalrous spirit! We went away then, Ilyusha and I, and our genealogical family tree remained forever imprinted on little Ilya's mind. No, sir, we cannot claim to be noblemen any more. Judge for yourself, sir. You've just been in our castle – what did you see there? Three ladies, sir, one a weak-minded cripple, another a hunchback cripple, and a third not crippled but too clever by half. A university woman, sir. Anxious to go back to Petersburg and look for the rights of the Russian women on the banks of the Neva. I say nothing about Ilyusha. He's only nine years old, sir. I'm all alone in the world, and if I die what will become of all of them – tell me that, sir! And if that's so, what's going to happen if I challenge him and he kills me on the spot? What will then become of them all? And if he doesn't kill me but only cripples me, it will be still worse: I shan't be able to work, but a mouth has to be fed, and who'll feed it, my mouth, that is, and who will feed all of them? Or should I send Ilyusha out to beg in the streets instead of sending him to school? So that's what challenging to a duel means to me, sir. It's a lot of silly talk, sir, and nothing else.'

'He will beg you to forgive him,' Alyosha cried again with burning eyes. 'He'll go down on his knees at your feet in the square!'

'I thought of summonsing him,' Snegiryov went on, 'but look up our code of laws, sir. Could I get much compensation from my assailant for a personal injury? And then Miss Svetlov, sir, sent for me: "Don't you dare to think of it," she shouted. "If you summons him, I'll see to it that the whole world gets to know that he beat you because of your own double-dealing, and then you'll be put on trial yourself!" And Lord only knows, sir, who was responsible for my double-dealing and at whose orders an insignificant worm like me acted – wasn't it at her own and Mr Karamazov's? "And what's more," she added, "I shall have nothing more to do with you and you'll never earn another penny from me. I shall also tell my merchant (that's what she calls her old man: my merchant), and he'll have nothing to do with you, either." Well, I think to myself, what's going to happen to me if the merchant, too, will have nothing to do with me? Who will provide me with a living then? Those two are the only ones left to me, for your father, sir, has not only stopped trusting me for quite a different reason, but he, too, wants to drag me into court, having obtained my signature to some receipts. As a result of it all, sir, I'm keeping quiet and you've seen our humble abode, haven't you? And now let me ask you: did he bite your finger badly? Ilyusha, I mean? You see, sir, I didn't want to go into it in my castle in front of him.'

'Yes, I'm afraid he did, rather. He was very angry. He was revenging himself on me as a Karamazov for you. I can see it now. But if you'd only seen how he was exchanging volleys of stones with his schoolfellows! It's very dangerous. They might kill him. They're children and stupid. A stone is thrown and somebody's head might get broken.'

'He was hit by a stone today, sir. Not on the head but on the chest, just above the heart. A big bruise, sir. He came home crying and groaning, and now he's ill.'

'And, you know, it's he who attacks them first. He's furious with them on your account. They say he stabbed a boy by the name of Krasotkin with a pen-knife the other day.'

'I've heard about that, too. It is dangerous, sir. Krasotkin is a civil servant here. I daresay there may be trouble.'

'I'd advise you,' Alyosha went on warmly, 'not to send him to school at all for a time until he quiets down and – his anger will pass.'

'His anger, sir!' Snegiryov repeated. 'That's just what it is, sir: anger! A great anger, sir, in a little creature like him. You don't know it all, sir. Let me explain this business in particular. You see, sir, after that incident all his schoolfellows began teasing him at school by calling him a bast-sponge. Schoolchildren are pitiless: singly they are angels, but together, especially at school, they're quite often pitiless. They began teasing him and this roused his spirit. An ordinary boy, a weak son, would have submitted. He would have been ashamed of his father. But Ilyusha stood up for his father – one against the lot of them. For his father, sir. For truth and justice. What he went through when he kissed your brother's hand and shouted to him: "Forgive my Daddy, forgive my Daddy!" – that only God knows, and myself, sir. And this is how our children – I don't mean yours but ours, sir, ours, the children of the despised but honourable poor, sir, learn about justice on earth even when they are only nine years old. The rich never get the chance; they will never explore such depths during the whole of their lives, but my Ilyusha, sir, grasped the whole meaning of truth at the very moment as he was kissing his hands in the square, at that very moment. That truth entered into him and crushed him forever,' Snegiryov said warmly and again as though in a frenzy, striking his right fist on his left hand, as if wishing to demonstrate how 'the truth' had crushed Ilyusha. 'That very day he lay in a fever and was delirious all night. He spoke little to me all that day. He was silent most of the time. Only I noticed that he kept looking at me from his corner, but mostly he kept turning to the window and pretending to be doing his homework. I could see, though, that his mind was not on his homework. Next day, sir, I'm afraid I got drunk, sinner that I am, to drown my sorrows, and I don't remember much. My wife, sir, started crying, too – I love my wife very much, sir – and, well, I spent my last penny on drink. Do not despise me, my dear sir: in Russia the drunkards are the most kindly people. The most kindly people in our country, sir, are the greatest drunkards. Yes, sir. Well, so there I was lying drunk and paying no attention to my little boy, and it was on that very day that the boys at school had made fun of him since morning: "Bast-sponge!" they shouted at him. "Your father was dragged out of the pub by his bast-sponge and you ran alongside asking for forgiveness." When the day after he came back from school again, I could see that he looked very pale. "What's the matter?" I asked. He did not reply. Well, sir, in my castle it's impossible to talk, for my wife and the girls interfere at once. Besides, the girls had by then got to know all about it. On the very first day, in fact. Varvara had begun grumbling already: "Buffoons, clowns, can you ever do anything sensible?" "Quite right," I said to her, "we can't do anything sensible!" That time I got away with it. In the evening, sir, I took my boy out for a walk. I used to take him out for walks every evening before tea, sir, the same way we are walking along now, from our gate to that big stone lying there alone by the wattle fence where the town pasture begins: a deserted and beautiful spot, sir. So there I was walking along with Ilyusha, his hand clasped in mine as usual: a tiny little hand, his fingers thin and cold: he suffers from a weak chest, you know. "Daddy," he says, "Daddy!" "What?" I asked. I could see his eyes flashing. "Daddy, how badly he treated you then, Daddy!" "I'm afraid," I said, "it can't be helped." "Don't make it up with him, Daddy, don't make it up. The boys at school say he's given you ten roubles for it." "No, my boy," I said, "I will never take any money from him for anything." The poor child trembled all over, took my hand in both his hands and kissed it again. "Daddy," he said, "Daddy, you must challenge him to a duel. They say at school that you're a coward and that you won't challenge him to a duel, but accepted ten roubles from him." "I'm afraid, my boy," I replied, "I can't challenge him to a duel," and I explained briefly to him what I've just told you. He listened to me and then he said: "But you shouldn't make it up with him all the same. When I grow up, I'll challenge him myself and kill him!" His eyes shone and glowed. Well, sir, I am his father and I had to tell him what was right, so I told him that it was a sin to kill a man even in a duel. "Daddy," he said, "Daddy, when I grow up I'll knock him down. I'll knock his sabre out of his hand with my own sabre. I'll hurl myself on him, throw him down, raise my sabre over him and say to him: 'I could kill you now on the spot, but I forgive you – there!'" You, you see, sir, what's been going on in his little head during the last two days. He must have been thinking of revenging himself with the sabre for a whole day and night and he must have been talking about it in his delirium at night. Yes, sir. But after that he began to come home from school badly beaten. I found out about it the day before yesterday, and you're quite right, sir: I shall not send him to that school again. When I learnt that he was standing up to his whole class and challenging them all by himself, that he'd become embittered and that his heart was full of resentment, I was frightened for him. We went out for a walk again. "Daddy," he asked, "Daddy, the rich are stronger than anybody else in the world, aren't they?" "Yes," I said, "there are no people in the world stronger than the rich." "Daddy," he said, "I'll get rich, I'll become an officer and I'll conquer everybody, and the Czar will reward me, and I'll come back here and no one will then dare to—" Then after a pause he said, his lips still trembling as before: "Daddy," he said, "what a horrid town this is, Daddy!" "Yes, darling," I said, "it isn't a very nice town." "Daddy," he said, "let's move to another town, to a nice town, where they don't know about us!" "Very well, Ilyusha," I said, "we shall as soon as I've saved up enough money." I was glad of the opportunity of distracting him from his gloomy thoughts, and we began dreaming how we would move to another town, buy a horse and cart. "We'll put Mummy and your sisters in it, cover them up, and you and I will walk beside it. I'll put you in the cart, too, now and then, and I'll walk beside, for we must take care of our horse and we can't all ride. That's how we will go." He was delighted with it, and especially that we would have a horse and cart of our own and he would ride in it. And it's a well-known fact, sir, that a Russian boy is born among horses. We chattered a long time and, "Thank God," I thought, "I've distracted and comforted him." This was the day before yesterday, in the evening, and yesterday evening everything was different again. He went to school in the morning and came back looking very gloomy, too gloomy for my peace of mind. In the evening I took him by the hand and we went out for a walk. He was silent and would not talk. It was getting windy, the sun had gone behind the clouds, there was a nip of autumn in the air, and anyway it was growing dark. We were walking along, feeling depressed both of us. "Well, my boy," I said, "let's see how we're going to get ready for the journey," thinking of how to resume our talk of the day before. He was silent. Only I felt his fingers trembling in my hand. Oh, thought I, it's bad, something new must have happened. We had reached this stone where we are now. I sat down on the stone. In the sky there were lots of kites, flapping and rustling. There must have been as many as thirty kites. For, you see, sir, it's the kite season now. "Well, Ilyusha," I said, "it's time we too got out our last year's kite. I'll mend it —where did you put it away?" My boy said nothing. He looked away, standing sideways to me. Just then the wind rose suddenly, whipping up the sand. He suddenly rushed up to me, threw his arms round my neck, and held me tight. You know, children who are silent and proud and who keep back their tears for a long time are liable to break down suddenly when in great trouble, and once they start crying, they dissolve into floods of tears. With those warm streams of tears he suddenly wetted my face. He sobbed as though in convulsions, trembling all over and clinging close to me as I sat on the stone. "Daddy," he kept crying out, "dear Daddy, how he humiliated you!" Well, sir, I burst into tears, too, and there we sat embracing each other and crying. "Daddy," he said, "Daddy!" "Ilya," I said, "my darling Ilya!" No one saw us there. No one, sir.

Only God saw it. Perhaps he'll put it on my service record. You must thank your brother, sir. No, sir, I shall not thrash my boy for your satisfaction!'

He finished again on his former note of shrill resentment. Alyosha, however, felt that he trusted him and that had there been someone else in his, Alyosha's, place, he would not have 'gone on' like that and would not have told what he had just told him. This encouraged Alyosha, who was moved almost to tears.

'Oh, how I'd like to make friends with your boy!' he exclaimed. 'If only you could arrange it. . . .'

'Why, yes, sir,' Snegiryov murmured.

'But now I must talk to you about something else, something quite different,' Alyosha went on excitedly. 'Listen, please. I've a message for you. That brother of mine, Dmitry, had also insulted his fiancée, a most high-minded girl, of whom you've probably heard. I have a right to tell you about her insult. Indeed, I must do so. For, you see, when she heard about the abominable way you'd been treated and about your unfortunate position, she commissioned me at once – this very afternoon – to offer you some assistance. But only from her alone and not from Dmitry, who had thrown her over. No, not from him and not from me, his brother, either, but from her alone! She begs you to accept her help – you've both been insulted by the same man. . . . In fact, she remembered you when she suffered a similar insult from him – an insult, that is, of equal force. It's as though a sister had come to the assistance of her brother. . . . Indeed, she asked me to persuade you to accept these two hundred roubles from her as from a sister. No one will ever know anything about it, there can be no question of any unjust gossip arising from it – I swear you must accept them, for otherwise – otherwise all men on earth must be enemies of one another! But there are brothers in the world, too. . . . You have a generous heart – you must understand that – you must!'

And Alyosha held out the two new rainbow-coloured hundred-rouble notes to him. They were both standing by the large stone just then, by the fence, and there was no one near. The notes seemed to have produced a tremendous impression on the captain: he gave a start, but at first apparently from sheer astonishment: he had never dreamt of anything of the kind and he had never expected such an outcome. Nothing could have been further from his thoughts than help from anyone – and so large a sum, too! He took the notes and for a whole minute he was almost unable to utter a word. Quite a new expression came into his face.

'Is that for me – for me? So much money – two hundred roubles! Good Lord, I haven't seen so much money for four years – dear me! And she says it's from a sister – is it true, true?'

'I swear that all I told you is the truth!' cried Alyosha.

Snegiryov coloured.

'Look here, sir, look here, if I take it, I shouldn't be acting like a scoundrel, should I? I shouldn't be a scoundrel in your eyes, sir, should I? No, sir, please, listen, listen,' he went on rapidly, touching Alyosha with both hands. 'You're persuading me to accept it by telling me that "a sister" sends it, but inside, deep inside you – you won't feel contempt for me if I take it, will you, sir?'

'No, no, of course not! I swear to you by my salvation I won't. And not a soul will ever know about it: only you, she, and I, and another lady, a great friend of hers. . . . '

'Never mind the lady! Listen, sir, listen carefully, for the time has now come when you have to listen carefully to what I have to say, because you can have no idea what these two hundred roubles mean to me,' the poor fellow went on, working himself up gradually into a kind of incoherent, almost wild enthusiasm. He seemed bewildered and spoke rapidly and hurriedly as though afraid that he would not be allowed to finish what he had to say. 'Apart from the fact that it has been honestly acquired from a highly respected "sister", sir, do you realize that now I shall be able to get medical treatment for my wife and my darling Nina – my hunchback angel – my daughter? Dr Herzenstube paid me a visit once out of the goodness of his heart and spent a whole hour examining them. "Can't make anything of it," he said, "but the mineral water which you can get at our local chemist's" (he left a prescription for it) "will certainly do her a lot of good," and he also prescribed some medicinal baths for her legs. The mineral water costs thirty copecks, and she'd have to drink forty jugs of it, perhaps. So I took the prescription and put it on the shelf under the icons, and it's still there now. And he prescribed hot baths for Nina with some kind of solution in them, twice a day, in the morning and in the evening, so where could we provide such treatment for her in that castle of ours, without a maid, without help, without a bath, and without water? Poor Nina has rheumatic pains all over. I didn't tell you that, did I? All her right side aches at night. She's in great pain and, you know, the dear angel bears it in silence so as not to trouble us. She doesn't groan so as not to waken us. We eat anything we can get, but she'll only take what's left over, what one would only give to a dog: "I'm not worth it, I'm taking it away from you, I'm a burden to you" – that's what her angelic look is meant to express. We wait on her, but she can't bear it: "I'm not worth it, not worth it, I'm a contemptible, useless cripple." Not worth it! Why, she'd obtain salvation for us all by her angelic meekness. Without her, without her gentle words, it would be hell in our house. She mollified even Varvara. And you mustn't blame Varvara, either, sir. She, too, is an angel. She, too, has been hardly done by. She came to us in the summer. She had sixteen roubles on her which she had earned by giving lessons and put away for her fares so that she could go back to Petersburg in September, that is, now. And we took her money and spent it and she has nothing to go back with now. That's how it is, sir. And she can't go back, for she works her fingers to the bone for us, for we've harnessed her like a mare. She looks after us all, mends, washes, sweeps the floor, puts her mother to bed, and her mother is capricious, her mother is tearful, her mother is insane, sir! But now I can engage a maid with this money, you understand, sir. I can afford medical treatment for my dear ones. I can send our student back to Petersburg. I can buy beef. I can get decent food for them all. Good heavens, why, it's a dream!'

Alyosha was terribly glad that he had brought so much happiness and that the poor man had consented to be made happy.

'Wait, sir, wait!' Snegiryov snatched at a new daydream that had just occurred to him and he again babbled away with frenzied rapidity. 'Do you realize that Ilyusha and I can really carry out our dream now? We'll buy a horse and a buggy, a black horse, he set his heart on a black horse, and we'll be off as we had planned the other day. I know a lawyer in the Kursk province, a very old friend of mine, and he let me know by a trustworthy person that if I were to go there he'd get me a job at his office as his clerk, and – who knows – perhaps he would too. . . . So I'd put mother and Nina in the buggy, let Ilyusha drive, and run on foot beside it, and I'd get them all there.

Why, sir, if I could only get one debt that's owing me paid up, I would be able to afford that, too!'

'You would, you would!' cried Alyosha. 'Miss Verkhovtsev will let you have more money, as much as you like. And, you know, I have money, too. Take as much as you like, as you would from a friend, from a brother. You'll pay me back afterwards. . . . You'll get rich, yes, rich! And, you know, you couldn't have thought of anything better than to move to another province! That would be the saving of you and, above all, of your boy. And, you know, you must go quickly, before the winter, before the cold, and you could write to us from there, and we will always be brothers. . . . No, it is not a dream!'

Alyosha was about to embrace him, so pleased was he. But, glancing at him, he stopped short. Snegiryov stood with outstretched neck, protruding lips, and a frenzied, pale face, his lips moving as though he were going to say something; but no sound issued from them, though he kept moving them. It was ghastly.

'What's the matter?' asked Alyosha, with a sudden start.

'You, sir. I —' Snegiryov muttered, faltering and looking at him with a strange, wild, fixed stare, like a man who had made up his mind to throw himself down a precipice, and at the same time with a strange smile on his lips. 'I, sir – you, sir —Would you like me to show you a lovely trick, sir?' he suddenly said in a rapid, firm whisper, his speech no longer faltering.

'What sort of trick?'

'A lovely trick, sir, a hocus-pocus,' Snegiryov kept whispering.

His mouth was twisted on the left side, his left eye was screwed up, and he kept staring fixedly at Alyosha, as though he were chained to him.

'But what is the matter with you?' cried Alyosha in real alarm. 'What kind of trick?'

'This kind,' Snegiryov suddenly squealed. 'Look!'

And showing him the two rainbow-coloured notes, which he had kept by one corner between thumb and forefinger during their conversation, he suddenly snatched them up in a kind of frenzy, crumpled them and squeezed them tightly in his right hand.

'See, sir, see!' he shrieked at Alyosha, pale and beside himself, and, raising his fist suddenly, he flung the two crumpled notes violently on the sand. 'You see, sir?' he shrieked again, pointing to them. 'Well, that's what I'm going to do!'

And raising his right foot, he began trampling the notes under his heel with wild fury, gasping for breath and exclaiming as he did so: 'So much for your money, sir! So much for your money! So much for your money!'

Suddenly he leapt back and drew himself up to his full height before Alyosha. His whole figure expressed indescribable pride.

'Tell those who sent you that the bast-sponge does not sell his honour!' he cried, raising his hand aloft.

Then he turned away quickly and began to run; but he had not run five yards before he turned round and blew Alyosha a kiss. He ran another five yards and turned round for the last time. But this time his face was no longer contorted with laughter. On the contrary, it was quivering all over with tears. In a tearful, faltering, choking voice he cried rapidly:

'And what would I say to my son if I took money from you for my disgrace?'

Having said it, he ran away, this time without turning back.

Alyosha looked after him with inexpressible sorrow. Oh, he understood that the poor man had not realized till the last moment that he would crumple and fling away the notes. He did not turn back once. Alyosha knew he would not. He did not want to run after him and call him, and for a very good reason. When Snegiryov was out of sight, Alyosha picked up the two notes. They were only badly crumpled, crushed and pressed into the sand, but were not damaged and even rustled like new ones when Alyosha unfolded and smoothed them out. Having done so, he folded them up, put them in his pocket and went to Katerina to report on the outcome of her commission.

BOOK FIVE: PRO AND CONTRA

I

The Engagement

MRS KHOKHLAKOV was again the first to meet Alyosha. She was in a hurry. Something important had happened: Katerina's attack of hysterics had ended in a fainting fit, followed, Mrs Khokhlakov informed him, 'by a terrible, awful weakness. She lay down, turned up her eyes and became delirious. Now she has a temperature and I've sent for Herzenstube and her aunts. The aunts are already here, but Herzenstube hasn't arrived yet. They're all sitting in her room and waiting. Something terrible is bound to happen. She's unconscious. What if it should be brain fever?'

Exclaiming this, Mrs Khokhlakov looked genuinely alarmed. 'This is serious, serious!' she added at every word, as though everything that had happened to her before was not serious. Alyosha listened to her sadly. He began telling her of his adventures, but she interrupted as soon as he had begun. She had no time to listen and she asked him to sit with Lise and to wait for her.

'Lise, my dear Alexey,' she whispered almost in his ear, 'Lise has given me a strange surprise just now, but she has also moved me deeply, and that is why I find it in my heart to forgive her for everything. Just fancy, as soon as you had gone, she began to be really sorry for having apparently laughed at you yesterday and today. But she was not really laughing. She was only joking. She was so sorry that she almost burst into tears. I couldn't help being surprised at her. She had never been sorry for anything so much before when she was laughing at me, but always made a jest of it. And, you know, she's always laughing at me. But now she's serious. Everything with her now is serious. She thinks highly of your opinion, Alexey, and try not to be offended with her or bear a grudge against her. I myself do all I can to spare her because she's such a clever girl. Don't you think so? She's been telling me just now that you were a friend of her childhood – "the truest friend of my childhood". How do you like that? The truest friend – and what about me? She had most sincere feelings about that, and even memories, but what is so remarkable are the phrases and words she uses, particularly the words which are most unexpected. You have no idea what she's going to say next and suddenly out it comes. There was, for instance, that thing she said about a pine-tree the other day. There used to be a pine-tree in our garden when she was very little. Perhaps it's still there so that there's no need to talk of it in the past tense. Pine-trees aren't people and they remain the same for a long time. "Mother," she said to me, "I've such a vivid recollection of the pine as if I pined for it." You see, "pine as if I pined". I mean, she may have expressed it differently, because I think I got it all muddled. Pine is such a silly word. But she said something so original about it that I simply can't repeat it. Besides, I can't remember it. Well, good-bye. I'm terribly upset and I shouldn't be surprised if I went out of my mind. Oh, dear Alexey, I've gone out of my mind twice in my life and I had to have medical treatment. Go to Lise and cheer her up as you always do it so charmingly. Lise,' she cried, going up to her daughter's door, 'I've brought you Alexey whose feelings you've hurt so badly. He isn't at all angry, I assure you. On the contrary, he's surprised that you should have supposed he was!'

'Thank you, Mother. Come in, Alexey.'

Alyosha went in. Lise looked somehow embarrassed and all of a sudden she blushed all over. She seemed to be ashamed of something, and, as always happens in such cases, she began talking very rapidly about something else, as though that was the only thing she was interested in at that moment.

'Mother has just told me the whole story about the two hundred roubles, Alexey, and about your commission to – to take them to that poor officer and – and she told me the terrible story of how he had been insulted and, you know, though Mother told it in such a jumbled-up way, jumping from one thing to another, I couldn't help crying when I heard it. Well, did you give him the money and how is the poor man now?'

'That's just the trouble, I didn't give it to him, and it's a long story,' replied Alyosha, as though what worried him most was that he had not handed over the money, and yet Lise was perfectly well aware that he, too, looked away and that he, too, was trying to talk about something else.

Alyosha sat down at the table and began to tell his story, but at his first words he completely lost his embarrassment and engaged Lise's interest, too. He spoke under the influence of strong emotion and of the powerful impression he had just received, and he succeeded in telling his story well and circumstantially. He had even before, as a boy in Moscow, liked to come to her and tell her what had just happened to him, what he had read or remembered of his days as a child. Sometimes they even used to daydream together and invent all sorts of stories, mostly cheerful and amusing ones. Now they seemed both to have been transported back to the old days in Moscow, two years before. Lise was very touched by his story. Alyosha knew how to describe 'little Ilya' to her with warm feeling. But when he finished telling her of the scene when the unhappy man had trampled on the money, Lise clasped her hands and exclaimed with unrestrained feeling:

'So you didn't give him the money! You let him run away without it! Oh dear, you should have run after him and overtaken him.'

'No, Lise, it's better not to have run after him,' said Alyosha, getting up from his chair and pacing the room with a worried look.

'Why better? How is it better? Now they can't afford to buy bread and they'll die of starvation!'

'They won't, because they will get the two hundred roubles in spite of everything. I'm sure he'll accept the money tomorrow. Yes, I'm quite sure of it,' Alyosha repeated, pacing the room thoughtfully. 'You see, Lise,' he went on, suddenly stopping short before her, 'I made one mistake, but that mistake, too, is for the best.'

'What mistake? And why is it for the best?'

'I'll tell you why. He is a timid man, a man of weak character. He's worn out with suffering and he's very good-natured. I keep on wondering why he should suddenly have become so offended and trampled on the money. He did it, I assure you, because up to the very last moment he did not know that he was going to trample on the notes. And I can't help feeling that there were lots of things he took offence at and – and it couldn't be otherwise in his position. . . . First of all, he resented having been so happy over the money in front of me and not having concealed it. If he'd been pleased, but not so much, if he hadn't shown it, but given himself airs, as others do when accepting money, if he'd dissembled, then he could have borne it and accepted the money. But he'd shown his joy too openly and that was why he felt so badly. Oh, Lise, he's a truthful and kindly man, and that's the whole trouble in a case like this! All the time he was talking to me his voice was so weak and feeble, and he spoke so fast, he kept chuckling in such a funny way, or he was crying – yes, he was crying, so delighted was he and – and he talked about his daughters and – and the job he hoped to get in another town. . . . But no sooner had he poured out his heart than he felt ashamed of having opened up his heart like that to me. That's why he conceived such a hatred for me at once. He's one of those awfully reserved poor people. But what he resented most of all was that he accepted me as his friend too quickly and gave in to me too soon. At first he sprang at me and tried to intimidate me, but as soon as he saw the money he began embracing me. For he did almost embrace me. He kept touching me with his hands. That was how he came to feel how humiliating it all was and it was just then that I made that mistake, that very serious mistake. You see, I suddenly told him that if he hadn't enough money to move to another town, he would be given more money, and indeed that I myself would give him as much as he liked of my own money. It was this that struck him suddenly as rather peculiar: for why should I, he thought, rush forward to help him? You know, Lise, it's awful for a man who's been through a great deal of trouble when everyone looks at him as if they were his benefactors. . . . I've been told of that. The elder told me about it. I don't know how to put it, but I've seen it often myself. Besides, you know, that's exactly how I feel, too. And the interesting thing is that though up to the last moment he did not know that he would trample on the notes, he did have a premonition of it. I'm sure of that. It's just because he had this premonition that he was so highly delighted. And yet though it's turned out so badly, it's all for the best. Indeed, I think that nothing better could have happened. . . . '

'Why, why could nothing better have happened?' Lise cried, looking in great surprise at Alyosha.

'Because, Lise, if he had taken the money and not trampled on it, he would have wept at his humiliation an hour after getting home. Yes, that would most certainly have happened. He would have wept and perhaps have come to me early tomorrow morning and flung the notes at me and trampled on them as he did today. But now he's gone off feeling very proud and triumphant, though he knows that he has "ruined" himself. Which, of course, means that there's nothing easier now than to make him accept the two hundred roubles to-morrow, because he has vindicated his honour by trampling on the money. He couldn't possibly have known when he did it that I would take him the money again tomorrow. And yet he needs the money badly. Though he may be proud today, he'll be thinking even today of what he has lost. He will be thinking of it even more at night, he will be dreaming of it, and tomorrow morning, I expect, he'll be ready to run to apologize to me. And just then I will appear and say: "You are a proud man and you've proved it. Now take the money and forgive us." Then I'm quite sure he'll take it!'

Alyosha uttered the last sentence: 'And then I'm quite sure he'll take it!' with a kind of rapture. Lise clapped her hands.

'Oh, it's true, it's true! Oh, I understand it all now so awfully well! Alyosha, how do you know all this? You're so young and you can see into people's minds. I should never have thought of it!'

'What we must do now is to convince him that he is on the same level with all of us, in spite of the fact that he's taking money from us,' Alyosha went on rapturously. 'And not only on the same level, but even on a higher level.'

'On a higher level – excellent, Alexey, but go on, go on!'

'I'm afraid I've put it rather badly. I mean, about the higher level – but it doesn't matter, because —'

'Oh, of course it doesn't matter in the least! I'm sorry, Alyosha dear. . . . You know, I hardly respected you till now. I mean, I did respect you, but on the same level, but now I shall respect you on a higher level. . . . Darling, don't be angry with me for "making puns",' she added at once with strong feeling. 'I'm an absurd little girl, but you, you — Listen, Alexey, don't you think our reasoning – I mean, yours – no, better say ours – don't you think it shows that we regard him – that unfortunate man – with contempt? I mean that we analyse his soul like this, as though from above? I mean that we're so absolutely certain that he'll accept the money. Don't you think so?'

'No, Lise, it doesn't show any contempt,' Alyosha replied firmly, as though he had been prepared for this question. 'I thought of that myself on my way here. Just think, what sort of contempt can it be if we ourselves are the same as he, if everyone is like him. For we are the same as he, you know. Not a bit better. And even if we were better, we'd be just the same in his place. I don't know about you, Lise, but I can't help feeling that in many ways I am small-minded. And he is not. On the contrary, he's very sensitive. No, Lise, there's no question of any contempt for him! You know, Lise, my elder said that one had to care for people as one would for children, and for some people as though they were patients in a hospital.'

'Oh, darling Alexey, let's care for people as we would for the sick!'

'Yes, let's, Lise. I'm willing, but I'm afraid I'm not quite ready for it. Sometimes I'm very impatient and at other times I don't seem to be able to see things. You're different.'

'Oh, I don't believe it! Alexey, I'm so happy!'

'It's nice of you to say that, Lise!'

'You're awfully nice, Alexey, but sometimes you're a bit of a prig. And yet you're not really a prig. Please, go to the door, open it gently, and see whether Mother is listening,' Lise suddenly said in a hurried, nervous whisper.

Alyosha went, opened the door a little and reported that no one was listening.

'Come here, Alexey,' Lise went on, blushing more and more, 'give me your hand – so. Listen, I have to make a great confession: I didn't write you yesterday's letter as a joke, but in earnest. . . .'

And she covered her eyes with her hand. One could see that she was greatly ashamed of this confession. Suddenly she seized his hand and kissed it impulsively three times.

'Oh, Lise,' Alyosha cried joyfully, 'that's all right then! I was quite sure that you had written it in earnest.'

'Quite sure – fancy that!' she cried, pushing away his hand without, however, releasing it, colouring terribly and laughing a little, happy laugh. 'I kissed his hand, and he says "that's all right!"'

But she was unfair to reproach him: Alyosha, too, was greatly embarrassed.

'I want you always to like me, Lise, but I don't know how to make you,' he murmured, also blushing.

'Alyosha, darling, you're cold and cheeky. How do you like that? He did me the honour of choosing me as his wife and that's enough for him! He's sure I was in earnest – really! Why, that's cheek – that's what it is!'

'Why, was it bad of me to be sure?' Alyosha laughed suddenly.

'Why no, Alyosha, it was awfully good of you,' said Lise, gazing tenderly and happily at him.

Alyosha was still standing beside her, holding her hand in his. Suddenly he bent over her and kissed her full on the mouth.

'Really Alexey! What's the matter with you?' exclaimed Lise.

Alyosha was thrown into utter confusion.

'I'm sorry if I shouldn't have. . . . Perhaps it was awfully stupid of – of me — You said I was cold, so I kissed you. Only I can see that it was stupid. . . .'

Lise laughed and hid her face in her hands.

'And in your cassock!' she cried between her bursts of laughter, but suddenly she stopped laughing and became very serious, almost stern. 'I think we'd better postpone our kisses, because we don't really know how to kiss and we shall have to wait a long time yet,' she concluded suddenly. 'You'd better tell me why you want to marry such a little fool as me, such a sickly little fool, you who are so clever, so intellectual, so observant? Oh, Alyosha, I'm awfully happy, for I don't deserve you a bit.'

'You do, Lise. I shall be leaving the monastery for good in a few days. If I go out into the world, I shall have to marry. That at least I know. He told me to marry, too. And whom could I marry better than you and – and who would marry me except you? I've been thinking about it. First of all, you've known me since childhood and, secondly, you've a great many qualities I haven't. You're a much more cheerful person than I and, what's more, you're much more innocent than I, for I've already come in contact with many, many things. Oh, you don't know, but I, too, am a Karamazov! I don't care if you laugh and joke, and at me too! On the contrary, go on laughing – I'm so glad of it. . . . But you laugh like a little girl and you think like a martyr. . . .'

'Like a martyr? How's that?'

'Yes, Lise. You see, your question whether we do not despise that unhappy man by dissecting his soul was the question of a person who has suffered a lot. I'm afraid I don't know how to put it properly, but a person to whom such questions occur is himself capable of suffering. Sitting in your invalid chair, you must have thought over many things already. . . .'

'Alyosha, give me your hand, don't take it away,' Lise said in a small voice, weak with happiness. 'Listen, Alyosha, what clothes are you going to wear when you leave your monastery? Don't laugh and don't be angry, please. It's very, very important to me.'

'I haven't thought of it yet, Lise, but I'll wear any clothes you like.'

'I'd like you to have a dark blue velvet coat, a white piqué waist-coat, and a soft grey felt hat. Tell me did you really think I didn't love you when I said I didn't mean what I wrote yesterday?'

'No, I didn't.'

'Oh, you impossible, incorrigible man!'

'You see, I suspected that – that you perhaps cared for me, but I pretended to believe you so that you – you shouldn't feel uncomfortable.'

'That makes it worse! Worse and better than everything, Alyosha. I love you awfully! Before you came I said to myself: shall I ask him for my letter? If he took it out calmly and gave it back to me (which could always be expected of him), then he doesn't love me at all, he doesn't feel anything, he is simply a stupid, good-for-nothing boy, and I am done for. But you left the letter in the monastery cell and that made me feel better. You did leave the letter behind so as not to give it back because you had a feeling that I'd ask for it, didn't you? You did, didn't you?'

'Oh, Lise, I'm afraid you're quite wrong. You see, I've got the letter on me now, and I had it on me before, too. It's in this pocket. Here it is.'

Alyosha pulled the letter out laughingly, and showed it to her at a distance.

'Only I'm not going to give it to you. Look at it from here.'

'Oh? So you told a lie, you – a monk?'

'I suppose I did,' Alyosha, too, laughed. 'I lied because I didn't want to give you back the letter. It's very dear to me,' he added suddenly with strong feeling, blushing again. 'It always will be and I shan't ever give it to anyone!'

Lise looked at him with admiration.

'Alyosha,' she murmured again, 'have a look at the door. Is Mother listening?'

'All right, Lise, I'll look. Only wouldn't it be better not to? Why suspect your mother of such meanness?'

'Meanness? What meanness? She has a right to eavesdrop on her daughter. It's not mean at all,' cried Lise, flushing. 'You may be sure, sir, that when I am a mother and have a daughter like myself, I shall most certainly be eavesdropping on her.'

'Would you really, Lise? It's wrong.'

'Goodness, what kind of meanness is it? If it had been some ordinary society gossip, I shouldn't dream of eavesdropping, for that would be mean. But if my own daughter were shut up with a young man — Listen, Alyosha, I shall be spying on you, too, after we're married, and you may as well know now that I intend to open all your letters and read them. You may as well be forewarned. . . . '

'Why, of course, if that's how —,' Alyosha murmured. 'Only it's not right.'

'Oh, what contempt! Darling Alyosha, don't let's quarrel the very first day. But I'd better be quite frank with you: it's of course very wrong to eavesdrop and, of course, I'm wrong and you're right, but I shall eavesdrop all the same.'

'By all means,' said Alyosha, laughing. 'Only you won't catch me doing anything wrong.'

'But will you do as I tell you, Alyosha? That, too, we'd better settle beforehand.'

'Very gladly, Lise. I most certainly shall, except in the most important things. If you don't agree with me in the most important things, I shall still do as my duty tells me to.'

'So you should. But I'd like you to know that I'm ready to submit to you not only in the most important things but in everything else, and I'm willing to take an oath on it now – in everything and all my life,' Lise exclaimed fervently. 'And I'll do that gladly, gladly! And what's more, I swear I shall never eavesdrop on you, never once – nor read a single letter of yours, for you're right and I'm wrong. And though I'd awfully like to eavesdrop – I know that – I shan't do it for all that because you don't consider it honourable. I shall look upon you now as my Providence. Listen, Alexey, why have you been so sad all this time – yesterday and today? I know you've had a lot of troubles and worries, but I can see that something is worrying you especially. It isn't some secret grief, is it?'

'Yes, Lise, it is,' Alyosha said sadly. 'I can see you love me, if you've guessed that.'

'What sort of grief? What is it about? Can't you tell me?' Lise asked with timid entreaty.

'I'll tell you later, Lise, later,' said Alyosha, looking embarrassed. 'If I told you now, you would not understand. Besides, I'm not sure I know how to tell you about it.'

'I know your brothers and your father are worrying you too.'

'Yes, my brothers too,' said Alyosha, as though sunk in thought.

'I don't like your brother Ivan, Alyosha,' Lise suddenly remarked.

Alyosha was somewhat surprised at that remark, but did not comment on it.

'My brothers are destroying themselves,' he went on, 'and my father, too. And they are destroying others together with themselves. What we have here is "the earth-bound Karamazov force", as Father Paissy expressed it the other day, earth-bound, unrestrained, and crude. I don't even know whether the spirit of God moves over that force. All I know is that I, too, am a Karamazov. I a monk, a monk? Am I a monk, Lise? I believe you said I was a monk a moment ago.'

'Yes, I did.'

'And yet I don't think I even believe in God.'

'You don't believe? What's the matter with you?' Lise said softly and guardedly.

But Alyosha made no answer. There was something very mysterious and very subjective in these sudden words of his, something that he perhaps did not understand himself, but that undoubtedly worried him.

'And, on top of that, my friend is passing away. The best man in the world is leaving the earth now. Oh, if only you knew, Lise, if only you knew how bound up, how closely knit I am spiritually with him! And now I shall be left alone. . . . I shall come to you, Lise. . . . In future we shall be together. . . . '

'Yes, together, together! From now on always together and for the rest of our lives! Listen, kiss me. I'll let you.'

Alyosha kissed her.

'Well, you can go now. Christ be with you' (and she made the sign of the cross over him). 'Go quickly to *him* while he is still alive. I think it was cruel of me to keep you. I shall pray for you and for him today. Alyosha, we shall be happy. Shall we be happy? Shall we?'

'I believe we shall, Lise.'

On going out of Lise's room, Alyosha did not think it necessary to go to see Mrs Khokhlakov and he went downstairs without taking leave of her. But as soon as he opened the door and began to descend the stairs, Mrs Khokhlakov suddenly appeared before him. Alyosha guessed from the first word she uttered that she had been waiting for him there on purpose.

'Alexey, this is terrible! It's all a lot of childish nonsense. It's ridiculous. I hope you won't take it into your head to dream of — It's foolishness, foolishness, nothing but foolishness!' she pounced on him.

'Only don't tell her that,' said Alyosha, 'or she'll be upset and that's bad for her.'

'I'm glad to hear a sensible word from a sensible young man. Am I to understand that you agreed with her only out of compassion for her ailing condition? Because you didn't want to make her angry by contradicting her?'

'Oh no, not at all,' Alyosha declared firmly. 'I spoke quite seriously with her.'

'Seriousness is out of place here, it's unthinkable, and, first of all, I shall never be at home to you again, and, secondly, I shall go away and take her with me. Make no mistake about that.'

'But why?' said Alyosha. 'It's still so far off. We may have to wait another sixteen months.'

'Oh, Alexey, that's quite true, of course, and I daresay in sixteen months you'll have time to quarrel a thousand times and to drift apart. But I'm so unhappy, so unhappy! Maybe it is all nonsense, but it's such a blow to me. Now I'm just like Famussov in the last scene of *The Misfortune of Being Clever*. You're Chatsky, she's Olga, and just imagine I've run on purpose to meet you on the stairs, and in the play, too, the tragedy happens on the stairs. I heard everything, I could hardly restrain myself. So that's the explanation of all the horrors of last night and of her hysterics! Love to the daughter and death to the mother. I might as well be in my grave. Now another thing and most important of all: What is the letter she's written to you? Show it to me at once, at once!'

'I'm sorry I can't. Tell me how is Katerina. I must know.'

'She's still delirious and hasn't regained consciousness yet. Her aunts are here, but they do nothing but sigh and turn up their noses at me. Herzenstube came and he was so alarmed that I didn't know what to do with him and how to calm him. I nearly sent for a doctor. I had him driven home in my carriage. And to crown it all – you and this letter! It's true all this cannot happen for a year and a half. I implore you, Alexey, in the name of all that's holy, in the name of your dying elder, to show me, her mother, this letter! If you like, you can hold it in your hand and I'll read it like that.'

'No, I won't show it to you, Mrs Khokhlakov. Even if I had her permission to show it, I wouldn't show it to you. I shall come tomorrow and if you like I shall talk many things over with you, but now – good-bye!'

And Alyosha ran downstairs and out into the street.

2

Smerdyakov with a Guitar

BESIDES, he had no time to lose. Even while he was saying good-bye to Lise a sudden idea occurred to him – an idea of how he might catch Dmitry, who was evidently hiding from him, by some clever stratagem. It was already rather late, three o'clock in the afternoon. Alyosha was longing with all his heart to go back to the monastery to his 'great departing friend', but the necessity of seeing Dmitry outweighed every other consideration: the conviction of some impending terrible catastrophe was growing stronger and stronger in Alyosha's mind with every hour. What the nature of the catastrophe was and what he meant to say to his brother just then, he could not perhaps tell himself. 'Let my benefactor die without me, but at least I shall not have to reproach myself all my life with being able to prevent something and not doing so, but passing by and hurrying back home. In doing this, I'm acting in accordance with his great precept. . . .'

His plan was to catch his brother Dmitry unawares by climbing over the fence, entering the garden as he had on the day before, and concealing himself in the summer-house. 'If he isn't there,' he thought, 'I shall wait in the summer-house till the evening, if necessary, without telling Foma or the women of the house. But if, as before, he is lying in wait for Grushenka, he will most likely come to the summer-house. . . . ' Alyosha, however, did not give much thought to the details of the plan, but decided to carry it out even if it meant that he could not go back to the monastery that day.

Everything happened without hindrance: he climbed over the fence almost in the same spot as the day before and got to the summer-house without being seen. He did not want to be seen: both the women of the house and Foma (if he were there), might be on his brother's side and carry out his instructions, that is to say, refuse to let Alyosha into the garden, or warn his brother betimes that he was being sought and asked for. There was no one in the summer-house. Alyosha sat down on the same seat as on the day before and began to wait. He examined the summer-house and for some reason it looked to him more dilapidated than the day before. It seemed such a wretched place this time. The day, though, was as fine as the day before. On the table there was the circle left by his brother's glass of brandy which had evidently spilt over. Idle and futile thoughts kept drifting into his mind as always in time of tedious waiting: for instance, why, having come there, had he sat down precisely in the same place as the day before and not in another? At last he felt very depressed – depressed by anxious uncertainty. He had not been sitting there for more than a quarter of an hour when he suddenly heard the strum of a guitar somewhere very near. Some people were sitting or had only just sat down somewhere in the bushes not more than twenty yards away from him. Alyosha suddenly recalled that, after he had left his brother in the summer-house the day before, he saw, or just caught a glimpse of, an old low green garden seat on the left by the fence among the bushes. Some new arrivals must have sat down on it now. But who? A male voice suddenly began to sing in a sugary falsetto a verse from a popular song, accompanying himself on a guitar.

> My devotion to my love
> All my life I shall prove,
> Lord have mer-r-cy
> On her and me!
> On her and me!
> On her and me!

The voice ceased. It was a lackey's tenor and the fanciful way of singing was also that of a lackey. Another voice, a woman's, suddenly asked caressingly and rather timidly, but in an affected, mincing voice:

'Why haven't you been to see us for so long? Why do you always turn your back upon us?'

'Not at all,' replied a man's voice, politely, though with unmistakably firm and emphatic dignity.

It was clear that the man was the master of the situation and the woman was making advances to him. 'The man must be Smerdyakov,' thought Alyosha. 'At least the voice is his, and his lady friend must be the daughter of the house, who has come from Moscow and who wears a dress with a train and goes to Marfa for soup.'

'I'm ever so fond of poetry, especially if it rhymes,' the woman's voice continued. 'Why don't you go on?'

The voice sang again:

> For an emperor's crown I cannot,
> If my dear one but keep her health,
> Lord, have mer-r-rcy,
> On her and me!
> On her and me!
> On her and me!

'Last time it was ever so much nicer,' the woman's voice observed. 'After the crown you sang "If my dearest darling but keep her health". It was ever so much more tender. I suppose you've forgotten it today.'

'Poetry's rubbish!'

'Oh, no, I'm very fond of a nice bit of poetry.'

'If it's poetry, it's absolutely rubbish, my dear. Consider yourself: have you ever met a person who talks in rhyme? And if we all started talking in rhyme, even at the order of the authorities, how much, do you think, should we say? Poetry's of no use, my dear.'

'How clever you are!' the woman's voice was growing more and more ingratiating. 'How did you get to know so many things?'

'I could have done lots of things and I could have known lots of things, too, if I wasn't born unlucky. I'd have shot a man in a duel, I would, if he'd called me a bastard because I'm the son of that stinking idiot woman and haven't got no father. In Moscow, my dear, they used to throw it in my teeth and all because the story got round to them thanks to Grigory. Grigory rebukes me for rebelling against my birth. "You've torn apart her thighs," he says. Well, I don't know about her thighs, but I'd have let myself be killed in the womb rather than come into the world at all. They used to talk about it in the market place, they did. And your mother, a very indelicate lady your mother is, my dear, she started telling me that she used to walk about with the hair of her head in a tangled mat and that she was four feet tall and a *wee* bit over. Why say a *wee* bit, when she might have said a *little* bit, like everyone else. Wanted to move me to tears, I suppose, but them's the sort of tears you would expect from a peasant, my dear – crude peasant feelings. Aye, that's what it is. Can a Russian peasant have feelings like an educated man? He can't have no feelings, and why? Because he's ignorant, that's why. Even as a child when I heard people say "a wee bit" I felt like knocking my head against a brick wall. I hate all Russia, my dear.'

'You wouldn't have talked like that, I'm sure, if you was a handsome cadet in the army or a dashing young hussar officer. You'd have drawn your sword to defend all Russia.'

'Far from wishing to be a dashing hussar officer, my dear, I'd have liked to do away with all soldiers.'

'But who'd defend us against an enemy then?'

'There's no need to, my dear. In 1812 there was a great invasion of Russia by the French Emperor Napoleon the First, the father of the present one, and it would have been a good thing if them Frenchies had conquered us. A clever nation, my dear, would have conquered a stupid one and annexed it. Things would have been different then, my dear.'

'As if they're so much better in their country than we are! Why, I'd never dream of exchanging one of our really handsome young gentlemen for three young Englishmen,' Maria Kondratyevna said in a tender voice, no doubt accompanying her words with a most languorous glance.

'It depends who you love, my dear.'

'But you're just like a foreigner yourself. Just like a real foreign gentleman. I'm telling you that even if it makes me blush.'

'If you really want to know, my dear, our folk here and theirs there are all alike when it comes to vice. They're all rogues, except that the rogues there walk about in patent-leather boots, and our scoundrels here wallow in their filth and see nothing bad in that. The Russian peasant, my dear, must be flogged, as Mr Karamazov quite rightly said yesterday, mad though he is, and all his children.'

'But you told me yourself that you've a great respect for Mr Ivan Karamazov.'

'Well, my dear, he called me a stinking lackey. He thinks I might turn against them, but he's mistaken, my dear. If I had a tidy sum of money in my pocket, I'd have cleared out long ago. Dmitry's worse than any lackey the way he goes on. He's poor and he isn't clever. He's no damn good for anything, but everyone respects him all the same. I may be only a broth-brewer, but with a bit of luck I could open a café-restaurant in Moscow, in Petrovka, because my cooking's something special and there's no one in Moscow, except the foreigners, whose cooking's something special, too. Dmitry's as poor as a church mouse, but if he was to challenge the son of the first count in Russia, he'd fight a duel with him. But how is he better than me? For, you see, my dear, he's so much stupider than me. Think of the money he's poured down the drain without getting anything for it!'

'Oh, I think a duel is ever so nice!' Maria Kondratyevna observed suddenly.

'How so, my dear?'

'Oh, it's so thrilling and brave, especially when two dashing young army officers with pistols in their hands fire at one another for some lady. It's lovely! Oh, if only they let girls go and look, I'd love to see it.'

'It's all very well if you're the chap what's doing the shooting, but if someone else is pointing a pistol straight at your mug, you'd feel pretty silly, I can tell you. You'd run away, you would, my dear.'

'You don't mean to say you'd run away, too?'

But Smerdyakov did not deign to answer. After a short pause he struck another chord on the guitar and burst into the last couplet of the song in his reedy falsetto:

> Whatever you say,
> I shall go away,
> Be mer-r-ry and gay . . .

> For the great city I'll leave,
> And shall not grieve,
> Never shall I grieve,
> Never again do I mean to grieve!

At this point something unexpected happened. Alyosha suddenly sneezed. The people on the garden seat at once fell silent. Alyosha got up and walked towards them. It was, indeed, Smerdyakov, dressed up, his hair pomaded and almost curled, and wearing patent-leather shoes. His guitar lay on the garden seat. The woman was Maria Kondratyevna, the daughter of the woman of the house, who was wearing a light blue dress with a train two yards long. She was a very young girl and she would have been quite good-looking if her face had not been a little too round and terribly freckled.

'Will my brother Dmitry be back soon?' Alyosha asked as calmly as he could.

Smerdyakov rose slowly from the seat; Maria Kondratyevna also got up.

'What makes you think I know about Mr Dmitry Karamazov's movements?' Smerdyakov replied quietly, in measured tones and with a scornful air. 'It isn't as if I was his keeper, is it?'

'Why, I simply asked you if you knew,' explained Alyosha.

'I knows nothing about his whereabouts, sir, and I don't want to know.'

'But my brother told me that it was you who let him know about all that went on in the house and promised to let him know when Miss Svetlov came.'

Smerdyakov slowly raised his eyes and looked at him imperturbably.

'And how,' he asked, looking intently at Alyosha, 'did you manage to get in here, seeing as how the gates was bolted an hour ago?'

'I came in from the lane over the fence and went straight to the summer-house. I hope,' he turned to Maria Kondratyevna, 'you don't mind. I was in a hurry to find my brother.'

'Of course we don't mind,' drawled Maria Kondratyevna, flattered by Alyosha's apology. 'For, you see, sir, Mr Dmitry Karamazov, too, often goes to the summer-house that way. We don't even know he's here, and there he's sitting in the summer-house.'

'I'm trying to find him now. I'm very anxious to see him, or to learn from you where he is now. I assure you it's a matter of the highest importance to him.'

'I'm afraid, sir, he never tells us,' Maria Kondratyevna murmured.

'Though I'm coming here to see some friends,' Smerdyakov began again, 'he's been worrying me something cruel even here by his constant questions about the master: how is he, what's going on in the house, who's coming and who's going, and what else I could tell him. Twice he even threatened to kill me.'

'Kill you?' cried Alyosha in surprise.

'It don't mean nothing, sir, to a man of his character. As you was so good as to observe yourself yesterday. If, he says to me, you let Miss Svetlov in and she spends the night here, you'll be the first to die. I'm terribly afraid of him, sir, and if I wasn't even more afraid of telling the police about him, I'd have gone and done it. God only knows, sir, what he may not do!'

'He told him the other day: I'll pound you in a mortar,' added Maria Kondratyevna.

'Well, if it's in a mortar, it may be only talk,' observed Alyosha. 'If I could meet him now, I might say something to him about it too.'

'All I can tell you, sir,' Smerdyakov seemed at last to have made up his mind to say, 'is that I'm coming here to visit my friends and neighbours. There's nothing wrong in that, is there? On the other hand, Mr Ivan Karamazov sent me early this morning to his lodgings in Lake Street, without a letter but with a message to be sure to go and dine with him at the restaurant in the square. I went but your brother was out, though it was eight o'clock. "He's been in," they told me, "but he's gone out for the whole day," those were his land-lady's very words, sir. It's just as though there was some kind of plot between them. I suppose they must be dining at the pub now, for Mr Ivan Karamazov hasn't been home to dinner, and the master had his dinner an hour ago by himself and is having his nap now. But I'd like to ask you, sir, not to say a word about me and about what I've told you to him, for he'd kill me for nothing at all.'

'My brother Ivan asked Dmitry to dine with him at an inn today?' Alyosha inquired quickly.

'Yes, sir.'

'At the "Metropolis" in the square?'

'That's right, sir.'

'That's very possible!' cried Alyosha in great excitement. 'Thank you, Smerdyakov. That's important. I'll go there at once.'

'Don't give me away, sir,' Smerdyakov called after him.

'Don't worry, I won't. I'll look into the restaurant as though by accident.'

'But where are you going?' Maria Kondratyevna cried. 'I'll open the gate for you.'

'No, it's much nearer this way. I'll climb over the fence again.'

The news about his brothers was a great shock to Alyosha. He ran to the inn. It was improper for him to go into the inn in his cassock, but he could ask for them on the stairs and call them down. But as soon as he reached the inn, one of the windows was thrown open and his brother Ivan called down to him from it.

'Alyosha, can you come up here to me or not? I shall be very grateful.'

'Of course I can, only what about my dress? . . .'

'I'm in a private room. Come up the steps to the entrance, and I'll come down to meet you.'

A minute later Alyosha was sitting beside his brother. Ivan was alone. He was having his dinner.

3

The Brothers Get Acquainted

IVAN was not, however, in a separate room. It was merely a place by the window separated from the rest of the bar by a screen, so that those sitting there could not be seen by the other people in the inn. It was the first room from the entrance with a bar along the opposite wall. Waiters were continually running to and fro in it. There was only one customer in the room, an old retired army officer who was drinking tea in a corner. But there was the usual bustle going on in the other rooms of the inn, people were calling for the waiters, beer bottles were being opened, billiard balls were clicking, the organ was droning. Alyosha knew that Ivan did not as a rule visit the inn and was not generally fond of inns. So he must have come there, he thought, to keep an appointment with Dmitry. Yet Dmitry was not there.

'Shall I order fish soup or something else for you? You don't live on tea alone, do you?' cried Ivan, evidently very pleased to have got hold of Alyosha. He had finished dinner and was drinking tea.

'Yes, let me have fish soup and tea afterwards,' said Alyosha gaily. 'I'm famished.'

'What about cherry jam? They have it here. Remember how you used to love cherry jam when you were little and living with Polenov?'

'You remember that? Let me have the jam, too. I still love it.'

Ivan rang for the waiter and ordered fish soup, tea, and jam.

'I remember everything, Alyosha. I remember you till you were eleven. I was fifteen then. There's such a difference between fifteen and eleven that brothers are never real friends at those ages. I don't even know whether I was fond of you or not. When I went away to Moscow I never even thought of you. Then, when you came to Moscow yourself, we met only once, I believe. And now I've been living here for over three months and we've scarcely exchanged a single word till now. Tomorrow I'm going away and I was thinking as I sat here how I could arrange to see you to say good-bye, and there you were passing by.'

'Did you want to see me very much?'

'Yes, very much. I want to get to know you once for all, and I want you to know me. And then to say good-bye. I think the best time to get to know people is before you part from them. I've seen how you've been looking at me during these three months. There was a sort of look of continual expectation in your eyes, and it was that I couldn't bear. That was why I've kept away from you. But in the end I learnt to respect you: this little fellow, I said to myself, has a firm hold on life. Mind you, though I'm laughing now, I'm speaking seriously. You do have a firm hold on life, haven't you? I like people who are firm like that, whatever it is they stand by, and even if they are such little boys as you. I didn't dislike your expectant look in the end; on the contrary, I grew fond of it. I believe you are fond of me for some reason, aren't you, Alyosha?'

'Yes, Ivan, I am. Dmitry says about you: Ivan is as silent as the grave, but I say about you: Ivan is a riddle. You're still a riddle to me, but something about you I already understand, and that, too, only since this morning!'

'What's that?' Ivan laughed.

'You won't be angry, will you?' Alyosha, too, laughed.

'Well?'

'I mean that you're just as young as all the other twenty-three-year-old young men. Just as young. Just a very young, fresh, and nice boy – just a young and inexperienced boy, in fact! You're not offended, are you?'

'On the contrary, you've surprised me by a coincidence!' Ivan cried gaily and warmly. 'You know after our last meeting at her place all I could think of was that I was just a young, inexperienced boy, and you seem to have guessed it now and begin with that. I was sitting here just now and do you know what I was saying to myself? I said to myself: if I didn't believe in life, if I lost faith in the woman I love, if I lost faith in the order of things, if I were convinced that everything was, on the contrary, a disorderly, damnable, and perhaps devil-ridden chaos, if I were completely overcome by all the horrors of man's disillusionment – I'd still want to live and, having once raised the cup to my lips, I wouldn't tear myself away from it till I had drained it to the dregs! However, I shall probably fling it away at thirty, even if I haven't emptied it, and turn away – where I don't know. But till I'm thirty, I know for certain that my youth will triumph over everything – every disappointment and every disgust with life. I've asked myself many times: is there in the world any despair that would overcome this frenzied and, perhaps, indecent thirst for life in me, and I've come to the conclusion that, perhaps, there isn't. But, of course, that holds true only till I'm thirty. After that I shall not want to go on myself – that's how I feel now. Some snivelling trivial moralists, poets especially, often call this thirst for life a base thing. It's to some extent a Karamazov characteristic. That's true. You, too, in spite of everything, have this thirst for life. But why is it a base thing? There's still a great deal of the centripetal force on our planet, Alyosha. I want to live and I go on living, even if it is against logic. However much I may disbelieve in the order of things, I still love the sticky little leaves that open up in the spring, I love the blue sky, I love some people, whom, you know, one loves sometimes without knowing why, I love some great human achievement, in which I've perhaps lost faith long ago, but which from old habit my heart still reveres. Here's your fish soup. Eat it. It's excellent. They know how to make it here. I want to travel in Europe, Alyosha, and I shall be going abroad from here. And yet I know very well that I'm only going to a graveyard, but it's a most precious graveyard – yes, indeed! Precious are the dead that lie there. Every stone over them speaks of such ardent life in the past, of such a passionate faith in their achievements, their truth, their struggles, and their science, that I know beforehand that I shall fall on the ground and kiss those stones and weep over them and – and at the same time deeply convinced that it's long been a graveyard and nothing more. And I shall not weep from despair, but simply because I shall be happy in my tears. I shall get drunk on my own emotion. I love the sticky little leaves of spring and the blue sky – yes, I do! It's not a matter of intellect or logic. You love it all with your inside, with your belly. You love to feel your youthful powers asserting themselves for the first time. . . . Do you understand anything of all this rigmarole, Alyosha, or don't you?' Ivan suddenly laughed.

'I understand it too well, Ivan: one longs to love with one's inside, with one's belly – yes, you put it excellently and I'm terribly glad you have such a longing for life!' cried Alyosha. 'I think everyone must love life more than anything else in the world.'

'Love life more than the meaning of it?'

'Yes, certainly. Love it regardless of logic, as you say. Yes, most certainly regardless of logic, for only then will I grasp its meaning. That's what I've been vaguely aware of for a long time. Half your work is done, Ivan: you love life. Now you must try to do the second half and you are saved.'

'So you're already saving me, though I may not be lost at all! And what does this second half of yours consist of?'

'Why, to raise up your dead who have perhaps never died at all. Well, let's have tea now – I'm glad, Ivan, that we're talking at last!'

'I see you're in a sort of inspired mood. I do like such *professions de foi* from such – novices. You're a steadfast fellow, Alexey. Is it true that you want to leave the monastery?'

'Yes, my elder sends me into the world.'

'We shall see each other, then, in the world. We shall meet before I'm thirty, before, that is, I begin to tear myself away from the cup.

Father doesn't want to tear himself away from his cup till he's seventy. He even means to hang on to it till he's eighty. He told me so himself. He's quite serious about it, though he's a clown. Stands on his sensuality as though it were a rock – though after thirty, I suppose, that is the only thing one can stand on. But it's disgusting to hold on to it till the age of seventy. It's much better till one is thirty: one could then retain "the outward show of nobility" by deceiving oneself. You haven't seen Dmitry today, have you?'

'Afraid not, but I saw Smerdyakov.'

And Alyosha told his brother rapidly and in detail of his meeting with Smerdyakov. Ivan suddenly began listening with a very preoccupied air and even asked Alyosha to repeat some of his statements.

'Only he begged me not to tell Dmitry what he had told me about him,' added Alyosha.

Ivan frowned and sank into thought.

'Are you frowning because of Smerdyakov?' asked Alyosha.

'Yes, because of him. But to hell with him. I really did want to see Dmitry, but now there's no need,' Ivan said reluctantly.

'And are you really going away so soon?'

'Yes.'

'But what about Dmitry and father? How will it all end?' Alyosha asked anxiously.

'You're still harping on it! What have I got to do with it? I am not my brother Dmitry's keeper, am I?' Ivan snapped irritably, but suddenly he smiled bitterly. 'Cain's reply to God about his murdered brother – eh? Perhaps that's what you're thinking now, aren't you? But, damn it all, I can't very well stay here to be their keeper, can I? I've finished what I had to do and I'm going away. You don't think I'm jealous of Dmitry, that I've been trying to filch his beautiful Katerina from him for the last three months, do you? Damn it, I had business of my own. I've finished it and I'm going away. I finished it just now, as you saw yourself.'

'At Katerina's?'

'Yes, and I've done with it once and for all. And, really, what is all the fuss about? What have I to do with Dmitry? It doesn't concern Dmitry at all. I had my own business to settle with Katerina. And you know yourself that Dmitry behaved as though he'd been in a plot with me. I never asked him. It was he himself who solemnly handed her over to me and gave us his blessing. The whole thing's too funny for words. Oh, Alyosha, if only you knew how happy I am now! I sat here having my dinner and, believe me, I felt like ordering some champagne to celebrate my first hour of freedom. Dear, oh dear, six months almost – and suddenly I got rid of it all at once. Why, even yesterday I never dreamt that I had only to wish and the whole thing would be over and done with!'

'Is it your love you're speaking of, Ivan?'

'My love, if you like. Yes, I fell in love with a young lady, a boarding-school miss. I had an awful time with her, and she, too, gave me an awful time. Spent hours with her . . . and now suddenly it's all over! This morning I spoke on the spur of the moment, but as soon as I got away I burst out laughing. You don't believe me? Honestly, I did. I mean every word of it.'

'Why, you seem to be happy about it even now,' observed Alyosha, looking closely at his face, which really had grown much more cheerful.

'How was I to know that I did not love her at all? Ha, ha! Well, it seems I didn't. But I did feel attracted to her! Even when I was making my speech this morning I felt attracted to her. Even now, you know, I like her awfully, and yet I don't mind leaving her a bit. You don't think I'm bragging, do you?'

'No, only perhaps that it was not love.'

'Dear Alyosha,' Ivan laughed, 'don't you get involved in arguments about love. It doesn't become you. The way you rushed in this morning! Dear me! I've forgotten to kiss you for it. . . . But what a dance she led me! It was certainly a case of incurable heartache. Oh, she knew well enough that I loved her! She loved me and not Dmitry,' Ivan insisted cheerfully. 'Dmitry was only a case of heartache. Everything I told her today was absolutely true. But, you see, the trouble is that it will take her perhaps fifteen or twenty years to realize that she didn't love Dmitry at all, that she loved only me, whom she only tortures. And I daresay she'll never realize it in spite of her lesson today. Well, it's best like that: get up and go away for good. Incidentally, how is she now? What happened there after I had gone?'

Alyosha told him about her hysterical fit and that she was apparently still unconscious and delirious.

'Mrs Khokhlakov isn't imagining it all, is she?'

'I don't think so.'

'I'll have to make inquiries. Still no one has ever died of hysterics. So she had hysterics – what does it matter? The good Lord gave hysterics to women out of love. I won't go back there. Why thrust myself upon her again?'

'But you did tell her this morning that she never loved you, didn't you?'

'I did so on purpose. Alyosha, let me order some champagne and let's drink to my freedom. Oh, if you knew how glad I am!'

'No, I don't think we'd better drink,' Alyosha said suddenly. 'Besides, I feel rather sad.'

'Yes, you've been feeling sad for some time. I noticed it long ago.'

'So you've quite made up your mind to leave tomorrow morning?'

'Tomorrow morning? I didn't say I was going to leave in the morning. Still, I might leave in the morning. You know, I dined here today only to avoid dining with the old man – I detest him so much. If it had only been him, I'd have left long ago. And why are you so worried about my going away? We've plenty of time before I go. A whole eternity of time – immortality!'

'What kind of eternity is it if you're leaving tomorrow?'

'But what does that matter to us?' Ivan laughed. 'We shall have plenty of time to talk over the things that interest us, the things we've come here to talk over, shan't we? Why do you look so surprised? Tell me: what have we come here for? To talk about Katerina's love? About the old man and Dmitry? About going abroad? About the calamitous position of Russia? About the Emperor Napoleon? Have we come for that?'

'No, not for that.'

'Very well, then. You know, therefore, what for. Others have their own subjects of conversation, and we, greenhorns, have ours. We have first of all to solve the eternal problems. That's our worry. Young Russia is talking of nothing but the eternal problems now. Now especially, for the old men have suddenly become preoccupied with practical problems. Why did you look so expectantly at me for all these three months? To ask me, "What do you believe or do you not believe at all?" That was the meaning of your glances for the last three months, my dear fellow, wasn't it?'

'I suppose it was,' Alyosha smiled. 'You're not laughing at me now, are you?'

'Me laughing at you? Why, I should hate to disappoint my little brother who'd been looking at me with such expectation for three months. Alyosha, look straight at me: am I not exactly the same little boy as you, except, of course, that you are a novice? For what have Russian boys been doing up to now? Some of them, I mean? Well, take this stinking pub, for instance. They meet here and sit in a corner for hours. They haven't known each other all their lives and when they leave the pub they won't meet again for another forty years. But, tell me, what are they going to talk about while snatching a free moment in a pub? Why, about eternal questions: is there a God, is there immortality? And those who do not believe in God? Well, those will talk about socialism and anarchism and the transformation of the whole of mankind in accordance with some new order. So, you see, they're the same damned old questions, except that they start from the other end. And thousands of the most original Russian boys do nothing nowadays but talk of eternal questions. Isn't that so?'

'Yes,' said Alyosha, looking at his brother with the same gentle and probing smile, 'to real Russians the questions whether there is a God and whether there is immortality, or, as you say, the questions that start from the other end, of course come first, and so they should.'

'Look here, Alyosha. Sometimes it isn't at all clever to be a Russian, but all the same it's impossible to imagine anything sillier than the way Russian boys spend their time now. But one Russian boy called Alyosha I'm awfully fond of.'

'How beautifully you got that in,' Alyosha laughed suddenly.

'Well, tell me what to begin with – give the order yourself – with God? Does God exist? Is that it?'

'Begin with anything you like, even "from the other end",' Alyosha said, looking searchingly at his brother. 'Didn't you declare at father's yesterday that there was no God?'

'I said that on purpose to tease you yesterday at dinner at father's and I saw how your eyes glowed. But I'm not at all averse from discussing it with you now and I mean it very seriously. I want to be friends with you, Alyosha, because I have no friend. I want to try to. Well, this may surprise you, but perhaps I accept God,' Ivan laughed. 'You didn't expect that, did you?'

'Of course I didn't, if, that is, you're not joking now.'

'Joking? They said I was joking at the elder's yesterday. You see, my dear chap, there was an old sinner in the eighteenth century who delivered himself of the statement that if there were no God, it would have been necessary to invent him: *S'il n'existait pas Dieu il faudrait l'inventer*. And, to be sure, man has invented God. And what is so strange, and what would be so marvellous, is not that God actually exists, but that such an idea – the idea of the necessity of God – should have entered the head of such a savage and vicious animal as man – so holy it is, so moving and so wise and so much does it redound to man's honour. So far as I'm concerned, I made up my mind long ago not to speculate whether man has created God or God has created man. Nor, of course, am I going to analyse all the modern axioms laid down by the Russian boys on that subject, all of them based on European hypotheses; for what is only an hypothesis there, becomes at once an axiom with a Russian boy, and not only with the boys but, I suppose, also with their professors, for Russian professors are quite often just the same Russian boys. And for this reason I'm going to disregard all the hypotheses. For what is it you and I are trying to do now? What I'm trying to do is to attempt to explain to you as quickly as possible the most important thing about me, that is to say, what sort of man I am, what I believe in and what I hope for – that's it, isn't it? And that's why I declare that I accept God plainly and simply. But there's this that has to be said: if God really exists and if he really has created the world, then, as we all know, he created it in accordance with the Euclidean geometry, and he created the human mind with the conception of only the three dimensions of space. And yet there have been and there still are mathematicians and philosophers, some of them indeed men of extraordinary genius, who doubt whether the whole universe, or, to put it more widely, all existence, was created only according to Euclidean geometry and they even dare to dream that two parallel lines which, according to Euclid, can never meet on earth, may meet somewhere in infinity. I, my dear chap, have come to the conclusion that if I can't understand even that, then how can I be expected to understand about God? I humbly admit that I have no abilities for settling such questions. I have a Euclidean, an earthly mind, and so how can I be expected to solve problems which are not of this world. And I advise you too, Alyosha, my friend, never to think about it, and least of all about whether there is a God or not. All these are problems which are entirely unsuitable to a mind created with the idea of only three dimensions. And so I accept God, and I accept him not only without reluctance, but, what's more, I accept his divine wisdom and his purpose – which are completely beyond our comprehension. I believe in the underlying order and meaning of life. I believe in the eternal harmony into which we are all supposed to merge one day. I believe in the Word to which the universe is striving and which itself was "with God" and which was God, and, well, so on and so forth, *ad infinitum*. Many words have been bandied about on this subject. So it would seem I'm on the right path – or am I? Anyway, you'd be surprised to learn, I think, that in the final result I refuse to accept this world of God's, and though I know that it exists, I absolutely refuse to admit its existence. Please understand, it is not God that I do not accept, but the world he has created. I do not accept God's world and I refuse to accept it. Let me put it another way: I'm convinced like a child that the wounds will heal and their traces will fade away, that all the offensive and comical spectacle of human contradictions will vanish like a pitiful mirage, like a horrible and odious invention of the feeble and infinitely puny Euclidean mind of man, and that in the world's finale, at the moment of eternal harmony, something so precious will happen and come to pass that it will suffice for all hearts, that it will allay all bitter resentments, that it will atone for all men's crimes, all the blood they have shed. It will suffice not only for the forgiveness but also for the justification of everything that has ever happened to men. Well, let it, let it all be and come to pass, but I don't accept it and I won't accept it! Let even the parallel lines meet and let me see them meet, myself – I shall see and I shall say that they've met, but I still won't accept it. That is the heart of the matter, so far as I'm concerned, Alyosha. That is where I stand. I'm telling you this in all seriousness. I deliberately began our talk as stupidly as I could, but I finished it with my confession, because that's all you want. You didn't want to hear about God, but only to find out what your beloved brother lived by. And I've told you.'

Ivan concluded his long tirade suddenly with a sort of special and unexpected feeling.

'And why did you begin "as stupidly as you could"?' asked Alyosha, looking thoughtfully at him.

'Why, first of all, for the sake of proving to you that I'm a Russian: Russian discussions on these subjects are all conducted as stupidly as possible. And, secondly, the stupider, the more to the point. The stupider, the clearer. Stupidity is brief and artless, but intelligence shifts and shuffles and hides itself. Intelligence is a knave, while stupidity is straightforward and honest. I've brought my argument down to my despair, and the more stupidly I presented it, the better for me.'

'Will you explain to me why you do not accept the world?' said Alyosha.

'Why, by all means. It isn't a secret. That's what I've been leading up to. My dear brother, it's not you I want to corrupt and push off the firm foundations on which you stand, it's me, perhaps, that I'd like to be healed by you,' Ivan said, smiling suddenly just like a little gentle child. Alyosha had never seen him smile like that before.

4

Rebellion

'I MUST make a confession to you,' Ivan began. 'I never could understand how one can love one's neighbours. In my view, it is one's neighbours that one can't possibly love, but only perhaps these who live far away. I read somewhere about "John the Merciful" (some saint) who, when a hungry and frozen stranger came to him and begged him to warm him, lay down with him in his bed and, putting his arms round him, began breathing into his mouth, which was festering and fetid from some awful disease. I'm convinced that he did so from heartache, from heartache that originated in a lie, for the sake of love arising from a sense of duty, for the sake of a penance he had imposed upon himself. To love a man, it's necessary that he should be hidden, for as soon as he shows his face, love is gone.'

'The elder Zossima has talked about it more than once,' observed Alyosha. 'He, too, declared that a man's face often prevented many people who were inexperienced in love from loving him. But then there's a great deal of love in mankind, almost Christ-like love, as I know myself, Ivan. . . . '

'Well, I'm afraid I don't know anything about it yet and I can't understand it, and an innumerable multitude of people are with me there. You see, the question is whether that is due to men's bad qualities or whether that is their nature. In my opinion, Christ's love for men is in a way a miracle that is impossible on earth. It is true he was a god. But we are no gods. Suppose, for instance, that I am capable of profound suffering, but no one else could ever know how much I suffer, because he is someone else and not I. Moreover, a man is rarely ready to admit that another man is suffering (as if it were some honour). Why doesn't he admit it, do you think? Because, I suppose, I have a bad smell or a stupid face, or because I once trod on his foot. Besides, there is suffering and suffering: there is humiliating suffering, which degrades me; a benefactor of mine, for instance, would not object to my being hungry, but he would not often tolerate some higher kind of suffering in me, for an idea, for instance. That he would only tolerate in exceptional cases, and even then he might look at me and suddenly realize that I haven't got the kind of face which, according to some fantastic notion of his, a man suffering for some idea ought to have. So he at once deprives me of all his benefactions, and not from an evil heart, either. Beggars, especially honourable beggars, should never show themselves in the streets, but ask for charity through the newspapers. Theoretically it is still possible to love one's neighbours, and sometimes even from a distance, but at close quarters almost never. If everything had been as on the stage, in the ballet, where, if beggars come in, they wear silken rags and tattered lace and beg for alms dancing gracefully, then it would still be possible to look at them with pleasure. But even then we might admire them but not love them. But enough of this. All I wanted is to make you see my point of view. I wanted to discuss the suffering of humanity in general, but perhaps we'd better confine ourselves to the sufferings of children. This will reduce the scope of my argument by a tenth, but I think we'd better confine our argument to the children. It's all the worse for me, of course. For, to begin with, one can love children even at close quarters and even with dirty and ugly faces (though I can't help feeling that children's faces are never ugly). Secondly, I won't talk about grown-ups

because, besides being disgusting and undeserving of love, they have
something to compensate them for it: they have eaten the apple and
know good and evil and have become "like gods". They go on
eating it still. But little children haven't eaten anything and so far are
not guilty of anything. Do you love little children, Alyosha? I know
you do and you will understand why I want to talk only about them
now. If they, too, suffer terribly on earth, they do so, of course, for
their fathers. They are punished for their fathers who have eaten the
apple, but this is an argument from another world, an argument that
is incomprehensible to the human heart here on earth. No innocent
must suffer for another, and such innocents, too! You may be surprised at me, Alyosha, for I too love little children terribly. And note,
please, that cruel men, passionate and carnal men, Karamazovs, are
sometimes very fond of children. Children, while they are children,
up to seven years, for instance, are very different from grown-up
people: they seem to be quite different creatures with quite different
natures. I knew a murderer in prison: in the course of his career he had
murdered whole families in the houses he had broken into at night
for the purpose of robbery, and while about it he had also murdered
several children. But when he was in prison he showed a very peculiar
affection for them. He used to stand by the window of his cell for
hours watching the children playing in the prison yard. He trained
one little boy to come up to his window and made great friends
with him. You don't know why I'm telling you this, Alyosha? I'm
afraid I have a headache and I'm feeling sad.'

'You speak with a strange air,' Alyosha observed uneasily, 'as
though you were not quite yourself.'

'By the way, not so long ago a Bulgarian in Moscow told me,'
Ivan went on, as though not bothering to listen to his brother, 'of
the terrible atrocities committed all over Bulgaria by the Turks and
Circassians who were afraid of a general uprising of the Slav population. They burn, kill, violate women and children, nail their prisoners'
ears to fences and leave them like that till next morning when they
hang them, and so on – it's impossible to imagine it all. And, indeed,
people sometimes speak of man's "bestial" cruelty, but this is very
unfair and insulting to the beasts: a beast can never be so cruel as a
man, so ingeniously, so artistically cruel. A tiger merely gnaws and
tears to pieces, that's all he knows. It would never occur to him to

nail men's ears to a fence and leave them like that overnight, even if he were able to do it. These Turks, incidentally, seemed to derive a voluptuous pleasure from torturing children, cutting a child out of its mother's womb with a dagger and tossing babies up in the air and catching them on a bayonet before the eyes of their mothers. It was doing it before the eyes of their mothers that made it so enjoyable. But one incident I found particularly interesting. Imagine a baby in the arms of a trembling mother, surrounded by Turks who had just entered her house. They are having great fun: they fondle the baby, they laugh to make it laugh and they are successful: the baby laughs. At that moment the Turk points a pistol four inches from the baby's face. The boy laughs happily, stretches out his little hands to grab the pistol, when suddenly the artist pulls the trigger in the baby's face and blows his brains out. . . . Artistic, isn't it? Incidentally, I'm told the Turks are very fond of sweets.'

'Why are you telling me all this, Ivan?' asked Alyosha.

'I can't help thinking that if the devil doesn't exist and, therefore, man has created him, he has created him in his own image and likeness.'

'Just as he did God, you mean.'

'Oh, you're marvellous at "cracking the wind of the poor phrase", as Polonius says in *Hamlet*,' laughed Ivan. 'You've caught me there. All right. I'm glad. Your God is a fine one, if man created him in his own image and likeness. You asked me just now why I was telling you all this: you see, I'm a collector of certain interesting little facts and, you know, I'm jotting down and collecting from newspapers and books, from anywhere, in fact, certain jolly little anecdotes, and I've already a good collection of them. The Turks, of course, have gone into my collection, but they are, after all, foreigners. I've also got lovely stories from home. Even better than the Turkish ones. We like corporal punishment, you know. The birch and the lash mostly. It's a national custom. With us nailed ears are unthinkable, for we are Europeans, after all. But the birch and the lash are something that is our own and cannot be taken away from us. Abroad they don't seem to have corporal punishment at all now. Whether they have reformed their habits or whether they've passed special legislation prohibiting flogging – I don't know, but they've made up for it by something else, something as purely national as ours. Indeed, it's so national that it seems to be quite impossible in our country, though I believe it is taking root here too, especially since the spread of the religious movement among our aristocracy. I have a very charming brochure, translated from the French, about the execution quite recently, only five years ago, of a murderer in Geneva. The murderer, Richard, a young fellow of three and twenty, I believe, repented and was converted to the Christian faith before his execution. This Richard fellow was an illegitimate child who at the age of six was given by his parents *as a present* to some shepherds in the Swiss mountains. The shepherds brought him up to work for them. He grew up among them like a little wild animal. The shepherds taught him nothing. On the contrary, when he was seven they sent him to take the cattle out to graze in the cold and wet, hungry and in rags. And it goes without saying that they never thought about it or felt remorse, being convinced that they had every right to treat him like that, for Richard had been given to them just as a chattel and they didn't even think it necessary to feed him. Richard himself testified how in those years, like the prodigal son in the Gospel, he was so hungry that he wished he could eat the mash given to the pigs, which were fattened for sale. But he wasn't given even that and he was beaten when he stole from the pigs. And that was how he spent all his childhood and his youth, till he grew up and, having grown strong, he himself went to steal. The savage began to earn his living as a day labourer in Geneva, and what he earned he spent on drink. He lived like a brute and finished up by killing and robbing an old man. He was caught, tried, and sentenced to death. There are no sentimentalists there, you see. In prison he was immediately surrounded by pastors and members of different Christian sects, philanthropic ladies, and so on. They taught him to read and write in prison, expounded the Gospel to him, exhorted him, tried their best to persuade him, wheedled, coaxed, and pressed him till he himself at last solemnly confessed his crime. He was converted and wrote to the court himself that he was a monster and that at last it had been vouchsafed to him by God to see the light and obtain grace. Everyone in Geneva was excited about him – the whole of philanthropic and religious Geneva. Everyone who was well-bred and belonged to the higher circles of Geneva society rushed to the prison to see him. They embraced and kissed Richard: "You are our brother! Grace has descended upon you!" Richard himself just wept with emotion: "Yes, grace has descended upon me! Before in my childhood and youth I was glad of pigs' food, but now grace has descended upon me, too, and I'm dying in the Lord!" "Yes, yes, Richard, die in the Lord. You've shed blood and you must die in the Lord. Though it was not your fault that you knew not the Lord when you coveted the pigs' food and when you were beaten for stealing it (what you did was very wrong, for it is forbidden to steal), you've shed blood and you must die." And now the last day comes. Richard, weak and feeble, does nothing but cry and repeat every minute: "This is the happiest day of my life. I'm going to the Lord!" "Yes," cry the pastors, the judges, and the philanthropic ladies, "this is the happiest day of your life, for you are going to the Lord!" They all walked and drove in carriages behind the cart on which Richard was being taken to the scaffold. At last they arrived at the scaffold: "Die, brother," they cried to Richard, "die in the Lord, for His grace has descended upon you!" And so, covered with the kisses of his brothers, they dragged brother Richard on to the scaffold, placed him on the guillotine, and chopped off his head in a most brotherly fashion because grace had descended upon him too. Yes, that's characteristic. That brochure has been translated into Russian by some aristocratic Russian philanthropists of the Lutheran persuasion and sent gratis to the newspapers and other editorial offices for the enlightenment of the Russian people. The incident with Richard is so interesting because it's national. Though we may consider it absurd to cut off the head of a brother of ours because he has become our brother and because grace has descended upon him, we have, I repeat, our own national customs which are not much better. The most direct and spontaneous historic pastime we have is the infliction of pain by beating. Nekrassov has a poem about a peasant who flogs a horse about its eyes, "its gentle eyes". Who hasn't seen that? That is a truly Russian characteristic. He describes how a feeble nag, which has been pulling too heavy a load, sticks in the mud with its cart and cannot move. The peasant beats it, beats it savagely and, in the end, without realizing why he is doing it and intoxicated by the very act of beating, goes on showering heavy blows upon it. "Weak as you are, pull you must! I don't care if you die so long as you go on pulling!" The nag pulls hard but without avail, and he begins lashing the poor defence-

less creature across its weeping, "gentle eyes". Beside itself with
pain, it gives one tremendous pull, pulls out the cart, and off it goes,
trembling all over and gasping for breath, moving sideways, with a
curious sort of skipping motion, unnaturally and shamefully – it's
horrible in Nekrassov. But it's only a horse and God has given us
horses to be flogged. So the Tartars taught us and left us the whip as a
present. But men, too, can be flogged. And there you have an educated and well-brought-up gentleman and his wife who birch their
own little daughter, a child of seven – I have a full account of it.
Daddy is glad that the twigs have knots, for, as he says, "it will
sting more" and so he begins "stinging" his own daughter. I know
for a fact that there are people who get so excited that they derive a
sensual pleasure from every blow, literally a sensual pleasure, which
grows progressively with every subsequent blow. They beat for a
minute, five minutes, ten minutes. The more it goes on the more
"stinging" do the blows become. The child screams, at last it can
scream no more, it is gasping for breath. "Daddy, Daddy, dear
Daddy!" The case, by some devilishly indecent chance, is finally
brought to court. Counsel is engaged. The Russian people have
long called an advocate – "a hired conscience". Counsel shouts in
his client's defence: "It's such a simple thing, an ordinary domestic
incident. A father has given a hiding to his daughter and, to our
shame, it's been brought to court!" Convinced by him, the jurymen retire and bring in a verdict of not guilty. The public roars with
delight that the torturer has been acquitted. Oh, what a pity I wasn't
there! I'd have bawled out a proposal to found a scholarship in the
name of the torturer! . . . Charming pictures. But I have still better
ones about children. I've collected a great deal of facts about Russian
children, Alyosha. A father and mother, "most respectable people of
high social position, of good education and breeding", hated their
little five-year-old daughter. You see, I repeat again most emphatically that this love of torturing children and only children is a peculiar
characteristic of a great many people. All other individuals of the
human species these torturers treat benevolently and mildly like educated and humane Europeans, but they are very fond of torturing
children and, in a sense, this is their way of loving children. It's just
the defencelessness of these little ones that tempts the torturers, the
angelic trustfulness of the child, who has nowhere to go and no one

to run to for protection – it is this that inflames the evil blood of the torturer. In every man, of course, a wild beast is hidden – the wild beast of irascibility, the wild beast of sensuous intoxication from the screams of the tortured victim. The wild beast let off the chain and allowed to roam free. The wild beast of diseases contracted in vice, gout, bad liver, and so on. This poor five-year-old girl was subjected to every possible torture by those educated parents. They beat her, birched her, kicked her, without themselves knowing why, till her body was covered with bruises; at last they reached the height of refinement: they shut her up all night, in the cold and frost, in the privy and because she didn't ask to get up at night (as though a child of five, sleeping its angelic, sound sleep, could be trained at her age to ask for such a thing), they smeared her face with excrement and made her eat it, and it was her mother, her mother who made her! And that mother could sleep at night, hearing the groans of the poor child locked up in that vile place! Do you realize what it means when a little creature like that, who's quite unable to understand what is happening to her, beats her little aching chest in that vile place, in the dark and cold, with her tiny fist and weeps searing, unresentful and gentle tears to "dear, kind God" to protect her? Can you understand all this absurd and horrible business, my friend and brother, you meek and humble novice? Can you understand why all this absurd and horrible business is so necessary and has been brought to pass? They tell me that without it man could not even have existed on earth, for he would not have known good and evil. But why must we know that confounded good and evil when it costs so much? Why, the whole world of knowledge isn't worth that child's tears to her "dear and kind God"! I'm not talking of the sufferings of grown-up people, for they have eaten the apple and to hell with them – let them all go to hell, but these little ones, these little ones! I'm sorry I'm torturing you, Alyosha. You're not your-self. I'll stop if you like.'

'Never mind, I want to suffer too,' murmured Alyosha.

'One more, only one more picture, and that, too, because it's so curious, so very characteristic, but mostly because I've only just read about it in some collection of Russian antiquities, in the *Archives* or *Antiquity*. I'll have to look it up, I'm afraid I've forgotten where I read it. It happened in the darkest days of serfdom, at the beginning

of this century – and long live the liberator of the people! There was
at the beginning of the century a General, a very rich landowner
with the highest aristocratic connexions, but one of those (even then,
it is true, rather an exception) who, after retiring from the army, are
almost convinced that their service to the State has given them the
power of life and death over their "subjects". There were such
people in those days. Well, so the General went to live on his estate
with its two thousand serfs, imagining himself to be God knows how
big a fellow and treating his poorer neighbours as though they were
his hangers-on and clowns. He had hundreds of hounds in his ken-
nels and nearly a hundred whips – all mounted and wearing uni-
forms. One day, a serf-boy, a little boy of eight, threw a stone in
play and hurt the paw of the General's favourite hound. "Why is
my favourite dog lame?" He was told that the boy had thrown a
stone at it and hurt its paw. "Oh, so it's you, is it?" said the General,
looking him up and down. "Take him!" They took him. They took
him away from his mother, and he spent the night in the lock-up.
Early next morning the General, in full dress, went out hunting. He
mounted his horse, surrounded by his hangers-on, his whips, and his
huntsmen, all mounted. His house-serfs were all mustered to teach
them a lesson, and in front of them all stood the child's mother. The
boy was brought out of the lock-up. It was a bleak, cold, misty autumn
day, a perfect day for hunting. The General ordered the boy to be
undressed. The little boy was stripped naked. He shivered, panic-
stricken and not daring to utter a sound. "Make him run!" ordered
the General. "Run, run!" the whips shouted at him. The boy ran.
"Sick him!" bawled the General, and set the whole pack of borzoi
hounds on him. They hunted the child down before the eyes of his
mother, and the hounds tore him to pieces! I believe the General was
afterwards deprived of the right to administer his estates. Well,
what was one to do with him? Shoot him? Shoot him for the satisfaction of our moral feelings? Tell me, Alyosha!'

'Shoot him!' Alyosha said softly, raising his eyes to his brother
with a pale, twisted sort of smile.

'Bravo!' yelled Ivan with something like rapture. 'If you say so,
then – you're a fine hermit! So that's the sort of little demon dwelling
in your heart, Alyosha Karamazov!'

'What I said was absurd, but —'

'Yes, but – that's the trouble, isn't it?' cried Ivan. 'Let me tell you, novice, that absurdities are only too necessary on earth. The world is founded on absurdities and perhaps without them nothing would come to pass in it. We know a thing or two!'

'What do you know?'

'I understand nothing,' Ivan went on as though in delirium, 'and I don't want to understand anything now. I want to stick to facts. I made up my mind long ago not to understand. For if I should want to understand something, I'd instantly alter the facts and I've made up my mind to stick to the facts. . . . '

'Why are you putting me to the test?' exclaimed Alyosha, heart-brokenly. 'Will you tell me at last?'

'Of course I will tell you. That's what I was leading up to. You're dear to me. I don't want to let you go and I won't give you up to your Zossima.'

Ivan was silent for a minute and his face suddenly became very sad.

'Listen to me: I took only children to make my case clearer. I don't say anything about the other human tears with which the earth is saturated from its crust to its centre – I have narrowed my subject on purpose. I am a bug and I acknowledge in all humility that I can't understand why everything has been arranged as it is. I suppose men themselves are to blame: they were given paradise, they wanted freedom and they stole the fire from heaven, knowing perfectly well that they would become unhappy, so why should we pity them? Oh, all that my pitiful earthly Euclidean mind can grasp is that suffering exists, that no one is to blame, that effect follows cause, simply and directly, that everything flows and finds its level – but then this is only Euclidean nonsense. I know that and I refuse to live by it! What do I care that no one is to blame, that effect follows cause simply and directly and that I know it – I must have retribution or I shall destroy myself. And retribution not somewhere in the infinity of space and time, but here on earth, and so that I could see it myself. I was a believer, and I want to see for myself. And if I'm dead by that time, let them resurrect me, for if it all happens without me, it will be too unfair. Surely the reason for my suffering was not that I as well as my evil deeds and sufferings may serve as manure for some future harmony for someone else. I want to see with my own eyes the lion lie down with the lamb and the murdered man rise up and embrace his murderer. I want to be there when everyone suddenly finds out what it has all been for. All religions on earth are based on this desire, and I am a believer. But then there are the children, and what am I to do with them? That is the question I cannot answer. I repeat for the hundredth time – there are lots of questions, but I've only taken the children, for in their case it is clear beyond the shadow of a doubt what I have to say. Listen: if all have to suffer so as to buy eternal harmony by their suffering, what have the children to do with it – tell me, please? It is entirely incomprehensible why they, too, should have to suffer and why they should have to buy harmony by their sufferings. Why should they, too, be used as dung for someone's future harmony? I understand solidarity in sin among men, I understand solidarity in retribution, too, but, surely, there can be no solidarity in sin with children, and if it is really true that they share their fathers' responsibility for all their fathers' crimes, then that truth is not, of course, of this world and it's incomprehensible to me. Some humorous fellow may say that it makes no difference since a child is bound to grow up and sin, but, then, he didn't grow up: he was torn to pieces by dogs at the age of eight. Oh, Alyosha, I'm not blaspheming! I understand, of course, what a cataclysm of the universe it will be when everything in heaven and on earth blends in one hymn of praise and everything that lives and has lived cries aloud: "Thou art just, O Lord, for thy ways are revealed!" Then, indeed, the mother will embrace the torturer who had her child torn to pieces by his dogs, and all three will cry aloud: "Thou art just, O Lord!", and then, of course, the crown of knowledge will have been attained and everything will be explained. But there's the rub: for it is that I cannot accept. And while I'm on earth, I hasten to take my own measures. For, you see, Alyosha, it may really happen that if I live to that moment, or rise again to see it, I shall perhaps myself cry aloud with the rest, as I look at the mother embracing her child's torturer: "Thou art just, O Lord!" But I do not want to cry aloud then. While there's still time, I make haste to arm myself against it, and that is why I renounce higher harmony altogether. It is not worth one little tear of that tortured little girl who beat herself on the breast and prayed to her "dear, kind Lord" in the stinking privy with her unexpiated tears! It is not worth it, because her tears remained unexpiated. They must be expiated, for otherwise there can be no harmony. But how, how are you to expiate them? Is it possible? Not, surely, by their being avenged? But what do I want them avenged for? What do I want a hell for torturers for? What good can hell do if they have already been tortured to death? And what sort of harmony is it, if there is a hell? I want to forgive. I want to embrace. I don't want any more suffering. And if the sufferings of children go to make up the sum of sufferings which is necessary for the purchase of truth, then I say beforehand that the entire truth is not worth such a price. And, finally, I do not want a mother to embrace the torturer who had her child torn to pieces by his dogs! She has no right to forgive him! If she likes, she can forgive him for herself, she can forgive the torturer for the immeasurable suffering he has inflicted upon her as a mother; but she has no right to forgive him for the sufferings of her tortured child. She has no right to forgive the torturer for that, even if her child were to forgive him! And if that is so, if they have no right to forgive him, what becomes of the harmony? Is there in the whole world a being who could or would have the right to forgive? I don't want harmony. I don't want it, out of the love I bear to mankind. I want to remain with my suffering unavenged. I'd rather remain with my suffering unavenged and my indignation unappeased, *even if I were wrong*. Besides, too high a price has been placed on harmony. We cannot afford to pay so much for admission. And therefore I hasten to return my ticket of admission. And indeed, if I am an honest man, I'm bound to hand it back as soon as possible. This I am doing. It is not God that I do not accept, Alyosha. I merely most respectfully return him the ticket.'

'This is rebellion,' Alyosha said softly, dropping his eyes.

'Rebellion? I'm sorry to hear you say that,' Ivan said with feeling. 'One can't go on living in a state of rebellion, and I want to live. Tell me frankly, I appeal to you — answer me: imagine that it is you yourself who are erecting the edifice of human destiny with the aim of making men happy in the end, of giving them peace and contentment at last, but that to do that it is absolutely necessary, and indeed quite inevitable, to torture to death only one tiny creature, the little girl who beat her breast with her little fist, and to found the edifice on her unavenged tears — would you consent to be the architect on those conditions? Tell me and do not lie!'

'No, I wouldn't,' Alyosha said softly.

'And can you admit the idea that the people for whom you are building it would agree to accept their happiness at the price of the unjustly shed blood of a little tortured child and having accepted it, to remain for ever happy?'

'No, I can't admit it. Ivan,' Alyosha said suddenly with flashing eyes, 'you said just now, is there a being in the whole world who could or had the right to forgive? But there is such a being, and he can forgive everything, everyone and everything and *for everything*, because he gave his innocent blood for all and for everything. You've forgotten him, but it is on him that the edifice is founded, and it is to him that they will cry aloud: "Thou are just, O Lord, for thy ways are revealed!"'

'Oh, "the only one without sin" and his blood! No, I have not forgotten him, and indeed I could not help being surprised at you all the time for not bringing him in, for in all your arguments you usually put him forward first of all. You know, Alyosha – don't laugh, but I made up a poem about a year ago. If you can spare me another ten minutes, I'll tell you about it.'

'You wrote a poem?'

'Oh, no, I didn't write it,' Ivan laughed. 'And I've never composed two lines of poetry in my life. But I made up this poem and I remembered it. I made it up in a moment of inspiration. You will be my first reader, I mean, listener,' Ivan grinned. 'Shall I tell you or not?'

'I'd be glad to hear it,' said Alyosha.

'My poem is called "The Grand Inquisitor". It's an absurd thing, but I'd like to tell you about it.'

5

The Grand Inquisitor

'I'M afraid here, too, it's impossible to begin without an introduction, that is, a literary introduction – oh, dear,' Ivan laughed, 'what a rotten author I'd make! You see, the action of my poem takes place in the sixteenth century and in those days, as you no doubt know from your lessons at school, it was the custom in poetical works to bring heavenly powers down to earth. Not to mention Dante, in France court clerks as well as monks in monasteries performed plays in which the Madonna, the angels, the saints, Christ, and even God himself were brought on the stage. In those days it was all done very artlessly. In Victor Hugo's *Notre Dame de Paris*, an edifying play, to which the people were admitted without charge, was performed at the Paris town hall in the reign of Louis XI to celebrate the birth of the French Dauphin. It was called *Le bon jugement de la très sainte et gracieuse Vierge Marie*, and she appeared in person and pronounced her *bon jugement*. We occasionally had almost identical performances of plays, based on Old Testament stories, in Moscow before the time of Peter the Great. But in addition to plays, there were in those days a great many stories and "poems" in which, whenever required, holy angels and all the heavenly powers took part. In our monasteries monks were also occupied with translating, copying, and even composing such poems – and even under the Tartars. There is, for instance, one such monastery poem (translated from the Greek, of course): *The Holy Virgin's Journey Through Hell*, with descriptions as bold as those of Dante's. Our Lady visits hell and is shown round "the torments" by the archangel Michael. She sees the sinners and their sufferings. There is there, incidentally, a highly diverting category of sinners in a burning lake: those who are thrown into this lake can never swim out of it, and these "God forgets" – an expression of extraordinary depth and force. And so the Mother of God, shocked and weeping, kneels before the throne of God and begs for a free pardon for all in hell, for all she has seen there, without distinction. Her conversation with God is extraordinarily interesting. She beseeches, she refuses to go away, and when God points to the stigmata on the hands and feet of her Son and asks her: "How am I to forgive his torturers?" – she bids all the saints, all the martyrs, all the angels and archangels to kneel with her and pray for a free pardon for all without distinction. It ends by her obtaining from God a respite from torments every year from Good Friday to Trinity Sunday, and the sinners in hell at once give thanks to the Lord and cry out to him: "Thou art just, O Lord, in that judgement!" Well, then, my little poem would also have been of that kind had it appeared at that time. In my poem he appears, though, it is true, he says nothing, but only appears and passes on. Fifteen centuries have passed since he gave the promise to come into his kingdom, fifteen centuries since his prophet wrote: "Behold I come quickly." "Of that day and hour knoweth no man, not the angels of heaven, but my Father only," as he said himself while still on earth. But mankind awaits him with the same faith and the same yearning. Oh, with greater faith even, for fifteen centuries have passed since the pledges given to man from heaven have ceased:

> Trust what thy heart doth tell thee,
> Trust no pledges from above.

'And only the faith in what your heart tells you remains! It is true there were many miracles in those days. There were saints who worked miraculous cures; according to their "lives", the Holy Mother of God herself came to visit some holy men. But the devil does not slumber, and many people were already beginning to doubt the truth of those miracles. Just then there appeared in the north of Germany a dreadful new heresy. A great star, "burning as it were a lamp" (that is, the church), "fell upon the fountains of waters and they became wormwood". Those heresies began impiously to deny the existence of miracles. But those who remained faithful believed all the more ardently. The tears of mankind rose up to him as before, they waited for him, they loved him, they put their hope in him, they yearned to suffer and die for him as before. . . . And for countless ages mankind prayed with fiery faith, "Oh Lord our God, appear unto us." They called upon him for so many ages that he, in his infinite mercy, longed to come down to those who prayed to him. He had come down and had visited before that day some saints, martyrs, and holy hermits while they were still on earth, as is written in their "lives". In our own country, the poet Tyutchev, who believed sincerely in the truth of his words, proclaimed that:

> In slavish habit, the Heavenly King,
> By the burden of the Cross weighed down,
> Through my native land went wandering,
> Showering blessings upon village and town.

And I can assure you that it really was so. And now the time came when he wished to appear to the people, if only for a moment – to the tormented, suffering people, to the people sunk in filthy iniquity, but who loved him like innocent children. The action of my poem takes place in Spain, in Seville, during the most terrible time of the Inquisition, when fires were lighted every day throughout the land to the glory of God and

> In the splendid autos-da-fé
> Wicked heretics were burnt.

Oh, of course, this was not the second coming when, as he promised, he would appear at the end of time in all his heavenly glory, and which would be as sudden "as the lightning cometh out of the east, and shineth even unto the west". No, all he wanted was to visit his children only for a moment and just where the stakes of the heretics were crackling in the flames. In his infinite mercy he once more walked among men in the semblance of man as he had walked among men for thirty-three years fifteen centuries ago. He came down into the hot "streets and lanes" of the southern city just at the moment when, a day before, nearly a hundred heretics had been burnt all at once by the cardinal, the Grand Inquisitor, *ad majorem gloriam Dei* in "a magnificent auto da fé", in the presence of the king, the court, the knights, the cardinals, and the fairest ladies of the Court and the whole population of Seville. He appeared quietly, inconspicuously, but everyone – and that is why it is so strange – recognized him. That might have been one of the finest passages in my poem – I mean, why they recognized him. The people are drawn to him by an irresistible force, they surround him, they throng about him, they follow him. He walks among them in silence with a gentle smile of infinite compassion. The sun of love burns in his heart, rays of Light, of Enlightenment, and of Power stream from his eyes and, pouring over the people, stir their hearts with responsive love. He stretches forth his hands to them, blesses them, and a healing virtue comes from contact with him, even with his garments. An old man, blind from childhood, cries out to him from the midst of the crowd, "O Lord, heal me so that I may see thee", and it is as though scales fell from his eyes, and the blind man sees him. The people weep and kiss the ground upon which he walks. Children scatter flowers before him, sing and cry out to him: "Hosannah!" "It is he, it is he himself," they all repeat. "It must be he, it can be no one but he." He stops on the steps of the Cathedral of Seville at the moment when a child's little, open white coffin is brought in with weeping into the church: in it lies a girl of seven, the only daughter of a prominent citizen. The dead child is covered with flowers. "He will raise up your child", people shout from the crowd to the weeping mother. The canon, who has come out to meet the coffin, looks on perplexed and knits his brows. But presently a cry of the dead child's mother is heard. She throws herself at his feet. "If it is thou," she cries, holding out her hands to him, "then raise my child from the dead!" The funeral cortège halts. The coffin is lowered on to the steps at his feet. He gazes with compassion and his lips once again utter softly the words, "Talitha cumi" – "and the damsel arose". The little girl rises in the coffin, sits up, and looks around her with surprise in her smiling, wide-open eyes. In her hands she holds the nosegay of white roses with which she lay in her coffin. There are cries, sobs, and confusion among the people, and it is at that very moment that the Cardinal himself, the Grand Inquisitor, passes by the cathedral in the square. He is an old man of nearly ninety, tall and erect, with a shrivelled face and sunken eyes, from which, though, a light like a fiery spark still gleams. Oh, he is not wearing his splendid cardinal robes in which he appeared before the people the day before, when the enemies of the Roman faith were being burnt – no, at that moment he is wearing only his old, coarse, monk's cassock. He is followed at a distance by his sombre assistants and his slaves and his "sacred" guard. He stops in front of the crowd and watches from a distance. He sees everything. He sees the coffin set down at *his* feet, he sees the young girl raised from the dead, and his face darkens. He knits his grey, beetling brows and his eyes flash with an ominous fire. He stretches forth his finger and commands the guards to seize *him*. And so great is his power and so accustomed are the people to obey him, so humble and submissive are they to his will, that the crowd immediately makes way for the guards and, amid the death-like hush that descends upon the square, they lay hands upon *him* and lead him away. The crowd, like one man, at once bows down to the ground before the old Inquisitor, who blesses them in silence and passes on. The guards take their Prisoner to the dark, narrow, vaulted prison in the old building of the Sacred Court and lock him in there. The day passes and night falls, the dark, hot and "breathless" Seville night. The air is "heavy with the scent of laurel and lemon". Amid the profound darkness, the iron door of the prison is suddenly opened and the old Grand Inquisitor himself slowly enters the prison with a light in his hand. He is alone and the door at once closes behind him. He stops in the doorway and gazes for a long time, for more than a minute, into his face. At last he approaches him slowly, puts the lamp on the table and says to him:

' "Is it you? You?"

'But, receiving no answer, he adds quickly: "Do not answer, be silent. And, indeed, what can you say? I know too well what you would say. Besides, you have no right to add anything to what you have said already in the days of old. Why, then, did you come to meddle with us? For you have come to meddle with us, and you know it. But do you know what is going to happen tomorrow? I know not who you are and I don't want to know: whether it is you or only someone who looks like him, I do not know, but tomorrow I shall condemn you and burn you at the stake as the vilest of heretics, and the same people who today kissed your feet, will at the first sign from me rush to rake up the coals at your stake tomorrow. Do you know that? Yes, perhaps you do know it," he added after a moment of deep reflection without taking his eyes off his prisoner for an instant.'

'I'm afraid I don't quite understand it, Ivan,' said Alyosha, who had been listening in silence all the time, with a smile. 'Is it just a wild fantasy, or has the old man made some mistake, some impossible *qui pro quo*?'

'You can assume it to be the latter,' laughed Ivan, 'if our modern realism has spoilt you so much that you can't bear anything fantastic. If you prefer a *qui pro quo*, then let it be so. It is true,' he laughed again, 'the old man was ninety and he might have long ago gone mad about his fixed idea. He might, too, have been struck by the Prisoner's appearance. It might, finally, have been simply delirium. A vision the ninety-year-old man had before his death, particularly as he had been greatly affected by the burning of a hundred heretics at the auto-da-fé the day before. What difference does it make to us whether it was a *qui pro quo* or a wild fantasy? The only thing that matters is that the old man should speak out, that at last he does speak out and says aloud what he has been thinking in silence for ninety years.'

'And is the Prisoner also silent? Does he look at him without uttering a word?'

'Yes,' Ivan laughed again, 'that's how it should be in all such cases. The old man himself tells him that *he* has no right to add anything to what had already been said before. If you like, this is the most fundamental feature of Roman Catholicism, in my opinion at any rate: "Everything," he tells him, "has been handed over by you to the Pope and, therefore, everything is now in the Pope's hands, and there's no need for you to come at all now – at any rate, do not interfere for the time being." They not only speak, but also write in that sense. The Jesuits do at any rate. I've read it myself in the works of their theologians. "Have you the right to reveal to us even one of the mysteries of the world you have come from?" my old man asks him and he replies for him himself. "No, you have not. So that you may not add anything to what has been said before and so as not to deprive men of the freedom which you upheld so strongly when you were on earth. All that you might reveal anew would encroach on men's freedom of faith, for it would come as a miracle, and their freedom of faith was dearer to you than anything even in those days, fifteen hundred years ago. Was it not you who said so often in those days, 'I shall make you free'? But now you have seen those 'free' men," the old man adds suddenly with a pensive smile. "Yes, this business has cost us a great deal," he goes on, looking sternly at him, "but we've completed it at last in your name. For fifteen centuries we've been troubled by this freedom, but now it's over and done with for good. You don't believe that it is all over? You look meekly at me and do not deign even to be indignant with me? I want you to know that now – yes, today – these men are more than ever convinced that they are absolutely free, and yet they themselves have brought their freedom to us and humbly laid it at our feet. But it was we who did it. And was that what you wanted? Was that the kind of freedom you wanted?" '

'I'm afraid I don't understand again,' Alyosha interrupted. 'Is he being ironical, is he laughing?'

'Not in the least. You see, he glories in the fact that he and his followers have at last vanquished freedom and have done so in order to make men happy. "For," he tells him, "it is only now (he is, of course, speaking of the Inquisition), that it has become possible for the first time to think of the happiness of men. Man is born a rebel, and can rebels be happy? You were warned," he says to him. "There has been no lack of warnings and signs, but you did not heed the warnings. You rejected the only way by which men might be made happy, but, fortunately, in departing, you handed on the work to us. You have promised and you have confirmed it by your own word. You have given us the right to bind and unbind, and of course you can't possibly think of depriving us of that right now. Why, then, have you come to interfere with us?" '

'And what's the meaning of "there has been no lack of warnings and signs"?' asked Alyosha.

'That, you see, is the chief thing about which the old man has to speak out.

' "The terrible and wise spirit, the spirit of self-destruction and non-existence," the old man went on, "the great spirit talked with you in the wilderness and we are told in the books that he apparently 'tempted' you. Is that so? And could anything truer have been said than what he revealed to you in his three questions and what you rejected, and what in the books are called 'temptations'? And yet if ever there has been on earth a real, prodigious miracle, it was on that day, on the day of the three temptations. Indeed, it was in the emergence of those three questions that the miracle lay. If it were possible to imagine, for the sake of argument, that those three questions of the terrible spirit had been lost without leaving a trace in the books and that we had to rediscover, restore, and invent them afresh and that to do so we had to gather together all the wise men of the earth – rulers, high priests, scholars, philosophers, poets – and set them the task of devising and inventing three questions which would not only correspond to the magnitude of the occasion, but, in addition, express in three words, in three short human sentences, the whole future history of the world and of mankind, do you think that the entire wisdom of the earth, gathered together, could have invented anything equal in depth and force to the three questions which were actually put to you at the time by the wise and mighty spirit in the wilderness? From those questions alone, from the miracle of their appearance, one can see that what one is dealing with here is not the human, transient mind, but the absolute and everlasting one. For in those three questions the whole future history of mankind is, as it were, anticipated and combined in one whole and three images are presented in which all the insoluble historical contradictions of human nature all over the world will meet. At the time it could not be so clearly seen, for the future was still unknown, but now, after fifteen centuries have gone by, we can see that everything in those three questions was so perfectly divined and foretold and has been so completely proved to be true that nothing can be added or taken from them.

' "Decide yourself who was right – you or he who questioned you then? Call to your mind the first question; its meaning, though not in these words, was this: 'You want to go into the world and you are going empty-handed, with some promise of freedom, which men in their simplicity and their innate lawlessness cannot even comprehend, which they fear and dread – for nothing has ever been more unendurable to man and to human society than freedom! And do you see the stones in this parched and barren desert? Turn them into loaves, and mankind will run after you like a flock of sheep, grateful and obedient, though for ever trembling with fear that you might withdraw your hand and they would no longer have your loaves.' But you did not want to deprive man of freedom and rejected the offer, for, you thought, what sort of freedom is it if obedience is bought with loaves of bread? You replied that man does not live by bread alone, but do you know that for the sake of that earthly bread the spirit of the earth will rise up against you and will join battle with you and conquer you, and all will follow him, crying 'Who is like this beast? He has given us fire from heaven!' Do you know that ages will pass and mankind will proclaim in its wisdom and science that there is no crime and, therefore, no sin, but that there are only hungry people. 'Feed them first and then demand virtue of them!' – that is what they will inscribe on their banner which they will raise against you and which will destroy your temple. A new building will rise where your temple stood, the dreadful Tower of Babel will rise up again, and though, like the first one, it will not be completed, yet you might have prevented the new tower and have shortened the sufferings of men by a thousand years – for it is to us that they will come at last, after breaking their hearts for a thousand years with their tower! Then they will look for us again under the ground, hidden in the catacombs (for we shall again be persecuted and tortured), and they will find us and cry out to us, 'Feed us, for those who have promised us fire from heaven have not given it to us!' And then we shall finish building their tower, for he who feeds them will complete it, and we alone shall feed them in your name, and we shall lie to them that it is in your name. Oh, without us they will never, never feed themselves. No science will give them bread so long as they remain free. But in the end they will lay their freedom at our feet and say to us, 'We don't mind being your slaves so long as you feed us!' They will, at last, realize themselves that there cannot be enough freedom and bread for everybody, for they will never, never be able to let everyone have his fair share! They will also be convinced that they can never be free because they are weak, vicious, worthless, and rebellious. You promised them bread from heaven, but, I repeat again, can it compare with earthly bread in the eyes of the weak, always vicious and always ignoble race of man? And if for the sake of the bread from heaven thousands and tens of thousands will follow you, what is to become of the millions and scores of thousands of millions of creatures who will not have the strength to give up the earthly bread for the bread of heaven? Or are only the scores of thousands of the great and strong dear to you, and are the remaining millions, numerous as the sand of the sea, who are weak but who love you, to serve only as the material for the great and the strong? No, to us the weak, too, are dear. They are vicious and rebellious, but in the end they will become obedient too. They will marvel at us and they will regard us as gods because, having become their masters, we consented to endure freedom and rule over them – so dreadful will freedom become to them in the end! But we shall tell them that we do your bidding and rule in your name. We shall deceive them again, for we shall not let you come near us again. That deception will be our suffering, for we shall be forced to lie. That was the meaning of the first question in the wilderness, and that was what you rejected in the name of freedom, which you put above everything else. And yet in that question lay hidden the great secret of this world. By accepting 'the loaves', you would have satisfied man's universal and everlasting craving, both as an individual and as mankind as a whole, which can be summed up in the words 'whom shall I worship?' Man, so long as he remains free, has no more constant and agonizing anxiety than to find as quickly as possible someone to worship. But man seeks to worship only what is incontestable, so incontestable, indeed, that all men at once agree to worship it all together. For the chief concern of those miserable creatures is not only to find something that I or someone else can worship, but to find something that all believe in and worship, and the absolutely essential thing is that they should do so *all together*. It is this need for *universal* worship that is the chief torment of every man individually and of mankind as a whole from the beginning of time. For the sake of that universal worship they have put each other to the sword. They have set up gods and called upon each other, 'Give up your gods and come and worship ours, or else death to you and to your gods!' And so it will be to the end of the world, even when the gods have vanished from the earth: they will prostrate themselves before idols just the same. You knew, you couldn't help knowing this fundamental mystery of human nature, but you rejected the only absolute banner, which was offered to you, to make all men worship you alone incontestably – the banner of earthly bread, which you rejected in the name of freedom and the bread from heaven. And look what you have done further – and all again in the name of freedom! I tell you man has no more agonizing anxiety than to find someone to whom he can hand over with all speed the gift of freedom with which the unhappy creature is born. But only he can gain possession of men's freedom who is able to set their conscience at ease. With the bread you were given an incontestable banner: give him bread and man will worship you, for there is nothing more incontestable than bread; but if at the same time someone besides yourself should gain possession of his conscience – oh, then he will even throw away your bread and follow him who has ensnared his conscience. You were right about that. For the mystery of human life is not only in living, but in knowing why one lives. Without a clear idea of what to live for man will not consent to live and will rather destroy himself than remain on the earth, though he were surrounded by loaves of bread. That is so, but what became of it? Instead of gaining possession of men's freedom, you gave them greater freedom than ever! Or did you forget that a tranquil mind and even death is dearer to man than the free choice in the knowledge of good and evil? There is nothing more alluring to man than this freedom of conscience, but there is nothing more tormenting, either. And instead of firm foundations for appeasing man's conscience once and for all, you chose everything that was exceptional, enigmatic, and vague, you chose everything that was beyond the strength of men, acting, consequently, as though you did not love them at all – you who came to give your life for them! Instead of taking possession of men's freedom you multiplied it and burdened the spiritual kingdom of man with its sufferings for ever. You wanted man's free love so that he should follow you freely, fascinated and captivated by you. Instead of the strict ancient law, man had in future to decide for himself with a free heart what is good and what is evil, having only your image before him for guidance. But did it never occur to you that he would at last reject and call in question even your image and your truth, if he were weighed down by so fearful a burden as freedom of choice? They will at last cry aloud that the truth is not in you, for it was impossible to leave them in greater confusion and suffering than you have done by leaving them with so many cares and insoluble problems. It was you yourself, therefore, who laid the foundation for the destruction of your kingdom and you ought not to blame anyone else for it. And yet, is that all that was offered to you? There are three forces, the only three forces that are able to conquer and hold captive for ever the conscience of these weak rebels for their own happiness – these forces are: miracle, mystery, and authority. You rejected all three and yourself set the example for doing so. When the wise and terrible spirit set you on a pinnacle of the temple and said to you: 'If thou be the Son of God, cast thyself down: for it is written, He shall give his angels charge concerning thee: and in their hands they shall bear thee up, lest at any time thou dash thy foot against a stone, and thou shalt prove then how great is thy faith in thy Father.' But, having heard him, you rejected his proposal and did not give way and did not cast yourself down. Oh, of course, you acted proudly and magnificently, like God. But men, the weak, rebellious race of men, are they gods? Oh, you understood perfectly then that in taking one step, in making a move to cast yourself down, you would at once have tempted God and have lost all your faith in him, and you would have been dashed to pieces against the earth which you came to save, and the wise spirit that tempted you would have rejoiced. But, I repeat, are there many like you? And could you really assume for a moment that men, too, could be equal to such a temptation? Is the nature of man such that he can reject a miracle and at the most fearful moments of life, the moments of his most fearful, fundamental, and agonizing spiritual problems, stick to the free decision of the heart? Oh, you knew that your great deed would be preserved in books, that it would go down to the end of time and the extreme ends of the earth, and you hoped that, following you, man would remain with God and ask for no miracle. But you did not know that as soon as man rejected miracle he would at once reject God as well, for what man seeks is not so much God as miracles. And since man is unable to carry on without a miracle, he will create new miracles for himself, miracles of his own, and will worship the miracle of the witch-doctor and the sorcery of the wise woman, rebel, heretic and infidel though he is a hundred times over. You did not come down from the cross when they shouted to you, mocking and deriding you: 'If thou be the Son of God, come down from the cross.' You did not come down because, again, you did not want to enslave man by a miracle and because you hungered for a faith based on free will and not on miracles. You hungered for freely given love and not for the servile raptures of the slave before the might that has terrified him once and for all. But here, too, your judgement of men was too high, for they are slaves, though rebels by nature. Look round and judge: fifteen centuries have passed, go and have a look at them: whom have you raised up to yourself? I swear, man has been created a weaker and baser creature than you thought him to be! Can he, can he do what you did? In respecting him so greatly, you acted as though you ceased to feel any compassion for him, for you asked too much of him – you who have loved him more than yourself! Had you respected him less, you would have asked less of him, and that would have been more like love, for his burden would have been lighter. He is weak and base. What does it matter if he does rebel against our authority everywhere now and is proud of his rebellion? It is the pride of a child and of a schoolboy. They are little children rioting in class and driving out their teacher. But an end will come to the transports of the children, too. They will pay dearly for it. They will tear down the temples and drench the earth with blood. But they will realize at last, the foolish children, that although they are rebels, they are impotent rebels who are unable to keep up with their rebellion. Dissolving into foolish tears, they will admit at last that he who created them rebels must undoubtedly have meant to laugh at them. They will say so in despair, and their utterance will be a blasphemy which will make them still more unhappy, for man's nature cannot endure blasphemy and in the end will always avenge it on itself. And so, unrest, confusion, and unhappiness – this is the present lot of men after all you suffered for their freedom! Your great prophet tells in a vision and in an allegory that he saw all those who took part in the first resurrection and that there were twelve thousand of them from each tribe. But if there were so many then, they, too, were not like men, but gods. They had borne your cross, they had endured scores of years of the hungry and barren wilderness, feeding on locusts and roots – and you can indeed point with pride to those children of freedom, freely given love, and free and magnificent sacrifice in your name. But remember that there were only a few thousand of them, and they, too, gods. But what of the rest? And why are the rest, the weak ones, to blame if they were not able to endure all that the mighty ones endured? Why is the weak soul to blame for being unable to receive gifts so terrible? Surely, you did not come only to the chosen and for the chosen? But if so, there is a mystery here and we cannot understand it. And if it is a mystery, then we, too, were entitled to preach a mystery and to teach them that it is neither the free verdict of their hearts nor love that matters, but the mystery which they must obey blindly, even against their conscience. So we have done. We have corrected your great work and have based it on *miracle, mystery, and authority*. And men rejoiced that they were once more led like sheep and that the terrible gift which had brought them so much suffering had at last been lifted from their hearts. Were we right in doing and teaching this? Tell me. Did we not love mankind when we admitted so humbly its impotence and lovingly lightened its burden and allowed men's weak nature even to sin, so long as it was with our permission? Why, then, have you come to meddle with us now? And why are you looking at me silently and so penetratingly with your gentle eyes? Get angry. I do not want your love because I do not love you myself. And what have I to hide from you? Or don't I know to whom I am speaking? All I have to tell you is already known to you. I can read it in your eyes. And would I conceal our secret from you? Perhaps it is just what you want to hear from my lips. Well, then, listen. We are not with you but with *him:* that is our secret! It's a long time – eight centuries – since we left you and went over to *him.* Exactly eight centuries ago we took from him what you rejected with scorn, the last gift he offered you, after having shown you all the kingdoms of the earth: we took from him Rome and the sword of Caesar and proclaimed ourselves the rulers of the earth, the sole rulers, though to this day we have not succeeded in bringing our work to total completion. But whose fault is it? Oh, this work is only beginning, but it has begun. We shall have to wait a long time for its completion and the earth will have yet much to suffer, but we shall reach our goal and be Caesars and it is then that we shall think about the universal happiness of man. And yet even in those days you could have taken up the sword of Caesar. Why did you reject that last gift? By accepting that third counsel of the mighty spirit, you would have accomplished all that man seeks on earth, that is to say, whom to worship, to whom to entrust his conscience and how at last to unite all in a common, harmonious, and incontestable ant-hill, for the need of universal unity is the third and last torment of men. Mankind as a whole has always striven to organize itself into a world state. There have been many great nations with great histories, but the more highly developed they were, the more unhappy they were, for they were more acutely conscious of the need for the world-wide union of men. The great conquerors, the Timurs and Ghenghis-Khans, swept like a whirl-wind over the earth, striving to conquer the world, but, though unconsciously, they expressed the same great need of mankind for a universal and world-wide union. By accepting the world and Caesar's purple, you would have founded the world state and given universal peace. For who is to wield dominion over men if not those who have taken possession of their consciences and in whose hands is their bread? And so we have taken the sword of Caesar and, having taken it, we of course rejected you and followed *him.* Oh, many more centuries are yet to pass of the excesses of their free mind, of their science and cannibalism, for, having begun to build their Tower of Babel without us, they will end up with cannibalism. But then the beast will come crawling up to us and will lick our feet and will bespatter them with tears of blood from its eyes. And we shall sit upon the beast and raise the cup, and on it will be written:

'Mystery!' And then, and only then, will the reign of peace and happiness come to men. You pride yourself upon your chosen ones, but you have only the chosen ones, while we will bring peace to all. But that is not all: how many of those chosen ones, of those mighty ones who could have become the chosen ones, have at last grown tired of waiting for you and have carried and will go on carrying the powers of their spirit and the ardours of their hearts to another field and will end by raising their *free* banner against you? But you raised that banner yourself. With us, however, all will be happy and will no longer rise in rebellion nor exterminate one another, as they do everywhere under your freedom. Oh, we will convince them that only then will they become free when they have resigned their freedom to us and have submitted to us. And what do you think? Shall we be right or shall we be lying? They will themselves be convinced that we are right, for they will remember the horrors of slavery and confusion to which your freedom brought them. Freedom, a free mind and science will lead them into such a jungle and bring them face to face with such marvels and insoluble mysteries that some of them, the recalcitrant and the fierce, will destroy themselves, others, recalcitrant but weak, will destroy one another, and the rest, weak and unhappy, will come crawling to our feet and cry aloud: 'Yes, you were right, you alone possessed his mystery, and we come back to you – save us from ourselves!' In receiving loaves from us, they will, of course, see clearly that we are taking the loaves made by their own hands in order to distribute them among themselves, without any miracle. They will see that we have not made stones into loaves, but they will, in truth, be more pleased with receiving them from our hands than with the bread itself! For they will remember only too well that before, without us, the bread they made turned to stones in their hands, but that when they came back to us, the very stones turned to bread in their hands. They will appreciate only too well what it means to submit themselves to us for ever! And until men understand this, they will be unhappy. And who, pray, was more than anyone responsible for that lack of understanding? Who divided the flock and scattered it on unknown paths? But the flock will be gathered together again and will submit once more, and this time it will be for good. Then we shall give them quiet, humble happiness, the happiness of weak creatures, such as they were created. Oh, we shall at last persuade them not to be proud, for you raised them up and by virtue of that taught them to be proud; we shall prove to them that they are weak, that they are mere pitiable children, but that the happiness of a child is the sweetest of all. They will grow timid and begin looking up to us and cling to us in fear as chicks to the hen. They will marvel at us and be terrified of us and be proud that we are so mighty and so wise as to be able to tame such a turbulent flock of thousands of millions. They will be helpless and in constant fear of our wrath, their minds will grow timid, their eyes will always be shedding tears like women and children, but at the slightest sign from us they will be just as ready to pass to mirth and laughter, to bright-eyed gladness and happy childish song. Yes, we shall force them to work, but in their leisure hours we shall make their life like a children's game, with children's songs, in chorus, and with innocent dances. Oh, we shall permit them to sin, too, for they are weak and helpless, and they will love us like children for allowing them to sin. We shall tell them that every sin can be expiated, if committed with our permission; that we allow them to sin because we love them all and as for the punishment for their sins – oh well, we shall take it upon ourselves. And we shall take it upon ourselves, and they will adore us as benefactors who have taken their sins upon ourselves before God. And they will have no secrets from us. We shall allow or forbid them to live with their wives and mistresses, to have or not have children – everything according to the measure of their obedience – and they will submit themselves to us gladly and cheerfully. The most tormenting secrets of their conscience – everything, everything they will bring to us, and we shall give them our decision for it all, and they will be glad to believe in our decision, because it will relieve them of their great anxiety and of their present terrible torments of coming to a free decision themselves. And they will all be happy, all the millions of creatures, except the hundred thousand who rule over them. For we alone, we who guard the mystery, we alone shall be unhappy. There will be thousands of millions of happy infants and one hundred thousand sufferers who have taken upon themselves the curse of knowledge of good and evil. Peacefully they will die, peacefully will they pass away in your name, and beyond the grave they will find nothing but death. But we shall keep the secret and for their own happiness will entice them with the reward of heaven and eternity. For even if there were anything at all in the next world, it would not of course be for such as they. They declare and prophesy that you will come and be victorious again, that you will come with your chosen ones, with your proud and mighty ones, but we shall declare that they have only saved themselves, while we have saved all. It is said that the whore, who sits upon the beast and holds in her hands the *mystery*, will be put to shame, that the weak will rise up again, that they will rend her purple and strip naked her 'vile' body. But then I will rise and point out to you the thousands of millions of happy babes who have known no sin. And we who, for their happiness, have taken their sins upon ourselves, we shall stand before you and say, 'Judge us if you can and if you dare.' Know that I am not afraid of you. Know that I, too, was in the wilderness, that I, too, fed upon locusts and roots, that I, too, blessed freedom, with which you have blessed men, and that I, too, was preparing to stand among your chosen ones, among the strong and mighty, thirsting 'to make myself of the number'. But I woke up and refused to serve madness. I went back and joined the hosts of those who have *corrected your work*. I went away from the proud and returned to the meek for the happiness of the meek. What I say to you will come to pass and our kingdom will be established. I repeat, tomorrow you will behold the obedient flock which at a mere sign from me will rush to heap up the hot coals against the stake at which I shall burn you because you have come to meddle with us. For if anyone has ever deserved our fire, it is you. Tomorrow I shall burn you. *Dixi!*" '

Ivan stopped. He had got worked up as he talked and he spoke with enthusiasm; but when he had finished, he suddenly smiled.

Alyosha, who had listened to him in silence, tried many times towards the end to interrupt him, restraining his great agitation with an effort. But now he suddenly burst into speech, as though carried away beyond control.

'But,' he cried, reddening, 'this is absurd! Your poem is in praise of Jesus and not in his disparagement as — as you wanted it to be. And who will believe you about freedom? Is that the way to understand it? Is that the way it is understood by the Greek Orthodox Church? It's Rome, and not the whole of Rome, either — it's not true. They are the worst among the Catholics — the Inquisitors, the

Jesuits! . . . And, besides, there could never have been such a fantastic person as your Inquisitor. What are those sins of men they take upon themselves? Who are these keepers of the mystery who have taken some sort of curse upon themselves for the happiness of men? When have they been seen? We know the Jesuits, people speak ill of them — do you really think they are the people in your poem? They are certainly not the same at all. . . . They are simply the Romish army for the future establishment of a universal government on earth, with the Emperor — the Pontiff of Rome — at its head. That is their ideal, but without any mystery or lofty sadness about it. . . . It's the most ordinary lust for power, for filthy earthly gains, enslavement — something like a future regime of serfdom with them as the land-owners — that is all they are after. Perhaps they don't even believe in God. Your suffering Inquisitor is nothing but a fantasy. . . .'

'Wait, wait,' Ivan laughed, 'don't be so excited! You say it's a fantasy — very well, I don't deny it. Of course it's a fantasy. But, look here, you don't really think that the Catholic movement in the last few centuries is really nothing but a lust for power for the sake of some filthy gains. . . . It isn't by any chance Father Paissy's teachings, is it?'

'No, no, on the contrary, Father Paissy once said something of the same kind as you, but,' Alyosha suddenly recollected himself, 'of course, it's not the same thing at all. Not the same thing at all!'

'A very valuable piece of information all the same in spite of your "not the same thing at all". What I'd like to ask you is why your Jesuits and Inquisitors have united only for some vile material gains? Why shouldn't there be among them a sufferer tormented by great sorrow and loving humanity? You see, let us suppose that among all those who are only out for filthy material gains there's one, just one, who is like my old Inquisitor, who had himself fed on roots in the wilderness, a man possessed, who was eager to mortify his flesh so as to become free and perfect; and yet one who had loved humanity all his life and whose eyes were suddenly opened and who saw that it was no great moral felicity to attain complete control over his will and at the same time achieve the conviction that millions of other God's creatures had been created as a mockery, that they would never be able to cope with their freedom, that no giants would ever arise from the pitiful rebels to complete the tower, that the great idealist had not in mind such boobies when he dreamt of his harmony. Realizing that, he returned and joined – the clever fellows. That could have happened, couldn't it?'

'Whom did he join? What clever fellows?' cried Alyosha, almost passionately. 'They are not so clever and they have no such mysteries and secrets. Except perhaps only godlessness, that's all their secret. Your inquisitor doesn't believe in God – that's all his secret!'

'Well, suppose it is so! At last you've guessed it! And, in fact, it really is so. That really is his whole secret. But is that not suffering, particularly for a man like him who had sacrificed his whole life for a great cause in the wilderness and has not cured himself of his love of humanity? In his last remaining years he comes to the clear conviction that it is only the advice of the great and terrible spirit that could bring some sort of supportable order into the life of the feeble rebels, "the unfinished experimental creatures created as a mockery". And so, convinced of that, he sees that one has to follow the instructions of the wise spirit, the terrible spirit of death and destruction. He therefore accepts lies and deceptions and leads men consciously to death and destruction. Keeps deceiving them all the way, so that they should not notice where they are being led, for he is anxious that those miserable, blind creatures should at least on the way think themselves happy. And, mind you, the deception is in the name of him in whose ideal the old man believed so passionately all his life! Is not that a calamity? And even if there were only one such man at the head of the whole army of men "craving for power for the sake of filthy gains" – would not even one such man be sufficient to make a tragedy? Moreover, one man like that, standing at the head of the movement, is enough for the emergence of a real leading idea of the entire Roman Church with all its armies and Jesuits – the highest idea of this Church. I tell you frankly it's my firm belief that there was never any scarcity of such single individuals among those who stood at the head of the movement. Who knows, there may have been many such individuals among the Roman Pontiffs, too. Who knows, perhaps this accursed old man, who loves humanity so obstinately in his own particular way, still exists even now in the form of a whole multitude of such individual old men, and not by chance, either, but by agreement, as a secret society formed long ago to guard the mystery. To guard it from the weak and unhappy, so as to make them happy. I'm sure it exists and, indeed, it must be so. I can't help feeling that something of the same kind of mystery exists also among the freemasons at the basis of their organization. That is why the Catholics hate the freemasons so much, for they regard them as their competitors who are breaking up the unity of their idea, while there should be only one flock and one shepherd. However, I feel that in defending my theory I must appear to you as an author who resents your criticism. Let's drop it.'

'You're probably a freemason yourself!' Alyosha cried, unable to restrain himself. 'You don't believe in God,' he added, but this time in great sorrow. He imagined, besides, that his brother was looking mockingly at him. 'How does your poem end?' he asked suddenly, his eyes fixed on the ground. 'Or was that the end?'

'I intended to end it as follows: when the Inquisitor finished speaking, he waited for some time for the Prisoner's reply. His silence distressed him. He saw that the Prisoner had been listening intently to him all the time, looking gently into his face and evidently not wishing to say anything in reply. The old man would have liked him to say something, however bitter and terrible. But he suddenly approached the old man and kissed him gently on his bloodless, aged lips. That was all his answer. The old man gave a start. There was an imperceptible movement at the corners of his mouth; he went to the door, opened it and said to him: "Go, and come no more – don't come at all – never, never!" And he let him out into "the dark streets and lanes of the city". The Prisoner went away.'

'And the old man?'

'The kiss glows in his heart, but the old man sticks to his idea.'

'And you together with him?' Alyosha cried sorrowfully. 'You too?'

Ivan laughed.

'Why, goodness me, Alyosha, it's all a lot of nonsense! It's only a stupid poem of a stupid student, who has never written two lines of poetry in his life. Why do you take it so seriously? You don't think I'm going to go straight there, to the Jesuits, to join the company of men who are correcting his work? Good Lord, what do I care? I told you all I want is to live to thirty and then – dash the cup to the floor!'

'And the sticky little leaves, the precious tombs, the blue sky, the woman you are in love with? How will you live? How will you love them?' Alyosha exclaimed sorrowfully. 'How could you with such a hell in your heart and your head? Oh no, that's just what you're going away for – to join them. And if you don't, you will kill yourself. You won't be able to endure it!'

'There is a force which can endure all!' said Ivan, this time with a cold smile.

'What force?'

'A Karamazov one – the force of the Karamazov baseness.'

'You don't mean to wallow in vice, to stifle your soul in corruption, do you?'

'I daresay, only till I'm thirty I'll perhaps escape it, and then —'

'Escape it? How will you escape it? It's impossible with your ideas.'

'That, too, à la Karamazov.'

'You mean, "everything is permitted"? Everything is allowed. That's it, isn't it?'

Ivan frowned and suddenly turned strangely pale.

'Oh, you're repeating the phrase I used yesterday which so offended Miusov and – and which Dmitry so naïvely and so eagerly repeated?' he asked with a wry smile. 'Yes, I daresay, "everything is permitted", since the words have been uttered. I won't deny it. And Mitya's version isn't bad, either.'

Alyosha looked at him in silence.

'You see, old man, I thought that when I went away I would have you at least in all the world,' Ivan said suddenly with unexpected feeling. 'But I can see now, my dear anchorite, that there's no place for me in your heart. I shall never repudiate the formula of "everything is permitted", but you will repudiate me for it, won't you?'

Alyosha got up and, without uttering a word, kissed him gently on the lips.

'Plagiarism!' cried Ivan, suddenly looking very delighted. 'You've stolen it from my poem! Thanks all the same. Get up, Alyosha, it's time we went, you and I.'

They went out, but stopped at the steps of the inn.

'Look here, Alyosha,' said Ivan in a firm voice, 'if I really have time enough to enjoy the sticky little leaves, I shall only love them in memory of you. It's enough for me that you're somewhere here, and I still shan't lose my desire for life. Does that satisfy you? If you like, take it as a declaration of love. And now you go to the right and I to the left – and that's enough – do you hear? – that's enough. What I mean is that if I do not go away tomorrow (I think I certainly shall), and we happen somehow or other to meet again, don't say a word to me on all these subjects. I ask you particularly. And, please, I ask you particularly, never even attempt to speak to me again about Dmitry,' he suddenly added irritably. 'We've got everything thrashed out. We've exhausted the subject, haven't we? And, for my part, I'll also make you a promise in return: when at the age of thirty I want "to dash the cup to the floor", I shall come once more to have a talk with you about it wherever you may be – even though it were from America. I want you to know that. I'll come on purpose. It will be very interesting to have a look at you, too, by that time – to see what sort of a chap you'll be then. You see, it's rather a solemn promise. For, as a matter of fact, we may be parting for seven or ten years. Well, go to your *Pater Seraphicus* now. I hear he's dying. If he dies without you, you will probably be angry with me for having detained you. Good-bye, kiss me once more – so – and now go. . . .'

Ivan turned suddenly and went his way without turning round. It was very similar to the way Dmitry had left Alyosha the day before, though the parting the day before had been quite different. This strange coincidence flashed like an arrow through Alyosha's wistful mind, sorrowful and grief-stricken at that moment. He waited a little, gazing after his brother. For some reason he noticed that Ivan swayed from side to side as he walked and that, when looked at from behind, his right shoulder appeared to be lower than his left. He had never noticed it before. But suddenly he, too, turned and almost ran to the monastery. It was getting very dark and he suddenly felt almost frightened; some new feeling was growing up inside him, something he could not explain. The wind had risen as on the previous evening, and the age-old pine-trees rustled gloomily round him when he entered the hermitage wood. He was almost running. '*Pater Seraphicus* – he must have got that name from somewhere – where from?' it flashed through Alyosha's mind. 'Ivan, poor Ivan, when shall I see you again? . . . Here's the hermitage. Good Lord! Yes, yes, it is he, it is *Pater Seraphicus*! He will save me – from him and for ever!'

Afterwards in his life he wondered several times in great perplexity how, after parting from Ivan, he could have entirely forgotten Dmitry whom only a few hours earlier that morning he had decided to find without fail and not to go back without having done so, even if he were unable to return to the monastery that night.

6

So Far Still a Very Obscure One

ON taking leave of Alyosha, Ivan went home to his father's house. But, strange to say, he suddenly felt terribly depressed and, what's more, his depression grew stronger and stronger with every step he took towards the house. It was not his depression that was so strange as the fact that Ivan could not for the life of him tell what was the cause of it. He had often been depressed before and it was not surprising that he felt like that at a moment when he had made a clean break with everything that had brought him here and was making ready to make a completely new start in life next day and enter upon a new and completely unknown future; he would again be as lonely as before, hoping for many things without any definite idea of what exactly he was hoping for, expecting many, too many things from life, but quite unable to give an account of his expectations or even his desires. And yet at that moment, though the apprehension of the new and unknown really did oppress his heart, it was not that at all that worried him. 'Is it disgust with my father's house?' he thought to himself. 'Looks like it. I loathe it so much, and though I shall cross its horrible threshold for the last time today, I can't help loathing it. . . . ' But no, it was not that, either. Was it his parting from Alyosha and the conversation he had had with him? 'I've kept silent for so many years with the whole world and thought it beneath my dignity to speak, and suddenly I've talked such a lot of rubbish. . . . ' And, as a matter of fact, it might have been a young man's annoyance at his youthful inexperience and youthful vanity. He was annoyed at having failed to speak frankly of his opinions and, particularly, to a fellow like Alyosha on whom he undoubtedly counted a great deal in his heart. Of course, that, too, that is, his annoyance had contributed to his depression. Indeed, it had to, but that was not it, either. No, it was not it. 'I feel sick with depression, but it's quite beyond my powers to tell what I want. Perhaps I'd better not think. . . .'

Ivan tried 'not to think', but that, too, was of no avail. What was so annoying about that depression of his and what irritated him so much about it, was the odd feeling that it was accidental and had nothing whatever to do with him. It was as if some person or thing were standing and obtruding itself somewhere, just as sometimes something obtrudes itself on your eye, and, immersed in your work or in some heated conversation, you are not aware of it for a long time, and yet it is quite obviously getting on your nerves and worrying you till at last it occurs to you to remove the offending object, often a very trifling and ridiculous one, some article left lying about in the wrong place, a handkerchief on the floor, a book not replaced in the book-case, and so on. At last Ivan, in a most vile and irritable temper, reached his father's house and, suddenly, about fifteen paces from the gate, he looked up and all at once realized what was disturbing and worrying him so much.

On a bench by the gate sat the servant Smerdyakov enjoying the cool of the evening. As soon as he caught sight of him Ivan realized that Smerdyakov was at the back of his mind and that it was this man he could not stand. A sudden light flooded his mind and everything became clear. When Alyosha had been telling him about his meeting with Smerdyakov a short while before, something gloomy and loathsome suddenly filled his heart and immediately evoked a responsive feeling of anger. Afterwards, during their talk, he had forgotten about Smerdyakov for a time, but he had stayed in his mind, and as soon as he parted from Alyosha and went home alone, the forgotten sensation at once began to emerge quickly into his consciousness again. 'Surely this wretched blackguard cannot worry me so much!' he thought with unendurable exasperation.

As a matter of fact, Ivan had recently, and especially during the last few days, taken an intense dislike to this man. He even began noticing this growing feeling of almost hatred for the man. Perhaps the process of hatred had grown so acute just because at the beginning, just after the arrival of Ivan Karamazov in our town, something quite different had been happening. At that time Ivan had suddenly taken a particular interest in Smerdyakov and had even found him very original. He himself encouraged him to talk to him, always, however, feeling surprised at a certain incoherence or rather restlessness of Smerdyakov's mind and unable to understand what it was exactly that so constantly and persistently worried the 'contemplative fellow'. They discussed philosophical questions and even how there had been light on the first day when the sun, the moon, and the stars were only created on the fourth day, and how that was to be understood; but Ivan soon found out that what interested Smerdyakov was not the sun, the moon, and the stars, and that though he was undoubtedly interested in the subject, it was only of secondary importance to him and it was something else he was after. Whether that was so or not, he began to display quite an inordinate vanity and an injured vanity, too. Ivan disliked that very much and that was the beginning of his aversion to him. Later on there were all sorts of rowdy scenes in the house. Grushenka had made her appearance, the quarrels with Dmitry had begun, there were all sorts of troubles. They discussed that, too. Smerdyakov was always very agitated when talking about it, but, again, it was very difficult to find out what exactly he hoped to get out of it. Indeed, one could not help being surprised at the illogicality and the confusing character of some of his desires, which he involuntarily betrayed and which were always rather obscure. Smerdyakov was always trying to ferret out information. He put certain indirect, but obviously carefully thought out questions, but he never explained why, and usually suddenly fell silent at the most interesting point of his inquiries or changed the subject. But what at last angered Ivan most and filled him with such revulsion was the sort of peculiar and revolting familiarity which Smerdyakov began more and more undisguisedly to show towards him. Not that he ever forgot himself so much as to be rude; on the contrary he always spoke very respectfully. But Ivan got himself into such a position that Smerdyakov began, goodness only knows why, to consider himself in some sort of league with him. He always spoke in a tone of voice that suggested that the two of them had some secret understanding about something, something that had at some time been said on both sides and that was only known to the two of them and was quite beyond the comprehension of the other mortals who were crawling round them. But even then Ivan failed for a long time to understand the real cause of his growing revulsion, and it was only quite recently that he had realized what it was all about. With a feeling of disgust and irritation he now tried to pass through the gate without speaking and without looking at Smerdyakov. But Smerdyakov got up from the bench, and by the way he did it Ivan at once guessed that he wished to talk to him about something special. Ivan glanced at him and stopped, and the fact that he stopped so suddenly and did not walk past, as he had meant to only a moment before, infuriated him. He looked with disgust and anger at Smerdyakov's eunuch-like, haggard face with the hair combed back from his temples and the fluffed-up little tuft of hair on the top of his head. His left eye was screwed up, and it winked and smiled ironically, as if to say, 'Where are you going? You won't pass by. Don't you see that two clever people like us have something to discuss?' Ivan shook with fury.

'Away, you scoundrel! What sort of company do you think I am for you, you fool?' he was about to say, but, to his utter astonishment, what he did say was something quite different: 'Is Father asleep or is he awake?' he said softly and humbly to his own surprise, and suddenly, again quite unexpectedly, sat down on the bench.

For a moment he was almost frightened – he remembered that afterwards. Smerdyakov stood facing him, his hands clasped behind his back, and looking at him with self-assurance, almost severity.

'He's still asleep, sir,' he said unhurriedly. ('You were the first to speak, not I', he seemed to say.) 'I'm surprised at you, sir,' he added after a short pause, dropping his eyes demurely, putting his right foot forward and playing with the toe of his patent-leather boot.

'Why are you surprised at me?' Ivan asked abruptly and sternly, doing his utmost to restrain himself and realizing all of a sudden with disgust that he was feeling intense curiosity and that he would not go away without satisfying it.

'Why don't you go to Chermashnya, sir?' asked Smerdyakov, raising his eyes suddenly and smiling familiarly.

'And you ought to understand yourself why I smile, if you're a clever man,' his screwed-up left eye seemed to say.

'What do I want to go to Chermashnya for?' Ivan asked in surprise.

Smerdyakov was silent again.

'Why, sir, didn't your father himself ask you to go?' he said at last unhurriedly and as though not thinking very highly himself of his question: 'I'm putting you off,' as it were, 'with a secondary reason, just to say something.'

'Damn you, man, speak more clearly! What do you want?' Ivan cried at last angrily, passing from humility to rudeness.

Smerdyakov put his right foot to his left, drew himself up, but continued to look with the same calm air and the same sweet smile.

'I've nothing important to tell you, sir. I was just passing the time of day, sir.'

Again there was silence. They did not speak for almost a minute. Ivan knew perfectly well that he ought to get up at once and explode angrily, and Smerdyakov stood before him as though waiting to see whether he would be angry with him or not. So at least Ivan thought. At last he made a movement to get up. Smerdyakov seemed to seize the moment.

'I'm in a terrible position, sir, I don't know what to do,' he said suddenly, firmly and distinctly, heaving a sigh at his last words. Ivan at once resumed his seat.

'Both of them are quite crazy, sir,' Smerdyakov went on. 'They seem to be behaving like a couple of kids. I'm speaking of your dad, sir, and your brother Dmitry. As soon as he gets up in the morning now, your dad, that is, sir, he at once starts pestering me every minute: "Hasn't she come? Why hasn't she come?" and he'll go on like that till midnight, and even later, I daresay, sir. And if Miss Svetlov don't come, for I don't think, sir, she intends to come at all, he'll be at me again next morning: "Why hasn't she come? What can have kept her away? When will she come?" as if, sir, I was to blame for it. And, on the other hand, sir, this is the sort of thing that happens: as soon as it gets dark, or even earlier, your brother comes from next door with a gun in his hands: "Take care," he says to me, "you dirty rogue, you broth-brewer, you, if you miss her and don't let me know she's come, I'll kill you before anyone else." When the night's over, in the morning, he, too, like your dad, sir, starts worrying me to death: "Why hasn't she come? When will she show up?" and here, too, sir, it's as if I was to blame that his lady-friend hasn't shown up. And every day and every hour, sir, they gets angrier and angrier, both of 'em, so that I begin to think, sir, sometimes, that I'd be better dead rather than be bullied like that. You see, sir, I can't trust them at all.'

'And why did you get mixed up with it?' Ivan said irritably. 'Why did you have to start spying for Dmitry?'

'And how could I help getting mixed up with it, sir? And I didn't get mixed up with it at all, if you wants to know the whole truth, sir. I never said a word from the very beginning, I didn't, sir. I daren't answer, you see. It was him, sir, who appointed me his page, in a manner of speaking. And since then all he says to me is, "I'll kill you, you dirty rogue," he says, "if you miss her!" I'm quite sure, sir, that I'm going to have a long epileptic fit tomorrow.'

'What's a long epileptic fit?'

'It's a long fit, sir. Goes on for a long time, it does, sir. For a couple of hours or more, or, as like as not, for a day or two. Once it went on for three days. I fell from the loft that time. The convulsions stop for a time, then start again. And for three days I didn't come back to my senses. Mr Karamazov, sir, sent for Herzenstube, our local doctor, and he put ice on my head and tried some other remedy, too. I might have died, I might, sir.'

'But I'm told with epilepsy it's impossible to tell beforehand at what time a fit is coming. What then makes you say that you'll have one tomorrow?' Ivan inquired with a peculiar and exasperated curiosity.

'That's right, sir. It's impossible to tell beforehand.'

'Besides, you fell from the loft then.'

'I climbs up to the loft every day, sir, and I might fall from the loft again tomorrow. And if it isn't from the loft, sir, I might fall down the cellar, for I have to go there every day, too, sir.'

Ivan gave him a long look.

'You're talking a lot of nonsense, I see, and I'm afraid I don't quite understand you,' he said quietly, but somehow menacingly. 'You don't mean to pretend tomorrow to have a fit lasting three days, do you?'

Smerdyakov, whose eyes were fixed on the ground and who was again playing with the toe of his right foot, set his foot down, putting his left foot forward instead, raised his head and said with a grin:

'Even if I was to play such a trick, sir, I mean, to pretend to have a fit, which isn't at all difficult for a man with experience of that sort of thing, I have a perfect right to use such means to save my life. For, you see, sir, even if Miss Svetlov comes to see his dad when I'm ill in bed, he can't very well come and ask a sick man why he hasn't told him. He'd be ashamed to.'

'Damn it,' cried Ivan, his face contorted with anger, 'why are you always in such a funk for your life? All my brother's threats are only words uttered in a passion and nothing more. He won't kill you. He will kill someone, but it won't be you!'

'He'll kill me like a fly, sir. Me first of all. But I'm more afraid of something else, sir. I'm afraid of being taken for an accomplice of his when he does something horrible to his dad.'

'Why should you be taken for his accomplice?'

'They'll take me for his accomplice, sir, because I told him the signals as a great secret!'

'What signals? Whom did you tell? Damn you, man, speak more plainly!'

'You see, sir, I must confess,' Smerdyakov drawled with pedantic composure, 'I've got a secret understanding with Mr Karamazov. As you knows yourself (if you do know it), he has for several days now locked himself in as soon as night or evening comes. Lately you've been going up to your room early every evening, sir, and yesterday you didn't go out at all and that's why perhaps you don't know how careful he's been to lock himself in at night. And though Grigory himself was to come, he'd only open the door if he recognized his voice. But Grigory, sir, never comes, and that's why I waits on him in his rooms alone – that's the arrangement he made himself ever since he started that business with Miss Svetlov. But at night, you see, sir, I goes away, by his orders, to the cottage as usual, but on condition that I don't go to bed till midnight, but keep watch, getting up and walking round the yard, waiting for Miss Svetlov to come, for he's been expecting her for the last few days, sir, just as if he was mad. He argues this way, sir: she's afraid of him, of your brother Dmitry, that is, of that puppy Mitya, as he calls him, and so she'll be coming the back way late at night. You look out for her, he says to me, till midnight and later. And if she comes, you run and knock on my door or on the window from the garden twice at first, very softly, so: one-two, then three times more quickly: knock-knock-knock. Then, he says, I'll understand at once that she's come and will open the door to you quietly. He told me of another signal in case something special happens: at first I have to knock quickly twice: knock-knock and then, after a short interval, knock again once, but much louder. Then he'll understand that something unexpected has happened and that I must see him at once, and he'll open the door and I'll go in and report to him. That's in case Miss Svetlov can't come herself but sends someone with a message. Besides, your brother Dmitry might also turn up, so I must let him know that he is near. He's terribly afraid of your brother Dmitry, sir, so that even if Miss Svetlov had come and was locked in the room with him and your brother Dmitry was in the meantime to turn up anywhere near, I have to report to him at once about it, knocking three times. So that the first signal of five knocks means: Miss Svetlov has come, the second signal of three knocks – "must see you at once". So he has taught me himself several times how to give the signals and explained them to me. And seeing as how it's only him and me in the whole world who knows about them signals, he will without the slightest doubt and without calling out (for he's terrified of calling out aloud), open the door. And it's them signals that your brother Dmitry knows all about now.'

'How does he know about them? Did you tell him? How dared you tell him?'

'It's because I'm so terrified, sir. And I would never dare hold it back from him, sir. Your brother Dmitry, sir, keeps bullying me every day. "You're deceiving me. You're hiding something from me, aren't you? I'll break both your legs for you, I will!" Well, sir, that's when I told him those most secret signals, so that he might at least see that I'm devoted to him like a slave and that he might be satisfied that I'm not deceiving him and that I'm doing my best to tell him everything I know, sir.'

'If you think he'll make use of the signals and try to get in, you mustn't let him.'

'But if I was to be laid up with a fit, sir, how am I not to let him in then, sir? Why, sir, I couldn't do nothing to stop him then even if I dare not let him in, knowing how desperate he is, sir.'

'Oh, hang it all! How can you be so sure that you're going to have a fit, damn you? You're not laughing at me, are you?'

'Why, sir, would I dare laugh at you? And, anyways, I don't feel like laughing, I can tell you, seeing as how I'm so frightened. I have a feeling I'm going to have a fit, sir. I have such a feeling. It will come from fright alone, sir.'

'Oh, hell! If you're laid up, Grigory will be keeping watch. Warn Grigory beforehand. He'll most certainly not let him in.'

'I'm afraid, sir, I'd never dare tell Grigory about the signals without master's orders. And as for Grigory hearing him and not letting him in, he's been ill ever since yesterday and Marfa intends to give him treatment tomorrow. They've arranged it today, sir. And her treatment, sir, is a fair treat. You see, sir, Marfa knows the recipe of a kind of infusion, and always keeps some. It's very strong, made from some herbs – she's got the secret of it. And she treats Grigory with this secret medicine of hers three times a year, sir, every time his lumbago gets so bad that he can't move, just as though he was paralysed, sir. Yes, sir, three times a year. When this happens, she takes a towel, dips it in the infusion and rubs his back with it for half an hour, till it's bone dry and goes quite red and swollen. Then what's left over in the bottle she gives him to drink with a special prayer, sir. Not all of it, though, for she leaves a drop or two over for herself, seeing as how it's such a rare occasion, sir, and she drinks it, too. And both being strictly teetotal, sir, they just drops off and they sleeps very soundly for a very long time. When Grigory wakes up, he's almost always well after it, but when Marfa wakes up she always has a headache from it, sir. So if Marfa carries out her plan tomorrow, sir, he won't hear nothing and he won't be able to stop your brother Dmitry from going in. He'll be asleep, sir.'

'What rot! And everything's going to happen all at once, as though on purpose! You'll have your epileptic fit and they'll both be unconscious!' cried Ivan. 'You're not by any chance planning it all to happen like that?' it escaped him suddenly and he knit his brows menacingly.

'How do you mean I've been planning it, sir? And how could I be planning such a thing if it all depends on your brother Dmitry and what he's a mind to do. If he has a mind to do something, he'll do it, and if he hasn't, I'm not going to bring him here on purpose to push him into your dad's room, am I?'

'But why should he go to father, and surreptitiously too, if as you say Miss Svetlov won't be coming at all?' Ivan went on, turning pale with anger. 'You say so yourself and all the time I've been living here I've felt sure that the old man was just imagining it all and that that slut will never come to him. Why, then, should Dmitry have to burst into the house if she doesn't come? Speak! I want to know what's at the back of your mind.'

'You knows yourself why he'll come, sir. It don't much matter what I'm thinking, does it? He'll come just out of spite or because he might get suspicious on account of my being ill, for instance. He'll think it's a trick and he'll come to search the rooms impatient-like, as he did yesterday, to make sure she hasn't slipped past him somehow or other. And, besides, sir, he knows very well that the master has a big envelope, sealed with three seals, with three thousand roubles in it. Tied round with a ribbon it is, sir, and on it is written in his own hand: "To my darling Grushenka, if she comes". Three days later, sir, he added: "And to my little chicken". So that's what makes me so suspicious, sir.'

'Nonsense!' cried Ivan, almost beside himself. 'Dmitry won't come to steal the money and kill father to get it. He could have killed him yesterday for Grushenka, like the crazy, frenzied fool he is, but he'll never steal!'

'He wants money very badly now, sir. He just has to have it. You've no idea, sir, how much he needs it,' Smerdyakov went on to explain with the utmost composure and with extraordinary explicitness. 'Besides, sir, he considers the three thousand roubles to be his own. He told me so himself. "My father," he says to me, "still owes me exactly three thousand," he says. And quite apart from that, sir, if you considers it carefully, that is, there's something else that's quite true. I mean, it's quite on the cards, if you don't mind my saying so, sir, that Miss Svetlov could, if she had a mind to, make the master himself, that is, your father, sir, marry her, if she had a mind to, of course. And for all you know, sir, she may have a mind to do just that. You see, sir, I've just said she won't come, but she, sir, may perhaps want something more than that. I mean, she may want to be the mistress, sir. I knows myself that her merchant Samsonov told her quite openly that it might not be such a bad thing at that, and he laughed, he did, as he said it. And she isn't such a fool, neither, sir. It's not in her interest to marry a beggar like your brother Dmitry, sir. And you've only to take this into account, sir, to see that if that was to happen neither your brother Dmitry, nor yourself, sir, nor your brother Alexey wouldn't get nothing after your dad's death. Not a penny, sir. For Miss Svetlov would only marry him to get everything settled on herself and have all his money made over in her name. Yes, sir. But if your dad was to die now, sir, while nothing of this has happened, each of you would get at least forty thousand at once. Even your brother Dmitry, sir, whom your dad hates. For, you see, sir, he hasn't made a will. And your brother Dmitry knows that, he does and all.'

A sort of spasm passed over Ivan's face. He suddenly flushed.

'So why in that case,' he interrupted Smerdyakov, 'do you advise me to go to Chermashnya? What did you mean by that? Suppose I go and all this happens here?'

Ivan drew his breath with difficulty.

'Quite right, sir,' Smerdyakov said, quietly and soberly, watching Ivan intently, however.

'What do you mean by "quite right"?' Ivan repeated, restraining himself with an effort, his eyes flashing menacingly.

'I said that because I feels sorry for you, sir. In your place, if I was here I'd chuck it all, sir, rather than stay on when such things might be happening,' replied Smerdyakov, looking with an air of the utmost frankness into Ivan's flashing eyes.

They were both silent.

'You seem to be a complete idiot and, of course, an – an awful blackguard!' said Ivan, rising suddenly from the bench.

He was about to pass straight through the gate, but he suddenly stopped and turned to Smerdyakov. What happened then was rather strange: Ivan, suddenly, as though in a spasm, bit his lips, clenched his fists and – in another moment would, of course, have flung himself on Smerdyakov. Smerdyakov, at any rate, noticed it at once. He gave a start and recoiled with his whole body. But the moment passed harmlessly for Smerdyakov, and Ivan turned back to the gate in silence, but as though in a sort of perplexity.

'I'm leaving for Moscow tomorrow, if you care to know – early tomorrow morning – that's all!' he said suddenly in a loud voice, spitefully and distinctly, surprised at himself afterwards that he had to tell Smerdyakov that at the time.

'That's the best thing you can do, sir,' Smerdyakov at once put in, as though he had expected to hear it. 'Except, of course, sir, that you might be summoned by telegram to come back, if anything happened.'

Ivan stopped again and again turned quickly to Smerdyakov. But something seemed to have happened to Smerdyakov. All his familiarity and casualness had gone completely; his whole face expressed extraordinary attention and expectation but this time timid and obsequious. 'You wouldn't say something more? You wouldn't add something, would you?' could be read in the intent look of his eyes fixed unblinkingly on Ivan.

'And wouldn't I be summoned from Chermashnya, too, if – if anything happened?' Ivan yelled suddenly, raising his voice to a shout for some unknown reason.

'Yes, sir, you would – er – be inconvenienced in Chermashnya, too,' muttered Smerdyakov almost in a whisper, as though he had lost his nerve, but continuing to look very intently into Ivan's eyes.

'Except that, I suppose, Moscow is further away and Chermashnya is nearer, and you are, no doubt, worried about my fares. That's why you're so keen on my going to Chermashnya, isn't it? Or do you take pity on me because I'll have to make such a long journey?'

'Quite right, sir,' Smerdyakov muttered in a faltering voice, with an odious smile and again making ready convulsively to jump back in time. But, to Smerdyakov's surprise, Ivan suddenly laughed and went quickly through the gate, continuing to laugh. If anyone had glanced at his face, he would most certainly have concluded that he was not laughing because he felt happy. Besides, he could not possibly have explained himself what he was feeling at that moment. He moved and walked as though he had no control over his actions.

7

'It's Nice to Have a Chat With a Clever Man'

AND he spoke like that, too. Meeting his father in the drawing-room, just as he entered it, he suddenly shouted at him, waving his arms: 'I'm going upstairs to my room, and I'm not coming in, good night!' and went past without even glancing at his father. Very possibly the old man was too hateful to him at that moment, but such an uncere-monious display of hostile feelings was most unexpected even to Mr Karamazov. And the old man evidently wanted to tell him some-thing at once, and that was why he had gone to meet him on purpose in the drawing-room; but hearing himself addressed in so courteous a manner, he stopped short in silence and followed with an ironical look his darling son's progress upstairs to his room in the attic till he passed out of sight.

'What's the matter with him?' he promptly asked Smerdyakov, who had followed Ivan into the room.

'He's angry about something,' Smerdyakov muttered evasively. 'You never can tell with him, sir.'

'Oh, to hell with him! Let him be angry! Let's have the *samovar* and clear out! Be quick about it! Any news?'

There followed a number of questions of the same kind as those Smerdyakov had just complained of to Ivan, that is, all about the expected visitor, and we will omit them here. Half an hour later the house was locked up, and the crazy old man kept walking from one room to another in tremulous expectation of hearing any minute the five prearranged knocks, peering through the darkened windows from time to time and seeing nothing but blackness outside.

It was very late, but Ivan was still not asleep. He lay awake think-ing. He went to bed late that night, at two o'clock. But we will not describe the trend of his thoughts, and, besides, this is not the time to analyse his soul: its turn will come. And even if we attempted to describe some of his thoughts, we should have found it very difficult, because they were not really thoughts, but something very vague and, above all, too excited. He felt himself that he had lost his bear-ings. He was also worried by all sorts of strange and almost unex-pected desires. For instance, after midnight he felt an insistent and unbearable desire to go downstairs, open the front door, go to the cottage and give Smerdyakov a good thrashing, but if he were asked why, he would have been at a loss to give a precise reason, except perhaps that the servant had become as hateful to him as a man who had insulted him more mortally than anyone he could think of in the whole world. On the other hand, he was overcome more than once that night by a sort of inexplicable and humiliating timidity which – and he felt it – seemed to deprive him suddenly of all his physical strength. His head ached and swam. A feeling of hate kept gnawing at his heart, just as though he were preparing to avenge himself on someone. He even hated Alyosha, as he recalled the conversation he had had with him, and at moments he hated himself intensely, too. He almost forgot to think of Katerina, and was very greatly surprised at it afterwards, all the more so as he remembered distinctly how when he had boasted that morning so boldly at Katerina's that he would leave for Moscow next day, he had whispered to himself in his heart: 'But that's all nonsense! You won't go. It won't be so easy to tear yourself away as you're boasting now.' Remembering that night long afterwards, Ivan recalled with particular disgust how he would suddenly get up from the sofa and quietly, as though terribly afraid to be seen, open the door, go out on the landing and listen to his father moving about and walking in the rooms on the floor below – he had listened for a long time, for about five minutes, with a sort of strange curiosity, with bated breath and a thumping heart. But why he had done all this, why he was listening, he did not of course know himself. That 'action' of his he called 'contemptible' all his life afterwards; and deep inside him, in the most secret recesses of his heart, he thought of it as the vilest action of all his life. He did not even feel any particular hatred for his father at those moments, but was for some reason only intensely curious to know why he was walking about down there and what he would be doing in his room. He pictured to himself how he must be looking through the darkened windows and then suddenly stopping in the middle of the room and waiting, waiting to hear if anyone were knocking. Ivan went out twice on the landing to listen like that. When everything was quiet and his father had gone to bed, Ivan, too, went to bed about two o'clock, firmly determined to go to sleep at once, for he felt terribly exhausted. And, to be sure, he slept like a log and without dreams, but he woke up early, at about seven, when it was already daylight. On opening his eyes, he felt, to his amazement, such an extraordinary surge of energy in himself that he quickly jumped out of bed and, dressing quickly, pulled out his trunk and, without wasting any time, began hurriedly to pack. As luck would have it, he had got his linen back from the laundress the previous morning. Ivan even smiled at the thought of how perfectly everything had worked out and that there was no needless delay to prevent his sudden departure. And his departure certainly was sudden. Though Ivan had said the day before (to Katerina, Alyosha, and afterwards to Smerdyakov) that he would be leaving next day, when he went to bed – he remembered that well – he had not thought of going away, at least he had never thought that the first thing he would do on getting up in the morning would be to pack his trunk. At last the trunk and bag were ready. It was about nine o'clock when Marfa came in with her usual question: 'Where will you have your breakfast, sir, in your room or downstairs?' Ivan went downstairs, looking almost cheerful, though there was something hurried and distracted in his words and gestures. Greeting his father affably and even inquiring particularly after his health, he announced at once, without bothering to listen to the end of his father's answer, that he was leaving for Moscow in an hour for good and asked him to send for the carriage. The old man heard the announcement without betraying the slightest surprise, most indecently forgetting to say how sorry he was to hear of his darling son's departure; instead of doing that, he suddenly became very flustered, remembering in time a most important business of his own.

'Oh, dear, what a funny fellow you are, to be sure! You didn't tell me yesterday but – never mind, we'll manage it now all the same. Do me a great favour, dear boy, and stop at Chermashnya on the way. It's only about ten miles from Volovya station. Turn to the left and there it is – Chermashnya!'

'I'm sorry, I can't. It's about fifty miles from here to the railway station and the train leaves for Moscow at seven o'clock in the evening. I'll just be in time to catch my train.'

'You can catch your train tomorrow, or the day after, but please turn off to Chermashnya today! Won't cost you anything to put your father's mind at rest, will it now? If I hadn't business to attend to here, I'd have run over long ago, because, you see, it's rather an important deal and it has to be done in a hurry, and I can't leave here just now. You see, I have a wood there in two plots, in Begichov and in Dyachkina, on a waste plot of land. The merchants Maslov, father and son, are only offering me eight thousand for the timber, and only last year I happened to run across a customer who offered me twelve thousand for it, but then he wasn't a local man – that's the point! For you can't sell anything to the local fellows because old

Maslov and his son, who're worth hundreds of thousands, have a monopoly of everything here. With them it's take it or leave it, because no local man dares to compete with them. Now, the priest at Ilyinskoye wrote to me last Thursday that a man I know, Gorskin by name, also a lousy merchant, has just arrived there. The beauty of it is, you see, that he isn't a local man but from Pogrebov, and so he isn't afraid of the Maslovs, because, you see, he isn't a local merchant. He offers me eleven thousand for the timber. Eleven thousand, do you hear? And he'll only be there, the priest writes, for a week. So if you were to go, you'd be able to clinch the deal, see?'

'Why not write to the priest? He'll clinch the deal.'

'He can't, that's the trouble. He has no eye for business. An excellent fellow, mind you. I'd trust him with twenty thousand to take care of for me any time without a receipt, but he has no eye for business. Just as if he weren't a grown-up man at all. A crow could deceive him. And yet he's a learned man – can you imagine it? Now this Gorskin fellow looks like a peasant, walks about in a blue peasant coat, but he's a rogue, if ever there was one. That's the trouble with all of us. He's a liar – that's his chief characteristic. Sometimes he tells you such lies that you wonder why he does it. Told me a tall story the year before last about his wife having died and his having married another, and there wasn't a word of truth in it! His wife never died. She's still alive and she beats him regularly every other day. So, you see, what we have to find out now is whether he's lying or speaking the truth when he says that he wants to buy the timber and is ready to pay eleven thousand for it.'

'I'm afraid I, too, shan't be of any use to you. I've no eye for business, either.'

'Wait a minute, will you? You'll do all right because I'm going to tell you how to deal with him, with Gorskin, I mean. I've done business with him a long time. You see, you have to watch his beard. He's got a nasty, thin, reddish beard. If his beard shakes when he talks and gets cross, then it's all right: he's telling the truth and means business. But if he strokes his beard with his left hand and grins, well, then he's trying to cheat you, the swindler. Never look into his eyes. You won't find out anything from his eyes. It's like looking through muddy water – the damned rogue – look at his beard! I'll give you a note and you show it to him. His name's Gorskin, but he isn't really

Gorskin, but Lyagavy – a "kicker". Only don't tell him that he's nicknamed Lyagavy or he'll be offended. If you come to terms with him and see it's all right, drop me a line at once. All you have to write is that he's not lying. Hold out for eleven thousand, one thousand you can knock off, but no more. Just think of it, my boy: there's a difference of three thousand between eleven and eight thousand. It's as good as finding three thousand. It's not so easy to find a purchaser, and I'm in desperate need of money. When I hear from you that it's a deal, I'll run over myself and clinch it. I'll snatch the time somehow. But what's the use of my rushing off there now if the whole thing is just the priest's idea? Well, are you going or not?'

'I'm sorry, I've no time. I'd rather you didn't ask me.'

'Come, do your father a favour. I shan't forget it! You've no heart, any of you – that's what it is! What's a day or two to you? Where are you off to now? To Venice? Your Venice will keep for two days. I'd have sent Alyosha, but what does Alyosha know about such things? I'm asking you because you're a clever fellow. Do you think I don't realize that? You're not a dealer in timber, but you've got a pair of eyes. All you have to do is to find out whether the man is serious or not: look at his beard, if it shakes, he's serious.'

'You're driving me to that damned Chermashnya yourself, aren't you?' cried Ivan with a malicious smile.

Karamazov did not or would not notice the malice, but he seized on the smile.

'Then you will go, won't you? I'll scribble a note for you at once.'

'I don't know whether I'll go or not. I'll decide on the way.'

'Why on the way? Decide now. Come on, my boy, decide! If you clinch the deal, drop me a line. Give it to the priest, and he'll send on your note to me at once. After that I won't keep you any more – go to Venice, if you like. The priest will send you back to Volovya station in his own carriage.'

The old man was simply overjoyed. He scribbled the note and sent for the carriage. Some snacks and brandy were brought in. When the old man was pleased, he always became expansive, but this time he seemed to hold himself in. For instance, he did not say a word about Dmitry. Nor was he in the least moved by the parting. Indeed, he seemed to be at a loss what to say. Ivan noticed it at once: 'He must be thoroughly sick of me,' he thought. It was only when seeing his son off on the front steps that the old man seemed to get a little excited. He even tried to kiss him, but Ivan quickly held out his hand, obviously anxious to avoid his kisses. The old man understood at once and instantly checked himself.

'Well, good luck, good luck!' he kept repeating from the steps. 'Will you ever come back while I'm still alive, I wonder. Well, if you do, I'll always be glad to see you. Well, Christ be with you!'

Ivan got into the carriage.

'Good-bye, Ivan,' his father cried for the last time. 'Don't be too hard on me!'

All the servants came out to see him off: Smerdyakov, Marfa, and Grigory. Ivan gave them ten roubles each. When he had taken his seat in the carriage, Smerdyakov rushed up to put the rug straight.

'You see I – I am going to Chermashnya,' the words escaped Ivan suddenly, again as the day before, against his will, and with a sort of nervous little laugh. He remembered it long after.

'Yes, sir,' Smerdyakov replied firmly, looking meaningfully at Ivan, 'people are quite right when they say that it's nice to have a chat with a clever man.'

The carriage started and drove off. The traveller felt troubled in his mind, but he looked eagerly around him at the fields, the trees, the flock of wild geese flying high overhead across a cloudless sky. And all of a sudden he felt so happy. He tried to talk to the driver and something in the peasant's answer interested him immensely. But a moment later he realized that he had missed most of what the driver had said and that, as a matter of fact, he had not even understood his answer. He fell silent. It was pleasant as it was: the air was fresh, pure, and cool, the sky was clear. The faces of Alyosha and Katerina flashed through his mind – but he smiled gently and blew gently on the dear phantoms and they vanished; 'Their time will come,' he thought. They reached the post station quickly, changed horses and galloped off to Volovya. 'Why is it nice to have a chat with a clever man? What did he mean to say by that?' he thought, and suddenly his breath failed him. 'And why did I tell him that I was going to Chermashnya?' They arrived at Volovya station. Ivan got out of the carriage and the coachmen surrounded him. They bargained with him over the fares for the journey of ten miles to Chermashnya. He told them to harness the horses. He went into the

station house, looked round, glanced at the station-master's wife, and
suddenly went out again.

'I won't go to Chermashnya. I won't be late for the seven o'clock
train, will I?'

'No, sir. We'll get you there in time. Shall we harness the horses?'

'Yes, at once. Will any of you be in town tomorrow?'

'Why, yes, sir. Mitry here will.'

'Can you do me a service, Mitry? Go to my father, Mr Fyodor
Karamazov, and tell him I haven't gone to Chermashnya. Can you
do it?'

'Of course I can, sir. I've known Mr Karamazov a long time.'

'Well, here's your tip, for I don't think he will give you anything,' Ivan laughed gaily.

'So he won't,' Mitry laughed too. 'Thank you, sir. I'll be sure to
do it.'

At seven o'clock in the evening Ivan got into the train and set off
for Moscow. 'Away with the past. I've finished for ever with my old
life and I don't want to hear of it again. To a new world, to new
places, and no looking back!' But instead of delight, his soul was
suddenly filled with such gloom and his heart ached with such anguish as he had never known in his life before. He lay awake thinking
all night; the train flew on, and it was only at daybreak, when he
was entering Moscow, that he seemed suddenly to come to.

'I'm a blackguard!' he whispered to himself.

Meantime, Karamazov, having seen off his son, was very pleased
with himself. For two whole hours he felt almost happy as he sipped
his brandy; but suddenly a most annoying and disagreeable thing
happened which at once threw him into utter confusion and dismay:
Smerdyakov, who had gone to fetch something from the cellar, fell
down from the top of the steps to the bottom. It was a good thing
Marfa happened to be in the yard at the time and heard it in time.
She did not see the fall, but she heard his scream – the strange, peculiar
scream she had long known, the scream of the epileptic falling in a
fit. It was impossible to say whether the fit had come on him when
he was descending the steps, so that he must have fallen down at once
unconscious, or whether it had been brought on as a result of the fall
and the shock, Smerdyakov being well known to be liable to epileptic fits. They found him lying at the bottom of the cellar steps,

writhing in convulsions and foaming at the mouth. At first they thought that he might have broken something – an arm or a leg – and hurt himself, but 'God has preserved him', as Marfa put it; nothing of the kind had happened, but it was difficult to get him out of the cellar. But they asked the neighbours to help and managed it somehow. Karamazov himself was present at the whole ceremony and lent a helping hand himself, looking frightened and rather lost. The sick man, however, did not recover consciousness: the attacks ceased for a time, but then began again, and they all concluded that the same thing would happen as had happened the year before when he accidentally fell from the loft. They remembered that ice had been put on his head that time. There was no ice in the cellar and Marfa took steps to get some, while towards the evening Karamazov sent for Dr Herzenstube, who arrived at once. After subjecting the patient to a thorough examination (Dr Herzenstube, an elderly and most estimable man, was the most careful and conscientious doctor in the province), he concluded that the fit was a very violent one and might have 'serious consequences', but that for the time being he, Herzenstube, could not quite make it out. If, however, the present remedies were of no avail, he would try something else next morning. The sick man was taken to the cottage and put to bed in the room next to Grigory's and Marfa's. But poor Mr Karamazov had to suffer one misfortune after another during the whole of that day. Marfa cooked the dinner, and compared with Smerdyakov's, the soup was 'just like slops' and the chicken was so dried up that it was quite impossible to chew it. In reply to her master's bitter, though justified, reproaches, Marfa maintained that the chicken was a very old one to begin with and that she had never been trained as a cook. In the evening more trouble came: Karamazov was informed that Grigory, who had been feeling ill for the last two days, was almost completely laid up with lumbago. Karamazov finished his tea as early as possible and locked himself in the house. He was in a state of terrible alarm and suspense. As a matter of fact, he was expecting Grushenka to arrive almost for certain; at least early that morning he had received an assurance from Smerdyakov that she 'had promised to come without fail'. The perverse old man's heart was beating uneasily. He kept pacing up and down his empty rooms and listening. He had to be on the alert: Dmitry might be on the watch for her somewhere and as soon as she knocked on the window (Smerdyakov had assured him two days before that he had told her where and how to knock), he had to open the door as quickly as possible and not keep her for a second longer in the hall, or else – which God forbid – she might get frightened and run away. It was a trying time for Karamazov, but never had his heart been full of such sweet hopes: why, this time it was practically certain that she would come!

I

The Elder Zossima and His Visitors

WHEN Alyosha entered the elder's cell with an anxious and aching heart, he stopped short almost in amazement: instead of a dying sick man, who was perhaps already unconscious, as he had feared to find him, he saw him sitting in his armchair, though looking weak and exhausted, but with a bright and cheerful face, surrounded by visitors and conversing quietly and lucidly with them. But actually he had only got up from his bed about a quarter of an hour before Alyosha's arrival; his visitors had gathered in his cell earlier and waited for him to wake, having received Father Paissy's firm assurance that 'the teacher will certainly get up to converse once again with those dear to his heart as he himself promised in the morning'. Father Paissy believed implicitly in this promise, and indeed in every word of the dying elder, so much so that if he had seen him unconscious and no longer breathing but had his promise to get up again to take leave of them, he would not perhaps have believed in death itself, but would still have expected the dying man to carry out his promise. In the morning, before he fell asleep, Father Zossima had told him positively: 'I shall not die without once again tasting to the full the joy of talking to you, beloved ones of my heart, looking at your dear faces and pouring out my heart to you once again.' The monks, who had gathered for this probably last conversation with the elder, were his oldest and most devoted friends. There were four of them: the senior monks Father Joseph and Father Paissy, Father Mikhail, the prior of the hermitage, and Brother Anfim. Father Mikhail was neither very old nor very learned. He was of humble origin, but steadfast of spirit and of firm and simple faith, outwardly stern, but of great tenderness of heart, though he obviously concealed it even to the point of being ashamed of it. Brother Anfim was a very old and ordinary little monk, of the poorest peasant class, almost illiterate, quiet and taciturn, very rarely speaking to anybody, the humblest among the most humble monks, who looked as though he had been frightened by something great and terrible beyond his comprehension. The elder Zossima was very fond of this man, who seemed always to walk in fear and trembling, and treated him all his life with extraordinary respect, though there was perhaps no other man to whom he had spoken less, in spite of the fact that he had spent many years wandering all over holy Russia with him. That was a long, long time ago, about forty years before, when Father Zossima first began his hard life as a monk in a poor and little known monastery in the Kostroma province and when, shortly after that, he had accompanied Father Anfim on his wanderings to collect funds for their poor, small monastery. All of them, the host and his visitors, were sitting in the elder's second room, where his bed stood, a room which, as has been described before, was very small, so that there was scarcely room for the four monks (in addition to the novice Porfiry, who remained standing) to sit round the elder's armchair on chairs brought from the first room. It was already getting dark and the room was lighted by the lamps and wax candles before the icons. Seeing Alyosha, who stood in the doorway looking embarrassed, the elder smiled joyfully at him and held out his hand:

'Welcome, my gentle one, welcome, my dear boy, here you are at last. I knew you'd come.'

Alyosha went up to him, prostrated himself before him and wept. Something surged up in his heart, his soul trembled, he felt like sobbing.

'Come, come, it's too early to mourn for me,' the elder said, smiling and putting his right hand on his head. 'You see I'm sitting here and talking. Perhaps I shall live for another twenty years as the dear, kind woman from Vyshegorye, with her little girl Lizaveta in her arms, wished me yesterday. Bless, O Lord, the mother and the little girl Lizaveta!' (He crossed himself.) 'Porfiry, did you take her offering where I told you?'

He was referring to the sixty copecks donated by the cheerful woman for 'someone poorer than me'. Such donations are offered as a voluntarily imposed penance and always with money earned by one's own work. The elder had sent Porfiry the evening before to a poor widow with two children whose house had been burnt down lately and who had gone begging after the fire. Porfiry hastened to reply that he had carried out the elder's commission and that he had given the money, as instructed, 'from an unknown bene-factress'.

'Get up, my dear boy,' the elder went on to Alyosha. 'Let me have a look at you. Have you been home and seen your brother?'

It seemed strange to Alyosha that he asked so firmly and precisely about one of his brothers only – but which one? So it was for that brother that he had perhaps sent him out yesterday and today.

'I've seen one of my brothers,' replied Alyosha.

'I'm talking of your elder brother to whom I bowed down to the ground yesterday.'

'I only saw him yesterday,' said Alyosha. 'I could not find him today.'

'Make haste and find him. Go again tomorrow and make haste. Leave everything and make haste. Perhaps you'll still be in time to prevent something terrible happening. I bowed down yesterday to the great suffering that is in store for him.'

He fell silent suddenly and seemed to be pondering. His words were strange. Father Joseph, who had seen the elder's deep bow yesterday, exchanged glances with Father Paissy. Alyosha could not restrain himself.

'Father and teacher,' he said in great excitement, 'your words are too obscure. . . . What sort of suffering is in store for him?'

'Don't be too curious to know. I seemed to see something terrible yesterday, just as if his whole future were expressed in the look in his eyes. There was such a look in his eyes that I was instantly horri-fied at what that man is preparing for himself. Once or twice in my life I've seen such an expression on a man's face, an expression that seemed to foreshadow the fate of that man, and his fate, alas, came to pass. I sent you to him, Alexey, in the hope that your brotherly face would help him. But everything is from God and all our destinies. "Except a corn of wheat fall into the ground and die, it abideth alone: but if it die, it bringeth forth much fruit." Remember that. And you, Alexey, I have blessed in my mind many times in my life for your face, know that,' said the elder with a gentle smile. 'This is what I think of you: you will go forth from these walls, but you will live in the world like a monk. You will have many adversaries, but even your enemies will love you. Life will bring many misfortunes to you, but it is in them that you will find happiness and you will bless life and make others bless it – which is what matters most. But that is how you are. Fathers and teachers,' he turned to his visitors with a tender smile, 'I have never till this day told even him why the face of this youth is so dear to me. Now I will tell you: his face has been, as it were, a reminder and a prophecy to me. At the dawn of my days, when I was a little child, I had an elder brother who died before my eyes when he was only a boy of seventeen. And afterwards, in the course of my life, I came gradually to the conclusion that that brother of mine had been, as it were, a guidance and a predestination from above, for if he had not come into my life, if he had not existed at all, I should never perhaps, so I think, have followed the calling of a monk and not entered upon this precious path. He appeared to me at first in my childhood, and now at my journey's end there seems indeed to be a repetition of it. It is strange, fathers and teachers, that, while he bears but a remote resemblance to him, Alexey seemed to me to be so much like him in spirit that many times I looked on him as that young man, my brother, who had come back to me mysteriously at my journey's end as a reminder and an inspiration, so that I was even surprised at myself and at this strange dream of mine. Do you hear that, Porfiry?' he turned to the novice who waited on him. 'Many times I've noticed a look of distress in your face that I love Alexey more than you. Now you know why that was so, but I love you too, know that, and many times I grieved that you should be distressed. I should like to tell you, dear friends, about that young man, my brother, for there was nothing in my life more precious, more prophetic and touching. I feel deeply touched at heart and at this moment I am contemplating my whole life as though living it all over again. . . . '

*

Here I must note that this last conversation of the elder with his visitors on the last day of his life has been partly preserved in writing. It was written down from memory by Alexey Karamazov a short time after the elder's death. But whether it was all the conversation on that evening or whether he added to it from his notes of his former talks with his teacher, I cannot say for certain. Besides, the elder's speech in his account seems to go on without interruption, just as though, in addressing his friends, he had been telling his life in the form of a story, while from other accounts of it there can be no doubt that it all happened somewhat differently; for the conversation that evening was general, and though the visitors did not interrupt the elder frequently, they did occasionally speak up for themselves and intervene in the conversation. Indeed, it is quite likely that they told something of themselves, too. Moreover, there can be no question of any uninterrupted narrative on the part of the elder, for sometimes he was gasping for breath, his voice failed him, and he even lay down to rest on his bed, though he did not fall asleep and his visitors did not leave their seats. Once or twice the conversation was interrupted by the reading of the Gospel by Father Paissy. It is remarkable, too, that none of them thought that he would die that night, particularly as on that last evening of his life, after his profound sleep in the day, he seemed suddenly to have acquired new strength, which sustained him during the whole of this long conversation with his friends. It was, as it were, the last expression of his tender feelings for his friends which kept up his incredible animation, but only for a short time, for his life was cut short suddenly. . . . But of that later. Now I should like to add that I have preferred to confine myself to the elder's story according to Alexey Karamazov's manuscript, without giving a detailed account of the conversation. It will be shorter and not so fatiguing, either, though, of course, let me repeat, Alyosha took a great deal from previous conversations and added them to it.

2

From the Life of the Departed Priest and Monk, The Elder Zossima, taken down from his own words by Alexey Karamazov

BIOGRAPHICAL DATA

(a) About Father Zossima's Young Brother

BELOVED fathers and teachers, I was born in a remote northern province, in the town of V. My father was a nobleman, but was neither a person of quality nor of high rank. He died when I was only two years old, and I do not remember him at all. He left my mother a small wooden house and some capital, not large, but sufficient to live on with her children without being in need. There were only two of us: my elder brother, Markel, and I, Zinovy. He was eight years older than I, short-tempered and irritable, but good-natured and not sarcastic, and quite unusually taciturn, especially at home, with my mother, myself, and the servants. He made good progress at school, but did not get on with his schoolmates, though he never quarrelled with them – so at least my mother remembered him. Six months before his death, when he was seventeen, he began visiting a man who led a very solitary life in our town, a political exile, who had been banished from Moscow for freethinking. That exile was a great scholar and a distinguished university philosopher. He got very fond of Markel for some reason and was glad to see him. Markel used to spend whole evenings with him all through that winter until he was summoned back, at his own request, to Petersburg to take up a post in the civil service, as he had influential friends there. It was the beginning of Lent, but Markel refused to fast. He swore and laughed at it: 'It's all nonsense,' he said, 'and there is no God,' so that my mother and the servants were horrified. And though I myself was only a small boy of nine, I too, hearing his words, was very frightened. Our servants were serfs, the four of them, all bought in the name of a landowner we knew. I can still remember how my mother sold one of the four, our cook Afimya, an elderly lame woman, for sixty roubles, and engaged a free servant in her place. In the sixth week of the fast my brother was taken seriously ill. He was never very well, he had a weak chest, a weak constitution, and a predisposition to consumption; he was rather tall, thin and delicate, but had a very handsome face. I don't know whether he caught a cold, but the doctor came and soon whispered to my mother that he had galloping consumption and that he wouldn't live through the spring. My mother began weeping and asking my brother very guardedly (chiefly so as not to alarm him) to fast and then go to church and take holy communion, for he was still walking about then. Hearing this, he got angry and swore at the church, but he grew thoughtful: he realized at once that he was seriously ill and that that was why his mother was sending him to church to confess and take the sacrament while he still had strength to go there. He had of course known that he had been ill for a long time and a year before had calmly observed to my mother at table: 'I shan't live long among you, perhaps I shan't last another year,' and it looked as though he had himself predicted it. Three days passed and Holy Week had come. And beginning with Tuesday my brother began fasting and going to church. 'I'm doing it really for your sake, Mother,' he said to her, 'to please you and set your mind at rest.' My mother wept with joy and with grief, too: 'His end must be near,' she thought, 'if there's such a sudden change in him.' But he was not able to go to church long. He took to his bed, and he confessed and was given extreme unction at home. Easter was late and the days were clear, sunny, and full of the fragrance of spring. I remember he used to cough and hardly slept all night, but in the morning he always dressed and tried to sit up in an armchair. And that's how I remember him: sitting in his chair, calm and gentle, smiling, looking cheerful and joyous, in spite of his illness. He was spiritually transformed – such a wonderful change suddenly took place in him! Our old nurse would come in and say: 'Let me light the lamp before the icon, dear.' Before he would not let her do it and he even used to blow it out. But now he would say to her: 'Light it, light it, my dear. I was a beast not to let you before. You pray to God when lighting the lamp, and I'm praying when I rejoice looking at you. So we are praying to one and the same God.' Those words of his sounded strange to us, and Mother would go to her room and weep, but coming back she would dry her tears and try to look cheerful. 'Don't cry, Mother darling,' he used to say, 'I shall live for a long time yet. I shall have lots of fun with you. Life is so joyful and gay!' 'Oh, my dear, how can you feel joyful when you are burning with fever at night, coughing as though your chest would burst?' 'Mother,' he replied to her, 'don't cry. Life is paradise and we are all in paradise, only we don't want to know it, and if we wanted to we'd have heaven on earth tomorrow.' And we all marvelled at his words, he spoke so strangely and so positively; we were deeply touched and wept. When friends came to see us, he would say to them: 'Dear ones, what did I do to deserve your love? Why do you love me, wretch that I am? And how is it I did not know and appreciate it before?' When our servants came in he would always say to them: 'Dear ones, why are you waiting on me? I don't deserve to be waited on. If God spared me and let me live, I'd wait on you, for we all must wait upon one another.' Listening to him, my mother would shake her head: 'Darling,' she would say, 'you talk like that because you're ill.' 'Darling Mother,' he would reply, 'there have to be masters and servants, but let me be the servant of my servants. Let me be the same as they are to me. And let me tell you this, too, Mother: every one of us is responsible for everyone else in every way, and I most of all.' Mother could not help smiling at that. She wept and smiled at the same time. 'How are you,' she said, 'most of all responsible for everyone? There are murderers and robbers in the world, and what terrible sin have you committed that you should accuse yourself before everyone else?' 'Mother, my dearest heart,' he said (he had begun using such caressing, such unexpected words just then), 'my dearest heart, my joy, you must realize that everyone is really responsible for everyone and everything. I don't know how to explain it to you, but I feel it so strongly that it hurts. And how could we have gone on living and getting angry without knowing anything about it?' So he used to get up every day, feeling more and more joyful and tender towards everyone and all vibrating with love. When the doctor, an old German called Eisenschmidt, called, 'Well, doctor,' he used to joke with him, 'how long do you give me? One more day?' 'Not one day,' the doctor would reply, 'you're good for many days yet, and for many months and years too.' 'Why years and months?' he would cry. 'Why count the days, when one day is sufficient for a man to experience all happiness. My dear ones, why do we quarrel? Why do we boast to one another? Why do we bear a grudge against each other? Why not go straight into the garden and walk and enjoy ourselves, love, praise and kiss one another, and bless our life?' 'Your son hasn't long to live,' the doctor said to my mother, when she saw him off at the front door. 'I'm afraid his illness is affecting his brain.' The windows of his bedroom looked out on to the garden, and our garden was full of shade, with old trees; the spring buds were beginning to swell on the trees, and the early birds had arrived and were chirruping and singing at the windows. And, looking at them and admiring them, he began suddenly to beg them, too, to forgive him: 'Heavenly birds, happy birds, forgive me, for I have sinned against you, too.'

That no one could understand at the time, but he wept with joy. 'Yes,' he said, 'there was such glory of God all around me: birds, trees, meadows, sky, only I lived in shame, I alone dishonoured everything, and did not notice the beauty and the glory of it all.' 'You take many sins upon yourself,' my mother used to say, weeping. 'Mother, joy of my heart, it's for joy, not for grief that I am crying. You see, I want to be responsible for them myself, only I can't explain it to you, for I don't know even how to love them. I may have sinned against everyone, but that is why they will all forgive me, and that is paradise. Am I not in paradise now?'

And there was a great deal more that I cannot remember or describe. I do remember going into his room one day when there was no one there. It was a bright evening, the sun was setting, and the whole room was lighted up by its slanting rays. He beckoned to me as soon as he saw me and I went up to him. He took me by the shoulders with both hands and looked tenderly and lovingly into my face. He said nothing, but just looked at me like that for a minute. 'Well,' he said, 'now run away and play, live for me!' I went then and ran to play. And many times afterwards in the course of my life I remembered with tears how he had told me to live for him. He said many more such wonderful and beautiful things, though we did not understand them at the time. He died in the third week after Easter. He was fully conscious, though he did not speak any more; but he did not change up to the last hour; he looked joyful, there was gladness in the eyes with which he sought us, smiled at us, called us. Even in our town they talked a great deal about his death. I was shaken by it all at the time, but not too much, though I did cry a lot at his funeral. I was very young then, a child, but it left an indelible impression in my heart, a feeling that lay dormant for years. It was to come to life and respond in time. And so it happened.

(b) Of the Holy Writ in the Life of Father Zossima

I was left alone with my mother. Soon her good friends advised her that, as she had only one son left and as we were not poor but had enough money, she ought to follow the example of other people and send me to Petersburg, for by keeping me with her she might deprive me of a brilliant future. And they persuaded my mother to send me to Petersburg and enter me in the Cadet Corps that I might afterwards join the Imperial Guard. My mother could not make up her mind for a long time: she could not bring herself to part with her only remaining son; but at last she decided to send me to Petersburg, though not without many tears, thinking that she was doing it for my good. She took me to Petersburg and entered me in the Cadet Corps, and after that I never saw her again; for three years later she died, grieving and mourning all during those three years for both of us. From the house of my parents I have brought nothing but precious memories, for there are no memories more precious than those of one's early childhood in one's own home, and that is almost always so, if there is any love and harmony in the family at all. Indeed, precious memories may be retained even from a bad home so long as your heart is capable of finding anything precious. To my memories at home I add also my memories of the stories from the Holy Scriptures, which, though a child, I was very eager to learn at home. I had a book of stories from the Holy Scriptures with beautiful illustrations called *One Hundred and Four Sacred Stories from the Old and New Testaments*, and I learnt to read from it. It is still lying on my shelf here, and I keep it as a precious keepsake of my childhood. But even before I learned to read, I remember how I was first moved by deep spiritual emotion when I was eight years old. My mother took me alone to church (I don't remember where my brother was at the time), to morning mass on the Monday before Easter. It was a sunny day, and I remember now, just as though I saw it again, how the incense rose from the censer and floated slowly upwards and how through a little window from the dome above the sunlight streamed down upon us and, rising in waves towards it, the incense seemed to dissolve in it. I looked and felt deeply moved and for the first time in my life I consciously received the first seed of the words of God in my soul. Then a boy stepped forth into the middle of the church carrying a big book, so big that I thought at the time that he could hardly carry it, and he laid it on the lectern, opened it, and began to read. And it was then that I suddenly understood for the first time, for the first time in my life, what they read in church. There was a man in the land of Uz, and that man was perfect and upright, and he had so much wealth, and so many camels, and so many sheep and asses, and his children feasted and he loved them very much and he prayed for them: perhaps they had sinned in their feasting. Now Satan came before the Lord among the sons of God, and he said to the Lord that he had been going to and fro in the earth and under the earth. 'And hast thou considered my servant Job?' God asked him. And God boasted to Satan, pointing to his great and holy servant. And Satan laughed at God's words. 'Hand him over to me and thou wilt see that thy servant will murmur against thee and curse thy name.' And God handed over the righteous man he loved so well to Satan, and Satan smote his children, and his cattle, and scattered his wealth, everything all at once, as with a thunderbolt from heaven. Then Job rent his mantle and fell down upon the ground and said, 'Naked came I out of my mother's womb, and naked shall I return into the earth: The Lord gave and the Lord hath taken away: blessed be the name of the Lord now and for ever!' Fathers and teachers, forgive my tears now, for my childhood days rise up again before me, and I breathe now as I breathed then, with the chest of a child of eight, and I feel, as I felt then, wonder and dismay and gladness. And my imagination was so forcibly struck by the camels, and by Satan who talked like that with God, and by God who gave up his servant to destruction, who cried, 'Blessed be thy name, though thou chastiseth me', and then the soft and sweet singing in the church: 'Hearken unto my prayer,' and again the incense from the priest's censer and the kneeling in prayer! Since then – even yesterday I took it up – I have never been able to read this sacred tale without tears. And how much that is great, mysterious, and inconceivable is there in it! Afterwards I heard the words of the scoffers and reprovers, proud words: how could God give up the most loved of his saints to Satan to play with, take his children from him, smite him with sore boils so that he scraped the corruption from his sores with a potsherd, and why? Just to be able to boast to Satan: 'See how much my saint can suffer for my sake!' But it *is* great – just because it is a mystery – just because the passing image of the earthly and eternal justice are brought together here. The act of eternal justice is accomplished before earthly justice. Here the Creator, just as in the first days of creation he ended each day with praise: 'That which I have created is good,' looks upon Job and again boasts of his creation. And Job, praising the Lord, serves not only him but all his creation for generations and generations and for ever and ever, since for that he was fore-ordained. Lord, what a book it is and what lessons it contains! What a book the Holy Bible is! What a miracle and what strength is given with it to man! Just like a sculpture of the world and man and human characters, and everything is named there and everything is shown for ever and ever. And how many solved and revealed mysteries: God raises Job again, gives him wealth again, and many years pass by and he has other children and he loves them. Good Lord, but how could he love those new ones when his old children were no more, when he had lost them? Remembering them, how could he be completely happy as before with the new ones, however dear they were to him? But he could, he could: the old sorrow, through the great mystery of human life, passes gradually into quiet, tender joy; the fiery blood of youth gives place to the gentle serenity of old age: I bless the rising sun each day, and my heart sings to it as of old, but I love its setting much more, its long slanting rays and, with them, my quiet, gentle, tender memories, the dear images of the whole of my long and blessed life – and over it all Divine Justice, tender, reconciling and all-forgiving! My life is drawing to a close. I know that, I feel it. But I also feel every day that is left to me how my earthly life is already in touch with a new, infinite, unknown but fast-approaching future life, the anticipation of which sets my soul trembling with rapture, my mind glowing, and my heart weeping with joy. . . . Friends and teachers, I have heard more than once, and now for some time past it can be heard more often, that our priests and, particularly, our village priests are everywhere complaining bitterly of their small stipends and their degradation, and they go so far as to declare plainly, even in print – I have read it myself – that they are unable to expound the Scriptures to the people now because their stipends are so small, and that if Lutherans and heretics come and drive away the flock, then let them do so, for their stipends, you see, are so small. Heavens above, I think to myself, may the stipends that are so precious to them be increased by all means (for their complaint is certainly just), but verily I say: if anyone is to blame for it, half the fault is ours! For even if he has no time to spare, if he is right in saying that he is overwhelmed all the time with work and church services, it is not all the time, he still has at least an hour a week in which to remember God. And his work does not go on all the year round. If at first he gathered only the children once a week, in the evening, their fathers would hear of it and they, too, would begin to come. And there is no need to build marble halls for this work, let him simply take them into his cottage; he need not be afraid, they won't make a mess in his cottage, for he will only have them for one hour. Let him open the Book and begin reading it without learned words and without conceit, without any feeling of superiority towards them, but gently and tenderly, rejoicing that he is reading to them and that they are listening to him with understanding, loving those words himself, and pausing only from time to time to explain some words that simple peasants do not understand. Don't worry, they'll understand it all, the orthodox heart will understand it all. Read to them about Abraham and Sarah, about Isaac and Rebecca, about how Jacob went to Laban and wrestled with the Lord in his dream and said, 'How dreadful is this place', and you will greatly impress the devout mind of the peasant. Read to them, and especially to the children, how the brothers sold their own brother, the sweet youth Joseph, a dreamer of dreams and a great prophet, into bondage and told their father that a wild beast had devoured him and showed him his bloodstained coat. Read to them how his brothers afterwards went down to Egypt for corn, and Joseph, already a great courtier, unrecognized by them, tormented them, accused them, kept his brother Benjamin, and all the time loving them, loving them: 'I love you, and loving you, I torment you.' For he remembered his whole past life how they had sold him in the parched desert, by the well, to some merchants and how he, wringing his hands, wept and besought his brothers not to sell him as a slave in a foreign land, and now, seeing them again after so many years, he again loved them beyond measure, but he tormented and plagued them, loving them. And then he left them at last, unable to bear the suffering of his heart, flung himself upon his bed and wept; then he wiped his tears and went out to them looking bright and radiant, and announced to them: 'Brothers, I am your brother Joseph!' Let him read further how happy old Jacob was when he learnt that his darling boy was still alive, and how he went to Egypt, even leaving his own country, and how he died in a foreign land, having uttered in his testament a great prophecy, which lay hidden mysteriously in his gentle and timid heart all his life, that from his descendants, from Judah, will come the great hope of the world, its Peace-maker and Saviour! Fathers and teachers, forgive me and do not be angry with me for talking like a child about something you knew long ago and can teach me a hundred times better and more skilfully. I am saying this only from rapture, and forgive my tears, for I love that Book! Let him too weep, the priest of God, and he will see how the hearts of those who listen to him will be shaken in response. Only a little seed is needed, a tiny seed: drop it in the soul of a peasant and it will not die. It will live in his soul all his life. It will be hidden inside him amidst the darkness, amidst the stench of his sins, as a bright spot, as a great reminder. And it is not necessary, it is not necessary to teach and expound a lot. He will understand it all simply. Do you think the peasant will not understand? Try and read to him further the moving and pathetic story of the fair Esther and the haughty Vashti; or the wonderful story of the prophet Jonah in the whale's belly. Don't forget either the parables of Our Lord, mostly from the Gospel of St Luke (that is what I did), and then from the Acts of the Apostles the conversion of Saul (that above all, above all!) and, finally, from the Lives of the Saints, let us say, the Life of Alexey the man of God, and the greatest of the great, the happy martyr and the seer of God and the bearer of Christ, Mary of Egypt – and you will pierce his heart with these simple tales. And only one hour a week, regardless of his small stipend, only one hour. And he will see for himself that our people are kind and grateful and will repay him a hundredfold; mindful of the zeal of their priest and his moving words, they will voluntarily help him in his fields and in his house and will treat him with more respect than ever before – and in this way his stipend will be increased. It is so simple a matter that sometimes we are afraid even to mention it for fear of being laughed at, and yet how true it is! He who does not believe in God, will never believe in God's people. But he who has faith in God's people, will also behold his Glory, though he had not believed in it till then. Only the common people and their future spiritual power will convert our atheists, who have torn themselves away from their native soil. And what is Christ's word without an example? The people will perish without the word of God, for their hearts yearn for the Word and for all that is good and beautiful. In the days of my youth, a long time ago, almost forty years ago, Father Anfim and I wandered all over Russia, collecting alms for our monastery, and one night we spent on the bank of a big navigable river with some fishermen. A handsome-looking young peasant, a lad of about eighteen, joined us. He was in a hurry to get to his job next day, dragging a merchant's barge along the tow-path. I saw him looking before him with clear and tender eyes. It was a warm, bright, still July night. The river was broad, a mist was rising from it and from time to time we could hear the soft splash of a fish. The birds were silent. All was still and beautiful, all was praying to God. Only we two were not asleep, the peasant lad and I, and we began to talk of the beauty of God's world and the great mystery of it. Every blade of grass, every small insect, ant, golden bee, all of them knew so marvellously their path, and without possessing the faculty of reason, bore witness to the mystery of God, constantly partaking in it themselves. And I saw the dear lad's heart glowing with emotion. He told me that he loved the woods and the wild birds; he was a bird-catcher, could distinguish each bird-call and knew how to decoy each bird; 'I know nothing better than to be in a wood,' he said, 'though all things are good.' 'Truly,' I replied, 'all things are good and beautiful, because all is truth. Look,' I said to him, 'at the horse, that great animal that is so near to man, or at the sad and pensive ox which feeds him and works for him, look at their faces: what meekness, what devotion to man, who often beats them mercilessly, what gentleness, what trustfulness and what beauty! It is touching to know that there is no sin in them, for all but man is perfect and without sin, and Christ has been with them even before us.' 'But,' asked the lad, 'can Christ really be with them?' 'How could it be otherwise,' I said to him, 'since the Word is for all; all creation, all creatures, every leaf are striving towards the Lord, glorify the Lord, weep to Christ, and unknown to themselves, accomplish this by the mystery of their sinless life? Out there in the forest,' I said to him, 'wanders the terrible bear, menacing and ferocious, and yet innocent of it all.' And I told him how a bear once came to a great saint, who was seeking salvation in a little hut in a forest. And the great saint was filled with tenderness for it, went up to it fearlessly and gave it a piece of bread: 'Get along with you,' he said to the bear, 'Christ be with you.' And the ferocious beast went away obediently and meekly, without doing him any harm. And the lad was deeply moved that the bear had gone away without doing any harm and that Christ was with him, too. 'Oh, how good that is,' he said, 'how all God's work is good and beautiful!' He sat musing softly and sweetly. I could see that he understood. And he slept beside me and his sleep was light and sinless. May God bless youth! And I prayed for him before I went to sleep myself. O Lord, send peace and light to the men thou hast created!

(c) *Recollections of Father Zossima's Adolescence and Manhood while He was Still in the World. The Duel*

I spent a long time, almost eight years, in the Cadet Corps in Petersburg, and my new education there stifled a great many of the impressions of my childhood, though I forgot nothing. Instead, I picked up so many new habits and even opinions that I was transformed into a cruel, absurd and almost savage creature. I acquired a surface polish of politeness and society manners together with a knowledge of the French language, but all of us, myself included, treated the soldiers, who waited on us at the college, like brutes. I treated them perhaps worse than anyone, for I was more susceptible to everything than any of my fellow-cadets. When we received our commissions we were ready to shed our blood for the honour of our regiment, but scarcely any of us knew anything about the meaning of real honour, and if anyone had known it, he would have been the first to jeer at it. Drunkenness, debauchery and daredevilry we almost prided ourselves on. I don't say we were bad; all those young men were good fellows, but they behaved badly, and I worst of all. The trouble was that I had come into money and gave myself up to a life of pleasure with all the enthusiasm of youth, and threw myself headlong and without restraint into it. But the strange thing was that I read many books then and even derived great pleasure from them; the Bible, however, was the only book that I almost never opened at that time, though I never parted from it and always carried it about with me: in truth I was keeping the Book, without knowing it myself, 'for an hour, and a day, and a month and a year'. After four years of this kind of army life, I found myself at last in the town of K., where my regiment was stationed at the time. The social life in the town was varied and gay; there were many rich people there who entertained on a grand scale. I was well received everywhere, for I was by nature of a cheerful disposition and, besides, I was reputed to be well-off, which means not a little in society. Then something happened that was the beginning of everything. I formed an attachment to a young and beautiful girl, high-minded and intelligent, of a noble and serene character, the daughter of a highly respected family. They were well-to-do and influential people of good social position. They received me warmly and cordially. I imagined that the girl cared for me, and I worked myself up into a fever of excitement at the mere thought of it. Afterwards I realized myself, and, indeed, was quite sure that perhaps I was not so passionately in love with her at all, but only respected her intelligence and lofty character, which was quite natural. My selfishness, however, prevented me from proposing to her at the time: I felt it was hard and unfair to have to give up the temptations of my free and licentious bachelor life while I was still so young and, besides, had plenty of money. I did, however, drop a hint as to my intentions, though I put off taking any decisive step for a time. Then we were suddenly ordered off to another district for two months. On my return two months later I was astonished to learn that the girl had in the meantime married a rich landowner, who had an estate in the vicinity of the town, a man who was still quite young, though considerably older than I, with excellent connexions in Petersburg and in high society, which I did not possess. He was an exceedingly nice man and of excellent education, and education was something I lacked completely. I was so startled by this unexpected turn of events that I lost my senses. The worst of it was that, as I learned then, the young landowner had been engaged to her a long time and that I myself had often met him at her house, but, blinded by my high opinion of myself, I had noticed nothing. And it was this that hurt me most: what a fool I was! Everyone had known about it, only I knew nothing! That I could not bear: I was filled with sudden fury. With a flushed face I began recalling how many times I was on the point of telling her that I loved her, and as she never stopped me or warned me, I could only conclude that she must have been laughing at me. On thinking it over afterwards, I realized of course that she had not laughed at me at all; on the contrary, whenever I began talking to her about my feelings, she invariably broke off the conversation with a jest and changed the subject. But at the time I was quite unable to see it and I was overcome by a burning desire to revenge myself. I remember with astonishment that my anger and desire for revenge were extremely painful and repugnant to me because, being easy-going by nature, I never could be angry with anyone for long. For that reason I had to work myself up artificially and became revolting and absurd in the end. I bided my time till one day I succeeded in insulting my 'rival' among a large company for a supposedly quite different reason by ridiculing an opinion he had expressed on some rather important public event. (It was in the year 1826.) I managed to ridicule him, so people said, very cleverly and wittily. Then I demanded an explanation from him and treated him so rudely that he accepted my challenge in spite of the great difference in our social positions, for I was not only younger, but also a man of no consequence and of low rank. Later on I learnt positively that he had accepted my challenge because he, too, for some reason, had felt jealous of me: he had been a little jealous of me before on account of his wife, while she was still engaged to him; now he thought that if she got to know that he had put up with my insult and had not the courage to challenge me, she could not help despising him and would waver in her love for him. It did not take me long to get a second, a fellow-officer, a lieutenant of our regiment. Although duels were forbidden and severely punished in those days, they were rather in fashion among the military – to such an extent do savage prejudices sometimes spread and get firmly established among people. It was the end of June, and our meeting was to take place at seven o'clock next day on the outskirts of our town. But something happened to me just then that had a decisive influence on the whole of my future life. In the evening I returned home in an ugly and ferocious mood. I lost my temper with my batman Afanasy and slapped his face twice, as hard as I could, so that it was covered in blood. He had not been in my service long and I had sometimes struck him before, but never with such brutal ferocity. And, believe me, dear fathers, though forty years have passed since then, I remember it still with shame and pain. I went to bed, slept for three hours, and woke up when day was breaking. I did not want to sleep any more, got up immediately, went up to the window, opened it – it looked out on to the garden – and watched the sun rising. It was warm and beautiful, the birds began to sing. 'What,' I thought to myself, 'can be the meaning of that strange feeling of shame and disgrace in my heart? Is it because I am going to shed blood? No,' I thought, 'I don't think it's that at all. Am I afraid of death? Afraid to be killed? No, it is not that, it is not that, either.' And then I suddenly realized what it was: it was because I had given Afanasy a beating the evening before! And I saw it all happen again, as though for the second time: there he stood before me and I was slapping his face as hard as I could, and he was standing stiffly to attention, his head erect, his eyes fixed blankly on me as though on parade, shuddering at every blow but not daring to raise his hands to protect himself – and that was what a man had been brought to, that was a man beating a fellow-man! What a horrible crime! I felt as though my heart had been transfixed by a sharp needle. I stood there as though I had lost my reason, and the sun was shining, the leaves were rejoicing and reflecting the sunlight, and the birds – the birds were praising the Lord. . . . I covered my face with both my hands, flung myself on my bed and burst out sobbing. And then I remembered my brother Markel and his last words to our servants: 'My dear ones, why do you love me? Do I deserve to be waited on?' 'Yes, do I deserve it?' it flashed suddenly through my mind. And, really, what had I done to deserve that another man, a man like me created in God's image, should wait on me? So for the first time in my life this question pierced me to the core. 'Mother, my dearest heart, every man is responsible for everyone, only people don't know it. If they knew – it would be paradise at once!' Dear Lord, I thought as I wept, could that, too, be untrue? Yes, indeed, I was perhaps more responsible than anyone for all and certainly worse than any other man in the world! And I became suddenly aware of the whole truth in its full light: what was I about to do? I was about to kill a man, a good, intelligent and honourable man, who had done me no wrong, and by killing him I should deprive his wife of her happiness for ever, torture and kill her, too. I lay like that stretched out on the bed with my face buried in the pillow and did not notice how time was passing. Suddenly my second, the lieutenant, came in with the pistols to fetch me. 'Oh,' he said, 'I see you're up already. That's fine! It's time we were off. Come along!' I rushed about the room completely at a loss what to do, but we went out to get into the carriage. 'Wait here a minute,' I said to him, 'I'll be back in a moment. I forgot my purse.' And I rushed back alone to my flat and went straight to Afanasy's little room. 'Afanasy,' I said, 'I struck you twice in the face yesterday, please forgive me,' I said. He gave a violent start, as though he were frightened, and stared at me. I saw that it was not enough, not enough, and I suddenly threw myself down at his feet, in full uniform as I was, with my forehead touching the ground. 'Forgive me!' I said. At that he looked utterly confounded. 'Sir,' he stuttered, 'sir, you shouldn't – I – I'm not worth it . . .' and he burst into tears himself, as I had done before and, covering his face with his hands, turned to the window and shook all over with sobs. I ran out to my fellow-officer and jumped into the carriage. 'Lead on,' I cried. 'Ever seen a conquering hero? Well, look at him now!' I was in such an ecstasy that I went on laughing and talking, talking all the way. I don't remember what I was talking about. He looked at me: 'Well, old man,' he said, 'you've certainly got pluck. I can see you won't let the regiment down!' So we arrived at the place, and they were already there waiting for us. We took up our positions, twelve paces apart. He had the first shot. I stood facing him, looking happy, without batting an eyelid. I looked at him lovingly, for I knew what I was going to do. He fired and just grazed my cheek and ear. 'Thank God,' I cried, 'you haven't killed a man!' I seized my pistol, turned round and, flinging it high into the air, threw it into the wood. 'That's the place for you!' I cried. Then I turned to my opponent and said: 'Forgive a stupid young fellow, sir, for having insulted you without any provocation on your part and now forcing you to shoot at him. I'm ten times worse than you and, perhaps, even more. Tell that to the person whom you respect more than anyone in the world.' As soon as I said this, they all began shouting at me: 'Really,' said my opponent – he got angry in good earnest, 'if you didn't want to fight, why did you trouble me to come here?' 'Yesterday,' I replied gaily, 'I was still a fool, but I'm wiser today.' 'As to yesterday,' he said, 'I believe you, but as to today, I find it difficult to agree with your opinion.' 'Bravo,' I cried, clapping my hands, 'I agree with you there, too. I've deserved it!' 'Are you going to fire, sir, or not?' 'I'm not,' I replied, 'but if you like, you can fire at me again, but it would be better for you not to fire.' The seconds were shouting, too, mine especially. 'How can you disgrace your regiment like that, sir, facing your opponent and asking for his forgiveness? If I'd only known this!' So I stood there in front of them all, no longer laughing. 'Gentlemen,' I said, 'is it really so extraordinary in these days to find a man who will acknowledge his own stupidity and apologize in public for the wrong he has done?' 'But not during a duel,' my second cried again. 'Ah,' I said, 'that's right, that's what's so surprising, for I should have apologized as soon as we got here, before he had fired a shot, and not led him into a great and mortal sin. But,' I went on, 'we ourselves have brought things to such an awful pass in society that it was almost impossible to do that, for it was only after I had faced his shot at a distance of twelve paces that my words could have any meaning for him. Had I told him that as soon as we arrived here and before he had fired, he would have simply said that I was a coward, that I had taken fright at the pistols and that it was no use listening to me. Gentlemen,' I cried suddenly straight from my heart, 'look round you at God's gifts: the clear sky, the pure air, the tender grass, the birds. Nature is beautiful and without sin, and we, we alone, are godless and foolish and we don't understand that life is paradise, for we have only to want to understand and it will at once come in all its beauty and we shall embrace and weep.' I would have said more, but I couldn't. My breath failed me. Everything was so fresh and sweet, and my heart was full of such happiness as I had never felt before in my life. 'It's all very nice and proper,' my opponent said to me, 'and you certainly are a most original person.' 'You may laugh,' I said to him, laughing too, 'but afterwards I'm sure you'll approve of me yourself.' 'Why,' he said, 'I'm quite ready to approve of you now. Let's shake hands, for I believe you really are a sincere person.' 'No,' I said, 'not now, afterwards when I've become a better man and deserved your esteem, then shake hands with me and you'll do well.' We went home, my second swearing at me all the time, while I kept kissing him. As soon as my fellow-officers heard of it, they met to pass judgement on me the same day: 'He's disgraced the uniform,' they said, 'and now let him resign his commission.' There were some who defended my action: 'He did face the shot,' they said. 'Yes, he did, but he was afraid of other shots and apologized during a duel.' 'But,' my defenders retorted, 'if he'd been afraid of being shot, he'd have fired first himself before apologizing, but he threw his loaded pistol into the wood. No, there's something else here, something original.' I listened and felt happy looking at them. 'My dear friends and comrades,' I said, 'don't worry about my resigning my commission, because I've sent in my resignation already, and when I receive my discharge from the army I shall enter a monastery at once. That's why I've resigned my commission.' As soon as I said it, they all burst out into loud laughter. 'Why didn't you tell us that before? Well, that explains everything. We can't try a monk.' They laughed and could not stop themselves. Not sarcastically, but kindly and gaily. They all grew suddenly fond of me, even my most fierce accusers, and they seemed to make a fuss of me during the whole of the following month before my discharge came. 'Oh, you monk!' they said. And everyone said a kind word to me, tried to dissuade me from entering a monastery, even began to pity me: 'What are you doing to yourself?' 'No,' they said, 'he's a brave fellow, he faced the fire, and he could have fired himself, but the night before he dreamed that he became a monk, and that's why he did it.' Almost the same thing happened with the people of the town. Before, they were scarcely aware of my presence, though they received me cordially enough, but now they were all suddenly eager to know me and began inviting me to their houses: they laughed at me themselves, but they could not help loving me. I may observe here that although everyone in the town was discussing the duel, the army authorities hushed it up, for my opponent was a near relation of our general, and as the whole thing came to nothing, as no blood was shed and as I resigned my commission, they just looked upon the whole thing as a joke. And I began then to speak aloud and fearlessly, regardless of their laughter, for, after all, it was a kindly and not a malicious laughter. All these discussions took place mostly at parties, in the society of ladies, for it was the ladies who were most eager to listen to me and they made the men listen too. 'But how is it possible that I should be responsible for everyone?' they all would laugh in my face. 'Can I, for instance, be responsible for you?' 'But,' I replied, 'how can you possibly understand it when the whole world has long been following a different road and when we accept a downright lie as truth and, indeed, demand the same lie from others? Here I have for once in my life done something sincerely, and what happens? Why, you look upon me as though I were an imbecile. You may be fond of me,' I said, 'but you laugh at me all the same.' 'But how can we help being fond of you?' my hostess said, laughing. She had a great many visitors at the time. All of a sudden I caught sight of the young woman whose husband I had challenged and whom I had been planning to make my bride. I had not noticed that she had just arrived at the party. She rose, came up to me and held out her hand. 'Let me tell you,' she said, 'that I am the first not to laugh at you, but, on the contrary, I want to thank you humbly and express my respect to you for the way you acted then.' Her husband, too, came up, and then they all surrounded me and almost kissed me. I felt so happy then, but my attention was especially caught by a middle-aged man who also came up to me. Though I knew him by name, I had never made his acquaintance and never exchanged a word with him till that evening.

(d) The Mysterious Visitor

He had long been a member of the civil service in our town, where he occupied a very important position. He was respected by everyone, he was rich, he was well known for his charitable works, having donated a considerable sum to the almshouse and orphanage, and spent a great deal of money on charity in secret, without publicity, all of which came to light after his death. He was about fifty and had a rather forbidding appearance and was not very talkative. He had been married for about ten years. His wife, who was still young, had borne him three children. On the following evening I was sitting alone in my room when the door suddenly opened and this gentleman walked in.

I think I ought to explain that I was no longer living in my old lodgings, but had moved to others after sending in my resignation from the regiment. My new landlady was an old woman, the widow of a civil servant, who had let me a room in her house with service. I had moved from my old quarters simply because on my return from the duel I had sent Afanasy back to his company, for I was ashamed to look him in the face after the way I had apologized to him – so prone is an unprepared man of the world to be ashamed even of some of his most just actions.

'I've listened to you with great interest in different houses for the last few days,' said the gentleman who had just entered my room, 'and I'd like to make your personal acquaintance, as I am anxious to discuss things with you in greater detail. Can you do me such a great service, sir?' 'Why,' I said, 'with the greatest pleasure, sir. Indeed, I shall consider it an honour.' I said this, but I felt almost dismayed, so greatly did he impress me from the first moment of his appearance in my room. For although people listened to me and were interested in what I had to say, no one had ever approached me before with such a serious and stern air of deep, personal concern. And that man had come to see me of his own accord. He sat down. 'I can see,' he said, 'that you're a man of great strength of character, for you were not afraid to serve truth in a matter in which you risked incurring the contempt of all.' 'I think, sir,' I said, 'that you are greatly exaggerating the importance of what I've done.' 'No,' he said, 'I'm not exaggerating. Believe me, it is much more difficult to do a thing like that than you think. It's that really that impressed me so much and that's what I have come to see you about. Can you describe to me, please, if, that is, you don't think I'm being unduly inquisitive, what you felt at the moment when you decided to apologize at the duel, if you can still remember it? Don't think me frivolous. On the contrary, in asking you this question I have a secret motive of my own, which I will perhaps explain to you later on, if it please God to make us more intimately acquainted.'

All the while he was saying this I was looking him straight in the face, and I suddenly felt that I could trust him implicitly. Besides, my curiosity was powerfully aroused, for I realized that there was some peculiar secret in his soul.

'You asked me what exactly I felt at the moment when I apologized to my opponent,' I answered, 'but, to begin with, I'd better tell you something I haven't yet told anyone else.' And I told him all that had passed between Afanasy and me and how I had prostrated myself before him. 'From that you can see for yourself,' I concluded, 'that it was easier for me at the time of the duel, for I had made a beginning at home, and once I had started on that road, the rest was not only easy, but also a source of joy and happiness to me.'

After hearing me out, he gave me a very friendly look. 'All this,' he said, 'is extremely interesting and I'll come to see you again and again.' And after that he began visiting me almost every evening. We would have become very close friends if he had also talked to me about himself. But he scarcely ever said a word about himself, but always kept asking me about myself. In spite of that I became very fond of him and spoke to him with perfect frankness about my feelings, for, I thought to myself, 'What do I care about his secret when I can see that he's a righteous man?' He was, besides, such a serious-minded man and so much older than I, and yet he came to see a youngster like me and treated me as his equal. And I learned many useful things from him, for he was a man of high intelligence. 'That life is paradise,' he said to me suddenly, 'of that I've long been convinced.' And he added quickly: 'In fact, that's the only thing I am convinced of.' He looked at me and smiled. 'I'm more convinced of it than you,' he said. 'You'll find out why later.' 'I expect,' I thought to myself, 'he wants to reveal some secret to me.' 'Paradise,' he said, 'is hidden in every one of us. It is hidden in me, too, now, and I have only to wish and it will come to me in very truth and will remain with me for the rest of my life.' He was speaking with great feeling and looking mysteriously at me, as though questioning me. 'And as for every man being responsible for every other man and for everything, apart from his sins, you were perfectly right about that and it's remarkable how you could have grasped that idea in all its implications. And it is indeed true that when people grasp this idea the Kingdom of Heaven will become a reality to them and not just a dream.' 'But,' I cried bitterly, 'when will that come to pass, and will it ever come to pass? Isn't it just a dream?' 'Oh,' he said, 'I can see you don't believe it. You preach it and you don't believe it yourself. Know, then, that this dream, as you call it, will undoubtedly come to pass – you can be sure of that, but not now, for every action has its own law. It's a spiritual, a psychological process. To transform the world, it is necessary that men themselves should suffer a change of heart. Until you have actually become everyone's brother, the brotherhood of man will not come to pass. People will never be able to share their property and their rights fairly as a result of any scientific advance, however much it may be to their advantage to do so. Everything will be too little for them and they will always murmur, envy and destroy each other. You ask me when will it come to pass? It will come to pass, but first the period of human *isolation* will have to come to an end.' 'What sort of isolation do you have in mind?' I asked. 'Why,' he replied, 'the sort of isolation that exists everywhere now, and especially in our age, but which hasn't reached its final development. Its end is not yet in sight. For today everyone is still striving to keep his individuality as far apart as possible, everyone still wishes to experience the fullness of life in himself alone, and yet instead of achieving the fullness of life, all his efforts merely lead to the fullness of self-destruction, for instead of full self-realization they relapse into complete isolation. For in our age all men are separated into self-contained units, everyone crawls into his own hole, everyone separates himself from his neighbour, hides himself away and hides away everything he possesses, and ends up by keeping himself at a distance from people and keeping other people at a distance from him. He accumulates riches by himself and thinks how strong he is now and how secure, and does not realize, madman that he is, that the more he accumulates the more deeply does he sink into self-destroying impotence. For he is used to relying on himself alone and has separated himself as a self-contained unit from the whole. He has trained his mind not to believe in the help of other people, in men and mankind, and is in constant fear of losing his money and the rights he has won for himself. Everywhere today the mind of man has ceased, ironically, to understand that true security of the individual does not lie in isolated personal efforts but in general human solidarity. But an end will most certainly come to this dreadful isolation of man, and everyone will realize all at once how unnaturally they have separated themselves from one another. Such will be the spirit of the time, and everyone will be surprised at having remained so long in darkness and not having seen the light. And then the sign of the Son of Man will appear in the heavens. . . . But till then we must still keep the banner flying and, even if he has to do it alone, a man has to set an example at least once and draw his soul out of its isolation and work for some great act of human intercourse based on brotherly love, even if he is to be regarded as a saintly fool for his pains. He has to do so that the great idea may not die. . . .'

It was in such fervent and high-spirited talk that we spent our evenings, one after another. I even gave up my social calls and visited much less frequently the homes of my friends and acquaintances, apart from the fact that I was no longer in fashion to the same extent as before. I'm not saying this in condemnation of my friends, for they continued to like me and treat me good-humouredly, but simply to point out that fashion, in fact, wields no small sway in society, and that must be admitted, much as we may dislike doing so. But I began at last to regard my mysterious visitor with admiration, for, apart from enjoying his high intelligence, I could not help feeling that he was nourishing some secret plan in his heart and was perhaps preparing himself to do something great. Perhaps the thing he liked about me, too, was that I betrayed no curiosity about his secret and did not question him about it, either directly or indirectly. But at last I noticed that he himself seemed to be anxious to reveal something to me. At any rate, this became pretty obvious about a month after he first began visiting me. 'Do you know,' he asked me once, 'that people are beginning to be very curious about us in the town and are wondering why I'm visiting you so frequently. But let them wonder, for *soon everything will be explained.*' Sometimes he would suddenly become very agitated, and when that happened he would almost always get up and go away. Sometimes he would look, as it were, penetratingly at me for a long time and I could not help thinking that he was about to say something immediately, but he would suddenly avert his gaze and begin talking about something ordinary and familiar. He also began complaining frequently of headaches. And then one evening, after he had been talking with great fervour for a long time, he suddenly and to my great surprise turned pale, his face became contorted and he fixed me with a motionless stare.

'What's the matter?' I said. 'Are you ill?'

He had, in fact, been complaining of a headache.

'I – you know – I – I am a murderer!'

He said this and smiled, but was as white as chalk. 'Why is he smiling?' the thought pierced my heart suddenly before I had time to realize anything properly. I turned pale myself.

'What are you talking about?' I shouted at him.

'You see,' he said with the same pallid smile, 'how much it has cost me to utter the first word. Now I've uttered it and, I think, I'm on the right path. I'll follow it.'

For a long time I did not believe him, and I didn't believe him when he first told me about it, but only after he had been to see me three days running and told me everything in detail. My first thought was that he must be mad, but I ended by being at last convinced, to my great grief and astonishment, that what he had told me was true. He had committed a great and terrible crime fourteen years earlier. He had murdered the rich widow of a landowner, a young and beautiful woman, who owned a house in our town. He fell violently in love with her, made her a declaration of love, and tried to persuade her to marry him. But she had already given her heart to another, an army officer of high rank and good social position, who was on active service at the time, but whom, however, she was expecting to return soon. She rejected his proposal and asked him not to call on her again. Having ceased to visit her, but knowing his way about her house, he gained admission into it through the garden and by the roof with great daring, for he ran the risk of being discovered. But as so often happens, all crimes committed with extraordinary daring are more often than not successful. Entering the loft of the house through the skylight, he made his way downstairs by descending the ladder from the loft, knowing that the door at the bottom of the ladder was, through the carelessness of the servants, not always locked. He had relied on this oversight and so it happened. Having made his way to the inhabited part of the house, he went in the dark into her bedroom where a light was burning before the icon. And, as though on purpose, her two young maids had gone without asking permission to a birthday party in the same street. The other servants slept in the servants' quarters in the basement and in the kitchen. At the sight of her asleep, his passion was aroused in him and then his heart was overcome by vindictive, jealous anger and, beside himself, he went up to her bed like a drunken man and plunged a knife into her heart, so that she did not even utter a cry. Then with fiendish and criminal intent he contrived it so that the suspicion should fall on the servants: he did not scruple to take her purse, he opened the chest of drawers with the keys from under her pillow and took some things from it, just as some ignorant servant might have done, leaving the valuable securities and taking only money. He also took away some of the larger gold articles and left the smaller articles that were ten times more valuable. He took some other things, too, as keepsakes for himself, but of that later. Having done this dreadful thing, he went back the way he had come. Neither the next day, when the alarm was raised, nor at any time in his life, did it occur to anyone to suspect the real criminal! Besides, no one knew that he was in love with her, for he had always been of a taciturn and unsociable disposition and had no friend to whom he might open up his heart. He was simply regarded as an acquaintance of the murdered woman, and not even a close acquaintance, for he had not visited her during the previous fortnight. Suspicion fell at once on her serf-servant Peter and, as it happened, all the circumstantial evidence pointed to him, for he knew, and his mistress had made no secret of it, that, having to send a recruit to the army from her peasants, she intended to send him, as he had no relations, and his conduct, besides, was bad. People had heard him, when drunk in a public house, angrily threaten to kill her. Two days before her death he ran away and lived in town at some unknown address. On the day after the murder he was found lying dead drunk on the high road outside the town, with a knife in his pocket, and his right hand for some unknown reason was stained with blood. He claimed that his nose had been bleeding, but no one believed him. The two servant girls, on the other hand, confessed that they had gone to a party and that the front door had been left open till they returned. There were many other similar clues which pointed to the innocent servant and led to his arrest. He was put on trial for murder, but a week later he fell ill with a fever and died in hospital without regaining consciousness. That was the end of the matter, and everyone – the authorities, the judges, and society at large – was convinced that the crime had been committed by no one but the servant who had died during his trial. And after that the punishment began.

The mysterious visitor, now my friend, told me that at the beginning he was not in the least troubled by pangs of conscience. He was unhappy for a long time, but not because of that, but because he was sorry he had killed the woman he loved, a woman he would never see again and that, having killed her, he had also killed his love, while the fire of passion was still in his veins. But he never gave a thought at the time to the shedding of innocent blood and the murder of a human being. He could never reconcile himself to the thought that his victim could have become the wife of another man, and that was why he was for a long time convinced at heart that he could not have acted otherwise. He was worried at first by the arrest of the servant, but the prisoner's illness and death set his mind at rest, for, he argued at the time, the man quite obviously died not because of his arrest or his fright, but because of a chill he had contracted while he was on the run, when for a whole week he had lain dead drunk on the ground all night. The theft of the articles and the money troubled him little for (he argued again) the theft had been committed not for gain but to avert suspicion. The sum stolen was small and he even donated it all, and even more, to the almshouse which had been founded just then in our town. He did this on purpose to set his mind at rest about the theft, and the remarkable thing about it was that for a time, for a long time, in fact, he really was at peace with himself – he told me so himself. He began just then his very active career in the civil service. He volunteered for a very troublesome and difficult job, which occupied him for two years, and, being a man of strong character, he almost forgot about the crime he had committed; when he did remember it, he tried to dismiss it from his thoughts. He also did a great deal of philanthropic work, founded and endowed all sorts of charities in our town, became known in Moscow and Petersburg, too, and was elected a member of philanthropic societies there. But in spite of all that he fell to brooding painfully over his past and the strain of it was too great for him to bear. It was just then that he was attracted by a beautiful and sensible girl and soon married her in the vain hope that marriage would dispel his lonely desolation and that, by entering upon a new life and by zealously performing his duty towards his wife and children, he would escape his old memories altogether. But the opposite of what he expected happened. Already during the first month of his marriage he began to be worried continually by the thought. 'My wife loves me, but what if she knew?' When she told him that she was going to have a baby, their first child, he looked troubled: 'I'm giving life, but have taken life away.' Children came: 'How dare I love them, teach them, and bring them up? How can I speak to them of virtue, I who have shed blood?' His children were beautiful and he longed to caress them: 'But I can't look at their bright innocent faces: I'm not worthy of it.' At last he began to be bitterly and menacingly haunted by the blood of his murdered victim, by the young life he had destroyed, by the blood crying out for revenge. He began to have fearful dreams. But, being a man of stout heart, he bore his suffering a long time: 'I shall atone for everything by this secret agony of mine.' But that hope, too, was vain: the longer it went on, the more intense did his suffering become. In society he was beginning to be respected for his philanthropic work, though people were daunted by his stern and gloomy character, but the more they respected him, the more unendurable it was for him. He told me he had been thinking of killing himself. But instead of that, he became obsessed by another dream, a dream which he considered insane and impossible at first, but which finally gripped his heart so strongly that he could not shake it off. He dreamed of getting up, going out before the people and publicly confessing that he had committed a murder. For three years he nurtured that dream in his heart and he thought of all sorts of ways of carrying it out. At last he believed with all his heart that by making a public confession of his crime, he would most certainly restore his peace of mind and set it at rest once and for all. But, having come to this conclusion, his heart was filled with terror, for how was he to carry out his decision? And suddenly the incident at my duel took place. 'Looking at you I have made up my mind,' he said to me. I looked at him.

'But is it possible,' I cried, throwing up my hands, 'that such an unimportant incident could arouse such resolution in you?'

'My resolution has been growing for three years,' he replied. 'That incident of yours only supplied it with the necessary impetus. Looking at you, I reproached myself and envied you,' he said to me almost in a stern voice.

'But I don't think they'll believe you,' I observed. 'It happened fourteen years ago.'

'I have incontestable proofs. I'll present them.'

And I wept then and kissed him.

'Tell me one thing, one thing!' he said to me (as though everything depended on me now). 'What about my wife and children? My wife will probably die of grief, and though my children will not lose their rank as noblemen nor their estate, they'll be the children of a convict serving a life sentence in a Siberian prison. And what a memory, what a memory I shall leave in their hearts!'

I said nothing.

'And what about leaving them? Leaving them for ever? It is for ever, you know, for ever!'

I sat still, praying in silence. At last I rose to my feet. I felt frightened.

'Well?' he asked, looking at me.

'Go,' I said, 'and confess in public. Everything will pass, only the truth will remain. When they grow up your children will understand how much nobility there was in your great resolution.'

He left me that time and it looked as though he had really made up his mind. But for over a fortnight he kept visiting me every evening, still preparing himself, but unable to make up his mind. He worried me to death. One day he would come determined and say with deep feeling:

'I know it will be paradise for me, that it will come as soon as I confess. Fourteen years I've been in hell. I want to suffer. I shall accept suffering and begin to live. You can go through life under false colours and there's no turning back. Now I dare not love my neighbours, let alone my children. Dear Lord, surely my children will understand what I've been through and will not condemn me! God is not in strength but in truth.'

'Everyone will understand your great act of expiation,' I said, 'if not now, then afterwards. For you have served truth, the higher truth, not of the earth. . . .'

And he would go away, as though comforted, but next day he would come again, pale and angry, and say ironically:

'Every time I come into your room, you look at me with such curiosity, as though to say: "Not confessed yet?" Wait a little longer. Don't despise me too much. It's not as easy as you think. Perhaps I won't do it at all. You wouldn't denounce me then, would you?'

But, as a matter of fact, far from looking at him with foolish curiosity, I was afraid even to glance at him. I was so worn out that I felt ill, and my heart was full of tears. I even lost sleep at night.

'I've just come from my wife,' he went on. 'Do you understand what a wife is? My children shouted to me as I went out: "Good-bye, Daddy. Hurry back to read *The Children's Stories* to us." No, you don't understand that! Another man's misfortune cannot make any-one wiser.'

His eyes flashed and his lips quivered. Suddenly he struck the table with his fist so that the things on it jumped. He was such a mild man, it was the first time he had done such a thing.

'But is it necessary at all?' he cried. 'Must I do it? No one has been condemned. No one has been sentenced to hard labour for me. The servant died a natural death. And I've been punished by my suffering for the blood I shed. Besides, they'll never believe me. No proof will ever convince them. Must I confess? Must I? I'm ready to suffer all my life for the blood I've shed, if only my wife and children are spared. Will it be just to ruin them with me? Are you sure we're not making a mistake? Who can tell what's right? And will people recognize it? Will they appreciate it? Will they respect it?'

'Heavens,' I thought to myself, 'he's thinking of people's respect at such a moment!' And I felt so sorry for him then that I was almost ready to share his fate if only it would make it easier for him. I could see he was beside himself. I was appalled, realizing with the whole of my being and not only with my reason what such resolution meant.

'Decide my fate!' he exclaimed again.

'Go and confess,' I whispered to him. My voice failed me, but I whispered it firmly. Then I took up the New Testament from the table, the Russian translation, and showed him the Gospel of St John, Chapter 12, Verse 24: 'Verily, verily, I say unto you, Except a corn of wheat fall into the ground and die, it abideth alone; but if it die, it bringeth forth much fruit.'

I had read that verse before he came in. He read it.

'That's true,' he said, but he smiled bitterly. 'Yes,' he said after a short pause, 'it's awful the things you come across in these books. It's easy to push them under your nose. And who wrote them? Not men, surely?'

'The Holy Spirit wrote them,' I said.

'It's easy for you to talk,' he said, smiling again, but almost with hatred this time.

I took the book again, opened it in another place, and showed him the Epistle to the Hebrews, Chapter 10, Verse 31. He read: 'It is a fearful thing to fall into the hands of the living God.'

He read it and flung down the book. He was shaking all over.

'A dreadful verse,' he said. 'You've picked out a good one, I must say.' He got up from the chair. 'Well,' he said, 'farewell. Perhaps I shan't come again. . . . We shall meet in heaven. So it's fourteen years since I've "fallen into the hands of God". That is what we must call the fourteen years, mustn't we? Tomorrow I shall entreat those hands to let me go.'

I wanted to embrace and kiss him, but I did not dare – so distorted was his face and so sombre did he look. He went out. 'Dear Lord,' I thought, 'the things that man has to face now!' I fell on my knees before the icon and wept for him before the Holy Virgin, our swift mediator and helper. I had been kneeling like that for half an hour, praying in tears. It was already late, about midnight. Suddenly I saw the door open and he came in again. I was astounded.

'Where have you been?' I asked.

'I think,' he said, 'I – I've forgotten something – my handkerchief, I think. . . . Well, even if I haven't forgotten anything, you won't mind my sitting down, will you?'

He sat down on a chair. I stood over him. 'Won't you sit down, too?' he said. I sat down. We sat like that for two minutes. He looked at me intently and then he suddenly smiled – I remember that well. Then he got up, embraced me warmly and kissed me.

'Remember, old man,' he said, 'how I came to see you for a second time. Do you hear? Remember that!'

It was the first time he had addressed me so familiarly. And he went out. 'Tomorrow,' I thought.

And so it was. I had no idea that evening that the next day was his birthday. I had not been out for the last few days, so I couldn't have found it out from anyone. On that day he always gave a big party and the whole town went to it. They went to it now, too. And so after dinner, he walked into the middle of the room, a paper in his hand – a formal statement to the head of his department. And as the head of his department was present at his party, he read it there and then aloud to the whole gathering. It contained a full description of the crime, in all its details. 'I cast myself out from the society of men as a monster,' he concluded his statement. 'God has visited me – I want to suffer!'

Then he brought out and put on the table all the articles he thought would prove his crime, which he had kept for fourteen years: the gold articles that belonged to the murdered woman, which he had taken to avert suspicion from himself, her locket and cross he had taken from her neck – with a portrait of her fiancé in the locket, her diary and, finally, two letters: her fiancé's letter to her with the news of his speedy arrival and her reply to his letter, which she had begun but left unfinished on the table, intending to post it next day. He had carried off those two letters – why? Why had he kept them for fourteen years instead of destroying them as evidence against him? And now this is what happened: they were all amazed and horrified, but no one would believe it, though they all listened with intense curiosity. They all thought that he was ill, and a few days later it was definitely decided and agreed in every house that the unhappy man was mad. The legal authorities could not refuse to start criminal proceedings against him, but they soon dropped them, though the articles and letters he had produced gave them cause to think. But it was decided that even if they turned out to be authentic, it was impossible to prefer a charge of murder only on the basis of that evidence. Besides, he could have obtained all those things from her as a friend of hers and as a person who had acted as her legal adviser. I heard afterwards, however, that the authenticity of the articles was proved by many of the murdered woman's friends and acquaintances, and that there was no doubt about them. But, again, the whole thing came to nothing in the end. Five days later all had learnt that the poor man was ill and that his life was in danger. What he had fallen ill of, I can't say. It was rumoured that he had had a heart attack, but it also became known that, at the insistence of his wife, the doctors had examined his mental condition and had come to the conclusion that he showed signs of insanity. I disclosed nothing, though they rushed to question me, but for a long time they would not let me visit him, his wife especially. 'It is you,' she said to me, 'who have unsettled him. Before, too, he was melancholy, and last year everyone noticed that he was unusually excited and did strange things, and then you came and ruined him. It was your reading to him that drove him out of his mind. For the last month he never left your room.' And it was not only his wife. Everyone in town pounced upon me and blamed me. 'It's all your fault,' they said. I said nothing, and indeed I rejoiced in my heart, for I could plainly see God's mercy to the man who had turned against himself and punished himself. I could not believe in his insanity. At last they let me see him, for he insisted on taking leave of me. I went in and saw at once that not only his days but also his hours were numbered. He was weak, his face was sallow, his hands trembled. He gasped for breath, but he looked joyful and his eyes were full of deep emotion.

'It's done!' he said to me. 'I've long been yearning to see you. Why didn't you come?'

I did not tell him that I was not allowed to see him.

'God has had pity on me and is calling me to him. I know I'm dying, but I feel happy and at peace for the first time after so many years. As soon as I'd done what had to be done I felt paradise in my heart. Now I dare to love my children and kiss them. No one believes me. Neither my wife nor the judges believed me. Nor will my children ever believe me. I see in that a sign of God's mercy to my children. I shall die and my name will be without a stain for them. Now I feel that God is near, my heart rejoices as in paradise. . . . I have done my duty.'

He could not speak. He gasped for breath, but pressed my hand warmly, looking ardently at me. But we did not talk long. His wife kept looking into the room while I was there. But he managed to whisper to me:

'Do you remember how I came back to you for a second time at midnight? I told you to remember it. Do you know what I came back for? I came back to kill you!'

I gave a violent start.

'I went out from you that time in the darkness, walked about the streets, struggling with myself. And suddenly I hated you so much that I couldn't bear it. Now, I thought, he's the only one who stands in my way. He's my judge, and I can't refuse to face my punishment tomorrow because he knows everything. It wasn't that I was afraid you'd inform the police (I never even thought of that), but I kept thinking, how am I going to face him, if I don't make a clean breast of it? And even if you'd been at the other end of the world, so long as you were alive it would have made no difference to me. I couldn't have borne the thought that you were alive and condemning me. I hated you as though you were the cause of it all and were to blame for it all. I came back to you that time, for I remembered that you had a dagger lying on the table. I sat down, asked you to sit down, and turned it over in my mind for a whole minute. If I had killed you, I should have been done for even if I hadn't made known my first crime. But I was not thinking of that at all. I didn't want to think of it at that moment. I just hated you and longed to revenge myself on you for everything. But the Lord vanquished the devil in my heart. I want you to know, however, that you were never nearer death.'

He died a week later. The whole town followed his coffin to the grave. The priest made a moving speech. They all bewailed the terrible illness that cut short his days. But after the funeral the whole town turned against me and they even stopped receiving me. It is true that some, a few at first, but more later on, began to believe in the truth of his confession, and started visiting me often and questioning me with great interest and eagerness, for people love to see the downfall and disgrace of a righteous man. But I kept silent and soon left the town for good, and five months later I entered by the grace of God upon the straight and glorious path, blessing the unseen finger which had shown it to me. And the much-suffering servant of God Mikhail I have remembered daily in my prayers to this day.

3

From the Discourses and Sermons of Father Zossima

(e) Something about the Russian Monk and his Significance

FATHERS and teachers, what is a monk? Among the educated this word is nowadays uttered with derision by some people, and some even use it as a term of abuse. And it is getting worse as time goes on. It is true, alas, it is true that there are many parasites, gluttons, voluptuaries and insolent tramps among the monks. Educated men of the world point this out: 'You are idlers and useless members of society,' they say. 'You live on the labour of others. You are shameless beggars.' And yet think of the many meek and humble monks there are, monks who long for solitude and fervent prayer in peace and quiet. These attract their attention less and they even pass them over in silence, and how surprised they would be if I told them that the salvation of Russia would perhaps once more come from these meek monks who long for solitary prayer! For they are verily prepared in peace and quiet 'for an hour, and a day, and a month, and a year'. In their solitude they keep the image of Christ pure and undefiled for the time being, in the purity of God's truth, which they received from the Fathers of old, the apostles and martyrs, and when the time comes they will reveal it to the wavering righteousness of the world. That is a great thought. That star will shine forth from the East.

That is what I think of the monk, and is it false, is it arrogant? Look at the worldly and all those who set themselves up above God's people on earth, has not God's image and God's truth been distorted in them? They have science, but in science there is nothing but what is subject to the senses. The spiritual world, however, the higher half of man's being, is utterly rejected, dismissed with a sort of triumph, even with hatred. The world has proclaimed freedom, especially in recent times, but what do we see in this freedom of theirs? Nothing but slavery and self-destruction! For the world says: 'You have needs, and therefore satisfy them, for you have the same rights as the most rich and most noble. Do not be afraid of satisfying them, but multiply them even.' That is the modern doctrine of the world. In that they see freedom. And what is the outcome of this right of multiplication of needs? Among the rich *isolation* and spiritual suicide and among the poor envy and murder, for they have been given the rights, but have not been shown the means of satisfying their needs. We are assured that the world is getting more and more united and growing into a brotherly community by the reduction of distances and the transmission of ideas through the air. Alas, put no faith in such a union of peoples. By interpreting freedom as the multiplication and the rapid satisfaction of needs, they do violence to their own nature, for such an interpretation merely gives rise to many senseless and foolish desires, habits and most absurd inventions. They live only for mutual envy, for the satisfaction of their carnal desires and for showing off. To have dinners, horses, carriages, rank, and slaves to wait on them is considered by them as a necessity, and to satisfy it they sacrifice life, honour, and love of mankind. Why, they even commit suicide, if they cannot satisfy it. We see the same thing among those who are not rich, while the poor drown their unsatisfied needs and envy in drink. But soon they will drown it in blood instead of in drink – that's where they are being led. I ask you: is such a man free? I knew one 'fighter for an idea', who told me himself that when he was deprived of tobacco in prison he was so distressed by this privation that he nearly went and betrayed his 'idea' just to get a little tobacco! And it is such a man who says, 'I'm fighting for humanity'! How can such a man fight for anything and what is he fit for? For some rash action, perhaps, for he cannot hold out long. And it is no wonder that instead of gaining freedom, they have fallen into slavery, and instead of serving the cause of brotherly love and the union of humanity, they have, on the contrary, sunk into *separation* and isolation, as my mysterious visitor and teacher said to me in my youth. And that is why the idea of service to humanity, of brotherhood and of the solidarity of men is more and more dying out in the world. Indeed, this idea is even treated with derision, for how can a man give up his habits, where can such a slave go, if he is so used to satisfying his innumerable needs which he has himself created? He lives in isolation, and what does he care for the rest of mankind? And they have now reached the point of having more and more things and less and less joy in life.

The monastic way is different. People even laugh at obedience, fasting and prayer, and yet it is through them that the way lies to real, true freedom: I cut off all superfluous and unnecessary needs, I subdue my proud and ambitious will and chastise it with obedience, and, with God's help, attain freedom of spirit and with it spiritual joy! Which of them is more capable of conceiving a great idea and serving it – the rich man in his isolation or the man *freed* from the tyranny of material things and habits? The monk is reproached for his solitude: 'You have sought solitude to find salvation within the walls of the monastery, but you have forgotten the brotherly service of humanity.' But we shall see which will be more zealous in the cause of brotherly love. For it is they and not we who live in isolation, but they don't see that. In the olden times leaders of men came from our midst, so why cannot it happen again now? The same meek and humble monks, living a life of fasting and silence, will rise again and go forth to work for the great cause. The salvation of Russia comes from the people. And the Russian monastery has from time immemorial been on the side of the people. If the people are isolated, then we too are isolated. The people believe as we do. An unbelieving leader will never achieve anything in Russia, even if he were sincere at heart and a genius in intelligence. Remember that. The people will meet the atheist and overcome him, and Russia will be one and orthodox. Therefore, take care of the people and guard their heart. Educate them quietly. That is your great task as monks, for this people is a Godbearer.

(*f*) *Something about Masters and Servants and whether it is possible for them to become Brothers in Spirit*

Good Lord, no one can deny that there is sin in the common people too. And the fire of corruption is spreading visibly every hour, working its way from the top. Among the common people, too, isolation is coming: *kulaks* and village usurers are growing in number; the merchant, too, is getting more and more eager for honours and strives to show that he is an educated man, though he has no education whatever, and to prove it he basely scorns ancient customs and is even ashamed of the faith of his fathers. He pays visits to princes, though he is only a peasant spoilt. The common people are rotting in drunkenness and cannot give it up. And what cruelty to their families, their wives and even their children! All from drunkenness. I've seen in the factories children of nine years of age: weak, sickly, bent and already depraved. The stuffy workshop, the racket of machines, work all day long, bad language and drink, drink, and is that what the soul of a little child needs? He needs sunshine, games, a good example everywhere, and just a little bit of love. There must be no more of this, monks, no more torturing of children – rise up and preach that at once, at once! But God will save Russia, for though the ignorant peasant is corrupt and cannot give up his foul sins, he knows that his foul sin is cursed by God and that he does wrong in sinning. So that our people still believe in righteousness, have faith in God and shed tears of tender devotion. It is different with the upper classes. Following science, they wish to live a life based on justice by their reason alone, but without Christ as before, and they have already announced that there is no crime, there is no sin. And they are right according to their views: for if you have no God, then why worry about crime? In Europe the common people is already rising up against the rich with violence, and the leaders of the people lead them everywhere to bloodshed and teach them that their wrath is righteous. But 'cursed is their wrath, for it is cruel'. God will save Russia as he has saved her many times. Salvation will come from the people, from its faith and its meekness. Fathers and teachers, take care of the people's faith, and this is no dream: all my life I have been struck by the true and splendid sense of dignity in our great people. I have seen it myself and I can bear witness to it. I have seen it and I have marvelled. I have seen it in spite of the foul sins and the destitute appearance of our people. It is not servile, and that after two centuries of slavery. It is free in appearance and bearing, but without offence. It is neither revengeful nor envious. 'You are noble, you are rich, you are intelligent and talented – all right, may God bless you. I respect you, but I know that I too am a man. By respecting you without envy, I show you my dignity as a man.' And, truly, if they do not say this (for they don't know how to say this yet), they *act* like this. I have seen it myself, I have experienced it myself, and you would not believe it, but the lower and poorer our Russian peasant is, the more noticeable is that splendid truth in him, for the rich among them, the *kulaks* and the usurers, are to a large extent corrupted already, and our own negligence and oversight is responsible for a great deal of it! But God will save his people, for Russia is great in her meekness. I dream of seeing our future, and I seem to see it clearly already: for it will come to pass that even the most corrupt of our rich will end by being ashamed of his riches before the poor, and the poor, seeing his humility, will understand and yield to him, and respond with gladness and kindness to his magnificent shame. Believe me, it will end like that: everything points to it. Equality is to be found only in the spiritual dignity of man, and that will be understood only among us. Let there first be brothers, and there will be brotherhood also, and before we have brotherhood there can never be any fair share-out. We preserve the image of Christ and it will shine forth like a precious diamond over the whole world. . . . It will be so, it will be so! . . .

Fathers and teachers, a most moving incident befell me once. In my wanderings I came across my former batman Afanasy one day in the chief provincial town of K. This happened eight years after I had parted from him. He saw me accidentally in the market place. He recognized me, ran up to me and was so delighted to see me that he almost fell on my neck. 'Good gracious, sir, is it you? Is it really you I see?' He took me to his home. He had left the army, was married and had two little children. He and his wife earned their living as stallholders in the market. His room was poor, but clean and cheerful. He made me sit down, set the *samovar*, sent for his wife, just as though my visit called for a special celebration. He brought his children to me: 'Bless them, Father.' 'Who am I, an ordinary, humble monk, to bless them?' I replied. 'I'll say a prayer for them, and as for you, Afanasy, I've been praying for you every day since that very day, for you,' I said, 'are the cause of it all.' And I explained it to him as well as I could. And what do you think he did? He looked at me unable to believe that I, his former master, an army officer, was now before him in so humble a state and wearing such clothes: he cried even. 'What are you crying for,' I said to him, 'you who are always uppermost in my thoughts? Better rejoice over me, my dear fellow, for my way is bright and joyful!' He did not say much, but just sighed and shook his head over me tenderly. 'What did you do with all your money?' he asked. 'I gave it to the monastery,' I replied. 'We live a communal life there.' As I was taking leave of him after tea, he took out fifty copecks and gave them to me as an offering for the monastery, and I saw him thrusting another fifty copecks into my hand hurriedly. 'That's for you,' he said, 'the pilgrim; you may find it useful in your travels, Father.' I accepted his fifty copecks, bowed to him and to his wife and went away rejoicing, thinking on the way: 'I suppose both of us, he at home and I on the road, are sighing now, and yet we are smiling happily, in the gladness of our hearts, shaking our heads and remembering how God has brought us together.' And I never saw him again after that. I was his master and he my servant, but now when we had kissed each other lovingly and in the joy of our spirits, a great human bond had grown up between us. I have thought a great deal about it, and now what I think is: is it so inconceivable that the same kind of great and simple-hearted union could also occur everywhere in due time between all the Russian people? I believe that it will and that the time is near at hand.

And about servants I will add this: as a young man I was often angry with servants: 'The cook had served a meal too hot, the batman had not brushed my clothes.' But something I heard my brother say when I was a child suddenly came back to me: 'Do I, such as I am, deserve to be waited on by another and lord it over him because he is poor and ignorant?' And I marvelled at the time that such very simple and, indeed, obvious ideas should occur to our minds so late in life! It is impossible to carry on in the world without servants, but you must see to it that your servant should be freer in spirit than if he were not a servant. And why can't I be a servant to my servant and in such a way that he should see it, and that without any pride on my part and no scepticism on his? Why should not my servant be like a relation of mine, so that I may take him into my family at last and rejoice in doing so? Even now it can be done, and it may serve as the basis for the magnificent union among men in future, when man will no longer look for servants for himself and will no longer desire to turn men like himself into servants, as it is done nowadays, but, on the contrary, will long with all his heart to become every-body's servant himself, according to the Gospels. And is it really a dream that in the end man will find his joy only in great deeds of light and mercy and not in cruel pleasures as now – in gluttony, fornication, ostentation, boasting, and envious superiority of one over the other? I firmly believe that it is not, and that the time is near at hand. People laugh and ask: 'When will this time come and is it likely that it will ever come?' But I think that with Christ we shall accomplish this great work. And how many ideas have there not been on earth in the history of man which were unthinkable ten years before and which, when their mysterious hour struck, suddenly appeared, and spread all over the earth? So it will be with us too, and our people will shine forth in the world, and all men will say: 'The stone which the builders refused, the same is become the head stone of the corner.' And those who scoff at us, we shall ask: if our idea is a dream, then when are you going to erect your building and organize your life justly by your reason alone, without Christ? And if they them-selves assert that they, on the contrary, are advancing towards unity, it is the most simple-minded of them who really believe it, so that one cannot help marvelling at such simplicity. Truly, their imagina-tion is more romantic than ours. They think to organize their life justly, but by rejecting Christ they will end up by drowning the world in blood, for blood cries out for blood, and he who un-sheathes his sword will perish by the sword. And if it were not for Christ's solemn promise, they would have destroyed each other to the last two men on earth. And even those two would in their pride not have been able to restrain each other, so that the last man would have destroyed the one before the last, and then destroyed himself. And that would have come to pass but for Christ's solemn promise that for the sake of the meek and the humble this shall never happen. I began at that time, after my duel, while I was still wearing my officer's uniform, talking in society about servants and they were all, I remember, surprised at me. 'What do you want us to do?' they asked. 'Make our servants sit down on the sofa and offer them tea?' And I answered them: 'Why not? Even if you did it only once in a while.' They all laughed at the time. Their question was frivolous and my answer vague, but I can't help thinking that there was a grain of truth in it.

(g) Of Prayer, of Love and of Contact with Other Worlds

Young man, do not forget to say your prayers. If your prayer is sincere, there will be every time you pray a new feeling containing an idea in it, an idea you did not know before, which will give you fresh courage; you will then understand that prayer is education. Remember also: every day and whenever you can repeat to yourself, O Lord, have mercy upon all who appear before thee today. For thousands of people leave life on this earth every hour and every moment and their souls stand before God – and how many of them depart this life in solitude, unknown to anyone, in anguish and sorrow that no one feels sorry for them and does not even care whether they live or die. And so from the other end of the earth your prayer, too, will perhaps rise up to God that his soul may rest in peace though you knew him not nor he you. How deeply touching it will be to his soul, standing in fear before God, to feel at that moment that he has someone to utter a prayer for him, that there is one human being on earth left who loves him. And God also will look upon you both more benignly, for if you have had so much pity on him, how much greater will God's pity be on you, for God is infinitely more merciful and more loving than you. And he will forgive him for your sake.

Brothers, be not afraid of men's sins. Love man even in his sin, for that already bears the semblance of divine love and is the highest love on earth. Love all God's creation, the whole of it and every grain of sand. Love every leaf, every ray of God's light! Love the animals, love the plants, love everything. If you love everything, you will perceive the divine mystery in things. And once you have perceived it, you will begin to comprehend it ceaselessly more and more every day. And you will at last come to love the whole world with an abiding, universal love. Love the animals: God has given them the rudiments of thought and untroubled joy. Do not, therefore, trouble it, do not torture them, do not deprive them of their joy, do not go against God's intent. Man, do not exalt yourself above the animals: they are without sin, while you with your majesty defile the earth by your appearance on it and you leave the traces of your defilement behind you–alas, this is true of almost every one of us! Love children especially, for they, too, like the angels, are without sin, and live to arouse tender feelings in us and to purify our hearts, and are as a sort of a guidance to us. Woe to him who offends a child! Father Anfim taught me to love children: in our wanderings he, kind and silent man, would buy sweets and cakes for them with the farthings given to us; he could not pass a child without being deeply moved: that is the sort of man he is.

At some ideas you stand perplexed, especially at the sight of men's sins, asking yourself whether to combat it by force or by humble love. Always decide: 'I will combat it by humble love.' If you make up your mind about that once and for all, you may be able to conquer the whole world. Loving humility is a terrible force, the strongest of all, and there is nothing like it. Every day and every hour, every minute, examine yourself and watch over yourself to make sure that your appearance is seemly. You pass by a little child, you pass by spitefully, with foul language and a wrathful heart; you may not have noticed the child, but he has seen you, and your face, ugly and profane, will perhaps remain in his defenceless heart. You may not know it, but you have perhaps sown an evil seed in him and it may grow, and all because you did not exercise sufficient care before a child, because you did not foster in yourself a discreet, active love. Brothers, love is a teacher, but one must know how to acquire it, for it is acquired with difficulty, it is dearly bought, one must spend a great deal of labour and time on it, for we must love not only for a moment and fortuitously, but for ever. Anyone can love by accident, even the wicked can do that. My young brother asked forgiveness of the birds: it may seem absurd, but it is right nonetheless, for everything, like the ocean, flows and comes into contact with everything else: touch it in one place and it reverberates at the other end of the world. It may be madness to beg forgiveness of the birds, but, then, it would be easier for the birds, and for the child, and for every animal if you were yourself more pleasant than you are now – just a little easier, anyhow. Everything is like an ocean, I tell you. Then you would pray to the birds, too, consumed by a universal love, as though in a sort of ecstasy, and pray that they, too, should forgive your sin. Set great store by this ecstasy, however absurd people may think it.

My friends, ask God for gladness. Be glad as children, as the birds of heaven. And let not men's sins trouble you in your work. Fear not that it will obliterate your work and prevent it from being accomplished. Do not say: 'Sin is powerful, wickedness is powerful, bad environment is powerful, while we are lonely and helpless. Bad environment will destroy us and prevent our good work from being done.' Fly from that despondency, children! You have only one means of salvation: take hold of yourself and make yourself responsible for all men's sins. My friend, believe me, that really is so, for the moment you make yourself responsible in all sincerity for everyone and everything, you will see at once that it really is so and that you are, in fact, responsible for everyone and everything. And by throwing your own indolence and impotence on to others, you will end up by sharing Satan's pride and murmuring against God. As for Satan's pride, this is what I think of it: it is difficult for us on earth to grasp it, and that is why it is so easy to fall into error and share it, even imagining that we are doing something great and beautiful. Besides, many of the strongest feelings and forces of our nature we cannot so far comprehend on earth. But be not tempted by this, either, and do not think that this may serve as a justification for you for anything, for the Eternal Judge will call you to account for what you can comprehend and not for what you cannot. You will be convinced of that yourself hereafter, for then you will see everything in its true light and you will no longer argue about it. On earth, however, we seem, in truth, to be walking about blindly, and, but for the precious image of Christ before us, we should have perished and lost our way altogether, like the human race before the flood. Many things on earth are hidden from us, but in return for that we have been given a mysterious, inward sense of our living bond with the other world, with the higher, heavenly world, and the roots of our thoughts and feelings are not here but in other worlds. That is why philosophers say that it is impossible to comprehend the essential nature of things on earth. God took seeds from other worlds and sowed them on this earth, and made his garden grow, and everything that could come up came up, but what grows lives and is alive only through the feeling of its contact with other mysterious worlds; if that feeling grows weak or is destroyed in you, then what has grown up in you will also die. Then you will become indifferent to life and even grow to hate it. That is what I think.

(h) Can One be a Judge of One's Fellow-creatures? Of Faith to the End

Remember particularly that you cannot be a judge of anyone. For there can be no judge of a felon on earth, until the judge himself recognizes that he is just such a felon as the man standing before him, and that perhaps he is more than anyone responsible for the crime of the man in the dock. When he has grasped that, he will be able to be a judge. However absurd that may sound, it is true. For if I had been righteous myself, there would, perhaps, have been no criminal standing before me. If you are able to take upon yourself the crime of the man standing before you and whom your heart is judging, then take it upon yourself at once and suffer for him yourself, and let him go without reproach. And even if the law itself makes you his judge, then act in the same spirit as much as you can, for he will go away and condemn himself more bitterly than you have done. If, however, he goes away indifferent to your kisses and laughing at you, do not let that influence you, either; it merely means that his time has not yet come, but it will come in due course; and if it does not come, it makes no difference: if not he, then another in his place will understand and suffer, and will judge and condemn himself, and justice will be done. Believe that, believe it without a doubt, for therein lies all the hope and faith of the saints.

Carry on with your good work without ceasing. If you remember at night as you go to sleep that you have not done what you should have done, get up at once and do it. If the people around you are spiteful and callous and refuse to listen to you, fall down before them and ask them for forgiveness, for in truth you are responsible for their refusing to listen to you. And if you find it impossible to talk to the malevolent ones, serve them in silence and in humility, never giving up hope. But if they will all abandon you and drive you away by force, fall upon the earth, when left alone, and kiss it, drench it with your tears, and the earth will bring forth fruit from your tears even if no one has heard or seen you in your loneliness. Believe to the end, even if it should so happen that all men on earth were led astray and you were the only one to remain faithful: sacrifice yourself even then and give praise to God – you who are the only one to be left. And if two of you should meet – then that will be the world entire, the world of living love, and embrace each other with great tenderness and give praise to God: for though only in two of you, his truth has been manifested.

If you yourself have sinned and are grieved even unto death for your sins, or for your sudden sin, rejoice for others, rejoice for the righteous, rejoice that, though you have sinned, he is righteous and has not sinned.

But if the evil-doing of men should arouse your indignation and uncontrollable grief, even to make you wish to revenge yourself upon the evil-doers, fear most of all that feeling; go at once and seek suffering for yourself just as if you were yourself guilty of that villainy. Accept that suffering and bear it, and your heart will be appeased, and you will understand that you, too, are guilty, for you might have given light to the evil-doers, even as the one man without sin and you have not given them light. If you had, you would have lighted a path for them too, and he who had committed the felony would not have committed it if you had shown him a light. And even if you showed a light but saw that men are not saved even by your light, you must remain steadfast and doubt not the power of the heavenly light; believe that if they were not saved now, they will be saved afterwards. And if they are not saved afterwards, their sons will be saved, for your light will not die, though you were to die yourself. The righteous man departs, but his light remains. People are always saved after the death of him who came to save them. Men do not accept their prophets and slay them, but they love their martyrs and worship those whom they have tortured to death. You are working for the whole, you are acting for the future. Never seek reward, for your reward on earth is great as it is: your spiritual joy which only the righteous find. Fear not the great nor the powerful, but be wise and always worthy. Know the right measure, know the right time, get to know it. When you are left in solitude, pray. Love to fall upon the earth and kiss it. Kiss the earth ceaselessly and love it insatiably. Love all men, love everything, seek that rapture and ecstasy. Water the earth with the tears of your joy and love those tears. Be not ashamed of that ecstasy, prize it, for it is a gift of God, a great gift, and it is not given to many, but only to the chosen ones.

(i) Of Hell and Hell Fire, a Mystical Discourse

Fathers and teachers, I am thinking, 'What is hell?' And I am

reasoning thus: 'The suffering that comes from the consciousness
that one is no longer able to love.' Once, in the infinitude of existence,
which cannot be measured by time or space, it was given to some
spiritual being, on its appearance on earth, the ability to say: 'I am
and I love.' Once, only once, was there given him a moment of
active *living* love, and for that earthly life was given him, and with it
times and seasons. And what happened? That happy being rejected
the priceless gift, prized it not, loved it not, looked scornfully upon
it and remained indifferent to it. Such a one, having left the earth,
sees Abraham's bosom and talks with Abraham, as it is told in the
parable of the rich man and Lazarus, and contemplates heaven, and
can go up to the Lord, but what torments him so much is that he will
go up to God without ever having loved and come in contact with
those who love and whose love he has scorned. For he sees clearly
and says to himself, 'Now I have the knowledge and though I yearn
to love, there will be no great deed, no sacrifice in my love, for my
earthly life is over, and Abraham will not come even with a drop of
living water (that is to say, again with the gift of former active
earthly life) to cool the fire of the yearning for spiritual love which
burns in me now, having scorned it on earth; there is no more life
and there is no more time! Though I would gladly give my life for
others, I can do it no more, for the life I could have sacrificed for
love is over and now there is a gulf between that life and this existence.' Men speak of material hell fire: I do not go into that mystery
and I dread it, but I think that even if there were material fire, they
would be genuinely glad of it, for I fancy that in material agony the
much more terrible spiritual agony would be forgotten, even though
for a moment. And, indeed, it is quite impossible to take that spiritual
agony away from them, for it is not outside but within them. And
even if it were possible to take it away, I cannot help thinking that
their unhappiness would be more bitter because of it. For though the
righteous ones in heaven, contemplating their torments, would have
forgiven them, and called them to heaven in their infinite love,
by doing so they would have multiplied their torments, for they
would arouse in them still more strongly the fiery yearning for
responsive, active, and grateful love, which is no longer possible. In
the timidity of my heart, however, I cannot help thinking that the
very consciousness of this impossibility would at last serve to allevi-

ate their suffering, for by accepting the love of the righteous without the possibility of repaying it, by this submissiveness and the effect of this humility, they will at last acquire a certain semblance of that active love which they scorned in life, and a sort of activity which is similar to it. . . . I am sorry, my friends and brothers, that I cannot express it more clearly. But woe to those who have destroyed themselves on earth, woe to the suicides! I don't think there can be anyone more unhappy than they. We are told that it is a sin to pray for them, and outwardly the Church seems to reject them, but in my heart of hearts I think that we may pray even for them. For Christ cannot be angry with love. I have prayed inwardly all my life for such as those, I confess it to you, fathers and teachers, and I am still praying for them every day.

Oh, there are some who remain proud and fierce even in hell, in spite of their certain knowledge and contemplation of irrefutable truth; there are some fearsome ones who have joined Satan and his proud spirit entirely. For those hell is voluntary and they cannot have enough of it; they are martyrs of their own free will. For they have damned themselves, having damned God and life. They feed upon their wicked pride, like a starving man in the desert sucking his own blood from his body. They will never be satisfied and they reject forgiveness, and curse God who calls them. They cannot behold the living God without hatred and demand that there should be no God of life, that God should destroy himself and all his creation. And they will burn eternally in the fire of their wrath and yearn for death and non-existence. But they will not obtain death. . . .

*

Here Alexey Karamazov's manuscript ends. I repeat: it is incomplete and fragmentary. The biographical data, for instance, cover only the elder's early years. His teachings and views have been grouped together, as if they formed one whole, though it is obvious that they were uttered at different times and on different occasions. What the elder said during the last hours of his life is not stated precisely, but the spirit and character of his last talk can be gathered from what has been quoted in Alexey's manuscript of his former teachings. The elder's death came quite unexpectedly. For although those who had gathered in his room that last evening fully realized that his death was near, they never imagined that it would come so suddenly; on the contrary, his friends, as I have mentioned earlier, seeing him that night apparently so cheerful and talkative, were quite convinced that there had been a marked improvement in his health, for a short time at least. Even five minutes before his death, as they afterwards recounted with surprise, it was quite impossible to foresee it. He seemed suddenly to feel an acute pain in his chest, he turned pale and pressed his hand to his heart. They all got up from their seats at once and rushed up to him; but though in great pain, he gazed at them with a smile, sank slowly from his chair on to the floor, knelt and then fell on the ground face downwards, stretched out his arms and, as though in joyful rapture, kissing the ground and praying (as he had bidden them do), quietly and joyfully gave up his soul to God. The news of his death spread immediately through the hermitage and reached the monastery. Those nearest to the departed one, as well as those whose duty it was in accordance with their monastic rank, began laying out his body according to the ancient rites, and all the monks gathered in the cathedral church. And even before dawn, as it was rumoured afterwards, the news of the elder's death reached the town. By the morning almost the entire town was talking of the event, and many citizens flocked to the monastery. But of this we shall tell in the next book; here we shall only add that before a day had passed, something so unexpected happened and, from the impression it made in the monastery and in the town, so strange, so disturbing and so confusing, that even after so many years that day, so upsetting to many people, is still vividly remembered in our town. . . .

◆ PART THREE ◆

BOOK SEVEN: ALYOSHA

I

The Odour of Corruption

THE BODY OF THE DECEASED PRIEST AND MONK FATHER
Zossima was prepared for burial in accordance with the established
ritual. It is a well-known fact that monks and ascetics are not washed.
'If any one of the monks depart in the Lord [it is said in the Prayer
Book], the appointed monk [that is to say, the monk whose duty it is]
shall wipe his body with warm water, first making the sign of the cross
with a sponge on the forehead of the deceased, on the breast, on the
hands and feet and on the knees, and nothing more.' All this was performed by Father Paissy, who, after wiping his body, clothed him in
his monastic garb and wrapped him in his cloak, which he slit a little,
according to the rule, so as to be able to fold it round him in the form
of a cross. On his head he put a cowl with an octagonal cross. The cowl
was left open, but the face of the deceased was covered with the black
cloth used to cover the chalice. In his hands was put the icon of the
Saviour. So arrayed, he was put just before daybreak in his coffin
(which had been got ready long before). It was decided to leave the
coffin all day in the cell (in the first large room where the elder used
to receive the monks and lay visitors). As the deceased was, according
to his rank, a priest and a monk, leading a life of the strictest monastic
rules, the Gospel, and not the Psalter, had to be read over him by
monks who were ordained priests or deacons. Immediately after the
requiem service Father Joseph began the reading; Father Paissy, who
had expressed the wish to read later on all day and night, was for
the present very busy and preoccupied, as was the Father Prior of the

Hermitage, for something extraordinary, an unheard-of and 'unseemly' excitement and impatient expectation, became suddenly apparent among the monks as well as among the laymen who arrived in crowds from the monastery inns and the town. As time went on, this excitement grew more and more intense. Both the prior and Father Paissy did all they could to calm as much as possible the excited and bustling crowds. When it was broad daylight, people began arriving from the town with their sick, especially children, just as though they had been waiting expressly for this moment, evidently hoping for the power of healing which, according to their faith, would be immediately manifested. And it was only now that it became apparent to what an extent everyone in our town had been accustomed to consider the deceased elder, even during his lifetime, as an incontestably great saint. And many of those who came did not by any means belong to the lower orders. This great expectation on the part of the believers, betrayed so hastily and so openly, and even with impatience and almost with insistence, seemed to Father Paissy a clear incitement to sin, and though he had long foreseen it, it actually greatly exceeded his fears. Coming across some of the monks who shared this excitement, Father Paissy even began to rebuke them: 'So great and immediate an expectation of something miraculous,' he told them, 'is sheer levity, admissible only among laymen, but unseemly in us.' But they paid little attention to him, and Father Paissy noticed it uneasily, though even he (to be quite truthful), exasperated as he was by this too impatient expectation, which he found both thoughtless and vain, secretly, at the bottom of his heart, expected almost the same thing as the excited crowds, which he could not but admit to himself. Nevertheless, he was greatly perturbed by the misgivings some of these people aroused in him. He could not help feeling that something untoward would happen. In the crowd in the dead man's cell he noticed with inward revulsion (for which he at once reproached himself) the presence, for instance, of Rakitin or the visitor from the remote Obdorsk monastery, who was still staying in the monastery. Of both of them Father Paissy for some reason felt suddenly suspicious, though they were not by any means the only ones he felt suspicious of. The Obdorsk monk stood out among the excited crowd as the most fidgety; he could be seen everywhere; everywhere he was asking questions, everywhere he was listening, everywhere he was whispering with a sort of strangely mysterious air. He looked most impatient and he even seemed to resent that the miracle they had all been expecting so long was so late in coming. As for Rakitin, he had arrived at such an early hour at the hermitage, as it appeared later, at the express request of Mrs Khokhlakov. As soon as that kindly but weak-willed woman, who could not herself be admitted to the hermitage, woke up and heard of the elder's death, she was seized by such intense curiosity that she at once sent Rakitin off to the hermitage to keep an eye on things and report to her in writing about every half hour *everything that took place*. She considered Rakitin to be a most religious and devout young man – so well did he know how to pull the wool over the eyes of people who could be of the slightest use to him. It was a clear, bright day, and many of the visitors were swarming round the graves, which were particularly numerous near the church and scattered all over the hermitage. Taking a walk round the hermitage, Father Paissy suddenly remembered Alyosha and that he had not seen him for some time, not since that night. And no sooner did he remember him than he caught sight of him in the farthest corner of the hermitage, by the wall, sitting on the tombstone of a monk who had died a long time ago and who was famous for his life of great piety. He sat with his back to the hermitage and his face to the wall, as though hiding himself behind the tombstone. Going up to him, Father Paissy saw that he was weeping quietly but bitterly, his face buried in his hands and his body shaking with sobs. Father Paissy stood over him for a few minutes.

'Come, dear son, come, my friend,' he said at last with feeling, 'what are you weeping for? Rejoice and do not weep. Don't you know that this day is one of *his* greatest days? Remember where he is now, at this moment – remember that!'

Alyosha looked up at him, revealing his face, which was swollen with crying like a little child's, but he turned away at once, without uttering a word, and again buried his face in his hands.

'Well, I daresay you're right,' said Father Paissy thoughtfully, 'I daresay you're wise to weep. Christ has sent you these tears. Your heart-felt tears,' he added to himself, walking away from Alyosha and thinking lovingly of him, 'are only a relief for your soul and will serve to gladden your dear heart.' He was in rather a hurry to move away, for he felt that, looking at him, he might burst into tears himself.

Meanwhile the time was passing and the monastery services and the requiem for the dead man followed in due order. Father Paissy again saw Father Joseph at the coffin and again took over the reading of the Gospel from him. But before three o'clock in the afternoon something took place, which I have already mentioned at the end of the last book, something so utterly unexpected by anyone and so entirely contrary to the general hope that, I repeat, the smallest detail of this trivial affair is still vividly remembered in our town and all over our district. Here I will add a personal remark, namely that I find it almost revolting to recall this trivial and reprehensible incident, though quite natural and unimportant, as a matter of fact, and I should, of course, not have mentioned it in my story at all, had it not exercised a most powerful influence on the heart and soul of the chief, though *future*, hero of my story, namely Alyosha, forming a crisis and a turning-point in his spiritual life, causing a violent shock, but finally strengthening his mind for the rest of his life and giving it a definite aim.

And so to return to my story: when before daybreak they put the elder's body, made ready for burial, into the coffin and took it out into the front room, which during his lifetime he used as a reception-room, the question whether or not to open the windows was raised among those who stood around the coffin. But the question, put casually and in passing by someone, remained unanswered and almost unnoticed – except that it was noticed, and that too without comment, by some of those present, but only in the sense that to expect putrefaction and the odour of corruption of the body of so great a saint was an utter absurdity, deserving pity (if not a smile) for the frivolity and lack of faith of the man who asked that question. For they expected something quite different. And then, soon after midday, something happened, which was accepted without comment by those who went in and out of the room, each one quite obviously being afraid to communicate the suspicion in his mind; but by three o'clock in the afternoon it could be detected so clearly and unmistakably that the news of it at once spread all over the hermitage and among all the visitors and monks in the hermitage and immediately penetrated into the monastery as well, throwing all the monks there into amazement, and, finally, reached the town in the shortest possible time and caused great excitement both among the believers and unbelievers. The unbelievers were delighted, and as for the believers, there were some among them who were even more delighted than the unbelievers themselves, for 'men love the downfall of the righteous and their disgrace', as the elder himself had said in one of his sermons. What happened was that an odour of corruption began to come from the coffin, growing more and more perceptible, and by three o'clock in the afternoon it could no longer be mistaken and was, indeed, becoming gradually stronger and stronger. And never in the whole history of our monastery had there been such a scandal, so vulgarly unrestrained and quite impossible in any other circumstances, which showed itself immediately after this discovery among the monks themselves. Many years afterwards, some of our more intelligent monks, recalling the events of the whole of that day, were amazed and horrified at the dimensions this scandal took on at the time. For before, too, it had happened that monks who had led righteous lives had died, God-fearing elders, whose righteousness was recognized by all, and yet from their humble coffins, too, the odour of corruption had come naturally, as from all dead bodies, but that had not given rise to a scandal, nor even to the slightest excitement. Of course, there had been in the old days some monks in our monastery whose memory has been preserved and whose remains, according to tradition, showed no signs of decomposition, a fact that had a moving and mysterious effect on the monks and was preserved by them as something wonderful and miraculous and as a promise of still greater glory from their tombs in the future, if only by the grace of God the time for it should come. One of these, Father Job, a celebrated ascetic renowned for his fasting and silence, whose memory was particularly cherished, died at the beginning of the present century at the age of a hundred and five. His grave was pointed out to all the pilgrims on their first visit to the monastery with special and quite extraordinary respect and mysterious hints of certain great hopes in this connexion. (That was the grave on which Father Paissy had found Alyosha sitting in the morning.) In addition to this long-since deceased elder, the memory of another famous priest and monk, Father Varsonofy, who had died comparatively recently, was also held in great reverence in the monastery. It was he Father Zossima had succeeded in the eldership and it was he whom all the pilgrims who arrived at the monastery regarded as a saintly fool. Those two, according to tradition, had lain in their coffins as though they were alive and were buried without showing any signs of decomposition, their faces looking happy and serene in their coffins. And some monks even insisted that a distinctly discernible sweet odour came from their bodies. But in spite of these impressive memories, it would still be difficult to explain the direct cause of so thoughtless, absurd, and spiteful a demonstration at the coffin of Father Zossima. So far as I am concerned, it is my opinion that all sorts of other causes were simultaneously responsible for what happened. One of these, for instance, was the deeply-rooted hostility to the institution of elders as a pernicious innovation, which was firmly embedded in the minds of many monks in the monastery. And, above all, there was, finally, of course, the jealousy of the dead man's saintliness, so firmly established during his lifetime that it seemed almost forbidden to question it. For although the late elder had won the love and affection of many people, and not so much by miracles as by love, and had gathered round him, as it were, a whole world of loving followers, none the less, or rather on that account, in fact, he had created many enviers and, subsequently, bitter enemies, both open and secret, not only among the monks in the monastery, but also among the laymen outside. He never did any harm to anyone, but, they asked, 'Why do they think him such a saint?' And that question alone, continually repeated, gave rise at last to a great surge of insatiable hatred. That was why, I think, many people, noticing the odour of corruption coming from his body, and so soon, too, for not a day had passed since his death, were so greatly delighted; just as there were some among the elder's devoted disciples who had hitherto revered him but who were almost outraged and personally offended by this incident. The whole thing gradually developed as follows:

As soon as decomposition set in, it was possible to tell from the very faces of the monks why they had come into the cell. They came in, stayed a little, and went out quickly to confirm the news to the crowd waiting outside. Some of these shook their heads mournfully, but others did not even attempt to conceal the delight which gleamed malevolently in their eyes. And no one thought of reproaching them any more, no one raised his voice in protest, which was rather strange, for, after all, the majority of the monks in the monastery were loyal to the elder: but apparently God himself had this time let the minority gain the upper hand for the time being. Soon laymen, too, for the most part educated visitors, went into the cell for the same purpose of spying. Few of the common people went into the cell, though large crowds of them gathered at the gates of the hermitage. What could not be denied was that after three o'clock the rush of lay visitors greatly increased just because of the scandalous news. People who would perhaps not have arrived that day at all and who had, indeed, never intended to come, now came deliberately, among them some of high rank. However, there was so far no breach of decorum, and Father Paissy, looking stern, went on reading aloud the Gospel slowly and firmly, as though unaware of what was happening, though he had, as a matter of fact, observed something unusual for some time. But presently voices, at first rather subdued, but gradually louder and more confident, began to reach him too. 'Seems God's judgement is not as man's', Father Paissy heard suddenly. The first to say this was a layman, an elderly civil servant of our town, a man known for his great piety, but what he said aloud merely repeated what the monks had for some time been whispering to each other. They had long before given voice to this despairing utterance, and the worst of it was that almost every moment a sort of triumphant note could be more and more perceived at the repetition of this sentence. Soon, however, even the pretence at decorum was beginning to be abandoned and everyone almost seemed to feel that he had a right to abandon it. 'And why should *that* have happened?' some of the monks said, at first with a certain show of regret. 'He had a small body, dried up, nothing but skin and bones, where would the odour come from?' 'Therefore,' others hastened to add, 'it must be a special sign from heaven.' And their opinion was at once accepted without question, for it was again pointed out that if the odour had been natural, as in the case of every dead sinner, it should have come later, at least after a lapse of twenty-four hours, and not with such apparent haste, for 'this is a violation of the laws of nature' and therefore it was undeniably God's doing and the finger of God was quite evident. He meant it as a sign. This opinion struck everyone as incontrovertible. Gentle Father Joseph, the librarian and a great favourite of the late elder's, attempted to reply to some of these backbiters that 'it is not by any means held everywhere', that the incorruptibility of the bodies of the righteous was not a dogma of the Orthodox Church, but only an opinion, and that even in the most Orthodox countries, at Mount Athos, for instance, they were not in the least upset by the odour of corruption and that there it was not the incorruptibility of the bodies that was considered to be the chief sign of the sanctification of the saved, but the colour of their bones when their bodies had lain many years in the earth and had decayed in it. 'And if the bones become as yellow as wax, that is the chief sign that the Lord has glorified the dead saint; but if they are not yellow but black, it means that the Lord has not deemed him worthy of such glory. That is what they believe on Mount Athos, a famed place, where the Orthodox doctrine has been preserved since olden times inviolate and in its brightest purity,' Father Joseph concluded. But the gentle Father's words made no impression and even evoked a sarcastic rejoinder. 'That's all pedantry and innovation,' the monks decided among themselves. 'It's no use listening to it. We stick to the old doctrine. There are all sorts of innovations nowadays. Are we going to ape them all?' 'We have had as many holy Fathers as they,' the most jeering of the monks joined in. 'They all live there under the Turks and they have forgotten everything. Even their Orthodox faith has long grown impure, and they have no church-bells, either.' Father Joseph walked away mournfully, particularly as he himself expressed his opinion not very confidently, but as though hardly believing in it himself. But he foresaw with distress that something highly unseemly was beginning and that disobedience itself was raising its head. One by one, after Father Joseph, all the sober voices fell silent. And somehow or other it just happened that all those who loved the late elder and had accepted the institution of elders with devout obedience suddenly became terribly frightened of something and, when they met, exchanged timid glances with one another. But those hostile to the institution of elders as an innovation, held up their heads proudly. 'There was no odour of corruption from the late Father Varsonofy, but a sweet odour,' they recalled maliciously. 'But he was deemed worthy of it not because he was an elder, but because he was a saint himself.' And this was followed by a flood of condemnations and even accusations against the newly-departed elder. 'His teachings were false. He taught that life was a great joy and not tearful self-abasement,' some of the more muddle-headed ones said. 'His faith was too modern, he did not recognize material fire in hell,' others, who were even more muddle-headed, joined in. 'He was not strict in fasting. He allowed himself sweet things. He took cherry jam in his tea. He loved it. Ladies used to send it to him. Is it fitting for an ascetic to gorge himself on tea?' some of the more envious declared. 'He sat in pride,' the most malicious ones said brutally. 'Considered himself a saint. People used to fall on their knees before him and he took it as his due.' 'He abused the sacrament of confession,' the fiercest opponents of the institution of elders added in a malicious whisper, and these were from among the oldest monks, strictest in their devotions, true adherents of a life of fasting and silence, who had kept silent during the life of the deceased elder, but whose lips were suddenly unsealed now, which was terrible, indeed, for their words had a great influence on the young monks whose views were still unsettled. The Obdorsk visitor, the little monk from St Sylvester, listened to all this avidly, heaving deep sighs and shaking his head. 'Aye,' he thought to himself, 'it seems Father Ferapont was quite right in what he said yesterday.' And at that very moment Father Ferapont made his appearance; he seemed to have come for the express purpose of increasing the confusion.

I have mentioned earlier that he rarely left his wooden cell by the apiary. Even in church he appeared very rarely and he was allowed that as a saintly fool upon whom the monastery rules were not binding. And to tell the truth, he was allowed that privilege out of necessity. For it seemed shameful to insist on burdening a man who was so dedicated to a life of fasting and silence and who spent all his days and nights in prayer (he even fell asleep on his knees), with the general monastic rules, if he refused to obey them himself. 'Why,' some monks might have objected, 'he's holier than any of us and follows much harder rules than the official regulations. As for his not going to church, he knows when he ought to go: he has his own rules.' It was because of these possible murmurs and the scandal that might ensue that Father Ferapont was left in peace. As was well-known to everyone, Father Ferapont disliked Father Zossima intensely; and now the news had reached him in his cell that 'God's judgement, it seems, was not the same as man's' and that what had happened was 'a violation of the laws of nature'. It may well be supposed that among the first to run to him with this news was the Obdorsk visitor, who had visited him the day before and had left him in terror. I have also mentioned the fact that Father Paissy, who was standing firmly and immovably reading the Gospel over the coffin, though unable to see or hear what was going on outside the cell, had foreseen most of it unmistakably in his heart, for he knew his monastery thoroughly. But he was not disturbed, but waited without fear, for what might still happen, watching with penetrating insight for the inevitable outcome of the excitement, which he could already apprehend with his inner eye. Suddenly an extraordinary noise in the passage, which was quite an unmistakable breach of decorum, burst upon his ears. The door was flung wide open and Father Ferapont appeared on the threshold. Behind him, as could be clearly seen from the cell, was a crowd of monks with some laymen among them, who had accompanied him and stopped at the bottom of the front steps. They did not, however, enter the cell or mount the steps, but waited to see what Father Ferapont would say and do, for they felt, and indeed feared, that in spite of his well-known arrogance he had not come for nothing. Stopping on the threshold, Father Ferapont raised his arms, and from under his right arm peeped out the sharp and inquisitive eyes of the Obdorsk visitor; he was the only one who, in his intense curiosity, could not restrain himself from running up the steps after Father Ferapont. All the others, on the contrary, were overcome with sudden terror and pressed further back the moment the door was flung open. Raising his hands aloft, Father Ferapont suddenly roared:

'Casting out, I cast out!' and at once began making the sign of the cross at each of the four walls and corners of the cell in succession. All who accompanied Father Ferapont at once understood his action; for they knew that wherever he entered he always did this and that he would not sit down or utter a word till he had driven out the evil spirits.

'Satan, get thee hence! Satan, get thee hence!' he repeated every time he made the sign of the cross. 'Casting out, I cast out!' he roared again.

He was wearing his coarse cassock girt with a rope. His bare chest, covered with grey hair, could be seen under his hempen shirt. His feet were bare. As soon as he started waving his arms, the iron chains he wore under his cassock began shaking and clanking. Father Paissy interrupted his reading, stepped forward and stood waiting before him.

'What have you come for, reverend Father? Why do you break

the rules of decorum? Why do you lead astray the meek flock?' he said at last, looking sternly at him.

'Why come I? Thou askest why? Oh, ye of little faith?' screamed Father Ferapont, playing the saintly fool. 'Dropped in to cast out your guests, the unclean devils. To see how many you've collected without me. Sweep them out with a birch broom, that's what I want.'

'You cast out the evil one, but perhaps you're serving him yourself,' Father Paissy went on fearlessly. 'And who can say to himself, "I'm holy"? Can you, Father?'

'I'm unclean, not holy,' Father Ferapont thundered again. 'I wouldn't sit in an armchair! I wouldn't crave to be worshipped like an idol! Nowadays folk destroy faith. The deceased, that saint of yours,' he turned to the crowd, pointing at the coffin with a finger, 'denied the existence of devils. Gave you physic to keep off the devils. And so they've multiplied like spiders in the corners. And now he's begun to stink himself. Behold God's great sign in that.'

And that really had happened once during Father Zossima's lifetime. One of the monks began seeing the evil one in his dreams and, later on, he seemed to see him also when awake. When, frightened out of his wits, he confided this to the elder, Father Zossima advised continual prayer and strenuous fasting. But when that, too, was of no avail, he advised him to take a certain medicine, without giving up his prayers and fasting. Many monks were scandalized at the time and discussed it excitedly among themselves, shaking their heads, and most of all Father Ferapont, to whom some of Father Zossima's detractors hastened to report his 'extraordinary' advice in so singular a case.

'Get thee hence, Father!' Father Paissy said imperiously. 'It is not for men but for God to judge. Perhaps we see "a sign" here which neither you nor I nor anyone else is able to comprehend. Get thee hence, Father, and do not lead the flock astray!' he repeated insistently.

'He did not keep the fasts according to the rules of his order, and that is why the sign has come. That's clear enough and it's a sin to hide it!' the fanatic, carried away by his zeal that outstripped his reason, refused to quiet down. 'Loved sweets, he did. Ladies brought them to him in their pockets. Partial to tea, he was, too. Lived for his

belly, filling it with sweetmeats and his mind with proud thoughts.
. . . That's why he was put to shame. . . .'

'You speak vain words, Father,' Father Paissy, too, raised his voice.
'I admire your fasting and your ascetic way of life, but you speak vain
words, such as some inconstant and callow youth in the world might
speak. Get thee hence, Father, I command thee!' Father Paissy thundered in conclusion.

'I will, don't worry!' said Father Ferapont, looking somewhat put
out, but without abating his animosity. 'You scholars! From the
height of your intellect you look down on a nobody like me. I came
here almost illiterate, and here I've forgotten the little I knew. God
himself has protected me, insignificant as I am, from your great
wisdom.'

Father Paissy stood over him, waiting resolutely. Father Ferapont
was silent for a moment and suddenly, looking woebegone and pressing his right hand to his cheek, said in a sing-song voice, gazing at the
coffin of the dead elder:

'Tomorrow they will chant "Our Helper and Defender" over
him – a glorious anthem – and over me, when I kick the bucket,
they'll only chant "What earthly joy" – a little canticle,' he said tearfully and pitifully. 'You're proud and stuck-up. This is a vainglorious
place!' he roared suddenly, like a madman, and, with a wave of his
hand, he suddenly turned round rapidly and quickly went down the
steps.

The crowd, waiting below, wavered; some followed him at once,
but others lingered, for the door of the cell was still open, and Father
Paissy, who came out after Father Ferapont, stood watching him
from the top of the steps. But the old man, still in a rage, had not
finished yet. After walking twenty steps, he suddenly turned towards
the setting sun, raised both his hands over his head and, just as though
someone had cut him down, fell to the ground with a mighty cry.

'My God hath conquered! Christ hath conquered the setting sun!'
he shouted frantically, raising his hands to the sun, and, falling face
downwards on the ground, he burst into sobs, like a little child,
shaken convulsively by his tears and stretching his hands out on the
ground. They all rushed up to him; exclamations were heard and
condoling sobs. . . . They seemed all to have been seized by a sort of
frenzy.

'It's he who is a saint! It's he who is righteous!' some cried, no longer afraid. 'It's he who should be an elder,' others added malevolently.

'He wouldn't be an elder,' others immediately put in. 'He'd refuse, he wouldn't be a party to an accursed innovation! He wouldn't ape their foolish tricks!'

And it is hard to imagine what the end of it would have been, had not the bell rung at that moment summoning them to service. They all began at once to cross themselves. Father Ferapont, too, got up and, repeatedly crossing himself, went back to his cell without looking round, still uttering cries, but they were completely incoherent now. A small number of monks followed him, but most of them began to disperse, hastening to the service. Father Paissy passed the reading of the Gospel on to Father Joseph and went out. He could not be shaken by the frenzied cries of the fanatics, but he suddenly felt sad at heart, which seemed to ache for something, and he felt it. He stopped and asked himself suddenly: 'Why am I sad even to despondency?' and perceived at once to his surprise that his sudden melancholy was evidently due to a very small and special cause: in the excited crowd of people clustering round the entrance to the cell he had noticed Alyosha and he remembered that, having caught sight of him, he had at once felt a sort of pain in his heart. 'Does that boy mean such a lot to me now?' he asked himself with amazement. At that moment Alyosha happened to walk past him, as though in a hurry to get somewhere, but he was not going in the direction of the church. Their eyes met. Alyosha quickly turned away his eyes, dropping them to the ground, and by his look alone Father Paissy realized that a great change was taking place in him at that moment.

'Have you, too, been led astray?' Father Paissy suddenly cried. 'Are you, too, with the men of little faith?' he added mournfully.

Alyosha stopped and gave Father Paissy a vague sort of look, but quickly turned away his eyes once more and dropped them to the ground. He stood sideways to Father Paissy and did not turn to him.

Father Paissy observed him closely.

'Where are you hurrying? They're ringing for service!' he asked again, but again Alyosha made no answer.

'Or are you leaving the hermitage? Without asking leave and without a blessing?'

Alyosha suddenly smiled wryly, raised his eyes with a strange, a very strange look to the questioning Father, to the man to whom his former guide had entrusted him before his death – the former ruler over his heart and mind, his beloved elder – and, suddenly, as before, without answering, with a wave of his hand, as though no longer caring even to show any respect, went with rapid steps through the gates and walked away from the hermitage.

'You will come back!' whispered Father Paissy, looking after him with mournful surprise.

2

An Opportune Moment

FATHER PAISSY was not, of course, wrong when he decided that his 'dear boy' would come back, and perhaps even (though not entirely, but perspicaciously all the same) penetrated into the real meaning of Alyosha's state of mind. Nevertheless, I frankly confess that I myself would find it very hard to explain the true significance of that strange, obscure moment in the life of the hero of my story, who is so young and whom I love so much. To Father Paissy's sorrowful question, addressed to Alyosha, 'Are you, too, with the men of little faith?' – I could, of course, reply firmly for Alyosha: 'No, he is not with those of little faith.' Moreover it was quite the opposite: all his confusion arose from the fact that he was of great faith. But there was confusion, it had arisen in spite of everything and it was so painful that long afterwards Alyosha thought of that sorrowful day as one of the most painful and fateful days of his life. If, however, I were to be asked frankly: 'Could all this distress and so great an anxiety have arisen in him simply because the elder's body, instead of beginning at once to exercise healing powers, was, on the contrary, showing sign of early decomposition?', I should reply without a moment's hesitation, 'Yes, it certainly was so.' I would only like to ask my readers not to be in too great a hurry to laugh at my young hero's pure heart. For my part, far from intending to apologize for him or excuse and justify his unsophisticated faith on the ground of his youth, or, for instance, the little progress he had made in his studies, etc., etc., I must, on the contrary, declare emphatically that I have genuine respect for the qualities of his heart. No doubt, some other youth, who responded cautiously to heartfelt impressions, who knew how to love not passionately, but lukewarmly, whose mind, though reliable, was a little too reasonable for his age (and, therefore, cheap), such a youth, I say, would have avoided what happened to my hero; but, as a matter of fact, in some cases it really is much more admirable to give way to an emotion, however unreasonable, which springs from a great love, than not to give way to it at all. And that is all the more so when one is young, for a youth who is invariably reasonable does not inspire much confidence and isn't worth much – that's my opinion! 'But,' sensible people will perhaps exclaim, 'surely not every young man can be expected to believe in such prejudices and your young man is no authority for others.' To this I reply again, 'Yes, my young man had faith and his faith was firm and inviolate, but still I am not going to apologize for him.'

You see, though I declared above (and, perhaps, a little too hastily) that I was not going to explain, justify or apologize for my hero, I feel that something has to be made clear for the understanding of the rest of my story. What I will say is that there is no question of miracles. There was no frivolously impatient expectation of miracles here. It was not for the triumph of his convictions that Alyosha needed any miracles at the time (that was certainly not so), it was not because of some former preconceived idea which he was anxious to triumph over some other idea, oh no, not at all: what he was concerned about here first and foremost was a person and only a person; the person of his beloved elder, the person of the righteous man whom he revered to the point of adoration. The real trouble was that all the love hidden in his young and pure heart for 'everyone and everything', seemed at that time, during the whole of the preceding year, to have been at times entirely concentrated, and perhaps wrongly, on one human being only, at least in the strongest impulses of his heart, namely on his beloved elder, now dead. It is true that being had so long been regarded by him as an indisputable ideal that all his youthful powers and all their aspirations could not but be directed exclusively towards that ideal, at moments even to the forgetting of 'everyone and everything'. (He remembered afterwards that on that painful day he had completely forgotten his brother Dmitry, about whom he was so worried and whom he had so longed to see the day before; he had also forgotten to take the two hundred roubles to little Ilya's father, which he had intended to do so eagerly also on the previous day.) But, again, it was not miracles that he needed, but only 'higher justice', which, according to his belief, had been violated, and it was this that dealt such a sudden and cruel blow to his heart. And what does it matter that this 'justice' had in Alyosha's expectations inevitably assumed the form of miracles to be performed immediately by the dust of his former beloved guide? Did not everyone in the monastery, even those whose intellects Alyosha admired, even Father Paissy himself, think and hope for the same thing? And so Alyosha, untroubled by any doubts, clothed his dreams in the same form as all the rest. Besides, all this had taken shape in his heart long since, during the whole year of his life in the monastery, and his heart had got into the habit of expecting it. But it was justice, justice that he hungered for, and not only miracles! And now the man who, according to his expectations, ought to have been raised above everyone else in the whole world, that very man, instead of receiving the glory that was his due was suddenly cast down and disgraced! What for? Who had judged him? Who could have decreed it? Those were the questions that all at once wrung his inexperienced and virginal heart. He could not bear without mortification, without bitterness even, that the most righteous of the righteous should have been exposed to such jeering and spiteful mockery of a crowd so thoughtless and so inferior to him. All right, even had there been no miracles, even had nothing wonderful occurred and had his immediate expectations not been justified – but why should this indignity have happened, why should this disgrace have been permitted, why this premature decomposition which was 'a violation of the laws of nature', as the spiteful monks said? Why this 'sign' which they were now so triumphantly pointing at together with Father Ferapont, and why did they believe that they had a right to point at it? Where was Providence and its finger? Why did it hide its finger at the most critical moment (thought Alyosha) and seem to be anxious itself to submit to the blind, dumb, and pitiless laws of nature?

That was why Alyosha's heart was bleeding, and, of course, as I have said already, what he was concerned about first and foremost was that the person he had loved more than anything in the world should be 'dishonoured' and 'disgraced'! Granted that my young hero's complaint was thoughtless and unreasonable, but, again, I repeat for the third time (and I am quite prepared to admit that my argument, too, is perhaps far from sound), I am glad my young hero did not turn out to be so reasonable at such a moment, for a man who is not a fool will have time enough to see reason, but if there is no love in a young man's heart at such an exceptional moment, then when will it come? I must not, however, forget to mention in this connexion another strange fact which, though only for a fraction of a second, occurred to Alyosha at that fatal and confused moment. This new 'something' that flashed through Alyosha's mind was the somewhat painful impression left by his conversation with Ivan the day before which kept recurring to him again and again now. Yes, even now. Oh, not that any of the fundamental and, as it were, elemental beliefs of his soul had in any way been shaken. He loved his God and believed in him firmly, though he did murmur against him suddenly. Yet a sort of vague but tormenting and evil impression left by his conversation with Ivan the day before again suddenly stirred in his mind and was demanding more and more insistently to come to the surface. It was beginning to get dark when Rakitin, who was on his way through the pine wood from the hermitage to the monastery, suddenly caught sight of Alyosha, lying motionless and apparently asleep under a tree with his face downwards on the ground. He went up and called him by name.

'Is that you, Alexey? Good Lord, have you—' he said in surprise, but stopped without finishing. He wanted to say, 'Have you *come to this?*'

Alyosha did not look up at him, but from a slight movement Rakitin at once realized that he heard and understood him.

'What's the matter with you?' he went on in a surprised tone of voice, but his surprise was already giving way to a smile, which was becoming more and more sarcastic.

'Listen, I've been looking for you for over two hours. You suddenly disappeared. But what are you doing here? What sort of stupid nonsense is this? You might look at me at least. . . .'

Alyosha raised his head, sat up and leaned with his back against the tree. He was not crying, but there was a look of suffering and irritation on his face. He did not look at Rakitin, however, but somewhere away from him.

'You know, your face is quite changed. No more of that famous meekness of yours in it. Not angry with someone, are you? Have they hurt your feelings?'

'Leave me alone!' Alyosha said suddenly, still without looking at him, with a weary wave of the hand.

'Oho, so that's how we are! Started shouting at people like other mortals, have you? And one of our angels, too! Well, Alyosha, old man, you have surprised me, you know. I mean it. It's a long time since I was surprised at anything here. You see, I've always looked upon you as an educated chap.'

Alyosha looked at him at last, but somehow absent-mindedly, as though he still scarcely understood what he was talking about.

'But, surely, you're not so upset because your old man is stinking the place out? You didn't seriously believe that he'd start pulling miracles out of the air?' Rakitin exclaimed, looking genuinely astonished again.

'I did believe, I do believe, and I want to believe!' Alyosha cried irritably. 'What more do you want?'

'Nothing at all, my dear fellow. But damn it all, a thirteen-year-old schoolboy doesn't believe in that now. Still, damn it . . . So you're angry with your God now, are you? Up in arms because he hasn't been promoted, that his name hasn't appeared in the Honours List! Oh, you fools!'

Alyosha screwed up his eyes and gave Rakitin a long look. There was an angry flash in his eyes, but it was not Rakitin he was angry with.

'I haven't taken up arms against God,' he said, with a sudden wry smile. 'I simply "don't accept his world".'

'You don't accept his world? What do you mean?' Rakitin asked, thinking over his answer for a moment. 'What rot is this?'

Alyosha did not reply.

'Well, enough of this nonsense. Now to business: have you had anything to eat today?'

'I don't remember – I think I have.'

'I can see by your face that you need something to eat. One can't help feeling sorry for you. You didn't sleep last night, either, did you? I understand you had a conference in there. And then all that silly rumpus . . . I expect all you had was a bite of holy bread. I've got some sausage in my pocket, brought it from the town just in case I felt hungry on my way here. Only you won't eat sausage, will you?'

'Let's have it.'

'Oho! So that's what you're like now! Open rebellion, I see. Barricades! Well, old man, we mustn't miss such a chance, must we? Come to my place. I'd be glad of a drop of vodka myself now. I'm dog tired. I don't suppose you'd agree to have a little vodka, or would you?'

'Let's have vodka too!'

'Dear me! Well, well!' Rakitin gave him a queer look. 'Well, one way or another, vodka or sausage, it's a damn good chance, and we mustn't miss it, must we? Come along!'

Alyosha got up in silence and followed Rakitin.

'If that dear little brother of yours Ivan could see it, he'd certainly have the surprise of his life! By the way, your brother Ivan went off to Moscow this morning. Do you know that?'

'Yes,' Alyosha replied apathetically, and suddenly his brother Dmitry's face flashed through his mind, but only for a fraction of a second, and though it did remind him of something, of some urgent business which must not be put off for a moment, some duty, some terrible obligation, this reminder made no impression on him, did not reach his heart, and immediately slipped his memory and was forgotten. But Alyosha remembered this long afterwards.

'Dear old Ivan delivered himself of a remark about me one day to the effect that I was "a third-rate liberal windbag". And on one occasion you, too, could not resist pointing out to me that I was "dishonest" . . . All right! Let's see what your great gifts and honesty will do for you now,' Rakitin concluded in an undertone to himself. 'Oh, hell, listen,' he said aloud, 'don't let's go through the monastery, let's take this path straight to town. As a matter of fact, I ought really to go round to Mrs Khokhlakov's. You see, I've written to tell her about everything that happened and, you know, she at once sent me a little note in pencil (she simply adores writing notes, the dear lady does) that she "never expected such *conduct* from such a highly respected elder as Father Zossima!" That was the very word she used: *conduct*! She, too, got very angry! Oh, what a lot of fools you all are! Wait!' he suddenly cried again, stopping and, taking Alyosha by the shoulder, made him stop too.

'Do you know, Alyosha, old man,' he said, looking searchingly into his eyes, completely under the impression of a new idea which dawned upon him suddenly, and though he was laughing outwardly, he seemed to be afraid of uttering this new sudden idea of his aloud, so hard did he still find it to believe the strange and unexpected mood in which he saw Alyosha now, 'do you know, Alyosha, old man, where we'd better go now?' he said at last, timidly and ingratiatingly.

'I don't care – anywhere you like.'

'Let's go to Grushenka, eh? Will you come?' Rakitin said at last, trembling all over with timid suspense.

'Let's go to Grushenka,' Alyosha replied at once calmly, and his prompt and calm agreement was so unexpected that Rakitin nearly started back.

'Well, I must say!' he cried in amazement, but all of a sudden seizing Alyosha firmly by the arm, he dragged him quickly along the path, still terribly afraid that his resolution might falter.

They walked along in silence, Rakitin being afraid even to utter a word.

'You can't imagine how glad she'll be, how awfully glad,' he muttered, but again fell silent.

And, indeed, it was not to please Grushenka that he was dragging Alyosha to her; he was a serious-minded man and never undertook anything without advantage to himself. He had two things in mind now, first, a wish to revenge himself on Alyosha, that is to say, to see 'the disgrace of the righteous one' and probably 'the downfall' of Alyosha 'from the saints to the sinners', a prospect he was already gloating over, and, secondly, he had in view a certain material advantage to himself, of which more later.

'So,' he thought to himself gaily and spitefully, 'the opportune moment has come and we shall jolly well catch it by the scruff of its neck, that moment, I mean, for it's certainly opportune for us!'

3

An Onion

GRUSHENKA lived in the busiest part of the town, near the cathedral square, in the house of the merchant's widow Morozov, in whose yard she rented a small wooden cottage. Mrs Morozov's house was a large two-storied stone building, old and very unattractive. Mrs Morozov, an old woman, lived a secluded life there with her two unmarried nieces, also rather elderly women. She had no need to let the cottage in the yard, but everyone knew that she had taken in Grushenka as a tenant, four years before, solely to please her relative, the merchant Samsonov, who was Grushenka's protector. It was said that in placing his 'protégée' with Mrs Morozov, the jealous old man's first idea was that the old woman should keep a sharp eye on the behaviour of her new tenant. But her sharp eye soon proved to be unnecessary, and in the end Mrs Morozov seldom met Grushenka and entirely stopped annoying her by her supervision. It is true that four years had passed since the old man had brought to this house the timid, shy, slender and melancholy girl of eighteen from the chief town of the province, and much water had flowed under the bridges since that time. Little was known of the life of this girl in our town, and what was known was rather vague; not much more had been learned during the last four years, even though many people had become interested in 'the great beauty' Miss Svetlov had been transformed into in four years. There were rumours that at the age of seventeen she was seduced by someone, supposedly an army officer, who immediately afterwards abandoned her. The officer was said to have gone away to another town and afterwards married, leaving Grushenka in poverty and disgrace. It was said, however, that though Grushenka had really been saved by her old man from a life of destitution, she came of a respectable family and was connected with the priestly class, being the daughter of a deacon or something of the sort. And now after four years the sensitive, betrayed, and pitiful little orphan had grown into a rosy-cheeked, plump Russian beauty, a woman of bold and determined character, proud and brazen, who knew the value of money, who was acquisitive, stingy, and careful, and who, by fair means or foul, had succeeded, as it was said about her, in scraping together a fairly substantial fortune of her own. They were all agreed on one thing, though: namely that it was difficult to get on intimate terms with Grushenka and that except for the old merchant, her protector, there had not been a single man who could boast of her favours during those four years. There could be no doubt whatever about that, for there had been a good many aspirants to her favours, especially during the last two years. But all their efforts had been in vain, and some of these aspirants had been forced to beat an undignified and even comic retreat, owing to the firm and mocking resistance they met from the strong-minded young woman. It was also known that the young woman had, especially during the last year, been dabbling in what is called 'business', and that she had shown quite a remarkable aptitude for it, so that in the end many people described her as no better than a Jew. Not that she lent money on interest, but it was known, for instance, that, in partnership with Fyodor Karamazov, she had for some time past actually been buying up bills of exchange for practically nothing, for a tenth of their value, and afterwards got ten times their value out of them. Samsonov, a sick man, a widower who during the last year had lost the use of his swollen legs, a man of large fortune, but niggardly and implacable, tyrannized over his grown-up sons, but had fallen greatly under the influence of his protégée, whom he had at first bullied and treated with a heavy hand, keeping her on short commons, 'on Lenten fare', as the wits of the town said at the time. But Grushenka had succeeded in emancipating herself, instilling in him, however, a boundless faith in her fidelity. This old man, a great businessman (now long since dead), was also quite a remarkable character. He was, above all, miserly and hard as flint, and though Grushenka had made such a strong impression on him that he could not even live without her (it had been so, for instance, during the past two years), he did not settle any considerable fortune on her and he would have remained unyielding even if she had threatened to leave him for good. But he did make over to her a small sum of money, and even that was a surprise to everyone when it became known. 'You've got your head screwed on the right way,' he said to her, when he settled eight thousand roubles on her, 'so go into business yourself, but I want you to know that except for your yearly allowance as before, you will get nothing more from me to the day of my death, and I will leave you nothing in my will, either.' And he kept his word: when he died, he left everything to his sons, whom, with their wives and children, he had treated like servants all his life. He did not even mention Grushenka in his will. All this became known afterwards. He did, however, help Grushenka a great deal with his advice how 'to go into business with her own capital' and put a great deal of business in her way. When Mr Karamazov, who first came across Grushenka accidentally, 'by way of business', ended to his own surprise by falling head over ears in love with her and seemed to lose his mind over her, old Samsonov, who was already at death's door at the time, was hugely amused. It is remarkable that throughout the whole of their acquaintance Grushenka was absolutely and even, as it were, affectionately frank with her old man, and he seemed to have been the only man in the world with whom she was so. During the last few months, when Dmitry, too, suddenly came on the scene with his love, the old man was no longer amused. On the contrary, one day he gave Grushenka a stern and serious piece of advice: 'If you have to choose between the two,' he said, 'father or son, then choose the old man, but only on condition that the old scoundrel most certainly marries you and settles some money on you beforehand. But have nothing to do with the captain, you won't get anything there.' Those were the very words of the old voluptuary, who knew at the time that he had not long to live and who actually died five months later. Let me also observe in passing that though many people in our town were aware of the absurd and monstrous rivalry of the Karamazovs, father and son, the object of which was Grushenka, hardly anyone understood what was really behind her attitude towards them. Even Grushenka's two maids (after the catastrophe, of which we will speak later) testified in court that Grushenka received Dmitry simply because she was afraid of him, because he seemed 'to have threatened to kill her'. She had two maidservants, an old cook, an ailing and almost deaf woman she had brought with her from her old home, and a sprightly young girl of twenty, her personal maid. Grushenka lived very economically and in far from rich surroundings. Her cottage consisted only of three rooms, furnished by her landlady with old mahogany furniture which was in fashion in the twenties. It was quite dark when Rakitin and Alyosha

entered her cottage, but there was no light in her rooms yet. Grushenka was lying in her drawing-room on the big, uncomfortable
sofa with a mahogany back. The sofa was hard and covered with
shabby leather, worn out long ago and in holes. Her head rested on
two white pillows taken from her bed. She was lying on her back,
stretched out and motionless, with her hands behind her head. She
was smartly dressed, as though expecting someone, in a black silk
dress, with a light lace cap on her head, which was very becoming;
over her shoulders was thrown a lace shawl, fastened with a massive
gold brooch. She was most certainly expecting someone and looked
impatient and bored, her face rather pale, her lips and eyes burning,
and tapped the arm of the sofa impatiently with the tip of her right
foot. At the appearance of Rakitin and Alyosha a slight commotion
ensued; from the passage they could hear Grushenka quickly jump
up from the sofa and cry in a frightened voice: 'Who's there?' But
the visitors were met by the maid, who at once called back to her
mistress:

'It's not him, madam. It's nothing. It's other visitors.'

'What's the matter with her?' muttered Rakitin, leading Alyosha
into the drawing-room.

Grushenka was standing by the sofa, still looking frightened. A thick
coil of her dark-brown hair suddenly tumbled from under her head-
dress and fell on her right shoulder, but she never noticed it and did
not tuck it up again until she had taken a good look at her visitors
and recognized them.

'Oh, it's you, Rakitin? You've frightened me. Who is this with
you? Good heavens, so that's whom you've brought!' she cried,
recognizing Alyosha.

'Come on, let's have some candles!' said Rakitin with the free and
easy air of a most intimate friend who had a right to give orders in
the house.

'Candles – yes, of course, candles . . . Fenya, fetch him a candle . . .
Well, you've chosen a fine time to bring him here!' she cried again,
nodding a greeting to Alyosha, and turning to the looking-glass, she
began rapidly to tuck in her plait. She seemed displeased.

'Why, have I done anything wrong?' asked Rakitin, instantly
almost offended.

'You frightened me, Rakitin, you idiot, that's what you did,' said

Grushenka, turning towards Alyosha with a smile. 'Don't be afraid of me, darling Alyosha. I'm awfully glad to see you. I didn't expect you at all. But you did frighten me, Rakitin. I thought Mitya was trying to get in. You see, I deceived him this afternoon. I made him promise to believe me and I told him a lie. I told him I was going to spend the whole evening with my old man Kuzma. Counting up his money with him till late at night. You see, I usually spend a whole evening a week with him making up his accounts. We lock ourselves in: he flicks the beads on the abacus and I enter it in the ledger – I'm the only one he trusts. Well, Mitya believes I'm there, while I've been sitting locked in here, expecting a message. Fenya should not have let you in. Fenya, Fenya! Run to the gate, open it and have a look whether the captain is anywhere to be seen. He may be hiding and spying – I'm scared to death!'

'There's no one there, ma'am. I've just had a good look round. Why, ma'am, I keep looking through a crack in the gate every minute. I'm all of a tremble myself, ma'am.'

'Are the shutters fastened, Fenya? And you should have drawn the curtains – so!' She drew the heavy curtains herself. 'Or he might dash in at once if he saw a light. I'm afraid of your brother Mitya today, Alyosha.'

Grushenka was speaking loudly, and though she was alarmed, she seemed to be almost delighted about something.

'Why are you so afraid of Mitya today?' Rakitin inquired. 'You don't seem to be particularly afraid when he's with you. He dances to your tune.'

'I tell you I'm expecting some news, a really good piece of news, so that I can certainly do without dear Mitya now. Besides, I'm sure he didn't believe I'd go to Kuzma. I feel it. I expect he must be sitting at the bottom of his father's garden, watching out for me. Well, if he *is* there, he won't be coming here. So much the better! As a matter of fact, I did go to Kuzma. Mitya took me there. I told him I'd be there till midnight and I asked him to be sure to come at midnight to take me home. He went away and I sat with my old man for ten minutes and then came back here. Goodness, I was scared to death. I ran all the way home so as not to meet him.'

'And why are you so dressed up? Going out somewhere? What a curious bonnet you've got on your head!'

'You're pretty curious yourself, Rakitin! I've told you I'm expecting some message. When it comes, I'll be off in a jiffy and you'll see no more of me. That's why I'm dressed up. To be ready.'

'And where will you be off to?'

'Ask me no questions and I'll tell you no lies.'

'Look at her! Happy, isn't she? I've never seen you like this before. All dressed up as if for a ball!'

Rakitin looked her up and down.

'A lot you know about balls!'

'Do you know a lot about them?'

'I've seen a ball. Two years ago Kuzma married off one of his sons and I watched from the gallery. But why should I be talking to you, Rakitin, when I've got such a prince standing here? What a wonderful visitor! Alyosha, darling, I look at you and can't believe my eyes! Goodness, whatever brought you here? To tell the truth, I never expected to see you and it never entered my head that you might come to see me. Though it's not really the proper time for a visit, I'm awfully glad to see you. Sit down on the sofa – here – that's right, my dear stranger. Really, I simply can't believe you're here . . . I say, Rakitin, what a pity you didn't bring him yesterday or the day before! Never mind, though, I'm glad as it is. Perhaps it's better he has come now, at such a moment, and not the day before yesterday. . . .'

She sat down gaily beside Alyosha on the sofa and gazed at him with unconcealed delight. And she really was glad. She was not lying when she said so. Her eyes glowed, her lips laughed, but good-naturedly, happily. Alyosha had never expected to see such a kind expression on her face. Till the day before he had met her seldom, he had formed a frightening impression of her, and the day before he had been so shocked by her malicious and treacherous attack on Katerina that he was very surprised now to see suddenly quite a startlingly different woman before him. And, crushed as he was by his own sorrow, he could not help gazing at her attentively. Her whole manner seemed to have changed for the better since yesterday: there was no longer that sugary inflexion in her voice or those dainty and affected movements – everything was simple and good-natured, her movements were rapid, direct and confiding, but she was greatly excited.

'My goodness, the things that are happening to me today,' she prattled on. 'And why I'm so glad to see you, Alyosha, I'm sure I don't know. If you asked me, I couldn't tell you.'

'Don't you really know why you're so glad?' asked Rakitin with a grin. 'Why did you pester me to bring him before? You had some reason for it, hadn't you?'

'Oh, I had quite a different reason before, but now that's over and done with. It's quite a different occasion. But I must offer you a drink, mustn't I? I'm a much kinder person now, Rakitin. Sit down, you, too, Rakitin. Why are you standing? Oh, you have sat down, have you? You never forget to look after yourself, do you, Rakitin dear? You see, Alyosha, he's sitting there opposite us, feeling hurt because I didn't ask him to sit down before you. Oh, he does take offence quickly, Rakitin does!' Grushenka laughed. 'Don't be angry, Rakitin. I'm feeling kind today. Why are you so sad, Alyosha, darling? You're not afraid of me, are you?' she asked, looking into his eyes with gay mockery.

'He's miserable. They haven't promoted him,' Rakitin said in a deep voice.

'Who hasn't been promoted?'

'His elder stank the place out!'

'What do you mean? You're talking a lot of nonsense. Want to say something nasty, I suppose. Shut up, you fool. Will you let me sit on your knee, Alyosha, like that?' And she suddenly sprang up and jumped, laughing, on to his knee, like an affectionate kitten, flinging her right arm caressingly round his neck. 'I'll cheer you up, my pious little boy. But are you really going to let me sit on your knee, darling? You won't be angry? Say the word and I'll get off.'

Alyosha was silent. He sat there, afraid to move. He heard her say, 'Say the word and I'll get off,' but he did not answer, just as though benumbed. But he did not feel what a man like Rakitin, for instance, who was watching him lasciviously from his corner, might have expected or imagined him to feel. The great grief in his soul swallowed up all the sensations that might have arisen in his heart, and if he could have given himself a full account of his feelings at that moment, he would have realized that he was now clad in the strongest armour against any temptation or seduction. Nevertheless, in spite of his utterly confused state of mind and the grief that oppressed him, he still could not help marvelling at a strange new sensation that was stirring in his heart: this woman, this 'terrible' woman not only did not arouse in him the fear he felt every time he thought of a woman, if such a thought ever appeared for a moment in his mind; on the contrary, this woman whom he feared more than any other woman and who was now sitting on his knee and embracing him, suddenly aroused in him quite a different, unexpected and peculiar feeling, a feeling of a kind of unusual, very intense and frank curiosity, and that without a trace of fear, without a trace of his former terror – that was the main thing, that was what he could not help being surprised at.

'Stop talking a lot of nonsense,' cried Rakitin. 'You'd better give us some champagne. You owe it to me. You know that, don't you?'

'Yes, I really do. You see, Alyosha, I promised him champagne, in addition to all sorts of other things, if he brought you. Let's have champagne and I'll have some too! Fenya, Fenya, bring us the champagne, the bottle Mitya left, and hurry! I may be stingy, but I'll stand you a bottle, not you, Rakitin, for you're a toadstool, but he's a prince! I've something else on my mind now, but so be it, I'll drink with you. I feel like having a good time!'

'But what is this occasion? What "message" are you expecting, may I ask? Or is it a secret?' Rakitin put in again, without concealing his curiosity, and pretending not to notice how he was being continually snubbed.

'Oh, no, it's no secret, and you know it, too,' Grushenka said in a worried voice, turning her head towards Rakitin and drawing a little away from Alyosha, though she still sat on his knee with her arm round his neck. 'My officer's coming, Rakitin. My officer's coming!'

'I heard he was coming, but is he so near?'

'He's at Mokroye now. He'll be sending a messenger from there. He wrote so himself. I got a letter from him today. I'm expecting the messenger any minute.'

'Good Lord! Why at Mokroye?'

'It's a long story. Anyway, I've told you enough.'

'Dear old Mitya will be in a state now – dear, oh dear! Does he know or doesn't he?'

'Of course he doesn't! How should he? If he knew, he'd kill me.

But I'm not afraid of that now. I'm not afraid of his knife. Shut up, Rakitin! Don't mention Dmitry to me. He's crushed my heart. I don't want even to think of it now. I can think of darling Alyosha. Darling Alyosha, I'm looking at him now. Come on, smile at me, darling. Cheer up. Smile at my foolishness, at my happiness! See how foolish and happy I am? He smiled, he smiled! See how affectionately he looks at me? You know, Alyosha, I've been thinking you're angry with me because of what happened the day before yesterday, because of that young lady. I was a bitch. Yes, that's what I was. Only it's a good thing it happened like that all the same. It was bad, but it was good, too,' Grushenka smiled thoughtfully suddenly, and there was a faint suggestion of cruelty in her smile. 'Mitya told me she kept screaming: "She ought to be flogged!" I hurt her feelings badly, I'm afraid. She sent for me, wanted to get the better of me, win me over with her cup of chocolate. Yes,' she smiled again, 'it's a jolly good thing it turned out like that. But I'm still afraid you'll be angry.'

'And she means it, too,' Rakitin put in suddenly with genuine surprise. 'She really is afraid of you, Alyosha, a fledgling like you.'

'He's a fledgling to you, Rakitin, and you know why? Because you've no conscience. That's why! You see, I love him with all my soul. I do, indeed! Alyosha, do you believe I love you with all my soul?'

'The shameless hussy! She's making you a declaration of love, Alexey!'

'What about it? I do love him.'

'And what about your officer? And the good tidings from Mokroye?'

'That has nothing to do with it.'

'Just like a woman!'

'Don't make me angry, Rakitin,' Grushenka cried warmly. 'It has nothing to do with it. I love Alyosha in a different way. It's quite true, Alyosha, I had designs on you. For I'm a low, violent creature, but there are times, Alyosha, when I look on you as my conscience. I go on thinking how a man like you must despise a bad woman like me. I thought so the day before yesterday as I ran home from that young lady's. I've thought that way a long time about you, Alyosha. Mitya knows it, too. I told him. Mitya understands. Would you believe it, Alyosha, sometimes I look at you and feel ashamed. I feel ashamed of myself. And how I began thinking about you like that, and since when, I don't know. I don't remember. . . .'

Fenya came in and put a tray with an uncorked bottle and three glasses of champagne on the table.

'Here's the champagne!' cried Rakitin. 'You're excited, my dear young woman, and not yourself. A glass of champagne and you'll start dancing. Oh dear, they've made a mess of this too!' he added, peering at the bottle. 'The old woman poured it out in the kitchen and the bottle has been brought in without a cork and warm. Oh well, never mind, let's have some . . .'

He went up to the table, took a glass, emptied it at one gulp and poured himself out another.

'It isn't often one gets the chance of having champagne,' he said, licking his lips. 'Come on, Alyosha, old chap, take a glass, show us what you're like. What shall we drink to? The gates of heaven? Take a glass, Grushenka, my dear, and drink to the gates of heaven, too.'

'What gates of heaven?'

She took a glass, Alyosha took his, had a sip and put it down.

'No, perhaps I'd better not,' he smiled gently.

'And you said you would!' cried Rakitin.

'Well, in that case, I won't either,' put in Grushenka. 'I don't feel like it, anyway. Drink the whole bottle alone, Rakitin. If Alyosha has some, I will, too.'

'What sloppy sentimentality!' Rakitin said tauntingly. 'And she's sitting on his knee, too! He's got something to be upset about, but what have you to worry about? He's rebelling against his God, he was going to eat sausage in Lent. . . .'

'Why's that?'

'His elder died today, the elder Zossima, the saint.'

'So Father Zossima's dead!' cried Grushenka. 'Good gracious, and I didn't know!' She crossed herself devoutly. 'Goodness, what have I been doing? Sitting on his knee like that now!' She started as though in dismay, jumped off Alyosha's knee at once and sat down on the sofa.

Alyosha gave her a long, surprised look and his face seemed to light up.

'Rakitin,' he said suddenly in a loud and firm voice, 'don't taunt me about having rebelled against my God. I don't want to feel angry with you and that's why I'd like you to be kinder, too. I've lost a treasure such as you've never had, and you can't judge me now. You'd better take an example from her: did you see how she took pity on me? I came here thinking to find a wicked soul – I felt drawn to wickedness because I was mean and wicked myself, but I've found a true sister. I've found a treasure – a loving soul. She took pity on me just now . . . I'm talking about you, Grushenka. You've just restored my soul.'

Alyosha's lips were quivering and he felt breathless. He stopped short.

'Saved you, has she?' Rakitin laughed spitefully. 'And she meant to swallow you up, did you know that?'

'Wait, Rakitin, you fool!' Grushenka jumped up suddenly. 'Shut up, both of you. Now I'll tell you everything: you, Alyosha, shut up because your words make me ashamed, for I'm wicked and not good – that's what I am. And you, Rakitin, shut up, because you're lying. I did have the mean intention of swallowing him up. But now you're lying. Now it's different . . . and don't let me hear another word from you, Rakitin!'

All this Grushenka said with extraordinary agitation.

'Look at them – gone crazy both of them!' Rakitin hissed, looking at them both with astonishment. 'Stark, staring mad – I feel as though I've got into a lunatic asylum. Lost their nerve, both of them. They'll be crying in a minute!'

'And I'm going to cry, I am, I am!' Grushenka went on repeating. 'He called me his sister and I shall never forget it, never! Only don't forget, Rakitin, I may be wicked, but I did give away an onion.'

'An onion? Damn it, they *have* gone crazy!'

Rakitin was surprised at their ecstatic enthusiasm and was annoyed and angry, though it might have occurred to him that everything had combined just then to arouse their deepest emotions, which does not happen often in a lifetime. But Rakitin, who was very sensitive to everything that concerned himself, was very insensitive when it came to understanding the feelings and sensations of his fellow-creatures, partly because he was young and inexperienced and partly because he was a great egoist.

'You see, Alyosha dear,' Grushenka suddenly laughed nervously, turning to him, 'I was boasting to Rakitin about having given away an onion, but I'm not going to boast to you about it. I shall tell you about it for another reason. It's only a fairy-tale, but it's a nice fairy-tale. I heard it from Matryona, who is my cook now, as a child. It's like this, you see. Once upon a time there was a very wicked old woman, and she died. And she did not leave a single good deed behind. The devils caught her and threw her into the lake of fire. But her guardian angel was wondering what good deed of hers he could remember to tell to God. Then he remembered and said to God: she once pulled an onion in her kitchen garden and gave it to a beggar woman. And God said to him: Well, take that onion and hold it out to her in the lake, let her catch hold of it and pull, and if you can pull her out of the lake, let her come to Paradise, but if the onion breaks, then the woman must stay where she is. The angel ran to the woman and held out the onion to her: come on, woman, he said, get hold of that and pull yourself out. And he began pulling her cautiously and was on the point of pulling her out when the other sinners in the lake, seeing that she was being pulled out, began catching hold of her so as to be pulled out with her. But the woman was terribly wicked and she began kicking them. 'It's me who's being pulled out,' she said, 'and not you. It's my onion, not yours.' The moment she said that, the onion broke. And the woman fell back into the lake and she's burning there to this day. And the angel wept and went away. So this is the fairy-tale, Alyosha, and I know it by heart, for I'm that wicked woman myself. I boasted to Rakitin about having given away an onion, but to you I'll say: I've given away only *one* onion in all my life, and that is the only good deed I've done. And don't you praise me for that, Alyosha. Don't think me good. I am wicked, terribly wicked, and if you praise me, you'll make me ashamed. Oh dear, I may as well confess everything. Listen, Alyosha: I wanted to get you to come here so much, and I pestered Rakitin so much about it that in the end I promised him twenty-five roubles if he brought you to me. One moment, Rakitin, wait!'

She went up quickly to the table, opened a drawer, got out a purse and took a twenty-five rouble note out of it.

'What nonsense! What nonsense!' cried Rakitin, taken aback.

'Take it, Rakitin! I owe it to you. I know you won't refuse. You asked for it yourself!'

And she threw the note to him.

'Refuse it?' Rakitin drawled in a low voice, obviously disconcerted, but concealing his sense of shame with a nonchalant air. 'It'll come in very handy. Fools are made for wise men's profit.'

'And now shut up, Rakitin. What I'm going to say now is not for your ears. Sit down in the corner there and shut up. You don't like us, so hold your tongue.'

'What should I like you for?' Rakitin snapped back, no longer concealing his malice.

He put the twenty-five rouble note in his pocket, and he most certainly felt ashamed before Alyosha. He had counted on receiving his payment afterwards, without Alyosha's knowledge, and now, feeling ashamed, he lost his temper. Till that moment he thought it discreet not to contradict Grushenka, in spite of all her snubs, for it was obvious that she had some pull over him. But now he, too, got angry.

'One loves people for a reason, but what has either of you done for me?'

'You should love for no reason at all, as Alyosha does.'

'What does he love you for? What has he shown you that you should make such a fuss about it?'

Grushenka was standing in the middle of the room, she spoke with heat and there was a hysterical note in her voice.

'Shut up, Rakitin, you don't understand anything about us! And don't you dare to be so familiar with me in future! I'm not going to let you and who, I'd like to know, gave you the right to talk to me like that? Sit down in that corner and keep still, just as though you were my footman! And now, Alyosha, I'm going to tell you the whole truth. I'm going to tell it to you alone, for I want you to see what a low creature I am. I'm telling it to you and not to Rakitin. I wanted to ruin you, Alyosha. That's the gospel truth. I'd made up my mind to do so. I wanted to so much that I bribed Rakitin to bring you. And why did I want to do such a thing? You, Alyosha, knew nothing about it. You used to turn away from me. Every time you passed, you dropped your eyes. But I've looked a hundred times at you before today. I began asking everyone about you. I couldn't forget your face: I carried it in my heart. He despises me, I thought to myself. He refuses even to look at me. And I resented it so deeply that in the end I couldn't help being surprised at myself for being so scared of a boy. I'll eat him up and laugh at him. I was livid with rage. I don't know if you'll believe me but nobody here dares to talk or to think of coming to see me, Agrafena Svetlov, with any nasty ideas in his mind. I've only got that old man of mine. I was bound to him, sold to him and Satan himself married us. But there's been no one else – no one. As I looked at you, I decided: I'm going to eat him up. Eat him up and laugh at him. You see what a wicked woman I am, I whom you called your sister! Now the man who seduced me has arrived and I am waiting for a message from him. And have you any idea what that man has been to me? Five years ago, when Kuzma brought me here, I used to hide my face from people. Didn't want anyone to see or hear me. I was such a silly slip of a girl. I used to sit here sobbing my heart out. Couldn't sleep a wink at night. I kept thinking, Where is he now, the man who wronged me? I suppose he's laughing at me with that other woman, but, I thought to myself, if ever I met him again, I'd pay him back. I'd pay him back. I used to lie sobbing into my pillow at night, in the darkness, planning it all, tearing my heart on purpose, feeding it with malice: "I'll show him! I'll pay him back!" That's what I used to scream in the darkness. But when I suddenly realized that I would do nothing to him at all, that he was laughing at me at that very moment or perhaps had completely forgotten me and didn't remember me at all, I'd fling myself from my bed on to the floor and go on weeping, weeping helplessly and lie shaking and shivering there till daybreak. In the morning I used to get up more spiteful than a dog, ready to tear the whole world to pieces! Then what do you think I did? I began hoarding money. I lost all pity. I grew fat – got more sense, you think? No, I did not. No one in the whole world saw it or knew about it, but as soon as it grew dark, I used to lie, as I did five years ago when I was a silly girl, gritting my teeth and crying all night, thinking, "I'll show him! I'll show him!" You've heard it all now. You can understand me now. A month ago the letter I told you about arrived: he was coming, he was a widower, he wanted to see me. It took my breath away. Goodness, I thought suddenly, if he comes and just whistles to me, if he calls me, I'll crawl back to him with the guilty look of a beaten dog! And even while I was thinking that, I couldn't believe myself: "Am I so contemptible or not? Shall I run to him or not?" And I felt so wild with myself all this month as I never felt five years ago. So you see, Alyosha, what a violent, what a vindictive creature I am! I've told you the whole truth! I was amusing myself with Mitya so as not to run away to the other one. Shut up, Rakitin. It's not for you to judge me. I wasn't telling it to you. Before you came, I was lying here, waiting, thinking, trying to decide what I was going to do, and you'll never know what I felt in my heart. Yes, Alyosha, tell your young lady not to be angry with me for what happened the day before yesterday. No one in the world knows how miserable I am now, and no one can ever know. That's why I may take a knife with me today when I go to him – I haven't made up my mind yet. . . .'

And having uttered that melodramatic phrase, Grushenka suddenly lost control of herself and, without finishing her confession, covered her face with her hands, flung herself down on the sofa, buried her face in the pillows and sobbed like a little child. Alyosha got up and went up to Rakitin.

'Don't be angry with me, Misha,' he said. 'She's hurt your feelings, but, please, don't be angry. You heard her just now, didn't you? One mustn't ask too much of a human heart. One must be more merciful. . . .'

Alyosha said this carried away by an irresistible impulse of his heart. He had to speak out and he turned to Rakitin. If Rakitin had not been there, he would still have said it. But Rakitin looked at him ironically, and Alyosha stopped short.

'They've loaded you with your elder this morning and now you've fired your elder at me, dear Alyosha, you little man of God,' Rakitin said with a smile of hatred.

'Don't laugh, Rakitin, don't jeer, don't talk of the dead man: he's higher than anyone in the world!' Alyosha exclaimed with tears in his voice. 'I haven't got up to talk to you as a judge. I'm myself the worst of the men in the dock. What am I beside her? I came here to seek my ruin. I was saying to myself: "Let it come! Let it come!" and all because of my cowardliness, but she, after five years of agony, as soon as someone came and said a sincere word to her, forgave everything, forgot everything, and is weeping! The man who ruined her comes back, he sends for her, and she forgives him everything and hurries to him with joy, and she won't take the knife, she won't! No, I'm not like that. I don't know if you are like that, Misha, but I'm not. I've learnt my lesson today – just now. Her love is higher than ours . . . Have you heard from her before what she has just told us? No, you haven't. If you had, you'd have understood everything long ago – and the person whose feelings were hurt the day before yesterday – she, too, must forgive her! And she will forgive her when she finds out . . . and she will find out . . . This soul is not yet at peace with itself. It must be spared. There may be a treasure buried in that soul. . . .'

Alyosha fell silent, because his breath failed him. In spite of his resentment, Rakitin looked at him with surprise. He had never expected such a tirade from the gentle Alyosha.

'Look at him! Some advocate! You haven't fallen in love with her, have you? Why, Grushenka, our pious anchorite has really fallen in love with you – you've made a conquest!' he cried with a coarse laugh.

Grushenka raised her head from the pillow and looked at Alyosha with a tender smile shining on her tear-stained face which seemed suddenly to have become swollen with crying.

'Don't take any notice of him, Alyosha, my sweet angel. You see what he's like. Your words are wasted on him. I was going to apologize to you, Mr Rakitin,' she turned to Rakitin, 'for having abused you, but now I've changed my mind again. Alyosha, come here, sit down beside me,' she motioned to him with a happy smile. 'That's right. Sit down here. Tell me,' she took him by the hand and peered, smiling, into his face, 'tell me, do I love that man or not? I mean the man who's wronged me. Do I love him or not? I was lying here in the darkness before you came and kept asking my heart whether I loved him or not. Settle this question for me, Alyosha. The time has come. It shall be as you decide. Am I to forgive him or not?'

'But you've forgiven him already,' Alyosha said with a smile.

'And so I have,' Grushenka said thoughtfully. 'Goodness, what a mean heart I have! To my mean heart!' she cried suddenly, snatching up a glass from the table.

She emptied the glass at a gulp, raised it and flung it on the floor. The glass broke with a crash. There was a touch of cruelty in her smile.

'And yet,' she said in a sort of menacing tone, dropping her eyes, as though she were speaking to herself, 'perhaps I haven't forgiven him. Perhaps my heart is only getting ready to forgive him. I'm afraid I shall still have to struggle with my heart. You see, Alyosha, I've grown terribly fond of my tears during these five years . . . Perhaps, it's the wrong I suffered at his hands that I love and not him at all!'

'Well, I certainly shouldn't care to be in his shoes,' Rakitin hissed.

'And you won't, Rakitin. You'll never be in his shoes. You'll be blacking my shoes, Rakitin. That's the use I'm going to make of you. You'll never have a woman like me. And neither will he, perhaps.'

'Won't he? Then why are you dressed up like that?' Rakitin taunted her maliciously.

'Don't sneer at me because of my fine dress, Rakitin. You don't know what's going on inside me! If I choose, I'll tear off my dress, tear it off this minute!' she cried in a ringing voice. 'You don't know why I've put on this dress, Rakitin. Perhaps I'll meet him and say, "Have you ever seen me look like this before?" For, you see, when he left me I was a thin, scrawny, seventeen-year-old cry-baby. I'll sit down beside him, make love to him, inflame his passions: "You see what I'm like now," I'll say. "Well, sir, have a good look, for that's all you'll get – there's many a slip between the cup and the lip!" That's perhaps what this dress is for, Rakitin,' Grushenka concluded with a malicious little laugh. 'I'm a wild and fierce one, Alyosha. I'll tear off my dress, I'll maim myself, destroy my beauty, burn my face, slash it with a knife, go begging in the streets. If I choose I shan't go anywhere now, not to anyone. If I choose I'll send Kuzma back all his presents tomorrow, all the money he's given me, and go charring myself! . . . You don't think I'd do it, Rakitin, that I'd dare to do it? I will do it! I will, I will! I could do it now – only don't exasperate me – and I'll send that one packing, snap my fingers at him – he'll never see me again!'

She shouted the last words hysterically, but broke down again, buried her face in her hands, flung herself on a pillow and again shook with sobbing. Rakitin got up.

'It's time we went,' he said. 'It's late. They won't let us into the monastery.'

Grushenka leapt up from the sofa.

'Surely you're not going, too, Alyosha?' she cried with grief-stricken astonishment. 'What are you doing to me? You've roused my feelings, you've tortured me, and now I'm to be left by myself all night again!'

'You don't expect him to spend the night with you, do you? But, of course, if he wants to, let him! I'll go alone!' Rakitin scoffed sardonically.

'Shut up, you spiteful fellow!' Grushenka shouted fiercely at him. 'You've never spoken to me as he has done today.'

'What did he say to you?' Rakitin muttered irritably.

'I don't know, I don't know what he said to me, except that it went straight to my heart. He wrung my heart . . . He was the first, the only one, to take pity on me – that's what it is! Why didn't you come earlier, my sweet angel?' she cried, falling on her knees before him as though in a frenzy. 'I've been waiting all my life for someone like you. I knew that someone like you would come and forgive me. I believed that someone would love me, too, nasty creature that I am, and not only use me for the satisfaction of his low desires!'

'What have I done to you?' replied Alyosha, bending over her with a tender smile and taking her affectionately by the hands. 'Why, I gave you an onion, just a tiny little onion, that's all!'

And having said it, he burst into tears himself. At that moment there was a sudden noise in the passage – someone came into the hall; Grushenka jumped to her feet, looking terribly frightened. Fenya rushed noisily into the room.

'Mistress, darling mistress,' she cried joyfully, panting for breath, 'the messenger has arrived. He's sent a carriage for you from Mokroye. Timofey the coachman, with three horses. They're changing the horses now. There's a letter, madam, a letter – here it is!'

There was a letter in her hand and she kept waving it in the air while she was talking. Grushenka snatched the letter out of her hand and took it to the candle. It was only a small note of a few lines and she read it in an instant.

'He wants me to come!' she cried, looking very pale and with a face contorted with a wan smile. 'He's whistled! Crawl to him, little doggie!'

But only for a fraction of a second did she hesitate; the blood suddenly rushed to her head and suffused her cheeks, which coloured deeply.

'I'm going!' she cried suddenly. 'Five years of my life! Good-bye! Good-bye, Alyosha, my fate is sealed . . . Go away, go away, go away, all of you now! I don't want to see you again! Grushenka is off to a new life! . . . Don't you, Rakitin, think badly of me, either. I may be going to my death! Oh dear, I feel as though I were drunk!'

She suddenly left them and rushed into her bedroom.

'Well, she's no time for us now,' growled Rakitin. 'Come on, or she'll start screaming again. I'm sick of these screams and tears!'

Alyosha let himself be led out mechanically. In the yard stood a low, open four-wheeler, the horses were being unharnessed, people were rushing about with a lantern, fresh horses were being led in through the open gates. But as soon as Alyosha and Rakitin went down the front steps, a window in Grushenka's bedroom was suddenly opened and Grushenka shouted in a ringing voice after Alyosha:

'Darling Alyosha, give my regards to your brother Mitya and tell him not to think badly of me, who treated him so badly. And, please, give him this message from me: "Grushenka has gone to a scoundrel, and not to a man of honour like you." And tell him, too, that Grushenka loved him only for one hour, for only one short hour she loved him – so let him remember this short hour all his life – say, Grushenka tells you to remember it all your life!'

She finished in a voice full of sobs. The window was shut with a bang.

'Ha, ha!' growled Rakitin, laughing. 'She's done in your brother Mitya and tells him to remember it all his life. What a man-eating tigress!'

Alyosha said nothing, just as though he had not heard it. He walked fast beside Rakitin as though in a terrible hurry; he seemed to be lost to the world and walked along mechanically. Rakitin felt a sudden stab of pain as though someone had touched his open wound with a finger. He had expected something quite different when he brought

Grushenka and Alyosha together; something quite different from what he had hoped for had happened.

'He's a Pole, that army officer of hers,' he began again, restraining himself. 'And he's no longer an army officer, as a matter of fact, but a customs officer. Served in the customs in Siberia, somewhere on the Chinese frontier, the dirty little Pole did, I think. He's lost his job now, I'm told. Heard Grushenka had got a tidy little sum, so he's come back. That's all there is to it.'

Again Alyosha did not seem to hear. Rakitin could restrain himself no longer.

'Well,' he laughed spitefully, turning to Alyosha, 'have you converted the sinner? Put the harlot on the right path? Cast out the seven devils, have you? So that's where the miracles we've been expecting so long have been performed!'

'Stop it, Rakitin,' Alyosha replied, deeply troubled in spirit.

'I suppose you "despise" me now for those twenty-five roubles, don't you? Sold my best friend, have I? But you're not Christ, you know, and I'm not Judas.'

'Good Lord, Rakitin, I assure you I'd forgotten all about it,' cried Alyosha. 'It was you who reminded me of it.'

But Rakitin had completely lost his temper.

'To blazes with all and every one of you!' he roared suddenly. 'And why the hell did I get mixed up with you? I don't want to know you any more. Go by yourself, there's your road!'

And he turned abruptly into another street, leaving Alyosha alone in the dark. Alyosha came out of the town and went across the fields in the direction of the monastery.

4

Cana of Galilee

IT was very late according to the monastery rules, when Alyosha arrived at the hermitage; the gate-keeper let him in by a special entrance. It had struck nine o'clock – the hour of general rest after such an anxious day for them all. Alyosha opened the door timidly and went into the elder's cell, in which his coffin was now standing.

There was no one in the cell except Father Paissy, who was reading the Gospel alone over the coffin, and the young novice Porfiry, who, exhausted after the discourse of the night before and by the disturbing events of the day, slept the sound sleep of youth, lying on the floor in the next room. Though he heard Alyosha come in, Father Paissy did not even look in his direction. Alyosha turned to the right of the door, knelt in the corner and began to pray. His heart was full of obscure feelings, and not one of them stood out clearly from the rest; on the contrary, one followed another in a sort of quiet and slow rotation. But his heart was at peace and, strange to say, Alyosha was not surprised at it. Again he saw that coffin before him, that covered-up dead man, so dear to him, but there was no weeping, gnawing, poignant compassion in his heart as in the morning. As he came in, he fell down before the coffin as before a holy shrine, but his mind and heart were full of gladness. One window of the cell was open, the air was fresh and cool. 'So the smell must have become stronger, if they decided to open the window,' thought Alyosha. But even this thought of the odour of corruption, which had seemed to him so dreadful and inglorious that morning, did not any longer arouse in him the former feeling of desolation and indignation. He began praying quietly, but soon he felt himself that he was praying almost mechanically. Fragments of thoughts flashed through his mind, caught fire like stars and died down again, to be succeeded by others. But his soul was full of something that was complete, firm, and satisfying, and he was conscious of it himself. Sometimes when he began praying ardently he felt a great desire to offer up thanks and to love. . . . But, having begun to pray, he suddenly passed to something else, or sank into thought, forgetting his prayer and what had interrupted it. He began listening to what Father Paissy was reading, but, feeling tired, he gradually began to doze. . . .

'And the third day there was a marriage in Cana of Galilee,' read Father Paissy, 'and the mother of Jesus was there: and both Jesus was called, and his disciples, to the marriage.'

'Marriage? What's that – marriage –' the words swept through Alyosha's mind like a whirlwind. 'There's happiness for her, too – she's gone to the feast. No, she has not taken the knife – not taken the knife – it was just a melodramatic phrase – Well – one must forgive melodramatic phrases – Yes, one must, one must – melodramatic phrases comfort the soul – without them grief would be too heavy to bear – Rakitin has walked off into the side-street. As long as Rakitin goes on thinking about his wrongs, he will always walk off into back-alleys. . . . And the road – the road is straight, bright, shining like crystal, and the sun is at the end of it. Eh? What is he reading?'

'*And when they wanted wine, the mother of Jesus saith unto him, They have no wine,*' Alyosha heard.

'Oh yes, I nearly missed that, and I didn't want to miss it. I love that passage: it is Cana of Galilee, it's the first miracle. . . . Oh, that miracle, oh, that lovely miracle! It was not grief but men's gladness that Jesus extolled when he worked his first miracle – he helped people to be happy. . . . "He who loves men, loves their gladness" – that was what the dead man had kept repeating, that was one of his main ideas. . . . Without gladness it is impossible to live, says Mitya. . . . Yes, Mitya. . . . Whatever is true and beautiful is always full of forgiveness – that also he used to say. . . .'

'*Jesus saith unto her, Woman, what have I to do with thee? Mine hour is not yet come. His mother saith unto the servants, Whatever he saith unto you, do it.*'

'Do it. . . . The gladness, the gladness of some poor, very poor people. . . . Yes, poor, of course, if they hadn't enough wine even at a wedding. . . . Historians write that the people living by the lake of Gennesaret and in all those places were the poorest that can possibly be imagined. . . . And another great heart of the other great being, his Mother, who was there at the time, knew that he had come down only for his great and terrible sacrifice, but that his heart was open also to the simple and artless joys of ignorant human beings, ignorant but not cunning, who had warmly bidden him to their poor wedding. "Mine hour is not yet come" – he said with a gentle smile (yes, he certainly smiled gently at her). . . . And, surely, it was not to increase the wine at poor weddings that he came down on earth. And yet he went and did as she asked him. . . . Oh, he is reading again:'

'*Jesus saith unto them, Fill the waterpots with water. And they filled them up to the brim.*

'*And he saith unto them, Draw out now, and bear unto the governor of the feast. And they bare it.*

'*When the ruler of the feast had tasted the water that was made wine, and knew not whence it was: (but the servants which drew the water knew;) the governor of the feast called the bridegroom.*

'*And saith unto him, Every man at the beginning doth set forth good wine; and when men have well drunk, then that which is worse: but thou hast kept the good wine until now.*'

'But what's this? What's this? Why do the walls of the room move apart? O yes, it's a wedding – the marriage – yes, of course. And here are the wedding guests, and here are the bride and groom and the merry crowd and – where is the wise ruler of the feast? But who is that? Who is it? Again the room moved apart. Who is rising there at the great table? What? Is he here too? But he's in the coffin. . . . But he is here too – he got up – he saw me – he's coming here – Lord!'

Yes, he went up to him, to him, the little dried-up old man, with little wrinkles on his face, joyful and smiling gently. The coffin was no longer there and he wore the same clothes as the day before, when he was sitting with them, when his visitors had gathered in his cell. His face was uncovered, his eyes were shining. So he, too, had been invited to the feast, to the wedding at Cana of Galilee. How was that?

'Yes, my dear boy, I too am invited, invited and bidden,' a soft voice was saying over him. 'Why have you hidden yourself here, so that no one can see you? Come and join us too!'

It was his voice, the elder Zossima's voice. And who else could it be, since he called? The elder raised Alyosha by the hand, and he rose from his knees.

'Let us make merry,' the dried-up old man went on. 'Let's drink new wine, the wine of new gladness, of great gladness. See how many guests there are here? And there's the bride and the groom, and there's the ruler of the feast, tasting the new wine. Why are you wondering at me? I have given an onion, and here I am. And many here have given only an onion, only one little onion. . . . What are our deeds? And you, my quiet one, and you, my gentle boy, you, too, have known how to give an onion today to a woman craving salvation. Begin your work, my dear one, begin your work, my gentle one! And do you see our Sun, do you see him?'

'I am afraid – I dare not look,' Alyosha whispered.

'Do not be afraid of him. He's terrible in his majesty, awful in his eminence, but infinitely merciful. He became like one of us from love and he makes merry with us, turns water into wine, so as not to cut

short the gladness of the guests. He is expecting new guests, he is calling new ones unceasingly and for ever and ever. There they are bringing the new wine. You see, they are bringing the vessels. . . .'

Something glowed in Alyosha's heart, something filled it suddenly
till it ached, tears of ecstasy were welling up from his soul. . . . He
stretched out his hands, uttered a cry and woke up. . . .

Again the coffin, the open window, and the soft, solemn, measured
reading of the Gospel. But Alyosha no longer listened to the reading.
It was strange, he had fallen asleep on his knees, and now he was standing up, and suddenly, as though torn from his place, he walked up
right to the coffin with three firm, rapid steps. He even brushed against
Father Paissy with his shoulder and did not notice it. Father Paissy
raised his eyes from the book for an instant, but at once looked aside,
realizing that something strange had happened to the boy. Alyosha
gazed at the coffin for half a minute, at the covered, motionless,
stretched-out dead man in it, with the icon on his chest and the cowl
with the eight-cornered cross on his head. Only a moment ago he
had heard his voice, and that voice was still ringing in his ears. He was
still listening, he was still expecting to hear it again – but suddenly,
turning away abruptly, he went out of the cell.

He did not stop on the steps, but went down rapidly. His soul, overflowing with rapture, was craving for freedom and unlimited space.
The vault of heaven, studded with softly shining stars, stretched wide
and vast over him. From the zenith to the horizon the Milky Way
stretched its two arms dimly across the sky. The fresh, motionless, still
night enfolded the earth. The white towers and golden domes of the
cathedral gleamed against the sapphire sky. The gorgeous autumn
flowers in the beds near the house went to sleep till morning. The
silence of the earth seemed to merge into the silence of the heavens,
the mystery of the earth came in contact with the mystery of the stars.
. . . Alyosha stood, gazed, and suddenly he threw himself down flat
upon the earth.

He did not know why he was embracing it. He could not have explained to himself why he longed so irresistibly to kiss it, to kiss it all,
but he kissed it weeping, sobbing and drenching it with his tears, and
vowed frenziedly to love it, to love it for ever and ever. 'Water the
earth with the tears of your gladness and love those tears', it rang in
his soul. What was he weeping over? Oh, he was weeping in his rap-

ture even over those stars which were shining for him from the abyss of space and 'he was not ashamed of that ecstasy'. It was as though the threads from all those innumerable worlds of God met all at once in his soul, and it was trembling all over 'as it came in contact with other worlds'. He wanted to forgive everyone and for everything, and to beg forgiveness – oh! not for himself, but for all men, for all and for everything, 'and others are begging for me', it echoed in his soul again. But with every moment he felt clearly and almost palpably that something firm and immovable, like the firmament itself, was entering his soul. A sort of idea was gaining an ascendancy over his mind – and that for the rest of his life, for ever and ever. He had fallen upon the earth a weak youth, but he rose from it a resolute fighter for the rest of his life, and he realized and felt it suddenly, at the very moment of his rapture. And never, never for the rest of his life could Alyosha forget that moment. 'Someone visited my soul at that hour!' he used to say afterwards with firm faith in his words. . . .

Three days later he left the monastery in accordance with the words of his late elder, who had bidden him 'sojourn in the world'.

I

Kuzma Samsonov

BUT Dmitry Karamazov, to whom Grushenka, before flying off to her new life, had 'ordered' Alyosha to give her last greetings and to bid him remember the short hour of her love for ever, knew nothing of what had happened to her. He was at that moment also in a state of great agitation and had his hands full of all sorts of things. During the last two days he had been in such an unimaginable state of mind that he really might have fallen ill with brain fever, as he himself admitted afterwards. Alyosha had not been able to find him the morning before, and Ivan had not been able to arrange a meeting with him at the inn on the same day. His landlady concealed his whereabouts at his request. He had spent those two days literally rushing from place to place, 'struggling with his destiny and trying to save himself', as he expressed it later himself, and even left the town for a few hours on some urgent business, in spite of the fact that he was terrified to go away and leave Grushenka even for a moment without keeping an eye on her. All this came to light afterwards in every detail and was confirmed by documentary evidence, but now we shall confine ourselves to the bare facts of his life which preceded the dreadful catastrophe that broke so suddenly upon him.

Though Grushenka had, it is true, loved him for a brief hour genuinely and sincerely, she sometimes also tortured him cruelly and mercilessly. The trouble was that he could not make out what her real intentions were; to get them out of her by force or kindness was also quite impossible: she would not have given in for anything, but would only have become angry and would have turned her back on him altogether, that he realized very well at the time. He suspected quite correctly that she was also passing through some sort of crisis herself, and was in a state of extraordinary indecision, that she was trying to make up her mind about something but could not bring herself to do so. That was why he supposed, not without good reason and with a sinking heart, that at times she must simply hate him and his passion.

Perhaps it was so, too, but what Grushenka was so miserable about he just did not understand. So far as he was concerned, the thing that worried him boiled down to the question whether it was to be he, Mitya, or his father. Here, incidentally, one indisputable fact must be noted, namely that he was absolutely convinced that his father would most certainly propose marriage to Grushenka (if, in fact, he had not done so already), and he did not believe for a moment that the old voluptuary hoped to get off with no more than his three thousand roubles. Mitya came to that conclusion from his knowledge of Grushenka and her character. That was why he could not help feeling at times that Grushenka's worries and all her indecision only arose from the fact that she did not know which of the two to choose and which one of them would be most to her advantage. As for the imminent return of the 'army officer', that is to say, the man who had exerted such a fatal influence on Grushenka's life and whose arrival she was expecting with such agitation and apprehension, he – strange to say – never thought of it for a moment during those days. It is true that Grushenka had never mentioned it to him during the last few days. And yet he had been told by Grushenka herself about the letter she had received from her seducer a month before, and he partly knew its contents, too. At the time Grushenka, in a fit of temper, had shown him the letter, but, to her surprise, he did not seem to regard it as of any importance. And it would be very hard to say why this was so; perhaps it was simply because, oppressed by all the hideous horror of his struggle with his own father for this woman, he could not imagine anything more dreadful or more dangerous for him, at any rate, at that time. As for her fiancé, who had suddenly appeared out of the blue after a five-years' disappearance, he simply did not believe in him, and still less in his impending arrival. Indeed, the first letter of 'the army officer', which had been shown to Mitya, contained only an indefinite hint of the arrival of this new rival: the whole letter was very vague, very high-flown and full of the most sentimental effusions. It must be observed that Grushenka had concealed from him the last lines of the letter, in which his return was mentioned in rather more definite terms. Besides, as Mitya recalled afterwards, he had at the time caught on Grushenka's face a certain expression of involuntary and proud contempt for that epistle from Siberia. After that Grushenka told Mitya nothing of all her further communications with that new rival of his. So it was that he gradually had completely forgotten about the existence of the officer. All he thought about was that whatever happened and whatever turn his relations with Grushenka took, his coming final clash with his father was too near and had to be decided before anything else. He was waiting every minute for Grushenka's decision with a sinking heart and still believed that it would come suddenly, on the spur of the moment. What if she suddenly said to him: 'Take me, I'm yours for ever' – then it would all be over: he would seize her and take her away at once to the end of the world. Oh, he would take her away at once, as far away as possible, if not to the end of the world, then somewhere to the farthest end of Russia. He would marry her there and live with her under an assumed name, so that no one should know anything about them, neither here, nor there, nor anywhere. Then, oh, then quite a new life would begin at once! About that different, new, and 'virtuous' life ('it must, it must be virtuous') he dreamed continuously and with a kind of frenzy. He yearned for that renewal and resurrection. He had sunk into a horrible bog of his own free will, and this weighed heavily on his conscience, and like many others in such cases, he believed most of all in a change of place: if only it were not for these people, if only it were not for these circumstances, if only he could get out of that damned place – everything would be different, everything would follow a new course! That was what he believed in and what he was pining for.

But that could only be in the event of the first, *happy* solution of the question. There was another solution, too. Another and this time terrible ending presented itself to him. What if she should suddenly say to him: 'Go away, I have just come to an understanding with your father, I'm going to marry him and I don't want you' – and then – but then. . . . Mitya, though, did not know what would be then. He did not know it up to the very last hour. One must be quite fair to him on that point. He had no definite intentions. He was not planning any crime. He was merely watching, spying, and worrying, but was preparing himself all the same only for the first, happy ending of his troubles. Indeed, he refused to contemplate anything else. But here he was faced with a new tormenting problem, a new circumstance that had nothing to do with the issue in question but that was no less fatal and insoluble.

For even if she were to say to him: 'I'm yours, take me away', how was he to take her away? Where was he to get the means, the money to do it? It was just at this time that all his resources, which depended entirely on the sums of money he had received for so many years without interruption from his father, had completely run dry. No doubt, Grushenka had money, but so far as that was concerned Mitya suddenly showed great pride: he wanted to take her away and begin a new life with her himself, at his own expense, and not at hers; he could not even imagine taking money from her, and the very idea of it sickened him to the point of agonized revulsion. I am not dilating on this fact or analysing it, but merely stating it: such was the state of his mind at that moment. All this could have arisen indirectly and, as it were, even unconsciously from the secret qualms of his conscience about the money he had dishonestly appropriated from Katerina: 'I've been a scoundrel to one of them and presently I shall show myself to be a scoundrel again to the other,' he thought at the time, as he confessed afterwards himself: 'Besides, if Grushenka hears of it, she will have nothing to do with such a scoundrel.' So where was he to get the means, where was he to raise the fateful money? Without it all would be lost and the whole thing would fall through, 'and simply because I hadn't enough money – oh, the shame of it!'

Let me say in anticipation that the whole trouble was that he did perhaps know where to get the money and that he did perhaps even know where he could find it. I shall not go into it at greater length just yet, for everything will become clear later; but his chief trouble, let me explain at once however obscurely, was that before he could take that money, before he could *have a right* to take it, he had first to return the three thousand to Katerina, for otherwise, he decided, 'I'm a pickpocket and a scoundrel, and I do not want to start a new life as a scoundrel.' That was why he made up his mind to turn the whole world upside down, if necessary, but to return the three thousand to Katerina without fail and *before everything else*. He had arrived at the final stage of this decision in, as it were, the last hours of his life, that is to say, after his meeting with Alyosha in the evening two days earlier, on the highway, after Grushenka had insulted Katerina and after hearing an account of it from Alyosha, he had admitted that he was a scoundrel and told his brother to tell Katerina so 'if that will in any way make it easier for her'. It was then, during that same night, that, having parted from his brother, he had felt in his frenzy that it would be better to murder and rob someone than fail to return his debt to Katya. 'I'd rather appear as a robber and murderer to the man I've robbed and murdered as well as to all men and go to Siberia,' he said to himself, 'than give Katya the right to say that I deceived her and stole her money and ran away with her money to begin a new, virtuous life with Grushenka! That I can't do!' So declared Mitya, gritting his teeth, and he might well have imagined at times that he would finish up by falling ill with brain fever. But for the time being he went on struggling. . . .

Strangely enough, one would have thought that, having taken such a decision, there was nothing left for him but despair; for where was a man like him, who was as poor as a church mouse, to raise such a large sum of money? And yet he kept hoping to the very last that he would get the three thousand, that they would somehow come to him of themselves, that they would drop from the sky, if there were no other way of getting them. But then that is exactly what does happen to people who, like Dmitry, spend all their lives wasting and squandering the money they have inherited and have no idea how to earn it. A most fantastic confusion arose in his head immediately after his parting from Alyosha two days before and played havoc with all his thoughts. It thus happened that he hit upon a perfectly wild enterprise. And, indeed, the most impossible and fantastic enterprises appear most practical to such men in such circumstances. He suddenly decided to go to the merchant Samsonov, Grushenka's protector, and put a certain 'plan' before him and by means of that 'plan' to obtain the whole of the required sum from him. He had no doubts at all about the value of his plan as a business proposition, but was not sure what Samsonov himself would think of his unconventional action, if he were to regard it not merely as a business proposition. Though Mitya knew the merchant by sight, he was not acquainted with him and had never spoken to him. But for some reason he had long been convinced that the old seducer, who was now at death's door, would perhaps not at all object now to Grushenka's marrying a 'reliable' man and settling down and leading an honest life. Not only would he not object, but he would be glad of it himself and, if the right opportunity presented itself, would be only too willing to help. He also concluded, whether because of what he had heard or from some chance remark of Grushenka's, that the old man would perhaps prefer him to his father for Grushenka. Possibly many readers of my story will think that in calculating on such help and in intending to take his bride, as it were, from the hands of her 'protector', Mitya behaved in too coarse and indelicate a manner. All I can say is that Mitya regarded Grushenka's past as something finished and done with. He looked upon her past with infinite compassion and resolved with all the ardour of his passion that once Grushenka told him that she loved him and would marry him, a new Grushenka would suddenly come to life, and, together with her, a new Dmitry Karamazov, free from every vice and endowed with all the virtues: they would both forgive each other and make a completely fresh start. As for Kuzma Samsonov, he regarded him as a man who exercised a fatal influence on Grushenka's past life, now finally over and done with, whom she never loved, however, and who – and that was the most important thing – was also 'done with', finished, so that he really existed no more. Besides, Mitya could hardly regard him as a man now, for everyone in the town knew that he was simply a sick wreck of a man, whose relations with Grushenka were, so to speak, only those of a father and not at all as they used to be in the past, and that this had been so for a long time, for almost a year. In any case, there was a great deal of simple-mindedness on Mitya's part, for with all his vices he was a very simple-minded man. As a result of this simple-mindedness of his, he was, incidentally, quite seriously convinced that old Kuzma, getting ready to depart to the other world, was sincerely sorry for his past relations with Grushenka, and that she had no more devoted protector and friend than this, now harmless, old man.

On the very next day after his conversation with Alyosha in the open country, after which he had scarcely slept all night, Mitya appeared at the house of Samsonov at about ten o'clock in the morning and asked the servant to announce him. It was a very large, bleak old house of two stories with outhouses and a cottage in the yard. The ground floor was occupied by Samsonov's two sons and their families, his old sister and his unmarried daughter. In the cottage lived his two clerks, one of whom also had a large family. Both the ground floor and the cottage were very crowded, but the old man lived on the upper floor by himself and would not let even his daughter, who looked after him, live with him, although, in spite of her asthma, she had to run upstairs to him many times a day and, indeed, any time he might call her. The 'top floor' consisted of a great number of large drawing-rooms, furnished in the old-fashioned merchant style, with long dull rows of mahogany armchairs and chairs along the walls, with cut-glass chandeliers in dust-covers, and gloomy mirrors on the walls between the windows. All these rooms were entirely empty and not lived in, for the sick old man kept only to one small room, his small bedroom at the far end of the house, where he was waited upon by an old maidservant with a kerchief on her head, and a 'lad', who spent most of his time sitting on a chest in the passage. Because of his swollen legs the old man could hardly walk at all and only rarely got up from his leather armchair when, supported under the arms by the old maidservant, he was led up and down the room once or twice. He was severe and taciturn even with this old woman. When he was informed of the arrival of the 'captain', he at once refused to see him. But Mitya persisted and sent up his name again. Samsonov questioned the lad at length: what he looked like and whether he was drunk and disorderly. He was told that Mitya was sober but would not go away. The old man again refused to see him. Then Mitya, who had anticipated it all and who had purposely brought a pencil and paper, wrote legibly on the piece of paper just one line: 'On most urgent business closely concerning Miss Svetlov', and sent it up to the old man. After a moment's reflection, the old man told the lad to take the visitor to the large drawing-room and sent the old woman down to tell his younger son to come up to him at once. This younger son, a man of over six foot and of exceptional physical strength, who was clean-shaven and wore European clothes (Samsonov himself wore a *kaftan* and a beard), came at once and without comment. They all trembled before their father. Samsonov had sent for the young fellow not because he was afraid of the captain, for he was by no means timid by nature, but just in case he needed him as a witness. Accompanied by the boy servant and his son, who supported him, he waddled at last into the drawing-room. It can be safely assumed that he was intensely curious himself. The drawing-room in which Mitya was waiting for him was a vast, gloomy, depressing room, with two large windows, a gallery, walls 'faced with marble', and three huge chandeliers in dust-covers. Mitya was sitting on a little chair at the door, awaiting his fate with nervous impatience. When the old man appeared at the opposite door, about sixty feet away, Mitya at once jumped up and with his long, military stride went to meet him. Mitya was well dressed, in a buttoned-up frock-coat, with a top hat and black gloves in his hands, just as he had been three days before at the elder's in the monastery, at the family meeting with his father and brothers. The old man waited for him, standing and looking stern and dignified, and Mitya felt at once that he had seen through him as he was approaching. Mitya was also very forcibly struck by Samsonov's face, which had swollen up enormously during the last few weeks: his lower lip, which had always been thick, hung down and looked like a crumpet. Samsonov bowed to his visitor in dignified silence, motioned him to sit down in an armchair by the sofa and, leaning on his son's arm and groaning painfully, began lowering himself on to the sofa opposite Mitya. Seeing his painful exertions, Mitya at once felt very sorry and deeply ashamed of his own insignificance in the presence of so dignified a personage whom he disturbed by his arrival.

'What can I do for you, sir?' asked the old man, slowly and articulately, but courteously, when he had at last seated himself.

Mitya gave a start, jumped up from his chair, but sat down again. Then he began at once speaking loudly, hurriedly and nervously, gesticulating and in an absolute frenzy. It was obvious that he was at the end of his tether, that he was facing ruin, looking desperately for some way out of his situation, and that if he did not find it, there was nothing left for him to do but to drown himself. Old Samsonov probably grasped all that in less than a second, though his face remained cold and immobile as a statue's.

'Sir, I expect you must have heard more than once of my disagreements with my father, who robbed me of my inheritance after the death of my mother – I mean, sir, since the whole town is talking about it – for here, sir, everyone talks about what doesn't concern them. . . . And, besides, it might have reached you through Grushenka – I'm sorry, through Miss Svetlov, the – er – lady I hold in the highest respect and esteem, sir. . . .'

So Mitya began and stopped abruptly almost as soon as he began. But we shall not quote his speech in full, but merely give the gist of it. The whole thing, he began, was really very simple. Three months ago, he, Mitya, had with express intent (he deliberately said 'with express intent' and not 'intentionally') taken the advice of a lawyer in the chief town of the province – 'a famous lawyer, sir, Pavel Korneplodov, I expect you must have heard of him – a man of great intellect, the mind of a statesman – he knows you, too, sir – spoke very highly of you –' Mitya stopped short a second time. But these gaps in his speech did not stop him. He jumped over them and rushed on and on. This Korneplodov, after questioning him at length and examining the documents, which Mitya had brought for his inspection (Mitya spoke rather vaguely about these documents, talking rather rapidly as he came to mention them), gave it as his considered opinion that the village of Chermashnya ought really to belong to him, Mitya, who should have inherited it from his mother, and that they could without a doubt take action for its recovery and jolly well take the wind out of the sails of that old hooligan of a father of his – 'for, you see, sir, not all the doors are closed and justice might yet find a loophole.' In fact, there was good hope of an additional six or even seven thousand roubles from his father, for Chermashnya was worth at least twenty-five thousand, that is, twenty-eight, in fact, 'thirty, thirty thousand, sir, and would you believe it, I didn't get seventeen from that cruel man!' Well, so he, Mitya, did nothing about this business at the time, for he knew nothing of the law, and, on coming here, was dumbfounded by a counter-claim against him (here Mitya got rather confused again and once more took a flying leap forward). 'So won't you, sir, take up all my claims against that monster and pay me only three thousand roubles. You can't possibly lose, sir, I swear on my honour, sir, on my honour. On the contrary, you may make six or seven thousand instead of three. . . .' Above all, he wanted it settled that very day. 'I could arrange to meet you at a notary's, or whatever it is. . . . In short, sir, I'm ready to do anything, let you have all the documents you want – I'll sign everything – and – er – we could draw up the agreement at once, and, if possible, I mean, sir, if it were really possible, this morning. . . . You could let me have the three thousand, sir, for – er – there's no man of substance in this rotten little town to compare with you, sir. . . . And in this way save me from – I mean, sir, save a poor fellow like me for a most honourable, a most high-minded action, if I may say so, sir – for I cherish the most honourable feelings for a certain person, whom you know well, sir, and in whom you take a fatherly interest. I wouldn't have come if – er – your interest had not been – er – fatherly. And, if you don't mind my saying so, sir, we're dealing here with a matter in which three persons have knocked their heads together, for fate, sir, fate is a most terrifying thing! Realism, sir, realism! And since you, sir, dropped out long ago, there are only two heads left. I'm afraid I've put it rather clumsily, but I'm not a literary chap. What I mean, sir, is that one of these heads is mine, and the other's that monster's. So you must make your choice: either the monster or I. Everything lies in your hands now, sir – the fate of three people and two lots to draw. . . . I'm sorry, I – I'm afraid I'm rather confused, but you understand – I see from your venerable eyes that you have understood. . . . And if you haven't then I'm done for – that's the position!'

Mitya broke off his absurd speech with the words, 'That's the position' and, jumping up from his seat, waited for an answer to his stupid proposal. At his last phrase he had suddenly become hopelessly aware that the whole thing had misfired and, above all, that he had been talking utter nonsense. 'A funny thing,' it suddenly flashed across his despairing mind, 'on the way here everything seemed all right, but now it's nothing but nonsense!' All the time he had been talking, the old man had sat motionless and had watched him with an icy look in his eyes. After keeping him for a moment in suspense, Samsonov at last declared in a most firm and cheerless tone:

'I'm sorry, sir, but we don't do such business.'

Mitya suddenly felt his legs giving way under him.

'But, sir, what am I to do now?' he murmured with a pallid smile. 'I'm done for now, don't you think so?'

'I'm very sorry, sir. . . .'

Mitya remained standing, staring motionlessly at Samsonov, and he suddenly noticed a slight movement in the old man's face. He gave a start.

'You see, sir, this is not really our line of business,' the old man said slowly. 'There will be courts, lawyers – one trouble after another! But if you like, there's a man here whom you might approach. . . .'

'Good Lord, who is he? You give me new hope, sir,' Mitya suddenly murmured.

'He's not a local man, sir, and he's not here just now, either. He's a former peasant, deals in timber. He's known as Lyagavy. He's been trying to buy the wood in Chermashnya from your father for the last year, but they can't agree on the price. You must have heard of it. Now he's come back again and is staying at the priest's in Ilyinskoye, about ten miles from the Volovya station, I believe. He wrote to me, too, about the business, about that wood, I mean. Asked my advice. Your father means to go and see him himself. So that if you got there before your father and made Lyagavy the same offer, he might —'

'A brilliant idea!' Mitya interrupted him enthusiastically. 'Yes, he's the very man! That would just suit him! He's anxious to buy it, he's being asked too much, and here I'm offering him the documents which will make him the owner of the property – ha, ha, ha!'

And Mitya suddenly burst into his short, dry laugh, which was so unexpected that even Samsonov gave a start.

'How can I thank you, sir?' Mitya cried ecstatically.

'Don't mention it, sir,' said Samsonov, inclining his head.

'But don't you realize? You've saved me! Oh, I knew you'd help me! So now to the priest!'

'You needn't thank me, sir.'

'I'm off at once. I hope I haven't injured your health, sir. I shall never forget it. A Russian says this to you, sir, a R-russian!'

'That's all right, sir.'

Mitya seized the old man's hand to shake it, but Samsonov's eyes flashed malevolently. Mitya drew back his hand, but at once reproached himself for his suspiciousness. 'He must be tired,' he thought.

'For her, sir! For her! You understand that it's for her, don't you?' he suddenly bawled in a loud voice, bowed, turned round sharply and, without looking back, strode quickly to the door with the same long military steps. He was trembling with delight. 'Everything was on the point of being lost,' he thought feverishly, 'and now my guardian angel has saved me! And if a big-business man like him (a most honourable old man, and what dignity!) suggested such a course, it's sure to come off. I must be off at once. I'll be back before nightfall and the thing's settled. Surely, the old fellow wasn't pulling my leg!' So Mitya was exclaiming as he walked back to his lodgings. And, indeed, he could scarcely have imagined anything else: either the advice was business-like (from such a business man), with a thorough understanding of business and with a thorough knowledge of that Lyagavy (what a funny name!), or – or the old man was pulling his leg! Alas, the second supposition was the only correct one! Afterwards, long afterwards, after the catastrophe had taken place, Samsonov admitted himself that he had made a fool of the 'captain'. He was a cold, spiteful, and sardonic man who, besides, was full of morbid antipathies. Whether it was the captain's rapturous look, or the foolish conviction of this 'rake and spendthrift' that he, Samsonov, could be taken in by such nonsense as his 'plan', or jealousy of Grushenka for whose sake this 'madcap' came to him with such a ridiculous story in the hope of getting money – I do not know what exactly induced the old man to act as he did, but at the moment when Mitya stood before him, feeling that his legs were giving way under him, crying idiotically that he was done for – at that moment the old man looked at him with intense hatred and decided to have a good laugh at him. When Mitya had gone, Samsonov, white with rage, turned to his son and told him to make sure that beggar was not seen in his house again, nor admitted into his yard, or else —

He did not finish his threat, but even his son, who had often seen him angry, trembled with fear. For a whole hour afterwards the old man was shaking with rage, and in the evening he fell ill and sent for the doctor.

2

Lyagavy

So Mitya had to set off 'at a gallop', and he had no money for the carriage, that is to say, he had forty copecks, but that was all that was left after so many years of prosperity! But at home he had his old silver watch which had long ago stopped. He took it to a Jewish watchmaker who had a little shop in the market-place. The watchmaker gave him six roubles for it. 'And I didn't expect that!' cried Mitya ecstatically (he was still in a state of ecstasy), grabbed the six roubles and ran back home. At home he added another three roubles which he borrowed from his landlady, who was pleased to give it to him, though it was the last she had, for she was very fond of him. In his excitement Mitya told the people of the house there and then that his fate would be decided that very day, and of course described to them in great haste practically the whole of his 'plan' which he had put before Samsonov, and Samsonov's suggestion, his own future hopes, etc., etc. Before that, too, these people had been let into many of his secrets and that was why they looked upon him as one of themselves, a gentleman who was not at all proud. Having thus collected nine roubles, Mitya sent for post-horses to take him to Volovya station. But it was in this way that the fact was remembered and established that 'on the day before a certain event, at midday, Mitya did not have a penny and, to obtain the money, he had sold his watch and borrowed three roubles from his landlady, and all in the presence of witnesses.'

I set down this fact beforehand and it will be explained later on why I do so.

Though on the way to Volovya station Mitya was radiant with the joyful anticipation that at last he would bring all these 'affairs' to a successful issue, he nevertheless trembled at the thought of what would happen with Grushenka in his absence. What if she should at last decide to go to his father? That was why he had gone off without telling her anything and warned his landlady not to disclose where he had gone if anyone came to ask for him. 'I must, I must be back this evening,' he kept repeating, as he jogged along in the cart, 'and I might as well bring that Lyagavy back with me to – to complete the deed of sale.' So Mitya dreamed with bated breath, but, alas, his dreams were not destined to be realized according to his 'plan'.

To begin with, he was late, having taken a rough country road from Volovya station, which meant driving for fifteen instead of ten miles. Secondly, when at last he arrived at Ilyinskoye, he found that the priest was not at home, having gone off to a neighbouring village. By the time Mitya, who had set off to the neighbouring village with the same exhausted horses, had found him, it was almost dark. The priest, a timid and kindly little man, explained to him at once that though Lyagavy had been staying with him at first, he was now at Sukhoy Possyolok, where he was spending the night in the forester's hut, for he was buying timber there too. At Mitya's earnest request to take him at once to Lyagavy and by doing so to 'save him', the priest at first hesitated, but at last agreed to conduct him to Sukhoy Possyolok, his curiosity having evidently been aroused; but, unluckily, he proposed that they should walk there as it was only about a mile 'and a bit' to the forester's cottage. Mitya, of course, agreed, and walked off with his long strides so that the poor priest almost ran after him. He was an extremely cautious, though not very old, little man. Mitya at once began discussing his plans with him, too, and heatedly and nervously asking advice about Lyagavy, talking all the way. The priest listened attentively, but was chary with his advice. He returned evasive answers to Mitya's questions: 'I don't know – oh, I'm afraid I know nothing about it, how am I to know about it,' and so on. When Mitya began to speak of his disagreements with his father over his inheritance, the priest grew quite alarmed, for he seemed to be in some way dependent on Karamazov. He did ask Mitya, however, with surprise why he called the peasant trader Gorskin, Lyagavy, and made it quite clear to Mitya that though he deserved his derogatory nickname, he should not address him by it, because he would be greatly offended at the name, but that he must be sure to call him Gorskin. 'Otherwise,' the priest concluded, 'you won't do any business with him, for he won't even listen to you.' Mitya could not help showing his surprise at that, and explained that Samsonov himself had called him by that name. On hearing this, the priest at once changed the subject, though he would have done well to explain at once his suspicions to Dmitry, namely, that if Samsonov had sent him to that peasant and called him Lyagavy, then he must have meant to pull his leg and was he sure there was not something wrong about it? But Mitya had no time to pause over 'such trifles'. He was in a hurry, he kept striding along, and it was only when he arrived at Sukhoy Possyolok that he realized that they had walked not a mile or a mile and a half, but a good three miles. This annoyed him, but he let it pass. They went into the hut. The forester, whom the priest knew well, lived in one half of the hut, and Gorskin had taken up his quarters in the other, the living-room across the passage. They went into this room and lighted a tallow candle. It was very hot. On the table was a *samovar* that had gone out, as well as a tray with cups, an empty bottle of rum, an almost empty pint bottle of vodka and a few crusts of white bread. Gorskin himself lay stretched out on a bench, with his coat bundled up under his head for a pillow, and snored heavily. Mitya stood looking perplexed. 'Of course, we have to wake him,' he said agitatedly. 'My business is too important. I was in a great hurry to get here and I'm in a hurry to get back today.' But the priest and the forester stood in silence, without giving their opinion. 'He's drunk,' Mitya decided, 'but what am I to do? Lord, what am I to do?' Suddenly, sick with impatience, he began pulling the sleeping man up by his hands and feet, shaking his head, raising him up and

trying to make him sit on the bench, but all he achieved by his prolonged exertions was that Gorskin began to grunt stupidly and utter
violent though inarticulate oaths.

'No,' said the priest at last, 'you'd better wait, because he's obviously not in a fit condition.'

'He's been drinking all day,' the forester put in.

'Good Lord,' cried Mitya, 'if only you knew how important it is
to me and how desperate I am!'

'No,' repeated the priest, 'I think you'd better wait till morning.'

'Till morning? But, good Lord, that's impossible!'

And in his despair he was almost on the point of making another
attempt to waken the drunken man, but stopped short at once, realizing the uselessness of his efforts. The priest was silent, the sleepy
forester looked gloomy.

'What terrible tragedies realism inflicts on people!' Mitya cried in
utter despair.

The perspiration was pouring down his face. Taking advantage of
the moment, the priest put it to him very reasonably that even if he
had succeeded in waking the sleeping man, Gorskin would in his
drunken condition be incapable of any conversation, 'and your business being so important,' he added, 'it would be much better to leave
it till the morning.' Mitya spread out his hands in a gesture of despair
and agreed.

'I'll stay here with the lighted candle, Father. I don't want to waste
a moment of my time. As soon as he wakes, I'll begin. . . . I'll pay you
for the candle,' he addressed the forester, 'and for the night's lodging,
too. You'll have good reason to remember Dmitry Karamazov. Only
I don't know what we're going to do with you, Father. Where are
you going to sleep?'

'Don't worry about me. I'm going back home. I'll take his mare,'
he pointed to the forester, 'and ride home. Now I must say good-bye
to you, sir. I wish you every success.'

So it was settled. The priest rode back home on the mare, glad to
be left in peace at last, but still shaking his head uneasily, wondering
whether he ought to inform his benefactor Karamazov in good time
of this curious incident, 'or else,' he thought, 'who knows, he might
find out, be angry and withdraw his favour.' The forester scratched
himself and went back to his room in silence, and Mitya sat down on

a bench not to waste, as he put it, a moment of his time. A deep depression hung about his soul like a heavy mist. A deep, fearful depression! He sat thinking, but could not arrive at any conclusion. The candle guttered, a cricket chirped, it was getting unbearably stuffy in the over-heated room. In his mind's eye he suddenly saw the garden, the path at the back of the garden, a door opening mysteriously in his father's house, and Grushenka running in through the door. . . . He jumped up from the bench.

'A tragedy!' he said, grinding his teeth, and, walking up mechanically to the sleeping man, he began looking at his face. He was a lean, middle-aged peasant, with an oblong face, fair, curly hair, and a long, thin, reddish beard. He wore a cotton shirt and a black waistcoat, from the pocket of which peeped out the chain of a silver watch. Mitya examined his face with intense hatred, and for some reason he found his curly hair particularly hateful. What was so insufferably galling was that he, Mitya, whose business was of such urgency, should be standing over him, all worn out, after having sacrificed so much and left matters of such great importance behind, while that good-for-nothing scoundrel 'on whom my entire future depends, snores as if nothing mattered, just as if he were an inhabitant of another planet'!

'Oh, the irony of fate!' exclaimed Mitya and suddenly, losing complete control of himself, fell to rousing the drunken peasant again. He tried to wake him in a kind of frenzy, pulled him about, pushed him, even beat him, but after five minutes of vain efforts he returned to his bench in helpless despair and sat down.

'It's stupid, stupid!' cried Mitya. 'And – how dishonourable it all is!' he added suddenly for some reason. His head had begun to ache terribly. 'Shall I give it up and go back?' it flashed through his mind. 'No, no, I'd better wait till morning. Yes, I'll stay on purpose, on purpose! What did I come here for, after all? Besides, I can't go back. I haven't got the money. How am I to get away from here? Oh, the absurdity of it!'

His head, however, ached more and more. He sat motionless and, hardly aware of it, dozed off and fell asleep as he sat. He must have slept for two hours or more. He awoke because of his quite unbearable headache, so unbearable that he could have screamed. His temples throbbed, the top of his head ached. Having come to, he could not grasp for a long time what had happened to him. At last he realized that the room was full of charcoal fumes and that he might even die. And the drunken peasant still lay snoring; the candle guttered and was about to go out. Mitya shouted and rushed, staggering, across the passage to the forester's room. The forester woke up very soon, but hearing that the other room was full of fumes, accepted the fact with such curious indifference that Mitya was surprised and annoyed.

'But he's dead, dead and then – what's going to happen then?' Mitya kept shouting to him in a rage.

They opened the doors, flung open the window and opened the flue. Mitya brought a pail of water from the passage, first wetted his head, then, finding some rag, dipped it into the water and put it on Lyagavy's head. The forester, however, went on treating the whole thing rather scornfully and, after opening the window, said sullenly, 'It will be all right now,' and went back to sleep, leaving Mitya a lighted iron lantern. Mitya busied himself with the poisoned drunkard for about half an hour, changing the wet rag on his head, and was seriously thinking of not going to sleep all night. But, feeling utterly exhausted, he sat down for a moment to take breath, and instantly closed his eyes and then unconsciously stretched himself out on the bench and slept like a log.

He woke up terribly late. It was about nine o'clock. The sun was shining brightly in at the two little windows of the hut. The curly-headed peasant was sitting on the bench dressed in his peasant coat. There was another *samovar* and another pint of vodka before him. He had finished yesterday's pint and more than half finished the new one. Mitya jumped to his feet and at once realized that the damned peasant was drunk again, well and truly drunk, and that nothing could be done about it. He looked at him for a minute with wide-open eyes. The peasant, on the other hand, kept looking silently and craftily at him, with a sort of offensive composure, even with a sort of contemptuous arrogance, as Mitya thought. He rushed up to him.

'I say – you see – I – I suppose you – er – you must have heard from the forester here in the other room – I – I'm Lieutenant Dmitry Karamazov, the son of old Karamazov, from whom you're buying the timber. . . .'

'You're a liar!' said the peasant suddenly, with the utmost composure and enunciating each word slowly and emphatically.

'A liar? What do you mean? Don't you know Mr Karamazov?'

'I don't know any Karamazov of yours,' said the peasant, in a rather thick voice.

'Why, you're haggling with him over the wood, the wood. Wake up, come to your senses. Father Pavel of Ilyinskoye brought me here. You wrote to Samsonov and he has sent me to you,' Mitya said breathlessly.

'You're l-lying!' Lyagavy again enunciated slowly and emphatically. Mitya's feet went cold.

'For pity's sake, this is no joke! Perhaps you're a little drunk. But you can speak and understand – or else – I don't understand anything!'

'You're a house painter!'

'For pity's sake, I'm Karamazov, Dmitry Karamazov. I have an offer to make to you – a profitable offer – a very profitable one – in connexion with the wood.'

The peasant stroked his beard importantly.

'No, you contracted for the job and turned out a scoundrel. You're a scoundrel!'

'I assure you you're mistaken!' Mitya cried, wringing his hands in despair.

The peasant went on stroking his beard and suddenly screwed up his eyes craftily.

'No, sir, you tell me this: tell me if there's a law that allows people to play dirty tricks. Do you hear? You're a scoundrel! Do you understand that?'

Mitya stepped back gloomily and suddenly it was as though 'something hit him on the head', as he put it afterwards himself. In a twinkling the truth dawned on him, 'a light was kindled and I grasped everything'. He stood dumbfounded, wondering how he, an intelligent man after all, could have yielded to such folly, how he could have got mixed up in such an adventure and gone on with it for almost a whole day and night, wasted his time with this Lyagavy, putting a wet rag on his head. 'Why, the man's drunk, dead drunk and he'll go on drinking for a whole week. . . . What am I waiting here for? And what if Samsonov sent me here on purpose? And what if she— Oh, Lord, what have I done?'

The peasant sat, looking at him and grinning. At any other time Mitya might have killed the fool out of sheer rage, but now he felt as weak as a child. He went up quietly to the bench, picked up his coat, put it on in silence and went out of the room. He did not find the forester in the other room. There was no one there. He took fifty copecks in small change out of his pocket and put it on the table for his night's lodgings, for the candle, and for the trouble he had given. On going out of the hut, he saw nothing but forest all round. He wandered along at random, not knowing which way to turn as he came out of the hut – to the right or the left: the night before, hurrying with the priest, he had not noticed the way. He had no revengeful feelings for anybody, not even for Samsonov. He strode along the narrow forest path, senselessly, lost, with his hopes shattered, without caring where he was going. A child could have knocked him down, so weak was he in body and soul. Somehow or other, however, he made his way out of the forest and there stretched before him for miles around a prospect of bare, harvested fields: 'What despair, what death all around!' he kept repeating, striding on and on.

He was saved by an old merchant who was travelling along the rough country road in a hired carriage. When it came alongside, Mitya stopped him to ask the way and it turned out that the merchant, too, was going to Volovya. After exchanging a few words, he agreed to give Mitya a lift to the station. Three hours later they arrived. At Volovya station Mitya at once hired post-horses to drive him to the town and suddenly realized that he was terribly hungry. While the horses were being harnessed, he ordered an omelette. He ate it at once, ate a huge chunk of bread, ate a sausage, which happened to be available, and drank three glasses of vodka. Having thus fortified himself, he felt much more cheerful and his heart grew light again. He drove along the road at a spanking pace, urging on the coachman, and suddenly he made a new and this time 'unalterable' plan how to obtain 'the damned money' that day and before the evening. 'And to think,' he cried scornfully, 'only to think that because of some rubbishy three thousand a man's life can be ruined! I shall settle it today!' But for his constant thought of Grushenka and of what might have happened to her, he would perhaps have become quite cheerful again. But the thought of her pierced his heart every minute like a sharp knife. At last they arrived, and Mitya at once rushed off to see Grushenka.

3

Gold-Mines

THAT was the visit about which Grushenka had told Rakitin with such terror. She had been waiting for the 'message' at the time and was very glad that Mitya had not been to see her that day or the day before, hoping to God that perhaps he would not come till she had gone. Then he suddenly appeared. The rest we know: to get rid of him, she at once persuaded him to take her to Samsonov's, where she pretended she had to go at once 'to do his accounts', and when Mitya accompanied her, she made him promise, as she took leave of him at the gate, to come for her at twelve o'clock to see her home again. Mitya, too, was glad of this arrangement, for if she was going to be at Samsonov's, she would not go to his father's, 'if only she is not lying,' he added at once. But from what he saw, he did not think she was lying. He was the sort of jealous man who, while he is away from the woman he loves, immediately starts inventing all sorts of terrible things that may be happening to her and how she may be 'unfaithful' to him, but when he runs back to her, crushed and heartbroken and absolutely convinced that she has succeeded in betraying him, he immediately recovers his spirits at the first glance at her face, the gay, laughing, affectionate face of the woman, and in a twinkling his suspicions are gone and he inveighs against himself for his jealousy. Having escorted Grushenka, he rushed home. Oh, he had so many things still to do that day! But at least he felt relieved. 'Except that I must find out from Smerdyakov at once whether anything happened there last night and whether she might not have been to see father last night – oh dear!' it flashed through his mind. So that even before he got home his jealousy again began to stir in his restless heart.

Jealousy! 'Othello is not jealous, he is trustful,' observed Pushkin, and this remark alone testifies to the extraordinary profundity of our great poet's mind. Othello's soul is shattered and his whole outlook on life is confused because *his ideal has been destroyed*. But Othello would not start hiding, spying, peeping: he is trustful. On the contrary, he had to be led on, pushed, excited by extraordinary efforts to make him suspect infidelity. Not so the truly jealous man. It is quite impossible to imagine the disgrace and moral degradation a jealous man is capable of putting up with without any qualms of conscience. And it is not as though all of them had sordid, vulgar minds. On the contrary, a man of most high-minded sentiments, whose love is pure and full of self-sacrifice, may at the same time hide under tables, bribe the vilest people and put up with the nastiest filthiness of spying and eavesdropping. Othello could never reconcile himself to infidelity – he could forgive it, but not reconcile himself to it – though his heart was as gentle and innocent as a babe's. It is different with a really jealous man: it is hard to imagine what some jealous men can descend to and be reconciled to and forgive! Jealous men are more ready to forgive than anyone else – every woman knows that! A jealous man is capable of forgiving extraordinarily quickly (after first making a violent scene, of course), he is capable of forgiving, for instance, infidelity that is practically proven, the embraces and kisses he has seen, if at the same time he could, for instance, be somehow or other convinced that it had been 'for the last time' and that his rival would vanish from that very hour, depart to the ends of the earth, or that he himself would carry her off somewhere where his terrible rival would never come. The reconciliation, of course, will be only for an hour, because even if his rival did really vanish, he would invent another one the next day, a new one, and would be jealous of him. And, one cannot help asking oneself, what is there in a love that has to be so watched over and what is a love worth that has to be so strenuously guarded? But that a truly jealous man will never understand, and yet there certainly are high-principled people with lofty hearts among them. It is remarkable, too, that though the very same high-principled people, while hiding in some cubbyhole, eavesdropping and spying, understand very well with their 'lofty hearts' how low they have sunk of their own free will, yet at that moment, at any rate, they never feel any pricks of con- science. At the sight of Grushenka, Mitya's jealousy disappeared, and for a moment he became trustful and generous, and even despised himself for his evil feelings. But that merely meant that in his love for this woman there was something much higher than he himself imagined, and not only carnal passion, not only the 'curve of her body', of which he had spoken to Alyosha. But, on the other hand, when Grushenka was away, Mitya at once began to suspect her of all the low and cunning stratagems of unfaithfulness, without feeling any pricks of conscience about it at all.

And so jealousy surged up in him again. In any case, he had to make haste. First of all he had to raise at least a little money as a short-term loan. The nine roubles had almost all been spent on his fares, and, as is well known, it is impossible to take a step without money. But already on his way back to the town in the cart he had thought over, together with his new plan, how he could raise a short-term loan. He had a brace of excellent duelling pistols with cartridges, and if he had not pawned them till then it was because he prized them more than anything he possessed. In the 'Metropolis' he had long since struck up a slight acquaintance with a young civil servant and had learnt by chance that this rather wealthy bachelor had a passion for weapons and bought pistols, revolvers, and daggers, hung them on the walls and, showing them to his friends, boasted of his ability to explain the mechanism of a revolver, of his knowledge how to load it, fire it, and so on. Without wasting any time, Mitya at once went to see him and offered to pawn his pistols to him for ten roubles. The civil servant was delighted and began trying to persuade him to sell them outright, but Mitya refused, and the young man gave him ten roubles, declaring that nothing in the world would induce him to take interest. They parted friends. Mitya was in a hurry to get to the summer-house at the back of his landlady's garden and to get hold of Smerdyakov as soon as possible. But in this way the fact was again established that only three or four hours before a certain event, of which more will be said later, Mitya had not a penny and had pawned something he greatly prized for ten roubles, though three hours later, thousands were suddenly found in his possession. . . . But I am running ahead. . . .

At Maria Kondratyevna's, Karamazov's neighbour, he was told the highly disturbing and surprising news of Smerdyakov's illness. He heard the story of Smerdyakov's fall in the cellar, followed by his epileptic fit, the doctor's visit, and his father's anxiety; he was also interested to learn of his brother Ivan's hasty departure for Moscow in the morning. 'He must have passed through Volovya before me,' thought Mitya. But he was greatly worried about Smerdyakov. What was he to do now? Who was going to keep watch for him?

Who was going to pass the word to him? He began to question the women eagerly whether they had noticed anything the evening before. They knew very well what he was driving at and completely reassured him: no one had been there, Ivan had spent the night in his father's house, everything had been perfectly all right. Mitya pondered: he had without a doubt to keep watch today, but where? Here or at Samsonov's gate? He decided that it had to be done both here and there, using his own discretion, and meanwhile, meanwhile. . . . What worried him was the new 'plan' he had devised while travelling in the cart, a plan that could not possibly fail and that could not possibly be put off. Mitya decided to sacrifice an hour to it. 'In an hour,' he thought, 'I shall settle everything, I shall find out everything, everything, and then, then I shall first of all go to Samsonov's, see if Grushenka is there, and immediately come back here, stay here till eleven, and then go to Samsonov's again to escort her home.' This was what he decided to do.

He rushed home, washed, combed his hair, brushed his clothes, dressed, and went to Mrs Khokhlakov's. Alas, the success of his 'plan' depended on her. He made up his mind to borrow three thousand from that lady. And the astonishing thing was that for some reason he suddenly felt absolutely convinced that she would not refuse to lend him the money. It may seem strange that he should not have gone to her, a woman who belonged to his own social set, as it were, in the first place if he felt so sure about it, but had gone to Samsonov, a man of a different mentality with whom he did not even know how to talk. But the fact was that he had practically broken off his relations with Mrs Khokhlakov during the last month, had never known her well before and, besides, knew perfectly well that she could not stand him. This lady had come to hate him from the very first simply because he was engaged to Katerina, while for some reason she wanted her to throw him over and marry 'the dear, chivalrously cultured Ivan Karamazov, who had such beautiful manners'. Mitya's manners she detested. Mitya, indeed, made fun of her and on one occasion expressed the view that this lady 'is as lively and pert as she is uneducated'. But that morning in the cart a most brilliant idea had struck him: 'If she really doesn't want me to marry Katerina and is so much against this marriage [he knew that she was almost hysterical on that subject], why should she refuse to lend me three thousand roubles to enable me to leave Katerina and clear out for good? If these spoilt society ladies get some idea into their heads, they will do anything to get what they want. Besides, she's so rich,' Mitya argued. As for his 'plan' itself, it was the same as before, that is to say, to offer her his rights to Chermashnya, but not, as with Samsonov the day before, with any commercial object, not trying to tempt the lady, as he had done Samsonov the day before, with the prospect of a hundred per cent profit on the deal, that is, with getting six or seven thousand for her three thousand, but simply as a gentleman-like security for a debt. As he worked out his new idea, Mitya was absolutely delighted with it, but it was always like that with him every time he took a sudden decision. He gave himself up to any new idea with passionate enthusiasm. All the same, when he mounted the front steps of Mrs Khokhlakov's house, he suddenly felt a shiver of fear run down his spine: it was at that moment that he fully realized, and this time with mathematical certainty, that this was his last hope, and that if he failed this time there was nothing left for him to do in the world except 'murder and rob someone for the three thousand....' It was half-past seven when he rang the bell.

At first fortune seemed to smile on him: as soon as he was announced he was received with quite unusual rapidity. 'Just as though she were expecting me,' it flashed through Mitya's mind, and then, as soon as he was shown into the drawing-room, Mrs Khokhlakov almost ran in and declared that she was expecting him.

'I was expecting you! Yes, I was, I was! Yet you must admit I had no reason to suppose that you'd come to see me, but I was expecting you! You may well marvel at my instinct, Mr Karamazov. I was absolutely convinced all the morning that you would come today.'

'It is, indeed, remarkable, madam,' said Mitya, sitting down awkwardly, 'but – er – I've come on a most important business, a business, madam, of the utmost importance to me, madam, to me alone and – er – I'm afraid I'm rather pressed for time. . . .'

'I know you've come on a most important business, and it's not a case of mere presentiment, not some half-hidden, retrograde desire for miracles (you've heard about Father Zossima, haven't you?). It's simply a case of a mathematical calculation: you couldn't help coming after all that has happened to Katerina. You couldn't, you couldn't! It's mathematically demonstrable!'

'The realism of actual life, madam, that's what it is! But let me explain, please.'

'Yes, sir, realism, indeed. I'm all for realism now. I've been taught a lesson so far as miracles are concerned. You've heard that Father Zossima is dead, haven't you?'

'No, madam, it's the first time I've heard of it,' Mitya sounded a little surprised. For a moment he thought of Alyosha.

'Last night and just imagine —'

'Madam,' Mitya interrupted, 'all I can imagine now is that I'm in an awful fix, and if you don't help me, everything will go to rack and ruin, and I first of all. Forgive the cliché, but I'm feeling so hot, I'm in a fever. . . .'

'I know, I know you're in a fever. You couldn't possibly be in any other state of mind, and whatever you may say, I know it all before-hand. I've long been thinking about your future, my dear Dmitry. I'm watching over it and studying it. . . . Oh, believe me, I'm an experienced doctor of the soul.'

'Madam, if you're an experienced doctor, then, for my part, I am an experienced patient,' said Mitya, making an effort to be polite, 'and I can't help feeling that if you are watching over my future like that, you will save it from being ruined. But, please, let me first explain the plan with which I've ventured to come to you and – er – what exactly I expect from you. I've come, madam —'

'Don't bother to explain. It's of minor importance. As for helping you, you're not the first I have helped. You've probably heard of my cousin Mrs Belmessov. Her husband was ruined, had gone to rack and ruin, as you so characteristically put it. Well, what do you think I did? I advised him to take up horse-breeding, and now he's simply flourishing. Do you know anything about horse-breeding?'

'Nothing at all, madam. Oh, madam, nothing at all,' cried Mitya with nervous impatience, even jumping up from his seat. 'I only im-plore you, madam, to listen to me, to grant me just two minutes of uninterrupted speech, so that I could first explain everything to you, the whole project with which I've come. Besides, I'm pressed for time and I'm in a terrible hurry,' Mitya exclaimed hysterically, feeling that she would start talking again and hoping to shout her down. 'I've come in despair – in the throes of despair – to beg you to lend me money, three thousand roubles, on good security, on the best possible security! Only, please, let me explain —'

'You can do it all afterwards, afterwards,' Mrs Khokhlakov waved her hands at him in her turn. 'And, anyway, I know everything you're going to tell me already. I've told you that, haven't I? You're asking for a loan, you must have three thousand roubles, but I'll give you more, immeasurably more: I will save you, my dear Dmitry. But first you must do as I tell you!'

Mitya leapt to his feet again.

'Madam, thank you, thank you. You are so kind!' he cried with great feeling. 'Good God, you have saved me. You have saved a man, madam, from a violent death, from a bullet. . . . My eternal gratitude —'

'I'll give you much more, infinitely more than three thousand!' cried Mrs Khokhlakov, gazing at Mitya's delight with a radiant smile.

'Infinitely? But I don't want so much. All I need is that fatal three thousand. And, for my part, I'm ready to guarantee you that sum with infinite gratitude and I propose a plan which —'

'Enough, it's as good as done.' Mrs Khokhlakov silenced him with the look of virtuous triumph of a benefactress. 'I've promised to save you and I will save you. I'll save you as I did Belmessov. What's your opinion of gold-mines, my dear Dmitry?'

'Gold-mines, madam? I've never thought anything about them.'

'Ah, but I've thought of them for you! I've been thinking and thinking of them. I've been watching you for the last month with that idea in my mind. I've looked at you a hundred times as you walked past and I've kept repeating to myself: here's an energetic man who ought to leave for the gold-mines. I've even studied the way you walked and I've come to the conclusion that you're the sort of man who will find many gold-mines.'

'From the way I walked, madam?' Mitya smiled.

'Why not? I can tell from that, too. Do you really deny that it's possible to tell a man's character from the way he walks? Natural sciences corroborate it. Oh, I'm now a realist, my dear Dmitry. From today, after all that affair in the monastery, which has upset me so much, I'm a complete realist and I want to take up practical work. I'm cured. Enough! as Turgenev has said.'

'But, madam, the three thousand which you so generously promised to lend me —'

'You'll get it, my dear Dmitry,' Mrs Khokhlakov broke in at once.
'The three thousand are as good as in your pocket, and not three
thousand, either, but three million, and within a short time, too! I'll
tell you what you have to do: you'll find gold-mines, make millions,
come back, become a public figure, put us on our mettle, too, and
make us work for the general good. We're not going to leave everything to the Jews, are we? You'll be putting up public buildings and
starting all sorts of enterprises. You'll help the poor, and they'll bless
you. This is the age of railways, sir. You'll become famous and indispensable to the Ministry of Finance, which is so badly off at present.
The depreciation of the paper rouble keeps me awake at night, my
dear Dmitry. People know so little of that side of me. . . .'

'Madam, madam,' Mitya interrupted again with a sort of uneasy
foreboding, 'I shall, indeed, perhaps, follow your advice, your wise
advice, ma'am, and – shall perhaps set off to – to those gold-mines
and – and I'll come again to discuss it with you – many times, but
now – the three thousand you so generously – Oh, they would untie
my hands, and if you could let me have it today – I mean, you see, I
haven't a minute – not a minute – to spare now —'

'Enough, sir, enough!' Mrs Khokhlakov interrupted determinedly.
'What I want to know is – are you going to the gold-mines or not?
Have you quite made up your mind? Answer yes or no.'

'I'll go, madam, afterwards. . . . I'll go anywhere you like – but
now —'

'Wait!' cried Mrs Khokhlakov and, jumping up from her seat,
rushed to her magnificent bureau with numerous drawers and began
opening and pulling out one drawer after another, looking for something in desperate haste.

'The three thousand!' Mitya thought with bated breath. 'And she's
going to give it me at once, without any papers, without formalities –
oh, that's doing things in a gentlemanly way! A splendid woman! If
only she didn't talk so much!'

'Here it is!' cried Mrs Khokhlakov joyfully, returning to Mitya.
'That's what I was looking for!'

It was a tiny silver icon on a cord, one of those one sometimes
wears near the skin with a cross.

'This is from Kiev, my dear Dmitry,' she went on reverently, 'from the relics of the Holy Martyr Varvara. Allow me to put it on your neck myself and with it give you my blessing for your new life and your new exploits.'

And she actually put the icon on his neck and began to set it right. Feeling greatly embarrassed, Mitya bent down and began helping her, getting it at last under his tie and the collar of his shirt on to his chest.

'Now you can set off!' said Mrs Khokhlakov, resuming her seat in triumph.

'Madam, I'm touched and – and I don't know how to thank you for – for such kind feelings, but – if only you knew how precious time is to me now! The sum of money which I'm waiting for so anxiously from – er – your generosity – oh, madam, if you are so kind, so touchingly generous to me,' Mitya exclaimed with sudden inspiration, 'then let me reveal to you – though, of course, you've known it for a long time – that I'm in love with someone here. . . . I've been false to Katya – Miss Verkhovtsev I should have said. . . . Oh, I've behaved inhumanly and dishonourably to her, but here I fell in love with another – a woman, ma'am, whom you perhaps despise, for you know everything already, but whom I cannot give up on any account, and that's why the three thousand —'

'Leave everything, sir!' Mrs Khokhlakov interrupted in a most emphatic tone. 'Leave everything, and especially women. Your goal is the gold-mines, and you don't want to take women there. Afterwards, when you come back rich and famous, you'll find the girl of your heart in the highest society. She'll be a modern girl, educated and without prejudices of any kind. By that time the woman question, which is only in its initial stages now, will have come to fruition and the new woman will have appeared.'

'Madam, that's not the point, that's not the point,' Mitya clasped his hands imploringly.

'It is the point, sir. It's just what you need, what you're longing for, without realizing it yourself. I'm not at all against the present woman question, sir. The development of women and even their political emancipation in the nearest future – that's my ideal. I have a daughter myself, my dear Dmitry. People don't know that side of me. I wrote to the author Shchedrin in that connexion. This writer has taught me so much, so much about the vocation of woman, that I sent him an anonymous letter last year of two lines: 'I kiss and embrace you, my dear author, for the modern woman, carry on!' And I signed myself: 'A mother'. I thought of signing myself, 'A contemporary mother', and hesitated, but finally wrote simply 'A mother'. There's more beauty in that, my dear Dmitry, and, besides, the word 'contemporary' would have reminded him of *The Contemporary*, a bitter reminder for him in view of our present-day censorship. Good heavens, what's the matter with you?'

'Madam,' cried Mitya, jumping up at last and clasping his hands in helpless entreaty before her, 'you'll make me cry if you delay any longer what you've so generously —'

'Do, do cry, sir! That's a fine feeling – you've such a long journey before you! Tears will relieve you, and afterwards you'll come back and rejoice. You'll come tearing along to me on purpose from Siberia to share your joy with me. . . .'

'But do let me put in a word, too,' Mitya roared suddenly. 'For the last time, I beseech you, tell me, can I have the sum you promised me today? If not, then when am I to come for it?'

'What sum, sir?'

'The three thousand you promised me so – so generously.'

'Three thousand? Roubles? Oh, no, I haven't got three thousand roubles,' Mrs Khokhlakov said with a kind of serene astonishment.

Mitya was stupefied.

'But, just now – you said – why, you – you said that it was as good as in my pocket —'

'Oh, no, you misunderstood me, my dear Dmitry. If that's what you mean, you misunderstood me. I was talking about the goldmines. It's true I promised you more, infinitely more than three thousand, I remember it now. But I had in mind the gold-mines.'

'But the money? The three thousand?' Mitya cried stupidly.

'Oh, well, if you meant money, I haven't got any. I've no money at all, my dear Dmitry. I'm fighting with my steward about it, and I borrowed five hundred roubles from Miusov myself the other day. No, sir, I have no money. And, to be quite frank with you, my dear Dmitry, if I had, I wouldn't give it to you. In the first place I never lend money to anyone. To lend money to people means quarrelling with them. But I wouldn't give it to you particularly. I wouldn't give it to you because I like you. I wouldn't give it to you because I want to save you, because all you want is the gold-mines, the gold-mines, the gold-mines! . . .'

'Oh, to blazes with you!' Mitya suddenly bellowed, bringing his fist down on the table with all his might.

'Help!' cried Mrs Khokhlakov in alarm, rushing to the other end of the drawing-room.

Mitya spat and walked rapidly out of the room, out of the house, into the street, into the darkness. He walked along like a madman, striking his breast on the same spot where he had struck himself two days before during his last meeting with Alyosha in the dark, on the highway. What those blows on his breast *on that spot* meant and what he wanted to express by it, that, for the time being, was a secret which no one in the world knew and which he had not revealed even to Alyosha. But that secret meant more to him than disgrace. It meant ruin and suicide. So he had already resolved, if he did not get hold of the three thousand to pay his debt to Katerina, and in that way remove from his breast, *from that spot on his breast*, the disgrace he carried upon it and that weighed so heavily on his conscience. All this will be fully explained to the reader afterwards, but now, after his last hope had vanished, this man, who was physically so strong, suddenly burst into tears like a little child after walking a few steps from Mrs Khokhlakov's house. He walked along and, completely unaware of what he was doing, wiped away his tears with his fist. In this way he reached the square and suddenly felt that he had stumbled upon somebody. He heard the whining wail of some old woman whom he had nearly knocked down.

'Lord, you nearly killed me! Why don't you look where you're going, you hooligan?'

'Is that you?' cried Mitya, recognizing the old woman in the dark.

It was the old maidservant who waited on Kuzma Samsonov and whom Mitya had noticed only too well the day before.

'And who may you be, sir?' the old woman said in quite a different tone of voice. 'I'm afraid I don't know you in the dark.'

'You live at Samsonov's, don't you? You're the servant there?'

'Yes, sir, I've just run out to Prokhorovich's. But why don't I seem to remember you?'

'Tell me, my good woman, is Miss Svetlov at your house now?'

said Mitya beside himself with suspense. 'I saw her as far as your place some time ago.'

'She's been there, sir. She came, stayed a little while and went away again.'

'What? Went away?' cried Mitya. 'When did she go?'

'Why, sir, she went away at once. Only stayed a minute. Told Mr Samsonov some story which made him laugh and ran away.'

'You're lying, damn you!' roared Mitya.

'Help!' shouted the old woman, but Mitya had vanished.

He ran as fast as he could to Mrs Morozov's house. It was only a quarter of an hour since Grushenka had gone to Mokroye. Fenya was sitting with her grandmother, the cook, in the kitchen when the 'captain' suddenly ran in. Seeing him, Fenya screamed at the top of her voice.

'You're screaming?' Mitya roared. 'Where is she?' But without giving Fenya, who was speechless with terror, time to answer, he suddenly fell down at her feet.

'Fenya, for Christ our Lord's sake, tell me where she is!'

'I don't know anything, sir, I don't know anything. Kill me, if you like, but I don't know anything!' Fenya protested violently. 'You went out with her yourself this afternoon. . . .'

'She came back!'

'She didn't, sir! I swear, she didn't!'

'You're lying,' cried Mitya. 'I can guess from the way you're frightened where she is!'

He rushed out. The terrified Fenya was glad to have got off so cheaply, for she realized very well that if he had not been in such a hurry, she would perhaps have paid dearly for lying to him. But, as he ran out, he surprised Fenya and old Matryona by an unexpected action: a brass mortar stood on the table with a brass pestle in it, a small brass pestle, only seven inches long. As he was running out, having already opened the door with one hand, Mitya suddenly snatched the pestle out of the mortar with the other and shoved it in his side-pocket. Then he was gone.

'Good Lord,' cried Fenya, clasping her hands, 'he's going to murder someone!'

4

In the Dark

WHERE did he run off to? There was only one place he could run
to: 'Where could she be except at Father's? She must have rushed
straight to him from Samsonov's. Now the whole thing is clear. The
whole intrigue, the whole deception is now obvious. . . .' All this
went whirling through his mind. He did not run to Maria Kondratyevna's yard. 'I mustn't go there. No, I mustn't do that. I mustn't
raise any alarm. They will at once let them know and betray me.
Maria Kondratyevna is obviously in the plot. Smerdyakov, too.
They've all been bribed!' He formed a different plan of action: he
crossed the lane and ran a long way round his father's house, ran up
Dmitrovskaya street, then over the little bridge, and got straight to
the deserted lane at the back of the houses. The lane was empty and
uninhabited, with the wattle fence of a kitchen garden on one side
and the strong high fence round his father's garden on the other.
There he chose a place, apparently the same place, according to the
story he knew so well, where Lizaveta Smerdyashchaya had once
climbed over the fence. 'If she could climb over it,' it flashed through
his mind, goodness only knows why, 'I can do it, too.' And, to be
sure, he jumped up and at once managed to catch hold of the top of
the fence, then he pulled himself up vigorously, climbed straight up
and sat astride it. The bath-house stood close to the fence, but he
could see the lighted windows of the house from where he was, too.
'I thought so! There's a light in the old man's bedroom. She's there!'
And he jumped down from the fence into the garden. Though he
knew that Grigory was ill and that Smerdyakov was perhaps also ill,
and that there was no one to hear him, he instinctively held his breath,
stood stock-still and began to listen. But there was dead silence
everywhere, and, as though on purpose, absolute stillness, not the
slightest breath of wind.

    'And naught but the silence whispers,' the line of poetry for some
reason flashed through his head. 'I only hope no one heard me jump
over the fence. I don't think anyone did.' He stood still for a minute,
then walked softly over the grass across the garden, skirting the

bushes and trees. He walked a long time, muffling his steps and listening intently to every step he took. It took him five minutes to reach the lighted window. He remembered that there were a number of large, thick, and high elder and guelder-rose bushes under the window. The back door from the house into the garden on the left-hand side was shut. He had made a point of looking at it carefully as he passed. At last he reached the bushes and hid behind them. He held his breath. 'I must wait now,' he thought. 'If they heard my footsteps and are listening now, I must give them time to reassure themselves. Must take care not to cough or sneeze. . . .'

He waited two minutes, but his heart was pounding violently and at moments he was almost choking. 'No, my heart won't stop pounding,' he thought. 'I can wait no longer.' He was standing behind a bush in the shadow; the front part of the bush was lighted up from the window. 'A guelder-rose, how red the hips are!' he whispered, not knowing why. Softly and noiselessly, step by step, he went up to the window and raised himself on tiptoe. The whole of his father's bedroom lay spread out before his eyes. It was not a large room, and was divided across by a red screen, 'Chinese', as Karamazov used to call it. 'Chinese,' it flashed through Mitya's head, 'and behind the screen is Grushenka.' He began scrutinizing his father, who was wearing his new striped silk dressing-gown, which Mitya had never seen, with a silk cord and tassels round the waist. A clean, expensive shirt of fine linen with gold studs peeped out from under the collar of the dressing-gown. His father's head was swathed in the same red bandage which Alyosha had seen. 'Dressed himself up,' thought Mitya. His father was standing near the window, apparently lost in thought. Suddenly he jerked up his head, listened a moment, and hearing nothing, went up to the table, poured himself out half a glass of brandy from a decanter and drank it. Then he took a deep breath, stood still again for a moment, walked up absently to the looking-glass on the wall between the two windows, raised the red bandage on his forehead a little with his right hand and began to examine his bruises and scars, which were still there. 'He's alone,' thought Mitya. 'In all probability alone.' His father moved away from the looking-glass, turned suddenly to the window and looked out. Mitya at once jumped back into the shadow.

'She's probably behind the screen, perhaps she's already asleep,' he thought, with a pang in his heart. His father moved away from the window. 'He was looking for her out of the window. So she isn't there. Why should he be staring into the dark? Must be eaten up with impatience. . . .' Mitya immediately stepped forward and began looking in at the window again. The old man was sitting at the table, looking quite obviously heartbroken. At last he put his elbow on the table and laid his right hand against his cheek. Mitya watched him eagerly.

'He's alone, alone!' he repeated again. 'If she'd been there, he'd look different.' Strange as it may seem, his heart was suddenly filled with an illogical, queer vexation that she was not there. 'Not because she is not there,' Mitya said to himself at once, realizing the true reason for his feeling, 'but because I can't find out for certain whether she is there or not.' Mitya remembered afterwards that at that moment his mind was extraordinarily clear and that he grasped everything to the smallest detail, seizing on every point. But a feeling of anguish, the anguish of uncertainty and indecision, was growing in his heart with incredible rapidity. 'Is she there or isn't she?' His heart boiled over with anger and, suddenly, he made up his mind, put out his hand and quietly knocked on the window frame. He gave the signal the old man had agreed on with Smerdyakov: twice slowly and then three times more quickly, knock-knock-knock – the signal that meant, 'Grushenka is here.' The old man gave a start, jerked up his head, jumped up quickly and rushed to the window. Mitya jumped back into the shadow. His father opened the window and thrust out his head.

'Is that you, Grushenka?' he said in a sort of trembling half-whisper. 'Where are you, darling? Where are you, my angel?' He was terribly excited and gasping for breath.

'He's alone!' Mitya decided.

'Where are you?' the old man cried again and thrust out his head farther, thrust it out to the shoulders, gazing in all directions, to the right and left. 'Come here! I've got a present for you. Come, I'll show you!'

'He means the envelope with the three thousand,' it flashed through Mitya's mind.

'But where are you! Not at the door? I'll open at once!'

And the old man almost climbed out of the window, looking to the right, where there was the door into the garden, and trying to catch sight of her in the darkness. A second later he would most certainly have run to open the door, without waiting for Grushenka's reply. Mitya was looking on from the side without stirring. The whole of the old man's profile, which he loathed so much, his pendulous Adam's apple, his hooked nose, his lips, twisted in a lewd smile of expectation, were all brightly lighted up by the slanting light of the lamp falling on the left from the room. A terrible, furious rage surged up in Mitya's heart: 'There he is, my rival, my torturer, the torturer of my life!' It was the onrush of that sudden, revengeful and furious anger, of which, as though foreseeing it, he had spoken to Alyosha in the summer-house four days before, when in answer to Alyosha's question, 'How can you say that you'll kill your father?' he had replied, 'I don't know, I don't know, perhaps I will kill him and perhaps I won't. I'm afraid he might become loathsome to me suddenly *with that face of his at that moment*. I hate his Adam's apple, his nose, his eyes, his shameless grin. I feel a physical aversion. That's what I'm afraid of. I may not be able to control myself. . . .'

His physical aversion was becoming unbearably strong. Mitya was beside himself and he suddenly pulled the brass pestle out of his pocket. . . .

*

'God,' as Mitya himself used to say afterwards, 'was watching over me then': just at that time Grigory woke up in his bed of sickness. In the evening he had undergone the treatment Smerdyakov had described to Ivan, that is to say, with the help of his wife he had rubbed himself all over with the very strong, secret infusion and had drunk what was left of it, while his wife whispered 'a certain prayer' over him, and had gone to sleep. Marfa, too, had drunk some of it, and, as an abstainer, slept like a log beside her husband. But quite unexpectedly Grigory woke up in the night, lay awake thinking for a moment and, though he immediately felt a sharp pain in the small of his back, sat up in bed. Then, again thinking about something, he got up and dressed quickly. Perhaps he was conscience-stricken at being asleep while the house was unguarded 'at such a dangerous time'. Smerdyakov, in a state of collapse as a result of his epileptic fit, lay motionless in the other room. Marfa did not stir: 'The old woman has had a drop too much,' thought Grigory, glancing at her, and, groaning, he went out on the front steps. No doubt, he only meant to have a look round from the top of the steps, for he was quite unable to walk, the pain in the small of his back and his right leg was unbearable. But he suddenly remembered that he had forgotten to lock the gate into the garden that evening. He was a most meticulous and punctilious man and observed religiously the once-established order and the habits of years. Limping and writhing with pain, he went down the steps and made for the garden. He was right: the gate was wide open. Mechanically he stepped into the garden: perhaps he fancied something or heard some faint noise, but, glancing to the left, he saw the open window of his master's bedroom, with no one looking out of it. 'Why is it open?' thought Grigory. 'It's not summer now.' And, suddenly, just at that very moment he caught a glimpse of something unusual in front of him in the garden. About forty paces in front of him a man seemed to have run past in the darkness. Someone's shadow was moving away very rapidly. 'Good Lord!' said Grigory, and, forgetting the pain in his back, rushed frantically to intercept the running man. He took a short-cut, the garden evidently being more familiar to him than to the stranger, who ran behind the bath-house and then rushed to the fence. Grigory followed without losing sight of him, running as fast as he could. He reached the fence at the very moment when the fleeing man was climbing over it. Grigory, beside himself, uttered a loud cry, rushed at the man and clutched at his leg with both hands.

Yes, his foreboding had not deceived him: he recognized the man, it was he, the 'monster', the 'parricide'!

'Parricide!' the old man shouted at the top of his voice, but that was all he had time to say; he suddenly collapsed on the ground, as though struck by lightning. Mitya jumped down into the garden again and bent over the prostrate figure of Grigory. In Mitya's hands was the brass pestle and he threw it mechanically into the grass. The pestle fell within two feet of Grigory, not in the grass, but on the path, in a most conspicuous place. He examined the figure lying before him for a few seconds. The old man's head was covered with blood; Mitya put out his hand and began feeling it. He remembered afterwards that he had wanted badly 'to find out for certain' whether he had fractured the old man's skull or merely 'stunned' him with the pestle. But the blood was flowing, flowing terribly, and at once poured over Mitya's fingers in a hot stream. He remembered pulling his clean white handkerchief, with which he had provided himself for his visit to Mrs Khokhlakov, out of his pocket, and putting it to the old man's head, trying stupidly to wipe the blood from the old man's face and forehead. But the handkerchief, too, became soaked in blood at once. 'Good heavens, what am I doing?' Mitya suddenly recollected himself. 'If I have fractured his skull, how can I find out now? And, anyway, what does it matter now?' he added suddenly, hopelessly. 'If I've killed him, I've killed him. . . . Bad luck, old man, you'd better stay here!' he said aloud, and suddenly rushing back to the fence, jumped over it into the lane and started running. The blood-soaked handkerchief was clenched in his right hand and, as he ran, he shoved it into the back pocket of his coat. He ran as fast as his legs would carry him, and several of the few passers-by who had met him in the dark, in the streets of the town, remembered afterwards that they had met a furiously running man that night. He was rushing back to Mrs Morozov's house. A few hours earlier, Fenya, as soon as he had gone, had rushed to the head porter, Nazar Ivanovich, and implored him 'by the Lord Christ' not to let the captain in again either that day or the next. The caretaker agreed to do so, but unfortunately he happened to be summoned suddenly upstairs to his mistress and, meeting on the way there his nephew, a lad of twenty, who had only recently come from the country, told him to stay in the yard, but forgot to tell him about the captain. Running up to the gates, Mitya knocked. The lad recognized him at once; Mitya had often tipped him before. He at once opened the gate, let him in, and, smiling cheerfully, hastened to inform him that Grushenka was not at home.

'Where is she, Prokhor?' Mitya asked, stopping suddenly.

'She drove off two hours ago to Mokroye with Timofey, sir.'

'What for?' cried Mitya.

'I don't know, sir. Seems to have gone to see some officer. Someone sent for her, sir. They also sent horses to fetch her. . . .'

Mitya left him and ran, like a madman, to Fenya.

5

A Sudden Decision

FENYA was sitting in the kitchen with her grandmother. They were both about to go to bed. Relying on the caretaker's promise, they had not locked themselves in. Mitya rushed in, pounced on Fenya and caught her violently by the throat.

'Tell me at once where she is? Who is she with now at Mokroye?' he bawled, beside himself.

The two women screamed.

'I'll tell you, sir, I'll tell you everything, I won't hide anything,' Fenya, frightened to death, cried, the words escaping her in a rapid stream. 'She's gone to Mokroye to her officer.'

'What officer?' roared Mitya.

'To her former officer, the one she used to know five years ago, the one who jilted her and went away,' Fenya jabbered, talking as fast as before.

Dmitry withdrew the hands with which he was squeezing her throat. He stood before her, pale as death, without uttering a word, but it could be seen from his eyes that he realized it all, all, from the first word, and that the whole situation had become clear to him in a flash. Poor Fenya, of course, was at that moment hardly in a condition to observe whether he understood or not. She remained sitting on the trunk as she had been sitting when he ran into the room, trembling all over and holding her hands in front of her as though in an attempt to defend herself and she remained motionless in that position. She stared at him without moving, with frightened, wide-opened eyes. And to make things worse, both his hands were stained with blood. On the way, as he ran, he must have touched his face, so that there were red blood-stained patches on his forehead and his right cheek. Fenya was on the verge of hysterics and the old cook had jumped up from her seat and was gazing at Mitya like a mad woman, almost unconscious with fright. Mitya stood for a moment and then mechanically sank on to a chair beside Fenya.

He sat there not so much thinking things over, as frightened out of his wits, in a sort of stupor. But everything was as clear as daylight: that officer – he knew all about him, he knew about him from Grushenka herself, he knew that she had had a letter from him a month before. So that this affair had been carried on behind his back in secret for a month, for a whole month, up to the very arrival of the new man, and he had never even thought of him! But how on earth could he not have thought of him? Why was it that he had forgotten about that officer at the time, forgotten as soon as he had heard of him? That was the question that rose before him like some monstrous spectre. And he did, indeed, contemplate that spectre in terror, frozen with terror.

But suddenly he began talking to Fenya softly and gently, like a gentle and affectionate child, forgetting that a moment before he had frightened her, hurt her, and worried her to death. He began questioning Fenya with a precision which was extraordinarily remarkable in his situation. And Fenya, too, though she stared wildly at his blood-stained hands, began answering his questions with extraordinary readiness and promptitude, as though in a hurry to tell him 'the whole truth and nothing but the truth'. Little by little and even as though she were really glad of it, she began to give an account of every detail, without wishing to torment him, but as though doing her very best with all her heart to do him a favour. She described to him all the events of that day in every detail, the visit of Rakitin and Alyosha, and how she, Fenya, had been keeping watch, and how her mistress had left and what she had shouted out of the window to Alyosha as her parting words to him, Mitya, that 'he should always remember that she had loved him for one little hour'. Having heard her last message, Mitya suddenly smiled and his pale cheeks flushed. At that very moment Fenya said to him, now not a bit afraid of showing her curiosity.

'What's the matter with your hands, sir? They're all covered with blood!'

'Yes,' Mitya replied mechanically, looking absent-mindedly at his hands and at once forgetting all about them and about Fenya's question. He again sank into silence. Twenty minutes had passed since he had run in. His recent feeling of fear was gone, but quite a new and inflexible resolution was evidently taking possession of him. He suddenly got up and smiled wistfully.

'What has happened to you, sir?' said Fenya, pointing to his hands again. She said it pityingly, as though she were now the closest human being to him in his grief.

Mitya looked at his hands again.

'It's blood, Fenya,' he said, looking at her with a strange expression. 'It's human blood and, Lord, why did it have to be shed? But – Fenya – there's a fence not far from here' (he looked at her as though setting her a riddle), 'a very high fence and terrible to look at, but – tomorrow at dawn when "the sun ariseth", dear old Mitya will jump over that fence. . . . You don't understand, Fenya, what fence? Well, never mind – it doesn't matter – you'll hear of it tomorrow and you'll understand everything – but now farewell! I won't stand in the way, I'll stand aside – I shall know how to stand aside. Live, my joy – you loved me for a little hour, so remember your darling Mitya Karamazov for ever! She always used to call me darling Mitya, remember?'

And with those words he suddenly went out of the kitchen. And Fenya was almost more frightened of the way he rushed out than she had been when he ran in and attacked her.

Exactly ten minutes later, Mitya went in to Peter Perkhotin, the young civil servant with whom he had pawned his pistols. It was half-past eight, and Perkhotin, having had his tea, had just put on his coat to go to the 'Metropolis' for a game of billiards. Mitya caught him coming out. Perkhotin, seeing him and his blood-stained face, cried in suprise:

'Good Lord, what's the matter?'

'Well,' Mitya said rapidly, 'I've come for my pistols and brought you the money. Thanks very much. I'm in a hurry. Please let me have them at once.'

Perkhotin grew more and more surprised: he caught sight of a thick wad of notes in Mitya's hand and, what was so strange, Mitya had walked in holding the money as no one walks in and carries money: he held all the notes in his right hand, as though for all to see, holding them straight before him in his outstretched hand. The civil servant's boy servant, who had met Mitya in the hall, said afterwards that he had gone into the hall holding the money in his hand, so that he must have carried it in his right hand like that in the street. They were all rainbow-coloured one-hundred-rouble notes, and he held them between his blood-stained fingers. In reply to the questions put to him by people interested in the affair, Perkhotin declared that it was difficult to tell at a glance how much money there was, two thousand, three thousand, perhaps, but it was a big bundle, 'a thick one'. Dmitry himself, as he also testified afterwards, was 'not quite himself, somehow, not drunk, but, as it were, in a state of exaltation, very absent-minded but at the same time also rapt in thought as though he were trying to solve some problem but could not. He was in a great hurry, replied abruptly, very strangely, and at moments did not seem to be upset at all but rather cheerful.'

'But what's the matter with you? What have you been up to just now?' cried Perkhotin again, looking wildly at his visitor. 'How did you manage to get so covered with blood? Have you had a fall? Look at yourself!'

He seized him by the elbow and led him to the looking-glass. Seeing his face covered with blood, Mitya started and knit his brows angrily.

'Damnation! That's the limit!' he muttered angrily, quickly changing the notes from his right hand to the left and agitatedly pulling the handkerchief out of his pocket.

But the handkerchief was also soaked in blood (he had used it to wipe Grigory's head and face): there was hardly a white spot on it, and it had not only begun to dry, but, somehow, hardened into a crumpled ball and could not be pulled open. Mitya flung it angrily on the floor.

'Damn it, have you got a rag of some sort to wipe it off?'

'So you're only stained, not wounded? Well, in that case you'd better have a wash,' said Perkhotin. 'Here's the wash-stand. I'll get you some water.'

'The wash-stand? That's good – but where am I to put this?' he asked in strange perplexity, indicating his bundle of hundred-rouble notes and looking questioningly at him, as though expecting him to decide where he should put his own money.

'Put it in your pocket or on the table here. They won't be lost.'

'In my pocket? Yes, in my pocket. That's good. . . . No,' he cried, as though recovering his senses, 'that's all nonsense! You see, we'd better settle our business first. Give me my pistols and here's your money – because I simply must have them and I – I haven't a minute to spare, not a minute.'

And taking a hundred-rouble note from the top of the bundle, he held it out to the civil servant.

'But I'm afraid I have no change,' Perkhotin observed. 'Haven't you got anything smaller?'

'No,' said Mitya, glancing at the bundle again and, as though uncertain of his own words, feeling two or three notes between his fingers. 'No, they're all the same,' he added, again looking questioningly at Perkhotin.

'But how have you got so rich all of a sudden?' Perkhotin asked. 'Wait a moment, I'll send my boy to Plotnikov. He closes his shop late. He may be able to change it. Here, Misha!' he called into the passage.

'To Plotnikov's shop – wonderful!' cried Mitya, too, as though a new idea dawned on him. 'Misha,' he turned to the boy as he came in, 'look here, run to Plotnikov and tell him that Dmitry Karamazov sends his compliments and will be at his shop presently. And listen: let him get ready, say, about three dozen bottles of champagne before I come, and have them packed as he did when I went to Mokroye. I took four dozen with me then,' he suddenly addressed Perkhotin. 'They know all about it. Don't you worry, Misha,' he turned to the boy again. 'And listen, let them put in cheese, Strasbourg pies, smoked whitefish, ham, caviare, and everything, everything they've got, up to a hundred roubles or a hundred and twenty as before. . . . And listen, don't let them forget fruits and sweets, bonbons, pears, two or three or four water-melons – no, no, one water-melon is enough, and chocolate, mint-drops, fruit-drops, toffee – in short, everything he packed for me when I went to Mokroye before, three hundred roubles' worth with the champagne. . . . Well, tell him to do the same now. And remember, Misha, if your name is Misha – his name is Misha, isn't it?' he turned to Perkhotin again.

'Wait a moment,' interrupted Perkhotin, listening and watching him uneasily, 'you'd better go yourself and tell him. He's sure to get it all wrong.'

'He will, I can see he will! Dear me, Misha, and I was going to kiss you for carrying out my errand. If you get it all right, I'll give you ten roubles. Off with you now and hurry, hurry! Champagne's the main thing. Let them get it out of the cellar, and – and brandy, too, and red and white wine, and all that, as before. They know what I had before.'

'But, look here,' Perkhotin interrupted, losing his patience, 'I'd rather he went now to change the note and told them not to close, and then you'll go and tell them yourself. Give me your note. Off with you, Misha, and be quick about it!'

It seemed that Perkhotin hurried Misha off because he stood staring at the blood-stained face and hands of the visitor, with the bundle of notes clasped between his trembling fingers, open-mouthed with fear and surprise and apparently understanding little of what Mitya was telling him to do.

'Well, now come and have a wash,' Perkhotin said sternly. 'Put the money on the table or shove it in your pocket. That's it. Now, come along. And do take off your coat!'

And he began helping him off with his coat.

'Look,' he cried again, 'your coat is covered with blood, too!'

'It's – it's not the coat. It's only a little here on the sleeve. And that's only where my handkerchief was. Soaked through the pocket. You see, I sat down on the handkerchief at Fenya's and the blood's soaked through,' Mitya at once explained to Perkhotin with quite astonishing trustfulness.

Perkhotin listened, frowning.

'What on earth have you been up to? Had a fight with someone, I suppose,' he muttered.

They began to wash. Perkhotin held the jug and kept pouring the water. Mitya was in a hurry and did not soap his hands properly. (His hands were trembling, as Perkhotin remembered afterwards.) Perkhotin at once told him to put more soap on and rub them harder. He seemed to take command of Mitya more and more as time passed. It may be observed, incidentally, that the young man was not easily frightened.

'Look, you haven't cleaned under your nails. Well, now rub your face – here on your temples and by the ear. You're not going in that shirt, are you? Where are you going? Look, all the cuff of your right sleeve is covered with blood.'

'So it is,' observed Mitya, examining the cuff of his shirt.

'You'd better change your shirt then.'

'I haven't time. You see,' Mitya went on with the same trustful air, drying his face and hands on the towel and putting on his coat, 'I'll turn the cuff up here and it won't show under the coat. . . . See?'

'Tell me now where did it all happen? Have you had a fight with someone? Not at the pub again, as before? It wasn't the captain again? You haven't been beating and dragging him along in the street again, have you?' Perkhotin reminded him reproachfully. 'What other person have you been beating or – killing perhaps?'

'Nonsense!' said Mitya.

'What do you mean – nonsense?'

'Never mind,' said Mitya and suddenly laughed. 'I just ran over an old woman in the square.'

'Ran over? An old woman?'

'An old man!' cried Mitya, looking Perkhotin straight in the face, laughing and shouting at him as though he were deaf.

'Damn it all, who was it? An old man or an old woman? You haven't killed anyone, have you?'

'We made it up. Had a fight and made it up. Somewhere. Parted the best of friends. A fool – he's forgiven me – I'm sure he's forgiven me now. If he'd got up, he wouldn't have forgiven me,' Mitya suddenly winked at him. 'Only damn him, I say, you know, damn him. No more of him! I don't want to talk about it just now!' Mitya snapped determinedly.

'What I mean is that you really oughtn't to pick quarrels with every Tom, Dick, and Harry, as – as you did that time with that captain. You've had a fight and now you're off on a spree – that's the kind of man you are! Three dozen bottles of champagne – where are you going to take it all?'

'Bravo! Now let me have my pistols. Honestly, I have no time. I'd have liked to have a chat with you, old man, but I can't spare the time. And there's no need for it, it's too late for talking. But where's the money? Where have I put it?' he cried and began rummaging in his pockets.

'You put it on the table yourself. There it is. Have you forgotten? Money is just dirt or water to you, it seems. Here are your pistols. It's funny, though. At six o'clock you pawned them for ten roubles and now – look at you – you've got thousands! Two or three, I suppose?'

'Three, I expect,' laughed Mitya, stuffing the money into the side pocket of his trousers.

'You'll lose it like that. You don't own gold-mines, do you?'

'Gold-mines? Gold-mines?' Mitya shouted at the top of his voice, roaring with laughter. 'Would you like to go to the gold-mines, Perkhotin? I know a woman here who'll let you have three thousand at once if only you'll go. She let me have it – she's so fond of gold-mines. Do you know Mrs Khokhlakov?'

'I don't, but I've heard of her and seen her. Did she really give you three thousand? You mean, just let you have it?' Perkhotin asked, eyeing him sceptically.

'Well, you go to her, to this Mrs Khokhlakov, as soon as the sun rises tomorrow, the ever-young Phoebus arises, praising and glorifying God, and ask her whether she did let me have the three thousand or not. Go and ask her.'

'I don't know how well you know her, but if you are so positive about it, I suppose she must have given it to you. And you've grabbed the money and instead of going to Siberia, you're off to spend the lot. But where are you really off to now, eh?'

'Mokroye.'

'Mokroye? But it's so late!'

'Tom a rich man was, pardie, today a beggarman he!' said Mitya suddenly.

'A beggarman? With all those thousands?'

'I'm not talking of the thousands. To hell with the thousands! I'm talking about a woman's heart —

> Credulous is the heart of woman,
> Inconstant and full of vice.

I agree with Ulysses. That's what he said.'

'I don't understand you.'

'You don't think I'm drunk, do you?'

'Drunk? No, much worse.'

'I'm drunk in spirit, old man, drunk in spirit, but enough, enough. . . .'

'What are you doing? Loading the pistol?'

'Yes, I'm loading the pistol.'

And, indeed, Mitya opened the pistol-case, unfastened the powder horn, carefully sprinkled in some powder and rammed in the charge. Then he picked up a bullet and before inserting it, held it up with two fingers in front of the candle.

'What are you looking at the bullet for?' Perkhotin asked, watching him with uneasy curiosity.

'Oh, just a fancy. Now if you intended to blow your brains out with this bullet, would you have looked at it before loading the pistol?'

'Why look at it?'

'It will go into my brain, so it's interesting to see what it looks like. However, it's all a lot of nonsense, a moment's folly. Now that's done,' he added, putting in the bullet and ramming in some tow on top of it. 'My dear fellow, it's all nonsense! And if only you knew what nonsense! Please give me a little piece of paper now.'

'Here's some paper.'

'No, a clean, plain piece of writing paper. That's it. Thank you.'

And taking a pen from the table, Mitya quickly wrote two lines on the paper, folded it in four and put it in his waistcoat pocket. He put the pistols in the case, locked it with a key and picked it up in his hand. Then he looked at Perkhotin with a slow, pensive smile.

'Now let's go,' he said.

'Go where? No, wait a minute. You're not going to blow your brains out with that bullet, are you?' Perkhotin said uneasily.

'Forget the bullet! I want to live. I love life! You bet I do. I love golden-curled Phoebus and his warm light. My dear chap, do you know how to keep away?'

'What do you mean – to keep away?'

'To make way. To make way for one you love and hate. So that the one you hate should be dear to you – to make way like that! To say to them, God be with you, go your way, pass by, while —'

'While you —?'

'Never mind, come on.'

'Upon my word,' said Perkhotin, looking at him steadily, 'I'll tell someone not to let you go there. What do you want to go to Mokroye now for?'

'There's a woman there, a woman, and that's enough for you, old fellow, and not another word!'

'Look here, you may be a savage, but I've always liked you somehow. That's why I can't help being worried.'

'Thanks, old man. You say I'm a savage. Savages, savages! That's what I'm always saying – savages! Ah, and here's Misha. I forgot all about him.'

Misha came running in with a bundle of small notes and reported that they were all 'rushing about' at Plotnikov's shop, fetching bottles, fish, and tea, and that everything would be ready presently. Mitya took a ten-rouble note and gave it to Perkhotin and then another ten-rouble note to Misha.

'Don't do that!' cried Perkhotin. 'You mustn't tip anyone in my house. Besides, it's merely spoiling them by setting a bad example. Put away your money. Put it here. Why waste it? It'll come in handy tomorrow when I expect you'll be coming to me for another loan of ten roubles. Why do you keep shoving the notes into your side-pocket? You're sure to lose them.'

'Look here, old man, why not come to Mokroye with me?'

'What do I want to go there for?'

'Listen, would you like me to open a bottle at once? Let's drink to life! I want a drink badly, and most of all to drink with you. I've never drunk with you, have I?'

'All right, I don't mind having a drink with you at the pub. Come on, I was going there myself.'

'I've no time for a pub. Let's have a drink at Plotnikov's shop, in the back room. Would you like me to ask you a riddle?'

'All right, ask away.'

Mitya took the piece of paper out of his waistcoat pocket, unfolded it and showed it to him. In a large, legible hand was written:

'I'm punishing myself for my whole life, my whole life I punish!'

'I really will tell someone,' Perkhotin said, after reading the paper. 'I'll go at once and report everything.'

'You won't have time, old man. Come, let's have a drink. Come on!'

Plotnikov's shop was only next door but one to Perkhotin's, at the corner of the street. It was the largest grocery shop in our town, belonging to rich merchants, and by no means a bad one. There was everything there you could get in a Petersburg shop, all sorts of groceries, wine 'bottled by Yeliseyev Bros', fruits, cigars, tea, sugar, coffee, etc. There were always three shop-assistants there and two errand-boys to deliver the customers' orders. Though our district had grown poorer, the landowners had left, and trade was slack, the grocery stores flourished as before and indeed more so every year: there was no dearth of purchasers for such goods. They were waiting for Mitya in the shop with impatience. They remembered very well how, three or four weeks ago, he had bought all at once in the same way all sorts of goods and wine to the value of several hundred roubles in cash (they would not let him have anything on credit, of course); they remembered that, in the same way as now, he had a whole bundle of rainbow-coloured notes in his hands, and threw them about regardless, without reflecting or caring to reflect what he wanted with so much wine, provisions, etc. They were saying in the town afterwards that, having dashed off with Grushenka to Mokroye at the time, he had squandered three thousand in one night and had returned to the town the following day without a penny in his pocket, 'as naked as on the day he was born'. He had picked up a whole gipsy camp (staying in our neighbourhood at the time) and in two days they relieved him of most of his money, while he was drunk, and drank most of his expensive wine. They used to tell, laughing at Mitya, that in Mokroye he made the boorish peasants drunk on champagne and the village women and girls sick from gorging themselves on his sweets and Strasbourg pies. They also laughed, especially in our public house (though not in his presence, of course, for it was a little dangerous to laugh at him to his face) at Mitya's frank avowal in public that all he had got out of Grushenka by this 'escapade' was that she let him 'kiss her foot' and that she would not let him do 'anything else'.

When Mitya and Perkhotin arrived at the shop, they found at the entrance a cart covered with a rug and drawn by three horses with bells on their harness, and Andrey the coachman, waiting for Mitya. In the shop they had almost finished packing one box of provisions and were only waiting for Mitya's arrival to nail it down and put it in the cart. Perkhotin looked surprised.

'How on earth did you get the cart in so short a time?' he asked Mitya.

'I met Andrey here as I was rushing to you and told him to drive straight to the shop. No use wasting time! Last time I drove there with Timofey, but Timofey has gone, drove off before me with a certain enchantress. Andrey, we're not going to be very late, are we?'

'They may get there an hour before us, sir, if that,' Andrey hastened to reply. 'An hour at most, sir. I got Timofey ready to start and I know which way he went. They're not as fast as we, they aren't sir, not by a long chalk. They won't get there an hour earlier, not them, sir!' Andrey, a lanky, gingery, middle-aged coachman, in a full-skirted, pleated coat and a long, peasant's overcoat over his left arm, declared warmly.

'I'll tip you fifty roubles if you're only one hour behind.'

'I can swear to that, sir. They won't be half an hour ahead of us, let alone an hour, sir.'

Though Mitya rushed about giving orders, he spoke and gave his orders strangely, somehow, disconnectedly and not consecutively. He started one thing and forgot to finish it. Perkhotin found himself obliged to come to his help.

'Four hundred roubles' worth, not less than four hundred roubles' worth, just like last time,' Mitya ordered. 'Four dozen bottles of champagne, not one bottle less.'

'What do you want with so much? What is it for? Wait a moment!' yelled Perkhotin. 'What's this box? What's in it? There isn't four hundred roubles' worth here, is there?'

The bustling shop-assistants at once explained to him in honeyed tones that there was only half a dozen bottles of champagne in the first box and 'the most indispensable articles', such as snacks, sweets, fruit-drops, etc. But 'the goods proper' would be packed and sent off, as on the last occasion, in a special cart and also with three horses and would be there in time 'at most an hour later than Mr Dmitry Karamazov'.

'Not an hour later,' Mitya insisted warmly, 'not an hour later, and don't forget to put in more fruit-drops and toffee, the girls there love it!'

'Toffee, all right! But what do you want four dozen bottles of champagne for? One's enough!' said Perkhotin, almost angrily.

He started bargaining, demanded the bill, and would not calm down. But all he managed to save was one hundred roubles. It was finally agreed that only three hundred roubles' worth of goods should be sent.

'Oh, to hell with you!' cried Perkhotin, as though changing his mind suddenly. 'What has it got to do with me? Throw away your money, if you got it for nothing!'

'Come this way, economical fellow, and don't be angry,' Mitya said, dragging him into the room at the back of the shop. 'They'll bring us a bottle here presently and we'll have a drink. Look here, old man, come along with me. You're such a nice fellow. I like fellows like you.'

Mitya sat down on a wicker chair in front of a tiny table, covered with a dirty table-napkin. Perkhotin found a place opposite, and the champagne appeared in no time. The gentlemen were asked if they would like oysters, 'first-class quality oysters, the last consignment in'.

'To hell with oysters,' Perkhotin snapped almost spitefully. 'I don't eat them and, anyway, we don't want anything.'

'No time for oysters,' observed Mitya, 'and I don't feel like them, anyhow. You know, old friend,' he said suddenly with feeling, 'I never have liked all this disorder.'

'Who does? Good Lord, three dozen bottles of champagne for peasants – it's enough to make anyone see red.'

'That's not what I meant. I'm talking of a higher order. There's no order in me, no higher order! But it's all finished and done with. No use crying over spilt milk. Too late, blast it! My whole life has been disorder and I must set it in order. A pun, eh?'

'You're raving, not punning.'

'Glory be to God on high,
Glory to God in me! —

that verse burst from my soul once – it's not a verse but a tear – I made it up myself, but – not when I dragged that captain by the beard.'

'Why bring him in all of a sudden?'

'Why do I bring him in? Oh, rot! Everything comes to an end, everything gets straightened out, you draw a line and the total is balanced!'

'I'm worried about those pistols of yours.'

'Pistols are rot, too! Drink and don't keep imagining things. I love life. I've loved life too much – that's what's so disgusting! Enough! Let's drink to life, old man, to life. I propose a toast to life! Why am I so satisfied with myself? I'm a rotter, but I'm satisfied with myself. And yet the thought that I am a rotter worries me, but I am satisfied with myself. I bless creation. I'm ready to bless God and his creation now, but – first I must destroy one stinking insect, to prevent it from crawling about and spoiling life for others. Let's drink to life, dear brother! What can be more precious than life? Nothing, nothing! To life and to a queen of queens!'

'All right, let's drink to life and to your queen, too, I suppose.'

They drank a glass each. Though Mitya was both highly excited and restless, he was melancholy, too, somehow. Just as though some overmastering, heavy anxiety preyed on his mind.

'Misha – is that your Misha who came in? Misha, my dear boy, come here, drink this glass to Phoebus, the golden-haired, of tomorrow morning. . . .'

'Why are you giving it him?' cried Perkhotin irritably.

'Please, let me. Please, I'd like to.'

'Oh Lord!'

Misha drank the glass, bowed and ran off.

'He'll remember it long afterwards,' observed Mitya. 'I love a woman, a woman! What is woman? The queen of the earth! I feel sad, I feel sad, old man. Remember Hamlet? "Alas, poor Yorick, I knew him, Horatio!" Perhaps Yorick that's me. Yes, I'm Yorick now, and a skull afterwards.'

Perkhotin listened in silence. Mitya, too, was silent.

'What kind of a dog is it you've got there?' he suddenly asked a shop-assistant absent-mindedly, noticing a pretty little lap-dog with dark eyes in a corner of the room.

'It's the mistress's lap-dog,' replied the shop-assistant. 'She brought it here a short while ago and forgot it. I'll have to take it back to her.'

'I saw one like that – in the regiment,' Mitya said thoughtfully. 'Only that one had its hind leg broken. . . . By the way, old man,' he turned to Perkhotin, 'I wanted to ask you something. Have you ever stolen anything in your life?'

'What sort of a question is this?'

'Oh, I didn't mean anything. From somebody's pocket, you see. Something that wasn't yours. I'm not talking of government money. Everyone steals government money, and you, too, of course. . . .'

'Oh, go to hell!'

'I mean something that's not yours: straight out of the pocket, out of a purse. Have you?'

'I did steal twenty copecks from my mother once. Took it from the table. I was nine years old at the time. Took it when no one was looking and held it tight in my hand.'

'Well, what happened?'

'Oh, nothing. I kept it three days, then I felt ashamed, confessed and gave it back.'

'And what happened then?'

'Well, I was thrashed. Why are you so interested? You've not stolen anything, have you?'

'I have,' Mitya winked at him slyly.

'What have you stolen?' inquired Perkhotin curiously.

'Twenty copecks from my mother when I was nine years old, and I returned it three days later.'

Having said this, Mitya suddenly got up.

'Won't you hurry up, sir?' Andrey cried suddenly from the door of the shop.

'Ready? Come along!' Mitya said, startled into activity. ' "One last tale more and my chronicle is ended" – a glass of vodka for Andrey for the road – hurry up! And a glass of brandy as well! Put that box (the one with the pistols) under my seat. Good-bye, Perkhotin, don't think badly of me!'

'But you'll be back tomorrow, won't you?'

'Certainly.'

'Will you pay the bill now, sir?' asked the shop-assistant, rushing up.

'Oh yes, the bill! Certainly!'

He pulled the bundle of notes again out of his pocket, took three rainbow-coloured notes from it, threw them on the counter and hurried out of the shop. They all came out after him and, bowing, took leave of him with the usual expressions of good wishes. Andrey cleared his throat from the brandy he had just drunk and jumped on the box. But before Mitya had time to take his seat in the cart Fenya suddenly and quite unexpectedly appeared before him. She ran up panting, clasped her hands before him with a cry, and plumped down at his feet.

'Please, sir, don't do anything to my mistress! And I told you all about it! And don't do anything to him, either. He was her first man. He is hers, sir! He's going to marry her now. That's why he's come back from Siberia. Please, sir, don't take the life of your fellow-creatures!'

'Aha, so that's what it is! Well, I expect you'll cause a lot of trouble there!' Perkhotin muttered to himself. 'Now everything's clear. I see it all now. Come on, old man, let's have the pistols, if you're anything like a man,' he cried aloud to Dmitry. 'Do you hear, Dmitry?'

'The pistols? Wait, old man, I'm going to throw them into a puddle on the way. Fenya, get up. Don't kneel before me. Mitya won't hurt anyone. The silly fool will not hurt anyone again. And another thing, Fenya,' he shouted to her, after having taken his seat. 'I hurt you just now, so please forgive me, forgive a scoundrel. . . . But if you won't, it doesn't matter. Because nothing matters any more now! Drive on, Andrey. Be quick about it and drive fast!'

Andrey drove away and the bells began to jingle.

'Good-bye, Perkhotin! My last tear is for you!'

'I don't think he's drunk, but what nonsense he talks!' Perkhotin thought as he watched him drive away. At first he thought of staying to see to the packing of the cart (also drawn by three horses) with the remaining wines and provisions, knowing perfectly well that they would cheat and defraud Mitya, but suddenly, feeling angry with himself, he swore and went to the public house to play billiards.

'He's a fool, though he's a good fellow,' he muttered as he walked along. 'I've heard something about that officer, Grushenka's first lover. Well, if he's turned up – a pity about those pistols, though! But, hang it all, I'm not his nurse, am I? Let them do as they like! It'll all come to nothing, anyway. They're a lot of bawlers, that's all. They'll get drunk and have a fight. Have a fight and make it up again. They're not men of action. "I'll keep away – I'll punish myself" – nothing will come of it! He shouted these fine phrases a thousand times when he was drunk in the pub. He's not drunk now – that's true. "Drunk in spirit" – how they love fine phrases, the scoundrels! I'm not his nurse, am I? But he certainly did have a fight – his mug was all covered with blood. Who with, I wonder. I shall find out at the pub. And his handkerchief was soaked in blood, too. . . . Damn it, he left it on the floor in my room – oh, to hell with it!'

He arrived at the public house in a filthy temper and at once made up a game. The game cheered him up. He played another game and at once began telling one of his partners that Dmitry Karamazov had plenty of money again, about three thousand, he had seen it himself, and that he had again gone off to Mokroye to have a good time with Grushenka. His listeners showed quite a surprising interest in his story.

And they all started talking about it, not laughing but looking strangely serious. They even stopped playing.

'Three thousand? But where could he have got three thousand?'

They began questioning Perkhotin further. The story of Mrs Khokhlakov's present was received sceptically.

'He didn't rob his old man, did he?'

'Three thousand? There is something wrong there.'

'He did threaten to kill his father, you know. We all heard him here. He did mention the three thousand, too. . . .'

Perkhotin listened and suddenly began giving dry and guarded answers to their questions. He did not say a word about the blood on Mitya's face and hands, and yet on the way to the pub he had meant to tell them about it. They began a third game and gradually the talk about Mitya petered out. But after finishing the third game, Perkhotin refused to go on playing, put down his cue and, without having supper as he had intended, left the public house. On coming out into the square, he stopped in perplexity, feeling rather surprised at himself. He suddenly realized that what he wanted to do was to go to Mr Karamazov's to find out if anything had happened there. 'Because of some nonsense, which is what it is quite sure to turn out, I'm going to wake up the household and create a row! Hell, am I their nurse, or what?'

He went straight back home in a very bad humour and suddenly remembered Fenya. 'Oh, hell, why didn't I question her just now?' he thought with annoyance. 'I'd have found everything out from her.' And so overcome was he suddenly by a strong and impatient desire to speak to her and find out everything from her that, though half-way home, he turned abruptly towards Mrs Morozov's house where Grushenka lived. On reaching the gates, he knocked, and the sound of the knock in the silence of the night seemed suddenly to sober him down and make him feel angry. Besides, no one answered him; everyone in the house was asleep. 'I'll create a row here too!' he thought, with a feeling of pain in his heart, but instead of going away, he suddenly began knocking at the gate again with all his might. The whole street resounded to his knocks. 'Well, then,' he muttered, 'I'm going to knock them up, I am!' And he got more and more furious with himself at each sound, but he went on knocking louder and louder at the gate.

6

Here I Come!

MEANWHILE Dmitry was speeding along the road. It was over fifteen miles to Mokroye, but Andrey's three horses galloped at such a spanking pace that they could cover the distance in an hour and a quarter. The fast driving seemed to revive Mitya. The air was fresh and cool; big stars twinkled in the clear sky. It was the same night and perhaps the same hour in which Alyosha fell on the earth and 'vowed ecstatically to love it for ever and ever'. But Mitya felt troubled, very troubled at heart, and though many things were lacerating his soul now, yet at that moment his whole being was yearning for her, for his queen, to whom he was flying now so as to look on her for the last time. I'll say this: his heart did not hesitate for a moment. I shall perhaps not be believed when I say that this jealous man did not feel the slightest jealousy of this new man, this new rival of his, this 'army officer', who had appeared out of nowhere. He would have been jealous at once of any other man, if such a one had appeared and, perhaps, would again have stained his terrible hands with blood – but for that man, for that 'first lover' of hers, he felt, as he sped along in his *troika*, no jealous hatred, no hostility even, though, it is true, he had not seen him yet. 'Here there can be no room for argument, here it was her right and his; this was her first love, which she had not forgotten after five years, which means that she had loved only him for those five years, and I – what have I got to do with it? Why should I come between them? Stand aside, Mitya, and make way! And, anyway, what am I now? Now even without the officer everything's at an end. Even if he had not turned up at all, everything would have been at an end, anyway. . . .'

It is in words such as these that he could have roughly expressed his feelings, if he had been capable of reasoning. But at that moment he was no longer capable of reasoning. His entire present resolution had arisen without any reasoning, in a flash, had been felt and accepted as a whole with all its consequences a few hours earlier, at Fenya's, at her first words. And yet, in spite of all his resolution, he felt troubled at heart, so much so that it hurt: even his resolution did not give him peace. He had left too much behind and it tortured him. And this seemed strange to him at moments: had he not himself written his own death sentence on paper: 'I punish myself and I punish my life'? And the paper was lying there in his pocket, ready. And his pistol was loaded and he had made up his mind how he would meet the first warm ray 'of Phoebus, the golden-haired' next morning. And yet he could not settle his account with his past, with all that was behind him, and that tortured him – he felt that agonizingly, and the thought of it pierced his heart with despair. There was one moment during his journey when he suddenly felt like stopping Andrey, jumping out of the cart, getting his loaded pistol and putting an end to it all, without waiting for the dawn. But that moment was gone in a flash. Besides, the cart, too, sped along 'devouring the distance', and the nearer he got to his destination, the more did the thought of her, of her alone, take his breath away, chasing away all the other fearful phantoms from his heart. Oh, he longed so much to look at her, if only for a fleeting moment, if only from a distance! 'She's now with *him*, well, I'll just have a look how she is now with him, her old lover, and that's all I want.' And never before had that woman, who was to have such a fateful influence on his life, aroused so much love in his breast, such new feelings he had never experienced in his life before, feelings that were unexpected even to himself, feelings that were tender to the point of supplication, to the point of complete self-effacement before her. 'And I will efface myself!' he said suddenly in a fit of almost hysterical rapture.

They had been driving for nearly an hour. Mitya was silent, and Andrey, though a talkative peasant, did not utter a word, either, just as though he were afraid to talk. All he did was to whip up his 'beauties', the lean, but mettlesome, swift bay horses. All of a sudden Mitya cried in terrible anxiety:

'Andrey, and what if they're asleep?'

This idea occurred to him suddenly: he had not thought of it before.

'I expect they must have gone to bed by now, sir.'

Mitya frowned as though in pain: what if that was so indeed – he would come rushing there – with such feelings – and they would be asleep – she, too, would be asleep, and – and perhaps beside him. . . . An angry feeling surged up in his heart.

'Faster, Andrey! Whip them up! Faster!' he cried in a frenzy.

'Perhaps they ain't gone to bed yet, sir,' Andrey decided, after a pause. 'Timofey said there were lots of 'em there.'

'At the station?'

'No, sir, not at the station. At Plastunov's, at the inn. It's a free station, sir. They hires out horses there.'

'Yes, I know. But why do you say there are lots of them there? Where would they all have come from? And who are they?' Mitya asked, terribly worried at this unexpected news.

'Well, sir, Timofey was saying they be all gentry, they be. Two from our town – who they be I can't say, only Timofey was saying as how they be our local gentlemen, and two others – them be strangers, and there may be more besides. I didn't ask properly. They be playing cards, Timofey says.'

'Cards?'

'Yes, sir, so maybe they ain't gone to bed if they starts playing cards. I don't expect it's gone eleven yet. Can't be later than that, sir.'

'Faster, Andrey, faster!' Mitya cried again nervously.

'I'd like to ask you something,' Andrey said again after a pause, 'only I'm afraid you'll be angry, sir.'

'What is it?'

'Well, sir, Fenya threw herself at your feet just now, sir, and begged you not to hurt her mistress and someone else, too. . . . And, well, sir, I mean, it's me, sir, taking you there. . . . I'm sorry, sir, I'm saying this because of my conscience – maybe what I've said is foolish.'

Mitya suddenly seized him by the shoulders from behind.

'Are you a driver? A driver?' he asked furiously.

'Yes, sir.'

'Then you know that you must make way. What sort of a driver is it who never makes way for anyone, who drives on regardless and runs over people? No, a driver must not run over people. One must not run over a man, one must not spoil people's lives, and if you've ruined someone's life, punish yourself and go away.'

All this burst from Mitya as though in an hysterical fit. Though Andrey was surprised at him, he kept up the conversation.

'Quite right, sir, you're quite right. One must not run over people or torture them, same as any other living creature, for every living creature, sir, is created by God, just as you might say a horse is. Because, you see, sir, some folks drives on regardless. Aye, sir, there's many a coachman who does that, too. There ain't no holding him, sir. He just goes dashing along regardless, dashing along regardless!'

'To hell?' Mitya interrupted suddenly and burst into his short, abrupt laugh. 'Andrey, you simple soul,' he again seized him firmly by the shoulders, 'tell me, will Dmitry Karamazov go to hell or not? What do you think?'

'Don't know, sir. It depends on you, sir, for you are — You see, sir, when the Son of God was crucified and died, he went straight down to hell and set free all the sinners who was tortured there. And there went up a great moan from hell, sir, for the devils, sir, they was thinking that nobody wouldn't come there no more, no sinners, I mean, sir. And then God says to them, he says, "Do not groan, hell, for all the great men, the rulers, the chief judges, and the rich shall come to you, and you shall be filled up as you've been all through the ages, until I come again." That's true, sir, them were his very words.'

'A folk legend! Wonderful! Whip up the left one, Andrey!'

'So you see, sir, who hell's for,' said Andrey, whipping up the left horse, 'but you're just like a little child, sir, that's what we think of you. And though there's no denying you're hot-tempered, sir, the Lord will forgive you for your being simple-hearted like.'

'And what about you, Andrey? Will you forgive me?'

'I got nothing to forgive you for, sir. You done nothing to me.'

'No, no. I mean for everyone, will you – just now – alone here on the road – will you forgive me for everyone? Tell me, you simple soul of a peasant.'

'Lord, sir, you talks so strange that I'm afraid to drive you. . . .'

But Mitya did not hear. He was praying frantically and whispering wildly to himself:

'O Lord, receive me with all my lawlessness, and do not judge me. Let me pass by without thy judgement. . . . Do not judge me because I've condemned myself. Do not judge me because I love thee, O Lord. I am vile, but I love thee: if thou sendest me to hell, I shall love thee there, and from there I shall cry that I love thee for ever and ever. . . . But let me, O Lord, love to the end – love to the end here and now, only five hours before thy warm ray of sunshine. For I love the queen of my heart. I love her and I can't help loving her. Thou seest what I'm like. I shall come and fall down at her feet and say, You are right to have passed me by. . . . Farewell and forget your victim – never trouble yourself about me again!'

'Mokroye!' cried Andrey, pointing ahead with his whip.

Through the pale darkness of the night there suddenly loomed a solid mass of buildings, scattered at a great distance from one another. The village of Mokroye had two thousand inhabitants, but at that hour they were all asleep, and only a few lights gleamed here and there in the darkness.

'Faster, Andrey, faster!' Mitya cried feverishly. 'Here I come!'

'They're not asleep, sir,' said Andrey again, pointing with his whip at Plastunov's inn at the very entrance to the village, the six windows of which were brightly lighted up.

'They're not asleep!' Mitya echoed, joyfully. 'Fill the air with the rattle of your cart, Andrey! Drive up at a gallop! Let the bells jingle! Drive up with a terrific dash! Let 'em know I've come! Here I come! Here I come!' Mitya shouted frenziedly.

Andrey whipped up his exhausted team into a gallop and, driving up to the front steps of the inn with a dash, pulled up his steaming, half-strangled horses. Mitya jumped down from the cart and just at that moment the innkeeper, who was, it is true, on his way to bed, looked up from the top of the front steps to see who had driven up in so dashing a manner.

'Is it you, Trifon?'

The innkeeper bent down, looked closely, ran headlong down the steps and rushed up obsequiously to the guest.

'Mr Dmitry Karamazov, sir! Do I see you again?'

The innkeeper was a thick-set, healthy peasant of medium height, with a rather fat face, of a stern and implacable appearance, especially when dealing with the peasants of Mokroye, but he possessed the gift of assuming a most obsequious expression when dealing with people he might profit from. He dressed in Russian style in a shirt with a tight collar fastening on one side and a long, pleated, full-skirted coat. He had amassed a considerable sum of money, but was constantly dreaming of better things to come. More than half the peasants were in his clutches, and all of them were entirely in his debt. He rented land from the neighbouring landlords, buying some outright, and the peasants cultivated the land for him to pay off their debts which they could never get rid of. He was a widower and had four grown-up daughters; one of them was already a widow and lived with her two small children – his grandchildren – at the inn, working for him like a charwoman. Another daughter of this peasant was married to a civil servant, a retired government clerk, and on a wall of one of the rooms of the inn could be seen among the family photographs a miniature photograph of this civil servant in uniform and civil service shoulder straps. On church holidays or when they went to pay visits, his two younger daughters wore blue or green dresses of the latest fashion, fitting tight at the back and with a train twenty-eight inches long, but next morning, as on any other day, they got up at dawn, swept out the rooms with birch-brooms, emptied the slops and cleaned up after the guests. In spite of the thousands of roubles he had saved up, Plastunov was very fond of fleecing a guest who was out on the spree. Remembering that not a month ago he had made two, if not three, hundred roubles in twenty-four hours out of Dmitry at his wild party with Grushenka, he welcomed him now joyfully and enthusiastically, scenting more loot from the dashing way Mitya had drawn up to the steps.

'Mr Dmitry Karamazov, sir, have you come to spend some time with us again?'

'One moment, Trifon,' Mitya began, 'first of all and most important of all – where is she?'

'Miss Svetlov, sir?' the innkeeper twigged at once, looking sharply into Mitya's face. 'Why, sir, she's – er – here, too.'

'Who with? Who with?'

'Some strangers, sir. One of them is a civil servant. A Polish gentleman, sir, to judge from his speech. It was he, sir, who sent the horses for her from here. And – er – the other gentleman is a friend of his or a fellow-traveller. Difficult to tell which, I'm afraid, sir. In civvies, both of them.'

'Well, are they having a party? Are they rich?'

'A party, sir? They're small fry, sir.'

'Small fry? And the others?'

'The others are from the town – two gentlemen, sir. They've come back from Cherny and are staying here. One of them is a young gentleman, a relative of Mr Miusov, I believe. I'm afraid I've forgotten his name – and I expect you know the other one, too. He's a landowner called Maximov. He's been on a pilgrimage to your monastery, he says, and is now travelling with the relative of Mr Miusov.'

'That's the lot?'

'Yes, sir.'

'One moment, Trifon. Now tell me the chief thing: what is she like? How is she?'

'Well, sir, she only arrived a short while ago and she's sitting with them now.'

'Gay? Laughing?'

'No, sir, I don't think she's laughing much. As a matter of fact, sir, she seems depressed. She's been combing the young gentleman's hair.'

'The Pole's? The officer's?'

'He's not so young and he isn't an officer, either. No, sir, not his, but the young gentleman's, Mr Miusov's nephew's – I'm sorry, I can't remember his name.'

'Kalganov?'

'Yes, that's it – Kalganov.'

'Very well, I'll see for myself. Are they playing cards?'

'They have been playing, sir, but they've stopped. They've had tea, and the civil servant has ordered liqueurs.'

'One moment, Trifon, my dear fellow, I'll see for myself. Now tell me the chief thing: are there any gypsies here?'

'No, sir, I'm afraid I haven't heard of any gypsies at all. The police have sent them away. But there are Jews here – playing the cymbals and the fiddles in Rozhdestvenskaya. You could send for them any time you like. They're sure to come, sir.'

'Yes, send for them, send for them at once!' cried Mitya. 'And we can get the village girls together as we did before, Maria especially, and Stepanida and Arina. Two hundred roubles for a choir!'

'Why, sir, for that money I'll raise you the whole village, though they're all asleep now. And, really, sir, are the peasants here worth such kindness or the girls, either? Waste so much money on such a rude and coarse lot? Is it proper for our peasants to smoke cigars? You gave them to them. Why, sir, they stink, the brigands. And the girls are all crawling with lice. Good Lord, sir, I'll get my own daughters up for you for nothing, let alone for such a sum. It's true they're asleep now, but I'll kick their backsides and make them sing for you. You gave the peasants champagne to drink last time, sir. Dear, oh dear!'

Trifon Plastunov was not really sorry for Mitya: he had stolen half a dozen bottles of champagne from him last time himself and had picked up a hundred-rouble note from under the table and clenched it in his fist, where it had remained.

'I spent more than a thousand here last time, Trifon. Remember?'

'So you did, sir. I remember it very well. I shouldn't be surprised, sir, if you hadn't left as much as three thousand here.'

'Well, I've come to do the same again now see?'

And he pulled out the bundle of notes and held it up before the innkeeper's nose.

'Now listen carefully: in an hour's time the wine will arrive, as well as snacks, pies, and sweets – bring it all up at once. The box Andrey's got is to be brought up at once, too. Open it and serve the champagne immediately. And, above all, the girls, the girls – Maria especially....'

He turned back to the cart and got out his box of pistols from under the seat.

'Now, then, Andrey, let's settle your bill. Here's fifteen roubles for your fares and fifty for your tip – for your willingness, your love.... Remember Karamazov!'

'I'm afraid, sir.' Andrew faltered. 'I'd be glad of a tip of five roubles, sir, but I won't take more. Mr Plastunov's my witness, sir. No offence meant, sir.'

'What are you afraid of?' Dmitry said, looking him up and down. 'Well, to hell with you, if that's what you want!' he cried, flinging him five roubles. 'Now, Trifon, show me in very quietly and let me have a good look at them first without them seeing me. Where are they? In the blue room?'

Trifon glanced warily at Mitya, but at once obediently carried out his request: he led him cautiously through the entrance hall, went himself into the first large room next to the one in which his guests were sitting, and took out the lighted candle. Then he led Mitya quietly in and put him in a corner of the dark room from where he could freely observe the people in the next room without being seen by them. But Mitya did not look long, and, indeed, he could scarcely see them: he saw her and his heart began pounding violently and a mist rose before his eyes. She was sitting in an armchair sideways to the table and next to her, on the sofa, was Kalganov, looking very young and handsome; she was holding his hand and was apparently laughing, while Kalganov, seemingly annoyed and not looking at her, was saying something in a loud voice to Maximov, who sat opposite Grushenka at the other side of the table. Maximov was laughing loudly at something. *He* sat on the sofa, and on a chair beside the sofa, against the wall, sat another man Mitya did not know. The man on the sofa was sprawling and smoking a pipe, and all Mitya was able to make out was that he seemed to be a fat, broad-faced little man, rather short and apparently angry about something. His friend, on the other hand, struck Mitya as extremely tall, but he could not make out anything more. His breath failed him. He could not hold out for another minute. He put the pistol case on a chest and feeling cold all over and with a sinking heart went straight into the blue room to join the company.

'Oh!' shrieked Grushenka, who was the first to see him, in alarm.

7

The First and Rightful One

MITYA walked up to the table with his long, rapid strides.

'Gentlemen,' he began in a loud voice and almost shouting, but stuttering at every word, 'I – er – I'm all right! Don't be afraid,' he cried. 'I'm not going to give any trouble,' he turned suddenly to Grushenka, who had recoiled in her chair towards Kalganov and clasped his hand tightly. 'I – I'm going away too. I'm here till morning. Gentlemen, as one traveller to another, may I stay here with you till morning? Only till morning, for the last time, in this room?'

The last sentence he addressed to the fat little man with the pipe, sitting on the sofa. The latter removed the pipe from his lips importantly.

'Sir,' he said gravely speaking with a thick, Polish accent, 'we're here in private. There are other rooms, I believe.'

'Why, it's you, Mr Karamazov!' Kalganov replied suddenly. 'Why, what's the matter? Sit down with us. How are you?'

'Hullo, my dear and – and most excellent fellow! I always thought a lot of you,' Mitya answered joyfully and enthusiastically, at once holding out his hand to him across the table.

'Ugh, not so tight! You've broken my fingers!' laughed Kalganov.

'He always squeezes your hand like that, always!' Grushenka remarked gaily, though with a timid smile, having come to the conclusion from Mitya's expression that he would not make a row and watching him with intense curiosity and still with some apprehension. There was something about him that surprised her greatly, and indeed she had never expected him to walk in and speak like that at such a moment.

'How do you do, sir?' Maximov, too, put in sweetly on the left. Mitya rushed up to him also.

'How do you do? So you're here too? I'm so glad you're here too! Gentlemen, gentlemen, I—' he turned again to the Pole with the pipe, evidently taking him for the most important person present. 'I flew here – I wanted to spend my last day and my last hour in this room, in this same room – where I too – er – adored – er – my queen! I'm sorry, sir,' he shouted frantically, 'I – I flew and as I flew I vowed — Oh, don't be afraid, it's my last night! Let's drink and be friends, sir. They'll bring in the wine presently. I brought this!' he pulled out his bundle of notes for some reason. 'Allow me, sir. I want music, a hell of a noise, just like last time. But, sir, the worm, the unwanted worm will crawl away across the earth and there'll be no more of him! Let me commemorate the day of my joy on this my last night!'

He was almost choking. There was much, much he wanted to say, but only strange exclamations escaped his lips. The Pole stared motionlessly at him, at his bundle of notes, then looked at Grushenka, and was obviously bewildered.

'If my queen commands —' he began.

'Queen? You mean me?' Grushenka interrupted suddenly. 'You do talk funnily, I can't help laughing at you all. Sit down, Mitya, and what are you talking about? Don't try to frighten me, please. You won't, will you? If you don't, I'm glad to see you. . . .'

'Me, me frighten you?' Mitya cried suddenly, throwing up his hands. 'Oh, you can all pass me by, walk past me, I won't stop you!'

And, suddenly, to everyone's surprise and, of course, to his own, too, he flung himself down on a chair and burst into tears, turning his head away to the opposite wall and throwing his arms round the back of his chair tightly, as though embracing it.

'There, there, you big silly!' Grushenka cried reproachfully. 'That's just how he used to come to see me. He'd burst into speech suddenly and I couldn't understand a word of what he said. He cried like that, too, once, and now again. . . . Aren't you ashamed of yourself? What are you crying for? Not that there's any reason for it!' she suddenly added enigmatically, emphasizing each word with a kind of exasperation.

'I – I'm not crying. . . . Well,' he turned round in a flash on his chair, 'how are you all?' and he burst out laughing suddenly, but not his abrupt, wooden laugh, but a sort of long, silent, nervous convulsive laugh.

'Well, again? . . . Come on, cheer up, cheer up!' Grushenka coaxed him. 'I'm very glad you've come, very glad, Mitya. Do you hear? I'm very glad. I want him to stay with us,' she addressed apparently all of them imperiously, though her words were obviously meant for the man sitting on the sofa. 'I wish it, I wish it! And if he goes, I'll go, too – so there!' she added with flashing eyes.

'What my queen commands is law!' the Pole said, gallantly kissing Grushenka's hand. 'Will you, please, join our company, sir?' he said, turning courteously to Mitya.

Mitya again jumped to his feet with the obvious intention of bursting out into another harangue, but what he actually said was different.

'Let's drink, sir!' he snapped suddenly instead of delivering a speech. They all laughed.

'Oh dear, and I thought he was going to make another speech!' Grushenka cried nervously. 'Listen, Mitya,' she added emphatically, 'don't jump up any more, but it's nice of you to have brought the champagne. I'm going to have some myself. I can't bear liqueurs. And it's a good thing you've come. I was awfully bored. But you haven't come here on the spree again, have you? For goodness sake, put your money in your pocket! Where did you get so much?'

Mitya, who had still been holding the crumpled notes in his hand, which had not failed to attract the attention of everyone in the room, and, especially, of the Poles, thrust them quickly and confusedly back into his pocket. He blushed. At that moment the innkeeper brought in an uncorked bottle of champagne and glasses on a tray. Mitya grabbed the bottle, but he was so bewildered that he did not know what to do with it. Kalganov took it from him and poured out the wine.

'And another bottle, another bottle!' Mitya cried to the innkeeper and, forgetting to clink glasses with the Pole, whom he had so solemnly invited to drink and be friends, he suddenly emptied his glass without waiting for anyone. His whole face suddenly changed. Instead of the solemn and tragic expression with which he had entered, there appeared an almost babyish look on it. He seemed suddenly to have grown gentle and subdued. He looked shyly and happily at them, breaking into a nervous titter now and again with the fawning and guilty expression of a lap-dog that had been let into the room and petted again. He seemed to have forgotten everything and was gazing at everyone with a rapturous, childish smile. He kept looking at Grushenka, laughing continuously and bringing his chair up close to her armchair. Gradually he got a pretty good idea of the two Poles, too, though he still did not know what they were after. The Pole on the sofa struck him by his dignified bearing, his Polish accent and, most of all, by his pipe. 'Well, what does it matter?' thought Mitya, contemplating him. 'Let him smoke a pipe if he likes.' The Pole's somewhat bloated, almost middle-aged face, with its very little nose and the very thin, dyed and impudent-looking moustache under it had not so far aroused the faintest doubts in Mitya. Nor was he particularly struck by the Pole's very cheap wig, made in Siberia, with love-locks absurdly combed forward over the temples. 'I suppose,' he went on contemplating it blissfully, 'it's all right, if he likes a wig.' As for the other Pole, sitting by the wall, who was younger than the Pole on the sofa and who was staring insolently and defiantly at the company and listening with silent contempt to the conversation, Mitya was only struck by his great height, which was terribly out of proportion with the Pole on the sofa. 'If he stood up, he'd be just under six foot ten,' it flashed through Mitya's mind. It also occurred to him that the tall Pole must be a friend and accomplice of the Pole on the sofa, a sort of 'bodyguard' of his, and that the little Pole with the pipe was, of course, the one who gave the orders. But even that seemed to Mitya to be perfectly all right and as it should be. The little lap-dog had lost all feeling of rivalry. He still could make nothing of Grushenka or the enigmatic tone of some of her words; all he did grasp with a throbbing heart was that she was kind to him, that she had 'forgiven' him, and let him sit beside her. He was beside himself with delight when he saw her take a sip from the glass of wine. He was, however, suddenly struck by the silence of the company and began gazing at them all with expectant eyes. 'What are you sitting like that for?' his smiling eyes seemed to say. 'Why don't you start something, gentlemen?'

'He goes on talking a lot of nonsense,' Kalganov began suddenly, as though divining his thought and pointing to Maximov, 'and we were all laughing.'

Mitya cast a quick glance at Kalganov and then at once at Maximov.

'Talking nonsense?' he said with his short wooden laugh, all at once delighted at something. 'Ha, ha!'

'Yes, you see, he maintains that in the twenties all our cavalry officers married Polish women. But it's awful nonsense, isn't it?'

'Polish women?' Mitya echoed again, this time with undisguised delight.

Kalganov had a pretty good idea about Mitya's relations with Grushenka and about her Pole, too, but all this did not interest him very much; indeed, it did not perhaps interest him at all; what interested him most of all was Maximov. He had arrived there with Maximov by chance and he met the Poles at the inn for the first time in his life. Grushenka he had known before and had even been to see her once with someone. But she did not like him very much at the time. Here, however, she kept looking very affectionately at him, and before Mitya's arrival she had even flirted with him, but, somehow, he remained unresponsive. He was a young man of no more than twenty, exquisitely dressed, with a very charming face, a fine complexion, and beautiful thick, fair hair. But the remarkable feature of his handsome face was his pair of beautiful light-blue eyes, with an intelligent and sometimes even a deep expression, rather surprising for a man of his age, particularly as he sometimes looked and spoke absolutely like a child, without being in the least ashamed or, indeed, aware of it himself. He was, on the whole, a very original, even capricious, person, though always kind. Sometimes there was something immobile and obstinate in his expression: he looked at you and listened to you, but seemed to be thinking obstinately of something else all the time. Or he would sometimes be listless and lazy and at other times he would grow excited for apparently the most trivial reason.

'You see,' he went on, drawling lazily, though without the slightest affectation but quite naturally, 'I've been taking him about with me for four days, ever since your brother – remember? – pushed him out of the carriage and sent him flying. That made me very interested in him at the time and I took him with me into the country, but now he keeps talking such nonsense that I'm ashamed to be with him. I'm taking him back.'

'The gentleman has never seen a Polish lady and what he says could never have happened,' the Pole with the pipe said to Maximov.

The Pole with the pipe spoke Russian fairly well, much better, in fact, than he let on. But whenever he used Russian words, he made them sound like Polish.

'Why,' Maximov tittered in reply, 'I was married to a Polish lady myself.'

'But you didn't serve in the cavalry, did you?' Kalganov put in at once. 'You were talking about the cavalry. Were you a cavalry officer?'

'Yes, indeed, was he a cavalry officer? Ha, ha!' cried Mitya, who was listening eagerly and transferring his questioning glance to every speaker in turn, as though expecting to hear goodness only knows what from each.

'No, sir, you see,' Maximov turned to him, 'what I'm driving at, sir, is that those Polish girls – and very pretty they are, too, sir – when they dance a mazurka with our Uhlans – I mean, sir, that no sooner does one of them finish a mazurka with a Uhlan officer than she jumps on his knee like a little kitten, sir, a lovely, white kitten, sir, and her father and mother look on and allow it, sir – yes, sir, they allow it, and next day, of course, the Uhlan goes and offers her his hand – yes, sir – he offers her his hand – hee, hee!' Maximov concluded with a titter.

'You're a good-for-nothing loafer, sir!' the tall Pole on the chair growled suddenly, crossing one leg over the other.

Mitya's attention was arrested for a moment by the Pole's huge greased boot with its thick, dirty sole. As a matter of fact, the clothes of both the Poles were rather greasy.

'So he's a good-for-nothing loafer now, is he? Why is he calling people names?' cried Grushenka, growing suddenly angry.

'Madam,' the Pole with the pipe observed to Grushenka, 'the gentleman saw serf-girls in Poland and not ladies of good families.'

'You can be sure of that,' the tall Pole on the chair snapped contemptuously.

'What next!' Grushenka snapped back. 'Let him talk! People talk – why interfere with them? It's fun to be with them.'

'I'm not interfering with you,' the Pole in the wig observed significantly, with a long look at Grushenka and, relapsing into dignified silence, began sucking at his pipe again.

'No, no, the Polish gentleman was quite right.' Kalganov grew excited again, as though the subject under discussion was really important. 'He's never been in Poland, so how can he talk about Poland? You weren't married in Poland, were you?'

'No, sir, I was married in the province of Smolensk. Only her Uhlan had brought her out of Poland before that, sir, my wife, that is, with her mother, her aunt, and another female relation with a grown-up son. Yes, sir, from Poland, he brought her from Poland, sir, and – and gave her up to me. A fine young fellow he was, too, one of our lieutenants. At first he wanted to marry her himself, but in the end he didn't, because she turned out to be lame. . . .'

'So you married a lame woman?' cried Kalganov.

'Yes, sir, I did. You see, both of them concealed it at the time and – er – deceived me a little. She kept hopping, you know, and I thought she did it because she was merry and gay. . . .'

'Because she was so happy to marry you?' Kalganov yelled in a sort of childishly ringing voice.

'Yes, sir. Because she was happy, sir. But it turned out to be for quite a different reason. Afterwards, when we were married, on the very evening after our wedding, she told me about it, sir, and apologized very sweetly to me. "I jumped over a puddle when I was a little girl," she said, "and injured my leg." Hee-hee!'

Kalganov burst into the most childish laughter and almost collapsed on the sofa. Grushenka, too, burst out laughing. Mitya was simply beaming with happiness.

'Do you know,' Kalganov exclaimed, addressing Mitya, 'he's speaking the truth now, he's not lying now! And, you know, he's been married twice – it's his first wife he's talking about, his second wife ran away from him and is still alive. Did you know that?'

'Did she?' Mitya turned quickly to Maximov, with an expression of intense astonishment on his face.

'Yes, sir,' Maximov confirmed modestly. 'She ran away, sir. I've had that unpleasant experience. With a Frenchman, sir. And what's worse, she had my little property transferred to her name before she did so. You're an educated man, she said to me, you'll always be able to earn a living. She cooked my goose, I can tell you. A venerable bishop once said to me in that connexion: "One of your wives was lame and the other lightfooted" – hee, hee!'

'Listen, listen!' Kalganov went on excitedly. 'If he does tell lies – and he often does – he does so only to give pleasure to people, and there's nothing wrong about that, is there? You know I like him very much sometimes. He's despicable, but it's natural with him, isn't it? What do you think? Some people behave despicably because they hope to get something out of it, but he does it because he can't help it, because it's his nature. Now, for instance, he claims (he was arguing about it all the way yesterday) that Gogol had him in mind in *Dead Souls*. You remember, there's a landowner by the name of Maximov there whom Nozdryov thrashed. He was put on trial for "inflicting a personal injury upon the landowner Maximov by birching him while under the influence of drink" – you do remember that, don't you? Well, you know, he claims that it was he and that it was he who was thrashed! Well, is that possible? Chichikov made his journey at the beginning of the twenties at the latest, so that the dates are all wrong. He couldn't have been thrashed then. He couldn't, could he?'

It was difficult to imagine what Kalganov was so excited about, but his excitement was genuine. Mitya was wholeheartedly on his side.

'Well, but what if they did thrash him!' he cried, roaring with laughter.

'They didn't thrash me exactly,' Maximov suddenly put in. 'It was only —'

'Only what? Did they or didn't they thrash you?'

'What's the time, sir?' the Pole with the pipe turned to the tall Pole on the chair, looking bored.

The other shrugged his shoulders in reply: neither of them had a watch.

'Why not talk?' Grushenka again exclaimed angrily, as though deliberately trying to provoke him. 'Let other people talk. Must nobody talk if you are bored?'

Something seemed for the first time to flash through Mitya's mind. This time the Pole replied with unconcealed annoyance:

'Madam, I said nothing against it. I didn't say anything.'

'All right, then. Go on,' Grushenka cried to Maximov. 'Why are you all silent?'

'Why, ma'am,' Maximov put in at once, looking obviously pleased and mincing a little, 'there's nothing to tell, because it's all so silly. And, anyway, Gogol too meant it all allegorically, because all his surnames are allegorical. Nozdryov wasn't really Nozdryov, but Nosov, and as for Kuvshinnikov – it bears no resemblance to his real name at all, for it was Shkvornyov. But Fenardi really was called Fenardi, only he wasn't an Italian, but a Russian, Petrov, ma'am, and Mam'selle Fenardi was a very pretty girl, ma'am, with her legs in tights, pretty little legs, and her dress was very short and covered with spangles, and she would whirl round and round, only not for four hours but for four minutes – yes, ma'am – and she turned everyone's head.'

'But what did they thrash you for?' yelled Kalganov. 'What did they thrash you for?'

'For Piron, sir,' replied Maximov.

'What Piron?' cried Mitya.

'The well-known French writer Piron, sir. We were all drinking then – lots of us, a large company – at an inn at that very fair. They had invited me, too, and the first thing I did was to start making up epigrams. "Is that you, Boileau? What a funny rig-out!" And Boileau replied that he was going to a fancy ball, that is, to the baths, hee, hee! And they thought I meant them. And I followed it up at once by another epigram, well known to all cultured people, a sarcastic one:

> You're Sappho, I'm Phaon,
> There's no doubt about it,
> But why the blame on me you lay on,
> When the way to the sea in vain you've scouted.

Well, they were still more offended and began calling me all sorts of offensive names, and to mend matters I told them, to my own undoing, a highly cultured anecdote about Piron, how they refused to elect him to the French Academy and how in revenge he wrote his own epitaph:

> Ci-gît Piron qui ne fut rien
> Pas même académicien.

So they thrashed me.'

'But what for? What for?'

'For being such an educated fellow. A fellow can be thrashed for all sorts of things, you see,' Maximov concluded, briefly and sententiously.

'Oh, I've had enough of it,' Grushenka cut them short suddenly. 'It's all a lot of nonsense. I thought it would be amusing.'

Mitya gave a violent start and stopped laughing at once. The tall Pole got up from his seat and, with the disdainful air of a man who is bored in a company he does not usually consort with, began pacing the room from one corner to the other, his hands behind his back.

'Look at him, pacing the room like that!' Grushenka murmured, looking at him contemptuously.

Mitya began to feel uneasy. Besides, he noticed that the Pole on the sofa was watching him irritably.

'Sir,' Mitya cried, addressing the Pole, 'let's drink, sir! And the other Polish gentleman, too – let's drink, gentlemen!'

He pushed three glasses together at once and filled them with champagne.

'To Poland, gentlemen! I'm drinking to your Poland, the land of Poland!' cried Mitya.

'With pleasure, sir, let's drink,' said the Pole on the sofa with dignity and some condescension, and he took his glass.

'And your friend, sir, what's his name? Hey, you, sir, take your glass!' Mitya cried.

'Vrublevsky,' prompted the Pole on the sofa.

Vrublevsky, swaying as he walked, came up to the table and took his glass.

'To Poland, gentlemen, hurrah!' cried Mitya, raising his glass.

The three of them drank. Mitya seized the bottle and again poured out three glasses.

'Now to Russia, gentlemen, and let's be friends!'

'Pour out some for me, too,' said Grushenka. 'I also want to drink to Russia.'

'Me, too,' said Kalganov.

'Why,' Maximov tittered, 'if you don't mind, I, too, will drink to dear old Russia, to our darling old granny.'

'All, all!' exclaimed Mitya. 'Landlord, fetch more bottles!'

The three other bottles Mitya had brought with him were fetched, and Mitya poured out the wine.

'To Russia, hurrah!' he repeated the toast.

All, except the Poles, drank, Grushenka emptying her glass at one gulp. The Poles did not touch theirs.

'What's the matter, gentlemen?' cried Mitya. 'Won't you drink at all?'

Vrublevsky took his glass, raised it and cried in a stentorian voice: 'To Russia within her borders of 1772!'

'That's right!' the other Pole cried, and both at once emptied their glasses.

'You're damn fools, gentlemen!' Mitya could not help exclaiming.

'S-sir!' the two Poles shouted threateningly, facing him like two fighting cocks.

Vrublevsky, especially, was boiling with rage.

'Isn't one to be allowed to love one's country?' he shouted.

'Shut up! Don't quarrel! I won't have any quarrelling!' Grushenka cried peremptorily, stamping her foot on the floor.

Her face coloured, her eyes flashed: the glass of champagne she had just drunk had taken effect. Mitya got terribly frightened.

'I'm sorry, gentlemen. It was my fault. It won't happen again. Mr Vrublevsky, sir, it won't happen again.'

'Oh, shut up, for goodness' sake!' Grushenka snapped at him in angry vexation. 'Sit down, you silly fool!'

They all sat down, they all fell silent, they all looked at one another.

'Gentlemen, it's all my fault,' Mitya, who did not discern anything in Grushenka's exclamation, began again. 'Well, what are we sitting like this for? What shall we do to – to cheer up, to be cheerful again?'

'Well,' mumbled Kalganov lazily, 'I certainly don't feel very cheerful.'

'Why not have another game of faro, as we had just now?' Maximov suddenly tittered.

'Faro? Excellent!' Mitya cried. 'If only the Polish gentlemen —'

'I'm afraid it's late, sir,' the Pole on the sofa declared in Polish as though unwillingly.

'That's true,' Vrublevsky assented.

'What do you mean?' asked Grushenka.

'It's late,' explained the Pole on the sofa in Russian. 'It's a late hour.'

'Everything is late with them,' Grushenka almost shrieked in vexation, 'and everything is too much trouble for them. They're bored themselves and they want everyone to be bored. Before you came, Mitya, they were just as silent and scowled at me.'

'My goddess,' cried the Pole on the sofa, 'I'm sorry, but I can't help feeling depressed seeing how unkind you are to me. I'm ready, sir,' he concluded, turning to Mitya.

'You start, sir,' Mitya said, pulling his notes out of his pocket and laying two hundred-rouble notes on the table. 'I'd be glad to lose a lot to you. Take your cards. You deal.'

'We'll get the cards from the landlord, sir,' the little Pole said, gravely and emphatically.

'That's the best way,' Vrublevsky backed him up.

'From the landlord? Good, I understand. We'll get them from the landlord. You're quite right, gentlemen. Cards!' Mitya gave the order to the landlord.

The innkeeper brought an unopened pack of cards and told Mitya that the girls were getting ready and the Jews with the cymbals would probably be there soon, too, but that the cart with the provisions had not yet arrived. Mitya jumped up from the table and ran into the next room to give the necessary orders. But only three girls had arrived and Maria was not among them. Besides, he did not know himself what orders to give or why he had run out. He only told them to get the sweets from the box and give them to the girls. 'And vodka for Andrey,' he ordered quickly, 'I've hurt his feelings.' At that moment Maximov, who had run out after him, touched him on the shoulder.

'Let me have five roubles,' he whispered to Mitya. 'I'd like to take a chance at faro, hee-hee!'

'Fine, excellent! Take ten!' cried Mitya, pulling all his notes out of his pocket again and picking out ten roubles. 'And if you lose, come again, come again. . . .'

'Thank you, sir,' Maximov whispered joyfully and rushed back into the drawing-room.

Mitya, too, returned at once and apologized for having kept them waiting. The Poles had already taken their seats at the table and opened the pack of cards. They looked much more amiable, almost friendly. The Pole on the sofa lighted another pipe and prepared to deal; there was even a certain solemnity in his face.

'Take your seats, gentlemen,' Vrublevsky cried.

'No,' said Kalganov, 'I'm not going to play any more. I've already lost fifty roubles to them.'

'The gentleman was unlucky,' the Pole on the sofa observed in his direction. 'The gentleman may be lucky this time.'

'How much in the bank? Enough to cover it?' Mitya asked excitedly.

'It all depends, sir. Perhaps a hundred, perhaps two, just as much as you will stake.'

'A million!' Mitya roared with laughter.

'Has the Captain perhaps heard the story about Podvysotsky?'

'Which Podvysotsky?'

'There was a bank in Warsaw and anyone could come and stake against it. In comes Podvysotsky, sees a thousand gold pieces and stakes against the bank. The banker says to him, "Mr Podvysotsky, are you laying down cash or is it on your word of honour?" "On my word of honour," says Podvysotsky. "So much the better, sir." The banker deals the cards, Podvysotsky takes the thousand gold pieces. "Wait, sir," says the banker, takes out a box and gives him a million: "Take it, sir, these are your winnings." "I didn't know that," says Podvysotsky. "Sir," says the banker, "you pledged your honour and we pledged ours." Podvysotsky took the million.'

'That's not true,' said Kalganov.

'Mr Kalganov, one doesn't say such things in decent society.'

'As if a Polish gambler would give away a million!' cried Mitya, but recollected himself at once. 'I'm sorry, gentlemen. It's my fault again. He would, he would give away a million on his word of honour, for the honour of Poland!' Mitya declared, imitating their Polish pronunciation. 'See how well I talk Polish, ha, ha? Here, I stake ten roubles, the knave leads.'

'And I put down a rouble on the little queen, the queen of hearts, the pretty one, my darling sweetheart, hee-hee!' Maximov tittered, putting down his queen and, as though wishing to conceal it from everyone, moving close to the table and quickly crossing himself under it.

Mitya won. So did Maximov.

'A corner!' cried Mitya.

'And I'll stake another rouble, one single little stake, a single tiny little stake,' Maximov murmured blissfully, terribly pleased to have won a rouble.

'Lost!' cried Mitya. 'A *double* on the seven!'

The *double*, too, was lost.

'Stop it!' Kalganov said suddenly.

'Double, double!' Mitya doubled his stakes, and any card he doubled lost. But the rouble stakes won.

'On the *double*!' Mitya bawled furiously.

'You've lost two hundred, sir. Are you staking another two hundred?' the Pole on the sofa inquired.

'What? Lost two hundred already? All right, then, another two hundred! All the two hundred on the *double*!'

And pulling out his money from his pocket, Mitya threw down two hundred on the queen, but Kalganov suddenly covered it with his hand.

'Enough!' he cried in his resounding voice.

'What are you doing?' Mitya glared at him.

'That's enough. I don't want you to go on. You're not going to play any more.'

'Why not?'

'Just because. Give it up and come away, that's why. I won't let you play any more!'

Mitya looked at him in amazement.

'Give it up, Mitya. He may be right. You've lost a lot as it is,' Grushenka, too, said with a strange note in her voice.

The two Poles suddenly got up, looking very hurt.

'Are you joking, sir?' the little Pole said, looking sternly at Kalganov.

'How dare you, sir!' Vrublevsky, too, shouted at Kalganov.

'Don't you dare to shout!' cried Grushenka. 'Oh, you turkey-cocks!'

Mitya looked at each of them in turn; but something in Grushenka's face struck him suddenly and at the same moment a new idea flashed into his mind – a strange new idea!

'Madam,' the little Pole, red with anger, began, when Mitya suddenly went up to him and tapped him on the shoulder.

'A word with you, sir!'

'What do you want?'

'Let's go to the other room. I've got something to tell you, something nice, something you'd like very much.'

The little Pole looked surprised and regarded Mitya apprehensively. However, he agreed at once, but only on condition that Vrublevsky went with them.

'Your bodyguard, you mean? All right, let him come, too. I want him, too. Yes, I certainly do want him!' cried Mitya. 'Come along, gentlemen.'

'Where are you going?' Grushenka asked in alarm.

'We shall be back in a jiffy,' replied Mitya.

His face glowed with a sort of courage, a sort of unexpected cheerfulness; it looked very different from what it had looked when he entered the room an hour ago. He led the Poles into the room on the right, not the large one where the girls' chorus was assembling and where the table was being laid, but into the bedroom with the trunks and boxes and two large beds with piles of cotton pillows on each. A candle burnt there on a little deal table in the corner. The little Pole and Mitya sat down opposite each other at the table and the huge Vrublevsky stood beside them with his hands behind his back. The Poles looked stern, but with evident curiosity.

'What can we do for you, sir?' the little Pole murmured.

'You can do this for me, sir,' Mitya said. 'I won't waste words. Here,' he pulled his notes out, 'take this money, take three thousand, if you like, and get out of here.'

The Pole looked searchingly at him, staring intently at Mitya's face.

'Three thousand, sir?'

He exchanged glances with Vrublevsky.

'Three, sir, three! Listen, old man, I can see you're a sensible fellow. Take three thousand and get the hell out of here, and take Vrublevsky with you – do you hear? But right now, this minute, and for good. Go through this door and never come back again. What have you got there – an overcoat, a fur-coat? I'll bring it out to you. I'll have a carriage ready for you in less than a minute and – good-bye, sir! Well?'

Mitya was waiting confidently for a reply. He did not doubt what it would be. A most determined look passed over the Pole's face.

'And the money, sir?'

'This is what we shall do about the money, sir: five hundred you'll get at once to pay your fares and by way of an advance, and two thousand and five hundred tomorrow in the town. I swear by my honour,' cried Mitya, 'I'll get it. I'll get it by hook or by crook!'

The Poles again exchanged glances. The little Pole's face assumed an ominous expression.

'Seven hundred, seven hundred, not five hundred, seven hundred at once, this minute, cash down!' Mitya raised his offer, feeling that something was wrong. 'What's the matter, sir? Don't you believe me? You can't expect me to give you the three thousand right away. If I give it, you may come back to her tomorrow. Besides, I haven't got the three thousand on me now. I've got it at home in the town,' Mitya babbled, faltering and losing courage with every word he uttered. 'I swear I've got them there. I've got them hidden there.'

In a flash a feeling of extraordinary personal dignity appeared on the face of the little Pole.

'You don't want anything else, do you?' he asked ironically. 'For shame, sir!' and he spat. Vrublevsky spat, too.

'You spit, sir,' Mitya said in despair, realizing that all was over, 'because you think you'll get more from Grushenka. You're a couple of blasted capons, both of you – that's what you are!'

'That is an insult, sir!' the little Pole turned as red as a lobster and left the room quickly, in terrible indignation, as though not wishing to hear anything more.

Vrublevsky followed him, swaying, out of the room, Mitya, crestfallen and completely dumbfounded, bringing up the rear. Mitya was afraid of Grushenka. He felt that the Poles would at once raise a cry. This was, indeed, what happened. The Pole entered the room and stopped before Grushenka in a theatrical pose.

'I've been insulted, madam!' he cried in Polish.

But Grushenka seemed suddenly to lose all patience, just as though she had been touched on a sore spot.

'Talk Russian, Russian!' she shouted at him. 'I don't want to hear a word of Polish. You used to speak Russian before. You haven't forgotten it in five years, have you? Speak Russian or I won't listen to you!'

She flushed with anger.

The Pole panted with offended dignity and, speaking in broken Russian, said rapidly and pompously:

'Madam, I came to forget the past and forgive it, to forget what has happened till today —'

'Forgive? You mean, you came here to forgive me?' Grushenka interrupted, jumping up from her seat.

'I did, madam. I'm not narrow-minded, I'm generous. But I was shocked when I saw your lovers. Mr Karamazov offered me three thousand in that room to go away. I spat in his face.'

'What?' Grushenka cried hysterically. 'He offered you money for me? Is it true, Mitya? How dare you? Am I for sale?'

'Sir, sir,' Mitya cried beseechingly, 'she's pure as the driven snow, and I've never been her lover! You're lying —'

'How dare you defend me to him?' Grushenka clamoured. 'I wasn't pure because I was virtuous or because I was afraid of Kuzma, but so that I might hold up my head to him and have the right to tell him he's a cad when I met him. Did he really not accept the money from you?'

'He did, he did,' cried Mitya, 'but he wanted the three thousand at once, and I only offered him an advance of seven hundred.'

'Why, of course, he heard I had money and that's why he came here to marry me!'

'Madam,' cried the Pole, 'I'm an honourable man, I'm a nobleman, and not a good-for-nothing loafer. I came here to make you my wife, but I see quite a different woman, not the one I knew, but a wilful and shameless one!'

'Well, go back where you came from!' Grushenka cried, beside herself. 'I'll tell them to kick you out of here and they'll kick you out. I was a fool, a fool, to have worried myself to death for the last five years! And I didn't do it for his sake, but out of spite! And this isn't him at all! Was he like that? It might be his father! Where did you get the wig from? He was an eagle, and this one is a drake. He used to laugh and sing songs to me. And I've been shedding tears for five years! What a damn fool I am! I'm a base, shameless creature!'

She sank into her armchair and covered her face with her hands. At that moment the choir of Mokroye girls, assembled at last, burst out into a rollicking dance song.

'Why, this is Sodom!' Vrublevsky roared suddenly. 'Landlord, throw the shameless hussies out!'

The innkeeper, who had been peeping through the door curiously for a long time, hearing shouts and realizing that his guests were quarrelling, at once entered the room.

'What are you hollering about?' he addressed Vrublevsky with quite inexplicable discourtesy.

'You swine!' Vrublevsky roared.

'Swine? And what sort of cards were you playing with just now? I gave you a pack and you hid it! You played with marked cards! I can have you packed off to Siberia for playing with marked cards – yes, sir, for it's the same as forged notes!'

And going up to the sofa, he thrust his fingers between the back of the sofa and the cushion and pulled out an unopened pack of cards.

'Here's my pack and it's unopened!' he said, holding it up and showing it to all in the room. 'I saw him from there shoving my pack between the back of the sofa and the cushion and substituting his for it – you're a card-sharper, sir, and not a gentleman!'

'And I saw the other one changing a card twice,' cried Kalganov.

'Oh, how disgraceful, how disgraceful!' cried Grushenka, clasping her hands and blushing with shame in good earnest. 'Lord, what has he come to!'

'I thought so, too!' cried Mitya.

But no sooner had he uttered the words than Vrublevsky, completely disconcerted and mad with fury, turned to Grushenka and, shaking his fist at her, shouted:

'You dirty prostitute!'

But no sooner had he said it than Mitya pounced upon him, seized him with both hands, lifted him in the air and in an instant carried him out of the room into the bedroom on the right, into which he had taken them a few minutes earlier.

'I've put him on the floor there,' he announced, coming back at once and breathless with excitement. 'He's putting up a fight, the blackguard, but I don't think he'll come back!' He closed one half of the door and, holding the other one wide open, cried to the little Pole: 'Won't you join your friend, sir? Be so good, sir!'

'Mr Karamazov, sir,' exclaimed the innkeeper, 'why don't you get back the money you've lost from them? Why, they've as good as stolen it from you.'

'I don't want my fifty roubles back,' Kalganov said suddenly.

'I don't want my two hundred, either,' cried Mitya. 'I won't have it back for anything. Let him keep it as a consolation.'

'Wonderful, Mitya, well done!' cried Grushenka, and there was a note of terrible spite in her exclamation.

The little Pole, purple with rage, though without losing his dignity, went to the door, but stopped on reaching it and said suddenly, addressing Grushenka:

'Madam, if you want to come with me, come, if not – good-bye!'

And, puffed up with indignation and self-importance, he went out of the door. He was a man of character: even after what had just happened, he still hoped that Grushenka would go with him – he had such a high opinion of himself. Mitya slammed the door after him.

'Lock them up,' said Kalganov.

But the key was turned on their side of the door: they had locked themselves in.

'Wonderful!' Grushenka cried again, spitefully and mercilessly. 'Wonderful! Good riddance to bad rubbish!'

8

Delirium

ALMOST an orgy began, a revel to end all revels. Grushenka was the first to demand champagne: 'I want to drink,' she cried, 'I want to get blind drunk, just as I was before when – remember, Mitya, remember? – we got to know each other so well here!' Mitya himself seemed to be in a delirium, feeling that his 'happiness' was now assured. Grushenka, however, kept sending him away from her: 'Go and enjoy yourself! Tell them to dance. I want them all to enjoy themselves – "let the stove and cottage dance" – like last time, like last time!' she went on saying. She was terribly excited. And Mitya rushed off to carry out her orders. The choir assembled in the next room. The room in which they had been sitting till that moment was too small, divided in two by a cotton curtain, behind which there was also a huge bed with a well-stuffed feather-bed and with an identical pile of cotton pillows. All the four 'drawing' rooms of the inn had beds in them. Grushenka settled herself at the door, Mitya placing an armchair for her there: she had sat in the same place 'last time', on the day of their first party and had watched the choir and dancing from there. The girls were the same as on that night. The Jewish band with the zithers and fiddles had also come, and the long-expected cart with the wines and provisions had at last arrived. Mitya was very busy. Other people, too, peasants and peasant women, came into the room to watch. They had all been asleep, but they had got up in the hope of another princely entertainment like the one they had enjoyed a month before. Mitya greeted and embraced those he knew, remembering their faces. He uncorked bottles and poured out wine to all and sundry. Only the girls showed a great interest in the champagne, the peasants preferred rum and brandy and, especially, hot punch. Mitya ordered hot chocolate for all the girls and saw to it that three samovars should be kept on the boil all night to provide tea and punch for anyone who cared to help himself. In short, what followed was utterly fantastic and chaotic, but Mitya seemed to be in his natural element, and the more fantastic it all became, the more his spirits rose. If any peasant had asked him for money at that moment, he would at once have pulled out his bundle of notes and begun distributing it right and left without counting. That was probably why the landlord, to protect Mitya, never for a moment lost sight of him, following him constantly about the room. He seemed to have given up the idea of going to bed that night, but he drank little (all he had was a small glass of punch) and kept a sharp watch over Mitya's interests, in his own way. Whenever it became necessary, he stopped him obsequiously and affectionately, tried to dissuade him from giving away 'cigars and Rhine wine' or, God forbid, money to the peasants as he had done before, and was very indignant with him for letting the girls drink liqueurs and eat sweets. 'They're a lousy lot, sir,' he said, 'I kick their backsides and tell them to regard it as an honour – that's what they're like!' Mitya remembered Andrey again and ordered punch to be sent out for him. 'I've offended him,' he kept repeating in a weak, tremulous voice. Kalganov did not want to drink, nor did he like the girls' choir very much at first, but after he had drunk a couple of glasses of champagne, he became very gay, strolled about the rooms, laughed and expressed his admiration for everything and everyone, songs and music. Maximov, drunk and looking blissful, never left him for a moment. Grushenka, who was also beginning to get drunk, kept pointing to Kalganov and saying to Mitya: 'What a nice boy he is! What a darling!' And Mitya ran delightedly to kiss Kalganov and Maximov. Oh, he was expecting great things! So far, she had said nothing to him to justify his hopes and, indeed, seemed to be deliberately refraining from saying it, looking at him only from time to time not only with affectionate but also with ardent eyes. At last she seized him firmly by the hand and drew him to her by force. She was sitting in the armchair by the door at the time.

'Goodness, if you knew what you looked like when you walked in! How you walked in! You gave me a terrible fright. What made you want to give me up to him? You did want to, didn't you?'

'I didn't want to destroy your happiness!' Mitya babbled to her blissfully.

But she did not need his answer.

'Well, go, have a good time,' she sent him away again. 'And don't cry, I'll call you back again.'

And he ran away, while she again began listening to the songs and looking at the dancing, following him with her eyes wherever he happened to be. But a quarter of an hour later she called him back again, and he ran back to her again.

'Well, sit down beside me now and tell me how you heard the news of my coming here yesterday? Who was the first to tell you?'

And Mitya began telling her all about it, incoherently, confusedly, feverishly, but rather strangely, too, often frowning suddenly and stopping abruptly.

'What are you frowning at?' she asked.

'Nothing. . . . I left a sick man there. I'd give ten years of my life for him to get well, to know he'll get well!'

'Oh, never mind, if he's ill. Did you really mean to shoot yourself tomorrow, you silly fellow? Whatever for? Oh, I love reckless men like you,' she murmured, articulating her words with some difficulty. 'So you'll do anything for me, will you? Did you really intend to shoot yourself tomorrow, silly? No, you wait, I may have something to tell you tomorrow – no, not today – tomorrow. You'd have liked it to be today, wouldn't you? No, I don't want to today. . . . Well, go along now, go – enjoy yourself.'

Once, however, she called him back to her, looking perplexed and troubled.

'Why are you sad? I can see you're sad. . . . Yes, I can,' she added, looking intently into his eyes. 'You may be kissing the peasants and shouting, but I can see something's wrong. No, go and enjoy yourself. I'm enjoying myself and I want you to enjoy yourself, too . . .

I love somebody here – guess who? Oh, look my little boy has fallen asleep, the darling's drunk.'

She was referring to Kalganov: he was, in fact, drunk and had dropped off to sleep for a moment, sitting on the sofa. And it was not only drink that had sent him to sleep; he felt suddenly sad for some reason or, as he used to say, 'bored'. He had been greatly disheartened in the end by the girls' songs, which, as the drinking went on, became more and more lewd and licentious. And so were their dances: two girls dressed up as bears, and Stepanida, a pert girl, with a stick in her hand, acting the part of the bear-leader, began 'to show them off'. 'Come on, Maria,' she cried, 'shake a leg, or you'll get the stick.' The bears, at last, rolled on the floor in a way that was far from decent amid the loud laughter of the closely packed company of peasants and their women. 'Well, let them, let them,' Grushenka kept saying sententiously with a blissful expression on her face. 'Why shouldn't people be happy when they're lucky enough to get a day to enjoy themselves?' But Kalganov looked as though he had soiled himself. 'It's filthy – all this folk revelry,' he remarked, as he moved away. 'These are their spring games when they keep watch for the sun all through midsummer night.' But he particularly disliked a 'new' song to a sprightly dance tune about how a country squire came and tried to find out whether his village girls loved him.

> A country squire his girls did ask:
> Do you love me or do you not?

But it seemed to the girls that they could not love their squire:

> The squire will beat me black and blue
> And I'll never be his lover true.

Then a gipsy came along and he, too, asked the girls:

> A gipsy man the girls did ask:
> Do you love me or do you not?

But they could not love the gipsy because –

> The gipsy he will always thieve,
> And all my life I'll have to grieve.

And all sorts of people came to ask the girls the same question, including a soldier:

> A soldier boy the girls did ask:
> Do you love me or do you not?

But they rejected the soldier with contempt:

> A soldier boy will wear full kit,
> And after him I'll run —

There followed a most unprintable expression, sung with absolute frankness, which created a furore in the audience. In the end a merchant came along:

> A merchant rich the girls did ask:
> Do you love me or do you not?

And it appeared that they did love him, because –

> The merchant riches great will gain
> And I his queen will be and reign. . . .

Kalganov grew positively angry:

'It's really an old folk song,' he said aloud, 'and who composes it for them, I wonder. I suppose if a Jew or a railwayman came along to try his luck with them, they'd have got the lot.'

And, almost as though he were offended, he declared at once that he was bored and, sitting down on the sofa, suddenly dozed off. His small, handsome face turned rather pale and his head fell back on the cushion of the sofa.

'Look, how handsome he is!' Grushenka said, taking Mitya up to him. 'I was combing his hair before you came; his hair's like flax and so thick! . . .'

And bending over him tenderly, she kissed him on the forehead. Kalganov instantly opened his eyes, looked at her, sat up and asked with a most worried expression where Maximov was.

'That's whom he wants,' Grushenka laughed. 'Sit with me for a minute. Mitya, go and fetch his Maximov.'

Maximov, it appeared, could not keep away from the girls, leaving them only occasionally to pour himself out a glass of liqueur. He had had two cups of chocolate. His face was red, his nose purple, and his eyes moist and amorous. He ran up to them and announced that he was wanted to dance a *sabotière* 'to a special tune'.

'You see,' he said, 'as a little boy I was taught all those well-bred society dances.'

'Go and have a look at him, Mitya, and I'll watch him dance from here.'

'I'm coming to look, too,' cried Kalganov in a most naïve way, rejecting Grushenka's offer to sit with her.

And they all went to look on. Maximov did, in fact, dance his dance, but, with the exception of Mitya, no one showed any particular enthusiasm for it. The whole dance consisted of a series of leaps and bounds and drawing up his feet behind him, and at every leap Maximov slapped the sole of his foot. Kalganov did not like it at all, but Mitya liked it so much that he kissed the dancer.

'Well, thank you, thank you. You're not tired, are you? What are you looking for here? Want a sweet? Or a cigar?'

'A cigarette, sir.'

'Don't you want a drink?'

'I'll have a liqueur, thank you. You haven't any chocolates, have you?'

'Why, there's a whole heap of them on the table. Choose any you like, you simple soul.'

'I'd like a vanilla one – they are for old people – hee, hee!'

'I'm sorry, we haven't got any of those.'

'I say,' the old man bent down to whisper in Mitya's ear, 'that pretty girl, there, Maria, hee, hee! Don't you think you could – er – introduce her to me? I'd consider it a great favour, you know. . . .'

'So that's what you want, is it? No, old man, you can't have that.'

'But I'm doing no harm to anyone,' Maximov whispered dejectedly.

'Oh well, all right. They only came to sing and dance here, old man. But, damn it, it might be arranged, only you'll have to wait. . . . Meanwhile eat, drink, and make merry. Want any money?'

'Later on, perhaps, sir,' Maximov smiled.

'All right, all right. . . .'

Mitya's head was burning. He went out into the hall and on to the wooden veranda which ran round the inner part of the house overlooking the yard. The fresh air revived him. He stood alone in the dark, in a corner of the veranda, and suddenly clutched his head in both hands. His disconnected thoughts suddenly sorted themselves out, his feelings merged and everything became clear to him in a flash of dazzling light. A terrible, dreadful light! 'If I am to shoot myself, why not now?' it ran through his mind. 'Go back for a pistol, bring it here, and make an end of everything in this filthy, dark corner.' For nearly a minute he stood still, unable to make up his mind. A short while earlier, when he was rushing here, he had left behind him disgrace, the theft he had committed and that blood, that blood! . . . But it was easier for him then, oh ever so much easier! For then everything was at an end: he had lost her, he had given her up, she was gone, lost to him – oh, the death sentence had been so much easier for him then, at least it had seemed inevitable and necessary, for what was there left for him to live for? But now? Was it the same as before? Now, at least, he had finished with one phantom, one horror: that 'first, rightful one', the man who had played such a fateful part in her life, had gone without leaving a trace behind him. The terrifying phantom had turned out to be so small, so comic; it had been carried into the bedroom and locked in. It would never return. She was ashamed and he could clearly see from her eyes now whom she loved. It was now that he should go on living, and yet it was impossible to go on living, impossible, oh, damnation! 'O Lord, bring to life the man I knocked down at the fence! Remove that terrible cup from my lips. Hast thou not wrought miracles for sinners like me, O Lord? But what, what if the old man is alive? Oh, I shall then blot out the shame of my other disgrace! I shall return the stolen money, I shall give it back. I'll get it by hook or by crook. . . . There will be no trace left of my disgrace except in my heart for ever! But no, no! Oh it's all an impossible, a cowardly dream! Oh, damnation!'

But there still was a faint ray of hope in the darkness. He rushed back to her, to her once more, to the queen, for ever! 'Isn't one hour, one minute of her love worth a lifetime of disgrace and agony?' That wild question clutched at his heart. 'To her, to her alone! To see her, to listen to her and think of nothing else! To forget everything, if only for this night, for an hour, for a moment!' At the very entrance to the hall, while still on the veranda, he ran across the landlord, who looked worried and gloomy and was apparently looking for him.

'What's the matter? Are you looking for me?'

'No, sir, not for you,' the innkeeper seemed to be taken aback. 'Why should I be looking for you? And where – where were you, sir?'

'Why are you so glum? You're not cross, are you? Wait a bit, you'll soon be able to go to bed. What's the time?'

'It'll be three o'clock, sir. Past three, I shouldn't wonder.'

'We'll be finishing soon, soon.'

'Good Lord, sir, I don't mind, I'm sure. You can go on as long as you like.'

'What's the matter with him?' Mitya wondered and rushed into the room where the girls were dancing. But she was not there. There was only Kalganov dozing on the sofa. Mitya looked behind the curtain – she was there. She was sitting in a corner, on a trunk, and, bending forward with her head and arms on the bed, she was crying bitterly, doing her utmost to stifle her sobs, so that she might not be heard. Seeing Mitya, she motioned him to her, and when he ran up to her, she grasped him tightly by the hand.

'Mitya, Mitya, I did love him,' she began in a whisper. 'I loved him so much, all those five years, all that time! Was it him I loved or only my own spite? No, him! Oh yes, him! It's not true that I loved only my spite and not him! Mitya, I was only seventeen then, and he was so nice to me, so gay, he used to sing songs to me. . . . Or did he seem so to me, a silly little girl, at the time? And now, goodness me, why, he isn't the same man, he isn't at all! His face isn't the same even, not at all the same. I shouldn't have recognized him by his face. When I drove here with Timofey, I kept thinking all the time, kept saying to myself all the way: "How am I going to meet him? What am I going to say to him? How shall we look at one another?" I couldn't wait to see him, and as soon as I arrived he seemed to have emptied a pail of slops over me. Speaks to me as though he were a schoolmaster, all so important and learned. He met me so importantly that I was taken aback. I couldn't get a word in edgeways. At first I thought he was ashamed of his big Pole. I sat looking at them and wondering why I didn't know what to say to him now. You know, I'm sure it was his wife who did it, the woman he threw me over for and married. It was she who made a different man of him. Oh, Mitya, think of the shame of it! Oh, I'm so ashamed, Mitya, so ashamed! I'm ashamed of my whole life! Damn, damn those five years, damn them!'

And she burst into tears again, but she did not let go of Mitya's hand, clasping it tightly.

'Mitya, darling, wait, don't go, I want to tell you something,' she whispered, suddenly raising her face to him. 'Listen, tell me who do I love? I love one man here. Who is that man? Tell me that.' A bright smile hovered over her face, swollen with weeping, and her eyes shone in the semi-darkness. 'Then a tall and handsome young man came in and my heart sank: "What a fool you are," my heart whispered to me at once. "That's the man you love!" You came in and everything became clear to me. What is he afraid of, I wondered. And you were frightened, weren't you? You were frightened to death. You could hardly speak. He couldn't be afraid of them, I thought, for you could not be frightened of anyone, could you? He's afraid of me, I thought, of me alone. For Fenya must have told you, you little idiot, how I cried to Alyosha out of the window that I'd loved darling Mitya for one little hour and that I was now going to love – another. Mitya, Mitya, how could I have been such a fool to think that I loved another after you? Do you forgive me, Mitya? Do you forgive me or not? Do you love me? Do you love me?'

She jumped up and clutched his shoulders with both hands. Mitya, dumb with rapture, kept gazing into her eyes, at her face, at her smile, and suddenly, clasping her tightly in his arms, began showering kisses upon her.

'Will you forgive me for having tormented you? I tormented you all from spite. It was from spite that I drove that horrible old man out of his mind. Remember how you drank at my house one day and smashed the glass? I remembered it today and I, too, smashed a glass, drinking to "my vile heart". Mitya, darling, why don't you kiss me? You kissed me once and stopped, and now you look at me and listen. Why listen to me? Kiss me, kiss me harder – so! If we are to love one another, then let's love properly! I shall be your slave now, your slave for the rest of my life. It is sweet to be a slave! Kiss me! Beat me, torture me, do what you like with me. . . . Oh, I deserve to be tortured. . . . Stop! Wait, later, I don't want to now,' she pushed him away suddenly. 'Go away, Mitya, I'll go and have some wine now. I want to get drunk, I'm going to get drunk and dance. Yes, I will!'

She tore herself away from him and disappeared behind the curtains. Mitya followed her, like a drunken man. 'I don't care what

happens now,' it flashed through his mind, 'for one minute I'll give
the whole world.' Grushenka actually did toss off a glass of champagne and got suddenly very drunk. She resumed her former seat in
the armchair with a blissful smile. Her cheeks flamed, her lips burned,
her eyes grew moist and there was an inviting, passionate look in
them. Even Kalganov's heart missed a beat and he went up to
her.

'Did you feel me kiss you just now when you were asleep?' she
murmured to him. 'I'm afraid I'm drunk now. . . . And aren't you
drunk? And why doesn't Mitya drink? Why don't you drink, Mitya?
I've drunk and you won't. . . .'

'I'm drunk! I'm drunk as it is – drunk with you, and now I'll get
drunk with wine, too.'

He drank another glass and – he thought it strange himself it was
only that last glass that made him drunk, suddenly drunk, for till then
he had been quite sober – he remembered it very well. From that
moment everything went whirling round him, as though in a delirium. He walked about, laughed, talked to everyone, and he did it
all without realizing what he was doing. The only thing he was aware
of every minute was the persistent, burning feeling inside him, 'just
like a burning coal in my heart', he recollected afterwards. He kept
going up to her, sitting down beside her, looking at her, listening to
her. . . . She, for her part, became very talkative, kept calling everyone to her, beckoned to some girl from the choir to come up to her,
and she would kiss her or let her go or make the sign of the cross over
her. Another moment and she would have burst into tears. The 'silly
old man', as she called Maximov, amused her very much. He kept
running up every moment to kiss her hand and 'every little finger',
and finished up by doing yet another dance to the tune of an old song
which he sang himself. He kicked up his heels with special enthusiasm
at the refrain:

> The little pig – oink, oink, oink, oink,
> The little calf – moo, moo, moo, moo,
> The little duck – quack, quack, quack, quack,
> The little goose – honk, honk, honk, honk,
> The little hen goes walking through the house,
> Cluck, cluck, cluck, cluck, she said,
> Oh, oh, she said!

'Give him something, Mitya,' Grushenka kept saying, 'give him a present, he's poor, you know. Oh, the poor, they've such a lot to put up with! . . . You know, Mitya, I think I'll enter a convent. Yes, I really shall one day. Alyosha said something to me today that I shall remember all my life. Yes. . . . But today let's dance. Tomorrow to a nunnery, but today we shall dance. I want to amuse myself, good people – and why not? God will forgive me. If I were God, I'd forgive everyone: "My dear little sinners, from today I forgive you all." And I'll go and beg forgiveness: "Forgive, good people, a silly woman." I'm a wild beast, that's what I am. I want to pray. I gave away an onion. Jezebel that I am, I want to pray. Mitya, let them go on dancing, don't interfere. Everyone in the world is good, everyone without exception. The world's a nice place. We may be bad, but the world's a nice place. We're good and bad, good and bad. . . . No, tell me, I ask you – come here everyone, I want to ask you something – tell me this: why am I so good? I *am* good, you know – I'm very good. Well, then tell me: why am I so good?' Grushenka babbled, getting more and more drunk. In the end, she declared that she was going to dance herself at once. She got up from her chair and staggered violently. 'Mitya,' she cried, 'don't give me any more wine – if – if I ask you for more, don't g-give me any. W-wine doesn't bring peace. And everything is going round and round, the stove and everything, I w-want to dance. Let them all see how I dance – how b-beautifully I dance. . . .'

And she really meant it: she took a white lawn handkerchief out of her pocket and held it up in her right hand by one corner to wave it in the dance. Mitya called everyone to order. The girls fell silent, ready to burst out into a dancing song at the first signal. Maximov, learning that Grushenka wanted to dance by herself, squealed with delight and went skipping in front of her, singing the refrain —

> Its legs thin, its sides trim,
> Its little tail all in a curl.

But Grushenka waved her handkerchief at him and drove him away.

'Sh-h! Mitya, why don't they come? Let them all come and see. . . . Why did you lock them up? Tell them I'm going to dance. I want them, too, to see how I dance. . . .'

Mitya went reeling drunkenly to the locked door and began knocking to the Poles with his fist.

'Hey, you there – Podvysotskys, come out! She wants to dance – she calls you.'

'Loafer!' one of the Poles shouted in reply.

'You're a dirty loafer yourself! You're a dirty little rascal – that's what you are!'

'I wish you'd stop jeering at the Poles,' Kalganov, who was also far gone, remarked sententiously.

'Keep quiet, boy! I told him he was a dirty rascal, but that does not mean that all Poles are rascals. One rascal doesn't make a Poland. Keep quiet, pretty boy, and eat your sweets.'

'What horrible people! Just as though they weren't human beings at all. Why don't they want to make friends?' said Grushenka, and went forward to dance.

The choir burst into a popular folk-song. Grushenka tossed back her head, half opened her lips, waved her handkerchief and, suddenly, swaying violently, stopped dead in the middle of the room, looking bewildered.

'I'm feeling awfully weak,' she said in a sort of exhausted voice. 'I'm sorry – I'm weak – I can't go on – sorry. . . .'

She bowed to the choir, and then began bowing in every direction in turn.

'I'm sorry – sorry. . . .'

'The lady's had a drop too much – the pretty lady has had too much to drink,' voices could be heard saying.

'She's drunk,' Maximov explained, tittering, to the girls.

'Mitya, take me away – take me, Mitya,' Grushenka said, weakly.

Mitya rushed up to her, grabbed her in his arms, and ran with his precious booty behind the curtain. 'Well,' thought Kalganov, 'now I'll certainly go,' and, going out of the blue room, he closed the two halves of the door behind him. But the party in the large room went thundering on and grew more and more noisy. Mitya put Grushenka on the bed and kissed her passionately on the lips.

'Don't touch me,' she murmured in an imploring voice, 'don't touch me, I'm not yours yet. . . . I've told you I'm yours, but don't touch me – spare me. . . . We mustn't while they're still here, not while they're so near. He's here. It's odious here. . . .'

'As you like! I wouldn't think of it – I worship you!' Mitya muttered. 'Yes, it is odious here – oh, it's contemptible.'

And, without freeing her from his embrace, he knelt on the floor by the bed.

'I know, you may be a brute, but you're honourable,' Grushenka said, enunciating the words with difficulty. 'It must all be open and above board – in future it shall be open and above board, and we, too, must be honest, we must be good, not brutes, but good. . . . Take me away, take me far, far away – you hear? I don't want to be here, but far, far away. . . .'

'Oh yes, yes, certainly!' Mitya assented, pressing her in his arms. 'I'll take you away – we'll fly away. . . . Oh, I'd give my whole life for one year now, if only I could find out about that blood!'

'What blood?' Grushenka repeated, bewildered.

'Nothing,' Mitya muttered, grinding his teeth. 'Grusha, you want it to be honest, but I'm a thief. I've stolen money from Katya. . . . It's disgraceful, disgraceful!'

'From Katya? You mean from that young lady? No, you haven't. Give it back to her. Take it from me. Don't shout at me! Now all I have is yours. What do we want money for? We'd squander it, anyway. People like us cannot help squandering it. We'd better go and work on the land. I want to scrape up the earth with my own hands. We must work – do you hear? Alyosha told me to. I won't be your mistress. I'll be a true wife to you, I'll be your slave, I'll work for you. We'll go to your young lady, bow down to her both of us, ask her to forgive us, and then we'll go away. And if she doesn't forgive us, we'll go away all the same. You take the money back to her, and love me. . . . Don't love her. . . . Don't love her any more. If you do, I'll strangle her. I'll scratch her eyes out with a needle. . . .'

'I love you, you alone. In Siberia I'll love you. . . .'

'Why in Siberia? Never mind, though. In Siberia, if you like. . . . We shall work there. . . . There's snow in Siberia. . . . I love driving in the snow and – we must have bells. . . . Listen, bells jingling. . . . Where are those bells jingling? Someone's coming. Now they've stopped jingling. . . .'

She closed her eyes, exhausted, and seemed suddenly to fall asleep for a moment. A bell had certainly been jingling in the distance and suddenly stopped. Mitya let his head drop on her breast. He did not notice that the bell had stopped jingling, nor did he notice that the songs had ceased suddenly and that, instead of the songs and the drunken uproar, a dead silence fell upon the whole house all of a sudden. Grushenka opened her eyes.

'What's the matter? Have I been asleep? Yes – the bells. . . . I've been asleep and dreamt that I was driving over the snow and the bells were jingling and I was dozing. I was driving with a man I loved, with you – far, far away. I was embracing you and kissing you, clinging to you. I was cold, and the snow glistened. . . . You know, when the snow glistens, and the moon looks down from the sky, I feel as though I were not anywhere on earth. . . . I wake up and my darling is beside me. Oh, how nice!'

'Beside you,' Mitya murmured, kissing her dress, her breast, her hands. Suddenly he had a strange feeling: it seemed to him that she was looking straight ahead of her and not at him, not at his face, but somewhere over his head, and with an intent and a strangely fixed gaze.

'Mitya, who is that looking at us?' she whispered suddenly.

Mitya turned round and saw that someone had indeed drawn the curtain and seemed to be watching them. And not one man, either. He jumped up and walked quickly up to the man who was watching them.

'Come along, sir, step into this room, please,' said a voice, not loudly, but firmly and insistently.

Mitya stepped to the other side of the curtain and stopped dead. The whole room was full of people, but quite new people, not those who had been there before. A cold shiver ran down his spine and he gave a start. He recognized all those men at once. That tall, fat old man, in an overcoat and a cap with a cockade was Mikhail Makarov, the police inspector. And that smartly dressed, 'consumptive-looking' man – 'always wearing such polished boots' – was the assistant public prosecutor. 'He has a chronometer worth four hundred roubles, he showed me it.' And that small young man in spectacles. . . . Mitya had forgotten his name, but he knew him, he had seen him: it was the examining magistrate, who had recently arrived from the 'school of jurisprudence'. And that one was the rural inspector of police, Mavriky Mavrikych – he knew that one very well, he was a good acquaintance of his. Well, and those fellows with the tin badges, what were

they doing here? And two more, peasants by the look of them. . . .
And there in the doorway were Kalganov and the innkeeper.

'Gentlemen, what is it all about?' said Mitya, but suddenly, as though
beside himself, as though not himself at all, he cried aloud, at the top
of his voice:

'I un-der-stand!'

The young man in the glasses suddenly stepped forward and going
up to Mitya, began with dignity, though hurriedly:

'We have something to – in short, I must ask you to come this way,
this way, to the sofa. We must absolutely insist on an explanation
from you, sir.'

'The old man!' cried Mitya in a frenzy. 'The old man and his
blood! I un-der-stand!'

And as though shot through the heart, he sank, almost fell, on the
chair standing beside him.

'You understand, do you? Understood, have you? Monster and
parricide! Your old father's blood cries out against you!' the old
police inspector roared suddenly, stepping up to Mitya.

He was beside himself, grew purple in the face, and shook all over.

'That's quite impossible!' the small young man cried, 'Mikhail
Makarych, this won't do, sir! I must insist on being allowed to speak
by myself. I'd never have expected you to behave like that, sir!'

'But this is delirium, gentlemen, delirium!' the police inspector kept
exclaiming. 'Look at him: at night, drunk, in the company of a disreputable woman, and with his father's blood on his hands. Delirium,
it's delirium!'

'I must beg you with all the force at my command to control your
feelings, sir,' the assistant public prosecutor whispered rapidly to the
old man. 'Otherwise, I shall be forced to take —'

But the little examining magistrate did not let him finish; he turned
to Mitya and said in a firm, impressive, loud voice: 'Retired Lieutenant Karamazov, it is my duty to inform you that you are charged with
the murder of your father, Fyodor Pavlovich Karamazov, which
was committed this night. . . .'

He said something else, and the public prosecutor, too, added a few
words, but though Mitya listened to them, he could no longer understand them. He stared at them all wildly.

I

The Beginning of Perkhotin's Civil Service Career

WE LEFT Peter Perkhotin knocking with all his might at the strong locked gates of Mrs Morozov's house, till, of course, they were eventually opened. Hearing the furious knocking at the gate, Fenya, who had been greatly frightened two hours before and who was still too excited and worried to go to bed, was again frightened almost to the point of hysterics: she imagined that it was Dmitry knocking again (in spite of the fact that she had seen him drive away herself), for no one but he could knock so 'impudently'. She rushed to the caretaker, who had been awakened by the knocking and gone out to the gate, and began imploring him not to open it. But the caretaker, having questioned Perkhotin and found out that he wanted to see Fenya on very important business, decided at last to open. On entering Fenya's kitchen (Fenya having first asked him to let the caretaker come in, 'to make quite sure'), Perkhotin began to question her and at once elicited a most important fact, namely, that when Dmitry had rushed out to look for Grushenka, he had snatched up the pestle from the mortar, and had returned without the pestle, but with his hands covered with blood: 'And the blood was still dripping from them, dripping, dripping all the time!' cried Fenya, who had evidently conjured up that dreadful image herself in her distraught imagination. But Perkhotin had himself seen those blood-stained, though no longer dripping, hands and had helped to wash them. The point, however, was not how long it would have taken the blood to dry, but where Dmitry had dashed off to with the pestle, that is, whether he had really gone to see his father, and what positive proof there was for it? Perkhotin kept harping on this point and though in the end he found out nothing definite, he was to all intents and purposes convinced that Dmitry could not have gone anywhere except to his father's house and that therefore *something* must have happened there. 'And when he came back,' Fenya added excitedly, 'and I told him everything I knew, I began asking him why there was blood on his hands, and he answered that it was human blood and that he had just killed a man – yes, sir, that's what he said. He admitted it all to me and then suddenly ran out of the house like a madman. I sat down and began thinking where he had dashed off to like a madman. He'll go to Mokroye, I thought, and kill my mistress there. So I rushed out at once to beg him not to kill her. I was running to his lodgings, but as I passed by Plotnikov's shop I saw him just about to drive off and that there was no blood on his hands no more.' (Fenya had noticed this and remembered it.) Fenya's grandmother confirmed Fenya's statement as far as she could. After a few more questions, Perkhotin left the house, feeling more worried and upset than when he had entered it.

It would seem that the most obvious and easiest thing for him to do now was to go straight to Fyodor Karamazov's house and find out whether anything untoward had happened there and, if it had, what it was exactly and, having been finally convinced, go to the police inspector, as he firmly made up his mind to do. But the night was dark, Fyodor Karamazov's gates were strong, and he would have to knock again, and if at last the gates were opened and nothing had happened there, Karamazov, whom he scarcely knew, would, in his sardonic fashion, go spreading the story all over the town how a stranger, a civil servant called Perkhotin, burst into his house to find out if anyone had killed him. What a disgrace! And public disgrace Perkhotin feared more than anything in the world. Nevertheless, the feeling that took hold of him was so strong that, stamping his feet angrily and swearing at himself, he rushed off again, but this time not to Karamazov's, but to Mrs Khokhlakov's. If she, he thought, denied having given three thousand roubles to Dmitry Karamazov at such and such an hour, he would go at once to the police inspector; if she did not, he'd put it off till next morning and go home. It was, of course, quite obvious that the young man's decision to go late at night, almost at eleven o'clock, to the house of a society woman he did not know and, perhaps, to get her out of bed in order to ask her a question, which in the circumstances was quite amazing, might have created a greater public scandal than if he had gone to see Karamazov. But that is what sometimes happens, especially in cases like the present one, with the decisions of the most precise and phlegmatic persons. And at that very moment Perkhotin was far from phlegmatic! He remembered all his life afterwards how the uncontrollable feeling of uneasiness that had gradually taken possession of him had at last reached a point of agonizing suspense and had driven him on against his will. Of course, he kept cursing himself all the way for going to that lady, but he said to himself for the tenth time, gritting his teeth, 'I'll get to the bottom of it, come what may!' – and he did: he carried out what he had set out to do.

It was exactly eleven o'clock when he entered Mrs Khokhlakov's house. He was admitted into the courtyard fairly quickly, but when asked whether his mistress was still up or had gone to bed, the caretaker could not say definitely, except that she usually went to bed at that time. 'You'd better go upstairs and send in your name, sir,' the caretaker said. 'If mistress wants to receive you, she will, if not – she won't.' Perkhotin went up, but things were not so easy there. The footman refused to take in his name, but, finally, called a maid. Perkhotin asked her politely but insistently to inform her mistress that a local civil servant wished to see her on some special business, and that if the business had not been so urgent he would not have ventured to come. 'Please,' he begged the girl, 'tell your mistress in those words, in those very words.' She went away and he remained waiting in the hall. Mrs Khokhlakov was in her bedroom, though she had not gone to bed yet. She had been greatly upset ever since Mitya's visit and felt that she would not escape the headache that night which usually followed incidents of that kind. She was very surprised at what her maid told her, and though the unexpected visit at such an hour of a 'local civil servant' she did not know greatly aroused her female curiosity, she declined irritably to see him. But this time Perkhotin stood his ground, stubborn as a mule: he asked the maid most emphatically to tell her mistress 'in these very words' that he wished to see her on 'a matter of great urgency' and that she might be sorry herself afterwards if she refused to see him now. 'I was in such a state that I didn't know what I was doing,' he described it afterwards. The maid looked at him in surprise and went to take his message to her mistress again. Mrs Khokhlakov was astonished, but, on thinking it over, she asked the maid what the gentleman looked like and was told that he was 'very smartly dressed, young, and ever so polite'. We may note, parenthetically, in passing that Perkhotin was a rather handsome young man and was aware of it himself. Mrs Khokhlakov decided to see him. She was in her dressing-gown and slippers, but she threw a black shawl over her shoulders. The 'civil servant' was asked to wait in the same drawing-room in which she had received Mitya a few hours earlier. Mrs Khokhlakov entered the room with a look of stern inquiry and, without inviting her visitor to take a seat, began straight with the question: 'What do you want?'

'I'm sorry to trouble you, madam, but it's a matter that concerns a mutual acquaintance of ours, Mr Dmitry Karamazov,' began Perkhotin.

But no sooner had he mentioned that name, than an expression of the most violent irritation came into Mrs Khokhlakov's face. She nearly shrieked and interrupted him furiously.

'How much longer,' she cried, beside herself, 'how much longer am I going to be worried by that dreadful man? How dare you, sir? How could you bring yourself to disturb a lady you don't know in her own house and at this unearthly hour and – and come to talk to her about a man who only three hours ago came to murder her in this very room, stamping his feet and going out of my house as no gentleman would ever leave a decent house. Let me tell you, sir, that I shall lodge a complaint against you, that I won't let it pass. . . . Kindly leave my house at once. I'm a mother – I – I —'

'Murder! So he tried to murder you, too?'

'Why, has he murdered someone already?'

'Do be so good, madam, as to listen to me for half a minute and I'll explain everything to you in a few words,' Perkhotin replied firmly. 'At five o'clock this afternoon Mr Karamazov borrowed ten roubles from me, as one friend from another, and I know for a fact that he had no money at the time, but at nine o'clock this evening he came to see me again with a bundle of hundred-rouble notes in his hands to the sum of I should say two or even three thousand roubles. His hands and face were covered with blood and he looked like a madman. When I asked him where he got so much money, he replied without hesitation that he had just received it from you and that you had given him a sum of three thousand roubles to go to the gold-mines. . . .'

An expression of painful and intense agitation suddenly appeared on Mrs Khokhlakov's face.

'Goodness, he must have murdered his father!' she cried, clasping her hands. 'I gave him no money. I didn't! Oh, run, run – don't say another word! Save the old man! Run to his father! Run!'

'One moment, madam. You say you gave him no money. Are you quite sure you did not give him any?'

'I didn't! I didn't! I refused to give it him because he wouldn't have appreciated it. He went out in a fury, stamping his feet. He tried to attack me, but I ran away from him. And I'll tell you something else, since I wish to hide nothing from you now. He spat at me – what do you think of that? But why are we standing? Do sit down, please. . . . I'm sorry, I— Or better run, run, you must run to save the unhappy old man from a terrible death!'

'But if he has killed him already?'

'Oh, goodness gracious, of course! So what are we to do now? What do you think we ought to do now?'

Meanwhile she had made Perkhotin sit down and sat down herself opposite him. Perkhotin gave her a brief, but fairly clear, account of the affair, that part of it at least of which he had been a witness himself. He told her also of his visit to Fenya and of the incident with the pestle. All these details produced a shattering effect upon the agitated lady, who kept uttering hysterical shrieks and covering her eyes with her hands.

'Just fancy, I had a feeling it would all happen like that! You know I have such a gift: whatever I imagine is going to happen, does happen. And the times I looked at that dreadful man thinking: that man will end up by murdering me. And now it's happened. I mean, if he hasn't killed me but only his own father, it's merely a visible sign of God's grace that protected me, and, besides, he was ashamed to kill me because, right here, in this very spot, I put round his neck the icon from the relics of the holy martyr, St Varvara. And to think how near I was to death at that moment, for I had gone up close to him and he had stretched out his neck to me! You know, Mr Perkhotin (I'm sorry, but you did say your name was Perkhotin, didn't you?), you know, I don't believe in miracles, but that icon and this unmistakable miracle with me now – it does shake me and I'm again beginning to believe in anything you like. Have you heard about the elder Zossima? But I don't know what I'm saying. . . . And would you believe it? He actually spat at me while wearing the icon round his neck! I admit, he only spat, he did not kill me, and – and dashed off there! But what are we going to do now? Where ought we to go? What do you think?'

Perkhotin got up and said that he was going straight to the police inspector and would tell him all about it and let him do what he thought fit.

'Oh, he's such a nice man! I know Mikhail Makarov. Yes, yes, do go to him. How clever you are, Mr Perkhotin, and how well you've thought it all out. You know I'd never have thought of it!'

'Particularly as I know the police inspector very well myself,' said Perkhotin, who was still standing and was obviously anxious to escape from the impetuous lady, who would not let him say good-bye to her and go away.

'And you know, you know,' she prattled on, 'you simply must come back and tell me what you find out there and – and what comes to light and – and what they decide to do with him and where he's going to be sent to serve his sentence. Tell me, we have no capital punishment, have we? But you simply must come back, even if it's at three o'clock in the morning, at four, at half past four. . . . Tell them to wake me, to shake me, if I don't get up. Oh dear, I shan't be able to go to sleep! I wonder if I oughtn't to come with you. What do you think?'

'N-no, I don't think so. But it wouldn't perhaps be amiss if you wrote three lines now to say that you did not give Mr Dmitry Karamazov any money – I mean, in case it's needed.'

'By all means,' cried Mrs Khokhlakov with enthusiasm, dashing to her bureau. 'And, you know, you amaze me, you simply shatter me by your resourcefulness and your skill in dealing with such affairs! Are you in the service here? How nice it is to know that you are in the service here. . . .'

And, while still talking, she scribbled in a large hand on half a sheet of notepaper the following lines:

'I never in my life lent to the unhappy Dmitry Karamazov (for he is unhappy now for all that) three thousand roubles today, and I have never given him any money at any other time – never! That I swear by all that's holy in the world. Katerina Khokhlakov.'

'Here's the note, sir!' she turned quickly to Perkhotin. 'Go, save him! It's a great thing you're doing, sir!'

And she made the sign of the cross three times over him. She even ran out into the hall to see him off.

'Oh, you don't know how grateful I am to you! You can't imagine how grateful I am to you for having come to me first! How is it we never met before? I should be very pleased to receive you in my house in the future. And how nice it is to know that you're in the service here – with such precision, such resourcefulness! . . . But they simply must appreciate you, they must after all esteem you, and if there's anything I can do for you, believe me. . . . Oh, I am so fond of young people! Our younger generation is the – the foundation of our dear, suffering Russia, her only hope. . . . Oh, go, go! . . .'

But Perkhotin had already run out of the house, or she would not have let him go so soon. However, Mrs Khokhlakov had made a rather agreeable impression on him, which even somewhat allayed his alarm at having got mixed up in such an unpleasant affair. Tastes differ, as we all know. 'And she isn't so old at all,' he thought, feeling rather pleased. 'Quite the contrary, I'd have taken her for her daughter.'

As for Mrs Khokhlakov, she was simply enchanted by the young man. 'Such *savoir faire*, such correctness, and in such a young man, too, and in our day! And all that with such nice manners and such a charming appearance! And there are people who say that our young men today can't do anything – here's an example for you!' and so on and so forth. So that she simply forgot this 'dreadful affair', and it was only as she was getting into bed that she suddenly remembered again how 'near death' she had been. 'Oh,' she exclaimed, 'it's dreadful, dreadful!' But she fell asleep at once and slept like a top. However, I wouldn't have enlarged on such trivial and irrelevant details, if the eccentric meeting of the young civil servant with the far from elderly widow I have just described had not afterwards turned out to be the making of the career of that correct and precise young man, which fact is still remembered with amazement in our little town and about which we shall perhaps have something to say when we have finished our long tale of the brothers Karamazov.

2

The Hue and Cry

OUR police inspector, Mikhail Makarov, a retired Lieutenant-Colonel, was a widower and a most excellent man. He had arrived in our town only three years previously, but had become a popular figure chiefly because he knew how 'to bring people together'. His house was always full of visitors and he could not apparently live without them. He had always a guest or two at dinner, and he never sat down to table without guests. He also gave dinner parties on any pretext, some-times on most surprising pretexts. The fare at his dinners, though not particularly dainty, was abundant, the fish soups were excellent, and the wines made up in quantity what they lacked in quality. In the large hall was a billiard table with all the necessary concomitants, that is to say, even with engravings of English race horses in black frames on the walls, which, as is well known, form the indispensable decora-tion of every bachelor's billiard-room. Every evening he and his guests played cards, even if it were only at one table. But quite often all the best society of our town – including mothers and their unmar-ried daughters – assembled at his house to dance. Though a widower, Inspector Makarov lived with his family, that is to say, with his widowed daughter, the mother of two girls, Makarov's grandchildren. The girls, who were grown up and had finished their education, were not bad-looking, and of a cheerful disposition, and though everyone knew that they would have no dowry, they attracted our young gentlemen to their grandfather's house. Inspector Makarov was far from efficient at his job, but he carried out his duties no worse than many others. To be quite frank, he was rather an uneducated man and was a bit lacking in a clear understanding of the limits of his adminis-trative powers. Though he had a pretty good idea of some of the reforms of the present reign, he was rather apt to misinterpret them badly sometimes, and that not because of any special incapacity, but simply because of carelessness, because he could not find time to study them properly. 'I am a soldier and not a civilian at heart, gentlemen,' he used to say of himself. He still did not seem to have a very clear and complete idea of the fundamental principles of the peasant reforms, and learnt about them, as it were, from year to year, accumulating his knowledge involuntarily and in practice, and yet he was himself a landowner. Perkhotin knew very well that he was sure to meet some visitors at Makarov's that evening, but did not know which in particular. But, as luck would have it, the public prosecutor and our district doctor, Varvinsky, a young man who had only recently arrived from Petersburg where he had graduated at the medical academy with distinction, were just then playing whist at the police inspector's. Ippolit Kirilovich, the public prosecutor, or rather the assistant public prosecutor, whom we all called the public prosecutor, was rather a peculiar man of only five and thirty, with a strong predisposition to consumption, married to a very fat and childless woman. He was vain and irritable, though extremely intelligent and, indeed, kind-hearted. It seems that all that was wrong with him was that he had a somewhat higher opinion of himself than his true accomplishments warranted. And that was why he always seemed restless. He had, indeed, some higher, and even artistic, pretensions; for instance, to psychology, to a special knowledge of the human heart, to a special gift of knowing the workings of the mind of the criminal and the motives of his crime. That was why he considered that he had been rather unappreciated and passed over in the service and was always of the opinion that in higher spheres he had not been appraised at his true worth and that he had enemies. In moments of depression he even threatened to resign his post and take up private practice as a lawyer in criminal cases. The unexpected Karamazov parricide case seemed to shake him up thoroughly: it was a case, he said to himself, that might become known all over Russia. But, I'm afraid, I am anticipating.

Our young examining magistrate, Nikolai Nelyudov, who had arrived in our town from Petersburg only two months before, was sitting in the next room with the young ladies. People could not help remarking afterwards with surprise that all these persons should, as though on purpose, have gathered on the evening of 'the crime' at the house of the executive authority. And yet the whole thing was very simple and happened quite naturally: the wife of the public prosecutor had had toothache for two days and he had to run away somewhere from her groans; as for the doctor, he could not, from his very nature, be expected to do anything but play cards in the evening. Nikolai Nelyudov, on the other hand, had been planning to drop in on Makarov for the last three days, as it were inadvertently, in order to startle his eldest grand-daughter Olga suddenly and perfidiously by the news that he knew her secret, that he was fully aware that it was her birthday and that she was trying to conceal it on purpose, so as not to have to invite the town to a dance. He anticipated a great deal of laughter and dark hints about her age and about her fear of revealing it, but now that he was in possession of her secret, he would tell everybody, and so on and so forth. The charming young fellow was very 'naughty' about such things and our ladies always spoke of him as 'a naughty man', which he seemed to like very much. He was exceedingly well-bred, however, of a good family, excellent education and feelings, and though leading a life of pleasure, his pleasures were very innocent and always highly proper. He was very short and of a weak and delicate constitution. On his white, slender fingers there always glittered a number of very big rings. But when carrying out his official duties, he became extraordinarily grave, as though realizing the sanctity of his position and of his responsibilities. He was particularly adept at throwing murderers and other criminals of the lower orders off their guard during an interrogation, and he certainly aroused in them a sort of grudging admiration, if not respect.

When he entered the police inspector's drawing-room, Perkhotin was simply staggered to find that everyone knew – indeed, they had risen from the card table and stood discussing the affair, and even Nelyudov had left the young ladies and joined them, looking very bellicose and ready for action. Perkhotin was met with the stunning news that old Fyodor Karamazov had really been murdered that evening in his own house, murdered and robbed. They had learned the news just before Perkhotin's arrival in the following manner.

Marfa, the wife of Grigory, who had been struck down near the fence, though soundly asleep in her bed, where she might well have slept till the morning, suddenly woke up. She was aroused, no doubt, by the dreadful epileptic scream of Smerdyakov, who was lying unconscious in the next room – the scream that always preceded his epileptic fits and that had always frightened Marfa terribly and had a painful effect on her. She could never get used to them. She jumped up and ran half awake into Smerdyakov's room. But it was dark there and all she could hear was the patient's terrible gasping and struggling. Marfa screamed herself and began calling her husband, but suddenly realized that when she got up Grigory did not seem to be in bed beside her. She rushed back to the bed and began feeling it with her hands, but the bed was really empty. He must have gone out then, but where? She ran out on the front steps and began calling him timidly. She got no answer, of course, but in the silence of the night she caught the sound of groans far away in the garden. She listened: the groans were repeated, and it was evident that they did actually come from the garden. 'Good gracious, just as it was with Lizaveta Smerdyashchaya!' it flashed through her distraught mind. She went gingerly down the steps and saw that the garden gate was open. 'He must be out there, the poor dear,' she thought, went up to the gate and then distinctly heard Grigory calling her, 'Marfa! Marfa!' in a weak, moaning, dreadful voice. 'Lord, help and preserve us!' Marfa whispered and ran towards the voice, and that was how she found Grigory. But she found him not at the fence, not at the place where he had been struck down, but about twenty yards from the fence. It appeared later that on coming to he had crawled away and kept crawling for a long time, losing consciousness again and again. She noticed at once that he was all covered with blood and she screamed at the top of her voice. Grigory was muttering softly and incoherently: 'He's murdered – his father – what are you screaming for, you fool – run, call someone. . . .' But Marfa went on screaming, and suddenly, seeing that her master's window was open and that there was a light in the bedroom, rushed up to the window and began calling Mr Karamazov. But, looking in at the window, she saw a terrible sight: her master was lying on his back on the floor, motionless. His light-coloured dressing-gown and white shirt were soaked with blood. The candle on the table brightly lit up the blood and Karamazov's motionless, dead face. Terrified out of her wits, Marfa rushed away from the window, ran out of the garden, unbolted the gates, and ran headlong by the back way to her neighbour, Maria Kondratyevna. Both mother and daughter were asleep, but they woke up at Marfa's screams and persistent and furious knocking at the shutters and rushed to the window. Marfa, still screaming shrilly and speaking incoherently, told them the main facts, however, and called for help. As it happened, the wanderer Foma was staying the night with them. They got him up at once and all three of them ran back to the scene of the crime. On the way Maria Kondratyevna remembered that at nine o'clock she had heard a terrible,

piercing cry from their garden, which, of course, was the cry of
'Parricide!' Grigory had uttered when he caught hold of the leg of
Dmitry who was already sitting astride the fence. 'Someone screamed
at the top of his voice and then was suddenly silent,' Maria Kondratyevna said, as she ran. On arriving at the place where Grigory lay, the
two women with the help of Foma carried him to the cottage. They
lighted a candle and saw that Smerdyakov was still having his fit in
his room, writhing in convulsions, his eyes turned almost inside out,
and foaming at the mouth. They washed Grigory's head with water
and vinegar and, recovering his senses completely, Grigory asked at
once: 'Has the master been murdered or not?' The two women and
Foma then went to have a look and, on entering the garden, saw this
time that not only the window, but also the door into the garden was
wide open, in spite of the fact that Karamazov had locked the door
every night for the last week and even forbade Grigory to knock on
it under any pretext. Seeing the door open, they were afraid – all three
of them – to go in 'in case anything should happen afterwards'. When
they returned, Grigory told them to run at once to the district police
officer. Maria Kondratyevna immediately ran to the police inspector's
and gave the alarm. She arrived only five minutes before Perkhotin,
so that he did not come just with his own theories and conclusions,
but plainly as a witness who by his story merely confirmed the
general theory as to who the criminal was (which, however, at the
bottom of his heart he had refused to believe up to the very last
moment).

It was decided to act immediately. The assistant police inspector of
the town was at once commissioned to get four witnesses, and according to the rules and regulations, which I am not describing here, they
all went into Fyodor Karamazov's house and carried out the investigation at the scene of the crime. The district doctor, an enthusiastic
man, new to this sort of work, almost insisted on accompanying the
district police inspector, the public prosecutor, and the investigating
magistrate. Let me just note briefly here: Fyodor Karamazov was
found to be quite dead, with a fractured skull, but with what weapon?
Most likely with the same weapon with which Grigory had been
struck down afterwards. And it did not take them long to find it, for
Grigory, who was given all the necessary medical assistance, gave
them in a weak and faltering voice quite a coherent description of how

he had been struck down. They began searching with a lantern by the fence and found the brass pestle, dropped in a most conspicuous place on the garden path. They found no special signs of disturbance in the room where Karamazov was lying, but behind the screen, near the bed, they picked up from the floor a large, thick envelope with the inscription: 'A little present of three thousand roubles to my angel Grushenka, if she comes,' and underneath had been added, probably afterwards by Fyodor Karamazov himself: 'and to my little chicken.' There were three large seals of red sealing wax on the envelope, but it had been torn open and was empty: the money had been removed. On the floor they also found a narrow pink ribbon, with which the envelope had been tied up. There was one thing in Perkhotin's evidence, incidentally, that made a tremendous impression on the public prosecutor and the investigating magistrate, namely his theory that Dmitry would most certainly shoot himself at dawn, that he had made up his mind to do so, had told Perkhotin about it, had loaded the pistol in his presence, had written a note, put it in his pocket, etc. etc. And when Perkhotin, who still refused to believe him, threatened to go and tell someone so as to prevent the suicide, Mitya himself had replied with a grin: 'You'll be too late.' It was therefore necessary to hurry to Mokroye to catch the criminal before he really took it into his head to shoot himself. 'That's clear! That's clear!' the public prosecutor kept repeating in great agitation. 'That's exactly the way such madcaps argue: I'll kill myself tomorrow, but before I do that, I'll have a jolly good time!' The story of how he got the wine and provisions at the shop only made the public prosecutor more excited than ever. 'Do you remember the fellow who killed the merchant Olsufyev, gentlemen? He robbed him of fifteen hundred roubles and went straight to have his hair curled and then, without bothering to conceal the money, almost in fact carrying it in his hands, too, went off to a brothel.' They were delayed, however, by the investigation, the search carried out in Karamazov's house, the formalities, etc. All that took time, and that was why, two hours before starting, they sent off to Mokroye the rural police officer, Mavriky Shmertsov, who had just arrived that morning in the town for his salary. Shmertsov was instructed that on arrival in Mokroye he should not raise the alarm, but keep the 'criminal' under observation unceasingly till the arrival of the proper authorities, as well as procure the witnesses, police constables, etc., etc. Shmertsov did that, keeping his incognito and taking only the innkeeper, an old friend of his, partly into his confidence. It was just a little later that Mitya met the landlord on the veranda in the dark, looking for him, and noticed that there was a curious change in his face and voice. So neither Mitya nor anyone else knew that he was being kept under observation and that his pistol case had been carried off by the landlord and put away in a safe place. The authorities, the district police inspector, the public prosecutor, and the investigating magistrate arrived in two carriages drawn by teams of three horses only at about five o'clock in the morning, almost at sunrise. The doctor remained at Karamazov's house with a view to carrying out a post-mortem on the body of the murdered man next morning. But what interested him most was the condition of the sick servant Smerdyakov: 'Such violent and protracted epileptic fits, which go on recurring uninterruptedly for two whole days, are seldom to be met with and are a matter of scientific interest,' he declared excitedly to his companions as they left, and they congratulated him laughingly on his find. The public prosecutor and the investigating magistrate remembered very well afterwards that the doctor had added in a most decisive tone that he did not expect Smerdyakov to live till the morning.

Now after this long but, I believe, necessary digression, we will return to that moment of our story at which we broke off in the last book.

3

The Journey Through Hell. The First Ordeal

AND so Mitya sat looking wildly at the people in the room, not understanding what they were saying to him. Suddenly he got up, flung up his hands, and cried in a loud voice:

'I'm not guilty! I'm not guilty of that murder! I'm not guilty of my father's murder. I meant to kill him, but I'm not guilty. It wasn't me!'

But no sooner had he said it than Grushenka rushed out from behind the curtain and flung herself straight at the district police inspector's feet.

'It's all my fault!' she cried in a heart-rending voice, tears streaming down her face, stretching out her hands towards them. 'I'm the guilty one, vile wretch that I am! It's because of me that he killed him! It was me who tortured him and drove him to it. I tortured the poor old man, too, out of spite and caused it all! I'm the guilty one – I'm guilty most of all!'

'Yes, you are! You're the chief criminal! You vicious harlot! You're most to blame!' the district police inspector shouted, shaking his fist at her, but at this point he was quickly and resolutely suppressed.

The public prosecutor even threw his arms round him.

'This is utterly irregular, sir,' he cried. 'You're absolutely hindering the investigation – you're ruining the whole thing,' he almost gasped.

'See that he doesn't interfere! See that he doesn't interfere!' cried Nelyudov, too, in great excitement. 'Otherwise it's absolutely impossible!'

'Put us on trial together!' Grushenka, still on her knees, went on screaming frantically. 'Punish us together. I'll go with him now even to the scaffold!'

'Grushenka, my darling, my only one, my treasure!' cried Mitya, falling on his knees beside her and holding her tightly in his arms. 'Don't believe her,' he shouted. 'She's not guilty of anything, of any murder, of anything!'

He remembered afterwards that several men had dragged him away from her by force, that she was led out, and that when he recovered his senses he was sitting at the table. The constables stood beside and behind him. Facing him across the table on a sofa sat Nelyudov, the examining magistrate, who kept asking him to have a drink of water out of a glass that stood on the table. 'That will refresh you, that will calm you,' he added very courteously. 'Don't be afraid, keep calm, keep calm!' Mitya, on the other hand (he remembered it well) became greatly interested in his large rings, one with an amethyst and another with a transparent bright yellow stone of fine brilliance. And long afterwards he remembered with astonishment that his eyes were irresistibly drawn to those rings even during the terrible hours of his interrogation, so that he could not for some reason tear himself away from them or forget them as something totally inappropriate to his situation. On the left, sideways to Mitya, in the place where Maximov had been sitting at the beginning of the evening, now sat the public prosecutor, and on the right, in the place where Grushenka had been, sat a rosy-cheeked young man in a sort of threadbare hunting jacket, with ink and paper before him. This was apparently the clerk of the examining magistrate, who had brought him with him. The district police inspector was now standing at the window, at the other end of the room, near Kalganov, who was sitting on a chair there.

'Have a drink of water!' the examining magistrate repeated gently for the tenth time.

'I had one, gentlemen, I had one, but – well, gentlemen, crush me, punish me, decide my fate!' cried Mitya, glaring at the examining magistrate with a terribly fixed look.

'So you positively assert that you are not guilty of the death of your father, Fyodor Karamazov?' asked the investigating magistrate gently but insistently.

'Not guilty, sir! I'm guilty of the murder of another old man, but not of my father. And I'm sorry for it! I killed, I killed the old man. Struck him down and killed him. . . . But it's hard to have to answer for that murder with another, a terrible murder of which I am not guilty. It's a terrible accusation, gentlemen, a stunning blow! But who has killed my father, who has killed him? Who could have killed him if not I? It's a mystery, an absurdity, an impossibility!'

'Yes, who could have killed him —' began the examining magistrate, but the public prosecutor (the assistant public prosecutor, but we shall call him the public prosecutor for brevity's sake), glancing at the examining magistrate, said, turning to Mitya:

'You needn't worry about the old man, the servant Grigory. I'd like you to know that he is alive, has recovered, and in spite of the terrible blow inflicted upon him by you, according to his own and your evidence, there is no doubt whatever that he will live. So at least the doctor says.'

'Alive? So he is alive!' Mitya shouted suddenly, clasping his hands. His face beamed with delight. 'O Lord, I thank thee for the great miracle thou has wrought for me, sinner and miscreant that I am, in answer to my prayer. Yes, yes, that was in answer to my prayer! I've been praying all night!' and he crossed himself three times. He was almost choking.

'It is from this same Grigory that we've received such important evidence concerning you that —' the public prosecutor went on, but Mitya again jumped up from his chair.

'One moment, gentlemen, for God's sake, one more moment. I'll go to her —'

'I'm sorry, sir, but at this moment it's quite out of the question!' Nelyudov, also jumping to his feet, almost shrieked. Mitya was seized by the constables, but he sat down of his own accord.

'What a pity, gentlemen! I wanted to see her only for a moment – I wanted to tell her that the blood that was weighing so heavily on my heart all night has been washed away and has gone and that I'm no longer a murderer! Why, gentlemen, she is my fiancée!' he said suddenly, ecstatically and reverently, looking round at them all. 'Oh, I thank you, gentlemen. You've restored me to life, you've made a new man of me in one moment! That old man – why, gentlemen, he used to carry me in his arms, washed me in the tub when I, a three-year-old child, was abandoned by everybody. He was like a father to me!'

'So, you —' began the examining magistrate.

'Please, gentlemen, please, one moment more,' Mitya interrupted, putting his elbows on the table and covering his head with his hands. 'Let me think for a moment, let me breathe, gentlemen. All this is a great shock to me. A man's soul is not a sheepskin drum, gentlemen!'

'Have some more water, sir,' Nelyudov murmured.

Mitya removed his hands from his face and laughed. He looked cheerful. In one moment he seemed to have completely changed. His whole bearing was changed: he was now again the equal of all these men, all these former acquaintances of his, just as if they had all met the day before, when nothing had happened, at some social gathering. Let us observe here, by the way, that when he arrived in our town Mitya was very cordially received at the district police inspector's, but that later on, especially during the last month, Mitya hardly ever visited him, and, when meeting him in the street, the police officer looked angry and frowned and returned Mitya's bow only out of politeness. Mitya had not been slow in noticing it. His acquaintance with the public prosecutor was even more distant, but he sometimes paid most respectful calls on the prosecutor's wife, the nervous and fantastic lady, without quite knowing himself why he called on her, and she always received him cordially, taking an interest in him up to the last. He had not had time to get acquainted with the examining magistrate, though he had met and spoken to him once or twice, each time about the fair sex.

'You're a most skilful examining magistrate, I can see, sir,' Mitya cried suddenly with a gay laugh, 'but I'll do all I can to help you now. Oh, gentlemen, I feel like a new man and – and don't be cross with me for addressing you so familiarly and openly. Besides, I'm afraid I'm a little drunk, I tell you that frankly. I believe I have had the honour – er – the honour and pleasure of meeting you, Mr Nelyudov, at my relative Miusov's. . . . Gentlemen, gentlemen, I don't pretend to be on equal terms with you. I – I quite understand my present position. If Grigory has given evidence against me, then I am – oh, of course – I am under suspicion of having committed a horrible crime! It's horrible, horrible – I quite understand that! But to business, gentlemen. I'm ready and I'm sure we shall finish it all now in a moment, because – listen, gentlemen, listen! If I know that I'm not guilty, then we can finish it all in a moment, can't we? Can't we?'

Mitya spoke much and rapidly, nervously and effusively, as though absolutely convinced that his listeners were his best friends.

'So for the present we shall write down that you absolutely deny the charge brought against you,' Nelyudov said impressively and, turning to his clerk, he dictated to him in an undertone what to write.

'Write down? You want to write it down? Why, by all means, write it down. I don't mind. I give you my full consent, gentlemen. . . . Only, you see. . . . Wait, wait! Write this: he is guilty of disorderly conduct, he is guilty of inflicting violent blows upon a poor old man – yes, he's guilty of that. And, well, there's something else in his heart of hearts that he is guilty of, but' (he turned suddenly to the clerk) 'you needn't write that down, for that, gentlemen, is my private life and has nothing to do with you, I mean what's in the depth of my heart. But of the murder of his old father – he's not guilty! The whole thing is absurd! Quite absurd! I'll prove it to you and you'll be convinced at once! You will laugh, gentlemen, you will roar with laughter at your suspicion!'

'Do calm yourself, sir,' the examining magistrate reminded him, as though wishing to allay Mitya's frenzied excitement by his own composure. 'Before carrying on with the interrogation, I'd like, if you don't mind, to hear from you a confirmation of the fact that you seem to have disliked your father and seemed to be having constant quarrels with him. . . . At least a quarter of an hour ago I believe you said that you even wanted to kill him. "I didn't kill him," you exclaimed, "but I wanted to kill him!"'

'Did I declare that? Oh, well, that may very well be so, gentlemen. Yes, unhappily, I did want to kill him many, many times – unhappily, unhappily!'

'You wanted to. Would you mind explaining your real motives for such hatred of the person of your father?'

'What is there to explain, gentlemen?' Mitya shrugged gloomily, looking down. 'I've never concealed my feelings. The whole town knows about it – everyone in the public house knows. Only a short time ago I told them about it in the cell of the elder Zossima. And the same day, in the evening, I attacked my father and nearly killed him. I swore in the presence of witnesses to come back and kill him. . . . Oh, thousands of witnesses! I kept shouting about it a whole month – lots of people will confirm it! . . . There's direct evidence of this fact, it speaks, it shouts for itself, but, gentlemen, feelings – feelings are quite a different matter. You see, gentlemen' (Mitya frowned), 'it seems to me you have no right to question me about my feelings. You may be empowered to do so – I quite understand that – but it's my own affair, my private, intimate affair. . . . But since I haven't concealed my feelings before – in the pub, for instance, where I've talked to everyone about it, I – I won't make a secret of it now. You see, gentlemen, I realize very well that the evidence against me in this affair is overwhelming: I told everyone that I'd kill him, and all of a sudden he's been killed: it couldn't, therefore, have been anyone but me, could it? Ha, ha! I don't blame you at all. I quite understand. You see, I'm completely bowled over myself, for who, after all, could have killed him, if not me? Isn't that so? If not me, then who, who? Gentlemen,' he exclaimed suddenly, 'I'd like to know, gentlemen, indeed, I demand to be told where he was murdered. How was he murdered? How and with what? Tell me,' he asked quickly, looking at the prosecutor and the investigating magistrate.

'We found him lying on the floor of his bedroom, lying on his back, with his head battered in,' said the public prosecutor.

'That's dreadful, gentlemen,' Mitya shuddered suddenly and, leaning on the table, covered his face with his right hand.

'Let's continue,' the examining magistrate interrupted. 'What prompted you in your feelings of hatred? You declared in public, I believe, that it was jealousy, didn't you?'

'Well, yes, jealousy, but not only jealousy.'

'Disagreements over money?'

'Yes, over money, too.'

'There was, I believe, a disagreement about three thousand roubles, which you claimed was owing to you as part of your inheritance.'

'Three thousand? More, more,' Mitya cried excitedly. 'More than six thousand, more than ten thousand, perhaps. I told everyone about it. I shouted about it to everyone! But I made up my mind to let it go at three thousand. I needed the three thousand desperately – so that I regarded the envelope with the three thousand which I knew he kept under his pillow ready for Grushenka as simply stolen from me. Yes, gentlemen, I regarded it as belonging to me, as my own property. . . .'

The public prosecutor glanced significantly at the examining magistrate and managed to wink at him unobserved.

'We'll come back to that later,' the examining magistrate said at once. 'You will, I hope, let us now note and write down this – er – little point, I mean, that you regarded the money in the envelope as your own property.'

'Write it down, gentlemen, write it down. You see, I realize that it's just another piece of evidence against me, but I'm not afraid of any evidence and I bring it against me myself. Do you hear? Myself! You see, gentlemen, you seem to take me for quite a different kind of person from what I am,' he added suddenly, gloomily and sadly. 'You're talking to an honourable man – a most honourable man, don't lose sight of that, above all – a man who's committed lots of mean actions, but who has always been and still is a most honourable human being, as a human being, inside, at bottom, and well, in short, I – I'm afraid I don't know how to put it. I mean, what has made me so unhappy all my life is that I longed to be an honourable man, to be, as it were, a martyr to honour and to seek for it with a lantern, with the lantern of Diogenes, and yet all my life I've been playing dirty tricks on people, like all of us, gentlemen – I mean, like me alone, gentlemen, not like all, but like me alone. I'm sorry, I was wrong – like me alone, me alone! . . . . Gentlemen, my head aches,' he knit his brows with pain. 'You see, gentlemen, I didn't like the way he looked. There was something dishonourable about him, boastful and trampling on everything sacred, jeering and lack of faith – horrible, horrible! But now that he's dead, I think differently.'

'Differently? How do you mean?'

'No, not differently, but I'm sorry I hated him so much.'

'You feel penitent?'

'No, not penitent. Don't write that down. I'm not very good-looking myself, gentlemen, that's the truth. I'm not very handsome, and that's why I had no right to consider him loathsome. Yes, that's it. You can write that down.'

Having said that, Mitya suddenly grew very melancholy. For some time now, gradually, as he kept replying to the investigating magistrate's questions, he had grown gloomier and gloomier. And just at that moment there was another unexpected scene. What happened was that, though Grushenka had been taken away, she had not been taken away far enough, only to the room next but one to the blue room where the interrogation was taking place. It was a small room with one window, next to the large room in which they had danced and made merry. She was sitting there with only Maximov to keep her company. Maximov was terribly confounded, terribly scared, and clung to her as though looking to her for deliverance. At the door of their room stood a peasant with a metal badge on his chest. Grushenka was crying, and then, suddenly, when her grief became too much to bear, she jumped up, threw up her hands, and with a loud wail, 'Oh, woe is me, woe is me!' rushed out of the room to him, to her Mitya, and so unexpectedly that no one was in time to stop her. Hearing her wail, Mitya trembled all over, jumped to his feet, and with a yell rushed headlong to meet her, as though beside himself. But again they were not allowed to meet, though they saw one another. He was violently seized by the arms: he struggled and tried to free himself and it took three or four men to restrain him. She, too, was seized and he saw her stretching out her arms to him as she was dragged out of the room. When the scene was over, he found himself again in the same place as before at the table, opposite the investigating magistrate, and he kept shouting to them:

'What do you want with her? Why do you torture her? She's innocent, innocent!'

The public prosecutor and the investigating magistrate did their best to calm him. Some time, about ten minutes, passed like that; at last Makarov, who had been away all this while, came hurriedly into the room, and said in a loud, excited voice to the public prosecutor:

'She's been taken away, she's downstairs. Will you permit me, gentlemen, to say one word to this unhappy man? In your presence, gentlemen, in your presence!'

'Do, sir,' replied the investigating magistrate. 'We have nothing against it.'

'Now listen to me, Dmitry, my dear fellow,' Makarov began, addressing Mitya, and there was an expression of warm and almost fatherly compassion on his excited face. 'I took your Grushenka downstairs myself, and handed her over to the landlord's daughters, and that old man Maximov is with her there, too, all the time. I prevailed with her – do you hear? – I prevailed with her and calmed her. I made her understand that you have to clear yourself and that she mustn't upset and hinder you, or you may get confused and say what you shouldn't – understand? Well, in short, I talked to her and she understood. She's an intelligent girl, old man. She's a good soul. She tried to kiss my hands in her eagerness to ask me to help you. She sent me here herself to tell you not to worry about her, and I have to go, old man, I have to go and tell her that you are calm and easy in your mind about her. So, calm yourself, please. Understand that I feel responsible for her, she's a Christian soul. Yes, gentlemen, she's a gentle soul and she's not to blame for anything. So what am I to tell her, my dear fellow? Will you keep calm or not?'

The kind-hearted fellow had said a great deal he shouldn't, but Grushenka's suffering, the suffering of a fellow-creature, went straight to his kind heart and tears even started to his eyes. Mitya jumped to his feet and rushed up to him.

'I'm sorry, gentlemen, but let me – oh, let me!' he cried. 'You've the soul of a saint, sir, the soul of a saint, and I thank you for her! I will, I will be calm, I will be cheerful. Tell her, in the infinite goodness of your heart, sir, that I am cheerful, cheerful, that I shall be laughing in a moment, knowing she has a guardian angel like you. I shall finish with all this any moment now, and, as soon as I'm free, I'll join her. She'll see. Let her wait. Gentlemen,' he turned suddenly to the public prosecutor and the investigating magistrate, 'I shall now open up my heart to you. I'll unburden myself to you, and we shall get it over in a moment. Let us finish it gaily and – we shall have a good laugh when it is all over, shan't we? But, gentlemen, that woman is the queen of my heart! Oh, permit me to say that, gentlemen. That I must reveal to you now. For I can see that I'm dealing with most honourable men. She's my light, she's the only thing I hold sacred – oh, if you only knew! You heard her cry "I'll go with him to the scaffold"? And what have I given her, I, a penniless beggar? Why such love for me? Do I, a clumsy, shameless brute, with my shameless face, deserve such love? Do I deserve that she should go to a Siberian prison with me? And a moment ago she was lying at your feet for me, she – a proud and innocent woman! How can I help adoring her? How can I help crying out and rushing to her as I did just now? Oh, forgive me, gentlemen! But now, now I am comforted!'

And he sank into his chair and, covering his face in his hands, wept aloud. But those were happy tears. He recollected himself at once. The old district police officer seemed very pleased, and, it seemed, the lawyers also. They felt that the interrogation was about to enter into a new phase. When the police officer was gone, Mitya looked absolutely gay.

'Well, gentlemen, I'm at your disposal now, entirely at your disposal. And – but for all these trifles, we'd come to an understanding at once. I'm speaking about trifles again. I'm at your disposal, gentlemen, but, I swear, there must be mutual confidence. You must trust me and I must trust you – otherwise we shall never get it finished. I'm saying this in your interests. To business, gentlemen, to business. Above all, don't probe into my heart like that. Don't lacerate it with trifles. Just ask me about facts and about what has a direct bearing on this business, and I'll satisfy you at once. To hell with trifles!'

So Mitya kept exclaiming. The interrogation was resumed.

4

The Second Ordeal

'YOU can't imagine, sir, how you reassure us by your readiness,' Nelyudov said with an animated air and with evident delight in his large, short-sighted, light-grey, protruding eyes, from which he had removed the spectacles a minute before. 'And you were quite right about our mutual confidence without which it is sometimes quite impossible to carry on in a case of such importance, provided, that is, the suspect really desires and hopes to clear himself and can clear himself. For our part, we shall do all we can, and, indeed, you can see for yourself how we are conducting the case. . . . You approve, sir?' he turned suddenly to the public prosecutor.

'Oh, without a doubt,' the public prosecutor replied a little drily, compared with Nelyudov's impulsiveness.

Let me note once and for all that the examining magistrate, who had arrived in our town only recently, had from the very outset felt quite an extraordinary respect for our public prosecutor and was almost on intimate terms with him. He was practically the only man who had implicit faith in the exceptional psychological and oratorical talents of our public prosecutor who had been treated in 'so unfair a fashion' by his superiors in the service, and he was fully convinced that he had really been treated unfairly. He had heard of him in Petersburg. On the other hand, our young examining magistrate, too, was the only man in the world for whom our 'unfairly treated' public prosecutor conceived a sincere liking. On the way to the inn they had managed to come to some agreement as to how to conduct the present case, and now, as he sat at the table, the keen mind of the examining magistrate was quick to interpret every indication and movement on the face of his senior colleague from a half-uttered word, a look, a wink.

'Gentlemen, let me tell my story in my own way and don't interrupt me with trifling questions, and I'll tell you everything in a moment,' cried Mitya excitedly.

'Excellent, sir. Thank you. But before we go on to your statement, you will, I hope, let me ascertain one more fact which is of great interest to us, I mean the ten roubles which you borrowed at about five o'clock yesterday on the security of your pistols from your friend Mr Peter Perkhotin.'

'I pledged them, gentlemen. I pledged them for ten roubles. What more do you want to know? That is all. As soon as I got back to town, I pledged them.'

'You came back to town? Had you been out of town?'

'I had, gentlemen, about thirty miles out of town. Didn't you know that?'

The public prosecutor and the examining magistrate exchanged glances.

'Why not begin your story with a systematic account of your movements since early yesterday morning? Can you tell us, for instance, why you left town, when you left, and when you came back and – and all those facts. . . .'

'You should have asked me that from the very beginning,' Mitya laughed loudly. 'Why, as a matter of fact I should really start not from yesterday but from the morning of the day before. Then you'll understand where, how, and why I went. I went in the morning of the day before yesterday, gentlemen, to our local merchant Samsonov to borrow three thousand roubles on excellent security – I simply had to have the money, gentlemen, I had to have it urgently. . . .'

'I'm sorry to interrupt you, sir,' the public prosecutor interposed courteously, 'but why did you have to have it urgently, and just such a sum, I mean three thousand roubles?'

'Oh dear, gentlemen, I wish you wouldn't bother about such trifles: how, why, and when, and why I had to have just so much money or not so much, and all that silly nonsense. Why, you'll want three volumes to write all that down, and an epilogue as well!'

All this Mitya said with the good-natured but impatient familiarity of a man who is anxious to tell the whole truth and is full of the best intentions.

'Gentlemen,' he seemed to recollect himself suddenly, 'you must not be offended with me for being so unco-operative. I beg you again: believe me I have the utmost respect for you and I understand the situation perfectly. Please, don't think I'm drunk. I'm quite sober now. And it wouldn't much matter if I were drunk. With me, you know, it's a case of —

> Sober and wise – he's stupid,
> Stupid and drunk – he's wise.

Ha, ha! However, I can see, gentlemen, it's improper for me to crack jokes with you now – not, that is, before we've come to an understanding. Do let me keep my self-respect, too, gentlemen. I quite understand the difference between us: in your eyes I'm a criminal and, therefore, far from being on an equal footing with you. It is your duty to watch me. Nor can I expect you to pat me on the back for Grigory, for one really can't go breaking old men's heads with impunity, can one? I suppose you'll put me on trial for that and jail me for six months or a year. I don't know what exactly the sentence for it is, but I hope without loss of civil rights, sir,' he turned to the public prosecutor. 'Without loss of civil rights. So, you see, gentlemen, I'm perfectly aware of the distinction between us. But you must also admit, gentlemen, that you can confuse God himself with such questions as where did you step? how did you step? when did you step? and what did you step on? If you go on like this, I'm sure to get confused, and you'll use every trifling remark I make as evidence against me and put it down in writing, and what do you think it will all lead to? It will lead to nothing! And even if what I've been saying now is all lies, please let me finish, and you, gentlemen, as men of honour and university education, must forgive me. Let me end with a request: do away, gentlemen, with the routine way of conducting an interrogation, I mean, at first, you see, starting with some ridiculous question of a trivial nature, such as how I got up, what I had for breakfast, how and where I spat, and "by putting the prisoner off his guard", suddenly catching him out with a startling question: "Whom did you murder? Whom did you rob?" Ha, ha! That's your routine, isn't it? That has become the rule with you. That's what all your cleverness is based on! But it's only peasants you take in by clever tricks like that, not me. I know the ropes. I've been in the service myself, ha, ha, ha! You're not angry with me, gentlemen, are you? You forgive my impertinence?' he cried, looking at them with surprising good nature. 'It's only Mitya Karamazov who said it, so you can excuse it, for what is inexcusable in a sensible man, is excusable in Mitya, ha, ha!'

The examining magistrate listened and laughed, too. The public prosecutor did not laugh, though. He was watching Mitya intently, without taking his eyes off him, as though not wishing to miss a single word, the slightest movement, the slightest tremor of a muscle on his face.

'But from the very beginning,' the examining magistrate said, still laughing, 'we never tried to confuse you with questions about how you got up in the morning and what you had for your breakfast. As a matter of fact, we began with questions of the utmost importance.'

'I understand. I realized and appreciated it, and I appreciate even more your present kindness to me, an unprecedented kindness worthy of your most generous hearts. The three of us who've met here are honourable men, so let's treat each other with the mutual confidence of educated and well-bred people who are linked by a common bond of noble birth and honour. Let me, at any rate, look upon you as my best friends at this moment of my life, at this moment when my honour is called in question! It's no offence to you, gentlemen, is it?'

'On the contrary, sir,' the examining magistrate assented with a look of dignified approval, 'you've put it all very beautifully.'

'And away with trivialities, gentlemen,' Mitya cried enthusiastically. 'Away with all these pettifogging trivialities. Or goodness only knows what will come of it. Isn't that so?'

'I shall follow your sensible advice entirely, sir,' the public prosecutor suddenly interposed, addressing Mitya. 'But I'm afraid I shall have to insist on an answer to my question. It is of the utmost importance for us to know why you needed such a sum, I mean exactly three thousand roubles.'

'Why I needed it? Oh, for all sorts of things – well, to pay a debt.'

'Who to?'

'That I absolutely refuse to answer, gentlemen. You see, I refuse to tell you not because I can't, or daren't, or am afraid to tell you, for the whole thing is of no importance whatever. In fact, it's quite a trivial matter. But – I won't tell you because it's a matter of principle: it's my private life and I won't allow anyone to poke his nose into my private life. That's my principle. Your question has nothing to do with the case, and everything that is in no way connected with the case is my private life! I wanted to pay a debt, a debt of honour, and I'm not going to say to whom.'

'You won't mind our writing this down, will you?' asked the public prosecutor.

'By all means. Just write down that I absolutely refuse to say. You can write, gentlemen, that I consider it dishonourable to say. Good heavens, the time you waste writing things down!'

'Let me caution you, sir,' the public prosecutor said in an emphatic and very severe tone of voice, 'and remind you once more that you have a perfect right not to answer the questions put to you now and that we, for our part, have no right whatever to extort any answer from you, if for one reason or another you decline to give it. That's entirely up to you. But it is, nevertheless, our duty, sir, as in all cases of this kind, to explain and point out to you the great harm that you will be doing yourself by refusing to give this or that piece of evidence. Now you may continue.'

'Gentlemen, I – I'm not angry – I –' Mitya muttered, a little put out by the reprimand. 'Well, anyway, you see, gentlemen, Samsonov to whom I went then —'

We shall, of course, not reproduce in detail his account of what is known to the reader already. Mitya was impatiently anxious to tell everything to the smallest detail and, at the same time, get it over as soon as possible. But as his evidence was written down as he went on, they had to interrupt him continually. Mitya objected to this, but submitted. He got angry, but did not lose his temper. It is true that sometimes he could not help crying: 'Gentlemen, this is enough to make the angels weep,' or: 'Gentlemen, do you realize that it's no good exasperating me?', but even while exclaiming in this way he remained in his genially effusive mood. He told them how Samsonov had 'cheated' him two days before. (He had fully realized by now that he had been cheated.) The sale of his watch for six roubles, which neither the examining magistrate nor the public prosecutor knew anything about, at once greatly aroused their interest and, to Mitya's intense indignation, they thought it necessary to write down this fact in detail as another confirmation of the circumstance that he had been practically penniless at the time. Little by little Mitya began to grow gloomy. Then, after describing his journey to see Lyagavy and the night he spent in the fume-laden hut, etc., he brought his story down to his return to the town, and here he began, without being prompted in any way, to give a detailed description of the agonies of jealousy he had gone through on account of Grushenka. They listened to him attentively and in silence, and they seemed to be particularly interested in the fact that he had an observation post in Maria Kondratyevna's house at the back of the garden to keep watch on Grushenka, as well as in the fact that Smerdyakov used to bring him information about the goings-on in their house: this they noted particularly and had it written down. Of his jealousy he spoke warmly and at great length, and though inwardly ashamed of exposing his most intimate feelings 'in public', he quite obviously tried to overcome his shame in order to be truthful. The cold severity with which the investigating magistrate and, especially, the public prosecutor stared at him while he told his story, disconcerted him greatly in the end. 'This boy Nelyudov, with whom I exchanged some silly remarks about women only a few days ago, and that sickly public prosecutor do not deserve to hear what I'm telling them,' he reflected mournfully. 'Oh, the disgrace of it! In humble patience hold thy peace,' he concluded his reflection with a line of verse, but he pulled himself together again and carried on with his story. When he came to tell of his visit to Mrs Khokhlakov, he even cheered up again and was about to tell them an amusing little anecdote about that lady, which had nothing to do with the case, but the investigating magistrate cut him short and suggested courteously that he should pass on 'to more essential things'. At last, after describing his despair and telling them how on leaving Mrs Khokhlakov he thought that he would get the three thousand even if he had to murder someone, he was stopped again and they wrote down that he had meant 'to murder someone'. Mitya let them write it down without protest. Finally, he reached the point of the story where he suddenly learnt that Grushenka had deceived him and had left Samsonov's house soon after he had brought her there, though she had told him herself that she would stay there till midnight. 'If I didn't kill that Fenya then, gentlemen,' he blurted out suddenly at that point in his story, 'it was only because I hadn't time.' That, too, was carefully written down. Mitya waited gloomily and went on to tell them how he ran to his father's garden, when the investigating magistrate suddenly stopped him and, opening his large brief-case, lying beside him on the sofa, took out the brass pestle.

'Do you recognize this object, sir?' he asked, showing it to Mitya.

'Oh, yes,' Mitya smiled, gloomily. 'I know it all right! Let's have a look at it. Oh, hell, I don't want it!'

'You've forgotten to mention it,' said the investigating magistrate.

'Oh, hell, I wouldn't have concealed it from you. We'd have come to it sooner or later, anyway, don't you think so? It simply slipped my memory.'

'Will you be so kind as to tell us exactly how you came to arm yourself with it?'

'Why, yes, gentlemen, I shall be so kind.'

And Mitya told them how he took the pestle and ran off with it.

'But what was your object in arming yourself with such a weapon?'

'My object? There wasn't any. I just grabbed it and ran off.'

'But why, if you had no object?'

Mitya was boiling over with vexation. He looked intently at 'the boy' and smiled gloomily and maliciously. He was beginning to feel more and more ashamed of himself for having told 'such people' the story of his jealousy in so sincere and so effusive a manner.

'To hell with the pestle!' he blurted out suddenly.

'All the same, sir!'

'Well, I took it to keep off the dogs. Or because it was dark, or just in case. . . .'

'But have you on any previous occasion, when going out at night, armed yourself, if you're so afraid of the dark?'

'Oh, to hell with it all! Really, gentlemen, it's quite impossible to talk to you!' cried Mitya, exasperated beyond endurance, and flushing with anger, he turned to the clerk and said to him with a sort of frenzied note in his voice:

'Write down at once – at once – that I took the pestle with me because I wanted to go and kill my father – Fyodor Karamazov – by hitting him on the head with it! Well, gentlemen, are you satisfied now? Have you got what you wanted?' he said, glaring defiantly at the examining magistrate and the public prosecutor.

'We realize very well, sir,' the public prosecutor replied drily, 'that the evidence you've just given was merely the result of your annoyance with us and of your exasperation with the questions we put to you, questions which you, sir, regard as trifling, but which, as a matter of fact, are of the utmost importance.'

'But, good Lord, gentlemen, what if I did take the pestle? Why does one pick up things at such moments? I'm sure I don't know. I grabbed it and ran off. That's all. For shame, gentlemen. *Passons*, or I swear I won't say another word!'

He leaned on the table with his elbows and propped up his head. He sat sideways to them and stared at the wall, trying to control his mounting exasperation. And, indeed, he was terribly anxious to get up and tell them that he wouldn't say another word 'even if you take me out to my execution'.

'You see, gentlemen,' he said suddenly, restraining himself with difficulty, 'you see – I listen to you and I seem to be haunted by a dream – you see, I sometimes have such a dream – a curious kind of dream – I often dream it – it keeps on recurring – that someone is chasing me – someone I'm terribly afraid of – chasing me in the dark, at night – looking for me, and I hide somewhere from him behind a door or a cupboard – hide myself so humiliatingly – and the worst of it is that he knows perfectly well where I've hidden myself from him, but he seems to be pretending deliberately not to know where I am, so as to prolong my agony, to enjoy my terror to the full. . . . That's what you're doing now! It's just like that!'

'Is that the sort of thing you dream about?' asked the public prosecutor.

'Yes, that's the sort of thing I dream about. Aren't you going to write that down?' Mitya smiled wryly.

'No, sir, we're not going to write that down. Still, I must say your dreams are certainly curious.'

'But now it isn't a dream! It's realism, gentlemen, the realism of actual life! I'm the wolf and you're the hunters. So you're just hunting the wolf down!'

'That's an unfair comparison, sir,' the examining magistrate began very gently.

'No, it isn't unfair, gentlemen, it isn't unfair!' Mitya flared up again, but having evidently relieved his mind by his outburst of sudden anger, he was again growing more good-humoured with every word he spoke. 'You may not believe a criminal or a prisoner at the bar, who is tortured by your questions, but, gentlemen, you cannot disbelieve, you've no right to disbelieve an honourable man, the honourable impulses of the heart – I say it boldly! – but —

> . . . heart be silent,
> In humble patience hold thy peace!

Well, shall I go on?' he broke off gloomily.

'Why, of course, sir, if you don't mind,' replied the examining magistrate.

5

The Third Ordeal

THOUGH Mitya began grimly, it was clear that he was trying more than ever not to forget or leave out a single detail of his story. He told them how he had jumped over the fence into his father's garden, how he had walked up to the window and about everything that had happened under the window. Speaking slowly and distinctly, as though weighing every word he uttered, he gave them a clear and precise account of the feelings that agitated him during those moments in the garden when he wanted so badly to find out whether Grushenka was with his father or not. But, strange to say, both the public prosecutor and the examining magistrate listened to him this time somehow with great reserve, looked coldly at him, and put many fewer questions. Mitya could not make out anything from their faces. 'They're offended and angry,' he thought. 'Well, to hell with them!' But when he told them how at last he decided to give his father the *signal* that Grushenka had come so that he should open the window, neither the public prosecutor nor the examining magistrate paid any attention to the word 'signal', as though they completely failed to grasp the significance of that word, which Mitya could not help noticing. Reaching at last the moment when, seeing his father leaning out of the window, he boiled over with hatred and snatched the pestle out of his pocket, he suddenly, as though on purpose, stopped short. He sat staring at the wall, knowing that their eyes were fixed upon him.

'Well, sir,' said the examining magistrate, 'so you pulled out the weapon and – and what happened then?'

'Then? Why, then I murdered him – hit him on the head and split his skull! That's what happened according to you, isn't it?' he asked, his eyes suddenly flashing.

All his suppressed anger suddenly rose up in him with extraordinary force.

'According to us,' the examining magistrate repeated. 'Well, and according to you?'

Mitya dropped his eyes and was silent for a long time.

'According to me, gentlemen, according to me, this is what happened,' he said quietly. 'Whether it was someone's tears, or my mother entreated God, or a bright spirit kissed me at that moment – I don't know, but the devil was vanquished. I rushed away from the window and ran back to the fence. . . . My father got frightened, he must have caught sight of me for the first time just then, and sprang back from the window with a cry – I remember it very well. And I ran across the garden towards the fence and – and it was there that Grigory caught me, when I was sitting on the fence. . . .'

At this point he raised his eyes to his listeners at last. They seemed to look at him with perfectly serene unconcern. A sort of spasm of indignation passed over Mitya's heart.

'I suppose you're just laughing at me at this moment, gentlemen,' he broke the silence suddenly.

'Why should you think that?' asked the examining magistrate.

'You don't believe a single word – that's why. I understand perfectly well that I've come to the crucial part of my story: the old man is lying there now with his skull smashed in, and I – having given such a melodramatic description of how I wanted to kill him and how I pulled out the pestle – I suddenly run away from the window. . . . A poem! In heroic couplets! As though you could take a fellow at his word! Ha, ha! You're laughing at me, gentlemen!'

And he swung round on his chair so violently that it creaked.

'And did you notice, sir,' the public prosecutor suddenly began, as though paying no attention to Mitya's agitation, 'did you notice when you were running away from the window whether the garden door at the other end of the house was open or not?'

'No, it was not open.'

'It was not?'

'It was closed. And who could have opened it? Oh, the door? One moment,' he seemed to recollect himself suddenly and almost with a start. 'Why, did you find it open?'

'Yes.'

'So who could have opened it if you did not open it?' Mitya asked, looking terribly surprised all of a sudden.

'The door was open and the murderer of your father quite certainly went through that door and, having committed the murder, went out by it,' the public prosecutor rolled out his words slowly, stressing every syllable. 'That is absolutely clear to us. The murder evidently took place in the room and *not through the window*, which becomes perfectly clear from the examination that has been made, from the position of the body, and from everything else. There can be no doubt whatever about it.'

Mitya looked terribly surprised.

'But that's impossible, gentlemen,' he cried, utterly at a loss. 'I – I never went in. . . . I tell you positively, I know for a fact that the door was shut all the time I was in the garden and when I fled from it. I only stood under the window and I saw him through the window, and that was all, all. . . . I remember everything to the last moment. And even if I didn't remember, I'd know it just the same, because the *signals* were only known to me and Smerdyakov and the dead man, and he would never have opened the door to anyone in the world without the signals.'

'Signals? What signals?' the public prosecutor cried with eager, almost hysterical, curiosity, and at once lost every trace of his dignified deportment.

He asked the question as if creeping furtively up on Mitya. He smelled an important fact, hitherto unknown to him, and at once felt terribly afraid that Mitya might be unwilling fully to disclose it.

'Oh, so you didn't know!' Mitya winked at him with a sardonic and malicious smile. 'And what if I won't tell you? From whom will you find it out then? You see, only the dead man, Smerdyakov and I knew about the signals – that's all, and, I suppose, Heaven knew it too, but it won't tell you. And it is a jolly interesting fact, isn't it? You could build goodness only knows what on it, couldn't you? Ha, ha! Don't worry, gentlemen, I'll reveal it. I can see you've all sorts of silly ideas in your heads. You don't know the man you're dealing with! You're dealing with a prisoner who gives evidence against himself, evidence that may do him harm! Yes, sir, for I'm a man of honour and you are not!'

The public prosecutor swallowed all the bitter pills. He was merely trembling with impatience to learn about the new fact. Mitya gave a full and precise account of everything that concerned the signals which had been invented by Fyodor Karamazov for Smerdyakov. He told them exactly what each knock on the window meant and even gave a demonstration of the different knocks on the table. And in reply to the examining magistrate's question whether Mitya, when knocking on the window, tapped out the signal, which meant: 'Grushenka has come,' he answered precisely that he had tapped out the signal that 'Grushenka has come'.

'There you are!' Mitya broke off, turning away from them with contempt. 'Now you can erect your tower!'

'And your dead father, you and Smerdyakov were the only people who knew of the signals. No one else?' the examining magistrate asked again.

'Yes, Smerdyakov and Heaven. Write down about Heaven. It may come in useful. And, if you ask me, you'll need God yourselves.'

And, of course, they began writing it down, but while they were writing it down, the public prosecutor said suddenly, as though quite a new idea had suddenly occurred to him:

'But if Smerdyakov, too, knew about those signals and you positively deny having had anything to do with the murder of your father, could it not have been he who tapped out the agreed signals, made your father open the door and then – committed the crime?'

Mitya looked at him sardonically, but at the same time also with intense hatred. He stared at him so long in silence that the public prosecutor blinked.

'Caught the fox again!' Mitya said at last. 'Caught the villain by the tail – ha, ha! I can see through you, sir! Through and through! You thought that I'd jump up at once, catch hold of your suggestion and scream at the top of my voice: "Yes, it's Smerdyakov! Smerdyakov is the murderer!" Confess that's what you thought, didn't you? Admit it, and I'll go on.'

But the public prosecutor admitted nothing. He kept silent and waited.

'You're mistaken,' said Mitya. 'I'm not going to shout, "It's Smerdyakov!"'

'Don't you even suspect him?'

'Do you?'

'He, too, is a suspect.'

Mitya fixed his eyes on the floor.

'Joking apart,' he said, gloomily, 'listen: from the very first, almost from the moment I came out to you from behind the curtain, the thought flashed through my mind: "Smerdyakov!" While sitting at the table here and shouting that I was not guilty of murder I kept thinking: "Smerdyakov!" I couldn't get him out of my mind. And just now, too, the same thought occurred to me: "Smerdyakov", but only for a second, for almost at once I thought: "No, not Smerdyakov!" It's not the sort of thing he'd do, gentlemen!'

'Is there anyone else you suspect, in that case?' the examining magistrate asked cautiously.

'I don't know who or what person, the hand of Heaven or of Satan but – not Smerdyakov!' Mitya declared emphatically.

'But why do you maintain so firmly and so emphatically that it isn't he?'

'From my conviction. From my impression. Because Smerdyakov is a man of the most despicable character and a coward. He's not a coward, but the sum and substance of all the different types of cowardice in the world that walks on two legs. He has the heart of a chicken. When talking to me, he always trembled for fear I should kill him, though I never raised a hand against him. He fell at my feet and wept, he literally kissed my boots, imploring me not to "frighten" him. Hear that? Not to "frighten" – what an expression to use! And I even offered him money. He's a sickly, chicken-hearted, and feeble-minded epileptic, whom an eight-year-old boy could thrash. Is that a man of character? No, gentlemen, it was not Smerdyakov. Besides, he doesn't care for money. He wouldn't accept any from me. . . . Besides, why on earth should he kill the old man? You see, he's probably his son. His natural son. Do you know that?'

'We've heard that story. But, then, you're your father's son, too, and yet you told everyone yourself that you meant to kill him.'

'A palpable hit, sir! And below the belt, too! But I'm not afraid! Oh, gentlemen, don't you think it's very mean of you to say that to my face? Mean because I told you that myself. Not only did I mean to kill him, but I could have killed him, and, in fact, I told you of my own accord that I nearly did kill him! But, then, I didn't kill him. My guardian angel saved me – that's what you haven't taken into account. . . . And that's why it's mean of you – mean! For I didn't kill him. I didn't, I didn't! Do you hear, sir,' he turned to the public prosecutor. 'I did not kill him!'

He was almost choking. He had never been so agitated during the whole of the interrogation.

'And what has Smerdyakov told you, gentlemen?' he added suddenly, after a pause. 'May I ask you that?'

'You may ask us about anything you like,' the public prosecutor replied with cold severity. 'About anything that has any bearing on the facts of the case and, I repeat, we are bound to answer every question you put to us. We found the servant Smerdyakov, about whom you inquire, lying unconscious in his bed in a very severe epileptic fit which had perhaps recurred for the tenth time. The doctor who was with us told us after he had examined him that he may not live till the morning.'

'Well, in that case the devil must have killed my father!' Mitya suddenly blurted out as though he had up to that very moment been asking himself whether it was Smerdyakov or not.

'We'll come back to it later,' the examining magistrate decided. 'Wouldn't you like to carry on with your statement now?'

Mitya asked for a rest. His request was courteously granted. Having rested, he carried on with his statement. But he obviously felt wretched. He was worn out, deeply hurt, and morally shaken. Besides, the public prosecutor, almost deliberately now, exasperated him every minute by harping on 'trivialities'. No sooner had Mitya described how, sitting astride the fence, he had hit Grigory, who had been hanging on to his left leg, on the head with the pestle and then had at once jumped down to see how badly he was hurt, than the public prosecutor stopped him and asked him to describe in greater detail how he was sitting on the fence. Mitya looked surprised.

'Well, I was sitting like this, astride, one leg on one side of the fence and one on the other.'

'And the pestle?'

'The pestle was in my hand.'

'Not in your pocket? You remember that clearly? Well, did you hit him hard?'

'I suppose so. What do you want to know that for?'

'Would you mind sitting on the chair just as you sat on the fence then and demonstrating to us how you flung your arms and in what direction?'

'You're not making fun of me, are you?' asked Mitya with a withering look at his questioner.

But the public prosecutor did not even blink. Mitya turned abruptly, sat astride the chair and swung his arm:

'That's how I hit him! That's how I killed him! What more do you want to know?'

'Thank you. Would you mind explaining now why you jumped down? With what object? What exactly had you in mind?'

'Well, damn it, I jumped down to have a look at the man I'd knocked down. I don't know what for!'

'Agitated as you were? And running away?'

'Yes, agitated as I was and running away.'

'You wanted to help him?'

'Good Lord, no! ... Well, I don't know. I may have wanted to help him, too. I don't remember.'

'You mean, you were not in a fit state to remember. You did not know what you were doing, in fact?'

'Oh, no, not at all. I remember everything. To the smallest detail. I jumped down to have a look and I wiped the blood off his face with my handkerchief.'

'We've seen your handkerchief. You hoped to restore him to consciousness, did you?'

'I don't know. I just wanted to make sure whether he was alive or not.'

'Oh, I see. You wanted to make sure. Well, did you?'

'I'm not a doctor. I wasn't sure. I ran away thinking I had killed him, and now he has recovered.'

'Excellent – thank you, sir,' the public prosecutor concluded. 'That's all I wanted to know. Please carry on.'

Alas, it never occurred to Mitya to tell, though he remembered it, that he had jumped down off the fence from pity and, standing over Grigory's prostrate body, even delivered himself of a few sorrowful words: 'Bad luck, old man – it can't be helped – well, you may as well lie here.' The public prosecutor, however, could only draw one conclusion, namely, that the man had jumped down 'at such a moment and in such agitation' only to make quite sure whether the *only* witness of his crime was alive or not. Which, of course, showed how great was the man's strength of mind, resolution, coolness, and sense of judgement that even at such a moment – and so on and so forth. The public prosecutor was pleased: exasperate a nervous man with 'trivialities' and he was sure to let the cat out of the bag.

Mitya, his mind in agony, went on. But he was at once stopped again, this time by the examining magistrate.

'How could you run to the servant Fenya with your hands so covered with blood and, as it appeared later, your face, too?'

'Why, at the time I never noticed that my hands and face were covered with blood!' replied Mitya.

'He's quite right,' the public prosecutor said, exchanging glances with the examining magistrate. 'It does happen like that.'

'I never noticed it, you've put it very well, sir,' Mitya suddenly expressed his approval of the public prosecutor's remark.

There followed the story of Mitya's sudden decision 'to step aside' and 'let the happy couple pass by'. But he could not any longer as before make up his mind to open his heart again and tell them about 'the queen of his heart'. He felt nauseated at the thought of talking about her to these cold-hearted people who were 'fastening on him like bugs!' And so, in reply to their repeated questions, he declared briefly and sharply:

'Well, so I made up my mind to kill myself. What was there left for me to live for? I could not help asking myself that question. Her first, rightful lover had come back, the man who seduced her but who had hurried back to offer her his love and to atone after five years for the wrong by marriage. I realized that it was all over for me. . . . And behind me disgrace and that blood – Grigory's blood. . . . What was there left for me to live for? So I went to redeem the pistols I had pawned, to load them and put a bullet through my brain at dawn. . . .'

'And have a high old time the night before?'

'A high old time the night before. Oh, damn it all, gentlemen, do finish it quickly. I was quite determined to shoot myself, not far from here, on the outskirts of the village, and I'd have done myself in at five o'clock in the morning. I had a note in my pocket. Wrote it at Perkhotin's when I loaded my pistol. Here it is. Read it. It's not for your benefit I'm telling this,' he suddenly added contemptuously.

He produced the note from his waistcoat pocket and flung it on the table. They read it with interest and, as is usual, added it to the exhibits.

'And you never thought of washing your hands even when visiting Mr Perkhotin? You weren't afraid of arousing suspicion, then, were you?'

'What suspicion? Suspect me or not, I'd have come here all the same and shot myself at five o'clock, and no one would have had time to do anything about it. For, but for what's happened to my father, you wouldn't have known anything about it and you wouldn't have come here. Oh, it's the devil who did it, the devil murdered father, and it was through the devil that you found it out so soon! How did you manage to get here so quickly? Marvellous, fantastic!'

'Mr Perkhotin informed us that when you came to see him you had your money in your hands – your blood-stained hands – a great deal of money, a roll of hundred-rouble notes, and that his boy servant saw it too!'

'Yes, gentlemen, that's quite correct, I believe.'

'Now, sir, we come to another little matter. Would you mind telling us,' the examining magistrate began very gently, 'where you got so much money from? For, as it appears from the evidence and even from the time at your disposal you could not possibly have gone back home for it?'

The public prosecutor frowned slightly at the question, put so point-blank, but he did not interrupt the examining magistrate.

'No, I didn't go home,' Mitya replied, apparently very calmly, though his eyes were fixed on the floor.

'In that case, let me repeat my question,' the examining magistrate went on, as though creeping up on Mitya. 'Where could you have procured such a large sum all at once when, on your own admission, at five o'clock that afternoon —'

'I was in need of ten roubles and pawned my pistols with Perkhotin, then went to Mrs Khokhlakov to borrow three thousand, and she didn't give it to me, and so on and so forth,' Mitya interrupted sharply. 'Yes, gentlemen, one moment I had no money and the next I'd suddenly got thousands – eh? You know, gentlemen, you're both in a devil of a funk now: what if he won't tell us where he got it? All right, then, gentlemen, I won't tell you. You've guessed it: you won't find out,' Mitya said emphatically, with extraordinary determination.

The examining magistrate and the prosecutor were silent for a moment.

'You must understand, Mr Karamazov, that it is absolutely necessary for us to know it,' the examining magistrate said quietly and suavely.

'I quite understand, but I won't tell you all the same.'

The public prosecutor intervened and again reminded the prisoner that, of course, he need not answer their questions, if he did not think it to be in his interest, and so on, but in view of the great harm he might do himself by his silence, especially in view of the great importance of such a question as —

'And so on and so forth, gentlemen,' Mitya again interrupted. 'Enough, I've heard that argument before! I realize myself how important it is and that this is a most essential point, but I'm not going to tell you for all that.'

'Well, sir,' the examining magistrate said nervously, 'I'm sure we don't care whether you answer or not. It's not our affair, but yours. You'll only be harming yourself.'

'You see, gentlemen, joking apart,' Mitya said, raising his eyes and looking firmly at them both, 'I felt from the very first that we should be at loggerheads on this point. But at first, when I began to give my evidence, all that was still far away, hidden in a mist, everything was still uncertain, and, indeed, I was so simple that I began with the suggestion of "mutual confidence" between us. I can see for myself now that there could be no question of such confidence, for we should all the same have come to this damned hurdle! And now we have come to it! I can't tell you and that's all there is to it! Still, I do not blame you, for I can't expect you to take me at my word – I understand that!'

He fell silent gloomily.

'But couldn't you, without altering your decision to say nothing about the chief point – couldn't you at the same time give us some slight hint at the nature of the motives which are so strong as to induce you to keep silent at such a critical stage in your evidence?'

Mitya smiled sadly and almost wistfully.

'I'm much more good-natured than you think, gentlemen, and I'll tell you my reason for withholding this information and give you that hint, though you don't deserve it. I'm saying nothing about it, gentlemen, because it's a matter that reflects on my honour. The answer to the question where I got the money from casts such a dishonour upon me that it cannot compare even with the murder and the robbing of my father, if I had murdered and robbed him. That's why I can't speak about it. I can't do it for fear of dishonouring myself. Why, gentlemen, you're not going to write that down, are you?'

'Yes, I think we'd better write it down,' the examining magistrate murmured.

'You ought not to write that down. About the "dishonour", I mean. I told you that only out of the kindness of my heart. I needn't have told you that at all. I've made you a present of it, and you're at once using it as evidence against me. All right, write, write anything you like,' he concluded contemptuously and with disgust. 'I'm not afraid of you and – I can still look you proudly in the face!'

'You couldn't tell us by any chance what kind of dishonour you have in mind?' the examining magistrate murmured.

The public prosecutor frowned terribly.

'No, no, *c'est fini*, don't trouble yourselves. And, anyhow, it's not worth while soiling myself. I've soiled myself enough, as it is, by talking to you. You don't deserve it. Neither you nor anyone else. Enough, gentlemen. Not another word.'

This was said a little too categorically. The examining magistrate did not insist any further, but from the expression in the public prosecutor's eyes he saw at once that he had not given up hope.

'Can't you at least tell us how much money you had in your hands when you went to see Mr Perkhotin – how many roubles, I mean?'

'I'm sorry I can't tell you that, either.'

'I believe you spoke to Mr Perkhotin of having received three thousand from Mrs Khokhlakov.'

'Perhaps I did. That's enough, gentlemen. I won't tell you how much money I had.'

'In that case would you mind telling us how you came here and what you've done since your arrival?'

'Oh, you'd better ask the people here about it. Still, why not? I'll tell you.'

He told them, but we will not repeat his story. He told it drily and cursorily. He said nothing about the raptures of his love. He did tell them, though, that 'in view of the new facts' he had given up his decision to shoot himself. He told his story without going into any motives or details. Besides, his interrogators did not worry him much this time: it was clear that they did not consider it to be of any vital importance.

'We shall check it all,' the examining magistrate concluded the interrogation, 'and we shall go back to it during the examination of the witnesses, which will, of course, take place in your presence. Now, I should like to ask you, sir, to put on the table everything in your possession and especially all the money you still have about you.'

'My money, gentlemen? All right, I understand that that is necessary. Indeed, I'm surprised you haven't asked about it before. It's true I couldn't have gone away anywhere. I'm sitting here where you all can see me. Well, here's my money. Count it, take it. That's all, I think.'

He took everything out of his pockets, even the small change, and pulled out two silver twenty-copeck pieces from his waistcoat pocket. They counted the money. There was altogether eight hundred and thirty-six roubles and forty copecks.

'And is that all?' asked the public prosecutor.

'That's all.'

'You've stated in your evidence just now that you spent three hundred roubles in Plotnikov's shop, you gave Perkhotin ten roubles, the coachman twenty, lost two hundred here at cards, then —'

The examining magistrate counted it all up again. Mitya helped him readily. They recollected every copeck and added it to the total and the examining magistrate quickly added it up.

'With this eight hundred you must have had about fifteen hundred at first?'

'I suppose so,' Mitya snapped.

'Why, then, does everyone assert that there was much more?'

'Let them assert.'

'But you asserted it yourself.'

'Yes, I, too, asserted it.'

'We'll check it over again with the evidence of the persons not yet examined. Don't worry about your money. It will be taken care of where – er – such things are usually taken care of, and will be returned to you at the end of – er – this business if – er – it appears or rather is proved that you have an undisputed right to it. Well, sir, and now —'

The examining magistrate suddenly got up and told Mitya firmly that it was his duty to carry out a thorough search 'of your clothes and everything else. . . .'

'Certainly, gentlemen, I'll turn out all my pockets if you like.'

And he really began turning out his pockets.

'I'm afraid you'll have to take off your clothes.'

'My clothes? You want me to undress? Damn it, can't you search me as I am? Can't you?'

'I'm afraid that's quite impossible, sir. You will have to take off your clothes.'

'As you like,' Mitya submitted gloomily. 'Only, please, not here, but behind the curtain. Who's going to search them?'

'Of course, behind the curtain', the examining magistrate inclined his head in assent. His small face wore an expression of quite exceptional gravity.

6

The Public Prosecutor Catches Mitya

WHAT followed was something quite unexpected and surprising to Mitya. He could never, even a moment before, have supposed that anyone would treat him, Mitya Karamazov, like that! And the worst of it was that there was something humiliating in it and, on their part, something 'arrogant and scornful'. He would not have minded if it were only a question of taking off his coat, but he was asked to undress further, and not asked, either, but actually ordered to – he understood that perfectly. From pride and contempt he submitted without protest. In addition to the examining magistrate, the public prosecutor, too, went behind the curtain, and there were also several peasants present, 'to use force, if necessary, of course,' thought Mitya, 'and perhaps for something else.'

'Well, have I got to take off my shirt too?' Mitya asked sharply.

But the examining magistrate did not reply: together with the public prosecutor, he was absorbed in the examination of Mitya's coat, trousers, waistcoat, and cap, and it was evident that they were both very interested in them: 'They don't seem to care a hang,' thought Mitya. 'They don't observe even the ordinary rules of politeness.'

'I ask you for the second time,' Mitya said even more sharply and irritably, 'do I have to take off my shirt or not?'

'Don't worry, we'll let you know,' the examining magistrate replied in a rather magisterial voice, or so at least it seemed to Mitya.

Meanwhile the examining magistrate and public prosecutor were conducting what seemed to be an important consultation in an undertone. There appeared to be huge blood-stains on the frock-coat, especially on the left skirt, at the back. They had gone dry and hard but still not crumbling. There were blood-stains on the trousers, too. In addition, the examining magistrate, in the presence of witnesses, passed his fingers along the collar, the cuffs, and all the seams of the coat and trousers, evidently looking for something – money, of course. They did not even bother to hide from Mitya their suspicion that he was capable of sewing money up in his clothes. 'Treat me quite unashamedly as a thief and not as an army officer,' Mitya muttered under his breath. Moreover, they confided their thoughts to one another in his presence with a frankness that was strange indeed. For instance, the clerk, who was also behind the curtain and who fussed about and helped them in their search, drew the examining magistrate's attention to Mitya's cap, which they were also fingering. 'Do you remember Gridenko, sir? The rural district clerk? Last summer he went to town to fetch the wages of the whole office and when he came back he declared that he had lost the money when drunk. And where was it found, sir? Why, in just these pipings of the cap, the hundred-rouble notes screwed up in little rolls and sewn into the piping.' They remembered Gridenko's case very well, both the examining magistrate and the public prosecutor, and so they put aside Mitya's cap and decided that all his clothes would have to be thoroughly examined later.

'I say,' the examining magistrate suddenly cried, noticing that the right cuff of Mitya's shirt was turned up and soaked in blood, 'I say, what's that – blood?'

'Blood,' Mitya snapped.

'I mean, what blood, sir? And why is it hidden inside the turned-up cuff?'

Mitya told them he had got his cuff soaked in blood while busying himself with Grigory and had turned it up while washing his hands at Perkhotin's.

'I'm afraid we shall have to take your shirt, too. It's very important as – er – material evidence.'

Mitya flushed and flew into a rage.

'You don't expect me to stay naked, do you?' he cried.

'Don't worry, sir. We'll see what we can do about it. Meanwhile take off your socks, please.'

'You're not joking? Is that really necessary?' cried Mitya with flashing eyes.

'I'm afraid we're in no mood for jokes!' the examining magistrate parried severely.

'Well, if it's necessary —' Mitya muttered and, sitting down on the bed, he began taking off his socks.

He felt terribly embarrassed: they were all dressed and he was undressed and, strange to say, without clothes he seemed to feel guilty in their presence and, what was worse, he was almost convinced himself that he really was inferior to them all and that now they were fully entitled to despise him. 'If everyone is undressed, you don't feel ashamed, but when only one is undressed and everyone else is looking at him it's a disgrace!' it flashed again and again through his mind. 'It's like a dream. I've sometimes dreamed of being in such a degrading situation.' But it was very painful for him to take off his socks: they were very dirty, and so were his underclothes, and now they all saw it. But the awful thing was that he disliked his feet and for some reason had all his life thought the big toes on both feet hideous, especially the coarse, flat, turned-in nail on the right foot, and now they would all see it. His unbearable feeling of shame made him suddenly and now deliberately more rude than ever. He tore off the shirt himself.

'You wouldn't like to carry out a search anywhere else if you're not ashamed, would you?'

'No, sir, not at present.'

'Well, am I to stay naked like this?' he added fiercely.

'Yes, sir, I'm afraid it is necessary for the time being. Please, sit down here for a while. Take a blanket from the bed and wrap it round you. I – I'll see to it all.'

All the things were shown to the witnesses, a report of the search was drawn up and, at last, the examining magistrate went out, and the clothes were carried out after him. The public prosecutor also went out, and Mitya was left alone with the peasants, who stood in silence without taking their eyes off him. Mitya wrapped himself in the blanket. He felt cold. His bare feet stuck out and, try as he might, he could not pull the blanket over so as to cover them. The examining magistrate did not come back for a long time for some reason. 'An excruciatingly long time. Treats me like a puppy,' Mitya muttered, grinding his teeth. 'That swine of a public prosecutor has also gone! Out of contempt, I suppose. Felt disgusted to look at a naked man.' Mitya still believed that after examining his clothes in another room they would return them to him. He was furiously indignant, therefore, when the examining magistrate suddenly came back with quite different clothes, carried in after him by a peasant.

'Well, here are the clothes for you,' the examining magistrate said casually, evidently well satisfied with the success of his mission. 'Mr Kalganov has kindly provided them for this emergency as well as a clean shirt. Fortunately, he had them all in his trunk. You can keep your socks and underclothes.'

Mitya flew into a terrible rage.

'I won't have other people's clothes!' he cried menacingly. 'Give me back my own!'

'I'm sorry, it can't be done.'

'Give me my own. To hell with Kalganov and his clothes!'

They spent a long time persuading him. Somehow or other, however, they calmed him down. It was pointed out to him that his clothes, being stained with blood, had to be included 'with the other material evidence' and that they had not 'even the right' to let him wear them 'in view of the possible outcome of the case'. Mitya at last grasped it. He fell silent gloomily and began to dress himself hurriedly. He remarked, though, as he put on the clothes, that they were much more expensive than his old ones and that he would not like 'to take advantage' of it. Besides, the coat was 'humiliatingly tight. Am I to play the clown in it for – your amusement?'

It was again pointed out to him that he was exaggerating, that though Mr Kalganov was taller than he, he was only a little taller, and that perhaps the trousers alone might be too long. But the coat turned out to be really tight in the shoulders.

'Damn it, can't button it properly,' Mitya muttered again. 'Please, do me a favour and tell Mr Kalganov at once from me that I didn't ask for his clothes and that I've been dressed up like a clown against my will.'

'I'm sure he understands that very well, sir, and is extremely sorry about – er – the whole thing,' the examining magistrate mumbled.

'I don't care a damn whether he's sorry or not! Well, where now? Or am I to go on sitting here?'

He was asked to go back to 'the other room'. Mitya went in scowling with anger and trying not to look at anyone. He felt himself totally disgraced in another man's clothes, even before the peasants and the landlord, whose face for some reason suddenly appeared in the doorway and vanished again: 'Came to have a look at the mummer,' thought Mitya. He resumed his old seat at the table. He had a feeling of something absurd and nightmarish; it seemed to him that he was not in his right mind.

'Well,' he said to the public prosecutor, grinding his teeth, 'what are you going to do now? Are you going to flog me? There's nothing else left for you to do!'

He did not want to turn to the examining magistrate, as though not vouchsafing even to talk to him. 'He examined my socks a little too closely,' he thought. 'Even had them turned inside out, the scoundrel! He did it on purpose. Wanted to show everyone how dirty my underclothes were!'

'I'm afraid we shall have to proceed to the examination of the witnesses now,' said the examining magistrate, as though in reply to a question by Mitya.

'Yes,' said the public prosecutor thoughtfully, as though he, too, were considering something.

'We've done what we could in your interest, sir,' went on the examining magistrate, 'but having received so categorical a refusal from you to explain where you obtained the money in your possession, we are at the present moment —'

'What's that stone in your ring?' Mitya suddenly interrupted him, as though awakening from some reverie and pointing to one of the large rings adorning the right hand of the examining magistrate.

'Ring?' the examining magistrate repeated with surprise.

'Yes, that one – on your middle finger – the one with the fine grains in it – what kind of stone is that?' Mitya persisted irritably, like a stubborn child.

'That's a smoky topaz,' said the examining magistrate with a smile. 'Would you like to have a look at it? I'll take it off.'

'No, no, don't take it off!' Mitya cried fiercely, recollecting himself suddenly and angry with himself. 'Don't take it off – there's no need. . . . Damn! Gentlemen, you've defiled my soul! Do you really think that I'd have concealed it from you if I had really killed my father, that I would prevaricate, lie, and hide myself? No, Dmitry Karamazov is not like that. He would never put up with it. And, I swear, if I were guilty, I shouldn't have waited for you to come or for the sun to rise, as I intended at first, but should have killed myself before then, without waiting for the dawn. I know it for certain now. I shouldn't have learned as much in twenty years of my life as I've found out during this damned night! And would I have behaved like that on this night or at this moment, sitting with you – would I have spoken like that, moved about like that, looked at you and the world like that, if I'd really been a parricide, when even the supposed murder of Grigory gave me no rest all night – and not because I was afraid, not because I was afraid of your punishment! Oh, the disgrace of it! And do you really expect me to be frank with such scoffers as you, men who see nothing and believe nothing, blind moles and scoffers, do you expect me to tell you of yet another mean action I've committed, another disgrace, even if it had saved me from your accusation? No, better penal servitude! The man who opened the garden door and went in through that door, that man killed my father, that man robbed him. Who was he? I'm racking my brains, I'm at my wits' end to think of someone, but I can tell you it was not Dmitry Karamazov – and that's all I can say to you – and that's enough, enough, don't pester me any more. . . . Send me to Siberia, hang me, but don't exasperate me any more. I've said all I had to say. Call your witnesses!'

Mitya uttered his sudden monologue as though he had made up his mind once and for all not to say another word again. The public prosecutor watched him the whole time and, as soon as he fell silent, suddenly said with a very cold and most composed air, just as though it were the most ordinary thing:

'Well, sir, about that open door you just mentioned, we are now able to inform you of a most interesting piece of evidence of the greatest importance to you as well as to us, which has been given by Grigory, the old man you have wounded. On recovering, he told us most emphatically in answer to our questions that the garden door, which you stated was closed when you were in the garden, was wide open. He noticed it as soon as he entered the garden through the open gate and even before he caught sight of you running away in the dark from the open window at which you saw your father. He, too, noticed the open window, but glancing to the left he also noticed at the same moment that the door, which was much nearer to him and which you declared was closed all the time you were in the garden, was open. Nor will I conceal from you that Grigory himself firmly declares and bears witness that you must have run out of that door, though, of course, he did not see you do so with his own eyes, noticing you for the first time at some distance from himself in the garden, running away towards the fence.'

Mitya jumped up from his chair half-way through this speech.

'Nonsense!' he yelled suddenly in a frenzy. 'An impudent lie! He couldn't have seen the door open because it was closed. He's lying!'

'I consider it my duty to repeat that he is absolutely sure of it. He doesn't waver. He swears by it. We've asked him again and again about it.'

'Yes, indeed,' the examining magistrate confirmed heatedly, 'I've asked him several times about it.'

'It's not true! It's not true! It's either an attempt to blame me or the hallucination of a madman,' Mitya went on shouting. 'He simply imagined it all in his delirium, when he came to, from loss of blood, from the wound. He's just raving.'

'Well, sir, he noticed the open door not when he came to after being wounded but before that, as soon as he entered the garden from the cottage.'

'But it isn't true, it isn't true, it can't be so!' Mitya shouted breathlessly. 'He's blaming me from spite. He couldn't have seen it. I didn't run out of the door.'

The public prosecutor turned to the examining magistrate and said to him impressively:

'Show him it.'

'Do you recognize this thing?' the examining magistrate asked, putting on the table a large thick envelope of the size used in government offices, on which the three seals were still intact. The envelope itself was empty and torn open at one end. Mitya stared open-eyed at it.

'I – I suppose it must be my father's envelope,' he muttered. 'The same that contained the three thousand roubles and – if there's an inscription – let me see, please – "To my little chicken" – here, you see? Three thousand,' he cried, 'three thousand! You see?'

'Of course, sir, we see, but we didn't find any money in it. It was empty and lying on the floor near the bed, behind the screen.'

For a few seconds Mitya stood as though thunderstruck.

'Gentlemen, it's Smerdyakov!' he suddenly shouted at the top of his voice. 'It's he who killed and robbed him! He alone knew where the old man had hidden the envelope. It's he – now that's clear!'

'But you, too, knew about the envelope and that it was under the pillow.'

'I never knew it. I've never seen it before. I see it now for the first time. I only heard of it from Smerdyakov. . . . Only he knew where the old man had it hidden. I didn't know,' Mitya declared, completely out of breath.

'And yet, sir, you stated in your evidence a short while ago that the envelope was under your late father's pillow. You most definitely stated that it was under the pillow. So you must have known where it was.'

'We've got it written down!' the examining magistrate confirmed.

'Nonsense! It's ridiculous! I hadn't the faintest idea that it was under the pillow. It might not have been under the pillow at all. I said it was under the pillow without thinking. What does Smerdyakov say? Have you asked him where it was? That's most important. I've told you lies against myself deliberately. I told you without thinking that it was under the pillow, and now you — Well, you know how one blurts something out without meaning it. Only Smerdyakov knew. Smerdyakov alone, and no one else! He did not tell me where it was, either. It was he! It was he! I have no doubt at all now that it was he who killed him. It's as clear as daylight to me,' Mitya kept exclaiming more and more frenziedly, repeating himself incoherently, getting more and more excited and embittered. 'Please understand that and arrest him at once, at once! I'm quite sure it was he who killed him after I had run away and while Grigory was lying unconscious. It's clear now. He gave the signals and father opened the door to him.

For he alone knew the signals and without the signals father would not have opened the door to anyone. . . .'

'But,' the public prosecutor observed restrainedly, but as though triumphing already, 'you again seem to forget the fact that there was no need to give the signal, if the door was already open while you were there, while you were still in the garden. . . .'

'The door, the door,' muttered Mitya, staring mutely at the public prosecutor.

He sank back exhausted in his chair. They were all silent.

'Yes, the door!' Mitya cried, staring vacantly in front of him. 'It's an apparition! God is against me!'

'Well, there you are,' the public prosecutor said gravely. 'You can judge for yourself now, sir: on the one hand, there's this evidence of the open door, from which you ran out, a crushing fact both for you and for us, and, on the other, your inexplicable, obstinate, and almost obdurate silence about the source of the money which appeared so suddenly in your hand when only three hours earlier, according to your own statement, you pledged your pistols to obtain only ten roubles! In view of all this, you can see for yourself that we don't know what to believe or what line to take in our investigation. And don't be angry with us for being "cold-blooded cynics and scoffers", who are incapable of believing in the noble impulses of your heart. Try to put yourself in our place. . . .'

Mitya was indescribably agitated. He turned pale.

'All right,' he cried suddenly. 'I'll tell you my secret. I'll tell you where I got the money! I'll reveal my shame so as not to blame either myself or you afterwards.'

'And believe me, sir,' the examining magistrate cried in a sort of touchingly joyful little voice, 'that every sincere and full confession of yours, and particularly at this moment, may afterwards have a tre- mendous influence upon the mitigation of – er – your sentence and, indeed, may besides —'

But the public prosecutor nudged him under the table and he man- aged to stop in time. It is true, Mitya was not even listening to him.

7

Mitya's Great Secret. He is Hissed Off

'GENTLEMEN,' he began, still in the same state of agitation, 'this money – I'd like to make a full confession – this money was *mine*.'

The faces of the public prosecutor and the examining magistrate fell: that was not at all what they expected.

'How do you mean it was yours?' the examining magistrate murmured. 'At five o'clock in the afternoon, on your own confession —'

'Oh, to hell with the five o'clock in the afternoon and my own confession – it doesn't matter now! That money was mine, I mean, stolen by me – not mine, that is, but stolen by me, and it was fifteen hundred, and I had it on me, I had it on me all the time. . . .'

'But where did you take it from?'

'I took it off my neck, gentlemen, off this neck of mine. It was there – round my neck, sewn in a rag and hanging from my neck. I've been carrying it about for a long time, for a month, round my neck, to my shame and disgrace!'

'But who did you – er – appropriate it from?'

'You were about to say "steal", weren't you? You can speak frankly now. Yes, I consider that I had as good as stolen it, or, if you like, really "appropriated". But in my opinion, I stole it. And last night I stole it in good earnest.'

'Last night? But you've just said that it's a month since you – er – got it?'

'Yes, but not from my father. Don't worry, not from my father. I did not steal it from my father, but from her. Let me tell you all about it and don't interrupt. It's not so easy, you know. You see, a month ago I was asked by Miss Katerina Verkhovtsev, my former fiancée, to go and see her. Do you know her?'

'Why, of course we do.'

'I know you do. She's a most noble soul, the noblest of the noble, but she's hated me for a long time, oh, for a long, long time – and with good reason, yes, she hated me with good reason!'

'Miss Verkhovtsev?' the examining magistrate asked with surprise.

The public prosecutor, too, stared at Mitya.

'Oh, don't take her name in vain! I'm a cad to get her mixed up in all this. Yes, I'd seen that she hated me – long ago – from the very first, from our first meeting at my lodgings. . . . But enough, enough, you don't deserve to know it even – I mustn't talk of it at all. All I need to say is that a month ago she asked me to call on her and gave me three thousand roubles to send to her sister and a relative of hers in Moscow (as though she couldn't have sent it off herself!) and I— You see, it was just at that fateful hour of my life when I — Well, in short, when I happened to fall in love with another, with *her*, my present fiancée, the one who's downstairs now – Grushenka. I carried her off then here, to Mokroye, and squandered half of that damned three thousand, that is, fifteen hundred here in two days, keeping the other half on me. Well, so the fifteen hundred which I'd kept, I carried about round my neck like an amulet and yesterday I undid it and spent it. Except, that is, for the eight hundred which are in your hands now, Mr Nelyudov. It's what's left over of the fifteen hundred.'

'But how is that possible? A month ago you spent three thousand and not fifteen hundred here. Everybody knows that.'

'Who knows that? Who counted the money? Who did I give it to to count?'

'But, good Lord, sir, you told everyone yourself that you had run through exactly three thousand that time.'

'Quite true, I did. I told the whole town, and the whole town talked about it, and everybody thought so, and here in Mokroye, too, everyone thought that it was three thousand. But all the same I did not spend three thousand, but fifteen hundred. The other fifteen hundred I sewed into a little bag. That's how it was, gentlemen. That's where I got that money yesterday. . . .'

'This is almost like a miracle,' the examining magistrate murmured.

'May I ask you, sir,' said the public prosecutor at last, 'whether you've told anyone about it before – er – I mean, that you had kept the fifteen hundred a month ago?'

'I told no one.'

'That's strange. Are you sure you've told absolutely no one?'

'Absolutely no one. No one – no one!'

'But why did you keep silent about it? What was your motive for making such a secret of it? Let me put it more plainly: you've told us your secret at last, a secret which, according to you, was so "shameful", though as a matter of fact – I mean, of course, comparatively speaking, this action, that is, the appropriation of three thousand roubles which did not belong to you and, no doubt, only for a time – this action is, in my opinion at least, a highly thoughtless action, but by no means so very disgraceful, especially when one takes into consideration your character. . . . But even supposing that it was a highly discreditable action, let's admit it, discreditable but not disgraceful. What I'm driving at is that many people have guessed during this last month that you had spent Miss Verkhovtsev's three thousand, even without your admitting it. I heard this story myself. Mr Makarov, too, for instance, had heard it. So that it isn't really a "story" any more, but the gossip of the whole town. Besides, there were indications that you, too, if I am not mistaken, confessed it yourself to someone, I mean, that the money was Miss Verkhovtsev's. That is why I am so surprised that till now, that is, up to this moment, you made such an extraordinary secret of the fifteen hundred which, you say, you put away, attaching a sort of feeling of horror to this secret of yours. It seems to me incredible that the confession of such a secret should cost you so much distress, for – for you were just shouting that you'd rather be sentenced to penal servitude than confess it. . . .'

The public prosecutor fell silent. He was excited. He did not conceal his vexation, almost anger, and gave vent to his accumulated resentment without bothering about the beauty of his style, that is, incoherently and almost confusedly.

'The disgrace was not in the fifteen hundred,' Mitya declared firmly, 'but in the fact that I separated it from the rest of the three thousand.'

'But,' the public prosecutor said with an exasperated laugh, 'what is there so disgraceful about having set aside, at your own discretion, half of the three thousand you had discreditably, or, if you prefer it, disgracefully appropriated? Surely, the important point is that you appropriated the three thousand and not what you did with them. By the way, why did you do that, I mean, why did you put away that half? What did you do it for? What was your object in doing it? Can you explain it to us?'

'Oh, gentlemen, the object was the chief point of it!' Mitya exclaimed. 'I put it aside because I was vile, or, in other words, because I had a selfish reason for it, and to have a selfish reason in such a case is vile. . . . And that vileness went on for a whole month!'

'I don't understand.'

'I'm surprised at you. However, I'll put it more plainly. Perhaps it really is difficult to understand. You see, listen carefully. I appropriate three thousand, entrusted to my honour, I spend it on a wild party, and having spent it all, I come to her next morning and say: "Katya, I'm sorry, I've squandered your three thousand." Well is that nice? No, it isn't. It's dishonest and cowardly, the man who does such a thing is a beast. He has no more self-restraint than a beast. Isn't that so? But he's still not a thief, is he? Not a downright thief, not a downright one, you must admit! He squandered the money, but he did not steal it! Now a second, a still more favourable, alternative – please listen carefully or I may get confused again – I'm afraid my head's swimming – so, here's a second alternative: I spend here only fifteen hundred out of the three thousand, that is, half of it. Next day I go to her and bring her that half: "Katya, take the fifteen hundred from me, blackguard and thoughtless scoundrel that I am, for I've squandered half the money and may therefore squander also the other half – so take it and keep me from temptation!" Well, what about such an alternative? Anything you like – a beast and a blackguard, but not a thief, not entirely a thief. For if I were a thief, I should certainly not have brought the other half, but would have appropriated that too. Here she would see that since I brought back half of her money, I'd also bring back the rest, that is, the money I had squandered, that I'd try to raise it all my life, that I'd work to get it and return it. I'd be a blackguard then, but not a thief. Not a thief, whatever you may say!'

'I daresay there is a certain difference,' said the public prosecutor with a cold smile. 'But it's strange all the same that you should regard it as such a vital difference!'

'Yes, I do regard it as a vital difference! Everyone can be a blackguard, and, I daresay, everyone is, but not everyone can be a thief, only an arch-blackguard can be that. Anyway, I'm afraid I'm not very good at these subtleties. . . . Only a thief is viler than a blackguard. I'm convinced of that! Now, listen: I carry the money about on me a whole month. Tomorrow I may decide to give it back and then I'm no longer a blackguard. But the trouble is that I can't make up my mind, though I make it up every day and though I egg myself on every day to do it: "Make up your mind, you dirty blackguard, make up your mind!" And yet for a whole month I can't make up my mind. Yes, sir! Well, what do you think? Is that nice?'

'I daresay it isn't so nice, I can understand that perfectly well, and I don't want to argue the point,' the public prosecutor replied with restraint. 'Anyway, let's leave all this wrangling about these subtleties and distinctions and, if you don't mind, let's get back to the point. And the point, sir, is that you have still not explained to us, although we've asked you, why, in the first place, you divided the three thousand into two equal parts, squandering one half and hiding the other. What exactly did you hide it for? What exactly did you mean to do with the fifteen hundred? I must insist on an answer to this question, sir.'

'Why, of course!' cried Mitya, striking himself on the forehead. 'I'm sorry to be such a nuisance to you. I haven't explained the main thing, or you'd have understood it at once. For, you see, it's in the motive, in the motive of it that the disgrace lies! You see, it was the old man, my late father, who kept worrying Grushenka, and that made me jealous. I had an idea at the time that she was hesitating between me and him. Every day I was thinking: what if she were to make up her mind all of a sudden, if she got tired of tormenting me, and were suddenly to say to me: "I love you and not him, take me away to the other end of the world"? I had only forty copecks – so how could I take her away? What could I do? I'd be lost! You see, I didn't know her then, I didn't understand her, I thought she wanted money and that she wouldn't forgive me my poverty. And so I craftily counted out the half of the three thousand and cold-bloodedly sewed it up with a needle, sewed it up intentionally, sewed it up before I was drunk, and having sewed it up, I was off to get really drunk on the rest! Yes, sir, that was vile! Do you understand now?'

The public prosecutor laughed aloud. The examining magistrate, too, laughed.

'Well, sir,' said the examining magistrate with a chuckle, 'in my opinion it was eminently sensible and highly moral of you to have restrained yourself and not to have spent the lot, for really, sir, what does it all amount to?'

'Why, that I stole it, that's what it amounts to! Oh, Lord, you horrify me by your lack of understanding! All the time I was carrying those fifteen hundred roubles sewn up on my chest, I kept saying to myself – every day and every hour I kept saying to myself: "You're a thief! You're a thief!" That's why I've been in such a rage all this month. That's why I had a fight in the pub. That's why I assaulted my father. It was all because I felt I was a thief. I didn't have enough courage, I dared not even tell Alyosha the truth about the fifteen hundred: so conscious was I of being a blackguard and a crook. But I want you to know that while I carried it about, I kept saying to myself at the same time every day and every hour: "No, Dmitry, you may not be a thief as yet. Why not? Because next day you may go and give back the fifteen hundred to Katya." And it was only yesterday, on my way from Fenya's to Perkhotin's, that I made up my mind to tear my amulet off my neck. Up to that moment I couldn't bring myself to do it, but as soon as I tore it off, at that very moment, I became definitely and finally a thief, a thief and a dishonest man for the rest of my life. Why? Because with the amulet I also destroyed my dream of going to Katya and saying to her: "I'm a blackguard, but not a thief!" Do you understand now? Do you?'

'But why was it just last night that you decided to do it?' the examining magistrate interrupted.

'Why? What a funny thing to ask: because I had condemned myself to die at five o'clock in the morning – here, at dawn. "What difference does it make," I thought, "whether I die a blackguard or a man of honour." But it seems I was wrong. It isn't the same thing! Believe me, gentlemen, what worried me most of all last night was not that I had killed the old servant and that I might be sent to Siberia and when? – at a time when my love was rewarded and Heaven was open to me again. Oh, that did worry me, but not so much. Not as much as the damned consciousness that I had at last torn the damned money off my chest and squandered it and had therefore become a downright thief! Oh, gentlemen, I repeat to you, and please believe me I mean what I say: I learnt a lot that night! I learnt not only that it is impossible to live a blackguard, but also that it is impossible to die a blackguard. . . . No, gentlemen, one must die an honest man!'

Mitya was pale. He looked utterly exhausted, in spite of being tremendously excited.

'I'm beginning to understand you, sir,' the public prosecutor drawled in a gentle and almost compassionate voice. 'But say what you like, it's all, in my humble opinion, just your overwrought nerves. Yes, sir. And why, for instance, should you not have saved yourself all this mental agony you've suffered for almost a whole month and gone to the lady who had entrusted the money to you and given her back the fifteen hundred roubles? Having explained everything to her, why shouldn't you, in view of your position, which, as you have described, was so awful, not have tried a solution which would so naturally have occurred to one's mind, I mean, why shouldn't you, after having honourably confessed your errors to her, have asked her to lend you the sum needed for your expenses? Seeing how unhappy you are, she would, I'm sure, in the generosity of her heart not have refused your request, especially if you had agreed to sign a promissory note or even offered the same sort of security as you did to the merchant Samsonov and Mrs Khokhlakov. You still consider that security valuable, don't you?'

Mitya suddenly blushed.

'You don't really consider me such an out-and-out blackguard, do you? You can't mean it seriously, sir!' he said, with indignation, looking the public prosecutor straight in the face, as though unable to believe his ears.

'I assure you I do mean it seriously. Why do you think I don't?' the public prosecutor was surprised in his turn.

'Oh, how base that would have been! Gentlemen, do you realize that you're tormenting me? Very well, I'll tell you everything. So be it. I'll confess all my fiendish plans to you. Just to make you ashamed of yourselves, and you'll be amazed to what depth of baseness a combination of human feelings can sink. Let me tell you that I had conceived that plan myself, I mean, the plan you spoke of just now, sir. Yes, gentlemen, I too had that idea in my mind during the whole of that damned month, so that I almost made up my mind to go to Katya – so vile was I! But to go to her, to tell her of my betrayal, and for the sake of that betrayal, to carry out that betrayal, to cover the expenses of that betrayal, to beg her, to beg Katya herself for money (to beg, do you hear, to beg!), and then go straight from her and run away with another, with her rival, the woman who hated and insulted her – why, sir, you must be out of your mind!'

'Well, not exactly out of my mind,' the public prosecutor said with a grin, 'but I admit, of course, that I was a little rash and did not quite take into account one woman's jealousy of another, if, indeed, there could be any question of jealousy here, as you say. . . . Yes, yes, I suppose there is something of the kind here. . . .'

'But that would have been infamous,' cried Mitya, bringing down his fist fiercely on the table, 'that would have stunk to high heaven! Why, do you realize that she was quite capable of giving me the money, and indeed she would have given it, she would quite certainly have given it, just to revenge herself on me, she would have given it, just to enjoy her revenge, to show her contempt for me, for she, too, is a fiendish woman, a woman of great wrath! I'd have taken the money, oh, I'd have taken it all right, and then for the rest of my life – oh, God! I'm sorry, gentlemen. I'm shouting like that because I had that idea in my mind quite recently, only the day before yesterday, the night I was having all that trouble with Lyagavy. And yesterday, too. Yes, all day yesterday. I remember it. Right up to the time when that happened. . . .'

'When what happened?' the examining magistrate put in, unable to suppress his curiosity, but Mitya did not hear it.

'I've made a terrible confession to you,' he concluded gloomily. 'Do appreciate it, gentlemen. And that's not enough. It's not enough to appreciate it. You must take it at its true value. If not, if you don't take it as truth, then you simply don't have any respect for me, gentlemen. That's what I have to tell you. And I'll die of shame at having confessed it to men like you. Oh, I'll shoot myself! Why, I can see, I can see already that you don't believe me! Good Lord, you're not going to write that down too?' he cried in dismay.

'Why, of course, your last statement,' the examining magistrate said, looking at him with surprise. 'I mean, that to the very last hour you were still meaning to go to Miss Verkhovtsev to beg her for that sum. . . . I assure you, sir, this is a very important piece of evidence in your favour. I mean, for the whole of this case and – and especially for you. It's particularly important for you, sir.'

'But for goodness' sake, gentlemen,' Mitya cried, throwing up his hands, 'don't write that down, at any rate. You ought to be ashamed of yourselves! Why, I have, so to speak, rent my soul in twain before you, and you take advantage of it and are probing with your fingers in the wounds in both the torn halves. . . . Oh, my God!'

He buried his face in his hands in despair.

'Don't be so upset about it, sir,' the public prosecutor concluded.

'Everything written down now will be read over to you afterwards and we'll alter everything you don't agree with. Now I should like to ask you a little question for the third time: are you quite sure that no one, positively no one, has heard from you about the money you sewed up? I must tell you I simply can't imagine it.'

'No one, no one! I told you so before, or you've not understood anything! Leave me in peace!'

'Just as you like, sir. This matter will have to be explained and there's plenty of time for it. But, meanwhile, I'd like you to think this over carefully: we have perhaps dozens of witnesses who will say that it was you who spread the story of the three thousand you had squandered, that you shouted everywhere about it, and that it was three thousand and not fifteen hundred. And even now, when you got hold of some money yesterday, you also gave many people to understand that you had brought three thousand with you.'

'You've not dozens but hundreds of witnesses, two hundred witnesses,' Mitya exclaimed. 'Two hundred people have heard me say that. A thousand!'

'Well, you see, sir, all, all bear witness to it. And the word *all*, sir, must mean something.'

'It means nothing. I've told a tall story and now all of them begin telling it.'

'But why did you have to tell "a tall story", as you put it?'

'Goodness only knows why. Perhaps to brag at – at squandering so much money. Perhaps because I wanted to forget about the money I'd sewn up – yes, that's it! Damn it, how often are you going to ask me that question? Well, I told a lie and that's all there is to it. Told a lie once and didn't want to correct it. Why do people tell lies sometimes?'

'It's very difficult to decide why people tell lies, sir,' the public prosecutor said impressively. 'Tell me, though, was the – er – amulet, as you call it, on your neck very big?'

'Oh, not big.'

'What size was it, for instance?'

'The size of a hundred-rouble note folded in two, I suppose.'

'Could you show us any scraps of it? You must have some somewhere.'

'Oh, hell! What nonsense! I don't know where they are.'

'But, look here, sir, can't you tell us where and when you took it off your neck? According to you, you didn't go home, did you?'

'I tore it off my neck and took out the money on my way to Perkhotin's from Fenya's.'

'In the dark?'

'I didn't want a light for it, did I? I did it with a finger in a minute.'

'Without scissors? In the street?'

'In the square, I think. What did I want scissors for? It was an old rag. It was torn in less than a second.'

'Where did you put it afterwards?'

'I threw it away there.'

'Where exactly?'

'Why, in the square. Anywhere in the square! I'm damned if I know where in the square. What do you want to know that for?'

'It's of the utmost importance, sir. Material evidence in your favour. Don't you see that? Who helped you to sew it up a month ago?'

'No one helped me. I did it myself.'

'Can you sew?'

'A soldier has to know how to sew. No special knowledge was needed for that, anyway.'

'Where did you get the material from? The rag, I mean, in which to sew the money up?'

'Are you pulling my leg?'

'Certainly not. We're not in the mood for pulling your leg, sir.'

'I don't remember where I got the rag from. Must have picked it up somewhere.'

'But, surely, sir, you ought to remember that.'

'Honestly I don't. I might have torn a bit off my linen.'

'That's very interesting. I expect we could find at your lodgings tomorrow the thing – a shirt, perhaps – from which you tore off a piece. What sort of rag was it: cotton or linen?'

'I'm damned if I know. Wait a moment, though. I don't think I tore it off anything, after all. It was a bit of calico. I believe I sewed it up in my landlady's cap.'

'Your landlady's cap?'

'Yes, sir. I took it from her.'

'Took it? How?'

'You see, I seem to remember now that I actually did take one of her caps for a rag, or, perhaps, to wipe my pen on. I took it without asking, because it was really just a rag of a thing. I tore it up and kept the bits, and, when I got the money, I sewed the fifteen hundred up in them. Yes, I think I did sew it up in that rag. It was a worthless old calico cap. Been washed thousands of times.'

'You're quite sure of it now?'

'Not quite. I think it was in the cap. Oh, what does it matter?'

'In that case your landlady could at least remember having lost the thing?'

'I don't think so. She never missed it. It was an old rag, I'm telling you. An old rag not worth a farthing.'

'And where did you get the needle and thread from?'

'I won't say another word!' Mitya got angry at last. 'Enough!'

'And don't you think, sir, it's rather strange that you should have so completely forgotten where you dropped that – er – amulet?'

'Why not order the square to be swept tomorrow?' said Mitya with a grin. 'Perhaps you'll find it. Enough, gentlemen, enough,' he declared in an exhausted voice. 'I can see plainly that you don't believe me! You don't believe a word I've said. It's my fault, not yours. I shouldn't have told you anything. Why, oh why have I besmirched myself by confessing my secret to you? It's just a laughing matter to you. I can see it from your eyes. It was you, sir,' he turned to the public prosecutor, 'who drove me to it! Sing a hymn of triumph to yourself if you can. Damn you, you torturers!'

He dropped his head and buried his face in his hands. The public prosecutor and the examining magistrate were silent. A minute later he raised his head and stared vacantly at them. His face expressed complete and hopeless despair. He seemed mute and forlorn and sat as though unaware of what was taking place around him. But it was time to bring the preliminary investigation to an end: they had to pass on to the interrogation of the witnesses. It was eight o'clock already. The candles had long been extinguished. Makarov and Kalganov, who had been coming in and out of the room during Mitya's interrogation, had now both gone out again. The public prosecutor and the examining magistrate, too, looked very tired. It was a dull morning. The sky was overcast and it was pouring with rain. Mitya gazed blankly at the windows.

'May I look out of the window?' he suddenly asked the examining magistrate.

'Oh, as much as you like,' he replied.

Mitya got up and went to the window. The rain came pelting against the little greenish window panes. He could see the muddy road just beneath the window, and farther away in the rainy haze the rows and rows of poor, black, unsightly peasant cottages, which looked even poorer and blacker in the rain. Mitya remembered 'Phoebus the golden-haired' and how he had meant to shoot himself at his first ray. 'I suppose it would have been much better on such a morning,' he grinned and, suddenly, with a downward wave of his hand, he turned to his 'torturers'.

'Gentlemen,' he cried, 'I can see that I'm done for. But what about her? Tell me about her, I implore you. Will she, too, be ruined with me? She is innocent. She was not in her right mind when she cried last night: "It's all my fault!" She had nothing to do with it. Nothing! My heart was heavy as I sat with you all night. Can't you – won't you tell me what you are going to do with her now?'

'You needn't worry at all on that score, sir,' the public prosecutor replied at once with evident alacrity, 'So far we have no grounds whatever for troubling the lady in whom you are so interested. I trust it will be the same in the later stages of this case. . . . On the contrary, we'll do everything in our power in this matter. You can set your mind completely at rest.'

'I thank you, gentlemen. I knew you were just and honest men in spite of everything. You've taken a load off my mind. Well, what are we going to do now? I'm ready.'

'Well, we certainly must hurry up. We must pass on at once to the interrogation of the witnesses. All that must take place in your presence and therefore —'

'Oughtn't we to have tea first?' the examining magistrate interrupted. 'I think we've earned it!'

It was decided that if tea were ready downstairs (in view of the fact that the district police inspector had certainly gone down 'to have a cup'), they would have a cup, too, and then 'carry on', and put off their proper breakfast and 'a drop of vodka' to a more favourable opportunity. Mitya at first refused the tea which the examining magistrate politely offered him, but afterwards asked for it himself and drank it greedily. He looked altogether astonishingly exhausted. One might have supposed that to a man of his herculean strength one night of drinking, even if accompanied by the most violent sensations, would not have meant a great deal. But he felt himself that he could hardly sit straight on his chair and at times everything in the room began to go round and round before his eyes.

'A little more and I'll begin seeing things,' he thought to himself.

8

The Evidence of the Witnesses. The Babby

THE interrogation of the witnesses began. But we shall not continue our story in such detail as we have been telling it till now. We shall therefore omit the description of how the examining magistrate impressed upon every witness called to tell the truth and nothing but the truth and that he would afterwards have to repeat his evidence on oath, or how every witness was required to sign his statement, etc., etc. We shall merely note the fact that the main point stressed again and again by the two officials was the same question of the three thousand, that is to say, whether the sum spent by Dmitry at Mokroye the first time he was there a month before was three thousand or fifteen hundred and whether Mitya spent three thousand or fifteen hundred the night before. Alas, the evidence given by every witness turned out to be against Mitya. Not one was in his favour, and some of the witnesses introduced new, almost overwhelming facts in refutation of his statements. The first witness to be interrogated was the innkeeper. He appeared before the two officials without the slightest indication of fear; on the contrary, he had an air of stern and grim-faced indignation with the accused, which undoubtedly made him appear quite extraordinarily truthful and full of his own dignity. He spoke little and with restraint, waited for the questions to be put to him and replied readily and after careful consideration. He testified firmly and without a moment's hesitation that a month before Mitya could have spent no less than three thousand, that all the peasants would bear witness that they had heard of three thousand mentioned by Mr Karamazov himself. 'The money he flung away on the gipsies alone! I suppose they must have got over a thousand at least.'

'I don't think I gave them as much as five hundred,' Mitya commented gloomily. 'Didn't count it at the time, though. I was drunk. A pity.'

This time Mitya was sitting sideways with his back to the curtains. He listened gloomily, looked tired and melancholy and seemed to be saying: 'Oh, say what you like! It's all one to me now!'

'You must have spent more than a thousand on them, sir,' the landlord refuted firmly. 'You flung your money about regardless and they picked it up. They're thieves and rascals, the lot of 'em. Horse-thieves. Been driven away from here or, I daresay, they'd have testified themselves how much they profited by you. I saw the money in your hands myself, sir. It's true I didn't count it, you never let me, but from what I could see, I'd say it was much more than fifteen hundred. Fifteen hundred indeed! Seen plenty of money in my time, I have, and I can judge, I can.'

As for the sum Dmitry had had on him yesterday, the landlord declared point-blank that as soon as he got off the cart Dmitry had told him himself that he had brought three thousand with him.

'Come now, are you quite sure?' Mitya objected. 'Did I say in so many words that I brought three thousand?'

'You did, sir. You said it before Andrey. Andrey is still here. He hasn't gone. You can send for him. And when you were treating the chorus in the drawing-room, sir, you shouted yourself that you was leaving your sixth thousand here – with what you spent before, that is, that's how it must be understood. Stepan and Semyon heard it, and Mr Kalganov, too, was standing beside you at the time. Perhaps he, too, remembers it.'

The evidence of the sixth thousand made a very great impression on the two officials. They liked the new version, three and three made six, which meant three thousand then and three thousand now – and there they had the six thousand – what could be clearer than that? All the peasants mentioned by the landlord were then interrogated; Stepan and Semyon, and the driver Andrey as well as Peter Kalganov. The peasants and Andrey confirmed the landlord's evidence without hesitation. In addition the officials wrote down, word for word, Andrey's account of his conversation with Mitya on the road and

Mitya's remark to the effect: 'Where am I going to get to – to heaven or to hell, and will I be forgiven or not in the next world?' The 'psychologist', that is, the public prosecutor, heard it all with a sage smile and ended up by recommending that Mitya's remark about where he would get to should also be added 'to the evidence'.

When his turn came, Kalganov came in reluctantly, looking sullen and capricious, and spoke to the public prosecutor and the examining magistrate as though he had met them for the first time in his life and not as old acquaintances whom he had been meeting every day. He began by declaring that he knew nothing about it and didn't want to know. But it seemed that he did hear of the 'sixth thousand' and he admitted that he had been standing beside Mitya at that moment. He couldn't tell 'how much money' Mitya had in his hands. He confirmed that the Poles had cheated at cards. He also explained, in reply to reiterated questions, that after the Poles had been turned out, Mitya's affair with Grushenka had certainly taken a turn for the better and that she had said herself that she loved him. He spoke of her with restraint and respect, as though she were a lady of the best society, and never once allowed himself to call her 'Grushenka'. In spite of his obvious repugnance to giving evidence, the public prosecutor interrogated him at great length and it was only from him that he learnt all the details of what made up Mitya's 'romance' that night. Mitya did not once stop Kalganov. At last the young man was allowed to go, and he left with unconcealed indignation.

The Poles, too, were examined. Though they had gone to bed in their little room, they did not sleep all night, and on the arrival of the authorities they hastily dressed, realizing that they would be sent for. They came in looking dignified, though rather apprehensive. The little Pole turned out to be a retired civil servant of the twelfth grade, who had served in Siberia as a veterinary surgeon. His surname was Mussyalovich. Vrublevsky turned out to be a dentist in private practice. On entering the room, in spite of the fact that the questions were put to them by the examining magistrate, they both addressed their answers to Makarov, taking him in their ignorance for the superior officer in charge of the proceedings and addressing him at every word as 'colonel'. And it was only after doing that several times and at the instigation of the district police inspector himself that they realized that they had to address their answers to the examining magistrate only. It turned out that they had an excellent command of Russian, except perhaps for the pronunciation of certain words. About his relations with Grushenka, past and present, Mussyalovich began to speak proudly and warmly, so that Mitya at once lost his temper and shouted that he would not allow 'the blackguard' to talk like that in his presence. Mussyalovich at once drew attention to the word 'blackguard' and asked it to be put on record. Mitya flew into a rage.

'He's a blackguard, a dirty blackguard! You can put that down, too. Put down that in spite of the record I still say that he's a dirty black-guard!' he shouted.

Though he put it on record, the examining magistrate showed a most praiseworthy and business-like flair for dealing with this un-pleasant incident: after sternly reprimanding Mitya, he at once put an end to any further inquiries into the romantic aspect of the case and turned hastily to the essential part of it. And the essential part of it contained a piece of evidence by the Poles which aroused the extra-ordinary interest of the two officials: it concerned Mitya's attempt to bribe Mussyalovich in the other room by offering him three thousand roubles if he gave up Grushenka, on condition that he agreed to take seven hundred down and the remaining two thousand three hundred 'next day in town', assuring them on his word of honour that he had not that sum at Mokroye, but that his money was in the town. Mitya, in his excitement, objected that he had never said that he would let them have the money in the town for certain next day but Vrublevsky confirmed his friend's evidence. Mitya himself, after thinking it over for a minute, frowningly agreed that it probably was as the Poles said, that he had been very excited at the time and might really have said that. The public prosecutor simply fastened on that piece of evidence: it seemed clear to the prosecutor (as, indeed, it came out afterwards) that half or part of the three thousand that had fallen into Mitya's hands could really have been hidden somewhere in the town or, indeed, somewhere in the inn at Mokroye, which might explain the fact, so awkward for the prosecution, that only eight hundred roubles had been found in Mitya's possession so far, the only fact that, rather insignificant as it was, to a certain extent told in Mitya's favour. But even that single piece of evidence in his favour was broken down now. Asked by the public prosecutor where he would have procured the remaining two thousand three hun-

dred roubles which he had promised on his word of honour to let the
Pole have the next day, in spite of the fact that he maintained himself
that he had only fifteen hundred, Mitya firmly replied that he had
not intended to offer 'the dirty Pole' money, but a formal deed of
conveyance of his rights to the estate of Chermashnya, which he had
offered to Samsonov and Mrs Khokhlakov. The public prosecutor
could not help smiling at 'the innocence' of Mitya's attempt 'to
wriggle out'.

'And do you really think that he'd have agreed to accept these
"rights" in place of two thousand three hundred roubles in hard cash?'

'He certainly would have agreed,' Mitya declared warmly. 'Why,
he could have made not two but four or even six thousand from such
a transaction! He'd have employed a whole regiment of pettifogging
lawyers, Jews, and Poles, and they'd have gone to court and got not
three thousand but the whole estate out of the old man.'

Mussyalovich's evidence was, of course, written down in the fullest
detail. The Poles were then allowed to go. No mention whatever
was made about their cheating at cards; the examining magistrate
was too grateful to them, as it was, and he did not want to worry
them with trifles, particularly as it was nothing but a stupid quarrel
between drunken men over cards. There had been enough wild
drinking and all sorts of shocking things going on that night. . . . So
the two hundred roubles remained in the pockets of the Poles.

Maximov was next sent for. He came in timidly, went up to the
table with little steps, looking very dishevelled and mournful. He
had been all the time downstairs with Grushenka, sitting mutely with
her and 'now and again', as Markov described afterwards, 'began
whimpering over her and wiping his eyes with his blue check handkerchief'. So that she herself had to calm and comfort him. The poor
old man at once said that he was sorry that 'being so poor' he had
borrowed 'ten roubles' from Dmitry and that he was ready to return
them. To the examining magistrate's direct question whether he had
noticed how much money Mr Karamazov had in his hands, since he
must have been able to see it better than anyone when he took the
ten-rouble note from him, Maximov replied most categorically:
'Twenty thousand, sir.'

'Have you ever seen twenty thousand anywhere before?' the examining magistrate asked with a smile.

'Yes, sir, I have: when my wife mortgaged my little property, sir. Only it wasn't twenty but seven. She just let me have a look at it from a distance. Boasted to me about it, she did, sir. A very big bundle it was, too, sir. All rainbow-coloured notes. Mr Karamazov's, too, were all rainbow-coloured.'

He was soon allowed to go. At last Grushenka's turn came. The public prosecutor and the examining magistrate were evidently apprehensive of the impression her appearance might produce on Dmitry, and the examining magistrate even murmured a few words of admonition to him, but, in reply, Mitya dropped his head in silence, giving him to understand that there would be 'no scene'. Grushenka was brought in by Inspector Makarov himself. She came in with a grave and gloomy face, outwardly almost composed, and sat down quietly on the chair pointed out to her opposite the examining magistrate. She was very pale. She seemed to be cold and she kept wrapping herself closely in her beautiful black shawl. Indeed, she was beginning to feel a light feverish chill coming on just then, the start of a long illness which she went through from that night. Her grave air, her frank and serious look, and her quiet manner produced a most favourable impression upon all. The examining magistrate was even 'taken' by her a little. He admitted himself, when talking about it to some people afterwards, that it was only then that he realized how 'beautiful' that woman was, for though he had seen her several times before, he had always considered her a sort of 'provincial hetaera'. 'She has the manners of the best society,' he blurted out, to his own dismay, enthusiastically in the company of some ladies. But they received his remark with great indignation and at once called him 'a naughty man', which pleased him very much. On entering the room, Grushenka only cast a cursory glance at Mitya, who, in turn, looked at her uneasily, but her face immediately set his mind at rest. After the first inevitable questions and admonishments, the examining magistrate, though hesitating a little, but preserving the most courteous manner, asked her what were her relations with the retired lieutenant Dmitry Karamazov. To this Grushenka replied quietly and firmly:

'He was an acquaintance of mine and it was as an acquaintance that I received him during the last month.'

To further inquisitive questions she replied plainly and with absolute frankness that though she liked him 'at times', she was not in love with him, but tried to get a hold on him as well as on 'the old man' from 'mean spite'. She had seen that Mitya was very jealous of his father and of anyone else, but that had only amused her. She had never intended to go to Fyodor Karamazov, but had only been laughing at him. 'I had no time for either of them all this month. I was expecting another man, the man who had wronged me. . . . But,' she concluded, 'I don't think there's any need for you to inquire into it or for me to answer your questions, for that's my own private affair.'

The examining magistrate acted upon it immediately: he again stopped insisting on the 'romantic' aspects of the case and passed on to the serious, that is, again to the main question about the three thousand. Grushenka confirmed that in Mokroye a month before Mitya had really spent three thousand roubles, and though she herself had not counted the money, she had heard from Dmitry himself that it was three thousand.

'Did he tell you that privately or before someone else, or did you only hear him speak about it to others in your presence?' the public prosecutor inquired.

To which Grushenka replied that she had heard him say it to her in the presence of other people, that she had heard him tell other people about it, and that she had heard him say it to her privately.

'Did he say it to you privately once or several times?' the public prosecutor inquired again, and was told that Grushenka had heard him several times.

The public prosecutor was very pleased with this evidence. Further questions elicited the information that Grushenka knew where that money had come from and that Dmitry had got it from Katerina.

'And didn't you hear even once that a month ago Mr Karamazov had spent not three thousand but less, and that he had saved half of that sum for himself?'

'No, sir,' Grushenka testified, 'I never heard that.'

It was disclosed further that during that month Mitya had, on the contrary, often told her that he had not a penny. 'He was always expecting to get some money from his father,' concluded Grushenka.

'And – er – did he ever say in your presence – er – er – just in passing, or in a moment of irritation, that he meant to make an attempt on his father's life?' the examining magistrate asked suddenly.

'Oh, I'm afraid he did!' sighed Grushenka.

'Once or several times?'

'He mentioned it several times, always in anger.'

'And did you believe he'd do it?'

'No, I never believed it!' she replied firmly. 'I had confidence in his honourable character.'

'Gentlemen,' Mitya cried suddenly, 'please let me say one word to Miss Svetlov in your presence.'

'You may speak,' the examining magistrate assented.

'Grushenka,' Mitya declared, getting up from his seat, 'believe me as you believe in God. I am not guilty of my father's murder last night!'

Having said this, Mitya resumed his seat. Grushenka got up, turned to the icon in the room and crossed herself devoutly.

'Thank God,' she said in a voice trembling with emotion, and without resuming her seat she turned to the examining magistrate and added: 'Believe what he has said just now! I know him. He may sometimes say something as a joke or out of stubbornness, but if it's against his conscience he'll never deceive anyone. He'll always tell the truth, you can believe it.'

'Thank you,' Mitya said in a trembling voice. 'You've given me new confidence.'

Asked how much money Mitya had the day before, she declared that she did not know, but had heard him tell several people that he had brought three thousand with him. As to the question where he got the money, he had told her alone that he had 'stolen' it from Katerina, and she had replied that he had not stolen it and that he must return the money next day. In reply to the public prosecutor's insistent question whether the money he said he had stolen from Katerina was what he had spent yesterday or a month before, she declared that he spoke of the money he had spent a month before and that that was how she understood him.

Grushenka was at last allowed to go, the examining magistrate telling her impulsively that she could go back to town any time she liked and that if, for his part, he could be of any assistance to her, with horses, for instance, or if she would like an escort, he – for his part —

'Thank you very much, sir,' Grushenka replied with a bow. 'I'll go back with the old man, the landowner. I'll take him back to town with me and, in the meantime, if you will permit, sir, I'll wait down-stairs to hear what you decide about Mr Karamazov.'

She went out. Mitya was calm and even looked quite cheerful, but only for a minute. All the time he felt overcome by a strange physical weakness which grew more and more perceptible as time went on. His eyes were closing with fatigue. The interrogation of the witnesses came to an end at last. They began working on the final draft of the official record of the evidence. Mitya got up, crossed over from his chair to the corner of the room by the curtains, lay down on the large chest covered with a rug and fell asleep at once. He dreamed rather a strange dream which was entirely out of keeping with the place and the time. He seemed to be driving somewhere in the steppes, where he had served long ago, while he was still a regular army officer, and he was being driven through the slush by a peasant on a cart drawn by a pair of horses. He was very cold. It was early in November, and snow was falling in large, wet flakes, melting as soon as it touched the ground. The peasant was driving him briskly, wielding his whip with a will. He had a long, fair beard. He was not an old man, about fifty perhaps, and he wore a peasant's grey homespun coat. Soon they caught sight of a village. He could see the grimy, black cottages, half of them burnt down, only their charred beams sticking up. As they drove in, there were peasant women drawn up along the road, lots of women, a whole row of them, all haggard and thin with strangely brown faces. One woman in particular, at the very end of the row, was very tall and bony; she looked forty but might have been only twenty, with a long thin face, and in her arms was a little baby crying, and her breasts were probably so dried up that there was not a drop of milk in them. And the baby cried and cried, holding out its little bare arms with its little fists quite blue from cold.

'Why are they crying? Why are they crying?' Mitya asked, as they dashed past them at a spanking pace.

'It's the babby, sir,' replied the driver. 'The babby's crying.'

And Mitya was struck by the fact that he had said 'babby', in the peasant way, and not baby. And he liked the peasant's way of saying 'babby': there seemed to be more pity in it.

'But why is it crying?' Mitya persisted stupidly. 'Why are its arms bare? Why don't they wrap it up?'

'The babby's chilled to the marrow, sir; its clothes are frozen and don't warm it.'

'But why is that? Why?' stupid Mitya still persisted.

'They're poor, sir. Burnt out. Ain't got no bread, sir. They're begging because their cottages have been burnt down.'

'No, no,' Mitya still seemed unable to understand, 'tell me why the burnt-out mothers stand there? Why are people poor? Why's the babby poor? Why's the steppe so bare? Why don't they embrace and kiss one another? Why don't they sing joyous songs? Why are they so black with black misfortune? Why don't they feed the babby?'

And he felt that, though he was asking wild and senseless questions, he could not help asking them and that, indeed, that was the way they had to be asked. And he felt, too, that strange and never before experienced emotions were surging up in his heart, that he wanted to cry, that he wanted to do something for everyone so that the babby should cry no more, that no one should shed tears from that moment, and that he ought to do it now, now, without delay and regardless of everything, with all the Karamazov impetuosity.

'And I'm with you, too,' he heard beside him the dear, deeply felt words of Grushenka, 'I shall never leave you now, I shall be with you now for the rest of my life.'

And his heart blazed up and rushed forward towards the light, and he longed to live and to live, to go on and on towards the new, beckoning light, and quickly, quickly – now, at once!

'What? Where?' he exclaimed, opening his eyes and sitting up on the chest, as though he had come to from a fainting fit, smiling brightly.

The examining magistrate was standing over him, asking him to hear the statement read out to him and sign it. Mitya realized that he had been asleep for an hour or more, but he did not listen to the examining magistrate. He was suddenly struck by the fact that there was a pillow under his head, a pillow which had not been there when he sank exhausted on the chest.

'Who put the pillow under my head? Who was that kind man?' he cried with a sort of rapturous, grateful feeling and with tears in his voice, as though goodness only knows what great favour had been shown him.

It was never discovered who that kind man was. It might have been one of the witnesses, or the examining magistrate's clerk had, out of compassion, seen to it that a pillow was put under his head. But his whole soul was shaken with tears. He went up to the table and said that he would sign anything they liked.

'I've had a good dream, gentlemen,' he said in a strange voice, looking transformed and his face radiant with joy.

9

Mitya is Taken Away

WHEN the statement had been signed, the examining magistrate turned solemnly to the accused and read him a Notice of Committal to Prison, to the effect that, on such and such a date and at such and such a place, the examining magistrate of such and such a district court, having examined so and so (that is, Mitya), accused of committing such and such crimes (all the charges were carefully stated), and taking into consideration the fact that the accused, while pleading not guilty to the charges made against him, had offered no evidence in his defence, whereas the witnesses (so and so and so) and the circumstances (such and such) show him to be guilty of the aforesaid charges, acting in accordance with such and such paragraphs of the Criminal Code, etc., has decided: in order to deprive so and so (Mitya) of any means of evading any further investigation and trial, to confine him to such and such a prison, of which the accused is to be notified and a copy of this Notice to be communicated to the assistant public prosecutor, etc., etc. Mitya, in short, was informed that he was a prisoner from that moment and that he would be at once taken to town where he was to be shut up in a very unpleasant place. Mitya listened attentively and merely shrugged his shoulders.

'Well, gentlemen, I'm not blaming you. . . . I'm ready. I understand that you could do nothing else.'

The examining magistrate explained to him gently that he would be taken to prison by the rural police inspector Mavriky Shmertsov, who happened to be still there.

'One moment, gentlemen,' Mitya suddenly interrupted him with a sort of uncontrollable feeling, turning to all of them in the room.

'We are all cruel, we are all monsters, we all make people weep, mothers and babies at the breast, but of all – let it be settled now once and for all – of all I am the most vile and despicable wretch! So be it! Every day of my life, beating my breast, I've vowed to turn over a new leaf, and every day I've done the same vile things. I realize now that such men as I need a blow, a blow of fate, to catch them as though with a lasso and bind them by a force from without. Never, never should I have risen of my own free will! But the lightning has struck. I accept the suffering of my accusation and of my public disgrace. I want to suffer and be cleansed by suffering! I will, perhaps, be cleansed, gentlemen, won't I? But listen to me for the last time: I am not guilty of my father's murder! I accept my punishment not because I killed him, but because I wanted to kill him and, perhaps, would, in fact, have killed him. . . . But I swear to fight you all the same and I'm telling you that. I shall fight you to the very end, and then God will decide! Farewell, gentlemen. Don't be angry with me for having shouted at you – oh, I was still so stupid then. In another minute I shall be a prisoner, but now, for the last time, Dmitry Karamazov, as a free man, holds out his hand to you. Saying goodbye to you, I say it to all men!'

His voice trembled and he really did hold out his hand, but the examining magistrate, who was nearest to him, suddenly, somehow, hid his hands behind his back with a sort of spasmodic movement. Mitya noticed it at once and gave a start. He let fall his outstretched hand immediately.

'The investigation is not over yet,' the examining magistrate murmured, looking a little embarrassed. 'We shall continue in the town and, for my part, I'm ready to wish you every success . . . in – er – obtaining an acquittal. I've always been disposed to consider you, sir, as a man who is, as it were, more sinned against than sinning. All of us here, if I may express an opinion on behalf of us all, are ready to acknowledge you to be an honourable young man at heart, but one who, alas, has been carried away to a rather excessive extent by certain passions. . . .'

The little figure of the examining magistrate was absolutely majestic by the time he finished his speech. The thought flashed through Mitya's mind that that 'boy' would at any moment take him by the arm, lead him to the other end of the room, and renew their recent conversation about 'girls'. But all sorts of irrelevant and inappropriate thoughts sometimes pass through the head even of a prisoner who is being led out to execution.

'Gentlemen, you are kind, you are humane, may I see *her*? May I take leave of her for the last time?'

'Certainly, but in view of – er – in short, now it's no longer possible except in the presence of —'

'By all means, be present if you must!'

Grushenka was brought in, but their parting was brief and of few words. It did not gratify the examining magistrate at all. Grushenka bowed low to Mitya.

'I've told you I'm yours and I will be yours. I'll be with you for ever, wherever they may decide to take you. Good-bye, dear, you've ruined yourself through no fault of your own.'

Her lips quivered and tears gushed from her eyes.

'Forgive me for my love, Grusha, for ruining you by my love!'

Mitya wanted to say something more, but he suddenly himself broke off and went out. He was at once surrounded by people who never let him out of their sight. Outside by the front steps, to which he had driven up with such a thunderous clatter the night before, in Andrey's *troika*, two carts were already waiting. The rural police inspector, a thick-set, stout man with a fat and flabby face, was exasperated by something, by an unforeseen irregularity of some sort, and he was short-tempered and shouting. He told Mitya a little too sternly to get into the cart. 'Before, when I used to stand him drinks at the pub, the man had quite a different face,' thought Mitya as he climbed into the cart. The innkeeper, too, came down the front steps. At the gate there was a crowd of people, peasants, women and drivers. They all stared at Mitya.

'Forgive me, good people!' Mitya suddenly shouted to them from the cart.

'Forgive us too,' two or three voices shouted back.

'Forgive me, too, Trifon!'

But the innkeeper did not even turn round; he was, perhaps, too busy. He was also shouting and fussing about something. It seemed that everything was not quite ready in the second cart, in which two constables had to accompany the rural police inspector. The little peasant who had been hired to drive the second cart was pulling on his homespun coat and kept arguing that it was not he but Akim who should by rights be driving. But Akim was not there. They were trying to find him and in the meantime the little peasant persisted and begged them to wait.

'You see what our peasants are like, sir,' cried the innkeeper, addressing the police officer. 'They've no shame! Akim gave you twenty-five copecks the day before yesterday, you've spent it on drink, and now you're shouting. Surprised I am at your kindness to our vile peasants, sir. That's all I can say!'

'But,' Mitya interposed, 'what do we want a second cart for? Let's go in one, old man,' he addressed the police officer. 'Don't worry, I won't give trouble. I won't run away from you. What do you want an escort for?'

'Would you mind addressing me as "sir" when speaking to me! I'm not "old man" to you. And keep your advice for another time!' the police officer cut Mitya short fiercely, as though he were glad to vent his anger on someone.

Mitya fell silent. He flushed all over. A moment later he felt terribly cold. The rain had stopped, but the dull sky was still overcast, and a sharp wind was blowing straight in his face. 'I think I've caught a chill,' thought Mitya, twitching his shoulders. At last the police officer, too, clambered into the cart, sat down heavily and, as though not noticing it, pushed Mitya to the edge of the cart. It is true, he was in a bad mood and very displeased with the task assigned to him.

'Good-bye, Trifon!' Mitya shouted again, but he felt himself that he had said it not from good nature, but from spite and against his will.

But the innkeeper stood proudly, his hands behind his back and staring straight at Mitya. He looked stern and angry and did not reply to Mitya.

'Good-bye, Mr Karamazov, good-bye!' cried Kalganov, who had appeared out of nowhere suddenly.

Rushing up to the cart, he held out his hand to Mitya. He had no cap on. Mitya had just enough time to shake his hand.

'Good-bye, my dear fellow, I shan't forget your generosity!' he cried warmly.

But the cart moved off and their hands parted. The bell jingled – Mitya was taken away.

Kalganov ran back into the hall, sat down in a corner, buried his face in his hands and wept. He sat there weeping for a long time, as though he were a little boy and not a young man of twenty. Oh, he was almost sure of Mitya's guilt! 'What sort of people are they?' he exclaimed incoherently, in bitter desolation and almost in despair. 'What sort of people can these be after that?' At that moment he had no wish to go on living. 'Is it worth it? Is it worth it?' the distressed young man kept exclaiming.

◆ PART FOUR ◆

BOOK TEN: THE BOYS

I

Kolya Krasotkin

EARLY NOVEMBER. THERE HAD BEEN ELEVEN DEGREES OF
frost in our town and the ground was crusted with ice. A little dry
snow had fallen on the frozen ground during the night, and a 'dry,
sharp' wind was lifting and blowing it along the dreary streets of our
little town and especially along the market square. It was a dull
morning, but the snow had ceased. Not far from the square, close to
Plotnikov's shop, there stood a small house, very clean inside and
out, belonging to the widow of the civil servant Krasotkin. The
provincial secretary Krasotkin himself had been dead a long time,
almost fourteen years, but his widow, a rather comely lady in her
early thirties, was living 'on her capital' in her clean little house. She
led a quiet and exemplary life and she was of an affectionate but
rather gay disposition. She was about eighteen when her husband
died, having lived with him for only a year and borne him one son.
Since then, from the day of his death, she had devoted herself entirely
to the upbringing of her darling boy Kolya, and though she had loved
him dearly during those fourteen years, she had, of course, far more
trouble than joy from him, trembling and dying with fear almost
every day, afraid that he might fall ill, catch cold, be naughty, climb
on a chair and fall off, and so on. When Kolya began going to school
and then to our grammar school, the mother began studying all the
subjects with him, in order to help him do his homework, began
making the acquaintance of his teachers and their wives, was nice to
Kolya's schoolmates and made up to them so that they shouldn't

touch Kolya, or make fun of him or beat him. She went so far that the boys really began making fun of him on her account and began teasing him with being 'a mother's darling'. But the boy knew how to stand up for himself. He was a brave little boy, 'terribly strong', as was rumoured and soon confirmed in his class; he was nimble, stubborn, daring, and resourceful. He was good at his lessons, and it was even said that he could beat his teacher, Dardanelov, at arithmetic and world history. But though the boy looked down upon everyone, his nose in the air, he was a good comrade and was not really conceited. He accepted the respect of his schoolmates as his due, but behaved in a friendly way to them. Above all, he knew where to stop, he could restrain himself when necessary and never overstepped a certain inviolate and sacred line beyond which every offence becomes a riot, a rebellion, and a breach of the law, and cannot be tolerated. And yet he certainly never missed a chance of playing some mischievous prank at any favourable opportunity like the wildest street urchin, and not so much to do something he shouldn't as to excel himself in doing something strange and wonderful, something 'extraspecial', to dazzle, to show off. Above all, he was very vain. He knew how to make even his mother submit to him and he treated her almost despotically. She submitted to him, oh, she had submitted to him long ago, and the one thought she could not bear was that her boy did not 'love her enough'. It always seemed to her that Kolya was 'unfeeling' to her and there were times when, weeping hysterically, she began reproaching him with his coldness. The boy did not like it, and the more heartfelt effusions she demanded from him, the more unyielding he deliberately became. But all this was not so much deliberate as involuntary – such was his character. His mother was wrong: he loved her very much, he merely disliked her 'sloppy sentimentality', as he put it in his schoolboy language. There was a bookcase left in the house after his father's death, which contained a few books; Kolya was fond of reading and he had read several of them by himself. It did not worry his mother, though she could not help wondering sometimes why, instead of running out to play, her boy spent hours by the bookcase poring over some book. In that way Kolya read some things which he should not have been given to read at his age. However, more recently the boy, though he took care not to overstep a certain limit in his pranks, began to do things which frightened his mother in good earnest; it is true they were not immoral, but certainly wild and reckless. It just happened that summer, in July, during the school holidays, that the mother and son went to another district, about forty-five miles away, to spend a week with a distant relative whose husband was an official at the railway station (the same station, the nearest one to our town, from which a month later Ivan Karamazov left for Moscow). There Kolya began by a thorough examination of the railway, making a study of the rules and regulations, in the hope of impressing his schoolmates with his newly acquired knowledge on his return. But there happened to be other boys there at the time with whom he made friends. Some of them lived at the station and others in the neighbourhood – boys between twelve and fifteen, altogether about six or seven of them, two of whom happened to be from our town. The boys played games together, and on the fourth or fifth day of Kolya's visit they made a quite absurd bet of two roubles: Kolya, who was almost the youngest among them and therefore rather looked down upon by the others, out of vanity and inexcusable recklessness, volunteered to lie down between the rails when the eleven o'clock train was due to arrive at the station and lie without moving while the train passed over him at full speed. It is true, they made a preliminary investigation which showed that it was indeed possible to lie flat between the rails in a way that the train would go over without touching, but all the same it would take some courage to lie there! Kolya insisted stoutly that he would. The other boys at first laughed at him, called him a little liar and boaster, but made him even more determined to carry on with his bet. What incensed him most was the way the fifteen-year-old boys turned up their noses at him and at first even treated him as 'a little boy' and refused to play with him, which he felt to be a quite intolerable insult. And so it was decided that they should go in the evening to a spot about half a mile from the station, so that the train might have time to gather full speed after leaving the station. The boys assembled. It was a moonless night, not just dark but almost pitch-black. At the fixed time Kolya lay down between the rails. The other five, who had accepted his bet, waited in the bushes below the embankment with sinking hearts and, finally, overcome with fear and remorse. At last there came in the distance the rumble of the train leaving the station. Two red lights gleamed out of the darkness and they could hear the roar of the approaching monster. 'Run, run away from the rails!' the terror-stricken boys shouted to Kolya from the bushes, but it was too late: the train rolled over him and thundered past. The boys rushed up to Kolya: he lay motionless. They began pulling at him and tried to lift him up. Kolya suddenly got up and went down the embankment in silence. He then declared that he had lain there as though unconscious on purpose so as to frighten them, but the fact was that he really had lost consciousness, as he confessed long after to his mother. Thus it was that his reputation as 'a desperate character' stuck to him for ever. He returned home to the station white as a sheet. Next day he had a slight attack of a nervous fever, but he was in high spirits, happy, and pleased with himself. The incident became known, though not immediately, but after their return to our town; it became known throughout the school and reached the ears of the authorities. But his fond mother at once went to beseech the school authorities on her boy's behalf and succeeded in persuading Dardanelov, one of the most respected and influential masters, to take his part and intercede for him, and the affair was hushed up. Dardanelov, a middle-aged bachelor, had been passionately in love with Mrs Krasotkin for many years, and about a year before, faint with fear and the delicacy of his sentiments, very respectfully ventured to offer his hand; but she refused him point-blank, considering that her consent would have been a betrayal of her boy, though from certain mysterious signs Dardanelov might perhaps have had some right to entertain the hope that he was not entirely objectionable to the charming but a little too virtuous and fond young widow. Kolya's mad prank seemed to have broken the ice, and as a reward for his intercession Dardanelov had been given a hint that there might still be some hope for him; the hint was rather vague, but for Dardanelov, who was a paragon of purity and delicacy, that was for the time being sufficient to make him perfectly happy. He was fond of Kolya, though he would have considered it humiliating to curry favour with him. He therefore treated him sternly and exactingly in class. But Kolya kept him at a respectful distance himself, he did his lessons well, was second in his class, treated Dardanelov coldly, and the whole class firmly believed that Kolya was so good at world history that he could easily 'beat' Dardanelov himself. And, indeed, when Kolya one day asked

Dardanelov who had founded Troy, the master replied in general terms about the movements and migrations of different peoples, the remoteness of the times, the legendary stories, but the question who had founded Troy, that is, what persons, he could not answer, and for some reason even found the question to be idle and of no importance. But the boys remained convinced that Dardanelov did not know who had founded Troy. Kolya had read about the founders of Troy in Smaragdov, whose history was among the books in his father's bookcase. In the end everyone, even the boys, became interested in the question who it was that had founded Troy, but Kolya would not tell his secret and his reputation for learning remained unshaken.

After the incident on the railway a certain change took place in Kolya's relations with his mother. When Mrs Krasotkin learnt of her son's exploit she nearly went out of her mind with horror. She had such terrible attacks of hysterics, lasting with intervals for several days, that Kolya, frightened in good earnest, gave her his solemn promise that he would never engage in such pranks again. He swore on his knees before the icon and by the memory of his father, at the demand of Mrs Krasotkin herself, and, overcome by his 'feelings', the 'manly' Kolya himself burst into tears like a six-year-old boy, and mother and son spent the whole of that day throwing themselves into each other's arms and sobbing their hearts out. Next morning Kolya woke up as 'unfeeling' as ever, but he became more silent, more modest, more sedate, and more thoughtful. It is true that a month later he got himself into trouble again and his name even reached the ears of our Justice of the Peace, but it was quite another kind of trouble, foolish and ridiculous, and it would seem that he was not responsible for it, but only got mixed up in it. But of that later. His mother continued to be worried and to tremble for him, and the more troubled she became, the more did Dardanelov's hopes increase. It must be noted that Kolya understood and was aware of Dardanelov's hopes, and, quite naturally, despised him greatly for his 'feelings'. Before, he had even been indelicate enough to reveal his contempt to his mother, hinting vaguely that he understood very well what Dardanelov was up to. But after the incident on the railway he changed his behaviour in this respect, too: he did not permit himself any more hints, even of the vaguest kind, and began speaking more respectfully of Dardanelov in the presence of his mother, which the sensitive Mrs Krasotkin at once appreciated with infinite gratitude in her heart; but at the slightest and quite inadvertent mention of Dardanelov by some visitor in Kolya's presence she would blush like a rose with shame. At such moments Kolya either stared, frowning, out of the window, or became absorbed in looking for holes in his boots, or began shouting fiercely for Perezvon, the rather big, shaggy, and mangy dog which he had acquired somewhere a month before, brought home and kept for some reason secretly indoors, not showing it to any of his friends. He bullied him terribly, teaching him all sorts of tricks, and reduced him to such a state that he howled whenever he was away at school and squealed with delight when he came home, rushed about like mad, begged, lay down on the ground and pretended to be dead, and so on, in fact, showed all the tricks he had been taught, no longer at a word of command but solely from the ardour of his rapturous feelings and his grateful heart.

Incidentally, I forgot to mention that Kolya Krasotkin was the boy whom Ilyusha, the son of the retired captain Snegiryov, already known to the reader, had stabbed with a penknife, in defending his father, whom the schoolboys had taunted with the name of 'bast-sponge'.

2

Kids

AND so, on that frosty, cold, and windy November morning Kolya Krasotkin was at home. It was Sunday and there was no school. But it now struck eleven and he simply had to go out 'on some very urgent business', and yet he was left alone in charge of the house, for it so happened that owing to some special and singular event the grown-up people of the house were all out. In Mrs Krasotkin's house, across the passage from her own flat, there was another small flat of two rooms, let to a doctor's wife and her two little children. The doctor's wife was of the same age as Mrs Krasotkin and a great friend of hers. Her husband, the doctor, had gone a year before to Orenburg and from there to Tashkent, and for the last six months there had been no news of him at all, so that but for her friendship with Mrs Krasotkin, which somewhat allayed the misery of the abandoned doctor's wife, she would have died of grief. And it just had to happen that, to add the finishing touch to fortune's blows, Katerina, the only maid of the doctor's wife, suddenly and to the great surprise of her mistress, told her on Saturday night that she proposed to give birth to a baby the next morning. How no one had ever noticed it before seemed almost a miracle to everyone. The astonished doctor's wife decided to take Katerina while there was still time to an establishment in our town kept for such emergencies by a midwife. As she valued her maid's services greatly, she promptly carried out her plan, took her to that establishment and remained with her there. In the morning, Mrs Krasotkin's friendly sympathy and help were urgently required, for she could, if necessary, give her moral support or ask someone else to take an interest in the case. Both ladies were, therefore, out that morning, and Agafya, Mrs Krasotkin's old maid, had gone to the market. And so Kolya was left for a time in charge of the 'silly kids', that is, the little boy and girl of the doctor's wife, who were left alone. Kolya was not afraid to guard the house and, besides, he had Perezvon, who had been ordered to lie flat on the floor under the bench in the hall 'without moving' and who for that very reason shook his head and gave two loud and ingratiating taps on the floor with his tail every time Kolya, walking through the rooms, came into the hall, but, alas, there was no summoning whistle. Kolya looked sternly at the unhappy dog, who relapsed again into obedient rigidity. The only thing that worried Kolya was the 'silly kids'. Katerina's unexpected adventure he, of course, regarded with the utmost scorn, but he was very fond of the abandoned 'kids' and had already taken them a children's book. Nastya, the elder, a girl of eight, could already read, and the younger boy, the seven-year-old Kostya, was very fond of hearing Nastya read to him. Krasotkin could, of course, have found some more interesting entertainment for them, that is, he could have made them stand side by side and played soldiers or hide and seek with them. He had done so many times before and was not ashamed to do it, so that even at school the news spread that Krasotkin played horses with the little lodgers at home, galloping and bending his head like a side-horse; but Krasotkin proudly parried this accusation, pointing out that to play horses with boys of one's own age, boys of thirteen, 'in our age' would certainly be disgraceful, but that he did it for the 'silly kids' because he was fond of them, and no one had a right to demand an account of his feelings. That was why the two 'silly kids' simply adored him. But this time he was in no mood for games. He had some very important business of his own to see to, something almost mysterious, and meanwhile time was passing and Agafya, in whose charge the children could be left, was still not back from market. He had several times crossed the passage, opened the door of the doctor's wife's flat, and looked anxiously at the 'silly kids', who, as he had told them, were sitting over a book. Every time he opened the door, they grinned at him, expecting him to come in and do something nice and amusing. But Kolya was worried and did not go in. At last it struck eleven and he made up his mind once and for all that if that 'damned' Agafya did not come back within ten minutes, he would go out without waiting for her, making the 'silly kids' promise him first not to be afraid, not to be naughty, and not to cry from fright. With that idea in mind, he put on his wadded winter overcoat with the cat-fur collar, slung his satchel over his shoulder and, in spite of his mother's repeated entreaties not to go out in 'such cold weather' without putting on his galoshes, merely glanced contemptuously at them as he crossed the hall, and went out only in his boots. Seeing him dressed for going out, Perezvon began tapping loudly on the floor with his tail, his whole body shaking nervously, and even emitted a plaintive squeal, but Kolya, seeing his dog's eager impatience, decided that it was injurious to his discipline, and kept him to the very last minute lying under the bench. It was only when he opened the door into the passage that he suddenly whistled for him. The dog leapt up madly and began bounding before him rapturously. Crossing the passage, Kolya opened the door to have a look at the 'silly kids'. They were both still sitting at the table, no longer reading but discussing something warmly. These two children very often discussed all sorts of exciting problems of everyday life with one another, Nastya, as the elder one, always getting the better of the argument; if Kostya did not agree with her, he always appealed to Kolya Krasotkin, whose decision was accepted by the two contending sides as the last word on the subject. This time Krasotkin became rather interested in the discussion of the 'silly kids' and he stopped in the doorway to listen. The children saw that he was listening and continued their dispute with redoubled enthusiasm.

'I shall never, never believe,' Nastya was saying heatedly, 'that midwives find babies among the cabbage beds in the kitchen garden. It's winter now and there are no cabbage beds, and the old woman couldn't have brought Katerina a baby daughter.'

'Whew!' Kolya whistled under his breath.

'Or perhaps they do bring them from somewhere but only to those who are married.'

Kostya looked intently at Nastya, listening with a wise air and thinking hard.

'Don't be such a fool, Nastya,' he said at last firmly and without heat, 'how could Katerina have a baby if she isn't married?'

Nastya got terribly excited.

'You don't understand anything,' she interrupted him irritably. 'Perhaps she has a husband, only he is in prison, and now she has a baby.'

'But are you sure her husband's in prison?' the practical-minded Kostya inquired gravely.

'Or perhaps,' Nastya interrupted impulsively, having given up and forgotten her first hypothesis, 'perhaps she has no husband, you may be right there, but she wants to get married, and she's been thinking of getting married, and she went on thinking and thinking about it till now she's got a baby and not a husband.'

'Oh, well, perhaps that's what it is,' Kostya, completely beaten, agreed. 'Why didn't you say so before? How was I to know?'

'Well, children,' said Kolya, stepping into the room, 'I can see you're a dangerous lot!'

'Have you got Perezvon with you?' grinned Kostya and began snapping his fingers and calling Perezvon.

'Look here, kids, I'm in a difficult position,' Krasotkin began importantly, 'and you must help me. I expect Agafya must have broken a leg, for she hasn't come back yet. I'm sure she has. But I simply have to go out. Will you let me go?'

The children looked anxiously at one another. Their grinning faces showed signs of uneasiness. But they still did not quite grasp what was expected of them.

'You won't be naughty while I'm away? You won't climb on the cupboard and break your legs? You won't start crying because you're frightened when you're left alone, will you?'

A look of terrible anxiety came into the children's faces.

'If you promise to be good I could show you something nice, a little copper cannon which you can fire with real powder.'

The children's faces brightened at once.

'Show us the little cannon,' said Kostya, beaming all over.

Krasotkin put his hand in his satchel and, taking out a little bronze cannon, stood it on the table.

'Show it to us indeed!' Krasotkin repeated. 'Look, it's on wheels,' he rolled the toy along the table. 'You can fire it off. Load it with shot and fire off.'

'Will it kill anyone?'

'It can kill everyone, all you have to do is to aim it at something,' and Krasotkin explained where the powder had to be put, where the shot had to be rolled in, showing them the little hole for priming and telling them about the recoil. The children watched with intense interest. What struck their imagination particularly was that the cannon recoiled after firing.

'And have you got any powder?' Nastya inquired.

'I have.'

'Show us the powder, too,' she begged with an imploring smile.

Krasotkin dived again into his satchel and pulled out a small bottle which contained a little real powder, and there was some shot, too, in a screwed-up bit of paper. He even took the cork out of the bottle and shook out a little powder into the palm of his hand.

'It's a good thing there's no fire about, or it would explode and kill us all,' Krasotkin warned them for effect.

The children looked at the powder with awe-stricken alarm, which intensified their enjoyment. But Kostya liked the shot most of all.

'The shot doesn't burn, does it?' he asked.

'No, the shot doesn't burn.'

'Give me a little shot,' he said in an imploring little voice.

'I will give you a little – here, take it, but don't show it to your mother before I come back or she'll think it's powder and die of fright and give you a hiding.'

'Mummy never canes us,' Nastya at once remarked.

'I know, I only said it because it sounds good. And don't you ever deceive your mother except this once – until I come back. And so, kids, can I go out or not? You won't be frightened and cry when I'm gone, will you?'

'We sh-all c-cry,' Kostya said, about to burst into tears.

'Yes, yes, we're quite sure to cry!' Nastya put in with timid haste.

'Oh, children, children, you're at such a dangerous age! Well, I suppose I'll have to stay with you for goodness knows how long. And, dear me, how time does fly!'

'Please, tell Perezvon to pretend to be dead,' asked Kostya.

'Well, I suppose I'll have to get Perezvon to do some of his tricks, too. Come here, sir!'

And Kolya began giving orders to the dog, who went through all the tricks he knew.

Perezvon was a shaggy, medium-sized mongrel with a sort of smoky-grey coat. He was blind in his right eye and his left ear had for some reason been torn. He yelped and jumped, begged, walked on his hind legs, threw himself on his back with his four paws in the air, and lay without moving as though he were dead. During his last trick the door opened and Agafya, Mrs Krasotkin's fat maid, a pock-marked peasant woman of about forty, appeared in the doorway, having returned from the market with a sackful of provisions in her hand. Holding the sack in her left hand, she stood watching the dog. Anxious as he was for her return, Kolya did not interrupt the performance, and, after keeping Perezvon dead for a certain time, at last whistled to him: the dog jumped up and started dancing about in his joy at having performed his duty.

'Well I never – what a dog!' Agafya said sententiously.

'And why are you late, woman?' Krasotkin asked sternly.

'Woman, indeed! Get along with you, you cub!'

'Cub?'

'Yes, sir, cub. What does it matter to you if I'm late or not? If I'm late, I've a good reason for it, you may be sure!' muttered Agafya, bustling about the stove, but not in a displeased and angry voice; on the contrary, she seemed quite glad of the opportunity of exchanging a few bantering words with her jovial young master.

'Listen, you silly old woman,' Krasotkin began, getting up from the sofa. 'Can you swear by all that you hold sacred in the world and by something else besides that you will keep an eye on the kids all the time I'm out. I'm going out now.'

'And why should I swear to you?' Agafya laughed. 'I'll look after them without it.'

'Oh no, not before you swear on your eternal salvation. I shan't go otherwise.'

'Don't go. What do I care? It's freezing cold outside, so you'd better stay at home.'

'Kids,' Kolya turned to the children, 'this woman will stay with you until I come back or until your mother comes back, for your mother, too, ought to have been back long ago. She will give you some lunch, too. You will give them something, Agafya, won't you?'

'That I will.'

'Good-bye, little ones, I go with a clear conscience. And you, granny,' he said gravely in an undertone as he walked past Agafya, 'won't, I hope, start telling them all your usual old wives' tales about Katerina. Spare their tender years. Here, Perezvon, here, sir!'

'Oh, get away with you,' Agafya snapped back at him, really angry this time. 'Funny, aren't you? You deserve a good hiding for saying such things, you do that!'

3

Schoolboys

BUT Kolya was not listening. At last he could go out. On going out of the gate he looked round, hunched up his shoulders and saying, 'It's freezing!' walked straight along the street and then turned to the right into a lane in the direction of the market square. When he reached the last house but one before the market square, he stopped, took a whistle out of his pocket and blew with all his might, as though giving a pre-arranged signal. He had to wait no more than a minute before a red-cheeked boy of eleven suddenly rushed out from the gate and ran up to him. The boy also was wearing a warm, clean, and even smart overcoat. It was Smurov, who was in the pre-paratory class (Kolya was two classes higher), the son of a well-to-do civil servant. He was apparently forbidden to have anything to do with Krasotkin, who was well known for his desperate escapades, so that Smurov had evidently rushed out of the house by stealth. Smurov, if the reader has not forgotten, was one of the group of boys who two months before had thrown stones across the ditch at Ilyusha and who told Alyosha Karamazov about him.

'I've been waiting for you for over an hour, Krasotkin,' Smurov said in a most emphatic tone of voice, and the boys walked towards the market square.

'I'm sorry to be late,' replied Krasotkin. 'I'm afraid I couldn't get away. You won't be thrashed for coming with me?'

'Good Lord, I'm not thrashed! Got Perezvon with you?'

'Yes.'

'Taking him there, too?'

'Yes, I am.'

'Oh, if only we had Zhuchka!'

'We can't have Zhuchka. Zhuchka doesn't exist. Zhuchka has vanished, disappeared without a trace.'

'Oh, but couldn't we do this?' Smurov suddenly stopped dead. 'You see, Ilyusha says that Zhuchka was a shaggy, smoky-grey dog like Perezvon, so couldn't we say that this is Zhuchka? He might believe it.'

'Boy, remember, don't tell lies, even if it's for a good cause. And, what's more, I hope you said nothing there about my coming.'

'Good Lord, no. I quite understand. But you won't comfort him with Perezvon,' Smurov sighed. 'I tell you what. His father, the captain, the bast-sponge, I mean, told us that he's bringing him a puppy today, a real Alpine mastiff pup, with a black nose. He thinks that will comfort Ilyusha. But will it?'

'And how is Ilyusha himself?'

'Oh, he's bad, bad. I think he has consumption. He's quite conscious, but he can hardly breathe. The other day he asked to be allowed to walk round the room. They put his boots on and he tried to walk, but he kept falling over. "Oh," he says, "I told you, Daddy, that my boots were no good. I couldn't walk in my old boots, either." You see, he thought he was falling over his feet because of his boots, but it was only because he was too weak to stand up. He won't live another week. Herzenstube comes to see him every day. Now they are rich again – they've lots of money.'

'The rogues.'

'Who are rogues?'

'The doctors and the whole dirty medical profession, generally speaking, and, of course, individually. I'm against medicine. A useless profession! I'm going to make a thorough investigation of it. What's all that sentimental nonsense, though? The whole class seems to be going there!'

'No, not the whole class. Just about a dozen of our chaps go to see him every day. That's nothing.'

'I'm surprised at the part Alexey Karamazov is playing in all this: his brother's going to be tried tomorrow or the day after tomorrow for such a crime, and yet he has so much time to waste on being sentimental with boys.'

'There's nothing sentimental about it. Aren't you, too, going to make it up with Ilyusha now?'

'Make it up with him? What a ridiculous expression! Still, I won't allow anyone to analyse my actions.'

'Ilyusha will be pleased to see you, I must say! He has no idea you are coming. Why didn't you want to come all this time? Why?' Smurov suddenly exclaimed warmly.

'My dear boy, that's my business, not yours. I'm going of my own free will, and you were all dragged there by Alexey Karamazov, so there's a difference, you see. And how do you know? Maybe I'm not going to make it up with him at all. A silly expression!'

'It wasn't Karamazov, it wasn't him at all. It's simply that our chaps started going there by themselves. At first, of course, with Karamazov. And there's been nothing of that sort – no silliness. First one went, then another. His father was awfully pleased to see us. You know, he'll simply go mad if Ilyusha dies. He can see that Ilyusha's dying. And he's so glad we've made it up with Ilyusha. He asked about you, Ilyusha did. He didn't say anything, though. He just asks about you and doesn't say anything more. I'm sure his father will go mad or hang himself. He behaved like a madman before, too. He's a very nice man, you know. It was all a mistake then. It was the fault of that murderer who beat him up then.'

'All the same, Karamazov is a riddle to me. I could have got acquainted with him long ago, but there are cases where I prefer to be proud. Besides, I've formed a certain opinion of him which has still to be verified and explained.'

Kolya lapsed into impressive silence; Smurov, too, was silent. Smurov, of course, worshipped Kolya Krasotkin and never even dreamed of putting himself on the same level with him. At that moment his interest was greatly aroused because Kolya had said that he was going 'of his own free will', for he could not help feeling that there must be some mystery in Kolya's taking it into his head to go to see Ilyusha just that day. They were walking across the market square which was that day full of all sorts of country carts and lots of live birds. The market women were selling buns, thread, etc., on their covered stalls. Such Sunday markets are naïvely known in our town as country fairs, and there were many such fairs in a year. Perezvon ran about in high spirits, rushing hither and thither in order to sniff at something. Whenever he met other dogs, he sniffed them all over with extraordinary zeal, according to all the canine rules and regulations.

'I like to watch realism, Smurov,' Kolya said suddenly. 'Have you noticed how dogs meet and sniff at each other? It seems to be a general law of nature with them.'

'Yes, it's a funny one, too.'

'Well, no, not funny. You're wrong there. There's nothing funny in nature, however much it may seem so to man with his prejudices. If dogs could reason and criticize, they would, I'm sure, have found many, if not more, things that seemed funny to them in the social relationships of men, their masters – if not more. I repeat this because I'm quite sure that we have a great many more silly things. It's Rakitin's idea. A remarkable idea. I'm a socialist, Smurov.'

'And what is a socialist?' asked Smurov.

'It's when all are equal, all hold property in common, there are no marriages, and religion and laws are according to everyone's liking, and, well, all the rest of it. I'm afraid you're too young to understand it. It's cold, though.'

'Yes, twelve degrees of frost. Daddy looked at the thermometer just now.'

'And have you noticed, Smurov, that in the middle of winter, when there are fifteen or eighteen degrees of frost, it doesn't seem to be as cold as it is now, for instance, at the beginning of winter when it's twelve degrees of frost and scarcely any snow. This means that people haven't got used to it yet. Everything is a matter of habit with people, everything, even their social and political relations. Habit is the prime mover. What a funny peasant, though!'

Kolya pointed to a peasant in a sheepskin, with a good-natured face, who was standing beside his cart beating his hands in long leather gloves to warm them. His long fair beard was covered with hoar-frost.

'The peasant's beard is frozen!' Kolya cried teasingly in a loud voice as he passed him.

'Lots of people's beards are frozen,' the peasant said calmly and sententiously in reply.

'Don't tease him,' said Smurov.

'Nonsense, he won't be cross. He's a good fellow. Good-day, Matvey!'

'Good-day, sir.'

'Are you Matvey?'

'Yes, sir. Didn't you know?'

'No. I guessed it.'

'Did you? You're a schoolboy, I suppose?'

'Yes.'

'Do they thrash you?'

'Just a little.'

'Does it hurt?'

'I'm afraid so.'

'Oh dear, what a life!' the peasant heaved a deep sigh.

'Good-bye, Matvey!'

'Good-bye. You're a good lad. Yes, sir.'

The boys walked on.

'That's a good peasant,' said Kolya to Smurov. 'I like to talk to peasants and I'm always glad to do justice to them.'

'Why did you tell him a lie about our being beaten at school?'

'Well, I had to say something to please him!'

'How do you mean?'

'You see, Smurov, I don't like being asked the same question twice, if I'm not understood the first time. It's difficult to explain some things to people. According to a peasant's idea schoolboys are beaten and must be beaten. What sort of schoolboy are you, if you're not beaten? That's what they think. And if I told him that boys were not beaten at our school, he might be upset. Still, I don't suppose you understand that. One must know how to talk to peasants.'

'But don't tease them, please, or there'll be a row again as with that goose.'

'Are you afraid?'

'Don't laugh, Kolya. Of course I'm afraid. Daddy will be awfully angry. I've been strictly forbidden to go out with you.'

'Don't worry. Nothing will happen now. Good morning, Natasha,' he shouted to one of the market women at the stall.

'I'm not Natasha, I'm Maria,' the market woman, who was quite young, answered shrilly.

'I'm glad you're Maria. Good-bye.'

'Oh, you little scamp, you can hardly see him and he's at it already!'

'Sorry, I'm in a hurry,' Kolya waved her away as though she had been pestering him and not he her. 'You'll tell me all about it next Sunday.'

'What am I going to tell you next Sunday? You started it, not me, you impudent little rascal,' Maria yelled. 'You should be whipped, you should! You always go about insulting people, you do!'

There was laughter among the other market women who had stalls next to Maria's. Suddenly an angry-looking man rushed out from the nearby arcade of shops. He was not a local tradesman, but a sort of merchant's clerk who had come to the fair. He was quite young, with a long, pale, pock-marked face and dark brown curly hair. He wore a long blue coat and a peaked cap. He seemed to be in a state of stupid excitement and at once began shaking his fist at Kolya.

'I know you,' he shouted irritably, 'I know you!'

Kolya stared at him. He, somehow, could not remember when he could have had a row with him. But he had been in so many scrapes in the streets that he could scarcely remember them all.

'Do you?' he asked him ironically.

'I know you! I know you!' the tradesman kept repeating like a fool.

'So much the better for you. Sorry, I'm in a hurry. Good-bye!'

'What are you creating a disturbance for?' the tradesman shouted.

'Creating a disturbance again, are you? I know you! Creating a disturbance again!'

'It's not your business, my good man, whether I'm creating a disturbance or not,' said Kolya, stopping and continuing to scrutinize him.

'Not my business?'

'No, not yours.'

'Whose is it then? Whose? Well, whose?'

'It's Trifon Nikitich's business, not yours.'

'What Trifon Nikitich?' the man stared at him with idiotic surprise, though still as excited as ever.

Kolya looked him up and down gravely.

'Have you been to the Church of the Ascension?' he asked him suddenly, sternly and emphatically.

'What Church of the Ascension? Whatever for? No, I haven't,' the man said, taken aback a little.

'Do you know Sabaneyev?' Kolya went on still more sternly and emphatically.

'What Sabaneyev? No, I don't know him.'

'Well, to hell with you then!' Kolya suddenly snapped and, turning sharply to the right, went quickly on his way, as though thinking it beneath his dignity to talk to a blockhead who did not even know Sabaneyev.

'Wait, you – hey! What Sabaneyev?' the man recollected himself, getting all excited again. 'Who is he talking about?' he turned suddenly to the market women, staring stupidly at them.

The women laughed.

'A funny boy,' said one of them.

'What Sabaneyev did he mean?' the man kept repeating furiously, waving his right arm.

'I suppose that must be the Sabaneyev what worked for the Kuzmichovs, that's who it must be,' one woman suddenly suggested.

The man stared wildly at her.

'Kuz-mi-chov?' another woman repeated. 'But his name ain't Trifon! He's Kuzma, not Trifon. And the lad called him Trifon Nikitich, so it ain't him.'

'That's not Trifon, that ain't. And not Sabaneyev, neither,' a third woman, who had kept silent till then, listening gravely, suddenly joined in. 'He's called Alexey Ivanovich. Chizhov, Alexey Ivanovich.'

'Aye, it's Chizhov all right,' a fourth woman confirmed.

The bewildered man kept looking from one to the other.

'But why did he ask, why did he ask, good people?' he exclaimed, almost in despair. 'Do you know Sabaneyev? How the devil am I to know who Sabaneyev is?'

'Why, you stupid fellow, I tells you it ain't Sabaneyev but Chizhov – Alexey Ivanovich Chizhov – that's who it is!' a market woman shouted at him impressively.

'What Chizhov? What? Tell me if you know!'

'Why, the long one. The one whose nose is always running. He used to sit in the market in the summer.'

'But what's your Chizhov got to do with me, good people, eh?'

'How do I know what Chizhov's got to do with you?'

'I'm sure I don't know what he's got to do with you,' another woman put in. 'You ought to know yourself what you wants him for, if you keeps hollering like that. He was telling you and not us, you silly man. Don't you really know him?'

'Who?'

'Chizhov.'

'Oh, to hell with Chizhov and with you too! I'll give him a hiding, I will. He was pulling my leg!'

'Give Chizhov a hiding? Take care he don't give you one! You're a fool, that's what you are!'

'Not Chizhov, not Chizhov, you bad, wicked old woman, you! I'll give the boy a hiding. Get him, get him – he was making fun of me!'

The women roared with laughter. But Kolya was striding along with a triumphant look on his face, a long way off. Smurov walked beside him, looking back at the shouting crowd in the distance. He, too, was in high spirits, though he was still afraid of getting mixed up in some scrape with Kolya.

'What Sabaneyev did you ask him about?' he asked Kolya, knowing very well what his answer would be.

'How do I know? They'll be screaming their heads off till the evening now. I like to shake fools up in every class of society. Here's another blockhead – that peasant there. Mind you, people say

"There's no one stupider than a stupid Frenchman," but you can recognize a Russian fool too by his face. Now, just have a look at that peasant – can't you see it written on his face that he's a fool?'

'Leave him alone, Kolya. Come on.'

'Not for anything in the world. I'm off now. Hey, there, good morning, peasant!'

A sturdy-looking peasant, who was walking slowly past them and who seemed to have had a drop already, with a round, simple face and a greying beard, raised his head and looked at the boy.

'Good morning if you're not joking,' he replied unhurriedly.

'And if I am?' laughed Kolya.

'If you are, you are. It don't matter to me. I don't mind, I'm sure. There's no harm in a joke.'

'I'm sorry, old chap. It was a joke.'

'Well, the Lord will forgive you.'

'Do you forgive me?'

'Yes, sir, I forgive you all right. Run along now.'

'I must say, you seem a clever peasant.'

'Cleverer than you,' the peasant replied unexpectedly and as gravely as before.

'Hardly,' Kolya said, taken aback a little.

'Aye, it's true all the same.'

'I suppose it is.'

'Yes, sir.'

'Good-bye, peasant.'

'Good-bye.'

'There are all sorts of peasants,' Kolya observed to Smurov after a short pause. 'How was I to know that I'd come across a clever one. I'm always ready to recognize intelligence in the common people.'

In the distance the cathedral clock struck half past eleven. The boys hurried along and the rest of the long way to the house of Captain Snegiryov they walked quickly and almost without speaking. Twenty yards from the house Kolya stopped and told Smurov to go on ahead and ask Karamazov to come out to him.

'I must sniff around first,' he remarked to Smurov.

'But why call him out?' Smurov objected. 'Go in, they'll be awfully glad to see you. What do you want to get acquainted with him in the frost for?'

'I know why I want him out here in the frost,' Kolya cut him short despotically (which he was very fond of doing with 'small boys'), and Smurov ran off to carry out his order.

4

Zhuchka

KOLYA leaned against the fence with an air of self-importance and waited for Alyosha to appear. Yes, he had wanted to meet him for a long time. He had heard a lot about him from the boys, but till now he had always assumed an air of contemptuous indifference every time they spoke to him about Alyosha, and even 'criticized' what he heard about him. But in his heart of hearts he wished very much to get acquainted with him: there was something sympathetic and attractive in all the stories he had heard about Alyosha. The present moment was, therefore, important; to begin with, he must do his best not to disgrace himself, and show his independence: 'Or else he'll think that I'm just a boy of thirteen and take me for the same sort of boy as the rest. And what does he want with those boys? I'll ask him when we are to become friends. It's bad, though, I'm so short. Tuzikov is younger than I and half a head taller. I have an intelligent face, though; I'm not good-looking, I know I've an ugly face, but it's intelligent. I must be careful, too, not to show how anxious I am to be friends with him, for if I throw myself into his arms at once, he may think. . . . Oh, it will be horrid, if he does! . . .'

So Kolya kept worrying, trying his utmost to assume a most independent air. The thing that upset him most was being so short, not so much his 'horrid' face as his small stature. At home, on a wall in the corner of his room, he had drawn a line with a pencil a year before to show his height, and since then he went up anxiously to the wall to measure himself every two months: how tall had he grown in the interval? But, alas, he grew very little and that at times simply threw him into despair. As for his face, it was not at all 'horrid'; on the contrary, it was rather attractive, with a fair, pale, freckled skin. His grey, small, but lively eyes had a fearless look and often glowed with feeling. His cheekbones were a trifle too broad, his mouth was small, his lips rather thin, but very red; his nose was small and most definitely turned up: 'Absolutely snub-nosed, absolutely snub-nosed!' Kolya muttered to himself every time he looked in the looking-glass, and always went away from it with indignation. 'And is my face intelligent, after all?' he thought sometimes, even doubtful about that. Still, it would be wrong to suppose that his anxiety about his face and his height occupied him to the exclusion of everything else. On the contrary, however bitter were the moments before the looking-glass, he quickly forgot all about them and for a long time, too, 'giving himself up entirely to ideas and the reality of life', as he defined his activity himself.

Alyosha appeared soon and walked up quickly to Kolya, who noticed even before he came up to him that Alyosha looked very happy. 'Is he so glad to see me?' Kolya thought with pleasure. Here, incidentally, we must note that Alyosha had changed very much since we saw him last: he left off his cassock and was now wearing a well-cut coat, a soft, round hat, and his hair had been cut short. All this was very becoming to him and he looked very handsome. His charming face always wore a cheerful expression, but his cheerfulness was rather gentle and quiet. To Kolya's surprise, Alyosha came out without an overcoat, and it was evident that he was in a great hurry. He held out his hand to Kolya at once.

'Here you are at last! We were all waiting for you!'

'There were reasons which you will know presently,' Kolya murmured, a little out of breath. 'Anyway, I'm glad to meet you. I've long been waiting for an opportunity. I've heard such a lot about you.'

'Why, we should have met anyway. I've heard a lot about you myself. It's here they've been waiting for you.'

'Tell me, how are things here?'

'Ilyusha is very bad. I'm afraid he's sure to die.'

'Really? You must admit, Karamazov, medicine is a low-down swindle,' Kolya cried warmly.

'Ilyusha has often, very often, mentioned you, even in his sleep, in delirium, you know. One can see you used to be very, very dear to him before – before that affair with – the knife. There's another reason, too. . . . Tell me, is that your dog?'

'Yes, Perezvon.'

'Not Zhuchka?' Alyosha looked sadly at Kolya. 'It's lost without trace, is it?'

'I know you'd all like to have Zhuchka, I've heard all about it,' Kolya smiled enigmatically. 'Listen, Karamazov, I'll explain it all to you. That's really why I came and that's why I asked you to come out, to explain the whole thing to you before we go in,' he began animatedly. 'You see, Karamazov, Ilyusha joined the preparatory class last spring. Well, you know what the boys in the preparatory class are – just kids. They began teasing Ilyusha at once. I'm two classes higher and, of course, I was watching it all from a distance, as an observer. I could see he was a small, weak boy, but he wouldn't give in to them, he even fought them, a proud boy, his eyes were full of fire. I like boys like that. But they kept teasing him worse than ever. The worst of it was that his clothes were so tattered, his trousers were too short, and his boots all in holes. They teased him about that, too. Humiliated him. Well, I don't like that, and I took his part at once and let them have it good and proper. You see, I beat them, and yet they adore me. Do you know that, Karamazov?' Kolya boasted unashamedly. 'But I'm very fond of kids, as a rule. I have two little ones on my hands at home – it's they who made me so late today. Well, so they stopped beating Ilyusha and I took him under my wing. I could see he was a proud boy. Yes, he certainly was proud, I tell you, but he became devoted to me like a slave, did everything I told him, obeyed me as though I were God, tried to copy me in everything. During the breaks at school he used to come to me at once and we'd go about together. On Sundays, too. At our school the boys laugh when an older boy becomes very friendly with a younger one, but that's a prejudice. If I take it into my head to be friends with a younger boy, I am friends with him, and that's that – don't you think so? I'm teaching him, cultivating his mind. And why, tell me, shouldn't I, if I like him? You, Karamazov, have made friends with all those little fellows, haven't you? And that means that you want to influence the younger generation, cultivate their minds, be useful to them, doesn't it? And I don't mind telling you that this trait in your character, which I knew from hearsay, appealed to me more than anything. However, to business. I noticed that the boy was beginning to acquire a sort of sensitiveness, sentimentality, and, you know, I've been a sworn enemy of all sloppy sentiments from the very day of my birth. Besides, there were those puzzling contradictions: he was proud and yet slavishly devoted to me – slavishly devoted, but all of a sudden his eyes would flash and he'd refuse to agree with me. Argued, flew into a rage. I used to propound certain ideas sometimes, and it wasn't that he disagreed with them. I could see that he was simply in open rebellion against me personally, because I was cool in responding to his blandishments. So, to train him to be a man, I grew colder the more he grew fond of me. I did it on purpose, out of conviction. I had in mind to train his character, to lick him into shape, to make a man of him – well, and so on – you get my meaning, don't you? All of a sudden I noticed that for three whole days he looked upset and was worried about something, but not about the way I repulsed his advances, but about something else, something more important, something higher. Well, I thought, what's all this tragedy? I pressed him and found out what was the matter with him. You see, he seemed to have made friends with Smerdyakov, your late father's servant (your father was still alive at the time), and Smerdyakov taught the little fool a silly trick, I mean, a beastly trick, an abominable trick – to take a piece of soft bread, stick a pin into it, and throw it to some stray dog, one of those who swallow anything without chewing because they're starving, and see what would happen. Well, so they got it all ready and threw a piece like that to Zhuchka, the shaggy dog they're now making such a fuss about, a watchdog that was never fed by the people who owned it and that kept barking all day long. (Do you like that stupid barking, Karamazov? I can't stand it.) Well, the dog pounced on the bread, swallowed it, began to squeal and spin round and round, then ran away, squealing all the time, and disappeared. So Ilyusha himself described it to me. He told me all about it and kept crying and crying, hugging me and trembling all over: "He ran and squealed, ran and squealed," he kept repeating – the sight must have made a deep impression on him. Well, I could see he was sorry. I took a serious view of it. You see, what I was chiefly concerned about was to teach him a lesson for his behaviour in the past, so that, I admit, I was rather cunning about it and pretended that I was much more indignant than I actually was: "What you've done is mean," I said to him. "You're a rotter.

I shan't let anybody know about it, of course, but I shall have nothing more to do with you for a time. I'll think it over and let you know through Smurov (the boy who has just come with me and who has always been loyal to me) whether I'm going to have anything to do with you in the future or whether I'll give you up for good as a rotter." That made a terrible impression on him. I must confess I felt at once that I had perhaps gone a bit too far, but that couldn't be helped: I did what I thought best at the time. Next day I sent Smurov to tell him that I was "not on speaking terms" with him any more. That's what we call it when two schoolfellows have no longer anything to do with one another. Secretly I meant to send him to Coventry for only a few days and then, seeing how sorry he was, to hold out my hand to him again. That was my firm intention. But what do you think he did? He heard Smurov's message and suddenly his eyes flashed: "Tell Krasotkin from me," he shouted, "that from now on I'll be throwing bits of bread with pins to all the dogs, all, all of them!" "Oh," I thought to myself, "so he's showing an independent spirit, is he? We'll have to smoke it out!" And I began showing the utmost contempt for him and every time we met I turned away or smiled ironically. And then that incident with his father occurred – you remember? – the bast sponge. You must understand that he had already been prepared by what had happened before for his terrible fit of exasperation. Seeing that I'd given him up, the boys all set on him and began taunting him by shouting: "Bast-sponge, bast-sponge!" And it was then that the fights between them started for which I'm terribly sorry, for I believe that on one occasion he was given a bad beating. One day he rushed upon them in the courtyard as they were coming out of school. I stood about ten yards away from him, looking at him. And I swear I don't remember laughing; on the contrary, I felt very sorry for him and in another minute I should have gone to his help. But he suddenly saw me looking at him; what he imagined I don't know, but he pulled out his penknife, rushed up to me and jabbed me in my thigh with it – just here, above my right leg. I did not budge. I don't mind saying, Karamazov, that I'm sometimes very brave. I just looked at him with contempt, as though to say, "If you'd like to stab me again for all my great friendship, then go on and do it!" But he did not stab another time. Couldn't keep it up. He got frightened himself, threw away his knife, burst out crying and ran away. I was not, of course, going to tell on him and I told all the boys to say nothing to anyone about it, so that it should not get to the ears of the masters. I didn't even tell my mother about it till the wound had healed up. It wasn't much of a wound, anyway. Just a scratch. Then I was told that he'd been throwing stones the same day and bit your finger – well, you can understand what a state he was in! But there was nothing to be done about it. I behaved like a fool: even when he was taken ill, I didn't go to forgive him – I mean, to make it up with him, and I'm sorry for it now. But then I had a special reason. Well, that's all there is to it – only I'm afraid I've behaved like a fool. . . .'

'Oh, what a pity,' Alyosha cried agitatedly, 'I didn't know of your relations with him earlier or I should myself have come to you long ago and asked you to go to him with me. You know, he talked about you in his delirium, when he was feverish. I had no idea how much you meant to him! And haven't you really found Zhuchka? His father and all the boys went looking for that dog all over the town. You know, since he's been taken ill, he told his father three times in my presence: "It's because I killed Zhuchka, Daddy, that I'm ill now. God is punishing me for it." He keeps harping on it! I can't help thinking that if you could have got Zhuchka now and showed him that he had not died it would make him so happy that he'd recover. We've all relied on you.'

'But tell me what reasons had you to rely on me to find Zhuchka, I mean, to think I'd be the one to find him?' Kolya asked, with intense curiosity. 'Why should you have counted on me and not on someone else?'

'There was a rumour that you were looking for him and that when you'd found him you'd bring him. Smurov said something to that effect. We are doing our best to make him believe that Zhuchka is alive and that he's been seen somewhere. The boys got him a tame rabbit from somewhere, but he just looked at it, smiled and asked them to set it free in a field. And so we did. Just now his father has come back and brought him a mastiff puppy which he got from somewhere, thinking to comfort him with that, but I believe it made things worse. . . .'

'Tell me another thing, Karamazov, what do you think of his

father? I know him, but what is he according to your definition: a clown, a buffoon?'

'Good Lord, no. There are people who feel deeply but who have been somehow crushed. Their buffoonery is merely a kind of resentful irony against those to whom they dare not speak the truth because they've been humiliated and intimidated by them. Believe me, Krasotkin, such buffoonery is sometimes extraordinarily tragic. Everything in the world for him is now centred on Ilyusha, and if Ilyusha dies, he'll either go out of his mind with grief or commit suicide. I'm almost sure of that when I look at him now.'

'I understand you, Karamazov,' Kolya said with feeling. 'I can see you have a good idea what human nature is like.'

'And as soon as I saw you with a dog, I thought that you had brought Zhuchka.'

'Wait, Karamazov, perhaps we'll find him, but this dog is Perezvon. I'll let him in now and perhaps he will amuse Ilyusha more than the mastiff pup. Wait, Karamazov, perhaps you'll find out something in a minute. Oh dear, why am I keeping you here?' Kolya cried suddenly, impulsively. 'You're wearing only your jacket in such cold, and I'm keeping you here! You see what an egoist I am! Oh, we're all egoists, Karamazov!'

'Don't worry. It's true it's cold, but I don't catch cold easily. Let's go in, though. Incidentally, what's your name. I know you're Kolya, but that's all.'

'Nikolai Krasotkin, or as they say officially, Krasotkin junior,' Kolya laughed for some reason, but suddenly added: 'Of course, I hate my name Nikolai.'

'But why?'

'It's so trivial, so official.'

'You are thirteen?' asked Alyosha.

'Fourteen, really. I shall be fourteen in a fortnight. Quite soon. I'd better confess a weakness of mine, Karamazov. I don't mind telling you at the very beginning of a weakness of mine, for I'd like you to see the sort of character I have at once. I hate being asked my age. Hate it more than anything. And – and, another thing, there's a libellous story going round about me that last week I played robbers with the boys of the preparatory class. Now, it's quite true that I did play that game with them, but that I played it for myself, I mean, for my own amusement, is an absolute libel. I have reason to believe that you've heard that story, but I wasn't playing for myself, but for the sake of the kids, because they couldn't think of anything by themselves. But they're always telling silly stories here. I assure you this town is interested in nothing but gossip.'

'But does it matter if you were playing for your own amusement?'

'Well, it does. You wouldn't be playing horses, would you?'

'Look at it this way,' smiled Alyosha. 'Grown-up people, for instance, go to the theatre, where the adventures of all sorts of heroes are performed on the stage – sometimes there are robbers and fighting – well, isn't it the same thing, in its own way, of course? And young people's games of soldiers or robbers during playtime are also a sort of burgeoning art, an awakening need of art in a youthful soul, and such games are quite often much better thought out than performances in the theatre, the only difference being that people go to the theatre to look at actors, while here the young people are themselves the actors. But that's only natural.'

'You think so? Is that really your opinion?' Kolya asked, looking intently at him. 'You know, you've expressed quite an interesting idea. When I go home, I'll think it over. I must say I knew that one could learn something from you. I've come to learn from you, Karamazov,' concluded Kolya in a voice full of deep feeling.

'And I from you,' smiled Alyosha, pressing his hand.

Kolya was extremely pleased with Alyosha. What struck him most was that Alyosha treated him as an equal and spoke to him as though he were 'quite grown up'.

'I'll show you a trick presently, Karamazov, a sort of theatrical performance, too,' he laughed nervously. 'That's what I've come for.'

'Let's go in first to the landlady's, on the left. That's where the boys leave their overcoats, because the room is small and hot.'

'Oh, but I'm only going to stay a moment. I'll go in in my overcoat. Perezvon will stay here in the passage and be dead. Here, Perezvon, lie down and be dead! You see, he's dead now. I'll go in and explore first and then I'll whistle to him at the right moment and you'll see he'll dash in like mad. I must see, though, that Smurov doesn't forget to open the door at the right moment. I'll arrange it all, and you'll see my trick. . . .'

5

At Ilyusha's Bedside

THE room, already familiar to the reader, in which the family of the retired captain lived, was at that moment both stuffy and crowded. Several boys had come to see Ilyusha that day and though all of them, like Smurov, were prepared to deny that Alyosha had reconciled and brought them and Ilyusha together, it was so all the same. The whole secret in this case was simply that he had brought them and Ilyusha together, one by one, without any 'sloppy sentimentality', but as though by pure chance and without premeditation. To Ilyusha, on the other hand, it brought great relief in his suffering. Seeing the almost tender affection and sympathy shown to him by all these boys, his former enemies, he was deeply touched. Krasotkin alone did not come to see him and that was a heavy weight on his heart. The bitterest of all Ilyusha's bitter memories was perhaps the whole episode with Krasotkin, his only friend and protector, whom he had attacked with a knife. That was also the opinion of the clever little boy Smurov, who was the first to make it up with Ilyusha. But Krasotkin himself, when Smurov hinted to him that Alyosha would like to see him 'on a certain matter', at once cut him short and put an end to the attempt at reconciliation by instructing Smurov to tell 'Karamazov' that he knew best what to do and did not ask any advice from anyone, and if he went to see Ilyusha, he would do so at the right time because he had 'his own reasons'. That was about a fortnight before this Sunday. That was why Alyosha had not gone to see him as he had intended. However, though he waited, he did send Smurov to Krasotkin twice again. But both times Krasotkin met him with a most determined and curt refusal, making it quite clear to Alyosha that if he came for him himself, he, Krasotkin, would never go to Ilyusha and that he did not want to be bothered any more. Up to the very last day Smurov himself did not know that Kolya had made up his mind to go to Ilyusha that morning, and it was only the evening before that Kolya, when parting from Smurov, told him brusquely to wait for him next morning, because he'd like to go with him to Snegiryov, but that he must not tell anyone about his coming as he wished his visit to be a surprise.

Smurov obeyed. The idea that he would bring back the lost dog
Zhuchka Smurov got from some words dropped casually by Krasotkin, to the effect that 'they're a lot of silly asses, all of them, not to
find the dog, if he's alive'. But when Smurov, taking advantage of a
favourable opportunity, hinted at his guess about the dog, Krasotkin
suddenly flew into a terrible rage: 'Do you think I'm such an ass as to
go looking for somebody else's dog all over the town when I've got
Perezvon? And could anyone really believe that a dog could be alive
after swallowing a pin? Sloppy sentimentality, that's what it is!'

Meanwhile Ilyusha had not left his little bed in the corner of the
room under the icon for almost two weeks. He had not been to school
ever since he met Alyosha and bit his finger. As a matter of fact, he
was taken ill the same day, though for a month afterwards he managed
to get up occasionally and take a walk round the room and the passage. But at last he got so weak that he could not take a step without
his father's help. His father was terribly worried about him. He even
gave up drinking and was almost out of his mind with fear that his
boy might die. Often, especially after taking his boy for a walk round
the room on his arm and putting him to bed again, he would suddenly rush out into the passage and, with his forehead pressed against
the wall, burst into an uncontrollable paroxysm of sobs, doing his
best to suppress them so that his boy might not hear them.

On returning to the room, he usually began doing something to
amuse and comfort his precious boy, telling him stories, funny anecdotes, or taking off all sorts of funny people he had happened to meet,
even imitating the funny howls or cries of animals. But Ilyusha hated
to see his father pulling faces and playing the fool. Though the boy
did his best not to show how much he disliked it, he was painfully
aware of his father's humiliating position in society and the memory
of the 'bast-sponge' and of that 'awful day' kept recurring again and
again in his mind. Nina, Ilyusha's quiet, gentle, crippled sister, also
disliked to see her father playing the fool (his eldest sister Varvara had
long before gone to Petersburg to resume her studies at the university), but his half-witted mother was hugely amused and laughed
happily when her husband began mimicking someone or pulling all
sorts of funny faces. That was the only thing that would cheer her up,
for the rest of the time she was always grumbling and complaining
that now everyone had forgotten her, that no one had any respect

for her, that everyone hurt her feelings, and so on. But during the last few days she, too, seemed to have completely changed. She kept looking at the corner of the room where Ilyusha was and seemed lost in thought. She was no longer talkative and grew more quiet, and if she started crying, she did so softly, so as not to be heard. Snegiryov noticed that change in her with mournful bewilderment. At first she disliked the visits of the boys and they made her angry, but later on their merry shouts and stories began to divert her and in the end she liked them so much that, if the boys had stopped coming, she would have been terribly depressed. When the children began telling something or playing games, she laughed and clapped her hands. She called some of them to her and kissed them. She became particularly fond of Smurov. As for Snegiryov, the appearance in his lodgings of the children who came to cheer up Ilyusha filled his heart from the very beginning with rapturous delight and he even hoped that now Ilyusha would get over his depression and, perhaps, get well quickly. Up to the last few days he never doubted for a moment that, in spite of his fears for Ilyusha, his boy would recover suddenly. He met his little visitors with reverence, followed them about, waited upon them, was ready to give them a ride on his back and actually did give them rides on his back, but Ilyusha did not like those games and they were given up. He began buying presents for them, ginger-bread and nuts, gave them tea and buttered their sandwiches. It must be noted that he had plenty of money all that time. He had accepted the two hundred roubles from Katerina Ivanovna, just as Alyosha had predicted. And afterwards Katerina, learning more about their circumstances and Ilyusha's illness, paid them a visit herself, made the acquaintance of the family and even succeeded in charming the captain's half-witted wife. After that she was not sparing of her acts of kindness, and Snegiryov himself, terrified at the thought that his boy might die, forgot all about his pride and humbly accepted her charity. All this time Dr Herzenstube, called in by Katerina, came to see the patient punctually every second day, but his visits were of little avail, though he kept dosing him with medicines. But on that day, that is to say, on Sunday morning, they were expecting a new doctor, a famous Moscow specialist. Katerina had sent for him specially from Moscow for a large fee – not for Ilyusha, but for someone else, of which more will be said at the appropriate time later on, but as he had come, she asked him to see Ilyusha, too, and Snegiryov had been told to expect him. He had no idea of Kolya Krasotkin's visit, although he had long wished that the boy who had caused so much worry to his son would come at last. At the moment when Krasotkin opened the door and came into the room, all of them, Snegiryov and the boys, crowded round Ilyusha's bed, looking at the tiny mastiff puppy which had just been brought. It had only been born the day before, though Snegiryov had bespoken it a week ago in order to comfort and amuse Ilyusha, who was still grieving for the vanished and, of course, dead Zhuchka. Ilyusha, who had heard three days before that he was to be given a puppy, and not an ordinary one, but a real Alpine mastiff puppy (which was, of course, terribly important), was anxious not to hurt his father's feelings and pretended that he was pleased with the present. But his father and the boys could not help seeing that the new puppy merely stirred up more violently in his little heart the memory of the unhappy Zhuchka he had killed. The puppy lay moving about restlessly beside him, and he, smiling painfully, stroked it with his thin, pale, wasted little hand. It was evident that he liked the puppy, but – it wasn't Zhuchka. Zhuchka was not there! If he could have had Zhuchka and the puppy, he'd have been completely happy!

'Krasotkin!' one of the boys, who was the first to see him enter, cried suddenly.

There was a general stir and the boys parted and stood at either side of the bed, so that he had a full view of Ilyusha. Snegiryov ran impetuously to meet Kolya.

'Come in, come in – I'm so glad you've come!' he cried. 'Ilyusha, Mr Krasotkin has come to see you. . . .'

But Krasotkin, shaking hands with him hurriedly, at once gave a demonstration of his knowledge of good manners. He first of all turned to Mrs Snegiryov, who was sitting in her armchair, greatly displeased with the boys and grumbling that by standing between her and Ilyusha's bed they prevented her from seeing the puppy, and very courteously scraped his foot and bowed to her and, then, turning to Nina, he made her, as a lady, a similar bow. This polite behaviour made an exceedingly favourable impression on the half-witted lady.

'You can recognize at once a well-brought-up young man,' she said aloud, with an eloquent gesture. 'Not like our other visitors, coming in one on top of another.'

'Not one on top of another, Mother! Surely, you didn't mean that!' Snegiryov murmured affectionately, but a little apprehensive of what 'Mother' might say.

'They do come in like that. They jump on each other's backs in the passage and come riding in astride each other, and in a respectable family, too! What sort of visitor is that?'

'But who came riding in like that, Mother? Who?'

'Why, that boy there came in today riding on that one's back, and this one on that one's. . . .'

But Kolya was already standing at Ilyusha's bed. The sick boy turned visibly pale. He sat up in the bed and looked intently at Kolya. Kolya had not seen his former little friend for two months, and he stood before him greatly struck by what he saw: he could never have imagined that he would see such a wasted, yellow face, such huge, feverishly burning eyes, such thin little hands. He observed with mournful surprise that Ilyusha's lips were so dry and that he was breathing so heavily and rapidly. He stepped close to him, held out his hand and, almost overcome with confusion, said:

'Well, old man, how are you?'

But his voice failed him, his jauntiness was gone, his face seemed to twitch suddenly, and the corners of his lips quivered. Ilyusha smiled ruefully at him, still unable to utter a word. Kolya suddenly raised his hand and for some reason passed it gently across Ilyusha's hair.

'Never mind!' he murmured softly to him, partly to cheer him up and partly because he did not know what to say.

For a minute they were silent again.

'Hullo! what's this? A new puppy?' Kolya asked suddenly in a most callous voice.

'Ye-es!' replied Ilyusha in a drawn-out whisper, gasping for breath.

'A black nose, which means that he'll be a very fierce dog, one of those one keeps on a chain,' Kolya observed gravely and firmly, as though all he were interested in was the puppy and its black nose.

The trouble was that he was still trying his utmost to overcome his impulse to burst out crying like 'a little boy', and was still unable to manage it.

'Yes,' he went on, 'when he grows up, you'll have to put him on a chain, I'm sure of that.'

'He'll be an enormous one!' one of the boys cried.

'Of course, it's an Italian mastiff. He'll be an enormous one, as big as that, as big as a calf,' several small voices cried all at once.

'As big as a calf, as big as a real calf!' Snegiryov said, rushing up. 'I got one like that on purpose. A very fierce one, and his parents are also huge and fierce, as high as that from the floor. . . . Do sit down here, on the bed beside Ilyusha, or here on the bench. I'm glad you've come. We've been expecting you for a long time. Have you come with Mr Karamazov?'

Krasotkin sat down on the bed, at Ilyusha's feet. Though on the way he had perhaps thought of a subject with which to begin the conversation in a casual manner, he completely lost the thread of it now.

'No – I came with Perezvon. . . . I've got a dog now – Perezvon. A Slavonic name. He's waiting for me outside the door. I have only to whistle and he'll rush in. I, too, have brought a dog, old man,' he turned suddenly to Ilyusha. 'Remember Zhuchka?' he suddenly bowled him over with the question.

Ilyusha's little face became distorted. He gave Kolya an agonized look. Alyosha, standing at the door, frowned and signalled stealthily to Kolya not to speak of Zhuchka, but Kolya did not or would not notice it.

'W-where is Zhuchka?' Ilyusha asked in a broken voice.

'Well, old man, your Zhuchka's vanished! Your Zhuchka's done for!'

Ilyusha said nothing, but just looked very intently at Kolya again. Alyosha, having caught Kolya's eye, again signalled to him vigorously, but Kolya turned away his eyes again, pretending not to have noticed.

'Must have gone off somewhere to die – of course, after such a meal!' Kolya went on pitilessly, and yet he seemed for some reason to be out of breath himself. 'But I've got Perezvon – a Slavonic name. I've brought him to you. . . .'

'I don't want him!' Ilyusha said suddenly.

'No, no, you must see him. . . . It will amuse you. . . . I brought him on purpose – he's as shaggy as the other one. You won't object to my calling in my dog, will you, ma'am?' he suddenly turned to Mrs Snegiryov with quite inexplicable agitation.

'I don't want him – I don't want him!' Ilyusha cried with a mournful catch in his voice.

There was a reproachful look in his eyes.

'You'd better,' Snegiryov suddenly jumped up from the chest by the wall, on which he had been sitting, 'you'd better – er – another time, sir,' he murmured.

But Kolya, persisting and in a great hurry, suddenly shouted to Smurov: 'Smurov, open the door!' and the moment it was opened, blew his whistle. Perezvon bounded into the room.

'Jump, Perezvon, jump! Dog, beg!' bawled Kolya, jumping up from the bed.

The dog, standing on his hind legs, drew himself up before Ilyusha's bed. Then something no one had expected happened: Ilyusha gave a start and suddenly lurched forward violently, bent over Perezvon and looked at it as though bereft of speech.

'It's – Zhuchka!' he suddenly cried in a voice breaking with suffering and happiness.

'And who did you think it was?' Krasotkin yelled with all his might in a ringing, happy voice and, bending over the dog, he seized him and lifted him up to Ilyusha.

'Look, old man, you see he's blind in one eye and his left ear is torn, exactly the same marks as you described to me. I found him by these marks! I found him almost on the same day. Didn't take me any time at all. You see, he did not belong to anyone, he didn't belong to anyone!' he kept explaining, turning quickly to Snegiryov, to Mrs Snegiryov, to Alyosha, and then back again to Ilyusha. 'He lived in Fedotov's back-yard. Made his home there, but they didn't feed him. He was a stray dog, he must have run away from some village. . . . So I found him. . . . You see, old man, he didn't swallow your piece of bread after all. If he had swallowed it, he would most certainly have died. Most certainly! So he must have spat it out, if he's still alive. You didn't see him spitting it out. Well, he spat it out but pricked his tongue – that's why he squealed. He ran away squealing and you thought that he had swallowed it. He could not help squealing loudly, for the inside of a dog's mouth is very tender – much tenderer than a man's, much tenderer!' Kolya kept exclaiming frantically, with a burning face, beaming with delight.

Ilyusha could not speak at all. He gazed open-mouthed at Kolya with his big eyes, which seemed almost to start out of his head, white as a sheet. And if only the wholly unsuspecting Krasotkin knew what a devastating and fatal effect such a moment might have on the health of the sick boy, nothing would have induced him to play such a trick on him. But Alyosha was perhaps the only person in the room who realized it. As for Snegiryov, he seemed to have been transformed into a little boy himself.

'Zhuchka? So this is Zhuchka?' he cried in a blissful voice. 'Ilyusha, darling, this is Zhuchka, your Zhuchka! Mother, look – this is Zhuchka!'

He was nearly crying.

'And I never guessed!' Smurov cried regretfully. 'Well done! Krasotkin! I said he'd find Zhuchka and he has found him!'

'He has found him!' some other boy put in joyfully.

'Well done, Krasotkin!' a third voice rang out.

'Well done, well done!' all the boys cried and they began clapping.

'But wait, wait,' Krasotkin tried to make himself heard above the din, 'let me tell you how it all happened. You see, the whole point is how it happened – that's the most important thing about it. I found him, took him home and hid him at once, locked him up and showed him to no one up to the last day. Only Smurov found it out a fortnight ago, but I made him believe that it was Perezvon and he never guessed it. And in my free time I taught him all sorts of tricks. You should see the tricks he knows! You see, old man, I taught him all that so as to bring you a dog well-trained and in fine condition and so as to be able to say to you, "See, old man, what your Zhuchka looks like now!" You haven't a piece of meat, have you? He'll show you a trick that'll simply make you die of laughing. Just a little bit of meat – haven't you got any?'

Snegiryov rushed headlong across the passage to the landlady's kitchen where their cooking, too, was done. Not to waste precious time, Kolya, in desperate haste, shouted to Perezvon: 'Dead!' The dog spun round and lay motionless on his back with his four paws in the air. The boys laughed and Ilyusha watched with the same agonized smile. It was 'Mother', however, who liked the way the dog 'died' most. She burst out laughing at the dog and began snapping her fingers and calling: 'Perezvon! Perezvon!'

'He won't get up for anything in the world, not for anything in the world,' cried Kolya, triumphantly and justly proud. 'You can shout as much as you like, but if I shout, he'll be up in a jiffy. Here, Perezvon!'

The dog jumped up and began bounding about, squealing with delight. Snegiryov ran in with a piece of boiled beef.

'It's not hot, is it?' Kolya inquired hastily and in a business-like tone of voice, taking the meat. 'No, it isn't. You see, dogs don't like hot things. Now then, watch all of you, watch, Ilyusha, old man, come on, why don't you watch? I've brought him and he isn't looking!'

The new trick consisted in making the dog stand without stirring with his nose thrust forward and putting the appetizing bit of meat on his nose. The poor dog had to stand motionless with the piece of meat on its nose as long as his master chose to keep him like that. He had not to move or stir for half an hour, if need be. But Perezvon was kept for only a few seconds.

'Catch it!' cried Kolya, and the piece of meat flew from Perezvon's nose into his mouth in the twinkling of an eye. The audience, of course, expressed enthusiastic surprise.

'And did you really stay away all this time only because you were anxious to train the dog?' Alyosha cried with involuntary reproach.

'Yes, just because of that,' Kolya cried with absolute ingenuousness. 'I wanted to show him in all his glory!'

'Perezvon! Perezvon!' Ilyusha suddenly snapped his thin little fingers, beckoning to the dog.

'Why, that's nothing! Let him jump on the bed. Here, Perezvon!' Kolya slapped the bed, and Perezvon flew like an arrow, to Ilyusha.

Ilyusha threw both his arms round the dog's head impulsively, and Perezvon in a flash licked his cheek. Ilyusha clung to him, stretched himself out in bed and hid his face from everybody in his shaggy coat.

'Lord, oh Lord!' Snegiryov kept exclaiming.

Kolya again sat down on the bed near Ilyusha.

'Ilyusha, I can show you something else. I've brought you a little cannon. Remember I was telling you about it and you said, "Oh, I wish I could see it!" Well, so I've brought it now.'

And, hurrying, Kolya pulled his bronze cannon out of his satchel. He was in such a hurry because he was feeling so happy himself: any other time he would have waited for the effect created by Perezvon to wear off, but now he was too much in a hurry to care for any such things: 'You're happy as it is, so I'll make you happier still!' He himself was absolutely transported with delight.

'I spied this thing for you long ago at Morozov's house. For you, old man, for you. He had no use for it. He got it from his brother. So I exchanged it for a book from father's bookcase: *A Kinsman of Mahomet or Healing Folly*. The book was published in Moscow a hundred years ago, when there was no censorship – a really bawdy book, and Morozov has a great liking for such things. He thanked me for it too. . . .'

Kolya held the little cannon in his hand so that all could see and admire it. Ilyusha sat up and, his right arm still round Perezvon, gazed with admiration at the toy. The effect produced reached its highest point when Kolya declared that he had powder and that he could fire the gun at once 'if it won't frighten the ladies'. Mrs Snegiryov at once asked to be allowed to look closer at the toy, and her request was immediately carried out. She liked the cannon on wheels very much and began rolling it about on her knees. Asked whether she would mind its being fired, she gave her consent at once, without any idea of what she had been asked. Kolya showed them the powder and shot. Snegiryov, as a former military man, loaded it himself, putting in a minute quantity of powder, and asking that the shot might be put off till another time. The cannon was placed on the floor, with its muzzle pointing to an empty part of the room, three grains of powder were put into the touch-hole and a match was put to it. The report that followed was absolutely magnificent. Mrs Snegiryov started, but at once laughed with joy. The boys looked in speechless triumph, but it was Snegiryov who, looking at Ilyusha, was the happiest man of them all. Kolya picked up the gun and immediately made a present of it to Ilyusha, together with the powder and shot.

'It's for you, for you!' he repeated again, overflowing with happiness. 'I've been keeping it for you a long time.'

'Oh let me have it! You'd better give me the little gun!' Mrs Snegiryov began begging like a small child.

Her face wore an expression of mournful anxiety for fear that she would not be given it. Kolya was embarrassed. Snegiryov fidgeted agitatedly.

'Darling Mother, darling Mother,' he cried, rushing up to her, 'the little gun is yours, yours, but let Ilyusha have it now, because it was given to him, but it's yours all the same. Ilyusha will always let you play with it. It will be yours and his, yours and his. . . .'

'No, I don't want it to be mine and his,' 'darling Mother' went on, on the verge of tears. 'I want it to be all my own and not Ilyusha's!'

'Mummy, take it! Here, take it!' Ilyusha cried suddenly. 'Krasotkin, may I give it to Mother?' he turned with an imploring air to Krasotkin, as though afraid to hurt his feelings by giving his present to someone else.

'Of course you may!' Krasotkin at once agreed, and taking the little gun from Ilyusha, he handed it himself with a polite bow to Mrs Snegiryov, who was so overcome that she burst into tears.

'Ilyusha, darling, you're the only one who loves your mother!' she cried, deeply moved, and at once began rolling the gun about on her knees.

'Darling Mother, let me kiss your hands,' her husband rushed up to her and at once did so.

'And the most charming young man here is this nice boy!' said the grateful lady, pointing to Kolya.

'And I'll get you as much powder as you like, Ilyusha. We make the powder ourselves now. Borovikov discovered the ingredients – twenty-four parts of saltpetre, ten of sulphur, and six of birchwood charcoal, pound it together, pour in some water, make a paste, and put it through a fine strainer and there you've got your powder.'

'Smurov has told me about your powder already,' said Ilyusha, 'but Daddy says it's not real powder.'

'Not real?' Kolya reddened. 'Well, it burns all right. I don't know, though. . . .'

'No, sir, I didn't mean it,' Snegiryov rushed up suddenly with a guilty expression. 'It's quite true I said that powder was not made like that, but that's nothing. It can be made like that, too.'

'I don't know. I suppose you know better. We lighted some in a stone pomatum crock and it burnt beautifully. It all burnt away, leaving only a little ash. But that's only the paste, if we'd put it through a strainer. . . . However, you know better. I don't know. . . . Belkin's father gave him a hiding for our powder, did you hear that?' he turned suddenly to Ilyusha.

'I did,' replied Ilyusha, who was listening to Kolya with immense interest and delight.

'We'd prepared a whole bottle of powder and he kept it under his bed. His father saw it. You could have blown us up, he said. And he thrashed him on the spot. He was going to make a complaint against me at school. Now he isn't allowed to go about with me. No one is allowed to go about with me. Smurov isn't allowed to, either. I've got a bad name with everyone. They say I'm a "desperate fellow",' Kolya smiled contemptuously. 'It all began with the railway incident.'

'Oh, we've heard all about that incident, too!' cried Snegiryov. 'How could you lie still there between the railway lines? And weren't you at all afraid, lying there under the train? Weren't you scared?'

Snegiryov fawned on Kolya terribly.

'N-not particularly,' Kolya replied carelessly. 'It's that damned goose that harmed my reputation more than anything,' he turned to Ilyusha again.

But though he assumed a careless air as he talked, he still could not quite control his excitement and seemed continually to lose the thread of his thoughts.

'Oh, yes, I heard about the goose, too!' Ilyusha laughed, beaming all over. 'They told me, but I didn't quite understand. Did you really have to appear in court?'

'Oh, it was a most idiotic, most trivial affair but, as usual, they made a mountain out of a molehill,' Kolya began casually. 'I was just walking across the market square one day when they had driven in some geese. I stopped and looked at the geese. Suddenly I noticed a fellow, Vishnyakov by name, he's now working as an errand-boy at Plotnikov's, looking at me. "What are you looking at the geese for?" he said to me. I looked at him: a round, stupid face, the silly ass must be twenty. But, you know, I never say anything against the common people. I – I always like to associate with them. . . . We're miles behind the common people, that's an axiom. . . . I believe you're laughing, Karamazov?'

'Good Lord, no, I'm listening to you with great interest,' Alyosha replied with the most good-humoured air, and the suspicious Kolya was at once reassured.

'My theory, Karamazov, is clear and simple,' he again hurried on at once happily. 'I believe in the common people and I'm always glad to do them justice, but without spoiling them, that's a *sine qua non*. . . . But I was talking about the goose, wasn't I? Well, then, so I turned to that fool and answered: "I'm trying to think what the goose is thinking about." He stared at me quite stupidly: "And what is the goose thinking about?" he asked. "Well, you see," I said, "there's a cart full of oats. The oats are dropping out of the sack and the goose has stretched out its neck right under the wheel and is pecking the grains – see?" "I sees it all right," he said. "Very well," I said. "Now if we were to push the cart a little forward, the wheel would break the goose's neck, wouldn't it?" "Aye," he said, "it would and all," and he grinned all over his face, looking greatly delighted. "Well, then," I said, "come on, my lad, let's do it!" "Let's do it," he said. And it didn't take us long to set about it. He took up his position un-obtrusively near the bridle, and I stood on one side to direct the goose. The peasant was busy at the time, talking to someone, so that I didn't have to direct the goose at all: it just stretched out its neck after the oats under the cart, straight under the wheel. I winked at the fellow and – c-crack, the goose's neck was broken in half! And as luck would have it, all the peasants noticed us at that very moment and started yelling all at once: "You done it on purpose!" "No, I didn't." "Yes, you did!" Well, so they clamoured: "To the Justice of the Peace with him!" They got hold of me, too. "You're in it, too," they shouted. "You was helping him! The whole market knows you!" And you know,' Kolya added, conceitedly, 'the whole market really does know me for some reason. So we all went off to the court and they took the goose with them, too. The young fellow was frightened out of his wits and started howling, howling at the top of his voice like a peasant woman. And the poultry keeper kept shouting: "They could kill any number of geese that way!" Well, of course, there were wit-nesses. The Justice of the Peace settled the whole thing in no time. The poultry man was to be paid one rouble for his goose and the fellow was to have the goose and he warned him not to play such jokes again. The fellow went on howling like a peasant woman. "It wasn't me," he said, "it's him what's made me do it," and he pointed to me. I replied very calmly that I hadn't suggested anything to him but had merely given expression to a fundamental truism. Merely spoken theoretically. The Justice of the Peace, Nefedov, smiled and got angry with himself at once for having smiled. "I shall at once report you to your school authorities," he said to me, "that you shouldn't entertain such theories in future, but sit over your books and do your lessons." Well, he didn't report me to the school authorities. That was just a joke. But the affair did become widely known and reached the ears of the authorities: they have long ears, you see! Our classics master, Kolbasnikov, was particularly outraged, but Dardanelov got me off again. Kolbasnikov is now furious with all of us, the silly ass. You know, Ilyusha, he's just got married. Got a dowry of a thousand roubles from the Mikhailovs, and his bride is an ugly old hag of the first rank and the last degree. The chaps in the third class at once made up an epigram on it:

> Striking news has reached our third class,
> Kolbasnikov has married a jenny-ass,

and so on. It's very funny, I'll bring it to you later. I say nothing against Dardanelov: he's a man of some learning. Yes, most decidedly of some learning. I respect such men, and not only because he got me off...'

'But you've scored off him about the founders of Troy,' Smurov suddenly put in, decidedly proud of Krasotkin at that moment. He was very pleased with the story about the goose.

'Have you really?' Snegiryov exclaimed, flatteringly. 'You mean about who founded ancient Troy? Yes, we heard how you'd scored off him. Ilyusha told me about it at the time.'

'He knows everything, Daddy, he knows more than any of us!' Ilyusha, too, put in. 'He only pretends to be like that, but he's top in all subjects.'

Ilyusha gave Kolya a look of infinite happiness.

'Oh, that thing about Troy is all nonsense, it's nothing!' Kolya said with deprecating modesty. 'I consider this question of no importance whatever.'

He had by that time completely regained his usual casual tone, though he was still feeling a little uneasy: he felt that he was greatly excited and that, for instance, he had told the story about the goose a little too frankly, while Alyosha had been silent all the time and had looked serious. The conceited boy was beginning to wonder unhappily whether Alyosha was silent because he despised him and because he thought that he, Kolya, was looking for praise from him. If he dared to think anything of the kind, he, Kolya, would —

'I consider this question of no importance whatever!' he snapped out again proudly.

'And I know who founded Troy,' a boy, who had hardly opened his mouth before, said quite unexpectedly.

He was a good-looking boy of eleven, called Kartashov, a shy and silent boy, who was sitting near the door. Kolya gave him a surprised and dignified look. As a matter of fact, the question who founded Troy had become a mystery to all the boys in all the forms and to solve it one had to read about it in Smaragdov's history, which no one but Kolya possessed. One day, when Kolya's back was turned, Kartashov quickly opened Smaragdov, which lay among Kolya's books, and at once lighted on the passage about the founders of Troy. It had happened a long time ago, but he was somehow too embarrassed and could not bring himself to announce publicly that he, too, knew who founded Troy. He was afraid of what might happen and that Kolya might somehow make him look foolish. But now he just could not restrain himself and blurted it out. Besides, he had wanted to for a long time.

'Well, who did found it?' Kolya asked, turning to him with haughty condescension.

He had guessed from the look on Kartashov's face that he really knew and, of course, at once made up his mind what attitude he should assume. There was, as it were, a discordant note in the mood of those present.

'Troy was founded by Teucer, Dardanus, Ilias, and Troas,' the boy replied at once in a firm voice and immediately blushed to the roots of his hair so that it was pitiful to look at him.

But all the boys stared at him for a whole minute, and then, suddenly, all the staring eyes turned at once to Kolya, who continued to look the impudent boy up and down with contemptuous composure.

'But,' he deigned at last to break the silence, 'how do you mean they founded it? And what, generally speaking does the foundation of a city or a State mean? What did they do? Did they go and each lay a brick?'

There was laughter. The poor boy turned from pink to crimson. He was silent and was about to burst into tears. Kolya held him like that for another minute.

'To talk of such historical events as the founding of a nation,' he rapped out sternly for his edification, 'one must first of all understand what it means. So far as I'm concerned, I do not consider any of these old wives' tales of the slightest importance, and I don't think very much of world history, in general,' he added in a casual tone of voice, addressing the company as a whole.

'World history?' Snegiryov inquired almost in alarm.

'Yes, sir, world history. It's just the study of a succession of human follies and nothing more. The only subjects I respect are mathematics and the natural sciences,' Kolya bragged, casting a quick glance at Alyosha.

It was only Alyosha's opinion he was afraid of. But Alyosha still said nothing and looked serious. If Alyosha had said something, that would have been the end of it, but Alyosha was silent and 'his silence might be an expression of his contempt', and that made Kolya feel more and more exasperated.

'Take those classical languages we have to learn: it's simply madness and nothing more. . . . I believe you don't agree with me again, Karamazov, do you?'

'I don't,' Alyosha smiled restrainedly.

'The classical languages, if you want to know what I really think of them, are nothing but a police measure. That's the only reason why they have been introduced,' Kolya was gradually beginning to get breathless again. 'They were introduced because they are boring and because they stunt one's intellectual abilities. It was boring before, so what could they do to make it even more boring? It was senseless before, so what could they do to make things even more senseless? So they thought of classical languages. That's my frank opinion of them and, I hope, I shall never alter it,' Kolya concluded sharply, two red spots appearing on his cheeks.

'That's true,' Smurov, who had been listening attentively, assented suddenly in a ringing tone of conviction.

'And yet he's top in Latin himself!' a boy shouted from the crowd.

'Yes, Daddy, he says that and yet he's first in Latin in his class,' Ilyusha, too, chimed in.

'Well, what does that prove?' Kolya thought it necessary to defend himself, though he was very pleased with the praise. 'I swot Latin, because I have to, because I promised my mother to pass my exam, and, in my opinion, if you do something, you must do it well, but at bottom I have the utmost contempt for classical studies and all that foul stuff. You don't agree, Karamazov, do you?'

'But why "foul stuff"?' Alyosha smiled again.

'Why, all the classics have been translated into all languages, and therefore it is not for the sake of studying the classics that they are so keen on Latin, but simply as a police measure and to stultify one's intellectual abilities. Isn't it foul stuff after that?'

'But who taught you all this?' Alyosha cried at last, looking surprised.

'In the first place, I'm quite capable of understanding it myself without being taught, and, secondly, let me tell you that Kolbasnikov himself said to the third form what I said just now about the classics having been translated.'

'The doctor has come!' Nina, who had been silent all the time, cried suddenly.

And indeed, the carriage belonging to Mrs Khokhlakov drove up to the gates. Snegiryov, who had been expecting the doctor all morning, rushed out headlong to meet him. Mrs Snegiryov sat up, put her dress in order and assumed a dignified air. Alyosha went up to Ilyusha and set his pillows straight. Nina watched him uneasily from her armchair putting the bed tidy. The boys began taking their leave hurriedly, some of them promising to come again in the evening. Kolya called Perezvon and the dog jumped down from the bed.

'I won't go away, I won't go away,' Kolya said hurriedly to Ilyusha. 'I'll wait in the passage and come in again after the doctor has gone. I'll come back with Perezvon.'

But the doctor was already coming in – an important-looking figure in a bearskin fur coat, with long, dark side-whiskers and a shining, closely-shaven chin. On crossing the threshold, he suddenly stopped, as though taken aback. He probably imagined that he had come to the wrong place. 'What's this? Where am I?' he muttered, without taking off his fur coat and his seal-skin cap with its seal-skin peak. The crowd of people, the poverty of the room, the washing hanging on a line in a corner of the room, confused him. Snegiryov was bowing low to him.

'It's here, sir, here,' he murmured obsequiously. 'It's here, sir, you were coming to my house, sir. . . .'

'Sne-gir-yov?' the doctor said in a loud and dignified voice. 'Are you Mr Snegiryov?'

'Yes, sir. That's me, sir.'

'Oh!'

The doctor cast another disdainful look round the room and threw off his fur coat. The high decoration round his neck flashed for all to see. Snegiryov snatched up the fur coat, and the doctor took off his cap.

'Where's the patient?' he asked in a loud, peremptory voice.

6

Precocious Development

'WHAT do you think the doctor will say to him?' Kolya asked rapidly. 'What a disgusting face, though, don't you agree? I can't bear medicine!'

'Ilyusha's going to die,' Alyosha replied sadly. 'It seems to me beyond doubt.'

'The frauds! Medicine's a fraud. I'm glad, though, to have met you, Karamazov. I've wanted to meet you for a long time. I'm only sorry we had to meet in such sad circumstances.'

Kolya would have very much liked to say something warmer and more effusive, but something about Alyosha seemed to stop him. Alyosha noticed it, smiled, and pressed his hand.

'I've long learned to respect you as a rare person,' Kolya murmured again, hesitantly and confusedly. 'I've heard you are a mystic and that you've been in a monastery. I know you are a mystic but – that hasn't put me off. Contact with reality will cure you. It's always like that with natures like yours.'

'What do you call a mystic? What will it cure me of?' Alyosha asked, looking a little surprised.

'Well – God and the rest of it.'

'Why, don't you believe in God?'

'On the contrary, I've nothing against God. Of course, God is only a hypothesis but – I admit that he is necessary for – for order – for world order and so on, and that if there were no God he'd have to be invented,' Kolya added, beginning to blush.

He suddenly fancied that Alyosha might think that he wished to show off his knowledge and let him see that he was 'grown up'. 'And I don't want to show off my knowledge to him at all!' Kolya thought indignantly. And he suddenly felt very annoyed.

'I must confess I hate entering into all these discussions,' he blurted out. 'One can love humanity without believing in God – don't you think so? Voltaire did not believe in God but he loved mankind, didn't he?' ('Again! Again!' he thought to himself.)

'Voltaire believed in God, but not, I suppose, very much, and I can't help thinking that he didn't love mankind very much, either,' Alyosha said, quietly, restrainedly and quite naturally, as though talking to someone of his own age, or, indeed, to someone much older than himself.

Kolya was at once struck by Alyosha's apparent diffidence about Voltaire's views and by the fact that he seemed to be leaving the question for him, little Kolya, to settle.

'Have you read Voltaire?' asked Alyosha, in conclusion.

'Well, not really. . . . I've read *Candide*, though, in a Russian translation, in an old, bad translation, a ridiculous translation.' ('Again! Again!')

'And did you understand it?'

'Oh yes, everything – that is . . . why do you suppose I shouldn't understand it? There are, of course, lots of obscenities in it. I'm, of course, quite capable of understanding that it is a philosophical novel, and written to propagate an idea,' Kolya had got thoroughly muddled by now. 'I'm a socialist, Karamazov, I'm an incorrigible socialist,' he broke off suddenly for no obvious reason.

'A socialist?' Alyosha laughed. 'But when have you had time to become one? You're only thirteen, aren't you?'

Kolya winced.

'First of all, I'm not thirteen, but fourteen, I shall be fourteen in a fortnight,' he declared, flushing. 'And, secondly, I completely fail to understand what my age has got to do with it? What matters are my convictions and not how old I am. Don't you agree?'

'When you're older, you'll understand how important age is for a man's convictions. It also seemed to me that you were not expressing your own ideas,' Alyosha replied quietly and modestly, but Kolya interrupted him hotly.

'Why, you want obedience and mysticism. You must admit that Christianity, for instance, has been useful only to the rich and powerful to keep the lower classes in slavery. Isn't that so?'

'Oh, I know where you read that,' exclaimed Alyosha. 'And I'm sure someone must have told you that!'

'Good Lord, why must I have read it? And no one told me anything. I can think for myself. And, if you like, I'm not against Christ. He was a very humane person, and if he were alive today, he would most certainly have joined the revolutionaries and would, perhaps, play a conspicuous part. I'm quite sure of that.'

'Good heavens, where did you get all that from? What fool have you had to do with?'

'You can't hide the truth, you know. It's true that I often talk to Mr Rakitin in connection with a certain affair, but, I'm told, old Belinsky used to say that too.'

'Belinsky? I don't remember. He hasn't written that anywhere.'

'If he didn't write it, I'm told he said it. I heard it from a – however, it doesn't matter.'

'And have you read Belinsky?'

'Well, you see, as a matter of fact, I haven't read him at all, but I did read the passage about Tatyana – why she didn't go off with Onegin.'

'Didn't go off with Onegin? Why, do you already understand – such things?'

'Good Lord, you must take me for that little boy Smurov,' Kolya grinned, irritably. 'Still, you mustn't think I'm such a terrible revolutionary. I often disagree with Mr Rakitin. If I mentioned Tatyana, it was not because I'm in favour of the emancipation of women. I'm of the opinion that a woman is a subordinate creature and must obey. *Les femmes tricottent*, as Napoleon said,' Kolya grinned for some reason, 'and in that at least I fully share the opinion of that pseudo-great man. I furthermore believe, for instance, that to run away to America from your own country is mean, and even worse than mean – stupid. Why go to America when we can do a great deal of good for humanity in our country, too? Especially now. A whole mass of fruitful activity. That's what I replied.'

'Who did you reply to? What do you mean? Has anyone already asked you to go to America?'

'I admit, they've tried to persuade me, but I refused. That's, of course, between you and me, Karamazov. Don't say a word to anyone about it, do you hear? I'm telling this to you alone. I certainly do not intend to fall into the clutches of the Secret Police and take lessons at the Chain Bridge.

You will ever remember,
The house at the Chain Bridge.

'Remember? Excellent! What are you laughing at? You don't
think I've been telling you lies?' ('And what if he finds out that there's
only one copy of *The Bell* in father's bookcase and that I haven't read
anything more of it?' Kolya thought with a shudder.)

'Good heavens, no! I'm not laughing and I don't think you've been
telling me lies. That's the trouble, you see, that I don't think so,
because all of it is, alas, only too true! But tell me, have you read
Pushkin, I mean, *Onegin*? You spoke of Tatyana just now. . . .'

'No, I haven't read it yet, but I want to read it. I have no prejudices,
Karamazov. I want to hear both sides. Why did you ask?'

'Oh, I just wondered.'

'Tell me, Karamazov, do you despise me very much?' Kolya asked
abruptly, drawing himself up to his full height before Alyosha, as
though taking up a position to meet any attack. 'Do me a favour, tell
me frankly.'

'Despise you?' said Alyosha, looking at him with surprise. 'Why
should I? I'm only sorry that a charming nature such as yours should
have been perverted by all this crude nonsense before you've begun
to live.'

'Don't worry about my nature,' Kolya interrupted not without
self-satisfaction, 'but it's quite true that I'm very sensitive. Stupidly
sensitive. Crudely sensitive. You smiled just now and I imagined that
you . . .'

'Oh, I smiled at something quite different. You see what I smiled
at was this: I recently read the opinion of a German who had lived
in Russia about our schoolboys today. "Show a Russian schoolboy,"
he writes, "a map of the stars, of which he had no idea before, and
he'll return it to you corrected next day." No knowledge and utter
self-conceit – that's what the German meant to say about the Russian
schoolboy.'

'Oh, but that's perfectly true!' Kolya suddenly burst out laughing.
'*Verissimo!* Exactly so! Bravo, German! But the damned foreigner
failed to notice the good side, eh? What do you think? Self-conceit –
I admit. That's a sign of youth, that will be corrected, if it has to be
corrected, but, on the other hand, there's also an independent spirit

almost from early childhood, and boldness of thought and convictions, and not their spirit of cringing servility before authority. . . . But, all the same, the German put it well! Bravo, German! Though Germans ought to be strangled for all that. They may be good at science, but they ought to be strangled. . . .'

'But why on earth strangle them?' smiled Alyosha.

'Oh well, I've been talking nonsense. Sorry, I agree. I'm a perfect child sometimes, and when something pleases me I can't control myself and talk a lot of nonsense. Look here, we're talking about all sorts of silly things here, while that doctor has been a very long time there. However, he may be examining Mrs Snegiryov and that poor cripple Nina. You know, I liked that Nina. She whispered to me suddenly as I walked past her: "Why didn't you come before?" And in such a reproachful voice! I think she's awfully good and so pathetic.'

'Yes, yes! When you come again, you'll realize what a nice girl she is. It'll do you a lot of good to know such people, for it will teach you to value many things you can find out from knowing them,' Alyosha observed heatedly. 'That more than anything will make you a different person.'

'Oh, I'm so sorry and I curse myself for not having come earlier!' cried Kolya, with bitter feeling.

'Yes, it's a great pity. You saw for yourself how glad the poor child was to see you! He was so upset because you did not come!'

'Don't tell me! You make me feel awful. Still, it serves me right: I didn't come, out of vanity, out of egoistical vanity and a beastly desire to lord it over people, which I can never get rid of, though I've been doing my best all my life to be different. I can see now that I've been a cad in lots of ways, Karamazov!'

'No, you've a charming nature, though it's been perverted, and I quite understand why you've had such an influence on this generous and morbidly sensitive boy!' Alyosha retorted warmly.

'And you say that to me!' cried Kolya, 'and, you know, I have thought several times – I've thought it just now – that you despise me! If only you knew how highly I think of your opinion!'

'But are you really so sensitive? At your age! You know, that was exactly my impression when I watched you telling your story in there. I couldn't help thinking that you must be very sensitive.'

'Did you? You see what an eye you've got! I bet it was when I was

telling about the goose. It was just then that I fancied that you must
despise me greatly for being in such a hurry to show what a fine fellow
I was, and I even hated you for it and talked a lot of rot. Then I fancied
(it was just now, here) that when I said that if there were no God he
had to be invented, that I was too much in a hurry to show how well
educated I was, particularly as I had got that phrase out of a book.
But I swear I was in such a hurry to show off not out of vanity but –
well, I really don't know why. . . . Out of joy, perhaps. Yes, I do
believe it was out of joy, though I admit it's a highly disgraceful thing
for a man to hurl himself at the heads of people out of joy. I know that.
But I'm quite convinced now that you don't despise me and that I'm
imagining it all. Oh, Karamazov, I'm terribly unhappy. I sometimes
imagine goodness knows what, that everyone is laughing at me, the
whole world, and then – then I'm simply ready to destroy the whole
order of things.'

'And you are horrid to everyone,' Alyosha smiled.

'And I'm horrid to everyone, to Mother especially. Tell me, Karamazov, am I making myself very ridiculous now?'

'Don't think about it, don't think about it at all!' cried Alyosha.
'And what does ridiculous mean? Does it matter how many times a
man is or seems to be ridiculous? Besides, today almost all people of
ability are terribly afraid of making themselves ridiculous and that
makes them unhappy. The only thing that surprises me is that you
should be feeling this so early, though I've noticed it for some time
now and not only in you. Today even those who are little more than
children have begun to suffer from it. It's almost a kind of insanity.
It's the devil who has taken the form of this vanity and entered into
the whole generation – yes, the devil,' added Alyosha, without smiling, as Kolya, who was staring at him, thought he would. 'You're
just like everyone else,' Alyosha concluded, 'that is, like many others.
Except that one ought not to be like everyone else. That's the important thing.'

'Even if everyone's like that?'

'Yes, even if everyone's like that. You ought to be the only one
who isn't like that. And as a matter of fact you are not like everyone
else: you weren't ashamed to confess a moment ago to something bad
and even ridiculous. And who confesses to that nowadays? No one.
People do not any longer even feel the need of admitting that they're

wrong. So don't be like everyone else, even if you are the only one who is not.'

'Excellent! I was not mistaken in you. You have the gift of comforting people. Oh, I was so anxious to know you! I have wished to meet you for such a long time! Have you really thought about me too? You did say just now that you had thought about me, too, didn't you?'

'Yes, I've heard about you and thought about you and – and if it's to a certain extent vanity that makes you ask, it doesn't matter.'

'You know, Karamazov, our talk has been like a declaration of love,' said Kolya in a sort of nervous and bashful voice. 'This isn't ridiculous, is it?'

'Of course not, and even if it were, it wouldn't matter a bit, because it's so splendid,' Alyosha smiled brightly.

'But, you know, Karamazov, you must admit that you feel a little ashamed yourself now. I can see it from your eyes,' Kolya smiled slyly, but also with undisguised happiness.

'What is there to be ashamed of?'

'Well, why are you blushing?'

'Why, it's you who made me blush!' laughed Alyosha and, indeed, he blushed all over. 'Well, yes, I am a little ashamed. Goodness knows why. I'm sure I don't,' he muttered, almost embarrassed.

'Oh, I love and admire you at this moment just because for some reason you feel ashamed. Because you're just like me!' Kolya exclaimed with genuine delight. His cheeks were burning, his eyes sparkled.

'Listen, Kolya, I can't help feeling that you'll be very unhappy in life,' said Alyosha suddenly without really knowing what made him say that.

'I know, I know. How you do know it all beforehand!' Kolya at once agreed.

'But on the whole you will bless life all the same.'

'Yes, indeed. Hurrah! You're a prophet. Oh, we shall be good friends, Karamazov. You know, what I like so much about you is that you treat me just as if I were your equal. And we are not equals, are we? No, we're not. You're higher than I. But we shall be friends. You know, during the past month I've been saying to myself: "We shall either be friends at once and for ever or we shall part enemies to the grave after our first meeting"!'

'And, of course, saying that, you loved me already!' Alyosha laughed gaily.

'Yes, I did. I loved you terribly. I've been loving you and dreaming about you! And how do you know everything beforehand? Ah, here's the doctor. Good Lord, what will he say, I wonder. Look at him!'

7

Ilyusha

THE doctor was coming out of the room, wrapped in his fur coat and with his cap on his head. He looked almost angry and disgusted, as though he were still afraid of dirtying himself. He glanced cursorily round the passage and, as he did so, glanced sternly at Alyosha and Kolya. Alyosha waved to the driver from the door and the carriage that had brought the doctor drove up. Snegiryov rushed out after the doctor and, bowing from the waist and almost grovelling before him, stopped him to have a last word. The poor fellow looked crushed and frightened.

'Sir, sir – isn't there —?' he began, but didn't finish, merely throwing up his hands in despair, though still looking at the doctor with mute entreaty, as though a word from him might change the poor boy's death sentence.

'I'm afraid I can't do anything. I'm not God,' the doctor replied in a casual, though his customary impressive tone of voice.

'Doctor – sir – and will it be soon, soon?'

'Be pre-pared for anything,' the doctor said, emphasizing every syllable and, dropping his eyes, was about to step over the threshold to the coach.

'For Christ's sake, sir,' Snegiryov stopped him again, looking frightened, 'can absolutely nothing be done to save him now?'

'It doesn't de-pend on me now,' the doctor said impatiently. 'However – h'm,' he stopped suddenly, 'if – er – you could perhaps – er – send your patient – er – at once and without delay' (the words 'at once' and 'without delay' the doctor uttered not so much sternly as almost angrily, so that Snegiryov even gave a start) 'er – to Sy-ra-cuse, then – er – as a result of the – er – favourable climatic conditions – er – there might – er – be – er —'

'To Syracuse!' cried Snegiryov, as though unable to understand a word.

'Syracuse is in Sicily,' Kolya suddenly blurted out.

The doctor looked at him.

'To Sicily, but, sir,' Snegiryov faltered, 'you've seen —', he waved his hands as though to draw his attention to the surroundings. 'And what about my wife, sir, my family?'

'N-no, your family should not go to Sicily but to the Caucasus – er – in the early spring. Your daughter to the Caucasus and – er – your wife after – er – after a course of the waters also in the Caucasus to cure – er – her rheumatism and – er – after that at once to Paris to – er – the clinic of the famous psychiatrist, Dr Lapelletier. I – er – could let you have a note to him and then – er – there might be —'

'But, doctor, can't you see?' Snegiryov again waved his hands, pointing in despair at the bare wooden walls of the passage.

'That's not my business, sir,' the doctor smiled. 'I only told you what sci-ence – er – could do as a last resort – er – for your family. As for the rest – er – I'm sorry, I – er —'

'Don't worry, doc, my dog won't bite you,' Kolya snapped out in a loud voice, noticing the doctor's rather uneasy glance at Perezvon, who was standing in the doorway.

There was an angry note in Kolya's voice. The word 'doc' instead of doctor he used intentionally and, as he declared afterwards himself, 'as an insult'.

'What's that, sir?' the doctor raised his head and stared in surprise at Kolya. 'Who's this?' he turned suddenly to Alyosha, as though demanding an explanation.

'This is Perezvon's owner, don't worry about me, doc,' Kolya said calmly.

'Bell [Zvon]?' the doctor repeated, not realizing that Perezvon was the dog's name.

'But where he cannot tell. Good-bye, doc, we shall meet in Syra-cuse.'

'Who's this? Who? Who?' cried the doctor, suddenly flying into a terrible rage.

'He's one of our schoolboys, doctor,' Alyosha said, frowning and speaking rapidly. 'He's a mischievous boy. Don't pay any attention to him, sir. Kolya,' he shouted to Krasotkin, 'hold your tongue! Don't take any notice of him, doctor,' he repeated a little more impatiently.

'Thrashed! Thrashed! He must be thrashed!' the doctor, who for some reason flew into a violent temper, shouted, stamping his feet.

'You know, doc, my Perezvon might bite after all!' said Kolya in a quivering voice, turning pale and with flashing eyes. 'Here, Perezvon!'

'Kolya, if you say another word I shall never have anything to do with you again,' Alyosha cried peremptorily.

'Doc, there's only one man in the whole world who can order Nikolai Krasotkin about – this is the man,' Kolya pointed to Alyosha. 'I obey him. Good-bye!'

He rushed to the door, opened it and went quickly into the room. Perezvon ran after him. The doctor stood still for five seconds more, staring at Alyosha as though in a stupor, then he spat and went out quickly to the carriage, repeating in a loud voice: 'This – this – this – I don't know what this is!' Snegiryov rushed after him to help him into the carriage. Alyosha followed Kolya into the room. Kolya was already standing beside Ilyusha's bed. Ilyusha was holding his hand and was calling for his father. A minute later Snegiryov, too, returned.

'Daddy, Daddy, come here – we —' Ilyusha murmured in violent agitation, but, apparently unable to go on, suddenly flung both his wasted arms round Kolya and his father, holding them, as well as he could, in one tight embrace and hugging them closely. Snegiryov suddenly shook all over with silent sobs and Kolya's chin and lips began to twitch.

'Daddy, Daddy! Oh, I'm so sorry for you, Daddy!' Ilyusha moaned bitterly.

'My darling Ilyusha – the doctor said you – you'd be all right and – and we'll be happy – the doctor —' Snegiryov began.

'Oh, Daddy, I know what the new doctor said to you about me – I saw!' cried Ilyusha, again hugging both of them tightly and hiding his face on his father's shoulder.

'Daddy, don't cry and – and when I die, get a good boy – another one – choose one yourself from all of them, a good one, call him Ilyusha and love him instead of me. . . .'

'Shut up, old man, you'll get well!' Krasotkin cried suddenly, as though in anger.

'And don't you ever forget me, Daddy,' went on Ilyusha. 'Come to my grave – and please, Daddy, bury me near the big stone, where we used to go for our walks, and come to me there with Krasotkin in the evening. . . . And Perezvon too. And I'll be waiting for you. . . . Daddy, Daddy!'

His voice failed him, and the three of them, united in one embrace, were silent. Nina, too, was crying quietly in her chair, and Mrs Snegiryov, seeing them all crying, burst into tears herself.

'My darling Ilyusha, my darling Ilyusha!' she kept exclaiming.

Krasotkin suddenly freed himself from Ilyusha's embrace.

'Good-bye, old man,' he said, speaking fast,' Mother is waiting dinner for me. I'm very sorry not to have told her. She'll be awfully worried. But after dinner I'll come back to you at once, for the whole day, the whole evening, and I'm going to tell you ever so many things, ever so many! And I'll bring Perezvon. He'll start howling if I'm not here and be a nuisance to you. So long!'

And he ran out into the passage. He did not want to cry, but in the passage he cried all the same. Alyosha found him like that.

'Kolya, you must keep your word and come, or he'll be terribly upset,' Alyosha said emphatically.

'I will! Oh, how I curse myself for not having come earlier,' Kolya murmured, crying and no longer ashamed of it.

At that moment Snegiryov seemed to leap out of the room and at once closed the door behind them. His face was contorted and his lips quivered. He stopped short before the two of them and flung up his arms.

'I don't want a good boy! I don't want another boy!' he said in a wild whisper, grinding his teeth. 'If I forget thee, Jerusalem, may my tongue —'

He did not finish, the words dying on his lips, and he sank helplessly on his knees beside the wooden bench. Clutching his head in his fists, he burst out sobbing, now and again whimpering absurdly, but doing his utmost not to be heard in the room. Kolya rushed out into the street.

'Good-bye, Karamazov! Will you be coming back?' he cried sharply and crossly to Alyosha.

'I'll certainly be back in the evening.'

'What was it he was saying about Jerusalem? What is it all about?'

'It's from the Bible: If I forget thee, Jerusalem, that is to say, if I forget all that is most precious to me, if I exchange it for anything, then —'

'I understand. That's enough! Don't forget to come. Here, Perezvon!' he shouted fiercely to the dog and almost ran home.

I

At Grushenka's

ALYOSHA walked in the direction of the Cathedral Square to Mrs Morozov's house to see Grushenka, who had sent Fenya early in the morning with an urgent message to call on her. Having questioned Fenya, Alyosha learnt that her mistress had been greatly upset since the day before. During the two months since Mitya's arrest Alyosha had been to see Grushenka often, both of his own accord and at Mitya's request. Three days after Mitya's arrest Grushenka fell seriously ill and was ill for nearly five weeks. For one of the five weeks she was unconscious. She had greatly changed, had grown thin and sallow-faced, though now for nearly two weeks she had been well enough to go out. But, in Alyosha's view, her face seemed much more attractive than before and he liked to meet her eyes when he went into her room. There seemed to be a look of firmness and greater comprehension in her eyes. There were signs of some spiritual change in her, of a resolution that appeared to be humble and unalterable, good and irrevocable. A small, vertical line had appeared between her eyebrows which lent her charming face a look of concentrated thoughtfulness, almost stern at the first glance. There was, for instance, no trace of her former frivolity. It also seemed strange to Alyosha that Grushenka had not lost her former youthful gaiety in spite of the terrible misfortune that had befallen the poor woman, the fiancée of a man who had been arrested for a terrible crime almost at the moment when she had promised to marry him, and in spite of her subsequent illness and the almost inevitable verdict of the court at the impending trial. There was a soft light in her once proud eyes, and yet – and yet they blazed with an ominous fire at times, too, when an old anxiety stole into her heart, an anxiety that had never abated, but had even grown stronger. The object of that anxiety was always the same: Katerina, whom she mentioned again and again during her illness and even in her delirium. Alyosha realized that she was terribly jealous of her, in spite of the fact that

Katerina had not once visited Mitya in prison, though she could have done so any time she liked. As a result of all this, Alyosha was faced with rather a difficult problem, for Grushenka confided her secret troubles to him alone and was constantly appealing to him for advice; and yet he was sometimes absolutely at a loss what to say to her.

He looked worried when he entered her flat. She was at home, having returned from a visit to Mitya half an hour before. From the rapid movement with which she jumped up from her chair at the table to meet him, he concluded that she had been expecting him with great impatience. There were cards on the table, and some of them had been dealt out for a game of 'fools'. On the other side of the table a bed had been made up on a leather sofa, and Maximov, in a dressing-gown and a cotton nightcap, lay on it, propped up on one elbow. He was evidently ill and weak, though he was smiling sweetly. On his return with Grushenka from Mokroye two months before, this homeless old man had stayed on at her house and was still living there. Having arrived with her in the rain and slush, he sat down on the sofa, soaked to the skin and frightened, and stared silently at her with a timid, beseeching smile. Grushenka, who was in terrible grief and already feverish, was so busy in the first half hour after her arrival that she had almost forgotten all about him. Suddenly she caught sight of him and looked at him intently: he raised his eyes and laughed a pitiful and forlorn little laugh. She called Fenya and told her to give him something to eat. The whole of that day he remained sitting in the same place almost without stirring. When it grew dark and the shutters were closed, Fenya asked her mistress:

'Is the old gentleman going to stay the night, madam?'

'Yes, he is,' Grushenka replied. 'Make up a bed for him on the sofa.'

Questioning him more in detail, Grushenka found out from him that he really had nowhere to go. 'Mr Kalganov, my benefactor,' he said, 'told me straight that I would not be received again at his house, and he gave me five roubles.' 'Well,' Grushenka decided in her grief, smiling compassionately at him, 'I suppose you'd better stay.' The old man was deeply touched by her smile and his lips quivered with gratitude as he barely restrained himself from crying. And so the wandering sponger had stayed with her ever since. Even when she was ill, he did not leave her house. Fenya and her mother, Grushenka's cook, did not turn him out and went on serving him meals and making up a bed for him on the sofa. Later on Grushenka got so used to him that, on returning from her visits to Mitya (whom she began visiting regularly even before she had completely recovered), she would sit down and begin talking to 'dear old Maximov' about all sorts of trifling matters, just to get over her depression and not to think of her grief. She discovered that occasionally the old man was rather good at story-telling, so that in the end she could not do without him. Except for Alyosha, who did not, however, come every day and who never stayed long, Grushenka scarcely received anyone. Her old merchant was already seriously ill at the time – 'breathing his last', as they said in the town, and, as a matter of fact, he did die a week after Mitya's trial. Three weeks before his death, feeling the end approaching, he called for his three sons and their wives and children and told them not to leave him again. From that moment he gave strict orders to his servants not to admit Grushenka and to tell her, if she came, that he wished her long life and happiness and asked her to forget him. Grushenka, though, sent almost every day to inquire after his health.

'You've come at last!' cried Grushenka, throwing down the cards and greeting Alyosha joyfully. 'Maximov kept frightening me saying that perhaps you wouldn't come. Oh, I need you so badly! Sit down at the table. Well, what will you have – coffee?'

'Thank you,' said Alyosha, sitting down at the table, 'I'm awfully hungry.'

'I thought so,' Grushenka cried. 'Fenya, Fenya, coffee! I've had it ready for hours for you. And bring some pies, Fenya, and mind they're hot. One moment, Alyosha. Before you say anything, I must tell you that we've had an awful row over those pies today. I took them to the prison for him, and he – would you believe it? – threw them back at me. He would not eat them. He threw one pie on the floor and stamped on it. I told him I was going to leave them with the warder. "If you don't eat them before the evening," I said, "then it means that it's your malicious spite alone that keeps you going." With that I went away. We've had another quarrel, you see. Every time I go, we quarrel.'

Grushenka said it all in the same breath, in agitation. Maximov at once became frightened and, dropping his eyes, went on smiling.

'What did you quarrel with him about this time?' asked Alyosha.

'Well, you know, I never expected it. Just fancy, he was jealous of my "first". "Why," he asked me, "are you keeping him? So you've begun keeping him, have you?" He's always jealous. Jealous of me all the time! Jealous of me when he eats and sleeps. He was even jealous of Kuzma one day last week.'

'But he knew about your first before, didn't he?'

'Of course he did. He's known about it from the very beginning. But today he suddenly got up and started calling me names. I'm ashamed to repeat what he said. The fool! Rakitin came to see him as I went out. Perhaps it's Rakitin who is inciting him against me. What do you think?' she added somehow absently.

'He loves you, that's what it is. He loves you very much. And, besides, his nerves are on edge now.'

'I should think so. His trial opens tomorrow. I went there today to say something to him about it, for, Alyosha, I tremble to think what's going to happen tomorrow! His nerves are on edge, you say. And what about my nerves? Aren't they on edge too? And he talks about the Pole! What a fool! I suppose he's not jealous of Maximov, or is he?'

'My wife was very jealous of me, too, ma'am,' Maximov put in his word.

'Was she now?' Grushenka laughed in spite of herself. 'Who was she jealous of?'

'Of the parlour maids, ma'am.'

'Oh, do be quiet, Maximov! I don't feel like laughing now. I feel so wild I – don't keep staring at the pies! I shan't give you any. And I won't give you any of my home-made liqueur, either. How do you like that?' she laughed. 'I've got him on my hands, too, just as if I kept an almshouse. Honestly!'

'I don't deserve your benefactions, ma'am, a worthless creature like me,' Maximov said in a tearful voice. 'You'd better lavish them on those who are of more use than I, ma'am.'

'Oh, everyone is of some use, Maximov, and how's one to tell which of us is of most use? I wish that Pole had never existed, Alyosha. He, too, took it into his head to fall ill. I've been to see him, too. Well, I'm going to send him some pies, too – on purpose! I hadn't sent him any and Mitya accused me of sending him some, so I'm

going to send him some now on purpose, on purpose! Oh, here's
Fenya with a letter! Yes, just as I thought! It's from those Poles
again. Asking for money again!'

Mussyalovich sent an extremely long letter, written in his usual
florid style, in which he asked for a loan of three roubles. He enclosed
a receipt for the money with a promise to repay it within three
months; the receipt was signed by Vrublevsky, too. Grushenka had
received many such letters from her 'first', enclosing similar receipts.
The letters had begun arriving a fortnight before, as soon as Grushenka had recovered from her illness. But she knew that the two
Poles had also been to inquire after her health during her illness. The
first letter was a very long one, written on a large sheet of notepaper
with a big family crest on the seal. It was written in so obscure and
florid a style that Grushenka read only half of it and threw it away,
unable to make head or tail of it. Besides, she had no time for letters
then. The first letter was followed by another one next day in which
Mussyalovich asked for a loan of two thousand roubles for a very
short period. Grushenka left that letter unanswered, too. Then there
followed a whole series of letters, which arrived regularly every day,
all of them written in the same grave and florid style, but in which the
amount of money they asked to borrow, gradually growing less,
dropped to one hundred roubles, then to twenty-five, to ten, and at
last Grushenka received a letter in which the two Poles asked her for
only one rouble and enclosed a receipt signed by both of them. It was
then that Grushenka suddenly felt sorry for them and, at dusk, went
round herself to see them. She found the two Poles in great poverty,
almost in destitution, without food or fuel or cigarettes, and in debt
to their landlady. The two hundred roubles they had won at cards
from Mitya in Mokroye seemed to have disappeared into thin air.
What surprised Grushenka, however, was that the two Poles had
met her with an air of insolent dignity and independence, with the
greatest ceremony and high-flown speeches. Grushenka just laughed
and gave her 'first one' ten roubles. On the same day she laughingly
told Mitya about it and he was not at all jealous. But since then the
Poles had seized on Grushenka and bombarded her with begging
letters every day and she had always sent them a little money. And
now Mitya suddenly took it into his head to be ferociously jealous
of her.

'Like a fool I went round to see him too for a minute on my way to Mitya, for, you see, he too is ill, my first one, my Pole,' Grushenka began again, hurriedly and nervously. 'I told Mitya laughingly about it. "Can you imagine it," I said, "that Pole of mine has taken it into his head to sing me his old songs to the guitar. He thinks I'll be touched and marry him!" Well, Mitya jumped up and began calling me names. . . . Well, then, if he carries on like that, I'm jolly well going to send them the pies! Fenya, have they sent the little girl? Here, give her three roubles and wrap a dozen pies up in a paper and tell her to take them. And you, Alyosha, don't forget to tell Mitya that I sent them the pies.'

'I wouldn't tell him for anything,' said Alyosha with a smile.

'Oh, you don't think he worries about it, do you?' Grushenka said bitterly. 'He was pretending to be jealous on purpose. He doesn't care a bit.'

'How do you mean – on purpose?' asked Alyosha.

'You're stupid, Alyosha darling. You don't understand anything for all your intelligence. I'm not offended that he should be jealous of a woman like me. I should have been offended if he wasn't. I'm like that. I'm not offended by jealousy. I have a cruel heart myself. I can be jealous too. If I'm offended it's because he doesn't love me at all and was now jealous *on purpose*. Do you think I am blind? Don't I see? He starts talking to me all of a sudden about that Katya of his. See what a nice woman she is, he says. She's sent for a doctor from Moscow, he says, and has engaged an eminent and learned Moscow counsel to save me. So I suppose he must love her if he keeps on praising her to my face, the shameless wretch! He got me into this mess, so now he attacks me and tries to put the whole blame on me alone. You were with that Pole before me, so why can't I make it up with Katya? That's what it is! He does it on purpose, I'm telling you, on purpose, but I'll —'

Grushenka did not finish saying what she would do, hid her eyes in her handkerchief and burst out sobbing bitterly.

'He doesn't love Katerina,' said Alyosha firmly.

'Whether he loves her or not, I'll soon find it out for myself,' Grushenka said with a note of menace in her voice, taking the handkerchief from her eyes.

Her face was distorted. Alyosha saw with distress how her face, hitherto so gentle and serenely happy, suddenly became sullen and spiteful.

'Enough of this nonsense!' she suddenly snapped. 'I didn't ask you to come for that. Alyosha darling, what's going to happen tomorrow? That's what worries me so dreadfully! And it seems to worry only me! I look at them all, and no one seems to be concerned about it at all. Are you thinking about it? Tomorrow he's to be tried! Tell me, how will he be tried? Why, it's the servant, the servant who killed him! Goodness, surely they're not going to find him guilty instead of the servant! Is there no one to take his part? They haven't even troubled the servant, have they?'

'He's been cross-examined severely,' Alyosha observed thoughtfully, 'but they all decided that it wasn't he. Now he's very ill. He's been ill ever since that attack of epilepsy. He really is ill,' added Alyosha.

'Oh dear, why don't you go to that lawyer yourself and tell him everything in confidence. I understand he's been brought from Petersburg at a fee of three thousand roubles.'

'We gave the three thousand together, Katerina, Ivan, and I, but she got the doctor from Moscow for two thousand herself. The counsel Fetyukovich would have charged more, but the case has created a sensation all over Russia, they write about it in all the papers and journals. Fetyukovich agreed to come more for the glory of the thing, for it's become so sensational a case. I saw him yesterday.'

'Well? Did you tell him?' Grushenka asked excitedly.

'He listened and said nothing. He merely said that he had already formed a definite opinion. But he promised to take my words into consideration.'

'Into consideration! Oh, the scoundrels! They'll ruin him! But what about the doctor? Why did she send for him?'

'As an expert. They want to prove that my brother is insane and committed the murder when he was not responsible for his actions,' Alyosha smiled gently. 'Only Mitya won't agree to that.'

'Oh, but it would be quite true if he had killed him!' cried Grushenka. 'He was mad then, quite mad, and it's all, all the fault of a vile creature like me! But, then, he didn't do it, he didn't do it! And they're all against him. The whole town is convinced that he did it. Even Fenya. Her statement seemed to show that he had done it. And the people in the shop, and that civil servant, and, before, the people in the pub had heard him threaten to kill his father! Everyone, everyone is against him. Everyone is screaming that he's guilty.'

'Yes,' Alyosha said gloomily, 'the evidence against him has greatly increased.'

'And Grigory, Grigory persists in saying that the door was open. Sticks to his story that he saw it. You can't shake him. I went and talked to him myself. He was rude, too!'

'Yes, that's perhaps the strongest evidence against him,' said Alyosha.

'As for Mitya being mad, he certainly seems so now,' Grushenka began suddenly with a sort of specially worried and mysterious air. 'You know, Alyosha, dear, I've been meaning to tell you about it before: I go to him every day and I simply can't help being surprised at him. Tell me, what do you suppose he's always talking about now? He talks and talks and I can't understand a word of it. I keep thinking he's talking about something very clever that a fool like me can't understand. Only he starts talking to me about some babby, that is, about some little baby. "Why," says he, "is the babby so poor? It's for the babby that I'm going to Siberia now. I didn't do it, but I must go to Siberia!" What is it all about, do you think? What babby is he talking about – I couldn't make any sense of it at all! I just burst out crying when he said it, because he spoke so nicely. He cried himself, and I cried, too. And then he suddenly kissed me and made the sign of the cross over me. What is it all about, Alyosha? Please, tell me what "babby" is it?'

'I expect it must be Rakitin, who's been seeing him often lately for some reason,' Alyosha smiled. 'And yet – I don't think it's Rakitin. I didn't see Mitya yesterday. I shall be seeing him today.'

'No, it's not Rakitin. It's his brother Ivan who's been getting him all confused. He's been going to see him and it's him. I'm sure of it,' said Grushenka, and suddenly stopped short.

Alyosha stared at her dumbfounded.

'Ivan? Has he been to see him? Mitya told me himself that Ivan hadn't been once.'

'Oh dear, I am a fool! I've let the cat out of the bag!' cried Grushenka, looking embarrassed and flushing all over. 'Wait, Alyosha, don't say anything! Very well, having said so much, I'll tell you the whole truth. He's been to see him twice, the first time as soon as he arrived. He came hurrying back from Moscow at once, you remember, before I was taken ill. And the second time was a week ago. He told Mitya not to say anything to you about it. Not to tell anyone, as a matter of fact. He came to see him secretly.'

Alyosha sat pondering deeply and considering something. He was obviously startled by the news.

'Ivan doesn't discuss Mitya's case with me,' he said slowly, 'and, generally, he has talked very little to me during the last two months. Every time I went to see him he looked so displeased that I haven't been to see him for the last three weeks. H'm. . . . If he visited him a week ago, then there's certainly been some sort of change in Mitya this week. . . .'

'Yes, a change, a change!' Grushenka put in quickly. 'They have a secret! They have a secret! Mitya told me himself that there was a secret and, mind you, it's such a secret that Mitya can't rest for a moment. He used to be so cheerful before, and, indeed, he's still cheerful, only when he starts tossing his head like that and pacing the room and rubbing the hair on his right temple with a finger, I know there's something worrying him – I know! He used to be so cheerful before – and he was cheerful today, too!'

'But you said he was irritable!'

'Well, yes, he was irritable and he was cheerful. He kept on being irritable for a minute, and then cheerful, and then irritable again. And, you know, Alyosha, I just can't help being surprised at him: there's this horror he has to face, and yet sometimes he roars with laughter at such silly things, just as if he were a baby himself.'

'But is it true that he told you not to tell me about Ivan? Did he actually say: don't tell him?'

'Yes, he did. You see, it's you Mitya's really afraid of. Because there's some secret here. He told me so himself. Alyosha, darling, go and find out what their secret is and come and tell me,' Grushenka suddenly besought him excitedly. 'Do it for me so that I should know the worst that is in store for me! That's what I wanted to see you about.'

'You think it concerns you in some way? But then he wouldn't have told you anything about the secret.'

'I don't know. Perhaps he wants to tell me, but doesn't dare to. Maybe he's just warning me. There is a secret, but what it is he didn't say.'

'What do you think yourself?'

'What do I think? It's the end for me, that's what I think. They've been plotting my end, the three of them, for that Katerina woman is in it, too. It's all her doing. It all comes from her. She's such a "splendid woman" – well, that means that I'm not. He's letting me know that in good time. He's warning me. He's thinking of throwing me over – that's the whole secret. They've planned it together, the three of them – Mitya, Katya, and Ivan. Alyosha, I've been meaning to ask you a long time: a week ago he suddenly told me that Ivan was in love with Katya because he goes to see her so often. Did he tell me the truth or not? Tell me honestly – don't spare me!'

'I won't tell you a lie. Ivan is not in love with Katerina. That's my opinion.'

'Well, that's what I thought, too! He's lying to me, the shameless wretch, that's what it is! And he was jealous of me just now so as to put the blame on me afterwards. You see, he's a fool, he can't conceal anything for long, he's so outspoken. Only I'll show him! I'll show him! You know what he said to me? "You think I did it!" That's what he said. That's what he reproached me with. Oh well, I don't mind! But I'll let that Katya have it good and proper in court! I'll say something there that – I'll tell them everything there!'

And again she cried bitterly.

'Now this I can tell you for certain, Grushenka,' Alyosha said, getting up. 'First, that he loves you. He loves you more than anyone in the world. And only you, believe me. I know. That I do know. Secondly, I must tell you that I do not want to worm the secret out of him, and if he does tell me today, I'll tell him frankly that I've promised to tell you. Then I'll come to you today and tell you. Only – I can't help thinking that Katerina has nothing to do with it at all, and that the secret is about something else. I'm sure I'm right. And it's not likely to be about Katerina. That's what I think. And now – good-bye.'

Alyosha pressed her hand. Grushenka was still crying. He saw that she had little faith in his consolation, but, at any rate, she felt better for having told him what was worrying her and got it off her chest. He was sorry to leave her in such a state, but he was in a hurry. He had many things to do still.

2

The Injured Foot

THE first of these things was at the home of Mrs Khokhlakov, and he hurried there so as to settle it as quickly as possible and not be late for Mitya. Mrs Khokhlakov had not been feeling well for the last three weeks: her foot had for some reason swelled up, and though she was not in bed, she was half-reclining on the settee in her boudoir in an attractive but decorous *déshabillé*. Alyosha had on one occasion said to himself with an innocent smile that in spite of her illness Mrs Khokhlakov was anxious to show off her clothes – topknots, ribbons, low-cut blouses, and he had an idea why she did it, but dismissed such thoughts as frivolous. During the last two months the young civil servant Perkhotin had become, among her other visitors, a very frequent caller. Alyosha had not called for four days and, on entering the house, was about to go straight up to Lise's room, for it was she he wanted to see. Lise had sent a maid to him the day before with an urgent request to go and see her at once 'on a very important matter', which, for certain reasons, had interested Alyosha very much. But while the maid went to announce him, Mrs Khokhlakov learnt of his arrival from someone and at once sent to ask him to come to her 'just for a minute'. Alyosha decided that he'd better first accede to the mother's request, for, if not, she'd be sending someone to Lise's room every other minute while he was there. Mrs Khokhlakov was lying on the settee, particularly smartly dressed and evidently in a state of extraordinary nervous excitement. She greeted Alyosha with cries of rapture.

'It's ages, ages since I saw you! A whole week – my goodness! Oh, I'm sorry, you were here only four days ago, weren't you? On Wednesday. You've come to see Lise, and I'm quite sure you wanted to tiptoe straight to her room, so that I shouldn't hear you. Dear, dear Alexey, if only you knew how worried I am about her! But of that later. It may be the most important thing, but of that later. Dear Alexey, I trust you with my Lise completely. Since the death of Father Zossima – God rest his soul,' (she crossed herself) 'I look upon you as a hermit, though you do look charming in your new suit. Where did you find such a tailor here? But no, no, that isn't very important. Of that later. You don't mind my calling you Alyosha sometimes, do you? I'm an old woman and I can permit myself such liberties,' she smiled coquettishly, 'but of that later, too. The main thing is that I mustn't forget the main thing. Please, remind me of it yourself the moment I begin talking of something else. You must say to me: "And what about the main thing?" Oh, but how am I to tell what the main thing is? Ever since Lise took back her promise – her childish promise, Alexey, to marry you – you've realized, of course, that it was only the playful fancy of a sick girl who has so long been confined to her wheel-chair – thank goodness, she can walk now. The new doctor Katerina got from Moscow for your unhappy brother, who will tomorrow – but why talk of tomorrow? I'm ready to die at the very thought of tomorrow! Of curiosity chiefly. . . . In short, this doctor was here yesterday and saw Lise. I paid him fifty roubles for the visit. But that's not what I want to talk to you about. Again it's not that. You see, I'm all mixed up now. I'm in such a hurry. Why am I in such a hurry? I'm sure I don't know. It's awful how I simply don't know now why I'm doing things. Everything seems to be tangled up in a kind of ball. I'm afraid you're so bored that you'll jump up and rush out of the room and I shan't see you again. Oh dear! Why are we sitting here and – first of all – coffee! Julia, Glafira, coffee!'

Alyosha hastily thanked her and said that he had just had coffee.

'Where?'

'At Miss Svetlov's.'

'At – at that woman's? Oh, it's she who's brought ruin upon everybody. And yet, I don't know. I'm told she's become a saint, though rather late in the day, I should think. She should have done it before, when it would have been of some use. But what's the use of it now? Not a word, not a word, dear Alexey, for I've got to tell you so many things that I'm afraid I shan't tell you anything. . . . This dreadful trial. . . . I shall certainly go, I'm getting ready for it. I'll be carried there in my chair. I can manage to sit up and, besides, I'll have people with me. You know, of course, that I'm one of the witnesses. How am I going to speak? Goodness, how am I going to speak? I simply don't know what I'm going to say. You see, I'll have to take an oath. I will, won't I?'

'Yes, but I don't think you'll be well enough to appear.'

'I can sit up. Oh, but you're confusing me! This trial, this wild act, and then they're all going to Siberia, others get married, and all this happens so quickly, so quickly, and everything's changing, and, at last, there's nothing! Everyone's old and everyone's at the brink of the grave. Well, it can't be helped, I suppose. Oh, I'm so tired. This Katya – *cette charmante personne*, has disappointed all my hopes: now she's going to follow one of your brothers to Siberia, and your other brother will go after her and live in a neighbouring town, and they'll all be torturing each other. It drives me out of my mind. But worst of all is the publicity: they have been writing about it scores of times in all the Petersburg and Moscow papers. Oh, by the way, they've been writing about me, too, can you imagine it? They've been saying I was your brother's "girl-friend" – I can't utter the horrid word. Imagine it! Just imagine it!'

'Impossible! Where did they write this about you? What did they write?'

'I'll show it to you in a moment. I got it yesterday – read it yesterday. Here, in the Petersburg paper *Rumours*. The paper began coming out this year. I'm awfully fond of rumours, and I've subscribed to it and that's what I got it for, that's the sort of rumour it is. Here, here, read it.'

And she held out to Alyosha a sheet of newspaper which she had kept under her pillow.

She was not so much upset as crushed and perhaps everything really had become tangled up in a ball in her head. The newspaper item was very typical and, of course, must have been a great shock to her. But, luckily, she was not capable of concentrating on any one subject at the moment, and so might forget all about the newspaper paragraph in a minute and start talking about something else. Alyosha had known for some time that the dreadful trial had become sensational news all over Russia and, good Lord, what wild reports and newspaper stories about his brother, the Karamazovs and even about himself he had read during those two months! One paper even reported that he had been so horrified by his brother's crime that he had entered a monastery and become a hermit; another denied this report and stated that he and Father Zossima had stolen the monastery funds and 'decamped from the monastery'. The report in *Rumours* was headed: 'From Skotoprigonyevsk (alas, that was the name of our little town, which I have so long concealed): The Karamazov Trial.' It was very brief, and Mrs Khokhlakov was not mentioned by name and, in fact, no names were mentioned at all. It was merely stated that the accused, whose forthcoming trial had created such a sensation, was a retired army captain of arrogant manners, a loafer and a serf-owner, who devoted all his time to all sorts of love affairs and exercised a particular fascination on 'certain ladies dying of boredom in solitude'. One of these ladies, a bored widow, who did her best to look young, though she had a grown-up daughter, had been so fascinated by him that only two hours before the murder she offered him three thousand roubles, provided he ran away with her at once to the gold-mines. But the villain preferred to murder and rob his father and so get the three thousand he wanted so badly, hoping to escape his punishment rather than drag himself off to Siberia with the middle-aged charms of this bored lady. This playful report concluded, as was to be expected, by expressing the correspondent's high-minded indignation at the immorality of the parricide and the recently abolished institution of serfdom. Alyosha read it with interest and, folding up the sheet, returned it to Mrs Khokhlakov.

'Well,' she rattled on, 'it is me, isn't it? It must be me, for barely more than an hour before I suggested gold-mines to him and all of a sudden "middle-aged charms"! That wasn't why I suggested it to him, was it? The correspondent did it on purpose! May the Eternal Judge forgive him for the middle-aged charms as I'm forgiving him, for you know who it is, don't you? It's your friend Rakitin.'

'Perhaps,' said Alyosha, 'though I've heard nothing about it.'

'It's he – he, there's no "perhaps" about it! You see, I turned him out of the house. You know all that story, don't you?'

'I know that you told him not to visit you in the future, but why you did so I – I didn't hear it from you, at any rate.'

'Oh, so you heard it from him! Well, does he abuse me? Does he abuse me very much?'

'Yes, he does, but then he abuses everybody. But why you turned him out I haven't heard from him. I don't see him often now, any-way. We are not friends.'

'Well, in that case I'll tell you all about it and, I suppose, I may as well confess that on one point I'm to blame too. But, mind, only on one small point, so small that it's hardly worth mentioning it. You see, my darling Alyosha' (Mrs Khokhlakov suddenly assumed a rather playful air and a charming, though enigmatic, smile played about her lips), 'you see, I suspect – I'm sorry, Alyosha, I'm talking to you like a mother – oh, no, no, I'm talking to you as to my own father because – er – mother is quite out of place here. . . . Well, let's say just as I would to Father Zossima at confession. Yes, that's it. That fits the occasion very well. I called you a hermit just now – well, that poor young man, your friend Rakitin (oh dear, I simply cannot be angry with him – I am angry and mad at him, but not very), in short, that thoughtless young man – just fancy! – suddenly took it into his head to fall in love with me! I noticed it later, only later, but at first, that is, a month ago, he began calling on me more often, almost every day, though of course we were acquainted before. I didn't suspect anything and – and suddenly the whole thing dawned on me and, to my astonishment, I began to notice things. . . . You know that two months ago I began receiving Mr Peter Perkhotin, a modest, charming, and worthy young man who is in the service here. You met him here many times yourself. And he is a serious, worthy young man, isn't he? He usually calls once in three days and not every day (though I shouldn't mind him coming every day), and he's always so well dressed. I'm generally very fond of young people, Alyosha, talented and modest young people, just like you, and he has almost the mind of a statesman. He talks so charmingly, and I'll certainly, most certainly, put in a good word for him. He's a future diplomat. On that terrible day he practically saved me from death by coming to see me at night. Well, and your friend Rakitin always used to come in such awful boots, and he would stretch his legs out on the carpet. . . . In short, he even began throwing out all sorts of hints, and one day, as he was leaving, he suddenly squeezed my hand very hard. And just as he squeezed my hand I had an awful pain in my leg. He had met Mr Perkhotin before and, you know, he was always jeering at him, always jeering at him. Just growled at him for some reason. I just used to watch them carrying on together and couldn't help laughing inwardly. Well, one day, as I was sitting here alone, no, I mean, lying down alone, Mr Rakitin came in suddenly and – just fancy! – brought me some verses, a short poem on my bad foot. I mean, a description of my foot in a poem. Wait, how did it go? —

> Sweet little foot, sweet little foot
> Why do you hurt so much? . . .

or something like that. I'm afraid I can never memorize poetry. I've got it here. I'll show it to you later. Oh, so charming, so charming! And it was not only about my little foot. It was a very edifying poem with a most charming idea, too, only I've forgotten it. In fact, it was just the thing for an album. Well, I naturally thanked him and he was evidently flattered. I'd hardly time to thank him when in came Mr Perkhotin, and Mr Rakitin suddenly looked as black as night. I could see that Mr Perkhotin had interfered with his plans, for he certainly wanted to say something after reciting his poem to me. I had a feeling he would, and just at that moment Mr Perkhotin came in. I at once showed Mr Perkhotin the poem without telling him who the author was. But I'm sure, I'm quite sure, that he immediately guessed, though he won't admit it to this day, but keeps saying that he didn't know. But he says that on purpose. Well, Mr Perkhotin immediately burst out laughing and began criticizing it: what awful doggerel! he said. Must have been written by some seminarist. And, you know, with such passion, with such passion! Instead of laughing, your friend suddenly flew into a rage. Good gracious, I thought to myself, they're going to have a fight! "I wrote it," Mr Rakitin said, "I wrote it as a joke, for I consider the writing of poetry degrading. . . . But my verses are good. They want to put up a monument to your Pushkin for his verses on women's feet, but my verses have a political significance and you," he said, "are a reactionary, an upholder of serfdom. You have no humanitarian feelings. You do not share any of our modern enlightened ideas, modern political development has passed you by," he said. "You're a civil servant," he said, "and you take bribes!" Well, here I began shouting and imploring them. But, you know, Mr Perkhotin is far from timid and he suddenly assumed a most gentlemanly tone: he looked sarcastically at him, listened and apologized: "I'm sorry," he said, "I didn't know. Had I known, I'd have praised it. Poets," he said, "are all so thin-skinned. . . ." In short, such derision delivered in a most gentlemanly tone. He explained to me himself afterwards that he had said it all ironically, and I thought he really meant it! Well, as I lay there, just as before you now, I thought to myself: would it or would it not be ladylike if I turned Mr Rakitin out for shouting so indecently at a visitor in my house? And – would you believe it? – I lay here with my eyes shut, thinking: would it be ladylike or not? I was awfully worried, and my heart was beating, but I just couldn't make up my mind whether to scream or not to scream. One voice kept telling me: Scream, and another: No, don't scream! But the moment the other voice had said it, I suddenly screamed and fainted. Well, of course, there was a terrible to-do. Then I got up and said to Mr Rakitin: "I'm sorry to have to say it, but I don't wish to receive you in my house again." So I turned him out. Oh, dear Alexey! I know myself I did wrong. I was lying. I wasn't angry with him at all. But I suddenly fancied, yes, suddenly – that's the main thing – that it would be such a wonderful scene. Only, you know, the scene was quite natural, because I even burst into tears, and I cried for several days afterwards, and then, after dinner one day, I suddenly forgot all about it. So he has stopped calling for the last fortnight, and I couldn't help wondering whether he wouldn't come again at all. That was yesterday and in the evening these "rumours" arrived. I read it and gasped. Who could have written it? Why, he, of course. He went home that afternoon, sat down and wrote it, sent it off and – they published it. You see, it only happened a fortnight ago. Only, Alyosha, goodness, what am I saying? I don't say what I mean, do I? Oh dear, I just can't help it!'

'I simply must be in time to see my brother today,' Alyosha murmured.

'Of course, of course! You've brought it all back to me. Listen, what is temporary insanity?'

'What sort of temporary insanity?'

'I mean a plea of temporary insanity. A kind of temporary insanity for which all is forgiven. Whatever you do – you'll be acquitted at once.'

'How do you mean?'

'This is what I mean – this Katya. Oh, she's such a charming girl, only I can't for the life of me make out whom she is in love with. She came to see me recently and I couldn't get anything out of her.

Particularly as she only talks about trivial things to me now. I mean, only about my health and nothing else, and in such a high and mighty tone, too. Well, I said to myself: All right, what do I care? Oh yes, the temporary insanity. That's why the doctor has come. You know that a doctor has come, don't you? Of course, you do. He's a specialist on mental disorders. You sent for him yourself, I mean, no, not you, but Katya. It's always Katya. Well, you see, a man may be perfectly sane and suddenly he has an attack of temporary insanity. He may be fully conscious and know what he is doing, and yet he's temporarily insane. Well, you see, Dmitry was probably suffering from temporary insanity. You see, as soon as our new courts were opened, they at once found out all about temporary insanity. This is the great benefit conferred by the new courts. The doctor has been to see me and he kept asking me about that evening, about the gold-mines, I mean. What was he like then? Why, of course, he was suffering from temporary insanity: he came in and started shouting: Money, money, three thousand, give me three thousand! And then he went away and suddenly committed the murder. "I don't want to murder him," he said, and off he went and murdered him. That's why they are going to acquit him – because he was fighting against it, and yet murdered him.'

'But he did not murder him,' Alyosha interrupted her a little sharply.

He was getting more and more overcome by uneasiness and impatience.

'I know. It's the old man Grigory who killed him.'

'Grigory?' cried Alyosha.

'Yes, yes! It was Grigory. Dmitry knocked him down, and then he got up, saw the door open, went in and killed Mr Karamazov....'

'But why, why?'

'Because he was suffering from temporary insanity. Dmitry hit him over the head, he came to, got an attack of temporary insanity, went in and killed him. And if he says he didn't, it's perhaps because he doesn't remember. Only, you see, it will be better, much better if Dmitry killed him. As a matter of fact, that's who it was, though I say it was Grigory. It was certainly Dmitry and it's better so, much better! Oh, it isn't better because a son has killed his father: I'm not in favour of that at all. Children should, on the contrary, honour their parents. But it's better all the same if it should be he, for then you needn't worry at all, for he did it without being aware of what he was doing, or rather being aware of everything but without knowing what was happening to him. Yes, let them acquit him: it's so humane! And also so that people may see the benefit conferred by the new courts. I knew nothing about it, but I'm told it's been like that a long time. When I heard about it yesterday, I was so struck by it that I wanted to send for you at once. And if he's acquitted, he must come and have dinner with me straight from the court. I'll invite my friends and we'll drink to the new courts. I don't think he'd be dangerous, do you? Besides, I'll invite a large number of friends, so that if he does start something, he could always be led out, and then he may perhaps become a Justice of the Peace or something in another town, for people who've been in trouble themselves make the best judges. And, anyway, who is not suffering from temporary insanity nowadays? You, I, everyone is temporarily insane, and there have been so many examples of it: a man sits singing a love song, suddenly something displeases him, he pulls out a pistol and kills the first person he happens to see, and then everyone forgives him for it. I read about it recently, and all the doctors confirmed it. The doctors are confirming it now, all of them are confirming it. Why, my Lise is also suffering from temporary insanity. She made me cry yesterday and the day before, but today I realized that she was simply temporarily insane. Oh, Lise makes me so unhappy! I'm sure she must be quite insane. Why did she send for you? She did send for you, didn't she? Or did you come to see her of your own accord?'

'Yes, she sent for me and I'm going to her now,' said Alyosha, getting up resolutely.

'Oh, dear, dear Alexey, that is perhaps the main thing,' cried Mrs Khokhlakov, suddenly bursting into tears. 'God knows that I trust Lise with you and it doesn't matter a bit that she sent for you without telling her mother about it. But I'm sorry to say I cannot trust your brother Ivan with my daughter so easily, though I still think him a most chivalrous young man. And yet, you know, he's been to see Lise and I knew nothing about it.'

'Has he? When?' Alyosha asked, looking terribly surprised. He did not resume his seat, but listened to her standing.

'I'll tell you. That's perhaps why I asked you to come, for I'm afraid I don't really know myself why I asked you to come. What happened was this: Ivan had been to see me twice after his return from Moscow. The first time he just called as a friend, and the second time quite recently. Katya was here and he came because he heard she was here. I naturally did not expect him to call often, for I knew how busy he was, as it is, *vous comprenez cette affaire et la mort terrible de votre papa*, but all of a sudden I learnt that he'd been here again, only not to see me, but Lise. That was six days ago. He came, stayed five minutes and went away. I got to know about it three days later from Glafira, so that it was a great shock to me. I sent for Lise at once, but she just laughed: he thought, she said, that you were asleep, so he came to ask me how you were. Well, that's what it was, of course. Only Lise, Lise, goodness, how she grieves me! Just fancy, one night, four days ago, just after you had gone the last time you came to see her, she suddenly had a fit. Cries, screams, hysterics! Why don't I ever have hysterics? Next day she had another fit, and the day after another and yesterday, yesterday that attack of temporary insanity. She suddenly shouted at me: "I hate Ivan and I demand that you shouldn't receive him! I want you to tell him never to call again!" I was dumbfounded at such an unexpected outburst and I said to her: "Why should I refuse to see such an excellent young man who is, besides, so well educated and so unhappy?" For, after all, what he had to go through so recently would make him unhappy rather than happy, wouldn't it? She suddenly burst out laughing at my words and, you know, so offensively. Well, I was glad, because I thought I had made her laugh and her fit would pass off now, particularly as I had a mind to tell Ivan not to call again, on account of his strange visits without my consent, and to demand an explanation from him. Only this morning Lise woke up and was annoyed with Julia and – just fancy! – struck her across the face. But that is monstrous, for, you know, I'm always very polite to my servants. Then, suddenly, an hour later, she was embracing Julia and kissing her feet. And she sent a message to me that she wasn't coming to see me and would never come to see me again, and when I dragged myself off to her, she started crying and kissing me and, while kissing me, pushed me out of the room without saying a word, so that I could not find anything out. Now, dear Alexey, I pin all my hopes upon you, and it goes without saying that the whole of my life is in your hands. I simply ask you to go to Lise now, find everything out from her, as only you know how, and come back and tell me, her mother. For, you understand, I shall die, I shall simply die if this goes on, or I shall run away. I can bear it no longer. I have patience, but I may lose it, and then – then anything may happen! Oh, dear me, here's Mr Perkhotin at last!' cried Mrs Khokhlakov, beaming all over, as she saw Perkhotin enter the room. 'You're late! You're late! Well, do sit down, please. Speak, put me out of my suspense. Well, what do you think about that lawyer? Where are you off to, Alexey?'

'To Lise.'

'Oh, yes! So you won't forget what I asked you, will you? It's a matter of life and death!'

'Of course I won't forget, if only it's possible – but I'm afraid I'm so late,' murmered Alyosha, beating a hasty retreat.

'No, you must, you must come and tell me, and not "if it's possible", or I shall die!' Mrs Khokhlakov called after him, but Alyosha had already left the room.

3

The Little She-Devil

ON entering Lise's room he found her half-lying in the chair in which she had been wheeled when she was still unable to walk. She did not attempt to get up to meet him, but her keen, sharp eyes were fixed on him intently. Her eyes were a little inflamed, her face was pale and sallow. Alyosha was surprised to see her so changed in three days. She even looked thinner. She did not hold out her hand to him. He touched her long, slender fingers which lay motionless on her dress, then sat down silently opposite her.

'I know,' Lise said sharply, 'that you are in a hurry to get to the prison, and that mother has kept you for two hours and has just been telling you about me and Julia.'

'How do you know that?' asked Alyosha.

'I was eavesdropping. What are you staring at me like that

for? If I want to eavesdrop, I eavesdrop. There's nothing wrong about it. I'm not sorry.'

'Are you upset about something?'

'Not at all, I'm very pleased. I've just been thinking for the hundredth time how fortunate it is that I refused you and won't be your wife. You're no good as a husband: if I were to marry you and give you a note to take to the man I fell in love with after you, you'd take it and most certainly give it to him *and* bring back his answer, too. And when you were forty, you'd still be carrying such notes for me.'

She suddenly laughed.

'There's something spiteful and at the same time innocent about you,' Alyosha smiled at her.

'The only thing that's innocent about me is that I'm not ashamed of you. And not only am I not ashamed of you, but I don't want to be ashamed of you, of you in particular. Alyosha, why don't I respect you? I love you very much, but I don't respect you. If I respected you, I wouldn't have said it without being ashamed, would I?'

'You wouldn't.'

'And do you believe that I'm not ashamed of you?'

'No, I don't.'

Lise again laughed nervously. She was talking very rapidly.

'I sent your brother Dmitry some sweets in prison. Alyosha, you know, you're so nice! I'll love you awfully for having so quickly given me your permission not to love you.'

'Why did you send for me today, Lise?'

'I wanted to tell you a certain wish of mine. I wish someone would tear me to pieces, marry me and then tear me to pieces, deceive me and leave me. I don't want to be happy.'

'You love disorder?'

'Oh no, I don't want disorder. I keep wanting to set fire to the house. I keep imagining how I'd go up and set fire to it by stealth. Yes, it must be by stealth. They'll be trying to put it out, but it will go on burning. And I'll know and say nothing. Oh, what silly nonsense! And how boring it is!'

She waved her hand with disgust.

'You're too well off,' Alyosha said quietly.

'Would it be better if I were poor?'

'Yes.'

'That's what your deceased monk told you. It's not true. What does it matter if I'm rich and everyone else poor? I'll be eating sweets and drinking cream and give nothing to anyone. Oh, don't say anything,' she waved her hand, though Alyosha never opened his mouth, 'don't say anything, you've told me all before. I know it all by heart. It's boring. If I were poor, I'd kill someone, and if I'm rich, I shall probably kill someone too. What's the use of sitting about and doing nothing. And you know what I want? I want to reap, to reap rye. I'll marry you and you'll become a peasant. A real peasant. We'll keep a colt. Would you like that? Do you know Kalganov?'

'Yes.'

'He's always going about and dreaming. He says: what's the use of living if you can dream? One can dream the most gay things, while to live is a bore. And yet he's going to be married soon. He has already made me a declaration of love. Can you spin tops?'

'Yes.'

'Well, he's just like a top: wind him up and let him spin, and then keep lashing at him, keep lashing at him with a whip. If I marry him, I shall spin him round and round all his life. You're not ashamed to sit with me?'

'No.'

'You're awfully angry because I don't talk about holy things. I don't want to be holy. What do they do to you in the next world for the greatest sin? You must know all about it.'

'God will censure you,' Alyosha said, looking at her closely.

'Well, that's just what I want. I'd come and I'd be censured, and I'd suddenly burst out laughing in their faces. Oh, I do so want to set fire to a house, Alyosha, to our house. You don't believe me?'

'Why not? There are children of twelve who long to set fire to something. And they do. It's a sort of illness.'

'It isn't true! It isn't true! There may be such children, but I'm not talking about that.'

'You take evil for good: it's a momentary crisis. Your former illness is perhaps responsible for it.'

'So you do despise me, after all! I simply don't want to do good. I want to do evil. And it's nothing to do with my illness.'

'Why do evil?'

'So that nothing should remain anywhere. Oh, how nice it would be if nothing remained! You know, Alyosha, sometimes I think of doing a lot of evil and everything that's bad, and I'd do it for a long time by stealth, and suddenly everyone would know about it. They would all surround me and point their fingers at me, and I'd look at them all. That would be very nice. Why would it be so nice, Alyosha?'

'Oh, I expect it's just a craving to crush something good or, as you said, to set fire to it. That, too, happens.'

'I wasn't only saying it. I'm going to do it.'

'I believe you.'

'Oh, how I love you for saying that you believe me. And you're not lying. You're not lying at all. Or do you think perhaps that I'm saying all this to you on purpose, just to tease you?'

'No, I don't think so. Though, I daresay, there's a little of that desire, too.'

'There is a little. I shall never lie to you,' she said, with strangely flashing eyes.

Alyosha was more and more struck by her seriousness: there was not a trace of mockery or jesting in her face now, though before gaiety and jesting never deserted her even in her most 'serious' moments.

'There are moments when people love crime,' Alyosha said thoughtfully.

'Yes, yes, you've expressed my thought. They love it. They always love it, and not only at "moments". You know, it's as though everyone had agreed to lie about it, and they have been lying about it ever since. They all say they hate evil, but in their heart of hearts they all love it.'

'And you are still reading bad books?'

'Yes, I am. Mother reads them and hides them under her pillow and I steal them.'

'How aren't you ashamed to destroy yourself?'

'I want to destroy myself. There's a boy here who lay down between the railway lines and the train passed over him. Lucky boy! Listen, your brother is being tried now for murdering his father, but everyone loves his having killed his father.'

'Loves his having killed his father?'

'Yes, they all love it! They all say it's horrible, but in their hearts they love it. I, for one, love it.'

'There's a grain of truth in what you say about everyone,' said Alyosha quietly.

'Oh, what wonderful ideas you have!' Lise shrieked in delight. 'And a monk, too! You wouldn't believe how I respect you, Alyosha, for never telling a lie. Oh, I'll tell you a very funny dream I had! I sometimes dream of devils. It's night, I'm in my room, and suddenly there are devils everywhere. In all the corners and under the table, and they open doors, and behind the doors there are crowds of them, and they all want to come in and seize me. And they are already coming near and taking hold of me. But suddenly I cross myself and they all draw back, they are afraid, only they don't go away, but stand near the door and in the corners, waiting. And then I'm suddenly overcome by a desire to begin cursing God in a loud voice, and I begin cursing him and they all rush at me again in a crowd, they're so pleased, and they're again about to lay hands on me, and I cross myself again and they draw back at once. It's great fun. Oh, it takes my breath away.'

'I've had the same dream, too,' Alyosha said suddenly.

'Have you?' Lise cried in surprise. 'Listen, Alyosha, don't laugh at me, it's awfully important: is it possible for two different people to have the same dream?'

'I suppose it is.'

'Alyosha, I'm telling you this is awfully important,' Lise went on with a sort of intense astonishment. 'It isn't the dream that is important, but that you should have had the same dream as me. You've never lied to me, don't lie to me now. Is it true? You're not laughing?'

'It is true.'

Lise was terribly struck by something and she was silent for half a minute.

'Alyosha, come and see me, come and see me more often,' she said suddenly in a beseeching voice.

'I shall always come to see you, all my life,' replied Alyosha firmly.

'You see, I'm telling this to you alone,' Lise began again. 'I'm telling it to myself and to you. To you alone in the whole world. And more readily to you than to myself. And I'm not a bit ashamed before you, not a bit. Alyosha, why am I not a bit ashamed before you, not a bit? Alyosha, is it true that Jews steal children at Easter and kill them?'

'I don't know.'

'I read it in a book about a trial somewhere, and that a Jew at first cut off a four-year-old child's fingers on both hands, and then crucified him, nailed him to a wall, and then said at his trial that the boy died soon, within four hours. Soon, indeed! He said the boy kept moaning and that he stood there enjoying it. That's good.'

'Good?'

'Good. I sometimes imagine that it was I who crucified him. He would hang on the wall and moan and I'd sit opposite him and eat stewed pineapples. I'm awfully fond of stewed pineapples. Are you?'

Alyosha looked at her in silence. Her pale, sallow face became suddenly distorted and her eyes glowed.

'You know, when I read about that Jew, I shook with sobs all night. I kept imagining how the little boy screamed and moaned (four-year-old boys understand, you know), and the thought of that pineapple *compote* kept hammering in my brain. Next morning I sent a letter to a man, telling him that he *must* come and see me. He came and I told him about the boy and the stewed pineapples, told him *everything*, *everything*, and said that it was "good". He suddenly laughed and said that it really was good. Then he got up and went away. He only stayed five minutes. Did he despise me? Did he? Tell me, tell me, Alyosha, did he or didn't he despise me?' she asked with flashing eyes, sitting up straight on the settee.

'Tell me,' Alyosha said agitatedly, 'did you send for that man yourself?'

'Yes.'

'You sent him a letter?'

'I did.'

'Just to ask him about that, about the child?'

'No, not about that at all. Not at all about that. But when he came in, I asked him at once about that. He replied, laughed and went away.'

'That man behaved decently to you,' Alyosha said softly.

'But did he despise me? Did he laugh at me?'

'No, because I suppose he believes in the stewed pineapples himself. He, too, is very sick now, Lise.'

'Yes, he does believe in it!' cried Lise with flashing eyes.

'He despises no one,' Alyosha went on. 'He merely doesn't believe anyone. But if he doesn't believe, he, of course, despises, too.'

'So he despises me also? Me?'

'You also.'

'That's good,' Lise cried, grinding her teeth. 'When he went out and laughed, I felt that it was good to be despised. And the boy with the cut-off fingers is good, and to be despised is good.'

And she laughed in Alyosha's face with a sort of feverish malice.

'Do you know, Alyosha, do you know, I'd like. . . . Alyosha, save me!' she cried, suddenly jumping up from the settee and, rushing up to him, she flung her arms tightly round him. 'Save me,' she almost moaned. 'Would I have said what I told you just now to anyone else in the world? And I spoke the truth, the truth, the truth! I'll kill myself because everything is so loathsome to me! I don't want to live, because everything is so loathsome to me! Everything is loathsome to me, everything! Alyosha, why don't you love me at all?' she concluded in a frenzy.

'I do love you!' Alyosha replied warmly.

'And will you cry for me? Will you?'

'I will.'

'Not because I didn't want to be your wife, but simply cry for me? Simply?'

'I will.'

'Thank you! All I want is your tears. Let everyone else punish me and trample me underfoot, everyone, everyone, not excepting *anyone!* Because I love no one. You hear, no one! On the contrary, I hate him! Go now, Alyosha. It's time you went to your brother!' She suddenly tore herself away from him.

'But how can I leave you like this?' Alyosha said almost in alarm.

'Go to your brother. The prison will be shut. Go! Here's your hat. Give Mitya my love. Go, go!'

And she almost pushed Alyosha out of the door by force. Alyosha looked at her in mournful perplexity, when he suddenly felt that a letter had been thrust into his hand, a little note, folded up tightly and sealed. He looked at it and instantly read the inscription: 'To Ivan Karamazov'. He glanced at Lise. Her face looked almost stern.

'Give it to him! Be sure to give it to him!' she ordered him in a frenzy, shaking all over. 'Today! At once! Or I'll poison myself! That's why I sent for you!'

And she quickly slammed the door. The bolt was shot noisily. Alyosha put the letter in his pocket and went straight downstairs without going in to see Mrs Khokhlakov, forgetting all about her, in fact. And as soon as Alyosha had gone, Lise unbolted the door, opened it a little, put her finger in the crack, and slamming the door, pinched her finger with all the force at her command. Ten seconds later, releasing her finger, she went back to her chair slowly and quietly, sat up erect in it, and began examining intently her blackened finger and the blood that oozed from under the nail. Her lips quivered, and she whispered rapidly to herself:

'Mean, mean, mean, mean!'

4

A Hymn and a Secret

IT was very late (a November day is not very long anyhow) when Alyosha rang at the prison gates. Dusk was beginning to fall. But Alyosha knew that he would be admitted to Mitya without hindrance. Things in our town are just like everywhere else. At first, of course, after the conclusion of the preliminary investigation, certain necessary formalities were still observed in admitting relations and a few other people to see Mitya, but later on the formalities were not so much relaxed as that certain exceptions were made for at least some of the people who came to visit Mitya. Indeed, sometimes even the interviews with Mitya in a room set aside for the purpose took place almost without the presence of warders. However, there were not many persons who enjoyed that privilege: there were only Grushenka, Alyosha, and Rakitin. But then the district police inspector Makarov was very favourably disposed towards Grushenka. The old man could not forgive himself for the way he had shouted at her in Mokroye. Having learnt the whole story about her afterwards, he completely changed his opinion of her. And, strange to say, though he was firmly convinced of Mitya's guilt, he had begun regarding him more and more tolerantly since his imprisonment: 'He is probably a good fellow at heart,' he thought, 'but he has ruined himself with drinking and leading a disorderly life.' His former horror gave place to pity. As for Alyosha, the district police inspector was very fond of him and had known him a long time; Rakitin, who had got into the habit of visiting Mitya very often during the last few weeks, was one of the closest friends of 'the police inspector's young ladies', as he called them, and was always to be found hanging about in their house. He, furthermore, gave lessons in the house of the prison governor, a good-natured old man, though a great stickler for formalities. Alyosha, on the other hand, was an old and particular friend of the prison governor, who liked to discuss 'abstruse' subjects with him. The prison governor, for instance, did not so much respect as fear Ivan Karamazov, and, chiefly, his opinions, though he was a great philosopher himself, having reached his conclusions through 'his own reasoning'. But he, somehow, felt powerfully attracted to Alyosha. During the last year the old man had happened to devote himself to the study of the Apocrypha and he constantly discussed his impressions with his young friend. Before, he even used to go and see him at the monastery and talked to him and the monks for hours on end. In short, even if Alyosha were late, he had only to go and see the prison governor and everything would be arranged. Besides, everyone in prison to the last warder had got used to Alyosha. The sentries, of course, did not interfere with him so long as he had the permission of the authorities. When summoned from his cell, Mitya always went downstairs to the room where the interviews took place. As he entered the room, Alyosha ran into Rakitin, who was just about to leave Mitya. Both of them were talking loudly. Mitya, as he saw him off, was roaring with laughter, while Rakitin seemed to be grumbling. Rakitin did not like meeting Alyosha, especially of late. He barely spoke to him and even greeted him stiffly. When he saw Alyosha coming in now, he knit his brows and looked away, as though preoccupied with buttoning his big warm overcoat with its fur collar. Then he began looking at once for his umbrella.

'Mustn't forget any of my things,' he muttered, simply to say something.

'Don't forget other people's things,' Mitya joked and at once burst out laughing at his own witticism.

Rakitin flared up at once.

'Tell that to your Karamazovs, the spawn of a slave-owner, and not to Rakitin,' he cried suddenly, shaking with fury.

'What's the matter? I was joking!' cried Mitya. 'Oh, hell! They're all like that,' he turned to Alyosha, nodding in the direction of Rakitin, who had rushed out of the room. 'A moment ago he was sitting here, looking cheerful and laughing, and now he suddenly flies into a rage! Didn't even nod to you. Have you fallen out with him completely? Why are you so late? I've not been so much waiting as longing for you all morning. But never mind. We'll make up for it now.'

'Why is he coming to see you so often now?' asked Alyosha, nodding at the door, behind which Rakitin had disappeared. 'You haven't become such great friends with him, have you?'

'Friends with Rakitin? No, not really. And, besides, he's a bloody swine! Thinks I'm a blackguard. They can't take a joke, either. That's their chief trouble. Never understand a joke. And they have arid souls, too, arid and trivial, just as mine was when I was driven up to the prison and looked at the prison walls. But he's a clever chap. Very clever. Well, Alexey, I'm done for now!'

He sat down on the bench and made Alyosha sit down beside him.

'Yes, the trial's tomorrow. Well, you haven't given up all hope, have you, Mitya?' asked Alyosha, timidly.

'What are you talking about?' said Mitya, looking rather vaguely at him. 'Oh, the trial! Oh, to hell with it! Up to now we've been talking about all sorts of trivial things, about that trial, for instance, and I said nothing to you about the most important thing. Yes, tomorrow's the trial, but I did not have the trial in mind when I said that I was done for. It's not I who am done for, but what's in me that's gone, finished, done for. What are you looking so critically at me for?'

'What have you in mind, Mitya?'

'Ideas, ideas, that's what it is! Ethics. What is ethics?'

'Ethics?' Alyosha repeated with surprise.

'Yes. Is it a science?'

'Yes, there is such a science, only I'm afraid I can't explain to you what kind of science it is.'

'Rakitin knows. Rakitin knows a lot, damn him! He won't be a monk. He's planning to go to Petersburg. There, he says, he'll be working as a critic, but a critic with a progressive tendency. Well, I suppose he may be of use and make a career for himself, too. Oh, they're all great at making careers. To hell with ethics. I'm done for, Alexey, my dear, simple-hearted fellow! I love you more than anyone. My heart aches for you – that's the truth. Who was Karl Bernard?'

'Karl Bernard?' Alyosha was surprised again.

'No, not Karl – wait, I made a mistake. Claude Bernard. What was he? A chemist or what?'

'He must be some sort of scientist,' replied Alyosha. 'Only I'm afraid I can't tell you much about him, either. I've heard he was a scientist, but what kind of scientist I don't know.'

'Well, to hell with him,' Mitya swore. 'I don't know, either. A blackguard of some sort most likely. They're all blackguards. But Rakitin will crawl through, he'll crawl through a crack – he's another Bernard. Oh, these Bernards! There are thousands of them!'

'But what is the matter with you?' Alyosha persisted.

'He wants to write an article about me, about my case, and start his literary career with it. That's what he comes here for. He told me so himself. Something with a political tendency. "He couldn't help committing a murder, he was a victim of his environment", and so on. He explained it to me. With a socialistic tendency. Well, damn him. If he wants a tendency, let him have his tendency, I don't care. He dislikes Ivan. Hates him. And he is not particularly nice about you, either. Well, I don't kick him out, because he's a clever chap. Thinks a lot of himself, though. I was telling him just now: "The Karamazovs aren't blackguards, but philosophers, for all real Russians are philosophers, but however much you may have studied, you're not a philosopher, you're a low-born fellow." He laughed. Maliciously. And I said to him: *De ideabus non est disputandum – de ideabus* is good, isn't it? At least, I've become a classical scholar, too.' Mitya suddenly burst out laughing.

'But why are you done for? You said so just now, remember?' Alyosha interrupted.

'Why am I done for? Well, as a matter of fact, if – if you take it as a whole – I'm sorry for God, that's why!'

'What do you mean – you're sorry for God?'

'Well, imagine: the nerves, in the head, I mean, the nerves in the brain – oh, damn 'em! – have sort of little tails, and, well, as soon as the little tails of those nerves begin to quiver – that is, you see, if I look at something with my eyes, like that, and they start quivering, the little tails, I mean, and as soon as they begin quivering, an image appears, not at once but after an instant, a fraction of a second, a sort of moment comes – no, not a moment to hell with the moment – an image, that is, an object or an event, or whatever it is – damn it – and that's why I contemplate and then think – because of the little tails, and not at all because I have a soul. I am some sort of image and likeness, all that sort of nonsense. That's what Rakitin explained to me yesterday, and it just bowled me over. Science is a wonderful thing, Alyosha! A new man is coming. That I understand. But all the same I'm sorry for God!'

'Well, that's a good thing, too,' said Alyosha.

'That I'm sorry for God? It's chemistry, Alyosha, chemistry! Can't be helped, your reverence, move up a little, make way for chemistry! Rakitin doesn't love God – oh, how he dislikes him! That's the sorest spot with all of them! But they conceal it. They tell lies. They pretend. "Well," I asked him, "will you develop these ideas in your critical articles?" "I don't think I'll be allowed to," he said, laughing. "But," I asked, "what's to become of man then? Without God and without a future life? Why, in that case, everything is allowed. You can do anything you like!" "Didn't you know that?" he said. He laughed. "A clever man," he said, "can do anything he likes. A clever man knows how to get about. But you," he said, "have put your foot in it. You've committed a murder and you're rotting in prison!" He says that to me, the dirty swine! I used to kick such fellows out, but now I'm listening to them. You see, he talks a lot of good sense, too. Damn clever at writing, too. A week ago he began reading me an article and I copied three lines out of it. Wait a minute. Here it is.'

Mitya took a piece of paper hurriedly out of his waistcoat pocket and read:

' "To solve this problem one must first of all put one's personality in opposition to one's reality." Do you understand that?'

'No, I don't,' said Alyosha.

He gazed attentively at Mitya and listened to him with curiosity.

'I don't understand it, either. It's dark and obscure, but damn clever. "They all write like that," he says, "because that's the sort of environment." They're afraid of the environment. He writes poetry, too, the dirty rotter. He's written one in praise of Mrs Khokhlakov's little foot, ha, ha, ha!'

'I've heard about it,' said Alyosha.

'Have you? And have you heard the poem?'

'No.'

'I've got it. Here it is. I'll read it to you. You don't know, I haven't told you, there's quite a story about it. The dirty rogue! Three weeks ago he tried to tease me. "You," he said, "have got yourself into a hell of a mess like a fool and all for the sake of three thousand, but I'm going to lay my hands on a hundred and fifty thousand. I'm going to marry a young widow and I'll buy a big house in Petersburg." And he told me that he was making up to Mrs Khokhlakov, who hadn't much sense when she was young and now at forty had lost what little sense she ever had. "Yes," he says, "she's very sentimental and that's how I'm going to get her. I'll marry her, take her to Petersburg and start a paper there." And there was such a disgusting, voluptuous spittle on his lips – his mouth was not watering for Mrs Khokhlakov but for the hundred and fifty thousand. And he made me believe it. He really did. Came to see me every day. "She is weakening," he kept saying. Beaming with delight he was. And then all of a sudden he was kicked out: Perkhotin got the better of him, stout fellow! I mean, I could kiss that silly old fool of a woman for having kicked him out! Well, it was while he was coming to see me that he made up that poem. "It's the first poem I've soiled my hands with writing," he said. "But it's for the sake of seducing a woman and, therefore, for something useful. Having got hold of the silly woman's fortune, I shall be able to be of some use to my fellow-citizens." You see, they justify every abomination they commit by appealing to their civic duties! "And anyway," he said, "it's a darn sight better than anything Pushkin ever wrote, for I've managed to shove civic sorrow into my ridiculous poem." I understand what he means about Pushkin. If only he really was a talented fellow and only wrote about women's feet! And how proud he was of his stupid verses! The vanity of these fellows – the vanity! "On the Recovery of My Beloved from a Poisoned Foot" – that's the sort of title he thought of – a wag of a fellow!

> What a darling little foot – how sweet!
> But swollen, alas, it must be said.
> Doctors come and seek to treat –
> Their skill but cripples her instead.
>
> 'Tis not indeed the feet I yearned,
> Let Pushkin sing their praises:
> 'Tis for the head I'm most concerned
> And for the problems that it raises.
>
> For though before it thought a little,
> Now the foot prevents it,
> For reason is a thing so brittle,
> The head can't mend till the foot be fit.

A swine, a bloody swine, but he put it very playfully, the rascal! And, to be sure, he did shove in "the civic sorrow". And how furious he was when she kicked him out! Gnashed his teeth!'

'He's taken his revenge already,' said Alyosha. 'He's sent in a story to a paper about Mrs Khokhlakov.'

And Alyosha told him briefly about the report in the paper *Rumours.*

'It's him, him!' Mitya agreed, frowning. 'It's him all right! These newspaper stories – I know – the horrible things that have been written – about Grushenka, for instance! And about the other one – about Katya. . . . Yes, indeed!'

He took a turn round the room, looking worried.

'I can't stay long, Mitya,' said Alyosha after a pause. 'Tomorrow will be a great, an awful day for you: the judgement of God will be passed on you and – and I can't help being surprised at you. You pace the room and instead of talking of what really concerns you, you go on talking about goodness only knows what. . . .'

'No, don't be surprised at me,' Mitya interrupted warmly. 'What do you want me to do? Talk about the stinking hound – the murderer? We've talked enough about it already. I don't want to talk any more of the stinking son of Stinking Lizaveta! God will kill him, you will see. Not another word about it!'

He went up to Alyosha excitedly and, suddenly, kissed him. His eyes lit up.

'Rakitin wouldn't understand it,' he began, in a kind of exaltation, 'but you, you will understand everything. That's why I longed for you so much. You see, I've been wanting to tell you so much for a long time here, within these peeling walls, but I haven't said a word about the most important thing: the time was not ripe for it, somehow. Now the time has come at last for me to pour out my soul to you. During these last two months, Alyosha, I've felt the presence of a new man in me – a new man has arisen in me! He was shut up inside me, but he would never have appeared, had it not been for this bolt from the blue! It's awful! And what does it matter if I spend twenty years in the mines hacking out ore with a hammer? I'm not afraid of that at all. It's something else I fear now – that the new man that has arisen within me may depart. One can find a human heart there also, in the mines, under the ground, next to you, in another convict and murderer, and make friends with him. For there, too, one can live and love and suffer! One can breathe new life into the frozen heart of such a convict. One can wait on him for years and years and at last bring up from the thieves' kitchen to the light of day a lofty soul, a soul that has suffered and has become conscious of its humanity, to restore to life an angel, bring back a hero! And there are so many of them, hundreds of them, and we are all responsible for them! Why did I dream of that "babby" just then? "Why is the babby poor?" That was a sign to me at that moment! It's for the "babby" that I'm going. For we are all responsible for all. For all the "babbies", for there are little children and big children. All of us are "babbies". And I'll go for all, for someone has to go for all. I did not kill my father, but I have got to go. I accept it! It all came to me here – within these peeling walls. And there are many of them, there are hundreds of them there, those who work under the ground with hammers in their hands. Oh yes, we shall be in chains, and we shall not be free, but then, in our great sorrow, we shall arise anew in gladness, without which man cannot live nor God exist, for God gives gladness. That's his privilege, his great privilege. . . . O Lord, may man dissolve in prayer! How can I be there under the ground without God? Rakitin's lying! If they banish God from the earth, we shall need him under the earth! A convict cannot exist without God, even less than a free man. And then shall we, the men beneath the ground, sing from the bowels of the earth our tragic hymn to God, in whom there is gladness! All hail to God and his gladness! I love him!'

In making this wild speech, Mitya was almost gasping for breath. He turned pale, his lips twitched, and tears rolled down his cheeks.

'No,' he began again, 'life is full, there is life under the ground, too! You wouldn't believe, Alexey, how much I want to live now, what a burning desire to live and to think has arisen in me just within these peeling walls! Rakitin doesn't understand it. All he wants is to build a house and let it out to tenants. But I've been waiting for you. And what, after all, is suffering? I am not afraid of it, however great it may be. Now I'm not afraid of it. Before I was. You know, perhaps I won't answer their questions at the trial at all. . . . And there seems to be so much strength in me now that I shall overcome all things, all suffering, so that I may say, say to myself every moment: I am! In thousands of agonies – I am, writhing on the rack – but I am! I may sit in prison but I, too, exist, I see the sun; and if I do not see the sun, I know that it *is*. And to know that the sun is – that alone is the whole of life. Alyosha, my angel, all these different philosophies drive me to despair – to hell with them! Ivan —'

'What about Ivan?' Alyosha interrupted, but Mitya was not listening.

'You see, I never had all these doubts before, but it was all hidden inside me. Perhaps it was just because all these ideas were raging inside me without my being aware of it that I drank and fought and raged. I fought so as to soothe them, to pacify them, to suppress them. Ivan is not Rakitin, there's an idea hidden in him. Ivan is a sphinx. He is silent, always silent. But God torments me. That's the only thing that is tormenting me. What if he doesn't exist? What if Rakitin is right that it's a fiction created by mankind. For if he doesn't exist, then man is the master of the earth, of the universe. Splendid! But how can he be virtuous without God? That's the question. I'm always harping on that. For whom will he love then? Man, that is. To whom will he be thankful? To whom will he sing a hymn? Rakitin laughs. Rakitin says that one can love humanity without God. Well, only a little snivelling half-wit can maintain that. I can't understand it. It's easy for Rakitin to go on living:

"You'd better see about the extension of civil rights today," he says, "or even that there's no increase in the price of beef. You'll show your love for humanity more simply and closely by that than by philosophies." I exposed the fallacy of that argument of his: "And without God," I said, "you'll put up the price of beef yourself, given the right opportunity, and make a rouble on every copeck." He lost his temper. For what is virtue? Answer me that, Alexey. It's one thing to me and another thing to a Chinaman – it's a relative thing. Or isn't it? Is it not relative? A shrewd question! You won't laugh if I tell you it kept me awake for two nights. I only wonder now how people can go on living and not think about it. Vanity! Ivan has no God. He has an idea. An idea that is beyond me. But he is silent. I think he must be a freemason. I asked him – he is silent. I wanted to slake my thirst from his spring – he is silent. Only once did he say something.'

'What did he say?' Alyosha took it up quickly.

'I said to him, "Then everything is permitted, if that's so?" He frowned. "Our dear father, Fyodor Karamazov," he said, "was an awful swine, but his reasoning was right." That's how he exposed the fallacy of my argument. That was all he said. That's going one better than Rakitin.'

'Yes,' Alyosha agreed bitterly. 'When was he here?'

'Of that later. I've something else to tell you now. I've said nothing to you about Ivan till now. I put it off to the last. When my business here is finished and the sentence has been passed, I'll tell you something, I'll tell you everything. There's a dreadful business here. . . . And you'll be my judge in it. But don't start asking me about it – not a word about it now. You talk of tomorrow, of the trial, but believe me I know nothing about it.'

'Have you talked to your counsel?'

'The counsel! I told him about everything. A soft-spoken rogue, a Petersburg rogue. A Bernard! Only he doesn't believe a word I say. He thinks I did it – imagine it! I can see that. "Why, then," I asked him, "have you come to defend me in that case?" To blazes with them. They've also got a doctor from Petersburg. Want to prove I'm insane. I won't let them! Katerina wants to do her "duty" to the last. However great the strain!' Mitya smiled bitterly. 'The cat! Cruel-hearted! She knows I said about her in Mokroye that she was a woman of "great wrath"! They told her. Yes, the facts against me are as many as the sand of the sea! Grigory sticks to his story. Grigory is honest, but he's a fool. There are many people who are honest because they are fools. That's Rakitin's idea. Grigory's my enemy. There are people who are more useful as enemies than as friends. It's Katerina I'm thinking of when I say this. I'm afraid, oh, I'm afraid she'll tell them in court about how she bowed low to me after those four thousand five hundred! She'll pay it back to the last penny. I don't want her sacrifice. They'll put me to shame at the trial! Oh, well, I'll put up with it, somehow. Go to her, Alyosha. Ask her not to speak of it in court. Or can't you do so? Oh, to hell with it! It doesn't matter. I'll put up with that, too! I'm sorry for her, though. She's asking for it herself. It serves her right if she suffers. I'll have my say, Alexey.' He smiled bitterly again. 'Only Grushenka – Grushenka – Grushenka – oh, God! Why should she have to suffer so much now?' he cried suddenly, with tears. 'It's Grushenka who is driving me to despair. It's the thought of her that's driving me to despair! She came to see me just now. . . .'

'She told me. She was very much upset by you today.'

'I know. Damn my character! I was jealous. I felt sorry as she was leaving. I kissed her. I didn't ask her to forgive me.'

'Why didn't you?' exclaimed Alyosha.

Mitya suddenly laughed almost gaily.

'May the Lord preserve you, my dear boy, from ever asking forgiveness from a woman you love, if you happen to be in the wrong. From a woman you love especially. Yes, especially. However much you may be in the wrong! For a woman, my dear fellow, is the devil only knows what sort of a creature. I am an expert on them, at any rate! But try to tell a woman that you're in the wrong – I'm sorry, it's my fault, forgive me, please – and she'll shower you with reproaches! She'll never forgive you frankly and openly, but will humiliate you to the last degree, bring up things that never happened, remember every little thing, forget nothing, add something of her own, and only then will she forgive you. And that's how the best of them, the best of them, will behave! She'll scrape the bottom of the barrel and put it all on your head – they'll flay you alive, I tell you, every one of them, every one of these angels without whom we cannot live! You see, my dear fellow, let me put it plainly and frankly: every decent man must be under the heel of some woman. That's my conviction – not conviction, but feeling. A man must be magnanimous, and that won't stain his reputation! It won't even stain the reputation of a hero, not even of a Caesar! But don't ever ask her forgiveness for anything all the same. Remember this rule: it was given you by your brother Mitya, who has been ruined by women. No, I'd better make it up to Grushenka somehow without asking her forgiveness. I worship her, Alexey, I worship her! Only she doesn't see it. No, she doesn't believe I love her enough. And she torments me, torments me with her love! It was different before. Before, I was only tormented by those infernal curves of hers, but now I've taken all her soul into my soul and through her I've become a man myself! Will they marry us? If they don't, I'll die of jealousy. I imagine something every day. . . . What did she tell you about me?'

Alyosha repeated all that Grushenka had said to him that day. Mitya listened attentively, made him repeat many things until he was satisfied.

'So she's not angry with me for being jealous,' he exclaimed. 'Just like a woman! "I have a cruel heart myself!" Oh, I love such cruel women, though I can't bear it if anyone is jealous of me! Can't bear it! We shall have fights. But I shall love her – I shall love her always. Will they marry us? Are convicts allowed to marry? That's the question. Without her I cannot live. . . .'

Mitya frowned as he took a turn round the room. It was getting almost dark. He suddenly became terribly worried.

'So there's a secret, she says, a secret? The three of us are plotting against her, and "the Katerina woman" is in it, too. No, Grushenka, old girl, you're barking up the wrong tree. You've made a mistake here. The usual silly mistake a woman makes. Alyosha, my dear fellow, oh, all right! I'll tell you our secret!'

He looked round, went up close to Alyosha, who was standing before him and began whispering to him with a mysterious air, though actually no one could hear them: the old warder was dozing in a corner on a bench, and the sentries were too far away to hear anything.

'I shall tell you all our secret,' Mitya whispered hurriedly. 'I meant to tell you afterwards, for how could I decide anything without you?

You're everything to me. Though I say that Ivan is superior to us, you are like an angel to me. Only your decision will decide it. Perhaps it's you who are really superior to us and not Ivan. You see, it's a matter of conscience, a matter of the highest conscience – the secret is so important that I could not possibly manage it myself and I've put it off till I could tell you about it. Still, it's a little early to decide now, because we have to wait for the verdict: as soon as the verdict is given, you shall decide my fate. Don't decide now. I'll tell you now, you'll hear it, but don't decide. Just stand still and say nothing. I won't tell you everything. I'll only tell you the idea, without details, and you say nothing. No questions, no gestures. Agreed? But, good Lord, what shall I do about your eyes? I'm afraid your eyes will tell me your decision, even if you are silent. Oh dear, I'm afraid of that! Alyosha, listen: Ivan suggested that I should *escape*. I won't tell you the details: everything has been taken into account, everything can be arranged. Don't say anything, don't decide. Escape to America with Grushenka. I can't live without Grushenka! But what if they won't let her go with me? They don't allow convicts to marry, do they? Ivan says they don't. And without Grusha what should I do there under the ground with – with a hammer? I could only smash my skull with the hammer! But, on the other hand, what about my conscience? I should have run away from suffering! There was a sign and I rejected it; there was a way of purification and I turned my back on it. Ivan says that a man "of good character" can be of more use in America than working under the ground. But what about our hymn under the ground? What is America? America is vanity again! And I daresay there's a lot of swindling going on in America, too. I run away from crucifixion! For I'm telling you this, Alyosha, because you alone can understand it and no one else, for others it's all nonsense, delirium. I mean, all I've told you about the hymn. They'll say that I've gone off my head or that I am a fool. But I haven't gone off my head and I'm not a fool, either. Ivan, too, understands about the hymn. Oh, he understands all right, only he says nothing about it, he is silent. He doesn't believe in the hymn. Don't speak, don't speak: I see how you look – you have already decided! Please, don't decide. Spare me. I can't live without Grushenka. Wait for the verdict!'

Mitya concluded, like one demented. He clutched Alyosha with both hands by the shoulders and stared intently at him with his yearning, inflamed eyes.

'They don't allow convicts to be married, do they?' he repeated for the third time in a beseeching voice.

Alyosha listened with intense surprise and was deeply shaken.

'Tell me one thing,' he said. 'Does Ivan insist on it very much and who was the first to think of it?'

'It was he. He thought of it first and he insists! He didn't come to see me all the time, and then, a week ago, he suddenly came and began straight with it. He insists on it terribly. He doesn't ask me, he orders me. He is sure I will do as he tells me, though I opened up my heart to him as I did to you and spoke to him about the hymn, too. He told me how he was going to arrange it, he has collected all the information, but of that later. He's absolutely mad on it. The chief thing is the money: he promised to give me ten thousand to escape and twenty thousand for America. "For ten thousand we'll arrange a wonderful escape for you," he says.'

'And he told you not to tell me on any account?' Alyosha asked again.

'To tell no one, but especially you. Not to tell you on any account! I suppose he's afraid you might stand before me as my conscience. Don't tell him I told you. For heaven's sake, don't!'

'You're right,' Alyosha made up his mind. 'It's impossible to decide before the verdict. After the trial, you'll decide for yourself. Then you'll find the new man in yourself and he will decide.'

'The new man or a Bernard who'll decide in his Bernard fashion! For it seems to me I'm a contemptible Bernard myself!' Mitya grinned bitterly.

'But have you really lost all hope of proving that you are not guilty?'

Mitya shrugged spasmodically and shook his head.

'Alyosha, my dear fellow, it's time you were going,' he said, with sudden haste. 'I can hear the governor talking in the courtyard and he'll be here soon. We're late and it's against the rules. Embrace me quickly. Kiss me and make the sign of the cross over me. Make the sign of the cross over me, for the cross I have to bear tomorrow. . . .'

They embraced and kissed.

'And Ivan,' Mitya said suddenly, 'advised me to escape, but he himself believes that I did it!'

A mournful smile hovered over his lips.

'Have you asked him whether he believes it?' asked Alyosha.

'No, I haven't. I wanted to, but I couldn't. I hadn't the strength. But it made no difference. I could see from his eyes. Well, good-bye!'

They kissed again hurriedly. Alyosha was on the point of leaving the room when Mitya suddenly called him back.

'Stand before me, please, like that – that's right.'

And he again seized Alyosha firmly by the shoulders with both hands. His face turned suddenly quite pale, so that in the almost dark room it was dreadfully noticeable. His lips twitched and his eyes were glued to Alyosha.

'Alyosha, tell me the whole truth as before God: do you believe that I did it or not? Do you in your own heart believe it? The whole truth, don't lie to me!' he shouted in a frenzy.

Alyosha seemed to sway and he felt distinctly a sharp pang in his heart.

'Good heavens, what are you saying?' he murmured, overcome with confusion.

'The whole truth, the whole truth, don't lie!' repeated Mitya.

'Not for a moment have I believed that you are the murderer,' the words came pouring out of his breast in a shaking voice, and he raised his right hand as if calling God to witness that he spoke the truth.

A look of intense happiness suddenly lighted up the whole of Mitya's face.

'Thank you!' he said in a drawn-out voice, as if letting out a sigh after recovering from a faint. 'Now you have made a new man of me. Believe me, till now I dreaded asking you this, you of all people! Well, go, go! You've given me strength for tomorrow, God bless you! Well, go now. Love Ivan!' he cried. It was Mitya's last word to him.

Aloysha went out in tears. Such mistrustfulness in Mitya, such lack of confidence even in him, in Alyosha, suddenly revealed to him such a depth of hopeless grief and despair in the soul of his unhappy brother as he had never suspected before. He was suddenly seized with a feeling of profound and infinite compassion, a feeling that drained all his strength out of him in an instant. His pierced heart ached terribly. 'Love Ivan!' he recalled Mitya's parting words. And he was going to Ivan. He should really have gone to see Ivan first thing in the morning. He was worried about Ivan no less than about Mitya, and more than ever now after his interview with his brother.

5

Not You! Not You!

ON the way to Ivan he had to pass the house in which Katerina lived. There was a light in the windows. He suddenly stopped and decided to go in. He had not seen Katerina for over a week. But it occurred to him now that Ivan might be with her, especially on the eve of such a day. He rang the doorbell and as he walked up the stairs, dimly lit by a Chinese lantern, he saw a man coming down and, as they met, he recognized his brother. Ivan, therefore, was coming from Katerina.

'Oh, it's only you,' Ivan said drily. 'Well, good-bye. Are you going to her?'

'Yes.'

'I shouldn't advise it. She's "in a state", and you'll upset her more.'

'No, no!' a voice suddenly shouted from a door that was flung open upstairs. 'Have you come from him, Alexey?'

'Yes, I've been to see him.'

'Has he given you any message for me? Come in, Alyosha, and you, too, Ivan. You must, you must come back! Do you hear?'

There was such a peremptory note in Katerina's voice that Ivan, after a moment's hesitation, decided to go up again together with Alyosha.

'She was eavesdropping!' he whispered irritably to himself, but Alyosha heard it.

'You won't mind my keeping my overcoat on, will you?' said Ivan, coming into the drawing-room. 'I won't sit down. I'll only stay a minute.'

'Sit down, Alexey,' said Katerina, remaining standing herself.

She had changed little during this time, but there was an ominous light in her dark eyes. Alyosha remembered afterwards that she had seemed to him extraordinarily beautiful at that moment.

'What did he ask you to tell me?'

'Only one thing,' said Alyosha, looking straight into her face. 'That you should spare yourself and say nothing in court about' (he faltered a little) 'what passed between you – er – at the time of your very first meeting in – in that town. . . .'

'Oh, he means that I bowed down to the ground to him for that money!' she said with a bitter laugh. 'Well, what do you think? Is he afraid for himself or for me? He said I should spare – whom? Him or me? Speak, Alexey.'

Alyosha was watching her intently, trying to understand her.

'Both you and him,' he said softly.

'I see!' she snapped spitefully and suddenly blushed.

'I'm afraid you don't know me yet, Alexey,' she said menacingly, 'and I don't think I understand myself, either. You may want to trample me underfoot after my cross-examination tomorrow.'

'You will, I'm sure, give your evidence honestly,' said Alyosha. 'That is all that's required.'

'A woman is often dishonest,' she said, grinding her teeth. 'Only an hour ago I thought I would be afraid to touch that monster – as though he were a reptile but – it seems I was wrong: he's still a human being to me! But did he do it? Did he?' she suddenly cried hysterically, turning quickly to Ivan.

Alyosha at once realized that she had put the same question to Ivan perhaps only a minute before his own arrival, and not for the first but for the hundredth time, and that they had ended by quarrelling.

'I've been to see Smerdyakov. . . . It was you, darling, it was you who persuaded me that he was a parricide. It's only you I believed!' she went on, still addressing Ivan.

Ivan forced a smile to his lips. Alyosha started at her familiar tone. He could not even have suspected such an intimate relationship between them.

'Well, that's enough, anyway,' Ivan cut her short. 'I'm going. I'll come tomorrow.'

And turning round at once, he went out of the room and walked straight to the staircase. Katerina suddenly seized Alyosha by both hands with an imperious gesture.

'Go after him! Overtake him! Don't leave him alone for a moment!' she whispered rapidly. 'He's mad. Don't you know that he's gone mad? He is in a fever, a nervous fever! The doctor told me so. Go, run after him. . . .'

Alyosha jumped up and rushed out after Ivan, who was only about fifty yards ahead of him.

'What do you want?' Ivan, seeing that Alyosha was overtaking him, turned round suddenly. 'She told you to run after me because I was mad. I know it all by heart,' he added irritably.

'She's, of course, mistaken,' said Alyosha, 'but she is right about your being ill. I was looking at your face just now. You look ill. You look very ill, Ivan!'

Ivan walked on without stopping. Alyosha followed him.

'But do you know, Alexey, how people go mad?' asked Ivan in a voice that was suddenly quiet and not at all irritable, a voice in which there was suddenly a note of the most good-natured curiosity.

'No, I do not. I imagine there are all kinds of insanity.'

'And is it possible to observe how one is going mad oneself?'

'I don't think it is possible to observe oneself clearly in a case like that,' Alyosha replied with surprise.

Ivan was silent for about half a minute.

'If you want to talk to me about something,' he said suddenly, 'then, please, change the subject.'

'By the way, I've just remembered, I've a letter for you,' Alyosha said shyly, and taking Lise's letter out of his pocket, he held it out to him.

They had just walked up to a lamp-post. Ivan at once recognized the handwriting.

'Oh, it's from that little she-devil!' he laughed spitefully and, without opening the envelope, he suddenly tore it into bits and threw it in the air. The bits were scattered by the wind.

'I don't believe she's sixteen yet and she's already offering herself!' he said contemptuously, striding along the street.

'Offering herself? What do you mean?' cried Alyosha.

'Just as loose women offer themselves, of course.'

'What are you saying, Ivan?' Alyosha protested warmly and sorrowfully. 'She's a child. You're insulting a child! She's sick. She's very sick. She's also perhaps going mad. I had to give you her letter. I had expected to hear something from you – I mean, that would save her.'

'I've nothing to tell you. If she's a child, I'm not her nurse. Shut up, Alexey. Don't go on. I'm not even giving it a thought.'

They were silent again for about a minute.

'She'll now be praying to the Holy Virgin all night to show her how to act in the court tomorrow,' he said sharply and spitefully again.

'You – you mean Katerina?'

'Yes. Should she save or ruin dear old Mitya? She'll be praying for a light from above. You see, she doesn't know herself. Hasn't had time to get ready. She, too, takes me for her nurse. Wants me to sing lullabies to her!'

'Katerina loves you, Ivan,' Alyosha said sadly.

'Perhaps. Only I'm not keen on her.'

'She's suffering. Why, then, do you sometimes say – things to her that give her hope?' Alyosha went on, with timid reproach. 'You see, I know you've given her hope. Forgive me for talking to you like this,' he added.

'I can't act towards her as I should – break off our relations and tell her so frankly,' Ivan said irritably. 'I must wait till the murderer has been sentenced. If I break off with her now, she'll ruin that rotten scoundrel in court tomorrow out of revenge, because she hates him and she knows she hates him. It's all lies here, lies on top of lies! But as long as I don't break off with her, she can still hope and she will not ruin that monster, knowing how anxious I am to get him out of trouble. And when will that damned verdict come?'

The words 'murderer' and 'monster' echoed painfully in Alyosha's heart.

'But how can she ruin Mitya?' he asked, thinking over Ivan's words. 'What could she say in her evidence that would ruin Mitya?'

'You don't know that yet. She has a document in dear old Mitya's own handwriting proving without a shadow of doubt that he killed father.'

'That's impossible!' cried Alyosha.

'Why impossible? I've read it myself.'

'There can't be such a document!' Alyosha repeated heatedly. 'There can't be, because he is not the murderer. It was not he who killed father, not he!'

Ivan suddenly stopped dead.

'Who, then, sir, is the murderer, in your opinion?' he asked, somehow coldly, apparently, and there was a sort of supercilious note in his voice.

'You know who yourself,' Alyosha said in a low, penetrating voice.

'Who? You mean that fairy-story about that crazy idiot, the epileptic? About Smerdyakov?'

Alyosha suddenly felt that he was trembling all over.

'You know who yourself!' the words escaped him helplessly. He was choking.

'But who? Who?' Ivan cried almost fiercely. All his restraint suddenly vanished.

'I only know one thing,' Alyosha said, still almost in a whisper. 'It was *not you* who killed father.'

'"Not you"? What do you mean by "not you"?' Ivan was dumbfounded.

'It was not you who killed father,' Alyosha repeated firmly. 'Not you!'

They didn't speak for half a minute.

'I know myself it wasn't I,' said Ivan, with a pale, distorted smile. 'Are you raving?'

He stared fixedly at Alyosha. Both were again standing under a street-lamp.

'No, Ivan. You've said several times to yourself that you are the murderer.'

'When did I say that? I was in Moscow. When did I say that?' Ivan murmured in utter confusion.

'You've said it many times to yourself, when you've been alone during these dreadful two months,' Alyosha went on, quietly and distinctly as before. But he was saying this, as it were, automatically, not of his own free will, as though in obedience to some irresistible command. 'You have accused yourself and have confessed to yourself that you and no one else is the murderer. But you did not do it. You are mistaken. You are not the murderer. Do you hear? It is not you! God has sent me to tell you this.'

They were both silent. The silence lasted for a whole minute. Both were standing and gazing into each other's eyes. Both were pale. Suddenly Ivan shook with anger and seized Alyosha firmly by the shoulder.

'You were in my room!' he said in an intense whisper. 'You were in my room at night when he came. . . . Confess, you saw him, didn't you?'

'Who are you talking about? Mitya?' Alyosha asked in bewilderment.

'No, not about him! To hell with the monster!' Ivan yelled, beside himself. 'Do you know he comes to see me? How did you find out? Speak!'

'Who is *he*?' Alyosha murmured, terrified. 'I don't know who you're talking about.'

'Yes, you do – how else could you – it's impossible that you should not know. . . .'

But suddenly he seemed to control himself. He stood still and seemed to be pondering over something. A strange grin contorted his lips.

'Ivan,' Alyosha began again in a shaking voice. 'I told you that because you'll believe me. I know that. I told you that it was *not you*, because I want you to remember it for the rest of your life. Do you hear? For the rest of your life. And it was God who put it into my heart to tell you so, even though you may hate me for ever from this hour. . . .'

But Ivan had now apparently regained complete control of himself.

'Alexey,' he said with a cold, ironical smile, 'I can't stand prophets and epileptics. Especially messengers from God. You know that only too well, sir. I shall have nothing to do with you from this moment, and, I think, for good. I ask you to leave me at once – at the cross-roads. And your lodgings, too, are down this lane, aren't they? Take particular care not to come near me today! Do you hear?'

He turned and walked straight ahead, with a firm step, without looking back.

'Ivan,' Alyosha shouted after him, 'if anything happens to you today, think of me first of all!'

But Ivan made no reply. Alyosha stood at the cross-roads by the street-lamp till Ivan had disappeared in the darkness. Then he turned and walked slowly down the lane towards his lodgings. Both he and Ivan occupied different lodgings: neither of them wished to live in their father's empty house. Alyosha rented a furnished room with a tradesman's family; Ivan lived at some distance from him, occupying a large and fairly comfortable flat in the wing of a house belonging to a well-to-do widow of a civil servant. But the only person to wait on him was an old woman, crippled with arthritis, who went to bed at six in the evening and got up at six in the morning. Ivan had become strangely undemanding during the last two months and liked very much to be left quite alone. He even tidied the room he lived in himself and very rarely went into the other rooms of his flat. On reaching the gate of his house and taking hold of the handle of the bell, he suddenly stopped. He felt that he was trembling all over with fury. Suddenly he let go of the bell, spat, turned round and walked quickly to the other end of the town, to a very small, tumble-down, wooden house, about a mile and a half from his flat. The house was occupied by Maria Kondratyevna, Fyodor Karamazov's neigh-bour, who used to come to his kitchen for soup and to whom Smer-dyakov had once sung his songs and played on the guitar. She had sold their little house and now lived with her mother in little more than a peasant's cottage, and Smerdyakov, ill and almost dying, had lived with them ever since Fyodor Karamazov's death. It was to see him that Ivan, drawn by a sudden and irresistible impulse, was going now.

6

The First Interview with Smerdyakov

THIS was already the third time Ivan had gone to talk to Smerdyakov since his return from Moscow. The first time, after the murder, he had seen and talked to him was on the very day of his arrival; then he had paid him another visit a fortnight later. But after that he had not visited him again, so that it was over a month since he had seen him and during that time he had scarcely heard anything of him. Ivan had returned from Moscow on the fifth day after his father's death, so that he was too late for the funeral which took place on the day before his arrival. The cause of his delay was due to the fact that Alyosha, having no precise knowledge of his Moscow address, asked Katerina to send his telegram, but she, not knowing his address, either, tele-graphed her sister and aunt in the hope that Ivan would visit them immediately on his arrival in Moscow. But he called on them only on the fourth day after his arrival and, having read the telegram, at once, of course, set off post-haste to our town. The first person he met was Alyosha, but after talking to him he was amazed to find that Alyosha did not suspect Mitya at all, but openly pointed to Smerdyakov as the murderer, which was quite contrary to the opinion held by everyone else in the town. Having next seen the district police inspector and the public prosecutor and having learnt all the details of the indictment and the arrest, he was even more surprised at Alyosha and ascribed his opinion to his greatly aroused feeling of sympathy for Mitya, of whom, as Ivan knew, he was very fond.

Incidentally, let us say a few words about Ivan's feelings for Mitya and dispose of the matter once for all: he positively disliked him and at most sometimes felt a compassion for him, but even that was mixed with great contempt, bordering on disgust. He found Mitya's personality and even his whole appearance unprepossessing in the extreme. Katerina's love for him filled Ivan with indignation. He did, however, go to see Mitya in prison also on the first day of his arrival and that meeting increased rather than weakened his conviction of his brother's guilt. He found Mitya in a state of restlessness and nervous excitement. Mitya had talked a lot, but he was very absent-minded and apt to change the subject rather abruptly. He spoke very sharply, accused Smerdyakov and was terribly muddled. He talked mostly about the three thousand roubles which he alleged his father had 'stolen' from him. 'The money belonged to me, it was mine,' Mitya kept repeating. 'Even if I had stolen it, I should have been within my rights.' He did not dispute the evidence against him, and if he interpreted some facts in his favour, he did so incoherently and absurdly, just as though he did not even wish to justify himself to Ivan or anybody else; on the contrary, he lost his temper, dismissed the charges against him scornfully, swore, and got excited. He merely laughed contemptuously at Grigory's testimony about the open door and declared that it was 'the devil who opened it'. But he could offer no coherent explanation of that fact. He even managed to insult Ivan at their first interview, telling him sharply that it was not for those who maintained that 'everything was permitted' to suspect and question him. He was generally very unfriendly to Ivan on that occasion. It was immediately after his meeting with Mitya that Ivan went to see Smerdyakov.

Already in the train, on his way from Moscow, Ivan had kept thinking of Smerdyakov and of his last conversation with him on the evening before his departure. There was a great deal that disconcerted him,
a great deal that seemed suspicious. But in his statement to the examining magistrate Ivan made no mention of that conversation. He put it
off till he had seen Smerdyakov, who was at that time in hospital.
Dr Herzenstube and Dr Varvinsky, whom Ivan met in the hospital,
in reply to Ivan's persistent questions, declared firmly that there could
be no doubt of the genuineness of Smerdyakov's epileptic fits and
were, in fact, astonished at Ivan's question whether Smerdyakov had
been shamming on the day of the murder. They gave him to understand that the fit was of quite unusual severity and kept recurring for
several days, so much so that the life of the patient was positively in
danger, and that it was only now, after all the necessary measures had
been taken, that it could be said definitely that the patient would live.
Though it was quite likely, Dr Herzenstube added, that his reason
would remain partially impaired 'if not permanently, then for rather
a considerable time'. To Ivan's impatient question whether that meant
that he was now mad, they replied that that was not the case in the
full sense of the word, but that 'certain abnormalities' could be perceived. Ivan decided to find out for himself what those abnormalities
were. At the hospital he was at once allowed to see the patient. Smerdyakov was lying in a bed in a separate ward. Not far from him was
another bed occupied by a very sick tradesman of our town, swollen
with dropsy, who was obviously going to die the next day or the
day after; he could be no hindrance to their conversation. Seeing
Ivan, Smerdyakov grinned mistrustfully and for the first moment he
seemed even to be frightened. So at least Ivan imagined. But it was
only for a moment. For the rest of the time, on the contrary, he was
struck by Smerdyakov's composure. From the first glance Ivan was
in no doubt whatever that he was very ill: he was very weak, he
spoke slowly, as though moving his tongue with difficulty, and he
had grown very thin and sallow. During the whole of the twenty
minutes of the interview he complained of a headache and of pain in
all his limbs. His eunuch-like, dried-up face seemed to have become
very small, the hair on his temples was tousled and, instead of his quiff,
a thin tuft of hair stuck up on top of his head. But the screwed-up
left eye, which seemed to be hinting at something, betrayed the old

Smerdyakov. 'It's nice to have a chat with a clever man,' Ivan at once recalled. He sat down on a stool at his feet. Smerdyakov stirred violently in bed with a painful effort, but he was not the first to speak; he was silent and did not appear to be particularly interested.

'Can you talk to me?' asked Ivan. 'I'm not going to tire you much.'

'Yes, sir, I can,' Smerdyakov mumbled in a weak voice. 'Been here long, sir?' he added condescendingly, as though encouraging an embarrassed visitor.

'No, I only arrived today. To clear up your mess here.'

Smerdyakov sighed.

'What are you sighing for? You know all about it, don't you?' Ivan blurted out.

Smerdyakov was stolidly silent for a moment or two.

'Couldn't help knowing it, sir. I could see it coming. Only how was I to know, sir, that it would come to that?'

'Come to what? Don't beat about the bush! You did foretell you'd have a fit as soon as you went down the cellar, didn't you? You told me yourself you'd have a fit in the cellar, didn't you?'

'You haven't mentioned it in your statement to the police, have you, sir?' Smerdyakov inquired calmly.

Ivan suddenly became angry.

'No, I haven't done so yet, but I certainly shall. You'll have to explain a lot to me now, my dear fellow. And I warn you I'm not going to let you play about with me!'

'But why should I, sir, seeing as how I put all my trust in you as in Almighty God?' said Smerdyakov in the same calm tone of voice and only closing his eyes for a moment.

'First of all,' Ivan began, 'I know that it's impossible to foretell an epileptic fit. I've made inquiries, don't you try to suggest anything to the contrary to me. It's impossible to foretell the day and the hour. How, then, did you tell me the day and the hour beforehand, and that it was going to happen in the cellar? How could you know beforehand that you would fall down the cellar steps in a fit, if you didn't deliberately sham such a fit?'

'I had to go to the cellar anyhow, sir,' Smerdyakov drawled unhurriedly. 'Several times a day, in fact. I fell off the attic ladder exactly like that a year ago, sir. It's quite true one can't foretell the day and the hour of an epileptic fit, but one can always have a presentiment of it.'

'But you did foretell the day and the hour!'

'You'd better ask the doctors here about my illness, sir. Ask them whether my fit was real or not. I've nothing more to say to you about it.'

'And the cellar? How could you know beforehand about the cellar?'

'You will keep on harping on that blamed cellar, sir! As I was going down the cellar that day I was not sure what was going to happen. I was so terrified. And the reason I was so terrified, sir, was because you was away and I could expect no protection from nobody in the world. So I goes down them cellar steps, thinking to myself: It's sure to come now, it's sure to strike me down. Am I going to fall to the bottom or not? And it was because I wasn't sure that the spasm that always comes before a fit caught me by the throat and – and, well, sir, down I flies. All that, sir, and all the talk I had with you at the gate the evening before, when I told you how frightened I was and about the cellar – all that I told Dr Herzenstube and Mr Nelyudin, the examining magistrate, and they writes it all down in my statement. And Mr Varvinsky, sir, the hospital doctor, made a special point of that. It was just the thought of it, he told them, that brought it on. Just because I was so nervous, that is, whether I might have a fall or not. Aye, it was just because of that that I had my fit. And they've written down, sir, that it was bound to happen, seeing as how I was so terrified.'

Having said that, Smerdyakov drew a deep breath as though utterly exhausted.

'So you've told them all that in your statement, have you?' asked Ivan, somewhat taken aback.

He had meant to frighten him by threatening to tell the examining magistrate about their conversation that evening, but it seemed that Smerdyakov had already told them everything himself.

'What have I to be afraid of, sir?' Smerdyakov said firmly. 'Let 'em write down the whole truth.'

'And have you also told them every word of our conversation at the gate?'

'No, sir. Not every word.'

'And did you tell them that you can pretend to have a fit, as you boasted to me that time?'

'No, sir. I didn't tell them that, neither.'

'Tell me now why you wanted me to go to Chermashnya?'

'I was afraid you might go to Moscow, sir. In Chermashnya you'd have been nearer, anyways.'

'You're lying You yourself suggested that I should go away. Get out of harm's way, you told me.'

'I told you that, sir, just out of friendship and out of a feeling of true devotion to you, foreseeing trouble in the house and feeling sorry for you. Only I felt even more sorry for myself, sir. I told you to get out of harm's way to make you understand that there would be trouble at home, so that you should stay behind to protect your father.'

'Why didn't you say so more plainly then, you fool!' Ivan suddenly flared up.

'How could I have said so more plainly, sir? It was only because I was afraid that I spoke to you, and, besides, you might have got angry. I might, of course, have suspected that your brother would make a row and carry off that money, for he looked upon it as his own. But how was I to know that it would end in murder? All I thought, sir, was that he'd carry off the three thousand that lay in an envelope under master's mattress. But he's gone and murdered him. You couldn't have guessed it yourself, sir, could you?'

'But if you say yourself that it couldn't be guessed, then how could I have foreseen it and stayed at home? What are you driving at?' Ivan said, thinking it over.

'Why, sir, you could have guessed it because I asked you to go to Chermashnya instead of to Moscow.'

'How on earth could I have guessed it from that?'

Smerdyakov appeared to be very tired and he was again silent for about a minute.

'You did ought to have guessed that I wanted you to be nearer, sir, just because I was trying to persuade you to go to Chermashnya and not to Moscow. For Moscow, sir, is a long way off, and your brother, seeing as how you was not far off, would not have dared to go on with it. And in case of anything happening, you could be back very quickly so as to protect me, too, for that was why I warned you of Grigory's illness and told you about me being afraid of having a fit. And the reason why I explained to you about the knocks by means of which one could get into your father's house and told you that your brother knew all about them through me was because I thought you'd guess yourself, sir, that he'd be quite sure to do something and that you wouldn't go even to Chermashnya but decide to stay.'

'He's talking very coherently,' thought Ivan, 'though he mumbles. What sort of impairment of his reasoning faculties was Herzenstube talking of?'

'You're trying to trick me, damn you!' Ivan cried angrily.

'And I don't mind admitting, sir, that I thought at the time that you guessed it all,' Smerdyakov parried with a most good-humoured air.

'If I'd guessed it, I'd have stayed!' cried Ivan, flaring up again.

'Well, sir, if you don't mind me saying so, I thought that, having guessed it all, you was most anxious to get out of harm's way as soon as possible, and that you was so afraid that you didn't mind where to run away to save yourself.'

'You don't suppose everyone is as great a coward as you, do you?'

'I'm very sorry, sir, but I did think you was just like me.'

'Well, of course, I should have guessed,' said Ivan excitedly, 'and as a matter of fact I did guess that you'd be up to some villainy. . . . Only you're lying, you're lying again,' he cried, suddenly recalling something. 'Do you remember how you went up to the carriage and said to me, "It's nice to have a chat with a clever man"? So I suppose you must have been glad I was going away since you were so pleased with me.'

Smerdyakov heaved a sigh, then another. His face seemed to colour slightly.

'If I was glad, sir,' he said a little breathlessly, 'it was only because you agreed to go to Chermashnya and not to Moscow. For, say what you will, sir, it certainly is nearer. And I never said them words to you because I was pleased with you, but by way of reproach, sir. You got it all wrong, sir.'

'What reproach?'

'Why, sir, that foreseeing such a calamity, you was leaving your own dad in the lurch and refusing to protect us, for, you see, sir, they might have arrested me any time for stealing the three thousand.'

'Damn you!' Ivan swore again. 'Wait a moment. Did you tell the public prosecutor and the examining magistrate about those signals, those knocks?'

'I told them everything as it was, sir.'

Again Ivan could not help being surprised inwardly.

'If I thought of anything at the time,' he began again, 'it was only of some nasty trick you might play. Dmitry might kill him, but that he would steal – that I never believed then. . . . But I expected you to play any dirty trick. You told me yourself that you could pretend to have an epileptic fit. Why did you say that?'

'I said that, sir, only because of my simplicity. Besides, I've never pretended to have a fit on purpose in my life. I only said it to boast to you. It was just stupidity, sir. I had got to like you very much then and I was just acting natural-like with you.'

'My brother accuses you openly of killing my father and stealing the money.'

'Well, sir, what else is there left for him to say?' Smerdyakov grinned bitterly. 'And who's going to believe him with all that evidence against him? Grigory saw the open door, and what better evidence do you want after that? But let him say what he likes. He's only doing it because he's afraid and is trying to save himself. . . .'

He fell silent calmly, and suddenly, as though realizing something, added:

'You see, sir, it's the same all over again. He wants to put the whole blame on me. Says it's my doing. I've heard that already. And now you, sir, say that I'm good at shamming epileptic fits. But would I have told you beforehand that I could do it, if I'd really been planning to murder your father just then? Had I been planning such a murder, I wouldn't have been such a fool as to give such evidence against myself beforehand, and to his son, too! Would I now, sir? Does it look likely? Would such a thing happen, sir? Why, of course not, sir. Now, take this conversation now between you and me, sir. No one hears it except Providence itself. But if you, sir, was to tell the public prosecutor and Mr Nelyudin about it, you'd provide me with the best defence you could think of. For what kind of criminal is it, sir, who's so artless beforehand? It stands to reason, sir.'

'Listen,' interrupted Ivan, getting up and greatly impressed by Smerdyakov's last argument, 'I don't suspect you at all and, indeed,

I think it's quite absurd to accuse you. On the contrary, I'm grateful to you for setting my mind at rest. I'm going now, but I'll come back. Good-bye for the present. Get well. Is there anything you want?'

'Thank you for everything, sir. Marfa, sir, does not forget me and lets me have anything I want. Very good she's always been to me, sir. Good people visit me every day.'

'Good-bye. By the way, I shan't say anything about your being able to sham a fit and – er – I should advise you not to say anything about it, either,' Ivan added suddenly for some reason.

'I quite understand, sir. And if you don't say nothing about it, sir, I won't say nothing of that conversation of ours at the gate, neither.'

Ivan went quickly out of the ward and it was only after he had gone about ten yards along the corridor that it suddenly occurred to him that there was some offensive meaning in Smerdyakov's last phrase. He was on the point of going back, but the idea had only flashed through his mind, and muttering 'Nonsense!' he walked rapidly out of the hospital. What pleased him most, he felt, was that he was relieved at the fact that it was not Smerdyakov but his brother who was guilty, though, it would seem, he ought really to have felt the opposite. He did not want to analyse the reason why he should have felt like that: indeed, he felt a reluctance to analyse his own sensations. He seemed to wish to forget something quickly. Then, during the following few days, as he acquainted himself more thoroughly with the depressing evidence against him, he became absolutely convinced of Mitya's guilt. There was the evidence of the most insignificant people, such as Fenya and her mother, for example, not to mention Perkhotin, the people in the public house and Plotnikov's shop, and the witnesses in Mokroye. It was the details that were so depressing. The information about the secret 'knocks' impressed the examining magistrate and the public prosecutor almost as much as Grigory's evidence about the open door. Grigory's wife, Marfa, in reply to Ivan's question, declared without a moment's hesitation that Smerdyakov had been lying all night behind the partition, 'within a few feet of our bed' and that though she had slept soundly, she woke up several times, hearing him moaning. 'He was moaning the whole time, continually moaning.' Talking it over with Herzenstube, Ivan told him that in his opinion Smerdyakov was not at all mad, but only very weak. But that only evoked a faint smile from the old man. 'Do you know how he spends all his time now?' he asked Ivan. 'Learning French words by heart. He has an exercise book under his pillow with French words written out for him in Russian letters by someone, ha, ha, ha!' Ivan at last dismissed all doubts. He could no longer think of Mitya without revulsion. One thing, though, was strange, namely that Alyosha stuck to his guns that Dmitry was not the murderer, but 'in all probability' Smerdyakov. Ivan always felt that Alyosha's opinion meant a lot to him, and that was why he was greatly puzzled by him. Another strange thing was that Alyosha did not try to talk to him about Mitya, that he never began talking about him himself, but only answered his questions. Still, at that time he was very much pre-occupied with quite a different matter: on his return from Moscow he gave himself up entirely to his mad and consuming passion for Katerina. This is not the place to begin to describe this new passion of Ivan's, which profoundly affected the rest of his life: all this could furnish the plot for another story, another novel, which I don't know if I shall ever write. But I cannot all the same pass over the fact that when, on leaving Katerina that night with Alyosha, Ivan, as I've already described, said to him: 'I am not very keen on her,' he was telling a terrible lie at that moment: he was madly in love with her, though it is quite true that at times he hated her so much that he could have killed her. There were many reasons for this: Katerina, deeply shocked by what had happened to Mitya, had thrown herself upon Ivan, who had returned to her, as though he were the only man who could save her. She was hurt, insulted, and humiliated in her feelings. And now the man had again appeared on the scene, the man who had loved her so much before – oh, she knew that too well! – and of whose mind and heart she had formed so high an opinion. But a girl of high moral principles like her did not give herself up entirely to him, in spite of the Karamazov vehemence of her lover's desires and the great fascination he exercised over her. At the same time she was continually tormented by remorse for having been unfaithful to Mitya, and during her violent quarrels with Ivan (and there were many of them) she told him so plainly. That was what, in his conversation with Alyosha, he had called 'one lie on top of another'. And, indeed, there were a great many lies in their relationship, and that angered Ivan more than anything. But of all this later. In short, he almost forgot about Smerdyakov for a time. And yet, a fortnight after his first visit to him, he began to be worried again by the same strange thoughts as before. It will suffice to say that he began continually asking himself the question: why did he, on the last night before his departure, in his father's house, creep silently like a thief on the stairs and listen to hear what his father was doing? Why did he recall it with revulsion afterwards? Why had he suddenly felt so miserable next morning, on the journey, and, as he arrived in Moscow, had said to himself: 'I am a blackguard'? And now he almost imagined that because of all these tormenting thoughts he might even forget Katerina, such a hold did they get on him! It so happened that while thinking this he met Alyosha in the street. He stopped him at once and suddenly put a question to him:

'Do you remember that day when after dinner Dmitry burst into the house and attacked father and I told you afterwards in the yard that I reserved "the right to desire" for myself – tell me, did you think then that I desired father's death or not?'

'I did,' Alyosha replied, softly.

'Well, so it was and there was not really anything left to guess. But didn't you think then that what I really wished for was that "one reptile should devour the other", that is, that Dmitry should kill father, and as soon as possible, too, and – and that I didn't mind helping to bring it about?'

Alyosha went pale a little and looked in silence into his brother's eyes.

'Speak!' cried Ivan. 'I must know what you thought then. I must. Tell me the truth, the truth!'

He drew a long breath, looking with suppressed anger at Alyosha even before he had time to answer.

'I'm sorry, but I did think that, too, at the time,' Alyosha whispered and fell silent without adding a single 'extenuating circumstance'.

'Thank you!' snapped Ivan and, leaving Alyosha, went quickly on his way.

After that Alyosha had noticed that his brother began avoiding him rather pointedly and even seemed to have taken a dislike to him, so that he stopped visiting him himself after that. But at that very moment, immediately after his meeting with Alyosha, Ivan went straight to see Smerdyakov again, without going home first.

7

The Second Interview with Smerdyakov

BY that time Smerdyakov had been discharged from the hospital. Ivan knew his new lodgings: they were in a tumble-down, little wooden house of two rooms, divided by a passage. Maria Kondratyevna and her mother lived in one of the rooms and Smerdyakov by himself in the other. Goodness only knows on what basis he lived with them: whether he paid for his room or not. Afterwards it was generally believed that he had taken up his quarters with them as Maria Kondratyevna's intended and was living there rent-free for the time being. Both the daughter and the mother respected him highly and regarded him as greatly superior to themselves. On the door being opened to his repeated knocks, Ivan went into the passage and, at Maria Kondratyevna's direction, went straight to the 'parlour' on the left, occupied by Smerdyakov. There was a tiled stove in the room and it was very hot. The walls were covered with blue paper, which was, it is true, in shreds and in the cracks under it cockroaches swarmed in great numbers, so that there was a continual rustling from them. The room was poorly furnished: two benches along the walls and two chairs by the table. The table, though of plain wood, was covered with a cloth with a pink pattern on it. There was a pot of geraniums in each of the two little windows and a case with icons in one corner of the room. On the table stood a very dented little copper *samovar* and a tray with two cups. But Smerdyakov had already had his tea and the *samovar* had gone out. He was sitting on a bench at the table and, looking at his exercise book, was scribbling something with a pen. There was a small bottle of ink beside him as well as a low, iron candlestick, but with a stearin candle. From Smerdyakov's face Ivan at once concluded that he had completely recovered from his illness. His face was much fresher and fuller, his quiff was brushed up and the hair on his temples plastered down. He was sitting in a multi-coloured, quilted dressing-gown, which was, however, very dirty and rather threadbare. He had spectacles on his nose, which Ivan had never seen him wearing before. That most trifling circumstance seemed suddenly to redouble Ivan's anger: 'A disgusting creature like that and wearing spectacles, too!'

Smerdyakov raised his head slowly and gazed intently at his visitor through his spectacles; then he removed them slowly and half-raised himself on the bench, but not in the least respectfully, almost lazily, in fact, just enough to observe the barest requirements of civility. All this flashed through Ivan's mind; he noticed it instantly and at once took it all in – and, particularly, Smerdyakov's unmistakably spiteful, unfriendly, and even disdainful look: 'What do you come barging in for?' it seemed to say. 'We settled everything there, so what have you come here again for?'

Ivan could hardly control himself.

'It's hot here,' he said, still standing, and unbuttoned his overcoat.

'Won't you take off your coat, sir?' Smerdyakov suggested politely.

Ivan took off his coat, threw it down on a bench, took a chair with trembling fingers, drew it up quickly to the table and sat down. Smerdyakov managed to sit down on his bench before him.

'First of all, are we alone here?' Ivan asked sternly and impulsively. 'Can anyone overhear us from the other room?'

'No, sir, no one can't hear nothing. You've seen for yourself: there's a passage.'

'Look here, my dear fellow: what was it you blurted out as I was leaving the hospital, I mean, that if I said nothing about how good you were at shamming an epileptic fit, you wouldn't tell the examining magistrate all about our conversation at the gate? What did you mean by "all"? What did you have in mind then? You weren't threatening me by any chance, were you? You don't imagine I've entered into a sort of league with you, do you? You don't think I'm afraid of you, do you?'

Ivan said it all in a perfect fury, letting Smerdyakov know openly and deliberately that he scorned any attempt at beating about the bush and that he was putting his cards on the table. Smerdyakov's eyes flashed spitefully, his left eye blinked, and, as was his custom, he at once gave his answer, slowly and restrainedly: 'You want plain speaking, well, then, you shall have it.'

'What I meant, sir, and why I said it then, was that, seeing as how you knew beforehand about this murder of your father, you didn't care a hang what happened to him, and I promised not to tell the authorities, so that people shouldn't think nothing bad about your feelings and, perhaps, of something else, besides.'

Though Smerdyakov said it all unhurriedly and apparently keeping himself completely under control, yet there was a note of firm determination, of malice and insolent defiance in his voice. He stared impudently at Ivan, who for a moment almost felt dizzy.

'What? What did you say? Have you gone off your head?'

'No, sir, I'm in full possession of my faculties.'

'But did I *know* of the murder then?' Ivan cried at last, bringing down his hand heavily on the table. 'What do you mean by "something else, besides"? Speak, you scoundrel!'

Smerdyakov said nothing and continued to stare impudently at Ivan.

'Speak, you stinking rotter, what is that "something besides"?' he bawled.

'By "something besides" I meant just now that you, too, sir, had probably greatly desired your father's death at that time.'

Ivan jumped up and struck him a violent blow on the shoulder with his fist, so that he fell back against the wall. In a twinkling tears rolled down his face, and saying, 'You ought to be ashamed to hit a sick man, sir,' he suddenly covered his face with a very dirty blue check handkerchief and began crying softly. A minute passed.

'That'll do! Stop it!' Ivan said peremptorily at last, sitting down on his chair again. 'Don't make me lose my patience completely!'

Smerdyakov removed the rag from his eyes. Every line on his shrivelled face reflected the insult he had just received.

'So you thought then, you blackguard, that I wanted to kill my father as much as Dmitry?'

'I didn't know what thoughts you had in your mind then, sir,' Smerdyakov said in a hurt voice. 'That's why I stopped you as you was coming through the gate, to sound you on that point.'

'To sound what? What?'

'Why, sir, on that very thing: whether you wanted your father killed as soon as possible or not.'

What Ivan resented most of all was the relentless, insolent tone which Smerdyakov stubbornly refused to abandon.

'It was you who killed him!' he exclaimed suddenly.

Smerdyakov smiled contemptuously.

'You knows very well, sir, that I did not kill him. I should have thought there was no need for a clever man to talk about it no more.'

'But what, what made you suspect me at the time?'

'Well, sir, as you knows already it was simply from fear. For I was in such a condition then that, shaking with fear, I suspected everybody. I decided to sound you, too, sir, for I thought that if you, too, wanted the same as your brother, then it was as good as done, and I, too, would be done for same as everybody else.'

'Look here, you didn't say that a fortnight ago.'

'The same thing was at the back of my mind when I talked to you in the hospital, only I thought you'd understand without me putting it into words. You see, sir, I thought that a clever man like you wouldn't care to talk of it openly.'

'Did you? But answer me, answer, I insist: what could I have said or done to put such a base suspicion into your mean soul?'

'If you mean murder, sir, then, of course, you couldn't have done it, and you didn't want to, neither. But you did want someone else to do it. Yes, sir, that you did.'

'And how calmly, how calmly he says it! But why should I have wanted it? Why the hell should I have wanted it?'

'How do you mean, sir? How the hell should you have wanted it? And what about the inheritance, sir?' Smerdyakov asked venomously and even, somehow, vindictively. 'Why, sir, after your father's death each one of you three would have got forty thousand at least and perhaps even more, but if your father married that woman, Miss Svetlov, she would have had all his capital made over to her immediately after the wedding, for she certainly isn't stupid, so that you wouldn't have got as much as two roubles, the three of you, after his death. And how far were they from a wedding? Not a hair's breadth, sir. The young lady had only to lift her little finger and he'd have run after her to church with his tongue hanging out.'

Ivan restrained himself with a painful effort.

'Very well,' he said at last, 'as you see, I haven't jumped up, I haven't struck you, I haven't killed you. Go on. According to you, then, I hoped that my brother Dmitry would do it, I had reckoned on him to do it.'

'Why, sir, you couldn't help hoping that he would do it. For if he killed him, he'd lose all his rights as a nobleman, as well as his rank and property, and be sent to Siberia. So that his share of the inheritance would be shared by you and your brother Alexey equally. Which means, sir, that each of you would get sixty and not forty thousand. Yes, sir, you certainly did reckon on your brother Dmitry.'

'The things I put up with from you! Listen, scoundrel, if I had reckoned on anyone then, it would have been on you and not on Dmitry and, I swear, I had a feeling then that you were up to something horrible – I – I remember my impression!'

'I also thought at the time for a moment that you was reckoning on me too,' Smerdyakov grinned sarcastically. 'So that you gave yourself away to me by that more than anything. For if, as you say, sir, you had such a feeling about me and went away at the same time, you as good as said to me: you can murder my father, I won't stand in your way.'

'You blackguard! So that's how you understood it?'

'And it was all because of Chermashnya, sir! Why, good Lord, sir, you was going to Moscow and you wouldn't hear of going to Chermashnya however much your father asked you to! And suddenly you agreed to go there just at a foolish word from me! And why, sir, did you have to agree to go to Chermashnya that time? If you didn't go to Moscow, but for no reason went to Chermashnya instead just because of something I said to you, then you must have expected something from me.'

'No, I swear, I didn't!' bawled Ivan, gritting his teeth.

'Didn't you, now? But, you see, sir, what you did ought to have done as a good son was to take me to the police station at once and have me flogged for such words or, leastways, boxed my ears good and proper there and then. But, good Lord, sir, you didn't do nothing of the kind. You was not a bit angry. Aye, you acted upon my words friendly-like at once. You acted at a foolish word from me and went off to Chermashnya, which, if you don't mind me saying so, sir, was very stupid of you, for you ought to have stayed to protect your father's life. So I couldn't help drawing my own conclusions from that, could I?'

Ivan sat scowling, his fists pressed convulsively on his knees.

'Yes, I'm sorry I didn't box your ears,' he said with a bitter smile. 'I couldn't have taken you to the police station, for who would have believed me and what charge could I have preferred against you? But I could certainly have given you a hell of a beating. A pity I didn't think of it. Though it's forbidden to box a servant's ears, I'd have reduced your ugly face to a gory mess.'

Smerdyakov looked at him almost with delight.

'Under ordinary circumstances,' he said in the self-satisfied, doctrinaire tone in which he used to taunt Grigory and argue with him about religion at Fyodor Karamazov's table, 'under ordinary circumstances the boxing of a servant's ears is really forbidden by law now, and, indeed, sir, people no longer do it, but in exceptional circumstances people still go on beating their servants not only in our country, but everywhere in the world, even in the Republic of France itself, just as in the time of Adam and Eve, sir. And they will never give it up, but you, sir, didn't dare beat me even in an exceptional case.'

'What are you learning French words for?' asked Ivan, nodding towards the exercise book on the table.

'And why shouldn't I learn them, sir? I want to improve my education in case I might one day go to the happier parts of Europe myself.'

'Listen, monster,' cried Ivan with flashing eyes, trembling all over, 'I'm not afraid of your accusations. Say what you like about me, and if I don't thrash you within an inch of your life now, it's only because I suspect you of the crime and I'm going to see that you're put on trial for it. I'll show you up.'

'And in my opinion, sir, you'd better keep quiet. For what can you accuse me of seeing as how I'm completely innocent? And who will believe you? Only if you starts anything, I will tell everything, too, for I have to defend myself, haven't I?'

'Do you think I'm afraid of you now?'

'Well, sir, even if the court don't believe all I've said to you just now, the public will, and you, sir, will be sorry.'

'It's nice to have a chat with a clever man – is that what you mean – eh?' snapped Ivan, grinding his teeth.

'You've hit the nail on the head, sir. And you'd better *be* clever, sir.'

Ivan got up, shaking all over with indignation, put on his overcoat, and without replying to Smerdyakov and even without looking at him, walked quickly out of the house. The cool evening air refreshed him. The moon shone brightly in the sky. A terrible nightmare of thoughts and sensations was surging in his soul. 'Go and tell the police at once about Smerdyakov? But what can I tell them? He's innocent, all the same. On the contrary, he will accuse me. And, really, why did I set off for Chermashnya then? What for? Whatever for?' Ivan asked himself. 'Yes, of course, I was expecting something and he's quite right. . . .' And, again, he remembered for the hundredth time how on his last night at his father's house he had listened on the stairs for a noise in his father's rooms, but he remembered it with such agony now that he stopped dead as though stabbed to the heart: 'Yes, it is true, I expected it then! I wanted the murder, I wanted it! Did I want it, did I? Smerdyakov has to be killed! If I don't dare kill Smerdyakov now, life is not worth living!' Without going home, Ivan went straight to Katerina and frightened her by his appearance: he was like a madman. He told her of his conversation with Smerdyakov, to the last detail. He could not be calmed, however much she tried, but kept pacing the room, talking abruptly, strangely. At last he sat down and, leaning his elbows on the table and resting his head on his hands, delivered himself of a strange aphorism.

'If Smerdyakov and not Dmitry murdered father, I'd be as guilty as he, for I put him up to it. Whether I put him up to it or not, I don't know yet. But if he killed him and not Dmitry, then, of course, I am a murderer, too.'

Hearing that, Katerina got up from her seat without a word, went up to her writing table, opened a box standing on it, took out a piece of paper and laid it before Ivan. This was the document which Ivan later told Alyosha was 'conclusive proof' that Dmitry had killed their father. It was a letter written by Dmitry to Katerina when he was drunk on the evening he met Alyosha outside the town, returning to the monastery after the scene at Katerina's, when Grushenka had insulted her. After parting from Alyosha, Mitya had gone to see Grushenka; whether he saw her or not is not known, but at night he found himself at the 'Metropolis' where he got dead drunk. It was then that he asked for pen and paper and wrote the document which was to have important consequences to himself. It was a frenzied, wordy, and incoherent letter, in fact, a 'drunken' letter. It was the sort of thing a drunken man, on returning home, begins with extraordinary heat to tell his wife, or one of his household, how he had just been insulted, what scoundrel had insulted him, what a fine fellow he is himself, and how he will pay that scoundrel back – and he goes on and on about it all, incoherently and excitedly, striking the table with his fists, and with drunken tears. The piece of paper they gave him to write his letter on in the public house was a dirty sheet of ordinary, cheap note-paper, with a bill scribbled on the back of it. There was apparently not space enough for his drunken verbosity, and Mitya not only filled the margins, but had written the last lines across the rest of his letter. The letter was as follows:

Fatal Katya, Tomorrow I'll get the money and return your three thousand to you, and good-bye – woman of great wrath, but good-bye my love, too! Let's make an end of it! Tomorrow I'll try and raise it from someone or other, and if I can't get it from them, I give you my word of honour, I shall go to my father and break his head and take the money from under his pillow, if only Ivan goes away. I'll give you back your three thousand if I have to go to Siberia for it. And to you – farewell! I bow down to the ground, for I've treated you like a scoundrel. Forgive me. No, you'd better not forgive me: it will be easier so for you and me! Better Siberia than your love, for I love another, and you've found out the sort of woman she is today, so how can you forgive me? I shall kill my thief! I shall go away to the East from you all so as not to know any of you again. Not *her*, either, for you're not the only one who torments me, she does too. Farewell!

PS. I am writing curses, but I adore you! I hear it in my breast. One string remains and it jangles. Better break, my heart, in twain! I'll kill myself, but first of all that cur. I'll tear three thousand from him and fling them to you. Though I've been a scoundrel to you, I'm not a thief! Expect three thousand. It's under the cur's mattress, a pink ribbon. I am not a thief, but I'll kill my thief. Katya, don't look disdainful: Dmitry is not a thief, but a murderer! He has murdered his father and ruined himself to be able to stand up to you and not have to put up with your pride. And not to love you.

PPS. I kiss your feet, farewell!

PPPS. Katya, pray to God that I get the money from someone. Then I shall not have blood on my hands, but if I don't get it – I shall! Kill me!

Your slave and your enemy,
D. KARAMAZOV.

When Ivan had read this 'document', he got up from the table convinced. So it was his brother and not Smerdyakov. And if it was not

Smerdyakov, then it was not he, Ivan, either. The letter suddenly assumed in his eyes the nature of a mathematical certainty. So far as he was concerned, there could no longer be any doubt of Mitya's guilt. Incidentally, there was no suspicion in Ivan's mind that Mitya might have committed the murder in conjunction with Smerdyakov. It did not fit in with the facts, either. Ivan was completely reassured. The next morning he only thought with contempt of Smerdyakov and his jeering remarks. A few days later he was even amazed how he could have been so deeply hurt by his suspicions. He made up his mind to take no notice of him and forget him. So a month passed. He made no further inquiries about Smerdyakov, but he happened to hear once or twice that he was very ill and out of his mind. 'He'll end up by going mad,' the young doctor Varvinsky said about him once, and Ivan remembered it. During the last week of that month Ivan himself began to feel very ill. He had already been to see the Moscow specialist who had been sent for by Katerina shortly before the trial. And it was just at that time that his relations with Katerina became acutely strained. They seemed like two bitter enemies in love with one another. Katerina's momentary but violent reversions to Mitya drove Ivan to complete distraction. Strange to say, to the very last scene described by us, when Alyosha brought Katerina the message from Mitya, he, Ivan, never during the whole month heard her express any doubts about Mitya's guilt, in spite of all her 'reversions' to him, which he hated so much. It is no less remarkable that, while feeling that he hated Mitya more and more every day, he realized at the same time that he hated him, not Katerina's 'reversions' to him, and that he hated him *because he had killed his father*! He felt and fully realized it himself. Nevertheless, ten days before the trial he went to see Mitya and proposed to him a plan of escape, a plan that he had apparently thought over long before. In addition to the main reason that prompted him to take such a step, he was also driven to it by the open wound in his heart left by Smerdyakov's remark that it was to his, Ivan's, advantage that his brother should be convicted, since that would increase his and Alyosha's inheritance from forty to sixty thousand. He therefore decided to sacrifice thirty thousand of his own money to arrange for Mitya's escape. On his return from the prison, he felt terribly depressed and disconcerted: he suddenly began to feel that he was so anxious for Mitya to escape not only because his wound would be healed by his sacrifice of thirty thousand, but for quite another reason: 'Is it because at heart I, too, am just such a murderer?' he asked himself. Deep, deep inside something seemed to sear his soul. And, what was worse, his pride suffered terribly all through that month, but of that later. When, after his talk with Alyosha, Ivan decided, his hand on the bell of his flat, to go and see Smerdyakov, he did so in obedience to a sudden and peculiar upsurge of indignation. He suddenly remembered how Katerina had only a few minutes before shouted to him in Alyosha's presence: 'It is you, only you who persuaded me that he [that is, Mitya] was the murderer!' Recalling this, Ivan was dumbfounded: never in his life did he persuade her that Mitya was the murderer; on the contrary, after he had returned from Smerdyakov he had told her that he might be guilty of his father's murder himself. It was *she*, she who had placed the 'document' before him and proved his brother's guilt! And now she suddenly exclaimed: 'I've been to see Smerdyakov myself!' When had she been to see him? Ivan knew nothing about it. So she was not at all convinced of Mitya's guilt! And what could Smerdyakov have said to her? What, what had he said to her? His heart was filled with terrible anger. He could not understand how he could, half an hour before, have let her words pass without protesting at once. He let go of the bell and rushed off to Smerdyakov. 'This time I shall, perhaps, kill him,' he thought on the way.

8

The Third and Last Interview with Smerdyakov

WHEN he was halfway to Smerdyakov's lodgings, a keen, dry wind that had been blowing early that morning arose again, and a thick, fine, dry snow began falling. It fell on the ground without adhering to it and the wind was whirling it about, and soon there was a regular blizzard. There were scarcely any street lamps in the part of the town where Smerdyakov lived. Ivan walked along in the darkness, paying no attention to the blizzard, and picking his way instinctively. His head ached and his temples throbbed painfully. His hands (he felt it) were twitching convulsively. A few yards from Maria Kondratyevna's little house he suddenly came across a solitary drunken little peasant, in a patched homespun coat, zigzagging along the road, grumbling and swearing, and suddenly leaving off swearing and beginning to sing in a hoarse drunken voice:

> Oh, Vanka's gone to Petersburg,
> And I won't wait for him!

But he kept breaking off at the second line and began swearing again, and then, again, suddenly began singing the same song. Even without thinking about him, Ivan had felt a terrible hatred for him, and, then, he suddenly became conscious of it. At once he felt an irresistible impulse to hit the little peasant with his fist and knock him down. Just at that moment he overtook him. The little peasant, swaying perilously, suddenly lurched heavily against Ivan, who pushed him back furiously. The little peasant went flying to the middle of the road and fell like a log on the frozen ground. He uttered one plaintive moan: 'Oh-h!' and fell silent. Ivan stepped up to him. He lay on his back, quite motionless and unconscious. 'He'll freeze to death!' thought Ivan and walked on to Smerdyakov's.

In the passage Maria Kondratyevna, who ran out to open the door with a candle in her hand, whispered to him that Pavel Fyodorovich (that is, Smerdyakov) was very ill. 'It's not as if he was laid up, sir, but he doesn't seem to be in his right mind. Told me to take away the tea, sir. Wouldn't have it.'

'He's not violent, is he?' Ivan asked bluntly.

'Why, no, sir! On the contrary, he's very quiet. Only,' Maria Kondratyevna begged him, 'don't talk to him too long, sir.'

Ivan opened the door and stepped into the room.

It was as hot as during his last visit, but certain changes could be observed in the room: one of the benches at the side of the wall had been taken out and an old mahogany sofa had been put in its place. A bed with fairly clean white pillows had been made up on it. Smerdyakov was sitting on the bed, wearing the same dressing-gown. The table had been moved in front of the sofa, so that the room seemed very crowded. A thick book in a yellow cover lay on the table, but Smerdyakov was not reading it. He sat there without doing anything. He greeted Ivan with a slow, silent gaze and was apparently not at all surprised at his coming. He was greatly changed:

his face had grown very thin and sallow. His eyes were sunken and there were blue patches under them.

'You really are ill, then?' said Ivan, stopping short. 'I'm not going to keep you long. I won't even take off my coat. Where can one sit down here?'

He walked up to the other side of the table, moved up a chair and sat down.

'Why are you looking at me without saying a word? I've come to ask you only one question and, I swear, I won't go unless I get an answer: has Miss Verkhovtsev been to see you?'

There was a prolonged silence, Smerdyakov still gazing quietly at Ivan. But all of a sudden he gave a despairing wave of the hand and turned his face away.

'What's the matter?' exclaimed Ivan.

'Nothing.'

'What do you mean – nothing?'

'Well, she's been here. What's it to you? Leave me alone.'

'No, I won't leave you alone! Tell me, when was she here?'

'Why, I've forgotten all about her,' said Smerdyakov, with a contemptuous smile, and, suddenly turning his face to Ivan again, he glared at him with eyes full of frenzied hatred, just as he had done at their last interview a month before.

'Seems to me you're ill yourself, sir,' he said to Ivan. 'Your face looks pinched. You look awful, sir!'

'Never mind my health. Answer my question.'

'And why are your eyes so yellow? The whites are quite yellow. Very worried, aren't you?'

He grinned contemptuously and suddenly laughed outright.

'Listen, I said I wouldn't go away without an answer!' Ivan cried in great exasperation.

'What are you badgering me for? Why do you torture me?' Smerdyakov said, with a pained look.

'Oh, hell, I don't care a damn about you. Answer my question and I'll go.'

'I've nothing to say to you!' Smerdyakov said, looking down again.

'I tell you I'll make you answer!'

'What are you so worried about?' Smerdyakov asked, staring at him again, not so much with contempt as with revulsion. 'Is it because the trial opens tomorrow? But nothing's going to happen to you. You can be quite sure of that! Go home, go to bed and don't worry. Don't be afraid of nothing.'

'I don't understand you – what have I got to be afraid of tomorrow?' Ivan said with surprise, and suddenly he really did freeze with terror.

Smerdyakov measured him with his eyes.

'You don't un-der-stand?' he drawled reproachfully. 'Don't you, now? Fancy a clever man like you trying to pull my leg like that!'

Ivan looked at him in silence. The quite unexpected and incredibly arrogant tone in which this former lackey was addressing him was in itself extraordinary. Even during their last interview he had not spoken to him in such a tone.

'I tell you you've got nothing to fear. I'm not going to say a thing against you. There's no evidence against you. Just look how your hands are shaking! Why are your fingers moving about like that? Go home, *it was not you who murdered him.*'

Ivan gave a start: he remembered Alyosha.

'I know it was not me,' he murmured.

'You know, do you?' Smerdyakov again put in quickly.

Ivan jumped up and seized him by the shoulder.

'Tell me everything, you dirty rotter! Tell me everything!'

Smerdyakov was not in the least frightened. He merely glared at him with eyes full of insane hatred.

'Well,' he whispered furiously, 'it was you who murdered him, if you really want to know!'

Ivan sank back on to his chair as though he had realized something. He smiled maliciously.

'Are you again harping on that? What you were talking about last time?'

'Aye, last time, too, you was standing before me and you understood everything. You understand it now, too!'

'All I understand is that you're mad.'

'How the man doesn't get tired of it! Here we are, the two of us, sitting alone in a room, so what's the use of fooling ourselves, pretending to each other? Or do you really want to put the whole blame on me to my face? You murdered him. You are the chief murderer. I was only your accomplice, your loyal page, and I done it because you told me to.'

'You *did* it? Did you murder him?' Ivan froze with horror.

Something seemed to give way in his brain. A cold shiver passed down his spine and he began shaking all over. Now Smerdyakov himself looked at him in surprise: the genuineness of Ivan's horror must have struck him at last.

'Didn't you really know nothing about it?' he muttered mistrustfully, staring at him with a wry smile.

Ivan kept looking at him; he seemed to be struck dumb.

> Oh, Vanka's gone to Petersburg,
> And I won't wait for him!

rang suddenly through his head.

'You know, I'm afraid you're a dream, you're a phantom sitting before me,' he murmured.

'No, sir, there ain't no phantom here, except the two of us, and another one, besides. No doubt he's sitting here between the two of us, the other one.'

'Who is he? Who's here? Who's the other one?' Ivan cried in terror, looking round the room, searching for someone in every corner.

'The other one's God, sir. Aye, Providence itself. It's here beside us, sir. Only you needn't look for it. You won't find it.'

'You lied! You didn't kill him!' Ivan cried frantically. 'You're either mad or you're taunting me as you did last time!'

Smerdyakov watched him searchingly as before without any sign of fear. He still could not overcome his feeling of mistrust; it still seemed to him that Ivan knew 'everything', but was merely pretending not to know in order 'to put the whole blame on me to my face'.

'Half a moment, sir,' he said at last in a weak voice and, suddenly, dragging his left leg from under the table, he began rolling up his trouser leg. He was wearing long white socks and slippers. Smerdyakov, without hurrying, took off his garter and put his hand into the bottom of his sock. Ivan looked at him and suddenly shook with convulsive horror.

'Madman!' he bawled and, jumping up quickly from his seat, he drew back so violently that he knocked against the wall and seemed to be glued to it, drawn up stiffly to his full height. He gazed at Smerdyakov with insane horror. Smerdyakov, not in the least disconcerted by his horror, was still fumbling about in his sock, as though trying to get hold of something with his fingers and pull it out. At last he got hold of it and started pulling it. Ivan saw that it was some papers or a bundle of papers. Smerdyakov pulled it out and put it on the table.

'Here it is, sir!' he said quietly.

'What is it?' asked Ivan, trembling.

'Won't you have a look, sir?' Smerdyakov said, still in the same soft voice.

Ivan stepped up to the table, took up the bundle and began unfolding it, but suddenly drew his hand away as though it had come into contact with some horrible, loathsome reptile.

'Your fingers keeps trembling, sir, just as if they was in convulsions,' observed Smerdyakov, and unhurriedly unfolded the bundle himself.

Under the wrapper were three rolls of rainbow-coloured hundred-rouble notes.

'They're all here, sir, all the three thousand, you needn't trouble to count them. Take them,' he said to Ivan, nodding at the notes.

Ivan sank on to his chair. He was as white as a sheet.

'You frightened me with – with your sock,' he said with a strange grin.

'Didn't you really know it till now?' Smerdyakov asked again.

'No, I didn't know. I was thinking of Dmitry all the time. Brother, brother – oh God!' He suddenly clutched his head in both hands. 'Listen, did you kill him alone? With or without my brother?'

'Only with you, sir. I killed him with your help, sir. Your brother's quite innocent, sir.'

'All right, all right. We'll talk about me later. Why do I keep on trembling? Can't utter a word.'

'You was brave enough then, sir. Everything, you said, is permitted, and look how frightened you are now!' Smerdyakov murmured in surprise. 'Won't you have some lemonade, sir? I'll ask for some at once. It's wonderfully refreshing, sir. Only I'd better hide this away first.'

And he motioned towards the bundles of notes again. He was about to get up to go to the door to call Maria Kondratyevna and ask her to make some lemonade and bring it to them. But, looking for something to cover the money with so that she might not see it, he first pulled out his handkerchief, but as it happened again to be very dirty, he took up the big yellow book that Ivan had noticed on entering the room and put it over the notes. The title of the book was: *Sayings of the Holy Father Isaac the Syrian.* Ivan had just time to read it mechanically.

'I won't have any lemonade,' he said. 'We'll talk about me later. Sit down and tell me how you did it. Tell me everything. . . .'

'You'd better take off your coat, sir, or you'll be all in a sweat.'

Ivan, as though he had only just thought of it, tore off his coat and flung it, without getting up from his chair, on the bench.

'Speak, please, speak!'

He seemed to grow calmer. He waited confidently, knowing for certain that Smerdyakov would tell him *everything* now.

'About how it was done, sir?' Smerdyakov sighed. 'It was done in a most natural way, sir, just as you said. . . .'

'About what I said later,' Ivan interrupted again, but no longer shouting as before, but enunciating each word distinctly, as though he had regained full control of himself. 'All I want is that you should tell me in detail how you did it. One thing after another. Don't forget anything. The details. Above all, the details. Please!'

'You had gone away and I fell into the cellar, sir.'

'Did you have a fit or did you sham one?'

'Of course, I shammed, sir. I shammed it all. Went down the steps quietly, I did, to the very bottom, lay down quietly, and as soon as I lies down, sir, I starts screaming. Writhing in convulsions till they carried me out.'

'One moment! Were you shamming all the time afterwards? In the hospital, too?'

'Why, no, sir. Next day, in the morning, before they took me to hospital, I had a real fit and such a violent one as I hadn't had for years. For two days I was quite unconscious.'

'All right, all right. Go on.'

'Well, sir, they puts me on the bed behind the partition as I knew all along they would, for whenever I was ill Marfa used to put me to bed behind that same partition in their cottage. Very kind to me she's always been, sir, ever since I was born. I moaned at night, only quiet-like. All the time I was waiting for your brother Dmitry to come.'

'Waiting for him to come? To you?'

'Why should he come to me, sir? I was waiting for him to come to the house, for, you see, sir, I had no doubt at all that he'd come that night, for seeing as how I wasn't there to meet him and having had no news, he would be sure to get into the house by climbing over the fence, as he knew how to and do what had to be done.'

'And if he hadn't come?'

'Then nothing would have happened, sir. I should never have made up my mind to do what I did without him.'

'All right, all right – speak more clearly. Don't hurry and, above all, don't leave anything out!'

'I expected him to kill Mr Karamazov. Yes, I was quite sure of that. For, you see, sir, I'd prepared him for it – er – during the last few days and – the chief thing was that he knew about the signals. With his suspiciousness and towering rage, which had been growing in him during all those days, he was quite sure to try to get into the house with the help of them signals. That was certain, sir. I was expecting him to do it.'

'Wait,' Ivan interrupted, 'if he'd killed him, he'd have taken the money and carried it off. That's exactly what you must have thought would happen. Well, what would you have got out of it? I don't see it.'

'You see, sir, he'd never have found the money. It was only me that told him that the money was under the mattress. But that wasn't true. No, sir. At first the money had been in a cash-box. That's where it was, sir. But afterwards I suggested to Mr Karamazov, who trusted me more than anyone in the whole world, to put the envelope with the money in the corner behind the icons, for no one would never have thought of looking for it there, especially if he was in a hurry. So that's where the envelope was, sir. In the corner behind the icons. You see, sir, it would have been silly to keep it under the mattress. He should at least have kept it in his cash-box under lock and key. But here they all believes now that it was under the mattress. Quite a silly notion, sir. So if your brother Dmitry had done the murder, he'd have found nothing and would either have run away quickly, afraid of every sound, as is always the case with murderers, or he'd have been arrested. So the next morning, or even on that same night, I could always go into the bedroom, go behind the icons and take the money, and your brother Dmitry would have been held responsible for it all. Yes, sir, I could always count on that.'

'But what if he hadn't killed him but only given him a beating?'

'If he hadn't killed him, then, of course, I shouldn't have dared to take the money and the whole thing would have fallen through. But, you see, sir, there was always the possibility that he'd beat him unconscious, so that I'd have time to take the money and then report to Mr Karamazov that your brother Dmitry had taken the money after beating him.'

'Wait – I'm getting all mixed up. So it was Dmitry, after all, who killed him and you only took the money!'

'No, sir, he didn't kill him. You see, sir, I could, of course, have told you even now that he done it, but I don't want to tell you no lies now, because – because I can see that you really haven't understood nothing till now and that you was not pretending to me so as to throw your undoubted guilt on me to my face. For it's you, sir, who're responsible for everything what's happened, because you knew about the murder and expected me to do it, and went away knowing all about it. That's why I'd like to prove it to you to your face this evening that you, you alone are the real murderer and not me, though it was me what killed him. Yes, sir, it's you who's the rightful murderer.'

'But why, why am I the murderer? Oh, God!' Ivan cried, unable to restrain himself any longer and forgetting that he had put off all discussion about himself till the end of their talk. 'You're still harping on that Chermashnya? Wait, tell me, what did you want my consent for, if you took Chermashnya for consent? How will you explain that now?'

'Well, sir, if I was sure of your consent, I'd have known that when you came back you wouldn't have raised a hullabaloo about the missing three thousand, even if for some reason the police had suspected me instead of your brother Dmitry, or thought that I was his accomplice. On the contrary, you'd have protected me from the others. And having got your inheritance, you might have rewarded me as soon as possible afterwards, and for the rest of my life, for it would be, after all, through me that you'd have got your inheritance, seeing as how otherwise your father would have married Miss Svetlov and you'd have got nothing at all.'

'Oh, so you intended to blackmail me afterwards – for the rest of my life, did you?' snarled Ivan. 'And what if I hadn't gone away then but had told the police about you?'

'What could you have told them? That I was persuading you to go to Chermashnya? Why, sir, that's just a lot of nonsense. Besides, after our conversation you'd either have gone or not. If you'd stayed, nothing would have happened. I'd have known that you didn't want to have anything to do with it and I shouldn't have undertaken anything. But as you went, it could only mean that you assured me that you wouldn't dare to give evidence against me in court and that you wouldn't mind me keeping the three thousand. And, anyway, sir, you couldn't possibly have prosecuted me afterwards, for I'd have told it all in court, not that I'd stolen the money or committed the murder – I shouldn't have told them that – but that you, sir, had incited me to steal and commit murder and that I wouldn't agree to it. That's why, sir, I had to have your consent then, so that you couldn't drive me into a corner afterwards, for where could you have got your proof? But I could always drive you into a corner by disclosing how eager you was for your father's death. And let me tell you, sir, the public would have believed it and you'd have been disgraced for the rest of your life.'

'So I was eager for it, was I?' snarled Ivan again.

'Yes, sir, without a doubt you was, and by your consent at the time you silently gave your approval for me to carry on with it,' said Smerdyakov, looking determinedly at Ivan.

He was very weak and he spoke softly and in an exhausted voice, but something deep inside him spurred him on. He evidently had some plan. Ivan felt that.

'Go on,' he said. 'Tell me what happened that night.'

'Well, sir, what is there to tell? So I lies there and I fancies I hears the master shout. Before that Grigory all of a sudden gets up and goes out, and suddenly I hears him yelling outside and after that all's quiet and dark. I lies there waiting, my heart's pounding, and I can't bear it no longer. So I gets up at last and goes out and I steals up to the bedroom window on the left to listen whether he's still alive there, and I hears the master rushing about the room and moaning – so he is alive all right. Damn! I thinks to myself. I goes up to the window and shouts to the master: "It's me, sir!" And he says to me, he says, "He's been here," he says, "he's been and he's run away!" That is, your brother Dmitry had been and gone. "He's killed Grigory," he says to me. "Where?" I whispers to him. "There, in the corner of the garden," he points. Whispering, too, he is. "Wait, sir," I says. So I goes to the corner of the garden to look for Grigory, and then I stumbles against him, lying by the wall, covered in blood and unconscious. So it's true, then, that your brother Dmitry has been here, I thinks to myself, sudden-like, and it was just then, sir, at that very moment, that I makes up my mind on the spot to finish it all without delay, for Grigory, even if he was alive, wouldn't see nothing of it, lying there unconscious. The only risk was that Marfa might suddenly wake up. I was aware of that at the moment, only I was so dead keen on going through with it that I could scarcely breathe. So off I goes back to the bedroom window and I says to the master: "She's here," I says, "she's come, Miss Svetlov has," I says, "and she asks to be let in." Well, sir, he just gives a violent start like a baby. "Where is she? Where?" he fairly gasps, but he don't believe me, you see. "There she is," I says, "open the door." He looks at me out of the window and he don't know whether to believe me or not, but he's afraid to open the door. Aye, I thinks to myself, he's afraid of me now. And, you know, sir, a funny thing: I suddenly takes it into my head to tap out them signals that Grushenka has come on the window frame before his very eyes. He didn't believe my words, but as soon as I taps out the signal, he ran at once to open the door. So he opens it. I tries to go in, but he stands there barring my way. "Where is she? Where is she?" he asks, looking at me and shaking all over. Well, I thinks, if he's as afraid of me as all that, it's bad! And, you know, my legs went limp with fright that he wouldn't let me in or that he'd call out or Marfa would run up or something or other might happen. I don't remember what exactly I was thinking just then, but I must have gone all pale in the face as I stood before him. I whispers to him, "Why, sir, she's there under the window! How is it you didn't see her?" "Bring her, bring her then!" "But she's afraid," I says, "she was frightened by the shouts and hid herself in the bushes. Go and call her yourself from the study," I says. So off he runs, goes up to the window, puts the candle on the window sill. "Grushenka," he cries, "Grushenka, are you there?" But though he called it out himself, he durstn't lean out of the window, he durstn't move away from me, because he was in a devil of a funk. He was so frightened of me, you see, sir, that he durstn't move away an inch from me. "Why, sir," I says (I walked up to the window and leaned right out of it), "there she is, there, in that bush. Can't you see her laughing at you?" Well, so all of a sudden he believes me, starts shaking all over – head over heels in love with her he was, sir – and leans right out of the window. So I grabs that there iron paper-weight from his table – do you remember, sir, must have weighed three pounds at least – and I raises it and hits him with the corner of it right on the crown of his head. He never even cried out. Slumped down on the floor suddenly, and I hits him over the head again and a third time. The third time I knows I've cracked his skull. It's then that he falls on his back, face upwards, covered all over with blood. I examines my clothes – not a drop of blood on me – it didn't spurt out, you see. So I wipes the paper-weight, replaces it, goes behind the icons, takes out the money, and throws the envelope on the floor, and the pink ribbon beside it. I goes out into the garden, shaking all over. Straight to the apple tree I goes, the one with the big hole in it – you knows the hole, sir, I'd had a good look at it long before and put a rag and a piece of paper in it – got it ready for an emergency. So I wraps the money in the paper and then in the rag and pushes it all deep down into the hole. There it lies for over a fortnight, all that money, sir, and I took it out only after I'd come out of the hospital. Anyways, so I goes back to my bed, lies down, and thinks to myself, fearful-like: "Now, if Grigory's been killed, it may turn out bad for me, but if he's not killed and comes to, it will be fine, for then he'll bear witness that your brother Dmitry has been here and, therefore, must have killed him and taken his money." So I starts moaning and groaning from uncertainty and impatience so as to wake Marfa as soon as possible. At last she gets up, rushes to have a look at me, but seeing all of a sudden that Grigory isn't there, runs out and I hears her screaming in the garden. Well, sir, then the hue and cry was raised, and it went on all through the night, and I was no more worried about anything.'

The speaker stopped. Ivan had listened to him in dead silence, without moving and without taking his eyes off him. Smerdyakov, on the other hand, only cast an occasional glance at him, as he went on talking, looking away most of the time. When he had finished his story, he was evidently agitated and was breathing hard. Beads of perspiration stood out on his face. It was impossible to say, however, whether he was feeling remorse or what.

'Wait,' Ivan cried, pondering. 'What about the door? If he only opened the door to you, then how could Grigory have seen it open before? For Grigory saw it before you, didn't he?'

It was remarkable that Ivan put his question in a most placid voice, in quite a different tone, in fact, in a tone that bore no trace of anger, so that if anyone had opened the door just then and looked at them from across the threshold, he would most certainly have concluded that they were discussing amicably some ordinary, though rather interesting, subject.

'About that door and Grigory's statement that he had seen it open, he just imagined it all, sir,' Smerdyakov declared with a wry smile. 'For let me tell you, sir, he's not a man, but just a stubborn mule. He never saw it, but only imagined he saw it – but you'll never shake his evidence. That's your luck and mine, sir, I mean, that he should have concocted it all, for his evidence alone is enough to convict your brother Dmitry.'

'Listen,' said Ivan, as though getting muddled again and trying hard to grasp something, 'listen. . . . I wanted to ask you lots of things, but I forget – I keep forgetting and getting muddled. Oh yes! Tell me just one thing: why did you open the envelope and leave it on the floor? Why didn't you simply carry off the money in the envelope? When you were telling me about it, it seemed to me that you spoke about the envelope as though that was the right thing to do. But why it was the right thing to do I can't understand.'

'Well, sir, I did that for a good reason. For if the man had been familiar with all the circumstances, he'd have known all about it, like me, for instance; he'd have seen the money before and perhaps put it into the envelope himself and seen it sealed and addressed with his own eyes. In that case, sir, why should he, if, that is, he had committed the murder, open the envelope afterwards, and in such a great hurry, too, seeing as how he knows for certain that the money must be in the envelope? On the contrary, if the robber had been someone like me, he'd simply shove the envelope in his pocket without bothering to open it and make his escape with it. Now, it's quite a different matter with a man like your brother Dmitry: he knew about the envelope only from hearsay, he never saw it himself, and as soon as he'd got it out from under the mattress, for instance, he'd open it at once to make sure the money was there. And then he'd throw the envelope down on the floor because he had no time to think that it could serve as evidence against him, because, you see, sir, he's an inexperienced thief, who's never stolen anything before, being a gentleman born and bred. And if he made up his mind to steal now, he did so on the ground that he was not stealing at all but only taking back what belonged to him, for he'd already let it be known all over the town and, indeed, boasted before everybody that he'd go and take his property from his father. I suggested this at my interrogation to the public prosecutor, but not in so many words, just hinting at it like, just as if I was not aware of its importance, and as if he'd thought of it himself and it was not I who suggested it to him. And what do you think, sir? The public prosecutor's mouth simply watered at that hint of mine. . . .'

'But did you really think it all out in the bedroom at the time?' cried Ivan, beside himself with surprise. He looked at Smerdyakov again with alarm.

'Really, sir, how can one think of it all at such a time? It was all thought out beforehand.'

'Well – well – in that case the devil himself helped you!' Ivan cried again. 'No, you're not stupid. You're much cleverer than I thought.'

He got up with the evident intention of taking a turn round the room. He felt terribly depressed. But as the table barred his way and he could just manage to squeeze through between the table and the wall, he merely turned round and sat down again. Perhaps the fact that he couldn't stretch his legs properly brought on a sudden fit of exasperation, for he shouted suddenly at the top of his voice almost in the same frenzy as before:

'Listen, you unhappy, contemptible wretch! Don't you realize that if I haven't as yet killed you, it's only because I'm anxious to hear what you will say at the trial tomorrow. God knows,' Ivan raised his hand, 'perhaps I, too, was guilty. Perhaps I really did wish secretly that – my father were dead. But I swear to you, I'm not as guilty as you think, and, perhaps, I didn't put you up to it at all. No, no, I didn't put you up to it! It makes no difference, though. I will give evidence against myself in court tomorrow. My mind is made up! I'll tell everything, everything. But I'll appear before the court together with you! And whatever you may say against me in court, whatever evidence you may give – I shall not shrink from it. I'm not afraid of you. I shall confirm it all myself! But you, too, must make your confession in court. You must, you must! We shall go together! It shall be so!'

Ivan said it forcefully and solemnly, and it could be seen from his flashing eyes that it would be so.

'You are ill, sir. I can see it. You're very ill, sir. Your eyes, sir, are quite yellow,' said Smerdyakov, but without a trace of sarcasm, even as though sympathizing with him.

'We shall go together!' Ivan repeated. 'And if you won't go, it doesn't matter. I shall confess alone.'

Smerdyakov said nothing, as though thinking it over.

'Nothing of the kind will happen, sir,' he decided at last, firmly. 'You won't go, sir.'

'You don't understand me!' cried Ivan reproachfully.

'You'll be too much ashamed, sir, if you takes it all upon yourself. And, what's more, it won't be of no use at all, sir. For I shall declare that I never said nothing of the kind to you, and that you're either suffering from some illness (and it looks like it, too) or that you're so sorry for your brother that you're sacrificing yourself to get him off and that you've invented it all against me, for all your life you thought of me as if I was a fly and not a human being. And who will believe you? And what single proof have you got?'

'Listen, you showed me the money just now to convince me, I suppose.'

Smerdyakov took *Isaac the Syrian* off the bundles of notes and put it aside.

'Take that money away with you, sir,' Smerdyakov said with a sigh.

'Of course, I'll take it! But why are you giving it to me if you committed a murder to get it?' Ivan asked, looking at him with intense surprise.

'I don't want it at all,' Smerdyakov said in a shaking voice, with a wave of the hand. 'I did have an idea of starting a new life in Moscow or, better still, abroad with that money, but that was just a dream, sir, and mostly because "everything is permitted". This you did teach me, sir, for you talked to me a lot about such things: for if there's no everlasting God, there's no such thing as virtue, and there's no need of it at all. Yes, sir, you were right about that. That's the way I reasoned.'

'Did you think of it yourself?' Ivan asked with a wry smile.

'With your guidance, sir.'

'And am I to understand that you believe in God now that you are returning the money?'

'No, sir, I don't believe,' whispered Smerdyakov.

'Then why are you giving it back?'

'Really, sir,' Smerdyakov dismissed the question with a wave of the hand, 'why bother to ask? You used to say yourself that everything is permitted, so why are you so upset now, sir? You even want to go and give evidence against yourself. . . . Only nothing will come of it! You won't go and give evidence!' Smerdyakov decided again firmly and with conviction.

'You'll see!' said Ivan.

'That will never be. You're much too clever, sir. You're fond of money. I knows that. You also like to be respected, because you're very proud, you likes women, beautiful women, too much, but what you likes most of all is to live in peace and comfort and not to have to bow and scrape before no one – that most of all. You won't want to spoil your life forever by disgracing yourself like that in court. You, sir, are more like Mr Karamazov than any of his other children. You've got the same soul as he, you have, sir.'

'You're not a fool,' said Ivan, as though amazed; the blood rushed to his face. 'I thought you were a fool. You're serious now!' he observed, as though suddenly regarding Smerdyakov in quite a different way.

'It's because you're so proud that you thought I was a fool. Take the money, sir.'

Ivan took the three rolls of notes and shoved them into his pocket without wrapping them up.

'I shall produce them in court tomorrow,' he said.

'Nobody will believe you, sir. You've lots of money of your own, so you could have taken it out of your cash-box and brought it into the court.'

Ivan got up from his chair.

'I repeat if I haven't killed you now it's only because I need you for tomorrow. Remember that. Don't you forget it!'

'You can kill me. I don't mind. Kill me now,' Smerdyakov said in a strange voice, looking strangely at Ivan. 'You won't dare do that even,' he added, with a bitter smile. 'You won't dare do nothing, sir, brave man as you was before!'

'Till tomorrow!' cried Ivan and he moved towards the door.

'Wait, sir, let me see them again.'

Ivan took out the notes and showed them to him. Smerdyakov gazed at them for ten seconds.

'Well, you can go,' he said with a wave of the hand. 'Mr Karamazov!' he called again suddenly after him.

'What do you want?' Ivan turned on the way to the door.

'Good-bye, sir!'

'Till tomorrow!' Ivan cried again, and walked out of the cottage.

The blizzard was still going on. He took the first steps boldly, but suddenly he seemed to stagger. 'It's something physical,' he thought, with a grin. A sort of gladness filled his soul now. He felt a sort of unbounded determination: an end to the vacillations which had tormented him so much all these last few weeks! He had taken a decision 'and it won't be changed now,' he thought, happily. At that moment he stumbled against something and nearly fell. Stopping, he made out at his feet the little peasant he had knocked down and who was still lying in the same place, unconscious and motionless. The snow had almost covered his face. Ivan suddenly seized him and dragged him along. Seeing a light in a little house on the right, he went up to it, knocked on the shutters and asked the tradesman, who had answered his knock and to whom the house belonged, to help him carry the peasant to the police station, promising to give him three roubles for his pains. The tradesman got ready and came out. I won't describe in detail how Ivan managed to get to the police station and arrange for the peasant to have a medical examination at once, providing 'for the expenses' with a liberal hand. I will only remark that the affair took a whole hour. But Ivan was very satisfied. His thoughts wandered and his mind worked continuously: 'If I hadn't taken such a firm decision for tomorrow,' he suddenly reflected with delight, 'I shouldn't have wasted a whole hour looking after the peasant, but should have passed by, without caring a damn whether he got frozen to death or not. . . . But how well I'm still capable of analysing myself,' he thought at the same moment with even greater delight. 'And they've decided that I'm going off my head!' On reaching his house, he stopped dead, suddenly asking himself: 'Ought I not to go and see the public prosecutor at once and tell him everything?' He answered the question as he turned back to his house: 'Tomorrow everything together!' he whispered to himself, and, strange to say, almost all his joy, all his self-satisfaction vanished in a moment. When he entered his room, he suddenly felt as though an icy hand had clutched his heart, as though a recollection, or, better still, a reminder of something horrible and agonizing that was in that room just at that very moment, and that had been there before. He sank down wearily on the sofa. The old woman brought in the *samovar*. He made tea, but did not touch it. He sent the woman away till the next morning. He sat on the sofa, feeling giddy. He felt that he was ill and helpless. He was on the point of dozing off, but he got up restlessly and paced the room to dispel sleep. At moments he imagined that he was delirious. But it was not his illness that interested him so much: sitting down again, he began looking round him as though trying to discern something. He did so several times. At last his glance was fixed intently on one spot. Ivan grinned, but an angry flush covered his face. He sat a long time in his place, his head leaning heavily on both hands and still looking out of the corner of his eyes at the same spot, at the sofa standing against the opposite wall. There was evidently something that irritated him there, some sort of object that worried and tormented him.

9

The Devil. Ivan's Nightmare

I AM not a doctor, and yet I feel that the moment has come when it is absolutely necessary for me to explain to the reader at least something of the nature of Ivan's illness. Running ahead, I shall merely say one thing: that evening there appeared the first symptoms of the nervous breakdown to which he completely succumbed, though he had offered strong resistance to the illness from which he had long been suffering. Having no knowledge of medicine, I venture to advance the theory that by a great effort of will he had perhaps succeeded in staving off his illness for a time in the hope, no doubt, of overcoming it completely. He knew that he was ill, but he was loath to be ill at this time, at these approaching fateful moments of his life, when he had to appear in court, when he had to put his case boldly and resolutely and 'justify himself to himself'. He had, however, paid one visit to the doctor, who had been summoned from Moscow by Katerina owing to a fantastic notion of hers, which I have already mentioned earlier. After listening to him and examining him, the doctor came to the conclusion that he was suffering from some mental disorder and was not at all surprised by an admission he had reluctantly made to him. 'In your condition,' the doctor declared, 'hallucinations are quite likely, though they have to be carefully checked. You must undergo serious medical treatment, without a moment's delay, or things will go badly with you.' But, on leaving him, Ivan did not carry out his sensible advice and refused to take to his bed and undergo a course of medical treatment: 'I'm walking about and I've still enough strength to carry on; if I collapse, it will be a different matter, then anyone who likes may give medical treatment to me,' he decided, dismissing the subject. And so he was sitting now, almost conscious himself that his mind was wandering and, as I have said already, staring at some object on the sofa at the wall opposite. Someone seemed to be sitting there. Goodness only knows how he had come in, for he had not been in the room when Ivan, on returning from Smerdyakov, came into it. It was a gentleman, or rather a Russian gentleman of a certain type, no longer young, *qui frisait la cinquantaine*, as the French say, with rather long, thick, dark hair, only just streaked with grey, and a small clipped, pointed beard. He was wearing a sort of brown coat, evidently cut by a good tailor, but rather threadbare, made about three years before and quite out of fashion now, in a style that had not been worn for two years by well-to-do men about town. His linen and his long scarf-like cravat were all such as were worn by smart gentlemen, but on closer inspection his linen was rather dirty and the wide scarf very threadbare. The visitor's check trousers were of an excellent cut, but again were a little too light in colour and a little too tight, such, in fact, as were no longer worn, and the same was true of his white fluffy felt hat, which was certainly not in season. In short, he gave the impression of a well-bred gentleman who was rather hard up. It looked as though he belonged to the class of idle landowners who used to flourish in the times of serfdom; he had evidently been received in good and fashionable society and had once had good connexions, which, no doubt, he still preserved, but after leading a gay life in his youth and after the recent abolition of serfdom, he had gradually turned into a sort of well-bred sponger, who was dependent on his kind old friends, who received him for his agreeable character as well as for being, after all, a decent fellow, who could be asked to sit down at dinner with anyone, though, of course, at the far end of the table. Such spongers, gentlemen of sociable character, who know how to tell a good story, make up a fourth at cards, and who are most decidedly averse from carrying out any commissions that may be forced upon them, are usually solitary men, either bachelors or widowers. They may, perhaps, have children, but their children are being brought up in a far-away province by their aunts, who are hardly ever mentioned in good society, as though these gentlemen are ashamed of such a relationship. They gradually lose touch with their children, only occasionally receiving a birthday or Christmas card from them and sometimes even answering it. The countenance of the unexpected visitor was not so much good-natured as, again, agreeable and ready to assume any amiable expression that occasion should demand. He had no watch, but he did have a tortoise-shell lorgnette on a black ribbon. On the middle finger of his right hand was a massive gold ring with a cheap opal stone. Ivan was resentfully silent and would not begin the conversation. His visitor waited and sat exactly like a hanger-on who had just come down from his room to keep his host company at tea, but who was discreetly silent in view of the fact that his host was preoccupied and thinking of something, knitting his brows; he was, however, ready to engage in any polite conversation as soon as his host began it. Suddenly a worried look passed over his face.

'I say,' he addressed Ivan, 'just to remind you: you went to see Smerdyakov to find out about Katerina, but you left without finding out anything about her. I expect you must have forgotten. . . .'

'Good Lord,' Ivan cried suddenly, and his face darkened with anxiety, 'yes, I'd forgotten! Still, it makes no difference now,' he muttered to himself, 'everything till tomorrow. As for you,' he turned irritably to his visitor, 'I should have remembered it myself presently, for it was that that made me feel so depressed! What did you have to interfere for? So that I should believe that you reminded me of it and I didn't remember it myself?'

'You needn't believe it,' the gentleman said, smiling affably. 'What's the good of believing against your will? Besides, so far as faith is concerned, no proofs are of any help, particularly material proofs. Thomas believed not because he saw that Christ had risen, but because he wanted to believe before that. Now, take spiritualists – mind you, I'm very fond of them – just imagine, they think they render a service to religion because the devils show them their horns from the other world. That, they maintain, is, as it were, material proof of the existence of another world. The other world and material proofs – dear me! And, after all, if you can prove the existence of the devil, does that prove the existence of God, too? I'd like to join an idealist society, and form an opposition in it. I'm a realist, I'll say, and not a materialist, ha, ha!'

'Listen,' said Ivan, suddenly getting up from the table, 'I seem to be delirious now – yes, no doubt about it. I am delirious – so you can talk any nonsense you like. I don't care! You won't drive me into a frenzy, as you did last time. I only feel ashamed of something. . . . I feel like pacing the room. . . . Sometimes I don't see you and I don't even hear your voice, as last time, but I always guess the absurd things you say because *it is I, I myself who am talking and not you!* Only I don't know whether I was asleep last time or whether I saw you while I was awake. I'm going to dip a towel in cold water and put it on my head and perhaps you'll disappear into thin air.'

Ivan went into the corner of the room, took a towel and did as he said, and with a wet towel on his head began walking up and down the room.

'I'm glad we're talking to each other like old friends,' began the visitor.

'Fool,' laughed Ivan, 'I'm not going to treat you as a stranger, am I? I'm in excellent spirits now, only I've got a pain in my temple and – and in my head. Only, please, don't philosophize, as you did last time. If you can't clear off, then talk of something amusing. Talk gossip. Why, you're a sponger, so talk scandal. I *would* have such a nightmare! But I'm not afraid of you. I'll get the better of you. They won't drag me off to a lunatic asylum!'

'*C'est charmant* – a sponger. Well, yes, I suppose I am just that. For what am I on earth if not a sponger? By the way, I'm listening to you and I can't help being a little surprised, you know: I could swear you're gradually beginning to take me for something that really exists and not only as a figment of your imagination, as you insisted on pretending last time. . . .'

'Never for a moment have I taken you for reality,' Ivan cried with a sort of fury. 'You're a lie, you're my illness, you're a phantom. I only don't know how to destroy you and I'm afraid I shall have to suffer for a time. You are my hallucination. You're the embodiment of myself, but only of one side of me – of my thoughts and feelings, but only the most vile and stupid. From that point of view you might even interest me, if only I had time to waste on you. . . .'

'Come, come, I'll prove to you that you are wrong. A few hours ago, at the lamp-post, when you flew at Alyosha, you shouted to him: "You learnt it from *him*! How did you learn that *he* comes to see me?" You were thinking of me then, weren't you? So that for a fraction of a second you did believe that I really existed, didn't you?' the gentleman laughed genially.

'Yes, that was a momentary weakness . . . but I couldn't believe in you. I don't know whether I was asleep or walking about last time. Perhaps I was only dreaming about you and didn't really see you at all. . . .'

'Why, then, were you so stern with him, with Alyosha, I mean? He's a nice boy. I'm afraid I feel guilty towards him over Father Zossima.'

'Don't talk of Alyosha! How dare you, you flunkey?' Ivan laughed again.

'You abuse me and laugh at the same time – a good sign. However, you're much more polite to me today than last time and I know why: that great decision of yours. . . .'

'Don't speak of my decision!' Ivan cried fiercely.

'I understand, I understand, *c'est noble, c'est charmant.* You're going to defend your brother tomorrow and sacrifice yourself – *c'est chevaleresque.*'

'Shut up or I'll kick you!'

'I'll be glad in a way, for my object will be attained. If you kick me, you must believe in my reality, for one doesn't kick a ghost. But joking aside, it makes no difference to me: abuse me if you like. All the same it's much better to be a little more polite, even to me. Fool, flunkey – really!'

'Abusing you, I abuse myself!' Ivan laughed again. 'You are I – I myself, only with a different face. You are merely putting my thoughts into words – and you can't say anything new to me!'

'If my thoughts are the same as yours, then it only redounds to my honour,' the gentleman declared with delicacy and dignity.

'Except that you only choose my worst thoughts, and the stupid ones to boot. You're stupid and vulgar. You're awfully stupid. No, I can't stand you! What am I to do? What am I to do?' cried Ivan, grinding his teeth.

'My friend, say what you like, but I prefer to be a gentleman and I want people to treat me like one,' the visitor began in an access of compliant and good-humoured pride, typical of a man who lived by sponging on others. 'I am poor but . . . I won't say very honest, but – in society they usually take it for granted that I'm a fallen angel. Honestly, I can't imagine how I can ever have been an angel. If ever I was, it was so long ago that I can be forgiven for forgetting it. The only thing I prize now is my reputation of being a decent fellow and I live as best I can, trying to be agreeable. I love people sincerely – oh, I've been terribly slandered! Here, when I come to live among you from time to time, my life does assume something in the nature of reality, and I must say I like it most of all. For, you see, like you, I, too, suffer from the fantastic and that's why I love your earthly realism. With you everything here is drawn in clear outlines, here everything is a formula, here everything is geometry, while with us everything is a sort of indeterminate equation! Here I can walk about and dream. I like dreaming. Besides, on earth I become superstitious – don't laugh, please: you see, to become superstitious is just what I like. I adopt all your habits here: I have grown fond of going to the public baths – can you imagine that? And I like to steam myself with merchants and priests. My fondest dream is to be reincarnated, but irrevocably and for good, into a fat, sixteen-stone wife of a merchant and to believe in everything in which she believes. My ideal is to go into a church and offer a candle from a pure heart – honestly, it is! That would be the end of all my sufferings. And I've also grown fond of medical treatment here: there was a small-pox epidemic in the spring and I went to a foundling hospital and got myself vaccinated – if only you knew how contented I felt that day: donated ten roubles in aid of our Slav brothers! But you're not listening. You know, you're not at all well today,' the gentleman paused a little. 'I know you went to see that doctor yesterday – well, how is your health? What did the doctor tell you?'

'Fool!' Ivan snapped.

'Ah, but you're so clever, aren't you? You're abusing me again? I didn't ask you out of sympathy, but just out of politeness. You needn't answer if you don't want to. People are beginning to suffer from rheumatism again now....'

'Fool,' Ivan repeated.

'You keep repeating the same thing, but I had such an attack of rheumatism last year that I still remember it.'

'A devil and rheumatism?'

'Why not, if I sometimes assume a human form. When I do, I suffer the consequences. Satan *sum et nihil humanum a me alienum puto.*'

'What did you say? Satan *sum et nihil humanum* – that's not bad for the devil!'

'I'm glad to have pleased you at last.'

'You didn't get it from me,' Ivan stopped dead suddenly, as though in amazement. 'That never entered my head – that's funny....'

'*C'est du nouveau, n'est-ce pas?* This time I'll be honest and explain to you. Listen: in dreams and particularly in nightmares, caused by indigestion or whatever you like, a man sometimes sees such artistic things, such a complex and actual reality, such events, or even a whole world of events, woven into such a plot, full of such astonishing details, beginning with the most exalted manifestations of the human spirit to the last button on a shirt-front that, I assure you, not even Leo Tolstoy could have invented it, and yet such dreams are sometimes seen not by writers but by the most ordinary people, civil servants, newspaper columnists, priests. . . . The whole thing, in fact, presents a most difficult problem: a Cabinet Minister admitted to me himself that his best ideas came to him when he was asleep. Well, that's what is happening now. Though I'm your hallucination, yet, as in a nightmare, I say original things which had not entered your head before, so that I don't repeat your thoughts at all, and yet I'm only your nightmare and nothing more.'

'You're lying. Your aim is to convince me that you exist as an independent entity and that you are not my nightmare. And now you admit yourself that you are a dream.'

'My dear fellow, today I've adopted a special method. I'll explain it to you later. Wait, where did I leave off? Oh yes. So I caught a cold, only not here but there. . . .'

'Where there? Tell me, are you going to stay here long? Can't you go away?' cried Ivan, almost in despair.

He stopped pacing the room, sat down on the sofa, again put his elbows on the table and clutched his head tightly in both hands. He tore off the wet towel and flung it away in vexation: it was evidently of no use.

'Your nerves have all gone to pieces,' the gentleman remarked in a carelessly casual, but very friendly tone. 'You're angry with me even for being able to catch cold, and yet it happened in a most natural way. I was in a hurry just then to get to a diplomatic reception given by a highly placed Petersburg lady, who was aiming at obtaining a ministerial post for her husband. Well, naturally, evening dress, white tie and tails, gloves, although I happened to be goodness knows where at the time and to get to your earth I had to fly through space. . . . Of course, it was only a matter of a second, but then even a ray of light from the sun takes eight minutes to get to earth, and there I was – imagine it! – in evening dress and open waistcoat. Spirits do not freeze, but once you have assumed human form – anyway, I did a silly thing and set off, and, you know, in those empty spaces, in the ether, in the water that is above the firmament – why, there's such a frost – you can hardly call it a frost – just imagine, one hundred and fifty degrees below zero! You know the sort of game village girls play: they ask a callow youth to lick an axe in thirty degrees of frost; his tongue freezes to it at once and the stupid fellow tears the skin off it so that it bleeds. Well, that is only in thirty degrees, and in one hundred and fifty you have only to put a finger to an axe and, I should think, there will be nothing left of it, if only – that is – there could be an axe there. . . .'

'And could there be an axe there?' Ivan suddenly interrupted absently and with a feeling of disgust.

He was doing his utmost not to believe in his mad dream and not to lose his reason completely.

'An axe?' the visitor repeated in surprise.

'Yes, what would happen to an axe there?' Ivan suddenly cried with a kind of fierce and insistent obstinacy.

'What would happen to an axe in empty space? *Quelle idée!* If it got far enough, it would, I think, begin circling the earth as a sort of satellite. The astronomers would calculate the rising and the setting of the axe, Gatzuk would put it in his calendar, and that's all.'

'You're stupid, you're awfully stupid!' Ivan said cantankerously. 'You'd better lie more intelligently or I won't listen. You want to get the better of me by realism. You want to convince me that you exist. But I don't want to believe that you exist! I won't believe it!'

'But I'm not lying. It's all true. Unfortunately, truth is hardly ever amusing. I can see that you positively expect something big from me and, perhaps, something beautiful, too. That is a great pity, for I only give what I can.'

'Don't philosophize, you ass!'

'How can you expect me to philosophize when the whole of my right side is numb and I'm moaning and groaning. I've consulted all sorts of doctors: they can diagnose excellently, they will tell you all your symptoms, they have your illness at their finger-tips, but they've no idea how to cure you. I happened to come across a very enthusiastic little medical student. "You may die," he told me, "but at least you'll have a very good idea of what illness you're dying of!" And, then again, the way they have of sending you to specialists. "We can only diagnose your disease," they tell you. "You'd better go to such and such a specialist and he'll be sure to cure you." I tell you the old-fashioned doctor who used to cure you of all illnesses has quite disappeared. Now there are only specialists and they all advertise in the papers. If there's something wrong with your nose, they will send you to Paris: there's a European specialist there who cures noses. You go to Paris, he examines your nose. "I'm sorry," he tells you, "I can only cure your right nostril, for I don't cure left nostrils, it's not my speciality. You'd better go to Vienna. There you'll find a special specialist who will cure your left nostril." What are you to do? I tried popular remedies. A German doctor advised me to rub myself with honey and salt on a shelf in a bath-house. I went just to get an extra bath: got myself covered all over with honey and salt, but it was no good at all. In despair I wrote to Count Mattei in Milan. He sent me a book and some drops – oh well, I don't blame him! And, just imagine, Hoff's malt extract cured me! I bought it by accident, drank a bottle and a half of it, and I was as fit as a fiddle – I could even dance if I wanted to! I made up my mind to publish my "thank you" to him in a letter to the press, my feeling of gratitude urged me to do it. And, well, you know, not a single newspaper would publish it and for quite an extraordinary reason! "It would be very reactionary," they said. "No one will believe it. *Le diable n'existe point*. You'd better publish it anonymously," they advised me. But what kind of "thank you" is it, if it's anonymous? I had a good laugh with the clerks at the newspaper office. "Why," I said to them, "it's reactionary to believe in God in our age. But I'm the devil. You can believe in me." "Quite right," they said, "who doesn't believe in the devil? But it can't be done all the same. It might harm the political tendency of our paper. You wouldn't like to publish it as a joke, would you?" Well, I didn't think it would be very witty to publish it as a joke. So it was not printed. And, you know, I still feel upset about it. My best feelings, gratitude, for instance, are formally denied me simply because of my social position.'

'Getting philosophical again, are you?' Ivan snarled malevolently.

'Good Lord, no, but one can't help complaining sometimes. I am a slandered person. Now, you too keep telling me every minute that I'm stupid. One can see you're young. My dear fellow, it isn't only brains that matter. I have a naturally kind and merry heart. I, too, you know, can enjoy all sorts of "gay farces". I'm afraid you're determined to take me for some elderly Khlestakov, but my fate has been a far more serious one. By some primordial decree, which I could never make out, I was appointed "to negate" while, as a matter of fact, I'm genuinely kind-hearted and not at all good at "negation". "Oh, no, you go and negate, for without negation there is no criticism," and what sort of periodical is it if it has no section for criticism? Without criticism there would be nothing but "hosannah". But "hosannah" alone is not enough for life. It is necessary that this "hosannah" should be tried in the crucible of doubt, and so on in the same vein. Still, it is none of my business. I didn't create the world, and I am not answerable for it. Well, so they have chosen their scapegoat, made me contribute to the section of criticism, and life was the result. We understand that farce: for instance, I frankly and openly demand annihilation for myself. No, they say, you must live because there'd be nothing without you. If everything on earth were rational, nothing would happen. Without you there would be no events, and it is imperative that there should be events. So I serve with a heavy heart so that there should be events and perform what is irrational by order. People accept all this farce as something serious for all their indisputable intelligence. That is their tragedy. Well, of course, they suffer, but – they live, they live a real and not an illusory life; for suffering is life. Without suffering, what pleasure would they derive from it? Everything would be transformed into an endless religious service: it would be holy, but a little dull. Well, and what about me? I suffer, but I do not live for all that. I am the x in an indeterminate equation – I am a sort of phantom who has lost all the beginnings and ends and who has even forgotten what his name is. You are laughing. . . . No, you are not laughing. You're angry again. You're always angry. All you care about is intelligence. But I tell you again that I'd give up all this life above the stars, all my ranks and honours, to be reincarnated into a sixteen-stone merchant's wife and offer candles to the Lord.'

'Do you mean to say you don't believe in God, either?' Ivan grinned malignantly.

'Well, how shall I put it, if only you are serious —'

'Is there a God or not?' cried Ivan again with fierce insistence.

'Oh, so you are serious! My dear fellow, I really don't know. There, I've said it!'

'You don't know, and yet you see God? No, you're not an independent entity. You are *I*, you *are* I and nothing more! You are rubbish. You are my fancy!'

'Well, if you like, I have the same philosophy as you. That would be fair. *Je pense donc je suis*, that I know for certain. As for everything else around me, all these worlds, God and even Satan himself – all that hasn't been proved to me. Does it all exist of itself or is it only an emanation of myself, a logical development of my *I*, which has existed as an entity for ever. . . . But I make haste to stop, for I can see you're spoiling for a fight.'

'You'd better tell me some amusing story,' Ivan said dismally.

'There's an amusing story and on our subject, too. I mean, not really a story, but a legend. You reproach me with unbelief: "You see," you say, "but you don't believe." But, my dear fellow, I'm not the only one like that. All our chaps there are in a muddle, and all because of your science. While there were still only atoms, five senses, five elements, it all still made some sense. There were atoms in the ancient world, too. But as soon as our chaps learnt that you've discovered "the chemical molecule" and "protoplasm" and the devil knows what else – they put their tails between their legs. There was a terrible confusion and, above all, superstition, gossip (you see, our chaps are as fond of gossip as you are, even a little more, in fact) and, finally, denunciations, for you see we, too, have a special branch where certain "information" is accepted. Well, anyway, that wild legend hails from our middle ages – not yours, but ours – and no one believes it even among us, except the sixteen-stone merchants' wives, and again I mean ours, not yours. Everything you have, we've got, too. I'm revealing one of our secrets out of friendship for you, though it is forbidden. The legend is about paradise. There was, so it goes, a certain thinker and philosopher here on your earth who repudiated everything, "laws, conscience, faith" and, above all, the future life. He died thinking he'd go straight to death and darkness, and, lo and behold, there was the future life before him. He was astounded and indignant. "This," he said, "is against my principles." So for that he was condemned – I'm sorry, you see, I'm only telling you what I heard myself, it's only a legend – so, you see, he was condemned to walk in darkness a quadrillion kilometres (we've adopted the metric system, you know), and when he had finished the quadrillion, the gates of heaven would be opened to him and all his transgressions would be forgiven. . . .'

'And what other tortures besides the quadrillion have you in the other world?' Ivan interrupted with a strange kind of animation.

'Tortures? Oh, you'd better not ask. Before we had all sorts, but now it's mostly moral ones, "pricks of conscience" and all that rot. This, too, we've adopted from you, from "the softening of your manners". And who do you think has gained by it? Only those who have no conscience; for what do they care for pricks of conscience, when they have no conscience of any kind? On the other hand, the decent people who have some conscience and a sense of honour left are in a worse plight than ever. So that's the sort of thing that happens to reforms when the ground has not been prepared for them and if, in addition, they've merely been copied from foreign institutions – nothing but harm! The hell-fire of old was much better. Well, so the man who was sentenced to the quadrillion kilometres stood still, looked round and lay down across the road: "I won't go! I refuse to go on principle!" Now, take the soul of an enlightened Russian atheist and mix it with the soul of the prophet Jonah, the chap who sulked in the whale's belly for three days and nights, and you get the character of the thinker who lay across the road.'

'What did he lie on there?'

'Oh, I suppose there must have been something to lie on. You're not laughing, are you?'

'Stout fellow!' cried Ivan, still with the same strange animation. Now he was listening with a sort of unexpected curiosity. 'Well, is he lying there still?'

'That's the whole point – he is not. He lay there for almost a thousand years, then he got up and off he went.'

'What a silly ass!' cried Ivan, laughing nervously, and still apparently thinking hard about something. 'What difference did it make whether he lay there forever or walked a quadrillion kilometres? Why, it would take him a billion years to walk that distance, wouldn't it?'

'Much longer. I'm sorry I haven't a pencil and paper or I'd have worked it out. But, you see, he walked it long ago, and that's where the story begins.'

'Did he? But where did he get the billion years to do it in?'

'You're thinking of our present earth: why, our present earth has probably repeated itself a billion times. I mean, it has become extinct, frozen, cracked, fallen to pieces, resolved itself into its component elements, again the water above the firmament, then again a comet, again a sun, again an earth from the sun – this evolution, you see, has repeated itself an infinite number of times, and all in the same way, over and over again, to the smallest detail. A most indecently tedious business. . . .'

'Well, what happened when he got there?'

'Why, the moment they opened the gates of paradise to him and he walked in, before he had been there even two seconds – and that is by his watch, by his watch (though, if you ask me, his watch should have dissolved in his pocket into its component elements on the way ages ago) – before he had been there two seconds, he exclaimed that for those two seconds he'd have gladly walked not only a quadrillion, but a quadrillion of quadrillions raised to a quadrillionth power! In a word, he sang a "hosannah", and overdid it so much that some people there with a more honourable trend of thought even refused to shake hands with him at first: he had jumped into the conservative camp a little too precipitously, according to them. The Russian temperament. I repeat, it's a legend. I give it to you for what it's worth. So that's the sort of ideas on all these subjects that we still have there.'

'I've caught you out!' cried Ivan with a sort of almost childish delight, as though remembering something at last. 'This amusing story about the quadrillion I made up myself! I was seventeen at the time. I was at a grammar school. I made up that story then and told it to a school-friend called Korovkin. That was in Moscow. The story is so characteristic that I couldn't have taken it from anywhere. I seemed to have forgotten it. But I recalled it now unconsciously – you didn't tell it to me, I told it to myself! One sometimes remembers thousands of things unconsciously even when one is taken to execution – I've remembered it in my dream. So you are that dream! You are a dream! You don't exist!'

'Judging by the vehemence with which you refuse to acknowledge my existence,' the gentleman laughed, 'I'm convinced that you believe in me all the same.'

'Not a bit! I don't believe a hundredth part in you!'

'But you do a thousandth part. Homeopathic doses, you know, are perhaps the strongest. Confess you believe, well, a ten-thousandth part.'

'Not for a moment!' Ivan cried furiously. 'I'd like to believe in you, though,' he added strangely.

'Oho! That *is* an admission! But I'm good-natured and I'll help you there, too. Listen, it's I who have caught you out and not you me! I deliberately told you the story you had forgotten so that you should lose your faith in me completely.'

'You're lying! The purpose of your appearance is to make me believe that you exist.'

'To be sure. But hesitations, uneasiness, the conflict between belief and disbelief – why, this is sometimes such a torture to a conscientious man like yourself that one would rather hang oneself. You see, knowing that you do believe in me a little bit, I made you disbelieve in me completely by telling you this story. I keep you dangling between belief and disbelief by turns, and I don't mind admitting that I have a reason for it. It's the new method, sir. For when you lose your faith in me completely, you will at once begin assuring me to my face that I'm not a dream, but do really exist. You see, I know you. And then I shall have attained my object, and my object is an honourable one. I shall sow a tiny grain of faith in you and it will grow into an oak tree – and such an oak tree that, sitting on it, you will long to join "the hermits in the wilderness and the chaste virgins", for at heart you long for it greatly; you will be feeding upon locusts and you will drag yourself off into the wilderness to save your soul!'

'So you're doing all this for the salvation of my soul, you scoundrel?'

'Well, one has to do a good deed sometimes, you know. You are in a bad temper, I can see that!'

'Clown! But did you ever try to tempt those who are feeding upon locusts, spend seventeen years praying in the wilderness, and are overgrown with moss?'

'My dear fellow, I've been doing nothing else. You will forsake the whole world and all the worlds and you will cleave to a man like that, for he is undoubtedly a very precious jewel. Why, one such soul is sometimes worth a whole galaxy of stars – you see, we have our own arithmetic. It's the victory over such a man that is so precious! And some of them, I assure you, are not inferior to you in intellect, though you may not believe it. They are capable of contemplating such depths of belief and disbelief at one and the same moment that you sometimes do, indeed, feel that another hair's breadth and your man will precipitate himself "head over heels", as the actor Gorbunov says.'

'Well, and did you have your nose put out of joint?'

'My friend,' the visitor observed sententiously, 'sometimes it's better to have one's nose put out of joint than to be without a nose altogether, as an ailing marquis (he must have been treated by a specialist) not so long ago said in confessing to his spiritual Jesuit father. I was present, and it was simply delightful. "Give me back my nose!" he said, and he smote his breast. "My son," quibbled the Jesuit, "according to the inscrutable decrees of Providence all things are accomplished and a great disaster sometimes leads to extraordinary, though imperceptible, benefits. If stern destiny has deprived you of your nose, it's to your advantage that no one for the rest of your life will dare tell you that your nose has been put out of joint." "Holy Father, that's no comfort!" the desperate man cried. "I'd be delighted to have my nose put out of joint every day provided it was only in its proper place!" "My son," the priest sighed, "you must not demand all blessings at once, for that is murmuring against Providence, which has not forgotten you even in this plight; for if you cry out, as you did just now, that you'd be delighted to have your nose put out of joint for the rest of your life, your wish has already been fulfilled indirectly: for, having lost your nose, you have, as it were, had your nose put out of joint by that very fact."'

'Dear me, how stupid!' cried Ivan.

'My friend, I only wanted to amuse you, but I swear that this is genuine Jesuit casuistry, and, I swear, it all happened just as I told you, word for word. It happened only recently and it gave me a lot of trouble. The unhappy young man, on his return home, shot himself that very night. I was there with him till the last moment. . . . As for those Jesuit confessionals, they really are my most delightful diversions at melancholy moments. Here's another incident that only happened the other day. A little blonde Norman girl of twenty comes to an old priest. She was a beauty, plump, and buxom, and everything nature lavishes to whet a man's appetite – make your mouth water. She bends down and whispers her sin to the priest through the grating. "Dear me, my daughter, have you fallen again already?" exclaims the priest. "O, Sancta Maria, what do I hear? Not with the same man? But how long is it to go on? And aren't you ashamed of yourself?" "*Ah, mon père,*" answered the sinner, penitent tears rolling down her cheeks, "*Ça lui fait tant de plaisir et à moi si peu de peine!*" Well, just fancy an answer like that! Here I just withdrew: it was the cry of nature and, if you like, better than innocence itself! I absolved her sin there and then and was about to go, but I was forced to go back at once. For I heard the priest making an assignation with her through the grating for the evening – an old man like him and hard as flint, and fell in a twinkling! Nature, the truth of nature asserting itself! Why, you're turning up your nose again? Not angry again? I don't know how to please you. . . .'

'Leave me, please, you are hammering on my brain like an excruciating nightmare,' Ivan moaned dismally, helpless before his apparition. 'I'm bored with you, unbearably and agonizingly bored! I'd give anything to be able to get rid of you!'

'I repeat, moderate your demands. Don't demand from me "everything great and beautiful" and you'll see how well we shall get on together,' the gentleman declared impressively. 'You are really angry with me because I haven't appeared to you in a red glow, "in thunder and lightning", with scorched wings, but have introduced myself in so modest a form. You are hurt, first of all, in your aesthetic feelings and, secondly, in your pride: how could such a vulgar devil come to visit such a great man? I'm afraid you do possess the romantic strain that has been so much derided already by Belinsky. It just can't be helped, young man. I did think, as I was getting ready to come to you, to appear, as a joke, in the guise of a retired Regular State Councillor, who had served in the Caucasus, with the star of the Lion and the Sun on my frock-coat; but, to tell the truth, I was afraid of doing it because you would most certainly have beaten me black and blue for having only pinned the Lion and the Sun to my coat instead of, at least, the Pole Star or Sirius. And you go on telling me that I am stupid. But, dear Lord, I don't claim to be your equal in intellect. Mephistopheles, when he appeared to Faust, introduced himself as one who desired evil but did only good. Well, that's as he pleases, but I'm quite the opposite. I'm perhaps the only man in the universe who loves truth and sincerely desires good. I was present when the Word, who died on the cross, ascended into heaven, carrying on his breast the soul of the thief who had been crucified on his right hand, and I heard the joyful cries of the cherubim, singing and shouting: "hosannah", and the thunderous shouts of rapture of the seraphim which shook heaven and all creation. And I swear by all that is holy I longed to join the chorus and shout "hosannah" with them all. The word had almost escaped me, it had almost burst from my chest – you know, of course, how sentimental and artistically sensitive I am. But common sense – oh, the most unhappy characteristic of my nature – kept me here, too, within the proper bounds, and I let the moment pass! For what, I thought at that instant, would have happened after my "hosannah"? Everything in the world would at once have been extinguished and no events would have happened after that. And so, solely from a sense of duty and my social position, I was forced to suppress the good moment and carry on with my loathsome work. Somebody else takes all the credit for what is good, and all the dirty work is left for me. But I do not envy the honour of living a life of deceit. I'm not ambitious. Why am I alone of all the creatures in the world doomed to be cursed by all decent people and even to be kicked? For, if I assume a human form, I have to run the risk of such consequences, too, sometimes. I know, you see, that there's a secret here, but they won't tell me the secret for anything because, having realized what it is all about, I might roar out "hosannah", and the indispensable minus sign would disappear at once, and good sense would reign all over the world, and once this happened, it would, of course, be the end of everything, even of newspapers and periodicals, for who would care to subscribe to them then? I know, of course, that in the end I shall be reconciled, that I, too, shall walk my quadrillion and learn the secret. But till that happens, I am making a nuisance of myself and reluctantly carry out my assignment to ruin thousands so that one may be saved. How many souls, for instance, have had to be ruined and how many honourable reputations discredited to get only one righteous Job, over whom they double-crossed me so cruelly in the days of yore! Yes, until the secret is revealed, there are two truths for me: one which is theirs, and which I know nothing about so far, and the other my own. And it is still on the cards which will turn out to be the better one. . . . Are you asleep?'

'I wish I were,' Ivan groaned angrily. 'Everything that is stupid in me, everything I've experienced long ago, everything I've thrashed out in my mind and flung aside like carrion, you present to me as something new!'

'So I haven't given satisfaction even here! And I thought to fascinate you by my literary style: that "hosannah" in heaven was not really so bad, was it? Why now this sarcastic tone à la Heine, eh? I'm right, am I not?'

'No, I was never such a flunkey! Why should my soul have begotten such a flunkey as you?'

'My friend, I know a most sweet and most charming young Russian gentleman: a young thinker, a great lover of literature and *objets d'art*, the author of a poem of great promise entitled *The Grand Inquisitor*. I had only him in mind.'

'I forbid you to speak of *The Grand Inquisitor*,' cried Ivan, colouring all over with shame.

'Well, and what about *The Geological Upheaval*? Remember? That was a lovely poem!'

'Shut up or I'll kill you!'

'Kill me? No, I'm very sorry but I will speak. I've come to treat myself to that pleasure. Oh, I love the dreams of my passionate young friends, quivering with a craving for life! "There are new men," you decided last spring, when you were about to come here, "who propose to destroy everything and start with cannibalism. The fools! They never asked my advice! In my opinion, there's no need to destroy anything. All that must be destroyed is the idea of God in mankind. That's what we ought to start with! Yes, we ought to start with that – oh, the blind fools! They understand nothing! Once humanity to a man renounces God (and I believe that period, analogous with the geological periods, will come to pass) the whole of the old outlook on life will collapse by itself without cannibalism and, above all, the old morality, too, and a new era will dawn. Men will unite to get everything life can give, but only for joy and happiness in this world alone. Man will be exalted with a spirit of divine, titanic pride, and the man-god will make his appearance. Extending his conquest over nature infinitely every hour by his will and science, man will every hour by that very fact feel so lofty a joy that it will make up for all his old hopes of the joys of heaven. Everyone will know that he is mortal, that there is no resurrection, and he will accept death serenely and proudly like a god. His pride will make him realize that it's no use protesting that life lasts only for a fleeting moment, and he will love his brother without expecting any reward. Love will satisfy only a moment of life, but the very consciousness of its momentary nature will intensify its fire to the same extent as it is now dissipated in the hopes of eternal life beyond the grave. . . ." And so on and so forth, in the same vein. Very charming!'

Ivan sat with his hands pressed against his ears and his eyes fixed on the ground, but he began trembling all over. The voice went on:

'The question now is, my young thinker thought, whether such a period will ever come. If it comes, everything is resolved and mankind will attain its goal. But as, in view of man's inveterate stupidity, it may not be attained even for a thousand years, everyone who is already aware of the truth has a right to carry on as he pleases in accordance with the new principles. In that sense "everything is permitted" to him. What's more, even if that period never comes to pass, and since there is neither God nor immortality, anyway, the new man has a right to become a man-god, though he may be the only one in the whole world, and having attained that new rank, he may lightheartedly jump over every barrier of the old moral code of the former man-slave, if he deems it necessary. There is no law for God! Where God stands, there is his place! Where I stand, there will at once be the first place – "everything is permitted" and that's all there is to it! All this is very charming; only, if you want to lead a life of crime, what do you want the sanction of truth for? But that's, I'm afraid, what our modern Russian is like: without that sanction he can't bring himself to lead a life of crime, so much is he in love with truth. . . .'

The visitor talked, evidently carried away by his eloquence, raising his voice more and more and throwing ironic glances at his host; but he did not succeed in finishing: Ivan suddenly grabbed a glass from the table and hurled it with all his might at the orator.

'Ah, mais c'est bête enfin!' the visitor exclaimed, jumping up from the sofa and flicking away the drops of tea from his clothes. 'He remembered Luther's ink-well! Thinks I am a dream and throws glasses at a dream! It's like a woman! I knew very well that you were only pretending to stop up your ears, but that you were listening all the time. . . .'

At that moment there was a loud and persistent knocking on the window-frame. Ivan jumped up from the sofa.

'Do you hear, you'd better open,' cried the visitor. 'It's your brother Alyosha who has come to tell you a most surprising and interesting piece of news, I promise you!'

'Shut up, deceiver! I knew it was Alyosha before you spoke, and of course he hasn't come for nothing – of course he's come "with news",' cried Ivan, beside himself.

'Open, open the window to him. There's a blizzard and he's your brother. *Monsieur, sait-il le temps qu'il fait? C'est à ne pas mettre un chien dehors. . . .*'

The knocking continued. Ivan was about to rush up to the window, but something suddenly seemed to fetter his hands and feet. He tried with all his might to break his fetters, but in vain. The knocking at the window became louder and louder. At last his fetters were broken and Ivan jumped up from the sofa. He looked wildly about him. The two candles had almost burnt out, the glass, which he had only just flung at his visitor, stood before him on the table, and there was no one on the sofa opposite. The knocking at the window, though it still went on persistently, was not as loud as it had seemed in his dream. On the contrary, it was very subdued.

'This wasn't a dream! No, I swear, it was not a dream! It all happened now!' cried Ivan and, rushing up to the window, he opened it.

'Alyosha, I told you not to come!' he shouted at his brother fiercely. 'Tell me quick what do you want? Quick, do you hear?'

'Smerdyakov hanged himself an hour ago,' Alyosha replied from the yard.

'Come round to the front door, I'll open at once,' said Ivan and went to open the door to Alyosha.

10

'It was He Who Said That!'

WHEN he came in, Alyosha told Ivan that just over an hour ago Maria Kondratyevna had been to see him and told him that Smerdyakov had committed suicide. 'I went into his room,' she said, 'to clear away the *samovar* and there he was hanging on a nail in the wall.' When Alyosha asked her whether she had informed the police, she replied that she had not, but had gone first straight to him, running all the way. She was beside herself, Alyosha declared, and was shaking like a leaf. And when Alyosha ran with her to the cottage he found Smerdyakov still hanging. On the table was a note: 'I put an end to my life of my own free will and no one should be blamed for it.' Alyosha left the note on the table and went straight to the district police inspector, where he made a statement, 'and from there I've come straight to you,' concluded Alyosha, looking intently into Ivan's face. He had not taken his eyes off him all the time he was telling his story, as though struck by something in the expression of his face.

'Ivan,' he cried suddenly, 'you must be terribly ill! You look at me, but you don't seem to understand what I'm saying!'

'It's good of you to have come,' said Ivan, as though he were thinking of something else and not hearing Alyosha's exclamations. 'I knew he had hanged himself.'

'From whom?'

'I don't know from whom. But I knew. Did I know? Yes, he told me. He told me just now.'

Ivan stood in the middle of the room and spoke still in the same pensive tone, his eyes fixed on the floor.

'Who is *he*?' asked Alyosha, looking round involuntarily.

'He's slipped away.'

Ivan raised his hand and smiled gently.

'He got frightened of you – of a gentle dove like you. You are "a pure cherub". Dmitry calls you a cherub. A cherub. . . . The thunderous shout of rapture of the seraphim! What is a seraph? A whole constellation, perhaps. And, perhaps, the whole of that constellation is just a sort of chemical molecule. Is there a constellation of the Lion and the Sun, do you know?'

'Ivan, sit down!' said Alyosha in alarm. 'For God's sake, sit down on the sofa. You're delirious. Put your head on the pillow – so. Want me to put a wet towel on your head? You'll feel better, perhaps.'

'Yes, give me the towel. It's there on the chair. I threw it down there a little while ago.'

'It isn't there. Don't worry, I know where it is – here,' said Alyosha, finding a clean towel, still folded and unused, at the other end of the room by Ivan's wash-stand.

Ivan looked strangely at the towel; his memory seemed to come back to him in an instant.

'Wait a minute,' he said, raising himself on the sofa. 'About an hour ago I took that same towel from there and wetted it. I put it on my head and threw it down here – how is it dry? There was no other towel.'

'You put this towel on your head?' asked Alyosha.

'Yes, and walked about with it about an hour ago. Why have the candles burnt down like that? What's the time?'

'Nearly twelve.'

'No, no, no!' cried Ivan suddenly. 'It was not a dream! He was here, he was sitting here – there, on that sofa. When you knocked at the window, I threw a glass at him – that one. Wait a minute. I was asleep before, but this dream is no dream. It's happened before, too. You see, Alyosha, I have dreams now – but they are no dreams. I am not asleep. I am walking about, talking and seeing and – and I'm asleep. But he was sitting here – he was here – on that sofa. . . . He's awfully stupid, Alyosha, awfully stupid,' Ivan laughed suddenly and began pacing the room.

'Who is stupid? Who are you talking about, Ivan?' Alyosha asked again, wistfully.

'The devil! He's taken to visiting me. He's been here twice, almost three times. He taunted me for being angry that he's just a devil and not Satan with scorched wings, appearing in thunder and lightning. But he is not Satan. He's telling lies about that. He's an impostor. He's just a devil, a rotten, insignificant devil. He goes to the baths. Undress him and you'll be sure to find a tail, a long, smooth tail, like a Great Dane's, a yard long, a brown colour. . . . Alyosha, you're cold. You've been out in the snow. Would you like some tea? What? It's cold, is it? Shall I tell her to make some? *C'est à ne pas mettre un chien dehors.* . . .'

Alyosha ran to the wash-stand, wetted the towel, persuaded Ivan to sit down again and put the wet towel round his head. He sat down beside him.

'What were you telling me about Lise last time?' Ivan began again. (He was becoming very talkative.) 'I like Lise. I said something bad about her. I was lying. I like her. I'm afraid for Katya tomorrow. I'm afraid for her more than anything. For the future. She'll throw me over tomorrow and trample me under her feet. She thinks I'm ruining Mitya because I'm jealous of her. Yes, she thinks that! But it's not so. Tomorrow the cross, but not the gallows. No, I shan't hang myself. Do you know, Alyosha, that I could never commit suicide? Is it because I am a rotter? I'm not a coward. It's because of my craving for life! How did I know that Smerdyakov had hanged himself? Yes, it was *he* who told me that. . . .'

'And are you quite sure that someone has been sitting here?' asked Alyosha.

'Yes, on that sofa, in the corner. You would have driven him away. Why, you did drive him away: he vanished as soon as you appeared. I love your face, Alyosha. Did you know that I loved your face? But *he* is me, Alyosha, *me*! All that is base, rotten, and contemptible in me! Yes, I'm a "romantic", and he noticed it – though it's a libel. He's awfully stupid, but that's his strong point. He's cunning, cunning like an animal. He knew how to madden me. He kept taunting me with believing in him, and that's how he made me listen to him. He fooled me like a boy. Still, he told me a great deal that was true about myself. I should never have said it to myself. You know, Alyosha, you know,' Ivan added very seriously and as though confidentially, 'I'd have liked very much that he should really be *he* and not me!'

'He has tired you out,' said Alyosha, looking with compassion at his brother.

'Taunted me! And, you know, cleverly, very cleverly. "Conscience! What is conscience? I invent it myself. Why, then, am I so unhappy? From habit. From the universal habit of mankind for the past seven thousand years. When we get rid of our habits, we shall become gods." It was he who said that. It was he who said that!'

'And not you, not you?' Alyosha cried uncontrollably, looking serenely at his brother. 'Well, let him, give him up, forget all about him! Let him take away with him all that you curse now, and don't let him come again.'

'Yes, but he's spiteful. He laughed at me. He was insolent, Alyosha,' Ivan said with a shudder of resentment. 'But he slandered me, he slandered me about lots of things. He told lies about me to my face. "Oh, you're going to perform a great act of virtue! You're going to declare that you murdered your father, that the servant killed him at your instigation."'

'Ivan, stop it,' Alyosha interrupted. 'You didn't do it. It's not true!'

'That's what he says. He! And he knows it. "You're going to perform a great act of virtue and you don't believe in virtue – that's what makes you so angry, that's what worries you, that's why you're so vindictive." That was what he said to me about myself, and he knows what he is talking about. . . .'

'It's you who are saying this and not he!' Alyosha cried, sorrowfully. 'And you say it because you are ill and delirious, tormenting yourself!'

'No, he knows what he is talking about. You are going, he says, out of pride. You'll stand up and say: "It was I who did it. Why do you look so horror-stricken? You are lying! I despise your opinion. I despise your horror." He's saying that about me, and then he suddenly says: "But you know you'd like very much to be praised by them: 'He's a criminal, a murderer, but what generous feelings he has. Wanted to save his brother, and confessed!'" That's a damn lie, Alyosha!' Ivan suddenly cried, with flashing eyes. 'I don't want the mob to praise me! He was lying, Alyosha! I swear, he was lying! That's why I threw the glass at him, and it broke against his ugly snout.'

'Calm yourself, Ivan! Stop!' Alyosha besought him.

'Yes, he knows how to torture, he's cruel,' Ivan went on, not listening. 'I always knew why he came. "All right," he said, "suppose you go out of pride, but there was still the hope that they'd convict Smerdyakov and sentence him to penal servitude in a Siberian prison, that they would acquit Mitya and condemn you only for a *moral* offence – [You hear? he laughed then!] and others would praise you. But now Smerdyakov is dead, he has hanged himself, so who will believe you alone in court now? But you're going, you're going. You will go for all that. You've made up your mind to go. What are you going for now?" This is terrible, Alyosha. I can't bear such questions. Who dares put such questions to me?'

'Ivan,' interrupted Alyosha, faint with terror, though there still seemed to be hope of bringing Ivan to his senses, 'how could he have told you about Smerdyakov's death before I came, when no one knew about it and there was no time for anyone to know about it?'

'He did tell me,' Ivan said firmly, not admitting the possibility of a doubt. 'He talked about nothing but that, as a matter of fact. "It would be all right," he said, "if you believed in virtue: don't let them believe me, I'm going for the principle of the thing. But you're a dirty rogue like your father, and what do you care for virtue? What then do you want to drag yourself off there for, if your sacrifice won't be of any use? The fact is you don't know yourself what you are going there for! Oh, you'd give a lot to learn why you go! And have you really made up your mind? No, you have not! You'll be sitting here all night trying to make up your mind whether to go or not. But you will go all the same and you know that. You know yourself that whatever you decide, the decision no longer depends on you. You will go because you won't dare not to go. Why you won't dare, you can guess for yourself – there's a riddle for you!" Then he got up and went away. You came and he went. He called me a coward, Alyosha! *Le mot de l'enigme* is that I am a coward. "It is not for such eagles to soar above the earth!" It was he who added that! It was he! And Smerdyakov said the same. He must be killed! Katya despises me. I've seen it for a month. And Lise, too, will start despising me! "You are going so that people should praise you" – that is a brutal lie! And you, too, despise me, Alyosha. Now I shall hate you again! And I hate the monster! I hate the monster! I don't want to save the monster. Let him rot in jail! He has begun singing a hymn! Oh, I'll go tomorrow, stand before them and spit in their faces!'

He jumped up in a frenzy, flung off the towel and began pacing the room again. Alyosha remembered the words he had uttered a short while ago: 'I seem to be awake in my sleep. I walk about, I talk and I see, but I am asleep.' That was exactly what was happening now. Alyosha did not leave him. The thought flashed through his mind to run for a doctor and bring him back, but he was afraid to leave his brother alone: there was no one with whom he could leave him. Little by little Ivan began to lose consciousness. He went on talking, he talked without stopping, but quite incoherently. He even articulated his words with difficulty and suddenly he staggered violently. But Alyosha was in time to support him. Ivan allowed himself to be led to his bed. Alyosha managed to undress him and put him to bed. He sat by his bedside for another two hours. The sick man slept soundly, without stirring, breathing softly and evenly. Alyosha took a pillow and lay down on the sofa without undressing. Before he fell asleep, he said a prayer for Mitya and Ivan. He began to understand Ivan's illness: 'The agony of a proud decision – a deep-seated conscience'. God, in whom he did not believe, and truth had gained a hold over his heart, which still refused to give in. 'Yes,' the thought passed through Alyosha's head, as he laid it on the pillow, 'yes, now that Smerdyakov is dead, no one will believe Ivan's evidence. But he will go and give it!' Alyosha smiled softly: 'God will conquer!' he thought. 'Ivan will either rise up in the light of truth or – perish in hate, revenging on himself and on everyone else the fact that he has served something he does not believe in,' Alyosha added bitterly, and again prayed for Ivan.

I

The Fatal Day

ON the day following the events I have described, at ten o'clock in the morning, our district court opened its session and the trial of Dmitry Karamazov began.

Let me make it quite clear at once that I am far from considering myself capable of describing all that took place at the trial, not only in full detail, but also in its proper order. It seems to me that if one were to recall and explain everything properly, it would fill a whole volume, and a large one at that. And so I trust that my readers will not complain if I describe only what struck me personally and what stuck in my mind. I may well have taken what was of only secondary importance to be the most important facts of the trial and even omitted altogether the most glaring and essential facts. However, I see that the best thing is not to offer any apologies. I shall do all I can and my readers will realize themselves that I have done all I could.

To begin with, before we enter the court-room, I must mention what surprised me particularly that day. As a matter of fact, I was not the only one to be surprised. Everyone, as it appeared afterwards, was surprised at it. What I mean is this: everyone knew that the affair had aroused the interest of a great many people, that everyone was burning with impatience for the trial to begin, that it had given rise to a great deal of talk, conjecture, excitement, and wild fancies in our society for the last two months. Everyone knew, too, that the case had become known all over Russia, but they still did not realize, as was proved that day in court, what a terrible and immense shock it had been to everyone not only in our town but all over Russia. People had arrived for the trial not only from the chief town of our province, but also from several other Russian towns as well as from Moscow and Petersburg. Among them were jurists and a number of distinguished personages as well as society women. All the tickets of admission had been snatched up. For the most illustrious and distinguished men visitors special seats were reserved behind the table at which the judges sat; a whole row of armchairs was placed there for various distinguished persons, which had never been permitted in our court-room before. There was a particularly large number of ladies, both from our town and visitors, not less than half, I believe. There were so many jurists alone that they did not know where to find places for them, for all the tickets had long been distributed, sought after, and changed hands. I saw myself how at the end of the court-room, behind the dais, a special enclosure was hurriedly put up behind which all the jurists had been admitted, and they thought themselves lucky that they could at least stand there, for, to gain room, all the chairs had been taken out and the whole crowd of them stood all through the trial, packed together shoulder to shoulder. Some of the ladies, especially those who arrived from other towns, appeared in the gallery very smartly dressed, but the majority of the ladies did not even bother to dress up. Their faces showed a hysterical, intense, almost morbid curiosity. The most characteristic feature of the entire public in the court which must be noted (it was established afterwards by many observers) was that almost all the ladies, at least the overwhelming majority of them, were on Mitya's side and in favour of his acquittal. Perhaps chiefly because of his reputation as a conqueror of female hearts. It was known that two women rivals would appear in the case. One of them, that is, Katerina, was an object of particular interest to everybody; all sorts of extraordinary tales were told about her, and quite surprising stories were current about her passion for Mitya, in spite of his crime. Her pride (she had paid scarcely any visits in our town) and her 'aristocratic connexions' were particularly stressed. It was said that she intended to appeal to the government to give her permission to accompany the criminal to Siberia and to be married to him somewhere in the mines. The appearance in the court of Grushenka, as Katerina's rival, was awaited with no less excitement. The meeting of the two rivals, the proud, aristocratic girl and the 'hetaera', was awaited with agonizing curiosity; Grushenka, though, was better known to our ladies than Katerina. They had seen her, 'the woman who had been the ruin of Fyodor Karamazov and his unhappy son', before and all without exception wondered how father and son could have fallen so passionately in love with this 'very ordinary and far from beautiful low-class girl'. In short, there was a great deal of talk. I know for a fact that in our town alone there were several serious family quarrels on account of Mitya. Many ladies had quarrelled violently with their husbands over differences of opinion about this terrible case, and it was only natural that the husbands of these ladies appeared in court not only ill-disposed towards the accused, but even bitterly prejudiced against him. Generally, it can be stated positively that the masculine, in contrast to the feminine, element was openly antagonistic to the accused. There was a great number of stern, frowning, and even vindictive faces. It is, of course, true that during his stay in our town Mitya had managed to offend many of them personally. No doubt, many of the people in court looked almost cheerful and were quite unconcerned about Mitya's fate, but not about the case as such; they were all interested in the outcome of it, and the majority of the men were most certainly in favour of a conviction, except perhaps the jurists, who cared nothing for the moral aspect of the case, but only, as it were, for the modern legal aspect of it. Everybody was excited by the arrival of the famous Fetyukovich. His talent was known everywhere, and it was not the first time that he had appeared in the provinces to act as counsel for the defence in sensational criminal cases. And after his defence such cases always became famous all over Russia and were long remembered. There were also several amusing stories told about our public prosecutor and the presiding judge. It was said that our public prosecutor was mortally afraid of an encounter with Fetyukovich, that they had been enemies ever since the beginning of their careers in Petersburg, that our vain prosecutor, who always considered himself hardly done by in Petersburg because his talents had not been properly appreciated, plucked up courage over the Karamazov case. He even dreamed that this case would restore his dwindling reputation, but was only afraid of Fetyukovich. The views expressed about his fear of Fetyukovich, however, were not quite fair. Our public prosecutor was not one of those men who lose courage in face of danger; on the contrary, he was one of those whose ambition increases and takes wings with the increase of danger. In general, it should be observed that our public prosecutor was much too excitable and morbidly susceptible. He would put his whole soul into some case and conduct it as though his whole life and his whole fortune depended on its outcome. In legal circles this gave rise to some laughter, for it was by just this trait of his character that our public prosecutor had won a certain notoriety, if not everywhere, then at least a much greater one than could be expected from his modest position. People were particularly amused by his passion for psychology. In my opinion, they were all wrong: our public prosecutor, both as a man and as a character, was, I think, much more serious than was generally supposed. But from the very outset of his legal career this ailing man never showed his real mettle and he failed to do so for the rest of his life.

As for the president of our court, all that can be said about him is that he was an educated and humane person, who had a good practical knowledge of his office and of the most progressive ideas of our days. He was rather vain, but he was not very concerned about his career. The main concern of his life was to be regarded as a man of advanced views. Besides, he had good connexions and a considerable fortune. He was, as it appeared later, intensely interested in the Karamazov affair, but only in a general sense. The case interested him as a social phenomenon. He was interested in its classification, and in the view that it was a product of our social conditions, throwing light on the Russian national character, etc., etc. So far as the personal aspect of the case was concerned, its tragic nature as well as the personalities of the people involved, beginning with the accused, his attitude towards it all was rather indifferent and abstract, as, indeed, it was perhaps right that it should be.

Long before the appearance of the judges, the court-room was packed to overflowing. Our court-room is the best hall in the town, spacious, lofty, and with excellent acoustics. On the right of the members of the court, whose seats were placed on a dais, a table and two rows of chairs had been reserved for the jury. On the left sat the accused and his counsel. In the middle of the court-room stood a table with 'the exhibits'. On it lay Fyodor Karamazov's blood-stained light silk dressing-gown, the fatal brass pestle, with which the murder was allegedly committed, Mitya's shirt with its blood-stained sleeve, his frock-coat covered with blood-stained patches at the back over the pocket in which he had put his blood-soaked handkerchief, the handkerchief itself, stiff with blood and by now quite yellow, the pistol Mitya had loaded at Perkhotin's and with which he had intended to commit suicide, and which the innkeeper in Mokroye had surreptitiously taken from him, the envelope with the inscription which had contained the three thousand for Grushenka, the narrow pink ribbon with which it had been tied round, and many other articles which I don't remember. At some distance away, in the body of the hall, were the seats for the public, but before the balustrade there were a few chairs for those of the witnesses who were to remain in court after giving their evidence. At ten o'clock the judges made their appearance – the president, one other judge, and an honorary justice of the peace. The public prosecutor, of course, came in immediately afterwards. The president was a stout, thick-set man of fifty, of less than medium height, with a sallow face, dark, greying, closely-cropped hair, and a red ribbon – I don't remember of what order. The public prosecutor struck me, and not only me but everyone else, as looking extraordinarily pale and almost green. He seemed for some reason to have suddenly grown much thinner, perhaps in a single night, for I had seen him looking his usual self only two days earlier. The president opened the proceedings by asking the usher whether all the members of the jury were present.

I can see, however, that I cannot go on like this, partly because some things I did not hear, others I failed to grasp the significance of, and others I have forgotten, but chiefly because, as I have said earlier, if I were to remember everything that was said and that took place, I should literally have neither time nor space to put it all down. All I know is that neither the counsel for the defence nor the public prosecutor objected to any of the jurymen. But I do remember the composition of the jury. Four of them were civil servants of our town, two were merchants, and six peasants and artisans. Long before the trial, I remember, people of the higher circles in our town, and especially the ladies, had been asking with some surprise how such a complex and subtle psychological case could be submitted for decision to some low-grade civil servants and, worst of all, to some peasants, and what could such a civil servant, let alone a peasant, make of it. And indeed the four civil servants of the jury were elderly people of no importance and low rank; only one of them being somewhat younger. They were little known in society, eked out a living on a miserable salary, probably had elderly wives, who could not possibly be introduced into decent society, and lots of children, who very likely ran about barefoot. Their only diversion was probably a game of cards for low stakes, and they certainly had never read a book in their lives. The two merchants looked respectable enough, but they were rather strangely silent and slow; one of them was close-shaven and wore European clothes; the other had a small, greyish beard and wore some medal on a red ribbon round his neck. There is no need to speak of the artisans and peasants. Our Skotoprigonyevsk artisans are almost indistinguishable from peasants, and even till the land. Two of them also wore European dress, and for that reason, perhaps, looked more unprepossessing and dirty than the other four. So that one really could not help wondering, as I did, for instance, as soon as I had a good look at them, what people like that could possibly make of such a case. Nevertheless, their faces made a strangely imposing and almost menacing impression: they were stern and frowning.

At last the presiding judge declared the case of the murder of the retired titular councillor Fyodor Karamazov open – I don't quite remember his exact words. The usher was ordered to bring in the accused, and Mitya made his appearance. A dead silence fell on the court-room, one could have heard a pin drop. I don't know how the others felt, but on me Mitya made a most disagreeable impression. The worst of it was that he came into court dressed up like a regular dandy in a brand-new frock-coat. I learnt afterwards that he had ordered the frock-coat in Moscow expressly for that day, from his tailor who had his measurements. He wore a pair of brand-new kid gloves and exquisite linen. He marched in with his yard-long strides, staring straight ahead of him, and sat down on his chair with a most nonchalant air. The famous defending counsel, Fetyukovich, came in immediately after him, and his appearance produced a sort of subdued hubbub in court. He was a tall, spare man, with long, thin legs, extraordinarily long, thin, pale fingers, a close-shaven face, demurely brushed short hair, and thin lips which from time to time twisted into something between a sneer and a smile. He looked about forty. His face would have been rather pleasant were it not for his eyes, in themselves small and inexpressive, but set so extraordinarily close together that the only thing that divided them was the thin line of his long thin nose. In short, his face had something curiously birdlike about it, and that was the first thing one was struck by. He wore a dress-coat and a white tie. I remember the presiding judge's first questions to Mitya, about his name, his rank, etc. Mitya replied sharply, but in a sort of unexpectedly loud voice, so that the presiding judge even tossed his head and looked at him almost in surprise. Then there was read out the list of names of the people who were to take part in the court proceedings, that is to say, the witnesses and experts. It was a long list; four of the witnesses failed to appear: Miusov, who was in Paris just then but who had given evidence at the preliminary investigation, Mrs Khokhlakov and the landowner Maximov, who were both ill, and Smerdyakov because of his sudden death, about which a statement from the police was presented. The news of Smerdyakov's suicide produced a violent stir and whispering in court. Many people, of course, knew nothing of his sudden suicide. But what really created a sensation in court was Mitya's unexpected outburst. As soon as the statement was read out, he shouted in a loud voice from his seat:

'A dog's death for a dog!'

I remember how his counsel rushed up to him and how the presiding judge addressed him, threatening to take severe measures if such an outburst were repeated. Mitya, nodding his head but showing no sign of repentance, repeated several times to his counsel in an undertone:

'I won't, I won't! It escaped me! I won't do it again!'

And, of course, this brief episode did not produce a favourable impression upon the jury or the public. His character became plain to everyone and it spoke for itself. It was under this impression that the act of indictment was read out by the clerk of the court.

It was rather short but circumstantial. It stated only the main reasons why so-and-so had been arrested and brought to trial, and so on. It did nevertheless produce a strong impression on me. The clerk read it distinctly in a loud and ringing voice. The whole tragedy seemed to have suddenly revealed itself again before everyone in clear outline and in a fatal and relentless light. I remember how immediately after it had been read, the presiding judge asked Mitya loudly and impressively:

'Prisoner, how say you, are you guilty or not guilty?'

Mitya suddenly got up from his place.

'I plead guilty to drunkenness and loose living,' he exclaimed again in a sort of unexpected and almost frenzied voice, 'to idleness and debauchery. I wanted to become an honest man for the rest of my life just at the moment when I was struck down by fate! But I am not guilty of the death of the old man, my father and my enemy! No, no. I am not guilty of robbing him, and could not possibly be guilty of it: Dmitry Karamazov is a scoundrel but not a thief!'

Having shouted this, he resumed his seat, visibly trembling all over. The presiding judge again addressed him with a brief but edifying admonition to answer only the questions put to him and not to indulge in irrelevant and frenzied exclamations. He then ordered the case to proceed. The witnesses were brought in to take the oath. It was then that I saw them all together. The prisoner's brothers, however, were not sworn in. After a brief address by the priest and the presiding judge the witnesses were led away and were offered seats as far away from each other as possible. Then they began calling them up one by one.

2

Dangerous Witnesses

I DO not know whether the witnesses for the prosecution and for the defence were separated into two groups by the presiding judge (I expect it was so), nor in what order they were supposed to be called up. All I know is that the witnesses for the prosecution were called in to give evidence first. I repeat, it is not my intention to give a full description of the examination of all the witnesses. Besides, such a description would have been partly superfluous, since in the speeches of the public prosecutor and the counsel for the defence all the facts of the case as well as the evidence before the court were summed up with clear and characteristic precision, and those two speeches I took down, at least parts of them, word for word and will quote them in due course, as well as one extraordinary and quite unexpected incident at the trial which occurred suddenly before the final speeches to the jury and which undoubtedly influenced its harsh and fatal outcome. I will only observe that from the very first moments of the trial a certain peculiar characteristic of the 'case' became clearly apparent and was noticed by everyone, namely, the unusual strength of the prosecution as compared with the evidence brought forward by the defence. Everyone in court realized that as soon as, in the hostile atmosphere of the court, the facts began to group themselves round one focal point and the whole horror of this terrible murder was gradually unfolded. Quite possibly everyone in court realized at the very outset that there could be no differences of opinion about the case, that the issue was never in doubt, that as a matter of fact no speeches for the defence or for the prosecution were needed, but were only a matter of form, and that the prisoner was guilty, manifestly guilty, guilty without a shadow of doubt. I can't help thinking that even the ladies in the court who were all without exception so eager for the acquittal of the fascinating prisoner were at the same time fully convinced of his undeniable guilt. What's more, I can't help thinking that they would have been greatly disappointed if his guilt had not been so fully established, for then the effect of the final scene of the criminal's acquittal would not have been so sensational. That he would be acquitted – that, strange to say, all the ladies were absolutely convinced of up to the very last moment: 'He is guilty, but he will be acquitted on humanitarian grounds, in accordance with the new ideas, the new sentiments that are in fashion now,' etc., etc. That was why they had all gathered there with such impatience. The men, on the other hand, were more interested in the contest between the public prosecutor and the celebrated Fetyukovich. They were all asking themselves with surprise what a great lawyer like Fetyukovich could possibly make out of a case that was obviously so hopeless and quite certainly lost, and that was why they followed his performance step by step with concentrated attention. But to the very end, up to his address to the jury, Fetyukovich remained an enigma to everyone. Men of experience felt that he had some system of his own, that he had already formed an idea of how to conduct his case, that he was doing it with some definite object in view, but what it was it was almost impossible to guess. There could, however, be no doubt whatever of his confidence and self-assurance. Besides, everyone noticed with pleasure at once that during his brief stay with us, only in about three days, perhaps, he succeeded in obtaining a thorough knowledge of the case and 'had studied it to a nicety'. People delighted in telling afterwards, for instance, how cleverly he had managed 'to outwit' the witnesses for the prosecution at the right moment and as far as possible to confuse them, and, above all, discredit their reputations and, consequently, their evidence, too. It was generally believed, however, that he did it mostly for fun, as it were, for the sake of showing off his forensic brilliance, to make sure that nothing was forgotten of the accepted legal methods: for everyone was convinced that he could not possibly obtain any great or conclusive advantage from these attempts 'to discredit' the witnesses. Indeed, it was quite likely that he himself realized it better than anyone, but that he had some idea of his own in reserve, a weapon of defence which he preferred to conceal for the time being, but which he would suddenly reveal at the right moment. But in the meantime, conscious of his strength, he was amusing himself. So, for instance, during the cross-examination of Grigory, Karamazov's former valet, who had given most damaging evidence about 'the open door into the garden', the counsel for defence, when his turn came to cross-examine the witness, stuck to him like a leech. It must be observed that Grigory stood up in the court-room with a composed and almost majestic air without being in the least overawed by the majesty of the law or the presence of a vast audience listening to him. He gave his evidence with as much confidence as though he had been talking to his wife Marfa, only, of course, more respectfully. It was impossible to shake him. At first he was questioned by the public prosecutor about all the facts of the family life of the Karamazovs. The family relationships emerged clearly. One could see and hear that the witness was artless and impartial. In spite of his profound respect for the memory of his late master, he declared, for instance, that he had been unjust to Mitya and had not brought up his children as he should. 'But for me,' he added in speaking of Mitya's early childhood, 'he would have been crawling all over with lice when he was a little boy. It wasn't right, either, of the father to wrong his son over his mother's family estate.' Asked by the public prosecutor what grounds he had for asserting that Karamazov had been unfair to his son in settling their accounts, Grigory, to everyone's surprise, had no convincing evidence to offer, but persisted in stating that Karamazov's settlement with his son was 'unfair' and that he ought 'to have paid him several thousand roubles more'. I must observe, by the way, that the public prosecutor repeated the question whether Karamazov had really owed some money to Mitya, with some persistence, to those witnesses who could be asked it, including Alyosha and Ivan, but obtained no satisfactory information from any of them; they all confirmed the fact, but no one could advance any clear evidence of it.

After that, Grigory described the scene at the dinner-table when Dmitry had burst in and beaten his father, threatening to come back and kill him. This made a very sombre impression on everyone in court, particularly as the old servant told his story calmly, without superfluous words in his own peculiar language, which turned out to be terribly effective. After describing how Mitya had struck him in the face and had knocked him down, he declared that he was not angry with him and had forgiven him long ago. Of the deceased Smerdyakov he observed, crossing himself, that the lad was not without ability, but that he was stupid and depressed by his illness, and, worse still, an infidel, and that it was Karamazov and his second son who had taught him not to believe in God. But he asserted almost with warmth that he had no doubt whatever about Smerdyakov's honesty and, to prove it, told the story of how a long time ago Smerdyakov, finding the money his master had dropped in the yard, had not concealed it, but taken it to his master who had given him 'a gold ten-rouble piece' and trusted him implicitly ever after. He confirmed emphatically that the door into the garden had been open. But he was asked so many questions that I find it quite impossible to remember them all. At last the counsel for the defence began his cross-examination, and he first of all wanted to know about the envelope in which Karamazov's three thousand roubles for 'a certain person' were 'supposed' to have been concealed. 'Did you see it yourself, you who were for so many years in your master's confidence?' Grigory replied that he had not seen it and had not even heard about the money from anyone 'up to the very moment when everyone began talking about it'. Fetyukovich put the same question about the envelope to every witness he could ask about it, and with the same persistence as the public prosecutor asked the question about the division of the property of Dmitry's mother. He got the same answer from everybody to the effect that none of them had seen the envelope, though many had heard about it. Everyone in court noticed the defence counsel's insistence on this question.

'Now, sir,' Fetyukovich asked quite unexpectedly, 'may I, if you don't mind, ask you what that balsam, or, rather, that infusion consisted of, with which, as appears from the preliminary inquiry, your wife rubbed your back in the hope of curing you of your attack of lumbago?'

Grigory looked blankly at the questioner and, after a short pause, muttered: 'There was sage in it, sir.'

'Only sage? Can't you remember anything else?'

'There was plantain in it, too.'

'And pepper, perhaps?' Fetyukovich queried.

'Yes, sir, and pepper.'

'And so on. And what did you pour on it? Good old vodka, I presume?'

'No, sir. Spirits.'

There was a faint sound of laughter in court.

'Well, well, so it was spirits, was it? And I presume that after rubbing your back you drank what was left in the bottle, uttering a certain pious prayer known only to your wife, didn't you?'

'Yes, sir.'

'How much approximately did you drink? Approximately? A liqueur glass or two?'

'A glassful, I suppose.'

'A whole glassful! Are you sure it wasn't a glass and a half?'

Grigory made no answer. He seemed to have grasped something.

'A glass and a half of neat spirits – not so bad, what do you think? You might have seen "the gates of heaven open", let alone the door into the garden, mightn't you?'

Grigory was still silent. There was some more faint laughter in court. The presiding judge stirred in his seat.

'Are you quite sure,' Fetyukovich persisted relentlessly, 'you were not asleep at the moment when you saw the open garden door?'

'I was standing on my feet, sir.'

'That is no proof that you were not asleep [more laughter in court]. Could you, shall I say, have answered at that moment, if anyone had asked you, well, for instance, what year it is now?'

'I'm afraid I don't know, sir.'

'And do you know what it is now – anno domini?'

Grigory stared steadily at his tormentor, looking utterly bewildered. It was certainly strange that he did not seem to know what year it was.

'But perhaps you can tell us how many fingers you have on your hands?'

'I'm not my own master, sir,' Grigory said suddenly in a loud and distinct voice. 'If the authorities think fit to make fun of me, I must put up with it.'

Fetyukovich seemed a little put out, but at this point the presiding judge intervened and reminded the counsel for the defence sententiously that he ought to ask more relevant questions. Fetyukovich bowed with dignity and declared that he had no more questions to ask. But, of course, both the public and the jury might very well have felt a certain doubt as to the value of the evidence of a man who was capable of seeing 'the gates of heaven' while under the influence of some quack cure and who, moreover, did not even know what year it was. The counsel for the defence, therefore, achieved his object in spite of everything. But before Grigory left the witness box another incident occurred. The presiding judge, turning to the accused, asked him if he had anything to say about the evidence of the witness.

'Except about the door,' Mitya cried in a loud voice, 'all he said is true. I thank him for combing the lice out of my head and I thank him for forgiving my blows. The old man has been honest all his life and as faithful to my father as seven hundred poodles.'

'Prisoner, be more careful in the choice of your words,' the presiding judge said, sternly.

'I'm not a poodle,' Grigory, too, muttered.

'Well, I'm a poodle, then, I am!' cried Mitya. 'If I've said anything offensive, I take it upon myself and I ask his pardon: I was a brute and cruel to him! I was cruel to that old dolt, too.'

'What old dolt?' the presiding judge again took him up sternly.

'I mean, to that Pierrot – to my father.'

The presiding judge again and again warned Mitya very sternly and impressively to be careful about the choice of his words.

'You are injuring yourself in the opinion of your judges.'

The counsel for the defence used the same clever tactics in his cross-examination of Rakitin. I might observe that Rakitin was one of the most important witnesses and one the public prosecutor set great store by. It appeared that he knew everything, that he knew quite an astonishing lot, that he had been everywhere, had seen everything, had spoken to everyone, and knew every detail of the biography of Fyodor Karamazov and all the Karamazovs. It was true, though, that he had only heard from Mitya about the envelope with the three thousand. On the other hand, he gave a detailed description of Mitya's exploits in the 'Metropolis', all his compromising words and gestures, and told the story of Captain Snegiryov's 'bast-sponge'. As to the rather important matter of Mitya's inheritance and whether or not Fyodor Karamazov owed Mitya anything on account of it, even Rakitin could say nothing definite and confined himself to generalities of a contemptuous character: 'Who could tell which of them was to blame,' he declared, 'or find out which of them was in debt to the other, considering the muddle-headed way in which the Karamazovs conducted their affairs, which none of them had any idea of?' The whole tragedy of the crime, he explained, was due to the ingrained habits of serfdom and to the disorderly state of affairs in Russia, suffering from the lack of proper institutions. In fact, he was allowed to express his opinions rather freely. With that trial Mr Rakitin for the first time showed the stuff he was made of and attracted public attention; the public prosecutor knew that he was preparing an article for a periodical on the case and in his speech afterwards (as we shall see) quoted several ideas from that article, which, of course, meant that he had seen it. The picture drawn by the witness was a sombre and fatal one and greatly strengthened 'the case for the prosecution'. Generally speaking, Rakitin's account appealed to the public by its independence of thought and the extraordinary nobleness of its scope. There were two or three spontaneous outbursts of applause, namely at those passages of his evidence in which he mentioned serfdom and the disorderly state of Russia. But, being still young, Rakitin made a little mistake, which the counsel for the defence at once turned to excellent account. Answering the familiar questions about Grushenka and carried away by his success, of which he was, of course, conscious, and the noble heights to which he had soared, he allowed himself to speak a little contemptuously of Grushenka as 'the mistress of the merchant Samsonov'. He would have given a lot afterwards to take back his words, for Fetyukovich at once caught him out over that. And all because it never occurred to Rakitin that Fetyukovich could have gained such an intimate knowledge of the case in so short a time.

'May I ask,' the counsel for the defence began with a most charming and even respectful smile, when his turn came to question the witness, 'may I ask if you are the same Mr Rakitin whose pamphlet, issued by the ecclesiastical authorities under the title of *The Life of the Deceased Elder Father Zossima*, so full of profound and religious reflections and containing such an excellent and devout dedication to the bishop, I have recently read with such pleasure?'

'I didn't write it for publication,' Rakitin murmured, as though suddenly taken aback and almost ashamed. 'It was published afterwards.'

'Oh, that's excellent! A thinker like you can and, I suppose, must take the widest possible point of view about every social problem. Thanks to the patronage of the bishop, your most useful pamphlet has had a wide circulation and has been of comparatively great benefit. But what I'm chiefly interested in is this: you have just declared that you were very closely acquainted with Miss Svetlov [*Nota bene:* Grushenka's surname was Svetlov. This I learnt for the first time that day in the course of the trial], didn't you?'

'I'm not responsible for all my acquaintances. I am a young man – and who can answer for all the people one meets,' replied Rakitin, flushing all over.

'I understand, I quite understand,' cried Fetyukovich, as though he, too, were embarrassed and anxious to apologize. 'You, like everyone else, might be interested, too, in an acquaintance with a young and beautiful woman who readily entertained the *élite* of the youth of this town, but – er – all I want you to tell me is this: we know that two months ago Miss Svetlov was very anxious to be introduced to Alexey Karamazov, the youngest of the Karamazovs, and promised you twenty-five roubles just for bringing him to her wearing his monastic clothes. That, we know, actually took place in the evening of the day which ended in the tragic catastrophe, which led to the present legal proceedings. You brought Alexey Karamazov to Miss Svetlov, but did you get the promised twenty-five roubles as a reward? That's what I should like to hear from you.'

'Oh, that was a joke. . . . I don't see why you should be so interested in it. I took it for a joke and – and I intended to give it back later. . . .'

'But you did take the money, didn't you? And you have not given it back as yet, have you?'

'Oh, it's just nonsense,' muttered Rakitin. 'I refuse to answer such questions. . . . I shall return it, of course.'

The presiding judge intervened, but Fetyukovich declared that he had no more questions to put to Mr Rakitin. Mr Rakitin left the witness-box somewhat discredited. The impression left by the noble sentiments of his speech was rather marred, and Fetyukovich, as he followed him with his eyes, seemed to say to the public in reference to him: 'That's what your high-minded accusers are like!' I remember that this, too, did not pass without an incident on the part of Mitya: enraged by the tone with which Rakitin had spoken of Grushenka, he suddenly shouted from his place: 'Bernard!' And when the presiding judge, after Rakitin's cross-examination, turned to the accused and asked him if he had anything to say, Mitya shouted in a stentorian voice:

'He's been cadging loans from me since I was arrested! He's a contemptible Bernard and a careerist. He doesn't believe in God and he cheated the bishop!'

Mitya was, of course, again called to order for the violence of his language, but that was the end of Mr Rakitin. Nor was Captain Snegiryov's evidence any more successful, but for quite a different reason. He appeared in tattered and dirty clothes, muddy boots and, in spite of all the precautions and the preliminary medical 'examination', he suddenly seemed to be dead drunk. Asked about the insult he had suffered at the hands of Mitya, he refused to answer.

'It's of no importance, sir. Ilyusha told me not to. God will repay me, sir.'

'Who told you not to? Who are you talking about?'

'Ilyusha, my little son, sir. "Daddy, Daddy, how he humiliated you!" He said this at that stone. Now he is dying. . . .'

Snegiryov suddenly burst out sobbing and flung himself at the feet of the presiding judge. He was quickly led away amid the laughter of the public. The effect prepared by the public prosecutor had not come off.

The counsel for the defence, on the other hand, went on making use of every means at his disposal and amazed everyone more and more by his knowledge of the smallest details of the case. So, for instance, the evidence of the Mokroye innkeeper at first produced quite a powerful impression and was, of course, highly unfavourable to Mitya. He had, in fact, counted up almost on his fingers that Mitya could not possibly have spent less than three thousand or 'at least very little less' during his first visit to Mokroye, a month before the murder. The money he had squandered on the gipsy girls alone! As for 'our lousy peasants', he didn't 'fling them just half a rouble in the street' but gave them at least twenty-five-rouble notes each, no less.

'And how much was simply stolen from him, sir! For the thief did not leave a receipt, so how was one to catch him, the thief, sir, when he was throwing his money about regardless! For our peasants, sir, are just robbers, they don't care for the salvation of their souls. And the money he threw away on our village girls! Aye, they've grown rich since then. Yes, sir! Before they were as poor as church mice!' In short, he remembered every item of expense and added it all up as though on an abacus. Thus, the theory that Mitya had spent only fifteen hundred and put the rest away in his 'amulet' became untenable. 'I saw it myself, sir. Three thousand I saw in his hands with my own eyes, sir. Me not know how to count money, sir?' the inn-keeper kept exclaiming, doing his level best to please 'the authorities'. But when the counsel for the defence began his cross-examination, he did not even attempt to refute the innkeeper's evidence. Instead he recalled an incident that happened when Mitya had first gone to Mokroye a month before his arrest. At that time the coachman Timofey and another peasant called Akim had picked up a hundred-rouble note from the floor in the passage of the inn, which Mitya had dropped when drunk, and had given it to the innkeeper, who had presented them with a rouble each for their pains. 'Well,' the counsel for the defence asked, 'did you return the hundred roubles to Mr Karamazov that night?' However much he tried to wriggle out of it, the innkeeper, after the two peasants had given evidence about finding the money, admitted to receiving the money, but added that he had returned it to Mitya that very night 'in all honesty, but I expect, sir, that, being dead drunk at the time, he wouldn't remember it'. But as he had stoutly denied receiving the money before the two peasants had been called to prove it, his evidence about returning the money to Mitya naturally became suspect. So one of the most dangerous witnesses for the prosecution had left the witness box under a cloud of suspicion and with his reputation greatly besmirched. The same thing happened with the Poles. These appeared looking proud and inde-pendent. They both bore witness loudly that, in the first place, both had been 'servants of the Crown' and that Mitya had offered them three thousand to sell their honour, and that they had seen a large sum of money in his hands. Mussyalovich introduced a great number of Polish words into his sentences and, seeing that this raised him in the estimation of the presiding judge and the public prosecutor, it greatly raised his spirits so that at last he began talking in Polish altogether. But Fetyukovich caught them also in his snares: however much the Mokroye innkeeper tried to wriggle, he had in the end to admit that Vrublevsky had substituted his pack of cards for his own and that, when dealing, Mussyalovich had cheated. That was confirmed by Kalganov in his evidence, and the two Poles left the court in disgrace and amidst the laughter of the public.

Then exactly the same thing happened with almost all the other most dangerous witnesses. Fetyukovich succeeded in sullying the reputation of every one of them and dismissing them with their noses somewhat out of joint. The jurists and legal connoisseurs did not conceal their admiration for Fetyukovich and merely wondered what positive results he hoped to obtain from it to bring about the acquittal of his client. For, I repeat, everyone in court felt that the case for the prosecution was water-tight, which was growing more and more tragically obvious. But from the confidence of 'the great magician' they saw that he was not in the least perturbed and they waited, for they were sure that he was not the sort of a man to come from Petersburg for nothing or to go back empty-handed.

3

The Medical Evidence and a Pound of Nuts

THE medical evidence, too, was not of great help to the accused. As a matter of fact, Fetyukovich himself did not seem to count a great deal on it, as, indeed, appeared afterwards. It was primarily due to the insistence of Katerina, who had sent for a celebrated medical specialist from Moscow on purpose. The defence, of course, could lose nothing by it and, with luck, could even gain something from it. However, the result of it was to some extent rather comic, owing to the difference of opinion among the doctors. The medical experts were the celebrated Moscow doctor, then our doctor, Herzenstube, and, finally, the young doctor Varvinsky. The last two appeared also as witnesses for the prosecution. The first to give evidence as an expert was Dr Herzenstube. He was an old man of seventy, grey and bald-headed, of medium height and sturdy build. He was greatly esteemed and respected by everyone in our town. He was a conscientious medical practitioner, an excellent and pious man, a member of the German Herrenguter community on the Volga or Moravian Brother, I don't quite know which. He had been living in our town for a great many years and carried himself with extraordinary dignity. He was a kind-hearted and humane man, treated his poor patients and peasants for nothing, went himself into their hovels and cottages and left money for medicine, but for all his goodness he was as stubborn as a mule. Once he got an idea into his head, it was impossible to get it out. Incidentally, almost everyone in our town knew that during the first two or three days of his stay with us the famous Moscow doctor had delivered himself of several exceedingly offensive remarks about Dr Herzenstube's medical ability. For although the Moscow doctor charged no less than twenty-five roubles for a visit, several people in our town were overjoyed at his arrival, did not grudge the expense, and rushed to consult him. All these patients, of course, had been previously treated by Doctor Herzenstube, and the famous doctor had criticized his treatment with extreme harshness. Indeed, in the end the first thing he asked a patient as soon as he entered his room was: 'Well, who has been messing about with you? Herzenstube? Ha, ha!' Dr Herzenstube, of course, got to know all about it. And now all the three doctors appeared one after the other to give evidence. Dr Herzenstube roundly declared that 'the abnormality of the mental faculties of the prisoner was self-evident'. Then, after producing the reasons for his statement, which I omit here, he added that the abnormality could be diagnosed chiefly not only from the prisoner's numerous previous actions, but even from his behaviour just now, at this moment, in court. When asked to explain how he could diagnose it just now, at this moment, the old doctor, with that straightforward naïvety of his, pointed out that, on entering the court-room, the prisoner had 'an extraordinary and, considering the circumstances, very strange air', that he had 'marched in like a soldier with his eyes fixed straight in front of him, while he should really have been looking to the left, where the ladies were sitting, for he was a great admirer of the fair sex and ought to have been thinking a lot of what the ladies would be saying about him now', the old man concluded in his peculiar language. I must add that he spoke Russian well and fluently, but somehow each sentence of his appeared to be phrased in the German way, which, however, never embarrassed him, for all his life he had a weakness for thinking that his Russian was a model of correctness, that it was 'even better than the Russians spoke it', and he was very fond of using Russian proverbs, maintaining every time that Russian proverbs were the best and most expressive of all the proverbs in the world. I may observe, furthermore, that in conversation, because of his absent-mindedness, he often forgot the most ordinary words, which he knew perfectly well, but which for some reason slipped his mind. Still, the same thing happened when he spoke German, and every time it happened he waved his hand in front of his face as though trying to catch the lost word, and no one could induce him to go on speaking till he had found it. His remark that the prisoner, on entering the courtroom, ought to have looked at the ladies provoked an amused whispering among the public. All our ladies were very fond of the old man. It was known, too, that, a confirmed bachelor all his life, he was religious and chaste and looked upon women as ideal and superior creatures. And that was why his unexpected remark struck everyone as extraordinarily funny.

The Moscow doctor, questioned in his turn, confirmed sharply and emphatically that he considered the prisoner's mental condition abnormal 'in the highest degree'. He talked a lot and cleverly about 'temporary insanity' and 'mania' and drew the conclusion that, according to all the collected facts, the prisoner had certainly been in a state of temporary insanity a few days before his arrest, and that if he had committed the crime, he had done so almost involuntarily, though he might have been conscious of it, being utterly unable to fight against the morbid compulsion that took possession of him. But apart from temporary insanity, the doctor also diagnosed mania which, according to his words, would quite certainly lead to complete insanity in future. (N.B. I reproduce his evidence in my own words, the doctor having expounded his views in very learned and highly technical language.) 'All his actions,' he went on, 'were contrary to common sense and logic. Quite apart from what I have not seen, that is to say, the crime itself and the whole catastrophe, during my talk with him the day before yesterday, the prisoner had an unaccountably fixed look in his eyes. Unexpected laughter when there was nothing to laugh at. Unaccountable and continuous irritation, strange words: Bernard, ethics, and others which were quite out of place.' But what the doctor thought especially significant about this mania was that the prisoner was quite unable to speak about the three thousand roubles, of which he considered himself cheated, without some kind of extraordinary irritation, while he could speak quite lightly about all his other failures and grievances. Finally, according to inquiries he had made, the prisoner had even before almost flown into a frenzy every time the three thousand roubles were mentioned, and yet he was said to be unselfish and disinterested where money was concerned. 'As for the view expressed by my learned colleague,' the Moscow doctor added ironically in concluding his speech, 'that on entering the court, the prisoner ought to have looked at the ladies and not straight in front of him, all I can say is that, apart from the facetiousness of such a conclusion, it is, moreover, radically unsound; for, though I quite agree that, on entering the court where his fate is being decided, the prisoner should not have looked so fixedly in front of him and that this could, in fact, have been considered a sign of his abnormal mental condition at that particular moment, I maintain at the same time that he ought not to have looked to the left at the ladies, but, on the contrary, to the right, in an attempt to find his counsel on whose help all his hopes rest and on whose defence his whole future depends.' The doctor expressed his opinion vigorously and emphatically. But the funny side of the difference of opinion between the two learned experts was emphasized by the quite unexpected conclusion drawn by Dr Varvinsky, who was the last to give evidence. In his view, the prisoner, now as before, was perfectly normal and though before his arrest he, no doubt, must have been in a nervous and highly excitable state, that could have been due to many most obvious reasons: jealousy, anger, continual drunkenness, etc. But that nervous condition had nothing whatever to do with 'temporary insanity', as had been asserted just now. As to the question whether the prisoner ought to have looked to the left or the right on entering the court, 'in his humble opinion' the prisoner, on entering the court, should most certainly have looked straight before him, as, in fact, he had done, for straight in front of him sat the president and the members of the court, on whom his whole fate now depended, 'so that by looking straight before him', the young doctor concluded his 'humble' evidence with some warmth, 'he proved his perfectly normal state of mind at that moment'.

'Bravo, medico!' cried Mitya from his seat. 'That's right!'

Mitya was, of course, pulled up, but the young doctor's opinion had a most decisive influence on the judges as well as on the public, for, as appeared afterward, everyone agreed with him. However, Doctor Herzenstube, when questioned again, but this time as a witness, quite unexpectedly gave evidence in Mitya's favour. As an old inhabitant of our town, who had known the Karamazov family for many years, he gave some evidence which was of great interest to the prosecution, but suddenly, as though something had just occurred to him, he added:

'And yet the lot of the poor young man might have been incomparably better, for he had a good heart both in childhood and afterwards, and I know it. But the Russian proverb says: "One head is good, but if a clever man comes to visit one, it will be better still, for there will be two heads and not just one." . . .'

'Two heads are better than one,' the public prosecutor prompted him impatiently, for he had long been aware of the old man's habit of talking in a slow and long-winded way, without caring for the impression he was making or for keeping his audience waiting till he had finished, but, on the contrary, being of a high opinion of his heavy, uninspired and always happily self-satisfied German wit. The old man was fond of cracking jokes.

'Oh, y-yes, that's what I said,' he went on stubbornly. 'One head is good, but two are much better. But no one with a good head on him came to see him, and so he lost his own head, too. . . . How did it happen? When did he lose it? I'm afraid I've forgotten the word for where he had lost his head,' he went on, waving his hand before his eyes. 'Oh, yes, *spazieren*.'

'Went for a walk?'

'Yes, yes, went for a walk. That's what I said. So his head went for a walk and came to such a deep place where he lost himself. And yet he was such a grateful and sensitive youth. Oh, I remember him very well when he was a little chap so high, abandoned by his father in the backyard, where he used to run about in the dirt without boots and his little breeches hanging by one button. . . .'

A note of deep tenderness suddenly came into the honest old man's voice. Fetyukovich gave a start as though anticipating what was coming and cottoned on to it at once.

'Oh, yes, I was a young man myself then. I – well, I was forty-five at the time, and I had only just arrived here. And I was sorry for the little boy and I asked myself why shouldn't I buy him a pound of – er – yes, a pound of – what do you call it? I've forgotten what it's called – a pound of what children are very fond of – now – what is it called? . . .' the doctor began waving his hands again. 'It grows on a tree and it's gathered and given as a present to everyone. . . .'

'Apples?'

'Oh, no, no! A pound! A pound! You buy apples by the dozen and not by the pound. . . . No, there are lots of them, and they're all very small, you put them in the mouth and c-c-rack!'

'Nuts?'

'Oh, yes, nuts, that's what I said,' the doctor declared very calmly, as though he had never been trying to think of the word. 'And I bought him a pound of nuts, for no one had ever bought the little boy a pound of nuts before, and I raised my finger and said to him: Boy, *Gott der Vater*, he laughed and repeated after me, *Gott der Vater*, *Gott der Sohn*, he laughed again and murmured, *Gott der Sohn – Gott der Heilige Geist*. Then he laughed again and said as best he could, *Gott der Heilige Geist*. So I went away. Two days later I passed that way again, and he shouted to me himself: Uncle, *Gott der Vater*, *Gott der Sohn*, and he had only forgotten *Gott der Heilige Geist*, so I reminded him, and I was again very sorry for him. But he was taken away, and I did not see him again. And now, twenty-three years later, I'm sitting one morning in my study, my hair already white, and suddenly a young man, looking the picture of health, whom I should never have recognized, walks in. But he raised his finger and said laughingly, "*Gott der Vater*, *Gott der Sohn und Gott der Heilige Geist*. I've just arrived and have come to thank you for the pound of nuts, for no one ever bought me a pound of nuts, and you were the only one to do it." And then I remembered the happy days of my youth and the poor boy without boots in the yard, and my heart turned over and I said, "You are a grateful young man, for you have remembered all your life the pound of nuts I gave you in your childhood." And I embraced him and blessed him. And I wept. He laughed, but he also cried – for a Russian often laughs when he should be crying. But he cried, I saw it. And now, alas! . . .'

'I'm crying now, too, German! I'm crying now, too, you dear old man!' Mitya suddenly shouted from his seat.

Be that as it may, but the story produced a certain favourable impression upon the public in court. But the chief effect in Mitya's favour was created by Katerina's evidence, which I will describe presently. And, as a matter of fact, when the witnesses *à décharge*, that is, the witnesses called by the defence, began to give evidence, fortune seemed suddenly to smile on Mitya in good earnest, and what was so remarkable, to the surprise even of the counsel for the defence. But before Katerina was called, Alyosha was examined, and he suddenly recalled a fact which seemed to furnish positive evidence against one of the most important points raised by the prosecution.

4

Fortune Smiles on Mitya

IT came as a great surprise to Alyosha himself. He was not required to take the oath, and I remember that from the very beginning of his examination both sides treated him very gently and sympathetically. It was clear that his good repute had preceded him. Alyosha gave his evidence modestly and with restraint, but his warm sympathy for his unhappy brother was manifest in every word he uttered. In reply to one question, he characterized his brother as a man of perhaps violent temper and carried away by his passions, but also as an honourable, proud, and magnanimous man who was quite ready to make any sacrifice, if this was demanded of him. He admitted, however, that because of his passion for Grushenka and his rivalry with his father, his brother had been in an intolerable position during the last few days before the murder. But he indignantly repudiated the suggestion that his brother was capable of committing a murder for the sake of a robbery, though he could not help admitting that the three thousand roubles had become a sort of obsession with Mitya, that he regarded them as part of the inheritance of which he had been cheated by his father and that, though he was not in the least interested in money, he could not even speak of the three thousand without flying into a violent temper. As for the rivalry of the two 'ladies', as the public prosecutor put it, that is to say, of Grushenka and Katerina, he answered evasively and was even unwilling to answer one or two questions altogether.

'Did your brother at least tell you that he intended to kill his father?' asked the public prosecutor, adding: 'You need not answer the question if you don't want to.'

'He never spoke of it directly.'

'Oh? Did he speak of it indirectly?'

'He spoke to me once of his personal hatred of Father and that he was afraid that – at a critical moment, at a moment when his loathing of him became unbearable, he – he might perhaps murder him.'

'And did you believe him when he told you that?'

'I'm afraid I did. But I was always convinced that when the fatal moment came some higher feeling would always save him as it actually did save him, because *it was not he who killed my father*,' Alyosha concluded firmly in a loud voice that could be heard all over the court-room.

The public prosecutor started like a war-horse at the sound of the trumpet.

'Let me assure you that I fully believe in the absolute sincerity of your conviction without attempting to explain it by, or identify it with, your affection for your unhappy brother. Your singular view of the whole tragic episode that took place in your family is known to us already from the preliminary investigation. I will not conceal from you that it is highly personal and contradicts all the other evidence obtained by the prosecution. And that is why I must insist on asking you what facts have led you to this firm conviction of your brother's innocence and of the guilt of some other person whom you mentioned at the preliminary investigation?'

'I only answered the questions put to me at the preliminary investigation,' Alyosha said quietly and calmly. 'I did not myself make any accusation against Smerdyakov.'

'But you did mention him, didn't you?'

'I did so because of what my brother Dmitry had told me. Even before my interrogation I was told what took place at his arrest and that he had pointed to Smerdyakov as the murderer. I believe absolutely that my brother is innocent. And if he did not commit the murder, then —'

'Then Smerdyakov did? But why Smerdyakov? And why are you so absolutely convinced of your brother's innocence?'

'I couldn't but believe my brother. I know he wouldn't lie to me. I could tell from his face that he wasn't lying to me.'

'Only from his face? Is that all the proof you have?'

'I have no other proof.'

'And you have no proof whatever of Smerdyakov's guilt except your brother's words and the expression on his face?'

'No, I have no other proof.'

At this point the public prosecutor broke off his examination. The impression made on the public by Alyosha's replies was most disappointing. People had been talking about Smerdyakov before the trial: someone had heard something, someone else had been pointing something out; it was said that Alyosha had collected some extraordinary proof of his brother's innocence and of the servant's guilt, and here there was nothing, no proofs, except certain moral convictions which were so natural in a brother of the accused.

But Fetyukovich began his cross-examination. He asked Alyosha exactly when it was that the prisoner had told him, Alyosha, that he hated his father and that he had felt like killing him. Had he heard it from him, for instance, at his last meeting before the murder? In answering, Alyosha seemed suddenly to give a start as though he had only just remembered and understood something.

'I've just remembered one circumstance, which I had quite forgotten and the full significance of which I did not grasp at the time, but now —'

And, evidently, only just at that moment struck by an idea, Alyosha recalled with animation how at his last meeting with Mitya, in the evening under the tree, on the road to the monastery, Mitya, smiting his breast, 'the upper part of the breast', had repeated several times that he had a means of restoring his honour, and that it was there, there – on his breast. 'I thought at the time that by striking himself on the breast he was referring to his heart,' Alyosha went on, 'that what he meant was that he could find strength in his heart to escape from some terrible disgrace which threatened him and which he did not dare even to confess to me. I must confess that I did think then that he was referring to Father and that he was shuddering, as though it were a disgrace, at the thought of going to see Father and doing some violence to him. And yet he seemed to be pointing to something on his breast, so that, I remember, the thought occurred to me that his heart was not in that part of his breast, but lower down, and that he struck himself much higher up, just here, below the neck, and kept pointing to that place. My thought seemed absurd to me at the time, but I expect he must, perhaps, have been pointing at the bag in which he had sewn the fifteen hundred roubles!'

'Yes, that is so, Alyosha,' Mitya suddenly cried from his place. 'I did strike it then with my fist.'

Fetyukovich, rushed up to him hastily, imploring him to keep calm, and at the same moment simply fastened on Alyosha. Alyosha, carried away by his recollection himself, warmly expounded his theory that what Mitya had meant by his disgrace was most probably the fact that he had on him the fifteen hundred roubles, which he could have returned to Katerina as half of what he owed her, but that he had made up his mind not to return it to her, but to use it for something else, namely, for his elopement with Grushenka, if she consented. . . .

'Yes, it is so, it most certainly is so,' Alyosha cried with sudden excitement. 'My brother did keep telling me that half, half of his disgrace (he repeated *half* several times!) he could at once get rid of, but that realizing how weak his character was, he would never do so – that he knew beforehand that he would not, that he had not the strength of will to do it!'

'And you remember quite clearly that he struck himself on just that part of the breast?' Fetyukovich questioned him eagerly.

'Yes, I remember it quite clearly, I'm quite sure of it, for I thought at the time: Why does he strike himself so high up on the breast when his heart is lower down, but at the time the thought seemed stupid to me. . . . I remember thinking it was stupid – it flashed through my mind. And that's why I remembered it just now. And how could I have forgotten it till now? It was that little bag he was pointing at when he said that he had the means, but that he would not return the fifteen hundred! And when he was arrested in Mokroye he cried – I know, I was told about it – that he considered it the most disgraceful act of his life that when he had the means of repaying half (yes, half!) his debt to Miss Verkhovtsev and no longer being a thief in her eyes, he could not bring himself to repay it, but preferred to remain a thief in her eyes rather than part with the money! And how he was worried, how he was worried by that debt!' Alyosha exclaimed in conclusion.

Of course, the public prosecutor, too, intervened. He asked Alyosha to describe again how it had all happened and insisted on repeating several times his question whether the prisoner had really been pointing at something when he beat his breast. Perhaps, he had simply been striking the breast with his fist?

'It was not with his fist at all!' exclaimed Alyosha. 'He kept pointing with his fingers, and he pointed here – very high up. How could I have forgotten it so completely till this moment?'

The presiding judge turned to Mitya and asked him what he had to say about Alyosha's evidence. Mitya confirmed that it had all happened just like that and that he had been pointing to the fifteen hundred which were on his breast just a little below his neck, and that, of course, it was a disgrace – 'a disgrace', he went on, 'which I do not deny! It was the most disgraceful thing I had done in all my life!' cried Mitya. 'I could have given it back, but I didn't. I preferred to remain a thief in her eyes rather than give it back. And the most disgraceful thing about it was that I knew beforehand that I wouldn't give it back! Alyosha is right! Thanks, Alyosha!'

So concluded Alyosha's examination. The important and remarkable thing about it was that one fact had at least emerged, one, it is true, very small proof, almost a hint at a proof, which nevertheless seemed to indicate, however vaguely, that the bag had existed, that there were fifteen hundred roubles in it, and that the prisoner had not been lying at the preliminary inquiry when he declared in Mokroye that the fifteen hundred were 'mine'. Alyosha was delighted. He went back to the place reserved for him with a flushed face. He kept repeating to himself: 'How could I have forgotten it? How could I have forgotten it? And how was it that I suddenly remembered it only now?'

The examination of Katerina Verkhovtsev began. The moment she appeared something extraordinary happened in the court. The ladies snatched up their lorgnettes and opera glasses, the men stirred in their seats, some getting up to have a better look at her. Everyone asserted afterwards that Mitya turned 'as white as a sheet' as soon as she entered. All in black, she modestly and almost timidly approached the place pointed out to her. It was impossible to tell from her face that she was agitated, but there was a gleam of resolution in her dark and sombre eyes. It must be observed that a great many people asserted afterwards that she looked particularly beautiful at that moment. She began to speak in a soft voice, but so clearly that she could be heard all over the court. She expressed herself very calmly or, at any rate, did her utmost to be calm. The presiding judge began putting his questions with great care and very deferentially, as though afraid to touch 'certain chords' and showing consideration for her great unhappiness. But Katerina herself, from the very first, declared firmly in reply to one of the questions put to her, that she had been engaged to the prisoner, 'till he left me of his own accord', she added softly. When she was asked about the three thousand she had entrusted to Mitya to post to her relations, she said firmly: 'I did not give it to him only to post. I felt at the time that he was in great need of money – just then. I gave him the three thousand on the understanding that, if he liked, he could send them off within a month. He needn't have tortured himself so much afterwards over that debt.'

I will not repeat all the questions put to her and all her answers in detail. I am only giving the gist of her evidence.

'I was firmly convinced,' she went on in answer to the questions, 'that he would have time to send off the money as soon as he received it from his father. I have always been convinced of his selflessness and his honesty – his scrupulous honesty in – in money matters. He was absolutely sure that he would get the three thousand from his father and he told me so several times. I knew that there was a feud between him and his father and I have always been of the opinion, and I am so now, that he had been unfairly treated by his father. I don't remember him threatening his father. In my presence, at any rate, he never said anything of the kind, he never uttered any threats. If he had come to me at the time, I should at once have set his mind at rest about those absurd three thousand roubles, but – he never came to see me again and – and I myself was put in such a position that – that I could not ask him to come to see me. Why,' she added suddenly, and there was a ring of determination in her voice, 'I had no right whatever to demand from him the repayment of that debt. I had once received a loan from him myself of more than three thousand and I accepted it in spite of the fact that I could not foresee at the time that I should ever be in a position to repay my debt.'

There seemed to be a note of defiance in her voice. It was just then that Fetyukovich began his cross-examination.

'That did not take place here but at the beginning of your acquaintance, did it not?' Fetyukovich asked, treading carefully, feeling at once something favourable. (I must note parenthetically that in spite of the fact that he had been summoned from Petersburg partly at the instigation of Katerina, he knew nothing about the episode of the five thousand Mitya had given her and of her 'bowing to the ground' to him. She did not tell him that. She concealed it from him. And that was remarkable. It may be confidently assumed that up to the very last moment she did not know herself whether she would tell about that episode in court and waited for some kind of inspiration.)

'No, I can never forget those moments!' She began to tell, she told *everything*, the whole of that episode Mitya had told Alyosha, her 'bowing to the ground' and her reasons, and about her father, and her visit to Mitya, and did not mention by one word or a single hint the fact that Mitya had himself proposed, through her sister, that 'Katerina should be sent to him for the money'. She generously concealed that and was not ashamed to declare in public that is was she, she herself, who had run to the young officer, of her own impulse, hoping for something or other – to obtain the money from him. It was stupendous! I turned cold and trembled as I listened. Everyone in the court held his breath, trying to catch every word. There was something so unexampled about it that it was almost impossible to expect even from so masterful and disdainfully proud a girl like her such frank and highminded a testimony, such sacrifice, such self-immolation. And for what? For whom? To save the man who had deceived and insulted her, and to do something, however small, to bring about his acquittal by creating a good impression in his favour? And, indeed, the character of the army officer who gave up his last five thousand roubles – all that he possessed in the world – and who bowed respectfully to an innocent girl, appeared in a very sympathetic and attractive light, but – my heart contracted painfully! I felt that it might give rise to calumny (and it did, it did!). People all over our town were saying afterwards with a malicious chuckle that her story was, perhaps, not quite exact, namely in her statement that the officer had let the young lady go 'with seemingly only a respectful bow'. It was hinted that something 'was left out there'. 'And even if nothing had been left out, if it were all true,' even the most respectable of our ladies asserted, 'even then it is still very doubtful whether it was nice for a young girl to behave like that, even for the sake of saving her father.' And, surely, Katerina with her intelligence and her morbid sensibility must have known very well that people would talk like that. She certainly must have known, and yet she made up her mind to tell everything. No doubt, all these sordid little suspicions as to the truth of her story only arose afterwards; at the first moment everyone was deeply moved by it. As for the members of the court, they listened to Katerina in reverent and, as it were, even shamefaced silence. The public prosecutor did not permit himself to ask a single question on the subject. Fetyukovich bowed very low to her. Oh, he was almost triumphant. A great deal had been gained: a man who on a generous impulse gives away his last five thousand roubles and the same man who afterwards murders his own father for the sake of robbing him of three thousand – such a thing was something that seemed almost incongruous. Fetyukovich could at least eliminate the charge of robbery. The 'case' suddenly appeared in quite a new light. There was a wave of sympathy for Mitya. But he – it was said about him that once or twice during Katerina's evidence he jumped up from his seat, but sank back again on the bench and buried his face in his hands. But when she had finished, he suddenly cried in a sobbing noice:

'Katya, why have you ruined me?'

And he burst into loud sobs, which could be heard all over the court. However, he controlled himself at once and shouted again:

'Now I am condemned!'

Then he seemed to sit rigid in his place, clenching his teeth and folding his arms tightly across his chest. Katerina remained in the court and sat down on the chair reserved for her. She was pale and sat with her eyes fixed on the ground. Those who were sitting near her declared that she kept trembling all over as though in a fever. Grushenka was the next to be examined.

I am now coming to the catastrophe which, coming so suddenly, was perhaps the real cause of Mitya's ruin. For I am quite sure, and everyone else, all the jurists, said the same thing afterwards, that, but for that episode, the prisoner would at least have been treated leniently. But of that in a moment. A few words first about Grushenka.

She, too, appeared in court dressed all in black, with her beautiful black shawl over her shoulders. She approached the dais with a light, noiseless step, swaying slightly, as plump women sometimes do. She gazed steadily at the presiding judge, looking neither to the left nor to the right. In my opinion, she was very beautiful at that moment and not at all pale, as the ladies afterwards declared. They also declared that she had a strained and spiteful expression. But I think she was only irritated and resentful of the contemptuous and inquisitive eyes of our scandal-mongering public. She was proud and could not stand contempt; she was one of those people who, as soon as they suspect anyone of contempt, flare up with anger and a desire to retaliate. There was, besides, also the fact that she was timid and inwardly ashamed of her timidity, so that it was no wonder that her evidence was given in an uneven tone of voice, angry at one moment, contemptuous and exaggeratedly rude at another, and with a sincere note of self-condemnation and self-accusation at a third. At times she spoke as though she were precipitating herself into some abyss: 'I don't care what happens, I'll say it all the same. . . .' Asked about her acquaintance with Fyodor Karamazov, she remarked sharply: 'That's all nonsense! Was it my fault that he kept badgering me?' And a moment later she added: 'It is all my fault. I was laughing at both of them – at the old man and at him – and I brought them both to this. It all happened because of me.' A reference was made to Samsonov. 'That's nobody's business,' she snapped with a sort of insolent defiance. 'He was my benefactor. He took me when I was running about bare-foot and when my family turned me out of the house.' The presiding judge, however, reminded her very courteously that she had to give concise answers to the questions without entering into unnecessary details. Grushenka blushed and her eyes flashed.

She had not seen the envelope with the money, but only heard from the 'villain' that Fyodor Karamazov had some envelope with three thousand in it. 'Only that was all nonsense. I just laughed. I wouldn't have gone there for anything.'

'Whom were you referring to just now as the "villain"?' asked the public prosecutor.

'The lackey, Smerdyakov, who murdered his master and hanged himself yesterday.'

She was, of course, asked at once what grounds she had for such a categoric accusation, but she, too, apparently, had no grounds for it.

'Dmitry Karamazov told me so himself. You must believe him. The woman who came between us has ruined him. Yes, she's the cause of it all,' added Grushenka, and she seemed to be convulsed with hatred, her voice ringing with a note of malice.

She was asked who she was hinting at.

'The young lady, Miss Verkhovtsev there. She asked me to go to see her, offered me a cup of chocolate, tried to charm me. She has no real shame, that's the trouble.'

At this point the presiding judge pulled her up sternly and asked her to moderate her language. But the jealous woman's heart was ablaze with hatred, and she did not mind what she said or did.

'When the prisoner was arrested in the village of Mokroye,' recalled the public prosecutor, 'everyone saw and heard you run out of the next room and shout: "It's all my fault! We'll go to Siberia together!" You must therefore have been certain at that moment that he had murdered his father, mustn't you?'

'I don't remember what I felt at the time,' replied Grushenka. 'They were all shouting that he had murdered his father, and I felt that it was my fault and that he had murdered him because of me. But when he said that he was innocent I believed him at once, and I believe him now and always shall believe him. He isn't the sort of man to tell lies.'

Fetyukovich began his cross-examination. Among other things, I remember, he asked her about Rakitin and about the twenty-five roubles 'you gave him for bringing Alexey Karamazov to see you'.

'There's nothing surprising about his taking the money,' Grushenka smiled with angry contempt. 'He was always coming to cadge money from me. He'd get thirty roubles a month sometimes and spend it on his own pleasures: he had enough for food and drinks without any support from me.'

'But what was your reason for being so generous to Mr Rakitin?' Fetyukovich was quick to ask, in spite of the presiding judge's attempt to intervene.

'Why, he's my cousin. My mother was his mother's sister. But he has always begged me not to tell anyone here about it. He was so terribly ashamed of me.'

This new fact was a complete surprise to everyone in court. No one in the town, nor in the monastery, not even Mitya, knew about it. It is said that Rakitin flushed crimson with shame. Before she came into court Grushenka had somehow got to know that Rakitin had given evidence against Mitya, and that was why she was angry. The whole of Mr Rakitin's speech, all its noble sentiments, all his attacks on serfdom and the political disorder of Russia – all its effect on the public was now finally destroyed and forgotten. Fetyukovich was satisfied: again his luck held. In general, Grushenka's examination did not last very long and, as a matter of fact, she could not have told them anything particularly new. She left a very disagreeable impression on the public. Hundreds of contemptuous glances were cast upon her when, having completed her evidence, she sat down in the court at some distance from Katerina. All through her examination Mitya was silent, as though turned to stone, his eyes fixed on the ground.

Ivan was next called to give evidence.

5

A Sudden Catastrophe

HE had been called, I ought, perhaps, to explain, before Alyosha. But the usher of the court informed the presiding judge that owing to a sudden attack of illness or some sort of fit, the witness could not appear just then, but that he was ready to give his evidence as soon as he felt better. But no one, somehow, seemed to have heard it and it only became known later. At first his appearance in court was almost un-noticed: the principal witnesses, especially the two rival young women, had already been examined; curiosity was for the time being satisfied. There was, indeed, a general feeling of fatigue among the public. A few more witnesses were still to be examined and, in view of what had already come out, they probably had nothing of particu-lar importance to reveal. Time was passing. Ivan approached the wit-ness stand quite surprisingly slowly, without looking at anyone and with his head lowered, as though thinking something over moodily. He was immaculately dressed, but his face produced, on me at least, a painful impression: there was something in his face that seemed to have been touched by decay, it looked like the face of a dying man. His eyes were glazed over; he raised them and looked slowly round the court. Alyosha suddenly jumped up from his seat and exclaimed: 'Oh!' I remember that. But few people noticed it.

The presiding judge began by informing him that, as a witness who was not on oath, he was free to answer or not to answer the questions put to him, but that, of course, whatever evidence he gave must be according to his conscience, etc., etc. Ivan listened and looked at him blankly; but suddenly his face began slowly to distend into a smile and as soon as the presiding judge, who looked at him in surprise, finished talking, he suddenly burst out laughing.

'Well, and what else?' he asked loudly.

There was dead silence in the court; everyone felt that something extraordinary was about to happen. The presiding judge began to feel anxious.

'Are you – er – perhaps still not feeling well?' he asked, searching for the usher with his eyes.

'Don't worry, sir, I'm well enough and I can tell you something interesting,' Ivan suddenly replied very calmly and respectfully.

'You have some special communication to make?' the presiding judge went on, still mistrustfully.

Ivan looked down, waited a few seconds and, raising his head again, replied as though hesitantly:

'No, sir – I haven't. I haven't anything special. . . .'

They began questioning him. He replied rather reluctantly, with extreme brevity, even with a sort of disgust which grew stronger and stronger, though his answers were sensible enough. Many questions he refused to answer, pleading ignorance. He knew nothing of his father's disagreements over money with Dmitry. 'I was not interested in it,' he said. He had heard the prisoner threaten to kill his father. He had heard about the money in the envelope from Smerdyakov.

'It's all the same thing,' he suddenly interrupted with a weary look. 'There's nothing particular I can tell the court.'

'I can see,' the presiding judge began, 'that you are unwell and understand your feelings. . . .'

He turned to the public prosecutor and the counsel for defence and asked them to cross-examine the witness, if they thought it necessary, when Ivan suddenly asked him in an exhausted voice:

'Please let me go, sir, I feel very ill.'

And without waiting for permission, he suddenly turned round and walked towards the door. But after taking four steps, he stopped, as though he was thinking something over, smiled quietly and returned to the witness stand.

'I'm just like that peasant girl, sir,' he said. 'You know how it goes: "If I wants to I gets up, if not, I doesn't." They follow her about with a *sarafan* or striped, home-spun skirt and beg her to get up so that they can put it on and take her to church to be married, but she keeps saying: "If I wants to I gets up, if not, I doesn't." . . . That seems to be a national characteristic of ours. . . .'

'What do you want to say by that?' the presiding judge asked sternly.

'This,' Ivan replied suddenly, taking out a bundle of notes. 'Here is the money – the same notes that lay in that envelope [he motioned to the table with the 'exhibits'] and for which my father was murdered. Where shall I put them? Usher, take them.'

The usher got up from his seat, took the bundle and handed it to the president of the court.

'How did you get hold of this money if – if it is the same money?' the presiding judge asked in surprise.

'I got them from Smerdyakov, from the murderer, yesterday. . . . I went to see him before he hanged himself. It was he and not my brother who murdered my father. He murdered him, and I told him to do it. Who doesn't wish his father dead?'

'Are you in your right mind?' the presiding judge cried involuntarily.

'Yes. I'm afraid that's the trouble that I'm in my right mind – and in the same vile mind as yourself and all these – ugly faces!' he turned suddenly to the public. 'My father has been murdered and they pretend to be horrified,' he snarled with furious contempt. 'Showing off before one another! The liars! They all wish their fathers dead. One reptile devours another. . . . If there had been no murder of a father, they'd all have got angry and gone home in a bad temper. . . . Circuses! "Bread and circuses!" Still I, too, am one to talk! Is there any water? For Christ's sake let me have a drink of water!' he cried, suddenly clutching at his head.

The usher at once went up to him. Alyosha suddenly jumped up and shouted: 'He's ill! Don't believe him! He's raving!' Katerina rose impetuously from her seat and, motionless with horror, gazed at Ivan. Mitya got up and looked at his brother and listened to him with a sort of wild, twisted smile.

'Calm yourselves, I'm not mad, I'm only a murderer!' Ivan began again. 'You can't expect eloquence from a murderer,' he added suddenly for some reason and laughed wryly.

The public prosecutor bent over to the presiding judge in evident dismay. The members of the court whispered agitatedly to one another. Fetyukovich pricked up his ears, listening attentively. The court-room was hushed in expectation. The presiding judge seemed suddenly to recollect himself.

'Witness, your words are incomprehensible and inadmissible here. Calm yourself, if you can, and tell us all about it if – if you really have something to say. How can you confirm your confession, if – if you are not raving?'

'Well, you see, the trouble is that I have no witnesses. That cur Smerdyakov will not provide you with evidence from the other world in – in an envelope. All you want are envelopes, but one's enough. I have no witnesses, except, perhaps, one,' he smiled wistfully.

'Who is your witness?'

'He has a tail, sir. I'm afraid you wouldn't consider that proper dress. *Le diable n'existe point!* Don't take any notice,' he added, suddenly leaving off laughing and as though confidentially, 'it's a paltry little devil. He's probably here somewhere – there under that table with the exhibits. Where else should he be sitting if not there? You see, listen to me: I said to him I won't be silent and he starts talking about geological upheavals – nonsense! Well, set the monster free – he's been singing a hymn. That's because he doesn't care! He's just like a drunken rascal bawling at the top of his voice how "Vanka to Petersburg has gone", and I'd give a quadrillion of quadrillions for two seconds of joy! You don't know me! Oh, how stupid everything is here! Well, take me instead of him! I didn't come here for nothing. . . . Why, why is everything in the world stupid? . . .'

And he began to look round the court-room again slowly and as though thoughtfully. But already the court was in a commotion. Alyosha rushed towards him, but the usher had already seized Ivan by the arm.

'How dare you?' Ivan cried, staring into the usher's face and, suddenly seizing him by the shoulders, hurled him on to the floor.

But the soldiers on guard were there in time. They seized him, and it was then that he uttered a piercing scream. And, shouting something incoherent, he went on screaming while he was being carried out.

The court was thrown into confusion. I cannot remember everything as it happened, for I was too agitated myself to see what was going on. All I know is that afterwards, when order had been restored and everyone realized what had happened, the usher was taken severely to task, though he quite rightly explained to the judges that the witness had been well all the time, that a doctor had seen him when an hour earlier he had a slight attack of giddiness, and that before he had come into the court he had talked coherently, so that it was quite impossible to foresee anything; that, on the contrary, he himself had insisted on giving evidence. But before anyone had calmed down and completely recovered, another scene followed immediately after the first. Katerina had an attack of hysterics. She shrieked loudly and burst into sobs, but refused to leave the court, struggled, entreated them not to remove her, and suddenly shouted to the presiding judge:

'I must give you some more evidence at once – at once! Here's a document, a letter – take it and read it quickly, quickly! It's a letter from that monster – that one, there!' she pointed to Mitya. 'It is he who murdered his father, as you will see presently. He wrote to me how he would kill his father! But the other one is ill, ill – he's mad! I could see for the last three days that he was mad!'

So she kept shrieking, beside herself. The usher took the document which she held out to the presiding judge. She herself collapsed on her chair and burying her face, began sobbing convulsively and noiselessly, shaking all over and stifling every moan for fear that she should be forced to leave the court. The document she had given to the usher was the letter Mitya had sent her from the 'Metropolis', which Ivan had described as a document of 'mathematical' certainty. Alas, its 'mathematical' nature was recognized, and but for that letter Mitya would not have been ruined, or, at any rate, not have been ruined so terribly. I repeat, it was difficult to follow every detail. Even now the whole thing seems utterly confused. I suppose the presiding judge must at once have communicated the new document to the judges, the public prosecutor, the counsel for the defence, and the jury. I only remember how they began examining the witness. Asked gently by the president whether she was sufficiently composed to give evidence, Katerina cried impulsively:

'I'm ready, ready! I'm quite able to answer your questions,' she added, evidently still terribly afraid that for some reason they would refuse to listen to her.

She was asked to explain in more detail what letter it was and under what circumstances she had received it.

'I received it on the day before the murder, and he wrote it the day before that at the public house, so that it was written two days before he committed the crime. Look, it is written on some sort of a bill!' she shouted, breathlessly. 'He hated me at that time because he himself had treated me disgracefully and had run off after that creature and – and also because he owed me those three thousand roubles! . . . Oh, it hurt him to owe me that money just because of his own baseness! This is what happened about the three thousand – please, I beg you, I implore you to hear me. Three weeks before he murdered his father he came to see me in the morning. I knew he needed money and I knew what he wanted it for – to entice that creature – yes, to entice her and carry her off. I knew at the time that he had been false to me and wanted to throw me over and I, I myself, offered him the money, I myself gave it him on the pretext of sending it to my sister in Moscow – and when I gave it him, I looked him in the face and said that he could send it whenever he liked, "even in a month's time". How then, how then could he have failed to understand that I was frankly telling him to his face: "You want money to betray me with that creature of yours, so here's the money for you, I'm giving it to you myself! Take it, if you're so dishonourable as to take it!" I wanted to show him up, and what did he do? He took the money. He took it and squandered it there with that creature in one night. . . . But he realized, he realized, I assure you, he realized very well that, by giving him that money, I was only trying to test him. I was trying to see whether he really was so dishonourable as to take it from me. I looked into his eyes and he looked into mine and he understood everything – everything, and he took the money! Took my money and carried it off!'

'That's true, Katya!' Mitya suddenly bawled. 'I looked into your eyes and I knew that you were trying to bring dishonour upon me, and I took the money for all that! Despise the blackguard, despise me all of you! I've deserved it!'

'Prisoner,' exclaimed the presiding judge, 'another word from you and I'll order you to be removed!'

'That money worried him,' Katerina went on with convulsive haste. 'He wanted to give it back to me. He wanted to, that's true, but he also wanted money for that creature. So he murdered his father, but didn't return the money to me all the same. Instead he went off with her to the village where he was arrested. There he again squandered the money he had stolen from the father he had murdered. And a day before he murdered his father he wrote me this letter. He wrote it when he was drunk. I saw it at once. He wrote it out of spite, knowing, knowing very well, that I wouldn't show the letter to anyone, even if he did kill him. He wouldn't have written it otherwise. He knew I wouldn't wish to revenge myself and ruin him! But read it, please. Read it carefully, as carefully as you can, please, and you will see that he described it all in the letter, all beforehand: how he was going to kill his father and where the money was kept. Look, please, don't miss anything. There's a phrase there: "I'll kill him, if only Ivan goes away." And that means that he had thought it all out beforehand how he would kill him,' Katerina prompted the court, venomously and with malicious joy. Oh, it was clear that she had studied the fatal letter with great care and knew every word of it. 'If he hadn't been drunk, he wouldn't have written to me. But look, everything is described there beforehand, everything exactly as it happened, how he committed the murder – the whole programme!'

So she kept exclaiming, beside herself, and, needless to say, regardless of all the consequences for herself, though she had, of course, foreseen them perhaps a month before, for even then, perhaps, quivering with anger, she had wondered whether to read it to the court or not. Now she had taken the fatal plunge. I think it was just at this point that the clerk read the letter aloud, and it created an overwhelming impression. Mitya was asked whether he admitted having written the letter.

'It's mine, it's mine!' exclaimed Mitya. 'If I hadn't been drunk, I shouldn't have written it! We've hated each other for many things, Katya, but I swear, I swear I loved you even while I hated you, but you never loved me!'

He sank back on his seat, wringing his hands in despair. The public prosecutor and the counsel for the defence began cross-examining her, chiefly in an attempt to ascertain what had induced her to conceal such a document and give evidence in a completely different tone and spirit from before.

'Yes, yes, I lied before,' Katerina cried madly. 'I was telling lies all the time against my honour and my conscience. But I wanted to save him because he has hated and despised me so much. Oh, he has despised me terribly, he has always despised me and, you know, you know he has despised me ever since that moment when I prostrated myself before him for that money. I saw it at once. . . . I felt it at once, but I refused to believe it for a long time. How many times have I read in his eyes: "But you came to me yourself that time all the same." Oh, he didn't understand, he didn't understand anything! He didn't understand why I came running to him then! He is capable of suspecting only base motives! He judged me by himself. He thought that everyone was like him,' Katerina cried furiously, completely beside herself. 'And the only reason he wanted to marry me was because I had inherited a fortune. Because of that, because of that! I always suspected that it was because of that! Oh, he is a beast! All his life he was convinced that I'd be trembling with shame before him because I went to him then, and that he could always despise me for that and for that reason have the whip hand over me – that's why he wanted to marry me! Yes, that's what it is! I tried to win him over by my love – a love that knew no limit. I tried even to put up with his betrayal, but he understood nothing, nothing! And how can he be expected to understand anything? He is a monster! I only received this letter the next evening. It was brought to me from the public house, and that very morning I had wanted to forgive him everything, everything, even his betrayal!'

The presiding judge and the public prosecutor, of course, tried to calm her. I am sure all of them were perhaps ashamed to take advantage of her frenzy and of listening to such avowals. I remember hearing them say to her: 'We realize how painful it is for you! Rest assured we are able to feel for you,' etc., etc. And yet they dragged the evidence out of the maddened, hysterical woman. Finally, she described with extraordinary clarity, which so often, though only for a moment, appears during such an overwrought condition, how Ivan had almost been driven out of his mind during the last two months in an attempt to save 'the monster and murderer', his brother.

'He tormented himself,' she exclaimed. 'He tried to minimize as much as possible his brother's guilt. He confessed to me that he didn't love his father himself and perhaps wanted him dead himself. Oh, he has a tender, a very tender conscience! It is his conscience that has driven him out of his mind! He told me everything, everything. He came to me every day and talked to me as his only friend. I have the honour to be his only friend!' she exclaimed suddenly, with flashing eyes, as though with a sort of defiance. 'He had been to see Smerdyakov twice. One day he came to me and said that if Smerdyakov and not his brother had committed the murder (for lots of people here spread the silly story that Smerdyakov had done it), then he, too, was guilty, because Smerdyakov knew that he didn't like his father and perhaps thought that he desired his death. Then I produced that letter and showed it to him, and he was entirely convinced that his brother had committed the murder, and that drove him out of his mind completely. He could not endure the thought that his own brother was a parricide! Already a week ago I could see that it was making him ill. When he came to see me during the last few days he was raving. I saw that he was going out of his mind. He walked about raving; he was seen talking to himself in the streets. At my request the doctor from Moscow examined him the day before yesterday and he told me that he was on the point of losing his reason – and all because of him, all because of this monster! And yesterday he learnt that Smerdyakov was dead and that was such a violent shock to him that he went mad – and all because of this monster, all because he wanted to save this monster!'

Oh, no doubt, it is only possible to talk like that and to make such confessions once in a lifetime – at the hour of death, for instance, when mounting the scaffold. But that, indeed, was in Katerina's character. She would do that at such a moment. It was the same impulsive Katya who had rushed to the young rake of an officer to save her father; the same Katya who, proud and chaste, had a short while before sacrificed herself and her maidenly modesty before all that crowd of people by telling them about the 'generous' way in which Mitya had treated her, so as to mitigate his sentence to some extent. And now she also sacrificed herself in exactly the same way, but this time for another, and perhaps it was only now, only at that moment, that she felt and fully realized how dear that other man was to her! She had sacrificed herself because she was terrified for him, for she realized all of a sudden that he had ruined himself by his evidence that it was he and not his brother who had committed the murder – she had sacrificed herself to save him, his good name and his reputation.

And yet one could not help being struck by a horrible doubt about it all: was she lying in describing her former relations with Mitya? – that was the question. No, no, she had not slandered him intentionally when she cried that Mitya despised her for bowing down to the ground to him! She believed it herself. She had been deeply convinced, perhaps ever since that scene in Mitya's room, that the simple-minded Mitya, who adored her even then, was laughing at her and despising her. And it was only out of pride that she had become attached to him with a hysterical love, a love full of heartache, out of injured pride, and her love was more like revenge than love. Oh, perhaps that love of hers, which was so full of heartache, would eventually have grown into real love. Perhaps Katya wished for nothing better than that. But Mitya had deeply insulted her by his betrayal, and she did not forgive him. The moment of revenge, however, had come upon her suddenly, and all that had for so long and so agonizingly accumulated in the breast of the wronged woman burst out suddenly and, again, quite unexpectedly. She betrayed Mitya, but she betrayed herself, too! And, to be sure, as soon as she had had her say, the tension was broken and she was overwhelmed with shame. She had another attack of hysterics and she collapsed, sobbing and screaming. She was carried out. At that moment Grushenka rushed up from her seat to Mitya so impetuously that there was no time to stop her.

'Mitya,' she cried, 'your serpent has ruined you! Now she has shown you what she's really like!' she shouted to the judges, shaking with anger.

At a sign from the presiding judge, she was seized and they tried to remove her from the court. She resisted and struggled to get back to Mitya. Mitya began shouting and also tried to get to her. He was overpowered.

Yes, I think our ladies must have been satisfied: the spectacle was certainly most magnificent. Then, I remember, the Moscow doctor

i

was recalled. It seems that the presiding judge had sent the court usher before to make sure that Ivan was given all the necessary assistance. The doctor informed the court that Ivan was suffering from a most dangerous attack of brain fever and that he ought to be taken away at once. In answer to the questions put to him by the public prosecutor and the counsel for the defence, he confirmed that the patient had been to see him of his own accord the day before yesterday and that he had warned him that such an attack was imminent, but that he had refused medical treatment: 'He was most decidedly not in his right mind and he told me himself that he sees visions when awake, meets people in the streets who have long been dead, and that Satan visits him every evening,' the doctor concluded. Having given his evidence, the celebrated doctor withdrew. The letter produced by Katerina was added to the exhibits. After consulting with one another, the members of the court decided to carry on with the trial and to put on record the two unexpected pieces of evidence (given by Katerina and Ivan).

But I am not going to describe the rest of the evidence. Besides, the evidence of the remaining witnesses was merely a repetition and confirmation of the previous evidence, though they all had their own characteristic peculiarities. But, I repeat, it will all be summed up in the speech of the public prosecutor to which I shall pass on at once. Everyone in court was greatly excited, everyone was electrified by the last catastrophe, and they were only waiting with burning impatience for the end: the speeches for the prosecution and for the defence and the sentence. Fetyukovich was evidently greatly shaken by Katerina's evidence. The public prosecutor, on the other hand, was triumphant. When the evidence of the witnesses was concluded, the court was adjourned for almost an hour. At last the presiding judge called upon the prosecutor and the counsel for the defence to deliver their speeches. I believe it was precisely eight o'clock when our public prosecutor began his speech.

6

The Public Prosecutor's Speech:
Characterizations

THE public prosecutor began his speech trembling all over with nervousness, his forehead covered in a cold sweat, and feeling hot and cold in turn. He said so afterwards himself. He regarded this speech as his *chef d'œuvre*, as the *chef d'œuvre* of his whole life, as his swan-song. It is true that nine months later he died of galloping consumption, so that, as it turned out, he really had the right to compare himself to a swan singing his last song, if he could have foretold his end beforehand. He put his whole heart and all the intelligence he possessed into that speech and quite unexpectedly proved that there was hidden in him both a feeling for civic duty and for the 'damned' questions, at least as much of them as our poor public prosecutor could accommodate. The chief reason why his speech had such a shattering effect lay in its sincerity: he sincerely believed in the prisoner's guilt and he accused him not merely because it was his duty to do so, and in calling for 'revenge' he was passionately moved by the desire 'to save society'. Even our ladies, who were, after all, hostile to the public prosecutor, had to admit that he made a tremendous impression on them. He began in a cracked, faltering voice, but very soon his voice grew stronger and rang all through the court, and so he went on like that to the end of his speech. But he almost fainted as soon as he had finished it.

'Gentlemen of the jury,' began the public prosecutor, 'this case has created a sensation all over Russia. But what, it would seem, is there to be surprised at or to be particularly horrified about? For us, for us, especially? For we are so used to all this. But the reason why we are horrified is that such dark deeds have almost ceased to horrify us! What we ought to be horrified about is that we have got so used to it, and not to the single crime of one individual or another. Where are we to look for the causes of our indifference, our almost lukewarm attitude to such crimes, to such signs of the times which predict an unenviable future for us? In our cynicism, in the premature exhaustion of the intellect and the imagination of our society, which is still so young and yet has grown so decrepit before it has had time to grow old? In our moral principles which are shattered to their very foundations or, finally, in the fact that perhaps we completely lack such moral principles? I'm afraid I cannot answer these questions, but they are disturbing nevertheless, and every citizen not only must but is in duty bound to be deeply concerned about them. Our young but still timid press, however, has done some good service to society, for without it we should never have learnt so fully about those horrors of unbridled licence and moral degradation which it is continually reporting in its pages to everyone and not only to those who attend our new public courts, granted to us in this present reign. And what do we read almost daily? Oh, about such things beside which even our present case pales into insignificance and appears almost to be something quite commonplace. But what is even more important is that a great number of our national Russian crimes bear witness to something which is of general significance, to a sort of general calamity which has struck root among us and against which, as against universal evil, it is difficult to fight. In one place a brilliant young army officer, a member of the highest society, practically at the very beginning of his life and career, foully and in an underhand manner murders, without any qualms of conscience, a low-grade civil servant, who had in a way been his benefactor, and his maidservant, to steal the promissory note he had given him as well as all his ready money: "It will come in jolly useful for my pleasures in high society and for my future career." After murdering them, he puts pillows under their heads and goes away. In another place, a young hero, decorated with crosses for bravery, kills, like a highwayman, the mother of his chief and benefactor on the high road and, in urging his companions to join him, assures them that she loves him "like a son" and "will therefore follow his advice and take no precautions". Granted that he is a monster, but now, at this time, I dare not say that he is the only monster in Russia. Someone else may not commit murder, but he will think and feel exactly like him and at heart be as dishonourable as he. In the dead of night, alone with his conscience, he perhaps asks himself: "What is honour and isn't the feeling against shedding of blood a prejudice?" Perhaps people will cry out against me and say that I'm morbid and hysterical, that it's a monstrous slander, that I'm raving, exaggerating. Let them, let them, and, good Lord, I'd be the first to rejoice if it were so! Oh, do not believe me, regard me as a sick man, but remember my words all the same: for if only a tenth or a twentieth part of what I say is true – it is dreadful even so! Look, gentlemen of the jury, look how young people shoot themselves in our country. Oh, they do so without asking themselves Hamlet's question about "the dread of something after death, the undiscovered country, from whose bourne no traveller returns". There is no hint of any such question, just as though this business about our spirit and about what awaits us beyond the grave has long been erased in their minds, buried and covered with sand. Have a look, finally, at our vice and at our sensualists. Fyodor Karamazov, the luckless victim in this case, was almost an innocent babe compared with some of them. And yet we all knew him, "he lived among us". . . . Yes, the greatest intellects in our country and in Europe will perhaps one day devote themselves to the study of the psychology of Russian crime, for the subject is worth it. But this study will come at some later date when the whole tragic mess of our present life will recede into the background so that it can be examined at leisure, more intelligently and more dispassionately than, for instance, people like me can do. Now we are either horrified or pretend to be horrified, while actually relishing the spectacle, like lovers of strong and morbid sensations which excite our cynically comatose apathy; or, finally, like little children, we wave the fearful phantoms away and hide our heads in the pillow until the dreadful apparition is gone so as to forget it at once and go back to our games. But one day we, too, must begin to live life soberly and in earnest; we, too, must regard ourselves as a society; we, too, must at least have some idea of our social life or at least make a beginning of trying to understand it. A great writer of the last epoch, at the end of the greatest of his works, comparing Russia to a dare-devil Russian *troika*, galloping no one knows whither, exclaims: "Oh, *troika*, birdlike *troika*, who invented you?" and he adds with proud enthusiasm that all the nations stand aside respectfully to make way for the *troika* galloping at break-neck speed. Well, gentlemen of the jury, that may be so, let them stand aside, respectfully or not, but in my humble opinion the great creative artist ended like that either in a fit of childishly innocent sentimentality or simply because he was afraid of the censorship. For if his own heroes, the Sobakeviches, the Nozdryovs and the Chichikovs, were harnessed into his *troika*, you would not get anywhere on such horses, whoever the coachman might be! And those horses belonged to an older generation; they cannot be compared to ours – ours are far worse. . . .'

At this point the public prosecutor's speech was interrupted by applause. The 'liberalism' of the portrayal of the Russian *troika* pleased the public. It is true the applause was very brief, so that the presiding judge did not even consider it necessary to address the public with the threat of 'clearing the court', and only looked sternly in the direction of the people who had clapped. But the public prosecutor was encouraged: he had never been applauded before! The man had been refused a hearing for so many years and now he was suddenly given an opportunity of speaking his mind before the whole of Russia!

'And, indeed,' he went on, 'what is this Karamazov family, which has all of a sudden gained such a sad notoriety throughout Russia? Perhaps I am exaggerating, but it seems to me that certain fundamental features of our contemporary educated society can to some extent be recognized in the picture of this far from admirable family. Oh, not all the features and they are reflected only in a microscopic way, "like the sun in a drop of water", but nevertheless something has been reflected, something of the sort is there. Consider that unhappy, licentious, and depraved old man, the head of a family, who has met with such a melancholy end. A nobleman born, who began his life as a poor hanger-on and who by the accident of an unexpected marriage came into a small fortune by means of his wife's dowry, at first a small rogue and a smooth-tongued clown, with undeveloped mental faculties which were fairly good, he was, above all, a money-lender. As the years passed, that is to say, as he grew richer, he plucked up courage. His obsequiousness and servility disappeared and all that was left was a sarcastic and malicious cynic and sensualist. The spiritual side of his character had been obliterated, while his appetite for life was quite extraordinary. As a result, he saw nothing in life but sensual pleasures, and it was this that he taught his children. He knew nothing of a father's spiritual duties. He laughed at them. He brought up his children in the back-yard and he was glad to be rid of them. Indeed, he forgot all about them. All the moral principles of the old man could be summed up in one phrase – *après moi le déluge*. He represented everything that is contrary to the idea of citizenship, a complete and even hostile separation from society: "Let the whole world perish in flames so long as I'm all right." And he was all right, he was completely satisfied, he was anxious to go on living in the same way for another twenty or thirty years. He cheated his own son and used his son's money, the money left by his mother, which he refused to let him have, to win over his mistress from him. No, I do not want to give up the defence of the prisoner to my learned and talented friend from Petersburg. I will speak the truth myself. I understand very well myself the great resentment he had piled up against him in his son's heart. But enough, enough of that unhappy old man. He has got what he deserved. But don't let us forget, however, that he was a father and one of the fathers of our own day. Shall I deceive society by saying that he is, indeed, typical of many of our fathers of today? Alas, there are many of our fathers of today who are like him, except that they do not express themselves in so cynical a fashion, for they have been better brought up and are better educated, but at bottom their philosophy is almost the same as his. But perhaps I'm a pessimist. Perhaps I am. We have agreed, haven't we, that you forgive me. Let us come to an understanding beforehand: I don't want you to believe me. I shall go on speaking, but you need not believe me. But let me say what I have to say all the same and, please, do not forget something of what I say to you. Now let us turn to the children of this old man, this head of a family: one of them is here in the dock before you. I shall speak of him at length presently; of the other two I shall say a few words now. The elder of the two is one of our modern young men, a man of brilliant education and a fairly powerful intellect who, however, no longer believes in anything. Like his father, he has rejected and expunged too much already from life. We have all heard him; he was given a friendly reception in our society. He did not conceal his opinions, quite the contrary, as a matter of fact, which emboldens me to speak rather frankly of him now, not, of course, as a private individual, but as a member of the Karamazov family. There died here yesterday by his own hand, on the outskirts of the town, an idiot, a chronic invalid, closely connected with this case, a servant and, perhaps, also the illegitimate son of Fyodor Karamazov, Smerdyakov. He told me with hysterical tears at the preliminary inquiry how the young Ivan Karamazov had horrified him by his complete lack of spiritual restraint. "Everything," he said, "is permitted, according to him, everything in the world, and nothing must be forbidden in future – that's what he taught me all the time." It seems that that idiot was completely driven out of his mind by this maxim, which he had been taught, though, of course, his epileptic fits and all this terrible catastrophe which had befallen their house had also affected his reason. But this idiot dropped a very interesting remark indeed, a remark that would have done credit to a much more intelligent observer, and that's why I've mentioned it. "If," he said to me, "any of the sons resembles Fyodor Karamazov in character, it is Ivan!" With this observation I conclude my characterization of him, thinking it indelicate to continue further. Oh, I do not want to draw any further conclusions and croak like a raven, prophesying only ruin to the young man's future. We've seen today in this court that an instinctive desire for truth still lives in his young heart, that the feelings of family loyalty have not yet been stifled in him by unbelief and moral cynicism, acquired by inheritance rather than by the true and painful application of his reasoning powers. Then there is the other son – oh, he is still very young, devout and modest, who, contrary to his brother's gloomy and corrupting outlook on life, seems to cling, as it were, to the "fundamental beliefs of the people", or to whatever is meant by that curious expression in some theory-infested circles of our thinking intelligentsia. He, you see, attached himself to the monastery; he almost became a monk himself. In him, it seems to me, that timid despair has unconsciously and so early found expression which drives so many people in our unhappy society, who are scared of cynicism and its corrupt influences and who mistakenly attribute all evil to European enlightenment, to go back to their "native soil", back, as it were, to the motherly bosom of their native country; like children, they are frightened by ghosts and long to fall peacefully asleep at the withered breasts of their frail and infirm mother and to sleep there all their lives, only not to see the horrors that terrify them. For my part, I wish the good and talented young man every success. I wish that his lofty but, I'm afraid, rather romantic idealism and his longing to go back to the fundamental beliefs of the common people may not afterwards, as so often happens, degenerate on the moral plane into gloomy mysticism and on the political plane into die-hard chauvinism – two tendencies that perhaps threaten our nation with a greater evil than premature corruption as a result of the misunderstood and gratuitous adoption of European civilization, from which his elder brother is suffering.'

Two or three claps were heard again in disapproval of chauvinism and mysticism. And, no doubt, the public prosecutor had been carried away and, besides, all this had little to do with the matter in hand, to say nothing of the fact that it was all rather vague, but the consumptive and embittered man was much too eager to have his say at least once in his life. It was afterwards asserted in our town that in his characterization of Ivan Karamazov he was influenced by a rather personal feeling, since Ivan had on one or two occasions got the better of him in a public argument and, remembering this, the public prosecutor was anxious to take his revenge. But I don't know whether it was fair to draw such a conclusion. In any case, all this was only an introduction. The rest of his speech dealt more closely and directly with the case.

'But to come back to the eldest son of the head of a modern family,' went on the public prosecutor. 'There he is, gentlemen of the jury, in the dock before you. We also have his exploits, his life and actions before us: the hour has struck and all has been displayed before the public gaze. As against the "Europeanism" and "the fundamental beliefs of the people" of his brothers, he seems to represent primitive Russia – oh, not all of it, not all of it – God forbid, if it were all of it! And yet, here she is, our dear old Russia, here we have the very smell of our dear old mother, here is the very sound of her. Oh, we are primitive, we are a wonderful mixture of good and evil. We are lovers of enlightenment and Schiller and at the same time we create brawls in pubs and tear out the beards of poor, confirmed drunkards, our boon companions. Oh, we too can be good and beautiful, but only when we ourselves feel good and beautiful. On the other hand, we can be obsessed – yes, obsessed – by the most noble ideals, but only if they come of themselves, if they fall from heaven for us, and, above all, if we can obtain them gratis, gratis, without having to pay a penny for them. For we simply hate paying for anything, but are very fond of receiving, and that is true of everything. Oh, give us, give us every possible good thing in life – yes, every possible, we shall not be content with anything less – and, most of all, do not interfere with our passionate natures in any way whatever, and then we will show that we, too, can be good and beautiful. We are not greedy, good heavens, no! But let us have money, more, more money, as much money as possible, and you will see how generously, with what contempt for filthy lucre, we shall squander it in one night of unrestrained dissipation. And if you won't give us any money, we shall show you that we know how to get it, if we want it very much. But of that later. Let us examine the events as they unfold themselves step by step. To begin with, we have before us a poor abandoned child running about "in the back-yard without boots", in the words of our worthy and esteemed fellow-citizen, alas, of foreign extraction! I repeat again, I shall not yield the defence of the prisoner to anyone! I am his prosecutor, but I am also his defender. Yes, gentlemen of the jury, we, too, have human feelings and we, too, are able to weigh the influence on character of the first impressions of home and childhood. But the boy grows up, he is a young man, an army officer. For his riotous acts and a challenge to a duel he is exiled to one of the remote frontier towns of our vast country. There he serves in his regiment, there he sows his wild oats, and, to be sure, a great ship asks deep waters. He must have money, money before everything. And so after long arguments he agrees with his father to settle his remaining claim on his mother's estate for six thousand, and the money is sent to him. Now, please note, gentlemen of the jury, he signed a document and a letter exists in which he practically renounces his claim to the rest and agrees to settle his dispute with his father over his inheritance on the receipt of the six thousand. It is at this time that his meeting takes place with the young girl of high character and good education. Oh, I wouldn't dream of repeating the details, you have just heard them: questions of honour and self-sacrifice are involved here, and I am silent. The character of a young man, frivolous and dissipated, who had bowed his head before true nobility and a higher ideal, appeared for a brief moment in a very sympathetic light before us. But immediately afterwards the reverse of the medal was shown to us quite unexpectedly in this very court. Again, I will not venture to conjecture and will refrain from an analysis of why this happened. But, I suppose, there were reasons why it did happen. With tears of long-suppressed indignation the same young girl told us that it was he, he in the first place, who despised her for her incautious and, perhaps, unrestrained impulse which, however, was lofty and generous for all that. It was he, the girl's fiancé, who was the first to look at her with that sardonic smile which she could not bear from him of all people. Knowing that he had already deceived her (he had deceived her in the conviction that now she had to put up with everything from him, even with treachery), knowing this, she deliberately offered him three thousand roubles and let him understand clearly, all too clearly, that she was offering him the money to deceive her: "Well, will you take it or not? Are you really as cynical as that?" her searching and accusing eyes said to him. He looked at her, saw clearly what was in her mind (he admitted himself here before you that he understood it all) and appropriated the three thousand without any more ado and squandered them in two days with his new lady-love. What are we then to believe? The first story – the impulse of high-minded generosity, which made the accused man sacrifice every penny he possessed in the world as an act of reverence to virtue, or the reverse of the medal, which is so revolting? It usually happens in life that when faced with two extremes, one has to look for truth somewhere in the middle; in the present case this is not so. The probability is that in the first instance he was genuinely noble and in the second as genuinely base. Why? Because we possess broad, unrestrained natures, Karamazov natures – that is just what I'm leading up to – capable of accommodating all sorts of extremes and contemplating at one and the same time the two abysses – the abyss above us, the abyss of the highest ideals, and the abyss below us, the abyss of the lowest and most malodorous degradation. Remember the brilliant remark made by Mr Rakitin, the young observer, who had made a close and profound study of the Karamazov family: "The feeling of the lowest degradation is as necessary to these unbridled and irrepressible natures as the feeling of the highest magnanimity." And that is true: they, in particular, continually and unremittingly need this unnatural combination. Two abysses, gentlemen of the jury, two abysses at one and the same moment – without them we are unhappy and dissatisfied, without them our life is incomplete. We are broad and unrestrained, gentlemen of the jury, as broad and far-flung as mother Russia. We can accommodate everything and put up with everything! By the way, gentlemen of the jury, we have just mentioned the three thousand roubles and I will take the liberty of running a little ahead. Can you really believe that a man like that, having received such a sum and in such a way, at the cost of so much shame and so much disgrace, can you really believe that he could have been capable on that very day of setting aside half that sum, sewing it into a little bag and of being strong-minded enough to carry it about round his neck for a whole month in spite of all the temptations and his great need of it? Neither during his drunken orgies at the pubs, nor when he had to fly from the town to get from goodness only knows whom the money he needed so badly to carry off his lady-love and prevent her from being tempted by his rival, his own father, did he muster enough courage to touch that little bag. Why, just because he was so anxious not to expose his lady-love to the temptations of the old man of whom he was so jealous, he should have undone his little bag and have stayed at home to keep constant watch over her, in expectation of the moment when she would say to him, "I'm yours", so as to escape with her as far as possible from the fatal situation in which they found themselves. But no, gentlemen of the jury. He did not touch the talisman, and for what reason? The principal reason, as I've just said, was that when she would say: "I'm yours, take me away anywhere you please," he had to have the money with which to take her. But that first reason, according to the prisoner himself, paled beside the second. "While I carry that money about on me," he declared, "I'm a blackguard but not a thief, for I can always go to my affronted fiancée and, laying down before her half of the sum I have fraudulently appropriated, I can always say to her, 'You see, I've squandered half of your money and shown that I'm a weak and immoral man and, if you like, a blackguard [I'm using the prisoner's own expression], but, though a blackguard, I'm not a thief, for if I'd been a thief, I should have appropriated the second half as I did the first.'" A marvellous explanation! This man, weak but of a most violent temper, who could not bring himself to resist the temptation of accepting the three thousand roubles at the price of such disgrace, this same man suddenly becomes conscious of such stoical firmness in himself that he carries about fifteen hundred roubles round his neck without daring to touch it! Is that at all consistent with the character we have analysed? No, gentlemen of the jury, it is not. Let me try to tell you how the real Dmitry Karamazov would have behaved in a case like that, if he really had made up his mind to sew his money into a little bag. At the first temptation – well, just to entertain his new lady-love with whom he had already squandered half the money, he would have unstitched his little bag and have taken from it, well, let us say, just a hundred roubles the first time, for why, indeed, must he return half the sum, that is, fifteen hundred roubles? Would not fourteen hundred be sufficient? For what difference would it make? He could still have said: "I'm a blackguard but not a thief, for I've brought back fourteen hundred, while a thief would have taken everything and brought back nothing." Then, after a little time, he would have unstitched the bag again and taken out another hundred, and then a third, and a fourth, and before the end of the month he would have taken out the last hundred but one, for even if he had returned only one hundred, he could still claim that he was a blackguard but not a thief. He had squandered two thousand nine hundred roubles, but returned the last hundred, and a thief would not have returned even that. Then, having squandered the last hundred but one, he would have looked at the last one and said to himself: "Why, it's not really worth while taking back one hundred, let's spend that also!" That's how the real Dmitry Karamazov, as we know him, would have behaved! As for the story about the little bag, anything more inconsistent with actual fact cannot be imagined. You can assume anything you like, but not that. But we shall return to that later.'

After a detailed resumé of what had been disclosed in the course of the trial about the financial disputes between father and son and their attitude towards one another, and after emphasizing again and again that, according to all the well-known facts, there was not the slightest possibility of deciding who cheated whom in the division of the property of Mitya's mother, the public prosecutor passed on to an examination of the medical evidence in connexion with Mitya's fixed idea about the three thousand roubles.

7

A Historical Survey

'THE medical experts have tried to prove that the prisoner is not in his right mind and that he is a maniac. I maintain that he is in his right mind, but that this, in fact, has perhaps turned out to be much worse for him: if he had not been in his right mind, he would perhaps have acted much more intelligently. As for his being a maniac, I would agree with that, but only in one point, the point emphasized by the medical experts, namely, in his idea about the three thousand which he claims his father still owed him. Nevertheless, it is my contention that one might find a more plausible reason to explain the prisoner's recurring fits of frenzy in connexion with the three thousand than his tendency to insanity. For my part, I'm in complete agreement with the view expressed by the young doctor who found that the prisoner was in full possession of his mental faculties, but was merely irritated and embittered. What it comes to is this: the reason for the prisoner's constant and frenzied bitterness was not the three thousand, not the sum itself; there was a special reason that aroused his anger. That reason was jealousy!'

Here the public prosecutor drew a detailed picture of the prisoner's fatal passion for Grushenka. He began from the moment when the prisoner had gone to see 'the young person' in order 'to give her a thrashing', to use his own words, explained the public prosecutor. But instead of thrashing her, he remained at her feet – that was the beginning of that love affair. At the same time the old man, the prisoner's father, took a fancy to the same person – an amazing and fatal coincidence, for both hearts were suddenly kindled with passion at one and the same time, though both had known and met her before – and both hearts were kindled with the most violent, most Karamazov-like passion. 'Here,' the public prosecutor went on, we have her own admission: "I was laughing at both of them," she said. Yes, she suddenly felt like laughing at both of them; before, she had not felt like it, but now the idea suddenly came into her head and – it ended by both of them lying conquered at her feet. The old man, who worshipped money as one worships God, at once set aside three thousand roubles, which he promised to give her only for going to his house, but was soon brought to a point where he would be happy to lay his whole fortune and his name at her feet, if only she agreed to become his lawful wife. We have cast-iron evidence for this. As for the prisoner, his tragic position is evident, it is before us. But such was the young person's "game". The "siren" gave the unhappy man no hope, for hope, real hope was given him only at the very last moment when, kneeling before his tormentress, he stretched out to her hands that were already stained with the blood of his father and his rival: it was in that position that he was arrested. "Send me to penal servitude in Siberia with him; I've brought him to this, I'm more to blame than anybody," this woman kept exclaiming at the moment of his arrest and at that moment with genuine remorse. The talented young man who has undertaken to write about this case, the same Mr Rakitin to whom I have already referred, summed up the character of this heroine in a few succinct and characteristic sentences: "Early disillusionment, early betrayal and fall, the treachery of her lover who had seduced and jilted her, then poverty, the curses of a respectable family and, finally, the protection of a rich old man, whom she still regards as her benefactor. Her young heart, in which there was perhaps much that was good, was filled with resentment at a time when she was still very young. All this led to the formation of a calculating character, a character given to hoarding money. She became bitter and was filled with a grudge against society." After such a characterization one can understand that she might laugh at both of them simply for the sake of amusement, malicious amusement. And so during this month of hopeless love, moral degradation, betrayal of his fiancée, appropriation of money entrusted to his honour, the prisoner was driven almost to frenzy, almost to madness by continual jealousy – and of whom? Of his own father! And the worst of it was that the crazy old man was enticing and tempting the object of his passion by means of that very three thousand which his son considered as belonging to him, as part of his inheritance from his mother, which he was accusing his father of stealing from him. Yes, I quite agree, it was hard to bear! Mania might well have been the result of a situation like this. It was not the money that mattered, but the fact that his happiness was being ruined by this money with such revolting cynicism!'

Next the public prosecutor went on to explain how the idea of parricide gradually arose in the prisoner's mind and traced its development step by step.

'At first we only shout about it in pubs – we shout about it all that month. Oh, we are fond of company and of airing our views in public, even our most fiendish and dangerous views. We are fond of sharing our views with people and, for some unknown reason, we demand at once that they should show us their fullest sympathy, that they should enter into all our worries and troubles, that they should agree with us about everything and should not put obstacles in the way of our passionate desires. Or else we shall fly into a temper and wreck the whole pub. [There followed the anecdote about Snegiryov.] Those who saw and heard the prisoner during that month felt at last that it was not just a matter of shouts and threats against his father, but that a man in such a frenzy might well turn the threats into action. [Here the public prosecutor described the meeting of the family at the monastery, the conversations with Alyosha, and the shocking scene in his father's house when the prisoner burst into it after dinner.] It is not my intention to assert,' the public prosecutor went on, 'that before that disgraceful scene the prisoner deliberately and with malice aforethought planned to murder his father. Nevertheless the idea had occurred to him several times and he had carefully considered it. We have facts to prove it as well as witnesses and his own admission. I must confess, gentlemen of the jury,' added the public prosecutor, 'that up to this very day I have been in two minds whether or not to attribute to the prisoner full and conscious premeditation of the murder that might have solved his problems. I was firmly convinced that he had many times contemplated in his mind the fatal moment before him, but merely contemplated it, merely pictured it to himself as a possibility, but had no definite idea as to when he might commit the murder or in what circumstances. But I was in two minds about it only till today, till that fatal document, presented to the court just now by Miss Verkhovtsev. You yourselves, gentlemen of the jury, heard her exclamation, "That is the plan, the programme of the murder!" That is how she described the unhappy "drunken" letter of the unhappy prisoner. And, indeed, the letter bears the stamp of premeditation and a programme. It was written two days before the crime, and so we now know for a fact that two days before carrying out his dreadful plan the prisoner swore that, if he could not get the money next day, he would murder his father in order to take the money "in the envelope with the red ribbon, if only Ivan goes away". Do you hear? "If only Ivan goes away!" Here, therefore, everything had been thought out and everything taken into account. And, to be sure, he carried everything out just as he had written it. There can be no doubt about the premeditation of the murder which was to be committed for the sake of robbing his father of the money: that is clearly stated, that is written and signed. The prisoner does not deny his signature. It will be said: it was written by a man who was drunk. But that does not belittle its importance; in fact, it increases it: he wrote when drunk what he had planned when sober. If he had not planned it when sober, he would not have written it when drunk. It may be said perhaps: then why did he shout in the pubs that he was going to kill his father? A man who *deliberately* plans such a thing is silent and keeps it to himself. That is true, but he shouted about it at a time when he had made no carefully worked out plan, when he had only a desire, when the idea of it was just beginning to mature in his mind. Afterwards he shouted about it less. On the evening he wrote that letter, after getting drunk at the inn "Metropolis", he was quite unusually silent, he did not play billiards, he sat in a corner, talked to no one, and only turned a local shop-assistant out of his seat, but he did that almost unconsciously, out of habit, because he could not enter a pub without picking a quarrel with someone. It is true that, having come to a final decision it must have occurred to the prisoner that he had been shouting too much about his plan all over the town and that that might lead to his arrest and conviction after he had carried out his plan. But he could do nothing about it. The thing was done and he could not take his words back, and, after all, something had always turned up whenever he had been in a tight spot before and the same was bound to happen again. We relied on our lucky stars, gentlemen of the jury! I must admit, though, that he did a lot to avoid taking the fatal step, that he did as much as he could to keep clear of bloodshed. "Tomorrow I'll try and raise three thousand from someone or other," as he writes in his peculiar language, "and if I don't get it, there will be bloodshed." And, again, he wrote it when drunk and, again, he carried it out as he had written it when sober!'

Here the public prosecutor proceeded to give a detailed description of Mitya's efforts to get the money in order to avoid committing the crime. He described his adventures at Samsonov's, his journey to Lyagavy – all in accordance with documentary evidence. 'Exhausted, made a fool of, hungry, after selling his watch to raise the fares for the journey (though he had fifteen hundred roubles on him – but had he, oh, had he?), tortured by jealousy of the young woman he loved whom he had left in the town, suspecting that in his absence she might go to his father, he returned at last to the town. Thank God, she had not gone to him! It was he, in fact, who accompanied her to her protector Samsonov. (Strange to say, he is not jealous of Samsonov and that is a highly characteristic psychological peculiarity in this affair!) Then he rushed back to his observation post in the "back-garden" and there – there he learnt that Smerdyakov had had an epileptic fit and that the other servant was ill – the coast was clear and he knew "the signals" – what a temptation! Nevertheless, he still resisted it. He went to see Mrs Khokhlakov, a lady highly esteemed by us all, who is temporarily in residence here. This lady, who had long felt deeply sorry for him, offered him the most sensible advice: to give up his riotous life, his disgraceful love affair, his hanging about pubs, the futile waste of his youthful energies and set off to Siberia to the gold-mines: "There you will find an outlet for your tempestuous energies and your romantic character, your thirst for adventure." '

After describing the result of that conversation and the moment when the prisoner suddenly received the news that Grushenka had not stayed at Samsonov's, the sudden frenzy of the unhappy, nerve-racked, jealous man at the thought that she had deceived him and was now with his father, the public prosecutor concluded by drawing attention to the momentous importance of chance.

'Had the maid had time to tell him that his lady-love was at Mokroye with her "first" and "rightful" lover, nothing would have happened. But she lost her head with terror, she swore and protested her ignorance, and if the prisoner did not kill her on the spot, it was because he rushed headlong in pursuit of the woman who had betrayed him. But note: beside himself with rage as he was, he did not forget to snatch the brass pestle. Why the pestle? Why not some other weapon? But if we contemplate committing a murder and making all the arrangements for it for a whole month, we snatch up the first thing that catches our eyes that could serve as a weapon. And that some article of that kind might serve as a weapon – that we had been picturing to ourselves for a whole month, too. That is why he had instantly and without hesitation recognized it as a weapon! And that was why it was not by any means unconsciously, not by any means involuntarily that he snatched up the fatal pestle.

And a short time afterwards he was in his father's garden – the coast was clear, there were no witnesses, the dead of night, darkness and jealousy. The suspicion that she was there in the house with him, with his rival, in his arms and, perhaps, laughing at him at that moment – took his breath away. And it was not mere suspicion, either: the time for suspicion had passed, the deception was plain, obvious: she was there, in that room, which was lighted up, she was there with him, behind the screen – and the unhappy man stole up to the window, peeped cautiously in, restrained himself like a good boy and withdrew discreetly, flying from trouble lest something untoward and immoral should happen – and that's what they want us to believe, us, who know the prisoner's character, who understand the state of mind he was in as shown by well-authenticated facts, and, moreover, that he had knowledge of the signals by which he could at once get into the house!'

Here, apropos of the signals, the public prosecutor for the moment interrupted his account of the crime to concentrate on the Smerdyakov episode with the intention of dealing exhaustively with the suspicion that Smerdyakov had committed the murder and dismissing it once and for all. He did this very circumstantially, and everyone realized that in spite of the contempt with which he discussed this theory, he considered it of the utmost importance.

8

A Treatise on Smerdyakov

'To begin with, how did the possibility of this suspicion arise?' the public prosecutor began with this question. 'The first to cry out that Smerdyakov had committed the murder was the prisoner himself at the moment of his arrest, and yet from that moment to this he has not brought forward a single fact to confirm the charge, and not only a fact but not even a suggestion of a fact that is consistent with ordinary common sense. Next, this charge is confirmed by three persons only: the two brothers of the accused and Miss Svetlov. But the elder brother of the accused expressed his suspicions only today, when he was ill and in an indisputably violent fit of madness.

Before, for the whole of the last two months, we know for a fact that he fully shared the conviction of his brother's guilt and did not even attempt to raise an objection against it. But we shall go into this thoroughly later. Next the younger brother of the accused has told us himself that he has not the slightest fact to support his theory of Smerdyakov's guilt, and has reached this conclusion only from the prisoner's own words and "from the expression on his face" – yes, that terrific piece of evidence has been brought forward twice today by his brother. Miss Svetlov expressed herself in an even more astounding manner: "What the prisoner tells you, you must believe. He is not the sort of man to tell a lie." This is all the actual proof of Smerdyakov's guilt produced by these three persons, who have all a personal interest in the prisoner's fate. And yet the imputation of Smerdyakov's guilt has been spread abroad and has been and is being maintained – incredible and inconceivable as it is!'

Here the public prosecutor thought it necessary to give a brief sketch of the character of the late Smerdyakov, 'who put an end to his life in a violent fit of madness'. He characterized him as a feeble-minded person with the rudiments of education, confused by philosophic ideas beyond his intelligence and frightened by certain modern ideas about one's duties and obligations which he had learnt thoroughly and practically from the reckless life of his master, who was probably also his father, and theoretically from various strange conversations with his master's second son, Ivan, who readily indulged in this diversion, probably out of boredom or out of a desire for amusement, having nothing better to do. 'He told me himself about his mental condition during the last days of his stay at his master's house,' the public prosecutor explained, 'but others, too, have borne witness to it: the prisoner himself, his brother, and even the servant Grigory, that is to say all who should have known him well. Besides, depressed by his epileptic fits, Smerdyakov was "chicken-hearted". "He fell at my feet and kissed them," the prisoner himself declared in his evidence at a time when he did not yet realize the damaging nature of such a statement. "He is a chicken suffering from epilepsy", he described him in his characteristic language. And it was he the prisoner chose for his confidant (as he had stated himself), and frightened him so much that at last he consented to act as his spy and informer. In this capacity of a domestic spy he betrayed his master and told the prisoner of the existence of the envelope with the money and of the signals with the help of which one could get into the house – and, indeed, how could he help telling him? "He'd have killed me, sir, I knew he would have killed me," he declared at the inquiry, trembling with fear even before us, in spite of the fact that the tormentor who had scared him out of his wits was himself under arrest at the time and could not come and chastise him. "He suspected me every minute, sir. Seeing as how I was in fear and trembling for my life, I hastened to tell him every secret to appease his anger, so that he might see for himself that I was treating him fairly and let me off alive." Those are his very words. I wrote them down and I remember them. "The moment he started shouting at me I'd just go down on my knees before him." Being by nature a very honest young fellow and having in this way gained the confidence of his master, who had rewarded him for his honesty when he had returned some money he had lost, the unhappy Smerdyakov, I suppose, must have suffered terribly from remorse at having betrayed his master, to whom he was greatly attached as his benefactor. People who suffer severely from epilepsy, so the greatest psychiatrists tell us, are always predisposed to continual and, needless to say, morbid self-condemnation. They worry over their feeling of "guilt", being convinced of having wronged someone in some way; they are tormented by remorse, often entirely without foundation; they exaggerate and even invent all sorts of faults and crimes against themselves. And such an individual actually becomes guilty of a crime from terror and intimidation. He had, besides, a strong feeling that something untoward was likely to happen out of the situation that was developing before his eyes. When Karamazov's second son Ivan was leaving for Moscow before the very catastrophe, Smerdyakov begged him to stay; but, being a coward, he had not the courage to tell him plainly and categorically what he feared. He merely confined himself to hints, but his hints were not understood. It must be noted that he regarded Ivan as a kind of protector, as a kind of guarantee that so long as he was at home nothing untoward would happen. Remember the expression in Dmitry Karamazov's "drunken" letter: "I shall kill the old man, if only Ivan goes away." So that Ivan's presence seemed to everyone a sort of guarantee of peace and quiet in the house. But Ivan went away, and barely an hour after the young master's departure Smerdyakov fell down the cellar steps in an epileptic fit. But that is perfectly intelligible. I must mention here that, oppressed by fears and, in a way, by despair, Smerdyakov had felt, especially during those last few days, that he would probably have an epileptic fit, which had happened to him before at moments of shock and moral tension. It is, of course, impossible to foretell the day and hour of such attacks, but every epileptic can feel beforehand that he is liable to have such an attack. That is the opinion of the medical profession. And so, as soon as Ivan had driven out of the yard, Smerdyakov, abandoned and unprotected, as it were, went to the cellar for something, descended the steps, thinking: "Will I have a fit or not, and what if it comes upon me now?" And just that mood of his, that fear of an attack, those questions he had been asking himself, caused the spasm in his throat that always precedes an epileptic fit, and down he fell, unconscious, to the bottom of the cellar steps. And in this perfectly natural occurrence people contrive to see something suspicious, a sort of indication, a kind of hint that he was *deliberately* simulating illness! But if it were done deliberately, the question arises: whatever for? What was his motive? What was his aim? Quite apart from the medical aspect: science, people say, is often wrong, science makes mistakes, the doctors could not distinguish between truth and pretence – all right, suppose it is so, but answer me the question: why should he have been shamming? Did he do it so that, having planned the murder, he should attract the attention of everyone in the house to himself by having the fit before? You see, gentlemen of the jury, on the night of the crime there were five people in Fyodor Karamazov's house: Karamazov himself – but he did not kill himself, that's clear; secondly, his valet Grigory, but he was almost killed himself; thirdly, the maid, Grigory's wife, Marfa, but to imagine her murdering her master would be simply shameful. There remain, therefore, only two suspects: the prisoner and Smerdyakov. But as the prisoner maintains that he did not do it, then Smerdyakov must have done it. There is no other alternative, for no one else can be found, there are no more suspects. So that's how this "crafty" and quite extraordinary accusation arose against the unhappy idiot who committed suicide yesterday! Yes, indeed. It arose simply because no other suspect could be found! Had there been a shadow of suspicion against anyone else, against some sixth person, I'm sure even the prisoner would have been ashamed to pick out Smerdyakov, but would have picked out that sixth person, for to accuse Smerdyakov of the murder is the height of absurdity.

'Gentlemen of the jury, let's put aside psychology, let's put aside medicine, let's even put aside logic, and let us turn to the facts, to the facts alone, and let us see what the facts tell us. Suppose Smerdyakov committed the murder, but how did he do it? Alone or together with the prisoner? Let's consider the first alternative, that is to say, that Smerdyakov did it alone. Naturally, if he did it, he must have done it for some reason, for some advantage to himself. But not having the faintest motive for the murder that the prisoner had, namely hatred, jealousy, and so on, Smerdyakov, no doubt, could only have done it for the sake of money, in order to appropriate the three thousand he had seen his master put in the envelope. And yet, having planned the murder, he tells another person, a person, moreover, who had a close personal interest in the matter, namely the prisoner, all the facts about the money and the signals: where the envelope lay, what was written on it, what it was tied round with, and, above all, above all, tells him about those "signals" by means of which he could gain an entry into the house. Did he do it just to betray himself? Or to find someone who might want to go into the house and get the envelope himself? Oh, I shall be told, but he told it all from fear. Did he? Do you really think that a man who did not hesitate for a moment to plan such an intrepid, brutal murder and then carry it out, would tell facts which only he in the whole world knew and which, if only he kept silent about them, no one in the whole world would ever have guessed? No, gentlemen of the jury, however cowardly a man might be, if he had planned such a crime, he would never have told it to anyone, at least not about the envelope and the signals, for that would have meant giving himself away beforehand. He would have invented something deliberately. He would have told some lie, if he simply had to say something, but he would have been silent about that! On the contrary, I repeat, if he had been silent about the money, no one in the world would ever have accused him, at any rate, of murder for the sake of robbery, for no one except him had seen the money or knew of its existence in the house. Even if he had been charged with murder, it would most certainly have been thought that he had committed it for some other motive. But as no one had ever suspected any such motives in him before, but, on the contrary, as everyone saw that his master was fond of him and honoured him with his confidence, he would, of course, have been the last to be suspected; for the man who shouted that he had such motives, who had not concealed them, who had told everyone about them, in a word, the son of the murdered man, Dmitry Karamazov, would have been suspected. Smerdyakov would have killed and robbed, but the son would have been charged with the murder and that, surely, would have been to Smerdyakov's advantage, wouldn't it? Well, and so Smerdyakov, having planned the murder, told the son, Dmitry Karamazov, beforehand about the money, the envelope and the signals – there's logic for you!

'The day of the murder planned by Smerdyakov comes, and what does he do? He falls down the cellar steps in a *simulated* epileptic fit. What for? Why, of course, to make sure, first of all, that the servant Grigory, who had been planning to take his cure, might put it off and remain on guard, seeing that there is no one to look after the house. Secondly, of course, that his master, seeing that there was no one to keep guard over the house and terribly afraid of his son's arrival, which he did not conceal, might redouble his suspiciousness and his vigilance. And, finally and above all, of course, that he, Smerdyakov, disabled by the fit, should be transferred from the kitchen, where he always slept apart from the rest and where he could come and go as he pleased, to the other end of the cottage, to Grigory's room, behind the partition, three paces from their own bed, as it invariably happened when he had an epileptic fit, in accordance with the arrangement made by his master and the kind-hearted Marfa. There, lying behind the partition, he would most likely, to keep up the appearance of being ill, of course, have begun moaning, that is, keeping them awake all night (as he actually did, according to the evidence of Grigory and his wife), and all this, all this to make it more convenient for him to get up and murder his master!

'But, I shall be told, perhaps he simulated illness so that he should not be suspected and that he told the prisoner about the money and the signals for the express purpose of tempting him to come and commit the murder and when he had murdered him and had gone away, taking the money with him, and perhaps also making a noise and waking the witnesses, he, Smerdyakov, would get up and go – to do what? Why, he would go to kill his master a second time and carry off the money that had already been carried off. Gentlemen of the jury, you are laughing? I'm ashamed to advance such suggestions myself, and yet, you know, that is exactly what the prisoner alleges: "After me," he declares, "after I had left the house, had knocked down Grigory and raised the alarm, he got up, went in, killed his master and stole the money." I need hardly ask how Smerdyakov could have possibly planned and foreseen it all beforehand, that is to say, that the exasperated and enraged son would come solely for the purpose of peeping in respectfully at the window and, though he knew the signals, beat a hasty retreat so as to leave Smerdyakov all the booty! Gentlemen of the jury, I ask you in all seriousness: at what exact time could Smerdyakov have committed the murder? Tell me the time, for unless you can do so you cannot accuse him.

'But, perhaps, the epileptic fit was real. The sick man suddenly came to, heard a shout, went out – well, and what then? He looked round and said to himself: "Let's go and murder the master"? But how was he to know what had happened? Had he not been lying unconscious till that moment? But, gentlemen of the jury, there is a limit even to flights of fancy.

' "You may be right," some astute people will say, "but what if both of them were in the plot, what if both of them murdered him and shared the money, what then?"

'Yes, indeed, such a theory is certainly worth considering and particularly as there seems to be weighty evidence in favour of it: one commits the murder and takes all the trouble, while the other, his accomplice, lies in bed, feigning an epileptic fit, I suppose for the sole purpose of arousing everyone's suspicion and alarming his master as well as Grigory. It would be interesting to know the motives that could have induced the two accomplices to hit upon such an insane plan. But, perhaps, so far as Smerdyakov is concerned, he was not expected to play an active, but, as it were, a passive part in the murder, one that a sick man like him could not help agreeing to. Perhaps, intimidated by the prisoner, Smerdyakov only agreed not to offer any opposition to the murder and, foreseeing that he might be accused as an accessory before the fact, for letting his master be killed and for not raising an alarm or offering any resistance, he had obtained permission from Dmitry Karamazov to stay in bed as though in an epileptic fit, "and you may murder him just as you like; it has nothing to do with me". But if that was what happened, then, again, that epileptic fit was bound to produce a commotion in the house, and, realizing this, Dmitry Karamazov could never have agreed to such a plan. But I concede you that point: suppose he did agree. In that case it would still follow that Dmitry Karamazov was the murderer, the actual murderer who had instigated the crime, while Smerdyakov was only a passive accomplice, and not even an accomplice, but one who merely connived at the crime out of fear and against his will. That would certainly have come out at the trial, but what do we see? As soon as the prisoner is arrested, he at once throws the blame on Smerdyakov, and accuses him *alone* of having committed the murder. He does not accuse him of being his accomplice, he accuses him *alone*: "He did it alone," he declares. "He murdered and robbed. It was his doing." But what sort of accomplices are they if they start at once accusing one another? Why, such a thing never happens! And think of the risk Karamazov was running: for it was he who committed the murder, while Smerdyakov merely connived at it and lay behind the partition, and now he throws all the blame on the invalid. Would not Smerdyakov have resented it and, to save his own skin, told the whole truth? "We both planned it, but I didn't do it! I only let him do it out of fear!" For he, Smerdyakov, might have realized that the court would at once differentiate between the degree of his guilt and he might, therefore, have reckoned that if he were punished, it would be much less severely than the principal murderer, who tried to throw the blame on him. But then he would have willy-nilly made a confession. That, however, he had not done. Smerdyakov did not so much as hint at any complicity in spite of the fact that the murderer went on accusing him and maintaining throughout that he alone was the murderer. And what's more, it was Smerdyakov who at the inquiry revealed that he himself had told the prisoner of the money and the signals and that but for him the prisoner would not have known anything about them. If he had really been an accomplice and guilty, would he have so readily told about it at the inquiry,

I mean, that he had told the prisoner everything? On the contrary, he would have tried to deny it and he would most certainly have distorted the facts and minimized them. But he neither distorted nor minimized them. Only an innocent man who was not afraid of being charged with complicity could have acted like that. And now, in a fit of morbid melancholy, arising out of his epilepsy and all this catastrophe, he hanged himself yesterday. He left a note, written in his peculiar language. "I put an end to my life of my own free will and no one should be blamed for it." What would it have cost him to add: "I am the murderer, not Karamazov"? But he did not add that: did his conscience prompt him to do one thing, but not the other?

'And what happens next? A short while ago, money, three thousand roubles, was brought into the court. "It is the same money," we were told, "that lay in the envelope, the one among the other exhibits on the table. I received them," said the witness, "from Smerdyakov yesterday." But, gentlemen of the jury, you remember the painful scene yourselves. I will not go into it at length, but I shall venture to make one or two comments, choosing the most trivial ones just because they are trivial and, therefore, might not occur to anyone and may be forgotten. To begin with, Smerdyakov gave back the money yesterday and hanged himself from remorse. (For if he had not felt any remorse, he wouldn't have given back the money.) And, no doubt, it was only yesterday evening that he confessed to having committed the crime to Ivan Karamazov, as Ivan Karamazov himself declared, or why else should he have kept silent till now? And so he confessed. But why, I repeat again, did he not tell us the whole truth in the letter he left behind, knowing that the innocent prisoner had to face his trial for murder the next day? The money alone is no proof. A week ago, for instance, the fact came to the knowledge of myself and of two other persons in this court that Ivan Karamazov had sent two five per cent bills of five thousand roubles each, that is, ten thousand in all, to the provincial capital to be exchanged. I merely mention it to show that anyone may have had ready cash in his possession on a certain date and that, having brought the three thousand, the witness could not possibly prove that it was the same money. I mean the money out of a certain box or envelope. Finally, having received such an important communication from the real murderer yesterday, Ivan Karamazov stayed calmly at home. Why shouldn't he have reported it at once? Why did he put it off till the morning? I think I have a right to conjecture why: for over a week he had been in bad health; he had admitted to a doctor and to his intimate friends that he was suffering from hallucinations and meeting people in the street who had long been dead; he had been on the verge of insanity and, in fact, had succumbed to it today; learning, therefore, suddenly of Smerdyakov's death, he at once said to himself: "The man is dead, I can say he did it and save my brother. I have money. I'll take a bundle of notes and say that Smerdyakov gave them to me before his death." You will say, this is dishonest, that it is dishonest to tell lies about the dead even to save a brother. So it is, but what if he lied unconsciously? What, if finally driven out of his mind by the news of the servant's sudden death, he imagined that it really was so? You saw the recent scene. You saw the state of mind of that man. He was standing up and talking, but where was his mind? After the poor madman's evidence there followed a document, a letter sent by the accused to Miss Verkhovtsev, written two days before the crime, with a detailed programme of the murder. Well, why, then, are we looking for the programme and those responsible for drawing it up? Everything happened exactly according to this programme and it was the man who drew it up who committed the crime. Yes, gentlemen of the jury, "it happened as written down"! And he did not run respectfully and timidly away from his father's window, at a time, too, when he was firmly convinced that his lady-love was with him. No, gentlemen of the jury, that is both absurd and improbable. He went in and – finished the business. Most probably he committed the murder in a rage, burning with resentment, as soon as he looked at his hated rival. But having killed him, which he must have done with one blow of the brass pestle, and having convinced himself after a careful search that she was not there, he did not, however, forget to put his hand under the pillow and take out the envelope with the money, the torn-up envelope which lies on the table with the other exhibits. I mention this fact because I want you to note one circumstance which, in my opinion, is highly characteristic. If he had been an experienced murderer, a murderer, that is, whose sole object was robbery, would he have left the envelope on the floor as it was found beside the dead body? Had it been Smerdyakov, for instance, committing a murder for the sake of robbery – why, he would have simply carried off the envelope with the money, without bothering to open it over his victim's dead body; for he knew for a fact that the money was in the envelope – it had been put in and sealed up in his presence – and if he had taken the envelope away with him, no one would have known whether there had been a robbery or not. I ask you, gentlemen of the jury, would Smerdyakov have acted like that? Would he have left the envelope on the floor? No, this is the sort of thing a man in a frenzy would do, a murderer who could not think clearly, a murderer who was not a thief and had never stolen anything before that day and who even then snatched the money from under the mattress not as a thief stealing it, but as a man taking away his own property from a thief who had stolen it, for that was Dmitry Karamazov's idea about the three thousand, an idea which had become almost an obsession with him. And so, having snatched the envelope, which he had never seen before, he tore it open to make sure that the money was there, then he ran away with the money in his pocket, even forgetting to reflect that he had left a most damning piece of evidence against himself in that torn envelope on the floor. And all because it was Karamazov and not Smerdyakov. He didn't think, he didn't reflect, and how should he? He ran away, he heard the loud cry of the servant who was overtaking him, the servant caught hold of him, stopped him, and collapsed on the ground struck down by the brass pestle. The prisoner jumped down to look at him – out of pity! Just imagine it, gentlemen of the jury: he assures us that he jumped down out of pity, out of compassion, to see whether he could do anything for him. But was that the moment to show such compassion? No, he jumped down to make sure whether the only witness of his crime was alive or dead. Any other feeling, any other motive would be unnatural! Please note that he took trouble over Grigory, he wiped his head with his handkerchief and, satisfying himself that he was dead, ran back to the house of his lady-love, dazed and covered with blood – how was it he never thought that he was all covered with blood and that he would be exposed at once? But the prisoner himself assures us that he did not even notice that he was covered with blood. That we may well believe, that is very possible, that always happens with criminals at such moments. Diabolical circumspection on one point and not enough discernment on another.

But at that moment his only thought was – where was *she*? He had to find out at once where she was, and so he ran to her lodgings and learnt an unexpected and most shattering piece of news: she had gone off to Mokroye to her "first" and "rightful" lover!'

9

Psychology Galore. The Galloping Troika. The End of the Public Prosecutor's Speech

HAVING reached this point in his speech, the public prosecutor, who had evidently chosen a strictly historical method of exposition, which is very popular with all nervous orators who deliberately seek to keep their own eloquence within strict limits in order to control their impatient enthusiasm, the public prosecutor expatiated particularly about Grushenka's 'former' and 'rightful' lover and gave expression to a number of highly diverting thoughts on this subject.

'Karamazov, who had been insanely jealous of everyone, all of a sudden, as it were, collapsed and vanished before the "former" and the "rightful" one. And that is all the more remarkable since before he had paid hardly any attention to this new danger to himself, which had suddenly materialized in the person of his unexpected rival. But he had imagined it to be still far off, and a Karamazov always lives in the present. Possibly he regarded him even as a fiction. But having realized at once with that sore heart of his that perhaps the woman had been concealing this newly arrived rival and had been deceiving him because for her he was everything and not just a fantasy or fiction, but the only hope of her life – having realized it at once, he resigned himself. Well then, gentlemen of the jury, I cannot pass over in silence the unexpected trait in the prisoner's character, which, it would seem, he was quite incapable of possessing. And suddenly he became aware of the inexorable necessity of truth, of a respect for woman, of a recognition of the rights of her heart, and when? – why, at the very moment when he had stained his hands with his father's blood for her sake! It was also true that the spilt blood was at that moment already crying out for revenge, for he who had ruined his soul and his whole future on earth could not help asking himself at that moment what he was and what he could be *now* to her, to the woman who was dearer to him than his own soul? What was he in comparison with her "former" and "rightful" lover, who had repented and come back to her, the woman he had once ruined, with new love, with honourable offers, with the solemn promise of a reformed and, this time, happy life? And he, unhappy man, what could he give her *now*, what could he offer her? Karamazov understood it all, he understood that his crime had closed all the doors to him and that he was only a criminal under sentence of death and not a man who had still his life to live! It was this thought that crushed and destroyed him utterly. And so he at once fixed upon one frantic plan which, to a man of Karamazov's character, could not but appear as the only possible way out of his terrible situation. That solution was suicide. He ran for the pistols he had pledged with the civil servant Perkhotin, and on the way pulled out of his pocket all the money for the sake of which he had stained his hands with his father's blood. Oh, now he needed money more than anything: if Karamazov is going to die, if Karamazov is going to shoot himself, this is going to be remembered! It is not for nothing that he is a poet, it is not for nothing that he has wasted all his life, burnt the candle at both ends. "To her, to her! And there I will give a most sumptuous feast, a feast that never was before, a feast that will be remembered and talked about for years! Amid the wild cries and the frenzied songs and dances of the gipsies I shall raise the glass and toast the woman I adore and shall congratulate her upon her new-found happiness and, then, there, at her feet, I shall blow my brains out and put an end to my life! She will remember Mitya Karamazov one day! She will see how Mitya loved her! She will be sorry for Mitya!" There is a great deal of picturesque, romantic frenzy in all this, a great deal of wild, unrestrained, Karamazov-like sentimentality, and, well, something else, gentlemen of the jury, something that clamours in his soul, throbs incessantly in his mind and poisons his heart unto death – that *something* is his conscience, gentlemen of the jury, it is its judgement, its terrible pangs! But the pistol will settle everything, the pistol is the only solution and there is no other, but *there* – I don't know whether Karamazov thought at that moment "*what will happen there*" or whether Karamazov could, like Hamlet, think of what would happen there. No, gentlemen of the jury, they have their Hamlets, but so far we still have our Karamazovs!'

Here the public prosecutor described in great detail Mitya's preparations, the scene at Perkhotin's, at the shop, and with the drivers. He cited a great number of words, sayings, and gestures, all confirmed by witnesses, and the picture he drew had a telling effect on his listeners. It was the agglomeration of facts that made itself felt in the end. The guilt of this frantically harassed man, who no longer cared what happened to him, was demonstrated clearly and beyond doubt. 'There was no need for him to take care,' said the public prosecutor. 'Once or twice he almost confessed, hinted at it and only just stopped himself in time from making a clean breast of it. [Here followed the evidence given by the witnesses.] He even shouted to the coachman on the way to Mokroye: "Do you know you are driving a murderer?" But it was, all the same, impossible for him to make a clean breast of it: he had first to get to the village of Mokroye and there finish his poem. But what was awaiting the unhappy man? The fact is that from the very first moment in Mokroye he saw and at last fully realized that his "rightful" rival was not so "rightful" after all and that his congratulations upon their new-found happiness and his toast to their health were not wanted and would not be accepted. But you already know the facts, gentlemen of the jury, from the evidence in court. Karamazov's triumph over his rival was incontestable and here – oh, here quite a new phase began in his soul, perhaps the most terrible phase his soul had gone through or will go through! It may most certainly be said, gentlemen of the jury,' exclaimed the public prosecutor, 'that outraged nature and the criminal heart take their own revenge more completely than earthly justice! And what is more, justice and punishment on earth even alleviate the punishment of nature, are even necessary for a criminal's soul at such moments to be saved from despair; for I cannot even conceive Karamazov's horror and his moral agonies when he learnt that she loved him, that she had rejected her "former" and "rightful" lover for his sake, that she was calling him, him, "Mitya", to follow her to a new life, that she was promising him happiness – and all this when? When everything was at an end with him and when nothing was possible! Incidentally, let me mention in passing a very important fact to explain the real position of the prisoner at that moment: this woman, this love of his, had up to the very last moment, up to the moment of his arrest been a being utterly beyond his grasp, passionately desired by him but unattainable. But why, why didn't he shoot himself then? Why did he give up his decision and even forget where his pistol was? Why, what held him back was just this passionate desire for love and the hope of satisfying it there and then. In the intoxication of the revelry he clung to his beloved, who was also enjoying the revels with him and whom he thought more lovely and more fascinating than ever. He did not leave her side for a moment, he feasted his eyes on her and forgot everything in the world in her presence. This passionate desire for her could, for a moment, not only banish his fear of arrest but also his pricks of conscience. For a moment, only for a moment! I can picture the prisoner's state of mind at that moment as being undoubtedly in complete subjection to three influences which crushed it utterly: firstly, the influence of drink, of the intoxication and noise of the party, the beat of the dance and the shrill noise of the songs, and of her, of her, flushed with wine, singing and dancing, drunk and laughing up at him! Secondly, the cheering thought at the back of his mind that the fatal end was still far off, at least not very near, and that they were not likely to come and take him till next day, till next morning. So he still had a few hours, and that was a lot, an awful lot! One can think of so many things in a few hours. I fancy he must have felt something a criminal feels when he's being taken to his execution, to the scaffold: there is still a long, long street to pass through, and at a walking pace, too, past thousands of people; then there will be a turning into another street and only at the end of that street the dreadful square! I can't help feeling that at the beginning of the journey the condemned man, sitting in his cart, must feel that he has infinite life still before him. But the houses recede, the cart moves on and on – oh, that's nothing, it's still a long way to the turning into the other street, and he goes on looking cheerfully to right and left at all those thousands of unconcernedly curious people whose eyes are riveted on him, and he still fancies that he is just such a man as they. But here is the turning into the other street – oh, that's nothing, nothing! There is still a whole street ahead of him. And however many houses he may have passed, he will still think: "There are lots of houses still left." And so to the very end, to the square itself. That is, I imagine, how it was with Karamazov then. "They haven't yet had time there," he must have thought. "I may still think of some-thing. Oh, there's still time to make up some plan of defence, to get the right answers, but now, now – now she is so lovely!" Deep inside him he feels confused and frightened, but he still manages to put aside half of his money and hide it somewhere – I cannot otherwise explain the disappearance of a whole half of the three thousand he had just taken from under his father's pillow. He had been in Mokroye before, he had made merry there for two days. The local inn, a big old house, was known to him with all its sheds and verandas. It is my view that he had hidden part of the money in that house not long before his arrest, in some chink, some crevice, under the floor-boards, in some corner, or under the roof. Why? How do you mean – why? Well, the catastrophe may happen at any moment! Of course, he hadn't formed any plan of how to meet it, he hadn't the time, his head was throbbing and all the time he was being drawn to *her*, and the money, why, the money was indispensable in any situation. A man with money was everywhere a man. Perhaps such foresight at such a moment may strike you as unnatural. But, then, he assured us himself that a month before, at an anxious and critical moment, he had set aside half his money and sewed it up in a little bag, and though that, of course, is not true, which we shall prove presently, the idea was familiar to Karamazov and he had been turning it over in his mind. What's more, when he later on assured the examining magistrate that he had put aside fifteen hundred in a little bag (which never existed), he must have invented the little bag at that very moment just because two hours earlier he had set aside half the money and hidden it somewhere in Mokroye, just in case it might come in useful, till morning, so as not to have it on him, on a sudden inspiration. Two abysses, gentlemen of the jury, remember that Karamazov can con-template two abysses, and both at one and the same time! We have searched that house, but we haven't found it. Perhaps the money is still there; on the other hand, it may have disappeared next day and is now in the possession of the prisoner. In any case he was arrested beside her, kneeling before her. She was lying on the bed, he was stretching out his hands to her and he was so oblivious of everything at that moment that he did not even hear the approach of the men who had come to arrest him. He had no time to prepare any line of defence in his mind. Both he and his reason were taken by surprise.

'And now he is facing his judges, the arbiters of his fate. There are moments, gentlemen of the jury, when, confronted with the execution of our duties, we feel almost terrified to face a man, terrified for the man! Those are moments when we are faced with the animal fear of the criminal who is already aware that all is lost but is still fighting, still intends to fight you. Those are moments when every instinct of self-preservation rises up in him all at once and, in an attempt to save himself, he looks at you with penetrating eyes, questioning and suffering eyes, catches your expressions and studies you, your face, your thoughts, waits to see on which side you will strike him, and, in a flash, frames thousands of plans in his distracted mind, but is still afraid to speak, afraid of giving himself away! These humiliating moments of a man's soul, this purgatory of the spirit, this animal craving for self-preservation are terrible, and sometimes arouse a shudder of horror and compassion for the criminal even in an examining magistrate! And all this we witnessed then. At first he was stunned and in his terror a few highly compromising words escaped him: "Blood! It serves me right!" But he quickly controlled himself. What to say, how to answer our questions – he had not got it all ready yet. All he had ready was an unsubstantiated denial: "I'm not guilty of my father's death!" That was so far the first fence behind which he took cover, and after that he might perhaps fix something up, throw up some barricade. Anticipating our questions, he hastened to explain his first compromising exclamations by declaring that he only considered himself guilty of the death of the servant Grigory. "I'm guilty of shedding his blood, but who has killed my father, gentlemen, who has killed him? Who can have killed him, *if not I?*" Do you hear that? He asked us, us, who had come to ask him that very question! Do you hear that anticipatory phrase: "if not I!", that animal cunning, that naïvety and that typically Karamazov impatience? "I did not kill him and you must not think I did: I meant to kill him, gentlemen, I meant to," he was in a hurry to admit (he was in a hurry, oh, he was in a terrible hurry), "but still I'm not guilty, it was not I who killed him!" He concedes to us that he meant to kill him: you can see for yourselves, he seems to say, how truthful I am; well, then, you should believe all the sooner that I didn't kill him. Oh, in such cases a criminal sometimes becomes incredibly thoughtless and gullible. And at that point he was asked the most simple question: "Are you sure it wasn't

Smerdyakov who killed him?" And it happened just as we expected: he became terribly angry that we should have anticipated him and caught him by surprise before he had time to prepare himself, to choose and catch hold of the moment when it would be most natural to bring in Smerdyakov. As was to be expected from a man of his character, he at once rushed to the other extreme and began assuring us that Smerdyakov could not have killed him, that he was incapable of committing a murder. But don't you believe him, that was only his cunning: he had no intention of giving up Smerdyakov; on the contrary, he was going to put him forward, for he had no one else to put forward, but he would do that at a more favourable moment because for the time being a spoke had been put in his wheel. He would bring him forward next day or even a few days later, waiting for the right moment when he could say to us: "You see, I was more convinced than you were that Smerdyakov didn't do it. You remember that yourselves, don't you? But now I am convinced: it was he who killed him and no one but he!" But for the time being he kept denying it gloomily and irritably. Impatience and anger prompted him, however, to resort to the most clumsy and improbable explanation of how he looked through his father's window and how he respectfully withdrew from it. Moreover, he did not as yet know of the facts of Grigory's recovery and how incriminating his evidence was. We proceeded to examine and search him. This angered but also encouraged him: we did not find the whole of the three thousand on him, only half of it. And, of course, it was at that moment of angry silence and denial that the idea of the little bag first occurred to him. I daresay he realized himself the utter improbability of his fictitious story and took great pains to make it sound as credible as possible, to tell it in such a way as to make a whole plausible story of it. In a case like that the chief task of the investigating authorities is first of all to prevent the criminal from getting ready his defence, to catch him unawares so as to make him reveal his most secret thoughts in all their incriminating simplicity, improbability, and contradictoriness. To make the criminal talk, however, is only possible by an apparently casual communication of some new fact, of some circumstance which is of the utmost importance, but of which he had hitherto no idea and which he could not possibly have foreseen. Such a fact we had in readiness, oh, for a long time: it was the evidence of the servant

Grigory about the open door through which the prisoner had run out. He had completely forgotten about that door and it had never even occurred to him that Grigory could have seen it. The effect of it was tremendous. He jumped to his feet and shouted: "It was Smerdyakov who killed him, Smerdyakov!" and so betrayed his secret, his basic idea in its most improbable form, for Smerdyakov could have committed the murder only *after* he had knocked down Grigory and run away. When we told him that Grigory had seen the open door *before* he was knocked down and that he had heard Smerdyakov moaning behind the partition as he left his bedroom, Karamazov was truly crushed. My colleague, our esteemed and able Mr Nelyudin, told me afterwards that he felt deeply sorry for him at that moment. And it was just then that, to improve matters, the prisoner hastened to tell us about that famous little bag: all right, then, now listen to this tale! Gentlemen of the jury, I have explained to you already why I consider this fictitious story about the money sewn up in a little bag a month before the murder not only absurd, but also the most improbable fabrication that could have been conceived in the present circumstances. Even if one were to wager what he could have said and brought forward that would be utterly improbable, one could hardly think of anything worse than that. The chief thing about a story of this kind is that the triumphant story-teller can be utterly confounded and reduced to silence by the details of the case, the same kind of details in which real life is so rich and which are always overlooked by these unfortunate and unwilling story-tellers and, indeed, never occur to them, just as if they were the most insignificant and useless trifles. Oh, at that moment they have other things to think of, their minds are bent on inventing something grandiose, and here they are offered such a trifle! But that's how they are caught! The prisoner is asked: "Well, and where did you get the material for your little bag? Who made it for you?" "I made it myself." "And where did you get the linen?" The prisoner begins to be offended, he considers it almost insulting to be questioned about such a trifle and, believe me, he is sincere, he's quite sincere about it! But they are all like that. "I tore it off my shirt." "Capital! So we shall find that shirt of yours among your linen tomorrow with a piece torn off." And just think, gentlemen of the jury, if we really had found that shirt (and how could we have failed to find it in his trunk or his chest of drawers if such a shirt had really existed?), then that would have been a fact, a palpable fact that would have proved his statements to be true! But he is incapable of grasping that. "I don't remember, perhaps it wasn't off my shirt. I sewed it up in my landlady's cap." "What sort of cap?" "I got it from her. It was lying about. An old cotton rag." "And do you remember it clearly?" "No, I don't remember it clearly." And he is angry, angry, and yet can you imagine him not remembering it? At the most terrible moments of a man's life, when he is being led to his execution, for instance, it is just such trifles that are remembered. He will forget everything but some green roof that has flashed past him on the way or a jackdaw on a cross – that he will remember. Why, he was hiding from the people in the house when sewing up his little bag, so he must have remembered how humiliating it was to be afraid that someone might come in and find him needle in hand, how at the first knock on his door he jumped up and ran behind the partition (there is such a partition in his room). . . . But, gentlemen of the jury, why do I tell you all this, all these details, all these trifles?' the public prosecutor exclaimed suddenly. 'Why, just because the prisoner persists stubbornly in sticking to his absurd story up to this very moment! During all these two months, ever since that disastrous night, he has not explained anything, he has not added one real, explanatory fact to his former fantastic statements: all that is trivial, you must take his word for it! Oh, we are glad to do that, we are eager to do it, even if it's only his word. We are not jackals thirsting for human blood, are we? Give us, show us a single fact in the prisoner's favour and we shall rejoice, but it has to be a palpable fact, a real fact, and not a conclusion drawn from the expression on the prisoner's face by his own brother, or the statement that when he smote his breast he must have been pointing to the little bag, and in the darkness, too. We shall rejoice at a new fact, we shall be the first to withdraw our charge, we shall hasten to withdraw it. But now justice cries out for satisfaction and we persist. We do not withdraw anything.'

The public prosecutor passed to his peroration. He seemed to be in a fever. He demanded loudly that the blood of the father shed by his son 'with the base motive of robbery' should be avenged. He pointed out the tragic and incontrovertible mass of facts. 'And whatever you may hear from the celebrated and learned counsel for the defence [he could not refrain from adding] and however eloquent and moving his words may be when he tries to appeal to your emotions, remember that at this moment you are in the holy of holies of our administration of justice. Remember that you are the champions of our justice, the champions of our holy Russia, her principles, her family, everything that she holds sacred! Yes, here at this moment you represent Russia, and your verdict will resound not only in this court-room but all over Russia, and the whole of Russia will hear you as her champions and her judges, and she will be encouraged or disheartened by your verdict. Do not disappoint Russia and her expectations. Our fateful *troika* dashes headlong on and, perhaps, to destruction. And for many, many years now the people of Russia have been stretching forth their hands and calling for a halt to its furious and reckless gallop. And if, for the time being, other nations stand aside from the *troika* galloping at break-neck speed, it may not be from respect, as the poet would have liked us to believe, but simply from horror. Remember that. From horror and perhaps also from disgust of her, and it is a good thing they stand aside, for one day perhaps they will no longer stand aside, but will stand like a wall before the on-rushing apparition and will themselves halt the frenzied gallop of our unbridled passions for the sake of their own safety, enlightenment, and civilization! We have already heard those alarmed voices from Europe. They begin to be heard already. Do not tempt them. Do not swell their chorus of ever-growing hatred by a verdict justifying the murder of a father by his son!'

In short, though the public prosecutor let himself be carried away, he wound up his speech on a note full of pathos, and, indeed, the effect produced by him was quite extraordinary. Having finished his speech, he hurried out and, I repeat, almost fainted in the adjoining room. The audience did not applaud, but the serious-minded people were content. Only the ladies were not so well content, but they, too, were pleased with his eloquence, particularly as they were not at all apprehensive of the outcome of the trial and relied entirely on Fetyukovich. 'He will, at last, speak and, of course, carry all before him!' They all kept looking at Mitya; he sat in silence all through the public prosecutor's speech, his hands tightly clasped, his teeth clenched and his eyes fixed on the ground. Only from time to time did he raise his head and listen. Especially when the public prosecutor spoke of Grushenka. When the public prosecutor quoted Rakitin's opinion of her, a contemptuous and spiteful smile passed over his face and he muttered quite audibly: 'The Bernards!' When the public prosecutor described how he interrogated and tortured him at Mokroye, Mitya raised his head and listened with intense curiosity. At one point in the speech, he even seemed about to jump up and shout something, but he controlled himself and only shrugged contemptuously. There was a great deal of talk in our town afterwards about the public prosecutor's exploits in Mokroye during the interrogation of the prisoner and people were rather apt to make fun of him. 'The man could not resist from boasting of his great abilities,' they said. The court was adjourned, but only for a very short time, for a quarter of an hour, or twenty minutes at most. There was a great deal of talk and exclamation among the audience. I remember some of them:

'A weighty speech,' a gentleman in one group observed, frowning.

'Too much psychology for my liking,' said another voice.

'But it was all true, undeniably true!'

'Yes, he knows his job.'

'He summed it all up.'

'And he summed us up, too,' a third voice chimed in. 'At the beginning of his speech, remember, when he said that we were all like old Karamazov.'

'And at the end. Only then he talked a lot of nonsense.'

'Yes, he was rather obscure.'

'Got carried away a little.'

'You're unjust, sir, unjust!'

'Well, no, it was clever all the same. He's had to wait a long time, poor fellow, and now he's had his say, ha, ha!'

'What will the counsel for the defence say, I wonder?'

In another group:

'He made a mistake in provoking the Petersburg fellow: "Trying to appeal to your emotions", remember?'

'Yes, that wasn't very clever of him.'

'He was too much in a hurry.'

'A nervous man, sir.'

'We laugh, but what must the prisoner be feeling?'

'Yes, sir, poor old Mitya! What must he be feeling?'

'I wonder what the counsel for the defence will say?'

In a third group:

'Who's that lady with the lorgnette? The fat one. Sitting at the end of the row.'

'That's the wife of a general. A divorcée. I know her.'

'Oh, so that's why she's got the lorgnette.'

'Looks common to me.'

'Not at all, a very tasty bit.'

'There's a little blonde two places from her. She's much prettier.'

'Caught him cleverly at Mokroye, didn't they?'

'I suppose so. Boasted of it again. He's been telling it all over the town hundreds of times.'

'Couldn't resist it now. Vanity.'

'A man with a grievance, ha, ha!'

'And quick to take offence. Lots of rhetoric, too. Long sentences.'

'Trying to frighten us, too. Did you notice? Always trying to put the fear of God into us. Remember about the "*troika*"? "There they have Hamlets, but so far we've still only Karamazovs." That was clever!'

'Trying to put himself right with the liberals. Afraid!'

'And he's afraid of the lawyer, too.'

'Yes, what will Mr Fetyukovich say?'

'Let him say what he likes, he won't get round our peasants.'

'Think so?'

In a fourth group:

'He put it nicely about the *troika*. I mean, when he was referring to the other nations.'

'And, you know, he was quite right when he said that the nations won't wait.'

'You mean?'

'Why, in the English House of Commons a member got up last week and, referring to the nihilists, asked the Minister whether it was not high time to intervene in the affairs of a barbarous nation and try to educate us. The public prosecutor had him in mind. I know he had. He was talking about it last week.'

'The silly fools will never do it.'

'What silly fools? And why not?'

'We'll seal up Kronstadt and not let them have any wheat. Where will they get it?'

'And what about America? They'll get it from America now.'

'Don't talk rot!'

But the bell rang and they all rushed back to their places. Fetyukovich mounted the rostrum.

10

The Speech for the Defence. A Double-edged Argument

A HUSH fell over the court when the first words of the celebrated orator rang out. The eyes of everyone in the audience were fastened on him. He began very straightforwardly, simply and with conviction, but without the slightest trace of arrogance. Not the slightest attempt at eloquence, pathos, or phrases full of emotion. He was a man speaking in an intimate circle of sympathetic friends. He had a beautiful voice, resonant and attractive, and there seemed to be something genuine and sincere in the very sound of it. But everyone realized at once that the orator could suddenly rise to true pathos and – 'thrill their hearts with incredible force.' He spoke perhaps less correctly than the public prosecutor, but without long sentences and, indeed, with greater precision. One thing, though, the ladies did not like: he kept bending forward, especially at the beginning of his speech, not so much bowing as rushing forward impetuously towards his listeners, bending almost double with his long spine, as though there were a hinge in the middle of it that enabled him to bend almost at right angles. At the beginning of his speech he seemed to jump from one subject to another, as though without a system, dealing with the facts at random, but in the end it all fell into place. His speech could be divided into two halves: the first was devoted to the criticism and refutation of the charge, sometimes malicious and sarcastic. But in the second half he seemed suddenly to have changed his tone and even his manner and all at once rose to pathos. The audience seemed to be waiting for it and quivered with delight. He went straight to the point and began by explaining that though his legal practice was in Petersburg, it was not for the first time that he was visiting provincial towns to defend prisoners but only those of whose innocence he was either convinced or was pretty well certain.

'The same thing happened to me in the present case,' he declared. 'Even from the first newspaper reports I was struck by something which greatly predisposed me in favour of the accused. In short, what interested me most was a certain juridical aspect which often occurs in legal practice but never, I believe, in so full and characteristic a form as in the present case. This aspect I ought to have formulated at the end of my speech, but I will do so at the very beginning, for it is my weakness, I'm afraid, to start with the main point without concealing my effects and economizing my impressions. That may be unwise on my part, but at least it is sincere. This idea of mine, this formula, is as follows: the overwhelming mass of facts is against the accused and yet there is not a single fact that will stand up to criticism, if considered singly, by itself! Following the case in the newspapers, and from the information I could gather elsewhere, I was more and more confirmed in my impression, and then I suddenly received an invitation from the relatives of the accused to take up his defence. I at once hurried here, and here I became completely convinced. So it was to destroy this terrible accumulation of facts and to show that each fact, taken separately, was unproven and fantastic that I undertook the defence of this case.'

So the counsel for the defence began and then he suddenly announced:

'Gentlemen of the jury, I'm a stranger here. I have no preconceived ideas. The prisoner, a man of violent and unbridled temper, has not insulted me as he has, perhaps, hundreds in this town, which explains why so many people are prejudiced against him beforehand. Of course, I, too, admit that the moral sentiment of local society is justly excited: the prisoner is violent and reckless. But he was received in society here. Indeed, he was even received and treated with every consideration in the family of my very learned friend, the public prosecutor. [*Nota bene:* At these words there were two or three laughs in the audience, quickly suppressed, but noticed by everyone. We all knew that the public prosecutor received Mitya against his will and only because he had for some reason been found interesting by his wife – a highly respectable and virtuous lady, but fanciful and self-willed, who liked on certain occasions to oppose her husband, especially in trifles. Mitya, however, visited them very rarely.] Nevertheless,' the counsel for the defence went on, 'I venture to suggest that even a man of so independent a mind and so just a character as my learned friend could form a rather wrong idea about my unhappy client Oh, that is so natural: the poor man certainly deserved to be treated with prejudice. Injured moral and, still more, aesthetic feeling is sometimes relentless. Of course, in the highly talented speech for the prosecution we have all heard a stern analysis of the prisoner's character and conduct and a sternly critical attitude towards the case as a whole; moreover, to explain the substance of the case to us, my learned friend has displayed such a profound psychological insight that, to achieve it, he could not possibly have been swayed by any deliberately malicious prejudice against the prisoner. But, then, there are things which are even worse and more fatal in such cases than the most malicious and deliberately hostile attitude. That is, I believe, true if, for instance, we are possessed by what, for lack of a better definition, I might call an artistic urge, the need for artistic expression, the desire to create, as it were, a work of fiction, especially if the good Lord has endowed us with a wealth of psychological gifts. While still in Petersburg, while still preparing for my journey to your town, I was warned, and, indeed, I was aware of it without any warning, that in my opponent here I should find a great and most subtle psychologist who had won quite a special kind of renown by this quality of his in our still young legal world. But, gentlemen of the jury, profound as psychology is, it is still a double-edged weapon. [Laughter in court.] Oh, you will, I'm sure, forgive me my trivial comparison; I'm afraid I'm not very good at making eloquent speeches. But let me illustrate my meaning by the first example that occurs to me from the public prosecutor's speech. The prisoner, running away in the garden at night, climbed over the fence and knocked down the servant, who had caught hold of his leg, with a brass pestle. Then he at once jumped back into the garden and busied himself for five minutes over the prostrate body, trying to find out whether he had killed him or not. Now, the public prosecutor refuses to believe that the prisoner was telling the truth when he stated that he had jumped down to Grigory out of compassion. "No," he says, "such sentimentality is impossible at such a moment. It is unnatural. He jumped down to find out whether the only witness of his crime was dead or alive and thereby proved that he had committed the crime, for he could not possibly have jumped down into the garden for any other motive, consideration, or feeling." There you have psychology. But let us take the same psychology and apply it to the case the other way round, and the result we shall get will be no less probable. The murderer jumped down as a precaution to find out whether the witness of his crime was alive or not, and yet, as the public prosecutor himself asserts, he had left in the study of his murdered father a most damning piece of evidence against himself in the shape of a torn envelope with an inscription that there had been three thousand roubles in it. "If he had carried away this envelope with him, no one in the world would have known that there existed such an envelope with the money in it and, hence, that the money had been stolen by the prisoner." Those are the public prosecutor's own words. Well, then, you see, one moment the prisoner shows a complete lack of caution, he loses his head, gets frightened and runs away leaving a clue on the floor, but two minutes later, he attacks and kills another man and at once displays a most inhuman and calculating feeling of precaution. But let us assume that this is what actually happened: after all, the whole point of psychological analysis is to prove that under such circumstances I'm as bloodthirsty and sharp-sighted as a Caucasian eagle one moment and the next as blind and timid as an insignificant mole. But if I'm so bloodthirsty and cruelly calculating that, having killed a man, I run back to him for the sole purpose of making sure whether the witness of my crime is alive or not, then why should I busy myself for five minutes over my new victim and, perhaps, run the risk of acquiring new witnesses? Why dip my handkerchief in blood, while wiping it off his head, so that it may serve as evidence against me later? If he were really so calculating and cold-hearted as that, would it not have been wiser to hit his victim again and again on the head with the same pestle so as to make quite sure he was dead, and having thus got a witness out of the way, relieve his heart of all anxiety? And, finally, he jumped down to make sure whether the witness against him was alive or not and left another witness on the path, namely that brass pestle he had taken from the two women which they could always identify afterwards as theirs and bear witness that he had taken it from them. And it isn't as if he forgot it on the path, dropped it through carelessness and in a moment of confusion: no, he flung it away, for it was found within fifteen paces of the place where Grigory lay. It may be asked why did he do so? Well, he did so because he was distressed at having killed a man, an old servant, and that was why he flung the pestle away in vexation and with a curse as a weapon with which a murder had been committed, for why should he otherwise have thrown it away with such force? But if he were capable of feeling pain and pity at having killed a man, it was, surely, because he had not killed his father. If he had, he wouldn't have jumped down to another victim from pity; he would have had no thought for pity but for self-preservation, and that, of course, is so. On the contrary, I repeat, he would have battered his skull and not busied himself with him for five minutes. There was room for pity and good feeling in his heart just because his conscience had been clear till then. So here you have a different kind of psychology. I have purposely resorted to the aid of psychology, gentlemen of the jury, to show clearly that you can prove anything by it. It all depends on who makes use of it. Psychology induces even the most serious people to indulge in romancing and that quite involuntarily. I'm speaking, gentlemen of the jury, of unnecessary psychology, of a certain abuse of it.'

Here again there was approving laughter in court, and all at the expense of the public prosecutor. I will not report the speech of the counsel for the defence in full, but will only quote some passages from it, some of the most important points.

I I

There Was No Money. There Was No Robbery

THERE was one point in the speech of the counsel for the defence that surprised everyone, namely his flat denial of the existence of the fatal three thousand roubles and, consequently, of the possibility of their having been stolen.

'Gentlemen of the jury,' the counsel for the defence began, 'every new and unprejudiced man must be struck by one characteristic peculiarity in this case, namely, the charge of robbery and, at the same time, the complete impossibility of proving what exactly has been stolen. It is alleged that money has been stolen, namely three thousand roubles, but no one seems to know whether they ever existed. Just consider: to begin with, how have we learnt that there were three

thousand roubles and who has seen them? The only person who saw
them and stated that they had been put in an envelope with an inscription was the servant Smerdyakov. It was he who had told the prisoner
and his brother Ivan about it before the tragedy. Miss Svetlov,
too, had been told about it. But not one of these three persons had
actually seen the money. Again it was only Smerdyakov who had seen
it, but here the question arises: if it is true that it did exist and that
Smerdyakov had seen it, then when did he see it for the last time?
What if his master had taken the money from under the mattress and
put it back in his cash-box without telling him? Observe that according to Smerdyakov's statement the money lay under the mattress; the
prisoner would have had to pull it out from under the mattress, and
yet the bed had not in any way been disturbed and that is carefully
recorded in the official statement of the investigating authorities. How
could the prisoner leave the bed completely undisturbed and, moreover, how could he fail to have soiled with his blood-stained hands
the fine and spotless linen with which the bed had that time been purposely made? But, I shall be asked, what about the envelope on the
floor? Well, it is worth saying a few words about that envelope. I
must say I was a little surprised just now: my learned friend, when
speaking of the envelope, himself – do you hear, gentlemen of the
jury – himself declared in his speech, referring to the absurdity of
supposing that Smerdyakov had killed his master: "Had it not been
for that envelope, had it not been left on the floor as a clue, had the
robber carried it away with him, no one in the world would have
known that an envelope had been there or that there had been money
in it, and that, consequently, the prisoner must have stolen the money."
So that, even by the admission of the counsel for the prosecution himself, only that torn scrap of paper with its inscription must be regarded
as proving the charge of robbery, for "otherwise no one would have
known of the robbery or that there was any money". But, surely, the
mere fact that that scrap of paper was lying on the floor is no proof
that there was any money in it and that that money had been stolen.
But, it may be objected, Smerdyakov had seen the money in the
envelope. But when, when was the last time he saw it, that's what
I should like to know. I talked to Smerdyakov and he told me that
he had seen it two days before the murder. But what, for instance,
prevents me from supposing that old Fyodor Karamazov, locked up

in his house and in the impatient and hysterical expectation of his beloved, suddenly took it into his head, having nothing else to do, to pull out the envelope and open it. "The envelope," he may have said to himself, "will not do the trick. She may not believe there is any money in it. But if I were to show her thirty rainbow-coloured hundred-rouble notes in one roll, it would, I'm sure, make a much greater impression on her, it would make her mouth water" – and so he tore open the envelope, took out the money, and threw the envelope on the floor, being fully entitled to do so as the owner and, of course, unafraid of leaving any clues. Don't you think, gentlemen of the jury, that there is nothing more likely than such a theory and such a fact? Why is it unlikely? But if anything of the sort could have happened, then the charge of robbery must fall to the ground, for if there was no money there could be no robbery. If the envelope on the floor is evidence that there had been money in it, then why may I not assert the opposite, namely that the envelope was on the floor because there was no money in it, the money having been taken out of it previously by its owner? "Yes, but where, in that case, is the money if Fyodor Karamazov took it out of the envelope and it was not found during the search of the house?" First of all, part of the money was found in the cash-box and, secondly, he could have taken it out that morning or even the night before, made some other arrangements concerning it, given it to someone, sent it away, or, finally, changed his mind, his plan of action, radically without thinking it necessary to inform Smerdyakov about it beforehand. And if there is only the barest possibility of such a supposition being true, how can the prisoner be so emphatically and positively accused of having committed the murder for the sake of robbery and, indeed, of having carried out the robbery? For in this way we are entering into the realm of fiction. For if it is maintained that a certain thing has been stolen, then the thing must be produced or, at any rate, it must be proved beyond a shadow of a doubt that it existed. And yet no one had even seen it. Not so long ago in Petersburg a lad of eighteen, a hawker, entered in broad daylight a money-changer's shop with an axe, and with extraordinary, typical boldness murdered the owner of the shop and carried off fifteen hundred roubles. About five hours later he was arrested and except for fifteen roubles, which he had already managed to spend, they found all the money on him. Moreover, the shop-assistant, on returning to the shop after the murder, informed the police not only of the stolen sum, but even of what it consisted of, that is to say, how many hundred-rouble, ten-rouble, and five-rouble notes, and how many gold coins and of what value there were in it, and those notes and coins were found on the murderer. In addition to all this, there was a full and frank confession by the murderer. That, gentlemen of the jury, is what I call evidence! There I know, I see and feel the money and I cannot say that it never existed. Is it the same in the present case? And yet it is a matter of life and death, of a man's fate. "This is all very well," it will be said, "but he was having a high old time that night, throwing his money about. Fifteen hundred roubles were found on him – where did he get them?" But, then, the very fact that only fifteen hundred were found on him and the other half of the sum could nowhere be found or discovered, this very fact proves that the money could not have been the same and that it had never been in any envelope. The most rigorous investigation of the prisoner's movements on the night of the crime carried out by the authorities at the preliminary inquiry showed beyond any doubt that after leaving the two maids he went straight to see the civil servant Perkhotin without going home or anywhere else, and that after that he was always in the company of people, so that he could not, consequently, have put aside half of the three thousand and hidden it somewhere in town. It was just this consideration that led the counsel for the prosecution to assume that he must have hidden it in some crevice at Mokroye. But why not in the dungeons of the Castle of Udolpho, gentlemen of the jury? Isn't this assumption too fantastic and too romantic for words? And please note that if that single assumption breaks down, the whole charge of robbery dissolves into thin air, for where else could the fifteen hundred have got to? By what miracle could they have disappeared, since it is proved that the prisoner went nowhere else? And with such romantic tales are we prepared to ruin a man's life? It will be said that for all that the prisoner was not able to explain where he got the fifteen hundred found on him and that, moreover, everyone knew that he had no money before that night. But who knew that? The prisoner has given a clear and circumstantial account of where he had got that money from, and if you like, gentlemen of the jury, if you like, nothing could ever have been more probable than that statement, quite apart from its being entirely in character. The counsel for the prosecution is pleased with his own romantic tale. A man of weak will, who had made up his mind to take the three thousand so offensively offered by his fiancée, could not, he claims, put aside half of it and sew it up in a little bag; on the contrary, if he had done so, he would have unstitched it every second day and kept dipping into it for a hundred at a time and so would have spent it all in one month. You will remember that all this was put to you in a tone that brooked no contradiction. Well, and what if the whole thing did not happen like that at all? What if you've made up the story and about quite a different person? That's the trouble, that you've invented quite a different person! I shall be told, perhaps, that there are witnesses that he squandered all the three thousand he had received from Miss Verkhovtsev in the village of Mokroye a month before the murder, and all in one night, so that he could not have put aside half of it. But who are these witnesses? The trustworthiness of the evidence of these witnesses has been shown up in this court already. Besides, a hunk of bread always seems larger in another man's hands. And, last but not least, no one of these witnesses counted that money, but merely judged it by sight. Did not the witness Maximov testify that the prisoner had twenty thousand in his hand? As you see, gentlemen of the jury, psychology is a double-edged weapon, so let me apply the other edge now and see what happens.

'A month before the murder the prisoner was entrusted by Miss Verkhovtsev with three thousand roubles to send off by post. But is it fair to say that they were entrusted to him in such an insulting and humiliating manner as was claimed here just now? In Miss Verkhovtsev's first statement on the subject it was different, quite different; in her second statement all we heard were cries of bitter resentment and revenge, cries of long-concealed hatred. But the very fact that the witness testified falsely the first time gives us the right to conclude that her second testimony, too, may have been false. The counsel for the prosecution does not want to, he dare not (those were his own words) touch upon that love affair. Very well, I won't touch upon it, either, but I will venture to observe that if a highly moral and pure person, as the highly esteemed Miss Verkhovtsev undoubtedly is, if such a person, I say, allows herself suddenly and all at once to go back on her first statement in court with the direct aim of ruining the prisoner, it is clear that her second statement has been made neither dispassionately nor coolly. Are we therefore to be deprived of the right to conclude that a woman who is out for revenge might have exaggerated much? Yes, indeed, she may have exaggerated the shame and disgrace of offering him the money. On the contrary, I suggest that it was offered in such a way that it could be accepted, especially by so thoughtless a man as the prisoner. The important point to remember is that he expected to receive shortly from his father the three thousand which, according to his calculation, were still owing to him. This may be thoughtless of him, but then it was just because he was so thoughtless that he was so firmly convinced that his father would give him the money and that he could, therefore, always post the money entrusted to him by Miss Verkhovtsev and repay the debt. But the counsel for the prosecution will not admit that he could have set aside half of the money on the day he received it and sewn it up in a little bag. That is not in his character, he claims, he could not have had such feelings. But didn't my learned friend himself shout about the prisoner's broad Karamazov nature and about the two abysses that a Karamazov could contemplate? Yes, Karamazov is just such a two-sided nature, a nature that could balance himself precariously between two abysses, one that when driven by the most uncontrollable craving for dissipation can pull itself up if something happened to strike it on the other side. And the other side is love, the new love that had blazed up like gunpowder, and for that love he needed money, oh, more than for giving the woman a good time. If she were to say to him, "I'm yours, I won't have your father," he would seize her at once and take her away – so he needed money to take her away. That was more important than giving her a good time. Could a Karamazov fail to understand that? Why, that was what he was so worried about! So what is there so improbable about his putting aside that money and hiding it in case he needed it? But time passed and Fyodor Karamazov did not give the prisoner the three thousand; on the contrary, the news reached the prisoner that his father was going to use the money to entice away the woman he, the prisoner, loved. "If my father doesn't give me the money," he thought, "I shall be a thief in Katerina's eyes." And so the idea occurred to him that he would go to Miss Verkhovtsev, lay before her the fifteen hundred roubles, which he still carried in the little bag round his neck, and say to her: "I'm a blackguard but not a thief." So here, therefore, we have a twofold reason for guarding the money as if it were the apple of his eye and for not unstitching the little bag and abstracting a hundred roubles at a time from it. Why should you deny the prisoner a sense of honour? Yes, he has a sense of honour, though maybe a mistaken one, and very often a false one, but it exists, he believes in it passionately, and he has proved it. But, unfortunately, the affair becomes more complicated, his torments of jealousy reach a climax and the same two questions take on a more and more agonizing shape in the prisoner's fevered brain: "If I return the money to Katerina, where shall I find the means to carry off Grushenka?" If he behaved like a madman, if he got drunk and created disturbances in the pubs during the whole of that month, it was perhaps because he felt sick at heart himself and was not able to bear it any longer. These two questions at last became so acute that they drove him to despair. He sent his younger brother to his father to beg him for the last time for the three thousand, but, without waiting for a reply, forced his way into the house, and ended by assaulting the old man in the presence of witnesses. After that there was no one he could get the money from, for the father he had assaulted would not give it him. The same evening he beat himself on the breast, on the *upper* part of his breast where the little bag was, and swore to his brother that he had the means of not being a blackguard, but that he would remain a blackguard for all that, for he could see that he would not use that means, that he would not have the strength of mind or character to do so. Why, why doesn't the prosecutor believe Alexey Karamazov's evidence, given so frankly and sincerely, so spontaneously and convincingly? Why, on the other hand, does he force me to believe in money hidden in some crevice, in the dungeons of the Castle of Udolpho? The same evening, after his talk with his brother, the prisoner wrote that fatal letter and that letter is the most damning evidence which seems to prove that the prisoner was guilty of robbery! "I shall beg from everyone, and if they refuse, I shall kill my father and shall take the envelope with the pink ribbon from under the mattress, if only Ivan goes away." A full programme of the murder, we are told, so it must have been he, mustn't it? "It all took place as he wrote it," the prosecution claims. But, in the first place, the letter was written when the prisoner was drunk and in a state of terrible irritation; secondly, he wrote of the envelope as he had been told by Smerdyakov, because he had not seen the envelope himself, and, thirdly, he certainly did write the letter, but how can it be proved that it took place as written? Did the prisoner get the envelope from under the mattress? Did he find the money? Did the money exist at all? And, moreover, was it the money that the prisoner ran off for? Just try to remember. He ran off in violent haste not to rob, but to find out where she was, where the woman was who had driven him to despair, so that he did not run off to carry out any programme, nor because of what he had written, that is to say, he did not run to carry out a premeditated robbery, but on a sudden impulse and in a jealous frenzy! Yes, I shall be told, but all the same he got there and, having murdered his father, took the money also. But did he murder him? The charge of robbery I repudiate with indignation: a man cannot be accused of robbery if it cannot be shown with accuracy what he has stolen – that is an axiom! But did he commit a murder, a murder without robbery? Has that been proved? Isn't that, too, pure fiction?'

12

And There Was No Murder, Either

'ALLOW me, gentlemen of the jury, to point out that a man's life is at stake and that one must exercise the utmost care. We have heard the prosecutor admit that up to the very last day, up to the day of the trial, he hesitated to accuse the prisoner of a premeditated murder, a murder committed with malice aforethought, that he hesitated till the very moment the fatal "drunken" letter was produced in court today. "It all took place as written!" But let me repeat once more: he ran to her, to find her, solely to find out where she was. That is an undeniable fact. If she had been at home, he would not have gone anywhere, but remained with her and would not have carried out what he promised in his letter. He ran off accidentally and on the spur of the moment and, perhaps, did not even remember his "drunken" letter at the time. "He snatched up the pestle," the counsel for the prosecution pointed out, and you will remember how we were treated to a whole psychological dissertation on that pestle, why he must have regarded the pestle as a weapon and snatched it up as such, and so on and so forth. Here a most ordinary idea occurs to me: what if the pestle had not lain where everyone could see it, not on the shelf from which the prisoner snatched it, but put away in a cupboard – then the prisoner would not have caught sight of it and he'd have run off without a weapon, empty-handed, and then, perhaps, he would not have killed anyone. How, then, am I to regard the pestle as a proof of premeditation, as proof that the prisoner had seized it as a weapon with which to murder his father? Yes, but he shouted in the pubs that he was going to kill his father, and two days earlier, on the evening when he wrote his drunken letter, he was quiet and only quarrelled with a shop-assistant "because, being a Karamazov, he could not help picking a quarrel". To which my answer is that if he was really contemplating such a murder, and according to a plan, too, according to his letter, he most certainly would not have quarrelled with the shop-assistant and, perhaps, would not have gone to the pub, for a man planning such a crime seeks quiet and self-effacement, seeks to disappear, so that he should not be seen or heard: "Forget my existence if you can," he seems to say, and he does so not from calculation, but from instinct. Gentlemen of the jury, psychology is a double-edged weapon, and we, too, know how to make use of it. As for all those shoutings in the pubs during the whole of that month, don't we often hear children or drunkards quarrelling with one another shout, "I'll kill you," but they don't kill, do they? And that fatal letter itself – isn't it just drunken irritability, too? Isn't it just the shout of a man leaving a pub: "I'll kill you, I'll kill the lot of you?" Why shouldn't it have been like that in this case? Why is that letter so fatal? Isn't it, on the contrary, just ridiculous? It is so because his father had been found murdered, because a witness saw the prisoner in the garden, armed and running away, and was himself knocked down by him, and so everything had happened as written, and therefore the letter, too, is not ridiculous but fatal. Thank God, we have come to the real point: "If he was in the garden, it means therefore that he killed him." On these two words: if he *was*, therefore it must *mean*, rests the whole case of the prosecution – "he was, therefore it means." But what if it does not *mean* that, even if he was there? Oh, I admit that the totality of facts, the series of coincidences, are, indeed, very impressive. But examine all these facts separately, without allowing yourselves to be impressed by their totality: why, for instance, does the prosecution refuse to acknowledge the truth of the prisoner's statement that he ran away from his father's window? Remember, too, the sarcasms which the counsel for the prosecution permitted himself about the respectfulness and the "pious" sentiments which suddenly came over the prisoner. But what if there really was something of the sort, that is to say, if not respectfulness, then at least a "piety" of sentiment. "I suppose my mother must have been praying for me at that moment," the prisoner stated at the inquiry, and so he ran away as soon as he had convinced himself that Miss Svetlov was not in his father's house. "But," the counsel for the prosecution objects, "he could not possibly convince himself by looking through the window." Why couldn't he? The window was opened at the signals given by the prisoner. Fyodor Karamazov might at that moment have uttered some word or some cry, and the prisoner might suddenly have become convinced that Miss Svetlov was not there. Why must we assume everything as we imagine or make up our minds to imagine? In real life thousands of things might happen that escape the attention of the most subtle novelist. "Yes, but Grigory saw the open door so that the prisoner must certainly have been in the house and, therefore, must have killed his father." Now, about that door, gentlemen of the jury. ... You see, we have only the evidence of one witness about the open door, a witness who was at the time in such a condition that ... But supposing the door was open, supposing the prisoner denied it, lied about it from an instinct of self-preservation, so understandable in his condition, supposing he did get into the house, was in the house – what about it? How does it follow that if he was there he must have killed his father? He might have burst in, rushed through the rooms, pushed his father aside and even hit him, but, having made certain that Miss Svetlov was not there, run away, rejoicing that she was not there and that he had not killed his father. That was, perhaps, why a moment later he jumped down from the fence to attend to Grigory, whom he had knocked down in his excitement. He did so because he was capable of a pure

feeling, a feeling of compassion and pity, because he had escaped
from the temptation of killing his father, because he felt that his
heart was pure and was glad that he had not killed his father. The
counsel for the prosecution described to us with terrible eloquence
the prisoner's state of mind at Mokroye when love came to him again,
calling him to a new life, and when he had no longer any right to
love because he had left the bloodstained corpse of his father behind
him, and beyond that corpse – retribution. And yet the counsel for
the prosecution did allow him love, which he explained in accordance
with his psychological method as "a state of drunkenness, a criminal
being taken to execution, a long time to wait", etc., etc. But let me
put the same question to my learned friend again: are you sure you
have not invented quite a different person? Is the prisoner so coarse and
soulless as to be able to think at that moment of love and of how to
prevaricate before the court, if his hands were really stained with his
father's blood? No, no, and no! As soon as he found out that she
loved him, called him to go away with her, promised him new
happiness, oh, then, I'm sure he must have felt the urge to commit
suicide doubled and trebled and he would most certainly have killed
himself if he had his father's murder on his conscience! Oh, no, he
wouldn't have forgotten where his pistols were! I know the prisoner:
the savage, callous heartlessness imputed to him by the prosecution
is inconsistent with his character. He would have killed himself, that
is certain; he did not kill himself because his "mother had been praying for him" and because he was innocent of his father's murder. He
was worried, he grieved that night in Mokroye only about old Grigory whom he had knocked down, and he was praying to God that
the old man would come to and get up, that his blow had not been
fatal, and that he would escape retribution for him. Why not accept
such an interpretation of events? What good proof have we that the
prisoner is lying? But, we shall again be told, what about his father's
dead body: he ran away, he did not commit murder – well, then,
who did murder the old man?

'I repeat, here you have the whole logic of the prosecution: who
murdered him, if not he? There's no one to put in his place. Gentlemen of the jury, is that so? Is there really, positively, no one who
could be put in his place? We have heard the public prosecutor count
on his fingers all the persons who were or who called that night at

that house. They were five persons. Three of them, I agree, could not possibly have been responsible: the murdered man himself, old Grigory, and his wife. There remain, therefore, the prisoner and Smerdyakov, and so the counsel for the prosecution exclaims dramatically that the prisoner pointed to Smerdyakov because he had no one else to point to and that if there had been a sixth person or even the ghost of a sixth person, the prisoner would at once have withdrawn his accusation against Smerdyakov, being ashamed of it, and would have pointed to the sixth person. But, gentlemen of the jury, why may not I assume the very opposite to be true? Two men are involved – the prisoner and Smerdyakov. Why can I not say that you accuse my client simply because you have no one else to accuse? And there is no one else because of your preconceived ideas – you have made up your minds that Smerdyakov could not possibly be guilty. Of course, it is true that only the prisoner himself, his two brothers, and Miss Svetlov have given evidence against Smerdyakov. But there are others, too, who did so: there is a rather vague feeling of discontent among the people of this town, a sort of suspicion, there is evidence of some vague rumours, there is a kind of expectation in the air. Finally, we have the evidence of certain very significant coincidences, though, I admit, rather inconclusive: in the first place, that epileptic fit on the day of the murder, a fit which the counsel for the prosecution has for some reason thought it necessary to defend and justify. Then we have Smerdyakov's sudden suicide on the eve of the trial. Then the no less sudden evidence in court today by the elder of the prisoner's brothers, who had hitherto believed in his guilt, but who has suddenly produced the three thousand roubles and who also proclaimed Smerdyakov to be the murderer! Oh, I'm entirely of the same opinion as the court and the prosecution that Ivan Karamazov is mentally sick and that his evidence may really be a desperate attempt, planned during his attack of insanity, to save his brother by putting the blame on the dead man. But, all the same, Smerdyakov's name was uttered, and again there seems to be something mysterious about it. Something, gentlemen of the jury, still remains to be said, something has been left unfinished. And perhaps it may still be said. But let's leave that for the moment. I shall come to it later. The court has decided to carry on with the hearing of the case, but for the time being I might say a few words about the characterization of the late Smerdyakov, sketched with such talent and subtlety by the counsel for the prosecution. But while admiring the talent of my learned friend, I cannot entirely agree with the main points of his sketch of Smerdyakov's character. I have visited Smerdyakov, I have seen him and spoken to him, and he made quite a different impression on me. It is true he was weak in health, but in character, in spirit – oh, no, he was not by any means the weak man the prosecution made him out to be. I certainly did not find a trace of timidity in him, that timidity which the counsel for the prosecution has so eloquently described. Neither was there any trace of simplicity in him; on the contrary, I found in him a terrible mistrustfulness concealed under a cloak of naïvety, and an intelligence that was capable of comprehending a great many things. Oh, my learned friend was too guileless in thinking him weak-minded. He made a very definite impression on me: I left him with the conviction that he was a spiteful man, excessively ambitious, vindictive, and violently envious. I collected some information: he hated his parentage, was ashamed of it, and gnashed his teeth every time he remembered that he was the son of "stinking Lizaveta". He treated Grigory and his wife, who had looked after him in his childhood, with disrespect. He cursed and jeered at Russia. He dreamed of going to France and becoming a Frenchman. He had talked a lot about it before and he often used to say that he had not the means to do so. I believe he loved no one but himself and that he had a strangely high opinion of himself. In his opinion, a cultured man was one who wore good clothes, clean shirt-fronts, and polished boots. Believing himself to be the illegitimate son of Fyodor Karamazov (and there are facts which confirm it), he might well have resented his position as compared with that of the legitimate sons of his master: they had everything and he had nothing, they had all the rights, they would get the inheritance, and he was only a cook. He disclosed to me the fact that he himself together with Fyodor Karamazov put the money in the envelope. The purpose of that sum of money – a sum that might well have made his career – was, of course, hateful to him. Besides, he saw three thousand roubles in bright rainbow-coloured notes (I asked him about it on purpose). Oh, never show an ambitious and envious man a large sum of money all at once, and it was the first time that he had seen such a large sum in the hands of one man.

The sight of the bundle of rainbow-coloured notes might well have made a morbid impression on his imagination, at first with no perceptible results. My learned friend outlined with extraordinary subtlety all the arguments for and against the theory of Smerdyakov's guilt and asked us in particular what motives he had in feigning an epileptic fit. But he need not have feigned it at all. The fit may well have happened quite naturally and the sick man may have recovered. Let us say that he could not have recovered completely, but he could have recovered consciousness sometime during the night, as happens with epileptics. The counsel for the prosecution asks at what moment could Smerdyakov have committed the murder. But it is very easy to point out that moment. He could have come to, got up from his deep sleep (for he was only asleep: after an attack of epilepsy the patient always falls into a deep sleep), just at the moment when old Grigory caught hold of the prisoner's leg and shouted at the top of his voice: "Parricide!" The shout must have been very loud in the stillness of the night and the dark, and it could have wakened Smerdyakov, whose sleep at that time might not have been very deep: he might have started coming out of his sleep naturally an hour before. Getting out of bed, he went almost unconsciously and without any definite purpose in the direction of the shout to see what was the matter. He still felt rather dazed and his mind was still only half awake, but in the garden he went up to the lighted windows and heard the terrible news from his master, who was, of course, very glad to see him. His mind at once began working feverishly. He learnt all the details from his frightened master. And so gradually an idea took shape in his disordered and sick brain – a terrible, but tempting and irresistibly logical idea: to kill his master, take the three thousand, and put the whole blame afterwards on his young master: everyone would naturally think that it was the young master who had done it, for who else could be accused of the murder in the light of the evidence that he had been there at the time? A terrible lust for money, for booty, might have seized hold of him together with the realization that now he could commit the murder with impunity without fear of being found out. Oh, those sudden and irresistible impulses come so often when a favourable opportunity presents itself and, most of all, they come on the spur of the moment to murderers who before that have never dreamt of committing a murder! And so Smerdyakov might well have gone in and carried out his plan. With what weapon? Why, with any stone he had picked up in the garden. But why? With what object? And the three thousand? Why, it meant a career for him! Oh, I'm not contradicting myself: the money may have existed. And perhaps Smerdyakov alone knew where to find it, where his master had put it. And the packet with the money, the torn envelope on the floor? A short while ago, when talking of this envelope, the counsel for the prosecution made the very subtle point that only an inexperienced thief like Karamazov would have left it on the floor, but not Smerdyakov who would never have left such incriminating evidence against himself, and, gentlemen of the jury, I couldn't help thinking that I was hearing something very familiar. And, just imagine, the very same point, the same conjecture of what Karamazov would have done with the envelope, I heard precisely two days ago from Smerdyakov himself. What's more, he rather astonished me by his explanation: it seemed to me that he was being a little too naïve, that he was putting it on, anticipating my questions, that he was foisting his idea on me so that I might think that it was my own, that he was, as it were, prompting me. Did he not suggest the same idea to the investigating authorities, too? Did he not by any chance foist it upon my learned friend, the counsel for the prosecution? I shall be asked: and what about the old woman, Grigory's wife? She heard the sick man moaning next door to her all night? She did, indeed, but that is an extremely debatable point of view. I knew a woman who complained bitterly that she had been kept awake all night by a dog in the yard. And yet the poor dog, as it appeared later, only barked once or twice in the night. And that is natural enough: if anyone is asleep and suddenly hears a groan, he wakes up, annoyed at being woken, but instantly falls asleep again. Two hours later there is again a groan, he wakes up again and falls asleep again, and two hours later again the same thing, altogether three times in the night. Next morning the sleeper gets up and complains that someone has been groaning all night and has kept waking him. And this is how it must seem to him; he has slept through the intervals of two hours and does not remember them, he only remembers the moments of waking and so he believes that he has been wakened all night. But why, why, the counsel for the prosecution exclaims, did not Smerdyakov confess in his last letter? Why should his conscience have made him confess one thing and not the other? But remember this: conscience means penitence, and the suicide may not have felt penitence but only despair. Despair and penitence are two quite different things. Despair may be spiteful and irreconcilable, and at the moment of committing suicide a man may have hated the people whom he had envied all his life twice as much. Gentlemen of the jury, beware of a miscarriage of justice! I put it to you: why is what I have described now so improbable? Find the error in my reasoning, find why it is impossible and absurd. And if there is a modicum of truth, a shade of probability in my propositions – do not bring in a verdict of guilty. And is there only a shade? I swear by everything I hold sacred that I fully believe in the explanation of the murder I have just put to you. But what troubles and horrifies me most is the thought that out of all this mass of facts piled up by the prosecution against the accused there is not a single one that is in any way precise or irrefutable and that the unhappy man may be ruined utterly simply because of this accumulation of facts. Yes, this mass of facts is terrible: the blood, the blood dripping from the fingers, the blood-stained linen, the dark night, rent by the cry of "parricide!", and the man who had uttered that cry sinking to the ground with a broken head, and then that mass of phrases, statements, gestures, cries – oh, it all exerts so much influence, it biases one's opinion so much! But, gentlemen of the jury, can it bias your opinions? Remember, you have been given immense power, the power to condemn and to acquit. But the greater the power, the more dreadful is its application! I do not retract anything from what I have just said, but let me for a moment, just for the sake of argument, agree with the prosecution that my unhappy client stained his hands with the blood of his father. This is merely an assumption. I repeat I do not for a moment doubt his innocence, but just let me assume for the sake of argument that the prisoner is guilty of parricide. Even if it were so, I beg you to hear what I have to say. I'd very much like to say something to you, for I feel that there is a great struggle in your hearts and minds. . . . Forgive me, gentlemen of the jury, for what I have just said about your hearts and minds. But I want to be truthful and sincere to the end. Let us all be sincere. . . .'

At this point the counsel for the defence was interrupted by rather

loud applause. Indeed, he uttered his last words with a note of such
sincerity that everyone felt that perhaps he really had something to
say and that what he was going to say now was, in fact, something
of the utmost importance. But the presiding judge, hearing the applause, threatened in a loud voice 'to clear the court' if 'a similar
incident' occurred again. A hush fell over the court and Fetyukovich
began in a sort of new, penetrating voice, quite unlike the tone of
voice he had used before.

13

Corrupters of Thought

'IT is not only the accumulation of facts that spells the doom of my
client, gentlemen of the jury,' he declared. 'No, what really spells
the doom of my client is only one fact: the dead body of his old
father! Had it been an ordinary case of murder, you would have
rejected the charge in view of the paltry and fantastic nature of the
facts and the impossibility of proving them beyond reasonable
doubt, if each of them is examined separately and not as part of a
whole; or you would at least have hesitated to ruin a man's life
merely out of the prejudice against him which, alas, he has only too
well deserved! But here we are not dealing with an ordinary murder
but with parricide! That impresses people and so greatly that the
very triviality and the lack of proof of the incriminating facts become
less trivial and far from lacking proof even to an unprejudiced mind.
How is one then to acquit such a prisoner? What if he did commit
the murder and goes off unpunished? That is what everyone feels
in his heart almost involuntarily, instinctively. Yes, it is a dreadful
thing to shed a father's blood, the blood of the man who has begotten
you, who has loved you, the blood of the man who has not spared
his life for you, who has worried over your illnesses from the days
of your childhood, who has been anxious all his life for your happiness, and who has lived only in your joys and your successes! Oh,
to murder such a father – why, it's not to be thought of! Gentlemen
of the jury, what is a father, a real father? What is the meaning of
that great word? What is the immensely great idea behind that

name? We have just given an indication of what it is and what a true father ought to be. But in the present case in which we are all now so deeply involved and over which we grieve so much, in the present case, gentlemen of the jury, the father, the late Fyodor Karamazov, did not at all come up to the idea of a father that has appealed so strongly to us just now. That is a misfortune. Yes, indeed, some fathers are a misfortune. Let us examine this misfortune a little more closely, for in view of the importance of your verdict, gentlemen of the jury, we must be afraid of nothing. We have a special reason now for not being afraid of any idea or, so to speak, waving it aside, like children or timid women, as my learned friend so happily expressed it. But in his heated speech my learned opponent (my opponent even before I uttered a word) exclaimed several times: "No, I shall not let anyone defend the prisoner, I will not yield his defence to the advocate who has come down from Petersburg – I am his accuser and I am his defender!" That is what he exclaimed several times, and yet he forgot to mention that if the terrible prisoner was so grateful for twenty-three years for only one pound of nuts he had received from the only man who had been kind to him as a child in his father's house, then, conversely, such a man could not help remembering for twenty-three years how he ran about barefoot in his father's backyard "in his little trousers hanging by one button", to quote the expression of the kind-hearted doctor Herzenstube. Oh, gentlemen of the jury, why examine this "misfortune" more closely, why repeat what everyone knows already? What did my client meet with when he arrived here at his father's house? And why, why depict my client as a man without feeling, an egoist, a monster? He is impetuous, he is wild and violent, and we are now trying him for that, but who is responsible for the circumstances of his life, who is responsible for his having received such an absurd upbringing in spite of his excellent propensities and his grateful and sensitive heart? Did anyone teach him to be sensible? Did he get any proper education? Did anyone love him ever so little in his childhood? My client grew up by the grace of God, that is to say, like a wild animal. He may have been eager to see his father after so long a separation. Remembering his childhood as though in a dream, a thousand times perhaps, he may have driven away the horrible phantoms that haunted his childhood dreams and longed with all his heart to justify and to embrace his father! And what happened? He was met by cynical sneers, suspiciousness, and attempts to cheat him out of the money that he claimed belonged to him. All he heard was sickening talk and hackneyed precepts delivered daily "over the brandy", and at last saw his father trying to entice away his mistress from him, his son, and with his own money. Oh, gentlemen of the jury, that was both abominable and cruel! And that same old man was complaining to everybody of his son's disrespect and cruelty, gave him a bad name in society, injured him, slandered him, bought up his IOU's in order to get him imprisoned! Gentlemen of the jury, these men, outwardly cruel-hearted, violent and uncontrollable, men like my client, are more often than not exceedingly tender-hearted, only they don't show it. Do not laugh, do not laugh at my idea! The learned counsel for the prosecution laughed mercilessly at my client a short while ago, pointing out that he loved Schiller, that he loved "the beautiful and the sublime". I should not have laughed at that in his place, in the place of a counsel for the prosecution! Yes, such hearts – oh, let me speak in the defence of these hearts, so often and so unfairly misunderstood, such hearts often long for what is tender, beautiful, and just, and they do so, as it were, in contrast to themselves, their violence, and their cruelty – they long for it unconsciously – yes, they long for it. Outwardly passionate and cruel, they are capable, for instance, of falling in love with a woman to a point where it becomes a torment to them, and their love is always high-minded and spiritual. Again do not laugh at me: this is more often than not the case with men of such natures! They only cannot hide their passion, sometimes very coarse passion – and that is what strikes people, that is what they notice, but they do not see what is taking place deep inside such men. Their passions, on the contrary, are quickly spent, but beside a noble and beautiful creature such an apparently coarse and cruel man seeks for regeneration, for a chance of reforming himself, for becoming a better, nobler, and more honourable man, for "the sublime and the beautiful", however much people may jeer at these words! I said a short while ago that I would not venture to touch upon my client's love affair with Miss Verkhovtsev. But I think I will say this: what we heard just now was not evidence but the scream of a frenzied and revengeful woman, and it is not she who should reproach him with betrayal, for she herself has betrayed him!

If she had had a little time to think things over, she would not have
given such evidence. Oh, don't believe her. No, my client is not a
"monster", as she called him. The crucified Lover of mankind, preparing for his crucifixion, said: "I am the good shepherd, and I lay
down my life for the sheep, so that not one of them might be lost. . . ."
Don't let us ruin a man's soul, either. I asked just now: what is a
father, and I said that it was a great word, a precious name. But,
gentlemen of the jury, words must be used honestly, and I venture
to call a thing by its right name, by its proper word. Such a father
as the murdered old Karamazov cannot and does not deserve to be
called a father. The love for a father who does not deserve such love
is an absurdity, an impossibility. One cannot create love out of
nothing, only God can create something out of nothing. "Fathers,
provoke not your children to anger," the apostle writes from a heart
burning with love. It is not for the sake of my client that I quote these
sacred words, but as a reminder to all fathers. Who empowered me
to preach to fathers? No one. But as a man and a citizen I make my
appeal – *vivos voco!* We are not long on earth, we do many evil deeds
and say many evil words. Let us, therefore, take advantage of the
favourable moment of our being together here to say a good word
to each other. That is what I am doing: while I stand here, I take
advantage of my moment. It is not for nothing that this tribune has
been given us by the highest authority – the whole of Russia hears us.
I am not saying this only for the fathers here, but I cry aloud to all
fathers: "Fathers, do not provoke your children to anger!" Let us first
carry out Christ's precept ourselves and only then venture to demand
it of our children. Otherwise we are not fathers, but enemies of our
children, and they are not our children, but our enemies and we ourselves have made them our enemies! "With what measure ye mete,
it shall be measured to you again," it is not I who am saying this, it is
an injunction of the Gospel: measure according to the same measure
as is measured to you. How, then, can we blame our children, if they
measure us according to our own measure? Recently in Finland a girl,
a housemaid, was suspected of having secretly given birth to a child.
She was watched and in the loft behind some bricks was found a box
of hers that no one knew anything about. It was opened and there
inside it was the body of a new-born baby she had killed. In the same
box were found the skeletons of two other babies she had killed,

according to her own confession, at the moment of their birth. Gentlemen of the jury, was she a mother to her children? It is true, she gave
birth to them, but was she a mother to them? Would any one of you
be so bold as to give her the sacred name of mother? Let us be bold,
gentlemen of the jury, let us be daring even! It is our duty to be so
at this moment and not to be afraid of certain words and ideas, like
the Moscow merchants' wives in Ostrovsky's comedy who are afraid
to say certain words they do not understand. No, let us, on the contrary, prove that the progress of the last few years has influenced our
development too, and let us say frankly: the man who begets a child
does not become its father unless he both begets it and does his duty
by it. Oh, no doubt, there's another meaning, another interpretation
of the word "father", which demands that my father, though he be
a monster, though he maltreat his children, still remains my father
simply because he begot me. But this meaning is, as it were, a mystical
one. I cannot grasp it by my mind, but can only accept it by faith, or,
better still, *on faith*, like many other things I do not understand but
which religion bids me believe. But in that case let it remain outside
the sphere of actual life. In the sphere of actual life, which not only
has its own rights but imposes upon us great duties, in that sphere, if
we want to be humane men and Christians, we must and, indeed, are
obliged to act upon convictions justified by reason and experience,
passed through the crucible of analysis, in short, we must act rationally
and not irrationally, as though in a dream or a delirium, so as to do
harm to no man, so as not to torture and ruin a man. It is only then
that it will be real Christian work, not only mystical, but rational and
truly philanthropic work. . . .'

At this point there was loud applause in many parts of the court,
but Fetyukovich waved his hands as though imploring them not to
interrupt but to let him finish his speech. A hush fell over the court at
once. The orator went on:

'Do you believe, gentlemen of the jury, that such questions can
escape our children, let us say, in their teens and when they begin to
reason? No, they cannot, and do not let us demand such self-restraint
from them! The sight of an unworthy father inevitably arouses painful questions in a boy's mind, especially when he compares him with
the worthy fathers of other children of the same age as he. He is given
the conventional answer to this question: "He begot you and you are

his flesh and blood and therefore you must love him." The boy cannot help reflecting: "But did he love me when he begot me?" he asks, wondering more and more. "Was it for my sake that he begot me? He did not know me, nor even my sex, at that moment, at that moment of passion, perhaps under the influence of drink, and, I suppose, all he transmitted to me was his propensity to drunkenness – those are all the benefits I got from him. . . . Why, then, ought I to love him? Just for begetting me and not caring for me all his life afterwards?" Oh, you may think these questions coarse and cruel, but you must not demand impossible restraint from a young mind: "Chase nature out of the door and she will fly in at the window," and most of all, most of all, don't let us be afraid of words we do not understand, but decide the question according to the dictates of reason and humanity and not as dictated by all sorts of mystical ideas. How then shall we decide it? Why, like this: let the son stand before his father and ask him: "Tell me, Father, why should I love you? Father, prove to me that I must love you!" And if his father is able to tell him that and prove it to him, then we are dealing with a real, normal family, based not merely on mystical prejudices, but on rational, responsible, and strictly humane foundations. If, on the other hand, the father cannot prove it, there is at once an end to the family relationship: he is not a father to him, and the son is free and entitled to look upon his father as a stranger, and even as his enemy. Our tribune, gentlemen of the jury, must be a school of truth and rational ideas.'

Here the speaker was interrupted by unrestrained and almost frenzied applause. Of course, it was not the whole audience that applauded, but half of it certainly did. The fathers and mothers applauded. Shrieks and screams were heard from the gallery where the ladies were sitting. They waved their handkerchiefs. The presiding judge began ringing his bell with all his might. He was visibly annoyed by the behaviour of the audience, but he dared not 'clear the court', as he had threatened earlier: even the eminent personages, old men with stars on their frock-coats, sitting behind the rostrum on specially reserved seats, applauded and waved their handkerchiefs, so that when the noise died down, the presiding judge was content merely to repeat his erstwhile stern threat to clear the court, and the triumphant and excited Fetyukovich went on with his speech.

'Gentlemen of the jury, you remember that awful night, of which so much has been said today, when the son climbed over the fence, got into the house and, at last, stood facing the man who had begotten him, his enemy and his persecutor. I insist with all the force at my command that he did not come for money just then: the charge of robbery is an absurdity, as I already explained. And it was not to murder him that he broke into the house – oh no! If he had planned to do that, he would at least have provided himself with a weapon beforehand, for the brass pestle he grabbed instinctively, without knowing why he did so. Let us suppose that he deceived his father by the signals and that he got into the house – I have said already that I do not for a moment believe this story, but, never mind, let us assume it to be true for a moment. Gentlemen of the jury, I swear to you by all that is holy, that if his persecutor had not been his father, but a complete stranger, he would have rushed through the rooms and, making sure that the woman was not in the house, have run off post-haste without doing any harm to his rival, except that he might have struck him, pushed him aside, but nothing more, for he had no thought and no time to spare for that, he had to find out where she was. But his father, his father – oh, the sight of his father, the man who had hated him from his childhood, his enemy, his persecutor, and now his unnatural rival, was the cause of everything! He was involuntarily seized by a feeling of hatred – irresistibly, there was no time for reflection: it all surged up in him in one moment! It was an impulse of madness and insanity, but an impulse of nature, avenging the violation of its eternal laws irresistibly and unconsciously, like everything in nature. But even then the prisoner did not kill him – I firmly maintain that – no, he merely struck him with the pestle in a burst of sickening indignation, without wishing to kill, not knowing that he would kill. But for that fatal pestle in his hand, he would, perhaps, have only assaulted his father, but not killed him. As he ran away, he did not know whether the old man he had knocked down was killed or not. Such a murder is not murder. Nor can the murder of such a father be called parricide. Such a murder can only be considered parricide by prejudice. But did such a murder actually take place? I appeal to you again and again from the bottom of my heart! Gentlemen of the jury, if we condemn him, he will say to himself: "These people have done nothing for me, for my upbringing, for my education, they have done nothing to make me better, to make a man of me. These people have not given me to eat and drink, they have not visited me naked in prison, and now they have sent me to penal servitude. I am quits, I owe them nothing now, and I don't owe anything to anyone for ever and ever. They are wicked and I shall be wicked. They are cruel and I shall be cruel." That's what he will say, gentlemen of the jury. And I assure you that by your verdict of guilty you will only make it easier for him, you will ease his conscience, he will curse the blood he has shed, but not be sorry for it. And at the same time you will destroy in him the man he could have become, for he will remain blind and wicked all his life. Would you not rather punish him fearfully, terribly, with the most dreadful punishment that could be imagined, but so as to save and regenerate his soul for ever? If so, then crush him with your mercy! You will see, you will hear how his soul will flinch and be horrified: "How am I to endure this mercy? Do I deserve so much love? Am I worthy of it?" – that is what he will exclaim. Oh, I know, I know that heart! It is wild, but generous, gentlemen of the jury. It will bow before your great act of mercy. It longs for a great act of love. It will blaze up and revive for ever! There are men who in their narrow-mindedness blame the whole world. But crush them with mercy, show them love, and they will curse their past deeds, for there are a great many potentialities for good in them. Their hearts will swell and they will see that God is merciful and that men are just and fair. Such a man will be horror-stricken, crushed by remorse and the great debt that he has to repay henceforth. And he will not say then, "I'm quits," but will say, "I am guilty in the sight of all men and I am more unworthy than all." With tears of penitence and poignant, tender emotion, he will cry: "Other people are better than I, for they wished to save me and not to ruin me!" Oh, you can perform this act of mercy so easily, for in the absence of evidence that is in any way convincing you would find it too difficult to pronounce: "Yes, guilty." Better acquit ten guilty men than punish one innocent man – do you hear, do you hear that majestic voice from the past century of our glorious history? Is it for me, insignificant person that I am, to remind you that a Russian court does not exist for punishment only, but also for the salvation of a ruined man? Let other nations adhere to the letter of the law and exact punishment, we will adhere to its spirit and meaning – the salvation and regeneration of the lost. And if that is so, if Russia and her courts of justice are really such, then let her go forward on her way, and do not frighten us with your frenzied *troikas* from which all nations stand aside with disgust! Not a frenzied *troika*, but the majestic Russian chariot will arrive, calmly and majestically, at its goal. The fate of my client is in your hands and in your hands is the fate of Russian justice. You will save it, you will vindicate it, you will prove that there are men who watch over it, that it is in good hands!'

14

The Dear Old Peasants Stood Up for Themselves

THAT was how Fetyukovich concluded his speech, and this time the enthusiasm of his listeners was as irrepressible as a storm. It was, anyway, quite impossible to suppress it: women wept, many men wept, too, and even a couple of important personages shed tears. The presiding judge gave in and was not even in any hurry to ring his bell: 'To encroach upon such enthusiasm,' as our ladies cried afterwards, 'would be to encroach upon something sacred.' The orator himself was deeply moved. And it was at such a moment that our public prosecutor rose again 'to voice some objections'. He was met with looks of hatred. 'What? What is he up to? How dare he object?' the ladies murmured. But even if the ladies of the entire world, headed by the public prosecutor's formidable wife, had murmured, he could not have been restrained at that moment. He was pale, he was shaking with excitement; the first words, the first phrases he uttered were even unintelligible: he gasped for breath, he enunciated his words badly, he floundered. However, he soon recovered himself. But I will quote only a few sentences from his second speech.

'. . . I'm reproached with having indulged in the invention of fictitious tales. But what about the counsel for the defence? Hasn't he been indulging in one romance after another? All that was wanting was poetry. Fyodor Karamazov, while waiting for his mistress, tears up the envelope and throws it on the floor. My learned friend even told us what he said during this remarkable incident. Is not this a whole poem? And what proof did my learned friend produce that he had taken out the money? Who heard what he said? The feeble-minded idiot Smerdyakov transformed into a sort of Byronic hero, who revenges himself upon society for his illegitimate birth – isn't that a poem in the Byronic style? And the son who bursts into his father's house, who murders him and yet does not murder him, that is not even a romance or a poem, but a sphinx setting a riddle which, needless to say, he cannot solve himself. If he murdered him, he murdered him, but how could he have murdered him and not murdered him – who can make any sense out of that? Then we are solemnly told that our tribune is a tribune of truth and sound ideas, and from this tribune of "sound ideas" an axiom is announced, strengthened by a solemn oath, that to call the murder of a father "parricide" is merely prejudice! But what will become of us if parricide is a prejudice, if every child were to ask his father: "Father, why must I love you?" What will become of the foundations of society? What will become of the family? Parricide, you see, is just an incomprehensible word that frightens Moscow merchants' wives out of their wits. The most precious, the most sacred precepts concerning the purpose and the future of Russian justice are presented in a perverted and frivolous form with the sole aim of obtaining a justification for something which cannot be justified. Oh, the counsel for the defence exclaims, crush him by mercy. But that is all the criminal wants, and tomorrow everyone will see how much he is crushed! And is not the counsel for the defence too modest in demanding only the acquittal of the prisoner? Why not ask for the founding of a scholarship in the name of the parricide to immortalize his exploit among the younger generation and posterity? Religion and the Gospel are amended: *that* is all mysticism, we are told, but ours, you see, is the only true Christianity, which has already passed the test of the analysis of reason and sound ideas. And so they set up before us a false image of Christ. "With what measure ye mete, it shall be measured to you again," cried the counsel for the defence, and in the same breath draws the conclusion that Christ teaches to measure as is measured to us – and that from the tribune of truth and sound ideas! We look into the Gospels only on the eve of making our speeches in order to show off our knowledge of what is, after all, a rather original work, which can come in useful to produce a certain effect when and as required! But Christ commands us not to do this, but to beware of doing this, because that is what the wicked world does, while we ought to forgive and to turn the other cheek, and not mete out in the same measure in which our persecutors measure to us. That is what our Lord teaches us and not that it is a prejudice to forbid children to murder their fathers. And it is not meet that from the tribune of truth and sound ideas we should correct the Gospel of our Lord, whom the counsel for the defence deigns to call only a "crucified lover of humanity", in opposition to all orthodox Russia, which calls upon him "For thou art the Lord our God!" . . .'

Here the presiding judge intervened and pulled up the over-enthusiastic counsel for the prosecution, asking him not to exaggerate, to keep within proper limits, and so on, as presiding judges always do in such cases. Besides, the audience, too, was getting restive. People were stirring in their seats and there were even cries of protest. Fetyukovich did not even think it necessary to reply. He only mounted the tribune, his hand pressed to his heart, to utter, in an injured tone, a few words full of dignity. He merely again touched lightly and ironically upon 'fictitious tales' and 'psychology' and interpolated at the appropriate place, 'Jupiter, thou art angry, therefore thou art wrong', which provoked a burst of approving laughter in the audience, for our public prosecutor certainly bore no resemblance to Jupiter. As for the accusation that he gave permission to the younger generation to murder their fathers, Fetyukovich observed with great dignity that he did not intend even to reply to it. As for the public prosecutor's remark about 'the false image of Christ' and that he had not deigned to refer to Christ as our Lord, but called him only 'the crucified lover of humanity' which was 'contrary to the orthodox faith and should not have been said from the tribune of truth and sound ideas', Fetyukovich hinted at an 'insinuation' and that in this court at least he had expected to be safe from accusations which were 'damaging to me as a citizen and a loyal subject'. . . . But at these words the presiding judge cut him short, too, and Fetyukovich concluded his reply with a bow, and went back to his seat to the accompaniment of an approving murmur of conversation in court. In the opinion of our ladies, the public prosecutor was 'crushed for good'.

Then the prisoner was asked if he had anything to say. Mitya stood up, but he said very little. He was terribly tired, both mentally and physically. The look of strength and independence with which he had appeared in court in the morning had almost disappeared. He seemed to have gone through an experience that day that he would not forget all his life, and that had taught him and made him understand something very important he had not understood before. His voice was weak. He no longer shouted as before. There was a new note of submission, defeat, and deep understanding in his words.

'What am I to say, gentlemen of the jury? My hour of judgement has come and I can feel the hand of God upon me. The end has come to a dissolute man! But as before God I tell you: of my father's death – no, I am not guilty! I repeat for the last time: it was not I who murdered him! I was dissolute, but I loved goodness. Every moment I was anxious to reform, but I lived like a wild beast. I thank the prosecutor. He told me many things about myself that I did not know. But it is not true that I murdered my father. There he was mistaken. I thank the counsel for the defence, too. I cried listening to him, but it is not true that I murdered my father and he need not have even assumed it! And don't believe the doctors: I am sane, only my heart is heavy. If you spare me, if you acquit me, I will pray for you. I will be a better man. I give you my word. I give it you before God. And if you condemn me – I shall break my sword over my head myself and kiss the pieces! But spare me. Do not deprive me of my God. I know myself, I shall murmur against him. My heart is heavy, gentlemen of the jury – spare me!'

He almost sank back in his seat, his voice faltered, and he could scarcely articulate the last sentence. Then the court proceeded to formulate the questions to the jury and both sides were asked to sum up their conclusions. But I will not describe the details. At last the jury got up to retire. The presiding judge looked very jaded and, therefore, his address to the jury was rather weak. 'Try to be impartial,' he said. 'Do not be swayed by the eloquence of the counsel for the defence, but still weigh the evidence carefully, remember that a great responsibility has been laid upon you,' and so on. The jury retired and the court was adjourned. It was now possible to get up, stretch one's legs, exchange one's accumulated impressions, and have a snack at the buffet. It was very late, almost an hour after midnight, but no one thought of going home. They all felt the strain so much that they were not in the mood for taking a rest. All waited with sinking hearts for the verdict, though, perhaps, this could not be said of the ladies, who were only in a state of hysterical impatience, but untroubled at heart, being quite certain of a verdict of not guilty. They all prepared themselves for the dramatic moment of general enthusiasm. I must admit that among the men, too, there were a great many who were convinced that an acquittal was inevitable. Some were pleased, others frowned, and others still walked about looking crestfallen: they were against an acquittal! Fetyukovich himself was quite confident of success. He was surrounded by people, who congratulated him and fawned upon him.

'There are invisible threads,' he said to one group, as it was reported afterwards, 'which connect the counsel for the defence with the jury. One feels during one's speech when this connexion is established. I felt it. These threads exist. We have won, don't worry.'

'But what will our dear old peasants say now?' a frowning, pock-marked, fat gentleman, a landowner of the neighbourhood, said, approaching a group of gentlemen who were engaged in conversation.

'But they aren't all peasants. Four of the jurymen are civil servants.'

'Yes, that's true,' said a member of the agricultural board, joining the group.

'And do you know Nazaryev, the merchant with the medal, one of the jurymen?'

'What about him?'

'A clever fellow.'

'But he never opens his mouth.'

'He doesn't, but so much the better. The Petersburg lawyer has nothing to teach him. He could teach all Petersburg himself. He's the father of twelve children. Think of that!'

'But, good heavens, won't they acquit him?' a young civil servant cried in another group.

'They're sure to acquit him,' a determined voice replied.

'It would be a shame and a disgrace if he were not acquitted,' the civil servant exclaimed. 'Suppose he did kill him, but there are fathers and fathers! And, after all, he was in such a state of frenzy. . . . He really may have just brandished the pestle and the old man fell down. A pity, though, they dragged that servant in. That was just an amusing episode. In Fetyukovich's place I'd have simply said: he murdered him, but he isn't guilty, and to hell with you!'

'But he did do that, except that he did not say "to hell with you".'

'No, sir, he practically said it,' a third voice put in.

'But, good heavens, gentlemen, was not an actress acquitted in our town during Lent of cutting the throat of her lover's wife.'

'But she did not cut deep enough.'

'It makes no difference. She started cutting it.'

'And how do you like what he said about the children? Splendid!'

'Splendid!'

'And what about mysticism? About mystical ideas, eh?'

'Oh, never mind mysticism,' someone else cried. 'Think of our poor public prosecutor! What do you think his life will be worth from now on? Why, his wife will scratch his eyes out tomorrow for the things he said about her darling Mitya!'

'She isn't here, is she?'

'No, of course not. If she'd been here she'd have scratched his eyes out already. She's at home with toothache. Ha, ha, ha!'

'Ha, ha, ha!'

In a third group.

'I suppose Mitya will be acquitted after all.'

'I expect he'll wreck the "Metropolis" tomorrow. He'll be drinking hard for the next fortnight.'

'The devil!'

'Aye, the devil's in it all right. Without him nothing would have happened. Where should he be if not here?'

'Gentlemen, I grant you eloquence is a fine thing, but, after all, you can't allow people to break their fathers' heads with blunt instruments, can you? Or what are we coming to?'

'The chariot, the chariot, remember?'

'Yes, he turned a cart into a chariot.'

'And tomorrow he'll turn a chariot into a cart. "All according to the requirements of the case!"'

'What clever fellows we've got nowadays. Is there any justice in Russia, gentlemen, or doesn't it exist at all?'

But the bell rang. The jury was away for exactly an hour, neither more nor less. As soon as the public had taken their seats, a dead silence fell over the court. I remember how the jury trooped back into the court. At last! I am not quoting the questions in order. I've forgotten them, anyway. I only remember their answer to the first and most important question of the presiding judge, namely, 'Did the prisoner commit the murder for the sake of robbery and with premeditation?' (I don't remember the exact words.) Everyone held his breath. The foreman of the jury, the civil servant who was the youngest member of the jury, announced in a loud and clear voice amid the dead silence of the court:

'Yes, guilty.'

And the same answer was returned to every question: guilty, yes, guilty, and without the slightest extenuating circumstance! That no one had expected. Almost everyone was convinced that there would at least be a recommendation for mercy. The dead silence of the court was not broken. Everyone, both those who longed for his conviction and those who longed for his acquittal, seemed literally turned to stone. But that only lasted a few minutes. After that a terrible commotion arose. There were many among the men who were very pleased. Some even rubbed their hands without concealing their glee. Those who were displeased with the verdict seemed crushed, shrugged their shoulders, whispered among themselves, but did not seem to have realized what had happened. But, dear me, our poor ladies! I thought they'd create a riot. At first they did not seem to believe their ears. And suddenly loud exclamations were heard all over the court: 'What's the meaning of this? What's all this?' They jumped up from their seats. They apparently believed that it was possible to change and reverse the verdict immediately. At that moment Mitya rose and shouted in a sort of heart-rending voice, stretching out his hands before him:

'I swear by God and His Last Judgement I'm not guilty of the murder of my father! Katerina, I forgive you! Brothers, friends, have pity on the other woman.'

He did not finish and burst out sobbing terribly in a loud, strange, and unnatural voice, a voice that did not seem to be his own and that could be heard all over the court. From the farthest corner of the gallery came a piercing shriek – it was Grushenka. She had besought someone to let her in before the beginning of the speeches of the two counsel. Mitya was taken away. The passing of the sentence was put off till next day. The whole court rose in a turmoil, but I did not wait or listen. I only remember a few exclamations on the steps outside the court.

'He'll get a taste of the mines for the next twenty years.'

'No less.'

'Yes, sir, our dear old peasants have stood up for themselves.'

'And put paid to dear old Mitya.'

I

Plans to Save Mitya

FIVE days after Mitya's trial, very early, at nine o'clock in the morning, Alyosha went to see Katerina to settle a matter of great importance to both of them and, in addition, to give her a message. She received and talked to him in the same room in which she had once received Grushenka; in the next room Ivan lay unconscious and in a high fever. Immediately after the scene in court Katerina had the sick and unconscious Ivan taken to her house, regardless of the inevitable gossip and the disapproval of society. One of her two relations who lived with her had gone to Moscow at once after the scene in court, the other remained. But even if both had gone, Katerina would not have changed her mind and would have gone on nursing the sick man and sitting by him day and night. He was attended by Varvinsky and Herzenstube; the Moscow doctor had gone back to Moscow, refusing to give an opinion as to the probable course the illness would take. Though the two doctors reassured Katerina and Alyosha, it was obvious that they could not hold out any definite hopes of recovery. Alyosha visited his sick brother twice a day. But this time he had some special and rather troublesome business, and he foresaw how difficult he would find it to broach it, and yet he was in a great hurry: he had other urgent business to see to that morning, at a different place, and he had to make haste. They had been talking for a quarter of an hour. Katerina was pale, very tired, and at the same time in a state of highly morbid excitement: she had a good idea why Alyosha had called on her now.

'Don't worry about his decision,' she said emphatically to Alyosha. 'One way or another he's sure to come to it: he must escape! That unhappy man, that paragon of honour and conscience – I don't mean Dmitry, but the man lying behind that door, who has sacrificed himself for his brother,' Katerina added with flashing eyes, 'told me the whole plan of escape long ago. You know, he has already entered into negotiations – I've told you something already. . . . You see, it will in all probability take place at the third stop when the party of convicts is taken to Siberia. Oh, it's still a long way off. Ivan has already been to see the man who will be in charge of the prisoners at the third stop. What we don't know yet is who will be in charge of the convicts, and it is impossible to find this out so far ahead. Tomorrow I will perhaps show you in detail the whole plan which Ivan left me on the eve of the trial, in case anything happened. . . . That was when – remember? – you found us quarrelling that evening; he was going down the stairs and, seeing you, I made him come back – remember? Do you know what we were quarrelling about that time?'

'I'm afraid I don't,' said Alyosha.

'Well, of course, he concealed it from you then: it was about the plan of escape. He had told me the main idea of it three days before that, and it was then we began quarrelling and went on quarrelling for three days. We quarrelled because when he told me that if Dmitry were convicted he'd escape abroad with that creature, I suddenly got angry – I can't tell you why because I don't know myself. . . . Oh, of course, I expect I got angry then because of that creature and just because she, too, would go abroad with Dmitry!' Katerina suddenly exclaimed, her lips quivering with anger. 'As soon as Ivan saw that I got angry because of that creature, he at once imagined that I was jealous of her and that I was therefore still in love with Dmitry. That was the reason for our first quarrel. I refused to give any explanations and I could not ask forgiveness; I resented the fact that such a man could suspect that I was still in love with this . . . And that after I had told him myself frankly that I did not love Dmitry and that I loved no one but him! I was angry with him out of resentment over that creature. Three days later, on the evening you came, he brought me a sealed envelope and asked me to open it at once if anything happened to him. Oh, he foresaw his illness! He told me that the envelope contained the details of the escape and that if he were to die or be taken dangerously ill, I should save Mitya alone. He left me the money, about ten thousand roubles – the bonds the public prosecutor mentioned in his speech, having learnt from someone that he had sent them to be changed. What struck me so forcibly at the time was that Ivan, though still jealous of me and still convinced that I was in love with Dmitry, should not have given up his idea of saving his brother and should have entrusted me with the plan of saving him. Oh, that was a sacrifice! No, Alexey, you will never be able to understand so great a sacrifice. I felt like falling down at his feet in reverence, but it suddenly occurred to me that he'd take it merely as an expression of my joy that Mitya would be saved (and he'd certainly have thought that!); so exasperated was I at the time at the mere possibility of such an unjust thought on his part that I got angry again and instead of kissing his feet, I made another scene! Oh, I'm so unhappy! That's what my character is like – my awful, unhappy character! Oh, you will see: I shall most certainly drive him to a point when, like Dmitry, he, too, will throw me over for another with whom he'll find it easier to get on, but then – oh, then I should not be able to bear it – I'd kill myself! And when you came that evening and I called to you and told him to come back, I was so enraged by the look of contempt and hatred he gave me that – you remember – I shouted to you that *he, he alone* made me believe that his brother Dmitry was a murderer. I said that awful thing about him to hurt him again, for he never, never made me believe that his brother was a murderer. On the contrary, it was I, I who persuaded him, Oh, my wild rage was the cause of everything, everything! It was I, I who planned that horrible scene at the trial. He wanted to prove to me that he was an honourable man and, though I might love his brother, he would not ruin him out of jealousy and revenge. That's why he appeared in court. . . . I'm the cause of it all! I alone am to blame!'

Katerina had never before made such confessions to Alyosha, and he felt that she had now reached that degree of unbearable suffering when even the proudest heart crushes its pride in agony and falls vanquished by grief. Oh, Alyosha knew still another terrible reason for her present agony, however much she had tried to conceal it from him all during those days since Mitya's conviction; but for some reason it would have been extremely painful to him if she had decided so to abase herself as to speak to him now about that, too. She was suffering for her 'treachery' at the trial, and Alyosha felt that her conscience was urging her to make a clean breast of it to him, Alyosha, especially, with tears, screams, hysterics, and writhings on the floor. But he dreaded that moment and wished to spare the sufferer. It made the message he had come to give her all the more difficult. He spoke again of Mitya.

'Oh, don't worry about him, he'll be all right,' Katerina began again, sharply and stubbornly. 'Everything with him only lasts a moment. I know him. I know his heart too well. You may be sure he'll agree to escape. And, anyway, it's not going to happen immediately. He'll have plenty of time to make up his mind. Ivan will be well by that time and will take charge of it himself, so that I won't have to do anything. Don't worry, he'll agree to escape. As a matter of fact, he has agreed already. You don't really think he'd give up that creature now? They won't let her join him in Siberia, so what else can he do but escape? It's you he's most afraid of. He's afraid that you won't approve of his escape on moral grounds. But you must generously *permit* it, if,' Katerina added venomously, 'your sanction *is* so necessary.'

She paused and smiled.

'He goes on talking,' she began again, 'about some hymns, some cross he has to bear, some duty. I remember Ivan telling me about it that evening and if only you knew how he spoke about it!' Katerina suddenly exclaimed with irrepressible feeling. 'If only you knew how he loved that wretched man at the moment he told me about him, and how he hated him, perhaps, at the very same moment! And I – oh, I listened to his story and watched his tears with a haughty smile. Oh, the horrible creature! It is I, I who am a horrible creature! It is I who am responsible for his brain-fever! But that one – the convict, is he ready to accept suffering? Do such as he suffer?' Katerina concluded irritably. 'Such as he never suffer.'

There was now an undisguised note of hatred and contemptuous disgust in her words. And yet it was she who had betrayed him. 'I suppose,' Alyosha thought to himself, 'it is because she feels so guilty towards him that she hates him at moments.' He would have liked it to be only 'at moments'. He felt there was a challenge in Katerina's last words, but he did not take it up.

'I asked you to come to see me this morning,' she said, 'to make you promise me to persuade him yourself. Or do you, too, think it dishonourable, or unheroic or – er – unchristian, perhaps, to escape?' Katerina added in an even more challenging tone.

'No, I don't,' Alyosha murmured. 'I'll tell him everything. He asked me to tell you that he'd like to see you today,' he suddenly blurted out, looking steadily into her eyes.

She gave a violent start and almost recoiled from him on the sofa.

'Me? Is it possible?' she murmured, turning pale.

'It is and it must be!' Alyosha declared emphatically, growing greatly animated. 'He needs you very badly, now especially. I wouldn't have mentioned it and worried you unnecessarily if it hadn't been so necessary. He's sick, he's almost out of his mind, he keeps on asking for you. It isn't to make it up with you that he wants you to come. All he wants is that you should go and show yourself at his door. A lot has happened to him since that day. He realizes how greatly he has wronged you. It isn't your forgiveness he wants – "I can't be forgiven," he declares himself, but merely that you should show yourself at his door. . . .'

'You've —' Katerina murmured. 'I had a feeling all this time that you'd come with that message. . . . I knew he would ask me to come. . . . It's impossible!'

'It may be impossible, but – please, do it. Remember it's the first time he's been struck by the thought that he's offended you. For the first time in his life. He had never realized it so fully before. He says that if you refused to come he'd be unhappy all his life. Do you hear? A convict sentenced to twenty years' hard labour still hopes to be happy – isn't that pitiful? Think of it: you will be paying a visit to a man who has been ruined, though he is innocent,' Alyosha blurted out, challengingly. 'His hands are clean, there's no blood on them. Go and see him now for the sake of his infinite suffering in the future. Go, see him off on his way into the darkness – stand at his door, that is all. . . . You must, you simply *must* do it!' concluded Alyosha, with great emphasis on the word 'must'.

'I must, but – I can't,' Katya said, in a sort of moan. 'He will look at me – I – I can't.'

'Your eyes must meet. How will you be able to carry on, if you won't make up your mind to see him now?'

'I'd rather suffer all my life.'

'You must go. You *must* go,' Alyosha again declared emphatically.

'But why today? Why now? I can't leave our patient. . . .'

'You can for a short time. It will only take a short time. If you don't come, he'll be delirious tonight. I wouldn't tell you something that wasn't true. Have pity on him!'

'Have pity on me!' Katerina reproached him bitterly and burst into tears.

'So you will!' Alyosha said firmly, seeing her tears. 'I'll go and tell him that you'll be coming presently.'

'No, don't tell him on any account,' Katerina cried in a frightened voice. 'I'll come, but don't tell him beforehand, because I may go but not go in. . . . I don't know yet. . . .'

Her voice failed her. She breathed with difficulty. Alyosha got up to go.

'But what if I should meet someone?' she suddenly said softly, turning deathly pale again.

'That's why you must go now so as not to meet anyone there. There won't be anyone, I'm certain of that. We shall be waiting for you,' he concluded emphatically, and went out of the room.

2

For a Moment a Lie Becomes Truth

HE hurried to the hospital where Mitya was a patient now. On the second day after the verdict, he had fallen ill with a nervous fever and was sent to the convict ward of our town hospital. But Dr Varvinsky, at the request of Alyosha and many others (Mrs Khokhlakov, Lise, etc.), put Mitya not with the convicts but in a separate little room, the same room in which Smerdyakov had been. At the end of the corridor, it is true, stood a sentry and there were bars on the window, so that Varvinsky could be easy in his mind about his not altogether legal concession; but he was a kindly and compassionate young man. He understood how hard it must be for a man like Mitya to pass over all at once into the company of thieves and murderers and that one had to get used to it gradually. The visits of relatives and friends were permitted by the doctor, the prison governor, and even by the police superintendent, though it was all done unofficially. But during these few days only Alyosha and Grushenka had visited Mitya. Rakitin had tried to see him twice, but Mitya told the doctor emphatically not to let him in.

Alyosha found him sitting on his bed in a hospital dressing-gown, slightly feverish, with a towel, soaked in vinegar and water, round his head. He looked rather vaguely at Alyosha as he entered the room, but there seemed to be something like fear in his eyes.

In general, he had become greatly preoccupied since the trial. Sometimes he was silent for half an hour, apparently trying hard and painfully to make up his mind about something, and quite oblivious of his visitor. Whenever he roused himself from his reverie and began to talk, he always did so, somehow, all of a sudden and he never said what he really wanted to say. He sometimes gazed at his brother with eyes full of suffering. He seemed to be more at ease with Grushenka than with Alyosha. It is true, he hardly ever spoke to her, but as soon as she entered his whole face lighted up with happiness.

Alyosha sat down silently on the bed beside him. This time he was waiting anxiously for Alyosha, but did not dare to ask him anything. He was quite sure Katerina would never consent to come and yet he could not help feeling that she could not but come. Alyosha understood his feelings.

'Trifon,' Mitya began nervously, 'Trifon, I'm told, has turned his whole inn upside down: taken up the floorboards, torn up the planks, pulled all his veranda to pieces. Looking for buried treasure all the time – the fifteen hundred roubles the public prosecutor said I'd hidden there. As soon as he got back home, I'm told, he began playing these silly tricks. Serve him right, the swindler! The hospital porter told me about it yesterday; he comes from there.'

'Listen,' said Alyosha, 'she will come, but I don't know when. Perhaps today, perhaps in a few days, I don't know, but she will come. She will, I'm sure of that.'

Mitya started. He was about to say something, but did not say it. The news affected him terribly. It was clear that he was very anxious to find out the details of Alyosha's talk with Katerina, but that he was afraid to ask: at that moment any cruel and contemptuous remark by Katerina would have been a mortal blow to him.

'By the way, she asked me to make your mind absolutely easy about escaping. Even if Ivan is not well by then, she'll arrange it all herself.'

'You've already told me about it,' Mitya observed musingly.

'And you've already spoken about it to Grushenka,' observed Alyosha.

'Yes,' Mitya admitted. 'She won't come this morning,' he went on, looking timidly at his brother. 'She'll be here only in the evening. As soon as I told her that Katerina was arranging things, she was silent, but made a wry face. She just whispered: "Let her!" She realized that it was something important. I dared not try her further. By now, I should think, she ought to have realized that the other one loves Ivan and not me, oughtn't she?'

'But does she?' Alyosha blurted out.

'Well, perhaps not. Only she won't come this morning,' Mitya hastened to explain again. 'I've asked her to do something for me. Listen, Alyosha, Ivan will surpass everyone. He ought to live and not us. I'm sure he will recover.'

'Well, you know, though Katerina is anxious about him, she hardly doubts that he will recover,' said Alyosha.

'This means that she's convinced he'll die. She's so sure of his recovery because she's afraid.'

'Ivan has a strong constitution,' Alyosha observed anxiously. 'I, too, have every hope that he will recover.'

'Yes, he will recover. But she's convinced that he'll die. There's no end to her grief. . . .'

There was a pause. Mitya was worried by something very important.

'Alyosha,' he said suddenly in a trembling voice, full of tears, 'I love Grushenka terribly.'

'They won't let her join you *there*,' Alyosha at once put in.

'And there's something else I wanted to tell you,' Mitya went on in a suddenly ringing voice, 'if they start flogging me on the way or *there*, I shan't let them. I'll kill someone and I'll be shot. And this is to go on for twenty years! Even here they talk to me contemptuously. The guards do. I've been lying here all night trying to arrive at a conclusion about myself: I'm not ready! I can't take it! I wanted to sing a "hymn", but I couldn't get over the contemptuous tone of the guards! For Grushenka I'd have put up with everything, everything except – beatings. But she won't be allowed to join me *there*.'

Alyosha smiled gently.

'Listen, Mitya, once and for all,' he said. 'This is what I think about it. And you know I wouldn't lie to you. Listen: you're not ready and such a cross is not for you. What's more, not being ready for it, you don't need such a martyr's cross. If you had killed Father, I'd be sorry that you should reject your cross. But you're innocent and such a cross is too much for you. You wanted to make a new man of yourself by suffering. Well, as I see it, all you ought to do is only to remember that other man always, all your life, and wherever you may run away to – and that will be enough for you. Not accepting the great suffering of the cross will only make your sense of duty stronger, and this constant feeling will help you in future, during the whole of your life, to find the new man in yourself perhaps much sooner than if you had gone *there*. For there you would not be able to bear it and you would rebel and, perhaps, really say at last: "I'm quits." The lawyer was right about that. Not everyone can bear heavy burdens; for some they are impossible. . . . That's what I think about it, if you really want to know. If others – soldiers or officers – would have to answer for your escape, I shouldn't have "permitted" it,' Alyosha smiled. 'But they say (the man in charge of the sleeping arrangements for the convicts assured Ivan himself) that, provided everything goes off without a hitch, the penalties won't be severe and that they can get off easily. Of course, bribing is dishonest even in such a case, but here I cannot possibly undertake to judge; for, in fact, if I were instructed by Ivan or Katya to make all the necessary arrangements for your escape, I know I should go and bribe whoever was to be bribed. I must be frank about it. And that's why I cannot set myself up as a judge of your actions. But I want you to know that I shall never condemn you. And it would be strange if I were to judge you in this, wouldn't it? Well, I think I've said all there is to say about it.'

'But I shall condemn myself!' cried Mitya. 'I shall run away. That has been decided without you: could Mitya Karamazov do anything but run away? But I shall condemn myself for it and I shall always pray that my sin should be forgiven. That's what the Jesuits say, isn't it? Just what we are saying now – eh?'

'Yes,' Alyosha smiled gently.

'I love you for always telling the whole truth and never hiding anything,' cried Mitya with a happy laugh. 'So that I've caught my Alyosha behaving like a Jesuit! I ought to kiss you for that! Now listen to the rest: I shall disclose the other half of my soul to you. That's what I planned and decided: if I run away, even with money and a passport, even as far as America, I'd be cheered by the thought that I'm not running away for a life of joy and happiness, but truly for a life of hard labour, no better, perhaps, than hard labour in Siberia. No better, Alexey, I tell you truly, no better! I hate America, the devil take it. I hate it already. Suppose Grushenka is with me. Well, what do you think? Can you imagine her as an American woman? She's Russian, Russian to the marrow of her bones. She'll be homesick for her native land, and every hour I'll see that she's miserable for my sake, that she's taken up the cross for me, and what has she done to deserve it? And do you think I could endure the common people there, even if every one of them is a better man than I? Oh, I hate that America even now! And though they were all of them there marvellous engineers, or whatever it is they are there – to hell with them! They are not my own people, they're not my sort. I love Russia, Alexey, I love the Russian God, though I'm a blackguard myself. Why,' he cried, his eyes flashing suddenly, 'I shall die like a dog there!'

His voice was trembling with tears.

'Well,' he began again, suppressing his excitement, 'this is what I've decided, Alexey. Listen. As soon as I arrive there with Grushenka we shall set to work, working on the land, in a far-away place, in solitude, with the wild bears. I expect there, too, we shall be able to find a place away from people. There are still Red Indians there, I'm told, somewhere on the edge of the horizon. Well, it's there we shall go, to the last of the Mohicans. And, well, we shall at once apply ourselves to the study of grammar, Grushenka and me. Work and grammar, and so for the next three years. And in these three years we shall learn to speak English like any Englishman. And as soon as we've learnt it – goodbye to America! We'll run back here, to Russia, as American citizens. Don't worry, we wouldn't come back to this hole of a town. We'll hide somewhere far away, in the north or in the south. I shall have changed by that time. She, too. There, in America, a doctor will make me a sort of wart – it's not for nothing that they're such good technicians! And if that can't be done, I shall put out an eye, grow a beard a yard long, a grey one (I shall go grey, homesick for Russia) – and it's ten to one they won't recognize me. And if they do, let them send me to Siberia. I don't care – it'll be just my luck! Here, too, we shall work on the land somewhere in the wilds, and I shall pretend to be an American all my life. But we shall die in our native land. That's my plan, and it shall be carried out. Do you approve?'

'I do,' said Alyosha, not wishing to contradict him.

Mitya was silent for a minute and said suddenly:

'And they got it all set at the trial, didn't they? How beautifully they got it all worked out!'

'If they hadn't, they would have found you guilty all the same,' Alyosha said with a sigh.

'Yes, the public here got sick of me. It can't be helped, I suppose, but it's hard!' Mitya moaned wretchedly.

They were again silent for a minute.

'Alyosha,' Mitya exclaimed suddenly, 'put me out of my misery at once. Tell me, is she coming or not? What did she say? How did she say it?'

'She said she would come, but I don't know whether she'll come today. It's hard for her, you know!' Alyosha looked timidly at Mitya.

'I should think so! I should think it's deuced hard for her! Alyosha, this is going to drive me mad. Grushenka keeps looking at me. She understands. Lord, chasten me: what is it I ask for? I ask for Katerina! Do I realize what I ask for? You can't restrain the impious Karamazov spirit! No, I'm not fit for suffering! I'm a blackguard, and that's all there is to it!'

'Here she is!' cried Alyosha.

At that moment Katerina suddenly appeared in the doorway. For an instant she stopped dead, gazing at Mitya with a sort of dazed expression. Mitya leapt to his feet at a bound. He looked scared and turned pale, but a timid, pleading smile appeared on his lips at once and, suddenly, he held out his hands impulsively to Katerina. Seeing this, she flew impetuously to him. She seized him by the hands and made him sit down on the bed almost by force. She herself sat down beside him, and, without letting go of his hands, pressed them tightly, spasmodically. Several times both tried to say something, but stopped short and again, as though unable to tear their eyes away from one another, gazed intently and in silence at one another with a strange smile; so two minutes passed.

'Have you forgiven me or haven't you?' Mitya murmured at last, and at the same instant, turning to Alyosha with a face distorted with joy, he cried to him: 'Do you hear what I'm asking? Do you hear?'

'It's because you're generous at heart that I loved you,' the words suddenly broke from Katerina. 'And you don't want my forgiveness

– it's I who want yours. But whether you forgive me or not – you'll always be a sore place in my heart and I in yours – that's how it should be,' she stopped to take breath. 'Why have I come?' she began again hurriedly and hysterically. 'I've come to embrace your feet, to press your hands – like this, till it hurts, as I used to do in Moscow, remember? And to tell you again that you're my god, my joy, to tell you that I'm madly in love with you,' she moaned in anguish and suddenly pressed his hand ardently to her lips.

Tears gushed from her eyes. Alyosha stood speechless and embarrassed; he had never expected to see what he was seeing.

'Love is over, Mitya,' Katerina began again, 'but what's over is terribly precious to me. I want you always to know that. But now, just for a little while, let what might have been come true,' she murmured with a drawn smile, gazing happily into his eyes again. 'You love another now and I love another, but for all that I shall always love you and you will love me – did you know that? Do you hear?' she exclaimed with an almost menacing catch in her voice. 'Love me, love me all your life!'

'I will love you and – you know, Katya,' Mitya said, drawing a deep breath at each word, 'you know, five days ago, on that evening I loved you. . . . When you fainted and they carried you out. . . . All my life! So it will be, so it will be always. . . .'

So they went on murmuring to one another almost meaningless, frantic, perhaps not even truthful, words, but at that moment it was all true, and they themselves believed implicitly what they said.

'Katya,' cried Mitya suddenly, 'do you believe I killed him? I know you don't believe it now, but did you believe it then – when you gave evidence. . . . Surely, surely you did not believe!'

'I did not believe it even then! I never believed it! I hated you and I suddenly persuaded myself – just at that moment. . . . When I gave evidence, I persuaded myself and I believed it, but when I had finished I ceased believing it at once. I want you to know all that. I've forgotten that I came here to punish myself,' she said suddenly with a kind of new expression, quite unlike her love-lorn chatter a moment before.

'It's hard for you, woman!' it escaped Mitya somehow quite uncontrollably.

'Let me go,' she whispered. 'I'll come again. I feel so wretched now.'

She got up, but suddenly uttered a loud cry and started back. Grushenka suddenly walked quietly into the room. No one had expected her. Katerina walked quickly towards the door, but as she drew near to Grushenka she suddenly stopped and, turning white as chalk, moaned softly almost in a whisper:

'Forgive me!'

Grushenka stared at her and, pausing for a moment, replied in a voice full of venomous hatred:

'We're wicked, my dear girl, you and I! We're both wicked! How then are we to forgive one another – you me and I you? Just save him and I'll worship you all my life.'

'Won't you forgive her?' Mitya shouted at Grushenka with wild reproach.

'Don't worry, I'll save him for you!' Katerina whispered quickly and ran out of the room.

'And how could you fail to forgive her after she herself had said – forgive me?' Mitya exclaimed bitterly again.

'Mitya, don't dare to reproach her,' Alyosha cried warmly. 'You have no right to.'

'It's her proud lips that spoke and not her heart,' said Grushenka with a sort of loathing. 'If she saves you, I'll forgive her everything.'

She fell silent, as though stifling something in her heart. She could not yet recover herself. She had come in, as it appeared later, quite by accident, without suspecting anything and not expecting to meet Katerina.

'Alyosha, run after her!' Mitya turned impetuously to his brother. 'Tell her – I don't know what – don't let her go away like that!'

'I'll come again before evening,' Alyosha cried and ran off after Katerina.

He overtook her outside the hospital walls. She was walking fast, she was in a hurry, but as soon as Alyosha caught up with her she said quickly:

'No, I cannot punish myself before that woman. I said "forgive me" to her because I wanted to punish myself to the end. She did not forgive me. . . . I like her for that!' Katerina added in a strangled voice and her eyes flashed with savage resentment.

'Mitya did not expect her at all,' Alyosha murmured. 'He was sure she wouldn't come.'

'No doubt. Don't let's discuss that,' she snapped. 'Listen, I can't go with you to the funeral now. I've sent them flowers. I believe they've still got some money. If necessary, tell them I'll never abandon them. . . . Now leave me, please. You're late as it is – the bells are ringing for late Mass. . . . Leave me, please!'

3

Little Ilyusha's Funeral. The Speech at the Stone

HE really was late. They had waited for him and already decided to bear the pretty, flower-covered little coffin into the church without him. It was poor little Ilyusha's coffin. He had died two days after Mitya was sentenced. Alyosha was met at the gate by the shouts of the boys, Ilyusha's school friends. They had been waiting impatiently for him and were glad that he had come at last. There were altogether twelve of them, and they had all come with their satchels and school-bags over their shoulders. 'Daddy will be crying,' Ilyusha had told them as he lay dying, 'stay with Daddy,' and the boys remembered it. Kolya Krasotkin was at the head of them.

'I'm so glad you've come, Karamazov,' he cried, holding out his hand to Alyosha. 'It's awful here. It really is painful to see. Snegiryov isn't drunk, we know for a fact that he hasn't had a drop today, but he looks as if he were drunk. . . . I'm always strong-minded, but this is dreadful. May I ask you one question, Karamazov, before you go in, if I am not keeping you?'

'What is it, Kolya?' Alyosha asked.

'Is your brother innocent or guilty? Did he kill his father or did the servant do it? As you say, so it will be. The thought of it kept me awake for four nights.'

'The servant did it, my brother is innocent,' replied Alyosha.

'That's what I said,' the boy Smurov cried suddenly.

'So he will be ruined, an innocent sacrifice to justice!' cried Kolya. 'He's happy, though ruined! I could almost envy him!'

'What are you saying? How can you? And why?' cried Alyosha, surprised.

'Oh, if I, too, could one day sacrifice myself for justice!' said Kolya with enthusiasm.

'But not in a case like that,' said Alyosha. 'Not with such disgrace and such horror.'

'Of course, I'd like to die for all mankind, and as for the disgrace, it makes no difference to me: may our names perish! I respect your brother.'

'And so do I!' the boy, who had once declared that he knew who had founded Troy, cried suddenly and unexpectedly from the crowd and blushed like a peony to the roots of his hair as he had done before.

Alyosha went into the room. Ilyusha, his hands folded and his eyes closed, lay in a blue coffin with a white frill of gauze round it. The features of his emaciated face were scarcely changed and, strange to say, there was almost no smell of decay from the corpse. The expression of his face was serious and seemingly thoughtful. His hands, crossed over his breast, were particularly beautiful, as though carved in marble. A bunch of flowers was placed in his hands, and, indeed, the whole coffin was covered, outside and inside, in flowers, sent early in the morning by Lise Khokhlakov. But there were flowers also from Katerina, and when Alyosha opened the door Snegiryov had a bunch of flowers in his shaking hands and was scattering them again over his darling boy. He barely glanced at Alyosha when he came in, and he would not look at anyone, in fact, not even at his weeping, crazed wife, his 'Mummy', who kept trying to raise herself on her crippled legs to have a closer look at her dead boy. The children had raised Nina on her chair and put it close to the coffin. She sat with her head pressed to it and was also apparently weeping softly. There was an animated but also bewildered and, at the same time, fierce look on Snegiryov's face. There was something crazy about his gestures and the words that escaped him from time to time. 'Old fellow, dear old fellow!' he exclaimed every minute, looking at Ilyusha. It was his habit when Ilyusha was still alive to call him affectionately: 'Old fellow, dear old fellow!'

'Daddy, give me some flowers, too,' the crazy 'Mummy' begged, whimpering. 'Take one out of his hands, that white one, and give it me!'

She had either taken a fancy to the little white rose in Ilyusha's hands or she wanted to have a flower from his hand to keep in memory of him, but she tossed about restlessly, stretching out her hands for the flower.

'I won't give it to anyone, I won't give you anything!' Snegiryov cried, callously. 'The flowers are his, not yours. Everything is his, nothing is yours!'

'Daddy, give Mother a flower,' Nina said suddenly, raising her tear-stained face.

'I won't give anything to anyone and least of all to her! She did not love him. She took away his little cannon and he gave it to her,' Snegiryov said, bursting into loud sobs as he remembered how Ilyusha had given up his cannon to his mother.

The poor crazed woman burst out crying softly, burying her face in her hands. At last, the boys, seeing that the father would not budge from the coffin and that it was time to carry it out, suddenly stood round it in a close circle and began to lift it up.

'I don't want him to be buried in the churchyard,' Snegiryov suddenly cried. 'I shall bury him by the stone, by our stone! That was Ilyusha's wish! I won't let him be carried there!'

For the last three days he had been saying that he would bury him near the stone; but Alyosha, Krasotkin, and the landlady, as well as the landlady's sister and the boys, had intervened.

'Fancy burying him by an unhallowed stone as though he had hanged himself,' the old landlady said sternly. 'In the churchyard the ground has been sanctified. There are crosses there. They will pray for him there. The singing can be heard from the church, and the deacon reads so clearly and so well that all the words will reach him every time just as though it was read over his grave.'

Snegiryov, in the end, gave it up in despair: 'Carry him where you like!' The boys lifted up the coffin, but as they carried it past the mother, they stopped and put it down for a moment so that she could take leave of little Ilyusha. But seeing suddenly the dear little face, which for the last three days she had only looked at from a distance, so close to her, she trembled all over and began jerking her grey head up and down over the coffin hysterically.

'Mother, make the sign of the cross over him, give him your blessing and kiss him,' Nina shouted to her.

But she went on jerking her head up and down like an automaton, without uttering a word, her face contorted with intense grief, and, then, she suddenly began beating her breast with her fist. They picked up the coffin again and carried it past Nina, who pressed her lips for the last time to her dead brother's lips. As he went out of the house, Alyosha turned to the landlady and asked her to look after the two invalid women. But she did not let him finish.

'Of course, I'll stay with them, we are Christians too!'

The old woman burst into tears as she said it.

They had not far to carry the coffin to the church. About three hundred yards, no more. It was a still, sunny day, with a slight frost. The church bells were still ringing. Snegiryov ran fussily and forlornly after the coffin in his short, old summer overcoat, his head bared and his wide-brimmed old felt hat in his hand. He seemed to be overcome by a sort of perplexed anxiety, stretching out his hand suddenly to support the head of the coffin and only interfering with the bearers or running alongside and looking for some place for himself there. A flower dropped down on the snow and he rushed to pick it up as though goodness only knew what might happen if the flower were lost.

'And the crust of bread, we've forgotten the crust of bread!' he cried suddenly in a terrible panic.

But the boys reminded him at once that he had taken the crust of bread and that it was in his pocket. He instantly pulled it out and, making sure he had it, calmed down.

'Ilyusha told me to, Ilyusha,' he explained at once to Alyosha. 'He was lying awake one night and I was sitting beside him, and all of a sudden he said to me, "Daddy, when they fill up my grave, crumble up a crust of bread on top of it so that the sparrows may fly down, and I shall hear and it will cheer me up not to be lying alone."'

'That's a very good thing,' said Alyosha. 'You must take some, often.'

'Every day, every day!' Snegiryov murmured, brightening up.

They arrived at last at the church and put the coffin down in the middle of it. All the boys stood round it and remained standing reverently like that all through the service. It was a very old and rather poor church, many of the icons were without settings, but somehow in such churches you pray more fervently. Snegiryov seemed to grow a little calmer during the service, though the same unconscious and seemingly perplexed anxiety came over him from time to time: he kept going up to the coffin to set right the cover or the wreath and when a candle fell out of the candlestick he rushed to put it back and busied himself a long time with it. Then he calmed down and stood still by the head of the coffin with a blank, worried, and bewildered expression. After the Epistle he suddenly whispered to Alyosha, who was standing beside him, that it had not been read *properly*, but he did not explain what he meant. During the hymn 'Like the Cherubim', he tried to join in the singing, but did not carry on with it and, kneeling, pressed his head to the stone floor and lay like that for a long time. At last they began the funeral service and candles were distributed. The distracted father started fidgeting again, but the deeply moving and heart-rending funeral chants stirred and thrilled his soul. He seemed suddenly to wilt and burst into rapid, short sobs, at first stifling his voice, but in the end whimpering loudly. When they began taking leave of the dead boy and closing the coffin, he threw his arms round it as though he would not let them cover Ilyusha, and began showering quick, greedy kisses on the lips of his dead boy. He was at last persuaded to desist and led down the steps, but he suddenly stretched out his hand impulsively and snatched a few flowers from the coffin. He looked at them and a new idea seemed to dawn on him, so that he apparently forgot what was happening all round him for a moment. Little by little he seemed to fall into a reverie and offered no resistance when the coffin was lifted and carried to the grave not far from the wall, close to the church. It was an expensive one and Katerina had paid for it. After the customary rites the grave-diggers lowered the coffin. Snegiryov bent down so low over the grave with the flowers in his hands that the boys caught hold of his coat and began pulling him back. But he no longer seemed to realize clearly what was happening. When they began filling up the grave, he suddenly began pointing anxiously at the falling earth and even started saying something, but no one could make out what he meant, and soon he fell silent himself. Then they reminded him that he had to crumble the bread and he grew terribly excited, pulled out the crust of bread and began tearing off bits of it and scattering them on the grave: 'Now, then, come on, little birdies, fly down, sweet little sparrows!' he mumbled anxiously. One of the boys observed that he must find it hard to crumble the bread with the flowers in his hands and suggested that he should let someone hold the flowers for a time. But he would not do so and even seemed suddenly alarmed for his flowers, as though they wanted to take them away from him. Then, casting a last look on the grave and having made sure that everything had been done and the bread scattered, he all of a sudden turned round unexpectedly and with the utmost composure walked off home. But his steps were getting faster and more hurried and soon he was almost running. The boys and Alyosha kept up with him.

'The flowers for Mummy! The flowers for Mummy! We've hurt Mummy's feelings!' he began exclaiming suddenly.

Someone shouted to him to put on his hat as it was very cold, but, hearing it, he flung his hat on the snow as though in anger and kept repeating: 'I don't want the hat, I don't want the hat!' Smurov picked it up and carried it after him. All the boys were crying, and Kolya and the boy who discovered Troy most of all. Though Smurov, with the captain's hat in his hands, was also crying bitterly, he managed, while running, to pick up a piece of red brick lying on the snow of the path and fling it at the flock of sparrows that was flying past. Of course, he missed them and went on crying as he ran. Half-way to his house Snegiryov suddenly stopped, stood still for half a minute as though struck by something and suddenly turned back to the church and started running towards the grave they had just left. But the boys at once overtook him and caught hold of him on all sides. Then, as though bereft of strength, as though struck down, he fell on the snow, and struggling, wailing and sobbing, began crying out: 'Ilyusha, old fellow, dear old fellow!' Alyosha and Kolya began raising him from the ground and did their best to persuade him to come home with them.

'Come, Captain,' Kolya murmured, 'a brave man must show courage!'

'You'll ruin the flowers,' Alyosha said. 'Remember "Mummy" is expecting them, she's sitting there crying because you didn't give her any of Ilyusha's flowers. And Ilyusha's bed is still there. . . .'

'Yes, yes, let's go back to Mummy,' Snegiryov suddenly recollected again. 'They'll make up his little bed, they'll make up his little bed!' he added, as though afraid that they would really make up the bed, and he jumped up and ran home again. But it was not far off now and they all arrived together. Snegiryov flung the door open and shouted to his wife with whom he had so callously quarrelled only a short time before:

'Mummy, oh, my poor crippled darling, Ilyusha has sent you these flowers!' and he held out the little bunch of flowers, frozen and broken while he was struggling in the snow.

But at that same moment he caught sight of Ilyusha's little boots which the landlady had put tidily together in a corner by the little bed – a pair of old, patched boots that had gone rusty and stiff. Seeing them, he raised his hands and, rushing up to them, fell on his knees, pressed his lips against them, and began kissing them greedily, crying: 'Ilyusha, old fellow, darling Ilyusha, where are your little feet?'

'Where have you carried him off? Where?' the crazy woman screamed in a heart-rending voice.

At this point Nina, too, burst out sobbing. Kolya rushed out of the room and he was followed by the other boys. At last Alyosha, too, went out.

'Let them have a good cry,' he said to Kolya. 'It's impossible to comfort them now. Let's wait a little and then go back.'

'Yes, it's impossible,' Kolya agreed. 'It's awful. Do you know, Karamazov,' he lowered his voice suddenly so that no one could hear him, 'I feel terribly sad and I'd give everything in the world to bring him back to life, if that were possible.'

'Oh dear, me too,' said Alyosha.

'What do you think, Karamazov? Ought we to come back here tonight? He'll be sure to get drunk.'

'Perhaps he will. Let's come back together, you and I and no one else, to spend an hour with them, with the mother and Nina,' Alyosha suggested. 'For if we all come together, we'd again remind them of everything.'

'The landlady is laying the table there now. There's going to be a wake, I suppose, and the priest is coming. Shall we go back there now, Karamazov?'

'Yes, certainly,' said Alyosha.

'It's all so strange, Karamazov. Such sorrow and all of a sudden pancakes – it's all so unnatural according to our religion!'

'They're going to have salmon, too,' the boy who discovered Troy suddenly observed in a loud voice.

'I'll thank you, Kartashov, not to interrupt again with your stupid remarks, especially when no one is talking to you or even cares to know whether you exist or not,' Kolya snapped irritably.

The boy flushed crimson, but he dared not say anything in reply. Meanwhile they were all walking slowly along the path, and suddenly Smurov exclaimed:

'Here's the stone under which he wanted to bury Ilyusha!'

They all stopped in silence at the big stone. Alyosha looked at it and the picture suddenly came back to him of what Snegiryov had told him the other day of how Ilyusha, crying and embracing his father, exclaimed, 'Daddy, Daddy, how he has humiliated you!' Something seemed to give way in his soul. He looked round with a serious and grave expression at the sweet bright faces of the school-boys, Ilyusha's friends, and suddenly said to them:

'Boys, I should like to say something to you here, at this place.'

The boys crowded round him and at once bent their eager, expectant glances upon him.

'Boys, we shall soon part. I'm staying here at present with my two brothers, one of whom is going to Siberia and the other is dangerously ill. But soon I shall leave this town, perhaps for a long time. So we may not see each other again. Let us, therefore, agree here, at Ilyusha's stone, never to forget, first, Ilyusha, and, secondly, one another. And whatever may befall us in life afterwards, even if we do not meet again for twenty years, we shall always remember how we buried the poor boy at whom we threw stones before at that little bridge – remember? – and how we all loved him so much afterwards. He was a nice boy, a good and brave boy. He was deeply conscious of his father's honour and the cruel insult to him, against which he had fought so stoutly. So, first of all, boys, let us remember him all our life. And though we may be occupied with most important things, win honours or fall upon evil days, yet let us never forget how happy we were here, when we were all of us together, united by such a good and kind feeling, which made us, too, while we loved the poor boy, better men, perhaps, than we are. My little doves – let me call you my little doves, for you are very like them, very like those pretty, bluish-grey birds, now, at this moment as I look at your kind, dear faces. My dear children, perhaps you will not understand what I'm going to say to you now, for I often speak very incomprehensibly, but, I'm sure, you will remember that there's nothing higher, stronger, more wholesome and more useful in life than some good memory, especially when it goes back to the days of your childhood, to the days of your life at home. You are told a lot about your education, but some beautiful, sacred memory, preserved since childhood, is perhaps the best education of all. If a man carries many such memories into life with him, he is saved for the rest of his days. And even if only one good memory is left in our hearts, it may also be the instrument of our salvation one day. Perhaps we may become wicked afterwards and be unable to resist a bad action, may laugh at men's tears and at those who say, as Kolya has just said: "I want to suffer for all mankind" – we may even jeer spitefully at such people. And yet, however wicked we may become, which God forbid, when we remember how we buried Ilyusha, how we loved him during these last days, and how we have been talking like friends together just now at this stone, the most cruel and the most cynical of us – if we do become so – will not dare to laugh inwardly at having been so good and kind at this moment! What's more, perhaps this memory alone will keep him from great evil, and he will change his mind and say, "Yes, I was good and brave and honest then." Let him laugh at himself – never mind, a man often laughs at what is good and kind; that is only from thought-lessness; but I assure you that as soon as he laughs, he will at once say in his heart: "No, I did wrong to laugh, for one should not laugh at such a thing!"'

'It will certainly be so, Karamazov!' Kolya exclaimed with flashing eyes. 'I understand you, Karamazov!'

The boys were excited and also wanted to say something, but they restrained themselves and looked intently and with emotion at the speaker.

'I am referring to our fear of becoming bad,' Alyosha went on, 'but why should we become bad – isn't that so, boys? Let us be, first and above all, kind, then honest, and then – don't let us ever forget each other. I say that again. I give you my word, boys, that I will never forget any one of you. I shall remember every face that is looking at me now, even after thirty years. Kolya said to Kartashov a moment ago that we did not care whether he existed or not. But how can I forget that Kartashov exists and that he doesn't blush now as when he discovered Troy, but is looking at me with his dear, kind, happy little eyes? Boys, my dear boys, let us all be generous and brave like Ilyusha, intelligent, brave, and generous like Kolya, who, I'm sure, will be much cleverer when he grows up, and let us be modest but also clever and kind like Kartashov. But why am I talking only about the two of them? You're all dear to me from now on, boys. I will find a place for you all in my heart and I beg you to find a place for me in your hearts also! Well, and who has united us in this good and kind feeling which we shall remember and intend to remember all our lives? Who did it, if not Ilyusha, the good boy, the dear boy, dear to us for ever and ever! Don't let us, then, ever forget him, may his memory live in our hearts for ever and ever!'

'Yes, yes, for ever and ever!' all the boys cried in their ringing voices, looking deeply moved.

'Let us remember his face and his clothes and his poor little boots, and his coffin, and his unhappy and sinful father, and how bravely he stood up for him alone against his whole class!'

'We will, we will remember!' the boys cried again. 'He was brave, he was kind!'

'Oh, how I loved him!' exclaimed Kolya.

'Oh, my dear children, my dear friends, do not be afraid of life! How good life is when you do something that is good and just!'

'Yes, yes,' the boys repeated enthusiastically.

'Karamazov, we love you!' a voice, probably Kartashov's, cried impulsively.

'We love you, we love you,' the other boys echoed. There were tears in the eyes of many of them.

'Hurrah for Karamazov!' Kolya shouted enthusiastically.

'And may the dead boy's memory live for ever!' Alyosha added again with feeling.

'May it live for ever!' the boys echoed again.

'Karamazov,' cried Kolya, 'is it really true that, as our religion tells us, we shall all rise from the dead and come to life and see one another again, all, and Ilyusha?'

'Certainly we shall rise again, certainly we shall see one another, and shall tell one another gladly and joyfully all that has been,' Alyosha replied, half laughing, half rapturously.

'Oh, how wonderful it will be!' Kolya cried.

'Well, now let us make an end of talking and go to his wake.

Don't let it worry you that we shall be eating pancakes. It is a very old custom and there's something nice about that,' Alyosha laughed. 'Well, come along! And now we do go hand in hand.'

'And always so, all our life hand in hand! Hurrah for Karamazov!' Kolya cried again with enthusiasm, and once more all the boys cheered.

THE END

FOR THE BEST IN PAPERBACKS, LOOK FOR THE 🐧

In every corner of the world, on every subject under the sun, Penguin represents quality and variety – the very best in publishing today.

For complete information about books available from Penguin – including Pelicans, Puffins, Peregrines and Penguin Classics – and how to order them, write to us at the appropriate address below. Please note that for copyright reasons the selection of books varies from country to country.

In the United Kingdom: Please write to *Dept E.P., Penguin Books Ltd, Harmondsworth, Middlesex, UB7 0DA*

In the United States: Please write to *Dept BA, Penguin, 299 Murray Hill Parkway, East Rutherford, New Jersey 07073*

In Canada: Please write to *Penguin Books Canada Ltd, 2801 John Street, Markham, Ontario L3R 1B4*

In Australia: Please write to the *Marketing Department, Penguin Books Australia Ltd, P.O. Box 257, Ringwood, Victoria 3134*

In New Zealand: Please write to the *Marketing Department, Penguin Books (NZ) Ltd, Private Bag, Takapuna, Auckland 9*

In India: Please write to *Penguin Overseas Ltd, 706 Eros Apartments, 56 Nehru Place, New Delhi, 110019*

In Holland: Please write to *Penguin Books Nederland B.V., Postbus 195, NL–1380AD Weesp, Netherlands*

In Germany: Please write to *Penguin Books Ltd, Friedrichstrasse 10–12, D–6000 Frankfurt Main 1, Federal Republic of Germany*

In Spain: Please write to *Longman Penguin España, Calle San Nicolas 15, E–28013 Madrid, Spain*

In France: Please write to *Penguin Books Ltd, 39 Rue de Montmorency, F-75003, Paris, France*

In Japan: Please write to *Longman Penguin Japan Co Ltd, Yamaguchi Building, 2–12–9 Kanda Jimbocho, Chiyoda-Ku, Tokyo 101, Japan*

GOGOL

DEAD SOULS

Translated by David Magarshack

Gogol, convinced of his messianic mission to save Russia, regarded *Dead Souls* as the means Providence had sent him for accomplishing this task. The first part of the novel, describing the attempts of Chichikov, a crook, to purchase dead souls whom he could then mortgage, was enthusiastically acclaimed, but Gogol's hopes were pinned on the second part, which was to depict Chichikov's spiritual regeneration. Persuaded by a religious fanatic, however, Gogol ultimately burnt the second part, and his life ended in insanity and suicide. His attempts to effect a final reconciliation of the hostile social and economic forces in Russia was a failure, as was proved by the abolition of serfdom eight years after his death. Despite this, the creations of his genius have achieved immortality as universal human types, making his name famous far beyond the borders of his own country.

Also translated by David Magarshack:

DOSTOYEVSKY

Crime and Punishment
The Devils
The Idiot

CHEKHOV

Lady with Lapdog and Other Stories

GONCHAROV

Oblomov